DATE			

LaVyrle Spencer

THREE COMPLETE NOVELS

Also by LaVyrle Spencer

NOVEMBER OF THE HEART
BYGONES
FORGIVING
BITTER SWEET
SPRING FANCY
MORNING GLORY
THE HELLION
VOWS
THE GAMBLE
A HEART SPEAKS
YEARS
SEPARATE BEDS
TWICE LOVED
HUMMINGBIRD
THE ENDEARMENT
THE FULFILLMENT

THREE COMPLETE NOVELS

LaVyrle Spencer

YEARS
TWICE LOVED
SPRING FANCY

G. P. PUTNAM'S SONS   NEW YORK

G. P. Putnam's Sons
Publishers Since 1838
200 Madison Avenue
New York, NY 10016

Published simultaneously in Canada

Library of Congress Cataloging-in-Publication Data

Spencer, LaVyrle.
[Selections. 1993]
Three complete novels / LaVyrle Spencer.
p. cm.
Contents: Years—Twice loved—Spring fancy.
ISBN 0-399-13842-0
1. Love stories, American. I. Title.
PS3569.P4534A6 1993 92-39606 CIP
813'.54—dc20

Printed in the United States of America
1 2 3 4 5 6 7 8 9 10

CONTENTS

YEARS

Chapter 1

1917

Linnea Brandonberg was neither asleep nor awake, but in a whimsical state of fantasy, induced—this time—by the rhythmic clatter rising through the floor of the train. Her feet rested primly together and often she glanced down to admire the most beautiful shoes she'd ever seen—congress shoes, they were called—with shiny, pointed patent leather toes giving way to smooth black kid uppers that hugged not only her foot but a good six inches of ankle as well. Miraculously, they had no buttons or ties, but slipped on tightly with a deep gusset of stiff elastic running from mid-shin to below the ankle bone on either side. But best of all they were the first shoes she'd ever owned with high heels. Though the heels added scarcely an inch to her height, they added years to her maturity.

She hoped.

He would be there at the station when she arrived, a dashing superintendent of schools who drove a fancy Stanhope carriage for two, drawn by a glossy blood-bay trotter. . . .

''Miss Brandonberg?'' His voice was rich and cultured, and a dazzling smile broke upon his handsome face as he removed a beaver top hat, revealing hair the color of rye at sunset.

''Mr. Dahl?''

''At your service. We're all so delighted you're here at last. Oh, please allow me—I'll take that valise!'' As he stowed the suitcase in the boot of the carriage she noticed the sleek fit of his black suit coat across nicely shaped shoulders, and when he turned to help her into the buggy, she noted the fact that his celluloid collar was brand new, stiff and tight for the occasion. ''Careful now.'' He had marvelous hands, with long pale fingers that solicitously closed over her own as he handed her up.

A reed-thin whip clicked above the trotter's head, and they sped away, with his elbow lightly bumping hers.

''Miss Brandonberg, to your left you'll note the opera house, our newest

establishment, and at the first opportunity I hope we can attend a performance together."

"An opera house!" she gasped in ladylike surprise while delicately steepling five fingers over her heart. "Why, I didn't expect an opera house!"

"A young lady with your looks will put the actresses to shame." His smile seemed to dim the sun as he approvingly scanned her narrow shoes, her new wool serge suit, and the first hat she'd ever owned without a childish wide brim. "I hope you won't think me too bold if I say that you have a definite flair for clothes, Miss Brandonberg. . . ."

"Miss Brandonberg?" The voice in her fantasy faded as she was roused by the conductor, who was leaning across the empty aisle seat to touch her shoulder. "Next stop Alamo, North Dakota." She straightened and offered the older man a smile.

"Oh, thank you!"

He touched the brim of his blue cap and nodded before moving away.

Outside, the prairie rolled by, flat and endless. She peered out the window but saw no sign of the town. The train lost speed as its whistle sounded, then sighed into silence, leaving only the *clackety-clack* of the wheels upon shifting steel seams.

Her heart thumped expectantly, and this time, when she placed a hand over it, there was no pretending. She would see it soon, the place that had been only a word on the map; she would meet them soon, the people who would become part of her daily life as students, friends, perhaps even confidantes. Each new face she'd meet would be that of a total stranger, and for the hundredth time she wished she knew just one person in Alamo. Just one.

There's nothing to be frightened of. It's only last-minute nervousness.

She ran a hand up the back of her neck, checking the hairstyle she wasn't yet adept at forming. Within the crescent-shaped coil around her head, the rat seemed to have slipped loose. With shaky fingers she tightened several hairpins, then checked her hatpin, smoothed her skirt, and glanced at her shoes for a last dose of confidence just as the train huffed out a final weary breath and shuddered to a halt.

Dear me, where is the town?

Lugging her suitcase down the aisle, she glanced through the windows, but all she could see was the standard small-town depot—a wood-frame building painted the color of a rutabaga with six-over-six windows flanking a center door that faced a waiting platform whose roof was held up by four square posts.

She eyed it again as she emerged from the dusky depths of the passenger car into the bright September sun, the metal steps chiming beneath her smart new heels.

She glanced around for someone who might look like a superintendent of schools and quelled her dismay upon discovering only one person in sight, a man standing in the shade of the depot porch. But judging from his mode of dress, he was not the man she sought. Still, he might turn out to be a parent of one of her students: she flashed him a quick smile. But he remained as before, with his hands inside the bib of his striped overalls and a sweat-stained straw hat shielding his eyes.

Forcing a confident air, she crossed the platform and went inside, but found only the ticket agent, busily clicking the telegraph behind his caged window.

"Excuse me, sir?"

He turned, pushed a green celluloid visor higher on his head, and smiled. "Yes, miss?"

"I am to meet Mr. Frederic Dahl here. Do you know him?"

"Know who he is. Haven't seen him around here. But have a seat—he'll probably show up soon."

Her stomach began to tighten. *What shall I do now?*

Too nervous to sit still, she decided to wait outside. She took up her station on the opposite side of the veranda from the farmer, set her valise down, and waited.

Minutes passed and no one came. She glanced at the stranger, caught him studying her, then self-consciously snapped her attention to the train. It huffed and hissed, spit out funnels of steam with each breath, but seemed to be taking an inordinate amount of time to be on its way again.

She chanced a peek at the man again, but the moment her eyes turned his way, his quickly darted toward the door of the train again.

Theodore Westgaard studied the train steps, waiting for the new teacher to emerge, but a full three minutes ticked by and the only person to alight was the thin young girl playing grownup in her mother's hat and shoes. His eyes were drawn to her a second time, but again she looked his way and self-consciously he shifted his attention toward the door of the train.

Come on, Brandonberg, let's get going. I've got harvesting to do.

From a pocket on his bib he withdrew a watch, checked the time, and shifted his feet impatiently. The girl glanced his way again, but their eyes barely met before her attention skittered down the train track as she crossed her wrists beneath a folded coat she was holding.

He studied her covertly.

Sixteen or so, he'd guess, scared of her own shadow and hoping nobody could tell. A cute little thing, though that hat with the bird wings looked ridiculous and she should still be in pigtails and flat-heeled shoes.

To Westgaard's surprise, before anyone else got off the train, the conductor picked up his portable step, stowed it inside the car, and waved an arm at the engineer. The couplings started clanging down the length of the train and it slowly groaned to life, then rumbled away, leaving a magnified silence broken only by the buzzing of a fly about the girl's nose.

She flapped a hand at it and pretended Westgaard wasn't there while he grew irascible at having made the trip to town for nothing. He took off his hat, scratched his head, then settled the brim low over his eyes while cursing silently.

City boy. Got no idea how a wheat man values every hour of daylight this time of year.

Angrily he stomped inside.

"Cleavon, if that young whelp comes in on the next train, tell him . . . aw, hell, forget it. I guess I'll just have to wait for it myself." Alamo offered no livery stable, no horses to rent. How else would the new teacher get out to the farm when he finally got here?

When Theodore clomped out the door again the girl was facing him with stiff shoulders and a frightened expression on her face. Her hands still clutched the coat, and she opened her mouth as if to speak, then closed it again, swallowed, and turned away.

Though he wasn't one to speak to strange girls, she looked all bird-eyed and about to break into tears, so he stopped and inquired, "Somebody supposed to meet you?"

She turned back to him almost desperately. "Yes, but it seems he's been detained."

"Ya, same with the fellow I was here to meet, name of L.I. Brandonberg."

"Oh, thank heavens," she breathed, her face suddenly rekindling a smile. "I'm Miss Brandonberg."

"You!" Her smile was met with a scowl. "But you can't be! L.I. Brandonberg is a man!"

"He is not . . . I mean, *I* am not." She laughed nervously, then remembered her manners and extended a hand. "My name is Linnea Irene Brandonberg, and as you can see, I most certainly am a woman."

At that his eyes made a quick pass over her hat and hair, and he gave a disdainful snort.

She felt the blood rush to her face, but stubbornly kept her hand extended, inquiring, "And whom do I have the pleasure of addressing?"

He ignored her hand and answered rudely, "The name's Westgaard and I ain't havin' no . . . *woman* livin' in my house! Our school board hired L.I. Brandonberg, thinkin' he was a man."

So this was Theodore Westgaard, at whose home she was to board and room. Disheartened, she dropped the hand he still ignored. "I'm sorry you were under that impression, Mr. Westgaard, but I assure you I didn't mean to deceive you."

"Hmph! What kind of female goes around callin' herself L.I.!"

"Is there a law against women using their initials as part of their legal signature?" she asked crisply.

"No, but there should be! Little city girl like you, probably guessed the school board would rather have a man and set out to deliberately hoodwink them."

"I did nothing of the kind! I sign all—"

But he cut her off rudely. "Teaching school out here's more than just scratchin' numbers on a slate, missy! It's a mile's walk, and buildin' fires and shovelin' snow. And the winters out here are tough! I don't have time to hitch up no team and haul a little hothouse pansy to school when it's thirty below and the snow's howlin' out of the northwest!"

"I won't ask you to!" She was enraged now, her face sour with dislike. How dare they send a garrulous old man like this to greet her! "And I'm not a hothouse pansy!"

"Oh, you ain't, huh?"

He eyed her assessingly, wondering how long a little thing like her would last when an Alaskan northwesterly smacked her in the face and the snow stung so hard you couldn't tell cold from hot on your own forehead. "Wall"—he drew the word out in a gruff note of disapproval—"the fact remains: I don't want no *woman* livin' at my house."

He could say the word *woman* the way a cowpoke said *sidewinder*.

''Then I'll board with someone else.''

''And just who might that be?''

''I . . . I don't know, but I'll speak to Mr. Dahl about it.''

Again he gave a grumpy, disdainful *hmph* that made her want to poke sticks up his nose. ''Ain't nobody else. We've always had the teachers livin' with us. That's just the way it is—cause we're closest to school. Only one closer's my brother John, and he's a bachelor, so his place is out.''

''And so what do you propose to do with me, Mr. Westgaard? Leave me standing on the depot steps?''

His mouth pinched up like a dried berry and his brows furrowed in stern reproof as he stared at her from beneath the brim of his straw hat.

''I ain't havin' no woman livin' under my roof,'' he vowed again, crossing his arms stubbornly.

''Perhaps not, but if not yours, you'd best transport me to someone less bigoted than yourself under whose roof I will be more than happy to reside, unless you want a lawsuit brought upon you.'' Now, where in the world had that come from? She wouldn't know the first thing about bringing a lawsuit upon anybody, but she had to think of some way to put this uncouth ox in his place!

''A lawsuit!'' Westgaard's arms came uncrossed. He hadn't missed the word *bigoted,* but the little snip was throwing threats and names out so fast he had to address them one at a time.

Linnea squared her shoulders and tried to make him think she was worldly and bold. ''I have a contract, Mr. Westgaard, and in it is stated that room and board are included as part of my annual salary. Furthermore, my father is an attorney in Fargo, thus my legal fees would be extraordinarily reasonable should I decide to sue the Alamo school board for breach of contract, and name you as a—''

''All right, all right!'' He held up two big, horny palms in the air. ''You can stop yappin', missy. I'll dump you on Oscar Knutson and he can do what he wants to with y'. He wants to be head of the school board, so let 'im earn his money!''

''My name is Miss Brandonberg, not *missy!*'' She gave her skirt a little flip in exasperation.

''Yeah, a fine time to tell me.'' He turned away toward a waiting horse and wagon, leaving her to grouse silently. *Dump me on Oscar Knutson, indeed!*

Reality continued to make a mockery of her romanticized daydreams. There was no fancy-rigged Stanhope carriage, no glossy blood-bay trotter. Instead, Westgaard led her to a double-box farm wagon hitched behind a pair of thick-muscled horses of questionable ancestry, and he clambered up without offering a hand, leaving her little choice but to stow her grip in the back by herself, then lift her skirts and struggle to the shoulder-high leaf-sprung seat unaided.

And as for gentlemen in beaver hats—ha! This rude oaf wouldn't know what to do with a beaver top hat if it jumped up and bit him on his oversized sun-burned nose! The nerve of the man to treat her as if she were . . . as if she were . . . *dispensable!* She, with a hard-earned teacher's certificate from the Fargo Normal School! She, a woman of high education while he could scarcely put one word before another without sounding like an uneducated jackass!

Linnea's disillusionment continued as he flicked the reins and ordered, ''Giddap.'' The cumbersome-looking horses took them through one of the saddest little bergs she'd ever seen in her life. Opera house? Had she really fantasized about an opera house? It appeared the most cultural establishment in town was the general store/post office, which undoubtedly brought *culture* to Alamo by means of the Sears Roebuck catalogue.

The most impressive buildings in town were the grain elevators beside the railroad tracks. The others were all false-fronted little cubicles, and there were few of them at that. She counted two implement dealers, two bars, one restaurant, the general store, a hotel, a bank, and a combination drug and barber shop.

Her heart sank.

Westgaard glared straight ahead, holding the reins in hands whose fingers were the size of Polish sausages, with skin that looked like that of an old Indian—so different from the long, pale fingers of her imagination.

He didn't look at her, and she didn't look at him.

But she saw those tough brown hands.

And he saw her high-heeled shoes.

And she sensed how he hunched forward and glared from under that horrible-looking hat.

And he sensed how she sat like a pikestaff and stared all persnickitylike from under those ridiculous bird wings.

And she thought it was too bad that when people got old they had to get so crotchety.

And he thought how silly people were when they were young—always trying their best to make themselves look older.

And neither of them said a word.

They drove several miles west, then turned south, and the land looked all the same: flat, gold, and waving. Except where the threshers had already been. There it was flat, gold, and still.

When they'd been traveling for half an hour, Westgaard pulled into a farmyard that looked identical to every other one they'd passed—weather-beaten clapboard house with a cottonwood windbreak on the west, the trees only half-grown and tipping slightly south by southwest; a barn looking better kept than the house; rectangular granaries; hexagonal silos; and the only friendly looking feature reigning over all: the slow-whirling, softly sighing windmill.

A woman came to the door, tucking a strand of hair into the bun at the back of her head. She raised one hand in greeting and smiled broadly.

''Theodore!'' she called, coming down two wooden steps and crossing the patch of grass that looked as golden as the fields surrounding them. ''Hello! Who do you have here? I thought you had gone to town to get the new schoolteacher.''

''This is him, Hilda. And he's wearin' high-heeled shoes and a hat with bird wings on it.''

Linnea bristled. How dare he make fun of her clothes!

Hilda stopped beside the wagon and frowned up at Westgaard, then at Linnea. ''This is him?'' She shaded her eyes with one hand and took a second look. Then she flapped both palms, pulled her chin back, and smiled as if with scolding humor. ''Oh, Theodore, you play a joke on us, huh?''

Westgaard jabbed a thumb at his passenger. "No, she's the one who played a joke on us. She's L.I. Brandonberg."

Before Hilda Knutson could respond, Linnea leaned over and extended a hand, incensed afresh by Westgaard's rudeness in failing to introduce her properly. "How do you do. I'm Linnea Irene Brandonberg."

The woman took her hand as if not actually realizing what she was doing. "A woman," she said, awestruck. "Oscar hired us a woman."

Beside her Westgaard made a throaty sound of ridicule. "I think what Oscar hired us is a girl dressed up in her mother's clothes, pretending to be a woman. And she ain't stayin' at my house."

Hilda's face sobered. "Why, Theodore, you always kept the teachers. Who else is gonna keep her?"

"I don't know, but it ain't gonna be me. That's what I come to talk to Oscar about. Where is he?" Westgaard's eyes scanned the horizon.

"I don't know exactly. He started with the west rye this mornin', but it's hard to tell where he is by now. You might see him from the road if you head on out that way though."

"I'll do that, but I'm leavin' her here. She ain't comin' to my house, so she might's well stay here with you till you find someplace else for her."

"Here!" Hilda pressed both hands to her chest. "But I got no spare rooms, you know that. Wouldn't be right stuffing the teacher in with the kids. You take her, Theodore."

"Nosirree, Hilda. I ain't havin' no woman in my house."

Linnea was incensed. The nerve of them, treating her as if she were the chamber pot nobody wanted to carry out back.

"Stop!" she shouted, closing her eyes while lifting both palms like a corner policeman. "Take me back to town. If I'm not wanted here, I'll be more than happy to take the next tr—"

"I can't do that!"

"Now see what you've done, Theodore. You've hurt her feelings."

"Me! Oscar hired her! Oscar's the one who told us she was a man!"

"Well, then go talk to Oscar!" She threw up her hands in disgust, then, belatedly remembering her manners, shook hands with Linnea again and patted the girl's knuckles. "Don't pay no attention to Theodore here. He'll find a place for you. He's just upset cause he's wastin' time out of the fields when all that wheat is ripe out there. Now, Theodore," she ordered, turning toward the house, "you take care of this young one like you agreed to!"

And with that she hustled back inside.

Defeated, Westgaard could only set out in search of Oscar with his unwanted charge beside him.

Like most Dakota farms, Knutson's was immense. Traveling down the gravel road, they scanned the horizon over his wheat, oat, and rye fields, but there was no sign of his team and mower crossing and recrossing the fields. Westgaard sat straight, frowning across the ocean of gold, peering intently for some sign of movement on the faraway brow of the earth, but the only thing moving was the grain itself and a flock of yapping blackbirds that flew overhead in ever-changing patterns before landing somewhere in the oats to glut themselves. The wagon came abreast of a shorn field, its yield lying in heavy plaits stretching as far as the eye could see. Drying in the sun, the grain gave up its sweet redolence to the sparkling air. With a subtle shift of the reins, Westgaard turned the horses off the gravel road along a rough grassy track leading between the cut field and another on their right whose grain was still straight and high. The track was bumpy, created chiefly for access to the fields. When the wagon suddenly lurched, Linnea grabbed her towering hat as it threatened to topple from its perch.

Westgaard angled her a silent glance, and for a moment one corner of his mouth tipped up. But her chin was lowered as she busily reset the hatpin to hold the infernal nuisance on.

They rocked and bumped their way up the track to a slight rise in the land. Reaching it, Westgaard intoned, ''Whoa.''

Obediently, the horses stopped, leaving the riders to sit staring at an eternity of Oscar Knutson's cut rye, with no Oscar in sight.

Westgaard held the reins in one hand, removed his hat and scratched his head with the other, mumbled something under his breath, then settled the hat back on with a disgruntled tug.

This time it was Linnea's turn to smile. Good enough for him, the rude thing! He agreed to keep me, now he can put up with me, whether he likes it or not.

''You'll have to come to my place till I can get this straightened out,'' Westgaard lamented, flicking the reins and turning the horses in the rye stubble.

''So I shall.''

He gave her a sharp, quelling glance, but she sat stiff and prim on the wagon seat, looking straight ahead.

But her ridiculous hat was slightly crooked.

Theodore smiled to himself.

They set off again, heading south, then west. Everywhere was the sound of the dry, sibilant grain. The heavy heads of each stalk lifted toward the heavens only momentarily before bending low beneath their own weight.

Linnea and Theodore spoke only three times. They had been traveling for nearly an hour when Linnea asked, ''How far from Alamo do you live, Mr. Westgaard?''

''Twelve miles,'' he answered.

Then all was still but for the birds and grain and the steady beat of the horses' hooves. Three times they saw mowing machines crawling along in the distance, pulled by horses who appeared minuscule from so far away, their heads nodding as they leaned into their labor.

She broke the silence again when a small once-white building with a belfry appeared on their right. Her eager eyes took in as many details as she could—the long narrow windows, the concrete steps, the flat yard with a grove of cottonwoods at its edge, the pump. But Westgaard kept the team moving with the same unbroken walk, and she gripped the side of the wagon seat and craned around as the building receded too fast for her to take in all that she wanted to. She whirled to face him, demanding, ''Is that the schoolhouse?''

Without turning his eyes from the horses' ears, he grunted, ''Yeah.''

Ornery, pig-headed cuss! She bunched her fists in her lap and seethed.

''Well, you could have told me!''

He rolled his eyes in her direction. His mouth twisted in a sardonic smirk as he drawled, "I ain't no tour guide."

Anger boiled close to eruption, but she clapped her mouth shut and kept her rebuffs to herself.

They rode on a little farther down the road, and as they passed a nondescript farm on their left, Theodore decided to rankle her just a little more. "This here's my brother John's place."

"How wonderful," she replied sarcastically, then refused to look at it.

Less than ten minutes from the school building they entered a long, curving driveway of what she supposed was Westgaard's place—not that he bothered to verify it. It was sheltered on its north side by a long windbreak of box elder trees and a parallel row of thick caragana bushes that formed an unbroken wall of green. As they rounded the windbreak, the farmyard came into view. The house sat to the left in the loop of the driveway. All the outbuildings were to the right, with a windmill and water tank situated between a huge weather-beaten barn and a cluster of other buildings she took to be granaries and chicken coops.

The wood-frame house was two stories high, and absolutely unadorned, like all they'd passed on their way from town. It appeared to have been painted white at one time, but was now the color of ashes, with only a flake of white appearing here and there as a reminder of better days. It had no porch or lean-to to relieve its boxlike appearance, and no overhanging eave to shade its windows from the prairie sun. The center door was flanked by long narrow windows giving it the symmetrical appearance of a face gaping at the vast fields of wheat surrounding it.

"Well, this is it," Westgaard announced in his own good time, leaning forward to tie the reins around the brake handle of the wagon. Bracing his hands on the seat and footboard, he vaulted over the side and would have left her to do the same, but at that moment an imperious voice shouted from the door of the house, "Teddy! Where are your manners! You help that young woman down!"

Teddy? thought Linnea, amused. *Teddy?*

A miniature whirlwind of a woman came hustling down the footpath from the kitchen door, her frizzy gray hair knotted at her nape, a pair of oval wire-rimmed glasses hooked behind her ears. She shook a finger scoldingly.

Theodore Westgaard made a dutiful about-face in the middle of the path and returned to the wagon to reach up a helping hand, but the expression on his face was martyred.

Placing her hand in his and leaping down, Linnea couldn't resist mocking sweetly, "Oh, thank you, Mr. Westgaard, you're too kind."

He dropped her hand immediately as they were joined by the bustling woman who made Linnea—only a little over five feet tall—feel like a giant. She had a nose no bigger than a thimble, faded brown eyes that seemed to miss nothing, and lips as straight and narrow as a willow leaf. She walked with her fuzzy knob of a chin thrust forward, arms swinging almost forcefully. Though her back was slightly bowed, she still managed to give the appearance of one leaning into each step with great urgency. What the woman lacked in stature, she made up for in energy. The minute she opened her mouth, Linnea realized she wasn't one to mince words. "So this is the new schoolteacher. Don't look like no man to me!" She took Linnea by both arms, held her in place while giving her a thorough inspection from hem to hat, and nodded once. "She'll do." The woman spun on Westgaard, demanding, "What happened to the fella?"

"She's him," Westgaard answered tersely.

The woman let out a squawk of laughter and concluded, "Well, I'll be switched." Then sobering abruptly, she thrust out her hand and pumped Linnea's. "Just what this place needs. Never mind that son of mine I should've taught more manners. Since he didn't bother to introduce us, I'm his ma, Mrs. Westgaard. You can call me Nissa."

Her hand was all bones, but strong. "I'm Linnea Brandonberg. You can call me Linnea."

"So, *Lin-nay-uh.*" She gave it an old country sound. "A good Norwegian name."

They smiled at each other, but not for long. It was becoming apparent Nissa Westgaard never did anything for long. She moved like a sparrow, each new action abrupt and economical. "Come on in." She bustled up the path, yelping at her son, "Well, don't just stand there, Teddy, get her things!"

"She ain't stayin'."

Linnea rolled her eyes toward heaven and thought, here we go again! But she was in for a surprise. Nissa Westgaard spun around and cuffed her son on the side of the neck with amazing force. "What you mean, she ain't stayin'? She's stayin' all right, so you can just get them ideas out of your head. I know what you're thinkin', but this little gal is the new schoolteacher, and you better start watchin' your manners around her or you'll be cookin' your own meals and washin' your own duds around here! I can always go and live with John, you know!"

Linnea covered her mouth with a hand to hide the smile. It was like watching a banty rooster take on a bear. The top of Nissa's head reached no higher than her son's armpit, but when she lambasted him, he didn't talk back. His face turned beet red and his jaw bulged. But before Linnea was allowed to watch any more of his discomfiture, the banty whirled around, grabbed her by an arm, and pulled her up the path. "Bullheaded, ornery thing!" she mumbled. "Lived too long without havin' no woman around. Made him unfit for human company."

It came to Linnea to say, "I couldn't agree more," but she wisely bit her tongue. It also occurred to Linnea that Nissa was a woman. But obviously, in these parts having a "woman" in the house did not mean living with your mother.

Nissa pushed Linnea through the open back door into a kitchen that smelled of vinegar. "It ain't much, but it's warm and dry, and with only three of us Westgaards livin' here, you'll have a room of your own, which is more than you'd have anyplace else around here."

Linnea turned in surprise. "Three of you?"

"Didn't he tell you about Kristian?"

Feeling a little disoriented from the woman's ceaseless speed and authoritative tone, Linnea only shook her head.

"What's the matter with that man! Kristian's his boy, my grandson. He's off cutting wheat. He'll be in at suppertime."

Linnea looked around for the missing link—the wife, the mother—but it appeared there was none. It also appeared she was not going to be told why.

"This here's the kitchen. You've got to excuse the mess. I been puttin' up watermelon pickles." On a huge round oak pedestal table fruit jars stood in rank and file, but Linnea scarcely had a chance to glimpse them before Nissa moved on through the room to another. "This is the front room. I sleep there." She pointed to one doorway leading off it. "And that's Teddy's room. You and Kristian are upstairs."

She led the way into the kitchen, and as they breezed through it to the doorway leading up, Linnea caught a glimpse of Theodore coming in with her suitcase. She turned her back on him and followed Nissa up a steep, narrow stairwell to the second floor. At the top was a cramped landing with matched double-cross doors leading both left and right. Her room was the one on the right.

Nissa opened the door and led the way inside.

It was the crudest room Linnea had ever seen. Nothing was pushed flush against the wall, for there were no walls, only the sharply pitched roof angling from its center ridgepole to the outer edges of the room. From underneath, the joists and beams and sub-roof were plainly visible, for the ceiling was neither plastered nor wainscoted. The only upright walls were the two triangular ones at either end of the room. But they, like the ceiling, were unfinished. Opposite the door, facing east, was a small four-paned window with white lace curtains tied back to the raw wood frame. Now, in late afternoon, the light coming through the panes was negligible, but from across the tiny landing the afternoon sun streamed through a matching window, warming Linnea's room slightly.

The floor was covered with linoleum bearing a design of large pink cabbage roses on a dark-green background. It did not quite reach the edges of the room, leaving a border of wide, unfinished floor planks exposed. To the right of the door, crowded beneath the roof-angle, was a single bed with a white-painted iron frame, covered with a chenille bedspread of bright rose. Across its foot lay a folded patchwork quilt and on the linoleum beside it a homemade rag rug tied with green warp. Beside the bed, on a square table with turned legs, a kerosene lantern was centered upon a white crocheted doily. Pushed against the opposite roof-angle was a chest-high dresser draped with an embroidered dresser scarf of snowy white cotton edged with crocheted lace. In the corner left of the door, the wide black stovepipe came up from the kitchen below and continued out to the roof. Across the way, beside the window, was a low stand holding a pitcher and bowl, with a door underneath that undoubtedly concealed the "nighttime facilities." On the wall beside the washstand hung a mirror in a tin frame with an attached bar holding a length of white huck toweling. Next to the tiny window was an enormous oak rocker with green and pink calico cushions on its seat and back.

Linnea's eyes moved from it to the rugged beams overhead, and she stifled her disappointment. Her own room at home was decorated with floral wallpaper and had two large windows facing two different directions. Every other spring her daddy gave the woodwork a fresh coat of ivory paint, and the oak floorboards were kept varnished until they shone. At home a large grate blew a steady stream of heat from the coal furnace, and down the hall was a newly installed bathroom with running water.

She looked at this raw-beamed, dark attic and searched for some comparison that would find it desirable. She glanced at the snowy-white dresser scarf and doily that were obviously starched and ironed with great meticulousness, at the hand-loomed and tied rug, at the linoleum that looked as if it had just been added for the new teacher, while beside her Nissa waited for some sign of approval.

''It's . . . it's so big!''

''Ya, big all right, but you'll be bumpin' your head on these rafters anyway.''

''It's far bigger than my room at home, and I had to share that with my two sisters.'' *If ever you wanted to be an actress, Linnea, this is the time.* Disguising her disappointment, she crossed the room, looking back over her shoulder. ''Do you mind if I try this out?'' Nissa crossed her hands over her stomach and looked pleased as Linnea sat on the padded chair and rocked widely, throwing her feet in the air. For added effect, she gave a little laugh, massaged the curved arms of the chair, and said truthfully enough, ''At home, with three of us in one room, there wasn't any space left over for rocking chairs.'' She tilted her chin up to look back at the miniature window, as if overjoyed. ''I won't know what to do with all this privacy!'' And she flung her arms wide.

By the time they headed downstairs again, Nissa was beaming with pride.

The kitchen was empty, but Theodore had left her suitcase by the door. Glancing at it, Linnea felt disappointment well afresh. He hadn't even the courtesy to offer to take it upstairs for her, as any gentleman would.

Nissa thoughtfully offered, but Linnea felt suddenly deflated by her dubious welcome into this home.

''Nissa, I don't want to cause friction between you and your son. It might be better if—''

''Nonsense, girl! You leave my son to me!'' And she would have taken the bag upstairs herself if Linnea hadn't quickly done so.

Alone for the first time in the room under the rafters, she set the suitcase on the rag rug and dropped disconsolately onto the bed. Her throat constricted and her eyes suddenly stung.

He's only one man. Only one crabby, bitter old man. I'm a qualified teacher, and an entire school board has approved me. Shouldn't that mean more than his bigoted opinion?

But it hurt.

She'd had such dreams of how it would be when she got here: the open smiles, the welcoming handshakes, the respect—ah, that she wanted most, for at age eighteen she felt she had truly earned the right to be honored not only as a teacher but as an adult. Now here she sat, blubbering like an idiot because the welcome she'd received hadn't matched her expectations. Well, that's what you get for letting yourself be carried away with all your silly imagining. Tears blurred the outline of her suitcase and the cabbage roses and the homemade rag rug.

You had to spoil it, didn't you, Theodore Westgaard?

But I'll show you.

I'll show you!

Chapter 2

The little missy was still upstairs when Theodore stalked out of the house and headed back for the fields. Women! he thought. The only thing worse than having one of them around was having a pair. And what a pair he had now!

He was infuriated by the way his mother had treated him in front of the girl, but what choice did he have except to stand there and take it? And how much longer would he have to put up with her bossing him around? His face burned yet with embarrassment.

She didn't have no right to humiliate him that way! He was a full-grown man, thirty-four years old. And as for her old threat about moving in with John—he wished to high heaven she would!

But at John's house there'd be nobody to butt heads with, and she knew it.

Still disgruntled, Theodore reached the place where two figures, guiding two teams, could be seen in the distance, mowing wheat. He paused and waited at the end of a windrow. There was a measure of ease to be found in watching John and Kristian change the profile of the field. The whirling blades of the sickles sliced away at the thick stand of grain, which appeared burnished gold on top, tarnished along its hewn edge. They cut parallel swaths, with John's rig slightly in the lead, Kristian's close behind, forming a steplike pattern on the edge of the grain as they crept along at a steady, relentless pace.

In time the pair became dots on the horizon, then swung about, returning in Theodore's direction, growing more distinct with each strenuous step the horses made. As they drew closer, he could hear the soft clatter of the wooden sickle bars as they met the bed knife. He watched the stalks topple, and inhaled—nothing sweeter than sweet wheat drying in the sun.

Sweet, too, was the price it would bring this fall. With the war on in Europe, each grain was pure gold in more than just color. Standing in the molten sunlight, watching the reapers bring it down, Theodore thought it a sacrilege that something so beautiful should end up in something so ugly as war. They said the day would come when that wheat might feed Yankee soldiers, but not the way things were going. Though American training camps bulged with restless recruits, word had it they had neither uniforms nor guns. Instead they drilled in civilian clothes armed with broomsticks. And with people all over the country singing songs like "I Didn't Raise My Boy To Be a Soldier," it seemed the only war Theodore had to worry about was the one between himself and that young whippersnapper of a teacher.

He was still pondering the thought when his brother drew up.

John reined in and called, ''Whoa, girls,'' then ponderously stepped down from the iron seat. The horses shook their heads, filling the still afternoon with the jingle of the harness.

''You're back,'' John said, sliding off his straw hat and wiping his receding hairline with a forearm.

''Yeah, I'm back.''

''Did you get him then?''

''Yeah.''

John nodded his head in his customary accepting way. He was a content man, not particularly bright, and not particularly minding. Thirty-eight years old, a little thicker than Theodore at the shoulder, thinner at the pate, and much slower at everything: from finishing chores to angering. He was built big and sturdy and moved with a singular lack of haste at once awkward and graceful. His frame was well-suited to bib overalls, dome-toed boots, and a thick flannel shirt. On the hottest of days he kept his shirt buttoned to the throat and wrist, never complaining about the heat as he never complained about anything, ever. His interests ranged only as far as the edges of the fields, and in them he earned his daily bread at his own unhurried pace. As long as he was able to do that, he asked little more of life. ''Mowin's goin' good,'' he observed now. ''The three of us oughta nearly finish this section before nightfall.'' John hunkered down, balancing on the balls of his feet, letting his eyes range over the field while he chewed a stem of wheat.

As always, it perplexed Theodore that his brother lacked curiosity about the goings-on around him. Yet he did. His contentment was such that it did not occur to him to question or defy. Perhaps it was because of this vagueness that Theodore loved him unquestionably and felt protective toward him.

What goes on in that mind of yours, John, when you hunker all motionless and gaze at the horizon?

''*He* turned out to be a *she,*'' Theodore informed his older brother.

John raised uncomprehending eyes but didn't say a word.

''She's a woman,'' Theodore explained.

''Who's a woman?'' The question came from Kristian who'd drawn abreast and was jumping down from the seat of his machine with a quickness totally opposite that of his uncle. Like the other two men, he was dressed in striped overalls, but beneath them his back was bare and on his head he wore no hat. He had wiry brown arms with dips at the biceps that had only become defined during the past half-year. The sudden spurt of growth had left his neck with a gangly appearance, for his Adam's apple had developed faster than the musculature around it. His face was long and angular, becoming handsomer as each day added flesh to the lengthened bone and brought him closer to maturity. He had his father's brown eyes, though they lacked the cynicism that often stole into Theodore's, and his mother's sensual lower lip, slightly fuller than the upper. When he spoke, his English pronunciation held the slight distortion of a Norwegian who has grown up speaking bilingually.

''The new schoolteacher,'' his father answered with an even more pronounced accent. Theodore paused and considered before adding, ''Well, not exactly a woman. More like a girl pretendin' to be one. She don't look much older than you."

Kristian's eyes widened. "She don't?" He swallowed, glanced in the direction of the house, and asked, "She stayin'?" He understood, without ever having been told in so many words, that his father had an antipathy toward women. He'd heard the old folks talking about it many times when they didn't think "little ears" were around.

"Your grandma took her upstairs and showed her her room, as if she was."

Again Kristian clearly understood—if Grandma said she was staying . . . she was staying!

"What's she like?"

Theodore's chin flattened in disapproval. "Wet behind the ears and sassy as a jaybird."

Kristian grinned. "What's she look like?"

Theodore scowled. "What do you care what she looks like?"

Kristian colored slightly. "I was just askin', that's all."

Theodore's scowl deepened. "She looks puny and mousy," he answered cantankerously, "just like you'd expect a teacher to look. Now let's get back to work."

Supper started late during harvest, for the men stayed out in the fields 'til the last ray of sunlight disappeared, stopping in the late afternoon to do the milking and eat sandwiches to tide them over until they came in for good.

Though Linnea had politely offered to lend a hand with the suppertime preparations, Nissa wouldn't hear of it, brushing her off with a terse declaration: "Teacher rooms *and boards* here. It's part of your pay, ain't it?"

So Linnea decided to explore the place, though there wasn't much to see. Tucked behind the L formed by two granaries she found a pig pen not visible from the house. The chicken coop, tool shed, corncribs, and silo offered little attraction, and it wasn't until she entered the barn that she found anything remotely interesting. It was not the immense, cavernous main body of the building that arrested her, but the tack room. Not even at the livery stable in Fargo had she seen so much leather! There seemed enough to supply a cavalry regiment. But for all the hundreds of loops and lines strung upon the walls, sawhorses, and benches, it had an orderliness and functionalism to rival that of a spider's web.

The tack room was glorious!

It had character. And redolence. And a fettle that made her wonder about the man who kept it so religiously neat. Not a single rein was draped over a narrow metal nail on which it might crimp or crack in time. Instead, they were hung fastidiously on thick wooden pegs with no loose ends allowed to touch the concrete floor. Smaller individual leather lines without hardware were coiled as neatly as lariats—no tangles or snags in sight. An assortment of oval collars trimmed one wall while a pair of saddles straddled a sawhorse wrapped with a thick swath of sheepskin to protect their undersides. A rough bench held tins of liniment and oil and saddle soap arranged as neatly as a druggist's shelf. Hoof trimmers, shears, and curry combs were hung upon their designated nails with fanatic neatness. Near a small west window sat an old scarred chair, stained almost black, with spooled back and arms. There were two paler spots worn in the concave seat, and its legs had been reinforced long ago with strong, twisted wire. Over one of its arms hung a soiled rag, folded precisely in half and draped as neatly as a woman drapes a dishtowel over a towel bar.

Punctilious person, she deduced. All work and no play, she imagined.

Somehow it was irritating to find perfection in such an irascible man. Waiting for him and his son to return from the fields, her stomach growling with hunger, Linnea imagined how she'd put him in his place some day.

With that thought in mind, she went to her room to wash up and recomb her hair before supper. Holding the brush in her hand, she leaned close to the oval mirror in the painted tin frame and whispered as if to more than just her reflection.

"You treat your horses better than you treat women. As a matter of fact, you treat your horses' harnesses better than you treat women!"

Linnea looked indignant at the imagined reply, then she cocked a wrist and touched her fingertips to her heart. *"I'll have you know, Mr. Westgaard, that I have been courted by an actor from the London stage and by a British aviator. I've turned down seven . . . or was it eight . . ."* For a moment her forehead puckered, then she flipped the brush back saucily and flashed a gainsome smile over her shoulder. *"Oh well,"* she finished airily. *"What difference does one little proposal make?"* She laughed in a breathy whisper and went on brushing the hair that fell to her shoulderblades.

"The British aviator took me dancing to the palace, at the special invitation of the queen, on the night before he flew away to bomb a German zeppelin shed in Düsseldorf." She hooked her skirt up high and swayed while tipping her head aside. A dreamy look came over her face. *"Ah, what a night that was."* Her eyes closed and she dipped left, then right, her reflection flashing past the small oval mirror. *"At the end of the evening we rode home in a carriage he'd assigned especially for the occasion."* She sobered and dropped her skirt. *"Alas, he lost his life in the service of his country. It was ever so sad."*

She mourned him a moment, then brightened heroically, adding, *"But at least I have the memory of swirling in his arms to the strain of a Vienna waltz."* She stretched her neck like a swan while lissomely stroking the hair back from her face. *"But then, you wouldn't know about things like that. And anyway, a lady doesn't kiss and tell."* She dropped the brush, picked up a comb, and parted her hair down the middle.

"And then there was Lawrence." Suddenly she spun, bringing her hips to the edge of the commode stand and leaning back provocatively. *"Have I ever told you about Lawrence?"*

The crash of splintering china brought Linnea out of her fantasy with chilling abruptness. The commode stand teetered in its angled place; the pitcher and bowl were no longer in sight.

From downstairs Nissa yelled, "What was that? Are you all right up there?" Footsteps sounded on the stairs.

Horrified, Linnea covered her mouth with both hands and bent over the commode. When Nissa reached the door she found the girl peering into the corner at the pieces of pottery that had been a pitcher and bowl only seconds before.

"What happened?"

Linnea whirled to face the doorway with a stricken expression on her face. "Oh, Mrs. Westgaard, I'm terribly sorry! I . . . I've broken the pitcher and bowl."

Nissa bustled in. "How in tarnation'd it get back there?"

"I . . . I accidentally bumped the stand. I'll pay for it out of my first month's salary." For only a second she wondered how much a pitcher and bowl cost.

"Lawsy, if that ain't a mess. You all right?"

Linnea lifted her skirts and looked down at the wet hem. "A little wet is all."

Nissa began pulling the commode out, but Linnea immediately took over. "Here, I'll clean it up!" When the piece of furniture was turned aside, she saw the shattered pottery and the water running underneath the linoleum, wetting its soft underside. "Oh, my . . ." she wailed, covering her mouth again while tears of embarrassment burned her eyes. "How could I have been so clumsy? I've probably ruined the linoleum, too."

Nissa was already heading downstairs. "I'll get a pail and rag." While she was gone Linnea heard voices outside and glanced through the window to see the men had arrived while she'd been daydreaming. Frantic, she fell to her knees, gathering broken pieces into a pile, stacking them, then using the side of her hand to press the water away from the edge of the linoleum. But the puddle had already made its way underneath, so she lifted the corner . . . which proved to be a mistake. Water sailed down the curve of the linoleum, wetting the skirt over her knees.

"Here, let me do that!" Nissa ordered from the doorway. "Drop them pieces in the pail."

Linnea set the broken pottery in the bottom of the pail with great care, as if gentle handling would somehow improve matters. She swallowed back the tears and felt clumsy and burdensome and disgusted with herself for letting childish whimsy carry her away again and get her into trouble, as it so often did.

When all the pieces had been picked up and Nissa sat back on her heels, Linnea reached to touch the woman's forearm with a woeful expression on her face.

"I . . . I'm so sorry," Linnea whispered. "It was stupid and—"

"Course you're sorry. Nobody likes to look like a fool when they're new to a place. But pitchers are—why, you've cut yourself!" Linnea jerked back her hand to find she'd left blood on Nissa's sleeve.

"Oh, now I've soiled your dress! Can't I do anything right?"

"Don't fret so. It'll wash out. But it looks like that hand is bound to bleed for a spell. I'd best get something to wrap it." She jumped to her feet and disappeared down the stairs. A moment later Linnea heard voices from the kitchen and her mortification redoubled as she realized Nissa was probably telling the men what had just happened.

But the old woman returned without a word of criticism, and wrapped the hand in a clean strip of torn sheet, tying it securely before heading for the steps again. "Fix up your hair now, and be downstairs in five minutes. The boys don't like to be kept waiting."

Unfortunately, Linnea was inexpert at arranging her hair in the new backswept style with *two* good hands; with one bandaged, she was inept. She did her best but was still fussing when Nissa called that supper was ready. Hands still frantically adjusting and ramming hairpins against her skull, Linnea glanced at her skirt—wet knees, wet hem, and no time to change. A peek in the mirror showed that the rat upon which she'd wrapped her hair was off-center. Blast it! She gave it a good yank to the left that only messed it further, and hurriedly reinserted three pins.

"Miss Brandonberg! Supper!"

The boys don't like to be kept waiting.

Giving up, Linnea headed for the stairs, hoping her clattering footsteps sounded jaunty.

When she came into the kitchen from the shadows of the stairwell, she was surprised to find *three* tall, strapping men turning to gawk at her.

The boys?

Theodore, of course, she'd already had the misfortune of meeting. He took one look at her red face, disobedient hair, and wet skirt, and a ghost of a smile tipped up one corner of his mouth. Dismissing him as an uncouth lout, she turned her attention to the others.

"You must be Kristian." He was half a head taller than herself and extremely handsome, with a far kinder and prettier mouth than his father, but with the same deep-brown eyes. His hair was wet and freshly combed, a rich golden brown that would probably dry to near blond. His face shone from a fresh washing, and of the three, he was the only one without a shirt or white line across the top half of his forehead. She extended a hand. "Hello. I'm Miss Brandonberg."

Kristian Westgaard gawked at the face of the new teacher. *Mousy and puny?* Cripes, what had the old man been thinking? He felt the color rush up his bare chest. His heart went *kawhump,* and his hands started sweating.

Linnea watched him turn the color of ripe raspberries as he nervously wiped both palms on his thighs. His Adam's apple bobbed like a cork on a wave. At last he clasped her hand loosely, briefly. "Wow," he breathed. "You mean *you're* gonna be our new teacher?"

Nissa passed by on her way to the table with a bowl of meat, and admonished, "Watch your manners, young man!" at which Kristian's blush rekindled.

Linnea laughed. "I'm afraid so."

Nissa interposed, "And this here's my son John. Lives just across the field over there but eats all his meals with us." She nodded east and moved back to the stove.

Linnea looked up into a face much like Theodore's, though slightly older and with a receding hairline. Shy, hazel eyes; straight, attractive nose, and full lips—nothing at all like Nissa's thin slash of a mouth. He seemed unable to meet her gaze directly or to keep from nervously shifting his feet. His face brightened to poppy red above the hat line, sienna-brown below. His timid eyes flickered everywhere but to her own. At their introduction, he nodded jerkily, decided to extend a hand, got it halfway out, and retracted it in favor of two more nods. By this time, Linnea's hand hung between them. At last he took it in a giant raw-boned paw and pumped once.

"Hello, John," she said simply.

He nodded diffidently, looking at his boots. "Miss." His voice rumbled soft and gruff and very, very bass, like thunder from the next county.

His face was shiny, fresh-scrubbed for supper, and his receding brown hair combed in a fresh peak down the center. He wore faded black pants and red suspenders. The collar of his red plaid shirt was buttoned clear up to the throat, giving him a rather sad, childish look for so big a man. Something warm and protective touched her heart the instant his enormous hand swallowed up her own.

The only one who hadn't spoken to her was Theodore. But she sensed him watching guardedly and decided not to let him off that easily. If he thought manners became inessential when a person aged, she'd show him that one was never too old to be polite.

"And hello again, Mr. Westgaard." She turned and confronted him directly, giving him no alternative but to recognize her.

"Yeah," was all he said, his arms crossed over a blue chambray shirt and black suspenders.

To vex him further, she smiled sweetly and added, "Your mother showed me my room and got me settled in. It'll do very nicely."

With the others looking on, he was forced to bite back a sharp retort. Instead he grumbled, "Well, we gonna stand here yammerin' all night, or we gonna have some supper?"

"It's ready. Let's sit," Nissa put in, moving to place one last bowl on the round oak pedestal table covered with snowy linen. "This'll be your chair." Nissa indicated one positioned between hers and John's, perhaps hoping a little distance between Linnea and Theodore might buffer his antagonism. Unfortunately it put them directly across from each other, and even before Linnea sat she felt his eyes rake her once with palpable displeasure.

When they were all seated, Theodore said, "Let's pray," and clasped his hands, rested his elbows beside his plate, and dropped his forehead to his knuckles. Everyone followed suit, as did Linnea, but when Theodore's deep voice began intoning the prayer, she opened her eyes and peeked around her knuckles in surprise. The prayer was being recited in Norwegian.

She pressed her thumbs against her forehead, watching the corners of his lips move behind his folded hands. To her dismay, he peeked back at her! Their eyes met for only a second, but even in that brief moment there was time for self-consciousness before his glance moved to her bandaged hand. Guiltily she slammed her eyes shut.

She added her amen to the others, and before she could even move her elbows off the tablecloth the most amazing action broke out. As if the end of the prayer signaled the beginning of a race, four sets of hands lashed out to capture four bowls; four serving spoons clattered against four plates—*whack, whack, whack, whack!* Then, like a precision drill, the bowls were passed to the left while each of the Westgaards took the one arriving from their right. Linnea sat agape. Apparently her delay in taking the bowl of corn from John threw a crimp into the works, for suddenly all eyes were on her as she sat empty-handed while John balanced two bowls in his big hands. Silently he nudged her shoulder with the corn bowl, and as she took it Theodore's eyes took in the bandaged hand again.

"What happened to her?" he asked Nissa.

Nissa clapped a mound of potatoes on her plate. "She broke the pitcher and bowl upstairs and cut her hand cleanin' it up."

How dare he talk around me as if I can't answer for myself! Linnea colored as four sets of eyes turned her way and perused the bandaged left hand holding the bowl of corn. The circus picked up again, bowls and spoons passing under her nose until finally it ended as abruptly as it had begun: four pairs of hands clunked down four bowls; four heads bent over four plates; four intense Norwegians started eating with an absorption so exceedingly rude that Linnea could only stare.

She was the last one holding a bowl, and felt as conspicuous as a clown at a wake. Well, manners were manners! She would display those that had been drilled into her all her life and see if a good example would faze these four.

She finished filling her plate and sat properly straight, eating at a sedate pace, using her fork and knife on the delicious beaten beefsteaks that were cooked in rich brown gravy and seasoned with allspice. When her knife wasn't in use, it lay properly across the edge of her plate. Potatoes, corn, coleslaw, bread, butter, and a bevy of relishes rounded out the meal.

The entire Westgaard family gobbled it with their napes up!

And the sounds were horrendous.

Nobody said a word, just dug in and kept digging until the plates began emptying and one by one they asked to have bowls passed to them again. But they did it with the manners of cavemen!

"Spuds!" Theodore commanded, and Linnea watched in disgust as the "spuds" were passed by John, who scarcely looked up while mopping up gravy with a slice of bread, then stuffing it into his mouth with his fingers.

A moment later Kristian followed suit. "Meat!"

His grandmother shoved the meat bowl across the table. Nobody but Linnea saw anything amiss. Minutes passed with more grunts and slurps.

"Corn!"

Linnea was unaware of the stalled action until the sudden silence made her lift her eyes from her plate. Everyone was staring at her.

"I said corn," Kristian repeated.

"Oh, corn!" She grabbed the bowl and shot it across the table to him, too disconcerted to take up the subject of manners on this first night in her new home.

Good lord, did they eat like this all the time?

They fell to their second helpings, giving her time to study them individually.

Nissa, with her little oval spectacles and gray pug head bent over her plate, too. As a mother she had been remiss in teaching manners, but she had indubitable control over her "boys" just the same. Had it been Nissa instead of Theodore who'd decided Linnea was not welcome, she wouldn't be sitting at the supper table now, Linnea was sure.

John. Sitting beside him she felt like a dwarf. His red plaid sleeve rested on the table and his broad shoulders bowed forward like a yoke. She recalled his hesitancy to shake her hand, the red flooding his face as he politely called her "Miss." She would never have to fear John.

Kristian. She had not missed his furtive glances throughout the meal. He'd been sneaking them at her ever since they sat down. He was so big! So grown-up! How awkward it would feel to be his teacher when he towered over her by half a head and had shoulders as wide as a plow horse. Nissa had referred to him as ''Theodore's boy,'' but he was no more boy than his father or his uncle, and it was obvious Kristian had been instantly smitten with her. She'd have to be careful not to encourage him in any way.

Theodore. What made a man so cantankerous and hard to get along with? She'd be a liar to deny she was afraid of this one. But he'd never know it, not if she lived in his house for five years and had to fight him tooth and nail all that time. Inside every hard person hid a softer one; find him and you might, too, find his soul. With Theodore that would undoubtedly be a difficult task, but she aimed to try.

Unexpectedly, he looked up, straight into her eyes, and she was startled to discover that Theodore was no old man. His brown eyes were clear and unlined except for a single white squint line at each corner. In those eyes she saw intelligence and pugnaciousness enough for two, and wondered what it would take to nourish the one and subdue the other. His hair was not the color of sunset over waving ripe rye, as she'd fantasized, but brown and thick, drying now after being slicked back with water, rebelliously springing toward his forehead in willful curls. And neither had he an oversized sunburned nose. It was straight and attractive and tan, like the rest of his face up to within an inch of the hairline where a band of white identified him as the farmer that he was. Unlike John, he wore his collar open. Inside it his neck was sturdy; above it no jowls drooped. When he stubbornly refused to break eye contact with her, she self-consciously dropped her gaze to his arms. Unlike John's, they were exposed to mid-forearm. His wrists were narrow, making both hands and arms appear the more mighty as they swelled above and below. Was he forty? Not yet. Thirty? Most certainly. He had to be to have a son Kristian's age.

Then, with a silent sigh Linnea decided she'd been right after all: somewhere between thirty and forty was very old indeed.

She peeked up again and found him bent low, eating, but still with his gaze pinning her. Flustered, she glanced around the table to find Kristian had been watching the two of them. She flashed him a quick smile and said the first thing that came to mind. ''So you're going to be one of my students, Kristian.''

Everyone at the table stopped forking and chewing while an immense silence fell. They all looked at her as if she'd sprouted fangs. She felt herself blush, but didn't know why. ''Have I said something wrong?''

The pause lengthened, but finally Kristian replied, ''Yes. I mean, no, you ain't said nothin' wrong and yes, you're gonna be my teacher.''

They all fell to eating again, dropping their eyes to their plates while Linnea puzzled over the silence. Again she broke it.

''What grade are you in, Kristian?''

Once again everyone paused, startled by her interruption. Kristian glanced furtively around the table and answered, ''Eighth.''

''Eighth?'' He had to be at least sixteen years old. ''Did you miss some school—I mean, were you ill or anything?''

His eyes were wide and unblinking as he stared at her and the color spread slowly up his chin. ''No. Didn't miss no years.''

"Any years."

"Beg pardon?"

"I didn't miss any years," she corrected.

For a moment he looked puzzled, then his eyes brightened and he said, "Oh! Well, me neither."

She could feel them all looking at her but couldn't figure out what it was they were so surprised about. She was only making polite supper conversation. But none of them had the grace to pick up the conversational ball she'd thrown out. Instead, they all clammed up and continued to stuff their gullets, the only sounds those of ostentatious eating.

Theodore spoke once, when his plate was cleared. He sat back, expanding his chest. "What's for dessert, Ma?"

Nissa brought bread pudding. Stupefied, Linnea watched everybody silently wait for their serving, then return to eating with reintensified interest. Glancing around, studying them, it finally dawned on her: eating was serious business around here. Nobody profaned the sacrosanct gobbling with idle chitchat!

Never in her life had she been treated so rudely at a table. When the meal was over, she was surrounded by a chorus of belches before they all sat back and picked their teeth over cups of coffee.

Not one of them said excuse me! Not even Nissa!

Linnea wondered how Nissa would react if she requested a tray in her room from now on. Most certainly she was disinclined to join them at this table and listen to them all carrying on like pigs at a trough.

But now, it seemed, the inviolable rite was done. Theodore pushed back and spoke directly to Linnea.

"You'll want to see the school building tomorrow."

What she really wanted to see tomorrow was the inside of a train taking her back home to Fargo. She hid her disillusionment and answered with as much enthusiasm as she could muster, "Yes, I'd like to see what books I'll have to work with, and what supplies I'll have to order."

"We milk at five and have breakfast right after. Be ready to go soon as breakfast is done. I can't waste time comin' in from the fields in the middle of the mornin' to haul you down there and give you no tour."

"I'll gladly walk. I *know* where the school building is."

He sipped his coffee, swallowed loudly, and said, "It's part of what they pay me for, showin' the new teacher the school building and telling him what his duties are soon as he gets here."

She felt the damnable blush creeping up, no matter how she tried to stop it. And though she knew it would have been better to ignore his jibe, she couldn't.

"He?" she repeated pointedly.

"Oh . . ." Theodore's eyes made an insolent tour of her lopsided hairstyle. "She. I forgot."

"Does this mean I'm staying? Or do you still intend to *dump me off* on Oscar Knutson when you manage to run him down?"

He sat back lazily, an ankle crossing a knee, and wielded the toothpick in a way that pulled his upper lip askew, all the while studying her without smiling.

At last he said, "Oscar don't have no room for you."

"*Doesn't* have *any* room for me." It was out before she could control the urge to set him down a notch.

He slowly pulled the toothpick from his mouth, and his lip fell into place, but it thinned in anger, and she saw with satisfaction the blush begin to creep up his face, too. Though she knew he fully understood he was having his speech corrected, she couldn't resist adding insult to injury. "Don't and no are double negatives, thus it's incorrect to say Oscar don't have no room. Oscar *doesn't* have any room for me."

The white stripe near his hairline turned brilliant red and he lunged to his feet, the chair scraping back on the bare wood floor as he pointed a long, thick finger at her nose. "He sure as hell don't, so I'm stuck with you! But stay out of my way, missy, you understand!"

"Theodore!" his mother yelped, but he was already slamming out the door. When he was gone, the silence around the table became deadly and Linnea felt tears of mortification sting her eyes. She glanced at the faces around her. Kristian's and John's were beet red. Nissa's was white with anger as she stared at the door.

"That boy don't know no manners atall, talking to you like that!" his mother ranted.

"I . . . I'm sorry. I shouldn't have goaded him. It was my fault."

"Naw, it was not," Nissa declared, rising and beginning to clear away the dishes with angry motions. "He just got ugly inside when—" She stopped abruptly, glanced at Kristian, who was staring at the tablecloth. "Aw, it's no use tryin' to straighten him out," she finished, turning away.

To Linnea's surprise, John made the one gesture of conciliation. He began to reach for her arm as if to lay a comforting hand on it, drew back just in time, but offered in his deep, slow voice, "Aw, he don't mean nothing by it, Miss."

She looked up into friendly, shy eyes and somehow realized that John's brief reassurance had been tantamount to an oration, for him. She reached out to touch his arm lightly. "I'll try to remember that the next time I cross swords with him. Thank you, John."

His gaze dropped to her fingers, and he flushed brilliant red. Immediately she withdrew her hand and turned to Kristian. "Would you mind taking me to the school tomorrow, Kristian? That way I won't have to bother your father."

His lips opened, but nothing came out. He flashed a quick glance at his uncle, found no help for whatever was bothering him, and finally swallowed and smiled broadly, growing pink in the cheeks yet again. "Yes, ma'am."

Relieved, she released a breath she hadn't realized she'd been holding. "Thank you, Kristian. I'll be ready directly after breakfast."

He nodded, watching her rise to pick up a handful of dishes. "Well, I'd better lend Nissa a hand with cleaning up."

But even before she'd gotten to her feet, she was being excused.

"Teachers don't clean up!" Nissa informed her. "Evenin's are your own. You'll need 'em for correctin' papers and such."

"But I have no papers to correct yet."

"G'won!" Nissa flapped a hand as if shooing away a fly. "Git out from underfoot. I'll tend to the cleanin' up. I always have."

Linnea paused uncertainly. "You're sure?"

Nissa peered up at her from behind her oval lenses while reaching for the empty cups and saucers. "Do I strike you as a person who ain't never sure of things?"

That made Linnea smile again. "Very well, I promised my mother I'd write to her immediately after I arrived and let her know I'd made it without mishap."

"Fine! Fine! You go do that."

Upstairs she lit the kerosene lantern and studied her room again, but it was as disappointing as ever. Nissa had replaced the pitcher and bowl with a blue-speckled wash basin. The sight of it brought back Linnea's disappointment not only in the room and the Westgaard family but in herself. She wanted so badly to act mature, had promised herself time and again that she'd give up those childish flights of whimsy that forever got her into trouble. But she hadn't been here thirty minutes and look what she'd done. She swallowed back tears.

From her first thirty dollars a month she'd have to pay the price of a new pitcher and bowl. But worse, she'd made a fool of herself. That was hard enough to face without having to confront Theodore's antagonism at every turn.

The man was truly despicable!

Forget him. Everyone told you becoming an adult wasn't going to be easy, and you're finding out they were right.

To put Theodore from her mind, she took up a wooden stationery box and sat on her bed.

> Dear Mother and Father, Carrie and Pudge,
>
> I have arrived in Alamo all safe and sound. The train ride was long and uneventful. When I arrived I searched the horizon for a town, but found to my dismay only three elevators and a handful of sorry buildings I would scarcely classify as a "town." Yes, Daddy, you warned me it would be small. But I hadn't expected this!
>
> I was met at the station by Mr. Westgaard, who escorted me to his farm, which appears to be of immense proportions like all the others out here, so big we tried to find one of his neighbors working in the field, but could not. Mr. Westgaard—Theodore is his first name—lives here with his mother, Nissa (a little bandy-legged spitfire whom I loved immediately), and his son, Kristian (who will be my eighth-grade student, but is half a head taller than I), and Theodore's brother, John (who comes here at mealtimes but the rest of the time lives at his own farm, which is the next one up the road to the east).
>
> We had a delicious first supper of steak and gravy, potatoes, corn, bread and butter and bread pudding and more relishes than I've ever seen on a table in my life, after which Nissa would not allow me to lift a finger to help her clean up—Carrie and Pudge, I know you're green with envy because I don't have to do dishes anymore! And now I'm settled into my very own private room with nobody to tell me to put out the light when I'd rather read a little longer. Imagine that, a room of my own for the first time in my life.

But then she glanced around that room, at the bare rafters overhead, the minuscule window, the commode where the new blue washbasin stood. She remembered the untarnished optimism she'd felt while riding toward her new home on the train, and her immediate disillusionment from the moment Theodore Westgaard had opened his mouth and declared, ''I ain't havin' no woman in my house!'' She glanced at the letter from which she had carefully winnowed all the disappointments and misgivings of her first six hours as the ''the new teacher,'' and suddenly the world seemed to topple in on her.

She curled into a ball and wept miserably.

Oh, Mother and Daddy, I miss you so much. I wish I was back home with all of you, where suppertime was filled with gaiety and talk and loving smiles. I wish I could pick up the dishtowel and complain loudly about having to help Carrie and Pudge before I was excused from the kitchen. I wish all three of us girls were back together, crowded into our pretty little flowered bedroom with the two of you siding against me when I wanted to leave the lights on just a little longer.

What am I doing out here in the middle of this godforsaken prairie, with this strange family, so filled with anger and reticence and a total disdain for manners?

I wish I had listened to you, Daddy, when you said I should stay closer to home my first year, until I knew how I liked independence. If I were there, I'd be sharing all this with you and Mother right now, instead of burying the hurts inside and sobbing out my sorrow in this sad little attic bedroom.

But she loved her family too much to tell them the truth and give them the burden of worrying about her when there was nothing they could do to comfort her.

And so, much later, when she discovered her tears had fallen upon the ink and left two blue puddles, she resolutely dried her eyes and started the letter again.

Chapter 3

By tradition, the school year officially began on the first Monday of September. Linnea had arrived on the Friday preceding it. Saturday hadn't quite dawned, when some faraway sound awakened her and she groggily checked her surroundings in the muted lavender light of the loft.

For a moment she was disoriented. Overhead were the unfinished beams of a roof. She groaned and rolled over. Oh yes . . . her new home in Alamo. She had slept poorly in the strange bed. She was tempted to drop off for a few more precious winks, but just then she heard activity below, and remembered the events of yesterday.

Well, Miss Brandonberg, drag your bones out of here and show 'em what you're made of.

The water in the basin was cold, and she wondered if she'd run into Theodore or Kristian if she sneaked down to warm it. Maybe nobody'd lit a fire yet: a glance at the window told her it was very early. She eyed the stovepipe, scurried out of bed, and touched it. Ah, someone had been up a while. She drew on her blue flannel wrapper, buttoned it to the throat, tied it at the waist, and took her speckled washbasin downstairs.

She tried to be very quiet, but the stairs creaked.

Nissa's head popped around the doorway. Her hair was already in its tight little bun, and she wore a starched white ankle-length apron over a no-nonsense dress of faded gray and red flowered muslin.

"You up already?"

"I . . . I don't want to keep anybody waiting this time."

"Breakfast won't be for a good hour yet. The boys got ten cows to milk."

"Are they . . ." She glanced above Nissa's head and pressed the basin tighter against her hip. "Outside already?"

"Coast is clear. Come on down." Nissa dropped her eyes to the bare toes curled over the edge of the step. "Ain't you got no slippers for them bare feet?"

Linnea straightened her toes and looked down. "I'm afraid not." She didn't want to mention that at home she'd only had to slip down the hall to reach the lavatory.

"Well, appears I better get out my knitting needles first chance I get. Come on down 'fore you fall off your perch. Water's hot in the reservoir."

In spite of Nissa's brusque, autocratic ways, Linnea liked her. The kitchen, with her in it, became inviting. She whirled around in her usual fashion, reminding Linnea of the erratic flight of a goldfinch—darting this way and that with such abrupt turns that it seemed she wasn't done with one task before heading for the next.

She lifted a lid from the gargantuan cast-iron stove that dominated the room, tossed in a shovelful of coal from a hod sitting alongside, rammed the lid back in place, and spun toward the pantry all in a single motion. Watching her, Linnea almost became dizzy.

In a moment Nissa breezed back, pointing to a water pail sitting on a long table against one wall. "There! Use the dipper! Take what you need! I draw the line when it comes to givin' the teacher a bath!"

Linnea laughed and thought if she had to put up with some nettlesome tempers around here, Nissa would more than make up for it. Upstairs again, all washed, with the bandage removed from her hand and her hair done in a perfect, flawless coil around the back of her head, Linnea felt optimistic once more.

She owned five outfits: her traveling suit of charcoal-gray wool serge with its shirtwaist of garnet-colored silk, a brown skirt of Manchester cloth bound at the hem with velvet and a contrasting white-yoked shirtwaist, a forest-green skirt of twilled Oxford with three inverted plaits down the back and a Black Watch plaid shirtwaist to match, a navy-blue middy dress with white piping around the collar, and an ordinary gray broadcloth skirt and plain white shirtwaist with no frills except a pair of narrow ruffles dropping at an inward angle from each shoulder toward her waist.

The suit was strictly for Sundays. The middy made her look childish. The Manchester cloth would be too warm yet, stiffened as it was with percaline. And she was saving the new green skirt for the first day of school because it had been a gift from her parents and was the most adult of all her outfits. So she chose the utilitarian gray skirt and plain white blouse. When she was dressed, she eyed herself critically.

Her hair was perfect. Her skirt was dry. Her bandage gone. Her clothing sensible, sober, even matronly. What could he possibly find to fault her for?

Suddenly she realized what she was thinking, and her chin took on a stubborn thrust. Why should I have to worry about pleasing an old grouch like Theodore? He's my *land*lord, not my lord!

She returned downstairs to find breakfast cooking, the table set, but the men still absent.

"Well, look at you! Now don't you look pretty!"

"Do I?" Linnea smoothed the front of her white shirtwaist and looked at Nissa uncertainly. "Do I look old enough?"

Nissa hid a smile and gave the girl a thorough inspection over the tops of her wire-rimmed spectacles. "Oh, you look old, all right. Why, I'd say you look at least . . . oh . . . nineteen, anyway."

"Do I really!"

Nissa had all she could do to keep from chuckling at the girl's pleased expression, then Linnea's tone lowered confidentially. "I'll tell you something, Nissa. Ever since I saw Kristian I've been awfully worried about looking younger than some of my students."

"Aw, go on," Nissa growled, pulling her chin low. "You might even look twenty in that crisp little skirt. Turn around here. Let me get a gander at the back." Linnea turned a slow circle while Nissa rubbed her chin studiously. "Yup! Twenty for sure!" she lied.

Again Linnea beamed, but the smile was followed by another sober expression as her hands pressed her waistband and she looked as if she were about to admit to a horrible crime. "I sometimes have . . . well, a little trouble, you might say. Acting grown up, I mean. My father used to scold me for being daydreamy and forgetting what I was about. But since I've been to Normal School I've been trying really hard to look mature and remember that I'm a lady. I thought the skirt helped."

Nissa's heart warmed toward the youngster. There she stood, all dressed in grown-up clothes, trying to act like she was ready to face the world, when she was scared out of her britches.

"I reckon you're going to miss your family. We're a strange bunch here, lots of new things to get used to."

"Why, no! I mean . . . well, yes, I'm sure I'll miss them, but—"

"You just remember," Nissa interrupted. "Ain't nothing stubborner nor bullheadeder than a bunch of hardheaded Norwegians. And that's about all there is around here. But you're the schoolteacher! You got a certificate says you're smarter than all the rest of 'em, so when they start givin' you sass, you just stand up square and spit in their eye. They'll respect *that!*"

Giving me sass? Linnea silently quailed. Were they all going to be like Theodore?

As if the thought materialized him, Theodore stepped through the door, followed by Kristian.

Catching sight of her, Theodore paused a moment before moving to the pail and washbasin. Kristian stopped in his tracks and openly stared.

"Good morning, Kristian."

"G . . . good morning, Miss Brandonberg."

"Goodness, you *do* get up early."

Kristian felt like he'd swallowed a cotton wad. Not a word came out while he stood rooted, admiring his teacher's fresh young face and pretty brown hair, all slicked up spruce and neat above a skirt and blouse that made her waist look thin as a willow whip.

"Breakfast is ready," Nissa advised, moving around him. "Quit your dawdling."

At the basin Theodore soaped his hands and face, rinsed, and turned around with the towel in his hands to find his son standing like a fencepost, gawking at the little missy who looked about thirteen years old again this morning. She even stood like a girl, her prim little shoes planted side by side. Her hair wasn't bad though, all hoisted up into a clever female puff that made her neck look long and graceful.

Theodore put a tight clamp on the thought and said, "The basin's yours, Kristian," then turned his back on the teacher again.

"Good morning, Theodore," she said, somehow managing to make him feel like a fool for not having said it first. He turned back to her.

" 'Morning. I see you're ready in time."

"Most certainly. Punctuality is the politeness of kings," she offered, and turned toward the table.

Punk-what? he thought, feeling ignorant and rightfully put in his place as he watched her take her chair.

"Didn't John help you this morning?" she asked, forcing him to talk to her when he didn't want to. He plunked himself down with a surly expression on his face, at the same chair he'd taken last night.

"John's got his own livestock to tend to. Kristian and me milk our cows, he milks his."

"I thought he ate all his meals here."

"He'll be along in a minute."

Nissa brought a platter of fresh bacon, another of toast, and five bowls containing something that looked like hot school paste. While Theodore said the prayer—again in Norwegian—Linnea stared down into her bowl and wondered what it was. It had no smell, no color, and no attraction. But when the prayer ended, she watched the others to see what she was supposed to do with the glutinous mess. They slathered theirs with pure cream and sugar, then decorated it with butter, so she followed suit and cautiously took a taste.

It was delicious! It tasted like vanilla pudding.

John came in shortly after the meal had begun. Though they all exchanged good mornings, Linnea's was the only one that included a pause in her eating and the addition of a smile. He blushed immediately and fumbled to his chair without risking another glance at her.

Like last night, the meal was accompanied by serious smacking and no conversation. Testing her theory, Linnea said, loud and clear, "This is very good."

Everybody tensed and stopped with their spoons halfway to their mouths. Nobody muttered a word. When their jaws started working again, she asked the table at large, "What is it?"

They all looked at her as if she were a dolt. Theodore chortled and took another mouthful.

"What do you mean, what is it?" Nissa retorted. "It's *romograut.*"

Linnea tipped her head to one side and peered at Nissa. "It's what?"

This time Theodore answered. "*Romograut.*" He gestured toward her bowl with his spoon. "Don't you know what *romograut* is?"

"If I did, would I have asked?"

"No Norwegian has to ask what *romograut* is."

"Well, I'm asking. And I'm only half Norwegian—my father's half. Since my mother was the cook, we ate a lot of Swedish foods."

"Swedish!" three people denounced at once. If there was a Norwegian born who didn't think himself one step better than any Swede on earth, he wasn't in this room.

"It's flour cereal," Linnea was informed.

They were in a hurry to get on with the day's work, so she was spared the burping session at the end of the meal. As soon as the bowls and platter were empty, Theodore pushed his chair back and announced peremptorily, "I'll take you to school now. Get your bird wings if you need 'em."

Her temper went up like a March kite. What was it about the man that gave him such pleasure in persecuting her? Happily, this time she had an answer she was more than elated to give.

"You won't have to bother. I've asked Kristian to take me."

Theodore's eyebrows lifted speculatively and his glance shifted between the two. "Kristian, huh?"

Kristian's face lit up like a beacon and he shuffled his feet. "It won't take long, and I'll hurry back to the field soon as I get her there."

"You do that. It'll save me the trouble." And without another word, he left the house. Linnea's glare followed him out the door, and when she turned, she found Nissa watching her shrewdly. But all Nissa said was, "You'll need cleaning supplies and a ladder to reach them windows, and I packed you a lunch. I'll get it."

Kristian drove her to school in the same wagon she'd ridden in before. They hadn't gone twenty feet down the road before Linnea totally forgot about Theodore. It was a heavenly morning. The sun was up a finger's width above the horizon, peering from behind a narrow strip of purple that dissected it like a bright ribbon, making it appear all the more orange as its golden rays radiated above and below. Its oblique angle lit the tops of the grain fields to a lustrous gold, making the wheat appear a solid mass, unmoving now in the windlessness of early day. The air was fragrant with the smell of it. And all was still—so still. The call of a meadowlark came lilting to them with clarion precision and the horses perked up their ears, but moved on as before, their rhythm never changing. In a field on the left several sunflowers lifted their golden heads.

''Oh look!'' She pointed. ''Sunflowers. Aren't they beautiful?''

Kristian eyed her askance. For a schoolteacher, she didn't know much about sunflowers. ''My pa cusses 'em.''

She turned to him, startled. ''Whatever for? Look at them, taller than all the rest, lifting their faces to the sun.''

''They're pests around here. Get 'em in a wheat field, and you'll never get rid of 'em.''

''Oh.''

They rode on. After a minute she said, ''I guess I have a lot to learn about farms and such. I may have to rely on you to teach me.''

''Me!'' He turned amazed brown eyes on her.

''Well, would you mind?''

''But you're the teacher.''

''In school. Out of school, I guess there's a lot I can learn from you. What's that?''

''Russian thistle,'' he answered, following the path of her finger to a patch of pale-greenish blossoms.

''Ah.'' She digested that a moment before adding, ''Don't tell me. Theodore cusses it too, right?''

''It's more of a pest than sunflowers,'' he verified.

Her eyes strayed behind, lingering on the blossoms as the wagon passed. ''But there's beauty to be found in many things, even when they're pests. We just have to take a second look. Perhaps I'll have the children paint pictures of Russian thistle before winter comes.''

He didn't quite know what to make of a girl—a woman?—who thought Russian thistle was pretty. He'd heard it damned all his life. Oddly enough, he found himself craning to look back at it. When she caught him, she smiled brightly and he felt confused. ''That there's John's place,'' he offered as they passed it.

''So I've been told.''

''I got aunts and uncles and cousins scattered all over around here,'' he volunteered, surprising himself because he'd always been tongue-tied around girls before. But he found he enjoyed talking to her. ''About twenty of 'em or so, not counting the greats.''

''The greats?''

''Great aunts and uncles. Got a few of them, too.''

''Crimany!'' she exclaimed. ''Twenty?''

His head snapped around in surprise and he smiled wide. He hadn't imagined a schoolteacher saying *crimany* that way.

Realizing what she'd said, she clapped a hand over her mouth. Realizing she'd clapped a hand over her mouth, she dropped it, looked at her lap, and nervously smoothed her skirt. ''I guess I have to watch myself, don't I? Sometimes I forget I'm the teacher now.''

And for the moment, Kristian forgot, too. She was only a girl he wanted to help down from a wagon when they drew up in the schoolyard. But he'd never done it before and wasn't certain how a man went about these things. Did he tell her to stay put while he hustled around to her side? What if she laughed? Some girls he knew would have laughed at him—girls laughed at the strangest things. The idea of taking Miss Brandonberg's hand made him feel all flustered and queer in the stomach.

In the end he deliberated too long and she leaped to the ground with a sprightly bounce, promising herself she'd do something about the manners of the Westgaard men if it was her only accomplishment here.

From the back of the wagon Kristian grabbed the ladder and followed her across the school grounds while she carried a bucket and rags.

At the door she spun to face him. "Oh, we forgot the key!"

He looked at her in amazement. "The door ain't locked. Nobody locks their doors around here." He leaned over and placed the ladder next to the foundation.

"They don't?" She glanced back at the door. In the city, doors were locked.

"Naw. It's open. You can go right in."

As she reached for the doorknob her heart lifted expectantly. She had waited for this moment for years. She'd known since she was eight years old that she wanted to be a teacher. And not in a city school. In a school just like this one, a building all her own, where she and she alone had responsibility for the education of her charges.

She opened the door and stepped into a cloakroom—a shallow room running the width of the building, with an unfinished wooden floor and a single window on each end. Straight ahead was a pair of closed doors. To the left and right of them were scarred wooden benches and above them metal hooks for coats and jackets. In the far left corner stood a square table painted pale blue upon which stood an inverted pottery jar with a red wing design baked into its side and a wooden spigot, much like a wine cask. The floor beneath the spigot was gray from years and years of drips.

She glanced to her right. In the corner leaned a broom, and from a nail above hung a big brush by its wooden handle. She glanced up. Above her head the bell rope hung from the cupola, the huge knot at its end looped over a nail beside the wide white double doors leading straight ahead to the main body of the school.

Slowly she set down her pail.

Just as slowly she opened the doors, then stood a moment, rapt. It was totally silent, totally ordinary. But it smelled of chalk dust and challenge, and if Linnea Brandonberg thought as a girl regarding many things, she embraced this challenge with all the responsibility of a full adult.

"Oh, Kristian, look . . ."

He had seen the schoolroom a thousand times before. What he looked at was the new teacher as her wide, eager eyes scanned the room.

The sun streamed in through the long narrow windows, lighting the rows of desks bolted to their wooden runners. Wall lanterns with tin reflectors hung between the windows. Dead center was a two-burner cast-iron stove, its stack new and glossy, heading up through the tin wainscot ceiling. At the front of the room was a raised platform that, to her disappointment, held no desk, but a large rectangular table holding nothing more than a single kerosene lantern. There was a wooden chair and behind it a tiny bookshelf filled with volumes whose spines had faded into pastel shades of rose, blue, and green. There was a globe, a retractable map—tightly rolled—and blackboards on the front wall, with recitation benches on either side.

Her heart tripped in excitement. It was no different from a thousand others like it in a thousand other similar country settings. But it was hers!

Miss Brandonberg.

The thought made her giddy, and she moved across the length of the room, her skirts lifting a fine layer of dust. Her footsteps startled a mouse that came running toward her, then darted quickly in the opposite direction.

She halted in surprise and sucked in a quick breath. "Oh look! It seems we have company."

Kristian had never before seen a girl who didn't yelp in fright at the sight of a mouse.

"I'll get a trap from home and set it for you."

"Thank you, Kristian. I'm afraid if we don't, he'll eat up the books and papers—if he hasn't already."

At random she chose a book from the shelf. She let it fall open where it would. Petroleum, it said. She forgot about the mouse hole chewed at the edge of the pages and faced Kristian while reading aloud, "The observation that Horace Greeley made that 'the man who makes two blades of grass grow where only one grew before is a benefactor to his race' finds an analogy in the assertion that he who practically adds to the space of man's life by increasing the number of hours wherein he can labor or enjoy himself is also a benefactor. The nineteenth century marked its course by a greater number of inventions, discoveries, and improvements, promotive of human civilization and happiness, than any like period that preceded it, and perhaps no feature of its record was more significant or beneficent than the improved methods of lighting our dwellings brought into use largely through the instrumentality of the great light bearer—petroleum."

She slapped the book closed and the sound reverberated through the room while she inhaled deeply, standing straight as a nail. He stared at her, wondering how a person could possibly learn to read such words, much less understand what they meant. He thought he had never known a smarter or prettier girl in his life, and welcomed the queer, light-bellied feeling that she inspired.

"I am going to love it here," she said with quiet intensity, pinning Kristian with a beaming blue-eyed look of great resolve.

"Yes, ma'am," Kristian answered, unable to think of anything else to say. "I'll show you the rest, then I got to get back to the fields."

"The rest?"

"Outside. Come on." He turned and led the way through the door.

"Kristian." At his name he stopped and turned.

"It's never too early to begin teaching each other, is it?"

"No, Miss Brandonberg, I guess not."

"Then let's begin with the oldest rule of all. Ladies first."

He blushed the color of a wild rose, hung a thumb from the rear pocket of his overalls, and backed up, waiting for her to pass before him. As she did, she said politely, "Thank you, Kristian. You may leave the door open behind us. It's stuffy in here."

Outside he showed her the pump and the empty coal shed, little more than a lean-to against the west wall of the building. The wheat fields crowded the edge of the school property to the north and east. To the west stood a tall row of cottonwoods, beneath which were the wooden privies with lattice walls guarding their entrances. The playground had two rope swings supported by a thick wooden spar, and a teeter-totter, also homemade of a rough plank. On the east side of the building was a flat grassy stretch that looked like it was used as a ball diamond.

When they'd explored the entire schoolyard, Linnea lifted her eyes to the tip of the cupola and said impulsively, "Let's ring the bell, Kristian, just to see what it sounds like."

"I wouldn't do that, Miss Brandonberg. Ring it and you'll have every farmer off his rig and running to help."

"Oh. It's a distress signal?"

"Yes, ma'am. Same as the church bell, but that's three miles in the other direction." He thumbed toward the west.

She felt childish once again for having made the suggestion. "I'll just have to wait until Monday then. How many students will I have?"

"Oh, that's hard to say. A dozen. Fourteen maybe. Most of 'em's my cousins."

"Your life's been a lot different than mine, growing up with so much family so close around. All of my grandparents are dead, and there are no aunts and uncles in this part of the country, so mostly it's been my parents and my two sisters and me."

"You got sisters?" he asked, surprised. He felt honored at being told something so personal.

"Two of them. One is your age—Carrie. The other one is four years younger. Her real name is Pauline, but she's at that age—you know—when girls sometimes get rather round and roly-poly." Suddenly she struck a pose, bulging out her cheeks with a big puff of breath until her lips almost disappeared and she waddled and pretended to hold a fat belly. "So we call her Pudge."

He laughed, and she did the same.

No, he really didn't know much at all about how girls changed. He'd never paid any attention to them before. Except to avoid them at every turn.

Until now.

Miss Brandonberg sobered and went on. "She doesn't like it when we tease her, and I suppose sometimes we do it too much, but both Carrie and I went through the same stage and had to put up with teasing, and it didn't hurt either of us."

It was hard for him to imagine her pudgy. She was thin and small-boned, one of the most perfect females he'd ever seen.

"Aw, you was never pudgy."

"*Were* never pudgy," she corrected automatically, then added, "Oh, yes I was. I'm glad you didn't see me then!"

Suddenly he realized how long he'd been here dawdling away the time with her. He glanced toward the fields, hooked his thumbs in his back pockets, and swallowed. "Well, if there's nothing else you need, I . . . I got to get back to help Pa and Uncle John."

She spun around quickly and motioned him away. "Oh, of course, Kristian. I can get along just fine now. I have plenty to do to keep me busy. Thank you for bringing me down and showing me around."

When Kristian was gone she went back inside and eagerly set to work. She spent the morning sweeping and scrubbing the floor, dusting the desks, and washing windows. At midday she took a break and sat on the front steps to dig into the lunch Nissa had packed for her in a small tin molasses pail. Munching a delicious sandwich made with some mysterious meat she'd never tasted before, Linnea relaxed in the sun and dreamed about Monday and how exciting it would be when she faced her first group of children. She imagined some would be eager, receptive, while others would be timid and needing encouragement, and still others would be bold and needing restraining.

The thought brought to mind John and Theodore, so different from one another. *Don't ruin your day with thoughts of Theodore,* she scolded herself. But when she had wandered down to the pump to get a drink of cold water to wash down her sandwich, she found herself gazing west. All the fields for as far as she could see belonged to the two of them. Somewhere out there they were cutting wheat, Kristian along with them.

The land out here was so vast, treeless for the most part. To some it would seem desolate, but Linnea, gazing at the clear blue sky and munificent plains, saw only bounty and beauty.

Her mother always told her she had the gift for finding the good in anything. Perhaps it had something to do with her imagination. In the worst of times she always had an escape ready at hand. Lately, her mother had agreed with her father that it was time to give up such child's play. But fantasy was magic. It took her places she'd never see any other way. It gave her feelings she'd never experienced any other way. And it made her happy.

She wiped the cool water from her lips with the back of a hand and did a dance step across the schoolyard. She leaped onto a swing, sending it into motion, then leaning back and pumping, let herself glide into her own magical world again.

"Well, hello, Lawrence. I hadn't expected to see you so soon again."

Lawrence was dressed like a real dandy today, in a spiffy straw hat, a red and white striped shirt, and bright scarlet sleevebands. He had a way of standing with all his weight on one leg, one hip jutting, that often provoked her to flutter her eyelashes.

"I came to take you on a picnic."

"Oh, don't be silly—I can't frolic off across a field to have a picnic with you. I have school to teach, and besides, the last time you left me with the mess to explain. I was very displeased with you." She pouted as prettily as possible.

Lawrence stepped behind the swing and stopped it, putting his hands on her waist as if to make her step down off the wooden seat.

"I know a place where nobody will find us," he said in a low, encouraging invitation.

She clung to the ropes and laughed teasingly, the sound lilting across the meadow . . .

Superintendent of schools, Frederic Dahl, guided his horse and buggy into the driveway of Public School 28 and found a most arresting sight waiting to greet him. A lissome young girl dressed in a full gray skirt and white shirtwaist clung to the rope of a swing high above her head, twisting it like a pretzel, first left, then right.

Across the grass he thought he heard a laugh, but a quick check of the surrounding area told him nobody else was in sight. The swing came unwound. She dipped her knees and set it in motion, then let her head hang back.

She was talking to someone—but to whom?

He halted the horse, secured the reins, and stepped from the carriage. As he approached, he could see that the girl was older than he thought, for with her arms upraised, he detected the shape of her breasts.

"Hello!" he called.

Linnea jerked upright and looked over her shoulder. *Crimany, caught again!* She leaped down, brushed at her skirts, and blushed.

"I'm looking for Mister Brandonberg."

"Yes, it seems like everybody is, but you'll have to settle for me. I'm *Miss* Brandonberg."

His face registered surprise, but no displeasure. "And I'm Superintendent Dahl. My mistake for not clarifying the point in our correspondence. Well, this is a pleasant surprise!"

Superintendent Dahl! Her face grew hotter and she immediately began rolling down the sleeves of her shirtwaist. "Oh, Superintendent Dahl, I'm sorry. I didn't realize it was you!"

"I've come to bring your supplies and make sure you're settled in all right."

"Oh, yes, of course. Come inside. I . . ." She laughed nervously and gestured at her rather soiled skirt. "I was cleaning, so excuse the way I look."

Cleaning? he thought, glancing back over his shoulder as they moved toward the building. But still he found nobody else about. Inside, a ladder leaned against the wall, and the raw wood floor was still damp. She whirled to face him, clasping her hands and exclaiming, "I love it! My first school, and I'm so excited! I want to thank you for recommending me to the school board here."

"You've earned your certificate. Don't thank me. Are you satisfied with your lodging at the Westgaards?"

"I . . . I . . ." She didn't want him to think he'd hired a complainer. "Yes, they're fine. Just fine!"

"Very well. I'm required to make an annual inspection of the property each year at this time, so you go about your work and I'll join you when I've finished."

She watched him walk away, smiling at the real Mr. Dahl, who was nothing at all like the dashing swain she'd imagined. He was scarcely more than five feet tall, about as big around as a rain barrel, and had balded so perfectly his head appeared tonsured. The circlet of hair he hadn't lost was bright rust colored and stuck out like a May Day wreath above his ears.

When he'd gone outside, she rested an arm across her stomach, covered her smile with one hand, and chuckled softly.

Some knights in shining armor you dream up, Miss Brandonberg. First Theodore Westgaard and now this.

He inspected the outside of the building, the coal shed, even the privies, before he returned inside to do the same. When he was finished, he asked, ''Has Mr. Westgaard mentioned the coal?''

''Coal?'' she asked blankly.

''Since the Blizzard of '88, when some schools were caught unprepared, there's been a law that there must be enough wood or coal on hand before the first of October to see you through till spring.''

She hadn't an inkling about the coal. ''I'm sorry, I didn't know. Does Mr. Westgaard supply the coal?''

''He always has in the past. That's got to do with an arrangement between him and the school board. They can pay whoever they want to bring in the coal, but it's my job to see that the arrangements are made.''

''Mr. Westgaard is working somewhere in the fields. You might be able to find him and ask him.''

He made a notation in a ledger he carried, and replied, ''No, that's not necessary. I'll be making my circuit again within two weeks, and I'll make a note here to remind myself to check on it then. In the meantime, I'd appreciate it if you'd remind him about it.''

She really didn't want to have to remind Theodore Westgaard about anything, but she nodded and assured Mr. Dahl she'd see to the matter.

He had brought her supplies: chalk, ink, and a brand-new teacher's grade book. She held it reverently, running a palm over its hard red cover. As he watched, he saw beyond the frivolous child who'd been daydreaming on the swing when he drove up. He had a feeling about this one: she'd be dedicated.

''As you know, Miss Brandonberg, school is in session from nine in the morning until four in the afternoon, and your duties include building the fire early enough to have the building warm when the children arrive, keeping it clean at all times, doing the necessary shoveling, and becoming an integral part of the community life around you so that you get to know the families whose children you teach. The last you'll find easiest of all. These are good people. Honest, hard-working. I believe you'll find them cooperative and helpful. If you're ever in need of something and can't reach me fast enough, ask them. I think you'll find nobody gets as much respect around here as the local teacher.''

As long as he's a man, she thought. But, of course, she didn't say it. They wished each other good-bye, and she watched Mr. Dahl walk back toward his buggy. But before he reached it, she shaded her eyes with one hand and called, ''Oh, Mr. Dahl?''

''Yes?'' He paused and turned.

''What happened to those teachers and students who ran out of fuel during the Blizzard of '88?''

He gazed at her steadily while the warm September sun beat down upon them benevolently. ''Why, don't you know? Many of them froze to death before help could get to them.''

A shiver went through her, and she remembered Theodore's admonition as they'd confronted each other at the train depot. ''Teaching school is more than just scratching numbers on a slate, missy! It's a mile's walk, and the winters out here are tough!''

So he hadn't been just trying to scare her off. His warning held merit. She gazed out across the waving wheat, trying to imagine the high plains denuded of all but snow, the arctic wind whistling out of the northwest, and fourteen children depending upon her for their very lives while they waited for help to come.

There'd be no solace to be found in fantasy then. She would need to keep her wits sharp and her head calm when and if that ever happened.

But it was hard to imagine, standing on the steps with the sun warming her hair and the striped gophers playing hide-and-seek in their holes and the meadowlarks singing and the finches feeding on thistle seeds and the grain waving slowly.

Still, she decided, she'd speak to Theodore immediately about the coal, and to Nissa about storing some emergency rations at the schoolhouse . . . just in case.

Chapter 4

There were times when Linnea remembered there was a war, but these were chiefly spawned by irritation or romanticized fantasy. Irritation when she had to do without the things she liked best such as sugar, bread, and roast beef, and romantic fantasy whenever it happened to beckon: soldiers kissing sweethearts good-bye as the train pulled from the station . . . those sweethearts receiving soiled, wrinkled letters filled with crowded words of undying love . . . nurses with red crosses on their scarves sitting at bedsides holding wounded hands . . .

Walking home from school that day she thought of the conflict going on in Europe. President Wilson had beseeched Americans to go ''wheatless and meatless'' one day each week to help keep supplies flowing to France. Glancing around at the endless miles of wheat and the large herds of cows in the distance, she thought, ''How silly, when we'll never run out!''

As always, even such a brief reflection on war was too distressing, so she put it from her head in favor of more pleasant thoughts.

The gophers and prairie dogs were hard at play, their antics delightful to watch as they scurried and chattered among the brown-eyed Susans. Stepping along at a sprightly pace, Linnea considered her new class list, which she'd found inside the teacher's grade book. Kristian hadn't been exaggerating when he said most of them were his cousins. Of the fourteen names on the list, eight of them were Westgaards! She couldn't wait to ask Nissa about each of them, and hurried along, eager to get home.

But before she was halfway, she realized her new congress shoes were far less practical than they were dapper. It seemed she could feel every pebble of the gravel road through her soles, and the elevated heels only served to make her ankles wobble when she stepped on rocks.

By the time she was trudging up the driveway, her feet not only hurt but the left one had developed a blister where the tight elastic joined the leather and rubbed her ankle bone. Nissa saw her hobble up and came to the kitchen door. "The walk a little longer than you 'spected?"

"It's just these new shoes. They're still rubbing in spots."

Nissa eyed them speculatively as Linnea climbed the steps and entered the kitchen. "Purty's fine, but sturdy's better out here."

"I'm beginning to see that," Linnea agreed, dropping to a kitchen chair with a sigh of relief. She lifted her ankle over her knee and winced.

Nissa stood with hands akimbo, shaking her head. "Got a blister, have ya?" Linnea looked up and nodded sheepishly. "Well, git 'em off and I'll take a look."

It took some doing to get them off. They were tighter than new cowboy boots, fitting securely well above the ankle. By the time Linnea had tugged and squirmed out of them, Nissa was chortling in amusement. "Don't know what you'd do if you had to get out of them things fast. You got others?"

Linnea's expression turned woeful. "I'm afraid not."

"Well, 'pears we better get you some straight up." She hustled off toward her bedroom and returned with a pair of heavy knit slippers of black wool and a Sears Roebuck and Company catalogue.

"Now, let's see that there blister."

To Linnea's chagrin, it was while Nissa was off fetching some gauze and salve to put on the blister that the men returned to do the milking. She was sitting with her bare foot pulled high up onto her lap, tenderly exploring the fat, bubbled blister when she felt somebody watching her.

She looked up to find Theodore standing in the door, one corner of his mouth hinting at amusement. She dropped her foot so fast it became tangled in her long skirts and she heard stitches pop. Color flooded her face as she covered one foot with the other and gazed up at him defiantly.

"Came for the milk pails," was all he said before moving into the kitchen and crossing to the pantry. Nissa arrived from her bedroom with a tin of ointment and went down on one knee before Linnea. Theodore stepped out of the pantry and asked, "What's wrong with her?"

"She got—"

"I have a blister from my new shoes!" Linnea retorted, suddenly not caring that her face was blazing red as she glared at Theodore. "And I've also got a Teacher's Certificate from the Fargo Normal School that says I'm quite capable of interpreting questions and answering them for myself, in case you're interested!" Angrily she grabbed the ointment and gauze out of Nissa's hands. "I can do that myself, Nissa, thank you." With an irritated twist she took the cover off the tin, wedged her foot sole up, and disregarded her audience while applying the unguent.

Theodore and Nissa exchanged surprised glances. Then Nissa pushed herself to her feet, handed over a needle, and advised dryly, ''While you're at it, better bust that thing before you cover it up.''

Linnea accepted the needle, raising her eyes no farther than Nissa's hand before tending to the unpalatable task. Nissa looked at her son and found him watching Linnea with an amused crook at the corner of his mouth. When he glanced up, his eyes met Nissa's and he shook his head—hopeless case, his expression said—then left the house with the milk pails swinging at his sides.

When he was gone, Linnea's heel hit the floor with an exasperated *klunk* and she glared at the door. ''*That* man can make me so angry!'' Suddenly realizing she was speaking to Theodore's mother, she mellowed slightly. ''I'm sorry, Nissa, I probably shouldn't have said that, but he's . . . he's so exasperating sometimes! I could just . . . just . . .''

''You ain't hurtin' my feelings. Speak your piece.''

''He makes me feel like I'm still in pinafores!'' She threw her arms wide in annoyance. ''Ever since he picked me up at the station and stood there almost laughing at my hat and shoes. I could see he thought I was little more than a child dressed up in grown-up clothing. Well, I'm not!''

''Course you're not. This here's just a misfortune, that's all. Why, anybody can get a blister. Don't pay no attention to Teddy. Remember what I told you about bullheaded Norwegians and how you got to treat 'em? Well, you just done it. Teddy needs that.''

''But why is he so . . . so cross all the time?''

''It goes a long way back. Got nothin' to do with you atall. It's just his way. Now you best get that padding on and let me go get some sandwiches made for them two. When they come in they don't want to waste no time.''

While Nissa made sandwiches, Linnea told her all about Superintendent Dahl's visit, then read the list of names from her red book while Nissa filled her in on each one.

The first name on the list was Kristian Westgaard, age sixteen.

''Kristian I already know,'' Linnea said. ''How about the next one—Raymond Westgaard, sixteen?''

''He's my oldest son Ulmer's boy. Him and Kristian've always been close. You'll meet Ulmer and his wife Helen and all the rest at church tomorrow. They live the next township road over.''

Linnea read the next two names. ''Patricia and Paul Lommen, age fifteen.''

''Them's the Lommen twins. They live just the other side of Ulmer's place. Sharp as whips, them two. Always fierce competition between 'em, which is natural, being twins and all. Patricia won the country spelling bee last year.''

Linnea noted it beside the name before reading on. ''Anton Westgaard, age fourteen.''

''That's little Tony. He belongs to Ulmer and Helen, too. He's shy like his uncle John, but got a heart the size of all outdoors. Tony had rheumatic fever when he was younger, and it left him a little weak, but he's got a good head on his shoulders nevertheless.''

Linnea noted his nickname, and a reminder about his health.

''Allen Severt, fifteen.''

''Allen's the son of our local minister. Look out for that one. He's a troublemaker.''

Linnea glanced up, frowning. ''Troublemaker?''

''I sometimes think he knows he can get by with it because there's only one person gets more respect around here than the schoolteacher, and that's the minister. If the teachers we had in years past had taken him to task like they should've, and told Reverend Severt some of the monkey business Allen's been up to, he might not be such a handful.''

''What sort of monkey business?''

''Oh, pushing the younger ones around, teasing the girls in ways that aren't always funny—nothing that could ever be called serious. When it comes to the serious stuff, he's crafty enough to cover his tracks so nothing can be pinned on him. But you watch him. He's mouthy and bold. Never cared for him much myself, but you form your own opinion when you meet him.''

Promising to do just that, Linnea went on to the next name. ''Libby Severt, age eleven.''

''That's Allen's sister. She pretty much gets ignored, cause Allen sees to it he gets all the attention in that family. She seems to be a nice enough child.''

''Frances Westgaard, age ten.''

''She's Ulmer and Helen's again. She's got a special place in my heart. Guess it's because she's slower than the rest. But you never saw a more willing or loving child in your life. You wait till Christmas time. She'll be the first to give you a present, and it'll have plenty of thought behind it.''

Linnea smiled, and sketched a flower behind the name. ''Norna Westgaard, age ten.''

''Norna belongs to my son Lars and his wife Evie. She's the oldest of five, and she's forever mothering the younger ones. Farther down your list there you'll find Skipp and Roseanne. They're Norna's younger sister and brother.''

Nissa became thoughtful for a moment before going on as if answering some silent question. ''Least I think Roseanne is starting school this year. They're good kids, all of 'em. Lars and Evie brought 'em up right, just like all my kids brought their own up right.''

Linnea smiled at the grandmotherly bias, lowering her face so Nissa couldn't see. The next name on her list was Skipp's, and she bracketed his name with those of his siblings while noting that besides Skipp there were two other eight-year-olds on her list—third grade would be her biggest. ''Bent Linder and Jeannette Knutson.''

''Bent belongs to my daughter Clara. She's my baby. Married to a fine fellow named Trigg Linder and they got two little ones. Expectin' their third in February.'' A faraway look came into Nissa's eyes, and her hands fell idle for a moment. ''Lord, where does the time go? Seems like just yesterday Clara was going off to school herself.'' She sighed. ''Ah, well. Who's next?''

''Jeannette Knutson.''

''She's Oscar and Hilda's—you know? The chairman of the school board?''

''Oh, of course. And I have two seven-year-olds. Roseanne and Sonny Westgaard.''

''Cousins. Roseanne I already told you belongs to Evie, and Sonny is Ulmer's. He's named after his pa, but he's always gone by 'Sonny.' ''

Linnea's notes were growing confused, just as she was. Her face showed it.

Nissa laughed, set a plate of sandwiches on the table, and returned to the stove, wiping her hands on her apron. "You'll keep 'em straight once you meet 'em all. You'll be callin' 'em by their first names in no time, and know which family they come from. Everybody knows everybody else around here, and you will, too."

"So many of them are your grandchildren," Linnea said with a touch of awe in her voice.

"Thirteen. Be fourteen when Clara has her next one. I always wondered how many more I'd have if John had got married and if Melinda hadn't . . ."

But just then the men clumped in and Nissa's mouth clapped shut. She threw a wary look across the room at Theodore, then abruptly hustled into the pantry to put away a butcher knife.

Who is Melinda, Linnea wondered. Theodore's wife? Kristian's mother?

If Melinda hadn't what?

Linnea covertly studied the father and son as they entered. She tried to picture Theodore with a wife. What would she have been like? Blond, which would account for Kristian's bright hair. And pretty, she decided, noting, too, the young man's attractive features. Was Kristian's shapely mouth and full lower lip inherited from his mother? More than likely so, for Theodore's mouth was shaped differently—wide, crisply defined, but not as bowed. Hard to imagine it ever smiling, for she'd never seen it do so.

From her seat at the table she watched him cross to the water pail, watched his head tilt back as he drank from the dipper. Suddenly he turned and caught Linnea studying him. Their eyes met as he slowly replaced the dipper in the pail, then even more slowly back-handed his lower lip. And something odd happened in her chest. A brief catch, a tightening that caused her to drop her gaze to the list of names in the open book on the kitchen table.

"Came for the sandwiches," he said to no one in particular. Momentarily he appeared beside her, picked up the stack of fat sandwiches, and handed two to Kristian. "Let's go."

"See you at supper," Kristian offered from the door, and she looked up to return his smile.

"Yes, see you at supper."

But Theodore bid no word of farewell, only followed his son out while Linnea wondered what it was that had just struck her. Embarrassment, she supposed, for somehow the man possessed the power to rattle her nearly every time the two of them were within speaking distance.

Nissa returned, set the coffeepot to the hottest part of the stove, and shifted a look to the doorway through which Theodore had just exited.

Linnea drew a deep breath for courage before asking, "Who is Melinda?"

"You want to order them shoes or not?" Nissa nodded toward the catalogue on the table.

"In a minute . . ." Linnea paused before repeating, quietly, "Who is Melinda?"

"She was Teddy's wife, but he don't like to talk about her."

"Why?"

Nissa took off her glasses, held them by the nosepiece, and dampened them with her breath. She lifted the skirt of her apron and paid great attention to their careful polishing while answering. "B'cause she run off and left him with a one-year-old baby and we never seen her in these parts again."

It took an effort for Linnea to withhold her gasp. "W . . . with a one-year-old baby?"

"That's what I said, ain't it?"

"You mean Kristian?"

"Don't see any other babies o' Teddy's 'round here, do you?"

"You mean she . . . she just . . . deserted them?" Something twisted inside Linnea, a twinge of pity, a compulsion to know more.

Nissa sat down, riffled the thick pages with one thumb, searching. The catalogue fell open. She licked a finger and with two flicks found the correct page. "These ones here . . ." She stretched her neck to peer at the row of black-and-white drawings through the polished lenses. "These ladies' storm boots. Good sensible lace-up ones. These'd be good for you." She tapped the page with a forefinger. The finger had skin the texture of jerky and wouldn't quite straighten anymore. Gently, Linnea covered Nissa's old hand. When she spoke, she spoke softly. "I'd like to know about Melinda."

Nissa looked up. The oval lenses magnified her faded brown eyes and accentuated the wrinkles in the lids. She studied Linnea silently, considering. From outside came the call of a crow and the disappearing sound of horses' hooves. She glanced toward the farmyard where father and son could no longer be seen, then withdrew her hand from Linnea's to push the catalogue back with two thumbs. "All right. You want to know, I'll tell you. Much as I know about it. You mind if I get a cup of coffee first?"

Was it Linnea's imagination, or did Nissa appear weary for the first time ever? She braced her knees and pushed herself to her feet, found a cup, and filled it. But when she returned to the table, it wasn't weariness alone that weighted her shoulders. There was in her eyes the unmistakable look of sadness.

"It was the summer of 1900. My man, my Hjalmar, he thought Theodore Roosevelt was just about the greatest person that ever walked this earth. All the people around here loved Old Four Eyes, you know, liked to think of him as their native son, ever since he ranched down at Medora those couple o' years. Add to that the fact that he'd just been down to Cuba with his Rough Riders and rode up San Juan Hill, and he was nothing short of a national hero. But there was nobody admired him like my Hjalmar.

"Then that summer Roosevelt decides to run for vice-president with McKinley, and Hjalmar heard they was coming through Williston on a campaign train. Never forget that day he comes poundin' in the house bellerin' 'missus'—that's what he used to call me when he was excited—'missus,' he bellered, 'get your gear packed, we're goin' to Williston to see Roosevelt!'

"Why, land, I couldn't believe it. I said 'Hjalmar, what're you talking about? You been samplin Helgeson's new batch of barley beer again?' Used to be this fellow named Helgeson, lived over in the next section and brewed homemade beer the two of them was always claimin' needed testin' . . ." A light of remembrance softened Nissa's eyes, and the ghost of a smile tipped up her lips. Abruptly she cleared her throat, took a gulp of coffee, and drew herself back to the main point of the story.

"So Hjalmar, he says no boy that was named after Teddy Roosevelt should miss the chance to see his namesake in the flesh when he was gonna be no more'n sixty miles away, and so we was all three going to Williston to meet that train."

Nissa made a gavel of her fist and brought it down lightly atop the open catalogue. "Well, say, that's just what we did. Rode on down to Williston, the three of us, and took a room in the Manitou Hotel and got all gussied up in our Sunday clothes and went to the depot to watch that train come in." She waggled her head slowly. "It was somethin' to see, I'll tell you." She pressed her fist to her heart. "There was this big brass band playin' all them marching songs and school children waving American flags, and then the train come in, all decked out with bunting . . . and there he was, Mr. Roosevelt himself, standin' on the last car with his hands in the air and his cheeks as red as the stripes on them flags and that band boomin' out patriotic songs. I remember lookin' up at my Hjalmar and seein' the smile on his face—he had a moustache just like Roosevelt's—and he had his arm around our Teddy's shoulder and was pointing at the great man and shoutin' somethin' in Teddy's ear."

Watching the expression on Nissa's face, Linnea could see and hear it all. Then Nissa looked up, caught herself wool-gathering, and dropped her hand from her heart to the handle of her cup. She sniffed, as if to clear more than just her nose.

"Well, she was there on the train somewhere, Melinda was. Her pa was on the McKinley/Roosevelt campaign committee and her ma was dead, so she went everywhere with him. As it turns out, they stayed in Williston for more than a whistlestop. Seems there was some rich fellow there by the name of Hagens who had donated plenty to the campaign, and there was a regular rally where the farmers could have a chance to talk to the candidates and pin 'em down to some promises. Afterwards there was a dinner at the Manitou and they spread all of McKinley's key people around at the tables to answer questions, and Melinda and her pa ended up at our table.

"I don't remember much about it and maybe it was Hjalmar's and my fault for not payin' much mind to them young people, but he was busy talkin' politics and I was gettin' my eye full of that fancy hotel. I do remember there was a band playin' again and once I nudged Hjalmar's shoulder and said 'Would you look at there,' because lo and behold, there was our Teddy dancing with that young girl. Course Hjalmar, he was caught up in arguing the goods and bads of Mr. Roosevelt's new civil service system, and I don't just remember what time it was but our Teddy he comes and tells us he and the young lady are going out for a walk. Sure, I was surprised, but Teddy, he was seventeen, after all."

Linnea tried to imagine Theodore at seventeen, but could not. She tried to imagine Theodore dancing, but could not. She tried to imagine him taking a young woman out for a walk with her hand on his arm, but could not. Having seen only his irascible side, these pictures seemed out of character.

"But seventeen or not, that boy had us in a tizzy fit before mornin'. We waited and we waited, and we checked with Melinda's pa, but she wasn't back either, and it wasn't till nearly five in the mornin' them two got back and when they come down the hall they was holdin' hands." Nissa peered over the tops of her glasses and crossed her arms over her chest. "Now, you ever seen what it's like when a weasel sashays into a hen house? That's about what it was like when we caught sight of them two in that hall. There was feathers flyin' in all directions, and some of 'em was from me. Granted, I was doin' my share of dressin' down, but, lord, I never heard such bawlin' and screamin' and shoutin' as when Melinda's pa hauled her off into their room down the hall, flingin' accusations at her. She was yowlin' fit to kill and claimin' they'd done nothin' to be ashamed of and that if she lived in a house and stayed put like other girls she wouldn't have to stay out all night to make new friends." Nissa rubbed her mouth, staring at the cold coffee in her cup. "I never asked where they was all that time, nor what they done. Truth to tell, I don't think I wanted to know. We hauled Teddy into our room and slammed the door while that girl was actin' like a wildcat in the hall yet, and heads was poppin' out of doors. Land, it was awful."

Nissa sighed. "Well, we thought that was the end of it and we hauled Teddy out of there in the mornin' without settin' eyes on Melinda again. But don't you know it wasn't a week later she showed up at my kitchen door, bold as brass—we was livin' in John's place then. That was the home place up there—said she wanted to see Teddy and would I please tell her where she could find him." Nissa shook her head disbelievingly. "I can see her yet, with that face lookin' like she wouldn't have the spunk to ask for second helpings, standin' there on my doorstep demanding to see my boy—it never fit, how she acted then and how she turned out to be. Guess it was just one of them crazy times of life some of us goes through when we're chafin' at the bit and think it's time to cut the apron strings."

Nissa faded off into memory again, pondering silently.

"What happened?" Linnea encouraged.

Nissa looked up, drew a deep sigh, and went on. "What happened is she marched right out there into the field where Teddy was cuttin' wheat with Hjalmar and the boys, and she says she had decided to come here and marry him after all, just like they talked about. Now, I never asked, but it appeared to me her showin' up sayin' that was as much of a surprise to Teddy as it was to the rest of us. But he never let on, and with a face like Melinda's, it was easy to see he was knocked off his pins.

"They married all right, and fast. Hjalmar, he give them this land here, and all the boys put up this house for them. We all wondered how it'd work out, but we hoped for the best. It come out later how she'd been fightin' with her pa about travelin' on the train with him, and I reckon what was actually behind it was she was nothin' more than a young girl being told to do one thing and decidin', by lizzie, she wasn't gonna be told what to do.

"So she married my boy. But she never suited." Nissa shook her head slowly. "Never. She was a city girl, and what she wanted with a farm boy I never could understand. First thing you know she got in a family way, and I can see her yet, standin' at the window staring at the wheat, sayin' it was drivin' her crazy. Lord, how she used to cuss that wheat. Trees, she said, there wasn't no trees out here. And no sound, she said. The sun gave her rashes and the flies drove her crazy and the smell of the barnyard give her headaches. How Teddy ever thought a woman like that could be a farm wife, I'll never know. Why, she had no sense about raisin' gardens—didn't like gettin' her fingernails dirty, didn't know how to put up vegetables.'' Nissa made a sound of humorless disdain: ''P'chee.'' Again she shook her head, crossed her arms. ''A woman like that,'' she ended, as if still mystified by her son's choice.

''I seen it happenin', but there wasn't nothin' I could do. Teddy, he was so happy when she first come here. And when he found out there was a baby comin', why, that boy was in his glory. But little by little her complainin' turned to silence, and she started actin' like she *was* gettin' a little tetched. At first, after Kristian was born, I could see she tried to be a good mother, but it was no good. Teddy never said so, but Clara used to come down here and play with the baby, and she'd come home and tell us how Melinda cried all the time. Never quit cryin', but what could he do about it? He couldn't change all that wheatland into woods. He couldn't put no city in the middle of this here farmyard for her.

''And then one day she just up and left. Left a note sayin' to tell Kristian she loved him and she was sorry, but I never saw it, nor did I ask to. It was Clara told me about it.'' Again her thoughts trailed off.

''And you took care of Kristian after that?''

A new sadness came into Nissa's eyes. ''Me and Clara did. You see, my man, my Hjalmar, he'd died that year. We'd been up to church one spring evenin' to help with the graveyard cleanin' like we always did every spring. We come home and was standin' just outside the kitchen door and I remember Hjalmar had his hands in his pockets and he looked up at the first star comin' out and he says to me, he says, 'Nissa, we got lots to be thankful for. It's gonna be a clear day tomorrow,' and just like that he pitches over and falls dead on our doorstep. He always used to say to me, Nissa, I want to die workin', and you know, he got his wish. He worked right up to the very hour he died at my feet. No pain. No sufferin'. Just a man counting his blessings. Now, I ask you, what more could a woman ask for than to see her man die a beautiful death like that?''

The room grew quiet except for a soft sigh of ash collapsing in the stove. Nissa's stiff old hands rested, crossed, beneath her drooping breasts. In her eyes was the bright sheen of remembrance as she stared, unseeing, at the red flowered oilcoth beneath the catalogue. A lump formed in Linnea's throat. Death was an entity she hadn't pondered, and certainly never as a thing that could be beautiful. Studying Nissa's downcast eyes, Linnea suddenly understood the beauty of lifelong commitment and realized that for those like Nissa it took more than death to negate it.

Nissa lifted the cup to her lips, unaware that the coffee was cold. ''The home place was never the same without Hjalmar, so I left it to John and came up here to take care of Teddy and the baby, and I been here ever since.''

''And Melinda? Where is she now?'' Linnea inquired softly, holding her breath for some inexplicable reason. She sat absolutely still while waiting for the answer.

''Melinda got run over and killed by a streetcar in Philadelphia when Kristian was six.''

Oh, I see. The words were unspoken, but buzzed in Linnea's mind as she released the lungful of air in small, careful spurts that slowly relaxed her shoulders. The room grew still except for the soft, absent tapping of Nissa's fingertips upon the forgotten catalogue. Her apron swagged between her spread knees, and the afternoon sun lit the soft fuzz on her cheeks. Suddenly it seemed the kitchen was being visited by two people long dead, and Linnea strove to see their faces, but all she made out was a white drooping moustache on one and the drooping shoulders of the other as she stared out the window at the fields where even now Theodore was cutting grain.

She glanced at the window. *So that's why you're bitter. You were so young and the wound was so deep.* She felt a twinge of guilt for her impatience and anger with him. She wished she could somehow undo it, but even if she could, what good would it do? It wouldn't change what he'd suffered in the past.

And Kristian, poor Kristian. Growing up without a mother's love.

"Does Kristian know?" Linnea asked sympathetically.

"That she run away? He knows. But he's a good boy. He's had me, and Clara, and plenty of other aunts. I know it ain't the same as his real ma, but he's got along fine. Well . . ." The mood was broken as Nissa threw a glance at the catalogue. "We ain't gettin' them shoes picked out now, are we?"

They chose the storm boots of pebbled black box calf that tied up the front to mid-calf, and while Linnea was filling out the mail-order blank, Nissa added one last postscript to the personal story. "I'd appreciate it if you didn't tell Teddy I told you. He don't talk about her much, and, well, you know how men can get. I figured you ought to know, being Kristian's teacher and all."

But Linnea didn't know how men could get. She was only now coming to learn. Still, the story had had great impact on her, and she found herself promising to treat Theodore more patiently in the future.

The men returned late again, and when they shuffled in, Linnea realized she was studying Theodore as if expecting to find some physical change in his appearance. But he looked the same as ever—powerful, somber, and unhappy. All through supper she was conscious of the fact that he had studiously refrained from glancing her way; neither had he spoken to her since she'd upbraided him earlier that afternoon. As they all took their places at the table, John offered his polite, self-conscious nod, accompanied by a shy, "Hello, miss." And Kristian angled furtive glances her way after a stumbling greeting. But Theodore concentrated on his plate and nothing else.

When the meal was half over, she could tolerate his disregard no longer and found herself overwhelmed by the need to end the enmity between them. Perhaps what she really wanted was to make up in some small way for Melinda.

He was taking a bite of mashed potatoes and gravy when she fixed her eyes on him and spoke into the silence. "Theodore, I want to apologize for the way I spoke to you this afternoon."

His jaws stopped moving and his gaze rested on her for the first time that evening while he tried to mask a look of total surprise.

Completely dauntless and wearing an open look of ingenuousness, she went on, "I'm certainly glad none of my students were here to see me, because I didn't make a very good example. I was sarcastic and snappy, which is really no way to treat people when it's just as easy to ask nicely. So I'm asking nicely this time. In the future, Theodore, would you please speak to me directly when I'm in the room, instead of talking over my head as if I'm not there?"

Theodore stared at her for a moment before his glance flickered to Nissa, then Kristian.

Kristian had stopped eating to stare in surprise at Miss Brandonberg taking his father down a notch, and all with the coolest of courtesy and a direct look that Theodore was having trouble meeting. Furthermore, she'd done it again—started talking in the middle of supper. Nobody around here cared much for talking on an empty stomach, and he could see Theodore's eagerness to get on with his meal in peace. But she was staring him down, second for second, sitting as pert and straight as a chipmunk while beneath her steady gaze his face turned pink.

"Somehow," she went on benevolently, "you and I managed to get off on the wrong foot, didn't we? But I think we can be more adult than that, don't you?"

Theodore didn't know what to say. The little missy had apologized—to the best of his memory the first time in his life any female had ever apologized to him—yet she seemed to be calling him childish at the same time. *Him!* When he was nearly old enough to be her father! He swallowed, feeling confused and wondering what sarcastic meant. Nissa, John, and Kristian were all watching and listening, nobody moving a hand, and finally Theodore had to say *some*thing!

He swallowed again and it felt like the potatoes were stuck in his throat. He stared at the little missy's fresh, wide-eyed expression and realized what a pretty young thing she was.

"Yeah, maybe we could at that. Now eat." And he gratefully dropped his attention to his plate.

She had won a round at last. Realizing it, Linnea felt John's gaze still lingering on her in amazement. She gave him a wide smile, making him dig into his meal again with self-conscious haste.

The little miss was something new to John. Someone who could make Teddy blush and back down when nobody'd ever been able to do that except their ma. But the way Ma did it was a lot different than the way Little Missy did it. In his dull-witted way, John wondered just how she'd managed it. He remembered one other woman who used to be able to soften up Teddy. Melinda. She'd been somethin', that Melinda, pretty and tiny and big-eyed as a newborn colt. All she used to have to do was turn those big eyes on Teddy and he'd get pink around the collar. A lot like he just did when Little Missy talked soft and serious and looked him square. And Melinda used to talk at the table, too. Always sayin' how she couldn't understand their Norwegian ways, how they all bottled things up inside and never talked about what really mattered.

Not being one who talked much, John never had understood that.

He glanced up and met Ma's eyes.

You remember, John, don't you? Nissa was thinking. That's the way he used to act around Melinda. She turned her gaze to her right, to the girl politely eating and totally unaware of the undertones she'd just caused, then to Teddy engrossed in his supper but frowning at his plate.

I think, my crotchety son, that you've met your match at last.

* * *

It was Saturday night. Nissa got down her galvanized washtub, set it near the kitchen stove, and began filling it with steaming water.

"We take turns," she announced. "You wanna be first?"

Linnea gawked at the tub, at the wide-open kitchen, glanced at the living-room doorway, from beyond which the voices of John and Theodore could be clearly heard, then back at the tub beside the stove.

"I think I'll just take some water upstairs in my basin."

She filled the small speckled basin and took it to her room, only to find the amount of water inadequate. Still, the all-over bath felt glorious. While she was washing, she heard John leave for home. The house grew quieter and quieter. She dried, dressed in her nightgown, and sat in her rocking chair to study the notes she'd made beside her students' names. Nissa took her bath first, then her voice carried clearly as she called upstairs to tell Kristian it was his turn. She heard him go downstairs with his clean clothes, and some time later, come back up wearing them, she presumed. She heard the third bath in progress, and tried to picture those long legs folded into the tiny tub, and smiled. A few minutes later she heard Theodore call Kristian downstairs to help carry the washtub outside.

Then nothing but silence.

John, Nissa, Kristian . . . Theodore, she thought. My surrogate family now. Each so individual, each raising a distinctly different reaction within her. She'd liked them all immediately. Except Theodore. So why was it she thought about him longest? Why did his unsmiling face and contrary disposition remain in her thoughts even after the lantern was out and she found it impossible to feel sleepy? Why was it *his* bare limbs she thought about in the washtub?

The house was quiet, the lingering smells of supper mixed with the scent of homemade lye soap in the dimly lit kitchen as Theodore and his son carried the washtub out to the yard.

When the water had been slewed, Theodore stood a moment, studying the sky, contemplating. After some time, he said thoughtfully, "Kristian?"

"What?"

He reviewed the word carefully before pronouncing it exactly as she had. "You know what sarcastic means?"

"No, Pa, I don't. But I'll ask Miss Brandonberg."

"No!" Theodore exclaimed, then consciously dropped the anxiety from his voice. "No, it don't matter. Don't go askin' her nothin' on my account."

They stood in the darkness, the sound of early-autumn crickets harmonizing through the night, the tub weightless now between their two hands. The moon was at three-quarter phase, white as fresh milk in a star-studded sky, throwing their shadows long and deep.

"She sure is pretty, ain't she?" Kristian murmured softly.

"You think so?"

"Well, she sure ain't mousy and puny, like you said. Why'd you say that, anyway?"

"Did I say that?"

"You sure did. But she's no more mousy and puny than Isabelle, and you seem to think Isabelle's all right."

Theodore harumphed. "I think you better take another look at Isabelle when she drives that cook wagon in here."

"Well, all right, there's a lot more to Isabelle compared to Miss Brandonberg, but still Miss Brandonberg isn't mousy and puny. She looks just right to me."

Theodore eyed his son askance, making out his clear, youthful profile beneath the bright moonlight. "You better not let her hear you say that, seeing as how she's your teacher."

"Yeah, I guess you're right," Kristian said dejectedly, dropping his glance to the dark earth, standing thoughtfully for a moment before suddenly lifting his face and asking more brightly, "You wanna know somethin' funny?"

"What?"

"She thinks Russian thistles are *pretty!* She said she's gonna have us go out in the field and paint pictures of them!"

Theodore grunted, then laughed once, joined by Kristian. "Yeah, well, she's a town girl. You know they ain't so smart about some things."

But later, when Theodore lay down in his double bed, where he'd slept alone for well over fourteen years, he tried to picture a Russian thistle blossom and realized he really wasn't sure what one looked like. For though he'd seen thousands upon thousands of them in his thirty-four years, he'd never looked at one with anything but contempt. He decided next time he saw one he'd take a second look.

Chapter 5

Linnea wasn't prepared for the change she saw in Kristian and Theodore on Sunday morning. They'd looked the same as always when they returned from doing the morning chores to have their breakfast. But afterward, when Nissa called up the steps, "Come on! Buggy's waiting!" Linnea dashed outside to find father and son dressed in formal black suits and ties and crisp white shirts, sitting side by side in the front seat of a black four-passenger surrey.

She came up short, assessing Theodore's formal black hat and Kristian's freshly combed hair, still wet at the sides and gleaming in the sun. They both wore tight, tight collars that appeared to be cutting into their jaws.

"My, don't you two look handsome," she said, pausing beside the rig. Kristian lit up while Theodore's eyes lazily lingered on her ridiculous high hat, then dropped to her feet to assess the high-heeled congress shoes. He'd give them about six weeks out here on these rocky roads.

Neither of them, however, remembered to help the ladies board. When Nissa made a move to do so unaided, Linnea halted her as inconspicuously as possible.

''I wonder, Kristian, if you'd mind giving your grandmother a hand up. Her knees are bothering her this morning.''

''My knees're as good—''

''Now, Nissa,'' Linnea hushed her with a light touch on the arm. ''You remember how you just said your knees seem to be out of joint this morning. Besides, a young man like Kristian is only too happy to display his manners and help us ladies board.''

He was down in a flash to hand up first Nissa then Linnea into the back seat, grinning widely. Theodore craned to observe, but said not a word. He just sat and watched the girl work her wiles on his son, who was falling all over himself to do her bidding. When everyone was seated, he caught the little missy's eye, lifted one brow sardonically, then turned to cluck at the horses, flick the reins, and order quietly, ''Hup there, Cub, Toots.'' The whiffletree leveled and they were off at a trot.

The ride was very pleasant, though Linnea couldn't help wondering at the reticence these people practiced during times when her own family would have been chatting pleasantly. Why, the weather alone made her spirits bubble. A slight breeze rustled the grasses at the edge of the road; the mid-morning sun was a golden caress. And the smell—pure, clean, the way she imagined it must smell a mile up into the clouds.

She glanced up. A few meringue puffs floated high to the north, but straight ahead the westerly sky was hard blue, a blue so rich it smote the senses.

Against it, she saw the white steeple long before they reached it. It seemed to be resting on Theodore's broad right shoulder. The bell pealed, drifting to them quietly on the soft autumn wind. Again it pealed, louder, then again, diminished, its reverberations waxing and waning at the whim of the wind. Twelve times it chimed, until its canticle at last ushered their carriage into the churchyard.

Here, as at school, the wheat pressed close, surrounding the scores of horses and rigs tied at the hitching posts. The churchyard was filled with the congregation, all outside taking in a few extra minutes of the wondrous morning. The men stood in groups with their thumbs caught in their waistcoat pockets discussing the weather and the crops. The women gathered together, their bonnets nodding, discussing their canning. The children, their freshly polished boots already coated with dust, chased each other around the women's skirts while being warned to stop before their shoes got dusty.

When the surrey halted, Linnea didn't have to remind Kristian of his manners. He was johnny-on-the-spot, helping both women with a newfound sense of pride. But as they walked toward the church steps, Nissa commandeered her grandson's arm and Linnea found herself beside Theodore. She neither took his elbow, nor did he offer it, but moved through the crowd with him, offering quick smiles when her glance met those of strangers.

Immediately she sensed people falling back to give her a respectful distance, watching as she made her way toward the door. There, Theodore introduced her to the minister, Reverend Martin Severt, a spare, handsome man in his mid-thirties, and his wife, an angular, well-dressed woman with prominent teeth and a ready smile. The Severts seemed a charming couple, their handshakes warm, their welcomes genuine, and Linnea couldn't help but wonder if their son was really the mischief-maker Nissa said he was.

Inside, John was already waiting in their pew. As they filed in to join him, Linnea ended up between Kristian and his father. When the service began, Kristian followed along in his prayer book, but Theodore sat for the most part with arms crossed tightly over his chest. Until the hymns began. She was amazed, then, to hear him sing out heartily in a clear, resonant baritone, as true as the tone of a tuning fork. Joining him in her equally true soprano, she allowed herself a cautious upward glance.

It was impossible, she decided, for a person to appear hard-bitten while singing a hymn.

For the first time, she saw all that his face could be. His lips, now open wide in song, appeared less harsh than ever before. His jaw, dropped low to hold a note, had lost its stubborn set. And his eyes, lit by morning light streaming through an arched window, sparkled with a mellow expression. Shoulders squared, he stood with eight fingertips lightly tapping the pew in front of them, adding his robust voice to those around him.

He glanced down and caught her—singing, too—peering up at him. For only a moment his eyes seemed to radiate the smile his open mouth could not. Obviously, he knew the words by heart, but the moment was too perfect to pass up the opportunity of proffering an olive branch. It took only the slightest leftward shift for Linnea to lift her hymnal and offer to share it. Her elbow bumped his arm. A ripple skipped up her skin. She felt his uncertain pause, then he angled his body toward her. His fingers took the far edge of the book and they finished the hymn together.

In those minutes, while their voices blended toward heaven, she felt a reluctant accord, but by the time the song ended, a barrier had tumbled.

When the amen faded, Theodore waited until she began folding toward the seat before following suit. The sermon began and she struggled to concentrate on it and not the smell of lye soap and hair dressing coming from her left.

The service ended with Reverend Severt announcing, "We're pleased to have with us today our new schoolteacher, Miss Linnea Brandonberg. Please take a minute to greet her and introduce yourselves and make her feel welcome." Dozens of heads turned her way, but she was uncomfortably aware of only one, the one directly to her left. Realizing Theodore was scrutinizing her at closer range than ever before, she wondered suddenly if her hat was straight, her collar flat, her hair tight. But a moment later the church began emptying and she was swept into the bright autumn day. She forgot about appearances and concentrated on the new faces and names.

They were all such ordinary people, but in that very ordinariness Linnea saw nobility. The men were built broad and strong, their hands hard and wide, all of them dressed in stern black and white. The women dressed simply with much more attention to comfort than to style. Their hats, unlike hers, were plain and flat, their shoes sensible. But to a number, they afforded Linnea an unmistakable diffident respect. The women smiled shyly, the men doffed their hats, and the children blushed when being introduced to "the new teacher."

She met all of her students, but the two who stuck in her memory after they turned away were the Severt boy—a looker like his father, but with an unsettling nervousness about him—and Frances Westgaard, because Nissa had said she was slow. Perhaps it was the innate teacher in Linnea that made her radiate toward any child who needed her most, but her first glimpse of the thin girl with freckles and a corona of braids sent her heart out to the child.

Alas, there were so many Westgaard children she soon gave up trying to remember who belonged to whom. The adults were a little easier. Ulmer and Lars were simple to spot because they looked so much like Theodore, though Ulmer, the eldest, was losing his hair, and Lars had a far more ready smile.

And then came Clara—bulging with pregnancy, laughing at something private her husband had just whispered in her ear, and with eyes that smiled even before her lips did. Her hair was coffee-brown and she had beautiful skin, though her features were far less classically attractive than her brothers'. Her nose was a little too long and her mouth a little too wide, but when she smiled one scarcely noticed these imperfections, for Clara had something much more lasting. Clara had the beauty of happiness.

Linnea knew the minute their eyes met, she was going to like this woman.

Clara clasped Linnea's hand, held it firmly and let a conspiratorial grin play at the corners of her lips. "So you're the one who put my brother in his place. Good for you. He probably needed it."

Linnea was so startled she couldn't think of a proper response.

"I'm Clara."

"Y . . . yes," Linnea's eyes swept down to her gently rounded belly. "I thought so."

Clara laughed, caressed her high stomach, and pulled her husband's elbow closer against her side. "And this is my Trigg."

Perhaps it was the way she said "my Trigg" that made Linnea like her even more. There was such obvious pride in her voice, and for good reason. Trigg Linder was probably the handsomest man Linnea had ever seen. His hair glinted in the sun like freshly polished copper, his sky-blue eyes had the kind of lashes women envy, and his Nordic features had flawless symmetry and beauty. But what Linnea noted about Trigg Linder that remained in her memory was that all the while his wife talked, he kept one hand lightly around the back of her neck and seemed unable to keep himself from enjoying her face.

"So Teddy gave you a hard time," Clara commented.

"Well, he . . . he didn't exact—"

Clara laughed. "You don't have to whitewash it with me. I know our Teddy, and he can be a royal Norwegian pain. Mule-headed, stubborn . . ." She squeezed Linnea's wrist. "But he has his moments. Give him time to adjust to you. Meantime, if he gets to you, come on over and let off some steam at my house. Coffee's always on and I sure could use the company."

"Why, thank you, I just might do that."

"And how about Ma? She treating you okay?"

"Oh, yes. Nissa's been wonderful."

"I love every wiry hair on her head, but sometimes she drives me plumb crazy, so if she gives you one too many orders and you have the urge to tie and gag her, come and see me. We'll talk about all the times I almost did."

She was already leaving when she turned back and added, "Oh, by the way, I love your hat."

Unexpectedly Linnea burst out laughing.

"Did I say something funny?"

"I'll tell you when I come for coffee."

Even pregnant, Clara moved briskly, but when she was gone Linnea was the one who felt breathless. So this was Clara, the one who'd been closest to Theodore. The one who'd known Melinda. And she'd invited Linnea's friendship. There was no doubt in Linnea's mind she'd take her up on the offer.

Just then Kristian appeared and announced, "Pa says to come and ask you if you're just about ready."

She looked across the churchyard and found Nissa already in the wagon and Theodore standing beside his rig looking displeased, his foot tapping nervously.

"Oh, am I holding you up?"

"Well, it . . . it's the wheat. Out here, when the weather's good and the wheat's ripe, we work every day of the week."

"Oh!" So she'd given her landlord fuel for the fire. "Let me just say good-bye to Reverend Severt." She kept her farewell short, but even so, as she crossed to Theodore's wagon she saw the irritation on his face.

"I'm sorry I held you up, Theodore. I didn't know you'd be going out in the fields today."

"You never heard of making hay while the sun shines, missy? Just get up there and let's move." He grasped her elbow and helped her up with a shove that was more rude than no help at all. Singed by his abrupt change after the closeness to him she'd felt in church, Linnea rode home in confusion.

As soon as they arrived there was a quick scramble to change clothes. Linnea was in her room removing her hatpin when she remembered the coal. The last thing on earth she wanted to do was bring up the subject and rile him further, but she had little choice.

She intercepted him as he came out of his bedroom into the parlor, dressed in freshly washed and ironed bib overalls and a clean faded-blue chambray shirt. He was setting his shaggy straw hat on his head when he came up short at the sight of her. His arm came down very slowly, and they stared at each other for a long, silent moment.

She recalled sharing the hymnal with him in church and how for those few minutes he had seemed . . . different. Approachable. Likable. Suddenly it became difficult to talk to him. But at last she found her voice.

"I realize how busy you are at this time of the year, but I promised Mr. Dahl I'd remind you about the school coal."

"Dahl always thinks a blizzard's gonna blow up in the middle of September and he'll lose his job if that coal shed's not filled. But Dahl ain't got wheat to get in."

"*Hasn't* got wheat to get in," she corrected.

"What?" His brows drew together.

"Hasn't got . . ." Her fingers went up to cover her lips. *Oh, Linnea, must your tongue always work faster than your brain?* "Nothing. N . . . nothing . . . I . . . I told him I'd remind you, now I have. Sorry I held you up." What was it about the man that could make her so twitchy at times?

"If Dahl comes around pesterin' you about it again, tell him I'll get to it when I can. While the sun shines, I cut wheat." And with that he shouldered around her and left the house.

The afternoon stretched before her endlessly, so she decided to go down to the schoolhouse. Knowing more about her students now, able to put a few faces to names, she sat down and mapped out the first week's lesson plans, perusing her limited textbooks. There was *Worcester's Speller, McGuffey's Reader, Ray's Mental Arithmetic, Monteith and McNally's Geography,* and *Clark's Grammar.* The other books on the shelf were on varied subjects and appeared to have been donated from homes over the years. Most, such as the one she'd randomly selected the day she read to Kristian—entitled *New Era Economics*—were far too advanced to be of much use for her students, especially the younger ones.

But there was one thing children were never too young to learn, and that was table manners. She needed no books to help her teach this! And it was high on her list of priorities.

When her lessons plans were done, she unfurled the American flag and hung it from its bracket up front, printed the words to the "Pledge of Allegiance" on the blackboard, then her name in large block letters: MISS BRANDONBERG. She stood back, surveying it with smiling satisfaction, brushing the chalk dust from her fingers, almost giddy at the thought of ringing the bell at nine o'clock tomorrow morning and calling her first class to order.

It was only mid-afternoon, and she hated to leave the pleasant schoolhouse just yet.

On a sudden inspiration she sat down and began drawing a series of large alphabet cards to augment the textbooks, each with a picture to represent the letter. On A she drew an apple. On B a barn. On C a cat. She enjoyed drawing, and took time over the task, stopping often to ponder long and hard over what symbol should represent each letter. Striving to make them pictures of things to which the children could relate, she made H a horse, rather misproportioned, but she did her best—M a mouse, and S a sunflower. And with a smile, she began next on a thistle.

But upon beginning, she realized she'd need to see the plant to capture the Russian thistle accurately.

She walked down the road with the sun beating hot on her hair, dreaming idle dreams while the cottonwoods tittered in the gentle afternoon breeze. Spying a gleaming amber rock in the middle of the road, she squatted, plucked it into her palm, and remained hunkered for long minutes, chin on knees, savoring the warmth of the stone—smooth and weighty in her palm. In places it glittered, and in the center bore a translucent stripe reminiscent of the color of Theodore's eyes. She closed her own and remembered the touch of his arm next to hers in church, the odd sense of unity she'd felt while singing with him. She had never before been to a church service with a man.

She rubbed the stone with her thumb, popped it into her mouth, tasting its warmth and good earthiness, then spit it into her hand and studied the brown stripe, wet now, gleaming, its color intensified to the deep amber of Theodore's eyes.

She smiled dreamily, hunkering yet in the center of the road.

"Lawrence," she murmured aloud, "isn't it funny, I've known you all this time yet I've never noticed the color of your eyes."

She stood up, squeezing the stone in her palm. She looked into Lawrence's eyes. "Oh," she noted disappointedly, "they're green." Then she forced herself to brighten. "Oh, well. Come on"—she grabbed Lawrence's hand—"I'll show you a Russian thistle."

She found one in the ditch not far up the road. It grew in a ball. In winter it rolled before the prairie wind and caught on barbed-wire fences, causing thick drifts to build up around it. Come spring, it had to be manually dislodged. But now, in September, it was a perfect orb of tiny green flowers. A pair of blue-green bottleflies buzzed around it, and a fat bumblebee came to dip into its flowers.

Linnea leaned her drawing pad against her waist and began sketching. *"Now tell me, Lawrence, don't you find that a pretty plant? Look how the bee drinks from it."*

Coming over the crest of a small rise of land in the wheat field to the northeast of the schoolhouse, Theodore raised his eyes to the small building in the distance. From here it appeared no larger than a dollhouse, but as the horses plodded along the gentle slope he made out the coal shed, the swings, the bell gleaming in the sunlight. A motion caught his eye and he noticed a figure some distance from the school, standing in the ditch near the far corner of the field. Unconsciously his spine straightened and his elbows came off his knees. Beneath the brim of his hat his brown eyes softened and a small smile lifted his lips.

What was she doing out there, the little missy? Standing in weeds up to her knees with something in her hands, something he couldn't make out from here. Such a child, dawdling in the ditch as if she had nothing better to do with her time. He gave a silent, indulgent chuckle.

He knew the moment she spied him. She straightened, alert, then lifted whatever she was holding to shade her eyes. An odd exhilaration fluttered within him as she suddenly flung both arms in the air and waved in wide arcs, jumping up and down several times.

He shook his head a little, smiling as he eased forward again, elbows to knees, and continued studying her.

Such a child, he thought. Such a child.

Linnea watched the three sickles cross the field, coming her way, but too far to tell who was in the lead. It was a stunning sight, and she wished she possessed the skill to capture it in a painting, in bright yellows and blues to duplicate those of the wheat and the sky. There was a magnificence about the men and horses, so small against the majesty of all that land, spread before her in vast oceans of undulating yellow. That they controlled it and made it bountiful increased her admiration. Something clutched her heart with a wondrous ferocity and the words of a song came with awesome clarity . . .

Oh, beautiful for spacious skies
For amber waves of grain . . .

Could there really be a war happening when before her lay nothing but beauty and bounty? And they said it was happening to preserve exactly what she was looking at. She thought of the flag she'd just hung, the words she'd just printed on the blackboard. She watched three men drive their teams through the thick stand of wheat. She breathed deeply. And leaped three times in sheer appreciation. And waved.

And one of them waved back.

Chapter 6

Linnea had slept in a state of excitement. Awakening the first morning of school, she heard a rooster crowing out a reveille. Dawn promised a clear day through her little square of window. Downstairs, Nissa was making noises in the kitchen. Linnea bounded from bed with vitality and an avidity to begin the real thing at last.

She took great care with her hair, parting it down the middle, forming the tight twist that began just behind her ears and contoured her nape in a crescent shape. She donned her new green skirt and the matching Black Watch plaid shirtwaist, buttoning it high up the neck, then stretching the thin waist ties from front to back where she formed a bow before twisting on tiptoe to check the results in the mirror.

Though the skirt fit snugly across the front, its rear plaits were deep and full, billowing slightly across her spine, giving a faintly bustled shape that lifted the gathered tail of the shirtwaist. Seeing her reflection, she felt adult and confident. Still on tiptoe, she struck a pose, arms elevated, wrists gracefully cocked.

"Why, thank you, Lawrence. How I wish I could, but you see, today is the first day of school, and I'll have a building full of children by . . ." She suddenly looked down at her chest and gave a chagrined laugh. "Oh, dear, I've forgotten my watch. You'll have to excuse me while I fetch it."

Dropping the whimsy, she moved to the dresser and took up a dainty gold pendant watch that hung suspended from a delicate bow-shaped pin. Over its face was a paper-thin gold cover etched with an all-over design of roses. It had been a graduation gift from her mother and father and was the first timepiece she'd ever owned. She pinned it just above the fullest part of her left breast, then stood back once again to admire herself with pride.

Yes, now I look the part. Miss Brandonberg, teacher.

With a smile, she went down to breakfast.

The others were there already, the men seated at the table while Nissa scuttled back and forth between it and the stove.

''Well, good morning, everyone! Mmm . . . that smells delicious, Nissa.'' Linnea sounded as cheerful as the wake-up rooster, and her step was sprightly as she crossed to her usual chair.

John pivoted in his, gave her a longer inspection than ever before, turned the color of a freshly cured ham, and seemed unable to find his tongue.

''John,'' she greeted, dipping her knees in a brief curtsy. ''Kristian.'' She swung his way with a gay smile and found him wide-eyed and gawking.

''Good—'' But his voice cracked and he had to start again. ''Good morning, Miss Brandonberg.''

''Theodore.'' She gave him her brightest smile, but he scarcely glanced up as he filled his plate.

''Mornin','' he mumbled.

Well, what have I done now, she wondered. Probably nothing. Theodore was just being his usual bright, sunny self.

''It looks like we're going to have a beautiful day for our first day of school,'' she chirped.

Nobody said a word except Nissa, who came to join them and offered, ''Sure does. Everybody's here so let's pray.''

Theodore again did the honors in Norwegian, and though Linnea tried several times to break the barrier of silence through the meal, she met with little success. She complimented Nissa on the breakfast, then brought up the subject of yesterday's lunch.

''If I keep eating this well, I'll be fat in no time. My sandwich Saturday was delicious, too.'' She looked up inquisitively. ''What was in it?''

''Tongue.''

Linnea felt her stomach lurch. ''T . . . tongue?''

''Beef tongue,'' Nissa clarified.

''Beef t—'' But she couldn't bring herself to say the word again. She gulped and felt slightly nauseated while four pairs of eyes slowly lifted to her.

''Never had tongue before?'' Nissa inquired.

''N . . . no, thankfully.''

''Thought you said you liked it.''

''I thought I did. But . . . *tongue?*''

''Hadn't you heard? There's a war going on. We don't waste no part of the cow around here, do we, boys?''

She could feel their amused gazes on her and suddenly felt foolish. Still, she had to ask. ''Did you put it in my sandwich again today?''

''Matter of fact, I did. It was the only cold meat I had. Course, I could fry you an egg and put it in there instead if you . . .''

''Oh, no . . . no,'' Linnea was forced to insist. ''I don't want to make any extra work for you. The t . . . tongue will be fine.''

For the first time that morning, Theodore's eyes rested on her for more than a flash. But they wore a glint of amused mockery as he said, ''Wait till you taste Ma's heart stew.''

A chuckle rippled around the table before the Westgaards returned to their eating, but Linnea found it impossible to take another mouthful.

Rising, she offered lamely, "If you'll excuse me, I have some things to get ready for school." She gestured limply toward the stairway, then made her getaway.

But not even the prospect of tongue sandwiches could daunt her later when she checked her watch and found it was at last time to set off down the road.

Nissa was waiting to bid her good-bye. Kristian must have been in his room changing clothes, and the other two had already gone off to the fields. At the door, Nissa said, "Kristian says to give you this. I put a chunk of cheese in your lunch pail to bait it with."

Linnea looked down at the mousetrap, accepted it gingerly between two fingers, and placed it on top of her grade book.

"Oh, he remembered. I'll thank him when I see him." She looked up and smiled, drew a deep breath, held it several seconds, then said, "Well, here goes. Wish me luck."

"You won't need it, I don't think. Just make 'em know you're boss and you'll do good."

Linnea set out on her twenty-minute walk eager and happy, her step animated as she strode along the crunching gravel. Beside the road the tall grasses were sleek with dew, glistening in the low sun, bending toward her in lissome arcs that scarcely quivered in the windless dawn. Beyond the ditches the fresh-cut grains dried in the long-stretching fields like a woman's freshly washed hair. And everywhere was the scent of harvest: a nutlike quality tinctured with the dusty smell of chaff that hung before the sun in gilded motes.

A red-tailed hawk drifted high on an updraft, its wings as still as the grasses below, only its tail occasionally twisting as it circled and searched for its breakfast. The world was resplendent, silent, its night sounds ceased in the flush of early morning. The sun was an orange ball of flame, hot and blinding, warming Linnea's front but leaving her back cool. Even squinting she could not make out the bell tower of the schoolhouse only half a mile away.

She passed John's place and studied the small weathered house behind its windbreak of columnar cedars. A number of black and white cows stood beside the barn. A flock of song sparrows fluttered about the latticed derrick of his windmill, whose lower third was covered with thick morning glories lifting their blue trumpets toward an equally blue sky. Halfway between the house and the windmill sat an old washtub over-flowing with bright pink and white petunias. Had he planted them? And the morning glories too? She felt a stab of loneliness for the shy, quiet man, then saw a patchwork cat sitting on the back step washing its white face with a gray paw. Somehow she felt better.

John, she thought. What a simple, dear man.

Theodore. She frowned. Anything but simple, and certainly not dear. How could two brothers possibly be so different? If only their personalities could in some way be homogenized—John could use some of Theodore's gall and Theodore some of John's shyness. Odd, how in spite of Theodore's boorishness—or was it because of it?—she couldn't stop trying to win him over. There were times when she detected humor emerging, but always he submerged it. How many days could a man go without smiling? Without laughing? Did he never indulge in gaiety? Surely he had when he was young, when he'd had Melinda.

You just wait, Theodore, you old sourpuss. I'll make you smile yet.

With that promise, she reached the schoolhouse. She paused in the driveway to relish the scene—white building, azure sky, emerald cottonwoods, gold wheat, birds singing somewhere in the grain, the awakening breeze brushing her ear, not a soul about . . . as if she were the only person arisen. Mine, she thought, filing away the memory, promising herself she would never forget these precious moments.

She walked to the concrete steps, touched the cool steel handrail, and opened the wooden door. *Mine . . . at last.*

She moved through the cloakroom and stopped just inside the double doors—everything was exactly as she'd left it. She clasped her hands beneath her chin, savoring the anticipation of her first school day. Golden light poured through the long, clean windows of the schoolroom. The shadows of the desks angled crisp and black against the unfinished oak floor from which Saturday's scrubbing had raised the smell of fresh wood. The shade pulls swayed lazily, their rings creating shifting oval shadows that undulated across a row of desks. Between the windows, the lamp chimneys gleamed. The flag hung motionless. The freshly blacked stove awaited its first fire, the inkwells their first filling, the words on the blackboard their first reading.

And the mouse was sitting in the middle of the floor.

She laughed. The sound sent the creature scampering toward the front of the room. ''Well, good morning to you, too.'' She watched as it scurried across the creaky floor and disappeared behind the bookcase. ''So this is where you hide,'' she said as she went down on one knee to peer behind the shelves. She stood up, brushed off her hands, and said aloud, ''I'll get you soon enough, but till I do, don't stick your nose out, do you hear?''

She sat at her desk, pried open the lid of her tin pail, and found the wedge of cheese Nissa had sent. But after she'd set the mousetrap, she glanced at the bookcase, back at the deadly steel spring, and at the bookcase once more. Finally she mumbled, ''Oh, all right, just one more day.'' She tripped the trap and set it on the floor, harmless, cheese and all.

Next she went outside and filled the water pail, lugged it inside, and transferred the water to the water crock. Last, she filled the inkwells then checked her watch impatiently. Fifteen minutes to wait. She glanced at the closed doors, tipped her head thoughtfully, then rushed across to open both the inner and outer ones, leaving them wide and welcoming.

From the door she studied her table. Then from her table she studied the door. She sat, clasped her hands on the scarred oak table, and studied the view: the west schoolyard and cottonwood windbreak framed by white walls and cleanly dissected by the black stovepipe.

She was sitting precisely that way when the first three heads appeared and peeked around the stovepipe.

''Good morning.'' Immediately Linnea was on her feet, moving toward them. Lars and Evie's children. Each of them held a theme book and a tin molasses pail, and they all stared at her. The boy was freckled, his hair parted on the side and severely slicked down. His dark-blue britches were held up by gray suspenders, and the toes of his boots hadn't a scuff mark on them. The taller girl held the hand of a younger one who tried to hide behind her sister's shoulder. The two girls were dressed similarly, in flowered cotton dresses reaching their high-top brown boots, which were obviously as new as their brother's. The younger girl wore a starched white pinafore over her dress. Both of them had their hair parted down the middle, slicked back into tight, neat pigtails bound by tiny yellow ribbons.

"Good morning, Miss Brandonberg," the older two sing-songed in unison.

Linnea's heart hammered as she tried desperately to recall their names, but dredged up only one. "You're Norna, aren't you? Norna Westgaard."

"Uh-huh. And this is Skipp and Roseanne."

"Hello, Skipp."

He nodded and colored while Roseanne stuck her finger in the side of her mouth and looked as if she were about to cry.

"Hello, Roseanne."

Norna nudged her with a knee and the little tyke recited the obviously rehearsed greeting. "Good morning, Mith Brandonberg." Norna leaned over and pulled her sister's finger from her mouth, ordering, "Say it nice now."

"Good morning, Mith Brandonberg." This time it came out a little more clearly, but with the same captivating lisp as the first time.

Linnea's heart melted immediately. She came forward, but not too near, afraid of rushing Roseanne. "Well, Roseanne, this is your very first day of school, I've heard."

Roseanne pulled out her cheek and nodded, her eyes never leaving Linnea's.

"Did you know it's mine, too? You're my very first students. And I'll tell you a secret if you promise not to tell anyone else." Linnea folded her hands, pressed them between her knees as she bent down, and confided, "I've been just a little bit nervous about meeting you."

Roseanne's finger came out of her mouth and she gazed up at Norna, who smiled down reassuringly.

Another figure came to the door just then. It was Frances Westgaard with a little brother in tow. Recognizing them as Ulmer and Helen's children, Linnea expected to see two older brothers join them momentarily. But as the children filed in to meet her, there were no older brothers.

After an exchange of greetings, they all went outside, the children to the playground and Linnea to the school steps to meet each student who came. She kept one eye on the road for the approach of the missing boys. But minutes passed and the oldest one to arrive was Allen Severt, who sauntered off to the playground where he immediately began pestering the older girls pushing the younger children on the swings.

At nine o'clock Linnea was still short of her four oldest male students and went back inside to check her class list to make sure she hadn't been mistaken about whom to expect.

But she couldn't be mistaken about Kristian! Where was he? Scouring her memory, she came up with a face to go with the name "Raymond Westgaard"—a tall, angular boy who, as soon as he'd been introduced to her on Sunday, had gone off with Kristian. And the Lommen girl had already arrived—she was the pretty one with trailing auburn hair and stunning, long eyelashes—but where was her twin brother? And who else was missing? Oh, yes—Linnea checked her list—Anton. Tony, Nissa had called him, and Linnea had marked his nickname in the margin. Tony Westgaard, age fourteen, was missing, too.

Linnea drew a deep breath and felt her stomach tense. Were they putting her to some test already, the older boys? Deliberately arriving late the first day just to see what her reaction would be?

Thinking of Kristian, she found it impossible to believe he'd be part of such maneuvering. But it was ten after nine already and she still hadn't rung the bell. Finally she looked over all the students and chose the one who looked the most sensible and trustworthy.

"Norna, may I speak to you a moment?" she called from the edge of the playground. Immediately Norna left the rest and came to stand before her.

"Yes, Miss Brandonberg?"

"It's ten after nine, and I'm missing four students. All the older boys. Would you happen to know where they are?"

Norna looked dumbfounded. "Oh, didn't you know?"

"Know? . . . know what?"

"They won't be coming at all."

"Won't be coming?" Linnea repeated disbelievingly.

"Well, no. Not till the wheat's in and threshing's done."

Confused, Linnea repeated, "The wheat? You mean today? Somebody's threshing today?"

"No, ma'am. Not only today, but at the end of the season. The boys got to help with the harvest."

As a glimmer of comprehension surfaced, Linnea feared she was beginning to understand only too well. "The harvest. You mean the whole thing?" She waved a hand at the vast fields around the schoolyard. *"All that?"*

Norna glanced nervously at her hands, then up again. "Well, they need the boys, else how would they get it all in and threshed before the snow flies?"

"Before the snow flies? You mean they intend to keep the boys out of school all that time?"

"Well . . . yes, ma'am," the girl answered with a worried expression.

Realizing she was making Norna uncomfortable, Linnea disguised her dismay and returned mildly, "Thank you, Norna."

But she was already seething as she gazed off toward the northwest, in the direction the boys had been cutting yesterday. Not a soul in sight. And when she stepped into the cloakroom and yanked the heavy knotted rope from its bent nail, she rang the bell with such vehemence that it pulled her feet completely off the floor on the upswing!

What a disastrous beginning to the day that she'd built up in her mind with such idealism. They really got by with it, year after year? Robbing the older boys of valuable school time to help them get their precious wheat in? Well, they'd better think again, because this year Miss Brandonberg was here and things were going to be a little different!

The incident ruined Linnea's entire day. Though she went through the motions of setting up a routine and getting acquainted with her charges, whenever they were busy and she was not, her thoughts turned sour and she couldn't wait to get home and tie into Theodore.

She assigned seats and drew herself a name chart, then had all the children who knew it say the "Pledge of Allegiance" to begin the day. After that they all took turns standing beside their desks, stating their names, ages, and the approximate place each had been working in various subjects when school ended last year. Most of the books the children used had no demarcation indicating grade level.

In an attempt to familiarize herself with each student, both personally and academically, she assigned the older ones the task of writing a short essay about any one member of their family. Those who were in the middle grades were assigned to write a list of ten words they thought described their family, and the younger ones were asked to draw pictures of their family. Meanwhile, she gathered her ''first grade'' around her—cousins Roseanne and Sonny Westgaard—and began teaching them the alphabet with her prepared flashcards.

It was tricky, Linnea found, keeping seven grade levels going at once, and there were times when it seemed she'd given one or a pair of her students enough to occupy their time for a full hour when—presto!—there they'd be, all finished and ready for the next lesson, long before she'd completed a task with another group.

She was grateful for the midmorning recess break and the lunch break at noon, though she couldn't force herself to choke down the tongue sandwich. She ended up discreetly throwing most of it away and spending the afternoon with a growling stomach.

Because the children worked alone so much of the time it was easy to tell who applied himself and who didn't, who was fast and who wasn't, who could work without constantly being watched and who couldn't be trusted.

Allen Severt was the worst of the lot.

His written work was slipshod, his attitude bordering on insolent, and his treatment of the other children boorish and inconsiderate. During the lunch break he went off to drown gophers—there was a bounty of gophers, Linnea learned, so gopher-catching was the boys' favorite noon activity—and brought back not only two tails but one tiny, furry foot, which he quietly laid on Frances Westgaard's shoulder after class resumed. When she discovered it, her shriek unsettled the whole schoolroom as she leaped to her feet and brushed the thing off onto the floor.

''Allen!'' Linnea ordered, ''you will apologize to Frances immediately, then take that vile thing outside and dispose of it!''

He slouched in his seat indifferently and demanded, ''Why? I didn't put it there.''

''Weren't you the one who caught the gophers at noon?''

Instead of answering, he let the cynical curl remain on his lips as he slowly dragged himself to his feet. He bent from the waist with a cheeky attitude and swished the gopher foot from the floor.

''Whatever you say, teacher,'' he drawled.

The way Allen said the word *teacher* was like a slap in the face. It took every bit of fortitude Linnea possessed to keep from giving him the smack he deserved. Their eyes clashed—his lazily victorious, hers snapping—then he hooked a thumb in his back pocket and began to turn away.

''The apology first,'' she demanded.

He stopped, one shoulder drooping lower than the other with an air of persecution, and barely took his eyes off Linnea. ''Sorry, twerp,'' he grunted.

"Outside!" Linnea snapped, realizing the psychological importance of getting in the last word. The boy shuffled to the door with a loose-jointed impudence, deliberately dragging his feet so they clunked on the hollow floor.

Thankfully, the incident happened near the end of the day, for it left Linnea in a state of trembling anger. She tried not to let it show as Allen shuffled back in and resumed his seat with the same bored attitude as before.

With a half hour to go before the dismissal bell, she sat at her table up front, going over the day's papers. Allen, who was part of the oldest group assigned to write the essays, had instead printed the list of words. Further angered by his willfulness, she read the list anyway, without taking him to task for deliberately disobeying instructions. The list itself revealed the boy's defiance:

boring
stoopid
prayers
pest (sister)
black
disterb

To Linnea's surprise he'd added two words totally incongruous with the rest:

choclat cookys

She looked up from the paper to find Allen slouched over his desk with his chin resting on one curled fist, staring at her. He was supposed to be reading, but his hands covered the open book.

Choclat cookys. His mother's chocolate cookies? Was there a glimmer of appreciation inside the boy after all? But what about the word *disterb?* Too disturbed herself to try to figure it out, she turned the paper face down and went on to the next. She felt Allen's eyes drilling the top of her head until she could stand it no more and checked her watch again.

The watch was retractable, its spring-wound cable concealed behind the gold bow. As she pulled it out and snapped the cover open she again felt a discomfiting scrutinization. She looked up to find Allen's eyes fixed on her breast where the fabric of her shirtwaist formed a point at the tug of the chain. A shiver rippled up her spine and she felt herself senselessly coloring, but then he turned his disinterested gaze out the window.

Don't be silly. He's only a fifteen-year-old boy, for heaven's sake.

She studied him covertly for a minute longer. He was gangly and thin, but tall and disproportionately wide at the shoulder, like a high building whose rafters are up and sturdy, but waiting for the walls to be fleshed out. He had none of Kristian's developing brawn, but then he didn't do strenuous work like the sons of farmers did. Still, approaching manhood could be seen in the bones of Allen's angular face and in his sardonic upper lip, which was already trimmed by a wispy shadow of soft whiskers matching those just below the hollows of his cheeks. His eyebrows appeared to be thickening, too, as if one day they would almost span the bridge of his nose. But when she considered what Allen would be like as a man, she shivered again, and quickly dropped her gaze as his head began turning her way again.

"Children, it's time to put your desks in order for the night. Please return your books to the front and wash your ink pens out in the pail in the cloak room. We'll go by grades—Jeannette, Bent, and Skipp, you may go first."

When the room was in order, she wished them all good afternoon and walked toward the cloakroom to ring the bell. But when her arms were lifted high above her head and the children were dashing past, Allen Severt alone took his slow, sweet time. He ambled toward her, heels dragging, and this time there was no question about it—he was openly eyeing her breasts. Immediately she released the bell rope, facing him with as much confidence as she could muster.

"Good-bye, Allen. Let's you and I try for a better day tomorrow."

He gave a single, mirthless huff and sauntered past without saying a word.

All of which did little to ameliorate her temper for her meeting with Theodore.

Theodore was troubled by the amount of time he spent thinking of Miss Brandonberg. It was a hazard of his occupation, thinking too much. How many hours of his life had been spent behind the plodding horses, thinking? And what else was there to do while riding along, watching their shiny rumps sweating in the sun and their large heads nodding? As a boy, working for his father, he'd done his share of dozing to the horses' steady strut. As an adolescent, maturing, he'd done his dreaming to the scrape of earth against an iron plowshare. As a disillusioned husband, he'd done his worrying to the constant *ch-r-r-r* of seeds falling from the grain drill. And as a greenhorn father, abandoned with a year-old son, he'd done his angering in this same place.

Over the years the vista hadn't changed at all: horses, harvest, and horizon.

He had communicated chiefly with the land and animals for so long that he'd grown introspective and dour and had quite forgotten how to communicate with human beings. Oh, there were Nissa and John, and even Kristian. But they, like him, were private, at home with their own company for the most part.

But this little missy, she was something else again. Forever babbling, bubbling. She sure didn't know how to put a button on her lip. The fellow who married her had better be ready to put up with plenty of sass. How was it she could rile him so? Loosen his tongue? Make him think of such foolishness as Russian thistle blossoms and the meaning of fancy words?

He smiled, imagining how surprised she must have been when Kristian didn't show up at school today. Yeah, she was going to be slinging words, first chance she got. Well, let her sling. Kristian was already acting fidgety, gazing off toward the schoolhouse every time he came to the crest of a hill. Theodore wasn't blind: a fool could see the boy was smitten with the schoolmarm and would have dropped the reins and run off to practice his three Rs at a moment's notice. Puppy love. The corner of Theodore's mouth lifted in a grin, but a moment later it faded as he recalled that he himself hadn't been much older than Kristian when he'd made that fateful trip to the city and met Melinda.

Melinda.

Dressed in butter yellow, with her black hair bound in a love knot, her green eyes flashing approval. From the moment he'd seen her on that railroad car, he'd been unable to look away.

He shifted restlessly, transferring the reins to his other hand. What in tarnation had come over him that he was thinking of Melinda lately? Melinda was a thing of the past, and the less he thought of her, the better. He'd learned that years ago.

Theodore squared himself in the iron seat and squinted at the sun, riding down the western sky. Milking time. He flexed and twisted, massaged the back of his neck, and thought of how good it would feel to climb down from this rig and stretch his legs. From the bib of his overalls he pulled a huge old silver stem-winder, checked the time, and slipped it away. Ahh, Ma would have sandwiches and a hot cup of coffee waiting. He signaled the others, pulled up at the edge of the field, and released the horses from the sickle. And as he guided the team toward the familiar windmill for a well-deserved drink, he wondered if the little missy would be home from school by this time.

She was waiting to pounce, standing by the derrick with her fists on her hips when Theodore and Kristian entered the yard on foot behind the horses.

Theodore eyed her from beneath the brim of his straw hat, but made no indication he noticed her. Instead, he called, "Slow down, you two," as the horses spied the water tank and lengthened their strides. Deliberately, he guided Cub and Toots within sniffing distance of her head, all the while ignoring the fact that she stood almost directly in his path.

"Mister Westgaard!" she accosted, turning to glare at his broad shoulders as he passed her without a word.

He'd come close enough to see sparks snapping in her blue eyes.

"Miss Brandonberg?" he replied, with deliberate coolness while she followed him, leaning forward, fists clenched and pumping with each step.

"I want to talk to you!"

"So talk."

"Your son was *not* in school today!"

Theodore nonchalantly dropped the reins and bent to loosen the cruppers.

"Course not. He was out in the fields with me."

"Well, what—pray tell!—was he doing there!"

"Doin' what every able-bodied boy around these parts was doing. Helpin' with the harvest."

"On your orders?"

Theodore straightened just as Kristian pulled up with his team, but the boy sensibly kept his mouth shut.

"It don't take no orders. Boy knows he's needed and that's all there is to that."

"*Doesn't* take *any* orders!" she exploded. "Just listen to yourself!" She gestured at Theodore's chest. "Your grammar is appalling, yet you want him to grow up talking that way? Well, that's exactly what he'll do if you don't let him come to school!" She shook a finger under his nose for good measure.

Theodore colored and his mouth became a thin slash. Just who did she think she was talking to? "What does it matter how he talks, long as he knows how to run a farm? That's what he's gonna do all his life."

"Oh, is it? And what does he have to say about that?" Her angry eyes snapped to Kristian, then back to his father. "Or does he have *anything* to say about it?'' Suddenly she turned and confronted Kristian directly. ''What do you say, Kristian? Is this what you plan to do all your life?''

The boy was so startled, he made no reply.

''See there!'' she continued. ''You've got him so brainwashed he can't even think for himself!''

''Missy, you'd better—''

''My name, when you are addressing me as your son's teacher, is Miss Brandonberg!''

Theodore glared at her, squared his shoulders, and began again. ''*Miss* Brandonberg . . .'' He let the pause ring mockingly before continuing, ''There's a couple things you'd better get straight. Around here we live by the seasons, not by no calendar set by no lord-high-mukky-muk school superintendent. We got wheat to get in, and when it's threshed and in the granaries is time enough for boys to go to school.'' He raised a finger and pointed to the horizon. ''We ain't tinkerin' in no old maid's garden here, you know. What you're lookin' at is fields measured in sections, not acres. Just when in the hell do you think he's gonna use all that fancy language when this land is his? His horses ain't gonna care one way or another if he talks proper or not.'' He thumbed over his shoulder at the horses whose noses were touching the water. ''All they care about is gettin' fed and watered and harnessed proper when we expect 'em to work for us. Cows, horses, pigs, and wheat! *That's* what matters around here, and you'd best remember it before you start preachin' education.''

She straightened and flung her palms up haughtily. ''So what was I hired for? If that's all that matters, you can teach him! I thought my job was to make literates out of children, to prepare them for the world beyond *Alamo, North Dakota,*'' she ended on a disparaging note.

If literate meant what he thought it did, the little snip had put him down again and he'd had about all of it a man could be expected to take from a wet-nosed brat sixteen years younger than himself!

''Alamo, North Dakota, *is* his world, and it always will be, so just be happy you get him for six months of the year instead of none.''

He turned away, but she hounded him. ''So you intend to jerk him out of school again in the spring, too, huh?''

Instead of answering, Theodore headed toward the barn. Incensed, she ran after him and caught him by an arm. ''Don't you dare turn your back on me, you . . . you ornery . . .'' She searched for an adequately scathing term, and finally spit, ''*Cynic!*''

Theodore had no idea what the word meant, and the fact riled him all the more. ''Watch who you're calling names, little missy.'' He yanked his elbow from her grasp.

''Answer me!'' she shouted. ''Do you intend to take him out of school to help you plant, too?''

Theodore's jaw grew stubborn. ''Six months for me, six for you. That's fair, ain't it?''

''For your limited information, there's no such word as *ain't,* and we're not talking about what's fair for me and you. We're talking about what's fair for your son. Do you want him to grow up without knowing how to read and write properly?''

"He knows enough to get by."

"Get by!" Frustrated beyond tolerance, she clutched her temples and spun away. "Lord, how did you get so dense!"

Theodore's anger rose swiftly, and he blushed a bright scarlet. "If I ain't smart enough to suit you, you can go find somebody else to give you a roof over your head. It's for sure the school district don't pay me enough to make up for the food you eat, much less heatin' the upstairs."

Again he turned away. This time she let him go. When he'd disappeared inside the barn, she became aware of Kristian, standing beside the horses with the reins forgotten in his hands, looking very uncomfortable.

Suddenly it struck her what she'd done.

"Kristian, I'm sorry. I didn't mean for you to witness that. I . . . I was totally out of line to call your father names. Please forgive me."

Kristian didn't know where to look. He glanced at the reins, back at Linnea, then at the tugs running along Nelly's rump. "Don't matter," he mumbled, absently laying a hand on the horse's shoulder.

"*Doesn't* matter," Miss Brandonberg corrected unconsciously, then added, "Yes, it does. I had no right to lose my temper that way, or to call him dense." She glared at the barn, made two fists, and hit her thighs. "But I just don't know how to make him realize the importance of education when all he sees is that he's done very well without it."

"He's right, you know." Kristian looked up and met her eyes. "I ain't going no place. This's where I'll probably live all my life. And anyway, I love this farm."

This time she didn't even bother to correct his grammar. Steeped in futility, she watched him walk toward the barn while from its far side came the sound of Theodore calling "Come, boss . . ." as he gathered the cows in for milking.

Chapter 7

Theodore tried to remember when he'd felt this angry. A long time ago, maybe as long ago as when Melinda abandoned him and the baby. Then, as now, he'd felt inadequate, which only increased his anger. There were a thousand more churning thoughts seething for release, but Theodore had had long practice at keeping his rage concealed. Throughout supper he ignored Miss Brandonberg, unable to look at her without feeling a suffocating sense of inferiority. The table was silent again and, by God, that's how it ought to be! He'd had all he could take of her high-handed back talk, and he wasn't about to speak another civil word to a sharp-tongued little snot like her who had no idea how to respect her elders.

The minute the tense meal was over, Theodore sought solace in the place he loved best. He pushed away from the table and without a word to anyone took his hat from the hook behind the door, lit a lantern, and walked through the darkness toward the barn. The night was throbbing with the trill of crickets, but he scarcely heard. The moon was nearly full, but he scarcely saw. Head bowed, footsteps automatic, he made his way through the living night.

The barn door squeaked when he opened it, the first thing to register on his troubled mind. He moved through the barn to the door of the tack room and lifted the lantern high. He glanced across the whitewashed walls where harnesses draped thick in garlands of heavy leather, the order as meticulously maintained as in any woman's pantry. Here was his domain. Here he had total control. Here nobody laughed at him or found him lacking.

The lantern turned his face to gold as he reached to hang it on an overhead hook, then the shadow of his hat darkened his scowling eyes. He let his inward rage run its course, externally calm while unconsciously moving to touch familiar things, finding an oil can and returning to oil the hinges of the barn door, scarcely aware of what he was doing.

Words at whose meanings he could only guess roiled through his thoughts.

Cynic. Literate. Sarcastic. Pondering them, he felt ignorant and impotent. How many times had he wished he could read English? He had grown up to the sound of Norwegian being spoken around him. His ma had taught him to read it when he was a boy, but in those days no other language was necessary here. Things had changed though. Laws had changed. Children were now versed in the language of the new country rather than the old, and only the old-timers clung to the language of their native land.

How did you get so dense? The blood rushed to his face afresh as he recalled the schoolteacher's words. Vehemently, he whacked the barn door shut, returned to the tack room, slammed the can down, then snatched a horse collar from the wall. He hooked it over the arm of the chair and found a thick needle. But as he threaded it with black whipcord, his hands shook. The frustrating sense of impotence came back stronger than ever, and he flung down the needle and thread, closed his eyes, hung his head, and pressed his palms hard against the top of the tool bench. *Dense. Dense. Dense.* It was true. She was nothing more than a child and already she knew more than he'd ever know in a lifetime. But how dare she throw it in his face!

His hands still trembled but somehow managed to thread the needle. Then he fell into the worn chair, took up the collar, and propped it on the floor between his feet. The seam of the leather had torn, exposing a line of pale wood within. He stared at it absently for a long time before patiently beginning to stitch.

There's no such word as ain't.

There ain't? he thought. She might be right, but everybody he knew said *ain't,* even Kristian, and he'd been to school to the seventh grade already!

"She *ain't* goin' to make me feel like an ass again," he vowed aloud, deliberately using the word, "cause I *ain't* going to talk to her and give her the chance."

His fingers fell still. He stared at the collar without seeing it. The light from the lantern fell upon his straw hat and slumped shoulders and threw a shadow over his hands and boots. Outside the crickets still sang. Inside, all was still. Then, hesitantly, he began speaking aloud once more.

"She . . . ain't . . ." He paused, thought, remembered the schoolteachers of the past and how they'd talked. "She's . . . not . . . goin' to make me feel like an ass again, cause I ain't . . . cause I'm not going to give her the chance."

He pondered again for some time, picked up the collar, and hung it over his crossed knees, continuing to mend it. "She ain't even dry behind the ears," he said to the collar, then amended, "She's . . . not . . . even . . . dry . . . behind . . . the . . . ears."

Her face appeared clearly, eyebrows angling, blue eyes intent and glistening as she stalked him with angry zeal and made *Alamo, North Dakota,* sound like the armpit of the earth. She was too good for Alamo, huh? Just like Melinda, though to Melinda's credit, she had never been nasty about it. But what did it matter now? She was gone.

What angered him now was the fact that the schoolmarm's coming had aroused his seething memories of Melinda, ones he'd successfully submerged for years.

He should have followed his initial instincts and tossed Linnea Brandonberg out on her smart little rump while he had the chance. He cut the whipcord, hung the collar up, and put the needle in its appointed place. *Well, when it comes right down to it, it don't matter. The schoolmarm will only be here one year, just like all the rest. She won't come back.*

He could ignore her for a year . . . couldn't he?

But when he'd hung around the tack room until weariness got the best of him, he found it impossible to ignore even so much as the fact that she was in his house. Making his way into the yard he eyed her tiny window. Though it was dark, lights burned yet in the kitchen. He halted, unnerved at the thought of running into her downstairs. *You ain't . . . you're not gonna let that little smarty-pants make you think twice about walkin' in your own house, are you, Teddy?* Resolutely he continued past the windmill toward the golden rectangle that threw an oblique slash of color into the yard. But he breathed a sigh of relief to find everyone had gone to bed. It must've been Ma who left the kerosene lantern on the kitchen table for him.

He took it along to his bedroom where he momentarily paused in the doorway. The room was simple, homespun, the furniture sturdy, old, but well-preserved. There was a mirrored dresser with bow-front drawers. It matched the heavy headboard of the bed, both stained as dark as a hickory nut. The bed was covered with one of Nissa's hand-stitched patchwork quilts in blue and red. The hand-loomed rag rugs brightened the wide pine floorboards, which were the color of coffee without cream. Upon the single window hung shirred lace curtains the color of coffee with cream.

Theodore crossed to the dresser whose top was protected by a white embroidered dresser scarf with blue crocheted edging. He stared at it a long time before setting the lantern down and touching an embroidered blue butterfly, remembering a woman's slim hands holding a needle and hoop, stitching, stitching, trying to stitch away her loneliness. He ran his fingers along the variegated edging until a callus caught the thread and pulled the scarf awry. Sadly, he straightened it, then with slow deliberation opened the top dresser drawer and searched beneath the clothing for the photograph he hadn't looked at in years. It was surrounded by a wooden oval frame with a domed-glass front and looked ridiculously feminine when contrasted against his wide, horny palm. The delicate likeness of a beautiful woman smiled up at him in sepia tones as colorless as she had become during the two precious years he'd had her.

A band of hurt cinched his chest. *Melinda. Aw, Melinda, I thought I'd gotten over you.*

He set the picture down atop the butterflies and flowers she had stitched, watching her as he drew his suspenders over his shoulders and methodically undressed. He turned down the lightweight patchwork quilt, folded back the coarse white sheet, extinguished the light, piled the goose-down pillows one on top of the other, and stretched out with both hands beneath his head. Even in the dark he could see her face smiling with the winsome appeal no woman had had for him before or since. He closed his eyes and swallowed hard, forcing himself to remain as he was, forcing his hands to cup the back of his head instead of running them over the empty half of the bed. Loneliness was a thing he usually accepted with the stoicism peculiar to his people and their way of life. But tonight it crept in stealthily, causing his heart to thump with a heavy ache he couldn't control. He was only thirty-four years old. Had he lived three-fourths of his life? Half? Had he thirty-four more years to sleep in this large bed alone? To come in from the fields at the end of the day to share a table with nobody but his ma and son and brother? And when Ma and Kristian were no longer there to share it, what then? Nobody but John, whom he loved—yes—but who could scarcely compensate for the void left by Melinda. Times were rare when he wished for a woman to replace her. Common sense told him that even if he wanted one there was none to be found around here, where half the women in the county were related to him and the other half either already married or old enough to be his mother.

He didn't understand what had brought on these thoughts of women. He didn't understand why this sadness had struck now at the height of the harvest season, which usually filled him with a sense of fullness and contentment. He didn't understand so many things, and if there was anything that made Teddy Westgaard feel stupid and inadequate, it was not understanding. He wished there was someone he could talk to about it, about Melinda, about the hurt she'd caused all those years ago, about how the hurt could be so intense yet when he'd thought it mastered. But who was there to talk to? And what man would ever resort to spilling out his feelings that way?

Nobody he knew.

Not a soul he knew.

In her bedroom upstairs, Linnea listened to the sounds of Theodore entering below, settling down for the night. She recalled his icy treatment of her at supper and the isolation she'd felt at being closed off that way. It made her feel like crying, though she didn't exactly understand why. Theodore was wrong and she was right. And just because she'd had a tiff with a bullheaded moose like him was no reason to bawl herself to sleep.

Resolutely she flopped over, burying her face in the pillow to stop the stinging in her eyes. Everything seemed so hopeless.

She recalled the conversation she'd had with Nissa right after her run-in with Theodore. She'd thought surely Nissa would see her side, but the older woman had offered little encouragement.

"We didn't tell you the boys wouldn't be in school 'cause we knew you'd be vexed," Nissa said. "And anyway, you ain't gonna change Teddy's mind. He's had the same fight with every schoolteacher that ever came here. Matter of fact, that's why most of 'em never come back a second year. Might as well get used to it. The boys won't be in school till the threshing crew's come and gone."

"And just when will that be?"

"Oh, about mid-October or so. Things move faster once the hired help comes in."

"Hired help?" Where were they going to get hired help when they were already using every available man and boy? And if Theodore could afford to hire help, why didn't he do it now when it would do Kristian the most good?

"Soon as the harvest is done in Minnesota, these boys come out here and hire on. We get some of the same ones, year after year."

So Linnea was alone in her fight to get the older boys the full nine months of education they deserved. Kristian was sixteen years old already and only in the eighth grade. Didn't they understand the reason was that he couldn't complete a full grade's work in six short months?

The tears were coming fast now. She blamed them on frustration and her shattered expectations and the trying day she'd had, what with her shortened roll and her confrontations with Allen Severt and Theodore. But when the tears turned to sobs it was not academics, or roll call, or Allen Severt of which she thought, but of Theodore Westgaard entering the kitchen, sitting at the table, eating an entire meal, and leaving the house without once glancing at her or acknowledging that she existed.

She was treated to more of the same whenever their paths crossed during the next several days. The only time he spoke to her was when she forced him to by greeting him first. But he never raised his eyes. And if she was in the room, he got out of it as fast as he could. On Sunday they ended up side by side in church, and she was conscious of the care he took to make sure his sleeve didn't brush hers. His enmity had by now become a winch about her heart. Each time he gave her the cold shoulder she wanted to clasp his arm and beg him to understand that in her position as a teacher she could not take any stand but the one she had. She wanted to bare her soul and admit that she was utterly miserable, living with his frigid detachment. She wanted him friendly again so the strain in the house would vanish.

Nothing like this had ever happened before in her life. She had never made an enemy of a friend—not that Theodore had ever really been her friend. But his point-blank snubbing was a far cry from the neutrality they'd managed to reach before she blew up at him and called him dense. To sit beside him, feeling his contempt, withered Linnea's heart.

Reverend Severt announced hymn number 203. The organ bellows swelled, the music spilled forth and the congregation got to its feet. It seemed providential that there was only one hymnal for each two people in a pew. Linnea picked one up and nudged Theodore's arm.

He stiffened. She peeked up from beneath her bird-wing hat and offered a hesitant smile. He realized she was offering much more than to share a songbook. He also realized he was in the House of the Lord—no place to practice hypocrisy. As he reached out to hold one edge of the book, he didn't consciously set out to dupe her into believing he could read the words between the stalves.

Though his antipathy seemed to mellow in church, he said nothing to her during Sunday dinner. He ate stolidly, then left the kitchen to change into work clothes. When he came back through the room on his way outside, he came up short at the sight of her staring at him from across the room. She twisted her fingers together and opened her lips as if struggling to speak.

He waited, feeling a curious weightlessness in his stomach, an expectancy that thrust up against the underside of his heart. Her blue eyes were wide and timorous. Two bright splashes of color highlighted her cheeks. The moment seemed to expand into an eternity, but then her lashes swept down. She swallowed and her lips fell closed. Disappointed, he passed through the room without uttering a word.

She spent the afternoon in her room, correcting papers and planning the week's classes. Downstairs, Nissa retired to her bedroom for a nap. The house grew quiet, the rafter room stuffy. Outside, the sun disappeared and the sky took on a green-gray tinge while off to the north, thunder groaned softly.

Immersed in misery and feeling less self-righteous by the hour, Linnea found her concentration straying from her schoolwork. She glanced at the window, noting the changing weather. Her thoughts wandered for the hundredth time to the fight she'd had with Theodore and the resulting antagonism neither of them seemed able to end. Having no one to discuss it with, she decided to tell Lawrence.

"Remember Theodore? Well, I'm afraid he and I are still at odds. We've had a terrible fight, and now he won't talk to me or look at me!" Dressed only in her chemise and petticoats, Linnea confronted her reflection in the mirror, pressing a hand to her breast, fingertips touching the pulse in her throat while an expression of utmost dismay covered her face. "What am I going to do, Lawrence?" She paused, fluttered her fingers and replied, "Well, I suppose we're both at fault. He's being bullheaded and I . . . well, I was terribly nasty to him." Suddenly her back arched and her chin came up defensively. "Well, he deserved it, Lawrence. He's such a stubborn moose!" She flung herself away, taking care not to bump the commode this time. "He thinks the rest of the world is at fault for wanting a higher education than he, and all the while he's tak—" She stopped abruptly and turned back toward the mirror. "Well, yes, I . . . I . . ." She flung her hands up, disgusted with Lawrence's unwillingness to place the blame where it belonged. "So I called him dense! So what?" She moved to the stack of papers she'd been correcting and fiddled with the corner of one, then swung around, wide-eyed. "Apologize? Surely you don't mean it! Why, he's the one who should be apologizing to me!"

* * *

At the first grumble of thunder Theodore turned toward the edge of the field. His backside was planted on solid metal, and in the middle of a wheat field he was a sitting duck in an electrical storm. A pale streak of yellow lit the gray horizon again, and he counted the seconds till the thunder reached his ears, then flagged the others in behind him.

He checked his watch. Four o'clock, and this would be the first day in well over three weeks they'd knocked off early. The break would do them all good, though if the rain came, it would cause delays in drying the wheat they'd already cut.

Back at the house Theodore left Kristian behind to water the horses. He stepped into the empty kitchen and crossed immediately to the stove to check for warm water. With the teakettle in hand he paused, cocking an ear. Now who in blazes could be here visiting with her in her room? He listened for another voice, but none came. There were pauses, then the soft muffled tones of the girl's voice. From a downstairs bedroom came the soft snuffle of Nissa's snoring, and with a puzzled glance at the ceiling, Theodore tiptoed to the stairway, the teakettle forgotten in his hand.

"I just don't know what I'd do without you, Lawrence. You're . . . well, you're absolutely the best friend I've ever had. Now be a dear and fetch my shirtwaist. It's suddenly grown quite chilly."

Theodore waited, but after that all was still. He heard the sound of her footsteps and his eyes followed them along the ceiling. *Lawrence? Who in thunder is Lawrence? And what was he doing in her room?* Again he cocked his head, waiting for a male voice to answer. But minutes passed and none came. What were they doing that could be done so quietly? Theodore poured water in the basin and scrubbed up as quietly as he'd ever done in his life, still curious, listening. But soon Kristian came in from the barn, slamming the screen door and awakening Nissa, who tottered out, hooking her glasses behind her ears and commenting on the brooding weather.

Theodore turned, drying his face and whispered. "Who's up there with her?"

Nissa stopped in her tracks. "Up there? Why, nobody."

"Then who's she talking to?"

Nissa listened intently for a moment. "She ain't talkin' to nobody."

"Oh, I thought I heard voices."

It didn't strike Theodore till he was on his way to the tack room that Ma had said *ain't.* Slipping both hands inside the bib of his overalls, he took on the appearance of a wise old monk as he walked along and corrected, "She's *not* talking to nobody."

The clap of the screen door and the conversation from below brought Linnea back to reality. Suddenly she became aware of how dark it had grown outside. Bracing her palms on the window frame she peered out and saw a flicker of lightning off to the north. So the men had come in early and wouldn't be going back out after the milking.

She plunked down on the edge of the bed and linked her fingers as they dangled between her knees. Flicking her thumb-nails together, she studied them morosely.

"You'd better be right, Lawrence," she said, then rose to tidy herself up.

She need not ask where Theodore might be; somehow she knew. The lightning had drawn nearer and the first knives of rain were riveting as she scurried to the barn. The outer door swung open soundlessly. As it closed behind her, she paused, letting her eyes adjust to the gloom. The long row of windows to her left gave off only the vaguest light, but enough to reveal that the barn was kept as fastidiously as Theodore's private little domain at the near end. Its door was open, spilling a flood of orange lantern light across the hem of her skirts.

She saw only half of Theodore's back. After church he had changed into overalls, but had left his white shirt on. It stretched taut over his shoulders, crossed by striped suspenders as he bent forward in the old chair with his elbows resting on wide-spread knees. He held something in his hands and appeared to be polishing it, his shoulders rocking rhythmically. He bent, dropping a hand to a can between his feet, and she tiptoed one step farther, bringing him fully into view. She watched the play of muscles in his arm below the rolled-up sleeve as he resumed his task. A strip of black leather dangled from his fingers and, as he worked it, its hardware set up a repetitive *ching*. The room was close, warm, and smelled of saddle soap and oil and horses.

He looked so at home in it, everything as tidily in place as when she'd inspected it before. But he looked lonely, too. His hands stopped moving, but he sat on as before, as if absently studying the rag in his hands. She held her breath and remained stark still. She could hear him breathing and wondered what he thought as he sat in solitude with his head bowed low.

''Theodore?''

He flew from the chair and spun to face her, sending the can skittering and the chair balancing on two legs. Even before it settled to the floor again he was blushing.

''Am I disturbing you?''

He'd been sitting there thinking of her, and having her appear silently behind him was disturbing, yes. Her hands were clasped behind her back, bringing her breasts into prominence, and even though he kept his eyes skewered on hers, he caught the wink of her gold watch hanging almost to the fullest part of the left one.

''No.''

''I didn't mean to startle you.''

''I didn't know you was standing there.''

''Were.'' It was out before she could stop it, and she bit her inner lip.

''What?''

''Nothing.'' It was her turn to blush.

Silence fell again, strained, as when they'd met and passed in the kitchen earlier.

''May I come in?''

''Oh, well.'' He waved the rag nervously, once. ''Yeah, sure. But there ain't much . . .'' He shifted feet. ''Isn't much room in here.''

His correction made her feel as uncomfortable as he. ''Enough for one more?'' she asked. When he made no reply, she eased into the room, affecting a casual air, with her arms overlapped behind her waist, glancing up at the wall wreathed with leather. ''So this is where you spend your spare time.''

"There ain't . . ." He tried to think up the right term, but somehow his mind seemed jumbled with her in the room. "No such thing on a farm."

"Mmm . . ." She perused the neatly hung harnesses, ignoring his grammar this time. "So what were you doing?"

"Polishing tack."

"Oh. Why?"

He stared at the side of her head as she tilted it to study things high above her. What a question. And *she* thought *he* was dense?

"Cause if you don't, the sweat from the horses'll rot it, and if that don't get it, the fumes from the . . . the fumes from out there will." He nodded toward the main part of the barn.

"Really?" She turned to face him, wide-eyes. "I never knew that before. That's interesting." Theodore had never before considered it interesting, only true. "But then, I guess you know absolutely everything there is to know about running a farm." She strolled farther into the room, and he watched, fascinated, unable to fathom why she'd come here. She ambled to the sawhorse, reached out to brush the sheepskin liner, and suddenly changed her mind.

"Oh! I almost forgot." She turned, producing a mousetrap from behind her back. "I have an unwanted guest at school. Kristian found the trap for me, but I'm afraid I didn't have much luck setting it. Could you show me how?"

He glanced at the mousetrap, then back at her, and she thought for an infinitesimal moment that he was going to grin. But he didn't, only thought for the second time in three minutes that for an educated woman she had her dense spots, too.

"You don't know how to set a mousetrap?"

She shrugged. "My father always did it in the store, so I never had to try before. Nissa sent some cheese in my lunch pail one day, but I kept springing the fool thing and I was scared I'd break a finger."

"What store?"

"My father owns a mercantile store in Fargo. The mice love to chew holes in the flour sacks."

His eyes narrowed slightly. "I thought your father was a lawyer."

She stared at him speechlessly, caught in her own lie. She dropped her eyes to the mousetrap, and when at last she spoke, there was contrition in her tone. "It was a fib. You . . . you rattled me so badly that day that I had to think up something quick, because I was . . ." She looked up appealingly, then dropped her eyes again. "Because I was afraid you weren't going to take me with you and I didn't know what else to say to change your mind."

So little miss righteous wasn't so righteous after all. But her cheeks were stained as bright as peonies and she concentrated on the mousetrap as if afraid to raise her gaze again. Her fingernails were neatly buffed and trimmed and she scratched at the stamped ink design around the edge of the wood.

He extended one wide palm. "So give it to me. It will be something new, me teaching you something."

Her head came up; and their eyes met. To her relief, she found in Theodore's a hint of amusement. She placed the mousetrap on his palm, and he stretched to pluck the lantern from its ceiling hook and took it to the workbench, presenting his back. But now that she'd come this far, she was reluctant to stand too close to him.

He looked back over his shoulder. "Well, are you coming?"

"Oh . . . yes."

They stood side by side, and she thought she had never seen hands so big as she watched them set the trap. He produced a tiny square of leather to use in place of cheese. "First you bait it. Here."

"Well, of course, there. I'm not *that* stupid."

He looked down. She looked up. They both came very close to smiling. She noted that he'd removed the celluloid collar from his dress shirt, which was open at the throat, and that for a man he had extraordinarily long eyelashes. He noted that the depths of her blue eyes held tiny flecks of rust, almost as bright as the burnished glow of the lanternlight reflecting off the gold watch on her breast. They forced themselves to concentrate on the lesson at hand.

"Hold it down flat and force the bow back to the other side."

"Force the bow back," she repeated and looked up again. "It's called a bow?"

"Yeah."

"Why?" He made the mistake of glancing into her eyes again, and the trap snapped and bounced off the top of the bench onto the floor.

She started giggling and he felt his face heating up.

"*I* can do it *that* well," Linnea teased. She bent over and retrieved the trap, then handed it to him with an expression of mocking tolerance.

Flustered, he took it and began again—found the square of leather, put it in place, and forced the bow back. "Put the locking bar into place beneath the little lip . . . " Carefully he withdrew his hands. "There." He was relieved to see he'd done it right this time. He reached to pluck a screwdriver from an orderly can of tools and tripped the trap with it. "Now you try." He slipped the screwdriver back into the can and pushed the trap her way.

"All right." He watched her hands perform the lesson, thinking of how the trap, if accidentally sprung, could bruise and probably break a finger that small. But she managed beautifully, and soon the baited trap lay on the workbench between their four hands.

Outside the storm had strengthened. In the little square of window their faces were reflected against a blue-black sky, while the tack room grew distractingly silent all of a sudden. The scent of leather, horses, and old wood sealed them in securely.

"Theodore?" She said it so quietly it might have been an echo. Rain was pelting against the window, but inside it was bright and dry. But not as dry as Theodore's throat, which suddenly refused to work as they both continued staring at each other's hands. "I didn't really come here to learn how to bait the mousetrap. I figured it out by myself on the second try. It was just an excuse."

He turned to look at her, but found himself staring at the part in her hair. Her head remained bowed as she went on. "I came to apologize to you."

Still he could think of nothing to say.

"I think I hurt you rather badly the other day when I ridiculed you for your improper grammar and called you dense. I'm very sorry I did that, Theodore."

He saw her chin lift and quickly glanced away before their eyes could meet. "Aw, it don't matter."

"Doesn't it? Then why have you refused to talk to me or even look at me ever since?"

He had no idea how to respond, so he stared at the piece of leather on the trap while an enormous clap of thunder made the sturdy barn shudder. But neither Theodore nor Linnea flinched.

"It's been very hard on me to share the same table with you and to pass you in the kitchen all the while you were trying to freeze me out. My family is very different from yours. We talk and laugh together and share things. I miss that very much since I came here. All week long, whenever you'd get all cold and stiff and turn away from me, I felt like crying, because I've never had an enemy before. Then today in church, I thought . . . well, I hoped maybe you'd warmed up a little, but when I thought about it a little more I realized you were probably very deeply hurt and if I wanted to be your friend again, I must apologize to you. Would you . . . would you look at me, please?" Their eyes met, his self-conscious, hers contrite. "I'm sorry. You're not dense, and I never should have said that. And I should have been more patient with you about your grammar. But, Theodore, I'm a teacher." Without warning she placed a hand on his arm and her expression became tender. Something awkward happened to his heart, and it felt like her light touch was singeing his skin. He tried to drag his gaze away but failed.

"Do you know what that means?" Her eyes glittered and he wondered frantically what he would do if she started crying. "It doesn't mean that I'm a teacher only when I'm in the schoolroom. I can't separate me into two different people—one who teaches when she's a mile down the road and one who forgets about it when she comes back here."

She gestured widely and, thankfully, he was free of her touch and of the threat of tears. "Oh, I know I'm impetuous sometimes. But it happens automatically. I hear people speaking improperly and I correct them. I did it again without even thinking, when I came in here. And I saw how uncomfortable it made you feel." He began to turn away, to pick up the rag and look busy, but she grabbed his shirtsleeve and forced him to stay where he was. "And I'll do it again . . . and again . . . and again before I'm through with you. Do you understand that?"

He stared at her mutely.

"So what harm can it do if you know that I don't mean to belittle you? There's no rule that says I must be a teacher only to children, is there?" When he made no comment, she twisted his sleeve impatiently and insisted, "Is there?"

She was an enigma. He wasn't used to dealing with directness such as this, and he waited too long, trying to decide what to say to her. She flung away his arm irritably. "You're being bullheaded again, Theodore. And while we're on the subject of bullheadedness, you certainly don't set a very good example for your son when you sulk around and pull your silent act. What do you think Kristian thinks about his father treating the schoolteacher that way? You're supposed to respect me!"

"I do," he managed at last.

"Oh, of course you do." She squared her fists on her hips and tossed a shoulder. "So far you've tried to pawn me off on the Dahls and freeze me out. But I can't live this way, Theodore. I'm just not used to that sort of enmity."

Out of the clear blue sky, Theodore made an admission such as he'd never expected to hear himself make. "I don't know what enmity means."

"Oh!" His admission went straight to her heart. Her eyes softened and she dropped her belligerent pose. "It means hostility . . . you know, like we're enemies. We're not going to be enemies for the next nine months, are we?"

He seemed unable to summon up his voice again. All he could think about was how fetching she looked in the lantern-light, and how her blue eyes came alight with those gold sparkles, and how he liked the pert tilt of her nose. She grinned and added, "Because I'll be plumb crazy before then."

What could a man say to a feisty little firecracker like her?

"You talk a lot, you know."

She laughed and suddenly swung across the room and mounted one of the saddles on the sawhorse. Astride, she crossed her hands on the pommel and hunched her shoulders. "And you talk too little."

"Quite a pair we make."

"Oh, I don't know. We were doing all right when I first came in here. Why, you were practically . . ." She grinned teasingly. "Rhapsodizing."

He leaned back against the workbench and crossed his arms over his bib. "So what does that mean?"

She pointed her nose at him and ordered, "Look it up."

Someplace in the house there was an English/Norwegian dictionary. Maybe he could puzzle it out or stumble across the word somehow.

"Yeah, maybe I'll do that." And maybe he'd see if he could find out anything about a few of the other words she'd harangued with him.

She took a big breath, puffed out her cheeks, and blew at her forehead. "Wow, I feel so much better."

She smiled infectiously, and Theodore found himself threatened with smiling back.

In her mercurial way, she slapped the saddle. "Hey, this is fun. Giddyup." With her heels she spurred twice. "I haven't been on a horse many times in my life. Living in town, we don't have any of our own, and whenever we travel, Father rents a rig."

A quarter grin softened his mouth as he leaned back, watching, listening. Forevermore, but she could babble! And she was, after all, really a child. No woman would sling her leg over a saddle that way while visiting a man in a tack room and run on about anything that popped into her mind.

"You know, little missy, it ain't . . . it's not good for a saddle to be set on that way when it's not on a horse."

"Sat on," she corrected.

"Sat on," he repeated dutifully.

She pulled a face and looked down at her skirts, then up at him while her expression changed to an impish grin. "Aww, it ain't?" Without warning, her foot flew over and she landed on her feet with a bounce. "Then next time maybe it better have one under it, wouldn't you say?" And with that she flitted to the door, pivoted, and waggled two fingers at him. ''Bye, Theodore. It's been fun talking.''

She left him studying an empty doorway as she ran out, heedless of the rain, and in her absence he found himself wondering again who Lawrence was.

Chapter 8

The following morning the rain had turned into a low-lying mist that clung to the skin and clothing and made hay cutting impossible. Kristian shivered, then sneezed twice as his feet went over the side of the bed. Even the linoleum felt damp. Over long underwear he drew on warm woolen britches, a long-sleeved undershirt, and an outer shirt of thick flannel. As he opened his bedroom door to go downstairs, Linnea Brandonberg opened hers to do the same.

Kristian's blood suddenly lost its chill.

Her hair wasn't combed yet but hung free to the middle of her back. She looked sleepy-eyed as she held the neck of her wrapper with one hand, the blue basin with the other.

''Good morning,'' she greeted.

''Good morning.'' His voice went from tenor to soprano in one crack. Flustered, he realized his shirt was only half-buttoned and hurriedly finished the job.

''Chilly, isn't it?''

''Damp, too.'' He'd never seen any woman besides Grandma in her wrapper and bare feet. The sight of his teacher in night-clothes made his throat feel queer and he wasn't sure where to let his eyes light.

''I guess you won't be able to go out to the fields today.''

''Ahh, no, I ahh, guess not.''

''You could come to school then.''

He shrugged, not sure what his father's reaction would be to that. ''One day wouldn't do much good, and the sun'll probably be out tomorrow.''

''One day is one day. Think about it.'' She turned and hurried down the stairs, giving him a better view of her cascading hair, which bounced with each step. What was happening to him lately? He never used to notice things like girls' eyes or what they were wearing or whether their hair was up or down. Girls were just troublesome brats who always wanted to tag along hunting gophers or swimming in Little Muddy Creek. When you let them they always spoiled your good time.

He clumped down the stairs behind her and pretended not to be watching as she greeted Nissa, filled her basin, and scurried back upstairs for her morning bath. He pictured it . . . and his chest felt like it was caving in.

She's the schoolteacher, you jackass! You can't go around thinkin' about the schoolteacher that way!

But he was still dwelling on how pretty she'd looked on the landing as he made his way to the barn to help with the morning milking.

Dawn hadn't yet arrived but would soon sneak in undetected. The farmyard, shrouded in mist, was redolent with the smells of animal and plant life. Cattle, pigs, chickens, mud, and hay—they were all out there in the damp shadows. The dense air muffled all but the faraway sound of roosting chickens throatily clucking their prelude to rising. Upon the spillpipe of the windmill droplets condensed, quivered, then fell to a puddle below with an uneven *plip*. Beyond the looming derrick a row of golden windows glowed a welcome.

Opening the barn door, Kristian sneezed.

Entering, he gave an all-over shudder, happy to be out of the damp. There was a pleasantness to the barn at this time of day that could always manage to take the edge off a man's early-morning grumpiness, especially when the weather was bad. Even when snow, sleet, or biting cold pressed against the windows, inside, beneath the thick, cobwebbed rafters with the doors sealed tightly, it was never chilly. The cattle brought with them a warmth that dispelled the most insidious dampness, the most oppressive gloom.

Theodore had already let them in. They stood docilely, awaiting their turns, rhythmically chewing their cuds, the grinding sound joining the hiss of the lanterns that hung from the rough-hewn rafters. The barn cats—wild, untamable things—had decided against mousing in the rain and watched from a safe distance, waiting for warm milk.

Kristian picked up his milk stool and wedged himself between two huge warm black and white bellies. When he sat and leaned his forehead against old Katy, he was warmed even further. He filled the sardine cans, set them at his side, and played the perennial game of waiting to see if the wary cats could be enticed that close. They couldn't. They held their ground with typical feline patience.

"You still asleep or what?" Theodore's voice came from someplace down the line, accompanied by the liquid pulsations of milk falling into a nearly filled pail.

Kristian flinched, realizing he'd been wool-gathering about Miss Brandonberg, whose hair was quite the same caramel color as one of the cats.

"Oh . . . yeah, I guess I was."

"All you took from Katy so far was two sardine cans full."

"Oh, yeah . . . well . . ." Guiltily, he set to work, making his own milk pail ring. Then, for long minutes, there was only rhythm . . . the unbroken cadence of milk meeting metal, of milk meeting milk, of powerful bovine teeth grinding against cuds, of the beasts' breaths throwing warmth into the barn with each bellowlike heave of their huge bellies.

Kristian and Theodore worked in companionable silence for some time before Theodore's voice broke in.

"Thought we'd drive over to Zahl today and get coal."

"Today? In this drizzle?"

"Been waitin' for a rainy day. Didn't want to waste a sunny one."

"Reckon you'll be wantin' me to hitch up the double box then."

"Soon as breakfast is over."

Kristian went on milking for some minutes, feeling the strong muscles in his forearms grow warm and taut. After pondering at length, he spoke again.

"Pa?"

"Yuh?"

Kristian lifted his forehead off Katy's warm side. His hands paused.

"Long as I'm gonna have the wagon all hitched up, would it be all right if I took Miss Brandonberg to school?"

In their turn, Theodore's hands stopped pumping. He recalled warning Miss Brandonberg that he didn't have time to be hauling her to school. He thought of her on that saddle last night and his neck seemed to grow a little warm. He'd readily admit she hadn't looked much like a hothouse pansy then. She'd looked . . . ahh, she'd looked . . .

Something happened within Theodore's heart as the picture of Linnea appeared. Something a man of his age had no business feeling for a young thing like her.

Resolutely, Theodore continued milking. "I told her when she come here I didn't have time to be cartin' her off to school when the weather got bad. I got things for you to do."

"But she'll be soaked through by the time she gets there!"

"Tell your grandma to find her a spare poncho."

Kristian's lips hardened and he vehemently lit into his milking. Damn the old man. He don't need me and he knows it. Not for the ten minutes it'd take me to drive her to school. But Kristian knew better than to press the point.

Linnea was all dressed for breakfast when she heard the thud of Kristian taking the steps two at a time. Two sharp raps sounded on her door, and she opened it to find him standing breathless on the landing.

For the second time that morning there was a look on his face that warned her to keep things very impersonal between them.

"Oh, hello. Am I late for breakfast?"

"No. Grandma's just putting it on. I . . . ahh . . ." He cleared his throat. "I just wanted you to know I'd give you a ride to school if I could, but Pa said he needs me right after breakfast. But Grandma's got a spare poncho for you to wear. And an umbrella, too."

"Why, thank you, Kristian, I appreciate it." She flashed him a second smile, attempting to make it appreciative but not encouraging.

"Well, I . . . um . . . I gotta wash up. See you downstairs."

When Linnea closed the door, she leaned back against it, releasing a huge breath. Goodness, this was one problem she hadn't foreseen. He was her student, for heaven's sake. How would she handle his obvious attraction for her if it kept growing? He was a sweet, appealing boy, but he was—after all—just a boy, and while she liked him as she liked all her students, that was as far as it went.

Still, she couldn't help being touched by his blossoming gallantry, his visible nervousness, and the fact that he'd asked permission to give her a ride to school. Neither could she help being piqued by the fact that the permission had been denied.

At breakfast, several minutes later, Linnea covertly studied Theodore. She'd hoped that last night had seen the last of his orneriness, but apparently not. Well, if one could be ornery, so could two.

"It's too wet to work in the fields today. No reason why Kristian can't come to school."

Theodore stopped chewing and leveled her with a chastising stare while she innocently went on spreading raspberry jam on a piece of toast.

"Kristian ain . . . isn't going to school today. We got other things to do besides cut wheat."

She glared at Theodore. Her mouth tightened like a draw-string purse. Their eyes met and clashed for several interminable seconds, then without another word, she pitched her toast onto her fried eggs, her napkin on the toast, and ejected herself from the chair. She made as much racket as possible as she clattered angrily up the stairs.

In her wake, John, Kristian, and Nissa, astonished, stared at the empty doorway, but Theodore went on calmly eating his bacon and eggs.

Less than fifteen minutes later Kristian watched her trudge off down the road through the drizzle and wished again he were going with her. Still stewing, he harnessed Cub and Toots, then clambered onto the wagon seat to wait in irate silence for his father. He sneezed twice, hunkered forward, and stared straight ahead when the old man came out of the house, dressed in a black rubber poncho and his tattered straw hat. The wagon seat pitched as Theodore climbed aboard, and Kristian sneezed again.

"You gettin' a cold, boy?"

Kristian refused to answer. What the hell did the old man care if he was getting a cold or not! He didn't care about anybody but himself.

Even before Theodore was seated, Kristian gave a shrill whistle and slapped the reins harder than necessary. The team shot forward, setting Theodore sharply on his rump. The older man threw a look at his son, but Kristian, churning, only pulled his hat down farther over his eyes, bowed his shoulders, and stared straight down the lines.

The day suited his mood—wet and cheerless. The horses plodded along through a sodden, colorless countryside devoid of moving life. Those fields already shorn looked dismal, their stubble appearing like tufts of hair on a mangy yellow dog. Those yet uncut bent low beneath their burden of rain like the backs of tired old people facing another hard winter. When Kristian had ridden in stony silence for as long as he could, he finally spouted, without preamble, "You shoulda let me give her a ride to school!"

Theodore cautiously studied his son, the profile set in lines of rebellion, the lips pursed in displeasure. Just when had the boy had time to become so dead set on squiring the schoolmarm around?

"I told her the first day I wasn't cultivating no hothouse pansies here."

Kristian glared at his father. "Just what is it you got against her?"

"I got nothin' against her."

"Well, you sure's hell don't like her."

"Better watch your mouth, hadn't you, boy?"

Kristian's face took on a look of intolerant disgust. "Aw, come on, Pa, I'm seventeen years old and if—"

"Not yet, you ain't!" In his ire Theodore realized he'd used *ain't,* and it angered him further."

"Two months and I will be."

"And then you figure it's all right to cuss a blue streak, huh?"

"Saying hell ain't exactly cussin' a blue streak. And anyway, a man's got a right to cuss when he's mad."

"Oh, a man is it, huh?"

"You don't ask that when you send me out to do a man's work."

The truth of the statement irritated Theodore further. "So what is it got you so nettled? And give me them reins. You ain . . . you're not doin' them horses' mouths any good." Theodore plucked the reins from Kristian's hands, leaving him to stare morosely between the horses' ears. Moisture gathered on his curled hat brim and dripped past his nose.

"You never ask me, Pa. You never even give me the choice about going to school or not. Maybe I want to be there right now."

Theodore had figured this was coming. He decided to confront it head on.

"To study?"

"Well of course to study. What else?"

"You tell me." Kristian shot his father a quick look, set his gaze on the hazy horizon, and swallowed pronouncedly. Theodore studied Kristian and remembered clearly the pangs of growing up. He forced his voice to calm, and asked without rancor, "Got feelings for the teacher, do you, boy?"

Surprised, Kristian again flicked a glance at his father, shrugged, then stared straight ahead. "I don't know. Maybe. What would you say if I did?"

"Say? Not much I can say. Feelings is feelings."

Having expected an explosion, Kristian was surprised at his father's calm. Having expected reticence, he was even more unprepared for Theodore's apparent willingness to talk. But they never talked—not about things like this. It was hard to get the words out, but there were so many things mixing up Kristian lately. His own anger calmed and much of his youthful confusion became audible in his tone. "How's a person supposed to tell?"

"Don't know if I can answer that. I guess it's different for everybody."

"I can't quit thinkin' about her, you know? I mean, I lay in my bed at night and think about stuff she said, and how she looked at supper, and I come up with things I wanna do for her."

The boy was smitten, but good, Theodore realized. Best tread soft.

"She's two years older than you."

"I know."

"And your teacher, to boot."

"I know, I know!" Kristian stared at his boots. Water funneled from the front of his hat brim and rain wet the back of his neck.

"Come on kind of fast, didn't it? She's only been here a couple weeks."

"How long did it take for you and my mother?"

What should he answer? The boy was growing up for sure, to be asking questions like that. Truth was truth, and Kristian deserved to know. "Not long—

I'll grant you that. I saw her standin' up there on that train beside her pa, wearin' a hat as yellow as butter, and I hardly looked at Teddy Roosevelt again.''

''Well then why couldn't it happen to me that fast?''

''But you're only sixteen, son.''

''And how old were you?''

They both knew the answer. Seventeen. In just two months Kristian would be seventeen. It was coming on faster than either of them was prepared for.

''What did it feel like, Pa, when you first knew how you felt about my mother?''

Like last night when I looked at the little missy sitting on that saddle. To Theodore's bewilderment the answer came at will. He was no more ready for it than for his son's imminent manhood.

''Feel like?'' The feeling was with him again, new and fresh. ''Like a strong fist in the gut.''

''And do you think she felt the same?''

''I don't know. She said she did.''

''She said she loved you?''

Slightly self-conscious, Theodore nodded.

''Then why didn't she stay?''

''She tried, son, she really tried. But right from the start she hated it here. Seemed like she was sad all the time, and after you were born it seemed to get worse. Oh, not that she didn't love you. She did. I'd find her layin' with you beside her on the bed in the middle of the afternoon. She'd be playing with your toes and talkin' and croonin' to you. But underneath, she was pure sad, like women get after birthings. She never seemed to get over it. By the time you were a year old she was still starin' out across the wheat fields, claimin' the sight of it wavin' and wavin' was drivin' her mad. There was no sound here, she said.'' Theodore shook his head disconsolately. ''Why, she never cared to listen. To her, sounds meant streetcars and motorcars clanging by on a cobblestone street and hawkers peddlin' and blacksmiths hammerin' and trains whistlin' through the city. She never heard the wind in the cottonwoods, or the bees in the caragana bushes.'' Theodore squinted at the vast prairie and went on as if talking to himself. ''She never heard them atall.

''She hated the stir of the wheat, she said after a while she hated it worse than she'd hated travelin' on that train with her pa. I watched the sparkle go out of her, and her laugh disappeared, and I knew . . .'' He looked at the runnels of rain slipping down his wet poncho. ''Well, I knew I wasn't the kind of man who could ever bring it back. She thought I was somethin' I wasn't, that night when we danced and talked in Dickinson. That was some kind of fairy tale to her, but this was the real thing, and she could never get used to it.''

Kristian sneezed. Wordlessly, Theodore lifted a hip, produced a handkerchief, and handed it to his son. When Kristian had blown his nose, Theodore went on.

''She just stared out over the wheat fields and got sadder and quieter, and pretty soon her eyes looked all dull and . . . well, nothin' like they were the day I first saw her on that train. Then one day she was gone. Just gone.''

Theodore's elbows rested on his knees. Sadly, he shook his head.

''Ah, that day. I'll never forget that day. Worst day of my life, I suppose.'' He shook off the memory and went on matter-of-factly, ''She left . . . but I never thought it was us she was leaving as much as it was the place. It hurt her to leave you. She said so in her note. Tell Kristian I love him, she said. Tell him when he's old enough."

Kristian had heard it before, but his heart swelled at the words. He'd always understood that his motherless family was different from those of his cousins and schoolmates, and though he'd never known a mother's love, there had always been Nissa. But suddenly he missed the mother he'd never known. Now, on the verge of manhood, he wished he had a mother to talk to.

"You . . . you loved her, didn't you, Pa?"

Theodore sighed, and kept staring at the horses' rumps. "Oh, I loved her, all right," he answered. "A man sometimes can't help lovin' a woman, even if she's the wrong one."

They rode on in silence through the weeping day, with Theodore's last words reverberating in their minds. And if those words brought to mind Linnea rather than Melinda, it was nothing either man could control.

They came at last to the coal fields of Zahl. Theodore pulled the wagon onto the scale and stopped the horses with the old Norwegian term that was somehow comforting today.

"Pr-r-r," he ordered, the word blending with the mood set by both the story and the falling rain. Nobody was about. They were surrounded by the smell of wet coal and the sound of dripping water. Theodore turned to his son, rested one hand on his shoulder, and said, "Well, she's a pretty little thing, all right. I'll grant you that." Abruptly, he changed moods. "So, here we are. You up to loadin' eight tons of coal, boy?"

Kristian wasn't. He was feeling worse all the time. The sneezes were coming one right after the other, and it was a toss-up as to which was dripping faster, his nose or his hat brim.

"I ain't got much choice, have I?"

Theodore gently scolded, "There's no such word as ain't, boy." Then he vaulted over the side of the wagon and went to find old man Tveit to get the empty wagon weighed, so they could start loading.

The vast farmland that had driven Melinda Westgaard into a state of depression and caused her to desert her husband and son was, that day, as bleak as she'd found it on the bleakest of days. The rain fell dismally over the flat coal fields of Zahl with not a single tree to break the monotony of the featureless horizon. Aesthetically, nature had been unkind to North Dakota. But though she'd robbed the state of trees to provide precious fuel, she had offered something in their stead: coal. Twenty-eight thousand square miles of it. Soft, brown lignite, so accessible that man could simply scrape away the thin covering of surface soil and harvest the fuel with pick axes and shovels.

And so Theodore and Kristian harvested it that wet September day.

The weather was so grim that old man Tveit hadn't even hitched his team to the fresno. Instead, the earth-scraper sat idle, collecting rain in its scoop.

As Kristian worked beside his father, he paused often to blow his nose and sneeze. The damp chill crept up his legs and down inside his poncho. The inside of his collar grew wet, sending a shiver straight to his marrow.

By the time the wagon was loaded, he was utterly miserable. But he still faced the hour-and-a-half drive back home. Long before they got there Kristian felt weak from sneezing. His nose was rubbed raw from Theodore's damp handkerchief and the chills were shaking his body. Halfway home a timid sun began separating the clouds, peering through like a jaundiced eye, but it did little by way of warming Kristian.

"I s'pect you're feeling as soggy as you look," Theodore noted.

Kristian's mouth was open, eyes closed, nostrils flaring as he felt another sneeze coming. He peered at the sun to bring it on. When it erupted, it doubled him over and left his eyes watering.

"I'll drop you at home before I go on over to school to unload."

"I can help," Kristian felt compelled to insist, but there was little zest in the words.

"The best place for you is in bed. I can handle one wagon of coal by myself."

Kristian had no thought of objecting, and Theodore left him tucked securely in bed with Nissa fussing over him like a mother cat.

By the time he started for school it was late afternoon. The sun had chased away the remaining clouds and lay upon the ripe wheat like a benediction. Troubled, Theodore went over his talk with Kristian.

You'd best tread light around the little missy, too. Kristian's got no idea she sets off a spark in you too, and he'd better not ever find out.

The schoolyard was empty as he pulled the horses up before the steps.

"Pr-r-r," he ordered softly, studying the door as he secured the reins and leaped down. Crossing before the team, he distractedly fondled Cub's nose and headed for the schoolhouse steps.

The door opened soundlessly. The cloakroom was deserted, its inner doors ajar. The lunch pails were gone from beneath the long benches. A drip of water fell from the water spigot into a bucket with a lazy, echoing *blip*. The heavy knot of the bell rope swayed before Theodore's eyes and he backhanded it aside, moving toward the double doors. Suddenly, from inside, came the sound of Miss Brandonberg's angry, feminine voice. With his hand on the door, he paused.

". . . next time I catch you up to your tricks, I fully intend to tell your parents about it. I will, in any case, be making visits to each home. You'd like me to have something good to report to your mother and father, wouldn't you, Allen?"

So the Severt kid was in there with her.

"You know, you've given me another one of those absolutely awful days. You and Theodore."

Theodore's eyebrows shot up and his chin drew in. Then he scowled. What business was it of the Severt kid's what went on between himself and the teacher?

"I do not understand that man. It wouldn't have hurt him one bit to let Kristian come to school today!" Her voice calmed and she added, *"But I guess that's none of your affair. You're excused, but tomorrow when you come to school it had better be with a changed attitude."*

Theodore backed away from the door, prepared to look as if he'd just entered the cloakroom when Allen walked past. But no footsteps sounded. No Allen appeared. Instead, all Theodore heard was the scrape and click of the chalk on the blackboard.

"All right, Theodore, he's gone and we can fight in peace!"

Theodore stiffened, chagrined at being caught eavesdropping. He was preparing to enter the schoolroom when her voice hurried on. *"Oh, all right, you know what I mean!"* Suddenly he realized she had no idea he was there, and smiled. So, what was she doing, *practicing* fighting with him? Apparently so, for she was putting plenty of gusto into her words as she scolded, *"It wouldn't have killed you to let Kristian come to school today, but no, you're too bull-headed stubborn to let me get one up on you, aren't you! So how did you keep him busy?"* Her voice turned sarcastic. *"Polishing harnesses in the tack room?"*

The chalk scraped on the board, and she started pronouncing disjointed words. *"Clock. Kite. Stuff. Fling. Wheel. Gullet."*

Theodore smiled and inched toward the double doors. Silently, he pushed one wider and peered inside. She was writing a list of words on the blackboard, putting dots above some of them with an angry smack of the chalk. She's going to chip that blackboard, he thought, amused. He watched her slim back as her hand moved along and the movement of her skirts as she slashed a crossbar across the top of a letter. Then she began long strings of words.

The *clock* hung on the wall, she wrote, murmuring along with each word, while Theodore's eyes followed. And next, The *kite* had a blue tail. She snapped straight and appeared to be studying the blackboard thoughtfully. Then, with brisk, sure motions, she wrote and pronounced very clearly, "I would like to stuff Theodore."

He smiled so big it was all he could do to keep from laughing aloud. She backed off and studied the sentence, forcefully underlined *stuff,* then propped her hands on her hips and snickered. "Oh, would I ever," she repeated, her voice rich with anticipation.

But when she wrote the next sentence, she chose not to repeat the words aloud, and Theodore's smile faded as he puzzled over the writing he couldn't read. Again she backed off and giggled, obviously enjoying herself at his expense before bending toward the board again.

When she'd finished the next sentence, she covered her mouth with both hands and laughed so hard it rocked her forward.

"Hello, teacher," he drawled.

Linnea whirled around, mortified. There stood Theodore, lounging against the back wall with one thumb hooked behind a suspender clip. Her face took on the appearance of a slice of watermelon, and she twirled back toward the blackboard, frantically erasing the words.

"Theodore, what do you mean by sneaking up on me that way?" She wielded the eraser so hard Theodore thought she might push the front wall off the schoolhouse.

"What do you mean, sneaking? I drove up with a team of horses making enough noise to raise the dead, but there was just so much racket in here you wouldn't've heard a mule train comin' through."

She swung around to face him with her palms pressed against the chalk tray behind her. "What do you want, Theodore? I'm busy," she finished superciliously.

His eyes lingered on the milky blackboard then came back to her as he tapped a pair of dirty leather gloves against his thigh. "Yeah, so I see. Getting ready for tomorrow's lesson?"

"Yes, I was, until you so rudely interrupted."

"Rude?" He touched the dirty gloves to his heart, as if unjustly maligned. "*I* am the rude one when I came to offer you a ride home from school?" That put her in a fine tizzy. She scowled like a great horned owl.

"Now's a fine time to offer me a ride home! Now that the sun's out and the rain has stopped! And where was your generous offer this morning, when you refused to let Kristian give me a ride to school?"

"He told you that?"

"He didn't have to tell me that. All he had to tell me was that he wanted to. And you don't fool me for one second. You didn't come to give this . . . this hothouse pansy any ride home, so what are you doing here?"

He pulled away from the back wall and clumped slowly up the left aisle, drawing on his gloves, all the time watching her. "Why, waitin' to get stuffed. Wasn't that what you said you wanted to do?" Reaching the edge of the teacher's platform, he spread his hands wide. "Here I am."

Linnea's embarrassment doubled, but her sense of theatrics came to save her. She pointed imperiously at the door. "And you can just turn around and head straight back out! I have no wish to either see or talk to you until you change your attitude about Kristian coming to school."

"My boy comes to school when I say he does, and not a minute sooner!"

She forgot theatrics and let her temper flare. "Oh, you . . . are . . . insufferable!" She stamped a foot and sent chalk dust swirling around her hem.

He lifted one boot to the edge of the platform and crossed both hands on his knee. "Yeah. And don't forget bullheaded."

"Well, you are, Theodore Westgaard."

"Yeah, I've been told that before, but who was the one that threw her napkin down and stomped out of the kitchen like a spoiled brat this morning? Not a very good example you set for your student."

Properly chastised, she faced the board and started erasing it more cleanly before listing the spelling words again.

"If all you came for is to criticize me, you may leave. And the sooner the better."

"That's not all I came for. I came with the load of coal."

"I could have used it this morning," she nagged, "my feet were squishing by the time I got here and the room was as chill as an icehouse."

The scrape of the chalk was the only sound in the room before his voice came again, kinder. "I'm sorry."

Her hand stopped moving over the blackboard. She peeked over her shoulder to see if he was serious. He was . . . and studying her feet. She turned to face him again, brushing the chalk dust from her hands. When their eyes met, she found only apology in his. Her gaze dropped to the soiled gloves, but even the sight of the aged, bruised leather became fascinating, simply because they encased his hands. How could he be so aggravating one moment and so appealing the next?

"You should be sorry. You made me so angry, Theodore, I did want to stuff you."

It was when she wasn't even trying that she achieved her goal: he reared back from the waist and broke into rich, resonant laughter. Never having seen him even smile before, she was unprepared for the impact. The sight was incredible; it completely changed him. She gazed at his beaming face with a feeling of profound discovery. She had not known his teeth were so beautiful, his mouth so handsome, his jaw so perfect, his throat so tan, or his eyes so sparkling. While his laughter filled the sunny schoolroom, the sight of him filled her heart. And suddenly she found herself incredibly happy. A first chortle of enjoyment left her throat, then a second, and soon her laughter joined his.

When the room stilled, they continued smiling at each other in mutual amazement. Her watch was lifting and falling very quickly upon her breast. He imagined that if he stepped close and placed his hand over it, he would find the gold warmed by her flesh.

He tried to swallow and couldn't.

She tried to think of something to say, but couldn't.

He tried to think of her as a child, but couldn't.

She tried to think of him as an older man, but couldn't.

He told himself she was the girl his son was falling in love with, but it didn't matter.

She told herself he was her student's father, she lived in his house, it wouldn't be fitting. But none of it mattered. None of it.

Common sense intruded, and Theodore withdrew his foot from the step. Briskly he tugged his gloves on tighter. "I'd better get that coal unloaded."

She stood with unformed words clogging her throat, watching him walk down the length of the room, noticing for the first time in her life how much narrower a man's hips are than a woman's, how beguiling bronze arms can be when protruding from rolled-up sleeves, how powerful a man's hands appear when sheathed in soft old gloves that have been with him through hours and hours of toil.

When he was gone, she tried returning to the sentences she'd been forming, only to be distracted time and again by the sight of him, just outside the window, shoveling coal. She moved closer. From her high vantage point she looked down upon his shoulders and the top of his head, captivated by the sight he made as he leaned to the task. How wide his shoulders, how spare his movements, how capable his muscles.

He paused, rested crossed wrists on the handle of the shovel, and she retreated one step into the shadows. The bright sun rained down on his rich walnut-brown hair, and she realized she rarely saw him without the straw hat he wore in the fields. She supposed it had gotten wet this morning and was at home, drying on the peg in the kitchen. He glanced in a circle, squinting, his face wearing a film of coal dust now. He was sweating, and she watched a droplet trickle along the edge of his hair, collecting black as it went. He pulled off one glove, searched his rear pocket, found no handkerchief, so donned the glove again and swabbed his forehead with a sleeve. Again he set to work, sending up a rhythmic clatter of coal falling upon coal.

He was so much a man, so much more mature than any of the boys to whom she'd ever been attracted. And he was attracted to her, too; she hadn't imagined it. For that brief, revealing second she had seen it in his eyes as clearly as she could now see the coal dust coating his handsome brown face. Something had sizzled between them while they'd stared at each other. Desire? Was that what it felt like? Her heart had caromed from the impact. She felt it yet. The awareness. The pull. The insistence.

But when he'd drawn the curtain over his eyes, she'd realized he still saw her as a child.

Most of the time.

Chapter 9

When the coal shed was full, he sailed the shovel onto the empty wagon bed and flexed his tired back. He wiped his forehead with an arm, checked the gray streak left there, tossed his gloves aside, and ambled across the school yard to the pump. Unhooking his suspenders, he sent them swinging, stripped off his shirt, and tossed it aside, then started pumping. With widespread feet he leaned over the stream of pure, icy water that splattered onto the dirt below. Alternately pumping and washing, he doused his face, splashed his chest, arms, and neck, then drank from his cupped palms.

When he straightened and turned, he found Linnea on the steps, watching him. She stood still as a stork with the fingertips of one hand lightly touching the iron handrail, the other palm clasping her elbow. Their gazes met and locked while he slowly wiped his mouth with the back of his hand, then became conscious of his bare, wet chest and the suspenders hanging down his thighs. He leaned from the hip and grabbed his flannel shirt from the ground, did a cursory toweling, then slipped it on and began buttoning it, all the while wishing she would move or at least stop staring.

But Linnea was intrigued by the sight of him. There were times she had seen her father's chest bare, but it hadn't nearly as much hair as Theodore's. And though her father, too, wore suspenders, they'd never dangled at his knees like dropped reins. And watching a father wash up was nothing whatever like watching Theodore pelt water over himself with such heedlessness that it went flying through the air, ran down his chest, and dripped from his temples and elbows.

But Theodore's heedlessness stopped abruptly when he spotted her.

She grew bemused by the sudden haste he showed in getting the shirt on and buttoned. He hung his head and half-turned away while stuffing the shirttails into his britches, snapping the suspenders back into place, and combing his hair with his fingers. At last he turned.

''Are you ready to go?'' he called.

She flashed him a saucy smile. ''Are you?''

She could have sworn Theodore began to blush, though he managed to hide it behind a wrist as he again swept a hand through his hair and broke into a purposeful stride.

''I'll bring the wagon around.''

When they were sitting side by side, heading home, all was silent. Theodore rode with his back sloped, elbows to knees, thinking of how strangely self-conscious he'd felt when he'd turned around and caught her watching him wash up. Linnea balanced her grade book on her knees and glanced at the passing countryside, thinking of how dark and curly the hair at the back of his neck became when it was wet. Neither of them looked at the other, and neither said a word until they were past John's place. Then, out of the clear blue sky, Theodore stated, ''Kristian caught a cold today. That's why he didn't come along to help unload the coal.''

Her head swiveled around, but he stared straight ahead, offering nothing further. How odd that he felt compelled to explain why he'd come alone. She searched for something clever to fill the gap, but her thought processes seemed to be confounded by the memory of that well water running into the hair on his chest. ''Oh, poor Kristian. It's much too beautiful a time of year to have a cold, isn't it?''

With the barest turn of the head he watched her study the landscape while she breathed deeply of the rarefied, fresh-washed air as if each breath were a blessing.

And he thought of how differently she studied the wheat than Melinda had.

Back at home he pulled up near the windmill. A soft breeze turned the vanes and a loose board rattled rhythmically above their heads. She craned to look up.

''There's something restful about a windmill, isn't there?''

''Restful?'' His eyes made the same journey hers did.

''Mmm-hmm. Don't you think so?''

He always had but would never have dreamed of saying so for fear of sounding silly.

''I reckon,'' he admitted, ill at ease with her so close.

''I see John planted morning glories around his,'' she recalled, while they both squinted up at the revolving blades behind which the sky was tinted the same vivid blue as John's flowers.

''I remember John and me helping Pa build this one.''

Linnea's gaze moved down the derrick to discover him still looking up. She found herself wondering what he'd looked like then, perhaps in the days just before full maturity set in, before he had whiskers and muscles and the brittle aloofness he preferred to display most times. Now, with his chin tilted, his jaw had the crisp angle of a boomerang. His lips were slightly parted as he squinted skyward, sending the fine white lines around his eyes into hiding. His eyelashes seemed long as the prairie grass, sooty, throwing spiky shadows across his cheek.

''Mmm . . . beautiful . . .''

''Melinda always said—'' Suddenly his lips clamped, his head came down with a snap, and he shot her a cautious sideward glance. Enjoyment fled his face. ''Got to fix that loose vane,'' he mumbled, then tied the reins and vaulted over the side of the wagon.

She clambered down right behind him and stood with her grade book against her breasts. ''Who is Melinda?''

Refusing to look at her, he busied himself loosening harness so the horses could drink. ''Nobody.''

She scratched on the red book cover with a thumbnail and rocked her shoulders slightly. ''Oh . . . Melinda always said. Only Melinda is nobody?''

He knelt, doing something under the belly of one of the horses. The top of his hair was flattened, messed, and dulled by coal dust, but still damp at temple and nape. She wanted to touch it, to encourage him to confide. He seemed to take a long time deciding. Finally he stretched to his feet. ''Melinda was my wife,'' he admitted, still refusing to meet Linnea's eyes while fussing with a strap just behind the horse's jaw.

Her shoulders stopped rocking. ''And Melinda always said . . .''

His hand fell still, spread wide upon Cub's warm neck. Linnea's eyes were drawn to that hand, almost as brown as the sorrel's hide, wider than any she remembered, and certainly far stronger.

''Melinda always said windmills were melancholy,'' he told her quietly.

Countless questions popped into Linnea's mind while the sound of the loose board rattled above their heads. She stood nearly shoulder to shoulder with Theodore, watching his blunt fingers absently comb Cub's mane. She wondered what he would do if she covered the back of his hand with hers, ran a finger along the inner curve of his thumb where the skin was coarse from years of diligent work. But, of course, she couldn't. What would he think? And whatever was making her conjure up these fanciful thoughts about a man his age?

''Thank you for telling me, Theodore,'' she offered softly, then, discomposed, swung away toward the house.

Watching her, he wondered if he knew another woman who could turn her back on such a topic without prodding further. And he knew she'd been as aware of him as a man as he'd been of her as a woman. Woman? Eighteen years old was hardly a woman.

But then that was the trouble.

At supper that night, Kristian was absent, but Linnea announced to the others, ''I've decided to visit all the homes of my students. Superintendent Dahl told me I should try to get to know them all personally.''

Theodore looked at her squarely for the first time since they'd been in the schoolroom together.

''When?''

''As soon as I get invited. I'll send letters home with the children, telling them I wish to meet their families, then wait to see what happens.''

''It's harvest time. You won't be meeting the men unless you go after dark.''

She shrugged, glanced at Nissa and John, then back to Theodore. ''So I'll meet the women.'' She spooned in a mouthful of broth, swallowed, then added, ''Or I'll go after dark.''

Theodore dropped his attention to his soup bowl while Linnea did the same. All was silent for several minutes, then to Linnea's surprise he spoke up again.

"You expect to be staying at their houses for supper?"

"Why, I don't know. I guess if I were invited I would."

Still giving all his attention to his soup bowl, he declared, "Dark sets in earlier these days. You'll need a horse."

Linnea stared at him in surprise. "A . . . a horse?"

"For riding." His eyes flicked to hers, then immediately away.

"If the children can walk, so can I."

"Clippa should do," he went on as if she hadn't spoken.

"Clippa?"

John and Nissa were observing the exchange with illconcealed interest.

"She's the best horse we got for riding. Calm."

"Oh." Linnea suddenly realized her folded hands were clasped between her knees and she didn't recall setting her spoon down. Jerkily she picked it up and lit into her vegetable soup again, the words *hothouse pansy* cavorting through her mind.

"You ever saddled a riding horse before?" Theodore asked presently.

They braved a quick exchange of glances.

"No."

Theodore reached across the table, stabbed a thick slab of bread with his fork, started buttering it, and didn't look at Linnea again. "Come down to the tack room after supper and I'll teach you how."

There was still some fading light left in the sky as she walked down to the barn. Across the prairie she made out the silhouette of John's windmill, and from somewhere far off came the lowing of a cow. The chickens had gone to roost, and the chill of evening had begun settling in.

The outer barn door was open and she stepped inside to the mingled scents, both pleasant and fecund, that were now a welcomed familiarity.

"Hello, I'm here," she called, peering around the doorway of the tack room before entering.

Theodore stood at the wall, reaching up for a piece of equipage. He was dressed as he'd been earlier, in black britches, a red flannel shirt, suspenders, and no hat. He glanced over his shoulder, plucked down a halter, and handed it to her, backwards.

"Here. You bring this."

He swung the smaller of the two saddles off the sawhorse, nodded toward the door, and said, "Let's go."

"Where?" She preceded him into the main part of the barn, casting questioning glances over her shoulder.

He grinned—just barely. "Got to catch the horse first."

He placed the saddle down beside a box stall, looped a lead rope in his hand, and ordered, "Grab that pail."

Carrying a galvanized pail of oats, she followed him outside into the dusky twilight, across the muddy barnyard with its strong scent of manure and damp earth. He opened a long wooden gate, waited while she stepped through, then closed it behind them. They stood now on firmer ground bearded with short yellow grass. Near a barbed-wire fence some distance away, a dozen horses clustered, feeding. Theodore whistled shrilly between his teeth. Their heads lifted in unison. Not one took a step.

"Clippa, come!" he called, standing just behind Linnea's shoulder with the bridle behind his back. The horses disinterestedly stretched their necks and returned to cropping grass.

"Guess you've lost your touch," she teased.

"You try it then."

"All right. Clippa!" She leaned forward, clicking her fingers. "Come here, boy!"

"Clippa's a girl," Theodore informed her wryly.

She straightened and clutched the pail handle with both hands. "Well, how was I supposed to know?"

He grinned teasingly. "All you have to do is look."

"I was born and raised in town."

Behind her she heard the ghost of a chuckle, then over her shoulder came his long arm. "Cub," he observed, pointing to the big sorrel workhorse that Linnea had never looked at closely. "Now he's a boy."

This time she looked closely, and even before Theodore's arm withdrew she felt her cheeks grow as pink as the streaks coloring the western sky behind them.

"Clippa, come here, girl," she tried again. "Sorry if I hurt your feelings. If you come over here I'm sure Theodore won't hurt you with that rope he's hiding behind his back. All he wants to do is take you to the barn."

Still the horse declined the invitation.

Greenhorn, Theodore thought, amused, watching as she leaned forward and talked to the horse as if it were one of her students, and all the while probably afraid the mare might decide to saunter over after all.

His eyes wandered down her slim back and hips. There's probably plenty I could teach her, he mused, and not only about catching horses.

Linnea straightened and declared petulantly, "She won't come."

"Bang the handle of the pail," Theodore whispered, almost in her ear.

"Really?" Her head swung around, catching him off guard, so close her temple almost bumped his chin. Her heart lurched at his nearness. "Will that work?"

"Try it."

"Here Clippa, come girl." At the first clatter of metal on metal, the horse came trotting, nose to the air, head bobbing. When Clippa's mouth hit the oat bucket, she caught the greenhorn unprepared and sent her thumping backward against Theodore. Instinctively his hands came up to steady her, and they laughed together, watching the horse bury her velvet nose in the grain. But when their laughter stilled and Linnea glanced over her shoulder, Theodore became aware of the warmth seeping through her sleeves. He dropped his hands with punctilious swiftness, then hastily moved around her to catch Clippa's bridle and snap the lead line to it.

Walking on either side of the mare, they led her back to the barn.

Inside, the shadows had grown deeper. Theodore lit a lantern and hung it safely above their heads, concentrating on the lesson at hand instead of the girl who seemed able to distract him far too easily. She stood close, watching intently, frowning and nodding as he demonstrated.

"Always tie the horse before you start 'cause you never know about horses. Sometimes they take to disliking the girth or the bit and get fractious. But if they're tied, they ain . . . they won't go no place."

"Anyplace. Go on."

He glanced at her sharply. She seemed unaware of having corrected him. Her concentration was centered on the lesson at hand.

"Anyplace," he repeated obediently before proceeding. "Make sure you pull the blanket well up past the withers so it pads the whole saddle and doesn't slip." When it was smoothed into place, he knelt on one knee, folded a strap back over the seat of the saddle, then looked up. "When you throw the saddle on, make sure the cinch isn't twisted underneath, or you'll have to take it off and throw it again. I reckon since this'll be the hardest part for you, you won't be wantin' to do it twice." He nodded at Clippa. "She's not as tall as some of the horses, so you oughta be able to handle it." He straightened with the saddle in his hands and tossed it on the mare as if it weighed no more than the horse blanket.

"Grab the cinch strap—" He ducked, and with a cheek pressed against the horse's side, reached beneath her belly. "—and bring it through this ring, then back up to the saddle ring as many times as you have to, till all you have left is enough to tie off. You tie it at the top . . . now watch." She moved slightly closer. "First take it to the back, then around, then up through. And make sure the knot is always flat—see?—then you give it a tug." With a few deft movements the knot was fashioned. One powerful tug made it secure, then his fingertips tucked the loose ends underneath.

"There. You think you can do that?"

He glanced down to find her studying the knot with a dismayed expression.

"I'll try."

He reversed the process, then stepped back to watch. It was the first time he'd ever seen her so nervous. Having been around horses his whole life, he'd forgotten how intimidating they could be. He smiled secretly, watching her sidle up to Clippa cautiously.

"She knows you're here. No sense sneaking."

"She's really big, isn't she?"

"As horses go, no. Don't be scared. She's a gentle one."

But when Linnea reached under Clippa's belly, the mare sensed someone strange and pranced sideways, rolling her eye to check who it was.

Linnea leaped back.

Immediately Theodore stepped forward, taking the bridle, rubbing the mare's forehead. *"Pr-r-r."* At the soft, rolling sound, the horse quieted. Linnea watched Clippa's brown hide twitch and tried to submerge her fear, realizing how little it had taken for Theodore to calm the animal. Still holding the bridle in one hand, his expression softened. "You're strange to her. She had to look you over a little bit first. Go ahead. She'll be still now."

She was, though it was with great diffidence that Linnea reached a second time under the thick belly. But things proceeded without a hitch until it was time to tie the knot. She tried it once, twice, then raised her eyes guiltily.

"I forgot."

He showed her again. Standing at his shoulder she watched his strong, brown fingers fold the leather into the shape he wanted, his broad thumbs flattening the knot before drawing the end of the strap behind and giving it its final tug.

Their arms brushed as she reached toward the saddle. Neither of them spoke as she took the cinch and began undoing Theodore's handiwork, studying it carefully in reverse. He noted how she held the tip of her tongue between her teeth while concentrating. She made a false start and mumbled under her breath.

"Have you ever tied a man's necktie?" he asked.

Her fingers stilled and she looked up at him. "No."

Her face was lit from above by the golden lantern light. He noticed for the first time the dusting of freckles across the crests of her cheeks. Coupled with her dark, studious eyes, they gave her a guileless look of innocent youth. Had she been laughing or angry his heart might not have fluttered. But her expression was sober, as if she approached the lesson with utter seriousness. It reminded him again of how truly young and inexperienced she was—so young she had never saddled a horse before, and certainly too inexperienced to have tied a man's necktie. He forced his attention back to the triangular knot.

"You have watched your father, haven't you?"

"Yes."

"So handle it like a necktie, keepin' it flat with your thumbs. Now start again."

She bit the tip of her tongue and started again. Halfway through, his thumb reached up and pressed hers. "No . . . flat," he ordered. His other hand clasped the back of hers and changed its angle. "The other direction."

Fire shot up her arm and she bit her tongue harder than she'd intended. But his hands fell away immediately and she was sure he had no idea how he'd affected her. "Now give it a good yank with both hands." She grabbed, gave a jerk, and secured a perfect knot.

"I did it!" she exclaimed jubilantly, smiling up at him.

His smile, when he turned it on full force, was numbing. It turned her bones to butter and made her heart dance. Had this been one of her daydreams, she would have awarded the heroine at least a hug of approval. But it wasn't, and Theodore only tapped the end of her nose with a fingertip and teased, "Yeah, you did, little missy. But don't get too smart yet. Not till you do it without help."

Little missy! Her cheeks grew pink with indignation at being treated like some adolescent in pigtails! She twirled toward the horse with a haughty lift of her chin and determination in each movement.

"I can and I *will* do it without your help!"

He stepped back and watched, grinning, while she not only untied the cinch, but reached up and whipped the saddle and pad off the horse's back. When her arms took the weight, it almost tipped her on her nose. Amused, he crossed his arms and waited for the show to go on. She narrated it in a piqued voice and never shot him so much as a glance.

"Blanket all the way up on the withers. Saddle ov-ver . . ." She grunted and puffed, lifting it off the floor. ". . . and make sh-shure . . ." She boosted it with one knee, but not high enough. He suppressed a smile and let her struggle.

"Make sure the cinch is . . . is . . ." She kneed the weighty load again and missed again, nearly pulling her arms from their sockets.

Theodore forced a sober expression and stepped forward, reaching to help.

"I'll do it!" At her angry glare he stopped cold, studied her puckered mouth, and backed off with a silent nod. Her shoulders weren't even as high as Clippa's back, but if the ornery little cuss wanted to prove she could do it, he wasn't about to stop her. There was a nice solid stool in the tack room for her to stand on, but he decided he'd let her suffer away until she grew tired and asked for his help. Meantime, he enjoyed the sight of her adorable mouth, pinched in irritation, and her dark eyes snapping like lightning bugs on a clear, blue night.

To Theodore's amazement, the saddle plopped over Clippa's back on the next throw, and his eyes took on a gleam of respect. She hung onto the stirrup for a moment, resting and panting, then stooped to capture the cinch. She executed a perfect flat knot, gave it a two-armed jerk, and spun to face him with her hands defiantly on her hips.

"There. What's next?"

The lanternlight caught in her dark pupils. She was breathing heavily from exertion. Theodore wondered what the law said about mature fathers making advances on their children's under-age teachers. With forced slowness he closed the space between himself and Clippa, nudging Linnea aside with an elbow. He slipped two fingers between the cinch and the horse's hide.

"This could've been tighter. She starts runnin', and you'll find yourself upside down, little missy."

"Theodore, I told you once, don't call me that!"

He casually rolled a glance her way with his fingers still beneath the girth.

"Yeah. Miss Brandonberg, then."

Her eyes blazed brighter and her fists clenched harder. "And don't call me that either. For heaven's sake, I'm not *your* teacher. Can't you call me Linnea?"

Calmly he untied her knot and tightened it.

"Probably not. Wouldn't be seemly—not when you're the schoolmarm. Around here teachers ain . . . are never called by their first name."

"Oh, that's absolutely ridiculous."

He turned to face her, reached around her shoulder, and sent her heart racing. But he only came away with the bridle from the edge of the stall behind her.

"What're you so riled up about?" he asked coolly.

"I'm not riled up!"

"Oh?" With exasperating calmness he moved to Clippa's head. "Guess I was mistaken. Here. You want to learn the rest?"

She glared at the metal bit resting across his palm, then whisked it up irately.

"Just show me what to do."

One last time he smiled at her charming display of temper, then showed her how to place the bit in Clippa's mouth, adjust the headstall, thread the mare's ears through the browband, and buckle the throatlatch.

"All right, she's ready to ride."

To his surprise, Linnea hung her head and said nothing. He studied her round shoulders and peeked around them. "What's wrong?"

Slowly she lifted her eyes. "Why do we fight all the time, Theodore?"

His throat seemed to close and blood surged through parts of his body that had no business coming to life around a girl of her age.

"I don't know."

Like hell you don't, Westgaard, he thought.

"I try very hard not to get angry with you, but it never seems to work. I always end up spitting like a cat whenever I'm around you."

He slipped his hands into his rear pockets and did his damndest to look platonic. "I don't mind." He certainly didn't. Being close to a riled Linnea was a good bit safer than being around one like this. Disconsolately she studied the rein draped over her palm, her lashes dropped like fans to her smooth cheeks.

"I wish I didn't."

Everything hung too heavy and silent between them. He gripped his own buttocks inside his pockets and tensed his leg muscles. When he knew he was in danger of touching her, he had to say something—anything to keep him from his own folly.

"You want to ride her?" He nodded toward Clippa.

Dejectedly, Linnea answered, "I guess not. Not tonight."

"Well, you better get up once, so I can adjust the stirrups for you."

For several seconds she stood still, silent. Finally she turned and reached up for the saddle horn. It was a long stretch, and to add to the difficulty her skirts got in the way. She hitched them up and hopped on one foot, making several false starts while Theodore fought the urge to put his hands on her backside and give her a boost. Persevering, she finally swung astride. But her skirts were caught, binding her legs. When she tried to stand and free them, her feet fell two inches short of the stirrups. She sat, waiting, looking down on Theodore's head as he adjusted first one stirrup, then walked around and adjusted the other.

She wished she were more experienced so she'd know how to handle the feelings that seemed to be springing up restlessly within her. She wanted to touch his gleaming hair, lift his chin and study his eyes at close range, hear his laugh and his voice speaking gently of what mattered most to him. She wanted to hear her name on his lips. But above all, she wanted to be touched by him. Just once, to find out if it would be as heady as she imagined.

He shortened the stirrups as slowly as possible, wanting to prolong their time together, wishing there were other favors he could do for her. It had been years since he'd felt this compulsion to be chivalrous. He'd thought it was something a man feels only when he's young and raring. What a shock to experience it again at his age. He felt her gaze following him as he moved about the horse, but controlled the urge to look up. To do so would be disastrous. But when he could think of nothing more to do for her, he stood staring at her delicate foot. How long had it been since he'd wanted to touch a woman this badly? But she wasn't a woman. Was she? Suppose he touched her—a simple touch, just once—what harm could come of that?

He reached for her ankle. It was warm and firm through the black leather of her new, sensible boots. His thumb bracketed her heel tendons, rubbing gently. There was no mistaking the touch for anything but what it was—a lingering caress. Nor was there any mistaking the fact that she sat with bated breath, waiting for him to look up, to go one step farther, to lift his hands and help her down. He thought of her name—Linnea—the name he refused to allow himself to call her lest it break down barriers better left unbroken. If he said it, if he lifted his eyes, he was certain of what would follow. Mistakes.

"Theodore," she whispered.

Abruptly, he dropped her foot and stepped back, realizing his folly. He stuffed his hands into his back pockets. When he looked up, his face was just as impersonal as usual.

"You're all set now. Make sure you put the saddle back in the tack room after you ride. I'll keep Clippa in the near pasture so you won't have to run clear to Dickinson to find her."

His attempt to lighten the atmosphere failed. There was too much burning between them.

"Thank you." Her voice held a faint reediness.

He nodded and turned toward the tack room with the pretext of searching for something, afraid if he stayed he'd reach up for her narrow waist to help her dismount and end up giving in to other urges.

By the time he returned she was removing the saddle.

"Here, I'll take that. You go on up to the house now. You probably got schoolwork to do yet."

When she was gone he turned Clippa out, then returned the saddle to its proper place. After throwing it over the sawhorse he stood a long time staring at it. He touched the curved leather. It was warm where she'd been sitting.

She's only eighteen and she's your boy's teacher. Closer to his age than to yours, Teddy, you fool. What would a girl like her want with a man damn near old enough to be her father?

A short time later, in her room beneath the rafters, Linnea prepared for bed with an odd feeling, like she'd swallowed a goose egg. Had she only imagined it all day long with him? No, she hadn't. He'd been aware of it, too. In the schoolroom. Then again when she'd watched him wash at the well. And tonight in the barn when he'd held her ankle.

It was awful.

It was awesome.

It was—she grew more certain by the hour—desire.

She blew out the lantern and went to bed to consider it. Flat on her back, she tucked the blankets painfully tight over her breasts, as if to keep the feeling from escaping. She could feel her heartbeat, heavy and fast against the strictures. She conjured up Theodore's naked back as he'd leaned to throw water on his shoulders . . . his chest when he'd turned around with water dripping into the mat of dark hair . . . his thick hair as he'd moved about the horse refusing to look up and meet her eyes.

The desire centered in her nether regions.

He'd felt it, too. That was why he was afraid to look up, to say her name, to answer when she'd spoken.

She closed her eyes and subtracted eighteen from thirty-four. Sixteen. He had lived and experienced almost twice as much as she. There were so many things she wanted to know and be for him that by virtue of her immaturity she could not know or be.

Suddenly she was smitten by a strong wave of jealously for his advanced age. Stubborn man that he was, he would probably never follow his instincts. Distraught, she rolled up on one elbow and gazed down at the white blot of her pillow in the dark.

"Teddy?" she queried in a soft yearning voice. Then she embraced the pillow tenderly and lowered her lips to his.

Chapter 10

Linnea's letters turned up immediate invitations to her students' homes, and within the week she began her visits. She chose Ulmer and Helen Westgaard's first because they had more children in school than any other family; also, because Ulmer was Theodore's brother. She'd developed a growing curiosity about anything relating to Theodore.

From the moment she stepped into their kitchen she sensed love present. The house was much the same as Theodore's, but far gayer and a lot noisier, with six children. The three oldest boys were out in the fields helping their father when Linnea arrived, the younger children helping their mother in the kitchen. But to Linnea's surprise, the field crew all came in for supper with their guest.

Eating, she observed, was as serious a business here as it was at Theodore's. They talked and laughed before the meal, and after. But while they ate—they *ate!*

However, several times during the course of the meal she looked up to find the oldest boy, Bill, studying her closely. Boy? He was no boy. He was a full-grown, strapping man of perhaps twenty-one or so, and he gave her a most disconcerting amount of overt scrutinization. His eighteen-year-old sister, Doris, also lived at home, though she was engaged and planning a January wedding. It seemed weddings, like education, had to be put off until after harvest season. Raymond and Tony, Linnea's missing students, treated her with diffidence, as though forewarned that she was displeased about their not coming to school. The two youngest, Frances and Sonny, smiled and giggled whenever she caught their eye, and she suspected they felt highly honored to have the teacher choose their home first.

She delayed bringing up the subject of the school calendar until after dessert. When she did, she introduced it calmly, stated her case, and left the subject open for discussion.

There was no discussion. She was told politely, but in no uncertain terms, that the boys would come to school when the wheat was in.

The family all came out into the yard to bid her good-bye, but Bill left the others and appeared at Clippa's head to detain Linnea.

"Miss Brandonberg?"

"Oh . . . did I forget something?"

"No. I just didn't want you to think it's anything personal against you, them keeping the boys out to help with harvesting. It's always been that way, you know?"

"Yes, I know. But that doesn't make it right. The boys need the full school year, just like the girls do."

Linnea was so tired of going over the same argument. But just when she expected it to continue, Bill seemed to forget all about it. He stood looking up at her with one hand on Clippa's bridle, his attractive green eyes issuing a message of undisguised interest.

"Do you dance?" he asked.

For a moment she was too startled to answer. "D . . . do I dance?"

"Yeah—you know, one foot, two foot."

She smiled. "I . . . well, yes, a little."

"Good, then I'll see you at one barn or another when the threshers come. There's always lots of dances then."

In her experience there had never before been anyone who so blatantly showed his interest. She grew flustered by his open regard and the fact that his family looked on, waiting for her to ride away. Frances and Sonny were giggling again, heads close together. Linnea stammered, "Y . . . yes, I . . . guess you will. Well, good night then."

Riding home, with the night air cooling her cheeks, she considered Bill Westgaard. Sun-streaked blond hair, eyes as green as spring clover, a rather upturned nose, and a smile revealing slightly crooked teeth. He was a curious combination of boyish features and manly brawn.

So what did you think of him? Handsome?

A little.

Appealing?

Somewhat.

Bold?

Bolder than any other fellow I've met before.

So will you dance with him?

Perhaps.

But when she imagined it, it was Theodore with whom she danced.

Her intentions had been to leave the Severt home until last, hoping to give Allen time to become more cooperative at school so that her own feelings wouldn't be negative when she paid the visit. But Allen continued instigating more classroom disruptions than anyone else. During school prayers he invariably created a disturbance by tapping his pencil or his boot against the desk. He pestered the younger children by boldly snatching their cookies and taking bites, then calling them cry babies before giving them back—if he gave them back at all. As if sensing that Frances and Roseanne were two of Linnea's favorites, Allen singled them out to persecute more than any of the others. He taunted Frances, calling her a dummy, and sometimes pulled her skirt up to peek at her underpants. He turned the wood block on the girl's privy door while Frances was inside, and stuck a garter snake through the moon-shaped cutout. The resulting fit of hysteria had Allen beaming with joy for the remainder of the afternoon. He looked satisfied each time he managed to rile one of his classmates, or the teacher. And he was very good at making people angry.

Linnea was dreading the visit to Allen's house, but decided to get it over with immediately. She left school early on the day of home visits, so it was well before suppertime when she arrived at the Severt home. To her surprise, Allen came out and asked to see to Clippa. Reverend Severt was busy in his study, but Linnea enjoyed a pleasant visit with his wife while she made the final preparations for the meal.

Lillian Severt was a meticulously groomed woman with a neat finger-waved upsweep of pure black hair, held in place by unadorned tortoise-shell combs. She had flawless ivory skin and a face that was marred only by her upturned nose with its rather overlarge nostrils. But one tended to forget her nose in view of her clear, hazel eyes and square-set mouth and chin. Instead of the customary starched cotton housedress, she wore a stylish garment of ribbed amber faille with a white collar of pierced, embroidered organdy. And earrings—nobody else around Alamo wore earrings. Hers were small gold apple blossoms, with tiny citrine gems centered in each. Unlike most farm wives who often smelled of homemade lye soap and whatever they were having for supper, Lillian Severt smelled of her bureau, of spearmint and tansy and saxifrage and whatever other fragrant herbs she had mixed into her potpourri.

Her house was different, too. The front parlor had a bound carpet covering most of the floor. The kitchen had a cabinet with a self-contained flour sifter. And there was a formal dining room with built-in glass-fronted china closets and a colonnaded archway dividing it from the front parlor.

The cherry-wood table was covered with ecru lace, the food served in covered tureens, the napkins bound with Belgian lace, and when Lillian Severt took her chair, she left her cobbler apron in the kitchen.

Though Allen was a hellion at school, at home it was another story. Around his parents he was so polite as to appear almost ingratiating, even pulling out his mother's chair as the meal began. He bowed his head reverently when grace was being said, displayed impeccable table manners, and his voice lost all its schooltime flippancy.

To Linnea's surprise, when supper was finished Martin Severt ordered, "Allen, now you help Libby clear the table, then the two of you are excused."

In a pleasantly modulated voice, Mrs. Severt countered, "Now, dear, you know doing dishes isn't a man's work. Libby will do them."

Reverend Severt's fingers tightened on his cup handle, his eyes confronted his wife's, and for a moment tension was palpable in the room.

Then Allen squeezed his mother's shoulder, kissed her cheek, and offered, "Supper was de-lish. Nobody makes pumpkin pie like you do, Mother."

She laughed, patted his hand, and ordered, "Off with you, you flatterer."

Before he could escape, his father interjected, "Did you fill the woodbox when you came home from school?"

Allen was already heading out of the room. "Didn't have to. It was already full.'' His footsteps sounded on the stairs leading up from the front parlor, presumably to his room. When he was gone Libby cleared the table, then disappeared, too.

''Would you like more coffee?'' Mrs. Severt inquired, refilling all three cups. A quiet fell upon the room. Linnea tried to screw up her courage to broach the subject foremost in her mind. She took a swallow of coffee and it seemed to drop twenty feet before it reached her nervous stomach.

''Mr. and Mrs. Severt . . .'' The minute the words were out Linnea wondered if she should have addressed him as Reverend. She pushed the doubt aside and did her job, unpleasant though it was at the moment. ''I wonder if we might talk for a while about Allen.''

Mrs. Severt beamed.

Reverend Severt frowned.

''What about Allen?'' he inquired.

Linnea planned her words carefully. ''Allen seems very different here at home than he does at school. He . . . well, he doesn't seem to get along with the other children very well, and I was wondering if you might offer some insight as to why not, and what we might do to help him.''

''We?'' Mrs. Severt repeated, raising one eyebrow. ''Allen has no trouble getting along anywhere else. If he's having difficulties, perhaps it's the school's fault.''

The implication was clear: *school* meant *Miss Brandonberg*. While the teacher was still adjusting to the rebuff, Allen's mother went on. ''I'm interested in what you see as . . . getting along.'' Her very inflection made the phrase sound suspect.

''Socially, it means he doesn't attempt to fraternize with the others, to join in the games, make friends. Academically, he doesn't always conform to the rules. He tends to . . . to ignore instructions and do things his own way.''

''Fraternize with whom, Miss Brandonberg? Until the older boys come to school there's nobody for him to fraternize *with*. Surely you don't expect a fifteen-year-old boy to be overjoyed about playing hopscotch with the second and third graders?'' Mrs. Severt's voice was a velvet ice pick chipping away at Linnea's self-esteem. Nerves prickled in places she hadn't realized she had them. She wished she were home at Nissa's where nobody talked at the table. Quivering inside, she nonetheless kept her voice placid.

''Perhaps fraternize isn't exactly the right term.'' Linnea searched for another, but none came, so she blurted out, ''Allen teases the other children a lot.''

''All children tease. I did when I was a child. I'm sure Martin did, too, didn't you, dear?''

But not all children take such perverse pleasure in it, Linnea thought, though she could hardly say so to the minister and his wife.

Reverend Severt ignored Lillian's question and posed one of his own. ''Specifically, what has he done?''

Linnea hadn't intended to name specifics, but it appeared Mrs. Severt had a blind eye where her son was concerned. If Allen was to be helped, Linnea must be frank. She related the incident about Frances and the garter snake.

Lillian Severt demanded, ''Did anyone *see* Allen put the snake through the moon?''

"No, but—"

"Well then." She settled back with a satisfied air.

Growing angrier by the minute, Linnea rushed on. "I was about to say that he was the only one not taking part in the kickball game that was going on in the playground at the time. And it happened right after he had stolen one of the cookies from Frances's lunch bucket and she'd complained to me about it."

Mr. Severt began, "Our Allen stole—"

"Frances?" his wife interrupted yet again. "You mean Frances Westgaard, that rather dim-witted child of Ulmer and Helen's?"

Under the table, Linnea's fists clenched in her lap. "Frances is not dim-witted. She's a little slow, that's all."

Lillian Severt took a ladylike sip of coffee. "Ah, slow . . . yes," she said knowingly, replacing her cup in its delicate saucer. "And you'd take the word of a child like that over the word of the minister's son?" One eyebrow raised in reproof, she let the question settle for several seconds, then brightened visibly. "And anyway," she flashed a smile at her husband, then at Linnea, "there would be absolutely no reason for Allen to steal someone else's cookies. I pack him an ample lunch myself every day, and as you just heard, he's more than appreciative of the sweets I make around here. Granted, he does love cookies, but I always see to it that he's well supplied."

Martin Severt leaned forward. "Miss Brandonberg, is there any chance you could be wrong about Allen stealing?"

Linnea turned to him with new hope. "This particular time, I'm afraid not. He snatched it from her while all the children were together, and gobbled it down before she could get it back. But there have been other times when he's managed to take bites and leave the cookies in their pails."

Again Mrs. Severt came to her boy's defense. "You may call that stealing, Miss Brandonberg, but I'd call it a childish prank."

"Given my vocation," the minister added, "you can well imagine that teaching the Ten Commandments has been of utmost importance to both Mrs. Severt and myself in raising our children. I know Allen isn't perfect, but stealing is a serious allegation against a boy who's been raised to read the Bible every night."

Allen's list of words came back to Linnea—*boring, stoopid, prayers, choclat cookys*. It had revealed more about Allen Severt than she'd realized at the time. She was beginning to see more and more reason to be concerned about Allen's behavior.

Sitting before his parents, feeling chastised and ineffectual, Linnea couldn't help but wonder what they'd say if she came right out and informed the Severts that their son spent an inordinate amount of time staring at her breasts. Undoubtedly, Lillian would intimate that Miss Brandonberg had done something to entice the boy. Having had a dose of the woman, Linnea wasn't too sure Mrs. Severt wasn't capable of costing a teacher her job on grounds much less serious than that.

Tact seemed prudent until she had gathered more substantial proof of Allen's misdeeds.

"Mr. and Mrs. Severt, I didn't come here to criticize how you raise your children. I wouldn't presume to do that, but I wanted you to be aware that things are not running smoothly for Allen at school. His attitude must change before he gets into even bigger trouble, and when I give him an order, I expect it to be carried out."

"Specifically what orders has he not carried out?" Mrs. Severt asked.

Linnea related the incident regarding the paragraph and the substituted list.

"And did the list tell you anything—now that you've seen his home?"

"Yes, but that's not—"

"The point is, Miss Brandonberg, Allen is an extremely bright boy. We've been told so ever since he began school. Bright children need constant challenge to perform at their best. Perhaps he isn't receiving that challenge under your tutelage." Linnea felt her face grow red and her anger multiply while Mrs. Severt went on almost indulgently. "You're new here, Miss Brandonberg. You've been with us less than a month and already you're labeling Allen a troublemaker. He's had five other teachers in the past, all of them older and more experienced than you . . . and men, I might add. Don't you find it strange that if our son *is* such a troublemaker we haven't heard about it before this?"

"Lillian, I don't think Miss Brandonberg—"

"And *I* don't think"—Lillian leveled her husband with a look that made Linnea expect a lightning bolt to come through the ceiling—"Miss Brandonberg has bothered to look for the positive traits of our son, Martin." If her words hadn't effectively silenced the minister, her condemnatory expression would have. "Perhaps she needs a little more time to do so. Let's hope that next time she comes to dinner her report will be less prejudicial."

To his credit, Martin Severt squirmed and blushed. Linnea wondered what to look at, and how long it would take to clear out of here so she could blow off the steam that was close to erupting.

"Yes, let's hope so," Linnea agreed quietly, then folding her napkin and pushing herself away from the table, added, "It was a delicious meal, Mrs. Severt. Thank you for having me."

"Not at all. You're welcome any time. The door of a minister's house is always open." She extended her hand, and though Linnea would rather have touched a snake, she took it and made her departure as gracefully as possible.

Upstairs, in the bedroom directly above the dining room, Allen Severt lay on his belly on the linoleum floor, his face directly above the heat register. Through its adjustable metal slats he clearly saw and heard what was going on in the room below.

"Allen, I'm gonna tell!" Libby whispered from the doorway. "You know you're not supposed to listen through the register. You promised Daddy you wouldn't."

Allen eased away from the grate slowly, so the floor wouldn't creak.

"Yeah, well, she's sittin' down there tellin' all kinds of damn lies about me, tryin' to make them think I cause trouble around school."

"You're not supposed to cuss either, Allen Severt. I'm tellin'!"

With a single insidious step he was at his sister's side, one hand painfully squeezing her arm. "Yeah, you just try it, pignose, and see what happens."

"You can't do anything to me. I'll tell Daddy and he'll make you recite verses."

Allen squeezed harder. ''Oh, yeah, smarty? Well, how'd you like that cat of yours to get her tail dipped in kerosene? Cats dance real good when they get kerosene up their ass. And when you touch a match to 'em—poom!''

Libby's chin quivered. Tears formed in her wide blue eyes as she tried to pull free. ''Ouch, Allen! Let go. You're hurting me.''

''Yeah, and just remember it when you wanna go tattle to the old man. When the teacher starts spreading lies about me it's not my fault what happens around school after that.'' He glared at the register, then gritted evilly. ''Just who does she think she is anyway?'' Then, as if he'd no further use for his sister, he thrust her aside.

''Lawrence, I swear I've never—never!—been so mad in my life! Why, that . . . that supercilious, misguided old bag! I swear to God, Lawrence, if she'd've made one more nasty crack, I would've pushed that flat snout of hers clear to the back of her skull!''

Linnea bounced along on Clippa's back, so infuriated her eyes teared. A lump of rage clotted her throat.

''Clippa, slow down, you mangy old nag! And, Lawrence, come back here!''

But Lawrence slunk away and Linnea needed someone with whom to vent her emotions. Perhaps it was fortuitous that only a quarter mile down the road she passed Clara and Trigg's mailbox.

''Whoa.''

She stared down their lane at the lights beaming from the windows, recalled Clara's invitation, and decided she had never before needed a friend as badly as she needed one now.

It was Trigg who answered the door.

''Why, Miss Brandonberg, what a surprise.'' He glanced beyond her and frowned. ''Is anything wrong at Teddy's?''

''No, everything's fine. It's just—''

''Come in, come in!''

At that moment Clara appeared behind her husband. ''Linnea! Oh, this is wonderful.'' She grabbed Linnea's hand and drew her inside. ''But the little ones are going to be so disappointed. They're already in bed.''

''Oh, this isn't an official visit. I was just passing by, and I remembered you said the coffee was always hot and . . .'' Suddenly Linnea gulped to a stop, blinking rapidly.

''Something's wrong. What is it?''

''I think I n . . . need a friend.''

The kitchen was warm, yellow, and cheerful, the welcome enthusiastic. Linnea's pent-up frustrations came to a head, and before she could stop them, tears glistened in her eyes. Clara immediately put an arm around the younger woman and drew her toward a round oak table where a kerosene lantern lit tomorrow's breakfast plates and cups already in place, upside down. While Clara urged Linnea into a chair, Trigg headed for the coffeepot.

''Your hands are cold. Where have you been, out there in the dark?'' Clara seated herself facing Linnea and rubbed her hands between her own.

''I'm sorry to come here this way and . . . and wail on your shoulder, but I'm so upset and I . . . I . . .''

"Is it Teddy?"

"No, it's Allen Severt."

Clara sat back, her expression wry. "Oh, *that* little turd."

Unexpectedly, Linnea laughed. She looked at the down-to-earth Clara and a weight seemed to lift from her chest. The tears that had been threatening suddenly evaporated and things didn't seem nearly as exasperating. She was going to love this woman.

"He really is. I wonder how many times I've wanted to call him that myself."

"Bent tells me plenty about what goes on around school. So what has Allen done now?"

"This time it isn't him so much as his parents." Linnea shook her head in exasperation. "His mother! Lord!"

Smiling wryly, Clara overturned and filled three coffeecups. "So you've met Lillian the Hun." Again Linnea laughed at the woman's outrageous candor. Clara tipped her head aside and grinned. "Well, I'm glad you can still laugh. Feeling better now?"

"Immeasurably."

"Then tell us what happened."

Linnea related the highlights of the confrontation and could see the anger growing in Clara.

"She called our Frances *what?*"

"Dim-witted. Can you imagine a minister's wife saying a thing like that?"

"Lillian thinks that being a minister's wife covers a multitude of sins. Like criticizing others to make herself look good. You ought to hear her at Ladies' Circle." Clara waved the memory away. "Well, I don't want to get into that, but you won't find anybody around here who has one good thing to say about her. She hasn't been liked since the first Sunday she stood beside the reverend on the church step and basked in reflected glory.

"But to think she'd have the gall to tell *you* that you're not doing your job at school when that devil of hers has been driving teachers crazy for years. I know more than one of them who didn't stay because of Allen.

"But that's neither here nor there. Listen, Linnea, the stories coming home from school with the children are all good. And don't you forget it! Lillian's been whitewashing that brat's foul streak her whole life. And she's gonna keep on till one of these days he'll pull one that she won't be able to wish away." Clara stopped, considered a moment, then asked, "Have you told Teddy about this?"

Startled by the question, Linnea grew wide-eyed. "No."

"Well, if Allen keeps it up, I think you should."

Linnea shook her head. "No, I don't think so. Theodore doesn't like to be bothered with school business."

"Oh. He's been grumpy lately, huh? Well, don't let that fool you. Underneath he cares about more than you'd guess. Take my word for it, if Allen keeps it up, the one to talk to is Teddy."

"All right. I'll think about it." The coffeepot was empty and Trigg was stifling a yawn. "It's late," Linnea said. "I've enjoyed this so much, but I really must go."

At the door she and Clara exchanged the customary parting niceties, but at the last minute they couldn't resist sharing an impetuous hug.

"You be careful riding home now."

"I will."

"Come anytime."

"I will. And you do the same."

At home, when Linnea reached the barn it was dark and silent. She lit a lantern, going over all of Theodore's instructions for putting away the tack and turning Clippa out into the near paddock. But she had scarcely begun working on the girth knot when Theodore appeared silently behind her.

"You're late!"

She jumped and spun, pressing a hand to her heart.

"Oh, Theodore, I didn't know you were there."

He'd been so worried. Pacing, listening for hoofbeats, wondering what could have happened to her. Her safe arrival brought relief, but along with it an irrational anger. "Haven't you got more sense than to stay out this long? Why, anything could've happened to you!"

"I stopped to visit Clara and Trigg."

He stood close enough to touch, but his face wore a mask of displeasure.

"This isn't the city, you know."

"I . . . I'm sorry. I didn't know you'd be up waiting."

"I wasn't up waiting!"

But he had been and they both knew it. While he scowled down at her she felt it again, that wild, wondrous new thing that filled her breast to bursting.

Blast it, girl, don't look at me that way, he thought, looking down into her somber face that hid little of what she was feeling. His heart pounded. His hands itched to touch her. He wanted to say he was sorry he'd shouted—it had little to do with her being out late. Instead, he reached for the girth knot.

"You go on up to the house," he ordered, more gently. "I'll see to Clippa."

"Thank you, Theodore," she replied softly.

He nodded silently, concentrating solely on his task.

She studied him as he turned away, but again he closed himself away from her. Why are you so afraid of what we're beginning to feel, she wondered. It's nothing to be afraid of. And you *were* waiting to see that I arrived home safely. You *were,* Theodore, whether you'll admit it or not.

But she kept her thoughts to herself and slipped quietly from the barn, leaving him to wrestle with his emotions.

During the days that followed, Linnea visited the homes of the rest of her students, sharing meals and getting to know the people whose lives were all so closely intertwined. She found them to be basic, hard-working, rather too introspective—the effervescent Clara was the exception—but flatteringly polite to the new teacher . . . if one disregarded table manners.

The Lommen twins had a charm all their own, stemming from their constant good-natured competition with each other. It was a positive force in their lives, one that spurred them to try to please, not only at school but also at home.

At Oscar Knutson's Linnea was startled to find the house so cluttered with litter, they seemed to live in the paths between piles. Linnea made a mental note to create a desk-check day at school in an attempt to teach Jeannette the value of orderliness. Aside from the messy house, however, the visit was a success.

Not only did Linnea enjoy a delicious meal, she had the chance to discuss such things as Christmas plays, county spelling bees, and a cakewalk she had in mind to raise funds for a real teacher's desk.

Her second visit to Clara and Trigg's house cemented the friendship between the two women, and Linnea went away considering Clara a confidante.

In making the rounds of the Westgaards, Linnea's respect for their mother grew. Nissa had raised sensible, loving children, with the possible exception of Theodore, who seemed the least pleasant, the least loving of the lot. Especially since that night in the barn. They'd said very little to each other since then, had managed to stay out of each other's way, but the fact that the older boys were still being withheld from school was like a rowel under Linnea's hide. Every time she sat down across the table from Theodore, she wanted to lash out at him and demand that he release his son into her daytime custody.

But October came and settled in with cooler weather, and still the older boys were missing.

At school, Allen Severt continued to persecute Rosie and Frances more than any of the others, but always sneakily enough to keep from getting caught. He hid Rosie's lunch pail, sometimes ate the choicest contents from it, then blamed it on someone else. When she ran to the teacher in tears, Allen taunted, mimicking her lisp in a singsong voice.

Systematically he worked on shortening Frances's left pigtail. Only her left. He did it in a way that could never be proven, somehow managing to trim off no more than a quarter inch at a time, leaving no fallen hair as evidence, no abrupt change in length to bring attention to what he was doing. It was only when Frances's pigtails began to look lopsided that it came to light.

Linnea found the ten-year-old crying in the cloakroom one day during noon recess. She was sitting in a dejected heap on one of the long benches, looking heartbreakingly forlorn with her pigtails drooping and her skinny shoulderblades protruding as she sobbed into her hands.

"Why, Frances, what is it, dear?"

Frances swiveled toward the wall and hid her face on a jacket hanging from a peg. But her shoulders shook. Linnea couldn't resist sitting down and turning Frances into her arms. Unadvisable as it was to have favorites, Linnea couldn't resist Frances. She was a sweet child, quiet, untroublesome, one who strove to please in every way, no matter how difficult it was for her academically. As if realizing her shortcomings in that department, she tried to make up for it with little kindnesses: a favorite cookie left on Linnea's grade book; a crisp, red apple placed on the corner of the teacher's table; an offer to collect the composition books or pass out crayons or tie the boot strings of the younger ones who didn't know how yet.

"Tell me what's made you so unhappy."

"I c . . . can't," the child sobbed.

"Why can't you?"

"B . . . because . . . you'll th . . . think I'm d . . . dumb."

Linnea gently pressed Frances back and looked into her puffy, downcast face. "Nobody here thinks you're dumb."

"Allen d . . . does."

"No, he doesn't."

"He d . . . does, too. He c . . . calls me d . . . dimwit all the t . . . time."

Linnea's anger flared, and with it protectiveness. "You are *not* dumb, Frances, so just put that out of your head. Is that what made you cry? What Allen said?"

Woefully, Frances shook her head.

"What then?"

It all tumbled out at last, the secret that "teacher" wasn't supposed to know, but part of which she already did. Frances's greatest wish was to be an angel in the Christmas play, because the angels always wore long white gowns and let their hair flow loose with a sparkly tinsel halo adorning it. But instead of growing, her hair was getting shorter, and not only did she fear missing the chance to be an angel, she was afraid she was going bald.

It took great self-control for Linnea not to laugh at this astounding revelation. She hugged Frances hard, then drew back to wipe the girl's cheek. Forcing a sober expression, Linnea cajoled, "Here now, have you ever heard of little girls going bald? Only grandfathers go bald."

"Th . . . then why is my h . . . hair getting sh . . . shorter?"

Linnea perkily turned the child around to investigate. "Doesn't look any shorter to me."

"Well, it is. But only one of my pigtails."

"Only one?"

"This one." She pulled the left braid over her shoulder.

Upon closer scrutiny, it was obvious the hair had been trimmed—and none too neatly. Linnea took the end of it and teasingly brushed Frances's nose. "Maybe you ate it off yourself. Isn't that the one you suck on when you're trying to figure out your arithmetic problems?"

Frances dipped her chin to her chest with a coy smile she couldn't quite hold back, though her cheeks were still tearstained.

"I have an idea," Linnea said, adopting a thoughtful air. "Until you find out if you're really going bald or not, and until you find out why it's happening to only one side of your head, why not have your mother tuck your pigtails up in a coil—like mine, see?"

Linnea twisted around, showing the child the back of her head, then faced her again, lifting the brown pigtails experimentally. "All it takes is a couple of hairpins, and they're tucked safely away so nobody can see how long or short they are."

Frances showed up the following day proudly displaying her new corona of braids, which Allen Severt could no longer crop. The change settled the symptom but not the problem, for only two days after that *somebody* drilled a peek hole through the back wall of the girls' privy.

Linnea felt certain the villain was Allen, but had no proof. And not only were his pranks growing more serious, she had the uneasy feeling he enjoyed seeing others suffer.

She decided to talk to Theodore about it.

Chapter 11

She sought him out that night and found him in the tool shed fashioning a new vane for the windmill. One of his knees held a wooden slat across a barrel top, and he faced the rear of the building as she approached.

She stopped outside the high-silled door and watched his shoulders flexing, then glanced around the interior of the shed.

Here, as in the tack room, neatness reigned. She studied the almost fanatic tidiness, smiling to herself. Hilda Knutson could take a lesson from Theodore. The shed was cozy. The lantern created enough heat to warm the tiny, windowless building, which smelled of fresh-cut pine and linseed oil. A stack of paint cans took up one corner. On the wall hung snowshoes, traps, and a variety of pelt stretchers. There were two small nail kegs and a neat coil of barbed wire. In a near corner leaned a worn broom. Linnea's eyes fell to the sawdust drifting onto Theodore's boot, and she imagined him sweeping it up the moment the chore was finished. His penchant for neatness no longer irritated her as it had when she'd first arrived. Now she found it admirable.

"Theodore, could I talk to you a minute?"

He swung around so suddenly the board clattered to the floor. His cheeks turned crimson.

"Seems you and I are always startling each other," she ventured.

"What're you doing out here?" He hadn't meant to sound so displeased. It was just that he'd been doing his best to avoid her lately. The sight of her made his palm feel slippery on the saw handle.

"May I come in?"

"Not much room in here," he replied, retrieving the fallen board and setting back to work.

"Oh, that's all right. I'll stay out of your way." She entered and perched herself on an upturned keg.

"Theodore, I have a problem at school and I wondered if I could talk to you about it. I need some advice."

The saw stilled and he looked up. Nobody ever asked Theodore for advice, least of all women. His ma was a dictator and Melinda hadn't bothered letting him know that she was going to show up at his doorstep expecting to get married. Neither had she informed him she was running away two years later. But there sat Linnea, rattling Theodore with her mere presence, posed like a nymph on the nail keg, with her hands clasping her knees. Her big blue eyes were wide and serious, and *she* wanted *his* advice.

Theodore set aside his work and gave her his full attention.

"About what?"

"Allen Severt."

"Allen Severt." He frowned. "He giving you trouble?"

"Yes."

"Why come to me?"

"Because you're my friend."

"I am?" he asked, surprised.

She couldn't hold back a chuckle. "Well, I *thought* you were. And Clara said if Allen kept it up, I should talk to you."

Theodore had never had a friend before. His only friends were his brothers and sister and those they'd married. It sounded good, having a friend, though he wasn't sure how well being Miss Brandonberg's would work. But if Clara thought he should know, he'd listen. He set aside his saw, straddled the barrel, and crossed his arms.

"So what has Allen been up to?"

"Not much I can prove, but plenty I can't. He's been a troublemaker right from the first day of school—teasing the younger children, openly defying me, creating disturbances. Just little irritating things. Hiding lunch pails, taking bites of cookies. But now he's started in on Frances and I—"

"Frances? You mean *our* little Frances?" His shoulders squared and his arms came partially uncrossed. As he bristled defensively everything about him became more masculinely imposing.

So Frances was one of the things he cared about. Linnea found it touching that he'd referred to the child as *ours*.

"He calls her dimwit all the time. He's very good at picking out the children's weaknesses and teasing them. But that isn't the worst of it. I suspect he's the one who's been cutting off Frances's braid, and one day he locked her in the outhouse and stuck a snake through the hole in the door. Now the girls have found a peek hole drilled in the back of the outhouse wall. I can't prove any of it, but there's something about Allen that . . ." She shrugged, then rubbed her arms and shivered.

Theodore's air of displeasure doubled. Forcing himself to remain seated, he pressed the heels of both hands to the barrel edge between his thighs.

"Has he done anything to you?"

She glanced up quickly, not having intended to say that much. Her personal misgivings about Allen were too nebulous to put to voice. And besides, she'd feel utterly foolish telling Theodore that Allen stared at her breasts. All boys reached an age where they became interested in the development of girls. With Allen it wasn't the fact that he stared, but *how* he did so; trying to put this into words would be difficult.

"Oh, no, he hasn't *done* anything. And it's not even so much what he does to the others. So far it's been little things. But they're getting more serious all the time. And what I'm most concerned about is that I think he enjoys being . . . well, malicious . . . making people squirm."

Theodore rose in one swift movement. He gave the impression that he wanted to pace but was unable to in the confined space. His brow beetled, he swung on Linnea. ''You talk to his folks about this when you were at their place for dinner?''

''I tried. But I saw immediately that Allen's mother wasn't going to believe a word I said about her golden boy. She has him so spoiled and herself so deluded that there's no reaching her. I thought for awhile I might get some cooperation from Reverend Severt, but . . .'' She shrugged. ''He seems to think that if Allen reads the Bible all his life it'll keep him a saint.'' Linnea chuckled ruefully, looking at the floor.

''Martin's not a bad sort. It's just that that wife of his has led him around by the nose for so long he don't know how to stand up to her.''

''Doesn't,'' she corrected absently.

''Doesn't,'' he repeated without a second thought.

Linnea looked up appealingly. ''I'm not sure I can handle Allen without their help.''

A warning stirred in Theodore. He pressed his hands more tightly against his armpits.

''You afraid of Allen?''

''Afraid?'' Her gaze held his for a moment, then flickered aside. ''No.''

He didn't believe her. Not entirely. There was something she wasn't telling him, something she didn't want him to know. And even if she was telling him everything, there was still little Frances to consider. She had always been one of Theodore's favorites, the one who never forgot her Uncle Teddy at Christmas. One year she had given him a pomander ball for his bureau—a pomander ball, of all things. He'd taken one sniff of the feminine thing and wondered what his brothers would think when he showed up smelling like orange and cloves in his clean overalls. But he'd slipped it into his bottom drawer until Frances smelled the fruit and spice on him one time and grinned wide in toothless approval. Then and only then had he removed it from his drawer.

With the recollection fresh in his mind, he made a sudden decision.

''I want you to tell everything you just told me to Kristian, then pick out a desk for him 'cause he'll be in school Monday morning. After that Allen better watch out if he decides to pick on Frances. But Monday's the soonest I can spare him.''

Linnea's lips dropped open in surprise.

''K . . . Kristian?'' she repeated.

Theodore—stubborn—was a sight to behold! His eyes darkened to the color of wet Zahl coal, his jaw jutted, and his chest looked invincible as he stood like a Roman gladiator with his shoulders thrust back, lips narrowed with resolve. ''What that little pip-squeak Severt needs is somebody bigger than he is to take him down a notch every now and then.''

She stared at him while a smile spread slowly upon her face. ''Why, Theodore!''

''Why Theodore what?'' he grumbled.

''You'll give up your field hand to protect someone you care about?''

He dropped the warrier's pose and gave her a quelling frown. ''Don't look so self-satisfied, teacher. Frances gave me a pomander ball for Christmas one year and—''

"A pomander ball!" Linnea squelched a giggle.

"Wipe that smile off your face. We both know Frances isn't nearly as bright as the rest of the kids, but she's got a heart of gold. I'd like to shake that Severt brat myself a time or two for pestering her. But don't worry. From now on Kristian'll be there to keep an eye on things."

On Monday not only Kristian showed up at school, but all the other older boys as well. It appeared they'd been simultaneously released from field work as if by some mystical force.

Their coming brought a distinct change to the schoolroom. It seemed pleasantly full, taking on a busy air, a new excitement. It was especially apparent in the younger students, who idolized the older ones. There was a wonderful and unexpected camaraderie between the oldest boys and the very youngest children. Instead of shunning the small ones, the big boys indulgently included them, helped them, soothed them if they fell and hurt themselves, and, in general, tolerated their immature concerns with good-natured forebearance.

On the playground things were livelier. Gopher-hunting was finished for the season, and it wasn't uncommon during noon recess for the entire school, including the teacher, to take part in a ball game.

Linnea loved it. There was a wholly different feeling to a country school than to a town school. She'd never experienced anything like it before. It was wholesome and rich with sharing, much the same as in an extended family. Watching a sixteen-year-old boy pick up and dust off a howling seven-year-old girl who'd hit the dust during a game of red rover was a rewarding experience. And watching an older girl teach a younger one the intricacies of making French braids brought a smile to Linnea's lips. One day, looking on, she realized something astounding.

Why, they're learning to be parents!

And as long as they were, they'd better learn right.

Now that all the boys were present, she took up the subject she'd been dying to introduce.

"Shakespeare may have said 'Unquiet meals make ill digestions,' but Shakespeare, I daresay, never sat down to the table with a bunch of hungry Norwegians. We shall today take up the topic of table etiquette, including the social amenity of making graceful mealtime conversation."

The boys looked at each other and snickered. Steadfastly, she went on, pacing back and forth in front of the room, hands clasped dramatically at her waist. "But before we get to that, we will start with the subject of burping."

When the laughter died down, the students suddenly realized Miss Brandonberg was not laughing with them. She was standing with sternly controlled patience, waiting. When she spoke again, not a student in the room doubted her earnestness. "I will have it clearly understood that this schoolroom has heard the last unrestrained belch it will ever hear as long as I'm the teacher here."

No more than five seconds of silence had ticked by when, from the direction of Allen Severt, came a loud, quick rifle shot of a burp that echoed to the rafters.

Laughter followed, louder than before.

Linnea strode down the aisle, stopped calmly beside Allen's desk, and with a movement as quick as the strike of a rattler smacked his face so hard it nearly knocked him out of his seat.

The laughter stopped as if a guillotine blade had fallen.

In the quietest of voices, the teacher spoke. "The proper words, Mr. Severt, are, 'I beg your pardon.' Would you say them to your classmates, please."

"I beg your pardon," he parroted, still too stunned to do otherwise.

It was, indeed, the last burp Linnea ever heard at P.S. 28, but Allen Severt didn't forget the slap.

October settled in, bringing the first frosts and the first hired hands. Linnea ambled out of the house one afternoon to find a stranger in conversation with Nissa by the windmill.

"Linnea, come on over! Meet Cope!"

Cope, it turned out, had been coming to work for the Westgaards for twelve years. A stubby, ruddy Polish farmer from central Minnesota, he took his nickname from the round can of Copenhagen snuff ever present in his breast pocket. Doffing a flat wool cap, he shook Linnea's hand, called her something sounding like "a pretty little sitka," spit out a streak of brown tobacco juice, and asked where them other bums was.

Cope was followed by Jim, then Stan, and a string of six others. Five of the men were repeaters, three of them new to the Westgaards.

One of the first-timers was a young buck who had drifted through from Montana wearing scarred cowboy boots, a battered Stetson, and a platter-sized silver belt buckle bearing a Texas longhorn. His hair was as dark and shiny as polished onyx, his smile as teasing as a Chinook wind.

As Cope had been, he too was talking with Nissa the first time Linnea saw him. She returned from school one afternoon with her grade book and papers to find the two of them outside, near the kitchen door.

"Well, who's this now?" he drawled as she approached.

"This here's Miss Brandonberg, the local schoolteacher. She boards with us." Nissa nodded sideways at the man. "This here is Rusty Bonner, just hired on."

From the moment her eyes met his, Linnea became flustered. In her entire life she'd never met a man so blatantly sexual.

"Miss Brandonberg," he drawled, slow as cool honey. "Happy t' meetcha, ma'am." When he spoke, one could almost smell sagebrush and whang leather. With one thumb he pushed his Stetson back, revealing arresting black eyes that hooked downward at the corners as he grinned, and untamable black locks that teased his forehead. In slow motion he extended one hand, and even before she touched it, she knew what it would feel like. Wiry and hard and tough.

"Mister Bonner," she greeted, attempting to keep the handshake brief. But he clasped her hand a moment longer than was strictly polite, squeezing his rawhide-textured hand against her much softer one.

"Name's Rusty," he insisted in that same drawn-out way.

The only rusty thing about him was his skin. Burned by the sun to a rich, deep mahogany, it framed his dark, lazy smile in a way that must have left a string of broken hearts from the Texas panhandle to the Canadian border. He was a head taller than Linnea, lean as a drought year, and put together mostly with sinew.

"Rusty," she repeated, flashing a nervous smile first at him, then at Nissa.

"Well now, you're a right pretty lady, Miss Brandonberg. Makes me wonder what I missed when I dropped out o' school to go rodeoin'."

Flushing, she dropped her gaze to his scarred boots and the bedroll lying on the ground beside them. He stood in the hipshot pose of a self-assured ladies' man, one knee bent, grinning at her lazily with those devilishly handsome eyes that looked as if they were figuring her body dimensions and her age.

Nissa sensed that Linnea was out of her league and ordered, "You can put your roll in the barn. You'll bunk with the other boys in the hayloft. Wash water'll be hot one hour before sunrise and breakfast'll be served in the kitchen till the cook wagon gets here."

Inveterate charmer that he was, Rusty Bonner wasn't choosy about whom he showered that charm on, long as she was female. He swung his laconic gaze to Nissa with no perceptible change in appreciation, doffed his hat, and drawled, "Why, thank y', ma'am. That's most obligin' of y'."

Then he swung down lazily to snag his bedroll and sling it over his shoulder by one finger. Tipping his hat brim low over his eyes, he sauntered off toward the barn, hips swinging like pines in a slow breeze.

"Whew!" Nissa puffed, shaking her head.

"Whew is right!" Linnea seconded, watching Rusty's back pockets undulate on his tight blue Levi Strauss britches.

Eyeing Linnea, Nissa declared, "I think I mighta just made a big mistake by hirin' that one on." She swung and aimed a finger at Linnea's nose. "You keep away from him, you hear?"

"Me?" Linnea's eyes widened innocently. "*I* didn't do anything!"

Disgruntled, Nissa turned back toward the house. "With his kind a woman don't have ta."

It was Sunday, the last lull before the roar of the steam threshers broke over the prairie. Down along the creek bottom the poplars were already dropping gold coins into the Little Muddy. The cottontails were fat as Buddhas, and as the muskrats went about filling underwater larders, their pelts were so thick they stood out like ruffs about their necks.

In the wind it was chilly, but in the shelter of the uncut millet, with the sun pouring into their own private bowl, Kristian and Ray lazed like a pair of contented coon hounds, their bellies to the sun. The boys were shaped alike, all length and angles, with too much bone for the amount of muscle they'd grown. Cradling their heads, elbows up, they studied the puffy white clouds scudding along the cobalt-blue sky.

"I'm gonna go after mink this year," Kristian announced.

"Mink?" Ray chuckled knowingly. "Good luck. You're better off goin' for muskrats."

"There's plenty of mink left. I'll get 'em."

"You'll get one for every ten of my muskrats."

"That's okay. It's gotta be mink."

Something in Kristian's voice made Ray roll his head to squint at his cousin. "What's gotta be mink?"

Kristian shut his eyes and mumbled, "Nothin'."

Ray eyed him a little longer, then settled back again, staring at the sky. From far away came a faint sound like old nails being pulled from new wood. It amplified into the unmistakable rusty squawk of Canadian honkers, heading toward the Mississippi flyway. The boys watched them grow from distant dots to a distinct flock.

"Hey, Ray, you ever think about the war?"

"Yeah . . . some."

"They got airplanes over there. Lots of 'em. Wouldn't it be somethin' to fly in one of those airplanes?"

The wedge of geese came on, necks pointing the way toward Florida, wings moving with a grace that forced a silent reverence upon the boys. They watched and listened, thrilling to a sound that stirred their blood. The cacophony became a clatter that filled the air over the millet field, then drifted off, dimmer, dimmer, until the graceful creatures disappeared and the only sound remaining was the rustle of the wind in the grass and their heartbeats against the backs of their heads.

"Someday I'm going to see the world from up there," Kristian mused.

"You mean you'd go to France and fight, just to fly in an airplane?"

"I don't know. Maybe."

"That's stupid. And besides that, you're not old enough."

"Well, I will be soon."

"Aww, it's still stupid."

Kristian thought about it a while and decided Ray might be right. It probably was stupid. But he was anxious to grow up and be a man.

"Hey, Ray?"

"Hmm?"

"You ever think about women?"

Ray let out a honk of laughter as raucous as the call of the geese. "Does a wild bear shit in the forest?"

They laughed together, feeling manly and wonderful sharing the forbidden language with which they'd only recently begun experimenting.

"You ever think about giving a woman something to make her look different at you?" Kristian asked, as if half asleep.

"Like what?"

It was quiet for a long time. Kristian cast a single wary glance at his cousin, returned to cloud-watching, and suggested, "A mink coat?"

Ray's head came up off the millet. "A mink coat!" Suddenly he clutched his stomach and bawled with laughter. "You think you're gonna trap enough mink to have a mink coat!"

He howled louder and rolled around like an overturned turtle until Kristian finally boosted up and punched him in the gut. "Aw, shut up. I knew I shouldn'ta told you. If you say anythin' to anybody I'll stomp you flatter'n North Dakota!"

Ray was still winding down, breathless. "A . . . m . . . mink coat!" Overdramatizing, he flopped spread-eagled, wrists to the sun. "You might just get enough mink by the time you're as old as your pa."

Kristian laced his fingers over his belly and crossed his ankles, scowling straight up. "Well, that was just a daydream, you jackass. I *know* I ain't . . . I mean, I'm not gonna get enough for a mink coat, but I could get enough to give her mink mittens, maybe.''

Suddenly it dawned on Ray that his cousin was serious. He came up on one elbow, giving Kristian his wholehearted attention.

''Who?''

Kristian grabbed a blade of dry millet and split it with a thumbnail. ''Miss Brandonberg.''

''Miss Brandonberg?'' Ray sat up, shifting his weight to one hip and raising one knee. ''Are you crazy? She's our teacher!''

''I know, but she's only two years older than we are.''

Too startled to be amused, Ray gawked at his cousin. ''You *are* crazy!''

Kristian flung the millet away and crossed his hands behind his head. ''Well, there's nothin' wrong with thinkin' about her, is there?''

Ray stared at Kristian as if he'd just sprouted horns. After a long stretch of silence, he flung himself onto his back and exclaimed, ''Sheece!'' in a breathy rush of excitement.

They lay flat, unmoving, thoughtful, staring at the sky to give themselves an air of controlled casualness while underneath their blood was running faster than Little Muddy Creek.

Ray broke the silence at last. ''Is that what you meant when you asked if I think about women? You think about the teacher . . . like *that?*''

''Sometimes.''

''You could get in trouble, Kristian,'' Ray declared dourly.

''I said, all I do is think.''

Minutes passed. The sun dipped behind a cloud, then came back out to bake their hides and turn their thoughts hot.

''Hey, Kristian?'' came a furtive inquiry.

''Hmm?''

''Anything ever . . . well, *happen* when you think about . . . well, about women?''

Kristian squirmed a little, as if trying to settle his shoulder-blades more comfortably. When he answered, he tried his best to sound offhand. ''Well . . . yeah. Sometimes.''

''What?''

Kristian considered for a long time, formulating answers, disqualifying them before they were spoken. Looking askance, he saw Ray's head roll his way and felt his eyes boring for the truth. He met Ray's eyes squarely.

''What happens to you?''

The millet whispered around their heads. The silent clouds rolled on. A slow grin appeared at one corner of Ray's mouth, and an answering grin came to Kristian. The grins became smiles.

''It's great, isn't it?'' Kristian put in.

Ray made a fist, socked the air, flailed one foot, and gave a banshee yell. ''Eeeeeee-yowww-eeee!''

Together they fell back and laughed and laughed, reveling in being almost sixteen and full of sap.

After a while Kristian asked, ''You ever kissed a girl?''

''Once.''

''Who?''

''Patricia Lommen.''

''Patricia Lommen! That brain?''

''Aw, she ain't so bad.''

''Yeah? So how was it?''

''Nothin' great, but that was a while ago. I wouldn't mind tryin' it again, except Patricia's the only one around here who's not my cousin, and I think she'd rather kiss you than me.''

''Me?'' Kristian popped up in surprise.

''Open your eyes, Westgaard. Every time you walk into the schoolroom she gawks at you like you were the eighth wonder of the world.''

''She does?''

''Well, doesn't she?'' Ray sounded a little envious.

Kristian shrugged, puffed out his chest like a strutting cock, and flapped his wings. Ray landed him a mock punch that doubled Kristian over. They shared a round of affectionate fisticuffs before the talk got serious again.

Kristian inquired curiously, ''You ever think about your ma and pa together—you know?''

''Doin' it, you mean?''

''Yeah.''

''Naw, I think they're too old.''

''Mmm . . . I don't know. They might not be, cause I think my pa . . .''

When Kristian drew up short, Ray became all ears. ''What? Come on, tell me.''

''Well, I don't know for sure, but I've been thinking about every fall, when Isabelle comes.''

''Isabelle!'' Ray was flabbergasted. ''You mean that fat woman who drives the kitchen wagon?''

''She's not exactly fat.''

''You mean, you think your pa does it with her? Why, they're not even married!''

''Oh, don't be such an infant, Westgaard. Not everybody's married when they do it. Remember that girl who used to live over on the other side of Sigurd's place, the one that got pregnant and nobody knew who got her that way?''

''Well, yeah, but . . . but . . . that was a girl and . . . well . . .'' His reasoning became muddy as he tried to puzzle it out. ''You really think your pa does it with Isabelle?''

''I don't know, but every year during threshin', while she's got her cook wagon around here, my pa isn't in the house much at night. I can remember him not comin' in till it was nearly milkin' time, and when he did, if he wasn't sneakin', you could've fooled me. Now where would he be spendin' the night besides in Isabelle's wagon?''

They pondered the possibility for a long time, till the sun went under and their lair grew chilly. They thought of women . . . those mysterious creatures who suddenly didn't seem like nuisances any more. They thought of flying in airplanes as high up as the wild geese had flown.

And they wondered how soon they'd be men enough to do it all.

Chapter 12

Isabelle Lawler's cook wagon, driven by the lady herself, rolled in the following morning. An ungainly looking thing, longer than a prairie schooner and fully as clumsy, it appeared on the road like a ramshackle railroad car that had somehow lost its tracks. From its roof projected a black stovepipe, and along its sides dangled pails and basins that sang out like glockenspiels whenever the cook wagon hit a pothole. The sight of its unvarnished boards rocking down the gravel road turned heads in every field it passed. The field hands waved a greeting and received a return flourish from Isabelle, who rode high atop the wagon, hunkered forward with her knees widespread, a battered felt ''John B'' perched on frizzy hair that blazed in the sun with the same hue and uncontrollability as a prairie fire.

There were those still alive who remembered the notorious Calamity Jane from down Deadwood way, who'd made her circuit through these parts many times with the Wild West shows in the 90s. Some said Isabelle and Jane would have been kindred spirits, had they met.

The only thing feminine about Isabelle was her name. She stood five foot eight in her bare feet. With four inches of wiry frizz on top of her head she appeared to tower over most men. She had the strength of a draft horse, the invincibility of a mule, and less grace than either, which led men to treat her like ''one of the boys.''

She rode alone, claiming her only home was the prairie, and when harvest season was over, nobody knew where she holed up for the winter. Asked about her origins, Isabelle was fond of bawling uproariously, ''I was sired by the devil when he tangled with a she-buffalo.'' She never failed to raise gusty laughs when she pulled her hat off to display her blinding hair and crowed, ''Devil give me m' fire and the buffalo give me m' shape!'' Then she'd slap some fellow's shoulder with her misshapen felt hat, clap it back on her gaudy hair, and stand foursquare with both hands planted on her beefy hips while laughter roared around her.

It took a woman like Isabelle to do what she did. The team she drove was a pair of cantankerous bay mules, the rig they pulled not only a mobile kitchen and dining room, but her rolling home as well. Maneuvering the clumsy cook wagon with such a pair of block-headed creatures would have daunted many men. Isabelle, however, took it all in stride, just as she did the enormous task of feeding four robust meals a day to threshing crews numbering up to twenty.

On most farms this was done by an army of cooks, but Isabelle did it single-handedly, bringing the food to the workers instead of the workers to the food. Breakfast and supper were served somewhere near the barn or bunkhouse, while midday dinner and afternoon sandwiches were served out in the vast wheat fields, near the steam engine, saving precious hours in transportation time. Those who hired her services provided the meat and vegetables, which Isabelle cooked and served right in her wagon at the long bench table that dominated its interior.

She'd been coming to Theodore's for nine years. The sight of her carrot-colored hair and splayed knees with the skirts drooping between them like a hammock brought smiles not only to the Westgaards but to most of the hired hands, who'd shared many a meal and laugh with her.

As her wagon appeared, bumping along the rough track at the edge of the field where the steam engine was already chugging, Theodore pushed his hat back. He rested his hands on the handle of his pitchfork and watched her progress. The expression on his mouth softened.

"Belle's back," John noted, turning to watch the wagon whose singing hardware was drowned out by the huff and puff of the steam engine behind them.

"Yeah, Belle's back," Theodore seconded.

"That Belle's a good cook," John praised simply.

"That's for sure."

Belle hauled the mules to a halt, got to her feet, and stood with the reins in one hand, waving her hat exuberantly.

The field hands set up a cacophony of calls, hoots, and whistles. "Hey, Belle honey! You still got the best shanks this side o' the Rockies?"

Belle glanced at her thighs, cupped her mouth, and bawled back in a voice like a guitar pick on a metal washboard, "You wanna talk about my shanks, you come up here where I can slap your mouth, you mangy little varmint!"

"*Beef* shanks, Belle!" the man called back.

"Beef shanks, my eye! You're talkin' about buffalo, and I know it!" Belle stood square on the high wagon, silhouetted against the pale-blue sky. Her fists were planted on her hips. At that moment, every man there loved her.

"Hey, Belle, you find that man who could throw you over his shoulder like a sack o' corn yet?"

"Hell no! I'm still single. Threw a few over m' own shoulder since I last seen y' though!"

She howled at her own joke as the men broke into gales of laughter, then another one called, "I get the first dance, Belle. You promised me last year!"

"Promises, hell! You git in line with the others!"

"Belle, you learn how to make potato dumplin's yet?"

"Who's that? That you, Cope, you little piss ant?" She shaded her eyes and leaned forward.

"It's me, Belle!"

"You still got that foul smellin' wad o' cow shit tucked in your cheek? Think I c'n smell it from clear over here!"

Cope bent over and laconically spit a brown streak, then hollered, "That's right. And I can still nail a grasshopper from twelve feet!"

Belle leaned back and bellowed with laughter, lifted one knee, and whacked it hard enough to put it out of joint, then yelled, ''Hey, Theodore, you pay these lazy no-counts to stand around jawin' with the cook?''

Theodore, who'd been standing aside enjoying the ribald interchange, only shook his head at the ground, centered his hat, and smilingly turned back to work, followed by the others, all of them refreshed and ready to roll.

Every year when Belle arrived it was the same: both the work and the fun could begin in earnest. The work was taxing, but lightened by the camaraderie she fostered in them all. Winter was coming, and soon they'd be back in their own homes, sealed in by snow. But for now there was the rhythmic rasp of the steam engine and the promise of hearty food and laughter around Belle's table. There would be dances, too, and more teasing, and at the end of it all, full pockets. So they labored in the autumn sun sharing a oneness of purpose and the grand sense of conviviality that came so naturally on the wake of Belle's arrival.

The morning had been rimed with hoarfrost, but long before noon the men were sweating in the sun as they fed bundles of wheat into the machine that separated grain from chaff and spewed the two out in separate directions. Periodically a full wagon of wheat would leave the field, headed for the granaries in the yard. And with each laden wagon the residual haystacks grew.

At noon Belle stepped out of her wagon and clanged a dishpan with a wooden spoon. The men dropped their pitchforks, wiped their foreheads, and headed for the welcome basins of warm water she had waiting beside the wagon. They washed beneath the sun while enticing aromas drifted out through the horizontal hinged doors that were lifted back along both sides of the wagon, giving them a view of its interior. At the front Belle scurried about before the big black cookstove, bellowing in her outrageously grating voice, ''You spit that cud out before you put foot in my kitchen, Cope! Cause if you don't, I'm gonna take my potato masher and make it disappear, and you ain't gonna be too happy about where!''

Cope obliged, while the men nudged him and grinned.

Again came Belle's outrageous orders. ''And I don't wanna hear no more mention of potato dumplin', you hear me, Cope? When you're done eating what I put on this table, if you can eat a potato dumplin', I'll sling you over m' shoulder and personally carry you onto that dance floor Saturday night!''

When the men clumped inside they were still chuckling. They filled the benches along the length of the table and dug into the generous meal amid more good-natured teasing and laughter. There was roast pork and beef, snowy mashed potatoes and succulent gravy, green beans and yellow corn, crusty buns and tart cole slaw, apple cobbler and strong coffee. And throughout its disappearance, there was always Belle, moving behind the men's benches, urging them to eat up, tossing out bawdy retorts, refilling bowls, slapping a shoulder here, pulling a hank of hair there.

She treated Theodore no differently from the rest. He took his share of teasing and back slapping, even added bits of wry humor now and then.

But that night, when the others had bedded down in the hayloft, on new, sweet wild hay, Theodore took a pail of cold water and a bar of soap to the tack room, closed the door, bathed, and donned fresh clothes. Buttoning his blue chambray shirt, he wondered if the others suspected what there was between

Belle and himself. Then he put it from his mind, drew his suspenders over his shoulders, and pulled on a plaid wool jacket against the cool night.

When he slipped from the barn, the light from Belle's wagon glowed softly out beside the caragana bushes. As he'd known she would, Belle had lowered the hinged doors, hooking them tightly at the bottom, leaving only a tiny square of brightness glowing from the window on the rear door.

He knocked softly, then slipped both hands into the deep pockets of his jacket, studying the knee-level step.

The door opened and he lifted his head. The rich light filtered through Belle's hair, turning it the color of sunset before it fell across Theodore's upraised face. She wore a fresh muslin nightdress surrounded by a pale-green shawl, which she held together at her breast. Her face was in shadow as she leaned out and held the door wide in welcome. All traces of the salty, loud-voiced harridan were gone. In her place was a mellowed woman, her coarse facade replaced by a quiet dignity, neither shy nor bold.

"Hello, Belle," Theodore said softly.

"Hello, Ted," she replied. "Been expecting you."

Briefly, over his shoulder, he glanced at the quiet farmyard. "It's a nice night. Thought we might talk a while."

"Come in." She moved back, and Theodore stepped up and inside, closing the door quietly behind him, glancing slowly around in a circle, both hands still in his pockets. The benches were pushed beneath the table, the table against one wall. Upon it was spread her bedding: two thick goose-down ticks and a single fluffy pillow. With the shutters secured, the interior of the wagon was cozy and private. A teakettle sizzled softly on the cookstove, and beside the entry door a kerosene lantern sat on the seat of the room's only chair.

"Looks the same," he said, his eyes returning to her and sliding on past.

"It is the same. Nothing changes. Have a chair."

He moved as if to sit, noted the lantern, and straightened again.

"Here, I'll set it out of the way," she said, brushing near him in the limited confines to take the lantern and set it on one of the benches, which she pushed from under the table to the opposite wall. Theodore bent his frame to the chair, and she boosted herself up onto the edge of the makeshift bed. For a full minute neither of them said a word.

"So, how have you been?" she asked at last.

He flicked her a nervous look, his elbows resting on his widespread knees. "Fine . . . fine. Had a good year." Again he studied the floor between his feet.

"Yeah. Me, too. I see you got most of the same boys back."

"Yeah, they're good workers, Cope and the rest. Got a couple new ones though." Still he studied the floor.

"So I see. So how they workin' out?"

"Good . . ." Then quieter, with a nod of the head, ". . . good."

"That boy of yours is sure growin' up."

Theodore braved a brief meeting of her eyes, smiling with banked pride. "Yeah, only an inch more and he'll be as tall as me."

"Gettin' to look more like you all the time, too."

Theodore chuckled silently, a little shyly.

"I notice he didn't come to help with the threshing till afternoon."

Theodore cleared his throat and met her eyes at last. "No, he's started school already. The new schoolmarm, she pitched a fit cause I was keepin' him out, so I finally let him go."

"Ah, I see."

Theodore put in quickly, "Course, he comes home and helps right after school."

That subject died, and when neither of them could think up a new one, Theodore dropped his eyes to the floor again. After some moments he rubbed the back of his neck.

Isabelle noticed and explained, "Gets a little warm in here when I close up. You want to take your jacket off, Ted?"

He stood to do so and found Belle there to help him. When she turned away to lay the garment on the bench, he watched her shoulders and the side of her breast, crisscrossed by the lattice stitches of the green shawl. When she straightened and turned, her eyes met his directly.

"I've thought about you, Ted."

"I've thought about you, too."

"You're not married yet?"

"Naw." He shook his head, dropping his gaze.

"You would be if I ever gave up this crazy life and decided to plant myself."

"Aw, Belle . . ."

"Close the curtain, Ted."

He looked up, and his Adam's apple bobbed once. Without further ado he crossed to the rear door and drew the little blue and red patterned curtain together on its drooping string. When he faced her again he found Belle back on the edge of her bed, still with her shawl on.

"You know what I always liked best about you, Ted?" She neither expected nor got an answer, only his dark, uncertain eyes that caught the orange lantern light as they lifted, then blinked. "You never take me for granted."

He moved to stand before her, raised one big hand to her temple, and touched the bright hair which she'd drawn back and tied at her nape with a wilted white ribbon. The hair was damp, as if she'd just washed it, and she smelled of the only perfume she ever used—ordinary vanilla extract. Wordlessly he took the shawl from her shoulders, folded it in half, and carefully laid it on top of his jacket. He took the ribbon between his fingers and slipped the bow free. When he laid the limp scrap of white atop the green shawl, he did it with as much care as if it were a jeweled tiara.

Returning to the edge of the makeshift bed, he took Belle's face in both hands, tipped it up, and lowered his mouth to hers with singular lack of haste.

When the kiss ended, he drew back and gazed into her plain, clean face. "A person gets hurt, takin' others for granted," was his reply. Then he kissed her again and felt her hands reaching for his suspenders to push them down and open his shirt before gathering him close and urging him with her onto the feather ticks where, together, they found ease.

Afterward, relaxed and lazing, he rested with Belle's head in the crook of his shoulder. Her hand lay across his chest, and he lightly brushed his fingertips up and down her arm.

"What's the matter with the women around these parts? Why doesn't one of them nab you?"

"I don't want to be nabbed."

"What a shame, when you're so good at what we just finished."

He smiled at the ceiling. "Am I?"

"Why, of course you are. You think any of those other galoots care about what I'm really feeling? How lonely it gets in this stuffy wagon night after night, year after year?"

"Then why don't you get married, Belle?"

"You askin' me, Ted?" His hand stopped moving on her arm, and she playfully swatted his chest. "Oh, no need to tense up so. I was only teasin'. You know a gypsy like me'll never take to settlin' down. But now and then I like to dream of it. Now and then a woman likes to feel like a woman."

His hand detoured for a light pass over her breast. "You feel like a woman, that's for sure."

She chuckled, then absently studied the glowing lantern and sighed against his chest. "You ever stop to think, Ted, about how different you and me are on the outside than we are on the inside?"

"A time or two, I have."

"I don't think another man on earth sees anything in me but the width of two axe handles, a lot of red hair, and too much sass. All these years I been meanin' to thank you for takin' time to look a little deeper."

He spanned her with both arms, kissed the crown of her head, and said, "You're a good woman, Belle. And I was thinkin' lately, you're probably the only friend I've ever had besides my brothers."

She raised her chin and peered up at him. "Really?"

He grinned down and squeezed her lightly. "Really."

"You reckon that's a sign we're growin' old, Ted? Cause I been spendin' some time lately dwellin' on the same thing. Never stayed in one spot long enough to make friends. Guess that's why I'm always so anxious to get back here every year."

"And I'm always here a-waitin'."

She tucked her head against his shoulder again, pondered silently for some moments, and asked, "You think what we do is wrong, Ted?"

He studied the circular impression from the lip of the lamp chimney thrown onto the ceiling in a wavering ring. "The Good Book says it is. But who we hurtin', Belle?"

"Nobody I know of. Unless, of course, your boy found out. Might not be so good if he did. Do you think he suspects?"

"I thought about it some before I came out here tonight. He's growin' up in more ways than just one. Lately he's been moonin' over that new teacher, and when that starts, boys usually get pretty observant about the birds and the bees."

"I can see why he'd moon over her. She's a pretty little thing, isn't she?"

Oddly enough, Isabelle's observation seemed to cause more reaction in his heart than anything else she'd said or done tonight.

"She's all right, I guess. Never really looked at her close."

"All right! Why, Ted, where's your eyes? A woman like me'd give what good teeth she had left in her head just to look like her for one day." While

Ted chuckled, Belle rolled across his chest, reached beneath the table, and came up with a tablet of cigarette papers and a drawstring bag of tobacco. Laying back down, she expertly filled, licked, and rolled herself a smoke, closed the drawstring bag with her teeth, then pressed herself across Theodore again to come up with a wooden match and a sauce dish. She struck the match against the edge of the table, beneath the overhanging feather ticks, then laid back with the sauce dish on her chest, thoughtfully watching the smoke drift toward the ceiling.

He patiently waited until she was settled before observing dryly, "There's nothin' wrong with your teeth, Belle, nor with your face either."

She smiled and blew a perfect, round smoke ring. "That's why I like you, Ted, cause you never seem to notice what's wrong with me."

He watched her smoke half the cigarette, trying his best to keep the images of Linnea from popping into his mind and making comparisons. When he failed, he reached over and took the cigarette from Belle's lips, transferred it to his own, and took a single deep drag. Finding it as distasteful as ever, he tamped it out, rocking the sauce dish on Belle's chest.

"Got some time to make up for and I'm gettin' a mite impatient, Isabelle."

He set the sauce dish on the floor. Rolling to his back, he found Belle grinning at him with a hooded look about her eyelids. As her strong arms and legs reached to reel him in, she declared in her gruff contralto, "Yessir, there's some mighty stupid women around here, but I sure hope they never wise up, Ted, cause once they do—"

"Shut yourself up, Belle," he said, then his mouth did it for her.

It was Saturday night. The first dance of the harvest season would start at eight o'clock in Oscar Knutson's barn, the one with the emptiest hay mow.

Linnea had devoted the entire afternoon to preparing for the event. She could have done it in far less time if Lawrence hadn't constantly interrupted, circling her around the bedroom floor while violins and cellos played Viennese waltzes—and she in her petticoat!

He sat in her rocking chair now, watching as she experimented with two combs, catching her hair back this way and that, frowning at herself in the mirror.

"I suppose you're going to be the belle of the ball. Probably dance with Bill and Theodore and Rusty and—"

"Rusty! Oh, don't be silly, Lawrence. Just because he smiled at me and called me 'right pretty' doesn't mean—" Linnea angled closer to the mirror and ran four fingertips from jaw to chin, studying her reflection critically. "Do you think I'm pretty, Lawrence? I always thought my eyes were too wide apart. It makes me look like a calf." She covered one incisor with an index finger. "And this tooth is crooked. I've always hated it." She closed her lips and smiled, then frowned again at what she saw in the mirror.

"You wouldn't be fishing for compliments now, would you?"

She spun around with her hands on her hips. "I am not fishing for compliments! And if you're going to tease me, you can just go away." She swung back to the mirror. "Which you'd better do anyway, or I'll never get this hair ready."

She had washed and given it a vinegar rinse, and now that it was dry, curled it with the curling iron. Heating the barrel over the kerosene lamp, she hummed and pondered hair arrangements. She tried piling it up on the crown of her head, leaving little sausage curls to drift from the cluster. But it was too long; the weight of the tresses pulled out the curls and left them looking like stringy cows' tails. Next, she put it up in a loose topknot, leaving trailing tendrils around her face and on her neck. But it was difficult to get the topknot loose enough without losing it entirely—she could just see herself spinning around the dance floor with the hairpins flying. By the time she had tried and ruled out the two styles, she had to curl it all again.

This time she decided on a simple, girlish fashion, letting the back hang free and catching the sides up high in a crisp navy-blue grosgrain ribbon. Assessing the final results, she smiled and moved to the next decision: what to wear.

Looking through her limited wardrobe, she ruled out the wools, which would be too warm, and decided on the white-yoked shirtwaist and the green twill skirt because, with its three back plaits, it was sure to billow as she swirled around the dance floor.

On her face she smoothed a single precious dollop of Almond Nut Cream, which she saved for very special occasions. On her lips and cheeks she spread three dots of liquid rouge. Standing back, she looked at herself and giggled. *You look like a tart, Miss Brandonberg. What are the parents of your students going to think?*

She tried to rub the rouge off, but it had already stained her skin. She succeeded only in roughing up her cheeks and making them brighter. She licked and sucked her lips, but they, too, were tinted fast.

A knock sounded and Linnea glanced at the mirror, perplexed. Her lips were not only red, but puffy now! *How do women ever mature and become self-assured?* Realizing it was too late to do anything about her face, she went to answer the door.

"Why, Kristian! Look at you! Are you going, too?"

There he stood, all decked out in his Sunday trousers and a white shirt and shiny shoes, his hair slicked back with brilliantine and shaped into a peak at the top like a rooster comb. And he smelled absolutely fatal! Like a funeral parlor full of carnations. Whatever he'd put on, he'd put too much. Linnea submerged the urge to pinch her nose shut.

"Course I am. I've been goin' since last November, when I turned sixteen."

"Goodness, does everybody around here start dancing so young?"

"Yup. Pa started when he was twelve. But when I turned twelve he said things had changed a lot since he was a boy, so me 'n' Ray had to wait till we was sixteen."

"Were sixteen."

He colored, shifted his feet, and repeated meekly, "Were sixteen."

Noting his discomfort, she flapped a hand. "Oh, blast me! Do I always have to be a schoolteacher? Just a minute while I get my coat."

He watched her move away.

Jumping Jehoshaphat, look at her! That hair—all loose and curling-like. If you put your finger in one of those locks, it'd twine right around and grab a-hold, like a baby's fist. And her face—what had she done to her face? It was all pink and soft-looking, and her lips were puffed out like she was waiting for somebody to plant a kiss on them. He tried to think of what a grown-up man would say at a time like this to let a woman know he liked her more than spring rain. But his mind was a total blank and his heart hammered in his chest.

Returning, she took one look at the rapt expression on his face and thought, oh no, what should I do now? But she was still his teacher and there definitely were things he needed to learn, and if one of them was that helping a woman with her coat didn't constitute an act of intimacy, so be it.

''Would you mind, Kristian?''

He stared at the wool garment, hesitant to touch it.

''Kristian?'' She cocked her head, waiting.

''Oh!'' He jumped and jerked his hands from his pockets. ''Oh, sure.''

He'd never held a woman's coat before. He watched her shrug into it, then reach up to free her hair from inside the collar—women sure moved different than men.

She lowered the lantern wick and preceded him down the steps with brisk, businesslike footsteps.

Downstairs, they collected Nissa, another surprise.

''You're coming, too?'' Linnea asked.

''Just try and get away without me. M' limbs ain't rusted up yet, and dancin's more fun than rockin'!'' She was gussied up in a navy-blue dress with a white lace collar, joined in the front by a ghastly brooch. And she was rarin' to go.

Outside, Theodore sat on the seat of a buckboard loaded with laughing men and the garish redheaded cook, who was regaling them with a loud story about somebody named Ole who could break wind on command.

As the trio approached from the house, Rusty Bonner leaped down, smiling with half his mouth. He tipped back his hat brim and hooked both thumbs beside his gleaming belt buckle. ''Evenin', Mrs. Westgaard, Miss Brandonberg. Allow me?''

He presented a palm to Nissa first.

''To do what?'' she crackled, and ignoring his hand informed him, ''I'll ride up front with Theodore. These old bones can still dance, but hunkerin' on that hay'd jar m' sockets.'' While the men laughed she hotfooted it to the front of the wagon, leaving Linnea facing Rusty, whose hand was now waiting for hers.

''Ma'am?'' he drawled. What else could she do but accept it?

Theodore cast a baleful eye over the proceedings as Bonner turned on the charm and, smooth as rendered lard, captured her waist and lifted her bodily onto the straw. He followed with a long-legged leap that showed off his wiry agility to great advantage. Theodore scowled as Bonner settled himself about as close as he could get to Linnea's side.

Theodore turned away. ''Giddyup!'' It was none of his business if Rusty Bonner flirted with every woman whose breasts didn't sag—he glanced askance at his mother—and some whose did!

But the little missy would be easy pickin's for a smooth mover like Bonner. She's got no pa to look after her here, so she's your responsibility! Bonner'll have her in a haystack faster than a weasel on a hen's neck, and she won't even know what he's aiming for till it's too late!

Riding, Linnea felt Rusty Bonner's hip and thigh press hers. Across the wagon, the boisterous cook was telling a story about skinning a bullhead fish with her teeth. The men roared. But from her right, she felt Kristian's outrage burning at Bonner. They sat with their backs against the sideboards, knees updrawn. She tried to ease over and put an inch between herself and Bonner, but when she did she encountered Kristian, and that certainly wouldn't do! She centered herself as best she could, but Bonner let his leg loll wider and stalk hers. She was conscious that he was the only man here wearing tight denim britches, so tight they were nearly indecent. They added to his sinewy look and that air of banked sexuality that made her feel awkward and a little frightened. She sensed him watching her from beneath the shadow of his cowboy hat while his shoulders slumped indolently, his knees lolled wide, and his wrists dangled lazily against his crotch.

Nissa's words came back clearly: *With his kind a woman don't have to.*

By the time they arrived at Oscar's place, Linnea's stomach was jumping. Rusty was johnny-on-the-spot to help her alight. But once she was down, he stepped back politely, then touched his hat brim in parting. "Y'all be sure to save me a dance, ma'am." Turning away from his unnerving grin, Linnea felt enormously relieved.

Theodore saw to the horses and entered the barn just as Linnea was taking her turn up the ladder to the loft. He watched furtively as Rusty Bonner stood back, eyeing her skirts and ankles as she made her way up. Theodore pressed his palms beneath his armpits and waited until Bonner, too, had gone up, then followed them and immediately searched out John.

"I got to talk to you." He took John's arm and angled him away from the crowd. "Keep your eye on Bonner."

"Bonner?" repeated John.

"I think he's got eyes for the little missy."

"The little missy?"

"She's awfully young, John. She's no match for a man like that."

John's face was an open book. When he became displeased it showed plainly.

"She all right?"

"She's all right. But tell me if you see him hounding her, will you?"

John wasn't bright, but his loyalty, when he bestowed it, was unshakable. He liked Linnea, and he loved Theodore. Nothing Rusty Bonner tried would escape his watchful eye.

The band was already tuning up—fiddle, squeeze-box, and harmonica, and it wasn't long before the music was in full swing. To Theodore's relief, the first one to ask Linnea to dance was his nephew, Bill. He watched her face light up with surprise as they stood talking for a moment.

"Hello, again," Bill said.

"Hello."

"Want to dance?"

Her gaze followed a smoothly moving couple. "I'm not very good. You might have to teach me."

He smiled and took her hand. "Come on. This one's a two-step. It's easy."

When he swung her onto the floor, he added, "I wondered if you'd be here."

"Where else would I be? Everybody's here." She looked around. "But how did they all know where the dance was going to be?"

"Word gets around. So, how have you been?"

"Busy—Oops!" She tripped on his toe and broke their rhythm. "I . . . I'm sorry," she stammered, feeling foolish, then blushing as she saw Theodore standing on the sideline, looking on. She dropped her eyes to her feet. "I wasn't raised doing fancy steps like that."

"Then I'll have to show you." He softened the turns, shortened his steps, and gave her time to adjust to his style.

"I'll have a lot of catching up to do if what Kristian says is true. He said some of you started going to dances when you were thirteen."

"Fourteen for me. But don't worry—you're doing fine."

She watched their feet for some time, then he playfully shook her a little. "Relax and you'll enjoy it more."

He was right. By the end of the dance, her feet were negotiating the patterns much more smoothly, and when the music ended she smiled and clapped enthusiastically.

"Oh, this is fun!"

"Then how about the next one?" Bill invited, smiling down appreciatively.

Bill was a smooth and artful dancer. Linnea was soon laughing and enjoying herself with him. Halfway through the second dance, she swirled around in his arms to confront Theodore, not six feet away, dancing with the redheaded cook. Though she knew she was gaping, Linnea found it impossible not to. Why, whoever would have thought Theodore could dance that way? He sailed around on the balls of his feet like some well-balanced clipper ship, guiding—what was her name again?—Isabelle . . . Isabelle Lawler. Guiding Isabelle Lawler with an easy grace that transformed them both. He caught Linnea's eye and nodded with a smile, then swung around leaving her to stare at his crossed suspenders and his incredibly wide shoulders with Isabelle Lawler's freckled arm spanning them. In another moment they were lost in the crowd. Linnea's gaze followed until all she could see was a glimpse of his outstretched right arm with the white sleeve rolled up to the elbow. Then even that was gone.

The song ended. She danced next with some stranger named Kenneth, who was about forty years old and had a pot belly. Then with Trigg, who said his wife would dance only on alternate songs, because she tired easily. Linnea found Clara looking on and waggled two fingers. Clara waggled back and they exchanged fond smiles. She'd intended to talk to Clara when the song ended, but Kristian appeared before her, wiping his palms on his thighs while asking her to dance. Goodness, was it all right for a teacher to dance with her students? She glanced at Clara for help. Clara shrugged, palms up, and smiled.

Dancing with Kristian, Linnea began to realize that rhythm came built into these Norwegians. Even he, with only a year's experience, made her feel like a bumbling beginner.

"Why, Kristian, you're as smooth as your father!"

"Oh, have you danced with him already?"

"No! No . . . I only meant. I can see he's very good."

Theodore was dancing with a buck-toothed woman now, laughing at something she'd said, and Linnea felt a small spurt of jealousy. But just then another couple danced by, distracting Linnea. "Oh, look at Nissa!"

They followed her as she whirled around on John's arm.

"And, mercy! John, too!"

Kristian laughed at her wide-eyed amazement. ''Ain't much . . .'' This time he stopped himself. ''Isn't much else to do around here all winter except dance and play cards. We're all pretty good at both of them.''

As the evening wore on, Linnea was paired off with one after the other of the Westgaard men, their helping hands, the fiddler (who took a conspicuous break), several neighbors she'd never met before, and even school-board chairman Oscar Knutson. They were all good, but none were as good as Theodore, and she was dying to dance with him. But he asked every woman in the place except her.

Once during a break between songs they nearly ran into each other in the crowd.

''You having a good time?'' he asked.

''Wonderful!'' she said, forcing a smile. She *was* having a wonderful time. So why did she have to force a smile?

She danced with John—he was almost as smooth as Theodore, but not quite—then twice more with Bill and even with Raymond. She visited with Clara while the redheaded cook was back on the dance floor with Theodore again. Her eyes met his across the noisy hay mow, and she flashed him what she hoped was an innocent smile of invitation, but he only twirled his partner away.

Blast you, Theodore, get over here and ask me!

When the song ended, he did cross to them, making Linnea's heart leap, but when he got there it was Clara he led back onto the floor. Next he chose the buck-toothed one again. A woman who could eat corn through a picket fence! *So what does he intend to do, ignore me all night?*

While Linnea was still seething, Rusty Bonner appeared before her, tipping his hat and smiling his crooked smile, the corners of his eyes hooking downward.

''Dance, ma'am?''

She'd been standing on the sidelines for two songs while Theodore blatantly ignored her.

Watch this, Theodore!

''That sounds fun.''

When he swung her into his arms, he immediately held her closer than the others, and instead of sticking to the basic box waltz, he languidly shifted from foot to foot with a ''one-two'' rocking motion that gently pumped her arm. He leaned forward from the waist and held his elbows high in a fashion that made her feel out of her depth. He was nothing whatever like the other men. Even his shoulders felt different inside a streamlined denim jacket that matched his jeans. Beneath it he wore a red and white checked shirt with a red bandanna tied about his throat. When he turned his eyes directly to hers, she found his face so close that she could count the hairs in his sable eyelashes. He had a way of allowing his eyelids to droop half-closed that made her stomach start jumping again. She returned a quavering smile and he shifted his arms, locking both hands at the small of her back. She felt his big silver belt buckle graze her waist and sucked in her belly.

''You enjoyin' yourself, Miss Brandonberg?'' he drawled, and she had the feeling he was indulgently laughing at her.

''Y . . . yes.''

"You dance very well."

"No, I don't. The other women are much better than I am."

"To tell the truth, I haven't been watching them much, so I really wouldn't know."

"Mister Bonner—"

"Rusty." He smiled that lazy, melting smile, and nudged her thighs with his. "And what's your first name?"

"Linnea."

"Lin-nay-uh." He rolled it from his tongue, syllable by syllable, as if tasting it. "Now isn't that pretty?" Everything about him made her feel like somebody had just rammed a finger into the hollow of her throat, and she thought, *Damn you, Theodore, for making me do this!*

She was surprised when her voice came out smoothly.

"Are you from around here, Rusty?"

"No, ma'am. Drifted in from Montana, and before that Idaho and Oklahoma."

"M . . . my, that's a lot of drifting."

He laughed, giving a glimpse of straight white teeth, tipping his head back, then letting his indolent gaze drift to her face again.

"I ride the rodeos, mostly. It's a driftin' kind of life, Linnea."

"So what are you doing here harvesting wheat?"

"The rodeo season is over. Got to have a dry bed and three square ones a day."

It struck her why he was so honed-looking: more than likely there'd been many a day he hadn't had three square ones, living the life he did. She suspected he'd danced this way with strange women in every western state of the union.

"So tell me. Do you win at this rodeoing?"

"Yes, ma'am." His drawl was thick and teasing as he settled a little closer so that her breasts brushed the front of his jacket. "When I let you go, you take a look at my belt buckle. Won it for riding the steers down in El Paso last season."

She tried to pull away but couldn't; he'd drawn her so close she had to lean back to see his face.

"You ever seen a man ride the steers?"

She swallowed and tried to breathe normally. "N . . . no."

"You ever seen a man ride anything?"

"O . . . only horses."

"Broncs?"

She shook her head in two nervous jerks while he poured that molten, sexy grin over her at far too close a range.

"N . . . no. Just saddle horses."

"You notice my belt buckle?"

Her throat closed tightly and her face turned the color of his shirt. His arms were strong and commanding, his shoulders hard as hickory. His fingers trailed on her spine and fired warning shivers down her thighs. He chuckled, throaty and low, and fit his chin against her temple . . . and her breasts against his chest . . . and his Texas longhorn against her stomach.

Theodore, come and get me, please!

Lazily, he tilted his shoulders back and smiled down into her eyes, leaving his hips cradled squarely against hers.

"Your cheeks're all pink. You warm, honey?"

"A little," she managed in a reedy voice.

"Cooler outside. Want to go see?"

"I don't think—"

"Don't think. Just follow me. We'll check out the stars."

She didn't want to, but Theodore was laughing with Isabelle Lawler again, and before she could dream up an excuse, Rusty had tugged her to the ladder. He went down first, then looked up. "Sssst! Come on."

She glanced down at his face and wondered if Theodore would miss her if she disappeared. Suppose he did, and asked her where she'd been. It would feel mighty sweet to be able to tell him she'd been outside looking at the stars with Rusty Bonner.

"Hey, you comin' or what?"

Three feet from the floor, Linnea felt Rusty catch her waist and lift her down. She gave a surprised squeal as she felt herself suspended in his strong hands. Then he settled her against his hip, looped an arm over her shoulder and ushered her toward the door.

Outside, the harvest moon smiled down so brightly it faded the stars by comparison. The air felt good against her heated cheeks.

"Oh, it *was* warm dancing," she breathed, covering her face with both palms, then dropping them to shake back her hair.

"Thought you said you were a beginner."

"Oh, I am. It's just that you're—well, it was easy following you."

"Good. Then follow me some more." He captured her hand and tugged her around the corner of the barn, where the moonbeams couldn't find them. In the shadow of the building he stopped, clasped her upper arms, and turned her to face him, rocking her lightly.

"So . . . you haven't danced much. And you never saw a man ride a bull or a bronc. Tell me, Miss Linnea Brandonberg, pretty little country school teacher . . . have you ever been kissed?"

"Wh . . . why, of course, I've been kissed. And more than once!" she lied, inexplicably excited at the prospect of finding out what it was like to really kiss a man—at last.

"I reckon you're pretty good at it, then."

"I reckon," she replied, trying her best to sound confident.

"Show me . . ."

Her heart caromed and a thrill of the forbidden shot through her as his head slowly tipped and his mouth touched hers. It was warm and firm and not wholly unpleasant. It rested lightly against her closed lips for some time before he backed away a mere inch. She opened her eyes to only the black shadow of his face and the underside of his hat brim. "More than once?" he murmured teasingly, bringing the blood surging to her cheeks. Again he covered her mouth with his, and this time the hot, wet tip of his tongue touched her. *What was he doing? Oh, mercy, he was licking her!* The shock sizzled down to her toes. Instinctively she drew back, but he captured her head in both hands, clasping her ears and threading his fingers into her hair as he drew her almost on to tiptoe. He ran his tongue around the entire rim of her lips until they were wet and sleek. She pushed against his chest, but he only released her mouth long enough to order, "Open your lips . . . come on, I'll show you more . . ."

"No . . ." she tried to argue, but his forceful tongue found the break in her lips and thrust inside. She struggled against him, but he shoved her flat against the cold stone barn wall and clasped one breast to hold her in place. She pulled at his wrist, but it was as taut as new wire fence, and while panic gripped her, so did Rusty Bonner. Again and again and again, squeezing her breast while she whimpered against his driving tongue and a stone painfully pressed her skull.

"Stop . . ." she tried to say, but again his mouth stifled the plea. She twisted violently and managed to free her mouth. "Stop! What are you doing?"

He caught her elbows and pinned them hard against the wall and ground his hips against hers until she felt dirty and more scared than she'd ever been before. Wildly she struggled to break free, but he'd ridden down broncs and Brahmas—one skinny little schoolteacher was nothing for Rusty Bonner.

"You said you'd been kissed before. More than once."

Mortified by what his hips were doing, she felt tears burn her eyes. "I lied . . . please, let me go."

His wrists were hard and corded and could not be budged.

"Easy, honey . . . easy. There now, you're gonna like this . . ."

She choked back a sob as he filled his hands with her breasts, nearly lifting her off her feet.

Then Theodore's quiet voice intruded. "Miss Brandonberg, is that you?"

The pressure on her breasts disappeared and her heels touched the ground.

Relief made her want to cry and take refuge against Theodore's solid bulk. But shame made her wish she could disappear from the face of the earth.

"Y . . . yes, Theodore, it's m . . . me."

"What you doing out here?"

Rusty's voice was thoroughly unruffled as he turned indolently and answered, "We're just talkin' about Texas bull ridin'. Any objection, Mr. Westgaard?"

Suddenly Theodore thrust himself forward, grabbed Linnea's wrist, and yanked so hard she thought her shoulder would come unhinged. "You little fool! What's the idea of coming out here with him like this? Don't you care what people think?"

"Now whoa, just a minute, Westgaard," the Texan drawled.

Theodore spun on Bonner, still gripping Linnea's wrist. "She's eighteen years old, Bonner! Why don't you pick on somebody your own age?"

"She wasn't objecting," Bonner returned in that same easy tone.

"Oh, wasn't she? That's not how I heard it. And if she's not, I am. You're done here, Bonner. Pick up your pay in the morning and that's the last I want to see of you." Bonner shrugged and moved as if to pass Theodore and head back toward the dance. "And you're not goin' back in there. I don't want anybody at that dance suspecting she was out here with you." Theodore turned on his heel, yanked Linnea along after him, and ordered, "Come on."

"Theodore, let me go!" She tried to squirm free, but his angry strides reverberated through her arm and made her head snap.

"I'll let you go when you learn some common sense. For now, you're coming with me. We're going back up there and make them think you were outside talking to me. And if you do one thing to make them think otherwise, so help me, I'll haul you into Oscar's toolshed and blister your rear end, which your own father would do if he was here!"

"Theodore Westgaard, you let me go this very minute!" Outraged at being treated like a recalcitrant child, she tried to pry his thumb loose from her wrist, but it was useless. He stalked across the barn, then gave her a push that nearly put her nose against the third rung of the ladder.

"Now get up there, and act like you ain't about to bust into tears!"

Angrily, she climbed the ladder, tripping on her skirts and cursing under her breath. All she'd done was exchanged one bully for another. By what right did Theodore Westgaard order her around?

Upstairs, he grabbed her elbow in a bruising grip, thrust her toward the dance floor, yanked her to face him, and started them waltzing without so much as a "May I?" She moved like a walking stick while he impressed a waxen smile on his face. Through gritted teeth he observed, "You're moving like a scarecrow. Pretend you're enjoying it."

She loosened up, let her feet follow his, and faked a smile. "I can't do this, Theodore, please let me go."

"You'll dance, little missy. Now get on with it."

She had wanted to dance with him, but not this way. Her stomach was quaking. Her eyes glittered dangerously. She was choking with the need to cry. Theodore's hand on her back was stiff with anger, the other clasping her fingers with suppressed fury. But their feet moved to the music, and her skirts flared out as he swirled her in circles, pretending that they were having a wonderful time.

She held up for as long as she could, but when the lump in her throat grew too large to contain, when the tears grew too plump to hide, she begged in a quavering voice, "Please, Theodore, please let me go. If you don't, I'm going to cry and embarrass us both terribly. Please . . ."

Without another word he turned her by an elbow and walked her directly to Nissa. "Linnea isn't feeling well. I'm driving her home, but I'll be back."

In a moment she was at the foot of the ladder again, crossing the barn with Theodore at her heels. Breaking into a run, she headed for the door, and once outside, dropped her face into her hands as a wretched sob broke from her throat. Uncertainly Theodore stood behind her, still angry, but moved by her tears more than he wanted to be. He finally touched her shoulder, but she spun away, burying her face in an arm and leaning against the barn wall.

"Linnea, come, let's get away from here."

She was too miserable to realize he'd called her Linnea for the first time. He led her, still sobbing, toward a grove of cottonwoods where the wagons waited. She stood drooping, crying, while he fought the urge to hold and comfort her.

"He'll be gone in the morning. There's nothing to be scared of now."

"Oh, Th . . . Theodore, I'm, s . . . so ash . . . shamed."

He stuck his hands hard into his pockets. "You're young. I don't suppose you knew what he'd do."

She lifted her face. He saw the silver tracks of tears on her cheeks and heard the plea in her voice. "I d . . . didn't. Oh, Theodore, honest, I didn't."

A cinch seemed to tighten about his heart. He trembled everywhere and felt his anger dissipating.

"I believe you, little one. But you must be careful around strange men, didn't your parents teach you that?"

"Y . . . yes." She hung her head until her hair covered her face. "I'm s . . . sorry, Theodore. H . . . he said we'd j . . . just go outside and c . . . cool off, b . . . but th . . . then he k . . . kissed me and I . . . I only w . . . wanted to know wh . . . what it was l . . . like." A sob lifted her shoulders and she bobbed her head. "S . . . so I l . . . let him." At the memory of what followed, she covered her face with both hands and leaned her forehead against Theodore's chest.

His hands came out of his pockets and caught her shoulders. "Shh, little one. There's nothing to cry about. So you've learned a lesson."

Against his chest she spluttered, "B . . . but ev . . . everyone will know, and I'm th . . . the schoolt . . . teacher. I'm supposed t . . . to set a g . . . good example."

"Nobody will know. Now stop crying." His thumbs stroked her arms, but he stood erect, barrel-chested, trying to keep some distance between them. With each sob, her hands bumped his chest. A damp blotch formed on his shirt, then stuck to his skin, and his resolution weakened. He chuckled, but the sound was strained. "You know, I'm pretty out of practice at handling crying women."

From beneath her trailing hair came a single choked laugh as she self-consciously tried to dry her cheeks. "My face is a mess. Have you got a hanky?"

He drew one from his back pocket and stuffed it into her hand, stepping back. When her face was cleaned he began to feel safer.

At last she looked up. In the dappled moonlight her eyes and lips appeared puffy, her hair in disarray. He thought of that bastard, Bonner, with his mouth and hands on her and felt the pagan urge to kill.

Without warning, she flung her arms about his neck and pressed her damp cheek to his. "Thank you, Theodore," she whispered. "I was never so happy to see anybody in my life as when you showed up outside the barn."

His eyes slammed shut. He stifled a groan and clasped her tightly to his breast. She clung tenaciously, pressing close, igniting his body. His hands found her back. Her skin smelled of almonds, and her soft, messed hair pressed against his jaw, her breasts against his throbbing heart.

Then he stiffened and gently pushed her away.

"Come, I'll take you home."

Obediently she withdrew but stared at the ground between their feet for a long time. At last she raised her head to gaze at him. The shadows couldn't quite hide the grave question in her eyes even before she spoke it.

"Why didn't you ask me to dance?"

He searched for an answer, but the truth was the last one he could give.

"You danced with everyone but me, and that's why I went outside with Rusty. To make you jealous."

''M . . . me?''

''Why didn't you ask me?''

He swallowed. ''We danced, didn't we?''

''That wasn't dancing, that was two people butting heads.'' She waited, but he backed a step away. ''All right then, why did you rescue me?'' She advanced a step and he put his hands out to stop her.

''Linnea.'' A warning.

''Why?''

''You know why, and it ain't good for either one of us.''

''Why . . . tell me, Teddy, why?''

The name went through him like flash fire. ''Linnea . . .'' He only meant to put his hands on her arms to stop her.

''Why . . .'' A whisper.

She was close enough that he could smell the almond on her skin again. She was insistent enough that he could feel the quivering in her arms beneath his hands. She was innocent enough that he knew, even as his hands tightened and drew her up, this was going to be one of the greatest mistakes he'd ever make.

''Because . . .'' He dropped his lips to her waiting mouth, and his heart was a wild thing in his breast. Her arms came up and their bodies meshed, close and warm and hard. She's still a child. She doesn't even know how to kiss. But her young breasts, crushed against him, her fingers on his neck, her sweet, closed, untutored lips were his for that moment. He let the feelings take him, and when common sense grew strong again, he finally found the strength to push her back.

Their breaths beat hard into the autumn night.

''It d . . . didn't feel like that when Rusty Bonner kissed me.''

''Shhh. Don't.''

''Kiss me again, please, Teddy.''

''No!''

''But—''

''I said no! I shouldn't have done it in the first place.''

''Why?''

''Have you got a couple of hours? I'll give you the whole list.'' He took her elbow and turned her toward the wagon. ''Up with you, now,'' he ordered briskly. But his voice rattled with emotion.

''Theodore—''

''No. Please, just get in the wagon.''

They hadn't realized they'd left their coats behind until they were headed home through the frosty night. Linnea shuddered and hugged herself. Theodore silently rolled his shirtsleeves down and buttoned his cuffs.

''You want to go back and get your coat?''

''No, just get me home.''

And though it pained him to watch her huddle, shivering, when he could have put his arm around her and kept her warm and shielded from the world, he didn't.

By all that was holy, he didn't!

Chapter 13

In the morning, Nissa stayed in bed later than usual, and Theodore was headed upstairs to awaken Kristian just as Linnea was headed down for water. They both halted at once. He looked up and felt his heart race. She looked down and felt the same. In that instant they relived the impact of the single kiss they'd shared the night before, and neither could think of a thing to say. For long moments they only stared.

Her toes were bare and she held her wrapper together at the throat. She's just climbed out from under the quilts, he realized, and his heart tripped faster at the thought.

He wore his heavy wool jacket, his nose was pink, and he hadn't shaved yet. He's already been out to do chores, she thought, and the sight of him, all rugged and masculine, made her toes curl over the edge of the step.

Suddenly they both realized they were standing in a narrow stairwell gawking at each other as if they'd been turned to pillars of salt. Linnea was the first to recover her voice.

"Good morning," she whispered.

"Good morning," he whispered back.

"You've been out already."

"I did the chores alone and let Kristian sleep."

"Oh."

This was silly. Couldn't they pass each other on the stairs without getting all fidgety?

"How are you this morning?" he asked.

"Tired. I didn't sleep much last night. How are you?"

"A little slow on the draw." He wondered what had kept her awake. Had she, like he, lain for hours thinking of that kiss? "We got home late. Looks like Ma and Kristian are in the same shape. But I better wake them or we'll be late for church."

Their hearts pounded harder as he moved up the stairs and she moved down. But when they finally passed each other, they made sure not so much as a thread of their clothing touched. As she reached the bottom step, he called down softly, "Linnea?"

She spun and looked up. She thought she would never grow tired of hearing him use her Christian name in that tone of voice. He stood with one hand on the knob of Kristian's door. She imagined what it would be like if he ever came to her door that way, and quietly spoke her name as he had a moment ago.

"Yes?"

"Bonner is gone."

But Bonner already seemed a hazy memory to Linnea, eclipsed by the imposing man above her. She could have stood all day, looking at him. But he turned away, opened Kristian's door, and disappeared.

Inside Kristian's room Theodore paused, staring at his boots. He remembered Linnea in her bare toes and wrapper, looking warm and tumbled and morning-mussed. It had taken fortitude to pass her on the stairs and not touch her. He sighed heavily. So damn young. Last night, when he'd hauled her out of Bonner's arms, he'd told himself he was acting in her father's stead, but it wasn't strictly true. All that anger hadn't been spawned by paternal protectiveness alone.

Aw, hell, Westgaard, you're just a middle-aged buck who feels like he's sipping from the fountain of youth whenever she's around. Are you forgetting you're a good five years older than Rusty Bonner, and you warned *Bonner* to pick on somebody his own age!

Theodore sighed and glanced at the bed. Kristian lay sleeping peacefully. His arms were thrown back and the quilt left part of his chest exposed. There was a fairly good crop of hair on it already. Now when had that happened? Next month he'd be seventeen. Seventeen already, and—Theodore had to admit—Kristian's seventeen to Linnea's eighteen was far less shocking than the sixteen years separating her from himself.

He recalled Kristian's uncharacteristic frankness in admitting he had feelings for the girl, and Theodore experienced a queer compulsion to sit on the edge of his son's bed and confess that he'd kissed her last night and ask the boy's forgiveness. Guilt. She'd only been here a month and she already had him feeling guilty. That was silly. Or was it? Kristian had marked her first, and had trusted Theodore enough to confide his feelings. Theodore considered the possible eventualities should his son ever find out what went on last night. Lord, suppose it got out and people started wondering what was going on over here with both father and son hankering after the same girl? Wouldn't they blow *that* all out of proportion?

You start anything with her, Westgaard, and you'll have one fine mix-up on your hands. She's too young for you and you know it, so leave her to your son and act your age.

The following night, who should show up at the door but Bill Westgaard, all spit-shined and brilliantined. The men were in from the fields and supper dishes were already put away when the knock sounded and Kristian went to answer it. When Bill stepped into the kitchen it was assumed this was nothing more than a family visit. They all sat around the table and Nissa brought out coffee cups and date cake and asked after Ulmer and Helen and the rest of the family. Bill politely gave an update and dutifully partook of the snack.

They talked about the war, President Wilson's military draft law, and how the American people were arguing about it everywhere. Few thought the nation's strength could be brought to bear on the battlefields of France in time to stave off an Allied disaster, and Theodore agreed. Bill, however, argued that with the

German armies already having driven Russia to the brink of collapse and the invading German and Austrian forces now inflicting smashing defeats on the Italians at Caporetto, we had to get behind Wilson's effort one hundred percent.

Linnea's eyes opened wide at the men's understanding of the happenings overseas. Even Kristian joined in the discussion, showing a vital interest in the subject of airplanes and the battles being fought in the air.

When the subject had run its course, they moved on to talk of winter trap lines, a fox that had been killing chickens in the area, and the possibilities of early snow.

They'd exhausted a variety of impersonal subjects when Bill announced, "I brought the rig. I thought you might like to go for a ride with me, Linnea."

An awkward silence fell. Linnea's eyes sought Theodore's. For an instant she saw startled disapproval, then he consciously wiped it away. What should she say?

"A ride. Oh . . . well . . ."

"We could go down along Holman's Bridge. It's pretty down along the creek, especially when there's a moon."

"It's rather chilly."

"I brought a lap robe," he added hopefully.

She glanced again at Theodore. His face was carefully blank, but across his belly his knuckles stood out like alabaster.

Nissa spoke up. "Sure, you young people go. Get out for a while."

"What do you say, Linnea?" Bill persisted.

And what could she say?

"That sounds wonderful. I'll get my coat."

They drove through the clear, cool night to Holman's Bridge, and counted the muskrat mounds on the river below. Bill was enjoyable to be with, polite and easy to talk to. He inquired about her Christmas holiday, her family, her plans for next summer. She asked about his plans for the future, and was shocked to hear that he was considering signing up for the army. The war, always so remote, was growing closer and closer, it seemed. Though she hadn't known Bill long, he was real flesh and blood, part of the Westgaard family. And he was thinking of going off to fight!

"Roosevelt said it was the thing to do, for us to join the Allies and declare war on Germany. Now that we have, I'd like to do my part."

Around here people paid more heed to Roosevelt than to Wilson.

"But you are doing your part. You're a farmer."

"There's plenty of men to raise wheat. What they need is a few more to fight."

Linnea pictured Bill in a trench with a bayonet in his hand . . . or in his heart . . . and shuddered. Guilelessly, she slipped her arm through his.

He chuckled, pleased. "Well, I'm not going yet, Linnea. I haven't even mentioned it to my folks."

"I don't want you to go, ever. I don't want anyone I know to go."

In less than an hour they were turning into the driveway again. When the horses stopped, Bill's gloved hand covered Linnea's.

"There'll be a dance again next Saturday night. Will you go with me?"

"I . . ." What should she say? She found herself comparing his upturned nose to Theodore's aquiline one, his clear green eyes to Theodore's brown ones, his blond hair to Theodore's plain brown. Bill's nose seemed too boyish, his eyes too pale, and his hair too wavy for her taste. Since the advent of Theodore in her life, no others seemed to measure up. He was the one with whom she wanted to go to the dance, but there was little hope for that.

"What do you say, Linnea?"

She felt trapped. What logical excuse could she concoct for refusing Bill? And maybe going with him would stir a reaction in Theodore. So she accepted.

Bill walked her to the house as if in no hurry to get there. Beside the back door he took her shoulders and gave her a single undemanding kiss. Yet it was lingering enough that if sparks were going to fly, they would have. None did. Absolutely none.

"Good night, Linnea."

"Good night, Bill."

"See you Saturday night."

"Yes. Thank you for the ride."

When he was gone she sighed, comparing his kiss to Theodore's. It wasn't fair that the kiss of a grouchy man should excite her more than that of a young interested buck like Bill.

Inside, a single lamp had been left burning low on the kitchen table. She felt tired and suddenly despondent, filled with endless questions about where her life was leading. And what about those she cared about? Would Bill really go off to war? Would other young men she knew? Absently she wandered around the table and rested her hands on the back of Theodore's chair. Thank God, if it came to that, he was too old to join.

"So, did you have a nice ride?"

Her blood fired at the sound of his voice in the shadows across the room. She turned to find him leaning against the living-room doorway, his arms crossed loosely. He wore black trousers and black suspenders over the top half of his union suit. He filled out the underwear like an apple fills its skin, each bulge and dip emphasized by the form-fitting cloth. His sleeves were pushed up to the elbow, revealing thick, muscular forearms shadowed with dark hair. At the open buttons near his throat more dark hair showed. He was so much more of a man than Bill.

"Yes," she replied, standing straight and still.

He waited, silent, willing away the jealousy, telling his heart to calm down. Her skin in the lamplight took on an apricot hue. Her lips were slightly parted. Her eyes seemed filled with challenge. And she made no effort to look as if she weren't caressing his chair. Damn girl didn't know what she was inviting.

"We rode down to the creek."

He knew perfectly well what she was up to, but leaned in the doorway with feigned indolence, pretending his vitals weren't wrenching him as he wondered what else they'd done.

"Pretty down there at night."

You stubborn Norwegian! Can't you tell what's in my heart?

"He asked me to the dance Saturday night."

"Oh? And what did you say?"

"I said yes."

For a long time Theodore stared at her, unmoving. Bill was young; he had the right. But that didn't make it any easier to accept. At length he forced himself to glance away. "That's good," he said, pulling away from the door.

She felt like bursting into tears. "Y . . . yes." She drew a deep breath and asked, "Will you be there?"

He seemed to consider for a long time before answering, "Guess I will."

"Will you dance with me this time?"

"You'd best dance with the young guys."

Her hand lifted in appeal. "Teddy, I don't wa—"

"Good night, Linnea." Swiftly he turned and left her standing in the kitchen.

In his bedroom he sat on the edge of the bed with his head in his hands. Her face glowed before him, that pretty young face with the expression that hid nothing. With those blue, long-lashed eyes that were incapable of concealing the truth. He flopped back, eyes closed, arms outflung. Lord, lord. He was the one with the age, the wisdom. It was up to him to hold her at arm's length. But how?

During the week that followed, the weather turned cold and the haymows began filling. Oscar Knutson stopped by on Thursday to let Linnea know Saturday's dance would be held in the schoolhouse.

"The schoolhouse?"

"You got a stove here, and we just pile the desks against one wall. Most of the dances'll be here till the haylofts get empty again, on toward spring. Just wanted you to know so you have them kids empty their inkwells. Generally Theodore comes down here to light the stove and get the place ready."

Theodore again. He hadn't said two words to her since she'd told him she was going to the dance with Bill—the last thing she wanted to do was ask him to come down and light the stove before the dance.

"Do I have to ask him?"

"No, it's all taken care of."

They all went down early, Bill and Linnea in one rig, Theodore, Nissa, Kristian, and all the hired hands in another, to light the fire and fill the water crock and push the desks aside.

The schoolhouse seemed cozy at night, with blackness pressing at the windows, the lanterns lit indoors. Linnea pushed her table against the front blackboard so the band could set up on the teaching platform. Nissa set up a refreshment table in the cloakroom, sliced a high lemon cake that would be joined by more cakes and sandwiches when the other women arrived. Kristian sprinkled cornmeal on the floor. Theodore got the fire lit, then sauntered around the edge of the room, tipping his head to study a line of childish drawings strung along the wall on a length of red yarn.

From behind him came a quiet voice. "Russian thistle."

He glanced over his shoulder to find Linnea observing him with her arms crossed. She was wearing a navy-blue middy dress tonight and looked no older than the young ones who'd drawn these pictures.

"I thought so, but on some of these it's hard to tell."

He turned back to study the clumsy attempts at artwork, thumbs hooked around his suspender clips, a benevolent smile on his lips. She idled along the line with him.

''The Halloween ones are a little better.'' She pointed. ''Pumpkins . . . corn shucks . . . ghosts.'' The farther along they moved, the more polished the work became, until it changed from outsized drawings to written compositions with smaller illustrations at the top.

''Kristian isn't much at artwork, but when it comes to rhetoric he shows great promise. Here, this is his.'' She removed a straight pin from the corner of one paper and proudly handed it to Theodore. ''Read it and you'll see.''

Read it? He gaped first at the paper, then at her, taken by surprise. Unable to think of what else to do, he reached out woodenly for his son's composition and stared at it while she waited at his elbow, beaming with pride. He stood beside her for several long minutes, feeling ignorant as a stump. He wondered what the paper said. The black writing on the white page reminded him of straight, parallel rows of corn stubble sticking out of a fresh snow, but beyond that it meant nothing. He was thirty-four years old and his son was smarter than he.

And now Linnea would know.

She tipped her head and pointed to a spot on the page. ''See what he chose to discourse on? Wouldn't you say that shows an inquisitive mind?''

The blood climbed Theodore's chest. It climbed his neck. It reached his ears and they seemed to grow hot enough to singe the hair above them. He hung his head, swallowed, and stared at the paper, mortified.

Blithely, she crossed her forearms behind her back, waiting for him to finish reading and offer some comment. When he didn't, she glanced up with a perky smile. ''Well, isn't it wonderful?''

One glimpse of his face and Linnea realized something was very wrong. He'd turned fiery red and refused to look up.

''I . . . I guess so,'' he stammered at last.

''Well, you don't seem . . .'' She glanced from his face to the paper and back again, her words slowing like an engine losing steam,''. . . very . . . impr . . .'' Something tripped in her mind. One hand came from behind her back and covered her lips. ''Oh . . .'' she breathed, the truth at last registering. ''Oh, Theodore . . . you can't read?'' They stood close, so close she heard him swallow convulsively while his thumbnail dented the right margin of the paper.

He shook his bowed head.

Oh my dear stubborn Theodore, why didn't you tell me? She was abashed for him. Her heart melted. She, too, felt herself blushing. They stood in a cocoon of discomfort that bound them mercilessly, while behind them the band started tuning up. Slowly, he handed her the paper, meeting her eyes at last, still red to the hairline.

''B . . . but what about the hymnal at church?'' she whispered.

''I know those songs by heart. I've been singing them for thirty-odd years now.''

''And the sentences on the blackboard?'' She recalled her own chagrin the day he'd caught her poking fun at him with all those outlandish insults. She empathized with him now when he was the one being found out.

His glance rested steady on her. ''The only one I understood was that you'd like to stuff Theodore.''

''Oh.'' She studied the toes of her shoes. ''When I heard you behind me that day, I thought you'd been standing there reading them all the while I was writing them, and I just wanted to die.''

''Not half as bad as I want to right now.''

She lifted her face and their eyes met, a little of the strain eased. The band struck up a first number. ''Theodore, I had no idea. I really didn't.''

''There was no school here when I was a boy. Ma taught me how to read a little Norwegian, but she never learned English herself, so she couldn't teach the rest of us.''

''But why didn't you tell me? Surely you didn't think I'd think any less of you.''

''After us arguin' about Kristian goin' to school? How could I?''

''Ah,'' she voiced knowingly, ''pride.'' She reached to hang the piece of paper on the yarn again. ''Men have such silly notions about it. So Kristian knows a little more than you do about the English language. But you know more than he does about a lot of other things.'' She faced him, gesturing toward herself. ''Why, for that matter, you know more than *I* do about a lot of things. The other night when you were talking about the war—Well, I had no idea you knew so much about what's been going on over there. And you know how to fix windmills and set mousetraps and . . . you taught me how to catch a horse and saddle him—''

''Her,'' he corrected.

Their eyes met. Something good happened between them. Something warm and rich and radiant that held the promise of enjoyment. Matching grins grew on their lips. Linnea bowed formally from the waist. ''I stand corrected again, sir. Her. Which proves my point exactly. Why, you don't have to feel—''

''There you are, Ted!'' It was Isabelle Lawler, appearing to interrupt the harmonious moment. ''My feet are itching and there's only one cure.'' Without troubling herself to apologize for the interruption, she appropriated Theodore and hauled him off to dance.

Linnea's happy mood turned sour. She glared after the outrageous redhead who seemed to follow no code of manners whatever. How dare that . . . that orange-haired hippopotamus commandeer a man that way, and trumpeting like a bull elephant yet! I'd like to get her into my etiquette class for just one day. Just one!

Suddenly something else struck Linnea.

Ted. She'd called him Ted!

''Come on. Let's dance.'' It was Bill, coming to claim his date. Linnea forced herself to smile and be gay, but she kept catching glimpses of *Ted* and the hippo and it practically ruined her evening. As before, Linnea had plenty of dance partners . . . with one obvious exception. Circling round and round the black stovepipe, she cast occasional furtive glances his way. Theodore was probably the best dancer in the place—damn his hide!—and he'd dance with that red-headed hussy till they'd have to put in a new schoolhouse floor! But he wouldn't dance with the *little missy* to save his soul. After what had passed between them last Saturday night, and earlier tonight, she'd hoped he'd finally begun looking at her as an adult. But apparently not, and she was sick and tired of being treated as if she were still wet behind the ears! But then, *she* wasn't built as wide as a gang plow. And *she* didn't have vocal chords like a mule skinner. And *she* didn't have hair the color of a Rhode Island rooster.

Petulantly, Linnea tried to turn a blind eye on them, but it didn't work. Finally, after Theodore had ignored her till nearly the end of the evening, she put on her best posture and most supercilious face, walked out on the floor, and tapped the redhead on the shoulder.

''I beg your pardon, Miss Lawler, may I cut in?''

To Linnea's acute embarrassment, the fool woman yelled in a voice loud enough to raise the dead, ''Why, I should say not! When I get my hands on a man, I make damn good use of him before I cut him loose!'' Then she collared Theodore in a death grip and whirled him away.

Linnea wanted to die on the spot. What could she do but withdraw to the edge of the room and burn? Just what did he see in that overblown floozy? She was rude and sweaty and she hauled Theodore around the dance floor puffing like an overweight draft horse.

Let him have her—it's no more than he deserves.

She was still standing petulantly at the edge of the dance floor when the song ended. She saw Theodore say something to Isabelle, then escort her to the cloakroom. Momentarily he reappeared alone, scanned the crowd, and crossed directly to Linnea. Her gaze shifted to the fiddler, and she tightened her mouth as if she'd just eaten a bad pickle.

''Come on, little missy, it's your turn.''

Her turn! As if she'd been pining away the whole evening until he could free a spot on his dance card.

''Don't bother yourself, Theodore.'' Haughtily, she turned up her nose.

''Well, you wanted to dance with me, didn't you?''

She glared at him, chagrined at how impotent she felt against his teasing. Give a man a few beers and a few dances with a redhead and he became noxiously jocular.

''Just wipe that smug expression off your face, Theodore Westgaard. No, I did *not* want to dance with you. I had something to tell you, that's all.''

Theodore had all he could do to keep from laughing aloud at the little spitfire. She was something when she got riled and turned up her saucy nose that way—looked about fourteen years old, too. Though he'd told himself to lay low when it came to the little missy, there was no danger in taking her around the floor a couple of times while the whole family looked on. As a matter of fact, dancing with every woman in the place but her might look more suspicious than giving her a turn.

''So come along. You can tell me now.''

He gave her no choice. He swung her onto the floor with loose-limbed ease and grinned down at her with the most annoying air of amusement.

''So, what was it you wanted to tell me?''

To dry up and blow away—along with that redheaded sweatbox! Linnea pursed her mouth and gazed over his shoulder pettishly. He tipped his head, bent his knees, and brought his eyes to the same level as hers.

''Cat got your tongue now that you finally got me?''

She glared at him, sizzling.

"Oh, quit treating me like a child. I don't like being condescended to!"

He straightened up and executed an adroit circle step, advising gaily, "You'll have to explain that one to me."

She punched him on the shoulder. "Oh, Theodore, you're exasperating! Sometimes I hate you."

"I know. But I sure can dance, can't I?"

Did the man have to be humorous just when she wanted to stay good and irritated with him? Her lips trembled, threatening a smile.

"You're a conceited pain! And if school were in session right now, I'd stand you in the corner of the cloakroom for treating me so rudely."

"You and what army?" he inquired with a devilish grin.

She laughed, unable to hold it back any longer. And when she laughed, he laughed. Then they forgot about bickering, and danced.

Mother MacCree, was he smooth. He even made *her* look good! He held her away from him, but guided her so masterfully that rhythm and pattern became effortless. How different he was on the dance floor than any other place. It was hard to believe this Theodore was the same one who'd greeted her that first day dressed in bib overalls and a battered straw hat, and had treated her so rudely he'd nearly sent her packing.

"So, are you going to tell me or not?"

They both leaned back from the waist while their feet glided effortlessly. "Tell you what?"

"Whatever it was you poked Isabelle's shoulder for."

"Oh, that!" She lifted her chin with an air of unassailability. "I'm going to teach you to read."

He grinned. "Oh, you are, huh?"

"Yes I am, huh," she mimicked.

"I'm gonna look pretty dumb tryin' to fit my knees under one of those toy desks."

"Not here, silly. At home."

"At home," he parroted sarcastically.

"Well, do you have something better to occupy your long winter evenings?"

He gave a snorting laugh and a slight lift of one eyebrow. "You sure you want to take me on? Men my age get pretty thick-headed and forgetful. I might not soak things up as fast as your first and second graders."

"Honestly, Theodore, you talk as if you're in your dotage."

"Prett' near."

She cast him a quelling look. "Men in their dotage have rheumatism. You don't dance like you've got a rheumatic bone in your body."

"No, by golly, my bones are pretty wonderful, at that, aren't they?" He preened and admired his elbow.

"Straighten up and be serious!" she chided, trying not to snicker. "When the schoolteacher is lecturing, you can't be making smart cracks."

His amused eyes met hers while they went on dancing smoothly, enjoying each other more all the time. "And what if I do, what's the little whippersnapper gonna do about it?"

"Whippersnapper!" she retorted indignantly, and stamped her foot. "I'm not a whippersnapper!"

But at that very moment the music had stopped. Quiet descended upon them while her words carried like a Swiss bell over a fjord. Several inquisitive heads turned their way. Linnea felt herself beginning to blush, but thankfully he guided her from the floor by an elbow. In parting, however, he added insult to injury by saying, "Thank you for the dance, little missy. Don't stay out too late now."

For two cents she would have kicked him in the seat of his britches!

She was still stiff and prickly as a new rope when Bill saw her home. As soon as the carriage stopped, he put an arm around her shoulders, pressed her back against the leather seat, and kissed her. She was just angry enough at Theodore to capitulate and hope to high heaven the kiss would raise some reaction in her heart. But it raised nothing.

"I've wanted to do that all night long."

"You have?"

"Mmm-hmm. Mind if I do it again?"

"I . . . I guess not." Not if Theodore's going to keep thinking of me as a child. Maybe this will become more fun.

But it became just the opposite when Bill's tongue entered her mouth and he rolled to one hip and tried to insert his knee between her legs. She jerked back and let out a squawk.

"I have to go in."

"So soon?"

"Yes, right now. Bill, don't!"

"Why not?"

"I said, don't!"

"Nobody ever done this to you before?"

Lord, how many hands did he have? "Stop it!" She shoved him so hard he clunked his head on a bonnet brace.

"Well, all right! You don't have to get pushy!"

"Good night, Mr. Westgaard!" With a jerk of her coat front, she leaped down.

"Linnea, wait!"

He caught up to her halfway to the house, but she shrugged his hand from her arm.

"I don't appreciate being mauled, Bill."

"I'm sorry . . . listen, I promise I—"

"No need for promises. I won't be going out with you again."

"But, Linnea—"

She left him spluttering in the path. Inside the kitchen she closed the door and leaned back against it, relieved. She felt her way up the stairs, undressed in the dark, and huddled under the covers, shuddering.

She wanted very badly to cry, but tears didn't come as easily as they used to. Wasn't this supposed to be a carefree, fun time of her life? But it wasn't carefree and certainly not much fun. What was she doing, anyway, kissing men like Rusty Bonner and Bill Westgaard when the only one she really wanted to kiss was Theodore?

But in the days that followed, he treated her like nothing more than a child. Always a child.

Linnea arose one morning shortly thereafter to a wind that whistled out of Saskatchewan bringing with it the chill promise of snow. Dutifully she drew on warm cotton snuggies and long wool leggings, but the walk to school seemed twice as long as it had when the reapers could be seen in the distance.

Arriving at school, she stood in the cloakroom doorway, studying the familiar room. Odd, how it took on different personalities under the different situations. On a sunny morning there was no place cheerier. On the night of a dance, no place more exciting. But today, totally devoid of children's voices, and with gray clouds churning beyond the long, bare windows, the little room brought an icy shiver.

She hurried outside for coal. The wind formed a funnel near the door of the coal shed and plucked at her scarf tails. She wondered how soon they'd see their first snow. Back inside she kept her mittens on while loading the stove, the sounds of the clanging lids and lifter resounding eerily through the school-room. When the fire was finally going, Linnea lingered near it a long time, warming her toes. Finally she forced herself back to the cloakroom, where she discovered the water crock topped with a disc of ice. She chipped it free and returned outside to the pump, feeling again the immense difference between doing this chore on a sunlit September morning and a dismal November one.

When Kristian arrived, she was terribly happy to have his company. Together they moved the water table to a rear corner of the main schoolroom. He and several of the other children brought potatoes to lay on the fender of the stove for their lunches, and by mid-morning the room was fragrant with the aroma. At recess time only half the students chose to go outside. The other half turned their potatoes and passed the time visiting or drawing on the blackboard.

On the way home that afternoon, a few dry, hard snowflakes were falling. The brown grass in the ditch shivered and seemed to hunch low, preparing for its winter mantle. There was a menacing look to the clouds. They gamboled faster across the slate sky, their underbellies dark and heavy.

She entered the yard and discovered Isabelle Lawler's cook wagon gone. She glanced around, but there were no hired hands in sight. Somehow she knew they were gone and wouldn't be back till next year.

It was quiet in the house.

''Nissa?'' she called. Nobody answered. ''Kristian?'' The kitchen was warm and smelled of roasting pork and new squash, but the only sound to be heard was the wind soughing bleakly outside. ''Nissa?'' she called again, searching the front room, but finding it empty, too. Cautiously, she peered into Nissa's bedroom. It was shadowed and unoccupied, the chenille spread tucked neatly beneath the pillows and everything in perfect order. Upon the dresser stood a gallery of photographs—her children as infants, toddlers, youngsters; on their confirmation days with Bibles in hand; on their wedding days with their spouses posing stiffly beside them. Without conscious volition, Linnea moved toward the dresser, bending to study them at closer range.

And there was Theodore with his bride. His hair was cropped painfully close above the ears and his face looked almost childish in its thinness. His neck appeared half its present girth, and his left ear seemed to lap over slightly at the tip. Funny, she'd never noticed it before.

Linnea's eyes moved to the image of the woman sitting erect on a straight-backed chair just in front of him. She had a face as serene and delicate as a violet blossom. Her eyes were very beautiful and her lips the kind—Linnea supposed—that men found dainty and vulnerable.

So you're Melinda. She studied the pretty face a moment longer. They don't say much about you around here, did you know that?

In keeping with the day, she shivered, then backed from the room. She paused, staring at the door to the adjacent bedroom. Unlike Nissa's, which had been left wide, it stood only slightly ajar. She had never seen what lay behind it.

"Theodore?" she called softly. His door was painted ecru, like all the woodwork in the house, and was of double-cross design with a white porcelain knob on a black metal escutcheon. "Hello?" She rested five fingertips on the wood and pushed. The door swung back soundlessly; as with everything, Theodore kept the hinges well oiled.

Guilty, but curious, she stared.

This room was lonelier than the last. The bed appeared to have been put into order this morning by Theodore himself. The spread was thrown over the pillows but not tucked beneath them as a woman would have done. There was no closet, only a hook board on one wall holding his black Sunday suit on a hanger, his overalls by their straps. On the floor his best boots nestled side by side like a pair of sleeping coots. Looking at them, she felt a ripple of guilt run through her—there was something so personal about abandoned shoes. She glanced away.

The wallpaper was floral and faded. Beside the nightstand perched a low, miniature footstool with a hand-creweled cover that must have belonged to Melinda. It seemed the kind of thing a shy-looking violet like her would have liked. It looked very sad and out of place in the dim room, as if waiting for the return of the woman who was gone forever.

On the bulge-fronted dresser lay a photograph in an oval frame, the kind that should have been hanging on a wall. Unable to make it out from her oblique angle, Linnea moved closer.

There was Melinda again, only more beautiful—if that were possible—than in her wedding picture. Linnea's hands were drawn to the photograph. She lifted it, touched the domed glass. Such melancholy eyes, such haunting exquisiteness. How hard it must be for a man to forget a woman like that. Melinda had been so young when the photograph was taken—as least as young as Linnea was now. The thought saddened her and she rued the years that separated now from then, and her own youth, which she'd gladly forfeit if she could make Theodore look at her just once as he must have looked upon this woman.

Sighing, she replaced the likeness in the exact spot where it had been before. Once more she glanced at the double bed, then stealthily withdrew from the room, setting the door at the same angle she'd found it.

The house felt lonely, and Linnea suddenly didn't want to be in it without the others. She wanted to find them and shrug off the lingering effects of the brooding weather, the photos and the deserted feeling lying over the whole farm. She tightened the wool scarf beneath her chin and headed out the door.

The cook wagon was really gone. Funny she should miss it when she'd been so jealous of Isabelle Lawler. Just the caragana bushes remained, dressed only in their long banana-shaped pods that clicked together forlornly in the wind. It wasn't the cook wagon she missed, but the passing of the season it represented. What was between Theodore and Isabelle? If there really was something, how could a man be attracted to her when she was so diametrically opposite of Melinda?

The wind pressed Linnea's coat against the backs of her legs as she turned toward three diminutive figures in a distant paddock. Even from here she could tell it was Theodore, Kristian, and Nissa. What were they doing out there by the horses? Again she tugged her scarf tighter and sailed downwind, buffeted by the Saskatchewan nor'westerly. It appeared that all of Theodore's horses were gathered in one spot, their tails lifting like spindrift while they shifted restlessly. As Linnea approached, she saw Theodore caressing the broad dappled nose of a mare named Fly.

"Is anything wrong?" she called.

The three turned. Kristian answered. "No, just saying good-bye."

"Good-bye?" Puzzled, she looked from one face to the next.

"This is the day we turn the horses loose. Harvest is all done. The crew is gone," Nissa explained.

"Turn them loose?"

"Yup."

"Where?"

"Open range."

"Range? You mean, they just run free?"

"Yup."

"But how can you do that? They're worth a lot of money."

This time Theodore answered. "We've been doing it for years. They always come back in the spring, just like clockwork, when it's time to get the fields plowed."

Linnea's face reflected amazement. "But how can they know when that is?"

Theodore jerked his head out of harm's way as Fly threw her powerful head up and shook her mane.

"They're smart. They know where they belong and what their jobs are."

"But why turn them loose?"

"To save on feed. They'll be back all fat and sassy, come April."

"And you've never lost one?"

"Never."

She watched the three Westgaards take turns scratching Fly's nose, sensing their subdued sadness at the good-bye. Such trust, she thought, to free the creatures who meant so much to their livelihood.

"Do they all have to go?"

"All but old Cub and Toots," Theodore answered. "I keep them in every winter, just like my pa did. Got to have a way to get into town and to church. They always seem to know they're being kept behind and get a little let down."

There were twelve horses in the paddock. They shifted constantly, tossing their heads and whickering into the wind while Cub and Toots thrust their noses over the fence from the adjoining padlock where they were confined. A sturdy buckskin named Chief pranced around the pack, rearing once, then neighing as if to scold Theodore for delaying their release.

''Guess they're getting impatient. They know what's gonna happen.'' Theodore grabbed Fly's halter. ''Don't you, girl?'' He glanced at Kristian. ''Well, I guess we better do it, huh, son?''

''I guess.''

Linnea moved closer to Nissa, watching as the men circulated through the stirring herd, removing bridles. The animals shook their heads, their restlessness growing more palpable as the moment of release grew closer. ''You want to let 'em out?'' Theodore asked Kristian.

Without replying, Kristian transferred his bridles to Theodore's arm, then Theodore stepped to Linnea's free side.

They watched silently while Kristian opened the pole gate on the far side of the paddock, then circled the herd and flapped his arms, giving a sharp whistle through his teeth. The sound pierced the steely late afternoon and set twenty-four equine ears up straight. For one infinitesimal moment the animals stood still, caught in relief against the roiling leaden sky that seemed to personify their moods. Linnea shivered in appreciation. It was one of those moments of sterling clarity, a niche out of her life that would, in memory, forever remain as rich and real as the moment in which it was happening. Theodore on her left, Nissa on her right, Kristian with the herd, tiny bites of snow pelting her skin, the horses pawing, their nostrils dilated. There was a raw beauty to the scene that made Linnea swallow thickly.

Then the horses moved. Out through the gate and off to freedom, all tails and rumps and flexing flesh. The thunder of their hoofbeats came up through the soles of Linnea's shoes. Cub and Toots trotted to the far fence, their heads high, whinnying as if to call, ''Wait for us!'' They ran the fence line back and forth, back and forth, bugling in distress.

Standing between Nissa and Theodore, so close their shoulders nearly touched, Linnea hugged her arms. It wasn't the cold. It was the rapport she felt with all three of the Westgaards at that moment. She had never before stopped to think of the skein of feeling between a farmer and the beasts who fed him, clothed him, kept him safe from peril, but she felt it now intensely. It was beautiful . . . and sad . . . and poignant.

Good-bye, horses. Keep safe.

Linnea leaned forward just enough to press her arm to Theodore's. He neither pulled away nor returned the pressure, but stood with his hands in his pockets, watching his horses gallop off to their winter world of freedom.

''Where will they go?'' she asked quietly.

''Down to the bottomland first, probably, along the creek. We let the hay grow wild down there, and we put in a crop of millet that we don't cut. They love the millet.''

''And after that?''

Theodore shrugged.

''How far away do you suppose they get?''

''Eight, ten miles or so. There's a lot of government land and school sections, plus what we all leave unfenced.''

''Are you sure they'll have enough food?''

Theodore looked down at her head. The red plaid scarf was tied in a double knot beneath her chin, making her look more like a little girl than ever. But her concern came from the heart and made her seem as much an adult as he. He thought again of the wonderful gift Linnea had for finding beauty in things others sometimes took for granted. So different from Melinda.

She looked up and found him studying her, and they both returned to watching the horses move off. ''They'll have enough. When the millet and hay run out, they'll start in on the stacks we left out in the fields.''

''They look so cold, don't they?''

''Don't worry about them. They're off to find the others, and they'll bunch up thirty or more in a herd. When the blizzards come, they'll huddle in a coulee someplace and press up close to keep each other warm.''

Suddenly Linnea realized her arm was pressed close and warm against Theodore's. He felt it, too, and stayed where he was.

''Will we see them at all till spring?'' she asked.

''Might, now and then. They make a sight, with their coats all shaggy, churning through the snow on a gray and windy afternoon like this one. Only the ground will be all white until you can't tell it from the whirlwind they leave behind. There's nothing prettier.''

At his words, she looked up, he looked down. They felt the pull again, strong, undeniable, elemental. She thought of the woman whose picture remained on his dresser and wondered what it would take to get him to put it away and never bring it out again. He thought of how welcome her warmth felt, through his jacket sleeve, and realized they had shared an accord here today that went far beyond anything he and Melinda had ever shared.

Then they both became aware of Nissa's presence and cautiously drew apart. They returned their gazes to the horizon, but the horses had disappeared.

Chapter 14

The end of harvest truly signaled the onset of winter. They awakened one morning in early November to a world of white. Linnea peered out her tiny window and gasped in delight. Overnight North Dakota had been transformed into a pristine fairyland.

But before she was halfway to school, she stopped considering the snow as quite so romantic and began looking upon it as a nuisance. Trudging along, she moved with all the agility of a freshly wrapped mummy. Lord, couldn't somebody invent something better than these miserable leggings to keep the snow out?

The leggings weren't the only problem. Underneath them she'd donned thick long underwear that covered her from waist to ankle, and over these, full-length black wool knit stockings rolled at the top around a tight rubber ring that pinched and cut into her groin. Over all this bulk went the khaki-colored canvas leggings—stiff, unbending things with stays running from ankle to knee, the entire contraption lashed together at the sides with eyelets and strings that cut off her blood supply even further. Added to it all were rubber overshoes. She felt as if she were walking in kegs!

At school the snow brought excitement. And puddles. And the smell of wet wool. And runny noses. And a mess in the cloakroom, where leggings lay strewn beneath the benches and wool scarves fell onto the dirty floor and got wet and mittens got lost and overshoes mismatched. After recess came the worst smell of singed wool from the mittens drying on the fender of the stove.

Linnea assigned a cloakroom monitor, gave orders that no child was to come to school without a handkerchief, and made a mental note to ask Superintendent Dahl about a wooden folding clothes rack.

But the snow brought gaiety, too. At recess they played fox and goose, Linnea running the rim of the wheel with as much exuberance as the first graders. The younger children made "angels" in the snow and chattered about Thanksgiving, which was just around the corner. The older boys made plans to run trap lines down along the creek bottom in the hope of earning money over the winter.

With the arrival of snow, things were different at home, too. The routine around the farm changed. Everything relaxed. The family was all together at mealtime again, and Kristian was beginning to show a marked improvement in table manners. In the mornings, the kitchen smelled milky. The cream separating was done inside now instead of outside. Two of the barn cats took up residence underneath the kitchen stove. In the evenings, Nissa was often seen with knitting needles in her hands. Linnea, taking her cue from the cats, corrected papers in the kitchen instead of in her drafty upstairs room.

The weather turned frigid. Like her students, Linnea wrapped a warm woolen scarf around her face when she walked, and even in thick knit mittens her fingers were often numb before she reached P.S. 28.

She returned home from school one day to find Theodore and John working by a small shed near the well. She crossed the yard, pulled her scarf down, and greeted them. "Hello, what are you two doing?"

"Getting ready for butchering," John answered, his breath a white cloud.

"In *here?*" The shed was only six feet square, built of wood, with a crude floor in the middle of which was a square hatch.

Theodore and John exchanged smiles. Sometimes the little missy asked the most ridiculous questions. "No," Theodore clarified, "this is where we store the meat. Gotta make the ice before we kill the cow."

"Oh."

They were busily pumping water into a deep, square hole beneath the floor. The following day she observed the ingenious efficiency of the meat house when she found them spreading a layer of clean straw over the huge solid block of ice, all now in readiness for the freshly cut beef.

The next afternoon, butchering day, she came home to a kitchen that quite turned her stomach. The two men were busy sawing up the carcass of a cow right on the kitchen table, and Nissa was busy with the sausage stuffer.

Walking in on the messy operation, Linnea turned a little green. Theodore grinned and teased, "So where did you think beef came from, missy?"

She hustled through the kitchen and burned a trail up the stairs in her haste to get away from the nauseating sight.

That evening, after supper, Theodore, Nissa, and Kristian sat at the table patiently cutting thin, long strips of beef and dropping them into a keg of brine.

"What's that now?"

"Gonna be jerky when we're through," Nissa replied without looking up. "Soak 'em a couple weeks, hang 'em in the granary to dry—ain't nothin' better."

The kitchen smelled delicious the following night, and at suppertime Linnea was passed a bowl containing a thick concoction of meat, potatoes, carrots, onions, and gravy. She buttered a slice of Nissa's fresh-baked bread, loaded her bowl with the scrumptious-smelling stew, and dug in. It was absolutely delicious. And how much more pleasant mealtime was around here now that they'd learned how to talk!

Kristian asked Nissa where Thanksgiving dinner was going to be held this year.

"Ulmer and Helen's turn," Nissa answered.

"Aw, Aunt Helen's dressing isn't as good as yours, Grandma. I like it best when we have Thanksgiving here."

"Christmas'll be here. You'll be eating my dressing then."

John put in, "Ma's dressing's good, but it can't hold a candle to this heart stew."

"Heart stew?" Linnea's jaw dropped and her eyes fell to her bowl.

"One of the biggest beef hearts I ever seen this year," added Nissa. "Eat up."

Linnea's innards seemed to roll and pitch violently. The spoon slipped from her fingers while she gaped at the half-finished serving before her. What was she going to do with the mouthful she was holding?

Just then Theodore spoke up. "I don't think Miss Brandonberg holds with John's opinion."

Every eye turned to her. She drew a deep breath, steeled herself, and bravely swallowed. Immediately the heart stew tried to come back up. She grabbed her coffee, sucked in a huge gulp, and burned her mouth. Her eyes started watering.

"Somethin' wrong with the heart stew?" Nissa inquired, peering at Linnea over her oval spectacles.

"I . . . I . . ."

"I don't think it's good table manners for her to answer, Ma," Theodore put in archly, hiding a grin.

"E . . . excuse me," Linnea managed in a weak, shaky voice. She pushed her chair back, dropped her napkin, and made a beeline for the stairs, running like a coon before a pack, a hand covering her mouth.

Upstairs, her door slammed.

The four at the table exchanged meaningful glances. "She's a fussy one at the table, ain't she?" Nissa observed wryly, and calmly went on eating.

"I reckon we should've told her. Especially after the tongue sandwiches," Theodore said, but inside he smiled.

"Thought she was Norwegian. Never heard of no Norwegian bein' so fussy."

"She's only half Norwegian," Kristian reminded them. "The other half's Swedish. Remember?"

"Oh. That must be the fussy half then," Nissa decided.

Upstairs Linnea curled on her bed, motionless. Each time she pictured the unsavory sights in the kitchen yesterday and thought of a big pumping beef heart, the queasiness peaked. She forced her thoughts to more pleasant things: the horses running free in a cool, fresh wind; the morning glories climbing John's windmill; the children playing fox and goose in the fresh, clean snow.

A gentle knock sounded on her door.

"Yes?" she answered weakly.

"Miss Brandonberg, are you all right?" It was Kristian—thoughtful, considerate Kristian.

"Not exactly."

"Can I do anything for you?"

"I'm afraid the heart stew already did it."

"Are you really sick?"

She drew a deep lungful of air. "Close."

Looking at her closed door, Kristian couldn't help smiling. "Grandma says to tell you if it's bad, you can take some peppermint extract."

"Th . . . thank you, Kristian."

"Well, g'night then."

"Good night."

That night, as he lay in bed, Theodore couldn't help smiling again at the memory of Linnea's face when she heard what she was eating. It was times when she appeared youngest that he was most attracted to her: when she balked at strange foods, when she stood looking down at an ice hole with her scarf tied tightly beneath her chin, when she stood in a middy dress with her arms crossed behind her back, when she caught her hair up in a crisp wide ribbon and let it fall free over her high collar. And, of course, when she looked at him across a dimly lit kitchen with innocent blue eyes that refused to admit the obvious reasons why the two of them must fight the attraction they felt for one another.

Since that night there'd been no further opportunities to be alone with her. Thank heaven.

But at bedtime, when he lay flat on his back staring at the ceiling, he pictured her in the room above. Sometimes he allowed himself to imagine what it would be like if she were thirty, or even twenty-five. The thoughts made him miserable. He ended up rolling to his stomach, groaning into his pillow, wishing for sleep to clear his mind of forbidden wishes.

Linnea's thoughts were far different. As the days went by, she found their age difference mattering less and less. Theodore's maturity only made him grow more desirable in her eyes. His body, fleshed out, honed by years of hard work, held far more attraction for her than the thin ones of younger men. The pair of creases that bridged his eyes only added character to his attractive face. And she knew how to make him laugh so they'd disappear. Though he didn't know how to read, he had knowledge of things that mattered more than written words: of horses and crops and weather and machinery and the thousand things about farm life she found fascinating. The few times she'd shared these with him only made her want to share more.

She thought of him sleeping below her, and remembered the night he'd kissed her. She closed her eyes and let the feelings sweep through her vibrant young body. Kissing her pillow no longer sufficed as a substitute for the real thing, and she was bound and determined to have more of the real thing.

On a night in mid-November the entire Westgaard family piled into Theodore's house for an impromptu card party. In no time at all the house was overrun with relatives. The adults set up several tables in the kitchen while the youngsters holed up in Kristian's and Nissa's rooms and the front parlor. While the children giggled, played paper dolls, or organized card games of their own, Linnea was invited to join in the adults' game of "smear."

In it, bids were announced as each hand began. Partners went for designated points: high, low, jick, jack, joker, and total game points. Linnea ended up as John's partner and sat across from him at a table of four, Lars on her right and Clara on her left.

As the cards were being dealt, she asked, "What's jick?"

"Left jack," John answered, scooping up his cards. "You never played before?"

"Oh, yes, but we never had anything called 'jick.' "

"Opposite jack of the same color as trump," he explained succinctly. She blinked at John, surprised. When play commenced she saw immediately that though he was slow at most things, cards wasn't one of them. Together they made an unbeatable team. In no time at all she and John were creating a sensation by winning nearly every hand. They took the first game easily, and as the evening wore on they remained consistent winners.

Between games, Ulmer passed out tiny glasses of a transparent liquid, placing one at Linnea's elbow, just as he did at everyone else's. She sipped and gasped, then fanned her open mouth.

"Aquavit," John informed her, grinning over his cards.

"Ah . . . ah . . . aquavit?" she managed, catching her breath. "What's in it?"

"Oh, a little potatoes, a little caraway seed. Pretty harmless, huh, Lars?" Linnea caught the devilish grin that passed between the two brothers. John tipped up his glass, downed the potent Norwegian liquor in one gulp, and closed his mouth tightly for a full ten seconds before breathing again.

Linnea expected to see the top of his head blow off. Instead, when he finally opened his eyes, he smiled appreciatively and nodded in satisfaction.

As the night rolled on, the glasses were refilled time and again, and though Linnea drank far less than the men, she mellowed at the same rate as everybody in the room. She couldn't say when the mood went from mellow to silly, then from silly to boisterous. But it all seemed to work in rhythm with the accelerating excitement over the card game. They whooped and hollered and leaped to their feet on big plays. Often a card would be played with a slam of the fist that sent the table jumping clear off the floor. Then everyone would roar with laughter or cuss good-naturedly.

Behind Linnea, Trigg bawled, "Damn you, Teddy, I figured you had that jack hiding someplace!" Linnea looked over her shoulder to see Theodore smiling like a new moon, his face flushed from the liquor, a hank of hair coiling down his forehead.

He caught her eye as he played another winning card and gave her a broad wink while scooping up the trick.

She spun to face her partner again, but she spun too fast and the room became a little bit tilted. The bottle labeled LINJE AKEVITT made the rounds again. By this time Linnea realized she was pleasantly drunk, and two-thirds of her students were in the house to witness it! She stopped imbibing, but the damage was already done. She giggled often and seemed to be observing everything through a golden haze.

Still, she and John continued winning. At the end of one close hand, Lars leaned his chair back on two legs and bellowed at Nissa, "Hey, Ma, we could use a little heart stew over here!"

Linnea's head snapped up—at least she thought it snapped, but everything seemed to be moving in slow motion now.

Without even looking up, Nissa called, "Why? You got somebody you wanna get rid of, Lars?"

Obviously, they had all heard of her green-faced flight from the supper table, and she wondered who'd spread the tale. She focused on Theodore, but he wore a tight-lipped grin. "All right, who's the loudmouth?" she demanded.

"John," Theodore accused, pointing a finger at his brother.

"Theodore," John accused, pointing back.

They all began chuckling, and suddenly the whole heart-stew episode became hilarious to Linnea. She giggled and giggled while the whole kitchen broke into an uproar of laughter.

It had been years since Linnea had laughed so much. When they let down their hair, these Westgaards really knew how to have a good time. She felt as much a part of the big, boisterous family as if she bore their name.

Midway through the evening everybody stretched, took a nature break, then returned to form up new tables.

"What do you say there, Heart Stew, you wanna take me on?"

Linnea turned around to find Theodore at her shoulder, grinning, the lock of hair still trailing down his forehead, his eyes dancing mischievously.

She lifted one brow cockily. "You think you're good enough . . ." She paused before adding, "Teddy?"

He pressed a hand to his chest and looked injured. "Me! Good enough? Why, I been playin' smear since before I had whiskers."

"Since before you had whiskers?" She gave a mock frown and pursed her lips. "Tsk! Tsk! Tsk! What a l-o-o-ong time! You're probably too good for me. And anyway, Trigg has already asked me to be his partner. But have a chair and we'll give you a chance to beat us." She pulled out the one at a right angle to hers. ''Come on, Trigg. Let's show this big talker who knows how to smear whom!''

The playing began again. With Theodore so close, Linnea was conscious of his every movement. Occasionally he sipped aquavit, studying her from the corner of his eye. Sometimes he rested his elbows on the table, other times he tipped his chair back on two legs, knees splayed, considering his cards. Then he'd narrow his gaze, studying her over his hand as if to determine her next play before making his. Occasionally he'd flip a card out as if there were no question that it would take the trick. And sometimes she'd come back with a better one, loudly snapping the corner of her card on the table before pushing the trick toward Trigg to collect.

Linnea and Trigg took four games over Teddy and Clara's two. When the games ended, Theodore tipped back and called to John, ''I get Heart Stew for my partner next week, John.''

''I don't think so,'' John called back. ''I found her first.'' Under cover of the noise and confusion of pushing chairs and clearing the tables, Theodore and Linnea exchanged a brief burning glance, then she murmured, low enough for only his ears, ''Yes, he found me first,'' and turned away.

They cleaned away the cards and spread out lunch on the great oak table, and all the while she felt Theodore's eyes on her. ''Lunch'' was a regular feast: deep-fried cookies called *fattigman,* tasty cheese known as *gammelost,* and a suspicious-looking entry they referred to as *blodpose.*

Turning up her nose, Linnea inquired archly, ''And what does *blodpose* mean?''

She directed the question to Theodore, expecting some teasing retort. Instead, he only sipped his coffee and glanced away. John answered instead. ''She caught you this time, Ma.''

Chuckles sounded, but Theodore remained sober. ''What does it mean?'' Linnea asked, clutching John's arm.

''Blood sausage.''

''Blood sausage!'' She groaned and did her best swooning heroine, grabbing her stomach and pitching forward across the table dramatically. Everyone laughed except Theodore.

When the lunch was cleared away, the adults collected their sleepy children, tucked them in the hay-filled wagons, and headed their horses home.

Kristian, who'd been tippling on the sly, immediately disappeared upstairs to escape the close scrutiny of his grandmother. Nissa made ''the long walk'' out back in the cold, and when she returned, Linnea did the same.

On her way back to the house, she tried to puzzle out the abrupt change in Theodore's mood. But her mind wasn't working well. She dropped her head back and sucked in deep breaths, trying to neutralize the effects of the potent aquavit. But in spite of the food, coffee, and fresh air, her head was still light and buzzing.

Back in the house the lamp had been left on the kitchen table for her. Not trusting herself to carry it up the steps in her tipsy condition, she lowered the wick until blackness settled over the room. As she tiptoed toward the stairway, Nissa's bedroom door opened, casting a pale gold splash of lantern light across the living room and into the dim recesses of the kitchen.

''Nissa?'' Linnea inquired softly.

''No.''

Linnea drew a sharp breath and held it as Theodore appeared around the doorway and stopped in her path. His feet were bare and he'd removed his outer shirt. In the muted glow the top of his underwear became a pale blur. She made out the silhouette of his suspenders, trailing beside his knees as they had that day by the school well, and the neck placket of his underwear, with several buttons open. His face was in shadow, but she sensed belligerence in the wide-set feet, the stiff arms at his sides.

''Oh, it's you.''

''You weren't really expecting Nissa anyway, were you?''

''I wasn't *expecting* anyone!'' She edged around him and stalked toward the stairs, but hadn't touched the first step before he spun her around by an arm.

''Oh, weren't you?''

In the dark confines of the narrow landing, their chests almost touched. His grip was bruising.

''What's gotten into you all of a sudden, Theodore, you're hurting my arm. Let go!''

Instead, he gripped it tighter. ''Little missy, if you can't keep level-headed when you drink aquavit, maybe you should stick to milk. It's better suited to somebody your age anyway!''

''My age! I'm eighteen years old, Theodore Westgaard, how dare you treat me like a child!''

''Eighteen, and all grown up, is that it?'' he mocked.

''Yes!'' She spit in a whisper, enraged at being unable to shout at him, but afraid of waking the house. ''Not that you've noticed!''

He laughed derisively, his voice low. ''Just because you left home and wear a bird-wing hat and drink aquavit doesn't make you grown up, little missy.''

''Stop calling me that! I told you before—''

''What was the idea of flirting with John tonight?'' Two hands clamped her upper arms and drew her almost to tiptoe. ''He's not very bright, don't you know that? But just because he's not doesn't mean he hasn't got feelings. So what do you think you're doing, teasing him that way? And if he falls for your shenanigans, then what? He's not like other men—he won't understand when you tell him that you were only fooling.''

''You're crazy! I wasn't flirting with John!''

''Oh, what would you call it then? All that hanging on his arm and being his partner and claiming John found you first?''

She suddenly saw how it must have looked to Theodore. ''B . . . but I didn't mean anything by it.''

''That's not how it looked. That's not how it looked at all.'' He gave her a little shake that further threatened her equilibrium. ''A lesson, huh? What happens when a little girl tries to act like the grown-ups and drinks too much aquavit.''

She neither fought nor conceded, but let him grip her arms until she knew there'd be a string of black-and-blue marks on each. She sighed. ''Oh, Theodore, you're so blind,'' she said softly, resting her fingertips against his chest. ''When will you see that I'm not a little girl any more than you're an old man?''

His hands fell from her as if she'd turned into a living torch. She grabbed the front of his underwear to hold him. Beneath her knuckles his heart knocked crazily. "Admit it, Theodore."

He clutched her wrists and forced them down. "You've had too much to drink, Miss Brandonberg."

"Have I?" she asked calmly.

His head loomed over her. His grip was deathly on her wrists, his voice tight with anger. "First John and now me. Brother against brother, is that it?"

"Don't," she begged softly, understanding his need to erect barriers. "Please . . . don't."

They stood poised in the clutches of a tension more powerful than anything either of them had ever experienced before. His fingertips sank into the soft skin of her wrist where her pulse thrummed hot and fast. The shadows of the stairwell hid all but the vague outlines of their faces as they stared at each other in silence. The night seemed to throb about them with a seductive insistence all its own.

Suddenly, with a soft, mewling sound, Linnea pulled free, flung her arms around his neck, and pressed her lips to his. He made absolutely no response, holding himself rigid, with his lips sealed tightly for a full ten seconds. Then his hands came down on her shoulders, trying to force her away. But she clung to him, fervent and eager, knowing she would die of humiliation if he remained stubborn and refused to return the kiss. His thumbs dug into her shoulderblades, his fingers into her back. He pushed and she clung until they both trembled in silent combat, their breathing heavy.

Suddenly he gave in. His powerful hands drew her up until their chests touched. With a groan of reluctant capitulation he slanted his head and began returning the kiss, moving his lips over hers without restraint, opening his mouth to graze his tongue along her childishly locked lips. At the first touch she stiffened slightly, then shuddered with surprise. Against her lips he whispered, "You asked for it, little missy, so open your mouth and learn to kiss the way a woman does."

His tongue returned insistently, and at its touch Linnea realized a sharp difference between this kiss and those she'd experienced before. The others had slightly revolted her. This one asked to be answered in kind. She opened her lips experimentally and felt the wondrous shock of heat and wetness as Theodore's tongue boldly entered her mouth and slipped in a full, voluptuous circle around its confines. Shyly, she followed his lead, returning the intimacy, tasting him, sampling his texture—all sleek and heated and flavored of aquavit and coffee. Her body came alive with sensations more compelling than any she'd known before.

So this is what it's supposed to be like! Oh, Teddy, Teddy, teach me more.

She strained closer and he crushed her against the wool texture of his underwear for altogether too short a time. Even before she could tell if Theodore's heart hammered as wildly as her own, he drew back and lifted his head, holding her away. His breath pelted her face, beating back a loose strand of hair from her forehead while her vitals pulsed, unrequited. When he spoke, the words were wrenched out angrily from between clenched teeth.

"You're playing with fire, little girl."

Then he was gone, leaving her shaken. She touched her moist, trembling lips, her heart, her stomach. Confused, aroused, she stumbled up the stairs, into the safe familiarity of her icy attic room, to lay beneath the covers and shiver. Her breasts ached pleasantly and her head spun crazily. But it wasn't all from aquavit.

Linnea awakened the following morning with the kiss still fresh on her mind. She touched her lips, as if the imprint of it remained. She flung her arms above her head, closed her eyes, and saw his face as it had looked when he'd winked at her last night, flushed, merry, with the lock of hair trailing down his forehead. A handsome face whose smile she'd come to crave, in whose gaze she longed to lose herself. The thought of him filled her with a giddiness to see him again. But when she did, what would she say to him? What did one say to a man the morning after you'd forced him to kiss you thoroughly?

They met at breakfast and she stared at him with open fascination, as if she'd never seen him before, feeling her cheeks grow hot.

For a fraction of a moment his footsteps paused when he saw her across the kitchen. The aquavit had left his head thumping with a slow, incessant ache. The pain increased at the sight of her, looking rather breathless and uncertain, her hands clasped just below her breasts.

Move, fool, before Ma sees the two of you gawking this way.

"Morning," he said, forcing himself to turn away from her bright, expectant face.

"Morning."

For the first time ever, he felt self-conscious washing up in front of her. This is crazy, he thought. Yet he avoided her eyes all during breakfast. And he avoided her all during the day.

But Linnea had something she wanted to say to him. She finally tracked him down to the tack room in the late afternoon. He sat in his worn wooden chair, rubbing soap on a saddle, unaware that she stood behind him. She drew a deep, shaky breath, and tried for a steady voice.

"Hello, Theodore."

The sound of her voice created havoc in his heart, but he forced himself not to jump. It was risky business, stealing kisses in the dark with a girl like her. One of them had to come to his senses and there seemed only one way to do it. He gave her a desultory half-glance over his shoulder and kept on working.

"Oh, it's you."

"I'm sorry about last night."

He looked over his shoulder once more, unsmiling.

"For what?"

She was stunned. *For what?* He could sit there looking as unemotional as one of his field horses and ask, For what? She dropped her eyes to the floor and said softly, "You know."

"Oh, you mean you drank too much, too?" He turned back to his task, hunching over the saddle. "My head still feels like there's a steam engine running inside it."

She gulped and stared at his broad shoulders. "You mean you . . . you don't remember?"

He chuckled softly, remembering everything. Vividly. "Not much. You were my partner for the second set, weren't you?"

The blood surged to her face, but he didn't turn around to see it.

"Yes, I was. And you got upset with me because I agreed to be John's partner next week. Don't you remember that either?"

"Afraid not. That aquavit is powerful stuff. Today I pay the piper."

Linnea stood rooted for several more seconds, abashed that he should have forgotten something that had rocked her to her very core, no matter how much aquavit she'd drunk! Suddenly her eyes narrowed and a spurt of anger flicked through her. Why, he's lying! The stubborn Norwegian mule is lying! But why?

The answer was obvious: the kiss had affected him as deeply as it had affected her.

Stiffening, she spun on a heel and slammed out of the barn.

He swiveled on his chair, frowned at the empty doorway, then stretched to his feet. He stepped over the saddle and flung the oily rag down. Bracing his hands on the edge of the tool bench, he stared out the small window at the snowy paddock, remembering her pressing warmly against his arm the day they'd turned the horses loose, and last night, feeling her breasts flattened against his chest, and her arms clinging to his neck . . . her mouth offered freely . . . tempting . . . innocent . . .

He clamped his jaw. The muscles of his cheeks twitched.

Wet behind the ears! Didn't even know how to kiss yet!

Grim-faced, he rammed a fist down on the rough-hewn tool bench. But it didn't help a bit. It didn't make her any older or himself any younger.

The extended Westgaard family was much closer than Linnea had at first realized. It had only been harvesting that had kept them apart. Now that winter had set in she grew used to seeing them often. Quite naturally they gravitated toward Nissa, so Theodore's house became the gathering spot more often than the others'.

Linnea came to learn their individual places within the family clan. Of Ulmer, the oldest, the others most often asked advice. John, being slow, was the most protected and cosseted. Theodore received their gratitude for giving "Ma" a home. He also received their sympathy, for they knew he was the one, ironically, whom Nissa had always picked on the most and made work the hardest. Lars was the happiest, the one who brought out the humor in all the rest. Clara, being the baby, and the only girl, and pregnant to boot, was doted on shamelessly by all her brothers. But it hadn't spoiled her one bit. The longer Linnea knew Clara, the better she liked her and the greater grew her urge to confide more deeply in Theodore's sister.

There were countless reactions roiling within Linnea since the night she'd kissed Theodore. Chagrin, curiosity, irritation, and fascination. Theodore was fascinated, too—Linnea could tell. There were times when she'd glance up unexpectedly and find him watching her across the room. Times when they met in a doorway and he stepped back too quickly to keep a safe distance as she passed. And once, getting settled in their chairs at the table, when their backsides bumped and his face turned scarlet. But there were other times when he acted as if he were irritated simply by being in the same house with her. Others when he seemed unaware of her existence. She had no idea from day to day what thoughts churned behind his silent scowl or flat expressionlessness.

As her frustration mounted, she felt drawn toward Clara. But Clara was Theodore's sister. Perhaps it was unseemly of Linnea to want to air her feelings with someone so close to him. But there was no one else, and when Linnea found herself becoming short tempered with the children at school, she realized they should not be the ones to pay for her frustration. She *must* have a confidante.

She walked over to the Linder farm one Saturday, and Clara herself answered the door. After a fond hug of greeting the two sat at the kitchen table, where Clara resumed cleaning eggs with a sanding block. She picked up a brown egg from the wire basket. As she stroked it with the sandpaper, it made a soft *shh-shh* in the cozy room.

Linnea fidgeted on the edge of her chair, staring at Clara's busy hands, wondering how to begin.

''How about some coffee?'' Clara asked.

''No, thanks. I . . .'' Linnea folded her hands between her knees. ''Clara, could I talk to you?''

''So tense. It must be something serious.''

''It is. To *me* anyway.''

Clara waited. Linnea shifted nervously. *Shh-shh. Shh-shh.*

''You're going to wear the varnish off the edge of that chair. Now what is it?''

''Remember the night I got a little tipsy on aquavit?''

Clara chuckled. ''Of course. Some of your students haven't quit talking about it yet.''

''I suppose I made a fool of myself.''

''No more than the rest of us.''

''Maybe not while you were there, but later I did.''

''Later?'' Clara selected another egg from the basket. The sandpaper rasped rhythmically again.

Linnea felt as if the egg were in her throat. Before she could lose her courage, she gulped and stated baldly, ''I kissed Theodore.''

The sanding block stopped in mid-air. ''You kissed Theodore?'' Clara's eyes widened. ''*Our* Theodore?''

''Yes.''

Clara leaned back and gave a full-throated whoop of laughter. ''Oh, that's wonderful.'' She rested the hand holding the egg on top of her head. ''What did he do?''

''Kissed me back, then got mad at me.''

''Why?''

Linnea shrugged, joined her hands on the table, and fit her thumbnails together. Scowling at them, she answered, ''He says I'm too young for him.''

Clara began sanding again. ''And what do you think?''

''I guess I didn't think. I just felt like doing it so I did.''

Clara noted the younger woman's frown. She couldn't resist grinning. ''So, how was it?''

Linnea's head came up. Their eyes met. *Clara wasn't upset!* Her grin evaporated Linnea's fears and left her feeling free to confide what she would.

"Better than with Rusty Bonner, I can tell you that."

Again Clara acted surprised. "You kissed Rusty Bonner, too?!"

"The night of the barn dance. But Theodore discovered us and got upset. That's why Rusty disappeared so suddenly the next day. Theodore threw him off the place."

Clara fell back against her chair and gave up cleaning eggs. "Well, I'll be."

"You aren't mad? About me kissing Theodore, I mean?"

"Mad?" Clara chuckled. "Why should I be mad? Teddy gets too broody. He needs somebody to liven him up a little bit, and I think you're just the one who can do it."

Linnea hadn't realized how concerned she'd been about what the family would think of her interest in Theodore until Clara accepted it so blithely.

If only Theodore would accept it as blithely.

He didn't. He remained stubbornly aloof.

Linnea and Clara visited again on a Sunday when the Linders dropped in for an afternoon visit. When they arrived, Linnea was in her frigid room correcting papers because Theodore was sitting downstairs at the kitchen table. A light tap sounded, then Clara's head popped around the door.

"Hi, am I disturbing you?"

"No, I'm just correcting papers. Come in!"

"Heavens, it's cold up here." She rubbed her arms as she entered.

"Too cold for you?" Linnea glanced at Clara's popping stomach. "I mean, is it all right if you stay a while?"

Clara's eyes followed Linnea's. She fondled her belly and laughed. "Oh, heavens, yes, it's all right." Inquisitively, she prowled the edge of the room. "I haven't been up here in years. Are you sure I'm not disturbing you?"

Linnea set her work aside and tucked her stiff fingers between her knees. "Believe me, it's a pleasure to be disturbed when you're correcting papers."

Clara lifted the top paper, studied it absently, then set it back down. "You know, a lot of times I envy you, having the job you've got, being away from home and on your own."

"*You* envy *me?*"

"Well, why not? I've never been farther away from here than Dickinson. Your life is . . . independent. Exciting."

"And don't forget scary."

"I haven't seen you scared too many times."

"No? Well, I hide it well, I guess."

Clara laughed.

"Did I ever tell you how your brother scared me the day he picked me up at the station?"

"Teddy?" Clara chuckled, strolled to the dresser, and glanced at Linnea's personal items. Among them was an agate bearing a beautiful translucent stripe of amber color. She held it up to the light. "Oh, Teddy's just an old softie underneath—what'd he do, make you carry your own bags?" She replaced the agate and looked back over her shoulder.

"Worse than that. He told me I'd have to find someplace else to room and board because he didn't want any *woman* living in his house."

"Probably because of Melinda."

Linnea's eyes grew wide, interested. "He never mentions her. What was she like?"

Clara dropped to the edge of the bed, pulled one knee up, and became thoughtful for several seconds. "Melinda was like two people. One was gay and gusty—that was the one we saw first, when she came here unannounced, saying she was going to marry Teddy. The other was the opposite. Quiet and broody. I was only eleven at the time, so I didn't realize it then, but I've thought about it since I've grown up and had children of my own. I think part of Melinda's problem was that she was hit harder than most by the baby blues and—"

"Baby blues?" Linnea interrupted, puzzled.

"You don't know what that means?"

Linnea shook her head.

Clara rested one hand on her mounded stomach and leaned back on the other. "Baby blues is after the baby is born when a woman gets real sad and cries all the time. It happens to all of us."

"It does?" Linnea's eyes dropped to Clara's burden. The sight of it filled her with awe.

"Strange, isn't it?"

"B . . . but, why? I mean . . . it seems to me that would be one of the happiest times of your life, right after a new baby is born."

Clara smoothed the skirts over her abdomen and smiled down wistfully. "Seems that way, doesn't it? But for a while after the birth you get so very sad, and you feel foolish because you know you have everything in the world and should feel lucky, but you just want to cry and cry. Husbands just hate it. Poor Trigg, he always hangs around feeling helpless and clumsy and asks over and over what he can do for me." She spread her palms and let them drop. "Only there's nothing. It's just got to run its course."

"And Melinda cried and cried?"

"Did she ever. Seemed like she'd never stop. I guess she hated it here. Claimed the wheat was driving her crazy. Then that fall, when the wheat was all in and the hired hands left, she disappeared, too."

"Oh!" Linnea drew a sharp breath and covered her lips. "You mean she . . . she ran away with one of them?"

"That part I don't know. If she did, they made sure I never heard the details. We lived in John's house then. That was the home place up there when Pa was alive. But Pa had been dead two years already. John was able to handle the home place alone and Teddy needed somebody to look after Kristian, so Ma and I moved in here. This used to be my room then. I can remember bringing Kristian up here and tucking him into bed with me when he was just a little mite." A soft smile crossed Clara's face. "Oh, he was the sweetest little thing you ever—" Suddenly she drew a sharp breath, closed her eyes, and tensed backward, one palm pressed to her stomach.

Linnea's eyes rounded in fright.

Momentarily, Clara relaxed again. "Oh, that was a hefty one."

Mystified, Linnea asked, "What happened?"

"The baby kicked."

"K . . . kicked?" She couldn't stop staring at Clara's protruding stomach, wondering about all the mysteries of childbearing.

"Don't you know anything about pregnant women?"

Linnea's gaze lifted, dropped again. "No . . . you're the first one I've ever talked to."

"The baby's alive already, you know. He's moving around in there."

"He is?" Linnea jerked as if from a reverie, and added, "I mean, of course he is. Otherwise how could he have kicked?" Fascinated, she had to learn more. "What does it feel like?"

Clara laughed, then invited, "Want to feel?"

"Oh, could I?"

"Come on. He'll move again. He always does, once he gets rolling."

Diffidently, Linnea perched beside Clara and reached out a timid hand.

"Oh, don't be shy. It's just a baby."

Shyly, Linnea touched. Clara was hard, and warm, and carrying a precious life. When it moved beneath her hand, Linnea's eyes widened in surprise, then a smile spread upon her face.

"Oh, Clara. Oh golly . . . feel."

Clara chuckled. "Believe me, I feel. More than I want to sometimes."

"But what does it feel like—I mean inside you when he rolls like that?"

"Oh, kind of like a gas pain rumbling around."

They laughed together. Linnea dropped her hand, envying Clara her head start on her family.

"Thank you for letting me feel."

"Oh, don't be silly. A woman's got to know these things, otherwise she's in for some big surprises once she gets married."

Linnea pondered for a moment, thinking of Theodore touching Melinda's stomach as she'd just touched Clara's, feeling his child's movements, holding his child for the first time. Birth . . . the greatest miracle of all. She tried to comprehend the depth of sadness a man would feel at being deserted by a wife with whom he'd shared that miracle.

"I guess what happened pretty much soured Theodore on women," she ventured, running her thumbnail between the rows of chenille on the bedspread.

"A lot of questions about Teddy today."

Linnea's gaze lifted. "I was just curious, is all."

Clara studied the young woman's face closely, inquiring, "So how are things going between you two?"

"About the same. He's grumpy most of the time. Treats me as if I had the bubonic plague." Suddenly Linnea jumped up and stamped one foot. "He treats me like a child all the time and it makes me so mad!"

Clara studied Linnea's back, surprised by her vehemence. So she wants to be treated like a woman. Well, well.

"You *do* have some feelings for our Teddy, don't you?"

Linnea slouched, returned to the bed, and dropped down disconsolately. "Lordy, I don't know." She lifted pleading eyes to her friend. "I'm so mixed up."

Clara recalled feeling mixed up herself during the days when she and Trigg had courted. She reached out to touch Linnea's hand, convinced of the young woman's affection for her brother. "Could it be you're still doing a little growing up?"

"I guess I am." Linnea's expression turned doleful. "It's awfully confusing, isn't it?"

"We all go through it. Thank heavens only once, though. But I suspect that it's a little harder when you find yourself falling for someone like Teddy." Clara sat back and asked casually, "So what is it you want to know about him?"

"Has he ever had anyone else besides Melinda?"

"I've had my suspicions about that Lawler woman, but I'm not sure."

"So have I."

Clara cocked her head. "You jealous?"

"No, I'm not jealous!" Linnea at first appeared defensive, then dropped the facade. "Yes, I am," she admitted more quietly. "Isn't that absolutely silly? I mean, he's sixteen years older than I am!" Exasperatedly, she flung her hands up. "My mother would absolutely lay an egg if she knew."

"Knew what?"

"That I kissed him."

"Ah, that."

"Yes, that. I don't understand him, Clara. He kissed me as if he enjoyed it, too, but afterward he got so angry, as if I did something wrong. But I don't know what," she finished in a near wail.

Clara squeezed Linnea's hands, then dropped them. "More than likely it's himself he's upset with, not you. It's my guess that Teddy is feeling a little guilty because you're so young. And he's probably wondering what people would think—you living in this house like you do."

"But that's silly! We haven't—"

"Of course it's silly. No need to explain to me. But there's one other thing you should remember. He's been hurt awfully bad. I lived here after Melinda ran away. I saw how he suffered, and I'm sure it isn't easy for him to break down and get close to someone again. He's probably a little scared, don't you think?"

"Scared? Theodore?" She'd never thought about him being scared before. Not the way he blustered around all the time. The idea was sobering. "I'm probably making too much out of just a couple of kisses. Like I said, he still treats me as if I'm in pinafores. But, Clara, please don't tell anybody I told you."

"Of course not."

"And thank you for telling me about Melinda and about your condition."

"You're almost like one of the family now. And being Kristian's teacher, you should know about his mother. As far as the other questions go—about personal matters—you can ask me anything, anytime. How are you supposed to know what to expect when you get married if you don't ask questions?"

In the weeks that followed their first confidential exchanges, Linnea voiced countless other questions. As the two women grew closer, Linnea learned more about a woman's body than she'd ever imagined there was to learn. There were times Clara shared some of the deeper intimacies of her marriage, revelations that sent Linnea's imagination spinning.

Each time after such a heart-to-heart talk, Linnea would lie in bed at night—still in her leggings and covered to the eyes—and try to imagine herself and Theodore doing what Clara and Trigg had done to get their babies. Oh, she'd heard rumors about copulation before, but never from any such reliable source as Clara, who should certainly know!

After all Clara had done it with Trigg *three times!*

Then in one of their confidential exchanges, Clara revealed that it was something men and women did together much more often than when they wanted to have babies. It was too much fun to reserve only for begetting!

They rolled their eyes at each other and giggled.

But Linnea went away feeling even more confused than before. She spent hours wondering about the logistics of such an act, and how on earth two people ever brought themselves to begin it. Did the man just say it was time and then you crawled in bed with him and did it? And *how,* for heaven's sake? Picturing it, she was sure it would be awkward and clumsy and grossly embarrassing, even if you loved the man. She recalled how repulsed she'd been by Rusty's groping, and how angry the night Bill had tried to wedge his knee between hers. Yet, the two times when she'd been pressed against Theodore—oh, mercy, it had been grand.

But to take off her clothes and let him do what Clara had talked about? Not on her life! In the first place, the size Theodore was, he'd squash her dead!

November waned and Kristian turned seventeen. At school, everybody geared up for the Thanksgiving and Christmas holidays. Linnea began planning the Christmas program, and she spent her evenings writing the script for the nativity play, conveniently forgetting about Theodore's reading lessons since they were still avoiding each other at every turn.

One day at noon recess the boys came back with a rabbit they'd snared. Excitedly, they asked Miss Brandonberg's permission to dress it then and there. Linnea reluctantly approved, though she steered clear of the coal shed where they skinned and gutted the poor creature.

When the job was done, Raymond, Kristian, Tony, and Paul came back, bright-eyed and eager. "Miss Brandonberg?" Tony acted as spokesman. "We were wondering . . . well, since we caught the rabbit ourselves, could we cook him?"

"Cook him? You mean here?"

"Yeah, see, we thought maybe if you'd let us we'd bring a frying pan and ask our mas how to do it, and we'd fry him up to go with our potatoes tomorrow."

Linnea's stomach turned at the thought of possibly being offered a hunk of rabbit meat, cleaned and cooked by four proud novices. Wasn't there such a thing as rabbit fever one could get from eating the creatures?

"I . . . well, goodness!" she exclaimed evasively.

"Please!" went up the chorus.

What could she do but consent, hoping that one small rabbit wouldn't go far, and she'd escape having to eat any?

"Well, all right." Hastily she added, "Provided you go home and find out exactly how to do it, and how long it has to be cooked to make sure it's safe. *And* clean up after yourselves.''

They cut up the carcass, cleaned Paul's lunch pail, and packed it inside, then left it in a corner of the cool cloakroom overnight. The next day Raymond arrived with a cast-iron skillet. The boys had a consultation and approached their teacher, shifting their feet nervously.

''Well, what now? Did you forget the onion?'' She had made sure to ask Nissa directions for cooking rabbit so things would be done properly.

This time Kristian had been elected to speak. ''We thought, if it was all the same to you, we'd save the one rabbit we got and freeze him while we go out lookin' for more. Then, when we get enough, we'll fix them for the whole school. One won't hardly be enough,'' he reasoned.

Dear, no, Linnea thought, feeling her gorge rise in anticipation.

''But there are fourteen of you,'' she reminded them, carefully excluding herself.

Tony beamed. ''Fifteen, countin' you, Miss Brandonberg.''

Linnea despaired, unable to deny them permission when their intentions were so forthright and generous. She remained silent for so long that Raymond took up their plea.

''See, we were thinking how all the girls always get to learn to cook cause their mas teach them. But us boys, nobody ever teaches us.''

''We boys,'' Linnea corrected automatically, her thoughts on the bloody patch of snow near the coal shed and the pinker patch beneath the pump.

''Yeah, we boys,'' Raymond repeated dutifully, rushing on eagerly. ''We might end up living alone some day, like Uncle John, then where would we be if we didn't have our ma close by like Gram, to cook for us?''

How could she argue with that? What more important duty had any teacher than to prepare young people for life—whatever that life might bring?

''All right. You have my permission.''

They howled in approval, socked the air, then babbled excitedly as they hit for the door.

''And boys?''

The four turned back.

''If you do a good and a neat job of it, there'll be extra credit for you at grade time. We shall call it 'domestics.' ''

It took the boys a week to catch four rabbits. During that time there was much whispering and secretiveness. Linnea suspected some of the girls were in on the plans, too, because every day during afternoon recess, Patricia Lommen and Frances Westgaard had their heads together with the boys, talking animatedly, occasionally breaking out in excited giggles, then quieting suddenly when a loud ''Shh!'' would go up from the group.

Raymond finally announced that they had all the rabbits they needed—by now they were frozen in several tightly covered pails in the snow by the coal shed—but informed Miss Brandonberg that they were saving the meal for the day before Thanksgiving, so could she set that day aside and give them a little longer dinner break than usual?

Libby Severt was somehow in on the act, too. She asked permission to take the smaller children aside for one hour of secret consultation early in Thanksgiving week. While Linnea sat at her desk, correcting arithmetic papers and trying her best not to appear inquisitive, a giggle went up from the youngsters in the back corner. She glanced up to see Roseanne and Sonny jumping up and down and clapping excitedly.

Then, with only one day to go before the event, another special request was made: they needed to use the cloakroom for a while and be left alone. Would Miss Brandonberg please stay out until they were done?

By this time Linnea was so curious it was all she could do to stay at her desk while the door opened and closed repeatedly and children came in and took things from their desks, then ran back and slammed the door. The cloak room was so cold they'd donned their jackets, yet nobody seemed to mind in the least.

At last the big day arrived and it was impossible to carry on normally with reading, writing, and arithmetic lessons. The children were simply jittering with excitement.

At mid-morning the older boys started frying rabbits in two enormous iron frying pans. Potatoes ringed the entire fender of the stove, and soon the savory scent of cooking onions filled the schoolroom. Skipp and Bent proudly marched to the cloakroom and came back with a metal corn-popper on a long handle and set to work popping corn. Jeannette and Roseanne produced a reasonable facsimile of a basket—woven by their own immature hands?—of fresh, dry cornstalks, into which the popcorn was dumped. Several of the children took over pushing the rows of desks back against the walls. They swept the floor, then ringed the stove with fifteen plates and forks confiscated from their mothers' pantries. A fruit jar of bright, golden butter appeared, and salt and pepper shakers.

Roseanne marched up to Linnea's desk and announced, very soberly, "We know the Pilgrimth din't have plates, but we—"

"Shh! Roseanne!" Libby came by and almost yanked Roseanne off her feet. A moment later the cloak room door slammed behind them.

Next, Norna came out and ran up to the big boys by the stove, whispering urgently into Kristian's ear. Kristian, Ray, and Tony followed her back into the cloakroom and returned moments later sporting wide white Pilgrim collars made of paper, and black paper hats that made them look more like warlocks than Pilgrims.

Finally, when Linnea's excitement was as great as that of her students, Bent and Jeannette came out of the cloakroom, marched with all due pomp and importance to "teacher's desk," and escorted her to the place of honor near the stove—one with a perfect view of the cloakroom door.

Libby Severt stepped out, closed the door, and announced clearly, "The first Thanksgiving." There followed a brief recitation on the history of the Pilgrims at Plymouth Colony in 1621, then Libby took her place on the floor next to Miss Brandonberg. Linnea squeezed her hand and solemnly returned her attention to the cloakroom door.

Out stepped Skipp and Jeannette nervously glancing at each other for a cue, taking deep breaths, then reciting in unison: "Thanksgiving was to give thanks for a good harvest or for rain after a drought." Each of them carried a sheaf of wheat in their arms. In procession they marched forward and laid the symbolic wheat on the floor within the circle of plates. When they were seated, Raymond hustled forward and whisked one bundle a safer distance from the stove, and at Jeannette's crest-fallen expression assured her in a loud whisper, "You did just fine, Jeannette." Then he gave her a broad wink, which staved off her tears.

Linnea controlled the urge to chuckle, truly touched by the solemnity with which the children carried out their parts in the pageant.

Next came Frances, dressed in a brown blanket, with a chicken feather in her hair. "The Indians brought gifts of food," she announced importantly. Behind her entered four other Indians in feathers and blankets. First came Norna.

"Corn," she announced, bearing forth a lopsided basket of popcorn.

Then came tiny Roseanne.

"Nutth!" she blasted, so loud it raised an undertone of laughter. The sound faded as she solemnly came into the room with a dishtowel tied neatly in a bundle. Kneeling at the circle, she tried to untie it. When the knot refused to budge, she glanced with a trembling lip toward Patricia—obviously the play director—hovering near the cloakroom door. Patricia hustled over to lend a hand, and together she and Roseanne opened the towel, revealing a pile of crisp, brown walnut meats.

Roseanne settled down cross-legged, and the next Indian entered.

"Wild fruits." Sonny's offering was a wooden bowl full of quartered apples.

"And berries," Bent ended. Another series of snickers arose as he came forward with two quart jars of home-canned raspberry sauce, explaining, "We couldn't find no fresh berries." The younger children covered their mouths and giggled.

Libby rose to her feet and recited, "The Pilgrims taught the Indians about God, and they all asked for thanks together, for the year had been bountiful and they had food enough to see them through till spring."

To Linnea's surprise, Allen Severt stepped from the cloakroom, looking completely out of character in one of his father's white collars, which hung around his neck like a band around a chicken's leg. He held a Bible and grudgingly mumbled his way through the Thanksgiving Psalm, then sat down.

Again, Libby began, "And they all sang—"

Over by the stove, Kristian interrupted, "And they all decided that they would sing the Thanksgiving song later so the rabbit wouldn't be burned to a crisp."

They broke into gales of laughter. Then Tony and Paul passed around piping-hot potatoes, followed by the fruit jar of butter. Kristian and Raymond served the rabbit, and there was cold milk for everyone. They had all brought cups from home, and Miss Brandonberg got the one from the water jug.

When the food was all served and the big boys seated, Linnea sat back and smiled at them all, tears flooding her eyes. She reached for the hands of those closest to her. Never in her life had she experienced a feeling like this. These wonderful children had done this all for her. Pride shone in their eyes. A lump formed in her throat.

As they all joined hands in a circle, she found room in her heart to love every one of them.

"I give thanks for each and every one of you dear, dear children. You've given me a Thanksgiving I shall never forget." A tear trembled and rolled over her lashes, followed by another. She unashamedly let them fall. The children gazed at her in awe, and nobody seemed to know how to end the awkward moment.

Then, Roseanne, with her uncanny sense of timing, lightened the mood by informing ''teacher'' with all due seriousness, ''Thkipp, he forgot the disheth for the rathberrieth, tho we can't really eat 'em.''

When the laughter died down, Linnea suggested, ''Maybe we don't need dishes if we finish our milk first and put our sauce in the cups.''

The Thanksgiving feast began, and a queasy Miss Brandonberg had her first bite of rabbit. She chewed cautiously, raised her eyebrows, licked her lips, and declared in genuine amazement, ''Why, it taste just like chicken!''

And it really did!

Chapter 15

They were all in the front parlor at Ulmer and Helen's house, gathered around a Thanksgiving table so long the far end seemed to vanish in the distance. It was much more formal than Linnea had expected. The table was set all in white: white china on white damask linens. The only color came from a luscious ribbon of translucent jellies, relishes, and preserves that lined the length of the table and caught the sun like a strand of jewels spread upon the snow. In the center was a glorious crown of tomato aspic.

When everyone was seated, Ulmer said grace. A moment later Helen swept in, triumphantly bearing a wide silver platter of steaming *lutefisk* glistening with drawn butter.

Oh no, Linnea thought. The Curse of Norway!

It passed from hand to hand accompanied by oohs and ahs while Linnea frantically wondered where the turkey was. But no turkey appeared. She watched the malodorous steaming cod come closer with all the eagerness of St. Joan watching the firebuilder search for a match.

When it reached her, she passed it on to Frances as unobtrusively as possible.

Frances bellowed, ''You mean you don't want any *lutefisk?*''

''No thank you, Frances,'' Linnea whispered.

''But you have to eat *lutefisk!* It's Thanksgiving!''

Frances might as well have hired a barker. Everyone turned horrified glances on the recalcitrant Miss Brandonberg.

''I never learned to like it. Please, just . . . just pass it on to Norna.''

At her left, Clara—bless her heart—was snickering. Across the table Linnea saw Theodore hide his smile behind a finger. The hostess bustled in with the next Norwegian delicacy, *lefse,* a flat potato bread that had, in Linnea's opinion, all the attraction of a platter of gray horsehide. Every eye in the house surreptitiously watched to see if the little missy would commit her second sin of the day. But this time she took a piece and plopped it on her plate to satisfy them. She slathered it with butter and lifted it to her lips. Looking up, she found Theodore lifting his own *lefse*—wrapped around a hunk of *lutefisk.* She bit into hers. He bit into his. She crossed her eyes and made a disgusted face. He chewed with exaggerated relish, then licked his lips ostentatiously while his eyes twinkled at her from across the table. It was their first friendly exchange since the night they'd kissed. Suddenly the *lefse* tasted nearly tolerable.

When the *lutefisk* and *lefse* courses were completed—ah, bliss—the turkey and dressing arrived. It was accompanied by snowy whipped potatoes, scalloped corn, peas in thick cream, and a rich apple and walnut salad in whipped cream.

Throughout the meal Linnea was conscious of Theodore's eyes roving her way again and again, but whenever she glanced up, he looked somewhere else.

When the meal ended she helped the women with the dishes while the men sprawled out and one by one drifted off to sleep.

When the dishes were finished Linnea peeked into the front parlor. The table had been taken down. The children had disappeared. John was snoozing in a rocker, Trigg was on his back on the floor. All was quiet except for the sound of soft snoring and the women settling at the kitchen table to chat. At one end of the horsehair sofa Lars was stretched out, eyes closed, hands laced across his stomach. At the opposite end, Theodore looked like his brother's bookend. Between them was the only available wedge of sitting space in the room, wide enough only for a small throw pillow that nobody had nabbed.

Her eyes traveled over Theodore. His suit jacket and tie were gone, his collar and vest buttons were open, white sleeves rolled to the elbow. His tan had begun fading; the pale strip of skin at the top of his forehead contrasted less sharply with the rest of his face than it had two months ago. His lips were parted, his chin was on his chest, his fingers relaxed, scarcely holding together as they lifted and fell with his slow breathing. He looked serene, imperturbable, even a little vulnerable.

She crossed the room, picked up the square pillow, and sat down. Theodore opened his eyes, smacked his lips, and sighed gently.

"Didn't mean to wake you," Linnea said quietly. "This is the only place left to sit."

"I wasn't really asleep." He closed his eyes again.

"Yes you were. I was watching you."

He grinned with one corner of his mouth, chuckled, and closed his eyes. "Oh you were, huh?"

She hugged the pillow and slouched down, resting her head on the sofa back. "You haven't been saying much to me lately."

"You haven't been saying much to me either."

"I know."

She rested her chin on the pillow and studied his shiny Sunday boots, crossed at the ankle, then his bare arm, where brown skin met white cotton, the sun-bleached hair beginning to come in darker.

He opened his eyes slightly and watched her without moving another muscle. "You still mad?"

"What's there to be mad about?"

Desultorily, he rolled his head toward her. "Don't know. You tell me."

She felt her cheeks warming and lowered her voice to a murmur. "I'm not *mad* at you."

A full thirty seconds passed while their gazes held and the sound of the men's soft snuffling continued through the peaceful room. At last he said, in a voice so low it was barely audible, "Good." Then he settled his head squarely again and went on. "I hear you had quite a feast at school yesterday."

"And you're gloating, no doubt."

He feigned an injured expression and they grinned at each other. "Gloating. Me?"

"About the rabbit."

"Would I gloat?" But he arched one eyebrow, inquiring, "How was it?"

"I bow to your peculiar tastes. Delicious."

He chuckled. "But you couldn't quite bring yourself to bow to our peculiar tastes today, could you?"

"Nothing against Helen's cooking, but there wasn't any way I could bring myself to eat that . . . that Norwegian atrocity."

Theodore laughed so unexpectedly his heels came up off the floor. Beside them, Lars shifted. Across the room John's snoring halted, he snuffled, rubbed his nose, and slept on. Theodore grinned at Linnea with pure enjoyment.

"You know, I might learn to like you yet, even though you don't eat *lutefisk*."

"Only a Norwegian would come up with a ridiculous standard like that. I suppose if I suddenly discovered I loved that rotten-smelling stuff, I'd pass muster, huh?" He took his sweet time deliberating until finally she advised wryly, "Don't strain yourself, Theodore. I wouldn't want to be responsible for your committing any ethnic sins."

He inquired, good-naturedly, "What's that mean, then—ethnic?"

"Ethnic . . ." She gestured searchingly. "You know—peculiar to your nationality."

"I didn't know sins came in Norwegian. I thought they was all the same in any country."

"Were all the same."

"Well, I see you're back to correcting me. That must mean you got over whatever had you all dandered."

"I was not dandered. I told you—"

"Oh, that's right. I forgot." He wriggled into a more comfortable position with an air of disinterest that made her want to knock him off the edge of the sofa. How was a girl supposed to get his attention?

"Theodore, you know what I wish you'd do?" He didn't even bother to grunt. "Go soak your head in the *lutefisk* barrel!" She hugged the pillow, crossed her ankles, and slammed her eyes closed. If he was grinning at her, let him grin, the damn fool! She'd lay there till she turned into a fossil before she'd let him see how his teasing riled her!

Several minutes passed. Her eyelids started twitching. Theodore sighed, wriggled down more comfortably, and let his arm touch Linnea's. Her eyes flew open. Sure enough, he was grinning at her.

"I was thinking about your offer to teach me to read. When can we start lessons?"

She jerked her arm away and huffed, "I'm not interested."

"I'll pay you."

"Pay me! Don't be ridiculous."

"I can afford it."

"That's not what I meant."

"Oh. What did you mean?"

"Friendship cannot be bought, Theodore."

He considered a moment, then told her, "You look about twelve years old when you stick out your bottom lip like that."

She sucked it in, sat up, produced her most syrupy smile, and pointed. "The *lutefisk* barrel is that way." She was half off the sofa when he grabbed her arm and hauled her back with a bounce. To her utter amazement, all his teasing disappeared.

"I want to learn to read. Will you teach me, Linnea?"

When he said her name that way she'd have done anything he asked. He had beautiful eyes, and when they rested on hers without teasing she wanted more than anything in the world for them to see her as a woman instead of a girl.

"Will you promise never to call me little missy again?"

Before speaking, he released her arm. "I promise."

"All right. It's a bargain."

She stuck out her hand and he shook it—one sure, powerful pump.

"Bargain."

She smiled.

"Miss Brandonberg," he added.

"Theodore!" she scolded petulantly.

"Well, you're my teacher now. Got to call you like your kids call you."

"I *meant* I wanted you to keep calling me Linnea."

"We'll see about that," was all he'd promise.

They began their lessons the following night. As soon as the supper dishes were done, Nissa settled down with her mending in a rocker by the stove. Kristian took a book to the kitchen table where he was joined by his father and Linnea.

Linnea was accustomed to facing a class full of fresh-scrubbed childish faces. It felt odd having to teach the ABCs to a full-grown man whose jaw showed the day's growth of whiskers, whose enormous hands dwarfed a pencil, and whose brawny chest and arms filled out a red plaid flannel shirt the way fifty pounds of grain fills a seed bag. On the other hand, she didn't have to put up with the attention lapses and fidgeting inherent with younger children. She couldn't have asked for a more eager or attentive student.

"We'll start with the alphabet, but I'll try to make it interesting by giving you something to spur your memory on each letter." Having left all her books at school, Linnea took out a large tablet. After a minute's thought she filled the first sheet with a sketch of a half-filled bottle, giving it a tall, narrow neck. In the upper right corner she formed a capital and small A.

She turned the tablet to face Theodore. ''A . . . is for aquavit.'' Her eyes met his over the thick pad. A slow smile spread over his face, a soundless chuckle formed in his chest.

''A is for aquavit,'' he repeated obediently.

''Very good. Now don't forget it.'' She tore off a sheet of paper and formed two perfect A's. ''Here, you make each letter as you learn it. Make a row of them.''

He bent over the paper and began following orders while she explained. ''A has several different sounds. A is for aquavit, and apple, and ace. Each word starts with an A, but as you can hear, they all have different sounds. A is for arm, and for always, and for automobile. Now you name me one.''

''Autumn.''

''Exactly. Now one that starts with a sound like apple.''

''Alfalfa.''

''Right again.''

''Now one with a sound like ace.''

''Eight.''

Linnea threw up her hands and let them flop to the table. ''You should be right, and the dictionary should be wrong, but the first thing you have to learn about the English language is that its rules seem to have been made only to be broken. Eight starts with E, but we'll get to that later. For now, just remember what A looks like, both capital and small.''

While Theodore worked on his small A's, Linnea sketched a string of link sausages, forming them into a capital B.

''B is for blood sausage,'' she announced, flashing the picture at him.

''Blood sausage?'' he repeated, surprised again by her quick wit. She turned up her nose in distaste. ''B is for bad, blukky, buckets of blood sausage!''

''B . . . blukky?'' He laughed. Her sense of humor made the lesson anything but dull.

Across the table, Kristian listened and watched the proceedings with a grin, wishing it had been this much fun when he'd been in first grade.

Next Linnea ordered, ''Name me a word that starts with B.''

Theodore's answer was immediate. ''Bird wings.''

She feigned an injured expression, then scolded, ''B is also for brat, so watch yourself, Theodore.''

Nissa peered over the top of her glasses at the sound of her son's laughter, wondering when she'd last heard it. She glanced at Linnea, grinned appreciatively, and returned to her knitting. As the evening advanced, they laughed often. Nissa listened with one ear, yawning now and then.

C was supposed to be for Clippa, but Theodore declared that the horse Linnea drew looked more like a moose, so they changed C to coal. They progressed through the alphabet, searching for familiar items with which to associate the letters. D was for dipper. E was for eggs. F was for fence. G was for grain. H was for hymnal.

I was a little tougher. While they puzzled over it, Kristian began nodding heavily over his book. I became ice house as Nissa set aside her knitting, lumbered to her feet, and said, "Kristian, come along before you slip off your hand and break your chin." The two of them toddled off to bed as Linnea and Theodore agreed on jar for J.

Theodore watched while Linnea sketched a fruit jar and put the appropriate letters in the corner. The kitchen was quiet without the creak of Nissa's rocker and Kristian's page turning. The kerosene lamp hissed softly and the room was warm and cozy.

Then came K.

"K is for—"

Kiss. The word popped into Linnea's mind, and her blue eyes seemed to crash with the brown ones across the table. The memory came back, as vibrant and unnerving as if it had just happened, and she saw in his deep, dark eyes that he was remembering it, too.

"K is for—" he repeated quietly, his gaze unwavering.

"You think of one first this time," she returned, hoping her face didn't betray her thoughts. "It should sound just like the letter."

"You're the teacher."

Becoming flustered by his steady regard, Linnea frantically searched for inspiration. "K is for *krumkaka!*" she rejoiced.

"No fair. That's Norwegian."

"So is aquavit, but we used it. Besides, *krumkaka* is one Norwegian food I love, so allow me." She busied herself drawing the sweet Christmas delicacy she'd eaten so many times in her life, and came up with a perfect likeness of the delicate cone-shaped cookies.

Glancing at it, he praised, "Very good." But she had the impression his mind wasn't on *krumkaka* any more than hers was. In an effort to leaven their mood again, she went on to L.

"L is for all the worst ideas Norwegians ever produced. *Lefse,* liver loaf, and *lutefisk.* Pick one."

Theodore's eyes met hers, his face golden and attractive in the lamplight as he leaned back and laughed. "Let's make it *lutefisk.*"

She drew her lower lip between her teeth, concentrating, trying to block out the electricity between Theodore and herself while she made the illustration. When the picture was done, she held it up. His head was bent low over his paper, the pencil moving.

"Theodore?"

He looked up. The tablet covered her face from the nose down. She peered at him over her depiction of a serving platter heaped high with chunks of nebulous matter emanating waving stink lines.

"L is for *lutefisk,*" she reiterated.

He broke out laughing—how mischievous she looked, eyeing him from behind the silly sketch. She laughed, too, happier than she'd been in a long time. Then suddenly their laughter dwindled, fell away completely, and left a room so silent they could hear the cat breathe, curled up in Nissa's abandoned chair. They stared at each other, stirred by feelings neither could control. She laid the picture down as if it were made of spun glass, nervous under his watchful eyes, casting about for something to say to end the gripping awareness they suddenly felt with each other.

She looked up. He studied her as steadily as before, his jaw resting on one hand, the index finger along his cheek. Was that how he used to look at Melinda?

"It's late," she noted quietly.

"Oh . . . yes, I suppose it is."

He made fists, stretched them out at shoulder level, quivering and bowing backward against the chair.

"I'd best get upstairs." But instead she remained, bewitched by the sight of his flexed muscles, the fists bunched beside his ears, his trunk twisting while the chair went back on two legs. It was a heavenly spectacle.

The stretch ended.

She dropped an elbow to the table and propped her chin on a palm. "We worked a long time. I didn't mean to wear you out."

He grinned lazily. "I never knew going to school would be such fun."

"It's not always. I can be an old witch when I want to."

"That's not what Kristian says."

Her eyelids drooped with veiled curiosity. "Oh? And do you spend time talking to Kristian about me?"

"He's my son. It's my job to know what goes on down at school." She picked up a pencil and began absently fanning it across the tablet, sketching arc after arc.

"Oh."

Eyes locked with hers, Theodore set the chair rocking . . . backward . . . forward . . . backward . . .

The house, cozy, silent, wrapped them in privacy, making them seem the only two in the world. She hooked the nail of a little finger into the corner of her mouth, lifting and misshaping her lip in an unconsciously sensual fashion while studying him: white underwear beneath red plaid shirt, both opened at the throat, exposing a wisp of dark curling hair; six inches of underwear showing at the wrist beneath the rolled-up cuffs of red plaid; thumbs hooked behind brass suspender clips, black trousers hugging spread thighs that straddled the chair; the shadows of his eyelashes throwing darker shadows upon his upper lids as he watched her unflinchingly, continuing the mesmerizing rocking motion.

When he spoke, his voice was no louder than the creaking of his chair. "Kristian says you're the best teacher he's ever had. After tonight, I can believe him."

Something singular was happening here. She felt it in her vitals. The spark of a change in him, a change she liked immensely.

Quietly, she spoke. "Thank you, Teddy."

His chair stopped rocking. His lips opened slightly. Her pencil stopped fanning. "Is there something wrong with my calling you that?" she inquired innocently.

"I . . . I don't know."

"Everybody else does. Would you prefer I stick to Theodore?"

He carefully lowered the chair to all fours. "Suit yourself," he offered, not unkindly, but breaking the spell nevertheless. He reached for the papers and began shuffling them together.

Disappointment pressed heavily on Linnea's chest. "Here, I'll take care of those." She took the papers from his hands.

He got to his feet and pushed his chair in, then watched her tap the sheets into a neat stack. Tempted to touch. Tempted to end the evening the way they both wanted it to end. Instead, he turned and crossed the kitchen, lifted a stove lid, and slid in a scoop of coal. He heard her cross behind him and pause at the upstairs doorway. ''Well, good night, Theodore.'' Her voice held the faintest tremble, and a touch of disappointment.

He clinked the lid back on the stove and swallowed thickly, wondering if he could handle turning around and looking at her and still stay level-headed. In that moment it seemed he had to prove to both of them he could. He slipped both hands into his hip pockets and faced her, wiping all but a brotherly look from his countenance.

She held the papers in one hand, pressed against her ribs, the tiny watch peeking from above them on the fullness of her breast. He knew beyond a doubt that if he took a single step toward her those papers would go scattering to the floor and her watch would be ticking against his chest.

Their eyes clung while the decision hung in the balance.

''Good night,'' Theodore managed.

Her face became a curious mixture of disappointment and hope. ''Should we do the second half of the alphabet tomorrow night?''

He nodded.

''And I'll think up some good funny ones that'll be easy for you to remember.''

He nodded again, digging his fingers into his buttocks, thinking, Git upstairs, girl, go on!

''Well . . .'' She waggled two fingers, but they fluttered to a stop. ''Good night.''

''Good night.''

She turned and fled. Behind her, Theodore released a rush of breath, his shoulders sagged, and his eyes closed.

In the days that followed, Linnea found herself kissing things. The most curious things. Mirrors. The back of her own hand. Icy window panes.

One day little Roseanne caught her at it. Returning to school to get the lunch bucket she'd forgotten, Roseanne asked from the back of the room, ''What you doin', Mith Brandonberg?''

Linnea spun around, leaving two damp lip marks on the blackboard. ''Oh, Roseanne!'' She pressed a hand to her heart. ''Gracious, child, you scared me half to death.''

''What were you doin'?'' Roseanne persisted.

''Trying to get a thick chalk mark off, that's all. Really, though, it isn't a very sanitary way. You must never lick the blackboard. Promise? It's just so icy outside I didn't want to go out to the pump and wet a rag to wash it off.''

''You mean you was gonna lick off the whole thing?'' Roseanne screwed up her face in disgust.

Linnea tilted back, laughing. ''No, not the whole thing. Now, you'd better get what you forgot and scoot. The others will be waiting for you.''

After that Linnea worked harder at controlling her impulse to drift into fantasies of Theodore. At home the lessons continued, but the mood remained light and often comical: as long as they were laughing they were safe.

She taught him to recite the alphabet by teaching him a simple song she used with her first graders, sung to the tune of "Twinkle Twinkle, Little Star."

A, B, C, D, E, F, Geee . . .
H, I, J, K, L-M-N-O-Peee . . .
Q, R, S, and T, U, Vee . . .
Double-ewe, and X, Y, Zee . . .
Now I've learned my ABCs,
Tell me what you think of me.

"You expect me to *sing* that!" he balked.

"Well, of course. It's the easiest way to learn the letters."

By now she'd grown accustomed to his tilting the chair back on two legs and could read his every mood. This one was stubborn. His crossed arms were lashed around his chest. His brow puckered obstinately.

"Not on your life."

"You know what I do to my students when they cross me?"

"I'm thirty-four years old, for cryin' out loud!"

She smirked. "Never too old to learn."

The look he gave her could have singed hair at thirty feet.

She got him to sing it once, but never again, because Kristian made the mistake of snickering. But she suspected Theodore practiced it when he was alone in the tack room or working around the place, for once she came upon him in the kitchen, regluing the sole on one of Kristian's boots and whistling "Twinkle Twinkle" softly between his teeth.

She stood behind him, smiling, listening.

When he heard her humming along softly with him, the whistling stopped. He turned around to find her with her hands clasped behind her back, picking up where he'd left off. In a very soft, very teasing voice she sang, "Now I've learned my ABCs, tell me what you think of me."

He scowled and pointed the toe of Kristian's boot at her nose. "What I think is that you'd better watch yourself, missy, or—"

"Tut! Tut!" She pointed back at him warningly.

He backtracked. "I think you'd better watch yourself, *Linnea,* or you're going to lose your only thirty-four-year-old first grader!"

The lessons progressed rapidly. Theodore was a very fast learner. He grasped concepts quickly. Having marvelous recall, he scarcely had to be told things twice. Possessed of a desire to learn, he worked hard. Blessed with natural curiosity, he asked innumerable questions and recorded their answers carefully in his brain.

In no time at all he had memorized all the single consonants, so they moved on to combinations such as *ch* and *sh,* and began working with vowel sounds. Then came the first simple words, and once taught, they were rarely forgotten. Within two weeks he was writing and deciphering simple sentences. The first was, *The cat is mine*. Then, *The book is red.* And, *The man was tall.*

She taught him his name. Thus came the first personal sentence: *Theodore is tall.*

The night he wrote it, she said apologetically, "I'm afraid we'll have to forgo the lessons for a while." At his look of consternation, she hurried on. "It's the school Christmas program. I have so much to do to prepare for it."

"Oh . . . well . . . that's all right." But she sensed his disappointment.

"We'll pick up again right after New Year's."

His head snapped up, his face blank. "New Year's? But that's three weeks."

"I'm going home for the holidays."

His lips slowly formed a silent oh while he nodded. But the nod echoed his disappointment at the news. He ran a hand down the back of his head and studied his lap. "Well, I've been thirty-four years learning to read, what's a few more weeks?"

But it wasn't the lessons he was thinking of, it was Christmas without her. Odd, how lonely it suddenly sounded.

"I can bring a reader and speller home for you to keep during Christmas vacation, and Kristian can teach you some new words. Then when I get back, you can surprise me."

"Sure," he said, but his voice was curiously lackluster.

She got up and began clearing the table. He did the same. When she'd pushed her chair under the table, she stood with her hands resting on its back. Her voice came quietly. "Teddy?"

"Hmm?" He looked up distractedly.

"I'll need a favor."

"I'm not paying you for the lessons. I owe you more than one favor."

"A ride into town to catch the train."

The picture of her leaving on the train seemed to drain all the joy out of Christmas.

"When you planning to leave?"

"The Saturday before Christmas."

"Saturday . . . well . . ." All was quiet for some time, then Theodore remarked, "You never said you were going home for Christmas."

"I assumed you knew."

"You don't talk about your family much. You miss them?"

"Yes."

He nodded. "Christmas'll be here at our house this year."

"Yes, I know." She gave a wisp of a smile. "I found out the night of the heart stew, remember?"

"Oh, that's right."

He looked at his feet. She looked at the way he hooked his thumbs into his side pockets, his fingers tapping restlessly against his hips. It was bedtime. The same thing seemed to happen every night at bedtime. After a pleasant two hours of lighthearted study, the minute they got to their feet their talk grew stilted, then fell away entirely. She searched for a way to tell him she'd miss him, too, over the holidays.

"I wish a person could be in two places at once."

He forced a laugh, but its melancholy note made her heart trip faster. So many times she thought he was about to voice his feelings for her, but he always backed off. Linnea's own feelings were running stronger by the day, yet she was helpless to force him to make the first move. And until he did, she could only wait and wish.

"You seem very sad all of a sudden. Is something wrong?" she asked, hoping he'd offer her the consolation of admitting he'd miss her.

But he only drew in a quick sigh and answered, ''I'm tired tonight, that's all. We worked a little later than usual.''

She studied his downcast face, wondering what it was that kept him from displaying his feelings. Was it shyness? Didn't he like her as much as she thought? Or was it that damnable difference in their ages? Whatever the reason, he was caught in its clutches. It seemed she might wait fruitlessly if something wasn't done to prod him.

She reached out and touched his forearm. His chin lifted and his eyes took on a dark, probing intensity. Beneath the sleeve of his underwear the muscles tensed. A pulse raced in her throat as she declared simply, ''I'll miss you, Theodore.''

His lips parted, but no words came out.

Her fingers tightened. ''Say it,'' she requested softly. ''Why are you afraid?''

''Aren't you?''

''Oh, no,'' she breathed, lifting her eyes to his hair, his brow, returning to his familiar, stubborn, confused brown eyes. ''Never. Not of this.''

''And if I say it, then what?''

''I don't know. I only know I'm not afraid like you are.'' She watched him hover, considering the options, the probable outcomes.

''You teach children arithmetic. Maybe you should try doing a little yourself. Like subtracting eighteen from thirty-four.'' His hand closed over her wrist and placed it at her side. ''I want you to stop looking at me that way, you hear? Cause if you don't, these lessons are gonna stop permanently. Now go up to bed, Linnea.'' Her troubled eyes clung to his. Her heart clamored at the sound of her name falling softly from his lips.

''Theodore, I—''

''Just go,'' he interrupted with throaty urgency. ''Please.''

''But you—''

''Go!'' he barked, thrusting her away, pointing to the stairway. Even before she obeyed, tears stung her eyes. She wanted to run not from him, but to him. But if she was miserable, she had one consolation.

So was he.

Chapter 16

As winter neared her solstice, the weather grew bitterly cold. Linnea's morning treks to school seemed to grow longer and longer and start earlier and earlier. Trudging down the road in the murky, predawn hours, with her breath hanging frozen in the cold-white light of the setting moon and the snow cracking beneath her feet like breaking bones, it seemed the fields had never worn their coats of gold, nor the cottonwoods their capes of green.

At school, the morning chores were the worst part of her day. The wind whipped around the coal shed, lifting the ground snow into a swirling funnel. Inside, the little lean-to was dark and icy, the sound of the coal chilling as it rattled into the tin hod from her shovel. The schoolroom itself was cheerless. The stove lids rang eerily as she removed them to lay the fire. Shivering and hunching before the crackling kindling, it seemed the room would never warm.

If there was fresh or drifted snow, she had to shovel the steps and the path to the outhouses. Then she shuddered over the worst chore of all: getting the day's water in. Even through thick wool mittens the pump handle numbed her fingers, and sometimes, while transferring the water to the crock, she got her fingers wet. One morning she froze her little finger, and it hurt for the rest of the week. After that, it seemed more vulnerable to the cold than the rest of her body.

It was on a particularly bitter morning while pumping water that she had the idea about the soup: if the boys could cook rabbits, why couldn't the girls cook soup?

When she presented them with the idea, it caught on immediately, not only with the girls, but with the boys, too. So Fridays became soup days. They agreed to work by fours, two older ones and two younger ones, taking turns getting recipes from their mothers, bringing ingredients from home—beef bones, potatoes, rutabagas, carrots. In the process of the soup-making the children learned planning, cooperation, and execution. Linnea often smiled as she watched the younger ones plying a paring knife for the first time under the tutelage of an older student. And for their efforts they were given a grade. But the biggest bonus was the soup itself.

During those cold December days nothing smelled better or tasted more delicious than Friday's soup.

The work began in earnest on the Christmas play, both at home and in school. Everyone at P.S. 28 looked forward to that most special Friday of all, the last one before Christmas vacation.

Linnea prevailed upon Kristian to help her make a rough wooden cradle for the manger scene and begged Nissa's help in creating costumes for those who lacked enough originality or materials to make their own. At school the children worked on a backdrop made of a cast-off sheet with the Christmas star, palm trees, and desert dunes drawn upon it in colored chalk. Those with more artistic ability cut out cardboard sheep and camels and drew in their features.

Frances wore a smile from day's beginning to day's end: she was going to be an angel. Linnea chose Kristian to be Joseph—after all, she told the others, he had turned seventeen in November and was now the oldest boy in the school. Patricia Lommen, with her long, dark hair would make the perfect Mary.

Linnea's plea for musical instruments turned up nothing more than one accordion. When she asked for a volunteer to play it, the only one who raised his hand was Skipp. The best he could do was pick out the tune to "Silent Night" with a single finger.

A note went home with each student asking for a Christmas tree. Shortly after four the next afternoon the children were all gone and Linnea was writing the program of Christmas songs on the blackboard, when a shy knock sounded on the door. John's head appeared, wearing a red and black plaid cap with ear flaps.

"John! Well, hello!"

He doffed the cap and hovered half in the cloakroom half in the schoolroom. "H'lo, Miss Linnea."

She stepped down from the platform and briskly crossed the room with a pleased smile. "Well, this is a surprise."

"Heard you needed a Christmas tree."

"Word travels fast."

"Kristian, he told me."

Suddenly she caught a whiff of evergreen. "Oh, John, you've brought one?" Her eyes shone with excitement as she reached the door and opened it wider. With a dip of the knees and a single clap she exclaimed, "Oh, you have! Well, bring it in here, it's cold out there!" She nudged him inside and the tree along with him. Quickly slamming the door, she whirled to examine the tree, clapped once more, then impetuously raised up on tiptoe to peck John on the cheek. "Oh, thank you, John. It's a beauty."

John turned plum red, shuffled his feet, and tapped his cap against his thigh. "Shucks, no, it ain't, but it's the best I could do. Kinda scraggly on that there side, but I figgered you could turn that to the wall."

She made a full circle around the tree. "It is *too* a beauty!" she scolded cheerfully. "Or it will be by the time the children get the decorations on it tomorrow. And the smell!" She leaned close and sniffed. "Isn't it glorious, John?"

He watched her dance around all giddylike, looking as pretty as a brand-new china doll and wondered why Teddy didn't snap her up and marry her. She'd make a man a mighty fetching little wife, and it was plain as the nose on his face she had eyes for Teddy. You'd think Teddy'd see that.

"Sure is, Miss Linnea. Ain't nothin' smells prettier than a pine fresh brung in."

Gaily, she whirled off toward the front of the room. "Where should we put it, John? In this corner, or that one? Look, didn't the children do a wonderful job painting the Bethlehem star?"

John perused the star, the palm trees, the sheep, and gave two bearlike nods. "It's pretty, all right. You want I should bring the tree up there?"

"Yes, right here, on the left, I think." Suddenly she twirled to face him, wearing a look of dismay. "But what'll we put it in?"

John leaned it in a front corner and lumbered back toward the door. "Never you worry, I got the stuff to make a stand. It's out in the wagon."

He returned with hammer, saw, and wood, and set to work. Looking on, she observed, "I swear, you Westgaards can fix anything, can't you?"

On one knee, sawing over the edge of the desk platform, he answered, "Pretty 'bout."

John was one person whose grammar she never corrected. She enjoyed it just as it was.

"Theodore fixes everything from shoes to harnesses."

"Teddy's a smart one, all right."

"But he has a terrible temper, doesn't he?"

John looked up blankly. "He does?"

Surprised, she shrugged. "Well, I always thought so."

John scratched his head, then righted his cap. "Teddy, he never gets mad at me. Not even when I'm slow." He paused, thinking for a full ten seconds before adding, "And I'm pretty slow." He studied the saw blade a long moment, then leaned back into the work at his usual plodding pace. Watching, she felt a warm, sympathetic spot in her heart, different from the warm spot reserved for Theodore, but every bit as full. She had never before realized that John knew he was slower than most, or that it must bother him. She could sense in him the quiet love he felt for his brother, and because Theodore was patient with John, she suddenly had even more reason to love him.

"You're not slow, John, you're only . . . unrushed. There's a big difference."

He looked up, the wool flaps of his cap sticking out like broken wings above his ears, their wrinkled black ties dangling below. He swallowed and his raw-boned cheeks took on color. The expression on his face said her words had made him happier than any gift she might have wrapped and left beneath a tree.

"Will you be coming to the Christmas program, John?"

"Me? Sure thing, Miss Linnea. Never missed it since Kristian's been in it."

"And . . . and Theodore, too?"

"Teddy? Why, he wouldn't dream of missin' it. We'll all be here, don't you worry."

The night of the big event they were all there, just as John had promised. Not only her own "family," but the families of all her students. The schoolroom was filled to capacity. Even the recitation benches from up front and the boot-changing benches from the cloakroom were pressed into service to seat the crowd.

Linnea's stomach had butterflies.

The "curtain"—two sheets confiscated from Nissa's bureau drawer—was strung across the front of the stage and behind it Frances Westgaard's face beamed as brightly as her tinsel halo as she stood in a long white angel costume with her bright hair flowing past her shoulder blades. Little Roseanne began crying because she'd misplaced her halo. Norna was dispatched to find it, but just when that problem was solved Sonny stepped on the backdrop and jerked it from its string line above. Linnea's face fell, but Kristian lifted Sonny bodily, set him to one side, and reached up easily to secure the clothespins once again. From out front came the smell of coffee brewing on the stove, and hot chocolate heating. Linnea peeked between the sheets and felt all the trepidation of a stage director on opening night. Nissa and Hilda Knutson were setting out cups and arranging cookies and nut breads on a table. The younger brothers and sisters of her students were climbing on their mothers' laps, agitating for the program to begin. And there was Superintendent Dahl! And the lady beside him had to be his wife. Linnea found Theodore and her heart skipped. There was no denying, she wanted everything to go smoothly not only for the children's sake but to prove herself in his eyes.

Bent Linder tugged her skirt. "I can't get my head thing on right, Miss Brandonberg."

She leaned to take the red farmer hanky from Bent and twist it into a rope, then secure it around the white dishtowel on his head. After checking to make sure he had his sprig of "myrrh," she stood him in place.

"Shh!"

It was time to begin.

The program went off without a hitch, but through it all, Linnea clutched her fingers and waited for someone to forget their lines and start crying. Or for the shaky cradle to collapse, or for somebody to step on the backdrop again and send it to the floor. But they were flawless, her children. And when the last stroke of applause died and she stepped before the curtain, Linnea's heart felt filled to bursting.

"I want to thank you all for coming tonight, and for helping at home with the costumes and the cookies. It's hard to say who's been more excited about tonight, the children or I." She realized she was still clutching her hands. Glancing down, she separated them and gave them a nervous flip. The audience laughed. She picked out Mr. and Mrs. Dahl. "We're honored to have Superintendent Dahl and his wife with us tonight—an unexpected surprise. Thank you so much for coming." Her eyes sought out John. "A special thanks to John Westgaard for providing us with our Christmas tree this year, and for delivering it and building the stand." She gave him a warm smile; he hung his head and blushed a holly-berry red. "John, thank you."

Her gaze moved past the spot where Theodore had been sitting, backtracked at finding him gone, then moved on to Nissa. "And to Nissa Westgaard for letting me raid her linen supplies. And for putting up with me when any less patient person would have told me to quit bothering her and find my own costumes."

"I want to take this opportunity to wish each and every one of you a blessed Christmas. I'll be leaving in the morning to spend Christmas with my family in Fargo, so I won't be seeing you in church. But Merry Christmas, one and all. Now, before we enjoy the treats you mothers have provided, let's give the children one more round of applause for a job beautifully done."

The sheets were drawn aside on cue and she stepped back, reached for the hands of those in the center of the line, and they all took a final bow.

When the performers and director lifted their heads again in unison, Linnea's mouth dropped open. Coming in the rear door was a robust red-cheeked Santa Claus with an enormous bag slung over his shoulder. Down each red pant leg ran a string of sleigh bells that sang out merrily as he moved.

"Wh . . . why . . . who in the world . . ." she breathed.

From behind the white beard and mustache came a deep, chortling voice. "Merrrrrry Christmas, everybody! Santa smelled coffee!"

The young children started whispering and giggling nervously. One of the pre-schoolers in the audience stuck his finger in his mouth and began to cry. Linnea had all she could do to keep from bursting out laughing. Why, Theodore Westgaard, you lovable sneak!

He closed the cloakroom door with more jingling of bells while from beside her came a murmur of awe. "It'th Thantaaaa!"

She leaned over to find Roseanne and Sonny with eyes like full moons. She nudged the two seven-year-olds gently. "Why don't you go invite him in?" she whispered. Then she turned to include all the small children in her suggestion. "Go on, make him feel welcome. Remember your manners."

It was quite a sight to watch the younger set shyly make their way to the rear of the schoolroom and reach for Santa's hand, then lead him to the front.

Tony rushed forward. "I'll get teacher's chair for you, Santa!"

As Santa stepped up onto the stage, a familiar brown eye gave Linnea a covert wink.

"Santa's been riding a long time. A little set-down'd feel mighty good." He lowered himself into the chair with a great show of breathlessness, bending over his enormous belly and bracing his knees as he plopped back, letting the top of his bag fall over one thigh. The eye of every believer in the room followed it excitedly.

He played the part to the hilt, inquiring archly how many of them had been good little boys and girls. In the audience little sisters and brothers furtively sneaked from their mothers' laps and inched forward, drawn irresistibly. As the man in red reached for the drawstring bag, one voice piped up boldly, "I been good, Thanta!"

Roseanne.

All the adults tried to muffle their laughter, but Roseanne approached him confidently and stood in her angel gown, with her belly thrust out. "You have?" Santa exclaimed, then with exaggerated motions, lifted one hip and searched his pocket. "Well, now, let's see who we have here." He produced a long white paper, ran a finger down it, stopped momentarily to peer more closely at Roseanne's face from beneath bushy white eyebrows. She waited before him, composed, her adorable face drawn into a sober expression of respect. "Ahh, there it is. This must be Roseanne."

She laughed like a lilting songbird and turned to Skipp. "Thee? He knowth me!"

When she was perched on his knee, she peered inside the bag until her head got in Theodore's way, and everyone laughed again. Roseanne offered, "I can reach."

Linnea could tell Theodore was having trouble keeping a straight face. "Oh, well, you go ahead then." He held the sack open and Roseanne almost fell into it, leaning over and groping. She came up with a brown paper bag. On it a name was printed in black.

"Who's it for?" Theodore asked.

Roseanne studied the name, then shrugged and looked up angelically into his eyes. "I can't read yet."

"Oh, well, let Santa try." Theodore checked the name. "Says here Frances Westgaard."

"Theeth my cuzzint!" Roseanne exclaimed.

"She is! Well, what do you know about that."

Frances came forward to accept her bag, and Roseanne dipped in for another. There was one for each child in the room, even those not yet attending school. Each of the young ones sat on Santa's knee and was given his personal approval. Linnea watched one after the other dig into their gift bags and pull out rosy red apples, green popcorn balls, peanuts, and peppermint sticks. Someone—she realized, gratified—had done a lot of planning. And someone else—Linnea studied the Santa whose cheeks glowed red with rouge and whose eyes twinkled gaily as he doled out the sacks to the tiny tykes on his knee—had done some extra studying to be able to read all those names. Her eyes glowed with pride, not only for Theodore who made such a marvelous Santa, but for the older children who gamely played along. Even Allen Severt accepted a gift, though he dragged his feet as he went to get it. Linnea was watching him when she heard her name being called and looked up in surprise.

Her gaze met the familiar brown eyes beneath the bushy white eyebrows. ''Got one here says Miss Brandonberg on it,'' Theodore stated in a forced bass.

''For me?'' She pressed her chest with her hands and chuckled nervously.

Santa glanced conspiratorially at the cherubic faces around him. ''I think Miss Brandonberg should come up here on Santa's lap and tell him if she's been a good girl, don't you?''

''Yeah!'' they all chorused, jumping and clapping. ''Yeah! Yeah!''

Before she could protest, Linnea found her hands captured. Resisting all the way, she was led toward the merrily dancing eyes of Santa Westgaard. ''Come on up here, Miss Brandonberg.'' He patted his knee, snagged her hand, and hauled her onto his lap while she blushed so brightly she wished she could crawl into his sack and draw the string over her head. ''There now.'' Theodore bounced her a time or two and the bells jingled. She lost her balance and grasped his shoulder while his steadying hand stole to her waist. ''Tell me, young lady, have you been good?'' The children howled in laughter, joined by the adults.

She braved a look into his mischievous eyes. ''Oh, the very best.''

He glanced at the children for confirmation. ''Has she been good?''

They nodded enthusiastically and Roseanne piped up, ''Thee let uth make thoop!''

''Thoop?'' he repeated.

Everyone howled and Theodore's hand seemed to burn into Linnea's waist.

''Then she should get her present. But first, Miss Brandonberg, give Santa a little kiss on the cheek.''

She wanted to die of embarrassment, but she dutifully leaned over and pecked his warm cheek above the wiry whiskers that smelled strongly of mothballs. Under the guise of the kiss, she whispered, ''I'll get you for this, Theodore.''

When she pulled back he was handing her a rectangular brown package. His eyes glinted merrily and his lips looked rosy against the snowy beard and mustache. For a brief moment his hand squeezed her waist. Under cover of the noisy crowd he ordered, ''Don't open it here.''

He set her on her feet and the place broke into raucous applause as he grunted his way off the chair, took up the empty bag, then, escorted by the gleeful children, made his way to the door. There he paused, turned, gave them all a wave, and bellowed, ''Merrrry Christmas!''

There was no doubt about it: his appearance had made the evening an unqualified success. Children and adults alike were in gay, laughing moods as refreshment time came. Moving through the guests, sharing hellos and holiday greetings, Linnea kept one eye on the door. She found Superintendent Dahl and put in a request for a soup kettle and a wooden clothes rack, but while she was explaining what she needed them for, Theodore reappeared and her words trailed away into silence. His eyes sought her out immediately and she felt as if they were the only two in the room. His cheeks were shiny and bright, chapped pink—Lord, had he washed at that icy well? His hair was inexpertly combed and there was a bit of straw on the shoulder of his jacket—and had he changed clothes out on a wagon? It struck her that there were qualities in Theodore she had scarcely tapped. Never before had she guessed how good he'd be with little children. He would be that way with their own, if only . . .

She blushed, turned away and took a bite of marzipan.

They met near the refreshment table some minutes later. She sensed him at her shoulder and gave a quick backward glance, then poured him a hot cup of coffee. In an undertone she teased, "Santa Claus had *lutefisk* on his breath." Turning, she offered him the cup. "A little something to cover it up, and to take the sting out of those icy cheeks."

He laughed softly, looking down at her. "Thank you, Miss Brandonberg." She wished no one else were in the room, that she could kiss more than his cheek, in more than gratitude. She wondered what was inside the brown package, and if he'd miss her after all while she was gone. But she couldn't stand here all night, riveting her attention solely on him. There were other guests.

"Don't mention it, Mr. Claus," she returned quietly, then reluctantly moved off to visit with someone else.

In the cloakroom Kristian and Ray were secreted in a corner, rehashing the Santa Claus scene and Miss Brandonberg's part in it when a feminine voice intruded, "Excuse me."

They both swung around to find Patricia Lommen behind them.

The two boys glanced at each other, then stared at her. She wore her auburn hair caught up at the top of her head in a wide red bow. Her dress was gray and red plaid with a high round collar, and for the play she had rouged her cheeks and darkened her eyebrows slightly.

"Could I talk to you alone for a minute, Kristian?"

Raymond said, "Well, I'll just go in and have some hot chocolate," and left the two of them alone.

Kristian stuffed his hands into his pockets and watched Patricia as she made sure the door was closed then crossed to his corner of the cloakroom. "I have a Christmas gift for you, Kristian." She brought it from behind her back—a balsam-green package with a dotted-swiss bow.

"F . . . for me?"

"Yes." She looked up brightly.

"B . . . but why?"

She shrugged. "Does there have to be a reason?"

"Well . . . gosh, I . . . gee . . . for me?" He accepted the gift, gawking at it self-consciously. As he took the delicate box he became aware of how ridiculously big his hands seemed to have grown this last year, with knuckles the size of baseballs.

He looked up to find her staring into his eyes, and his heart lurched into a queer, dancing beat. He'd been noticing things about her lately—how good she was with the younger children while directing the Thanksgiving play; what a perfect madonna she made, standing on the other side of the cradle in the manger scene; how her pretty brown eyes tilted up at the corners and had thick, black lashes; how her hair was always washed and curled and her nails neatly trimmed. And she'd developed breasts the size of wild plums.

"I don't . . ." He tried to speak, but his voice croaked like a bullfrog at mating time. He tried again and managed in a soft, throaty voice, "I don't have anything for you, though."

"That's all right. Mine isn't much. Just something I made."

"You *made* it?" He touched the bow, gulped, then looked up again and whispered reverently, "Gosh, thanks."

"You can't open it now. You have to wait till Christmas Eve."

Her mouth seemed to be smiling even though it wasn't really. A gush of rapture sluiced down his body. Oh, jiminy, were her lips ever pretty. The tip of her tongue came out to wet them and his heart slammed into doubletime. She stood before him straight and expectant, her chin tilted up slightly, her hands crossed behind her back. There was a look in her eyes he'd never seen in any girl's eyes before. It sent his heart knocking. His eyes dropped to her lips. He gulped, drew a deep breath for courage, and bent toward her an inch. Her eyelids fluttered and she held her breath. Kristian felt as if he were choking. They tipped closer . . . closer . . .

"Patricia, Ma wants you!"

The pair in the cloakroom leaped apart guiltily. Her brother stood in the open doorway, grinning. "Hey, what're you guys doin' out here?"

"None of your business, Paul Lommen, just go back and tell Ma I'll be there in a minute."

With a knowing leer, he disappeared inside.

Patricia stamped one foot. "Oh, that dumb Paul! Why can't he mind his own business!"

"Maybe you'd better go in. It's awful chilly out here and you might catch a cold." He wondered how it would feel to reach out and rub her arms lightly, but the mood was shattered and he'd lost his courage. She hugged herself and he observed the lift of her breasts above her crossed arms. He looked into her eyes, thinking about braving it again. But before he could she answered.

"I guess so. Well, I'll see you at church, okay?"

"Yeah, sure." She turned away with ill-disguised reluctance.

"Patricia?" he called just before she opened the door.

"What?" She faced him eagerly.

He gulped and said the manly thing that had been on his mind ever since Christmas play rehearsals had started. "You made the prettiest madonna we ever had."

Her face broke into a radiant smile, then she opened the door and slipped inside.

When the schoolhouse lanterns had been doused and the door closed behind them, they all rode home together. Theodore and John sat up front on the cold, wooden seat; Nissa, Linnea, and Kristian in the back with a motley assortment of sheets, dishtowels, Nissa's soup kettle, tins of leftover *sanbakkels* and *krumkaka,* coffee cups, a bag of Christmas gifts Linnea had received from her students, and one Santa suit buried under the hay. Theodore had brought the buckboard tonight, its summer wheels replaced by wooden skids that squeaked upon the snow. The sleigh bells he'd worn on his legs were now strung around Cub's and Toots's necks and jangled rhythmically through the clear, star-studded night. The air was stingingly cold, cold enough to freeze the nostrils shut, but the group in the sled was in a spirited mood. Linnea had to endure a description of her blushing face while she was sitting on Santa's knee, and plenty of teasing about the entire charade. Theodore took his share of good-natured jest, too, and they all laughed about the fact that his beard smelled like mothballs. They rehashed Roseanne's remark about "thoop." They were still laughing when they dropped John at his house.

"We'll be by in the morning to pick you up on our way to town," Theodore reminded John as his brother stepped down from the wagon.

"Sure enough," John agreed as they said their good nights.

Linnea's heart fell. She'd hoped to be alone with Theodore on their ride into town, but it appeared he wasn't risking it. He could set her on his knee, squeeze her waist, and even let her kiss his cheek in front of the entire school population, but he took great care to keep her at arm's length when nobody was around. She realized the importance of traveling by twos out here in the winter and knew she shouldn't resent John's coming along to keep Theodore company on his way back, but when would she get a minute alone with Theodore before she left? It was really the only thing she wanted for Christmas.

At home, Theodore pulled up close to the back door and they all helped unload the wagon. She rehearsed the things she wanted to say to him if only she'd get the chance. But it was late, and when morning came there'd be chores, then breakfast with the entire family, then John beside them every minute.

Theodore came into the kitchen with a last armload and turned back toward the door to see to the horses. If she didn't act now, her chance would be lost.

"You two go on to bed," she advised Nissa and Kristian. "I want to talk to Theodore for a minute." And she followed him back outside.

He was already climbing onto the sleigh when she called, "Theodore, wait!"

He dropped his foot, turned, and asked, "What're you doing out here?" The way he was feeling, the last thing he needed was to be alone with her—tonight of all nights, when a two-week separation loomed like two years.

"I just wanted to talk to you for a minute."

He glanced surreptitiously toward the kitchen windows. "It's a little cold out here for talkin', isn't it?"

"This is nothing compared to pumping water at school in the morning." In Nissa's bedroom a lantern came on. "Let me come down to the barn with you."

Forever seemed to pass before he made his decision. "All right. Get in." He handed her up, followed, and sent the team plodding slowly along. In the milky moonlight the windmill stood tall and dark, casting a long, trellised shadow across the face of the snow. The outbuildings were black shadows with glistening white caps. The skids squealed softly, the sleigh bells jingled, the horses' heads nodded to the rhythm.

"You made a wonderful Santa Claus."

"Thank you."

"I wanted to choke you."

He laughed. "I know."

"Why didn't you tell me?"

"And spoil the surprise?"

"Do you do it every year?"

"We pass it around. But it's got to be somebody without little ones, else they'd recognize their pa."

"And you did very well reading all those names off the sacks. How did you learn them all so fast?"

"Kristian helped me."

"*When?*" she asked, surprised.

"We did it in the tack room."

"Oh." She felt a little cheated, but insisted, "Promise me you'll keep on practicing hard while I'm gone?"

His only reply was a quick smile. He guided the sleigh beneath a lean-to roof behind a granary. It was suddenly very dark with the moonlight cut off, but the horses pulled through the blackness and stood again with the white rays falling on their backs. Theodore hopped over his side, and Linnea followed suit. He moved around the horses, disconnecting them from the whiffletree, and she helped him spread a crackling canvas tarp over the sleigh.

"I'm surprised Roseanne didn't say you sounded just like her Uncle Teddy."

He chuckled. "So am I. She's a smart little cookie, that one."

"I know. And one of my favorite pupils."

"Teachers aren't supposed to play favorites."

She let the silence hang poignantly for several seconds before replying softly, "I know. But we're only human, after all."

He straightened. All movement ceased. They stood on either side of the team, staring at each other in the thick shadows of the lean-to.

Think of something, Theodore warned himself, anything, or you'll end up kissing her again.

"So John brought you the Christmas tree."

"Yes. He's so thoughtful."

He moved to the horses and she followed at his shoulder as he drove them toward the barn. Even in the sharp, fresh air she smelled like almonds. He was getting to like the smell altogether too much.

"He's smitten with you, you know."

"John! Oh, for heaven's sake, where did you get that preposterous idea?"

"John never took a Christmas tree to any of our men teachers."

"Maybe they didn't send out a plea for one."

Theodore chuckled sardonically and ordered, "Open the doors."

She folded back the big double doors, then closed them when he'd driven the team inside. Just as the latch clicked, a lantern flared and Theodore hung it overhead, then concentrated on removing the harnesses from Cub and Toots and turning them into their stalls. She was right on his heels.

"Theodore, I don't know where you get these ideas, but they're just not true."

"Then there was Rusty Bonner and Bill. Yup, you sure do collect 'em, Miss Brandonberg, don't you?" Nonchalantly he reached overhead for the lantern and took it away.

"Rusty Bonner!" she yelped. "He was a . . . a . . . Theodore, come back here! Where are you going?"

The lanternlight disappeared into the tack room, leaving her in near darkness. She stalked after him, with her fists on her hips. Did the infernal man always have to pick a fight with her when she wanted just the opposite?

"I don't *collect* them, as you put it, and I resent your implying that I do!"

He hung up the collars, looped the lines in neat circles, then turned with a leather bell strap in his hands. "And what about in Fargo? You got some more you're collectin' over there?" He stood with feet spread wide, knees locked, the string of sleigh bells doubled over his palm.

"There is nobody in Fargo. Nobody!" she declared vehemently.

With a sideward toss he threw the bells onto the workbench. They made a muffled *ching* before the room fell silent. Theodore rammed his fists into his pockets.

"Then who is Lawrence?" he demanded.

Linnea's belligerence abruptly disappeared.

"L . . . Lawrence?"

"Yes, Lawrence."

Her cheeks grew blotchy pink, then deepened to an all-over heliotrope. Her eyes rounded and her lips parted uncertainly.

"How do you know about Lawrence?" she finally managed in a choked whisper.

"I heard you talking to him one day."

She absolutely wished she could die. How long had it been since she'd fantasized about Lawrence? Why, she'd practically forgotten he'd ever existed. Now when she kissed windows and blackboards and her pillow, it was Theodore she kissed, not Lawrence! But how could she explain such childishness to a man who already considered her far too much of a child?

"Lawrence is none of your business."

"Fine," he snapped and turned away, taking a rag to a bell strap and rubbing it punishingly.

"Unless, of course, you're jealous."

He reared back and barked at the ceiling, "Hah!"

She stomped to within a foot of his back, wishing she could whap him a good one and knock some sense into his head. Lord, but he was such a chicken!

"All right, if you're not jealous, then why did you bring him up . . . and Rusty . . . *and* Bill?"

He flung down the bells and swung on her. "What would a man of my age be doing getting jealous over a . . . a whelp like you?"

"Whelp?" she shrieked. "Whelp!"

"Exactly!" His hand lashed out and turned down one of her ears. "Why lookit there, just like I thought, still wet back there!"

She twisted free, hauled off, and kicked him a doozy in the shin.

"I hate you, Theodore Westgaard! You big lily-livered chicken! I never saw a man so scared of a girl in my life." She was so angry tears stung her eyes and her breath lost control. "And furthermore, I c . . . came out here to thank you f . . . for the Christmas present and you . . . you . . . sp . . . spoil it all by p . . . picking a fight!" To Linnea's horror, she burst into tears.

Theodore cursed and grabbed his bruised leg as she whirled and ran from the barn.

Utterly miserable, he breathed a sigh of relief. What else was he supposed to do except pick a fight when she came following him with those big blue eyes all wide and pretty and tempting him to do things no honorable man would think of doing with a girl barely out of normal school?

He sank to his chair, dropping his face into his hands. Lord God, he loved her. What a fine mess. Old enough to be her father, and here he sat, trembling in a tack room like some boy whose voice was just changing. He hadn't meant to make her cry—God no, not cry. The sight of those tears had made him want to grab her close and apologize and tell her he hadn't meant a word of it.

But what about Lawrence? Who was he? What was he to her? Most certainly someone she'd left behind, judging from her reaction when his name was mentioned. Someone who made her blush like summer sunset and argue hotly that he was nobody. But no girl got that upset about a man unless he was *somebody.*

Theodore puttered around the tack room until he was certain she was safely in bed. Wretched, he wiped off the harnesses and the strands of bells.

He thought of her returning to her gay life in the city with all its conveniences and old friendships, comparing some young buck eighteen or twenty years old to an old cuss like himself. At length he stretched and sighed, feeling each and every one of his thirty-four years in the heaviness of his heart and the stiffness of his bones.

Let her go and make comparisons, he decided sadly. It's best for all concerned.

In the morning neither of them spoke during breakfast. Nor on the ride to John's house. Nor on the long ride to town. The sun beat down blindingly upon the glittering snow. The sleigh bells had been left in the tack room, and the horses seemed less spirited without them. As if he sensed the strain, John, too, remained silent.

At the train depot, both men accompanied Linnea inside, and when she made a move toward the barred window, Theodore unexpectedly clasped her elbow.

"I'll get it. Wait here with John."

She went into the ladies' room and replaced her scarf with her bird-wing hat, and upon returning to the waiting room, studied Theodore's broad shoulders and the upturned collar of his heavy wool jacket. Within her was a hollow space where her holiday spirit had been the night before. A single word from him would revive that spirit and take away this terrible urge to cry again. But he turned and handed her the ticket without so much as meeting her glance. John picked up her suitcase and they moved toward the long wooden waiting bench with its thirteen matched armrests. She sat, flanked by the two men. Her elbow bumped Theodore's and he quickly pulled away.

Somewhere in the station a pendulum clock ticked, but other than that it was dreadfully silent.

"Something wrong, Miss Linnea?" John asked.

She felt as if she'd swallowed a popcorn ball. The tears were very close to showing.

"No, John, nothing. I'm just a little tired, that's all. It was a big week at school, and we got home late last night."

Again they sat in silence. Askance, she saw Theodore's jaw working, the muscles clenched so tightly they protruded. His fingers were clasped over his stomach, the thumbs circling each other nervously.

"She'll be in any minute," the station agent announced, and they went outside to wait on the platform.

Theodore scowled up the tracks. The train bleated in the distance—once, twice.

Linnea reached to take her suitcase from John's hand and saw that his eyes were very troubled in his long, sad face. The tears were glistening in her eyes now—she couldn't help it. Impulsively she flung an arm around John and pressed her cold cheek to his. "Everything's okay, John, honest. I'm just going to miss you all so much. Thank you for the present. I'll open yours first." His arm tightened around her for a moment, and she kissed his cheek. "Merry Christmas, John."

"Same to you, missy," he returned with gruff emotion.

She turned diffidently to face Theodore. "Merry Christmas, Theodore," she said shakily, extending one gloved hand. "Thank you for the g . . . gift, too, it's p . . . packed in . . ." But as his hand came out slowly to clasp hers, she could continue no longer. His deep brown eyes, filled with unspoken misery, locked with hers. He squeezed her hand so hard, so long, it took an effort not to flinch. The tears splashed over her lashes and ran in silver streaks down her cheeks. He wanted to brush them away, but resisted. Her heart felt swollen and bruised, and it beat so heavily it seemed she felt the reverberations at the bottom of her boots.

Down the track to the west the train wailed into view beneath its bonnet of white steam.

Theodore swallowed.

Linnea gulped.

Suddenly he grabbed her wrist and yanked her after him so abruptly that she dropped her suitcase and her hat tipped sideways.

"Theodore, whatever—"

Across the platform and down the steps he strode, in footsteps so long it took two of Linnea's to make up one of his. His face was set and thunderous as he towed her along the tracks and around the end of the building. She had no choice but to stumble after him, breathless, holding her hat on with one hand. He hauled her between a baggage dray and the dun-colored depot wall, then swung her around without warning and scooped her into his arms, kissing her with a might and majesty rivaling that of the locomotive that came steaming past them at just that moment, drowning them in noise. His tongue swept into her mouth and his arms crushed her so tightly her back snapped. Desperately, wildly, he slanted his mouth over hers, clutching the back of her head and pressing her against the wall. The tears gushed down her cheeks, wetting his, too.

He lifted his head at last, his breath falling fast and hard on her face, his expression agonized.

His mouth moved.

"I love you," it said, but the train whistle blasted, covering the precious words she'd waited so long to hear.

"What?" she shouted.

"I love you!" he bawled in a hoarse, miserable voice. "I wanted to tell you last night."

"Why didn't you?"

They had to shout to be heard above the couplings clanging against each other as the train came to a stop. "I was scared, so I trumped up that nonsense about John and Rusty and Lawrence. Are you going to see him in Fargo?"

"No . . . no!" She wanted to cry and laugh at the same time.

"I'm sorry I made you cry."

"Oh, I'm just foolish . . . I . . . oh, Theodore—"

"*Boooooard!*" the conductor called from around the corner.

Theodore's mouth swooped down again, open and hungry, and this time she clutched him as desperately as he clutched her. Her hat was smashed under his left boot. A piece of siding on the depot wall creased the back of her head and the clip of her watch was stamping its shape into her left breast. But Theodore had said it at last!

As abruptly as he'd lunged, he pulled back, holding her face, searching her eyes with a harrowed look.

"Tell me."

"I love you, too, Teddy."

"I know. I've known for quite a while, but I don't know what we're going to do about it. I only know I've been miserable."

"Oh, Teddy, don't waste precious time. Kiss me again, please!"

This time it was sweet and yearning and filled with good-byes that were really hellos. Their hearts thrust mightily. Their bodies knew want. They tore their mouths apart long enough for her to cry, "I don't want to go."

"I don't want you to either," he returned, then impaled her mouth with his warm, wet tongue a last time.

John came barreling around the corner, yelling, "Are you crazy, you two? The train's leaving!"

Theodore twisted from her, pulling her practically off her feet as he headed for the moving train.

"My hat!"

"Leave it!"

They raced for the doorway of the silver car that was sliding away in a billow of steam, and at the last possible moment, Linnea caught the handrail and was lifted from behind and swung safely aboard.

She leaned out and waved, then threw two kisses to the receding figures with hands raised over their heads.

"Merry Christmas! Merry Christmas!"

It would be the happiest of her life. As she found her seat and fell back with her eyes closed, she wondered how she'd live through it.

Chapter 17

Linnea's father was waiting to greet her at the train station, smiling and robust. His hair was parted in the center and paralleled the sweeping line of his thick blond moustache. Wrapped in his strong arms, with her face pressed against his storm coat, she smelled the familiar bay rum on his jaw and felt tears spring to her eyes.

"Oh, Daddy."

"Dumpling."

She had worked so long and hard at acting grown up that it was an unexpected relief to be his child again.

"What's this? A tear?"

"I'm just so glad to see you." She kissed his jaw and held his elbow tightly as they went outside.

He had bought a brand-new Model T Ford touring car that nobody had told her about.

"What's *this?*" She stared at it, awestruck.

"A little surprise. Business has been booming."

"Y . . . you mean it's yours?"

"You betcha. Get in."

They drove down the streets of Fargo, startling horses, laughing, peering through the horizontal split in the windshield. It was thrilling, but at the same time the new automobile made Linnea feel she had been away for years instead of months. It created an odd, sad feeling she tried her best to hide. She wanted to come home and find everything as she'd left it.

"Do you want to stop by the store on our way?" he asked.

The store, where she'd been her father's clerk ever since she was old enough to make change. The store, with its intermingled smells of coffee and sweeping compound and oranges. The store would be the same.

"Let's," she answered excitedly.

But there were changes at the store, too. From the front window James Montgomery Flagg's frowning Uncle Sam pointed a bony finger at Fargo's men, admonishing, "I want you for the U.S. Army." A scratchy radio—a new addition—sat on a shelf, transmitting the new George M. Cohan song, "Over There." Beside the counter sat a collection barrel for empty tin cans. On the counter stood a "Blot it out with Liberty Bonds" poster. And behind the counter stood a total stranger.

''Here she is, Adrian, home from Alamo. Linnea, I'd like you to meet Adrian Mitchell, the fellow who took your place as my right hand. Adrian, my daughter Linnea.''

Resentment prickled even as Linnea shook hands across the counter. Mother had written that they'd hired a new ''boy,'' and here he was, measuring six feet tall and wearing a natty plaid bow tie.

''Pleasure, Miss Brandonberg.''

''Mr. Mitchell,'' she said politely.

''Adrian is a sophomore at the university this year. Putting himself through,'' announced her father with a discernible note of pride.

Adrian smiled at Linnea. ''And I understand this is your first year out of normal school. How do you like teaching so far?''

While they chatted she noticed he had an innate sense of cordiality, the most perfect teeth she'd ever seen, and a face almost unfairly handsome. It only made her resent him further for usurping her place.

The stop at the store was brief. Before long they were in the Ford again, heading home.

''I thought you said you hired a new *boy,*'' Linnea commented dryly.

Her father only chuckled.

''Well, where did you find him?''

''Walked in one day and said he needed a job to put himself through college, and he promised to increase my business by five percent within the first six months or he'd refund half his salary, and damned if he hasn't done it in three!''

To Linnea's resentment was added a tinge of jealousy. More than ever, she wanted to get home where things would be just as when she'd left.

Her mother was preparing her old favorite, fricasseed chicken, and Linnea's heart swelled with gratitude. Upstairs, Carrie and Pudge had their bedroom all spic-and-span, but when Linnea came back down to the kitchen and asked where they were, her mother answered, ''Oh, I'm afraid they're gone, but they'll be here in time for dinner.''

''Gone?'' repeated Linnea, disappointed. She'd expected them to rush her with a thousand questions displaying the same girlish awe they'd shown upon learning that their big sister was going out into the world.

''Their Girl Scout troop is cutting and stitching comfort bags for departing soldiers.''

Comfort bags? Her baby sisters?

''So did you stop at the store?'' her mother inquired.

''Yes, for a minute.''

''Then you met Adrian.''

''Yes.''

''What did you think of him?''

Linnea threw a suspicious glance at her mother, but Judith was busily shaping dumplings, dropping them into the kettle.

''I was only there five minutes.'' *Don't even think it, Mother. He's not my type.*

Carrie and Pudge arrived in time for dinner, overjoyed to see their big sister, but breathless and gushing about their own activities, scarcely asking about Linnea's. During the meal Linnea learned that their scout troop had spent weeks collecting peach stones to be burned into charcoal for gas-mask filters and was now engaged in a campaign to solicit soap, needles, thread, and other necessities for filling the comfort bags. Carrie was all excited about the fact that each individual who filled a bag was allowed to include a name card. She was hoping to hear from the soldiers who received hers. They bubbled on about the white elephants they were collecting for a rummage sale their school was planning to earn the $125 they'd pledged to the War Fund Drive.

Linnea was quite disconcerted. When she'd left home, the girls were climbing trees and skinning knees. Carrie had been clumsy. Now she wore a new willowy silhouette. Her honey-colored hair touched her shoulders and her blue eyes would soon start capturing the boys' attention. Pudge, too, had changed. Her nickname scarcely fit anymore. She was thinning out and her pigtails were gone, replaced by a fall of caramel-colored curls held by a ribbon. When she talked about their Girl Scout work her hazel eyes lit with excitement that gave Linnea a glimpse of the pretty young lady she would soon become. How could they have changed so much in four months?

Her mother's interests had changed, too. She was no longer sitting home darning socks in her spare time. She was in charge of the women's committee for the Belgian and Armenian Relief Fund at church, working with the Supplementary Military Aid committee to meet trains and provide meals for enlisted men passing through the city on their way to army camps. She was taking a Red Cross class to learn how to make surgical dressings and spent two evenings each week at the public library picking oakum.

"What's oakum?" Linnea asked, and they all looked at her as if she'd spoken a profanity.

But that wasn't all. Her father had spent a day recently with a group of citizens who'd laughingly dubbed themselves "The Amalgamated Order of Wood Sawyers." A river-bottom wood lot had been donated to the Red Cross by the Fargo Tile Company, and the men had spent the day felling the trees and sawing them into cordwood. It was auctioned off and $2,264 was raised for the war effort.

Her father, sawing wood?

Christmas would be less lavish this year, he said, because they were giving instead to the soldiers who needed so much so badly.

It wasn't that Linnea needed a lavish Christmas. She simply wanted things as they were. She had rather expected her return to be the axis upon which her family revolved while she was at home. Instead, their axis seemed to be the war effort.

That night, when she went to bed, she lay in the dark pondering her disappointment. Four months—not *even* four months, and it seemed she'd left no more vacancy in their lives than a cup of water drawn from a full barrel. Her emotions were in turmoil. She wanted nothing so badly as constancy from her family. But they were all so busy. So involved! She wanted to cry, but tears didn't come as easily as they had last summer, before she'd started her plunge into maturity.

At least the house hadn't changed. The bedroom she and her sisters shared was as bright and cheerful as ever with its flowery wallpaper and long double windows. When she got up in the mornings the floor wasn't icy beneath her feet, and she didn't have to walk down a snowy path to an outhouse, or bathe in a wash basin, or trudge a mile to school, or shovel coal, or build a fire or pump water.

But she missed it all terribly.

On Christmas Eve day her father asked her to come and help him at the store, as she used to. "So many of my customers ask about you; I know they'd love to see you. And I'd really appreciate the help today. It's going to be a race right up till closing."

"But you have the new boy."

"Adrian will be there, but there'll be enough business to keep us all busy. What do you say, dumpling?"

She couldn't resist her father when he called her the old pet name, and no matter how things had changed, she loved it at the store.

When they arrived Adrian was already there, dressed in natty collegiate clothes, sweeping snow off the front sidewalk.

"Good morning, Mr. Brandonberg!" he greeted, doffing a tweed golf-style cap, smiling at Linnea at the same time. "And Miss Brandonberg."

"Good morning, Adrian. I talked her into coming down and giving us a hand today."

"And we can certainly use it. Are you enjoying your vacation?"

Standing with his hands crossed on the broom handle, Adrian Mitchell chatted as amiably as if they were old friends. He had a wonderful smile, which he wore nearly all the time, and the kind of natural courtesy Linnea tried so hard to instill in her boys at school. He doffed his hat to passersby and bid each a pleasant good morning. When Linnea and her father moved toward the front door, he opened it for them before returning to his sweeping.

When he followed them inside minutes later, she watched him moved around the store. He hung his stylish coat and suit jacket on a coat tree in the back, then donned a starched white apron, whistling softly between his teeth as he doubled the ties around the front and secured them in back. He moved with a briskness and confidence that made him appear as much the proprietor of the store as the proprietor himself. He sprinkled sweeping compound on the floor and swept the whole place without so much as a word from her father. When the job was done and the pleasant oily smell clung to the air, he marched to the double front doors, pulled up the green shades to the tall windows, and turned over the OPEN sign.

The first customer was a little boy Linnea didn't recognize who had been sent by his mother to pick up a last-minute pound of lard. Before the boy left, Adrian dropped something into his bag and said, "Now you give that to your mother, Lonnie, okay?"

"What's he giving him?" Linnea whispered to her father.

"An egg separator. It was Adrian's idea, to give out some small kitchen item as a gesture of good will during the holiday season. Shows the customers we appreciate their business."

She studied her father's profile as he beamed at Adrian. Obviously the new employee was his golden boy.

The twinge of jealousy returned, but as the day progressed she came to see why her father valued Adrian so immensely. The customers loved him. He knew them all by name and inquired after their families and asked if they knew Miss

Brandonberg was here today, back from school and in just to say hello to all of them. As each customer left, he called, "Merry Christmas."

He had a way about him, all right. There were times when Linnea studied him covertly and wondered if it was phony. But long before the end of the day she'd decided he was strictly genuine, a natural-born businessman who loved people and wasn't afraid to let it show.

When the store closed at four that afternoon, Linnea's father gave Adrian a ham as a Christmas gift. Adrian had something hidden in the back room—a long, tall box—which he gave to his boss before the two exchanged a fond handshake. Then he turned to Linnea with his radiantly handsome smile.

"Miss Brandonberg, I hope we'll meet again while you're home. As a matter of fact, if it's all right with your father, I'd like to stop by the house some evening and pay a call."

He turned to seek Selmer Brandonberg's approval, and before Linnea could object, her father answered, "Anytime, Adrian. You just let Mrs. Brandonberg know and she'll set an extra place at dinner."

"Thank you, sir. I'll do that." Turning to Linnea, he added, "One evening next week then, after the Christmas rush slows down."

She was quite flabbergasted. He was so straightforward and confident that he hadn't really given her a chance to decline before he bid them a last holiday wish and left. Linnea stood gaping at the swinging shade pulls on the windows.

"So what do you think of him?" her father asked.

Hands on hips, she affected a scolding pout. "And you told me you'd hired a new *boy*. Why, he's no more boy than you are."

Selmer slipped on his coat, cocked one eyebrow, and grinned. "I know." Buttoning his coat, he repeated, "I asked what you thought of him."

Linnea threw him an arch, amused glance. "He isn't running for Congress yet, is he?"

Selmer laughed. "No, but give him time. I'm sure he'll get around to it."

"My point exactly."

They eyed each other a few seconds, then burst out laughing. But as they were leaving the store, Linnea pressed a gloved hand to her father's lapel.

"He's handsome and dynamic and a real up-and-comer, and though at first I was frightfully jealous of him, I can see what an asset he is to you. But I'm not looking for a boyfriend, Daddy."

He patted her hand and steered her out the door. "Nonsense, dumpling. You said it first—Adrian's no boy."

Immediately upon reaching home, Linnea was asked three times, "What did you think of Adrian?"

It was obvious the entire family fancied themselves matchmakers. They oohed and aahed upon discovering Adrian had given Selmer a bottle of fine Boston brandy, Selmer's favorite brand, but one he rarely bought because of its prohibitive price.

"Oh, Selmer," his wife crooned, "isn't that boy thoughtful? And while he's struggling to put himself through college yet."

Linnea had all she could do to keep from rolling her eyes. She wanted to tell them they were wasting their time trying to foist Adrian on her, because there was another man in her life.

She thought of Theodore and wondered what they'd say if she told them about him. Would they understand if she said that beneath his gruff exterior lay a man with deep vulnerabilities? That his greatest wish was to know how to read? That he defended his family, down to the last niece, with a quick, noble ferocity? That he could tease one moment and share a hymnal the next? That he grew heavyhearted when it was time to turn his horses loose for the winter?

But the fact remained that she had fallen in love with a thirty-four-year-old illiterate wheat farmer who wore bib overalls, still lived with his mother, and had a son nearly Linnea's age. How could she possibly make a man like that compare favorably to an enterprising twenty-one-year-old college student with brains, ambition, good looks, and charisma enough to charm the molars out of a mother's head?

Linnea was very much afraid she couldn't, and so she said nothing of Theodore Westgaard.

They opened gifts, and true to her word, Linnea chose John's first. She was truly touched by the hand-carved likeness of a cat with its paws curled beneath it, like the one she often saw sitting on his step. From Frances she received a homemade pin cushion fashioned from a puff of steel wool inside a piece of strawberry-colored velvet. Nissa's gift was a beautiful handcrocheted shawl of white wool shot with tiny threads of silver; Kristian's—she gasped—the most beautiful pair of mittens she'd ever seen in her life. They were made of mink, and when she slipped one on she realized she'd never felt anything as warm. The girls leaned over to have their cheeks stroked, and her mother tried one on, rubbed it on her neck, and cooed with delight.

"What a beautiful gift," Judith said, passing the mitten back. "How old did you say Kristian is?"

Linnea felt slightly uncomfortable and wondered if her cheeks were pink. "Seventeen."

Selmer and Judith Brandonberg exchanged meaningful glances. "Very thoughtful for a boy of seventeen," Judith added.

Linnea met her mother's eyes squarely, hoping to dispel the erroneous impression. "Kristian traps down on the creek bottom. That's how he got the mink."

"How resourceful." Her mother smiled, then pointed. "You have another gift left, dear. Who is it from?"

"Theodore." She had intentionally saved it for last. It was weighty, wrapped in the same brown paper as that in which the children's treats had been bagged. Caressingly, she ran a hand over it.

"Ah, yes, Kristian's father." Her mother's words brought Linnea from her reverie. She realized she'd been daydreaming while her whole family looked on. "Well, go ahead, open it!" demanded Pudge impatiently.

Removing the wrapping, Linnea remembered the teasing brown eyes of a Santa Claus as she'd sat on his lap, and the feeling of her lips against a firm rosy cheek above a scratchy white beard. And the whispered words, "Don't open it here." She wished, suddenly, that she were in a weather-beaten house on the snow-swept prairie at this moment.

It was a book of Tennyson's poems, beautifully bound in brown and gilt, with engravings of angelic beings in wispy gowns whose bare feet trailed in drifting roses.

On the endleaf, in ink, he had meticulously printed, "Merry Christmas, 1917. To Linnea Brandonberg from Theodore Westgaard. Some day I will know how to read all these too."

Linnea carefully hid her secret pleasure as she showed her family the beautiful book. "I'm teaching Theodore to read and write, but I didn't think he knew how to spell my name yet. Kristian must have helped him with the inscription." Her mother reached for the book, brushed her fingertips over the expensive gilt lettering on its cover, read the inscription, looked up at her daughter's wistful expression, and murmured, "How nice, dear."

Several times during Christmas dinner Judith glanced over to find Linnea staring into her plate with a faraway look in her eyes. It wasn't the first time she'd noticed it. There was an unusual reticence about Linnea since she'd been home, an occasional withdrawal totally unlike her.

Later that night, she asked Selmer, "Have you noticed anything different about Linnea since she's been home?"

"Different?"

"She's so . . . I don't know. Subdued. She just doesn't seem to be her old bubbly self."

"She's growing up, Judith. That was bound to happen, wasn't it? A young woman with adult responsibilities, off in the world away from her mother and father." He lifted his wife's chin and kissed her nose. "She can't stay our little girl forever, you know."

"No, I suppose not." Judith turned away and began undressing for bed. "Did she . . . well, did she say anything at the store today?"

"Say anything about what?"

"Not about what. About whom."

"About whom? Whom did you expect her to say something about?"

"That's the puzzling part. I'm not sure whether it's Kristian or . . . or his father."

"His father!" Selmer's fingers stopped freeing his shirt buttons.

"Well, did you see her face when she opened that book from him?"

"Judith, surely you're wrong."

"Let's hope so. Why, the man must be nearly forty years old!"

Selmer became visibly upset.

"Has she said anything to you?"

"No, but do you think she would, considering the man has a son almost as old as she is and she . . . she lives in his house?"

Selmer forced himself to calm down and took his wife by the arms. "Maybe we're wrong. She has a good head on her shoulders, and besides, she's always confided in you before. And I haven't told you the good news. Adrian Mitchell asked my permission to pay a call on her sometime this week."

"He did?" Judith brightened. "Did he really?"

"How do you feel about throwing an extra carrot in the soup for our daughter's dinner guest?"

"Oh, Selmer, really?" Her eyes lit up like Christmas candles as she clasped his hands tightly. "Can you imagine the two of them together? He'd be absolutely perfect for her."

"But we have to be careful not to push too hard," he scolded gently. "You know how single-minded that girl can be when she thinks she's being coerced. Still, it wouldn't hurt to have him over maybe a couple times before she has to go back, then this summer when she comes home to stay—who knows?"

Judith spun away and began pacing, one hand on her waist, the other squeezing her lower lip. "Let's see . . . I'll fix something splendid—stuffed pork chops maybe, and mother's hazelnut torte. We'll use all the best china and . . ."

Judith was still matchmaking when Selmer drifted off to sleep.

Adrian came on Wednesday, thoughtfully bringing his hostess a round tin of parfait mints to serve with after-dinner coffee. He sat and visited in the front parlor with the whole family until after ten P.M., then wished Linnea a polite good night when Judith insisted she see him to the door.

He came again on Thursday, around seven P.M., visited with the family for half an hour, then suggested that he and Linnea go for a walk.

"Oh, I don't—"

"That's a wonderful idea," Judith cut in. "Goodness, dear, all you've done since you've been home is sit here cooped up with us old folks."

"Linnea?" Adrian asked quietly, and she was too kind to embarrass him by saying no.

They walked around the bandstand in the city park and talked about their families, their jobs, his school, her school, and what they'd received for Christmas. She slipped once, and he took her elbow and walked her back home through the softly falling snow, then turned her to face him on the front porch and gave her a soft kiss on the mouth.

She pulled back. "Don't, Adrian . . . please."

"And how else should I state my case?" he asked pleasantly, still holding her arms.

"You're a charming man and I . . . I like you . . . but . . ." Discomfited, she fell silent.

"But?" He tipped his head.

"But there's someone else back in Alamo."

"Ah." They were quiet a while. She studied his chest while he studied her face, then asked, "Is it serious?"

"I think so."

"Are you promised to him?"

She shook her head.

"Well, in that case, would there be any harm in your coming to a party with me on New Year's Eve?"

She looked up. "But I told you—"

"Yes, there's someone back in Alamo. And I'll respect that, but I'd like your company just the same. And I'll bet you don't have any other plans, do you?" He tipped her chin up with one finger. "Do you?"

Good heavens, there was no justice in the world when one man could be so handsome.

"No."

"It's just some of my friends who are all about our age. We're going to go ice-skating, then go back to one of the girl's houses for something to eat. I'll have you home by one o'clock. What do you say?"

It sounded fun, and it had been so long since she'd been with people her age. And if she didn't go with him, she'd probably usher the new year in by lying in her bed wishing she'd said yes.

"No kissing at midnight?" she insisted.

He raised a palm, Boy Scout fashion. "Promise."

"And no laughing if I take a few spills on the ice?"

He laughed, flashing his dazzling white teeth. "Promise."

"All right. It's a date."

He brought her violets. Violets for a skating party! Where he managed to find them in the middle of winter in Fargo, North Dakota, remained a mystery, but they were the first flowers Linnea had ever received from a man, and as she accepted them she thought of Theodore and had a flash of guilt.

Adrian had borrowed his father's automobile for the evening, and getting into it with him redoubled her guilt, but as the night progressed, she found herself forgetting about Theodore and having a wonderful time.

They skated on the river, warmed themselves with hot apple cider, returned to the home of a girl named Virginia Colson and played parlor games, danced, and toasted the new year with a light champagne punch. But—true to his word—Adrian remained the consummate gentleman all night long.

When he took her home she tried to make a quick getaway, but he walked her to the porch, captured both of her hands, leaned one shoulder against the porch wall, and studied her with disconcerting thoroughness. "You're the prettiest thing I've ever met, you know that?"

She dropped her gaze to his chest. "Adrian, I really should go in."

"And you're all the things that your father said you'd be. I'd seen your picture, of course—he's so proud of you. But when you came into the store that day and I saw you in person for the first time, I thought right off the bat, that girl's for me." He paused, squeezed her hands, and said more softly, "Come here, Linnea."

Startled, she lifted her head. "Adrian, you promised."

"I promised no kisses at the stroke of midnight. It's now quarter to one."

He slowly eased his shoulder away from the porch wall while it struck her afresh how nature had played favorites with him. He was almost unfairly handsome. And she had never met a man who smelled better, nor one more polite, charming, or winning. Her parents were smitten with him. They were going to be outraged when she told them about Theodore. Suppose . . . just suppose she kissed Adrian back and discovered it was as shattering as it had been with Theodore? All her worries would be over . . .

His lips were soft and silky as they opened over hers. When his tongue slipped inside her mouth, hers hesitantly answered. When he wrapped her tightly in his arms, she let herself wilt against him. When his hands caressed her back, hers caressed his shoulders. But instead of her mind filling with skyrockets, she found herself analyzing the smell of his hair pomade and the starch his mother put in his collars. She let him have as long as he liked . . . waiting . . . waiting . . .

But nothing happened.

Nothing.

When Adrian lifted his head, his hands slipped discreetly to the sides of her breasts and he breathed on her lips, plucking at them gently—once, twice. "Linnea, darling girl," he whispered, "summer can't come fast enough."

But she knew that even in summer there would be no acceleration of her feelings for Adrian. If it were going to happen, it already would have.

Later, in bed, the guilt struck. She'd never kissed any man up until a couple months ago, and now she'd kissed four. She suspected all four really knew what they were doing, and wondered if kissing four men qualified her as a loose woman. She supposed it did, and that Theodore was too honorable to deserve a loose woman.

Yet her reaction to each had been decidedly different.

She shuddered at the thought of Rusty Bonner, so practiced in his approach. Rusty'd probably left a trail of bastard babies from the Rio Grande to the Canadian border! How naive she'd been. It was rather embarrassing to recall it now.

And Bill—every time she met up with him she thought of how he'd forced his knee between her legs, and got angry all over again.

And of course there was Adrian, perfect, flawless Adrian. She almost wished she'd felt that keen fire in her blood when he'd kissed her; it would have simplified everything. After all, he was the most logical choice.

Love, however, paid little heed to logic. And she loved Theodore. Only his kiss had the power to shake her to the soles of her feet, to make her feel right, and eager, as though their love had been destined. It mattered little his age, his illiteracy, his simple upbringing, the clothing he wore, or the fact that he'd been married before and had a son who was nearly Linnea's age.

What mattered was that he was honorable, and good, and at the thought of going home to him tomorrow her heart soared and her blood pounded.

In the morning she was packing to go when her mother came to the bedroom doorway, crossed her arms, and leaned against the door frame. The girls had gone off skating and the house was quiet.

"Linnea, I've been waiting for you to tell me about it ever since you've been home, but I guess if I don't ask, you won't say anything."

Linnea turned with a stack of freshly laundered underwear in her hands. "Tell you about what?"

"What's bothering you."

For a moment she considered a denial, then sank to the edge of the bed, staring morosely at the clothing on her lap. "How do you know when you're in love, Mother?" she asked plaintively.

"In love?" Judith straightened, then crossed the room to perch beside Linnea. She took her daughter's hand.

"With Adrian?" she asked hopefully.

Linnea only shook her bowed head disconsolately.

"With . . . with Kristian then?"

Again Linnea shook her head, then lifted it slowly to meet her mother's questioning eyes.

"Oh, dear . . ." Judith breathed, dropping Linnea's fingers and resting four of her own against her lips. "Not . . . not the father."

"Yes . . . and his name is Theodore."

Alarmed, Judith leaned forward to grasp Linnea's hand again. "But he's got to be—what?—thirty-some years old."

"Thirty-four."

"And he's been married."

"A long time ago."

"Oh, my child, don't be foolish. This can't be. How far has it gone?"

"It hasn't *gone* anywhere." Linnea jerked her hand away in irritation and rose to put the underwear in her suitcase. "He's fought it every inch of the way because he thinks I'm just a child."

Judith pressed her heart and exclaimed quietly, "Oh, thank goodness!"

Linnea swung around and flopped down dejectedly. "Mother, I'm so mixed up. I don't know what to do."

"Do? Well, for heaven's sake, child, put him out of your head. He's almost as old as your father! What you can *do* is continue to see Adrian Mitchell when you get back here next summer. He certainly seems interested enough." She stopped, beetled her brow, and inquired, "He is, isn't he?"

"I guess so." Linnea shrugged. "If kissing me means he's interested."

"He kissed you." Judith sounded pleased.

"Yes. And I think this was about as experienced as a kiss could get. I tried to put my heart into it—honest, Mother, I did—but nothing happened!"

Judith began to show renewed concern. "Nothing is *supposed* to happen till after you're married."

"Oh, yes it is. I mean, don't you ever watch Daddy just . . . well, just walk into a room, and your stomach goes all woozy and you feel like you're choking on your own spit?"

"Linnea!" Judith's eyes widened in shock.

"Well, don't you?"

Judith would have jumped from the bed, but Linnea detained her with a hand on her shoulder. "Oh, Mother," she went on urgently, "don't tell me it's not supposed to happen, because it does. Every time Teddy comes around a doorway. Every time I see him pulling the horses into the yard. It even happens when we're fighting!"

Befuddled, Judith only stared at her daughter and asked, "You . . . you fight with him?"

"Oh, we fight all the time." Linnea got up and resumed packing. "I think that for a long time he picked fights with me to keep himself from admitting how he felt about me. And because he knew I felt the same and it scared him to death. I told you, he thinks he's too old for me, of all the preposterous things."

Judith fought down the panic, got to her feet, and went to take her daughter by her shoulders. "He is, Linnea."

"He's not," the girl declared stubbornly.

"He has a son nearly your age. I was upset at the thought that it was the boy you had feelings for, but to even consider yourself in love with his *father!* Linnea, it's absurd."

Their troubled gazes locked. Then Linnea said quietly, ''I think you just want me to end up falling in love with Adrian and marrying him. I really wish I could—I mean it, Mother. But I'd better warn you right now, I don't think it's going to happen, not judging by what happened when he kissed me last night. Or rather, what didn't happen.''

''Puh!'' Judith huffed, releasing her daughter's shoulders with a slight shove. ''You've always been single-minded, and I suppose nothing I say is going to change that now. But you listen to me . . .'' She shook a finger beneath Linnea's nose. ''That . . . that *man,* that . . . that . . . Theodore? At least he's got some common sense. He knows better than you that there are too many years difference between you, and you'd best accept the fact before this thing goes any further!''

But Judith Brandonberg might as well have shouted down the rain barrel. Linnea only turned once more to do her packing with a stubborn set to her shoulders. ''I didn't choose to fall in love with him, Mother. It just happened. But now that it has, I'm going to do everything in my power to make him see that what we've been given is a gift we must not squander.'' She straightened, and Judith saw the determined look in her eyes. Linnea's voice softened to a wistful, womanly tone. ''He loves me, too, as much as I love him. He's told me so. And it's too precious to risk giving up, don't you see? What if I never find it again with a man my own age?''

Judith's troubled eyes lingered on Linnea with a sad, certain recognition. Yes, her little girl was growing up. And though her heart hammered in trepidation, Judith had no reasonable argument.

It was difficult to argue against love.

Chapter 18

It was overcast the following day as Linnea rode the westward train. Beyond the window the sky was the color of ashes, but it couldn't dull the excitement she felt: she was going home.

Home. She thought of what she had left behind. A cheery house, a mother, a father, two sisters, the city where she'd been born. All the familiar places and people she'd known her whole life . . . yet it wasn't home anymore. Home was what tugged at the heartstrings, and the steel wheels were drawing her closer and closer to that.

When the train was still an hour out, she pictured Theodore and John already on the road to town, but when she stepped down from the car onto the familiar worn platform of the Alamo depot, only Theodore was waiting. Their eyes met immediately, but neither of them moved. She stood on the train step, clutching the cold handrail. He stood behind a cluster of people waiting to board: his hands were buried in the deep front pockets of a serviceable old jacket buttoned to the neck with the collar turned up. On his head was a fat blue stocking cap topped with a tassle; in his eyes, an undisguised look of eagerness.

They studied each other above the heads of those separating them. Steam billowed. The train breathed in gusts. The departing passengers hugged good-bye. Linnea and Theodore were aware of none of it, only of each other and their buoyant hearts.

They began moving simultaneously, suppressing the urge to rush. He stepped around the group of passengers, she off the last step. Eyes locked, they neared . . . slowly, slowly, as if each passing second did not seem like a lifetime . . . and stopped with scarcely a foot dividing them.

"Hello," he said first.

"Hello."

He smiled and her heart went weightless.

She smiled and his did the same.

"Happy New Year."

"The same to you."

I missed you, he didn't say.

It seemed like eternity, she swallowed back.

"Did you have a nice ride?"

"Long."

Words failed them both while they stood rapt, until somebody bumped Theodore from behind and said, "Oh, excuse me!"

It brought them from their singular absorption with each other back to the mundane world.

"Where's John?" Linnea glanced around.

"Home nursing a cold."

"And Kristian?"

"Checking his trap line. And Ma said she wanted me out from underfoot anyway while she fixed you a come-home dinner."

So, they were alone. They need not guard their gazes or measure their words or refrain from touching.

"Home," she repeated wistfully. "Take me there."

He took her suitcase in one hand, her elbow in the other, and they moved toward the bobsled. He had missed her with an intensity akin to sickness. The house had been terrible without her and Christmas only a day to be borne. He had been silent and withdrawn from the rest of the family, preferring to spend his time in the tack room alone, where his memories of her were most vibrant. He had even imagined that once she got a fresh dose of her old life in Fargo, she might not come back. He had worried about Lawrence and how he himself would compare to any man she'd known in the city, how Alamo and the farm would compare.

But she *was* back, and he was touching her again—though only through her thick coat sleeve and his leather glove.

She glanced up as they walked, her smile sending currents to his heart. "You have a new cap."

He reached up and touched it self-consciously. "From Ma for Christmas." He stowed her grip in the rear of the wagon and they stood beside the tailgate, trying to get their fill of each other, unable.

"I love my book, Theodore. Thank you so much."

He wished he could kiss her right here and now, but there were townspeople about. "I love my new pen and ink stand and the slate, too. Thank you."

"I didn't know you knew how to write my name."

"Kristian showed me."

"I thought as much. Have you been working with the speller since I've been gone?"

"Every night. You know, that Kristian, he isn't such a bad teacher."

"Kristian isn't a bad teacher," she corrected. "Not Kristian *he* isn't a bad teacher."

He flashed her a lopsided grin. "First thing back and she's pickin' on me already." He tightened his grip on her elbow and handed her up. A moment later they were heading home.

"Well, you might think you collected the wrong girl if I didn't pick on you a little bit."

His slow smile traveled over her, and he took his sweet time before replying, "Naw, not likely."

Her heart danced with joy.

"So how was your family?" he inquired.

They talked unceasingly, it mattered little of what, riding along with their elbows lightly bumping. Though the sun remained a stranger, the temperature was mild. The snow had softened, gripping the runners like a never-ending palm. It was pleasant, gliding along to the unending squeak and the clop of hooves. All around, the clouds hung like old white hens after a dust bath. They sulked churlishly overhead. Where they met the horizon, little distinction was visible between earth and air, just a grayish-white blending with neither rise nor swale delineating the edge of the world.

Theodore and Linnea were a half mile east of the schoolhouse when he squared his shoulders, stared off to the north, and drew back on the reins. Cub and Toots stopped in the middle of the road, pawed the snow, and whinnied.

Warily, Linnea glanced at the team, then at Theodore. "What's wrong?"

"Look." He pointed.

"What? I don't see anything."

"There, see those dark spots moving toward us?"

She squinted and peered. "Oh, now I see them. What is it?"

"The horses." Then, excitedly, "Come, get down." He twisted the reins around the brake handle and leaped from the wagon, distractedly reaching up to help her alight. Down the ditch they went, and up the other side, giant-stepping through knee-deep snow until they stood at a double strand of barbed-wire fence. Standing motionless they gazed at the herd that galloped toward them, unfettered, across the distant field. In minutes the horses drew near enough to be distinguished, one from another. But only their heads. Their bellies were obscured by loose snow moving like an earth-bound cloud around them. Their hooves churned it up until it blent with the white-clad world below and the milky clouds above. The sight was stunning: a swirling, whirling mass of motion.

As they neared, Linnea could feel a faint tremor beneath her soles, a singing in the thin wire between her mittens. There must have been forty of them, their leader a proud piebald prince with streaming gray mane and thick dappled shoulders of gray and white that seemed an extension of the dirty-linen clouds behind him.

Sensing their presence, he whinnied and lifted his head, nostrils dilated and eyes keen. With a snort and lunge, he veered, taking the herd off in a new direction. What a majestic show of power and beauty they made, their hooves charging through whorls of white, tails trailing free, coats long and shaggy now in high winter.

No sleek Virginia trotters, these, but thick-muscled giants of questionable breed whose chests were massive, shoulders strapping, legs thick, beasts who knew the plow and harrow and had earned their temporary freedom.

The pair who watched shivered in appreciation. Absorbed, Linnea clambered up to the lower fence skein to get a better look. Balancing there, watching the horses thunder off, she was scarcely aware of Theodore's steadying arm around her hips. The reverberations faded. The cloud of snow became dimmer.

Theodore looked up.

She might have been one of the unbridled creatures, reveling in her freedom. He had the feeling she'd forgotten he was beside her as she stood on the lower rung of barbed wire with her knees pressed flat against the upper rung, neck stretched, nosing the air, straining for a last glimpse of the disappearing herd. He wondered if she even realized she'd climbed up there. She looked more childish than ever, with a plaid wool kerchief over her hair, knotted beneath her chin.

But it didn't matter. All that mattered was that she saw the majesty in the horses just as he did.

It struck him afresh, how much he'd missed this poppet of a girl in the childish scarf, whose nose was as red as a cherry and whose mitten rested on his shoulder.

He chuckled, hoping it would relieve the sudden tension in his loins.

She glanced down.

"Come down here before you topple over to the other side and I lose you in a snowdrift." He took her by the waist and she leaped down. They stood for a moment with her mittens resting on his breast pockets.

"Wasn't that something, Teddy?" She glanced wistfully after the horses once more. All had grown silent, as if the herd had never appeared.

"I told you we'd see them sometime."

"Yes, but you didn't tell me it would be this beautiful . . . this . . ." She searched for an adequate word. "This awesome! How I wish the children could draw them, just as they looked, all mighty and snorting and throwing snow up everywhere!" Without warning she bent and scooped up two handfuls and tossed it over their heads. It drifted down on her upraised face while he laughed and backed off to avoid it. "Chicken, Theodore!" she taunted. "Honestly, I never saw such a chicken."

"I'm no chicken. I just got more sense than some teachers I know who're gonna end up in bed with the sniffles, like John."

"Oh, phooey! What's a little snow gonna hurt?" She stooped over, scooped again, and took a bite. He could gauge almost to the exact second when she changed from woman back to child. It was part of why he loved her so much, these quicksilver changes of hers. Nonchalantly she began shaping a snowball, patting it top and bottom, transferring it from mitt to mitt, arching one eyebrow with devious intent.

"You just try it and you'll find out what it's gonna hurt," he warned, backing off.

"It's just clean snow." She took a second taste and advanced lazily. "Here, try a bite."

He jerked his head back and grabbed her wrists. "Linnea, you're gonna be sorry."

"Oh yeah? Bite . . . here . . . bite it, bite it, have a b—" They began struggling and laughing while she tried to push the snowball in his face. "Come on, Teddy, good clean *Nort* Dakota snow." She mimicked the Norwegian accent that sometimes crept into his words.

"Cut it out, you little twerp!" She nearly got him this time, but he was too quick, and much stronger.

"Don't you call me a little twerp, Theodore Westgaard. I'm almost nineteen years old!"

He was laughing unrestrainedly as they continued struggling in hand-to-hand combat. "Oh, how about that—she goes off for two weeks and comes home a year older."

She gritted her teeth and grunted. "I'm gonna get you yet, Theodore!" He only laughed, so she hooked a heel behind his boot, gave one mighty shove, and set him on his backside in the snow. There he sat, with an amazed expression on his face, sunk in up to his ribs and elbows while she covered her mouth and rocked with laughter. He picked up one hand and peered into the sleeve. Snow was packed against the lining. He gave it a slow, ponderous shake, all the while skewering her with a feral gleam. He picked up the other hand, dug the snow from around his wrist, and eased to his feet with deliberate slowness. Linnea started backing away.

"Theodore, don't you dare . . . Theodore . . ."

He dusted his backside and advanced, leering wickedly. "Now she begs when she knows she's in for it. What'sa matter, Miss Brandonberg, you scared of a little good clean *Nort* Dakota snow?" he teased.

"Theodore, if you do, I'll . . . I'll . . ."

Unfazed, he advanced. "You'll what?"

"I'll tell your mother!"

"Tell my mother! Ha ha ha!" He came on steadily.

"Well, I will!"

"Yeah, you do that. I'd like to know what she'd say." Suddenly he lunged, caught her wrists, and tried to knock her backward. She squealed and fought. He pushed harder and she braced deeper, struggling, laughing. "I didn't mean it, honest!"

"Ha ha!" He took another step and she grabbed his jacket to keep herself from going over, but she was too late. Whoosh! Back she went, hauling him with her into the puffy pillow of snow, landing in a tangle of arms and legs and skirts, with Theodore sprawled over her like a human quilt. He fell to his side, one leg trailing across her knees while they laughed and laughed and laughed.

As suddenly as it started, it ended. The world grew silent. The weight of his leg across hers grew heavy. A pulse seemed to rise up out of the earth itself, through the snow, into their bodies.

He braced up on an elbow and looked down at her. Their gazes grew intense. ''Linnea,'' he uttered in a queer, strained voice. Snow clung to the back of his collar, his shoulders. She saw him for a brief moment, his blue hat gone, his face framed by the pewter sky above him, his breath labored through open lips. Then his mouth took hers and his weight pressed her deeper into the snow. Their tongues met, mated, warm against their cold lips while he settled full length upon her and she drew him in with eager arms.

When he lifted his head, their hearts were crazy, erratic, and they knew an impatience to make up for lost time.

''I missed you . . . Oh, Teddy . . .'' He kissed her again, holding her head in both gloved hands, and it felt as if the herd galloped by once more and made the earth tremble. The kiss ended with the same reluctance as the first.

''I missed you, too.''

''I kept thinking of how I was home, but it didn't seem like home anymore because all I wanted was to get back here to you.''

''I wasn't fit to live with so I spent most of my time in the tack room.'' A dollop of snow fell from his collar onto her cheek and as he licked it away her eyes closed and her lips opened. His mouth slid back to hers, reclaiming it with a fervor that vitalized both of their bodies.

Reluctantly he rolled from her and lay on his back.

''I even thought you might not come back,'' he confessed.

''Silly.'' She felt denied with his weight gone, and rolled across his chest.

''Am I silly? I don't think I've ever been silly before.''

She kissed his eye, then lay with her lips there, breathing on him, smelling him—leather, wool, snow.

''Did you mean what you said at the station?''

''Oh, God, Linnea.'' He clutched her tightly, closing his eyes, wondering what to do.

She pushed back to see his face. ''Y . . . you mean, you didn't?'' Her fear sent another shaft of love to his heart.

''Yes, I meant it. But it's not right.''

''Of course it's right. How could love be wrong?''

He took her arms and pushed her up, and they sat hip to hip. He wished he could be young again, plunging into life with the same recklessness she had. But he wasn't, and he had to use the common sense she hadn't grown into yet.

''Linnea, listen. I told you I didn't know what to do about it and—''

''Well, I do. I've thought about it a lot and there's only one thing *to* do. We have to get—''

''No!'' He lunged to his feet, turning away. ''Don't go getting ideas. It just wouldn't work.''

She was up and at his shoulder in an instant, insisting, ''Why not?''

He picked up his hat from the snow and whacked it against his thigh. ''Linnea, for heaven's sake, use your head.''

She swung him around by an arm. ''My head?'' She gazed into his eyes, forcing him to look at her. ''Why my head? Why not my heart?''

''Have you thought about what people would say?''

''Yes. Exactly what my mother said this morning. That you're too old for me.''

''She's right.'' He settled his cap on his head and refused to meet her eyes.

''Theodore.'' She clutched his arm. ''What do years have to do with this feeling we have? They're just . . . just numbers. Suppose we had no way of measuring years and you couldn't say you're sixteen years older than I am.''

Lord in heaven, he loved her so. Why did she have to be so young?

He took her upper arms in his gloved hands and made her listen to reason. ''What about babies, Linnea?''

''Babies?''

''Yes, babies. Do you want them?''

''Yes. Yours.''

''I've had mine already and he's sixteen years old. Almost as old as you.''

''But, Teddy, you're only thirt—''

''What about Kristian? He's sweet on you, did you know that?''

''Yes.''

He'd expected her to deny it. When she didn't he was nonplussed. ''Well, don't you see what a mess that could make?''

''I don't see why it should. I've made it very clear in every way I know how that I'm his teacher and nothing more. I'm the first infatuation he's ever had, but he'll get over it.''

''Linnea, he *told* me. I mean, he came right out and told me the day we went to get coal together how he felt about you. He trusted me for the first time ever with his feelings! Imagine what he'd feel like if I tell him now that I'm going to marry you.''

But she sensed what was really bothering him. ''You're scared, aren't you, Teddy?''

''Y' damn right I'm scared, and why shouldn't I be?''

She held his face in her soft mink mittens, capturing his eyes with her own. ''Because I'm not Melinda. I won't run off and abandon you. I love it here. I love it so much I couldn't wait to get back.''

But she was too young to consider that if they had children, by the time they left home he'd be a very old man—if he lived that long. He swung away and strode toward the wagon. ''Come on. Let's go.''

''Teddy, please—''

''No! There's no use even talking about it anymore. Let's go.''

They rode in silence until they approached the driveway to P.S. 28.

''Could we stop at school for just a minute?''

''You need something?''

''No, I've just missed it.''

He looked her full in the face. ''Missed it?'' She'd actually missed this little bump on the big prairie?

''I missed a lot of things.''

He adjusted his cap and tended his driving again. ''We can stop for a minute, but not long. It's cold out here.''

When they pulled into the schoolyard, she exclaimed, ''Why, somebody's shoveled the walks!''

He drew the horses up, went over the side, but avoided her eyes. ''We had a little snow one day, and it drifted.''

''You did it?'' she asked in pleased surprise.

He came around to her side to help her down. They both recalled the first day she'd come here, how he'd claimed he had no time to be looking after hothouse pansies. ''How sweet of you. Thank you, Teddy.''

''If you wanna go inside, go,'' he ordered gruffly.

He watched her trot toward the door and shook his head at the ground. So young. What was he doing, fooling around in the snow with her when nothing could come of it and he knew it.

He followed her in and stood near the cloakroom door watching as she made a quick scan of the room. She observed it lovingly, and on her way to the front, touched the stove, the desks, the globe, as if they had feelings. The place was frigid, but she didn't seem to notice; her face wore a satisfied smile. What she'd said back there was true. She was nothing whatever like Melinda. But—hang it all!—she didn't stop to think that when she was thirty-four like he was now, he would be gray and long past his prime.

She mounted the teacher's platform, picked up a piece of chalk, and printed across the clean blackboard, ''Welcome back! Happy New Year, 1918!''

She set the chalk down with a decisive click, brushed off her palms, and marched back to Theodore, then turned to inspect the message.

''Can you read it?'' she asked.

He frowned, concentrating for several seconds. ''I can read back and New.'' He struggled with the first word. ''Wwww . . .'' When it dawned, his face relaxed. ''Welcome back.''

''Good! And the rest?''

She watched him trying to figure it out.

''The next word is Happy,'' she hinted.

''Happy New Year, 1918,'' he read slowly, then reread the entire message. ''Welcome-back-Happy-New-Year-1918.''

She smiled with pride. He *had* been busy studying. ''By the end of which you're going to be reading as well as my eighth graders.'' As he returned her smile the buildup of tension eased.

''Come on. Let's go home. Ma's waiting.''

Stepping into Nissa's kitchen was like taking off new dancing shoes and putting on worn carpet slippers. Everything was just the same—the oilcloth on the table, the jackets on the hook behind the door, the pail and dipper, the delectable smell coming from the stove.

Nissa was making meatballs and potatoes and gravy for supper, and the windows were thick with steam. The old woman turned from her task and came with open arms. '' 'Bout time you was gettin' back here.''

Linnea returned the affectionate hug. ''Mmm . . . it smells good in here. What're you cooking?''

''Heart stew.''

They laughed and Linnea pushed her away playfully. "I'll tell Theodore to take me back to the depot."

"Don't think you'd have much luck. Think he was a little lost without you."

"Oh, he was, was he?" She arched one brow in Theodore's direction. "I wouldn't have guessed. He pushed me into a snowbank on the way home."

"A snowbank!"

Across the room Theodore scowled. Just then Kristian, fresh back from his trap line, came barreling down the stairs and careened to a halt before Linnea, wearing a smile so wide it seemed to lift his ears. His cheeks were still rosy, his hair stood in peaks, and the red toes of his wool socks belled out. Linnea could almost feel the strain as he held back from hugging her. She would marry his father. She *would!* And this entire family had better get used to the fact that she didn't intend to tiptoe around Kristian feeling guilty every time she had the urge to touch him. She rested her mink mittens on his cheeks.

"Kristian, they're the warmest, most beautiful mittens I've ever seen. Did you make them?" He blushed and shifted his feet.

"They fit okay?"

"Perfectly. See?"

He thanked her for the rosewood brush and comb set, and she thanked Nissa for the slippers, and the awkward moment was behind them. Nissa quipped wryly, "Thank you, too, missy, but what's an old coot like me gonna do with that fancy lilac toilet water you give me? Ain't no man within forty miles'd wanna get close enough to sniff it." While they laughed and filled each other in on the last two weeks, Linnea set the table. Just before mealtime, John showed up, bundled in the new fine navy-blue wool scarf Linnea had given him for Christmas, though he wore it tied over his earlapper cap.

"John, I thought you were sick!"

"Was. Ain't no more."

Linnea gave him a quick hug then backed off to assess him critically. "You are too. Look at that red nose and those watery eyes. You shouldn't have walked clear over here in the cold."

Like Kristian, he self-consciously shuffled his feet and turned pink. "Didn't wanna miss out on anything."

Everyone laughed. Ah, how good it was to be back. This was what homecomings were supposed to feel like.

When they sat down to supper Linnea couldn't resist studying Theodore as he prayed—his bent head, his hair slightly flattened from the wool cap, his lowered eyelids, the corners of his lips behind his folded hands.

"Lord, thank you for this food, and for all You provided for us today, but especially for bringing our little missy back home safe. Amen."

He looked up and found her watching him, and they both knew perfectly well this was where she belonged, in this niche they had made for her in their lives.

Her gaze circled the table. Something sharp, very akin to pain, clutched her heart.

Why, she loved them. Not just Theodore, but all of them—Nissa with her gruff affection, Kristian with his quick blush of admiration, and John with his heart of gold and slow, plodding ways.

Theodore watched her eyes return to him. He quickly reached for the bowl of meatballs, though he'd been studying her ever since the prayer ended, thinking of how empty mealtimes had seemed without her. During her absence the family had reverted to their old accustomed silence, eating with the sole purpose of filling their bellies. But the minute she entered the house, gaiety came along with her, and they all seemed to find their tongues again.

He thought of spring, of her leaving, and the succulent meatballs seemed to turn to sawdust in his mouth.

When supper ended, Linnea said, "I'm anxious to see what you've learned. Care to show me?"

Though he answered off-handedly, "If you're not too tired," he came as close to fidgeting as he ever had when Ma said, "Teddy'll drive you home, John." John tugged on his over-shoes, buttoned his jacket, and buckled his earlappers like a snail with low blood pressure. Laboriously, he tied his new scarf over his head and patted his pockets, searching for mittens. Theodore stood with one hand on the doorknob, but didn't say a word. There was an additional delay while Nissa tucked a fruit jar of vegetable soup under John's arm and gave him orders to stay home in bed the next day.

By the time he got John home, returned, put the horses away, and entered the kitchen, Theodore was fairly jittering with excitement. Both Nissa and Kristian were sitting at the table with Linnea. The books and new slate were spread out in readiness, and Kristian had the speller opened to the last page they'd been working on, eager to demonstrate all he'd taught his father.

Theodore had worked insatiably on his reading while Linnea was gone. He had hounded Kristian to help him, and now, as Kristian proudly dictated a spelling test, he became totally immersed in writing the words. He formed each one carefully: Theodore, know, knee, blood, sausage, fence, Kristian, heart, Cub, Toots, since, sense, John, mother, stove, Linnea, *lutefisk.*

"*Lutefisk!* You taught him to spell *lutefisk?*"

"He made me."

Linnea laughed, but when Theodore began reading aloud to her, she realized what remarkable progress he'd made, partly due to his own determination and partly due to their unorthodox method of choosing words hither-thither.

"Why, Theodore, you're already reading as well as my fifth graders!"

"He nearly drove me crazy, that's why!" Kristian put in. "He barely left me enough time to check my traps." Theodore's face turned pink, but she could see how proud he was. "One day I even found him writing words in the snow with a stick."

"In the snow?" She glanced at Theodore and his blush brightened. His eyes met hers and flickered away.

"Well, I didn't have my slate and I couldn't remember how to spell a word and it was easier if I saw it."

The only other time she'd seen him so vivid and flustered was the night she'd discovered he didn't know how to read. When he blushed and acted bashful he looked so young it made her heart thump.

The following night they were at the table again with Kristian and Nissa sitting by when Linnea decided to try to stump him. She wrote on the slate, "Did I tell you my father bought an automobile?" She turned it around to face him, watched as he read along smoothly, then frowned over the last word. His lips moved silently as he tried to puzzle it out. After several seconds she flipped the board around and put a slash through the word—auto/mobile—then turned it to him again.

He mouthed the word and his face split in a smile. But instead of answering aloud, he took the slate, erased it, and wrote, "No. Did you ride in it?"

She erased it and wrote, "Yes, it was delightful."

He puzzled for a full minute and finally gave up. "I don't know that one," he said.

"Delightful."

"Oh." He suddenly grew pensive and forgot about the slate as he studied her.

An automobile, Theodore thought. She would be the kind to like an automobile. When spring came and she returned to her life in the city, with the family automobile and all the other conveniences, surely she would compare it to the life out here and find this backward. Why ever would she want to return next fall? And there was one other thing that he hadn't been able to get off his mind but had felt foolish to ask.

He rubbed the chalky rag over his slate, then wrote, "Did you see Lorents?" He pondered the question for a long moment, trying to dredge up the nerve to show her. He cast an eye at Nissa and Kristian across the table. But his mother was mending a sock and his son was bent over a book. Theodore looked up to find Linnea with one fist bracing her jaw as she waited idly to see what he'd come up with. Slowly—very slowly—he angled the board so only she could read it.

She studied it, frowning, puzzling it out. Did you see . . .

Her eyes flashed up to his and her jaw came off her fist. Her heart did a quickstep and she threw a cautious glance at the two across the table, but they were paying no attention whatever.

She eased the board from his fingers, but left his question and wrote beneath it, "Lawrence?"

Theodore studied the name, properly spelled, feeling awkward and a little warm around the neck. He erased *Lorents,* rewrote it correctly, turned it to her, and nodded.

For interminable seconds their dark, intense gazes locked above the slate. Kristian turned a page. Nissa's scissors snipped a thread. In the final moment before Linnea's hand went back to her slate, Theodore thought he saw a flicker of amusement in her eyes.

No, she wrote.

When he read it, he quietly released a long breath and his shoulders relaxed against the back of the chair.

Though neither of them said a word about the message exchanged on the board, it was on both of their minds as they went to bed that night.

It won't work, having her so close all the time. You either got to marry her or get her out of here.

It won't work, living under the same roof with him. If he won't marry you, you'll have to find someplace else to teach next year.

The following day, when Linnea returned from school, an envelope was propped against the potted philodendron in the middle of the kitchen table. The return address said Adrian Mitchell.

She came up short at the sight of it and suddenly felt a pair of eyes censuring her. She looked across the room to find Theodore standing in the doorway to the front room, glaring at her as if she'd just announced she was a German spy. Between them Nissa worked at the stove, ignoring them. The silence was broken only by the sound of onion spattering into hot grease. Theodore spun and disappeared, and Linnea thought, Oh, you don't want me for yourself, but nobody else can have me either, is that it?

She snatched the letter off the table and went bounding up the stairs.

Adrian was as good at writing letters as he was at handling customers and parents. Some of his compliments made Linnea blush. And his plans for summer made her hide the envelope beneath her underclothes in a drawer where Nissa wouldn't spot it when she came up to change the sheets.

That night as they sat over their lessons, the tension between Linnea and Theodore was palpable. He wished for once they could be alone and have words, but Nissa sat on her usual chair, knitting, and Kristian was mending a snowshoe and chewing jerky. When Theodore could stand it no longer, he wrote on his slate, "Who is Adrian?"

When he turned it to face Linnea, his eyes were hard, his lips set in a thin line.

"He works in my father's store," she wrote back.

Though no further personal messages were exchanged that night, Theodore was stiff and sulky. He did his writing exercises without once looking at her, and at the end of the evening, when she offered a good night, he refused to answer.

The following morning Linnea awakened to a thermometer reading of thirty-eight degrees below zero and a wind keening out of the northwest so forcefully it appeared the windmill was going to go flying off to Iowa.

They took turns washing in the kitchen: there was no question of doing it upstairs where the temperatures were nearly as cold as outdoors. The windows were so thick with ice it was impossible to see out. John didn't even show up for breakfast.

When the meal was done, Theodore pushed his chair back, reached for his outerwear, and without bothering to glance Linnea's way, ordered, "Get your things. I'll be taking you to school."

"Taking me?" She glanced up, surprised.

"That's what I said. Now get your things."

"But you said—"

"Don't tell me what I said! You wouldn't make it to the end of the driveway before your eyeballs froze." He jerked on his wool jacket, buttoned it, turned up the collar, and jammed a battered felt Stetson low on his head. Yanking the door open, he repeated cantankerously. "Get your things."

Obediently she hustled upstairs. Five minutes later, when she ran down the freshly shoveled path, she came up short at the sight of the strangest looking contraption she'd ever seen, hitched behind Cub and Toots. It appeared to be a small shed on runners, with a chimney stack sticking out its roof spouting smoke and reins stretching inside through a crude peek hole. Beside a small rear door

Theodore waited impatiently, a look of thunderous unapproachability upon his face.

"What is this thing?" Linnea asked, eyeing the warped roof.

"Get in!" He grabbed her arm and pushed her inside, then followed, closing the door. The interior was warm and dark. A fire gleamed through the minute cracks of the tiniest round iron stove she'd ever seen. It was no bigger than a cream can, but more than ample to heat the small space. A thin ray of daylight threaded in through the peek hole up front. She felt the floor rock as Theodore made his way past her, advising, "There's no seats, so you'd best stand up here by me and hang on."

Before she could follow orders, he slapped the reins and nearly set her on her backside. Rocking, she grappled forward and grabbed the edge of the peek hole, through which the horses' rumps were visible.

"What about Kristian?"

"He's doing the chores. I'll bring him later."

"But you always do the chores before breakfast."

"Had to put this thing together before breakfast," he stated in his grumpiest voice.

Immediately her temper sizzled. "You didn't *have* to do anything, Theodore. I could have walked!"

Staring through the peek hole, he retorted, "Ha."

"I didn't ask to be treated like some . . . some hothouse pansy!"

"You got any idea what wind like that does to bare skin when the temperature's thirty-eight below?"

"I could have covered my face with a scarf."

In the dim square of light that fell on his face, she watched him roll his eyes her way. He gave a deprecating chuckle, then glanced away again.

"I'm *sorry* I put you out," she said sarcastically. "Next time, before you build a wagon for me, you might ask me first if I need a ride."

"I didn't *build* a wagon for you," he returned in a tone that matched her own. "It breaks down and stores in the lean-to. All I had to do was stand it on the bobsled runners and hook it together."

She was getting angrier by the moment at his high-handedness and the insulting tone of his voice.

"Theodore, I don't know what in the world's the matter with you lately, but you're acting like some . . . some bear with a thorn in his paw!"

He threw her a withering glance but said nothing.

"Well, what did I do?" she demanded angrily, rocking with the motion of the vehicle, trying not to bump his arm.

His jaw bulged. He glared straight head. Finally he bit out, "Nothin'! You didn't do nothin'!"

They pulled into the schoolyard and she leaped out into the slicing wind, anxious to be away from him. But, to her surprise, he followed, grasping her elbow so hard she winced as they trudged through thigh-deep drifts. The wind was so ferocious it threatened to pluck off her scarf. Theodore held his hat on with his free hand. The edges of their footprints began blurring even before they reached the steps, which were buried beneath a drift so deep they had to search for footholds as they climbed.

She stumbled once and he mercilessly yanked her to her feet. The door was totally blocked by a wall of white. After attempting to open it and failing, Theodore plowed his way back down the steps toward the wagon. In a moment he returned with a shovel.

"I can do it!" she shouted as he came back to her. "Give it to me!"

She reached for the shovel handle. One of her mittens closed around it beside his worn leather glove. She pulled. He tugged. They glared at each other stubbornly. The wind flickered his hat brim and sent her scarf tails whipping like a flag. The tip of her nose was wet. The tops of his ears were red.

Wordlessly he wrenched the shovel from her grasp, then ground through his teeth, "Just get out of my way." He shouldered her rudely aside and rammed the shovel in the snowdrift with uncontrolled vehemence.

"Theodore, I said I can do it!"

It took no more than twelve flying shovelfuls to free the door. He jerked it open, grabbed her elbow, and thrust her inside.

"I will shovel the goddamn snow!" he bellowed, then slammed the door in her face.

She stared at it while tears scalded her eyes, then gave it a vicious kick. Angrily she swung inside to get the coal hod. But when she marched out with it he yanked it from her hand, jammed his shovel in a drift, did an about face, and without a word trudged around the corner of the building through knee-deep snow. She was standing rigidly with her back to the door when he clumped inside and cracked the pail down beside her with a force that shook the windows. Behind her his boots thudded like hammer blows, then both doors slammed.

She built the fire with enough banging and clanging to shake the teeth loose in his head—she hoped! When it was lit she tightened the ends of her scarf so hard it nearly choked her. She had just opened the cloakroom door and was heading for the water pail when he barged in from outside, with the same intent. Sour-faced, she watched him grab it and head outside. She slammed her door before he could slam his.

He was back in minutes. With her back to the door, arms crossed tightly, she stood by the stove and listened to him transfer the water to the crock in the corner. Next came the clap of the wooden cover, then he returned the pail to the cloakroom.

The inner door slammed.

Was he in or out?

She glared at the stovepipe for two full minutes, wondering. Nothing but silence. Curiosity finally got the best of her and she peeked over one shoulder. There he stood, hands on hips, glaring at her from under the brim of his Stetson.

She snapped around to the stove again.

"Well, are you going to tell me about him or not?" came his belligerent voice.

"Tell you about whom?" she retorted stubbornly.

"Whom?" He laughed derisively and his boots clunked slowly across the floor. He stopped no more than a foot behind her. "Adrian what's-his-name, that's who!"

"Mitchell. His name is Adrian Mitchell."

"I really don't give a damn what his name is. Are you going to tell me or not?"

"I told you, he works at my father's store," she spit.

"I'll bet," he returned sardonically.

She spun around. "Well, he does!"

His eyes were shadowed by the brim of his hat, but even so she could make out the anger gleaming in their depths. His jacket collar was turned up around his ears, his boots planted wide. "Another one for your collection?" he accused.

"And what do you care?" she retorted, making fists inside her mittens.

"Is he?" Theodore spit back, making fists inside his gloves.

"It's none of your business. How dare you question me about my personal life. All you are is my landlord!"

"What did you do, go out riding in *automobiles* with him?" Theodore sneered.

"Yes, as a matter of fact, I did. And I had fun, too. And he took me to a party, and ice-skating, and we danced and drank champagne punch, and he came to my house for supper. And you know what else he did, Theodore?" She thrust her nose closer, taunting him with bright, snapping eyes. "He kissed me. Is that what you want to know? Is it?"

She thrust even closer and squared her jaw while Theodore's face burned pepper-red between cold, mottled white spots.

"You're pushin' your luck, missy," he threatened in a low, gravelly voice.

She backed off and gave a derisive sniff. "Oh, don't make me laugh, Theodore. It would take a railroad locomotive to push you. You're scared of your own shadow." He took one threatening step forward, but she held her ground, blue eyes gone black with challenge. "Aren't you?"

They faced off, each looking for a weakness in the other, finding none. Finally Theodore demanded, "How old is he?"

"Twenty, twenty-one maybe. Now run, Theodore, run like you always do!"

He glared at her, the muscles in his neck so tense a pain shot up the back of his head. Then Theodore, who rarely cursed, growled his second curse of the day.

"Damn you." He jerked her forward by both elbows, dropping his mouth over hers in a savage kiss. Immediately her mouth opened, and she struggled as if to call out, but he ruthlessly held her, feeling her arms tensed to fight. Beneath his mouth she made a muffled sound as if trying to speak, but he refused to free her lips and let her rail at him again. His tongue thrust between her teeth and hers met it, full force. Only then did he realize she was struggling not to get away from him but to get *to* him. He eased his grasp on her elbows and immediately she flung her arms around his neck. Up on tiptoe she went, moving close, clinging. His arms circled her back, pulling her flush against him, the bulk of their woolen clothing forming a barrier.

He lifted his head abruptly, forcing her away from him, breathing hard. Her eyes were like chips of coal to which a match had been touched. They burned bright and intensely into his face.

"Teddy, Teddy, why do you fight it?" Her breath came in quick, driving beats.

He closed his eyes to get control, pressing her away by the arms. "Because I'm old enough to be your father. Don't you understand that?"

"I understand that you only use it as an excuse."

"Stop it!" he shot back, opening his eyes to reveal a tortured expression. "And think about what you're saying, what we're doing! You're eighteen years—"

"Closer to nineteen."

"All right, so you'll be nineteen next month. And I'll be thirty-five two months after that. What difference does it make? There'll still be sixteen years between us."

"I don't care," she insisted.

"Your pa would care." Immediately he saw that he'd touched a vulnerable spot. "Your pa, who probably has a young fellow named Adrian all picked out for you and already working in his store, isn't that right?"

"Adrian wrote to me. I didn't write to him."

"But you kissed him and did all those things with him and I'm jealous and I got no right to be, don't you see? You should be with young people like him, not with old bucks like me."

"You're not an old buck, you're way more fun to be around than he is, and when he kisses me nothing happens like when you—"

"Shh!" He covered her mouth with one gloved finger, the anger falling away as fast as it had come.

For a long moment their eyes locked, then she freed her lips from his hand and whispered, "But it's true."

"You live in my house. Don't you understand what people would say, what they might think?"

"That you love me?" she questioned softly. "Would that be so terrible?"

"Linnea, don't," he uttered, still pressing her away.

"Oh, Teddy, I . . . I love you so much I do crazy things," she admitted plaintively. "I kiss blackboards and windows and pillows because you won't kiss me."

Though he tried to steel himself against her, her ingenuousness made his mouth flicker in a sad smile. Trouble was, what he liked most about her were the very things that made her too young for him. No other girl he'd ever known had been so natural and unspoiled. He let his eyes drift to her hairline, the red plaid scarf tied severely around her face. Her sincere eyes. Her sweet mouth.

Much more softly she said, "I do love you, Teddy."

Lord, lord, girl, don't do this to me.

But when she raised her eyes to his once more, he gave up and drew her into his arms, gently this time. He closed his eyes and nestled her beneath his chin with one gloved hand holding the back of her head. "Don't," he requested in a dry, scratchy voice. She felt him swallow against the top of her head. "Don't try to grow up too fast and waste these precious years on me. Be young and foolish. Kiss blackboards and windows and talk to people who aren't there."

Chagrined, she burrowed deeper beneath his chin. "You guessed, didn't you?"

"That you talk to people who aren't there? Yes, after the day I surprised you at the blackboard here. And one other time I heard you upstairs, talking to your friend Lawrence. Are you ready to tell me who he is yet?''

He leaned back, the better to see her. She hung her head sheepishly. One leather-covered finger tipped her chin up until she couldn't avoid meeting his eyes. A blush appeared on the crests of her cheeks and she blinked wide. ''He's nobody,'' she admitted, ''I made him up.''

Theodore scowled. ''Made him up?''

''He's just a figment of my imagination. Somebody to take the place of the friend I didn't have when I first came out here. Actually, I invented him when I was about thirteen or so, when I first noticed the difference between boys and girls. He and I . . . well, I could just talk to him, that's all. Like I never could to a real boy.'' She dropped her chin and studied a pocket flap on Theodore's jacket.

He studied her nose, her eyebrows, the sweep of lashes dropped docilely over her pretty blue eyes. Her lips were delicate and slightly puffed, and he wanted worse than anything to kiss them and teach them the hundreds of ways of kissing back.

''What am I going to do with you, little one?'' he questioned softly.

She looked up and told him, ''Marry me.''

''I can't. No matter how I'd like to, I can't. It wouldn't be fair to you.''

Why should it be unfair of him to do something that would make her the happiest woman in the world?

''Fair? To me?''

''Linnea, think. Think about twenty years from now when you'd still be young . . . I'd be past middle age.''

''Oh, Teddy, you have an obsession with years. You're forever counting them. But don't you see it's more important to count happiness? Why, even in twenty years we could have more happiness than some people have in fifty. Please . . .''

Her eyes were so sincere and her mouth trembled as she stood a heartbeat away. When her gaze dropped to his lips his pulsebeat thudded out a warning, but he found it impossible to move as she slowly lifted on tiptoe, raised her slightly parted lips to his, then held both sides of his face between her sleek mink mittens. ''Please . . .'' she murmured, tipping her head and softly plucking at his mouth, then slipping her hands around his neck and pressing herself against him. ''Please . . .''

He steeled himself to resist, but her tongue glided over his lips, then shyly probed inside, over his teeth, and the sensitive skin of his inner lips. With a throaty sound he gathered her close, slanted his head and joined her fully. Their tongues met in a silken encounter and their bodies strained together. Their hearts seemed to collide, breast to breast, and arousal took them by storm.

He tasted faintly of morning coffee and smelled of winter air. The interior of his mouth was hot, moist, and more tempting than anything she had ever imagined. None of the kisses she'd experienced had ever moved her as this one did. She thought she would simply die if it couldn't be hers forever.

But suddenly he pulled back and jerked her arms from around his neck. The scarf had fallen back and lay in soft folds about her collar. Her eyes were wide and pleading, her lips parted, exuding small, panting breaths. His voice shook and his breath was driven.

"I have to go."

"But what about us?"

"The answer is still no."

She swallowed the lump in her throat and said shakily, "Then I'll have to go, too. I can't stay in that house with you any longer. Not the way I feel."

He'd known it would come down to this, but he hadn't expected it to hurt quite this much.

"No. I promise I wouldn't—"

She touched his lips to silence him. "I can't make the same promise, Teddy . . ." she whispered.

Everything in him seemed to hurt. Everything in him wanted. He wanted Linnea, but so much more—the rich, full life she could bring. He'd never known he could hurt so bad, want so bad.

"I'll be back for you at five o'clock and we'll talk about it then. You're not to start out for home, is that understood?"

"Yes," she whispered.

"When you need more coal, send Kristian out for it. Promise?" When she didn't respond he shook her a little, demanding softly, "Promise?"

"I promise."

"Fix your hair. I think I've messed it in the back." The words were gravelly as he stepped back, steadying her by her arms.

"I will," she replied woodenly.

Then he dropped his hands and left without looking back.

Chapter 19

Because the weather was so frigid, all the fathers delivered and picked up their children that day. Linnea left a note for Teddy on the schoolhouse door and rode home with Trigg and Bent. She took one look at Clara and the tears she'd held at bay since morning came gushing with a vengeance. A moment later she was in Clara's consoling arms.

"Why, Linnea, what is it?"

"Oh, Clara," she wailed, clinging.

Clara telegraphed a silent message to Trigg and he disappeared with Bent, who stared in astonishment as his teacher broke into sobs.

"Shh . . . shh . . . it can't be as bad as all that. Is it something with Allen again?"

Linnea withdrew, sobbing, searching out a hanky. "It's Th . . . Theodore."

"Ah, brother Theodore. What's he done this time?"

"Oh, C . . . Clara, it's j . . . just awful."

Clara drew back to see Linnea's face. "What's awful? I can't help you if you won't tell me."

"I l . . . love him."

The older woman controlled a smile. "That's awful?"

"He loves m . . . me too and he w . . . won't m . . . marry me."

Clara hugged Linnea again as a new rash of weeping wilted her. She rubbed her shuddering back and turned her toward the table. "You mean you asked him?"

Linnea nodded wretchedly and let herself be lowered to a chair. Clara couldn't help smiling. Poor Teddy, didn't he ever get the chance to do the proposing himself?

"You did, huh? Well, that took some courage. So exactly what did he say?"

"He th . . . thinks I'm too young f . . . for him, and he s . . . says he d . . . doesn't want any more b . . . babies and oh, Clara, wh . . . what am I g . . . going to do?" She laid her head on the table and let the misery flow.

Babies? thought Clara. They've already talked about having babies? Poor Teddy was already fated to Linnea and didn't know it.

"Cry it out, and when you've dried up a little we'll talk it all over."

That's exactly what they did. Linnea unburdened herself, relating all her feelings, all the complications Theodore insisted on throwing in their way. Clara listened, and sympathized, and soothed. And when the story was out and all that remained of Linnea's tears was the puffiness in her eyelids, the younger woman said, "Clara, I have to ask you something. It's awfully presumptuous of me, but you're the only one I can think of to ask."

"What is it? You can ask me anything, you know that."

"Could I come and stay here with you and Trigg? I just can't live there anymore, and the school board will pay you, and I don't eat much. I thought maybe with the baby coming I could help you with things around the house. And it'd only be till spring. I . . . well, I doubt that I'd be coming back in the fall."

It took Clara only a few moments' consideration to decide.

"Of course you can." She cupped Linnea's tear-shined cheek. "And I'll be only too happy for the help. I'm already so enormous it's an effort just to wobble around. Now . . ." She boosted herself to her feet and spoke brusquely. "You'll stay for supper, then Trigg can take you to Ma's to get your things. How does that sound?"

When Linnea and Trigg walked into Nissa's house a short time later, the atmosphere was funeral. The three members of Linnea's "family" all stood back, uncertain, unhappy, not knowing what to say while she explained that Clara needed her during this last part of her pregnancy, so Trigg was taking her back there.

"Tonight?" Nissa asked.

"Yes, as soon as I get my things together."

"A little sudden, ain't it?"

Linnea knew Theodore didn't believe her story, and it was questionable whether Nissa did, but all she wanted was to gather her things and escape as quickly as possible. She avoided Theodore's eyes, but sensed his stunned disbelief as he hovered in the background, staring at her, saying nothing. Kristian kept glancing at Nissa as if expecting her to stop Linnea, while Nissa put on her prune face and tried to decide if she should feel hurt or not.

There wasn't a lot for Linnea to pack—she hadn't much more than she'd come with, except a pair of mink mittens, a carved cat, a crocheted shawl, and a leather-bound volume of Tennyson. She forced herself not to dwell on them as she stuffed them into her valise.

When she came back down she wasn't sure she could manage the good-bye that was necessary. The tears were so close to the surface that the inside of her nose stung, and the clot of emotion in her throat made speaking an effort. But she did her best job of acting ever, pasting a bright smile on her face and injecting an excited bounce into her footstep.

The hug she gave Nissa was fleeting. "One less to cook for," she chirped.

The finger she pointed at Kristian's nose was playful. "Now see to it you do homework even when I'm not here at the table in the evenings."

The handshake she gave Theodore was convincing. "You'll do wonderfully with your reading, I know you will. Kristian can help you with it. Well, Trigg, all set."

She whirled out with all the apparent eagerness of a child approaching a candy store, but when she was gone the three remaining Westgaards looked at each other and didn't know what to say. Nissa finally broke the silence.

"Well, what do you know about this, Teddy?"

He swallowed and turned away. "Nothin'."

"Kristian?"

"Nothing."

"Well, that child had been cryin', and cryin' hard. She didn't fool me one bit. Tomorrow I intend to march over there and find out what's goin' on."

"Leave it, Ma."

"Leave it?"

"She wants to go there and live, let her. Like she said, it's one less mouth to feed."

But nothing was good without her. It was as it had been when she'd gone home for Christmas, only worse, because this time she wasn't coming back. Mealtime was a sullen ordeal. Nobody talked. They all stared at their plates and wondered why the food didn't taste good. They caught each other glancing at Linnea's empty chair and tried to pretend they hadn't been. John was back—his cold was better—but though he'd come out of his shell since Linnea had come into their lives, now that she was gone, he was more indrawn than ever. He shuffled in with his head down and shuffled out the same way. Though Kristian saw her at school every day, he came and went without a word about how she was. How is she doing, Theodore wanted to ask. Does she seem happy? What was she wearing? It took an effort to get up mornings and pretend the day had some meaning. Evenings were torture. Nobody brought out a book, nobody brought out a slate. Trigg took her to school these cold days; his rig passed regularly, morning and afternoon. But he had the warming house on, and if she was in it, she couldn't be seen. Theodore found himself hovering around the out-buildings at those times of day, straining for a glimpse of the vehicle that carried her.

At night he tossed in bed restlessly, pondering his future. Kristian was already sixteen. Ma was seventy. They wouldn't be around forever. And when they weren't, what then? Then there'd be him and John. Two old men batching it in their lonely prairie farmhouses, talking mostly to the animals, waving to wagons that passed on the road, hoping one of them would turn in and bring company.

He thought about Linnea, up there at Clara's, wondered how she was getting on, and if she missed him. Lord, she was strong, that girl. He'd never thought she'd up and leave like she did. He reckoned she was happy up there, with the kids always making some kind of excitement—she sure loved kids, no doubt about it. Loved Clara, too, and the two of them got along like peas in a pod. He supposed when the new baby came Linnea would be in her glory being around it.

He thought about babies. Girl like that deserved babies, but a man his age had no business having 'em. Still, he wondered what they'd look like, his and Linnea's. Blond, probably, and robust and full of energy like her.

He saw her at church on Sunday and got all goggle-eyed and tight-chested. But she looked happy as a lark, wearing a great big smile and her bird-wing hat. She said, "Oh, hi, Teddy. Where's Nissa?" Then she was gone before he could get his tongue unglued. After Sunday dinner he sneaked into his room and combed his hair, figuring they'd be here any time; Clara and Trigg always came to Ma's on Sunday. But they didn't come.

By late afternoon, when they hadn't shown up, he hid his slate under his jacket and went down to the tack room to see if a little schoolwork would relieve his wretchedness. But he wasted a good half hour staring at the saddle on the sawhorse, and another staring at the name he'd written on the slate. Linnea. Linnea. Linnea. Lord God almighty, what should he do? He hurt. Hurt. Love wasn't supposed to hurt like this. He wrenched himself to his feet and tried cleaning the tool bench, but it was already in perfect order. He reared back and threw a hoof trimmer so hard it knocked over three cans and sent horsehoe nails skittering to the floor. Then with a violent curse he swung, picked up the slate, and stormed from the room.

Nissa and Kristian were both in the kitchen when he came back in. They watched him but said nothing. He went to his bedroom, reappeared momentarily with his suspenders and underwear top turned down, filled the basin, washed, shaved for the second time that day, patted bay rum on his face, macassared his hair, combed it meticulously, disappeared once more, and returned shortly wearing his Sunday suit and a clean white shirt with a brand-new collar. He looked neither at his son nor mother but pulled on his coat, picked up the slate and speller, and announced, "I'm going up to Clara's, see if I can get on with my reading lessons."

When the door slammed behind him Kristian stared at it, speechless. Nissa's knitting needles didn't miss a beat as she studied her grandson over the rim of her spectacles.

"I could've given him a reading lesson," Kristian declared belligerently.

"Yup." *Clickety-snickety* went the knitting needles. Kristian's eyes swerved to Nissa's.

"Then why'd he have to go up to Clara's?"

She dropped her eyes to the stitches, though she could form them blindfolded. " 'Pears to me your pa's gone courtin'," she replied with a satisfied air.

At Clara's, Linnea was preparing Monday's lessons at the kitchen table, where the whole family sat eating popcorn. A sound filtered through the wall. "Somebody's coming." Trigg got up and squinted through the window into the dark. "Looks like Teddy."

Linnea's hand stopped halfway to her mouth and her heart jumped into doubletime. She scarcely had time to adjust to the announcement before the door was opening and there stood Theodore, turned out as if it were his burial day. He glanced at everybody in the room except Linnea.

"Howdy, Clara, Trigg, kids. Thought you'd come up't the house today. Decided to ride down and see if everything's okay."

"Everything's fine. Come on in."

"Cold out there."

Linnea felt a blush rise.

"Uncle Teddy! Uncle Teddy! We got popcorn!" Little Christine barreled against him, reaching up. He set her on his arm and chucked her under the chin, smiling. Finally he met Linnea's eyes above the child's blond head. His smile dissolved and he gave a silent nod. She dropped her attention to her schoolwork.

"Pull up a chair," Trigg invited, and stuck one between himself and Bent.

"What did you bring?" Bent inquired.

Theodore joined them at the table, with Christine on his knee. "My slate and speller." He laid them on the table. "I'm learning how to read."

"You *are?* Gosh, but you're awful old to—"

"Bent!" his parents scolded simultaneously.

The little boy glanced from one parent to the other, wondering what he'd done wrong. "Well, he *iii*s."

Linnea wanted to crawl beneath the table.

"A person's never too old to learn," Theodore told the eight-year-old. "What do you think, Miss Brandonberg?"

She met his eyes and not one blessed word came to her mind.

"If you can spare the time, I'd like to go on with the reading lessons."

Reading lesson? Dressed like that he came claiming he wanted reading lessons? How could she possibly concentrate on teaching him when her blood had set up such a singing in her head?

"I . . . well . . . sure, why not?"

He smiled and nodded and reached for some popcorn, and one of the children said something that diverted his attention. Linnea felt Clara's inquisitive scrutiny and wrote at the top of a paper, "Don't leave!" Silently she flashed it toward Clara, praying she'd heed the message. It would have looked utterly conspicuous for Clara and Trigg to disappear suddenly; the kitchen was the warmest room in the house, the gathering place on cold evenings like this. The front room was rarely used in winter.

Thankfully, Clara took Linnea's plea to heart. When the popcorn was gone, everyone shifted places so Linnea and Teddy could sit side by side, but everybody stayed. The children found a ball of yarn and played on the floor with Patches, their pet cat. Clara stitched on a baby quilt. Trigg read a *Farm Journal.* Linnea and Teddy tried to concentrate on a lesson that meant not a whit to either one of them. Though their elbows rested on the table, they made certain not to touch. When their knees bumped once beneath the table, they sat up straighter in their chairs. Though they studied each other's hands, they never looked directly at each other. They had been working for nearly two hours when Teddy silently pushed the slate across the table to her. On it were written three words.

Please come home.

A heart-burst of reaction flooded Linnea's body. Love, pain, renunciation. She glanced up sharply, but Trigg and Clara were occupied. Teddy studied her; she felt his eyes like a longing caress on her cheek. His knuckles were white as the chalk he gripped. It would be so easy to say yes, knowing how he felt about her. But he wasn't offering anything permanent, only a temporary solution to their misery.

She reached for the chalk, slipping it from his fingers and watching as he forcibly relaxed them. She wrote only two words—I can't—and for the first time that night, met his gaze directly.

Oh, Teddy, I love you. But I'll have it all or nothing.

She saw that he understood clearly. She saw how fast he was breathing. She saw him fight with himself. And everything in her rushed outward toward him in a silent plea.

But he closed his speller, set it atop the slate, and pushed his chair back. "Well, it's late, I'd best be going." He stretched to his feet and reached for his coat. "Can I come again tomorrow?"

"Why sure," Trigg answered.

"Linnea?"

She couldn't quite find the strength to say no. "If you'd like."

He nodded solemnly and said good night.

He came the next night, but not in his Sunday best. He wore a gray plaid flannel shirt with the sleeves rolled to the elbow and the throat open, revealing the sleeves and placket of the ever-present winter underwear. He looked utterly masculine. Linnea wore her hair caught up in a ribbon, flowing down her back. In her navy and white middy dress she looked utterly young.

She gave him a story to read and he settled down to do so, slunk low in his chair with his temple propped on two fingertips. She looked up once to find that over the top of the book he was studying her breasts, which rested over her crossed wrists on the edge of the table. Her face turned red, she sat back, and his eyes returned to the book.

The following night she told him to write a sentence using the word blue and he wrote, Linnea has beautifull blue eyes.

In a snap, Linnea's beautiful blue eyes met Theodore's beautiful brown ones. Her face became a blushing red rose and Teddy smiled. Flustered, she took refuge in grabbing the slate and correcting his spelling. Unperturbed, he erased the whole thing, applied the chalk again and wrote, You look pretty when you blush.

He came six nights and still she refused to return home. They sat at the table as usual, Clara and Trigg with them, and Theodore covertly studied Linnea. She corrected papers while he was supposed to be reading, but it was impossible. She had done something different with her hair tonight, gathered it up in a loose puff with a tiny pug knot in the back, like an egg in a fat nest. At her temples tendrils trailed and she caught one around her finger, winding and rewinding it abstractedly. Suddenly she giggled at something on the paper. "You have to see this." She angled it so they all could see. "It's a spelling test I gave today. This word is supposed to be sheet."

S-h-i-t, it said.

They all laughed and settled back. Theodore watched her giggles subside and her head bend over her work again. In time she finished and smacked the pile of papers straight, looked up, and caught him admiring her.

"Did you finish reading your assignment?"

He cleared his throat. "Ahh . . . no, not quite."

"Theodore!" she scolded, "you can read faster than that."

"Some nights."

"Well, you can finish it at home. It's time for a couple new words." She pulled out the slate and they began working, elbows and heads close. She smelled like almonds again. It created havoc with his concentration. He remembered dancing with her, smelling that almond flavor up close. He remembered kissing her, and how she had made him feel. Young. Alive. Bursting. Just looking at her brought it all back again, made his blood surge and his heart knock. He reached for the slate as if he had no choice in the matter, and though he felt fearful and even a little timid, he had to ask. He just had to. It was pure hell without her.

Can I pick you up for the dance tomorrow? he wrote.

This time she expressed no surprise. No blush lit her cheek. No excitement kindled her eyes. Only a sad resignation as their gazes met and she slowly shook her head.

He felt a brief flare of anger: what was she trying to do to him? But he knew, and he knew she was stubborn enough, strong enough to hold fast in her resolution to live the remainder of the year at Clara's. And next fall she wouldn't be back. He saw it all in her sad eyes as they confronted him, and suddenly his life stretched out before him like a bleak, eternal purgatory. He knew full well what he must do to turn that purgatory to heaven. He knew what she was waiting for.

He felt as if he were strangling. As if the walls of his chest would collapse at any moment. As if his heart would club its way out of his body—the hard ache beneath his ribs, the sweating palms and shaky hands. But he took the chalk anyway and wrote what all the common sense of the universe could not keep him from writing.

Then will you merry me?

There wasn't a sound in the room as he turned the slate her way and waited. The muscles in his belly jumped.

When she read it the shock passed over her face. Her lips dropped open and she took a sharp breath. Her eyes widened upon him and they stared at each other, breathing as if they'd just come up for the third time. Their faces were suffused with color and neither of them seemed capable of movement. At last she reached an unsteady hand for the chalk . . . and for once she didn't correct his spelling.

Yes, she wrote. Then the blackboard was jerked from her hand and clapped upside down on the table. In one swift, impatient leap Theodore was on his feet, reaching for his jacket, carefully refraining from looking at her.

"There's northern lights tonight. Linnea and I are going out and see 'em."

It seemed to take a year instead of a minute for them to button into their outerwear and close the door behind them. And the only lights they saw were those exploding behind their closed eyes as he swung her recklessly into his arms and crushed his mouth to hers. They kissed with a wild insatiability, until everything in the world seemed attainable, and life ran rampant in their veins. They freed their mouths, clutching each other till their muscles quivered, murmuring half-sentences in desperate haste.

"Nothing was good without . . ."

"I've been miserable . . ."

"Will you really . . ."

"Yes . . . yes . . ."

"I tried not to . . ."

"I didn't know how to get you to . . ."

"Oh God, God, I love you . . ."

"I love you so much I . . ."

They kissed again, unable to climb into each other's skins as they wanted to, striving nonetheless. They ran their hands over everything allowable and as close to the unallowable as they dared. They pulled back, giddy in the unaccustomed release brought by agreement. They kissed again, still astounded, then paused to find equilibrium.

She rested her forehead against his chin. "Remind me to teach you how to spell *marry*."

"Don't I know how?"

She pivoted her forehead against his chin: "No."

He chuckled. "Seems like it didn't make any difference."

She smiled and rubbed up and down his sides with both hands. "M-a-r-r-y spells will you marry me. M-e-r-r-y spells will you happy me."

"Ah, little one." He smiled and pulled her closer. "Don't you know that when you're my wife you'll do both?"

She had not known a heart could smile.

They kissed again, less hurried now—the initial rush was sated; they could explore at leisure. She caught his neck, drew his head down, tasting his warm, wet mouth with her own, savoring every texture, experimenting with seduction. His head moved in lazy circles, his hands kneaded her ribs. Impatience became a thing to be reckoned with and he forced himself to back off. "I said I was bringing you out here to look at the northern lights. Maybe we should take a look anyway."

"Bad idea," she murmured, crowding, kissing his neck.

He chuckled low. She felt it against her lips. "Such an unappreciative girl. Nature putting on a show like that and she doesn't even care."

"Nature's putting on another show right here and I'm trying to show you exactly how much I care."

But Theodore was noble, not heroic. He swung her around in his arms and planted her back against his chest, circling her from behind.

"Look."

She looked. And was awed.

The indigo sky to the north radiated an unearthly glow, shifting fingers of pinkish light that reached and receded in ever-changing patterns. The aurora borealis spread like the earth's halo lit from below, reflecting from the white-mantled land. At times not only the sky, but the earth itself seemed to radiate, creating a night vista much as if the earth's fiery core were glowing up through a vast opaque window. For as far as the eye could see the land lay sleeping, swaddled in snow. Flat, endless space, leading away to forever, like the rest of their lives together.

"Oh, Teddy," she sighed and tilted her head back against his shoulder. "We're going to be so happy together."

"I think we already are." He rocked them gently while they watched the sky brighten and dim, by turns.

"And we'll live to tell the story of this night to our grandchildren. I'm just sure of it."

He kissed the crest of her cheek, envisioning it.

She covered his arms with hers. "Do you think our horses are out there somewhere?"

"Somewhere."

"Do you think they're warm and full?"

"Mmm-hmm."

"Just like us."

That's what he loved about her: she never took joy for granted.

"Just like us."

"Some of the best moments we've shared have been like this, just looking at nothing . . . and everything. Oh, look!" The lights shifted, like fresh milk spilling upward. "They're beautiful!"

"The only place they're brighter is in Norway," Theodore told her.

"Norway. Mmm . . . I'd like to go there sometime."

"The land of the midnight sun, Ma calls it. When she and Pa first came here they thought they'd never get used to this prairie. No fjords, no trees, no water to speak of, no mountains. The only thing that was the same was 'the lights.' She said when they got to missing the old country so much they couldn't stand it, they used to stand just like we are now, and it got them through."

Somehow Theodore's hand had come to rest on Linnea's breast. It seemed right and good so she held his wrist to keep it there.

"I've missed Nissa this past week," she said.

"Then come home with me. Tonight."

They both realized where his hand was and he moved it. She turned to face him.

"Do you think that's wise?"

"With her and Kristian right there all the time?" He pressed her collar up, leaving his hands circling her neck. "Please, Linnea. I want you back there, and we'll be married as soon as Martin can heat up the church. A week. Two weeks at the most."

She wanted very badly to give in. She'd enjoyed her stay with Clara, but it wasn't home. And it was farther to school, and Trigg had put himself out to get her there these cold mornings. And she'd missed Theodore with an ache so fierce it was frightening. She raised up on tiptoe and hugged him, sudden and hard.

"Yes, I'll come. But they'll be the longest two weeks of our lives."

He crushed her to his sturdy chest and lowered his face to her almond-scented neck and thought that if he had no more than two score years with her he'd be grateful.

He singled out Kristian at the dance the following night. "I need to talk to you, son. Think we could go outside a minute?"

Kristian seemed to measure his father a moment before replying, "Sure."

They went out where the air was brittle and the moon no bigger than a fingernail paring. The surface of the snow crunched beneath their feet and they ambled with no apparent destination, until they found themselves near the clustered wagons. The horses stood asleep with hoarfrost trimming their coarse nose hairs. Unconsciously the two men gravitated toward their own Cub and Toots and stood before their great heads, silent for some time. Down in the barn the music stopped, and the only sound was that of the horses breathing like enormous bellows.

"No lights tonight," Theodore observed at length.

"Nope."

"Lots of 'em last night."

"Oh?"

"Yeah, Linnea and me we . . ." Theodore trailed off and started again. "Son, remember the day you and me we went to Zahl for coal?"

"I remember." Kristian knew already; it wasn't often Theodore called him son, and when he did it was something serious.

"Well, you told me that day how you felt about Linnea, and I want you to know I didn't take it lightly."

It was the second time he'd referred to her as Linnea when he'd never used her given name before.

"You're gonna marry her, aren't you?"

Theodore's heavy hand fell to Kristian's shoulder. "I am, but I got to know how you feel about it."

There was disappointment, but nothing like Kristian had expected. He'd had time to absorb the idea since Nissa's startling deduction.

"When?"

"Week from today if we can arrange it, two weeks if we can't."

"Wow, that's fast."

"Son, it rankled, knowing how you felt about her. I didn't set out to fall in love with her, you got to know that—I mean, after all, there's sixteen years difference between us—but it didn't seem to matter in how we felt. Guess we don't have much choice about who we fall in love with. When it happens it happens, but when it did I had plenty of guilt pangs since you'd set your cap for her first."

Kristian knew what he must say.

"Aw, she just thinks of me as a kid. I can see that now."

"It might surprise you to know that's not true. We've talked about you, and she—"

"You mean she knew how I felt about her?" Kristian's head came up in consternation. "You told her?"

"I didn't have to tell her. What you have to understand is that a woman can tell a thing like that without being told. She could see how you felt and she was scared it'd make for problems in the family." Theodore put his palm beneath Toots's nose, feeling the white puffs of breath push against his glove. "Will it?"

They wouldn't have any problems from Kristian no matter how tough it was for him to get used to her being his father's wife. "Naw. It was probably just puppy love anyway, like Ray says." Kristian strove to lighten the mood. "But I won't have to call her Mother, will I?"

Theodore laughed. "I hardly think so. She'll still be your friend. Why don't you call her Linnea?"

Kristian peered at his father. "Would you mind?"

Theodore was the one who'd come out here to ask that question. It struck him how lucky he was to have a son like Kristian, and he turned to do something he rarely did; he took Kristian in his arms and pressed him close for a minute.

"You'd do well, son, to try to get a boy like you someday. They don't come much better."

"Oh, Pa." Kristian's arms tightened against Theodore's back.

Behind them Cub set up a gentle snoring, and from the barn came the dim sound of a concertina starting another song. In another part of the world soldiers fought for peace, but here, where a father and son pressed heart to heart, peace had already spread its blessing.

Chapter 20

Theodore and Linnea were married on the first Saturday of February in the little country church where Theodore and most of the wedding guests had been baptized. Its pure white spire, like an inverted lily, was set off majestically against the sky's blue breast. The one-note chime of the bell reverberated for miles on the crisp, clean air. In the graveled patch before the building the hitching rails were crowded, but the curious horses turned their blinders toward the automobiles that arrived with sound unlike any whinny they'd ever heard and left a tracery of scent definitely not resembling any leavings of their kind.

Across the delphinium sky a raucous flock of blackbirds sent forth their incessant noise, while from a field of untaken corn came the tuneless roup of pheasants. A freshly fallen snow lay upon the shorn wheat fields like a fine ermine cape, and the sun poured into the modest prairie church through the row of unadorned arched windows, as if to add an omen of joyful promise to the vows about to the exchanged.

Almost all the people who mattered most to Theodore and Linnea were present in the congregation. The horseless carriages belonged to Superintendent Dahl and Selmer Brandonberg, who along with his wife and daughters had arrived early that morning. All the students from P.S. 28 were there, and all of Theodore's family except Clara and Trigg—she'd had a baby girl two days earlier and was still confined to bed. Kristian was Theodore's attendant; Carrie, Linnea's.

The bride wore a simple dress of soft oyster-white wool, brought by her mother from the city. Its hobble skirt was shaped like an unopened tulip bud, no wider at the hem than a ten-gallon barrel. Her matching wide-brimmed hat was wrapped with a frothy nest of white net that made it seem as if a covey of industrious spiders were artfully spinning homes about her head. On her feet were delicate satin pumps with high heels that brought her eyes to a level with Theodore's lips and elicited sighs of envy from all of her female students.

To Theodore, Linnea had never looked prettier.

The groom wore a crisp new suit of charcoal woolen worsted, white shirt, black tie, and a fresh haircut that accentuated his one lop ear and made his neck look like a whooping crane's. His hair was severely slicked back, revealing the remnants of his summer tan that ended an inch above his eyebrows.

To Linnea, Theodore had never looked handsomer.

"Dearly beloved . . ."

Standing before Reverend Severt, the groom was stiff, the bride eager. Speaking their vows, he was sober, she smiling. Bestowing the gold ring, his fingers shook while hers remained steady. When they were pronounced man and wife Theodore emitted a shaky sigh while Linnea beamed. When Reverend Severt said, "You may kiss the bride," he blushed and she licked her lips.

His kiss was brief and self-conscious, with their wedding guests looking on. He leaned from the waist, making certain to touch nothing but her lips while she rested a hand on his sleeve and lifted her face to him as naturally as a sunflower lifts its petals to the sun. Her eyelids drifted closed but his remained open.

In the carriage on the way to the schoolhouse, with her father's and Superintendent Dahl's automobiles spluttering along behind them, he sat stiff as an oak bole while she contentedly pressed her breast and cheek against his arm.

At the schoolhouse, throughout a dinner provided by all the church women, he was stiff and formal while conversing with her parents, acting as if he were scared to death to touch their daughter in front of them. When the dancing started he waltzed mechanically with Linnea, making certain their bodies stayed a respectable distance apart.

The most romantic thing he said all day was when Selmer and Judith congratulated them. "I'll take very good care of her. You don't have to worry about that, sir."

But at the dubious expression on her father's face and the crestfallen one on her mother's, Linnea could see they were not reassured.

She herself was rather amused by Theodore's uncharacteristic nervousness. There were times when she looked up and caught him studying her across the room, and to her delight, *he'd* be the one to blush. She watched him drinking beer and was fully aware of his taking care not to drink too much. And when she danced with Lars, or Ulmer, or John, she knew his eyes followed admiringly. But he was careful not to get caught at it.

Now they stood in the dusk of late afternoon with her father's car chugging off down the road and the new snow shimmering in the brilliant glow of a tangerine sunset. From inside the school building it sounded as if the fun were just beginning. Theodore buried his hands in his pockets as he looked at his wife. ''Well . . .'' He cleared his throat and glanced at the building. ''Should we go back in?''

The last thing in the world she wanted to do was go back in to mingle and dance like a pair of wooden Indians. They were husband and wife now. She wanted them to be alone . . . and close.

''For how long?''

''Well . . . I mean, do you want to dance?''

''Not really, Theodore. Do you?'' she inquired, gazing up fetchingly.

''I . . . well . . .'' He shrugged, glanced at the schoolhouse door again, tugged out his watch, and snapped it open. ''It's only a little after five,'' he noted nervously, then put the watch away.

Her eyes followed as it flashed in the waning daylight and disappeared inside the pocket of a tapered vest that had captivated her all day long, clinging to his ribs and pointing to his stomach.

''And people would think it was strange if we left at such an odd time of the day?''

Her bold conjecture corrupted his calm. He swallowed hard and stared at her, wondering exactly what people *would* say if they left now.

''Wouldn't they?'' he choked out.

Poor Teddy, suffering with buck fever on his wedding night. She could see she'd have to be the one to get things started.

''We could tell them we're going to stop by Clara and Trigg's, like we promised.''

''But we already did that on the way to the church.''

She stepped close and rested a hand on his breast. ''I want to go home, Teddy,'' she requested softly.

''Oh, well then, of course. If you're tired, we'll leave right away.''

''I'm not tired. I just want to go home. Don't you want to?''

At her request Theodore's skin grew damp in selective spots. Lord, where did she get the calm? His stomach felt as if it held a hundred fists that clenched tighter every time he thought about the night ahead.

''Well, I . . . yes.'' He worked a finger inside his celluloid collar and stretched his neck. ''It would feel good to get this thing off.''

She raised up on tiptoe, balanced eight fingertips against his chest, and kissed him lightly. ''Then let's go,'' she whispered. She heard the sharp hiss of indrawn breath as his palms dropped over her upper arms. He cast a cautious glance at the schoolhouse door and dropped a light kiss on her forehead.

"We'll have to say our good-byes."

"Let's say them then."

He turned her by an elbow and they moved around a horse and buggy and up the steps.

Kristian was having a wonderful time. He'd had a couple of beers, and danced with all the girls. It was plain as the pug nose on Carrie Brandonberg's face that she liked him. A lot. But every time he danced with her, Patricia Lommen's eyes followed every move they made. A song ended and he sought her out, teasing, "Next one's yours, Patricia, if you want it."

"Think you're special, don't you, Westgaard? Like you're the only boy in the place I'd care to waltz with."

"Well, ain't I?"

"Hmph!" She turned her nose in the air and tried to whip away, but he swung her into his arms without asking permission, and in seconds they were cozying up in a waltz. The longer they danced, the closer they got. Her breasts brushed his suit coat and one thing led to another, and somehow, by some magic, she was pressed against him. He thought nothing had ever felt so good in his entire life.

"You sure smell good, Patricia," he said against her ear.

"I borrowed my mother's violet water."

Her cheek rested on his jaw and the warmth of their skins seemed to mingle.

"Well, I sure like it."

"Smells like you got into your pa's bay rum, too."

They backed up and looked into each other's eyes and laughed and laughed. And both fell silent at once. And felt a wondrous tug in their vitals, and moved close again, learning what it feels like when two bodies brush.

When the song ended he held her hand. His heart slammed with the uncertainty of all first times. "It's kinda warm in here. Want to go cool off in the cloakroom for a while?"

She nodded and led the way. They had the chilly room to themselves, but moved to a far corner. From behind, he watched as she fluffed the hair up off her neck.

"Hoo! It *was* warm in there."

"You might get chilled. You want me to get your coat?"

She swung to face him. "No. This feels good."

"Hey, you're a good dancer, you know that?"

"Not as good as you, though."

"Yes, you are."

"No, I'm not, but I have better grammar. At least I don't say ain't."

"I don't say ain't anymore."

"You just did. When I was teasing you about being the only boy in the place I wanted to waltz with."

"I did?"

They laughed and fell silent, trying to think of something else to say.

"Last time we were in the cloakroom alone you gave me the scarf you made for me for Christmas. I felt bad cause I didn't have anything to give you back."

She shrugged and toyed with the sleeve of somebody's jacket hanging beside them. "I didn't want anything back."

She had the prettiest eyes he'd ever seen, and when she looked away shyly, as she was doing now, he wanted to raise her chin and say, "Don't look away from me." But he was scared to death to touch her.

Suddenly she looked smack at him. "My mother says—" Their gazes locked and nothing more came out. Her lips dropped open and his eyes fell to them—pretty, bowed lips; just looking at them made his heart churn like a steam engine gone berserk.

"What does your mother say?" he whispered in a reedy voice.

"What?" she whispered back.

They stared at each other as if for the first time and felt the thrum of fear and expectation beat through their inexperienced bodies. He leaned to touch her lips with his—a kiss as simple and uncomplicated as youth. But when he backed up he saw she was as breathless and blushing as he. He kissed her a second time and timidly rested his hands on her waist to pull her closer. She came without compunction, hooking her hands lightly on his shoulders. When the second kiss ended they backed off and smiled at each other. Then his eyes swerved to the corner and hers dropped to his chest while they both wondered how many kisses were allowable the first time. But in seconds their gazes were drawn together again. There was scarcely a moment's hesitation before her arms lifted and his circled, and they were as close as when they'd been dancing, with their lips sealed tightly.

The outside door opened and he leaped back, blushing furiously but gripping her hand without realizing it.

It was his father and Linnea.

As the newlyweds passed into the shadowed cloakroom they looked up in surprise as two startled figures untwined from an embrace.

"Kristian . . ." Linnea said. "Oh, and Patricia. Hello."

"Hello," they replied in unison.

Linnea felt Theodore halt at her shoulder, staring at his son, obviously perplexed about how to handle such a situation. She spoke into the breach with a naturalness that eased the guilt from Patricia's face and made her stop trying to free her hand from Kristian's nervous grip.

"Your father and I are going home now. Are you staying for the rest of the dance?"

Patricia lifted hopeful eyes to Kristian. The message in them could be read even across the dim confines of the cloakroom. The young man met her gaze, looked back at the pair who'd interrupted, and answered, "For a while, anyway. Then I'll be taking Patricia home. I thought I'd take the wagon, if that's all right with you, Pa."

"That's . . . that's fine. Well, you be careful then, and we'll see you in the morning."

Kristian nodded.

"Well, excuse us while we go in and say our good-byes," Linnea put in.

Kristian nodded once more.

When the farewells were said and they left, the cloakroom was empty. The familiar green wagon was absent from the schoolyard. Searching for it, Theodore frowned.

''Now where do you suppose they've went to?''

''They've *gone* to Patricia's house, in all likelihood. Wouldn't you have when you were their age and the place was deserted while the folks were at a wedding dance?''

He glanced up the road to the east. Standing beside their own black carriage she looked up at the freshly cut hair above his coat collar, his wide shoulders, and his distracted eyes. *The time has come, Theodore, for them and for us. Don't fight it.* Possessively, she slipped a hand under his arm and asked in a quite tone, ''Wouldn't you, *now* when the place is deserted and we have it all to ourselves?'' Nissa had gone back to Clara's right after the church service and would be there for at least a week.

He looked down at her, and from the expression on his face she knew Kristian and Patricia had fled his mind.

She made the short ride home beside a stiff, formal stranger, who dropped her at the door and left her to worry while he drove down toward the barn to see to the horse and buggy.

The kitchen was cold. She lit a lamp then sat on a hard chair at the table. Her clothes and personal items were still in her old bedroom upstairs. When would they be moved down? And who would move them?

The door opened and Theodore stepped inside, bringing a current of chill night air that made the lantern flame twist and flicker. He stood looking around the room as if it belonged to someone else. His eyes moved back to Linnea with her high net-swathed hat still on her head, her coat still buttoned, and her gloved hands folded in her lap.

''You're cold. I'll get a fire going.''

She sensed his great relief at having something to do as he made the stove clatter and chime. In no time at all he clapped the lid over the fire, and the room fell silent.

Linnea rose from her chair and Theodore wiped his palms on his thighs as she came to stand near him at the stove.

''Well . . .'' he said with an uncertain smile.

She wondered if she'd have to be the one to initiate every move throughout this night. What a disappointing thought. She'd imagined that a man who'd been married before would be very adept at this. Instead, Theodore flinched each time she drew near, and his eyes wandered from hers whenever she tried to catch his gaze.

Turning aside, she held out her hands toward the thin warmth from the fire. He studied the back of her hat, the froth of ivory net with its tiny slubs like morning dew caught in a spider web, the fine separations in her hair where built-in combs clung to hold the flowery concoction on her head. She dropped her chin and his glance was drawn to the proper little crescent hairstyle beneath the hat brim, the shallow well at her nape where several loose hairs caught on her wool collar. He let his eyes rove from her narrow shoulders to her hips to the hem of her coat, and he was clutched by an ache of arousal so fierce he rammed his hands beneath his armpits to keep from shocking her with what he wanted to do at this ungodly hour of the day. And in the kitchen yet.

''Well, everyone seemed to be having a good time at the dance,'' she said, though the dance was the farthest thing from her mind.

''Do you want your coat off now?'' he asked at the same moment.

''Oh, yes, I guess so.'' She tugged the new gray gloves from her fingers while he stood watching over her shoulder. She tucked them into her coat pocket, then unbuttoned the garment. He peeled it from her shoulders and stood uncertainly, wondering what to do with it. She had always kept it in her bedroom upstairs.

She glanced over her shoulder and their gazes collided for an electrified second. ''Well, I reckon I'll hang this in my room now.''

He turned into the front parlor and she listened to his footsteps snapping across the linoleum.

In the semi-dark he hung her coat on a hook, then stood for a moment clinging to the hook with both hands, recalling how carefully he'd dust-mopped the floor in here, and changed the bedding, and put the room in perfect order. Probably not as clean as Ma would have done, but the best he could do. He heaved a deep breath and headed back for the kitchen.

At the sound of his returning footsteps Linnea snatched up the teakettle and began industriously filling it from the water pail.

From the doorway he watched her move across the room with tiny, careful steps in the skirt too narrow to allow proper movement. Such foolishness. Last year bird wings, this year narrow skirts that seemed like shackles. He supposed he'd be paying for many feminine geegaws in his life. But he didn't mind. He wanted to do so much for her . . . so much. And besides, there was something about the skirt and the way it revealed her ankles that turned a man's head clean around.

''What's that called then, that skirt?''

''A hobble.''

''It's a mite skinny, isn't it?'' He watched from behind as she set the kettle on the stove, then swung around brightly.

''Mother says they're all the rage. A Harvard professor said narrower hems would save on wool for uniforms . . . so this is . . . the . . .''

Looking at him, her words trailed away. He stood staring at her, tallying the hours till their normal bedtime. God in heaven, some nights when they were studying they hadn't gone to bed till nearly eleven o'clock. That was a good five hours and more!

''Are you hungry?'' she asked, as if suddenly inspired.

''No.'' He tapped his vest buttons for effect. ''I ate plenty at the school.'' Guiltily, he remembered his manners. ''Oh, are you?''

''No, not a bit.'' She glanced around as if searching for something. ''Well . . .'' Now he had her doing it! An hour ago she'd been totally confident. Now his jitters were rubbing off on her. ''My things are all upstairs yet. Should I . . . I mean . . .''

''Oh, I'll get them. Might as well bring them down to my room, too.''

He practically leaped to the spare lantern in his eagerness to get out of the room. When she heard his footsteps halt above her she smiled, covered her mouth with one hand, and shook her head at the floor. Then she followed him up the stairs to find him standing in her doorway, rattled and uncertain.

"Excuse me, Theodore." He jumped aside to let her pass, then watched her move to the dresser, open drawers, and select things, piling them on her arm—everything white, some with wisps of eyelet and blue ribbon. From the dresser top she took a brass-handled brush, a comb, a hairpin holder, and a heart-shaped bottle of toilet water; from a hook behind the door, her blue chenille robe. Then, on last thought, she returned to the dresser for a small rock.

Joining him, she said brightly, "There. I guess that's everything I need. The rest can wait till tomorrow."

"What's that?" He pointed to her hand.

She opened her palm and they both looked down. "It's an agate I found on the road last fall. It has a stripe of brown the exact color of your eyes."

She looked into them and he was caught off guard, awed afresh by the fact that she was really his and that as long ago as last fall she'd been interested in the color of his eyes. But he stepped back as she moved through the door and down the steps, with the light from his lantern gilding the top of her hat. At his bedroom doorway she stopped politely and let him lead the way inside and set the lantern on the dresser.

Her eyes followed hesitantly, but the picture of Melinda was gone. Theodore opened a dresser drawer, then straightened to face her, eager to please. "You can put your things in here. I cleaned it out and threw some old things away to make room."

"Thank you, Theodore." She placed her collection in the drawer beside a stack of blue cambric work shirts and a pair of elastic sleeve holders he never used. His blood pounded, having her so close. It had been so long since he'd watched a woman do such things: smooth the clothes, shut the drawer, align her brush and comb on the dresser scarf, place the rock and the hairpin dish and the bottle of toilet water beside two spare celluloid collars, his own hairbrush and . . . and a handful of *rivets?*

His hand lashed out and scooped them up. "I was fixin' a harness yesterday," he explained sheepishly and dropped them into a drawer, then slammed it guiltily behind him.

With a tilting smile she stepped over and opened the drawer again, nudging him out of the way. She dug in the corner beneath a pile of winter underwear and found the metal pieces, and dropped them where they'd been before, on top of the dresser.

"This is still your room. If we're to share it, you may leave your rivets exactly where you did before you married me."

Had she recited a flowery poem, he could not have loved her more at that moment. He wondered again what time it was and if she'd think him perverted if he leaned over and kissed her and carried her to the bed as he wanted to, ignoring the fact that the rest of the world was either doing their milking or eating their supper right now. Or dancing at his wedding dance without him. What in God's name were they doing talking about rivets? How did a man lead up to the suggestion that his wife get ready for bed at five forty-five in the afternoon?

She looked around the room, all guileless and innocent, her top-heavy hat making her neck appear very fragile. The bodice of her dress disappeared beneath a form-fitting jacket with a high neck and tiny looped buttons running waist to throat. Lord, let it be a whole dress under there, he thought, as he suggested, "You might like to take your jacket and hat off and get more comfortable, so I'll leave you alone for a few minutes."

She'd had dreams of how this night should be. They had not included a painfully shy husband. She remembered things Clara had told her, and she greedily wanted it all. In a soft, quavering voice, she ventured, "I thought that was the husband's job."

Theodore's eyes shifted to the clock that stood on the bedside stand ticking, ticking, ticking into the sudden silence, the hour hand nearly touching six. He looked back into his wife's eyes. "Did you?"

She nodded twice, so slightly he had to watch closely to catch it. Her eyes were wide and lustrous in the lamplight as she stood with one hand resting on the edge of the dresser.

He took one step and her lips parted. He took a second and she swallowed. He took a third and her head tilted up, her eyes dark now, lifting to his from underneath the hat brim. They stood close, rapt, watching each other breathe. He kissed her once, very lightly, much more lightly than he wanted, then turned her around by the shoulders. In the mirror she saw only the top half of his face above the beehive of netting.

His blunt fingertips searched out the teardrop pearl and withdrew a nine-inch hatpin. He clamped it in his teeth and gently freed the combs behind her ears. As he lifted the hat free, one comb caught a blond strand and pulled it free. She reached up nervously to brush it back while he anchored the pin in the hat and set it down before her.

Their eyes met in the mirror, so dark neither appeared to have color beyond the sparkle of anticipation. The wisp of loose hair trailed free behind her ear. He stood so close his breath sent it waving like a strand of wheat in a summer breeze. He touched it, lifting and clumsily tucking it back in, then watched it drift stubbornly down her thin, sculptured neck. She waited breathlessly, willing him to go on. As if he divined her thoughts, his unaccustomed fingers probed the secrets of her chignon, finding celluloid pins hidden within, freeing them one by one until the mass of gold drooped, then tumbled under its own weight to lay in a furl on her shoulders. He combed it with callused fingers. Its fine texture caught on his horny skin. When had he last smelled a woman's hair? He bent and buried his face in the fragrant mass, and drew a prolonged breath. In the mirror she watched his face disappear then reappear as he straightened.

When their eyes met, a thousand pulsebeats seemed to fight for space in his throat. She had taken up the perfume bottle. Holding his gaze in the mirror, she slowly uncapped it, tipped it against a fingertip, then brushed the scent beneath her uptilted jaw. Once, twice, until lily of the valley had turned the room to a bower. She pushed back a cuff, exposing the delicate blue-veined skin of one wrist, scented it, then the other, and silently recapped the bottle, all the while holding him prisoner with her sapphire eyes.

Where had a girl her age learned to do a thing like that? All day long, each time he'd thought of this hour, his imagination had stalled at the thought of her inexperience. But her invitation was unmistakable.

He pressed her arms, pivoted her like a ballerina in a music box, then studied her shadowed eyes momentarily before reaching for the button at her throat. It was a quarter the size of his thumbnail, caught in a delicate loop that thwarted his fumbling fingers twice before he discovered how to manage it. Then slowly, slowly he worked his way down thirteen of the same.

Beneath the jacket her bodice fit taut over breasts that lifted and fell to the rapid beat of her breathing. He lifted his eyes to her delicate mouth, the lips parted and waiting.

How incredible—they were man and wife.

He bent to touch her mouth with his own, the shadow of her hair eclipsing his face as he cupped her jaws and kissed her with a first tender consideration—soft, plucking, plural kisses while the sleek warmth of his inner lips joined hers. She swayed toward him, her fingertips touching his lapels.

When at length he lifted his head, they were both breathing harder, their hearts dancing a rondo as they gazed into each other's eyes.

Wordlessly he removed her jacket, folded it, and laid it on the dresser.

She reached for his tie and collar button, determined to do her share.

Tick, tick, tick came from the bedside.

"It's only six o'clock," he reminded her in a strange, forced voice.

Her fingers fell still at his throat. Her clear, guileless eyes lifted and met his squarely.

"Is there a right and a wrong time?"

He'd never pondered the question before. In his whole life he'd never done anything like this except at bedtime, in the sheath of late hours and darkness. With something akin to surprise he realized he'd come here prepared to be the teacher, only to find himself being taught.

"No, I guess not," he replied, and his heart thrust hard as she proceeded, removing his tie, opening his collar, and freeing the top three shirt buttons until the vest stopped her progress. Glistening dark hair sprang into view, and she pressed her lips into the cleft, something she'd long imagined doing.

A ragged breath fanned the top of her hair and his arms came around her.

"Your jacket," she interrupted, and he pulled back and let her take it from him to hang on a wall hook beside her coat. Next, she freed his vest buttons, then took his watch in her hand and looked up at him.

"Let's never watch clocks, Teddy," she requested softly, then laid it on the dresser.

When she turned he was waiting to haul her near, slanting his mouth over hers with lips open, tongue searching out the treasures of her willing mouth. She pressed close, lifting, nestling. His arms swept her up commandingly and took her against muscle and sinew she'd touched too few times—ah, far too few.

The kiss twisted between them with wondrous urgency, his tongue slewing the interior of her mouth, hers probing in a wild, loving quest. She spread her fingers wide over the warm satin back of his vest, inquisitive to know each taut inch of him. His chest heaved against her breasts, making them yearn for more.

He ripped his mouth from hers, labored breath pouring on her ear. "Oh, Linnea . . ."

She backed away only far enough to search his eyes. ''What's wrong, Teddy? All day long you've been acting as if you're scared to death of me.''

''I am.'' He chuckled ruefully—a forced, pained sound in the lamplit room, then he scraped the hair back from her temples and held her head in two broad palms. ''You're so young. It keeps coming back to me, no matter how I try to put it from my mind.''

''I'm not. I'm a woman, and I'm ready for this. You have a fixation with time—clocks, years. What do they matter when there's love? Please . . . please . . .'' She dropped a nosegay of quick kisses on his chin, his cheek, his mouth. ''Please . . . count the love, not the years. I'm your wife now. Don't make me wonder any longer.''

One quick, unresolved kiss, then he drew back to search her dress for closures. Without a word she presented her back, lifting her hair aside while he released buttons to her spine. Inside she wore a sleeveless white cotton garment that disappeared into her petticoats. He watched, fascinated, as she unbuttoned the waistband of those petticoats, then shimmied the dress down her arms and let both drop over her slim hips.

When she turned to face him he saw her undergarment fully. It covered her from shoulder to mid-thigh, where it was banded with elastic on both legs. The waist was secured by a thin white cord tied in front. The scoop-necked bodice held another row of buttons—closed—revealing little more than the shadows at her collarbones.

His ma wore undershirts and snuggies, and in winter, long underwear. He'd never seen anything like the white bit his wife had on. Filmy stockings disappeared inside the pantaloonlike legs, and her calves were slender and shapely as she stood before him in the gleaming satin shoes that arched her foot daintily.

When his eyes rose from them to her face, both Theodore and Linnea were flushed and breathless.

A self-conscious smile winged past her lips and disappeared. His vest took a sudden ride down his arms and landed on the floor behind him, revealing crisp black suspenders that dented the shoulders of his starched shirt. He hooked them with his thumbs and sent them drooping, then yanked his shirttails out of his trousers and reached for her hand, holding it loosely while his eyes wandered to her breasts and he unconsciously freed his last few shirt buttons.

It was a glorious sight, watching him undress. Watching the play of shrugging shoulder muscles, and suspenders falling, and a sea of wrinkles appearing on a shirt bottom, and wrists twisting while cuffs were freed.

Then the shirt lay on the floor and Linnea couldn't withhold an exclamation of appreciation.

''Oh, Theodore . . .'' she breathed on a falling note. ''Look at youuu . . .'' Impulsively she reached out four fingertips and tested the dark hair that branched across his warm chest, then followed it halfway down his belly before realizing where she was heading. Quickly she retracted the curious hand and clasped it with the other. Her wide eyes flashed up. He captured her hand and placed it on the spot it had abandoned.

It played over him, tantalized.

How hard, how silky, how masculine. How wondrously different from herself he was. While she explored the hollow of his throat, the backs of his knuckles stroked her collarbone, then brushed down her front buttons.

She forgot how to breathe.

His hand moved back up and gently cupped a breast.

Her eyes dropped closed and she stood shadow still, steeped in sensation. Goose bumps climbed her arms, her belly, rippled the breast he gently kneaded. It hardened for him and changed shape beneath his palm. His tongue touched her lower lip, traced a wet, circular path, bringing him back to the point of origin, which he bit and sucked into his mouth, massaging it with only the tip of his tongue until she wriggled slightly and shivered. Up stole her hands to his chest, his neck, his hair, fingers spreading wide within it, caressing his skull as she pulled his head down to receive a bride's kiss.

Her tongue danced lustily within his mouth. Her body strained high, pulsing against him until he took both breasts and felt her driving the handfuls of flesh into his clasp. Around her back he reached, hands skimming down her buttocks, gripping hard to lift her high against him. Rhythm began, a sweet slow lolling that rocked them one against the other.

He set a river flowing in her body, flooding its banks. The sensation was so sudden it took the starch from her knees. As she drooped, their mouths parted with a soft succulent sound, and for a moment he bore her weight with a knee, until, astride, she knew a momentary relief from the pressures building within. The knee let her back to the floor, then slipped away.

His hands played over her spine. Their tongues and lips were joined when he first touched bare skin on her backside. His head jerked up in surprise.

"What is this thing?"

Arms looped around his neck, she tilted her head back, somewhat surprised, too. Truly, she thought he'd have known.

"A teddy."

"A what?" He backed away and looked down, holding her loosely by the waist.

"A teddy. The kind that's not named after Mr. Roosevelt."

He chuckled and gave it a second look.

"Mmm . . . a teddy, huh?" Kissing her again he buried his hand inside an open porthole that seemed to extend from the back of her waist to eternity. He soothed her curved flesh while wondering exactly how far the access extended, moved to explore her stomach, and sure enough, the open placket ran from belly to backside, under her legs.

But as his explorations continued, the construction of her garments ceased to matter. His fingers found their way inside the white cotton welt and flattened over her warm stomach to ride lower, lower, finally touching her intimately. At his entry she jumped once, then relaxed against the strong arm banding her waist. Worlds of wonder opened up in her mind's eye, worlds no amount of imagination had prepared her for. Colors danced behind her closed lids, from pastoral to passionate. She swayed and rocked against him, flowing into primal rhythm.

His touch went deeper, infusing her with delight in her own flesh.

"Oh, Teddy . . . Teddy . . ." she murmured, awash with desire.

He left her to move toward the lantern, and she called softly, "No!" He paused, turning. "Please . . . I've never . . . I mean . . ." Her cheeks pinkened and she looked down at her hands, then resolutely at him. "I want to see you."

His heart drummed heavily at her request. He had not thought of women that way—a new lesson for Theodore Westgaard.

Leaving the lantern glowing softly, he drew her to the side of the bed and leaned down to loosen his shoestrings. She followed suit, slipping the satin shoes from her heels and setting them neatly side by side. He reached beneath his trouser legs to peel off his stockings, and again she followed his lead, rolling her elastic garters to her ankles and taking the opaque stockings with them. He stretched to his feet, unbuttoned and doffed his trousers, but her eyes remained downcast as she realized he was standing before her naked.

"Linnea . . ."

She raised her eyes in an evasive sweep until they locked with his. The only sound in the room was the tick of the clock and the thunder of their hearts in their ears. He reached out a hand, palm up. She placed hers in it and he drew her to her feet and dispensed with the teddy without further delay.

Before she had time to grow self-conscious he swept her to the bed, dropping beside her in a full-length embrace. With their mouths joined, he rolled her to her back, finding her naked breast first with his hand, then with his tongue, murmuring low in his throat as it pearled up in nature's reach for more. He laved it, leaving it wet for the stroke of his thumb. He smiled down at it, then rubbed his soft, upturned lips over its ascended tip with infinite gentleness before turning his attention to its twin.

She twisted languorously, murmuring his name, lifting in invitation, threading his hair with her fingers. His wet tongue felt silken and profoundly powerful as he suckled, released, suckled again, drawing sensation from deep in her belly. She cried out, one ecstatic hosanna, as he tugged gently with his teeth. She lolled, immersed in pleasure, stretching her arms over her head until her belly went hollow and he stroked it with his hand, then gave it a lingering kiss before crushing her tightly, taking her on a rolling journey across the bed. She landed on top and shinnied down for more of his mouth. Her hair caught between them; he flicked it aside and kissed her almost roughly. She clung, returning stroke for stroke.

After long minutes she lifted her face.

He held the hair back from her temples with both hands, eyes glittering up at her with dark, intense passion. "Linnea, I love you. I used to lay here alone and think of this. So many nights, when you were upstairs, over my head. But you're better than you were in my wishes."

I love you . . .

I love you . . .

I love you . . .

Some of the words were his, some hers, indistinguishable one from the other as they sated themselves upon kisses until kisses would no longer suffice.

He rolled her to her back, leaning above her, studying her eyes while their hearts pounded with one accord. A brief kiss on her parted lips, a briefer one on her breast, a hand on her stomach, an intense flame leaping from his gaze to hers while he reached low, low . . .

He touched her with care, tutored her limbs to widen beneath his caress, her flesh to blossom to his exploration. And when she was lithe and lissome and fervid, he captured her hand and curled it inside his own, then placed it on his distended flesh and taught her some things a woman has to know.

He closed his eyes and groaned softly while his flesh slipped through her hand. His head dropped back, while she wondered at her power to bring such abandon to a man so strong and indomitable. When he trembled and his breathing grew ragged, there awaited that greatest pleasure of all. He hovered above her and his voice came shaken at her ear. ''If anything hurts, tell me and I'll stop. Now easy . . . easy . . .''

His entry was slow, sacred. His elbows trembled near her shoulders while he waited. She drew him deep.

''Lin, ahh, Lin . . .'' came his utterance as she lifted to impale herself.

Nature had planned nothing in vain; sword to sheath, key to lock—they fit with an arcane exquisiteness. He found her no girl, but all the woman he'd ever want. She taught him a new youth, a boundless thing of the heart rather than the calendar. Lying beneath the sinuous motion of his driving hips she followed his wordless commands and lifted in accommodation. She came to know the touch of his breath moving her hair and warming her neck; he the gentle grip of those strands as they coiled against his damp forehead. Together they discovered a timeless lovers' language fashioned of murmurs and rustles and sighs. She learned his capacity for gentleness; he her capacity for strength. Together they learned when to reverse roles. He found a joy in making her arch and gasp, she an equal joy in his shuddering call of release. She discovered that twice was possible for a man; he that thrice was not enough for some women.

And the keen, seeping pleasure to be found in the after minutes. Ahh, those weak, wilted stretches of time when their sapped bodies could do no more or no less than tangle together in sated exhaustion.

And years mattered little. All that mattered was that they were man and wife, consummate, that it was their wedding night and through it they gave each other the ultimate recompense for all of life's tribulations . . . again . . . and again . . . and again . . .

Chapter 21

It was a winter of great change, that winter of 1918. The changes happened not only within the Westgaard family, but within their newest member, and throughout the world at large. In her blissful, newly married state it would have been easy for Linnea to forget that American doughboys were going to France to make the world safe for democracy and to bask instead in the happiness that glowed within her heart. But the example set by her own family made her realize she, too, had an obligation, perhaps an even greater one in her position as a teacher. Linnea talked Superintendent Dahl into allowing the school to subscribe to the newspaper, and with the children she followed the events in Europe in an effort to understand.

The cry to defeat Germany was everywhere, but while in late January it was announced that the first U.S. troops were occupying front-line trenches, stateside military camps were still bulging with restless soldiers forced to drill in civilian clothes with broomsticks instead of rifles. Democratic fervor alone would not win the war. It would take supplies, and supplies took raw materials, and raw materials were limited. The War Board was formed to determine production priorities, and America cheerfully tightened up, cut back, and sang rousing patriotic songs. New factories sprang up overnight, turning out overcoats, shoes, rifles, gas masks, blankets, trucks, and locomotives, while all businesses not engaged in war contracts closed on Mondays. A ban was put on Sunday automobile driving. People were encouraged to use more sweaters and less coal, eat more bran and less wheat, more spinach and less meat, and adopt the ''gospel of the clean plate.'' But above all, Americans were asked to give.

What it gave most of was its men. A half million of them reached France by the spring of 1918, and one of the volunteers was Bill Westgaard. The church had a special service for him on the Saturday before he left, and from that day on a service flag bearing a single blue star hung in the nave, raising countless prayers that there never come a time when a gold star be sewn in its place. Shortly thereafter, Judith wrote with the news that Adrian Mitchell had received a draft notice and was already gone.

Bill and Adrian may have been rejected suitors, but it mattered little to Linnea. The war had touched her personally now, and she felt a zeal to do her part in whatever way possible.

There were countless things the children could do to help with the war effort; all they needed was organization. Noon knitting became the favorite pastime. Linnea herself sought Nissa's help in learning how, and each mother was asked to teach her daughters. At school a chart was posted, with a star for each stocking or muffler completed. To Linnea's amazement, Kristian and Ray showed up one day, each with a ball of yarn and a pair of needles. It caused a great deal of laughter when the boys awkwardly took up the craft, but soon they had every boy in the schoolhouse joining them. With the exception of Allen Severt, who adamantly called knitting ''sissy stuff'' and became an outcast because of his attitude.

But all the others were willing and eager to help with all of Linnea's plans. Patricia Lommen came up with the idea of piecing a quilt and everybody enthusiastically agreed to bring scraps of cloth from home. As the children watched it take shape, plans were begun for an auction sale at which to sell it, proceeds to be donated to the Red Cross. Word of the auction spread and the cloakroom began filling with a motley collection of donations, including several prime muskrat skins from Ray and Kristian. Libby Severt, who showed a promising talent in art, made two large posters advertising the event: one was hung in the church, the other in the Alamo General Store and Post Office. A farmer from a neighboring township volunteered a player piano and even offered to deliver it. From then until the day of the auction, the schoolhouse rang with music.

It was Nissa who suggested a cakewalk to go along with the auction, and soft-hearted Frances who read in the newspaper about clothing drives for refugees and shyly suggested taking up a collection for that cause along with all the rest.

The big day was dubbed "War Day," and as it approached excitement ran high and auction items overflowed into the main schoolroom. An auctioneer from Wildrose volunteered his services and old man Tveit brought an unexpected wagon of coal to put up for auction. By the time the day was over, P.S. 28 had earned $768.34 for the noble cause.

Theodore watched Linnea bloom throughout that winter. She took up her war project with characteristic enthusiasm and carried it to completion only to immediately begin another: this time a book drive for soldiers overseas. It was as successful as the auction sale had been. After the book drive came the making of scrapbooks for soldiers lying in European hospitals and the formation of a Junior League to sell liberty bonds. And when the state school board officially announced that the study of the German language was being dropped from all curricula, she stood up in church one Sunday and requested that in accordance with the current administration's fervor for Americanization, all table prayers be said in English instead of Norwegian. How could anyone refuse a woman who'd almost single-handedly raised $768 in the name of life, liberty, and the pursuit of happiness?

And if Linnea brought a fervid enthusiasm to her organizational abilities, she brought no less to her marriage. She turned nineteen in late February and was fond of whispering into Theodore's ear as she lay atop him in bed at night that she was learning more during her nineteenth year than in all the years of her life. And it was much more fun.

She was an ardent, uninhibited lover, insistent on "trying" things even Theodore had never tried before.

"How come you know about that?" he asked one night when the quilts were thrown back and the lantern was burning, as usual.

"Clara told me."

"Clara!"

"Shh!" She covered his lips and giggled.

He lowered his voice to a whisper. "You mean my little sister, Clara?"

"Your little sister Clara is a woman, in case you hadn't noticed, and she and Trigg have a wonderful time in bed. But if Clara ever finds out I told you, she'll kill me."

"Hmm . . . I'll have to remember to thank Clara next time I see her."

She socked him a good one. "Teddy, don't you dare!" He caught her wrists and flung her beneath him and bit her bottom lip.

"You wanna talk about it all night or you wanna try it, Mrs. Westgaard?"

Within minutes they were trying it.

Another time, after they'd made love, Linnea lay in the crook of Theodore's shoulder, thinking of how she used to wonder what lovemaking would be like.

She chuckled and admitted, "I used to think you'd squash me like a bug if we ever made love together."

A rumble of laughter sounded beneath her ear. "Oh? So you used to think about it?"

"Sometimes."

"How much?"

"Oh, I don't know."

"Come on . . . how much?"

"Oh, all right. A lot."

"When?"

"What do you mean, when?"

"I mean, how long before we were married?"

"Mmm . . . at least four years."

"Four—aw, you didn't even know me then."

"Yes I did. But your name at that time was Lawrence."

"Lawrence!"

"Oh, lay back down and don't get all huffed up. I had to name you *some*thing, since I didn't know who you were yet."

A powerful arm looped her neck in a lazy headlock. "Girl, you're a little bit crazy, you know that?"

"I know."

He chuckled again. "So tell me what you used to imagine."

"Oh . . . at first I used to imagine how it was to kiss a boy—I mean a man. I've kissed an awful lot of strange things in my day. Tables, icy windows, pillows—pillows work really well, actually, if you haven't got the real thing. Then there are blackboards, the back of your own hand, plates, doors—"

"Plates?"

"Well, sometimes when I'd be doing the dishes I'd imagine I'd just finished having supper with a man and he was helping me do the cleanup afterward. I mean, you look in this nice clean plate and there's this person looking back at you, and you close your eyes and pretend and . . . well, you've got to use your imagination, Theodore."

"Not anymore, I don't," he countered, and rolled her onto his belly to end the night as they ended each.

She was more than he'd ever hoped for. She was bright, happy, spontaneous. She made each day a joyous sharing, a cause for celebration, a span of hours so piercingly rich and full he wondered how he'd ever survived those solitary years without her. He took her to school each morning, and from the moment he kissed her good-bye beside the warming stove, he counted the hours till he could go back and collect her. He never knew what she'd come up with next. She saw things from a refreshingly youthful perspective that often made him laugh, and always made him happy she was as young as she was.

One particularly frigid morning as they stood beside the stove waiting for the building to warm up, the school mouse slipped out of hiding and cowered by the mop board.

"Didn't you ever catch that pest?"

"I never tried. I didn't have the heart to kill the poor little thing, so I've been feeding him cheese instead. He's my friend."

"Feeding him! Linnea, mice are—"

"Shh! He's cold . . . see? Be very still and watch."

They stood silently, unmoving, until the mouse timidly scuttled closer, drawn by the heat, and stood on the opposite side of the stove on his hind legs, warming his front feet as if they were human hands.

Theodore had never seen anything like it in his life.

''Do you two do this often?'' Theodore asked, and at the sound of his voice the creature retreated, stopped, and turned a bright-pink eye on them.

''There's enough death—don't you think—that we don't have to cause any more.''

He wondered if it were possible to love any stronger than he did at that moment. Life had never been more perfect.

But one day in late March Kristian shattered that perfection.

He'd been down along the creek bottom with Ray, hauling in their traps for the season, and at supper that night, Theodore could tell there was something on the boy's mind.

''Something bothering you, Kristian?'' he asked.

Kristian looked up and shrugged.

''What is it?''

''You're not gonna like it.''

''There's lots of things I don't like. That don't change 'em.''

''I've been talking with Ray about it for a long time, and I'm not sure if he's decided yet, but I have.''

''Decided what?''

Kristian set his fork down. ''I wanna enlist in the army.''

Eyelids could have been heard blinking in the room. All eating stopped.

''You want to *what?*'' Theodore repeated menacingly.

''I've been thinking about it for a long time. I want to do my part in the war, too.''

''Are you crazy? You're only seventeen years old!''

''I'm old enough to shoot a gun. That's all that counts.''

''You're a wheat farmer. The draft board ain't gonna get you. You're exempt from the draft—have you forgotten that?''

''Pa, you aren't listening.''

Theodore jumped to his feet. ''Oh, I'm listening, all right, but what I'm hearing don't make a lick of sense.'' Linnea had never seen Teddy so angry. He pointed a finger at Kristian's nose and shouted, ''You think all that's going on over there is them doughboys still pointing brooms at each other, well you're wrong, sonny! They're getting shot and killed!''

''I want to drive airplanes. I want to *see* 'em!''

''Airplanes!'' Theodore drove his hands into his hair, twisted away in exasperation, then rounded on Kristian again. ''What you'll drive is a pair of horses and a plow, because I won't let you go.''

''Maybe I want to do more with my life than drive horses and a plow. Maybe I want to see more than horses' rumps and smell more than horse droppings. If I enlist, I can do that.''

''What you'll see over there is the inside of a trench, and what you'll smell is mustard gas. Is that what you want, boy?''

Linnea touched Theodore's arm. ''Teddy—''

He shrugged it off violently. ''Keep out of this! This is between me and my boy! I said, is that what you want?''

''You can't stop me, Pa. All I have to do is wait till school's done and walk down that road, and you won't know where to find me. All I have to do is tell 'em I'm eighteen and they'll take me.''

''Now I raised a liar, too, as well as a fool.''

''I wouldn't have to be one if you'd give your okay.''

''Never! Not so long as I draw breath.''

Kristian showed profound control as he said quietly, ''I'm sorry you feel that way, Pa, but I'm going just the same.''

From that day forward the tension in the house was palpable. It extended into Theodore and Linnea's bedroom, too, for that night was the first since they'd been married that they didn't make love. When she touched his shoulder, he said gruffly, ''Let me be. I'm not in the mood tonight.''

Abashed that he'd turn away her offer of comfort when he most needed it, she rolled to her side of the bed and swallowed the tears thickening her throat.

At school, too, Linnea's placid days seemed to be over. As if the sap were rising in him as well as in every cottonwood on the prairie, Allen Severt started acting up again. He put pollywogs in the water crock, a piece of raw meat behind the books in the bookshelf, and syrup on Frances's desk seat. There were times when Linnea wanted to bash his head against the wall. Then one day he went too far and she did.

He was walking past her at the four-o'clock bell when he nonchalantly plucked her watch out and let it retract with a snap against her breast. Before her shock had fully registered, she grabbed two fistfuls of his hair and cracked his skull against the cloakroom wall.

''Don't you ever do that again!'' she hissed, an inch from his nose, pulling his hair so hard it lifted the corners of his eyes. ''Is that understood, *Mister* Severt?''

Allen was so stunned he didn't move a muscle.

The young children looked on saucer-eyed, and Frances Westgaard snickered softly.

''You're hurtin' me,'' Allen ground out through clenched teeth.

''I'll do worse than that if you continue with this sort of behavior. I'll have you expelled from school.''

With his eyes slanted back, Allen looked more malevolent than ever. She could sense the vindictiveness in those cold, pale eyes, something worse than heartlessness. It was a cruelty with which she simply did not know how to deal. And now she had embarrassed him in front of the other children for the second time. She could sense his vengefulness growing, and her hands shook as she released his head.

''Children, you are excused,'' she said to the others, her voice far from calm. Allen shrugged away from the wall and shouldered her roughly aside on his way to the door. ''Not you, Allen. I want to talk to you . . . Allen, come back here!''

But he swung around at the bottom of the steps and pierced her with a venomous glare. ''I'm gonna make you sorry, teacher,'' he vowed, low enough that only she could hear, then turned and marched away without a backward look.

She stared after him, realizing only after it was over how weak-kneed she was. She sank onto a cloakroom bench, hugging her shaky stomach. Well, he's backed you into a corner again, so what are you going to do, sit here quaking like a pup with the palsy or march down to his house and tell them what a devil they have on their hands?

She marched down to his house to tell them what a devil they had on their hands. Unfortunately, Martin wasn't home at the time, and his wife's response was "I'll speak to Allen about it." It was said dryly, condescendingly, with one eyebrow raised. Her lips were compressed into a superior moue as she held the door open for Linnea's exit.

I'm sure you'll speak to Allen, thought Linnea, while her own hope of having Allen dressed down on the spot went unsatisfied.

She walked home feeling more frustrated than ever and utterly ineffectual.

Two days later she found her mouse dead in a baited trap.

She told Theodore about it and he wanted to march right down to Severt's house himself and put a couple more dents in the kid's skull, but she said she could handle it, and he said are you sure, and she said yes, and something good came of it anyway, because they made love again as they used to, and afterward she begged him to talk to Kristian about going to war, only this time without anger. And he agreed to try.

But the attempt failed. The two of them talked down in the barn the next day, but Theodore's fear for his son's life manifested itself in anger once again, and the session ended with the two of them shouting and Kristian marching out and heading down the road without telling anybody where he was going.

He went to Patricia's house because lately it felt better to be with her than with anybody else he knew.

"Hi," he said when she answered the door.

"Oh . . . hi!" Her eyes brightened and a flush beautified her face.

"You busy?"

"No, just knitting. Come in!"

"I was wondering if you could come out instead. I mean, well . . . I'd like to talk to you. Alone someplace."

"Sure. Just let me get my coat. Ma?" she yelled, "I'm going for a walk with Kristian!" A moment later she appeared in a brown wool coat with a tan scarf looped over her head, its tails hanging over her shoulders. They both stuffed their hands into their pockets as they headed down the prairie road. Beside it the snow was already pithy and showed deep ruts. The north-westerlies had a milder breath—soon the snowdrops would blossom in the ditches. The days were growing longer and the late afternoon sun was warm on their faces.

He needed to talk, but not now. What he needed now was to simply walk along beside Patricia with their elbows softly bumping. She took her hand out of her near coat pocket and he followed suit. Their knuckles brushed . . . once . . . and again . . . and he took her hand. She squeezed his tightly and looked up at him with something more than a smile: a look of growing awareness and trust. She tipped her head against his shoulder for two steps, then they walked again without saying a word.

Not until they'd turned and were heading back did he speak.

"You ever get sick of looking at the same old road, the same old fields?"

"Sometimes."

"You ever wonder what it's like beyond Dickinson?"

"I've been beyond Dickinson. It looks just like it does around here."

"No, I mean *way* beyond Dickinson. Where there's mountains. And the ocean. Don't you wonder what they look like?"

"Sometimes. But even if I saw them, I'm sure I'd come back here."

"How can you be sure?"

"Because you're here," she answered guilelessly, looking up at him.

He stopped. Her blue eyes were clear and certain, her mouth somber. The tan scarf had fallen back and the March wind ruffled her hair. In his broad hand, hers felt fragile. He suffered a moment of doubt about the wisdom of going to war.

"Patricia, I . . ." He swallowed and wasn't certain how to put his feelings into words.

"I know," she replied to the unspoken. "I feel the same way."

He leaned down and kissed her. She went up on tiptoe and lifted her mouth, resting her hands against his chest. It was a chaste kiss, as kisses went, but it filled their hearts with the essence of first love, while all around them the land readied for spring, for that season of bursting renewal.

In time they moved on, back through her yard, but loath to part yet.

"Want to go in the corn crib?" she asked. "We could shell some corn for the chickens."

He smiled and she led the way to the far side of the farmyard, pulled a corncob from the hasp on a rough wooden door, and he followed her into semi-privacy. Inside the sun angled through the slatted walls against the steep hill of hard yellow ears. At the base of the corn sat a crude wooden box with a hand sheller attached, and beside it a seat made of nothing more than an old chopping block. Kristian sat down and fed an ear into the hopper and began turning the hand crank. Patricia leveled off the corn and sat down cross-legged on the lumpy ears, watching. It was warm in the corn crib, protected from the wind as it was, with the sun radiating off the wall of gold behind them. She flung off her scarf and unbuttoned her coat. He finished the first ear and she handed him another as the naked cob fell free. He watched the ear rotating as the teeth of the grind wheel gripped it; she watched his shoulders flexing as he cranked the wide fly-wheel. When the ear was only half clean, he dropped the handle and swung to face her. They hadn't come to the corn crib to shell corn, and they both knew it.

"What would your ma say if she knew we were out here?"

"She probably does. We walked right past the house."

"Oh." He wished she were closer, but felt uneasy about moving over beside her when they sat in a building where anybody could see right through the walls.

Their mutual hesitation hung heavy between them for a moment, then she laughed and plucked up a piece of dry, brown cornsilk. "Let's see what you'd look like in a moustache." The corncobs rolled as she moved to kneel before him and fit the tuft of cornsilk beneath his nose and lips.

It tickled and he jerked back, rubbing a finger across his nostrils.

She laughed and pulled him forward by the front panel of his jacket. "Here, don't be so twitchy. I want to see."

He submitted, letting her hold the cornsilk in place again and study him assiduously.

"Well, how do I look?"

"Gorgeous."

The sun threw bars of light and shadow across her face as she knelt between his knees, and the wind whistled softly through the slatted walls.

"So what do you think, should I grow one?" He hardly realized what he was saying; his thoughts were on her and how pretty she looked with her lips the color of sunset and her long-lashed eyes intent upon him.

"I don't know. I think I should kiss you first and then decide."

"So kiss me."

She did, with her finger and the cornsilk in the way, both of them giggling and the fine brown strands tickling terribly. Until she came up against his open legs and they pulled back, staring into each other's eyes.

"Oh, Kristian . . ." she murmured just as he, too, murmured her name. Then no excuse was needed. The cornsilk fell to his jacket collar as she flung her arms around him and they kissed fully, pressed as close as gravity would allow, with her stomach cradled by his warmest parts and their arms clinging tenaciously. He tightened his thighs against her hips and callowly explored her lips with his tongue. It took some coaxing before she realized what was expected of her and allowed her lips to slacken, and his tongue to probe inside.

The warm, sleek contact rocked them both, and when the kiss ended, they backed off to stare at each other, still somewhat overcome by discovery.

"I think of you all the time," she whispered.

He straightened a strand of her auburn hair that had caught on her forehead. "I think of you, too. But I need to talk to you about something, and when we start kissing I forget all about talking."

"Talk about what?"

"Me and my pa had a dilly of a fight—two of 'em, actually."

"About what?"

He swiveled around and started shelling corn again. Above the loud metallic grinding and the sound of the kernels falling she thought she heard him say "I want to enlist." But that was silly. Who'd *want* to go to war?

"What?"

This time he turned so she saw his lips move. "I want to enlist," he said louder, still cranking.

She put her hand on his and forced him to stop. "Enlist? You mean go fight?"

He nodded. "As soon as I graduate in the spring."

"But Kristian—"

"I suppose you're going to argue with me just like my pa did."

Crestfallen, she gulped and stared at him, then sat back and folded her hands between her thighs. "Why?"

"I want to fly airplanes and . . . and I want to see more of this world than Alamo, North Dakota! Oh, damn, I don't know." When he would have leaped to his feet she grasped his knees and made him stay.

"Couldn't you do that without becoming a soldier?"

"I don't know. My pa says I'm a wheat farmer and I guess I'm afraid that if I don't go now I probably will end up being a wheat farmer all of my life, and maybe I could be something more. But when I try to reason with my pa about it, he just gets mad and shouts."

"Because he's scared, Kristian, don't you see?"

"I know he is—so am I. But does he have to shout at me? Couldn't we just talk about it?"

She didn't know how to answer. She herself had had bouts with her own parents recently that seemed to flare out of nowhere.

"I think it's part of growing up, fighting with your parents."

She was so calm, so reasonable. And looking at her made him waver in his convictions.

"What would you think if I went?"

She studied him intently for a moment, and answered softly, "I'd wait for you. I'd wait for as long as it would take."

"Would you?"

She nodded solemnly. "Because I think I love you, Kristian."

He'd thought the same thing about her more than once lately, but hearing her say the words was like a blow to his senses. In a flash his hands were on her arms, drawing her up into his embrace again. "But we shouldn't say it," he said against her neck. "Not now, when I'm planning to leave. It'll make everything too hard."

She clung, pressing her breasts firmly against him. "Oh, Kristian . . . you might get killed." Her words were muffled by his coat collar before he forced her head around and their mouths joined. As they strained against each other, his trembling, uncertain hand slid inside her warm coat, glided over her back, her side, and finally sought her breast. Her breathing stopped and her mouth hovered close without meeting his.

"It's a sin," she whispered, her breath warm against his damp lips.

"So is war," he whispered in reply.

But she stopped his hand anyway and drew it to her lips and kissed his knuckles.

"Then stay," she pleaded.

But he knew as he kissed her one last time and backed away that she was part of what would keep him here his entire life if he didn't leave in June.

Chapter 22

Spring came to the prairie like a young girl preparing for her first dance, taking her time primping and preening. She bathed in gentle rains, emerging snowless and fresh. She dried with warm breezes, stretching beneath the benign sun, letting the wind comb her grassy hair until it lifted and flowed. Upon her breast she touched a lingering scent of earth and sun and life renewed. She put on a gay bonnet, trimmed of crocus and snowdrop and scoria lily, fluffed her red-willow petticoat, then tripped a trial dance step upon the stirring April breeze.

The animals returned as if on cue. The "flickertails"—striped gophers—perching beside their fresh-dug holes then chasing each other in playful caprice. The prairie dogs, barking and churring to their mates at twilight. The sharp-tailed grouse, drumming like thunder in lowland thickets. Mallards and honkers, heading north. And last but not least, the horses, heading home.

They came with the instinct of those who know their purpose, appearing one evening at the fence in the low pasture, whinnying to get in, to be harnessed, to turn the soil once again. All shaggy and thick, they stood in wait, as if the sharpening of plowshares had carried their tune across the prairies and beckoned them home. They were all there—Clippa, Fly, Chief, and the rest—two mares, Nelly and Lady, thick with foals.

They all walked down together to greet them, and Linnea observed the reunion with a renewed sense of appreciation for a farmer and his horses. Nose to nose, breath to breath, they communicated—beast and man happy to be together again. Teddy and Kristian scratched the horses' broad foreheads, walked in full circles around them, clapped their shoulders, checked their hooves. Linnea watched Teddy rub one big hand under Lady's belly, recollecting his voice raging, "I've had my family and he's damn near a full-grown man." What would he say when she told him, if what she suspected was true? She had missed one menstrual period and was waiting until she'd missed a second before giving him the news. They hadn't talked about babies again, but if it was true and she was expecting, surely he'd be overjoyed, as she was.

April moved on and the plowing began in earnest, but the older boys were present at roll call each day. Linnea wasn't certain whether it was due more to the fact that the schoolmarm was now Teddy Westgaard's wife or to the fact that he and Kristian still weren't talking.

In the fourth week of April Theodore turned thirty-five. He and Linnea were preparing for bed that night when she slipped her arms around him and kissed his chin. "You've been a little out of sorts today. Is anything wrong?"

He rested his hands on her shoulders and looked down into her inquiring eyes. "On the day I turn a year older? Do you have to ask?"

"I have a birthday gift for you that I think will cheer you up."

He grinned crookedly, held her by both ear lobes, and teasingly wobbled her head from side to side. "You cheer me up. Just having you here at night cheers me up. What do I want with gifts?"

"Oh, but this gift is special."

"So are you," he said softly, releasing her ears and kissing her lingeringly on the mouth. When the kiss ended she looked up into his earth-brown eyes and kept her stomach pressed close against him.

"We're going to have a baby, Teddy."

She felt the change immediately: he tensed and leaned back. "A b . . ."

She nodded. "I think I'm about two months along."

"A baby!" His surprise turned to outright displeasure and he pushed away. "Are you sure?"

Her heart thudded heavily. "I thought you'd be pleased."

"Pleased! I told you a long time ago I didn't want any more babies! I'm too old!"

"Oh, Teddy, you aren't. It's just a notion in your head."

"Don't tell me I'm not! I'm old enough to have one of my own going off to get himself killed in a war and you expect me to be happy about having another one so I can go through this agony again?"

She was so hurt she didn't know what to say. The disappointment was too intense to bring tears. She stood stiffly, wondering how to handle the huge lump of distress that seemed to lodge in her womb beside their growing fetus. All the excitement she'd felt dissolved and left only disillusionment.

"And besides," he went on peevishly, "you and I have barely had any time alone together. Three months—not even three months and you're pregnant already." Turning away, he cursed softly under his breath, folded himself on the edge of the bed, and held his head.

"Well, what did you expect to happen when we practically never miss a night?"

His head came up sharply, jutting. "Don't throw that up to me now, at this late date," he snapped. "You and your 'let's try this and let's try that,' " he finished on a mordant note.

Her hurt intensified. She pressed her stomach. "Teddy, this is your child I'm carrying. How can you not want it?"

He jumped to his feet in frustration. "I don't know. I just don't, that's all. I want things to go on like they were. You and me, and Kristian back in the fields where he belongs, and no more of this talk of war and . . . and . . . oh, goddammit all!" he cried and pounded from the room.

She was left behind to stare at the door, to press her hands to her stomach and wonder how someone who loved her so deeply could still hurt her equally as deeply. How could he have said such things about their lovemaking, as if he'd never felt the same wondrous compulsions she had?

She put on her nightgown and crept into bed, lying like a plank with the covers tightly under her arms, staring at the ceiling. Thinking. Sorrowing. Waiting. Odd, how tears didn't seem to accompany the most grievous hurts in life. She lay dry-eyed and stricken and praying that when he came back in he'd gather her into his arms and say he was sorry—he'd been unreasonable and he wanted their baby after all.

But he didn't. Instead, he blew out the lantern, undressed in the dark, got in beside her, and turned away. She felt his continued reproof as palpably as if he'd struck her.

The following day she walked to school alone. They hadn't spoken a word during breakfast and it was almost a relief to escape the tension.

It was Arbor Day; she and the children spent it doing the traditional outside cleanup. They had all brought rakes and put them to use tidying up from one end of the yard to the other. While the older boys painted the outhouses, the girls washed windows. It was a sunny day, so warm that some of the children had removed their shoes and stockings to go barefoot. When the yard work was all done they would go down to the creek bottom and select one sapling to dig up and transplant in the schoolyard.

They piled all the yard clippings on a sandy spot in the ditch and set them afire. Linnea was tending the blaze when she looked up to find Theodore and John passing by in a buckboard. Her heart skittered.

John waved and called, "Hello!"

"Hello!" She waved back. "Where you going?"

"To town."

"What for?"

"Get a share welded and buy supplies!"

"Have fun!"

She waved effusively. John waved back and smiled. Theodore gave a wan greeting with one palm, and she watched them move on down the road.

They finished the yard work by twelve-thirty, doused the embers with water, and headed for the lowlands with their lunch pails. Roseanne and Jeannette skipped along holding hands, singing, "Merrily in the Month of May." Allen Severt found a baby bullsnake and tormented the girls with it. Patricia Lommen walked beside Kristian, their arms touching.

They found a sunny glade beside Little Muddy and flopped in the grass to eat a leisurely lunch. Some of the children tried to wade, but the creek was still icy. They turned instead to exploring, searching for duck nests along the banks, probing into anthills, examining the locomotion of a pair of green inch-worms.

Finally Linnea checked her watch and decided they must find their tree if they were to make it back in time to replant it. They chose a straight, vigorous-looking sapling with bright silver bark and fat pistachio-colored buds. The older boys dug it up and put it in a pail to carry back.

They made a fetching sight, trooping over the prairie in a straggly line, the younger children skipping, chasing gophers, the older ones taking turns carrying the tree. They were crossing the stretch of wheat field just northeast of the school, the bell tower already in sight, when a frigid current of air riffled across the plain and a huge flock of blackbirds lifted, squawking raucously. The smaller children shivered; Roseanne pulled up her skirt and used it for a cape.

Ahead of Linnea, Libby halted in her tracks, pointed to the west, and said, "What's that?"

They all stopped to stare. A solid mass of white was rapidly moving toward them.

"I don't know," an awed voice answered. "Mrs. Westgaard, what is it?"

Grasshoppers? Linnea stiffened in alarm. She'd heard of grasshoppers coming in legion to devastate everything they touched. But it was too early for grasshoppers. Dust? Dust, too, could suddenly darken the sky out here. But dust was brown, not white. They all stood in fascination, waiting, as the wall of white moved toward them. Seconds before it struck, someone uttered, "Snow . . ."

Snow? Never had Linnea seen snow like this. It smote them like a thousand fists, instantly sealing them in a colorless void, bringing with it a wicked wind that tugged at the roots of her hair and pressed her clothing flat.

Two children screamed, unexpectedly cut off from the sight of all around them. Linnea stumbled over a warm body and knocked it off its feet, raising a cry of alarm. Dear God, she couldn't see five feet in front of her! She set the child on his feet and groped for his hand.

"Children, grab hands!" she shouted. "Quickly! Here, Tony, take my hand," she ordered the boy behind her. "Everyone back toward my voice and hold onto the person next to you. We'll all run together!" She had the presence of mind to take a hasty roll call before they moved. "Roseanne, are you here? Sonny? Bent?" She called all fourteen names.

Everyone accounted for, they followed the wheat rows, the small children crying now in their bare feet. Within minutes there were no wheat rows to follow, and she prayed they were heading in the right direction. All sense of perspective was lost in the white maelstrom, but they clung together in a ragged, terrified line and fought their way through it. These were not the usual fat, saturated snowflakes of late spring, the kind that land with a splat and disappear instantly. These were hard and dry, a mid-winter type of storm wrapped in a front of frighteningly frigid air.

They had no idea they were near the schoolyard until Norna ran headlong into one of the cottonwoods of the windbreak. She bounced off the tree and sat down hard, howling, taking two others down with her.

"Come on, Norna." Raymond was there to pick her up and carry her, while Linnea, Kristian, Patricia, and Paul herded the remaining youngsters blindly across the yard. How incredible to think they'd been blithely raking it only hours before.

There was no question of finding shoes that had been left on the grass. They were already buried. The shivering picnic party straggled up the steps, the barefoot ones stubbing toes and crying.

Inside, they stood in a trembling cluster, catching their breath. Roseanne plopped down, whimpering, to check a bruised toe. Linnea took a nose count, found all present and accounted for, and immediately started issuing orders.

"Kristian, are you good for one more trip outside?"

"Yes, ma'am."

"You get the coal." He was heading for the coal shed before she got the words out of her mouth.

"And Raymond, you get water."

He was right on Kristian's heels, grabbing the water bucket on his way out.

"Raymond, wait!" she shouted after him. In blizzards like this men were known to get lost between the house and barn, heading out to do the evening chores. "Kristian can follow the edge of the building, you can't. Climb the ladder and untie the bell rope."

"Yes, ma'am." Without hesitation, Raymond made for the cloakroom.

"Paul, you go with him and hold the end of the rope while he goes to the pump. Those of you with bare feet, take off your petticoats and dry them. Girls, share your petticoats with the boys. Don't worry about keeping them clean. Your mothers can wash them when you get home. And I know your toes are freezing, but as soon as Kristian has a fire going they'll be warm as toast again. How many of you have any lunch left in your pails?" Six hands went up.

A tiny voice quaked, "I lotht my lunth pail. Mama will thpank me."

"No she won't, Roseanne. I promise I'll explain to her that it wasn't your fault."

Roseanne began to wail nonetheless, requiring soothing before she'd settle down. Patricia and Frances were dispatched to oversee the smaller children and to take their minds off their discomforts.

Kristian returned and built a fire. Allen and Tony were given the job of periodically shoveling the steps to keep the door free.

When at last everyone was settled down as comfortably as possible, Linnea called Kristian aside.

"How much coal do we have?"

"Enough, I think."

"You think?"

It was late April. Who ever would have thought it would become a concern when wildflowers were already blooming on the prairie? Exactly how cold could it get this late in the year? And how long could a blizzard rage when May Day was just round the corner?

Kristian squeezed her arm. "Don't worry about it. This can't keep up for long."

But 1888 was heavy on her mind as Linnea stalwartly went to her table, took out a theme book, and made her first entry, hoping—praying—no one ever need see it: April 27, 1918, 3:40 P.M.—*Caught in a blizzard on our way back from the creek bottom, where we'd gone to dig an Arbor Day tree and have our picnic lunch. The day began with temperatures in the low 70s, so mellow some of the children went barefoot cleaning the schoolyard in the morning.*

Suddenly Linnea's pen stopped and her head snapped up.

Theodore and John!

She stared at the windows, which looked like they'd been painted white and listened to the wind howling down the stove-pipe and rattling shingles.

With her heart in her throat, Linnea swung a glance at Kristian. He was hunkering close to the stove with the other children, all of them talking in low voices. She got to her feet, feeling fear for the first time since the blizzard had struck. She moved to the window, touched its ledge, and stared at the white fury that beat against the panes. Already triangular drifts webbed the corners, but beyond all was an impenetrable mystery. Forcing a calm voice, Linnea turned.

"Excuse me, Kristian. Could you come here a moment?"

He glanced over his shoulder, rose, and crossed the room to her.

''Yes, ma'am?''

She tried to sound nonchalant. ''Kristian, while we were still cleaning the yard did you see your father and John pass by on their way home from town?''

He glanced at the window, then back at her. His hands came slowly out of his back pockets and concern sharpened his features.

''No.''

She affected an even lighter tone. ''Well, chances are they're still in town, probably at the blacksmith shop all snug and cozy around the forge.''

''Yeah . . .'' Kristian replied absently, glancing back to the window. ''Yeah, sure.''

She forced herself to wait a full five minutes after Kristian had rejoined the group before moving to the edge of the circle. ''Raymond, would you mind climbing back up to the cupola and tying the rope back on the bell again? It occurs to me that on a day like this we may not have been the only ones caught unawares by the blizzard. It might be a good idea to toll the bell at regular intervals.''

It was terribly hard to keep her voice steady, her face placid.

''But why you gonna do that?'' Roseanne inquired innocently.

Linnea rested a hand on the child's brown hair, looked down into an upturned face whose wide brown eyes were too young to understand the scope of true peril. ''If there's anyone out there, the sound might guide them in.'' Linnea scanned the circle. ''I'm asking for volunteers to stay in the cloakroom and ring the bell once every minute or so. You can take turns, two at a time, and we'll leave the cloakroom doors open so it won't be quite so cold in there.''

Kristian was on his feet immediately, followed by Patricia whose troubled eyes had been resting on him throughout the exchange.

Skipp Westgaard spoke up next. ''Mrs. Westgaard, don't you think our pas will drive to school to get us?''

''I'm afraid not, Skipp. Not until this snow lets up.''

''You mean we might have to stay in the schoolhouse overnight?''

''Maybe.''

''B . . . but where we gonna sleep?''

Allen Severt answered, ''On the floor—where else, dummy?''

''Allen!'' Linnea reprimanded sharply.

Allen demanded belligerently, ''What I wanna know is what we're gonna eat for supper.''

''We'll share whatever is left in the lunch pails, and I—''

''Nobody's gettin' my apple!'' he interrupted rudely.

Linnea ignored him and went on. ''I have emergency crackers and raisins on hand. There's water to drink and I have a little tea. But we'll worry about that if and when the time comes. For now, why don't you all think up a game to keep yourselves occupied? In case you hadn't guessed, school is over for the day.''

That brought a laugh.

Overhead the school bell sounded. Automatically Linnea checked her watch. She moved back to her desk to make a second entry: 3:55. *We will toll the school bell every five minutes to guide in any ships that might be lost in the night.*

But she couldn't sit at her desk a moment longer. The windows drew her, eerily. She stood staring out at the obscured world, shuddering within. With her back to the room she folded her hands on the sill and twisted her fingers together till the knuckles paled. Her eyelids slid closed, her forehead rested against the cold pane, and her lips began moving in a silent prayer.

The horses had been acting skittish all the way from town. Theodore continuously checked the sky, the horizon, the road behind, the road ahead, wondering at the animals' restlessness. Coyotes, he thought. You always had to be on the lookout for coyotes out here. They spooked the horses. Not that they'd attack, only make the horses bolt. That's why Theodore carried the gun—to scare the varmints off, not to kill them. Coyotes ate too many grain-eating critters to want to see them dead.

Seeing none, his thoughts turned to Linnea. He shouldn't have been so rough on her, but—hang it all!—she didn't understand. She was too young to understand! You raised a boy, pinned your hopes on him, watched him grow, nurtured him, provided love, sustenance, everything, only to find yourself helpless when he took a fool notion into his mind to jeopardize his life.

But he'd been unfair about the other part, too. It rankled, how he'd taken her to task for bringing about the pregnancy as if he'd had no part in it. Displeased with himself, he forced his mind to other things.

The burrowing owls were back, nesting in the abandoned badger holes from last year—a sure sign of spring come for good. The snowshoe rabbits had exchanged their white coats for brown. Ulmer said the trout were already biting down on the Little Muddy. Maybe the three of us, me and Ulmer and John, should try to get down there together one day soon and dip our lines.

"Ulmer says the trout're bitin'."

Beside him, John's eyebrows went up in happy speculation, though he didn't say a word.

"Sounds good, uh?"

"You betcha."

"We get an early start tomorrow and we could have the northeast twenty done by four or so."

They rode along, content, picturing fat, wriggling "rainbows" flopping on the creek bank, then sizzling in Ma's frying pan.

Cub shied.

"Whoooa . . . Easy there, boy." Theodore frowned. "Don't know what's wrong with them today."

"Spring fever, maybe."

Theodore chuckled. "Cub's too old for that anymore."

John noticed it first. "Somethin' up ahead."

Theodore's eyes narrowed. "Looks like snow."

"Naw. Sun's out." John leaned back and gave the blue sky a squint.

"Never saw snow that looked like that. But what else could it be?"

The first bank of chill wind struck them full in the face.

"Might be snow after all."

"That thick? Why, you can't see the road on the other side of it nor nothin' behind it."

They stared, intent now, puzzled. Theodore stated wryly, "Better turn your collar up. Looks like we're about to leave spring behind.'' Then he calmly rolled his sleeves down and settled his hat more firmly on his head.

When the wall of wind and snow struck, it rocked them backwards on the buckboard seat. The horses danced nervously, rearing in their traces while Theodore stared in disbelief. Why, he couldn't see Cub's and Toots's heads! It was as if somebody had opened a sluice gate that held back the Arctic. Like an avalanche it hit, a flaky torrent mothered by a fearsome wave of cold air that grew colder by the second.

Struggling, Theodore finally got the animals under control. Though they moved forward, he had no idea where to direct them, so he let them have their heads. ''You think it's only a snow squall, John?'' he shouted.

''Don't know. That air's like ice, ain't it?''

The air *was* ice. It bit their cheeks, pecked at their eyelids, and filtered into their collars.

''What you wanna do, John? Go on?''

''You think Cub and Toots can keep on the road?'' John shouted back.

Just then the team answered the question themselves by rearing and whinnying somewhere in the white blanket that kept them from sight.

''Giddap!'' But at the slap of the reins the horses only complained and shied sideways.

Cursing under his breath, Theodore handed the lines to his brother. ''I'll try leading 'em!'' He vaulted over the side, bent into the wind, and groped his way to the horses' heads. But when he grasped Toots's bridle, the team pranced and fought him. Theodore cursed and tugged, but Toots rolled her eyes and planted her forefeet.

Giving up, he made his way back to the wagon again and shouted up at John, ''How far you figure we are from Nordquist's place?''

''Thought we passed it already.''

''No, it's up ahead.''

''You sure?''

''I'm sure.''

''We could take Cub and Toots off the wagon and let them lead on. They might get us there.''

''But will we see the house when we're in front of it?''

''Don't know. What else we gonna do?''

''We could walk the fence line.''

''Don't know if there's any fence along here.''

''Hold on. I'll check.''

Theodore left the wagon behind, walked at a right angle from it, feeling with his hands. He hadn't gone five steps before he was swallowed up by the snow. He checked both sides of the road. There were no fences on either side. He had to follow the sound of John's voice back to the wagon. Sitting beside John again, he announced, ''No fences. Try the horses again.''

John shouted, ''Here, giddap!'' He slapped the reins hard. This time the horses lurched forward valiantly, but in moments they became disoriented and started shying again.

Theodore took the reins and tried coercing them. ''Come on, Cub, come on, Toots, old gal, on with y'.'' But they continued balking.

The temperature seemed to be dropping at a steady, relentless pace. Already Theodore's fingers felt frozen to the lines, and though he'd rolled down his shirt sleeves, they were little protection against Nature's unexpected wrath. The wind keened mercilessly, straight out of the west, smacking their faces to a bright, blotchy red.

Holding his hat on, Theodore took stock of the situation. "Maybe we better wait it out," he decided grimly.

"Wait it out? Where?"

"Under the wagon, like Pa did that time. Remember he told us about it?"

John looked skeptical, but his eyebrows were coated with white. "I ain't much for cramped spaces, Teddy."

Theodore clapped John's knee. "I know. But I think we got to try it. It's gettin' too cold to stay up here in the wind."

John considered a minute, nodded silently. "All right. If you think it's best."

Together they climbed down and released the traces with stiff fingers. They removed the singletree, laid it on the ground, and beside it piled flour, sugar, and seed bags, then did their best to kick away the snow and clear a place for themselves. When they overturned the wagon it landed atop the sacks, braced up far enough that they could shinny underneath the opening. They tied the horses to a wheel and Theodore went down on his knees.

His gun went under first, he next, on his side, shivering, hugging himself, watching John's heavy boots shuffling nervously on the far side of the opening.

"Come on, John. It's better out of the wind." Inside the cavern his words sounded muffled.

John's boots shuffled again, and finally he got down, rolled himself underneath, and lay facing the thin band of brightness with wide, glassy eyes.

Rocks and last year's dried weed stalks gouged into Theodore's ribs. In spite of their efforts to kick the snow away, some remained. It melted through the side of his shirt and clung to his skin in icy patches. Something with prickles scratched through his sleeve and bit the soft underside of his arm.

"Best try to get comfortable." Theodore raised up as best he could, tried to scoop the biggest pebbles and dried plant stalks from under his ribs, then lay down with an elbow folded beneath his ear. Beside him, John didn't move. Theodore touched his arm. "Hey, John, you scared?" John was trembling violently. Theodore made out the stiff shake of John's head in the dim light. "I know you don't like bein' cooped up much, but it probably won't be for long. The snow's bound to let up."

"And what if it don't?"

"Then they'll come and find us."

"Wh . . . what if they don't?"

"They will. Linnea saw us heading for town. And Ma knows we ain't back yet."

"Ma ain't rid a horse in years, and anyway how could she get through if we couldn't?"

"The snow could stop, couldn't it? How much snow you reckon we can have when it's almost May?"

But John only stared at the daylight seeping in beneath the wagon, petrified and shaking.

"Come on. We got to do our best to keep warm. We got to combine what little heat we got." Theodore shinnied over and curled up tightly against John's back, circling him with one arm and holding him close. John's arm came to cover his. The cold fingers closed over the back of Theodore's hand, clenching it.

When John spoke, his voice was high with panic. "Remember when Ma used to make us go down in the 'fraidy hole when there'd be a bad summer storm?"

Theodore remembered only too well. John had always been terrified of the root cellar. He'd cried and begged to be released the whole time they'd waited out the storm. "I remember. But don't think about it. Just look at the light and think about something good. Like harvest time. Why, there's no time prettier than harvest time. Riding the reaper off across the prairie with the sky so blue you'd think you could drink it, and the wheat all gold and shiny."

While Theodore's soothing voice rolled over him, John's unblinking eyes remained fixed on the reassuring crack of light. Occasionally miniature whirlpools of snow puffed in on a backdraft, touching his cheeks, his eyelashes. The wind whistled above, setting one of the wagon wheels turning. It rumbled low, reverberating through the wood over their heads.

After some time, Theodore gently loosened his hand from John's tight grip. "Put your hands between your legs, John. They'll keep warmer there."

"No!" John's fingers clutched like talons. "Teddy, please."

John was bearing the brunt of the cold, lying closer to the opening. But his fear of confinement seemed worse than his fear of freezing, so Theodore assured him, "I'm only going to put my arm over yours, okay?" He lined John's arm with his own and found the back of his hand like ice.

"Snow's a good insulator. Pretty soon we'll probably be snug as a cat in a woodbox."

Reassuring John kept Theodore's own panic at bay. But as soon as he fell silent, it threatened again. Think sensibly. Plan. Plan what? How to keep warm when we're dressed in thin cotton shirts and neither one of us smokes, so we don't even have any matches to burn the wagon if we need to? Even their long winter underwear had been discarded days ago when the weather turned mild. Short of the snow suddenly stopping, there was nothing that could help them. And if it didn't stop . . .

You shouldn't have tied the horses.

Oh, come on, Teddy. One of you panicking is enough. You've only been under here twenty minutes. Takes a little longer than that to freeze to death.

But it already felt like parts of him were frostbitten.

He laid and thought about the horses until he couldn't hold back any longer. "Listen, John," he said as casually as possible. "I gotta roll out a minute."

"What for?"

Damn you, John, after a lifetime of not asking questions, this is a fine time to start.

"Gotta make yellow snow," he lied. "But you stay here. I think I can roll over you."

Outside, he was alarmed to see how quickly the drift was building up around their makeshift shelter. Already it had stopped the free wheel from turning. He flicked the reins off the wagon wheel, and in spite of the cold, took a moment to affectionately brush each horse's muzzle, whispering into their ears, "You're a good old girl, Toots . . . You, too, Cub. Remember that.'' Their rumps were to the wind, head down. Snow glistened in their tangled manes and tails, but they stood patiently, unconcerned about whatever befell.

Just like John's done all his life.

But fatalistic thoughts did no good. Theodore pushed them from his mind and went down on one knee. As his palm pressed a sack of seed corn, he had an inspiration. He leaned low and peered through the opening. ''Roll to the back, John. Gonna give us something warmer to lay on.'' He took a jackknife from his pocket, plunged it into the bag, and tore a long gash. As the corn poured out he scooped it under the wagon with both hands. It was blessedly warm with trapped heat. ''Spread it in there, John.'' He had only three sacks to spare. The others were necessary to hold the wagon up and give them an escape hatch. But when the three bags were distributed, the corn made a more comfortable bed. Huddled again, belly to back, the two men wriggled into it, absorbing its warmth.

They'd been snuggled for some time when John asked, ''You didn't go out to pee, did you?''

Startled, Theodore could only lie. ''Course I did.''

''I think you went out to turn Cub and Toots loose.''

Again Theodore thought, *A fine time for you to get wise, big brother.*

''Why don't you close your eyes and try to sleep for a while. It'll make the time go faster.''

But time had never moved so slowly. After a while the corn shifted, leaving them lying on pebbles and sticks again. What little warmth they'd absorbed from it ended. The shudders began—first in John and eventually in Theodore. They watched the white of day fade to the purple of evening.

They'd been lying in silence for a long time when John spoke. ''Did you and the little missy have a fight, Teddy?''

A knot clogged Theodore's throat. He closed his eyes and tried to gulp it down, refusing to admit why John had brought up such a subject at a time like this.

''Yeah,'' he managed.

John didn't ask. John would never ask.

''She's pregnant and I . . . well, I got real ugly about it and told her I didn't want any more babies.''

''You shouldn't've did that, Teddy.''

''I know.''

And if they froze to death under this damn wagon, he'd never have a chance to tell her how sorry he was. Her image as he'd last seen her filled his mind—standing with a rake in one hand, her eyes shaded by the other, the children scattered all around her like a flock of finches, and the white building in the background with its door thrown wide. He recalled the row of cottonwoods coming in green at their tips, the ditch filled with wild crocus, Kristian raking near the edge of the ditch—the two people he loved most in the world, and he'd been ugly to both of them lately. Linnea had waved and called hello, but he'd been stubborn and had scarcely waved back. How he wished now he had. He ached and felt like crying. But if he cried, who'd keep John from giving up?

To make matters worse, John suddenly snapped. He thrust Theodore's arm away and shinnied on his belly toward freedom.

''I can't take it no more. I gotta get out of here for a while.''

Theodore grabbed the seat of John's overalls. ''No! Come on, John, it's bad under here but it's worse out there. The temperature is dropping and you'll freeze in no time.''

''Let me go, Teddy. Just for a minute. I just got to, before night falls and I can't see no more.''

''All right. We'll go out together, check the horses and the snow. See if it's lettin' up.''

But it wasn't. The horses were almost belly deep and the wagon was a solid hillock now. The only opening was on the leeward side, where the wind had swirled, creating a one-foot crawl space for their use. Standing in it, Theodore hugged himself, watching John stretch and breathe deeply, lifting his face to the sky. Damn fool would have frozen fingers if he didn't tuck his hands beneath his arms.

''Come on, John, we got to go back under. It's too cold out here.''

''You go. I'm just gonna stay here a minute.''

''Damn it, John, you'll freeze! Now get back under there!''

At the severe tone of the reprimand, John immediately became docile. ''A . . . all right. But I got to be closest to the opening again, okay, Teddy?''

His childlike plea made Theodore immediately sorry he'd scolded.

''All right, but hurry. If our hands aren't froze already, they will be soon.''

Back in their burrow, John asked, ''Can you feel your fingers anymore, Teddy?''

''Don't know for sure, but I'm not gonna think about it.''

They fell silent again. Soon the world beyond their shelter grew totally black.

''I think my nose is froze,'' John mumbled.

''Well, if you'd turn over here and face the inside or let me be on the outside for a while it might thaw. What difference does it make now anyway? It's night outside, just as black out there as it is in here.''

All John would say was, ''I got to have my air hole at least.''

Miraculously, they slept.

Theodore awakened and blinked, disoriented. At his side John was too still. Panic clawed through him. ''John, wake up! Wake up!'' He shook his brother violently.

''Huh?'' John moved slightly. Theodore reached for his face in the blackness. It felt frozen. But maybe what was frozen was his own hand.

''You got to roll over. Come on now, don't argue.'' This time John submitted. Theodore put both arms around him and held him as if he were a child, willing his own fright to subside. They couldn't die out here this way. They just couldn't. Why, when they left home Ma had had sheets hangin' on the line and bread rising in the oven. By now it would be baked and in the bread box. They were gonna go fishing with Ulmer one day this week. And Kristian was going to be graduating from the eighth grade in four more weeks. What ever would Kristian say if his pa missed the ceremony? And Linnea—oh, his sweet Linnea—she still thought he was mad at her. And she was going to have their baby. He couldn't die without seeing their baby. Lying in the inky blackness beneath an overturned wagon, with his brother shaking in his arms, Theodore found all these thoughts to be valid reasons why the blizzard couldn't win.

His ribs hurt terribly. There was no feeling in his toes, and his head throbbed when he tried to lift it off the corn. In spite of it, he dozed again, but some distracting thought kept him just short of sleeping fully—something he had to tell Linnea when he saw her next time. Something he should have told her last night.

He awakened again. John's breath was steady on his face. He wondered how much time had passed, if it was still the first night. But he felt disoriented and mysteriously weightless. As if his entire body were filled with warm, buoyant air.

He couldn't keep his thoughts clear. Was he close?

No!

He thrust John back.

"Wha . . ."

"Git up, John. Git out of here. We got to move, I think, else more of us is gonna freeze, if it isn't already."

"Not sure I can."

"Try, damn it!"

They rolled out, stumbling. The blizzard was worse than ever. It hit them with the same invincible wall of snow and wind as before. The horses were still there, loyally waiting. They whinnied, shook their heads, tried for a step forward but were thwarted by the drifts beneath their bellies.

The men fought their way to the animals. "Put your hands by Cub's nose. Maybe his breath will warm 'em." Theodore instructed.

They stood at the horses' heads, trying to warm themselves against anything that would provide the slightest bit of heat. But it was hopeless, and Theodore knew it.

In the eastern sky a dim light was beginning to glow through the driving snowfall. By it he tried to check his watch, only to find that his fingers could not handle the delicate catch to open its lid. He returned it to his pocket, held Toots's head, leaning his cheek on her forelock, wondering if a man knew when he'd stretched fate to its limits—the exact hour, the exact minute when destiny needed manipulation if he were to survive.

There was one possible way. But he resisted it, had been resisting it all through the cramped, fearful hours of the long night when he'd lain trying to warm his quivering body against his brother's, knowing that the rifle lay just behind his back. He hugged Cub's face with an apology the beast didn't understand. He pressed his icy lips to the hard bone just above her velvet nose. How many years had he known these horses? All his life. They'd been his father's even before he himself had grown old enough to take up the reins. Behind them he'd learned the terms and tones of authority. To their long, nodding gait he'd learned to control power great enough to kill, should it turn on him. Yet it never did. Cub. Toots. His prized pair. The ones he kept behind, winters. Older than all the others, but with so much heart there were times their understanding seemed almost human. They had, in their years, provided a good life. Could he ask them now to give him life at the cost of their own?

He stepped back, steeling himself, telling himself they were dumb animals, nothing more. "John, get my gun."

"Wh . . . what . . . y . . . you . . . g . . . gonna . . . d . . . do?" John's teeth were rattling like the tail of a snake.

"Just get it."

"N . . . no! I ain't g . . . gonna!" It was the first time in his life John had ever defied his brother.

With a muttered curse, Theodore knelt and fished the gun from beneath the wagon. He'd barely regained his feet when John's hand clamped the barrel and pointed it skyward. They stared into each other's eyes—haunted, both—neither of them feeling the icy black metal in their frozen fingers.

"Teddy, no!"

Theodore cocked the gun. The metallic clack bore the sound of doom.

"No, T . . . Teddy, you c . . . can't!"

"I got to, John."

"N . . . no . . . I'd r-r-rather f . . . freeze t . . . to d . . . death."

"And you will if I don't do it."

"I d . . . don't c . . . care."

"Think of Ma and the others. They care. *I* care, John." They stood a moment longer, gazes locked, while precious seconds ticked away and the blizzard raged on. "Let the gun go. Your fingers're already froze."

As John's hand fell, so did his head. He stood slumped, abject, unaware of the wind howling about his head, throwing fine shards of ice down the back of his collar.

Theodore stood beside Cub, his whole body trembling, jaw clenched so tightly it ached more than any other part of his body. In his throat was a wad of emotion he could neither swallow nor cough up. It lodged there, choking him. I'm sorry, old boy, he wanted to say, but could not. His heart slammed sickeningly as he raised the gun only to find he could not see down the sight. He lifted his cheek from the stalk and backhanded the tears away roughly, then took aim again. When he pulled the trigger he didn't even feel it; his finger was frozen. He fired the second shot rapidly, giving himself no time to think, to see.

Just do it, something said. Do what you got to do and don't think. He opened the pocket knife with his teeth because his fingers couldn't manage it. The blade froze to his tongue and tore off a patch of skin. Again, there was no feeling. He had closed himself off from it, moving with a grim determination that had hardened the planes of his face and turned his eyes flat and expressionless.

He plunged the knife to the hilt, shutting his mind against the gush of scarlet that colored the pristine snow at his knees. He ripped a hole two hands wide and ordered, "Get over here, John!"

When John remained rooted, Theodore lurched to his feet, jerked him around by the shoulder and gritted, "Move!" Ruthlessly, he gave his brother a shove that sent him to his knees. "Get your hands in there. This is no time to be queasy!"

Tears were coursing down John's cheeks as he slipped his hands into the sleek, wet warmth.

Mercilessly, Theodore turned to utilize the warmth of the second animal. While his hands thawed, he forced from his mind all thought of what pressed against his flesh. He thought instead of Linnea, her hair streaming in the wind, her face bright with laughter, the gold watch on her breast, the child in her womb. As the feeling returned to his hands, the pain grew intense. He clenched his teeth and rocked on his knees, swallowing the cry he could not let John hear.

But the worst was yet to come.

When his hands had warmed and he could hold the knife, he knelt beside the warm carcass, closed his eyes, and drew several deep, fortifying breaths, swallowed the gorge in his throat, and ordered John, "Get out your knife and gut 'er."

But even while Theodore set to work on his own grisly task, John knelt motionless, in a stupor. "Do it, John!" Terror, nausea, and pity tugged at Theodore's body while he performed woodenly, forcing the gruesomeness from his mind. Several times he had to struggle to his feet and turn away to breathe untainted air and gather fortitude. And all the while John knelt beside Toots's felled body, rattling now with shock, unable to perform the smallest task.

By the time Theodore finished, he was—unbelievably—sweating. It was arduous labor, the horse's carcass heavy and unwieldy. Much of the job had to be done by feel, leaning low, his cheek laying against the familiar brown hide while he slashed and pulled.

When at last he struggled to his feet, dizzy and weak, he knew John was incapable of helping either of them in any way.

"Get in, John. I'll help you."

Staring, glassy-eyed, John shook his head. Snow had made a fresh drift around his knees. His bloody hands rested motionless on his thighs.

Frantic, close to shock himself, Theodore felt tears of desperation form in his eyes. If they coursed down his face, he couldn't tell, for his cheeks were long since numb. "Goddammit, John, you can't die! I won't let you! Now get in!"

Finally, realizing John was incapable of making decisions, or of moving, Theodore rolled him off his knees and pushed him back, stood over him, and wedged the carcass open. "Double up. You'll fit if you roll up in a tight ball." The strain was immense, lifting the dead weight. Theodore's arms trembled and his knees quaked. If John didn't move soon, it would be too late.

Just when he thought he'd have to let go, John clenched his knees and backed in. A pathetic whimper sounded, but Theodore had no time to waste.

Gutting the second horse was more difficult than the first, for his energy had been sapped. Steel-willed, he struggled on, shutting out the smell and the sight of steam rising from the entrails in the snow and the sound of John's whimpers. Once he had to rest, near exhaustion, hands supporting himself, head drooping. The knife blade broke on a bone and he gave up the fight, unable to labor any longer. Through a dizzy haze, he crawled toward the life-giving warmth, but when he was struggling to get inside, his mind grew lucid for several seconds, and he finally remembered what it was that he had to tell Linnea.

On hands and knees he crawled through the snow, groping for the broken knife, taking it with him as he pulled himself underneath the wagon one last time.

Lying on his back in the murk, he pictured the letters, just as she'd taught them. L is for *lutefisk.* I is for ice. N is for—he couldn't remember what N was for, but he need not know. By now he could spell her name by heart.

"Lin," he carved blindly, "I'm sorry."

His ears buzzed. His head felt ten times its size. Somebody was crawling through the snow on bloody hands. Now why would anybody want to do a thing like that? On leaden limbs he reached his destination, unaware of the miasma or the gore or the fact that he tore his shirt and scraped both his belly and back as he squeezed inside. There, emotionally and physically exhausted, he lost consciousness.

* * *

In the school building six miles up the road a child rubbed her tear-filled eyes and wailed, "But I don't *like* raith-inth."

Linnea, her own eyes rimmed with red, forced patience into her voice and soothed Roseanne when all she wanted to do was cry herself. "Just eat them, honey. They're all we have."

When Roseanne toddled away still sniffling over her handful of sticky raisins, Linnea wearily pulled the bell rope again, then clung to it with both hands, eyes closed, forehead resting against the scratchy sisal while the woeful *clong-g-g* resounded like a dirge. Outside the wind picked up the shivering sound and carried it over the white countryside. One minute later it carried another . . . then another . . . and another . . .

Chapter 23

The blizzard lasted twenty-eight hours. In that time, eighteen inches of snow fell. The children were rescued just before dark on the second day by men on snowshoes, pulling toboggans. The first one to reach the school was Lars Westgaard. He rammed his snowshoes into a drift, opened the door and met a circle of relieved faces, three of them—his own children's—tearfully happy.

But as he held Roseanne, clinging to him like a monkey, and petted the heads of Norna and Skipp who hugged close, he met the haunted eyes of Linnea, waiting beside Kristian.

"Theodore and John?" she asked quietly.

He could only shake his head regretfully.

A sick, rolling sensation gripped her stomach and panic girthed her chest. She interlaced her fingers with Kristian's, squeezing hard and meeting his young, worried eyes.

"They're probably sitting at someone's place in town, worrying about us more than we're worrying about them."

Kristian swallowed pronouncedly and muttered, "Yeah . . . probably." But neither of them were convinced.

The other fathers straggled in, stomping off snow, and warmed themselves by the fire. When all had arrived, search plans were made, then the fire was banked and the little school-house closed. Someone had brought a spare toboggan and snowshoes for Linnea. Dressed in someone else's coat, scarf, and mittens, she was pulled home by Kristian.

Already the air was mellowing. In the western sky the red-gold eye of the sun squinted through purple clouds, sending long spans of gilt streaking across the transformed world. The shadows on the downside of the snowdrifts were the same deep purple as the westerly clouds that were already breaking and separating, shedding more sunny shafts and promising a clear day tomorrow.

They made a mournful little caravan, four toboggans pulled by Ulmer, Lars, Trigg, and Kristian, with Raymond walking beside. It had been decided, in the interest of expedience, that the Westgaard children would all be taken to Nissa's, which was closest, so the men could set out immediately on their grim errand. Even on the short walk home they were alert, watchful, each of them carrying a long cane pole, occasionally stopping to pierce a drift in several places. Each time, Linnea watched the latticed tracks of their snowshoes create cross-stitches on the snow, listened to their low, murmuring voices, and dreaded what they might find. She gazed in horrified fascination at the depth to which the cane poles sank and, holding her stomach as if to protect her unborn child from worry, said a silent prayer.

Poor Kristian. She herself was weary beyond anything she'd ever imagined, and he must be, too. Yet he stalwartly moved with his uncles over the suspicious-looking hillocks, watching while the poles disappeared again and again into the snow, leaving it pock-marked. Each time he returned to her toboggan, resignedly picked up the rope, and high-stepped behind the others, the sleds whining a mournful lament against the pristine surface of the snow.

When they reached Nissa's house the men had to shovel a drift from the back door. They worked to the continuous bawling of the cattle who stood near the barn in snowdrifts, with painfully bulging bags, waiting to be milked since last night at this time. But the cattle were ignored in light of the much greater urgency.

It was clear that Nissa hadn't slept at all. It was equally clear that she was one of those who functions well under stress, whose thought processes clarify in direct proportion to the necessity for clear thinking. She had gear all packed: quilts tied into tight bundles like jellyrolls; steaming coffee and soup in fruit jars bound with burlap; sandwiches wrapped in oilcloth; bricks in the oven and hot coals ready to be scooped into tins. Though her face appeared haggard, her movements were brisk and autocratic as she scurried about the kitchen, getting the boys outfitted and prepared to move out again. Recognizing the value of time, they wasted little of it on useless consternation. The only pause came when Kristian and Raymond insisted on going along. The men exchanged glances, but to their credit included them. "You sure?" Ulmer asked.

"My pa is out there," Kristian answered tersely.

"And I go with Kristian," Raymond stated unequivocally.

With Ulmer's nod, it was decided. Within minutes after their arrival, the men were gone again.

Nissa neither fretted nor watched them snowshoe away. Instead, she turned her attention to her grandchildren, for whom she'd prepared a pot of thick chicken noodle soup. There was fresh bread, too, and a batch of fresh-fried *fattigman,* evidence that she'd remained industrious during her worried hours alone.

How Linnea admired the scuttling little hen. No taller than her eight-year-old grandsons, Nissa didn't slow down a bit. She moved like heat lightning, rarely smiling. Yet all seven children instinctively knew she loved them as she tended to their needs and they babbled about their night at the school-house.

Somehow Roseanne's voice could be heard above all the others, shrill and lisping. "And Grandma, gueth what! Aunt Linnea made me eat raith-inth, and I *did* it! I can't wait to tell Mama." Her mobile face suddenly drooped. "But I lotht my lunch pail and Mama'th gonna thpank me for thure."

The jabber continued as soup bowls were emptied and refilled. When the children were stuffed, they seemed to droop in unison, and within minutes were asleep on the two downstairs beds.

The house quieted. From outside came the sound of snow melting off the roof, dripping rhythmically, even though the sun had gone down.

Nissa gripped the tops of both knees as if to navigate herself up from the hard kitchen chair. Her faded skirt drooped between her thighs like a hammock. She looked as if a deep sigh would have done her a world of good, but instead she sounded stern.

"Well, I guess I better try to give them cows some relief."

"I'll help you," Linnea offered.

"Don't think so. Milkin' cows is harder'n it looks."

"Well, I'd like to try, at least."

"Suit yourself." Nissa donned her outerwear without the slightest hint of self-pity. If a thing's got to be done, it's got to be done, her attitude seemed to say. For Linnea there was great reassurance in sticking close to the stubbornly determined little woman.

Dressed in Theodore's and Kristian's outsized overalls, they trudged through the snowdrifts to the barn.

Milking, as Nissa had declared, was "hardn'n it looked." Linnea was a total flop at it. So while Nissa milked, Linnea shoveled a path between the barn and the house. Together they carried the white frothing pails up, cleaned the children's soup bowls, then faced the dismal task of waiting with idle hands.

Nissa filled hers. She found a fresh skein of yarn and sat in the kitchen rocker, winding it into a ball. The rocker creaked in rhythm with her winding. Outside the sky was the color of a grackle's wing. Stars came out, and a moon thin as a scimitar blade. Not a breeze stirred, as if the last twenty-eight hours had never happened.

The rocker creaked on.

Linnea tried knitting, but couldn't seem to keep her hands steady enough to make smooth stitches. She glanced at the woman in the rocker. Nissa's blue-veined hands with their thin, shiny skin worked mechanically, winding the dark-blue yarn. It was the same color as the cap she'd knit for Teddy at Christmas. Was she thinking of that cap now, packed away in mothballs along with all of Theodore's and John's other woolen clothes?

"Nissa?"

The old woman looked over her spectacles, rocking, winding.

"I want you to know, I'm carrying Teddy's baby."

They both knew why Linnea had told her—if Teddy didn't make it, his child would. But Nissa only replied, "Then you oughtn't to have shoveled all that snow."

At that moment Roseanne toddled to the kitchen doorway, rubbing her eyes and her stomach. ''Grandma, I got a thtomach ache. I think I ate too much thoop.''

The blue yarn lost all importance. ''Come, Rosie, come to Grandma.'' The drowsy-eyed child padded into her grandma's open arms and let herself be gathered onto the warm, cushioned lap and settled beneath a downy chin. The old bones of the rocker creaked quietly into the room.

''Grandma, tell me about when you was a little girl in Norway.''

For long minutes only the chair spoke. Then Nissa started recollecting the story that had obviously been told and retold through the years, in terms sometimes strange to Linnea's ears.

''My papa was a crofter, a big strong man with hands as horny as hooves. We lived in a fine little glade. Our house and byre was strung together under a green-turfed roof and sometimes in spring violets blossomed right there on the—''

''I know, Grandma,'' Rosie interrupted. ''Right there on the roof.''

''That's right,'' Nissa continued. ''Some wouldn't call it much, but it had a firm floor that was always fresh-washed and Mama made me go out and collect fresh green sprays of juniper to spread on it after she swept. And at our front door was a fjord . . .'' Nissa looked down. ''You 'member what a fjord is, don't you?''

''A lake.''

''That's right, a lake, and at our back door was the purple mountains. Up a hill toward the woods and marshes was the village of Lindegaard. Sometimes Papa would take us there and we'd dress in dark homespun and the men wore plush hats, and off we'd go, maybe at Whitsuntide when the spinneys on the hills was only just tinged with pale green and the bare fields smelled like manure and the night never got darker than pale blue. And that was because Norway is called . . .'' Nissa waited.

''The land of the midnight thun,'' Roseanne filled in.

''Right again. There were alder trees and birch woods and heather—always heather.''

Roseanne looked up and rested a hand on her grandmother's neck. ''Tell about the time when Grandpa brought you the heather.''

''Oh, that time . . .'' The old one chuckled low in her throat. ''Well, that was when I was fifteen years old. Your grandpa picked me a bouquet so big a girl couldn't hold it in both arms. He delivered it in the back of a two-wheeled cart behind a jet-black pony—''

''I 'member the pony's name!'' put in the eager child.

''What?'' Nissa peered down through her oval spectacles.

''El-tha.''

''That's right. Else. I'll never forget the sight of your grandpa, leading that little mare up the lane, comin' to call. Course he had to sit politely and visit with my family a long time. And Mama brought out thick curdled cream with grated rusks and sugar on top as if that was all in the world he'd come to do was have sweets with us.'' Wistfully, Nissa rested her chin on Roseanne's head while the child picked at a button on her grandma's dress.

''He was a fisherman, like his papa. But the fishing off the Lofotons had failed four years running and there was talk of America. Sometimes in the evening when he'd come to call we'd sit in the door yard and talk about it, but, shucks, we never dreamed we'd come here.

"Oh, those evenin's were fine. There'd be black cocks callin' from the bird-cherries, and they'd be in blossom, and when the sun would set behind the snow-capped mountains the cottage windows would blaze like as if they was afire." Nissa rocked gently, a wistful expression on her face. "The woods to the north opened onto a peat bog, and in the spring of the year the air was filled with the smell of peat fires and roasted coffee beans, and always you could smell the sea."

"Tell about the grindstone, Grandma."

Nissa pulled herself from one reverie to another. "There was a grindstone at the back of the byre where my papa sharp—"

"I know, Grandma," the child interrupted again, leaning back to look up at the face above her. "Where your papa tharpened toolth and the thound wuth like the drone of a hundred beeth—*bth, bth, bth!*"

Nissa smiled down indulgently, wrapped her arms more securely around Roseanne, and went on. "And I had a Lapland dog . . ." She waited, knowing it was expected.

"Named King," put in Roseanne. "And you had to leave old King behind when you married Grampa and came on the boat to America."

"That's right, little one."

The name lit a warm flame in Linnea's heart. Theodore had called her by it at times, and she knew now from whom he'd learned it.

Sonny and Norna toddled out from their nests, and the old woman gathered them 'round, taking sustenance from their sleepy faces. One by one they all came, beckoned by some call none could divine—much as the horses had appeared when the fields needed them—to leave their cozy beds and gather at their grandmother's feet as she reached into the past for ease. They surrounded her chair, some sitting on its wooden arms, some sinking to their knees and resting their cheeks against her thigh. Nissa's fingers sifted through a head of silken hair. Watching, listening, Linnea felt a lump form in her throat. She understood, as she never had before, the why and wherefore of family, of generation leading to generation, flesh to flesh, past to future.

Posterity.

She said silently to the child she carried, Listen now, this is your legacy.

The tale went on, laced with more mysterious words: bannocks and moors and bilberries and brambles.

Much later the lights of bobbing lanterns showed in the east. Linnea stood at the window with dread thickening her throat. It buzzed through her veins and popped out in liquid pearls on her forehead. She stared into the night, loath to tell Nissa they were coming, giving her time—she was old and had too little of it left—all the time it was possible to give.

No horses—where were the horses?—but a pair of toboggans with two shadowed forms upon them, and downturned faces in the light of the gold lamps. Linnea despaired. Oh God, oh God, not both of them!

Nissa's voice lilted on. "There were fires in the hills on Whitsuntide, and they burned long into the night . . ."

Was it Linnea's own voice that finally spoke, so quiet, so calm, when it felt as if she herself were dying a little as each second passed?

"They're coming."

Nissa's story stopped. So did the rocker. Gently she pushed the young ones off her lap while her sons and grandsons trudged toward the house with their burdens trailing on the moon-washed snow. A blanket of dread worse than any she'd ever imagined pressed down on Linnea.

She opened the door and Lars came through first, his haunted eyes going directly to the rocking chair.

"Ma . . ." he croaked softly, voice breaking.

Nissa sat forward, pain flickering through her eyes.

"Both of them?" she asked simply.

"No . . . j . . . just John. We got to Teddy in time."

Nissa's softly-fuzzed cheeks collapsed into swags of sorrow. Her cry keened quietly through the room. "Oh no . . . oh, John . . . my son, my son . . ." She wrapped her body with one arm, covered her mouth with a hand, and rocked in short desperate motions. Tears rolled down, catching on the lower rim of her spectacles before finding the valleys of despair in her face and riding them to her chin.

"Ma . . ." Lars managed again and went down on one knee before her. Clinging, they grieved together. Watching, Linnea felt gratitude and grief conflicting within her breast. Teddy was alive . . . but John. Gentle John. Tears streamed from the corners of her eyes and her shoulders shook. The children, silent and uncertain, looked questioningly from their grandma to their teacher. Some of them understood but were hesitant to believe. Some of them still thought the worst hazard of a blizzard was having to eat raisins.

The men came in, carrying the toboggans like litters. They set the quilt-wrapped burdens by the stove and Kristian entered behind them, his face gaunt and pale. His stricken eyes immediately found Linnea's.

"Krist . . ." she tried, but the word tore in half.

He lunged into her arms, closing his eyes and swallowing hard against the tears he could contain no longer.

"Pa's alive," he managed in a guttering whisper.

She could only nod yes against his shoulder, her throat too constricted to speak. Kristian drew himself from her arms and she found Raymond beside them, watching, looking as drawn as all the others. She hugged him hard while across the room Nissa cried softly and Ulmer knelt on the floor beside the toboggans.

"Somebody get the children out of here," he ordered in a quivering voice.

Crushing back the need to see for herself that Teddy was alive, Linnea did what she knew was most needed.

"Come, ch . . . children . . ." She dashed a hand beneath her eyes. "Come w . . . with me upstairs."

They balked, sensing disaster, but she herded them ahead of her, up the squeaking steps into the gloom overhead. "Wait right where you are. I'll get a lamp."

What she saw when she turned back to fetch a lamp made her freeze in her footsteps. Ulmer had rolled back the quilts, revealing Theodore's body coiled into a fetal pose, his hands crossed and clutching his shoulders. His hair was plastered to his head and his clothes pasted to his body with a gruesome mixture of gore and entrails. On his face and hands was a film of liquid that looked like red oil. His eyes were closed and lips open as if in an eternal gasp, yet not a muscle moved. He looked as if he were the dead one.

A cry escaped Linnea's throat.

Ulmer looked up. "Take the children upstairs, Linnea," he ordered sternly.

She stared, horrified, her jaw working, mouth agape. "What—"

"He's alive. We'll take care of him, now get the lantern and go!"

With her stomach lurching she spun from the room.

Upstairs all seven children settled on her old bed, their knees crossed, their eyes wide and frightened. She fought helplessness, tears, and nausea. Theodore, oh dear God, what happened to you? What did you suffer out there in the wrath of the storm? Something more deadly than the blizzard itself? Something with teeth and jaws? She tried to recall where his skin was broken, but there'd been so much blood it was impossible to tell from where it had come. Shudders wracked her body as she hunkered on the edge of the mattress and hugged herself, rocking. What kind of animal stalks humans and attacks in the middle of a blizzard? Please, oh please, somebody, tell me what happened to him. Tell me he'll live.

What brought her out of her shock was the touch of a small hand on her back and a tiny, frightened voice.

"Aunt Linnea?"

She turned to find Roseanne kneeling behind her. Linnea saw the fear in the wide brown eyes and the downturned mouth, saw it reflected in the circle of faces with their big, wondering eyes and their still poses. She realized they relied upon her to keep their world secure right now.

"Oh, Roseanne, honey." She swept her arms around the child, kissed her cheek, and held her tightly to her breast, suddenly understanding even more fully why Nissa had welcomed having the children near during the last hour of her vigil. "All of you . . ." She opened her arms to include them all, and though they wouldn't all fit, they nestled as close as possible, seeking comfort, too. "I'm so sorry. I've been thinking only of myself. Of course you want to know what happened." Her troubled eyes scanned the circle of faces. "Let's hold hands now, all of us." As they had on Thanksgiving when there'd been so much to be grateful for, they formed a continuous ring of human contact while she told them the truth.

"Your uncle John is dead, and your uncle Teddy is . . . well, he's very . . . ill. They were caught in the blizzard yesterday on their way home from town. Now we'll all have to be very strong and help Grandma Nissa and Kristian and all of your papas and mamas. They'll be v . . . very s . . . sad."

But she could go on no longer. She let the tears roll unheeded down her cheeks, holding two small hands that felt like lifelines. She watched their faces change from fearful to respectful, and understood that most of them were dealing for the first time with death. What came as the greatest surprise was how they dealt with their sorrowing teacher. Their first concern was for her. Seeing her crying and in the throes of near shock frightened them worse than anything so far. In their inexperienced way, they tried to comfort. And during those minutes while they huddled on the bed, the bond of love among them drew even tighter.

Downstairs, Nissa staunchly set aside her grief and attended to the living. She insisted on bathing Teddy herself, washing his hair, while he lay on the toboggan beside the stove. Only after that did she allow his brothers to dress, lift, and carry him to his own freshly made bed. Throughout it all he remained unconscious, sealed in the protective security of natural escape.

It was near dawn when Kristian went upstairs to fetch his young cousins. In Linnea's old room a jumble of sleeping bodies huddled on the bed, leaning, tilting, curled together like a ball of spring angleworms. At their core sat Linnea, with her back to the bedstead, ear to shoulder, limp arms circling Bent and Roseanne, while the other children tangled as close as they could get.

He felt awkward waking her.

"Linnea?" He touched her shoulder.

Her eyelids flickered. Her head lifted. She winced and let her head ease down at an acute angle and slept again.

"Linnea?" He shook her gently.

This time her eyes opened slowly and her head stayed up. Disoriented, she looked into Kristian's eyes. Slowly things began to register—Kristian's hand on her shoulder, the children slumped around her, the pale light of dawn coming in her window.

She jerked to life and tried to get off the bed. "Oh, no, I didn't mean to fall asleep. I should have been down there—"

"It's all right. Grandma took care of everything."

"Kristian," she whispered, "how is he?"

"I don't know. He hasn't moved. They washed him and put him to bed. Now Ulmer and Lars are doing the milking, then they have to go home. Helen and Evie will be worried about the kids." He straightened, then glanced at the sleeping children strewn about her lap.

"I want to go see him."

Kristian sat heavily on the edge of the bed. "He looks bad."

She felt the same hideous fear as last night, but she had to know. "Kristian, what happened to them?"

He sucked in a deep, shaky breath and ran a hand through his hair. When he spoke his voice reflected the horror of the past night. "When the blizzard first hit they must have overturned the wagon and laid underneath it to get out of the wind. When that wouldn't protect them enough they . . ." He swallowed and she reached for his hand, clasped it tightly. "They shot the horses and g . . . gutted them and c . . . crawled inside."

The horror on his face was reflected in hers. "C . . . Cub and Toots?" Theodore's favorites. "Oh no . . ." Her stomach suddenly churned. A myriad of images flashed through her mind—the horses nodding along on their way to town on a mellow Arbor Day morning, the entire herd prancing away to freedom while Cub and Toots trumpeted to them from inside the pasture fence, the countless times she'd seen Theodore rub their noses. Oh, what it must have been like for him to slay the beasts he loved so well, and for Kristian to find them. She pressed the boy's cheek. "Oh, Kristian, how awful for you."

He sat perfectly still, tears coursing slowly down his cheeks, his eyes fixed on a point beyond her shoulder. She stroked the wetness with her thumb. In a choked voice, Kristian went on. ''It looked like Uncle John must've b . . .'' His Adam's apple bobbed twice. ''Been in . . . inside T . . . Toots, but he must not've b . . . been able to st . . . stand it, because we f . . . found him sitting beside her in the snow as if . . . aw, Jesus—'' Sobs overwhelmed him and he hunched forward, burying his face in his hands. He sobbed brokenly, shoulders heaving. Linnea was crying, too, as she dislodged herself from the sleeping children and struggled to the edge of the bed. On her knees she circled Kristian from behind, pressing her cheek against his trembling back, holding him tight.

''Shh . . . shh . . . it's all right . . .''

He found one of her hands, twined his fingers with hers, and pressed it hard against his aching heart. ''I can't f . . . forget all that r . . . red snow.''

She felt his heart beat heavy beneath her palm. ''Kristian . . .'' she sympathized, unable to come up with any words of ease. ''Kristian . . .'' Her tears left dark splotches on the back of his blue shirt. Then neither of them spoke. They let grief have its way, solacing each other.

In time Kristian heaved a long shuddering sigh and Linnea released her hold on him. He blew his nose and she dried her eyes with a sleeve.

''Grandma's with Pa. She could use a breather.''

''And you, too. You look like you're ready to tip over.''

He managed a weary smile. ''Tipping over sounds wonderful.''

''Help me wake the children, then you do just that.''

The young ones were half-carried, half-nudged downstairs to make the long rides home on toboggans behind their weary, heartsore fathers whose chores today would include making funeral arrangements for their brother as well as seeing after the carcasses of two dead horses and an overturned wagon. The only blessing—and it was an ironic one at best—was how quickly eighteen inches of snow had melted to nine.

The sun yawned awake, strewing the prairie with tardy warmth, painting sky and snow vivid pinks and oranges before stealing higher into a lustrous sky as clear as springwater.

It streamed into the east window of Theodore's room, while in the doorway, Linnea hesitated.

Beside the bed, Nissa slumped on a hard kitchen chair, her chin resting on her chest and her fingers laced loosely over her stomach. Linnea's glance moved to the bed. She stifled a gasp. He looked so haggard, so drawn . . . and undeniably old. The healthy color was gone, replaced by a wan, waxy tone. His eyes, behind closed lids, were surrounded by flesh tinted a faint blue. His cheekbones appeared to have sharpened into hooked blades that seemed as if they might slice through the flesh at any moment. His cheeks were sallow, and upon them shone lighter spots where frostbite had deadened the skin. His beard had grown for—for what?—two, almost three days. It seemed years since she'd waved his wagon off to town from the schoolyard. Studying the whiskered jaw and chin, she grieved afresh for all he'd been through.

Her gaze passed to Nissa. Poor, afflicted mother. How tragic to outlive your own children. Linnea moved into the room to touch the slumped shoulder.

''Nissa.''

Her head snapped up. The spectacles had slipped low on her nose.

"He took a turn for the worse?"

"No. He's the same. Why don't you go lie down in your own room and I'll sit watch for a while?"

She flexed her shoulders, wedged her fingertips beneath her glasses, and rubbed her eyes. "Naw . . . I'll be fine."

Linnea could see it would be useless to argue. "Very well, then I'll sit with you."

"I'd welcome the company. Ain't no other chairs in here, you'll have to—"

"This will be fine." Linnea snagged the small creweled footstool and brought it near Nissa's chair. She folded herself on it and drew her ankles in with both hands. The room smelled of camphor and liniment. Outside a rooster crowed and a robin boisterously heralded the morning. Inside, the regular beat of Theodore's breathing was soon joined by the heavier purr of his mother's soft snore.

Linnea glanced up to see the old woman threatening to topple from her chair. She awakened her again, gently. "Come on, Nissa. You're not doing Teddy any good when you can't keep your own eyes open." She gathered Nissa unresistingly against her side and guided her to the bedroom next door.

"Well . . . all right . . . just for a minute." Nissa dropped to the bed and rolled to her pillow without even bothering to remove her glasses. As Linnea slipped them from her nose, Nissa mumbled, ". . . chicken soup on the stove . . ."

"Shh, dear. I'll see to him. Rest now."

Before leaving the room, Linnea loosened Nissa's shoe-strings and slid off the high-topped black shoes, then gently drew a comforter to her shoulders.

Back in their own room she stood beside the bed, studying Theodore's haggard face. The silent cry was gone from his lips. With two fingertips she gently brushed his eyebrows, his temple. She leaned to kiss the corner of his mouth; his skin was cool and dry. She touched a strand of his hair—clean but disheveled, curling slightly at the tips. She watched his chest lift and fall. The blankets covered his ribs. Above was the exposed wool of his exhumed winter underwear, buttoned all the way up to the hollow of his throat where the morning shadows delineated the trip of his pulse. His hands lay atop the coverlets. She took one; it lay lax and unresponsive, its skin callused and hard. She thought of that hand lovingly mending harnesses, soothing the belly of the pregnant mare, turning down Cub's ear as he whispered into it . . . then grasping the haft of a knife and eviscerating his beloved beasts.

Tears burned her eyelids again, and this time when she kissed his temple she lingered, breathing in the scent of his living flesh and hair, feeling his reassuring pulsebeat beneath her lips. Oh, Teddy, Teddy, we came so close to losing you, the baby and me. I was so scared. What would I have done without you?

She stretched out beside him, on top of the covers, pressing her stomach close against his side, wrapping a protective arm around his waist, and for a while she slept, with their baby pressed between them.

His cough awakened her. She sat up, listening for signs of congestion, got off the bed, and pulled the covers up to his ears. On the chair beside the bed, she kept vigil. For the most part he lay quietly, but once he rolled to his side, not with the wild flinging of one experiencing haunted dreams, but with a slow, tired deliberation, as of one too exhausted to move quickly. He spoke not a word, no unconscious outcries prompted by the horror he'd suffered. For now, he seemed at peace.

He awakened near noon, as undramatically as he'd slept. He was flat on his back, hands on his stomach when he opened his eyes and rolled his jaw to the pillow. His pupils and mind tried simultaneously to focus, finally lighting on Linnea. When he spoke his voice sounded like nutshells cracking.

"John?"

Her throat and mouth filled. Her heart wrenched with pity. She'd feared being the one to whom he'd awaken and ask the question, yet perhaps it was best that Nissa and Kristian be spared answering it.

She took his hand. "John didn't make it."

"Tell him to get under the wagon," Theodore said very clearly. Struggling to brace up on both elbows, he ordered in an eerily normal tone, "John, get in," then made as if to get up and see to it.

Linnea sprang to her feet, pushed him back, and struggled to keep her tears hidden.

"Go to sleep . . . please, Teddy . . . shh . . . shh . . ."

He fell back, closed his eyes, and rolled toward the wall, again claimed by the blissful arms of sleep.

He was still dead to the world when Nissa came to spell Linnea. And later in the afternoon, when the men returned to discuss funeral arrangements. Linnea took Nissa's place again and was sitting beside the bed when Lars and Ulmer came to the bedroom door and knocked softly. Lars asked, "How is he?"

"Still sleeping."

The two men came in and quietly stood looking down at their sleeping brother. Ulmer reached to brush the hair from Teddy's forehead, then turned to rest a hand on Linnea's shoulders. "How you doing, young 'un?"

"Me? Oh, I'm fine. Don't waste your worries on me."

"Ma tells us you're in a family way."

"Just barely."

"Barely's enough. You take it easy, okay? We don't want Teddy to wake up to more bad news."

He glanced at Teddy again while Lars leaned over to give Linnea a kiss on the cheek. "That's wonderful, Linnea. Now how about a breath of fresh air?"

She glanced at Theodore. "I'd rather not leave him."

"We went out with a couple horses, cleaned up the mess, tipped over the wagon, and brought it back home. It's sitting down by the windmill. There's something carved in the bed of it we think you should see."

They let her go alone. On the fast-disappearing snow the shadow of the windmill stretched long. She ran through the late afternoon toward the parsley-green wagon with its bright red wheels. The words were easy enough to spot—after all, Theodore kept everything in shipshape, including the thick green paint on the wagon bed. The letters were slightly disconnected, but decipherable just the same.

Lin, I'm sorry.

More tears? How was it possible to feel more pity, more love than she already did? Yet she experienced as real a pain while reading the message as she imagined he had felt writing it. She ran her fingertips over the scarred paint, picturing him lying beneath the overturned wagon carving the words, afraid he'd die without saying them, without seeing his child.

Love welled up, combined with grief, despair, and hope, a mixture of emotions brought about by the random hand of fate choosing one life and sparing another.

That evening, when she was sitting beside Teddy, his eyes opened. She saw immediately he was lucid.

"Linnea," he said croakily, reaching.

She took his hand; his fingers twisted tight and pulled. "Teddy . . . oh, Teddy."

"Come here."

Gingerly, she sat beside him.

"No . . . under."

Sweater, apron, shoes, and all she got beneath the covers where it was warm and he was waiting to roll her tight against his stomach and hold her as if he were shipwrecked and she was a sturdy timber.

"I'm so sorry, Linnea . . . so sorry . . . I didn't think I'd—"

"Shh."

"Let me say it. I've got to."

"But I found the carving on the wagon. I know, love, I know."

"I thought I was going to die and you'd think I didn't want the baby, but when I was laying under that wagon thinking I'd never see you again I . . . I kept thinking that the baby was a godsend, only I'd been too stubborn to recognize it. Oh, Lin, Lin . . . I was such a fool." He could not hold her close enough, nor kiss her hard enough to convey all he felt. But she understood fully as his hand stole down to mold her stomach where his seed grew, healthy and strong.

"And I thought you'd die in the blizzard and I wouldn't get a chance to tell you I knew you hadn't meant it. But you're alive . . . oh, dear Teddy . . ."

"You feel so good, so warm. It was so cold under that wagon. Hold me."

She did, gratefully, until his tremors passed.

In time she whispered, "Teddy, John . . ."

"I know," came his voice, muffled against her chest. "I know."

He shuddered once, convulsively, then his hands clutched her sweater and he pulled her tightly against him while she cradled his head, her lips buried in his hair.

There were no words she could say, so she didn't try. She let him breathe of her warm, live, pregnant body, clutch it, draw from it, until the worst had passed. When he spoke, he spoke for both of them. "If the baby's a boy, we'll name it after him."

A life for a life—somehow they both found ease in the thought.

Chapter 24

John's funeral was held on May Day, the temperature reaching an unprecedented seventy-nine degrees. There remained no hint that the blizzard had ravaged the countryside save for the casket of the man who'd lost his life in it. Indeed, the wild crocus and buttercups blossomed euphorically. In the cemetery beside the little white country church a myriad of spring flowers were up and radiant beside the headstones—creeping phlox in carpets of purple, peonies in explosions of heliotrope, and bridal wreath in cascades of white.

But what a woeful scene at the graveside. On a day when the children should have been gathering those flowers for May baskets, they stood instead among them in a crooked flank, singing a farewell hymn in clear, piping voices while their teacher directed them with tears in her eyes. The family stood nearby, hemmed in close, their elbows touching.

When the song ended, Linnea took her place by Theodore's shoulder; he was still too depleted to stand through the ceremony, so sat instead on a plain wooden kitchen chair. It looked out of place with its spooled legs buried in the spring grass. It was the kind of chair usually seen with toddlers climbing on its seat, or with a man balancing it on two legs while considering what card to play, or with a work jacket carelessly flung over its back. The sight of it at the graveside brought Linnea's tears up again with new vigor.

But it wasn't really the chair at all. It was Theodore who made her cry, sitting upon it so wan and gaunt, dolefully formal, his legs crossed at neither ankle nor knee. The gentle breeze riffled his pant legs and fingered the hair on his forehead. He still hadn't shed a tear, though she knew his agony was even greater than her own. But all she could do was stand at his side and squeeze his shoulder.

And then there was Nissa, listening to Reverend Severt eulogize her son, breaking down at last and turning against Lars's broad chest for support until from somewhere a second kitchen chair was produced and she was gently lowered onto it.

The faces of John's siblings were vacant, each of them undoubtedly reliving their own private memories of the gentle, unassuming man they had protected all their lives.

The eulogy droned on. Funny, Linnea thought, but it didn't seem to touch on any of the important things: John, self-consciously shuffling his feet while peeking around a cloakroom door with a Christmas tree hidden behind him; John, blushing and stammering as he asked the new schoolmarm to dance; John, winking at his partner just before playing the winning card; John, planting morning glories by his windmill; John, saying, "Teddy, he never gets mad at me, not even when I'm slow. And I'm pretty slow."

Oh, how they'd miss him. How they'd all miss him.

The ceremony ended as Ulmer, Lars, Trigg, and Kristian lowered the coffin into the grave. When a symbolic spadeful of dirt was dropped upon it, Nissa collapsed in a rash of weeping, repeating woefully, "Oh, my son . . . my son . . ." But Theodore sat on as before, as if part of his own life had been snuffed out with John's.

During the hours following the service, while the mourners gathered at the house to share food, Theodore looked haggard and spoke little. When the house emptied at last and the quietude settled too thickly, Nissa sat at the kitchen table, listlessly tapping the oilcloth. Kristian went for a walk up the road with Patricia and Raymond. Linnea hung up wet dishtowels on the clothesline and returned to the tranquil house.

Nissa stared vacantly at the sunset sky, the budding caragana bushes, the windmill softly turning. Linnea stepped behind her chair and leaned to kiss the old woman softly on the neck. She smelled of lye soap and lavender salts. "Can I get you anything?"

Nissa heaved herself from her reverie. "No . . . no, child. Guess I've had about everything a body's got a right to expect."

The tears stung once more. Linnea closed her eyes, leaned back, and held a deep breath. Nissa sighed, squared her shoulders, and asked, "Where's Teddy?"

"I think he slipped away to the barn to be by himself for a while."

"You reckon he's all right out there?"

"I'll go down and check on him if it'll make you feel better."

"He's awful weak yet. Didn't see him eatin' much today either."

"Will you be all right alone for a few minutes?"

Nissa gave a dry laugh. "Y' start alone, y' end alone. Why is it that in between folks think y' always need company?"

"All right. I won't be long."

She knew where he'd be, probably slumped on his chair polishing harness that didn't need it. But when she came to the door of the tack room she found him instead with idle hands. He sat in the ancient chair, facing the door, with his head tipped back against the edge of the tool bench, eyes closed. On his lap, washing her chest, sat John's cat, Rainbow, with Theodore's hands resting inertly beside her haunches. Though he at first appeared to be asleep, Linnea saw his fingertips move in the soft fur, and from the corner of his eyes, tears seeped. He wept as he'd awakened—quietly, undramatically—letting the tears roll down his face without bothering to wipe them away.

Linnea had never seen Theodore cry before; the sight was devastating.

"Theodore," she said gently, "your mother was worried about you."

His eyes opened, but his head didn't move.

"Tell her I just wanted to be alone."

"Are you all right?"

"Fine."

She studied him, trying to keep her lips from trembling, her eyes from stinging. But he looked so forlorn and alone. ''Did Rainbow come down here by herself?''

With an effort he lifted his head to watch his fingers probe the cat's fur, the look on his face so desolate and lifeless it tore at her soul. ''No. Kristian went and got her. Figured she'd sit on John's doorstep meowing for food . . . t . . . till . . .'' But he never finished. His face suddenly furrowed into lines of grief. A single harsh sob rent the room as he dropped his head and covered his eyes with one hand. Rainbow started and leaped away while Linnea rushed across the concrete floor to squat before him, touching his knees.

''Oh, Teddy . . .'' she despaired, ''I need so badly to be with you right now. Please don't shut me out.''

A strangled cry left his throat as his arms lashed out to take her close. Then she was in his embrace, on his lap, holding him fiercely while his ragged sobs heaved against her breast, and hers upon his hair. Clutching, they rocked. Against her dress he brokenly uttered her name while she clung to him—consoled, consoling.

When the crying subsided, they were left limp, depleted, but feeling better and infinitely closer. A step sounded in the outer barn and though Teddy straightened, Linnea stayed where she was, with her arms around his neck.

Kristian stepped to the doorway, looking lost and lonely himself. ''Grandma was worried. She sent me down here after you two.''

They'd each had their time alone. Now it was time to draw strength from others. Linnea got to her feet, drew Theodore up, and said, ''Come. Nissa needs to be with us now.'' She looped one arm around his waist, the other around Kristian's, and followed by John's cat, they walked up past the sighing windmill toward the house.

Life went on. Theodore returned to the fields alone. Nissa started putting in her garden. P.S. 28 had been closed long enough.

How fast the school year was coming to a close. May seemed to pass in a blur. There was the county spelling been in Williston—won by Paul this year. Then came *Sytende Mai*—the seventeenth of May—the biggest Norwegian holiday of the year, celebrating the day the homeland had adopted its constitution. There were games and a picnic at school, followed by a dance, at which Linnea brought up the subject of Kristian's enlistment.

''He's not a child anymore.'' They watched Kristian and Patricia dancing, so close a gnat couldn't have come between them. ''If he's made his decision, I think you'll have to let him go.''

''I know,'' Theodore said softly, his eyes following the pair. ''I know.''

And so the end of the school year would bring additional heartache. But, come what may, the days marched on and Linnea felt both the exhilaration inherent with term's end and the sadness of realizing these were her last precious days as a teacher. She had been a good one; she felt no false sense of modesty about it and wished that when fall came she could somehow have both the baby and her old job back. But when she said good-bye to the children on the last day, she'd be bidding farewell to a phase of her life.

Final examinations were held, then it was time for the last-day picnic. The class had voted to hold it down by the creek so they could all swim.

The day turned out ideally—warm and sunny with little wind. Just perfect for a crew of excited children celebrating the end of school. They played games, swam, ate, explored. The boys fished downstream while the girls searched for wild-flowers and twined them in each other's French braids.

It was near the end of the afternoon when Norna approached Linnea with a frown, announcing, "I can't find Frances anyplace."

"She's with the others, picking flowers."

"She was, but she isn't anymore."

Linnea glanced upstream. Laughter floated down from the small group of girls who were busily engaged in making clover rings. But Frances wasn't with them.

Automatically, Linnea turned to the one she always seemed to turn to. "Kristian, have you seen Frances?" she called.

Kristian's head came up. He and Patricia were sitting quietly on the creek bank, talking. He glanced around. "No, ma'am."

"Have you, Patricia?"

"No, ma'am."

All four of them looked at the creek. But it wasn't deep enough here for Frances to drown. Quickly Linnea took a nose count. Her heart beat out a warning when she realized Allen Severt, too, was missing.

Frances Westgaard had been in and out of the creek four times that day. She had water in one ear that refused to be shaken out, and a bad case of shivers. Hugging herself, she made her way through the thick underbrush toward the place where the girls had left their clothes.

When she grew up, Frances decided, she was going to be a teacher, just like Aunt Linnea. She'd take her class on picnics like this all the time, at least once every week when the weather was good. And in the winter they'd cook soup, too. And rabbits on Thanksgiving and popcorn whenever the kids said they wanted it.

Her wet bathing drawers felt thick and sticky. They clung like leeches when she tried to pull them down. Hobbling around, she managed to work them to her hips, and finally to her knees, but even hopping one-footed she couldn't get them off completely. Finally she gave up and plopped down on the scratchy grass. Her teeth were chattering, her jaw dancing as she tried to work the clinging drawers over her ankles.

"Hey, Frances, whatcha doin'?" an unctuous voice drawled.

Frances jumped and tried to jerk the drawers back up, but they were rolled up tight as a new rope. "I'm changin' my clothes. You git outa here, Allen!"

Allen stepped out from behind a cottonwood with a smart-aleck expression on his mouth. "Why should I? It's a free country." Allen had had all year long to nurse his rancor for Mrs. Westgaard and Frances. Both of them had caused him embarrassment more times than he cared to count. There was no way for him to get back at his teacher, but he could even the score with this little dummy.

"You better get outa here or I'm gonna tell Aunt Linnea!" Frantically Frances fumbled with the drawers, trying to straighten them out, but Allen advanced and stood over her, pinning the wet garment to the ground between her ankles with his foot. "Oh yeah? What you gonna tell her?"

Allen's eyes raked Frances's bare skin and she shielded her lap with her hands.

"You ain't supposed to be here. This is where the girls change."

But Allen only gave a sinister laugh that struck a bolt of fear through the girl.

"Allen, I don't like you. I'm gonna tell on you!"

"You been tellin' on me all year, gettin' me in trouble all the time. Haven't you, snot?"

"No, I—"

"You have, too, and I'm gonna make you sorry . . . dummy!"

Before she could wiggle away Allen jumped her. The force of his body knocked her flat. She shrieked out, "I'm gonna tell!" before he clapped a hand across her mouth and slammed her head against the earth. Frances's eyes widened with fear and her mouth opened in a suppressed scream beneath his palm.

"You tell and I'll get you good, Frances!" he threatened in an ugly voice. "You tell and I'll do something worse to you next time. All I wanna do now is look."

Again Frances gave a muffled scream. She thrashed and kicked, but he was older than she and much bigger. "Frances, you shut up! You scream and they'll all come runnin' and I'll tell 'em you pulled your pants down right in front of me. You know what they do to girls who pull their pants down in front of boys?"

Terrified, Frances fell still, her heart hammering pitifully as Allen thrust a knee between her legs, trying to force them apart. But the wet drawers shackled her ankles, aiding her. Nose to nose, they struggled until Allen finally managed to wedge her knees open. Beneath him the frightened face had turned the color of chalk, only the dark, horrified eyes holding any color. Allen's breath came in a hard hiss. He squeezed her face till her cheek sliced against a tooth and she tasted blood. Struck afresh by terror, she squirmed harder. Twisting frantically, fighting for breath, Frances felt his weight shift as he yanked her wet shirt up. Behind his hand, she screamed again. His face contorted with ugliness. "You scream and you'll be sorry. Cuz once you do they'll all know you been doing dirty things with me." With the speed of a snake he shifted, got her by the neck, and squeezed, completely subduing her at last. Her fingers uselessly plucked at his stranglehold while he knelt between her legs and braced back.

The next moment he was jerked to his feet like a marionette, then a fist slammed into his face and sent him crashing against the trunk of a cottonwood.

"You filthy rotten son of a bitch!" This time the fist caught him in the solar plexus and doubled him over like a pocket knife. In a flash he was jerked erect and hammered again. Somebody screamed. Blood flew across the grass. Children came running. Sobs filled the air. Linnea shouted, "Kristian, stop it this moment! Kristian, I said *stop!*"

It ended as abruptly as it had begun.

Allen Severt held his bloody face in both hands and looked up to see Kristian spraddled above him like Zeus outraged. Linnea held a whimpering Frances in her lap. Libby Severt gaped at her brother in horrified disbelief. Raymond stormed onto the scene with fists clenched. "Get away from him, Kristian. It's my turn!"

"Mine, too!" echoed Tony, arriving on his brother's heels. Had the situation not been so grave it might have been humorous to see Tony, bristling mad, clenching his weak fists and squaring his skinny shoulders as if he had the power to do more than swat mosquitoes.

"Boys! That's enough!"

"That puny little bastard ain't gonna forget the day he laid hands on my little sister!" Raymond vowed, being restrained now by Kristian.

Transferring the weeping Frances into Patricia's arms, Linnea leaped to her feet and confronted the three angry boys. "Watch your language in front of the little ones, and don't raise your voice to me!" Her insides trembled and her knees had turned to aspic, but she hid it well. "Allen, get up," she ordered officiously. "You get back to school and wait for me, and so help me God, you'd better be there when I get there! Patricia, help Frances get dried and dressed. Raymond, you may carry your little sister back to school. Kristian, button your shirt and head cross country to our place and get Clippa for Raymond and Frances. The rest of you, change out of your wet things and collect your lunch pails."

Linnea's quick commands subdued them all, but she herself was still in a state of fury thirty minutes later when she marched up the lane to the Severts' front door. She followed Libby inside while Allen whimpered behind them, holding his jaw, blood congealed in one nostril and dried on his fingers.

"Mother?" Libby called, and a moment later Lillian Severt appeared in the far archway.

"Allen!" She scurried across the room. "Oh, dear Lord, what's happened to you?"

"He got precisely what he deserved," Linnea retorted, then went on coldly, "Where is your husband?"

"He's busy right now, in the church."

"Get him."

"But Allen's face—"

"Get him!"

"How dare you—"

"Get him!" Linnea's blast of outrage finally stunned Lillian Severt into compliance. She ran from the room, casting a baleful glance over her shoulder at Allen's bloody nose, while Libby dropped her chin. When Mr. and Mrs. Severt returned, Linnea gave them no chance to coddle their son. She made sure she had him sitting on a straight-backed chair with herself standing over him like a prison guard. His face was swollen, the right eye nearly shut. Lillian moved as if to console him, but Linnea stopped her by ordering, "All right, Allen, talk!"

Allen held his jaw and mumbled, "Can't . . . hurts."

She gave him a nudge that nearly knocked him off the chair. "I said, talk!" He dropped his head onto the table and cradled it in his arms. "Very well, I'll tell them myself." She pierced his parents with a glare. "Your son attacked Frances Westgaard today during the school picnic. He pulled her pants down and—"

"I did not!" howled Allen, coming up straight, but immediately he clutched his jaw and subsided into moans of pain.

"He followed her to the girls' changing spot when nobody else was around and attacked her. Pulled her pants down and threatened to get her again and do worse if she dared tell on him. He had her pinned to the ground by the throat when we found them.''

''I don't believe you!'' declared Lillian Severt, her eyes huge.

''You didn't believe me the last time I came to you, or the time before that. Not only didn't you believe me, you went so far as to intimate that the fault for Allen's misbehavior should be placed on me. You refused to see that his violations are much more than simple boyish pranks and that steps must be taken to help him. This time, I'm afraid you'll have no choice. The whole school witnessed it. I happened to have all the children out searching for them when it happened. Tell them, Libby.''

''I . . . he . . .'' Libby's terrified eyes flashed from her brother to her teacher.

''You needn't be afraid, Libby,'' Linnea said, softening for the first time, but she could see Libby's fear of retribution was greater than her fear of not answering. ''You know that to avoid telling the truth is as good as a lie, don't you, Libby?''

''But I'm scared. He'll hurt me if I tell.''

Martin finally spoke up. ''Hurt you?'' He came forward, reaching for Libby's hand.

''He always hurts me if I do anything to make him mad.''

His wife began, ''Martin, how can you be concerned with her when his nose is bleeding and—''

''Let her talk,'' Martin demanded, and encouraged his daughter. ''Hurt you? How?''

''He pinches me and pulls my hair. And he said he'd kill my cat. He said he'd put k . . . kerosene in her . . . in her . . .'' Chagrined, Libby hung her head.

''What a preposterous—''

''Quiet!'' Martin roared, spinning toward his wife. ''You've had your way with him for as long as you're going to. If I had stepped in years ago, this never would have happened.'' Gently he turned to Libby. ''So it's all true, what Mrs. Westgaard said?''

''Yes!'' she cried. ''Yes!'' Tears poured from her eyes. ''He was laying on top of poor Frances and he was choking her and her . . . pants were down and . . . and . . . everybody in the school saw it and then Kristian pulled Allen off and slugged him a good one and Raymond wanted to slug him, too, but Mrs. Westgaard wouldn't let him. But I wish he would've! I wish Raymond would've knocked his teeth clear out . . . because he's . . . he's mean and hateful and he's always teasing people and calling them names when they never did anything to him. He just hurts everybody to be sp . . . spiteful!'' When she broke into a rash of weeping and buried herself in her father's arms, Linnea took over.

''Mr. and Mrs. Severt, I'm afraid this time there will be serious repercussions. I'm going to recommend to Superintendent Dahl that Allen be officially expelled from school as of today. And I caution you to see to it that Allen does nothing to hurt Libby because she told the truth.''

Mrs. Severt's face had turned ashen, and for the first time ever she had nothing to say in defense of her darling. By the time Linnea left the house, Allen was howling in pain, but getting little sympathy.

She went directly to Ulmer and Helen's to find Frances already tucked into bed, being coddled by all her sisters and brothers. A moment after Linnea arrived, so did Theodore. He stalked into the house scowling, and announced, "Kristian told me. How's the little one?"

So naturally they banded together in times of distress. Without hesitation, without explanation. Seeing Teddy appear with Kristian at his side brought tears at last to Linnea's eyes. She'd been running on adrenaline for well over an hour, but now that Teddy was here and the incident was over, she felt like a piece of old rope.

"You okay?" Teddy asked, turning to her.

She nodded shakily. "Yes."

But he opened his arms anyway, and she went into them like a child to her mother. "I'm so glad you're here," she whispered against his chest. His shirt was stained beneath the arms and he smelled of sweat and horses, but she had never loved him more nor been more grateful for his support.

"This time we're gonna nail that little bastard," he vowed against her hair. He rarely cursed, and never in front of Kristian. Hearing him, she realized the depth of his concern. "I brought the wagon," he added, "figured you could use a ride over to Dahl's."

She looked up at him and smiled tenderly. "If I accept, will you think I'm a hothouse pansy?"

And there before all the others he did something he'd never done before: kissed her full on the lips.

Not only did Raymond and Kristian refuse to be shunted off from underfoot while the incident was discussed, they insisted on coming along to relate the tale as they'd seen it. They were old enough to be in on this and weren't going to budge until they were assured that Allen Severt got his comeuppance.

Though it took the remainder of the day, the outcome was decided before nightfall. Allen Severt was officially expelled from school and would not be allowed at the graduation ceremonies. Whether or not he would be allowed to attend next year would be decided by the school board at its next meeting.

The children tittered about the fact that if Allen were allowed to return, he'd undoubtedly do so not only much mollified, but also much thinner, for Kristian's first punch had broken Allen's jaw, and it would have to be wired shut for six weeks.

The graduation ceremony was held in the schoolyard on the last Friday evening in May. Mourning doves cooed their soothing vespers. The sun slanted down through the ticking leaves of the cottonwoods and dappled the scene with gray and gold. The smell of fecund earth lifted from the adjacent fields where wheat sprouted like a youth's first beard.

The parents came in wagons, bringing kitchen chairs again, setting them in neat rows upon the beaten grass of the schoolyard. The four- and five-year-olds scrambled among the recitation benches up front, pretending they were as old as their sisters and brothers.

Kristian delivered the valedictory speech with all due gravity. He spoke of the war in Europe and the responsibility of the new generation to seek and assure peace for all mankind. When it was over Linnea, with misty eyes, directed the children in "America the Beautiful."

Superintendent Dahl gave his windy oration at the end of which he surprised Linnea by declaring that her leadership had been superlative, her innovations noteworthy, and her personal conduct exemplary. So much so, he continued, that the state board of education had asked him on their behalf to bestow upon her an award for excellence for organizing the first official ''Domestics'' class in a school of this size in the state; also for her organizational ability on behalf of the war effort, for her cool-headedness during the blizzard, and her foresight in having stocked emergency rations beforehand. Mr. Dahl added with a grin, ''In spite of what some of the children might think of raisins as emergency rations.'' A ripple of laughter passed over the crowd, then he continued, earnestly, ''And last but not least, the State Board of Education commends Mrs. Westgaard for accomplishing what no other teacher has done before her. She has persuaded the P.S. 28 parents to agree to extend the school year to a full nine months for both girls *and* boys of all ages.''

Linnea felt herself blushing, but hid it as she rose to take the podium herself. Gazing out at the familiar faces, looking back on the rewards and heartbreak of the past nine months, she felt a lump form in her throat. There were few out there whom she couldn't honestly say she loved. Equally as few who didn't love her in return.

''My dear friends,'' she opened, then paused, glanced over their sunlit faces. ''Where should I begin?''

She thanked them for a year of wonderful experiences, for their support, their friendship. She thanked them for opening their homes and hearts to her and for giving her one of their own to be her own. And she announced that though she would gladly have come back next fall to teach another year, she'd be staying home to have a baby. She invited the children to come and visit her during the summer, and admonished them to start victory gardens. In the fall, should the war not have ended, they could work together with their new teacher on an autumn-harvest auction.

Lastly, with a lump in her throat, she asked them all to pray for world peace, and told them Kristian would be leaving the following day for Jefferson Barracks, Missouri, for voluntary enlistment into the army.

She thanked them one last time with tears in her eyes and turned the program back to Superintendent Dahl for the distribution of grade-achievement certificates and eighth-grade diplomas.

Afterward, they had apple cider and cookies, and Linnea found herself hugged by nearly every parent present, and to a number, her students told her they wished she were coming back next year. By the time the benches were carried into the building and stacked up against the side walls, it was dusk.

Kristian had gone off with Patricia, but Nissa and Theodore waited in the wagon.

Standing in the cloakroom doorway and looking at the shadowed room with its desks pushed against the side walls, its flag furled tightly in brown paper, its blackboard washed, and its stovepipe freshly cleaned, Linnea felt as if she were leaving a small part of her heart behind. Ah, the smell of this room. She'd never forget it. A little dusty, a little musty—like sweating heads—and perhaps tinged with the undying after scent of cabbage from their Fridays' soup.

''Ready?'' Theodore asked behind her.

''I guess so.'' But she didn't turn. Her shoulders sagged slightly.

He squeezed them, pulling her back against his chest. ''You'll miss it, huh?''

She nodded sadly. ''I grew up a lot here.''

''So did I.''

''Oh, Teddy.'' She found his hand and pulled it to her lips. The twilight settled upon their shoulders. Outside, the horses waited—Nelly and Fly now. Inside, memory's voices drifted back from yesterday—the children's, John's, Kristian's, the hired hands', their own.

''In six years one of ours will be coming here,'' he mused. ''And we can tell him the stories about when his mother was teacher.''

She smiled up at him over her shoulder, then raised up on tiptoe and kissed him.

He rested his hands on her waist. ''I know how much you'd like to come back . . . and it's okay. Cause I know you want the baby, too.''

''Oh, I love you, Theodore Westgaard.'' She linked her fingers behind his neck.

''I love you, too, little missy.'' He kissed the end of her nose. ''And Ma's waiting.''

With one last look, they closed all four doors and walked arm in arm to the wagon.

It was a breezeless night. The big dipper was pouring light into the northern sky and the moon in three-quarter phase lit the world like a blue flame. The first crickets had arrived and they sawed away dissonantly from the shadows, stopping momentarily at the sound of a horse passing, then tuning up again.

Clippa plodded unhurriedly along the grassy verge between two wheat fields, head down, backside swaying lazily. On her warm, bare hide Kristian rode with the reins loose in his fingers and Patricia's cheek pressed against his back, her hands hugging his belly. They'd been riding that way, aimlessly, for nearly an hour, loath to face the final good-bye.

''I should get you home.''

Her arms tightened. ''No, not yet.''

''It's late.''

''Not yet,'' she whispered fiercely. Beneath her palm she felt his heart beat, strong and sure. Against her thighs she felt his legs rub with the rhythm of the hoofbeats on the grass.

''We're almost to the creek.''

The branch of a black willow touched his face and he bent to avoid it, tilting her with him.

''Stop a minute.''

He reined in. Clippa obeyed instantly, her head drooping while the pair on her back sat still, listening. They could hear the purling water some distance off, and the pulsing duet of two bullfrogs. Kristian tipped his head back to look at the stars. It bumped hers and he felt her breath blowing warm through his shirt, heating his shoulder blade. He swallowed and closed his eyes, covering her arms with his own.

''We shouldn't've stopped.''

She kissed his shoulder blade once more. ''You could die, Kristian.''

''I'm not gonna die.''

''But you could! You could, and I'd never see you again.''

''I don't want to go either.''

"Then why are you?"

"I don't know. It's just something in me. But I aim to come back and marry you."

Behind him, he felt her straighten. "Marry me?"

"I've thought about it. Haven't you?"

"Oh, Kristian, you really mean it?"

"Course, I mean it." Her arms snaked around his belt and her breasts warmed his skin through the white cotton shirt. "Does that mean you would?"

"Of course I would. I'd marry you today if you'd let me." Her palms moved to rub the tops of his thighs where his trousers stretched taut over firm, young muscle. Abruptly he swung a leg over Clippa's head and slid off. Looking up, he reminded Patricia, "You aren't done with school yet. Better get that done first, don't you think?"

"I'm fifteen. My grandmother was married a year already by the time she was fifteen." In the moonlight her face was shadowed, but he understood the expression in her eyes even though he couldn't make it out. "Come on, let's walk." He reached for her waist, and she for his shoulders, but when she dropped from the horse their bodies brushed and neither of them moved. The night thrummed around them. Their heartbeats matched its rhythm. Their breaths came quick and heavy.

"Oh, Kristian, I'm going to miss you," she breathed.

"I'll miss you, too."

"Kristian . . ." She lifted to him, looping his neck with her arms, pressing close. When their lips met it was with the singular desperation only farewells can bring. Their bodies were tensile and straining, burgeoning with imminent maturity and the awesome need to lay claim to one another before tomorrow's separation. His arms bound her tightly and his tongue evoked an answer from hers. His hands began traversing her body, dreading the loss of it even before the gain.

He found her breasts—firm, small, upthrust—her curved feminine length against his hard, honed body. He set a rhythm against her and she answered, until they could not have come closer together but tried nonetheless. He went down to his knees, hauling her with him, falling to the thick, dry grass that whispered beneath them as they added a new, pulsing rhythm to those of the summer night around them.

When the rhythmic caress grew reckless, he hauled himself away. "It's wrong."

She brought him back on top of her. "One time . . . just once, in case you never come back."

"It's a sin."

"Against who?"

"Oh God, I don't want to leave you with a baby."

"You won't. Oh, Kristian, Kristian, I love you. I promise I'll wait for you, no matter how long it takes."

"Oh, Patricia . . ." Her body formed a cradle upon which he rocked. Their bodies fit with mysterious conformity unlike any they'd imagined. He rolled aside, touched her here, there, discovering. She was the answer to the myriad questions of his universe. "I love you, too . . . you're all soft . . . and so warm . . ."

She brushed her knuckles across his masculine secrets, discovering, too. "And you're hard and warm . . ."

When they undressed each other it was only by half, and haltingly. When their bodies sought each other it was with the fumbling uncertainty of all first times. But when their flesh linked, so did their souls, bound together in both a promise and prayer for the future.

"I love you, don't forget it," he said later, at her door. She was sobbing too hard to answer, able only to cling. "Tell me once more before I go," he said, wondering why he'd ever been so anxious to grow up when growing up hurt this much, wondering why he'd ever wanted to leave this place when it was all the things he loved.

"I l . . . love y . . . you, K . . . Kristian."

He forced her back, holding her head in both wide palms. "There, now you remember it. And pray for me."

"I w . . . will . . . I p . . . promise."

He kissed her hard, quick, then spun and mounted Clippa before he could change his mind again, sending the mare galloping at breakneck speed through the summer moonlight.

It was just past sunrise. Grandma waited at the door with six blood-sausage sandwiches wrapped in oilcloth.

Kristian looked down as she thrust them into his hands.

"Grandma, I don't need all that."

"You just take 'em," she said sternly, trying to keep her chin from trembling. "Ain't nobody in the army knows how to make blood sausage."

He took them, and the fresh batch of *fattigman,* too.

"Now, git! And hurry and take care of them Jerries so you can git back home where you belong."

Her little gray pug was neatly in place, her glasses hooked behind her ears, her apron clean and starched. He didn't ever remember seeing her any other way, not in all the years they'd lived in the same house. The morning sun lit the hairs on her chin to a soft, gilt fuzz, and reflected from the sparkle she couldn't keep from forming behind her oval spectacles. He scooped her against him so hard her old bones barely stayed intact.

"Good-bye, Grandma. I love you." He'd never said it before, but it suddenly hit Kristian how true it was.

"I love you, too, you durn fool boy. Now git going. Your pa's waiting."

He rode into Alamo on the seat of the double-box wagon, flanked by Theodore and Linnea, holding the sandwiches and cookies on his lap. In town, he studied the buildings as if for the first time. Too quickly they reached the depot. Too quickly the ticket was purchased. Too quickly the train wailed into sight.

It clanged in beside them and they stood in the white puffs of steam, all of them trying valiantly not to cry.

Linnea needlessly adjusted Kristian's collar. "There are more socks in your suitcase than any *two* soldiers could possibly need. And I put in some spare hankies, too."

"Thanks," he said, then their eyes met and the next moment they were hugging hard, parting with a swift kiss. "We love you," she whispered against his jaw. "Keep safe."

"I will. Got to come back and see my little sister or brother."

He turned from her tear-streaked face to Theodore's.

Jesus, Mary . . . Pa was crying.

"Pa . . ."

His face wracked with sorrow, Theodore clutched Kristian to his wide, strong chest. His straw hat fell from his head but nobody noticed. The conductor called "All aboard," and the father clutched his son's hale body and prayed he'd return the same way. "Keep your head low, boy."

"I will. I'm c . . . comin' back . . . you can c . . . ount on it."

"I love you, son."

"I love you, too."

When Kristian backed away they were both crying. They leaned toward each other one last time . . . straining . . . clasping each other's necks. As adults, they had never kissed; both of them realized they might never get the chance again. It was Theodore who leaned forward, kissing Kristian flush on the lips before the boy spun for the train.

It lumbered into motion, gathering speed, giving them a brief glimpse of Kristian waving from a window before whisking him away. The breath of its passing stirred the June air, lifting dust and Linnea's skirts as the caboose swayed eastward along the track.

She clutched Teddy's arm against the side of her breast, trying to think of something to say.

"We'd best get home. There's wheat to be planted."

The wheat . . . the wheat . . . always the wheat. But now they had a real reason to keep loaves going to Europe.

Chapter 25

Oh, that summer, that endless crawling summer while the war in Europe absorbed half a million doughboys and German submarines sank civilian barges and fishing schooners off America's east coast. In the Westgaard living room the newest addition was a gleaming mahogany Truphonics radio around which the family gathered each evening to hear the news from the front, via the scratchy transmissions from Yankton, South Dakota.

Linnea was shocked the day the age limits for the draft were extended to include men eighteen to forty-five. Why, most of the men she knew fell into that age bracket: Lars, Ulmer, Trigg . . . Theodore. Thankfully farmers were exempt, but it struck her that even her own father could be drafted! At church, where the service flag now held an additional blue star, she prayed more intensely, not only for Kristian and Bill, but that her father would not be called up. How would her mother survive if he went to war?

Poor Judith, bless her heart, whose husband had always owned a store with fresh and tinned goods available, had planted a victory garden. But her letters were filled with complaints about it. She hated every moment spent on her knees amid the weeds and cutworms. The cabbages, Judith complained, attracted little white butterflies and resembled Swiss cheese. The green beans ripened so fast no mortal could keep up with them, and the tomatoes got blight.

Linnea wrote back and advised her mother to leave the victory gardens to someone else and continue with the other war efforts at which she was so good. Meanwhile, she herself was learning the ins and outs of gardening from Nissa. Together they planted, weeded, picked, and canned. Linnea had never before realized how much work went into a single jar of perfect gold carrots gleaming like coins beneath their zinc lid. As the summer rolled on and Linnea's girth increased, the work became more arduous. Bending grew difficult, and straightening made her dizzy. Being in the sun too long made black dots dance before her eyes. Standing too long made her ankles swell. And she lost both the inclination and agility to make love.

Nighttimes, after listening to the radio and worrying about where and how Kristian was, she could not offer Theodore the consolation to be found in her body. She felt guilty because now, more than ever, he needed the temporary release. He worried about Kristian constantly, especially during his long hours alone, crisscrossing the fields behind the horses. They'd heard from Kristian—he'd completed his basic training and was assigned to the seventh division under Major General William M. Wright and had left for France on August eleventh after only eight weeks of training upon U.S. soil. Even with additional training in France, how could a farm boy who'd had to deal with nothing more belligerent than a shying horse be equipped for combat in so little time?

Then, as the summer drew to a close, news of another threat, more insidious than flamethrowers and mustard gas, made its way across the ocean to worry not only Theodore and Linnea, but all the fathers, mothers, wives, and sweethearts of the men fighting in Europe. This was an enemy who took no sides. It struck American, German, Italian, and Frenchman alike. With absolute impartiality it smote down hero and coward, experienced commander and pea-green recruit, leaving them sneezing and shivering and dying of fever in the trenches on the Marne and at Flanders Field.

The name of the threat was Spanish influenza.

From the time the news of it reached American shores, Theodore's restlessness and concern escalated. He became edgy and untalkative. And when the epidemic itself reached America and started spreading westward through its cities, the news affected everyone.

Meanwhile, Linnea grew enormous and ungainly, and looked in the mirror each day to find herself so unappealing she couldn't blame Teddy for paying her little attention lately. She loved going down to Clara's and holding baby Maren, telling herself *this* was what her payoff would be, and it would be well worth it.

One day, when Maren was asleep in her crib and Clara was rolling out crust for a sugarless apple pie, Linnea sat on a nearby chair like a beached whale. "I feel like a fat old ugly hippopotamus," she wailed.

Clara only laughed. "You're not fat and ugly and you're certainly not old. But if it's any consolation, we all get to feeling like that toward the end."

"You did, too?" Even at full term, Clara had always looked radiantly beautiful to Linnea, and had never seemed to lose her gaiety.

"Of course I did. Trigg just teased me a little more and made me laugh to keep my spirits up."

Linnea's spirits drooped further. "Not Teddy."

"He has been rather grouchy lately, hasn't he?"

"Grouchy—hmph!—there's got to be a worse word for it than that."

"He's got a lot on his mind, that's all. Kristian, and the baby coming, and threshing about to start."

"It's more than that. I mean, in bed at night he hardly even touches me. I know we can't do anything with the baby only six weeks away, but he doesn't even snuggle or . . . or kiss me or . . . well, he acts like he can't st . . . stand me." Linnea put her head down and started to cry, which she'd been doing with some regularity lately.

Clara dropped the rolling pin and wiped her hands on her apron, coming immediately to comfort the younger woman. "It's not you, Linnea. It's just the way men are. If they can't have it all, they don't want any. And they all get ornery without it. Teddy's acting like they all act, so you just get it out of your head that you're fat and ugly."

"B . . . but I am. I w . . . waddle around like a Ch . . . Christmas goose and all I do is bawl all the time, and oh, Clara . . . I don't think h . . . he likes m . . . me anymore!" she sobbed.

Clara rubbed her friend's shaking shoulders. "Now that's silly and you know it. Of course he likes you. Wait till that baby is born and you'll find out."

But before the baby was born someone else came along to lift Teddy's spirits and make him forget his cares temporarily: Isabelle Lawler.

Her cook wagon came rocking into the yard and Linnea's intestines seemed to tighten into knots. Isabelle was the same as ever—large, loud, and lusty. Same pumpkin-colored hair. Same face that looked like a bowl of half-eaten pudding. Same bawdy mule-skinner's voice. The transient cook was the farthest thing from a lady Linnea had ever seen. And even unpregnant, she outweighed Linnea by a good forty pounds. Why then the grin on Theodore's face the moment he saw her? From the time she and the threshing crew arrived, his crankiness mellowed. He smiled more, laughed with the hired hands, and took his meals in the cook wagon, as he had last year. He said the men expected it of him, but Linnea thought he had other reasons.

The night of the first dance, she counted: four times he danced with Isabelle Lawler. Four times! She kept no tally on the other women, so didn't realize he'd danced equally as many times with Clara, and with Nissa, and with plenty of others. She only knew that each time he took the cook onto the floor her own sense of inadequacy redoubled and she felt the embarrassing urge to cry. She was standing on the sidelines watching them when Clara found her.

"Whew! It's warm in here."

"Teddy's plenty warm—I can see that. Seems to be warming up more by the minute," she noted caustically.

Clara glanced at the dancing couple, then back at Linnea. "Isabelle? Oh, honey, don't be silly. He's just dancing with her, that's all."

"This is the fourth time."

"So what? That doesn't mean anything."

"Tell me what he sees in her, will you? Look at her. With those teeth she could eat corn through a picket fence, and that hair looks like somebody set fire to a haystack. But he's smiled more since she got here than he has in the last two months."

"He's always happy during threshing. All the men are."

"Sure. So how many times did Trigg dance with her? Or Lars?"

"Linnea, you're overreacting. Teddy just loves to dance, that's all, and he knows you tire easily now."

Though Clara's observation was meant to console Linnea, it only made her gloomier. "I feel like marching out there and telling that orange-headed tub of lard to find her own damn man and leave mine alone!"

"Well, if it'd make you feel better, why don't you do it?"

Linnea glanced at Clara to find her wearing a gamine grin and couldn't resist grinning back.

"Oh sure, and start everybody for forty miles around talking?"

"She's been coming here for—golly, what is it?—five years? Seven? I don't even remember anymore. Anyway, if there was something between them, don't you think people would have been talking long before this?"

Linnea's ruffled feathers were smoothed momentarily, but later that night, when Theodore flopped into bed beside her, she immediately sensed a difference in him. He rolled to his side facing her and lay a wrist over her hip.

"Come here," he whispered.

"Teddy, we can't—"

"I know," he returned, bracing on an elbow to kiss her, kneading her hip. He'd been drinking beer and the flavor of it lingered on his tongue. He pulled her close. Her distended stomach came up against his, then he found her hand and brought it to his tumescence, sheathing himself with her fingers.

She realized he'd been aroused even before he hit the bed.

Hurt, she whispered, "Who brought this on?"

"What?"

"I said who brought this on—me or Isabelle Lawler?"

His hand paused. Even in the dark she sensed him bristling. "Isabelle Lawler? Now what's that supposed to mean?"

"You've been bundling up on your own side of the bed for weeks, and now after dancing with her all night long you come to me hard as a fresh-dug rutabaga and expect me to take care of it for you? How dare you, Theodore Westgaard!"

She thrust his flesh away as if it were distasteful and flopped onto her back. He, too, rolled to his back angrily.

"Isabelle Lawler hasn't got a thing to do with this."

"Oh, hasn't she?"

"Come on, Linnea, all I did was dance with her."

"Four times. Four times, Theodore!"

He plumped his pillow and flounced over, presenting his spine. "Pregnant women," he mumbled disgustedly.

She grabbed his arm and tried to yank him onto his back again with little success. "Don't you 'pregnant woman' me, Teddy, not after you made me this way! And not after you've been walking around here smiling all week like some . . . some Hindu who just got his thirteenth wife!"

"Thirteenth . . ." Head off the pillow, he looked back over his shoulder, shrugged his arm free, then settled down with his back to her again. "Go to sleep, Linnea. You've got no reason to be jealous. You're just not feeling yourself these days."

This time she punched him on the arm. "Don't you go—"

"Ow!"

"—playing possum with me, Theodore Westgaard. Roll over here, because we're going to have this out! Now, don't tell me there's nothing between you and Isabelle Lawler, because I don't believe it!"

He folded his hands beneath his head, glared at the ceiling in the dark, and said nothing.

"Now tell me!" she insisted, sitting up beside him.

"Tell you what?"

"What there is between you and that woman?"

"I told you, there's nothing."

"But there was, wasn't there?"

"Linnea, you're imagining things."

"Don't treat me like a child!"

"Then don't act like one! I said there's nothing and I meant it."

"I can see the way she likes to hang around you. And you're the only one she never cusses with. And tonight before the dance you . . . you put on bay rum and you were humming."

"I put on bay rum before every dance."

Did he? She'd never watched him get ready for a dance before. She flounced onto her back and tucked the bedclothes beneath her arms. Picking at a knot of yarn on the quilt, staring at the moonlight on the opposite wall, she steeled herself to accept whatever he might say. Her voice became softer.

"You can tell me, Teddy, and I promise I won't get mad. I'm your wife. I've got a right to know."

"Linnea, why do you keep on this way?"

"Because, you know you were the first one for me."

"You already know there was Melinda."

"That's different. She was your wife."

He pondered silently for some time before going on. "And suppose it was true. Suppose there was a whole string of other women. What good would it do for you to know it now?"

She turned her head to face him and spoke sincerely. "There shouldn't be secrets between husbands and wives."

''Everybody's got a right to their own secrets.''

She was hurt at the thought that there were things he didn't share with her. She shared everything with him.

''What was there between you and Isabelle?'' she prodded.

''Linnea, drop it.''

''I can't. I wish I could, but I can't.''

He lay silently a long time, ran a hand through his hair, and wedged it behind his neck, emitting a long sigh.

''All right. Every year at threshing time I saw Isabelle in her wagon, after bedtime.''

The jealousy Linnea had felt before became pallid beside this gargantuan lump in her chest. ''You were . . . lovers?''

He drew a deep breath, let it out slowly, and closed his eyes. ''Yes.''

Now that the truth was out, she wished she'd left sleeping dogs lie, but some perverse instinct forced her to ask further questions. ''This year?''

''No, what do you think—''

''Last year then?''

A long silence, then, ''Yes.''

Rage burned through her. ''But that was after you met me!''

''Yes.'' He braced up on one elbow, looking down into her face. ''And we couldn't look at each other without snapping. And I thought you were too young for me, and that it was indecent to have stirrings about my son's school teacher. And I thought you couldn't stand my guts, Linnea.''

He tried to touch her but she jerked away. ''Oh, how could you!''

Typical woman, he thought, says she won't get mad, then bristles like a hedgehog. ''It's been fifteen years since Melinda ran away. Did you think there'd be nobody in all that time?''

''But she's . . . she's fat and . . . and uncouth and—''

''You don't know anything about her, so don't go casting stones,'' he returned tightly.

''But how could you bring her back here this year and parade her under my nose.''

''Parade her! I'm not parading her!''

''And what *else* are you doing right under my nose?''

''If you're insinuating—''

''Coming to bed hornier than a two-peckered goat when you and I haven't been able to make love for nearly a month. What am I supposed to think?''

''If you'd stop acting like a child, you'd realize that no man can go fifteen years without something . . . someone.''

''Child! Now I'm a child!''

''Well, you act like one!''

''So go to Isabelle.'' Tossing the covers back, Linnea leaped from the bed. ''With her build and her language, nobody'd ever mistake her for a child, would they?''

He sat straight up, jabbed a finger at the spot she'd left. ''I don't want Isabelle, now will you get back in this bed?''

''I wouldn't get back in that bed if my clothes were on fire and it was made of water!''

"Lower your voice. Ma's not deaf, you know."

"And you wouldn't want her to know about your little peccadilloes, would you?" she returned sarcastically.

He didn't know what "peccadilloes" meant and it made him all the angrier. He braced his elbows on his updrawn knees and ran both hands through his hair. "I should've known better than to tell you. I should've known you couldn't handle it. You're just too damn young to understand that everything in life isn't black and white. Isabelle and I weren't hurting anybody. She was alone. I was alone. We gave each other what we needed. Can you understand that?"

"I want that woman out of here tomorrow, do you hear?"

"And who's gonna feed the threshers? You, when you're eight months pregnant and can hardly make it to the end of a dance?"

"I don't care who does it, but it better not be Isabelle Lawler!"

"Linnea, come back here—where you going?"

At the door she paused only long enough to fling back, "I'm going to my old room!"

"You are not! You're my wife and you'll sleep in my bed!"

"You can expect me back in it when Isabelle Lawler disappears!"

When she was gone he sat staring at the black hole of the doorway, wondering how any woman could be so perverse. First she says she won't get mad, then she yells loud enough to wake the dead—much less, Ma—and marches off as if she expects him to go whimpering after her and apologize. Well, she'd wait till hell froze over cause he didn't have anything to apologize for! Last year had nothing to do with this year, and this year all he'd done with Isabelle was dance. And how could she think he'd be so faithless as to take Isabelle to bed just because he had to do without from his pregnant wife for a couple months?

Cut to the quick, Theodore lay on his back and stewed.

Just who did she think she was, that little snip, to dictate orders? Isabelle was a damn fine cook, and without her they'd be in a pretty pickle. She'd cook till the end of the threshing season, and if Linnea didn't like it, she could go right on bunking upstairs! He'd sleep better with her up there anyway; all she did all night long was make trips to the commode and wake him up.

Lord God . . . pregnant women, he thought again, flopping onto his side. Well, never again! He was too old to be going through this. This one baby and that was it . . . the end! And he hoped to high heaven when she had it she'd get over this testiness and life would get back to normal.

In the morning Nissa didn't say a word, though she most certainly must've heard the ruckus through the wall last night, and she knew Linnea had slept upstairs.

The three convened in the kitchen for breakfast.

"Fine mornin'," Nissa offered to no one in particular.

Nobody said a word.

"Ain't it?" she snapped, eyeing Linnea over the tops of her glasses.

"Yes . . . yes, it's a fine morning."

Theodore crossed the room with the milk pails, eyeing his wife silently.

"Need me a couple more pieces o' coal for the fire. Reckon I'll go out and get 'em, get me a sniff of this morning air."

When the old woman was gone, taking the half-full coal hod with her, he studied Linnea a little closer. He could tell she'd been crying last night. "Mornin'," he said.

"Morning." She refused to look at him.

"How'd you sleep?"

"Like a baby."

"Good. Me, too." It was a lie; he'd slept hardly at all without her beside him. His palms were damp. He wiped one on his thigh, intending to reach out and touch her arm, but before he could she spun away—"Excuse me. I have to comb my hair"—and flounced into the bedroom without once glancing his way.

All right, you stubborn little cuss, have it your way. It'll get colder than an eskimo's outhouse in that room before long and you'll come back wanting to snuggle. Meantime, the cook stays!

And she did.

Isabelle stayed through the entire week while Linnea refused to look at or speak to Theodore, unless he spoke to her first. By Saturday night the tension in the house was horrendous. Nissa was the only one getting a decent night's sleep. The other two managed only enough to get by, and the strain was showing in their faces.

There was a barn dance at their place Saturday night, and Teddy and Linnea spent the first hour laughing and dancing with everybody in the place but each other. Teddy slugged down two beers, eyeing her over the beer glass most of the time, thinking how pretty she looked pregnant. Some women got dowdy and washed-out looking when they were carrying babies. Not his wife. She glowed like someone had lit a candle inside her cheeks. He screwed up his courage to cross the hayloft and ask her to dance, and after several minutes, made his move. Before he reached her, his palms were sweating again.

With feined jocularity, he paused beside her, hooked his thumbs in his waistband and raised one eyebrow. "So what do you say, you wanna dance?"

She flicked him a glance of unadulterated feline haughtiness, shifted it pointedly to Isabelle Lawler, and replied, "No, thank you." Then, with a slight lift of her nose, she turned away.

So he danced with Isabelle. And one hell of a lot more than four times!

Linnea tried not to watch them. But Teddy was the best darn dancer in the county, and every corpuscle in her body was bulging with jealousy. Thankfully, Nissa offered an escape.

"Think I overdid it with the homemade wine," she said. "Either that or the spinning or both, but I feel a little dizzy. Would you walk me to the house, Linnea?"

Naturally, Linnea complied. Halfway there, Nissa took up reminiscing in an offhand manner, "I 'member once when my man brung home this new rag rug. I says to him, what you wanna go buy a rug for when I can make 'em myself? What you wanna waste your money on a thing like that for? He smiles and says he thought it'd be nice one time, me not having to make a rug, but just flop it down on the floor already warped, woofed, and tied. But me, I got mad at him cause one o' the boys—I can't remember which one—was near out of his shoes. Should've got new boots for the boy, I says, instead of throwin' your money away on rag rugs. He said there was a widow woman with two young ones peddling her rugs in town that day and he thought it'd help her out if he bought that rug.'' Nissa sniffed once. ''Me, well, I asks, what you doin' talkin' to widow women, and he says I might be his wife, but that don't give me the right to tell him who he can and can't talk to. So I asks who this widow woman was, and he tells me, and I recall these several times we was all at a barn-raising together and how he'd talked and laughed with her some, and my hackles got up and before you know it I asks how she's gettin' on without her husband, and where she's livin' now. And, by Jove, if he can't answer every one of my questions. And pretty soon I'm telling him I don't want his blame rag rug, not if he got it from her! As I recall, we didn't speak to one another for over a week that time. Rag rug laid on the floor and I refused to put a foot onto it, and he refused to pick it up and take it away.

''Then one day I went to town and happened to run into her on the street. She'd got tuberculosis and coughed all the time and was nothin' but a bag of bones, and when she saw me she says how grateful she was that my man bought that rug from her, and how one of her little ones had needed a pair of boots so bad, and when she sold that rug, she'd been able to buy 'em.''

Linnea and Nissa had reached the back door by this time, but the older woman stood on the steps a moment, looking up at the stars. ''Learned a thing or two that time. Learned that a man's heart can get broke if he's accused when he ain't guilty. Learned that some men got hearts o' gold, and gold, it don't tarnish. But gold . . . well, it's soft. It dents easy. Woman's got to be careful not to put too many dents in a heart like that.'' Nissa chortled softly to herself, turned toward the door, and opened it but hesitated a moment before stepping inside. ''As I recall, the night I finally told him I was sorry, he laid me down on that rag rug on the floor and put a couple rug burns on m' hind quarters . . . hmm . . . still got that old rug around here someplace. In a trunk, I think, with my wedding dress and a watch fob I braided for him out of my own hair when I was sixteen years old.'' She shook her head, touched her brow. ''Land, lookin' up like that makes a person dizzier than ever.'' Without glancing back, she continued into the house. ''Well, good night, child.''

Linnea was left with a lump in her throat and a thick feeling in her chest. She glanced toward the barn. The apricot lanternlight shone dimly through the windows. The distant strains of concertina and fiddle music drifted dimly through the night. Go to him, it seemed to say.

She glanced in the opposite direction. Nestled beside the caragana hedge the bulky form of the cook wagon hovered like a threatening shadow. The moon, like a half-slice of shaved cheese, threw its light across the yard while the night breeze played the dried seedpods of the caragana bushes like tiny drums. But it's he who should be apologizing, they seemed to say. He's the one who's dancing with somebody else.

Dully, she went inside and climbed the stairs to her old room once more, then lay beneath the covers, cold and lonely.

Each night she'd expected Theodore to come to her. She'd lain and imagined him opening the door silently, standing in the shadows and looking at her sleeping form, then kneeling beside the bed to awaken her, press his face to her neck, her breast, her stomach, and say, "I'm sorry, Lin, please come back."

But this was the eighth day and still he had not come. And he was down in the barn jigging with another woman while his pregnant wife lay in tears. Why, Teddy, why?

She was determined to stay awake until the dance ended and the wagons pulled out of the yard, then watch through the window to see if he came straight to the house. But in the end she fell asleep and heard nothing.

In the morning she awakened as if touched, her eyelids parting like two halves of a sliced melon. Something was wrong. She listened. No sound. Not so much as a tinkle of silverware or the crackle of an expanding stovepipe. Stretching an arm she found her watch on the table. Why wasn't Nissa up at seven-fifteen? Church would begin in less than two hours.

She heard footsteps on the stairs just as her heels touched the floor. Without wasting time on a wrapper she flung the door wide and met Theodore on the landing, his eyes dark with worry, hair tousled from sleep.

"What's wrong?"

"It's Ma. She's sick."

"Sick? You mean from blackberry wine?" Even as she spoke, Linnea was following Theodore down the stairs in her bare feet.

"I don't think so. It's chills and congestion."

"Chills and congestion?" Linnea's skin prickled as she rushed to keep up with Theodore. At the bottom of the steps she grabbed the shoulder of his underwear, swinging him to an abrupt half. "Bad congestion?"

His eyes and cheeks appeared gaunt with concern.

"I think so."

"Is it . . ." After one false start she managed to get the dread word past her lips. ". . . the influenza?"

He found her hand, clutched it hard. "Let's hope not."

But that hope was dashed when the doctor was summoned from town. When he left, a yellow and black quarantine sign was tacked on the back door, and Theodore and Linnea were given instructions that neither of them was to enter Nissa's room without a mask tied over both nose and mouth. The two stared at each other in disbelief. The influenza struck soldiers in the trenches and people in crowded cities, not North Dakota farmers with an endless supply of pure air to breathe. And certainly not old bumblebees like Nissa Westgaard who buzzed between one task and the next so fast it seemed no germ could catch up with her. Not Nissa, who only last night had been tippling wine and dancing the two-step with her boys. Not Nissa, who rarely even contracted a common cold.

But they were wrong.

Before the day was over Nissa's respiratory system was already filling with fluids. Her breathing became strident and chills racked her body, unmitigated by the quinine water they periodically forced her to drink. Theodore and Linnea watched helplessly as her condition worsened with fearful rapidity. They sponged and fed her, kept her propped up with pillows, and took turns sitting watch. But by the end of the first day it seemed they were fighting a losing battle. They sat at the kitchen table, disconsolately staring at the servings of soup neither of them felt like eating, their hands idle beside their bowls.

Their worried gazes locked and their own differences seemed inconsequential. He covered her hand on the red and white checked oilcloth.

"So fast," he said throatily.

She turned her hand over and their fingers interlocked. "I know."

"And there's nothing we can do."

"We can keep sponging her and feeding her the quinine. Maybe during the night she'll take a turn for the better." But they both suspected it was wishful thinking. The influenza preyed first upon the very old, the very weak, and the very young. Few of them who contracted it survived.

Theodore stared at their joined hands, rubbing his thumb over Linnea's. "I wish I could get you out of here where you'd be safe."

"I'm fine. I don't even have a sniffle."

"But the baby . . ."

"The baby's fine, too. Now you mustn't worry about us."

"You've put in a long day. I want you to rest."

"But so have you."

"I'm not the pregnant one, now will you do as I say?"

"The dishes . . ."

"Leave 'em. I can see you're ready to tip off that chair. Now, come on." He tugged her hand, led her to their bedroom, turned the bed down, sat her on the edge of it, then knelt to remove her shoes. His tender consideration wrenched her heart, and as she looked down at the top of his head it seemed she could scarcely contain her love and concern for him. He had suffered the loss of a beloved brother; his son was off fighting a war; must he now watch his mother die, too?

When her second shoe was off, Theodore held her foot, caressing it while raising his eyes to hers.

"Linnea, about Isabelle—"

She silenced his lips with a loving touch. "It doesn't matter. I was stupid and childish and jealous, but you've got enough on your mind without worrying about that now."

"But I . . ."

"We'll talk about it later . . . after Nissa gets well."

He tucked her in lovingly, securing the quilts beneath her chin, then sitting beside her on the edge of the bed. With hands braced on either side of her head, he leaned above her, studying her face as if in it he found the strength he needed.

"I want to kiss you so bad." But he couldn't; not while there was influenza in the house. He could only look at her and rue the past week of idiocy that had kept them alienated, that had made him do foolish things to hurt her when she was the last person in the world he wanted to hurt.

"I know. I want to kiss you, too."

"I love you so much."

"I love you, too, and it feels so good to be back in our bed again."

He smiled, wishing he could crawl in beside her and snuggle tight behind her with his hand cradling their moving child. But Ma was in the next room and she'd been untended long enough.

''Sleep now.''

''Wake me up if there's any change.''

He nodded, rested a palm on her stomach, turned off the lantern, and left.

Nissa's lungs filled with fluid and she died on the third day. Before the undertaker's wagon could come to bear her body away, Linnea's worst fears were realized: Teddy was stricken with the dread virus. She was left alone to nurse him, to mourn, and to worry, locked in a house with nobody to spell her bedside vigils or comfort her in her grief. Already depleted from three days of little sleep and weighted by despair, she was near exhaustion when a loud banging sounded on the door and Isabelle Lawler's voice came through. ''Mrs. Westgaard, I'm comin' in!''

Linnea called, ''But you can't, we're under quarantine.''

The door burst open and the redhead pushed inside. ''Makes no difference to a tough old buffalo like me. Now you need help and I'm the one's gonna give it to you. Lawsy, child, you look like that undertaker should've toted you off, too. You had any sleep? You eat?''

''I . . .''

The brazen woman didn't give Linnea time to answer. ''Set down there. How's Ted?''

''He's . . . his breathing isn't too bad yet.''

''Good. I can poke quinine down him just as easy as you can, but you got his young one to take care of and if I let somethin' happen to it or to you, I'm afraid I'd lose my cookin' job around here, years to come, so step back, chittlin'.'' While she spoke, Isabelle shrugged out of a heavy, masculine jacket. Linnea got up as if to take it.

''Set down, I said! You need a good meal under your belt and I'm just the one to see it gets there. I'm the best durn cook this side of the Black Hills, so don't give me no sass, sister. You just tell me what needs doin' for him, and how often, and if you're worried about me seein' him in his altogether, well, I seen him that way before, and you know it, so I ain't gonna blush like no schoolgirl and cover my eyes. And if you're thinkin' I got designs on your man, well, you can put that out of your head, too. What was between us is finished. He ain't the least bit interested in no loud, sassy moose like me, so where's the quinine and what would you like to eat?''

Thus the audacious Isabelle dug in for the duration.

She was nothing short of a heaven-sent blessing to Linnea. She mothered and pampered her with continued bumptiousness, and took her turns seeing after Theodore's needs with equal brashness. She was the most flagrantly bold woman Linnea had ever met, but her very outspokenness often made Linnea laugh, and kept her spirits up. Isabelle blew through the house like a hurricane, her rusty hair ever standing on end, her mannish voice loud even when she whispered. Linnea was utterly grateful to have her there. It was as if she forced the fates to accept her zest for life and to transfer a good bit of it to the ailing Theodore.

When he was at his worst, the two women sat together at his bedside, and oddly enough, Linnea felt totally comfortable, even knowing that in her own way, Isabelle loved Theodore. His breathing was labored and his skin bright with fever.

"Damn man ain't gonna die," Isabelle announced, "cause I ain't gonna let him. He's got you and the young one to see after and he won't be shirking his duty."

"I wish I could be as sure as you."

Another woman would have reached out a comforting hand. Not Isabelle. Her chin only jutted more stubbornly.

"A man as happy as he is about that baby and his new wife's got a lot o' reason to fight."

"He . . . he told you he was happy?"

"Told me everything. Told me about your fight, told me the reason you were sleepin' in the spare room. He was heartsick."

Linnea dropped her gaze to her lap. "I didn't think he'd tell you all that."

Isabelle spread her knees wide, leaned forward, and rested her elbows on them. "We could usually talk, Ted and I."

Linnea didn't know what to say. She found herself no longer able to harbor jealousy.

Isabelle went on, her eyes on Theodore while she leaned forward in her masculine pose. "It's nothin' you need to worry about, what me and Ted did together. You're young yet, you got things to learn about human urges. They just got to be satisfied, that's all. Why, shoot, he never loved me—the word never come up once." She sat back, reached in her pocket for cigarette makings, and started rolling herself a smoke. "But he's a kind man, a damn kind man. Don't think I don't know it . . . I mean, a woman like me, why . . ." Her words trailed away and she gave a single self-deprecating sniff, studying the cigarette as she sealed the seam, then stroked it smooth. She reached in her apron pocket and found a match, set it aflame with the flick of a blunt thumbnail, and sent fragrant smoke into the room. She leaned back, rested her crossed feet on the edge of the mattress, and puffed away silently, squinting through the smoke. After some time she said, "You're a damned lucky woman."

Linnea turned to study Isabelle. Her apron was filthy. Her stomach looked more pregnant than Linnea's. She held the cigarette between thumb and forefinger like a man would, and her chair was tilted back on two legs. But in the corner of her left eye Linnea thought she detected the glint of a single tear.

Impulsively, she reached and lay a hand on Isabelle's arm. The redhead looked down at it, sniffed again, clamped the cigarette between her teeth, patted the hand twice, then reached for the cigarette again.

"You'll be back next year, won't you?" the younger woman asked.

"Damn tootin'. I'll be dyin' to git a gander at Ted's young 'un."

On the seventh day they knew that Theodore would live.

Chapter 26

The very old, the very weak, the very young. Indeed, the Spanish influenza preyed first upon these, and it chose from the Westgaard family one of each. Of the very old it took Nissa. Of the very weak, Tony. And of the very young, Roseanne. Nissa died never knowing her grandchildren, too, had fallen ill.

It was a mercurial disease, indiscriminately ravaging home after home on the Dakota prairie, while leaving others totally untouched. There seemed no rhyme nor reason as to whom it took, whom it left. Its very unpredictability made it the more deadly. But as if Providence had better things in mind for Theodore and Linnea Westgaard, Theodore pulled through with nothing longer lasting than a ten-pound weight loss, and Linnea was untouched.

On the morning Theodore awakened clear-eyed and clear-headed, she was there alone beside the bed, asleep in a chair, looking as if she'd fought the war single-handedly. He opened his eyes and saw her—slumped, breathing evenly, hands folded over her high-mounded stomach. Linnea, he tried to say, but his mouth was so dry. He touched his forehead; it felt scaly. He touched his hair; it felt oily. He touched his cheek; it felt raspy. He wondered what day it was. Ma was dead, wasn't she? Oh, and Kristian—was there any news of him? And what about the wheat . . . the milking . . . Linnea . . .

He rolled to one side and touched her knee. Her eyes flew open.

"Teddy! You're awake!" She tested his forehead then gripped his hand. "You made it."

"Ma . . ." he croaked.

"They buried her over a week ago." She brought a cup to his lips and he drank gratefully, then fell back weakly.

"What day is it?"

"Thursday. You've been sick for two weeks."

Two weeks. He'd lain here two weeks while she looked after him. She and Isabelle. He had a vague recollection of Isabelle tending him, too, but how could that be?

"Are you all right?"

"Me, oh I'm fine. I've come through unscathed. Now no more questions until I get you something to eat and you feel stronger."

She would brook no more talking until she'd brought him strong beef broth and, after he'd drunk it, washed his face and helped him shave. She herself had found time to change her dress and comb her hair, but even so, he could see on her face the effects of her long vigil. When she was bustling about, cleaning up the room, he made her sit down beside the bed and rest for a minute.

"Your eyes look like bruises."

"I lost a little sleep, that's all. But I had good help." She glanced at her lap and toyed with the edge of her apron.

"Isabelle?" he asked.

"Yes. Do you remember?"

"Some."

"She refused to obey the quarantine sign. She came in and stayed for nine days and took care of both of us."

"And she didn't get it either?"

Linnea shook her head. "She's some woman, Teddy." Her voice softened as her gaze met her husband's. "She loves you very much, you know."

"Aww . . ."

"She does. She risked her own life to come in here and take care of you, and of me because she knew it would hurt you if anything happened to either me or the baby. We owe her a lot."

He didn't know what to say. "Where is she now?"

"Out in the cook wagon, sleeping."

"What about the wheat?"

"The wheat is all done. The threshing crew kept right on working."

"And the milking?"

"They took care of that, too. Now you're not to worry about a thing. Cope says he'll stay on until you're strong enough to take over again."

"Has there been any news from Kristian?"

"A letter came two days ago and Orlin read it from the end of the driveway." Orlin was their mail carrier. "Kristian said he hadn't seen the front yet, and he was just fine."

"How long ago did he write the letter?"

"More than three weeks."

Three weeks, they both thought. So many shells were fired in three weeks. She wished there were a way to reassure Theodore, but what could she say? He looked gaunt and pale and inutterably sapped. She hated to be the one to add new lines of despair to his face, but there was no escaping it. She leaned both elbows on the bed, took his hand in both of hers, turning the loose-fitting wedding ring around and around his finger.

"Teddy, there's more bad news, I'm afraid. The influenza . . ." How difficult it was to say the words. She saw the faces of those blessed children she'd come to love so much. Such innocents, taken before their time.

"Who?" Theodore asked simply.

"Roseanne and Tony."

His hand gripped hers and his eyes closed. "Oh, dear God."

There was nothing she could say. She herself ached, remembering Roseanne's lisp, Tony's thin shoulders.

Still with his eyes closed, Theodore drew Linnea down atop the coverlets. She lay beside him and he held her, drew strength from her.

"But they were so young. They hadn't even lived yet," he railed uselessly.

"I know . . . I know."

"And Ma . . ." Linnea felt him swallow against the crown of her head. "She was such a good woman. And sometimes, when she'd . . . when she'd get bossy and order me around I'd wish to myself that she wasn't here. But I never meant I w . . . wanted her to die."

"You mustn't feel guilty about thoughts that were only human. You were good to her, Teddy, you gave her a home. She knew you loved her."

"But she was such a good old soul."

So were they all, Linnea thought, holding him close. John, Nissa, the children. They'd lost so many . . . so many. *Lord, keep Kristian safe.*

"Oh, Teddy," she whispered against his chest, "I thought I was going to lose you, too."

He swallowed thickly. "And I thought the same thing about you and the baby. At times I'd wish I could die real quick, before you got it, too. Then other times, I'd come to and see you sitting there beside the bed and know I just had to live."

His heartbeat drummed steadily beneath her ear while she spoke a silent prayer of thanks that he'd been spared. Between them pressed the bulk of their thriving, unborn child and an old quilt that had been pieced and tied by Nissa's hands years and years ago. She who had passed on. He who was yet to come. A new life to replace an old.

"It's as if we and our baby were spared to carry on. To take the place of those who are gone," she told him.

And carry on is what they did, like many others who'd suffered losses. The epidemic ran its course. The quarantine signs disappeared one by one, and the Westgaards bid goodbye to Isabelle Lawler, waving her away while she bellowed that she'd be back next year to see the young 'un. Still, there were the dead to mourn, the living to console. The Lutheran church had a new minister now that the Severts had moved away. Reverend Helgeson held one bitterly sad memorial service for the seven members of his congregation who had died and been buried while their families were not allowed at the gravesides, and together they prayed for peace and gave thanks that the service stars on the church flag yet remained blue. The bereaved drew strength from above and lifted their eyes toward tomorrow.

There came a day in November when Theodore was outside beneath a chilly overcast sky, ballasting the foundation of the house with hay. It was a typical late-autumn day, dreary, with a bite to the wind. The leaves of the cottonwoods had long since fallen. The wind lifted topsoil and sent it against the legs of Theodore's overalls as he wielded the pitchfork, time and again. The job would normally have been done much earlier, but had been delayed this year due to his illness. But his strength had returned, and Cope had gone back home to Minnesota.

From overhead came the rusty carping of a tardy flock of Canadian honkers headed south. Theodore paused and glanced up, watching the birds fly in majestic formation. Kristian hadn't got to fly those airplanes like he'd wanted to. But he'd ridden in one, his last letter said. Theodore smiled, thinking of it. His boy riding up there as high as those geese. What was this world coming to? There was talk about those airplanes being the up-and-coming thing, and that when and if this war ever ended, they'd be used for something better than killing people.

Was Kristian still alive? He had to be. And when he came home Theodore wondered how he'd like to be set up in a business of his own, transporting goods by airplane maybe, like folks said was going to be the coming way. What the hell, he was a rich man. The war had forced wheat up to the landmark price of $2.15 a bushel. It had never seemed right, getting rich off the war, but as long as he was, he might as well share some of that wealth with his son who'd gone to fight it. Heck, Kristian didn't want to be no wheat farmer, and if that boy would just make it home, Theodore promised himself he'd never try to force him again, after all, it wasn't—

"Teddy! Teddy!" Linnea came flying out of the house, leaving the door open wide behind her. "Teddy, the war's over!"

"What!"

The pitchfork went clunking to the ground as she came barreling into his arms, shouting and crying all at once. "It's over! The news just came on the radio! The armistice was signed at five o'clock this morning!"

"It's over? It's really over?"

"Yes! Yes! Yes!" she rejoiced.

He spun her off her feet. "It's over! It's over!" They couldn't quit saying it. They danced around the yard and tripped on the pitchfork. Beside them Nelly and Fly stood before a wagonload of hay and turned curious heads to watch their antics. Nelly whickered, and Linnea flew out of Theodore's arms and kissed the horse on her nose. When she'd likewise kissed Fly, Theodore swooped her into his arms again and lifted her toward the wagon seat.

"We got to be with the others."

They were scarcely out of their driveway before the school bell began clanging in the east. They had not traveled one mile before it was joined by the church bell from the west. They met Ulmer and Helen on the road halfway to Lars's house and got down from the wagons to hug and kiss and listen to the bells resounding from both directions. While they were celebrating in the middle of the gravel road, Clara and Trigg appeared, with baby Maren swaddled warm but howling loudly, upset by all the unusual commotion. On their heels came others, including Lars and Evie, and old man Tveit, who was out delivering a load of coal.

"Everyone'll gather at the school," Ulmer predicted. "Let's go!"

And sure enough, by the time they got there, the building was already filling. The bell kept pealing. The crowd kept growing. The new teacher, Mr. Thorson, announced that classes were dismissed for the day. The children stood on their desk seats and clapped. Reverend Helgeson arrived and led them all in a prayer of thanksgiving, and the celebration continued on into the late afternoon.

By the time the rejoicing band broke up, the snow that had been threatening all day had begun in earnest. They drove their wagons home through the wind-driven flakes, carefree in spite of them, their joy undaunted by the prospect of a winter storm. The wheat was in. The world was at peace. There was much to be grateful for.

Linnea awakened with her first pain at one o'clock that morning. She wasn't certain what it was, so waited for another, which was some time in coming. She didn't wake Theodore until an hour had passed and she was certain.

"Teddy?" She shook him gently.

"Hmm?" He rolled over and braced on an elbow. "Something wrong?"

"I think my pains have started."

Immediately he was awake, straining toward her, reaching for her stomach. "But it's a month early."

"I know. I must have done too much dancing and shook things loose."

"How close together are they?"

"Fifteen minutes."

"Fifteen . . ." He was out of bed in a flash, reaching for his trousers. "I got to get to town and get the doc."

"No!"

"But you said it's—"

"No! Look out the window. I won't have you going out in that!"

From within the dark room it was easy to see how bright it was outside. The snow, still swirling, had whitened everything and gathered in the corners of the window ledges in thick white triangles.

"But, Linnea—"

"No. After John, no! This baby's gonna know his father!"

"But it's not a blizzard. It's just a regular snowfall."

She struggled from the bed and caught his arm as he reached for his shirt.

"Teddy, we can do it ourselves."

His muscles tensed beneath her hand. "Are you crazy? I've never delivered a baby."

"You've delivered horses, haven't you? It can't be too much different."

"Linnea, I'm wasting time."

"You're not going!" She clung to him tenaciously, pulling him back when he would have leaned for his boots. But suddenly she gasped. "Oh . . . Teddy . . . oh!"

"What is it?"

Terrified, he lit the lantern and turned to find her standing in the middle of the floor with her feet widespread, staring down.

"Something's coming out already. Oh, please don't leave me."

He gaped at the puddle between her feet, frantically wondering what to do. With Melinda it had taken hours . . . and Ma had been here to see to things.

"Your water broke. That means it . . . it won't be long."

"Wh . . . what should I do?" she asked, as if there were anything she could control.

In three steps he'd swept her off her feet and deposited her on the bed again. "Rest between pains, don't fight them when they come. I've got to light a fire and get some rope."

"Rope! Oh, Teddy, please don't go to town. We—"

"I'm not." He pressed her back, took a moment to soothe her, brushing her hair back from her forehead, kissing her wild eyes closed. "The rope's for you to hang onto. I'll be right back, all right? And I promise I won't go to town. But I have to go out to the barn. Just stay here and do like I said when the pains come."

She nodded in the brisk way of one too afraid to argue. "Hurry," she whispered.

He hurried. But—blast his hide!—why hadn't he got things ready before?

He'd thought he had another whole month, and even then, the doctor usually brought leather stirrups and sterilized instruments. He never thought he'd have to cut ropes and boil scissors. Damn these Dakota winters! What in tarnation would he do if complications set in?

The snow bit into his cheeks as he made his way back from the barn with the cleanest length of rope he could find. Linnea seemed frantic by the time he reached the bedroom.

"They're coming f . . . faster, Teddy, and I . . . I got the bed all wet."

"Shh, love, don't worry. The bedding can be washed."

In between pains he lit a fire, sterilized scissors, found string, and a clean blanket for the baby, and a washbasin and towel for its first bath. He lifted Linnea from the bed and lined it with a rubber sheet, then padded it with a soft, folded flannel blanket over which he stretched a new, clean sheet. He was holding her in his arms, transferring her back to the bed when she was hit by the most intense pain yet. She gasped and stiffened, and he held her, felt her body tense, her fingers dig into his shoulder through the worst of it. When it was over, her eyes opened and he kissed the corner of one. "Next time a war ends, not so much dancing, all right, Mrs. Westgaard?"

She gave him a quavering smile, but sighed and seemed to wilt as he laid her down again.

"I want a clean gown," she said when her breath evened.

"But what does it matter?"

"Our child will not be born while his mother wears a soiled nightgown. Now get me a clean gown, Theodore."

When she called him Theodore in that tone of voice, he knew he'd best not cross her. He flew to the dresser, wondering where the sudden show of spunk came from when a moment ago she'd been submerged in pain. Women, he thought. What did men really know about them after all?

The old gown was off, but the new one still rolled in his hands when the next pain struck. She fell back and arched, and he saw her stomach change shape with the contraction, saw her knees go up and her body lift of its own accord. Sweat broke out across his chest. Low across his belly he thought he felt the same pain she'd experienced. His hands shook when he helped her don the clean, white nightgown and folded it back at the waist.

He'd never tied knots so fast in his life. He slashed the rope into two three-foot lengths, secured each to the metal footboard of the bed, then fashioned the opposite ends into loops through which Linnea's legs could slip. The last knot wasn't quite finished when she gasped his name, reaching with both hands. She gripped his hands so hard he felt bruised, and drew on him with a force that made both their arms quiver. Sweet Jesus, those ropes would cut right through her flesh!

When the contraction ended, they were both panting.

He rushed to the kitchen and found two thick towels to pad the ropes for her legs. He moved the bedside table and kerosene lantern toward the foot of the bed where it shone on her exposed body. Gently, he lifted her feet and placed them through the ropes, then carefully slid them up behind her knees. The lanternlight threw a golden tint upon her white thighs. For the first time it struck him fully how vulnerable a woman is during childbirth.

Her bleary eyes opened. "Don't be scared, Teddy," she whispered. "There's nothing to be scared of." There remained no trace of the fear he'd sensed in her earlier. She was calm, prepared, confident in his ability to play the part of midwife. He moved to her side and bent over her, loving her more than ever before.

"I'm not scared." It was the first time he'd ever lied to her. Looking down into her flushed face he would gladly have taken her place if only he could. He stretched her arms over her head and gently placed her hands around the metal rods above her. "Now save your energy." He covered her fingers with his own. "Don't talk. Scream if you want, but don't talk."

"But talking takes my mind off the p—"

She grimaced and sucked in a deep breath. Heart pounding, he rushed to the opposite end of the bed, feeling uncertain and clumsy and even more frightened than when he and John had been trapped in the blizzard.

Her muscles strained. The ropes stretched taut. The iron bed rails chimed and bent inward. She growled deep and long while a trickle of pink flowed from her body. He stared at it, horrified at being responsible for bringing her to this travail, vowing, Never again. Never again.

Teeth clenched, he whispered, "Come on . . . come on . . ." as if the child could hear.

When Linnea's pain eased, Theodore's shirt was damp beneath the arms. She rested and he wiped her brow.

"How you doing?" he asked softly.

She nodded, eyes closed. "Tell me when—" she began, but this time the pain brought her hips higher off the bed than before. He watched the trickle of pink grow brighter and thought, oh God, she's dying. Don't let her die. Not her too! He was wracked by the need to do something for her, anything whatever to help. He placed his hands beneath her and helped her lift when lifting seemed what Nature intended.

"Come on, get out here," he muttered. "Scream, Lin, scream if you want to!"

But when a cap of blond appeared, he was the one who yelped, "I see the head!" Excitement rushed through his body. "Push . . . once more . . . come on, Lin . . . one more big one . . ."

With the next contraction the child came into his big callused hands in a squirming, slithering, slippery mass of warmth. At the sound of the child's lusty yowling, Theodore smiled as wide as a man can smile. He wanted to tell Linnea what it was, but couldn't see through his tears. He shrugged and cleared his eyes against his shoulders.

"It's a boy!" he rejoiced, and laid the wriggling bundle on Linnea's stomach.

"A boy," she repeated.

"With a little pink acorn." She chuckled tiredly and managed to lift her head. But it fell back weakly and her fingertips searched for the child's head.

By some miracle, Theodore had grown as calm as the eye of a tornado. It seemed he'd never in his life been so efficient as he tied the two pieces of string around the umbilical cord and severed it.

"There. He's on his own now."

Linnea laughed, but he could tell she was crying. He lifted the infant and stuck a finger into his mouth, to clear it of mucous.

"He's sucking already," he told Linnea, thrilled at the feel of the delicate tongue drawing on his little finger.

"Does he have all his fingers and toes?" she asked.

"Every one of 'em, but they're no bigger'n a sparrow's bones."

"Hurry, Teddy," she said weakly.

Forcing the afterbirth from her body hurt him as much as it hurt her, he was sure. Her stomach was soft and pliable as he pressed upon it with both palms. Once more he promised himself never to put her through this again. If they could take turns, he'd go through it. But not her. Not his precious Linnea.

It was the first time he'd ever given a baby a bath. Mercy, how could a human being be so tiny yet so perfect? Fingernails and eyelids so fragile he could see right through them. Legs so spindly he was afraid to straighten them out to dry behind the tiny knees. Eyelashes so fine they were scarcely visible.

He wrapped his son in a clean flannel blanket and placed him in Linnea's arms.

"Here he is, love. He's a tiny one."

"John," she cooed softly, in welcome. "Why, hello there, John."

Theodore smiled at the sight of her lips on the baby's downy head.

"He even looks a little like our John, doesn't he?"

He didn't of course. He had the look of all newborn babies: wrinkled, red, and pinched.

But Linnea agreed, anyway. "He does."

"And I think I see a little of Ma around his mouth."

His mouth was nothing whatever like Nissa's, but again Linnea agreed.

Theodore settled beside her, the two of them gazing at the miracle their love had created. Born into a family who had lost so many, he embodied the hope of new life. Born to a man who'd thought himself too old, he would bring renewed youth. Born to a woman who thought herself too young, he would bring about a glowing maturity. Conceived in a time of war, he brought with him a sense of peace.

Theodore nudged the baby's hand with his little finger and thrilled when his son's tiny fist closed around it.

"I wish they could see him," he said.

Linnea touched Theodore's hand, so big and powerful compared to the baby's fragile grasp. She looked up into his eyes.

"I think they do, Teddy," she whispered.

"And Kristian," Theodore said, hopefully. "Kristian's gonna love him, isn't he?"

Linnea nodded, her eyes locked with Theodore's, suddenly knowing in her heart that what they said was true. "Kristian's going to love him."

He kissed her temple, his lips lingering.

"I love you."

She smiled and knew a deep sense of fulfillment. "I love you, too. Always."

They listened to the prairie wind worrying the windows. And the sound of their son, suckling nothing. John's cat slipped around the doorway and stood looking curiously at the three. With a soft, throaty sound, it leaped to the foot of the bed, circled twice, and settled down to sleep on Nissa's old quilt.

The cantankerous wheat farmer who'd greeted the new schoolmarm at the station so gruffly the first time she'd appeared sat with his arm cradling her head. He wondered if it was possible to make her understand how much he loved her.

''I lied before. I *was* scared,'' he confessed.

''I could tell.''

''Seeing you like that, in so much pain—'' He kissed her forehead. ''It was awful. I'll never put you through that again.''

''Yes, you will.''

''No, I won't.''

''I think you will.''

''Never. So help me God, never. I love you too much . . .''

She chuckled and brushed her fingers over the fine hair on John's head. ''I want a girl next time, and we'll name her Rosie.''

''A girl . . . but—''

''Shh. Come. Lie down with us.'' With the baby in the crook of her elbow, she moved over and made room for him. He stretched out on top of the quilt and rolled to his side, folding an elbow beneath his ear and stretching a protective arm across the baby to Linnea's hip.

Outside, somewhere on the prairie, the horses ran free. And Russian thistles rolled before the wind. And upon the derrick of a windmill the dry, tan husks of last summer's morning glories still clung while the blades rapped softly above. But inside, a man and wife lay close, watching their son sleep, thinking of their tomorrows and the blessings to be reaped, the life to be lived to its fullest . . . the minutes, the days, the years.

TWICE LOVED

Chapter 1

1837

It had been five years, one month, and two days since Rye Dalton had seen his wife. In all that time only the salty kiss of the sea had touched his lips, only its cold, wet arms had caressed him.

But soon, Laura, soon, he thought.

He stood on the deck of the whaleship *Omega,* a two-masted schooner riding low in the brine just beyond the shoals of Nantucket Bay, her hold crammed with brimming oil casks, "bung up and bilge free," so that none of the precious cargo would be lost. The hand on the larboard rail was burnished to the shade of teak, as was the face that contrasted starkly with thick brows and unruly hair bleached almost colorless by years of sun and salt. That hair, badly in need of cutting, added a ruggedness to the bold Anglican features. A thick tangle of side-whiskers swooped almost to his jaw, emphasizing its squareness, then jutting toward the hollow of his cheek. A handsome man with a mariner's wide stance, he stood rock-ribbed and anxious, studying the distant shore.

Just short of Nantucket Shoals, the *Omega's* sails were reefed, her anchors dropped, and the lighters used for unloading were lowered from their davits. Her crew boarded the boats, babbling eagerly, their ribald banter laced with excitement. *They were home.*

The lighter slipped through the calm waters of Nantucket Bay, but across the sun-splashed surface it was difficult to make out the crowd awaiting their arrival at Straight Wharf. The May sun transformed the top of the water into a million gilded mirrors, each shaped like a tiny, flashing fish, blinding the blue eyes of the man who squinted quayward. He need not see her—she'd be there, he knew, just as most of the town would be. The watchtower out on Brant Point had spotted the *Omega* long since, and word would have spread; she was coming in, plowing deep: the voyage had been successful.

The bright reflection paled and the crowd came into view. Weeping women waved handkerchiefs. Old retired sea-dogs scraped crusty wool caps from graying pates and hailed the returning whalers with flapping arms, while lads with salt in their dreams gaped in awe, impatiently awaiting their day for becoming heroes.

The lighter thumped against the pilings, and Dalton's eyes scanned the crowd. Within minutes the wharf was a melee of happy reunion: sweethearts hugging, fathers holding children they'd never seen, wives dabbing happy tears from their eyes, while horse-drawn buggies and carriages waited to bear the arriving seamen away to their homes. Other lighters were already arriving from the *Omega,* and stevedores began unloading heavy wooden casks of whale oil and blubber, rolling them down a wooden gangplank with a rumble like low, constant thunder. Horse-drawn drays waited to haul the cargo off to warehouses along the waterfront.

At last Rye's boots touched solid planking that neither rolled nor pitched. He shouldered his heavy sea chest, caught his pea jacket under one arm, and moved through the crowd, searching anxiously. All about were skirts flared over baleen hoops and waists pinched tight by whalebone corsets. His gaze swept them cursorily, searching for only one.

But Laura Dalton was not there.

Frowning, Rye swayed up the length of Straight Wharf, picking his way between clusters of townspeople, his stride wide and balanced even under the weight of the sea chest. In his wake, matrons gaped at each other in stunned surprise. A pair of young girls tittered behind their palms, and old Cap'n Silas, knees crossed, back hunched against the weather-bleached wall of a bait shack, nodded silently to Rye, squinted at the tall young cooper as he moved up the street, puffed on his pipe, and grunted, ''Uh-oh!''

Leaving the excitement of the wharf behind, Rye passed warehouses redolent with tar, hemp, and fish. From the noisome tryworks where blubber was melted down into whale oil came its omnipresent reek, mingling with billows of gray smoke from the cauldrons.

But the rangy seaman scarcely noticed the stench, certainly not the occasional eye peering inquisitively at him from chandlery, ropewalk, and joiner's shop as he strode along the cobbled streets toward the heart of the village. At the head of the wharf he entered the lower square of Main Street itself. Before him, rising from the great harbor and ascending in gently rising slopes toward the Wesco Hills, spread the town where he'd been born. Ah, Nantucket, my Nantucket!

A lonely outcropping in the North Atlantic, the island lay thirty miles asea, off the clay cliffs of Martha's Vineyard, to the west and the windswept moors of Cape Cod, due north. The Little Gray Lady of the Sea, Nantucket had come to be called, and she certainly looked it today, sleeping beneath an arch of blue sky, her silvery cottages gleaming like rough-hewn jewels in the high May sun. The cobbled streets contrasted sharply with the startling green of new spring grass along the walkways, giving way to paler paths of sand and shells farther inland. Salt breezes swept across the open heath, carrying with them the fragrance of blossoming beach plums and bayberries, while in dooryards apple trees bloomed in scented explosions of white.

Rye paused long enough to pick one, hold it to his nose, and savor the delicate fragrance, made the more precious for being a product of land instead of sea. He drank deep, as if he might make up for the five-year dearth of such pleasure.

Then, thinking again of Laura, he frowned in the direction of home and strode on purposefully.

Within minutes he came to a quaint lane of startlingly white scallop shells. They clicked beneath the crush of his boots, and he hoisted the sea chest higher, reveling in the remembered sound, the scent of the apple blossoms, and the familiarity of the cottages he passed. A wild thrum of expectation pounded through his vitals at the thought that he was, at last, *walking* home.

He reached a *Y* in the path, the left branch leading away to Quarter Mile Hill, the right narrowing toward a gentle rise upon which rested a little story-and-a-half saltbox, typical of most on the island, its sides and roof sheathed in silvered shingles, unpainted, polished by wind and salt and time until each board gleamed like a lustrous gray pearl. Its leaded windows were long gone, melted down for bullets, decades before as a sacrifice to the Revolution, but on either side of the door small panes gleamed in wooden frames and white shutters spread like open arms to allow the spring day inside.

Geraniums—Laura's favorite—had already been set out beside the wooden step. A new line of evergreen shrubs bordered the west end of the house, where a lean-to—called a linter on Nantucket—snuggled against the fireplace wall. Surprised, Rye scanned its angled roof. The linter had been added on since last he was home.

As he crunched his way the last twenty feet up the shelled path, the noon clarion rang out from the tower of the Congregational church below. Fifty-two times a day it struck, and had for as long as Rye remembered. It now called Nantucket's citizens to take their midday meal, but the reverberations seemed to explode within Rye Dalton's heart as a personal welcome home.

Just short of the house, he stepped off the path to approach silently. The front door was open, and the smell of dinner drifted out as if in welcome. A thrill of expectation again lifted his heart, and suddenly he was grateful she'd chosen to await him in the privacy of their home instead of on the public wharf.

He set his sea chest beside the path, ran four shaky fingers through the bleached hair that lay about his face like tangled kelp, heaved a nervous sigh that momentarily lifted his chest, and stepped to the open doorway.

It faced south, leading directly to the yard from the keeping room into whose shadows Rye peered blindly, his eyes still dazzled by the brilliance outside. He made not a sound, though it seemed his heart clattered aloud and must forewarn her of his presence.

She leaned before a giant stone fireplace, dressed in a blue flowered floor-length dress and a white homespun apron, which she held like a potholder while stirring the contents of an iron cauldron hanging on the crane.

He stared at the back of her head with its heavy knot of nutmeg-colored hair, at her slender back, at the faint outline of hip beneath blue cotton. She was humming quietly to the accompaniment of the spoon clanking against the pot.

His palms went damp and he felt almost dizzy at finding everything so dearly close to the way he'd left it. In silence he watched her, basking in the simple familiarity of homing to such a woman, such a house.

She clapped the cover back on the pot and reached up to set the spoon on the mantel while he imagined the lift of her breasts, the coffee brown of her eyes, and the curve of her lips.

At last he knocked softly on the open door.

Laura Dalton looked over her shoulder, startled. A tall man was silhouetted in the door space, haloed by the blaze of noon light behind him. She made out broad shoulders, a full shock of hair, something bulky draped between wrist and hip, feet spraddled wide as if against a hearty wind.

"Yes?" She turned, wiping her palms on the apron, then lifting one to shade her eyes. She squinted, and moved forward with uncertain steps until the hem of her dress was lit by the sunlight slanting across the wooden floor. There she stopped, making out familiar blue eyes, copper skin, bleached brows and hair . . . and the first lips she had ever kissed.

She gasped, and her hands flew to her mouth. Her eyes widened in disbelief while she stiffened as if struck by lightning.

"R . . . Rye?" Her heart went wild. Her face blanched, and the room seemed to spin around crazily while she stared at him, shocked. At last her hands fluttered downward and she stammered again in a choked voice, "R . . . Rye?"

He managed a shaky smile while she struggled to comprehend the incredible: Rye Dalton, hale and vital, was standing before her!

"Laura," he got out, half choking on the word before continuing with gruff emotion. "After five years, is that all y've got t' say?"

"R . . . Rye . . . my God, you're alive!"

He dropped his pea jacket to the floor and took one long step, head bending, arms reaching, while she flew forward to be gathered high and hard against him.

Oh no, oh no, oh no! her thoughts protested, while those long-remembered arms hauled her close against a rough striped shirt that smelled of the sea. She pinched her eyes shut, then opened them wide as if to steady the senses that careened off kilter. But it was Rye! It was Rye! His embrace threatened to crack her ribs and his body with its wide-spread legs was pressed against the length of hers, his cheek of bronze very warm and rough, and very much alive! Her arms did what they'd done a thousand times before, what they'd ached to do a thousand times since. They circled his tough, wide shoulders and clutched him while her temple lay pillowed against his swooping sideburn and tears scalded her eyes. Then Rye lifted his head. Hard calluses framed Laura's face as he bracketed her jaws with broad hands and kissed her with an impatience that had been growing for five years. Wide, warm, familiar lips slanted over hers before reason interfered. His tongue came hungering, searching and finding the depths of her mouth as the years slid away into oblivion. They crushed each other with the sweet torment of reunion driving their hearts into a ramming dance as the embrace and kiss pushed all sense of time aside.

At last they separated, though Rye still held her face as if it were a precious treasure, gazing down into her eyes as he whispered in a racked voice, "Ah, Laura-love." Tiredly, he leaned his forehead against hers while his eyes sagged shut, and he basked in the scent and nearness of her, running his palms over her back as if to memorize its every muscle.

After a long moment she lifted his face, traversing it with fingertips and eyes, familiarizing herself with five added years of creases that webbed its bronzed skin. The days of gazing into high sun seemed to have bleached not only his hair and brows, but the very blue of his eyes.

With those eyes he drank her in, standing a small space away. He lifted one long palm, as tough as the leagues of rigging it had hauled, and lay it on her cheek, pink still from the heat of the fireplace. His other palm fell from her shoulder to the gentle hillock of her breast, caressing it as though to affirm that she was real, that he was here at last.

She reacted as she always had, pressing more firmly against his palm, letting her eyelids slide closed for a moment, cupping the back of his hand with her own as her heartbeat and breathing hastened. Then, realizing what she was doing, she captured his hand in both of hers, turned her lips into it, and pressed it instead to her face, while dread and relief raised a tempest of emotions within her.

"Oh, Rye, Rye," she despaired, "we thought you were dead."

He placed his free hand on the knot of hair at the nape of her neck, wondering how far down her back it would fall when he freed it. His rough palm caught in the fine strands he remembered so well, had dreamed of so many lonely times. Once more he circled her with both arms, holding her lightly against him while asking, "Didn't y' get any of my letters?"

"Your letters?" she parroted, gathering enough common sense to push at his inner elbows and back out of his embrace, though it was the last thing she wanted to do.

"I left the first one in the turtle shell on Charles Island."

There was, atop a certain rock in the Galapagos Islands, a large white turtle shell known to every deep-water whaling man in the world. No New England vessel passed it by without putting in to check for letters from home or, if heading eastward around Cape Horn, to pick up any seamen's letters it held and deliver them to loved ones in towns such as Nantucket or New Bedford. It often took months for these letters to reach the right hands, but most eventually did.

"Y' didn't get it?" Rye studied the brown eyes with long charcoal lashes that had seen him through a hundred storms at sea and brought him safely into harbor at last.

But Laura only shook her head.

"I left that first one in the winter of 'thirty-three," he recalled, frowning in consternation. "And I sent another with a first mate from Sag Harbor when we crossed paths with the *Stafford* in the Philippines. And another from Portugal . . . why, I know I sent you at least three. Didn't y' get any of them?"

Again Laura only shook her head. The sea was wet and ink was vulnerable. Voyages were long, destinies uncertain. There were myriad reasons why Rye's letters had failed to reach their destination. They could only stare at each other and wonder.

"B . . . but word came back that the *Massachusetts* went down with . . . with all hands." Unsmiling, she touched his face, as if to reaffirm he was no ghost. It was then she saw the small craters in his skin—several on his forehead, one that slightly altered the familiar line of his upper lip, and another that fell into the smile line to the right side of his mouth, giving him an appearance of rakishness, as if he wore a teasing grin when he did not.

Dear God, she thought. Dear God, how can this be?

"We lost three hands just this side of the Horn. They jumped ship, too scared t' face roundin' 'er after all. So we put into the coast of Chile t' sign on some shoalers and walked into an epidemic of smallpox. Eleven days later, I knew I had it, too.''

''But you took the cowpox inoculation before you left.'' She touched the scar on his upper lip.

''Y' know it's not foolproof.'' Indeed, it wasn't. The current method of inoculation was to let the pus of the cowpox scabs dry on the ends of threads, then apply the virus to a scratch in the skin. Though it didn't always prevent the disease, it nevertheless greatly reduced its severity.

''Anyway, I was one of the unlucky ones who caught it. At least, I thought I was unlucky when they put me off ship. But later, when I heard that the *Massachusetts* had piled up on Galapagos and gone down with all hands . . .'' A haunted look came into his eyes and he sighed deeply at his near brush with death and memories of his lost shipmates. Then he seemed to draw himself back to the present with a squaring of his shoulders. ''When the fever and rash were gone, I had t' wait for another ship in need of a cooper. I made my way t' Charles Island, knowin' they all put in there, and I got lucky. Along came the *Omega,* and I signed articles on her, then headed into the Pacific, all the time believin' my letter would reach y' and y'd know I was still alive.''

Oh, Rye, my love, how can I tell you?

She studied his beloved face—long, lean, handsome, and hardly marred by the scars. She counted each one—seven, she could find—and resisted the urge to kiss each of them, realizing that the physical scars of this voyage were nothing compared to the emotional scars yet to come.

His thick hair was the color of corn shocks darkening in the weather, and her eyes followed the L-shaped side-whiskers as they jutted toward his cheeks, then she lifted her gaze to his beautifully shaped eyebrows, far less unruly than his hair, which always seemed styled by the whims of the wind, even after he'd just combed it. She smoothed it now—ah, just this once—unable to resist the familiar gesture she'd performed so often in the past. And while she touched his hair she became lost in his eyes, those eyes that had haunted her so when she'd thought him dead. All she'd had to do was step to the doorsill and scan the skies on a clear day to know again the color of those pale, searching eyes of Rye Dalton.

She looked away from them now, haunted anew by all he'd suffered, by all he must yet suffer, through no fault of his own.

They had fought before he left, bitter arguments, with him promising to go whaling just this once, to return to her with his cooper's ''lay''—his share of the profits—and put them on easy street. She had begged and pleaded with him not to go, to stay and work the cooperage here on Nantucket with his father. Riches mattered little to her. But he'd argued, just one voyage—just one. Didn't she realize how much a cooper's lay could be if they filled all their barrels? She had expected him to be gone perhaps two years and at first had schooled herself to accept an absence of this duration. But the Nantucket whalers could no longer fill their barrels close to home. The entire world sought whale oil, baleen, as whalebone was called, and ambergris, a waxy substance used in making perfume; those who went in search of these products of the deep found them harder and harder to find.

''But five years!'' she half-moaned.

Moving again to cradle her face in his hands, he said now, "I'm not sorry I went, Laura. The *Omega* chocked off! Filled 'er hold! Do y' know how rich—"

But just then a small voice interrupted. "Mama?"

Laura leaped backward and pressed a hand to her hammering heart.

Rye spun around.

In the doorway stood a lad whose pale blond head reached no higher than Rye's hip. He peered up uncertainly at the tall stranger while one finger shyly tugged at the corner of a winsome mouth. A burst of emotion flooded Rye's chest. A son, by Jesus! I have a son! His eyes sought Laura's, but she avoided his questioning glance.

"Where've you been, Josh?"

Josh, Rye thought joyously. Shortened from my father's Josiah?

"Waiting for Papa."

Panic tore through Laura. Her mouth went dry, her palms damp. She should have told Rye immediately! But how do you tell a man a thing like that?

His face, alit with joy only seconds ago, suddenly lost its smile as he turned a quizzical expression to his wife. She felt the blood leap to her cheeks and opened her mouth to tell him the truth, but before she got the chance, steps crunched on the shell path outside and a square-built man stepped to the doorway. His attire was very formal: square-tailed black frock coat, bowed white cravat, and twilled pantaloons stretched faultlessly taut between hidden suspenders and the straps riding under his shoes. He removed a shiny beaver top hat and hung it on a coat tree beside the door in a smooth, accustomed movement. Only then did he look up to find Laura and Rye standing like statues before him. His hand fell still halfway down the row of buttons on his double-breasted topcoat.

Laura swallowed. The face of the man in the doorway suddenly blanched. Rye's glance darted from the dapper man to Laura, to the beaver hat on its peg, and back to the man again. The sound of stew bubbling in the pot seemed as loud as the roar of a nor'easter, so silent had the room become.

Rye was gripped by a sick feeling of dread, a dread much stronger than any he'd experienced while rounding Cape Horn in the jaws of two oceans that ripped at one another and threatened to dismember the ship.

Daniel Morgan was the first to recover. He forced a welcoming smile and came forward with hand extended. "Rye! My God, man, have you been regurgitated from the bowels of the sea?"

"Dan, it's good t' see you," Rye returned automatically, though the words were suddenly half lie, if his suspicions proved true. "The fact is, I wasn't aboard the *Massachusetts* when she went down. I'd been left ashore with a case of small-pox."

The men, dear friends all their lives, clasped hands and pounded each other's shoulders, but the hearty sincerity of the handclasp did little to lighten the strained atmosphere. Neither was certain of what the situation was.

"Saved . . . by smallpox?" Dan said.

The irony of it made them laugh as they broke apart. But the laugh drifted into uncomfortable silence and each glanced at Laura, whose eyes skittered from one to the other, then fell to Josh, who studied the three of them in puzzlement.

"Go out back and wash your hands and face for dinner," Laura ordered gently.

"But, Mama—"

"Don't argue, now. Go." She gave the child a nudge, and he disappeared out the rear door while the pale blue eyes of the seaman followed.

The tension was as thick as the shroud of fog that covered Nantucket one day out of four. Casting about, Rye took in the trestle table for the first time—it was set for three. A humidor stood on a finely made table of cherrywood beside an upholstered wing chair with a matching cricket stool. The bed that had been in the room when he left was no longer there. In its place was an alcove bed, a single bunk situated above a built-in storage chest, the entire setup fronted by folding doors, open now, revealing some carved wooden soldiers standing at attention upon the counterpane—obviously the child's bed. Rye's gaze moved to the new doorway that had been cut into the wall on the left side of the fireplace. It led to the linter room beyond, where a corner of the familiar double bed was visible.

Rye Dalton swallowed hard. "Y've come t' have lunch with Laura?" he questioned his friend.

"Yes, I . . ." It was now Dan Morgan's turn to swallow, and it appeared he didn't know where to put his hands.

Both men silently appealed to the woman, whose fingers were clenched tightly before her. The room had the kind of pall usually presaged by the news that someone had died, brought about now, ironically, by the news that Rye Dalton lived.

Laura's voice was strained, her cheeks blazing, as she worked her palms together nervously. "Rye, we . . . we thought you were dead."

"We?"

"Dan and I."

"Dan and you," Rye repeated expressionlessly.

Laura's eyes sought Dan's for help, but he was as speechless as she.

"And?" Rye snapped, looking from one to the other, his dread growing with each passing second.

"Oh, Rye." Laura reached a beseeching hand toward him, and her face seemed to melt into lines of pity. "They said *all hands*. How could we know? The log was never found."

They stood, appropriately enough, in a perfect triangle. Finally, Dan suggested quietly, "I think we should all sit down."

But being a man of the sea, Rye Dalton was used to facing calamities on his feet. He faced them both, challenging. "Is it . . . is it what it looks like here?" His eyes made a quick arc around the room, encompassing all the signs of Dan's residence in that single sweep, and came to rest on his wife. Her lips were open, trembling. Her hands were folded so tightly the knuckles were white. Her brown eyes were luminous with unshed tears and bore an expression of deep remorse.

Softly, she admitted, "Yes, Rye, it is. Dan and I are married."

Rye Dalton groaned and sank into a chair, burying his face in his hands. "Oh my God."

It was all Laura could do to keep from going to him, kneeling before him, comforting him, for she felt the keen agony as sharply as he. She wanted to cry out, "I'm sorry, Rye, I'm sorry!" But Dan stood there, too. Dan, Rye's best friend. Dan, whom Laura also loved, who had seen her through the worst times of her life; who had comforted her when the news of Rye's death came; who had been so much stronger than she in the face of their mutual loss; who had cheered her during her utterly despondent pregnancy and given her the will to go on; who had been her right hand whenever she needed the strength of a man for the thousand things she, as a pregnant woman, was unable to do; Dan, who had grown to love Rye Dalton's child as if he were his own, who had taken Josh as his son when he took Laura as his wife.

Josh came charging in now, face shiny, a rooster tail of hair standing straight up from the crown of his head. He ran directly to Dan, hugging the man's legs, gazing up his body with a cherubic smile that tore at Rye Dalton's heart.

"Mama made one of your favorites—guess what."

Rye watched Dan Morgan ruffle the boy's hair, then smooth down the rooster tail, which immediately popped up again.

"We'll play our guessing game at supper, son," he said without thinking, then immediately colored, and glanced up to meet the pained expression on Rye's face.

The pale blue eyes dropped to the boy—how old? Rye wondered frantically, Four? Five? But he couldn't tell.

His slumped shoulders straightened by degrees, and he raised his gaze to Laura, silently asking the question. But the boy was there, and Rye understood that she could not answer before him. He looked down at the lad again, wondering, Is he mine or Dan's?

The tension built and Laura felt like the rope in a tug-of-war. She felt lightheaded and nauseated and removed from herself, as if this farce must certainly be happening to someone else. Some sense of propriety surfaced and made her lips move to say, "You're welcome to stay for dinner, Rye." Even to her own ears it sounded strange, inviting a man to a table that was his own.

Rye Dalton heard her stilted invitation and held back a bark of tormented laughter that almost escaped his lips. For five years he'd sailed the seas, eating unsavory ship's biscuits, unpalatable lobscouse stew, and salt fish, all the while savoring the anticipation of his first meal at home. And now he was here; in his nostrils was the aroma of the meal he'd dreamed of. Yet he could not possibly sit and share it with Laura and her . . . her *other* husband.

Rye reeled to his feet, suddenly in a hurry to get away and sort out his thoughts. The boy still looked on, making questions impossible. "Thank you, Laura, but I haven't seen my parents yet. I think I'll go down and say hello t' them." His parents would know the truth.

Laura's heart seemed to drop to the pit of her stomach. She and Dan exchanged a secret glance while she telegraphed a silent plea for him to understand. "I'll walk a little way down the path with you, Rye," she offered.

"No . . . no, that's not necessary. I remember the way well enough."

Quickly, Dan interjected, "You go with him, Laura. I'll spoon up for Josh and me."

The tension grew while Rye pondered whether to gesture Laura ahead of him or insist again that she need not go.

Josh lifted his face to Dan, asking, "Is that man going to go for a walk with Mama?"

''Yes, but she'll be right back,'' Dan answered.

''Who is he?'' Josh inquired innocently.

''His name is Rye, and he's an old friend of mine . . . and your mother's.''

Josh perused the tall, strapping stranger whose clothes were whitened by salt rime, whose hair was streaked by sun, whose boots were soaked with whale oil, and whose speech was clipped and different from theirs.

''Rye?'' repeated the child. ''That's a funny name.''

With an effort, Rye smiled at the precocious child, taking in every freckle, every gesture, every expression, wondering yet if Josh was his.

''Yes, it is, isn't it? It's because m' mother's name was Ryerson when she was a girl.''

''I gots a friend, his name is Jimmy Ryerson.''

He's your cousin if you're my son, thought the man, whose blue eyes moved to Laura, only to have the answer forestalled once more while she knelt down on one knee to speak to the boy.

''You and . . . and Papa get started. I'll only be a minute.'' Hearing her own hesitation over the word *Papa,* Laura felt guilty, confused, and embarrassed. Dear Lord, what have I done? From the corner of her eye she saw Rye lean to scoop his pea jacket off the floor, then stand waiting.

As Laura preceded Rye out the door, Dan watched their backs, a tight-lipped expression on his face. He remembered the three of them as children, running the dunes together, barefoot and carefree. Down through his memory drifted his own voice, cracking into a high falsetto.

''Hey, Laura, wanna go with me and see if the wild strawberries are ripe?''

And Laura, calling after Rye's retreating back. ''Hey, Rye, you wanna come with us?''

Rye, looking over his shoulder, still walking away. ''Naw, think I'll go up to Altar Rock and watch for whalers.''

Then Laura again, choosing as she always chose. ''I'm gonna go with Rye. Strawberries prob'ly ain't ripe yet anyway.''

And Dan, following the two of them, hands in his pockets, wishing that just once Laura would follow him the way she followed Rye.

Outside, Rye again hefted his sea chest onto his shoulder and moved down the scallop-shell path beside Laura while both of them carefully kept their eyes straight ahead. But she was conscious of his salt-caked cuffs, and he of her sprigged skirts. It seemed an eternity before they were beyond earshot of the house, and he asked without preface, ''Is Josh my son?''

''Yes.'' She knew a wheeling jubilation at being able to tell him at last, even as uncertainties came to crowd out the momentary joy.

Rye's feet stopped moving. The sea chest slid off his back and landed on the shells with a crunch. They had reached the *Y* in the path. To their left was a grove of apple trees rioting with blossom. Patches of violet-colored crocus nodded in the sun. Below, the bay twinkled, bright and blue as the eyes that sought and held Laura's. ''He's really mine?'' Rye asked incredulously.

''Yes, he's really yours,'' she whispered, a tremulous smile lending her face a brief serenity while she watched the stunned reactions parade across Rye's face. Suddenly he plopped backward and sat on the sea chest, drawing deep breaths, as if recovering from having the wind knocked out of him.

"Mine," he repeated to the shells, then to her brown smiling eyes, "Mine," as if it were too incredible to grasp yet.

He reached for her hand, and she could no more deny her own hand its rightful place in his at this moment than she could turn the irreversible tides of fate that had brought them to this impasse. His broad, brown hand enfolded her much narrower, much lighter one, and he drew her closer, to stand within the vee of his thighs, then rested his palms on her hips while gazing up at her with a wealth of emotions in his eyes. With a slight pressure at her waist, he brought her still closer until her knees touched the juncture of his legs, then he softly groaned and pressed his face against her midsection.

"Oh, Laura . . ."

A pair of screeching gulls arced overhead, but she did not see them, for her eyelids were closed against the sight of the coarse, pale hair resting just below her breasts, the full crown of his skull, which she wanted so badly to pull securely against her.

"Rye, please . . ."

He lifted his pained eyes to search hers. "How long have y' been married to him?"

"It'll be four years in July."

"Four years." A succession of uninvited pictures flashed through Rye's head, of Laura and Dan and the intimacies they had inevitably shared. "Four years," he repeated, disheartened, staring at the hem of her skirt. "How could something like this happen? How!" Angrily, he leaped to his feet, turning his back on her, feeling helpless and thwarted. "And Josh . . . he doesn't know?"

"No."

"Y' never told him anything about me?" He turned to face her again.

"We . . . we didn't consciously keep it from him, Rye. It's just that . . . well, Dan's been here since Josh was born, since *before* Josh was born. He grew up loving Dan as a . . . a father."

"I want him t' know, Laura. And I want y' back, and the three of us livin' in that house the way it ought t' be!"

"I know, but give me time, Rye, please." Her face was etched with creases and her voice cracked. "This is . . . well, it's all so sudden, for all of us."

"Time? How much time?" He glowered.

Her eyes met his directly as she wondered exactly what it was he was asking. But seeing the intensity there, the determination, she dropped her gaze to his chest, and she didn't know how to answer.

"I've been waitin' five years for this day, and y' ask me t' give you time. How long do I have t' keep waiting?" He moved toward her.

"I don't . . . we shouldn't . . ." Her glance flickered past his lips. "I . . . please, Rye . . ." she stammered.

"Please, Rye?" With his eyes riveted on her mouth, he reached slowly for her elbow. "Please what?"

"We . . . we could be seen here." But her cheeks were flushed, her eyes bright. Her breath came fast between open lips.

"So what? You're my wife."

"I didn't walk down here with you for this."

"I did." His voice was throaty, and he tugged inexorably at her elbow, his gaze shifting to the top of the hill to make sure they could not be seen from the house. ''It's been five years, Laura. My God, do y' know how I've thought of y'? How I've missed y'? And all I've had is a single kiss when I want so much more.'' His eyes were an azure caress, his voice a husky temptation. ''I want to take y' right here under these apple trees, and the world be damned, and Dan Morgan be damned along with it. Come here.''

His fingers tightened. Her heart leaped crazily as he pulled her closer, closer, erasing the space between them while his blue eyes roved the features of her face and his broad hand found the curve of her waist. He pulled her flush against him, and though her elbows folded between them, she knew the instant their hips met, that Rye had blossomed as fully as the apple trees. His kiss was wide, wet, and demanding, a thorough invasion of her mouth, telling her without doubt that it would take only her acquiescence for him to invade the rest of her as well.

He groaned into her open mouth, his tongue dancing lustily over hers, his fingers feeling the sun's heat captured in her bountiful spice-brown hair, careful not to mess it, though he wanted nothing so much as to untether it and send it flying free in a circlet upon the grass as he possessed her the way he'd dreamed of doing for so long.

His hand drifted down her neck, found her shoulder blades, her back, her ribs—but there it encountered the firm lashing made of the very substance that had sent him onto the high seas to lose her: whalebone!

''Damn all whalers!'' he cursed thickly, tearing his mouth away from hers, examining the stays of her corset with his fingertips. They started just below her shoulder blades and extended to the lumbar regions of her spine, and he traced them through the blue cotton of her dress while his breath beat heavily against her ear.

She couldn't help smiling. ''Thank God for whalers right this minute,'' she declared shakily, backing away.

''Laura?''

It was the first she had admitted to wanting him. But when he would have tipped her chin up for another kiss, she would not allow it. ''Stop it, Rye! Anyone on the island could happen along here.''

''And see a man kissin' his wife. Come back here, I'm not through with y' yet.'' But again she eluded him.

''Rye, no. You must understand, this has got to stop until we can get this awful situation untangled.''

''The situation is clear. You were married t' me first.''

''But not longest.'' Difficult as it was to say, she had to make it clear she would not willfully hurt Dan.

The tumescence wilted from Rye's body with a suddenness that surprised him. ''Does that mean y' intend t' stay with him?''

''For the time being. Until we get a chance to talk, to—''

''Y're my wife!'' His fists bunched. ''I will not have y' living with another man!''

''I have as much to say about it as you do, Rye, and I'm not . . . not walking out on Dan in an emotional fit. There's Josh to consider, and . . . and . . .'' Frustrated, she clenched her hands together and began pacing in agitation, finally whirling on him and facing him head on. ''We've believed for more than four years that you were dead. You can't expect either of us to adjust to the fact that you're not, in one hour.''

Rye's jaw looked as hard as teak as he scowled out across Nantucket Bay. ''If y're goin' t' stay with him,'' he said icily, ''just give me the word, because—by God!—I won't stay around t' watch it. I'll be gone on the next whaleship that leaves port.''

''I didn't say that. I've asked you to give me some time. Will you do that?''

He turned his eyes to her once again, but it took extreme effort to be so close to Laura and not embrace her . . . kiss her . . . more. He gave a brusque New England nod, then gazed out at the bay again.

The lonely ringing of a bell buoy drifted up to them from the hidden sandbars of the shoals. The ever-present rush of the ocean to shore created a background music neither of them heard, after living their entire lives to its beat. The cry of gulls and the sound of hammers from the shipyards below became part of the orchestration of the island, taken in unconsciously, as was the scent of its heaths and marshes, the damp salt air.

''Rye?''

Belligerently, he refused to face her.

She lay a hand on his arm and felt the muscles tense beneath her touch. ''The reason I walked out here with you is that I wanted to talk to you before you walk down the hill.''

He still would not look at her.

''I'm afraid I have some . . . some bad news.''

He snapped a glance at her, then turned away again. ''Bad news?'' he repeated sardonically, then laughed once, mirthlessly. ''What could be worse than the news I've already got?''

Rye, Rye, her heart cried, you don't deserve to return to all this heartache. ''You said you were going down to see your parents, and I . . . I thought you should know before you got there . . .''

He began to turn his head, and there was a wary stiffness about his shoulders, as if he'd already guessed.

Laura's hand tightened on his arm. ''Your mother . . . she's not at home, Rye.''

''Not at home?''

But even though she sensed that he knew, the words seemed to stick in Laura's throat. ''She's down there on Quaker Road.''

''Qu . . . Quaker Road?'' He looked in its direction, then back to her.

''Yes.'' Laura's eyes filled, and her heart ached at having to deliver yet another emotional blow to him. ''She died over two years ago. Your father buried her in the Quaker cemetery.''

She felt a tremor pass through his body. He whirled about, ramming his hands hard into his pockets, squaring his shoulders while fighting for control. Through tear-filled eyes she watched the pale, pale hair at the back of Rye's neck fall over his collar as he raised his face to the blue sky and a single sob was wrenched from his throat.

''Is anything the way it was before I l . . . left here?''

She was torn by sympathy. It welled high in her throat, and she had a sudden overwhelming need to gentle and comfort. She moved close behind him and lay a hand on the valley between his shoulder blades. Her touch brought forth another sob, then another.

''Damn whaling!'' he shouted at the sky.

She felt his broad back tremble and suffered at the tormented sounds of his despair. Yes, *damn* whaling, she thought. It was an inhuman taskmaster who little valued life, love, or happiness. These a whaler was asked to forfeit in the pursuit of oil, bone, and ambergris. Windjammers plied the seven seas for years at a time, their barrels slowly filling, while ashore mothers died, children were born, and impatient sweethearts wedded others.

But homes glowed at night. And ladies perfumed themselves with scents congealed by ambergris. And they pretended that whalebone corsets could effectively guard their virtue because a stiff-spined queen across the Atlantic led the vanguard of prudishness that was spreading across the waves like a pestilence.

The inhumanity of it swept over Laura, and unable to hold herself apart from Rye any longer, she circled his ribs and held him fast, her forehead pressed against the small of his back. ''Rye darling, I'm so sorry.''

When his weeping had passed, he asked only one question. ''When will I see y' again?''

But she had no answer to ease his misery.

The May wind, heedless of human misery, too, scented with salt and blossom, ruffled his hair, then skittered on to dry the caulking of yet another whaleship being readied for voyages, and to carry away the smoke from the tryworks that brought prosperity, and sometimes pain, to the people of Nantucket Island.

Chapter 2

Whaling was the loom that wove together the warp of sea and the woof of land to create the tapestry called Nantucket. Not an islander was unaffected by it; indeed, most earned their living from it, whether directly or indirectly, and had since the late 1600s, when the first sperm whale was taken by a Nantucket sloop master.

The island itself seemed predestined by nature to become the home of whaling, a new economic force in Colonial America, for its location was close to the original migratory routes of the whales, and its pork-chop shape created a large natural anchorage area ideal for use as a waterfront and needing no modification. As a result, the town was laid out contouring the edge of the Great Harbor and virtually rising from the rim of the sea.

The pursuit of the sperm whale had become not only an industry on Nantucket, but a tradition passed down from generation to generation. The sons of captains became captains themselves; the sailmaker passed down his trade to his son; ships' riggers taught their sons the art of splicing the lines that carried the sails aloft; shipwrights apprenticed their sons in the trade of ship repair; ships' carvers taught their sons to shape the figureheads, believed to be good-luck charms, that would see the ships safely back to shore; the retired shipsmith often saw his son take his place with anvil and hammer aboard an outgoing whaler.

And so it was with Josiah Dalton. A fifth-generation cooper, he had passed down his knowledge of barrel making to his son and had watched Rye sail away as he himself had done when he was younger.

Barrels were constructed on shore, then dismantled and packed aboard ships to be reassembled as needed when whales were captured. Coopers, therefore, had the advantage of plying their trade either on land or aboard a whaleship, choosing the risk of a voyage for the chance of high stakes, for a cooper's portion of the profits—his lay—was fourth only to those of the captain and the first and second mates.

Josiah Dalton had, in his time, earned himself three substantial lays, but had, too, suffered the miseries of three voyages, so now he shaped his barrels with both feet on solid ground.

His back was hunched from years of straddling the shaving horse and pulling a heavy steel drawknife toward his knees. His hands were rivered with bulging blue veins and were widespread from clutching the double-handled tool. His torso seemed wrought of iron and was so muscular that it out-proportioned his hips, giving him the burly look of an ape when he stood.

But his face was gentle, seamed with lines reminiscent of the grains in the wood he worked. The left cheek was permanently rounded in a smile from accommodating the brierwood pipe that was never absent from between his teeth. His left eye wore a perennial squint and seemed tinted by the very hue of the blue-gray smoke that always drifted past it, as if through the years it had absorbed the fragrant wisps somehow. The frizzled hair about his head was gray and curly, as curly as the miles of wood shavings that had fallen from his knives.

Rye paused in the open double doors of the cooperage, peering in, taking a minute to absorb the sights, sounds, and scents on which he'd been weaned. Shelves of barrels lined the walls—plump-waisted barrels, flat-sided hogsheads, and an occasional oval, which could not roll with the pitch of a ship. Partially constructed barrels sat like the petals of daisies in their hoops, while the staves of the next wet barrel soaked in a vat of water. Drawknives were hung neatly along one wall while the grindstone sat below them in the same place as always. The croze—planes for cutting grooves at each end of the barrel stave—adzes with their curved blades, and jointing planes were up high off the damp floor, just as Josiah had always taught they must be.

Josiah. There he was—with a billow of fresh wood curls covering his boot, which pressed against the foot pedal of the shaving horse, clamping a stave in place as he shaped it.

He's grown much older, Rye thought, momentarily saddened.

Josiah looked up as a shadow fell across the door of his cooperage. Slowly, he raised his veined hand to remove the pipe from his mouth. Even more slowly, he swung his leg over the seat of the shaving horse and got to his feet. Telltale tears illuminated his eyes at the sight of his son, tall and strapping in the doorway.

The thousand greetings they'd promised themselves, if only they could ever see each other alive again, eluded them both now, until Josiah broke the silence with the most mundane remark.

"Y're home." His voice was perilously shaky.

"Aye." Rye's was perilously deep.

"I heard y'd docked aboard the *Omega*."

Rye only nodded. They stood in silence, the old man drinking in the younger, the younger absorbing the familiar scene before him, which he'd sometimes doubted he'd ever see again. The emotions peculiar to such homings held them each, for the moment, bound to the earthen floor, until at last Rye moved, striding toward his father with arms outflung. Their embrace was firm, muscular, crushing, for Rye's arms, too, had known their share of pulling drawknives. Clapping each other's backs, they separated, smiling—blue eyes gazing into bluer—quite unable to speak just yet.

An old yellow dog with graying muzzle filled the breach by shambling to her feet and lurching forward, her tail wagging in joyful welcome.

"Ship!" Rye exclaimed, going down on one knee to scratch the dog's face affectionately. "What're y' doing here?"

Ah, what a sight, his father thought, to see the lad's head bent over that dog again. "Beast seemed t' think y'd come here if y' ever made it back. Left the house on the hill and wasn't anybody gettin' 'er t' stay up there without y'. Been waitin' here these five years."

Rye lowered his face, one hand on either side of the dog's head, and the old Labrador squirmed as best she could, swiping her pink tongue at the man's chin as Rye laughed and backed away, then changed his mind and leaned forward for a pair of wet slashes from the tongue.

He'd had the dog since he was a boy, when the yellow Labrador was found swimming ashore from a shipwreck off the shoals. Put up for grabs, the pup had immediately been appropriated by young Rye Dalton and named Shipwreck.

Finding old Ship waiting, whining a loyal welcome, Rye thought: Here at last is something the same as it used to be.

The old man clamped his teeth around his pipestem, watching Rye and the dog, joyful at the boy's return, but sorrowed that Martha wasn't here to share the moment.

"So the old harpy didn't get y' after all," Josiah noted caustically, chuckling deep in his throat to cover emotions too deep to be conveyed any other way.

"Nay." Rye raised his eyes, still scratching the dog's ears. "She tried her best, but I was put off ship just before the wreck, with a case of smallpox."

The pipestem was pointed at Rye's face. "So I see. How bad was it?"

"Just bad enough to save my life."

"Ayup," Josiah grunted, scrutinizing with his squint-eye.

Rye stood up, rested his hands on his hips, and scanned the cooperage. "Been some changes around here," he noted solemnly.

"Aye, and aplenty."

Their eyes met, each of them saddened by the tricks five years had played on them.

"Seems we've each lost a woman," the younger man said gravely. The dog nudged his knee, but he hardly noticed as he gazed into his father's eyes, noting the new lines etched about them, the threatening tears glistening there.

"So y've already heard." Josiah studied his pipe, rubbing its warm bowl with his thumb as if it were a woman's jaw.

"Aye," came the quiet reply.

The dog reared up and leaned against Rye's hip, pushing him slightly off balance. Again he seemed not to notice. His hand unconsciously sought the golden head, moving on it absently as he watched his father rub the bowl of the brierwood pipe. "It won't seem the same, goin' upstairs without her there."

"Well, she had a good life, though she died sad to think y'd been drowned at sea. Seemed she never quite got over the news. Reckon she knew you was safe long before I did, though," Josiah said with a sad smile for his son.

"How'd she die?"

"The damps got her . . . the cold and damps. She got lung fever and was gone in three short days, burnin' up and shiverin' both at once. Wasn't a thing that could be done. It was March, and you know how gray the Gray Lady can be in March," he said. But he spoke without rancor, for anyone born to the island knew its foggy temperament and accepted it as part of life . . . and of death as well.

"Aye, she can be a wicked bitch then," Rye agreed.

The old man sighed and clapped Rye on the shoulder. "Ah well, I've got used t' life without y'r mother, as used t' it as I'll ever get. But you—" Josiah left the thought dangling as he studied his son quizzically.

Rye's glance went to the window.

"Y've been up the hill, then?" Josiah asked.

"Aye." A muscle tightened and hardened the outline of Rye's generous mouth, then he met his father's inquisitive eyes and the mouth softened somewhat.

"I've lost only one woman, lad, but y've lost two."

Again the mouth tensed, but this time with determination. "For the time bein'. But I mean t' reduce that number by half."

"But she married the man."

"Thinking me dead!"

"Aye, as we all did, lad."

"But I'm not, and I'll fight for her until I am."

"And what's she got t' say about it, then?"

Rye thought of Laura's kiss, followed by her careful withdrawal. "She's still in shock, I think, seein' me walk into the house that way. I think for a minute she believed I was a ghost." Rye turned his stubborn jaw toward his father again. "But I showed her I wasn't, by God!"

Josiah chuckled silently, nodding his head as his son colored slightly beneath his tan. "Aye, lad, I'll bet my buttons' y' did. But I see y've hauled y'r chest down here and set it on me floor as if y've come expectin' to share me bunk."

"It's Ship I've come t' bunk with, not you, you old salt, so y' can wipe the smirk off y'r briny face and have done with teasin'!"

Josiah broke into an appreciative roar of laughter, the pipe in jeopardy, scarcely anchored between his yellowing teeth. At last he removed it. "Haven't changed a bit, Rye, and it's my guess y'r woman's wonderin' what t' do with that spare husband of hers, eh? Well, stow y'r gear and welcome to y'. Ship and I are happy enough for y'r company. 'Tis been a quiet house f'r two years now. Even y'r sharp tongue will be welcome." Again he pointed at Rye's nose with his pipestem, and added, "Up to a point." Their eyes met and they shared the moment of levity—an aging parent and the child who'd grown taller and stronger than himself.

At the saltbox on the hill, Laura was still trembling from the shock of seeing Rye again, of kissing him. As soon as he disappeared down the path, none of it seemed real. But facing Dan made reality sweep back, along with the need to accept the bizarre truth and deal with it.

At the door, Laura closed her eyes for a moment, pressed a hand to her fluttering stomach, then stepped inside.

Dan sat at the table, but his elbows rested on either side of an untouched plate and his mouth was hidden behind interlaced fingers. His eyes followed her across the room, hazel eyes she'd known for as long as she'd had memory. Hazel eyes she now found difficult to meet.

She stopped beside the trestle table, wondering what to say, and if the man who sat studying her so silently was still her husband. His eyes moved to her hands, and she realized her fingers were nervously toying with the waistband of her apron, so she dropped them quickly and took her place on the bench across from Dan. Her nerves felt as if they were made of spun glass. The room was painfully silent, all but for the constant sounds of the island: hammers, gulls, bell buoys, and the faraway breath of a steam whistle from the Albany packet as it pulled into Steamboat Wharf below.

Suddenly Laura wilted, resting her elbows on either side of her own plate and burying her face in her palms. Several long, silent minutes passed before she raised her eyes to confront Dan again. He was absently toying with a spoon, pressing it firmly against the tabletop and cranking it around as if to screw it into the wood.

When he realized she was watching, he stopped, and his well-groomed hand fell still. He sighed, cleared his throat, and said, "Well . . ."

Say something, she berated herself. But she didn't know where to begin.

Dan cleared his throat again and sat up straighter.

"Where is Josh?" she asked quietly.

"He finished and went out to play."

"You haven't eaten anything," she noted, eyeing his plate.

"I . . . I wasn't very hungry." His eyes refused to meet hers.

"Dan . . ." She reached to cover his hand with her own, but his did not move. "He looks healthy as a horse, and very much alive."

She couched her hands in her lap, studying the plate that Dan had filled for her sometime while she was outside. ''Yes, he does . . . he . . . he is.''

''Was he here long?''

''Here?'' She looked up quickly.

''Here. In the house.''

''You know when the *Omega* came in.''

''No, not exactly. Nobody said a word to me about Rye's being on board. Funny, isn't it?''

Again she covered his hand with hers. ''Oh, Dan, nothing is changed . . . nothing.''

He jerked his hand free and spun to his feet, turning his back on her. ''Then why do I feel as if the world just dropped out from under my feet?''

''Dan, please.''

He turned and took a step nearer. ''Dan, please? Please what? Sit here . . . at *his* table, in *his* house, with *his*—''

''Dan, stop it!''

He whirled away again, the words *his wife* echoing through the room as distinctly as if he'd uttered them. Almost everything here was Rye Dalton's, or had been at one time—people and possessions both. Dan Morgan found himself floundering for a way to accept the fact that his friend was very much alive and had walked in here expecting to reclaim it all.

From behind, Laura watched as Dan grasped the back of his neck with one hand and dropped his chin onto his chest.

''Dan, come and sit back down and eat your dinner.''

His hand fell to his side and he turned to face her. ''Laura, I've got to get back to the countinghouse. Will you . . . are you going to be all right?''

''Of course.'' She rose and accompanied him to the door, where she held his jacket while he slipped it on. She watched as he retrieved his beaver top hat from the tree, but instead of donning it, he brushed his fingertips distractedly along its brim, his back to Laura. Studying his despondent pose, her throat constricted and her fingers twisted into a tight knot.

Dan took a step toward the open door, halted, drew a deep breath, then spun and clasped her against his chest so hard, the breath swooshed from her lungs. ''I'll see you at supper,'' he whispered in a tortured voice, and she nodded against his shoulder before he tore himself away and quickly stepped out the door.

As Dan Morgan moved down the scallop-shell path in the footsteps of Rye Dalton, it seemed to him that was where he'd been walking all his life.

When Dan was gone, Laura found tears in her eyes. She went back inside to find she must confront countless objects that bore witness to the curious melding of their three lives. At the trestle table she touched Dan's fork, which still rested in the unfinished food on his plate, realizing that years ago Rye, too, had eaten with this very fork; he very likely owned it. Distracted, she put away the remainder of the interrupted meal, but still the memories persisted. She closed the doors of the alcove bed, cutting off the sight of the place where Rye Dalton's son slept at night beside a row of wooden soldiers that had belonged to Dan Morgan as a boy. The humidor beside the wing chair had been a gift to Dan from Rye. The chair itself was one Dan had chosen after marrying Laura, though the cricket stool before it was a piece given to Rye and Laura by some guest at their wedding.

Almost against her wishes, Laura found herself at the door of the linter room, her eyes moving to the bed—how painful it was to look at it now—where she and Rye had conceived Josh and upon which Josh had been born and where Dan had come to sit beside the new mother and peer into the flannel blankets at the squirming pink bundle and predict, "He'll look just like Rye." Laura's eyelids trembled shut as she remembered Dan's words and how they'd been spoken because he'd sensed it was what Laura had needed to hear at that moment. This bed, above all, seemed a testimony to their convoluted history. It had been used by all three of them; the pineapple carving on its headposts had held the jackets of both men and the rails in between had been clasped by Laura's hands in the throes of both ecstasy and pain.

Her throat constricted and she turned away.

Which of them is still my husband? Above all, this question needed answering.

Thirty minutes later, Laura had her answer. She stepped out of the office of Ezra Merrill, the island's attorney, suddenly unable to face the house again, with all its reminders. And though she was twenty-four and a mother herself, Laura was smitten by the overwhelming urge to run to her own mother's arms.

Having left Josh at the Ryersons' house, Laura made her way to the silver-brown saltbox on Brimstone Street where she'd grown up. Returning to it, the memories grew stronger, of Rye and herself and Dan trooping in and out at will, in those days before commitments had been made. Nostalgia created a deep need to talk about those days and these, with someone who knew their beginnings.

But Laura had scarcely put foot inside her mother's keeping room before realizing Dahlia Traherne wasn't gong to be much help.

Dahlia could scarcely handle the everyday decisions of her own life, much less offer advice to others on how to handle theirs. An inveterate whiner, she had learned to get her way through chronic complaining about the most trivial problems; when trivialities failed to surface, she invented imaginary problems.

Her husband, Elias, had been island-born, a sailmaker who had sewn canvas all his life but had never sailed beneath it, for at the merest mention of his signing articles, Dahlia had come up with some new malady to make him promise never to leave her. He had died when Laura was twelve, and there were those who said Dahlia had driven him to an early grave with her habitual complaining and hypochondria, but that he'd probably gone to it gladly, to get away from her. Some said Dahlia should have stepped down a little harder on her daughter after Elias Traherne's death, for the girl ran free as a will-o'-the-wisp after her father was gone, tramping the island without curfew or call, following the boys, and learning the most unladylike habits while Dahlia sat home and made not the slightest effort to control her. And there were still others who condescendingly explained away Dahlia's weak nature by pointing out, "Well, after all, she's an off-islander."

No, Dahlia had not been born on the island, though she'd lived here for thirty-two years. But if she lived on Nantucket another hundred, she would still bear the stigma from which no mainland-born person could ever be free, for once an off-islander, always an off-islander. Perhaps it was because she sensed this wry disdain that Dahlia lost confidence and became so weak and puling.

Greeting her daughter now, she wheezed like the airy whine of a calliope. ''Why, Laury, I didn't expect to see you today.''

''Mother, could I talk to you?''

The expression on Laura's face made her mother suddenly suspect there was a problem, and the older woman hesitated, as if reluctant to invite her daughter in. But Laura swept inside, dropping to a bench at the table, heaving an enormous sigh, and saying in a shaking voice, ''Rye is alive.''

Dahlia felt a pain stab her between the eyes. ''Oh no.''

''Oh yes, and he's back on Nantucket.''

''Oh dear. Oh my . . . why it's . . . what . . .'' Dahlia's hands fluttered to her forehead, then massaged her temples, but before she could dredge up an ailment, Laura rushed on. The whole story tumbled out, and long before it ended, Dahlia's expression of dismay had intensified to one of alarm.

''You . . . you aren't going to . . . to see him, are you, Laury?''

Disheartened, Laura studied the woman across the table. ''Oh, Mother, I already have. And even if I hadn't, how could I avoid it on an island the size of Nantucket?''

''B . . . but what will Dan think?''

Laura resisted the urge to cry out, What about me? What about what I think? You haven't even asked me. Instead, she replied tonelessly, ''Dan's seen him, too. Rye came to the house.''

''To the house. . . . Oh my . . .'' Dahlia's fingertips fluttered from her temples to her quivering lips. ''Whatever will I say to people?''

Insecurity had always been Dahlia's fundamental problem. Laura realized her folly in expecting her mother to analyze a situation in which security was clearly personified by Daniel Morgan, who had been the stalwart in Laura's life for so long, while Rye had gone away and left her ''high and dry,'' as Dahlia had often said. But Laura couldn't help herself from admitting, ''I've already talked to Ezra Merrill and found out Dan is still my legal husband.'' She raised troubled eyes that needed comfort. ''But I . . . I still have feelings for Rye.''

Immediately, Dahlia presented her palms. ''Shh! Don't say such a thing. It will only cause trouble. You shouldn't even have *seen* him!''

Laura became exasperated. ''Mother, it's Rye's house. Josh is his son. I couldn't possibly keep him away.''

''But he could . . . could take everything from you!''

''Mother, how could you think such a thing of Rye!'' How typical of Dahlia to be concerned about such a thing at a time like this. Laura sprang to her feet and began pacing.

''Laury, you mustn't get yourself worked up. Are you feeling all right? I'll have to speak to Dan about getting you some drops to calm this—''

''There's nothing wrong with me!''

But to a woman who could conjure up a convenient ache at the mention of anything disagreeable, it seemed imperative to discover an ailment. She came forward, attempting to press a palm to Laura's forehead, but Laura adroitly sidestepped.

''Oh, Mother, please.''

The fussy hand dropped. The pinched face with its ever-present expression of suffering seemed to take on several new wrinkles. Frustrated by her mother's inability either to cope or sympathize, Laura felt perilously close to tears.

Oh, Mother, can't you see what I need? I need reassurance, your cheek against my hair. I need to go back with you into the past so that I can sort out the present.

But Dahlia had never been a calming influence; whatever had possessed Laura to believe she would be now? Dahlia's flustered twittering only made things worse, and Laura was not surprised when her mother drifted to a chair, rested the back of her hand against her forehead, and said, "Oh, Laury, I fear I have a frightful headache. Could you mix up a tisane for me? There . . ." She fluttered a hand weakly. "On the shelf you'll find some valerian root and anise. Mix it up . . . with some water . . . please." By now she was breathless.

Thus, Laura found herself administering to her mother instead of being comforted, and by the time she left the house on Brimstone Street, she herself had a headache. She returned home to pass a tense afternoon reflecting upon the past and worrying about the future.

When Dan returned at the end of the day, his eyes scanned the keeping room as if he half expected to find Rye there. He hung up his jacket and caught Laura's glance from across the room, but neither of them seemed able to speak.

Dan's stare followed Laura as she put supper on the table, but throughout the meal the strained atmosphere remained while they avoided the subject of Rye Dalton.

But in the evening, Josh, with the intuitive accuracy of a child, shot a question that hit two marks at once. Dan was sitting at a small oak desk with a pen in his hand when Josh leaned across his lap and asked, "Why did Mama get scared today when that man was here?"

The entry on the ledger sheet went awry. Then Dan's hand stopped moving over the page, Laura's over her crocheting. Their eyes met, then Laura dropped her gaze.

"Why don't you ask Mama?" Dan suggested, watching the red creep up Laura's cheeks while he wondered again what had gone on between the two of them when Rye first got here.

Josh galloped over and flung himself across his mother's lap. "Are you scared of that man, Mama?"

"No, darling, not at all." She ruffled Josh's hair.

"You looked like you was. Your eyes was big and you jumped away from him like you make me jump away when I get too close to the fire."

"I was surprised, not scared, and I did not jump away from him. We were talking, that's all." But guilt flared Laura's cheeks to an even brighter hue, and she could tell Dan was studying her carefully. She lit into her crocheting as if the doily had to be finished by bedtime. "I think it's time you marched your soldiers to the shelf and got your nightshirt on for bed."

"You and Papa wanna talk grown-up talk, huh?"

Laura couldn't hide her smile. Josh was a bright and witty child, though there were times when she'd cheerfully have gagged him for his innocent comments. But there was a new discomfort between Laura and Dan that would have been there with or without Josh's remark, and as the evening rolled on toward bedtime, it became more and more palpable. By the time they retired to their room, Laura felt as if she were walking on fishhooks. And to make matters worse, there was the problem of disrobing.

Clothing of the day was styled for ladies with maids; both dresses and whalebone corsets were laced up the back, so it was impossible to don or doff them without aid. Laura had protested when Dan insisted on her purchasing such dresses instead of making her own, but he had a fierce pride in his ability to provide for her, thus she'd obliged and bought the inconvenient garments, though twice daily she needed his assistance to get the infernal things on and off.

But tonight she felt a disquieting reluctance to ask the favor, though it had come to be part of their bedtime ritual, as automatic as the pinching of the last candlewick.

But tonight was different.

Dan set the candle on the commode table, untied his cravat and hung it on the bedpost, followed by his shirt. Laura, trussed up like a stuffed turkey ready for the spit, silently rebelled at women's plight. Why did women dress in such absurdly restrictive clothes? Men had no such inconveniences with which to contend.

How she wished she might unobtrusively slip out of her things and into her nightie and quickly duck beneath the covers. Instead, she was forced to ask, "Dan, would you loosen my laces please?"

To her horror, his face went red. She whirled to present her back. After nearly four years of unlacing her, Dan was blushing!

He released the brass hooks down the back of her dress and tugged at the laces, which were strung through metal grommets along the back of her corset. She felt him fumble, then he muttered under his breath. When at last she was free, she stepped from the garment, laid her corset over the cedar trunk, and unbuttoned her petticoat. That left only her pantaloons, which buttoned at the waist, and the chemise—it tied up the front with a satin ribbon.

The wrinkles of her chemise had been pressed into her skin all day, leaving a crisscross of red marks that itched terribly. Often Dan teased her when she slid into bed and immediately began scratching.

But tonight all was quiet after they'd dressed in nightgown and nightshirt—standing back to back—and lay beneath the coverlets, with only the after scent of candle smoke remaining. From outside came the incessant wash of sea upon land, and from nearer, the cluck of a whippoorwill that always precedes its song. Again it clucked, and Laura lay in the dark, equally as tense as Dan, telling herself there were many nights when they went to sleep without touching. Why was she so aware of it tonight?

She heard him swallow. Her ribs itched, but she forced her hands to be still. The silence stretched long, until at last, when the whippoorwill had called for the hundredth time, Laura reached for Dan's hand. He grasped it like a lifeline and squeezed so hard, her knuckles cracked softly, while from his side of the bed came a throaty sound, half relief, half despair. She heard the shush of the feather pillow as he turned to face her and ground his thumb into the back of her hand with possessive desperation.

When he finally spoke, his voice was guttural with emotion. "Laura, I'm scared."

A thorn seemed to pierce her heart. "Don't be," she reassured, though she was, too.

There were things he could not say, would not say, understood things that neither had ever admitted but that were suddenly implicit between them.

During their childhood and adolescence it had always been the three of them, forever comrades. But it had never been any secret that Laura had eyes only for Rye. When news of his death reached Nantucket, Dan had suffered with her, the two of them walking the windswept beaches, knowing that particular torment reserved for those who mourn without the benefit of a corpse. Helplessly, they'd wandered, needing the proof of death's finality. But that final proof was denied them by the greedy ocean, which cared little for man's need to lay a spirit to rest.

During those restless, roaming days, Dan's despair was shorter-lived than Laura's, for with Rye gone, he was free to court her as he'd always dreamed of doing. But he lived those days under a mantle of guilt, grateful that Rye's death had cleared the way for him, yet sickened by that very gratitude.

He had won Laura mainly by becoming indispensable to her.

She had awakened one morning to the sound of the ax in her back yard and had found Dan there, chopping her winter wood. When the crisp weather warned of imminent winter, he had come again, unasked, with a load of kelp with which to ballast the foundations of the house against the intrusive drafts of the harsh climate. When she grew cumbersome with pregnancy, Dan came daily to carry water, to fill the wood-box, to bring her fresh oranges, to insist that she put her feet up and rest when backaches riddled. And to watch her eyes fill with sorrow as she brooded before the fire and wondered if the baby would look like Rye. When she went into labor, it was Dan who fetched the midwife and Laura's mother, then paced the backyard feverishly, as Rye would have done had he been there. It was Dan who came to her bedside to peep at the infant and smooth Laura's brow with a promise that he would always be there when she and Josh needed him.

Thus, she grew to depend on Dan for all the husbandly support he was more than willing to give, long before he ever asked her to be his wife. They drifted into marriage as naturally as the bleached planks of ancient vessels drift to Nantucket's shores at high tide. And if intense passion was not a part of Laura's second courtship, security and companionship were.

As in most marriages, there was one who loved more, and in this one it was Dan. Yet he was secure at last, for the rival who'd once claimed Laura was no longer there. She was Dan's at last, and she loved him. He had never dissected that love, never admitted that much of it was prompted by gratitude, not only for his physical and financial support, but because he truly loved Josh as if the boy were his own and was as good a father as any natural father could be.

But when Dan had stepped into the house this noon and found Rye Dalton standing there, he'd felt the very foundation of his marriage threatened.

Lying beside Laura now, his throat ached with questions he did not want to ask for fear her answers would be those he dreaded hearing. Yet there was one he could not withhold, though his heart swelled with foreboding at the thought of putting it to her. His thumb ground against her hand. He swallowed and sent the question through the dark in a strange, tight voice.

"What were you and Rye doing when I walked in today?"

"Doing?" But the word sounded pinched and unnatural.

"Yes . . . doing. Why did Josh say you jumped when he walked in?"

"I . . . I don't know. I was nervous, naturally—who wouldn't be when a . . . a dead man has just walked in your door?"

"Quit hedging, Laura. You know what I'm asking."

"Well, don't, because it doesn't matter."

"Meaning he kissed you, right?" When she made no reply, he went on. "It was written all over your faces when I interrupted."

"Oh, Dan, I'm sorry, I really am. But he took me completely by surprise, and it didn't mean anything except hello." But she knew in her heart it did.

"And what about when you walked down the path with him—did he kiss you then, too?"

"Dan, please tr—"

"Twice! He kissed you twice!" He gave her hand a hurtful yank. "And what was the second time, another hello?"

She had never known jealousy from Dan before, for there'd never been cause. The vehemence of it quite frightened her as she frantically searched for a reply.

"Dan, for heaven's sake, you're hurting my hand." Though he eased his grip, he didn't release it. "Rye had no idea, when he walked in here, that we were married."

"Does he mean to take up his old place as your . . . husband?"

"You're my husband now," she said softly, hoping to placate him.

"One of them," he said bitterly. "The one you haven't kissed yet today."

"Because you haven't asked," she said even more softly.

He came up on one elbow, leaning over her. "Well, I'm not asking," he whispered fiercely. "I'm *taking* what's mine by rights."

His lips came down violently, moving over hers as if to punish her for circumstances that were not of her doing. He kissed her with a fierce determination to force Rye Dalton from her thoughts, from her life, from her past, knowing all the while that it was impossible to do.

His tongue plundered deep, wounding her with a lack of sensitivity she'd never before known from him. Hurt, she pulled sharply aside, making him suddenly realize how rough he'd been.

At once penitent, he scooped her tightly into his arms and crushed her beneath him, speaking raggedly into her ear. "Oh, Laura, Laura, I'm sorry. I didn't mean to hurt you, but I'm so afraid of losing you after all the years it took to finally have you. When I walked in here and saw him, I felt like I was back ten years ago, watching you trail after him like a love-sick puppy. Tell me you didn't kiss him back . . . tell me you won't let him touch you again."

He had never before admitted that he'd been jealous of Rye all those years ago. Pity moved her hands to the back of his neck to smooth his hair. She cradled him, closing her eyes, kissing his temple, suddenly understanding how tenuous his security was, now that Rye was back. Yet she was afraid to make promises she wasn't at all sure she could keep.

But this much she could say, and say with all truthfulness: "I love you, Dan. You never have to doubt that."

She felt a shudder run through him, then his hands started moving over her body. But at his touch came the wish that he would not make love to her tonight. Immediately, she was deluged with guilt for the thought. Never before had she even considered denying him. Dutifully, she caressed his neck, his back, telling herself this was the same Dan she'd made love with for three years and more;

that Rye Dalton could not come walking up the lane and give her the right to turn this man away.

Yet she wanted to—God help her, she wanted to.

He ran his hand down her hip, pulled her nightgown up, and she understood his need to reestablish himself. She opened her body to him and moved when she knew it was expected, and held him fast when he groaned and climaxed, and hid the fact that she felt faithless to another for what last night would have been the most natural and welcome act in the world.

In the loft above the cooperage, Rye Dalton lay on his back, disquieted by the emptiness of the womanless house. At each familiar piece of furniture he had pictured his mother, sitting, working, resting, her presence felt as much now as it had been when she was there in the flesh.

His first meal at home was an improvement over ship's fare, but fell far short of the tasty stews his mother or Laura would have prepared. His boyhood bunk, though larger than that on the *Omega,* was a sorry substitute for the large rosewood featherbed he'd thought to be sharing with Laura tonight. When he lay down, his body expected to ride the sway and swell it had known for five years; the steadiness of the bed beneath him kept Rye awake. Outside, instead of the whistle of wind in the rigging, he heard hooves on new cobbles, occasional voices, the crack of a whip, the closing of a street lantern's door.

Not disturbing sounds—just different.

He rose from his bunk and padded to the window facing south. Were it daybright, he could have seen the tip of his house, for trees here on the island were stunted things, pruned by the wind so that few grew taller than the edifices built by man.

But it was dark, the hill obliterated by a near-moonless night.

Rye imagined Laura in the bed he'd once shared with her, but lying in it now with Dan Morgan. He felt as if a harpoon had been thrust into his heart.

In his bed nearby, Josiah moved restlessly, then his voice came through the dark. "Thinking of 'er will do y' little good tonight, lad."

"Aye, and don't I know it. She's up there in bed with Dan this very minute, while I stand here making wishes."

"Tomorrow is time enough to tell her how y' feel."

"I needn't tell her—she knows."

"So she put y' off, did she?"

Rye leaned his elbow against the windowframe, frustrated anew. "Aye, that she did. But the lad was there, thinking Dan is his father, lovin' him as if he is, the way she tells it. That'll be somethin' t' reckon with."

"So she told y' about the boy?"

"Aye."

The incessant sound of the ocean seemed to murmur through the rough walls of the building while Rye remained as before, studying the dark square outside the window. When he spoke again it was quietly, but with inchoate pride nearly making his voice crack. "He's a bonny lad."

"Aye, with the look of his grandmother about his mouth."

Rye faced the spot where his father's bed was, though he could not clearly make him out. "Y've lost your grandchild just as I've lost my wife. Did she never bring him around for the two of y' t' get acquainted?"

"Aw, she has little business in the cooperage, and I doubt the lad lacks for grandparents' love, with Dan's folks playin' the part. I've heard they love him like their own."

The entanglements of the situation were ever increasing. Remembering days when he felt as free to run uninvited into the Morgans' house as he did into his own, Rye asked, "They're still well, then?"

"Aye, sound as dollars, both of 'em."

Silence followed again for a moment before Rye asked, "And Dan . . . what does he do t' keep her in such fancy furniture up there?"

"Works at the countinghouse for old man Starbuck."

"Starbuck!" Rye exclaimed. "You mean Joseph Starbuck?"

"One and the same."

The fact stung Rye, for Starbuck owned the fleet of whaleships that included the *Omega*. How ironic to think he himself had gone in search of riches only to lose Laura to one who stayed behind to count them.

"You see those three new houses up along Main Street?" Josiah continued. "Starbuck's buildin' them for his sons. Hired an architect clear from Europe to design 'em. The Three Bricks, he's callin' 'em. Starbuck's had good times. The *Hero* and the *President* came home chocked off, too, and he expects the same of the *Three Brothers*."

But Rye was barely listening. He was ruing the day he'd set out after riches—and riches he'd have, for his lay at one-sixtieth a share, would be close to a thousand dollars, no small amount of money by any man's standards. But the money could not buy Laura back. It was obvious she had a good life with Dan; he provided well for both her and the boy. Rye swallowed, peering through the dark to where the tip of his house must be, remembering his and Laura's bed in the new private linter room.

Damn! He takes her in my very own bed while I sleep in my boyhood bunk and eat bachelor's rations.

But not for long, Rye Dalton vowed. Not for long!

Chapter 3

The following day, fog had again settled over Nantucket. Its dank tendrils sniffed at Rye Dalton's boot tops like a keen-nosed hound, then silently retreated to let him pass untouched. As he strode toward Joseph Starbuck's countinghouse, the thick mist shifted and curled about his head while beneath his boots it turned the dull gray cobbles jet black and left them sheeny with moisture. On the iron bowl of the horse-watering fountain beads gathered, then ran in rivulets before dropping with irregular *blips,* each magnified into a queer resounding musical note by the enshrouding fog. Almost as an afterbeat came the click of Ship's toenails as she followed her master.

But in spite of the damp, gray day, Rye Dalton reveled in the unaccustomed luxury of being dry and clean after five years of being splattered by ceaseless waves and wearing oily, salt-caked "slops."

He was dressed in a bulky sweater Laura had knit for him years ago, its thick turtleneck hugging high against his jaw, nearly touching the side-whiskers that swept down to meet it. Those whiskers closely matched the color and texture of the tweedy wool, while down his sleeves twisted a cable knit that seemed to delineate the powerful curvature of the corded muscles it followed. His black wool bell-bottom trousers were waistless, rigged out with twin lacings just inside each hip, creating a stomach flap inside which his hands were pressed for warmth as he crossed the cobbles with long, masculine strides that parted the fog and sent it roiling behind him.

The salmon-colored bricks of the countinghouse appeared specterlike, a hazy backdrop for the dazzling white paint of its door, window casings, and signpost that stood out even under the leaden skies. When Rye's hand touched the latch, Ship dropped to her haunches, taking up her post with tongue lolling and eyes riveted on the door.

Inside, the fires had been lit to ward off the spring chill, and the place swarmed with activity, as it always did after a whaleship came in. Rye exchanged greetings with countless acquaintances while he was directed to the office of Joseph Starbuck, a jovial mutton-chopped man who hurried forward with hand extended the moment Rye appeared at his doorway.

Starbuck's grip was as firm as that of the cooper. "Dalton!" he exclaimed. "You've done me proud this voyage. Chocked off and bringing a dollar fifteen a gallon! I couldn't be happier!"

"Aye, greasy luck for sure," Rye replied, in the idiom of the day.

Starbuck quirked an eyebrow. "And are they makin' a landlubber of y' or will y' sail on the next voyage with the *Omega?*"

Rye raised his palms. "Nay, no more whaling for this fool. One voyage was enough for me. I'll be content t' make barrels with the old man for the rest of m' life, but right here on shore."

"Can't say I blame y', Dalton, though your lay is a healthy one. Are y' sure I can't tempt y' to try 'er one more time—say for a one-fifteenth share?" Starbuck kept a shrewd eye on Rye's face while he moved again to the enormous roll-top desk that dominated the room.

"Nay, not even for a one-fifteenth. This voyage has cost me enough."

A frown settled over Starbuck's features, and he hooked his thumbs in his waistcoat pockets as he studied the younger man. "Aye, and I'm sorry for that, Dalton. Hell of a mix-up for a man to come home to—hell of a mix-up." He scowled at the floor thoughtfully before looking up. "And be assured both Mrs. Starbuck and I extend our deepest sympathies at the loss of your mother, too."

"Thank y', sir."

"And how is your father?"

''Spry as ever, and cutting barrel staves over there faster than that punk apprentice of his can keep up with.''

Starbuck laughed robustly. ''Since I cannot convince you to cooper my ship on the ocean, perhaps I can convince you and your father to put up my order for barrels this time around.''

''Aye, we'd be happy t' do that.''

''Good! I'll be sending my agent over to agree on a price with you before the day is out.''

''Good enough.''

''I expect you've come to collect your lay.''

''Aye, that I have.''

''You'll have to see your . . . ah, friend . . . Morgan.'' Starbuck looked slightly uncomfortable. ''He's my chief accountant now, you know. His office is on the second floor.''

''Aye, so I've heard.''

Starbuck studied Dalton's face at the mention of Dan Morgan, but his expression remained unchanged, only a polite nod of the head acknowledging Starbuck's statement. Starbuck extracted a ten-cent cigar from a humidor, offered one to Rye, who refused, snipped the end, and soon blew fragrant smoke into the room.

''You know, Dalton, there are aspects of this business which I cannot say I relish. A man leaves his home with the best of intentions, tryin' to be a proper provider for his wife and family, but his rewards are often grim in the final outcome. Now it's not his fault, though neither is it mine. Yet I feel responsible, damnit!'' Starbuck thumped a fist on the elbow-worn arm of his captain's chair. ''Though it's small consolation, Mrs. Starbuck and I wish to show our appreciation by inviting the officers under my employ to a dinner party at our house Saturday night, to celebrate the return of the *Omega*. You'll come, won't you?''

''Aye, and happily.'' Rye grinned. ''Especially if Mrs. Starbuck plans t' serve anything my old man hasn't cooked.''

Though Dalton smiled and bantered, Starbuck realized what a hell of a shock the man had suffered, landing to the news that his wife had been usurped by his best friend. It was damn sure Dalton missed more than just his wife's cooking. There was little Starbuck could do about the situation, but being a fair man, the thought rankled, and he promised himself to see that Dalton received a generous contract on barrels.

Upstairs, Rye approached the broad pigeonholed desk before which Dan Morgan sat on a high stool. A candle in the hurricane lamp with a bowl-shaped reflector shed light onto the open books spread out on the desk, for though Nantucket lived by whale oil, ironically, it rarely lit itself by it. As the saying went, ''Why burn it up when you can sell it and get rich?''

Morgan glanced up as Rye's footsteps echoed on the oiled pine floor. His quill pen paused, and the corners of his mouth drooped. But he eased from the stool to greet Rye on his feet.

Rye stopped beside the desk, his feet planted wide in a new way to which

Dan was not yet accustomed, his thumbs caught up on his stomach flap. It seemed suddenly intimidating, this seaman's stance, so solid, so self-confident. And he was reminded that Rye was half a head taller.

Rye, too, assessed Dan. After five years he was still trim and fit. He was dressed in a stylish coat of twilled mulberry worsted, his neckpiece impeccably tied, and a striped waistcoat hugged his lean ribs. He was dressed like a man who enjoyed financial security and wanted to display it in even so reserved a fashion.

Momentarily, Rye wondered if Laura was equally as proud of Dan's natty mode of dress.

He extended his hand, thrusting jealousy aside, and for a moment he thought Dan would refuse to greet him civilly. But at last Dan's hand clasped Rye's briefly. Their touch could not help but bring back memories of their years of friendship. There was, within each, an ache to restore that friendship to its original vigor as well as the realization that it would never again be recaptured.

''Hello, Dan,'' the taller man greeted.

''Rye.''

They dropped hands. Clerks and subordinates moved around them, carrying on business within full view and earshot. Curious eyes turned their way, making their exchange cautious.

''Starbuck sent me up t' collect my lay.''

''Of course. I'll make out the bank draft for you. It'll only take a minute.'' Rye even talked in a new clipped seaman's vernacular, Dan noted.

Dan again sat down on his stool, pulled out a long ledger, and began making an entry. Standing above him, watching his hands, Rye remembered the hundreds of times they'd threaded bait for each other, gone gigging for turtles in Hummock Pond, or digging clams at low tide, sharing their catch over an open fire on the beach, often with Laura sitting between them. Rye stared at Dan's well-shaped hands as he penned the figures in the ledger, then wrote in an elegant, swirling English roundhand—square, competent hands with a faint spray of light hair on their backs—and he realized those hands had known as much of Laura as his own. The conflict between old loyalty and new rivalry created a maelstrom of emotion within Rye.

My friend, my friend, he thought, must you now be my enemy?

''Y've provided well for Laura, I can tell,'' he said, speaking quietly so nobody else could hear. ''I thank y' for that much.''

''There's no need to thank me,'' Dan replied without looking up. ''She's my wife.'' Here he did look up, a challenge in his eyes. ''What would you expect?''

They confronted each other silently for a moment, knowing well that each would suffer in the days ahead.

''I expect a hell of a good fight for her, from the looks of it.''

''I expect no such thing.'' Dan stood up and extended the check, scissored between two fingers. ''The law is on my side. You were reported lost at sea. In such cases there is what is legally referred to as an assumption of death, so in the eyes of the law, Laura is *my* wife, not yours.''

''Y' haven't wasted any time checkin' on legalities, have y'?''

''Not a day.''

So a fight it will be, Rye thought, disappointed at this new disclosure. Yet if Dan had gone to all that trouble, it meant Laura had cast some doubt into his mind about her intentions.

''And so the battle lines're drawn, old friend?'' Rye asked sadly.

''Put it as you will. I will not give up either Laura or my son.'' His meaning was clear. His posture was stiff.

So, that was how it was to be. But Rye could not resist placing one well-aimed barb as he pocketed the check and gave a brief salute.

''Give them both my love, will y', Dan?'' Then he turned on his heel and left.

But once outside, his jaunty attitude vanished. In its place came a worried frown as he paused to glower in the direction of Crooked Record Lane. Ship lifted her head off her paws and lumbered to her feet, raising patient eyes. Rye seemed unaware of the dog's rapt attention, but presently he slipped his palms inside his stomach flap and spoke softly. ''Well, Ship, it seems she's truly his wife after all. And what are we t' do about that, mate?''

The dog's mouth opened while she looked up Rye's length, waiting for some signal. At last the man turned away from the spot he'd been studying and strode off in the opposite direction, the click of canine toenails accompanying him across the square.

But the pair had not gone ten yards before approaching footsteps echoed eerily and came to a halt before them. Rye looked up and stopped in his tracks. The familiar creased eyes of Dan's father were relaxed on this sunless day, so the lines radiating from their corners were strikingly white in the mahogany face. He'd grown thinner, and there was less hair on his head than ever. For a moment neither spoke, then the pleasure at the sight of the long-loved man forced Rye to move forward again.

''Zach, hello.'' He extended a hand, and Zach came forward to take it. He had hard, horny hands, those of a fisherman who'd hauled both sail and nets all his life. They were burned by sun, cured by salt to the color and texture of brine-soaked ham.

''Hello, Rye.'' The handshake was brief and bone-crushing. ''I heard the news.'' Zachary Morgan lifted his eyes momentarily to the countinghouse behind Rye's shoulder where his son was working, then met Rye's again self-consciously. ''It's good to hear you're alive after all.''

''Aye, well, it's good to be back on dry land, I can say that for sure.''

But the unsaid hovered between the two men. They shared a history that commanded them to care, but there were new obstacles between them.

Zach bent to scratch Ship's head. ''Ah, and the old girl's glad to have you back, aren't you, Ship? Haven't seen you for a long time.'' The dog was a convenient diversion, but only temporary. When Zach straightened, they were ill at ease again. ''Sorry about your mother, Rye.''

''Aye, well . . . things change, don't they?''

Their eyes met, spoke silently. And now my boy is your grandson, Rye thought, and his mother your daughter-in-law. I won't be runnin' in and out o' your house like I used to. ''But the old man tells me your missus is healthy and spry.''

''Ayup, same as always.''

An enormous void fell, a void five years wide. It used to be so easy to talk to each other.

"You're not out fishin' today."

"Fog's too thick."

"Aye."

"Well . . ."

"Give my best to Hilda," Rye said.

"I'll do that. And say hello to Josiah."

They'd said nothing. They'd said everything. They'd said, Understand, this is hard for me—I love them both, too. They turned their backs on each other and their footsteps parted in the fog, then Rye turned to watch Zach disappear into the countinghouse, presumably to talk with his son about this queer quirk of fate.

The fog seemed the perfect accompaniment to Rye's morose mood. He and Ship plodded through its shreds, both with heads hung low. Along the silent streets the silvery saltboxes blended into the enveloping whiteness, their painted shutters the only glimmer of color in the otherwise bleak day. Occasionally those shutters were blue, the color reserved for captains of whaleships only. The close-pressed yards were surrounded by picket fences that soon gave way to those into which the ribs of whales were woven. Out near the tryworks the odor of putrefaction hung in the air, the gray smoke of decomposing blubber inescapable, locked as it was about the island by the veil of fog.

Whaling! It was everywhere, and suddenly the despondent Rye Dalton wanted to escape it.

Seeking the solace of isolation, he made for Brant Point Marshes. The low-lying land spread out like a sea of green, providing a nesting area for thousands of species of birds. Their voices lilted through the haze that pressed close above the cattails and sedge. There was a constant flutter of activity about the thickets of highbush cranberry as the birds fed, and the scene was lent a surreal quality by the swirling mists that were constantly on the move. How many times had three children come here in search of nests and eggs? Rye pictured the three of them as they'd been then, but immediately Laura's face alone emblazoned itself upon his memory, not as she'd been yesterday, surprised and stunned, but as in the days of their awakening sexuality, when she'd first looked at him through a woman's eyes—wondering and tremulous. Next he pictured her turning from the hearth with the spoon handle wrapped in her apron; then his son running in, heedless . . .

And a great loneliness overwhelmed him.

He moved on through the marshes, making useless wishes, wondering what she was doing at this very moment.

He stopped on a high bank where last year's sea oats now drooped, laden with heavy water droplets. The fog swirled about his knees and obscured the distant view of the shore. But from out of the lost beyond came the incessant throb of incoming waves while in the foreground the Brant Point Shipyard was vignetted by a frame of fog. There, below, the *Omega* was already undergoing a complete overhaul. Like a beached whale, she'd been hoisted onto the skeletal "ways" and careened—turned on her side for cleaning. Workers scurried over her like ants, scraping every inch of her hull, recaulking seams, holystoning, or scrubbing, and revarnishing decks. Already six new cedar whaleboats were being constructed for her davits, while in town, at the ropewalk, new hemp was being woven for standing rigging and manila for running rigging from which the ship's rigger waited to splice the intricate network of shrouds, sheets, and stays for the upcoming voyage. And in a sailmaker's loft above a chandlery on Water Street, needles and fids were flying as new sails were being stitched.

But on an embankment above Brant Point Shipyard, a lonely man stood beside his dog, forlornly contemplating the implacable cycle that never ceased in this whaling empire. *Whaling!* He clenched his fists.

Damn you, you merciless bitch! I have lost my wife to you!

He studied the *Omega* below, painfully considering whether it would be preferable to sign on another voyage rather than stay here to see Laura remain married to Dan.

But then, with a determined grimace, he turned back the way he had come, stalking the ocean path while seagulls squawked and hammers echoed through the shrouds of mists behind him.

Dan is at his desk in the countinghouse, and she is home alone.

The long stride grew longer, and the dog at his heels broke into a trot.

Laura Morgan had been expecting the knock, but when it came she started and pressed a hand to her heart.

Go away, Rye! I'm afraid of what you do to me!

The knock sounded again, and Laura caught her trembling lower lip between her teeth. Resolutely, she moved toward the door, but when it was opened, only stared transfixed at Rye, who stood outside with his weight slung on one hip, his hands tucked inside the stomach flap of his britches. A myriad of impressions danced across her mind, all too quick to grasp—he stands differently; he's wearing the sweater I made; his hair needs trimming; *he's* spent a sleepless night, too.

"Hello, Laura."

He didn't smile, but stood at ease, waiting patiently on the stoop. And it happened, as it had happened since she was fourteen—that total surge of gladness at the sight of him. But now caution tempered it.

"Hello, Rye." Resolutely, she held the edge of the door.

"I had t' come."

Somewhere in the recesses of her mind she noted the abbreviated speech he'd picked up on the high seas, realizing it added to his magnetism: a thing she needed to explore, for it made him somewhat a stranger. Her fingers clenched upon the door, but her eyes remained steadily on his.

"I was afraid you might."

At the word *afraid* his eyebrows puckered, and his lips seemed to thin. She noted again the pockmark on the top one and steeled herself against the urge to touch it with her fingertip.

He studied her as if she were a rare diamond and he a gemcutter.

She stared at him as if expecting him to rattle some ghostly chain. The Nantucket mists formed an appropriate background, as if they had levitated Rye Dalton and borne him to her, then hung back to watch what she'd do.

"Can I come in?"

How preposterous the question. This was his house! Outside it was damp and cold, and behind her a fire burned. Yet while he tucked his hands against his stomach for warmth, she hesitated like a gatekeeper.

She glanced nervously down the scallop shell-path, then dropped her hand from the door. "For just a minute."

As he stepped forward, the dog instinctively moved with him.

"Stay."

At the word, Laura noticed Ship for the first time. Immediately, she smiled and bent to greet the Lab.

"Ship . . . oh, Ship . . . hello, girl!" With a whine and a wag, Ship returned the greeting. Laura hunkered in the doorway, holding the dog's chin with one hand and scratching the top of her head with the other. Her pale gray skirt billowed wide, hiding Rye's boots as he stood studying the top of her head. But it was on the dog that she lavished her affectionate greeting.

"So you've come to see me at last, silly girl . . . and it's about time, too. You could have dropped by now and then . . ." There followed a chuckle as Laura was bestowed a brief whip of a pink tongue on her cheek. She jerked back, but laughingly invited, "No need for you to stay outside, girl. Your rug's still there."

Looking down at the two of them, it was all Rye could do to keep from pulling the woman up into his arms and demanding the welcome he, too, deserved.

She rose and led the way inside. When the door was closed, she faced it while Rye paused with his back to it, and they both watched Ship gave a brief sniff to the air, then circle twice before dropping to the braided rug beside Rye's ankles, with a grunt of satisfied familiarity.

The blue eyes of Rye Dalton lifted to meet the brown ones of Laura. The sense of homecoming was overwhelming. Ship lowered her chin to her paws with a sigh while Rye once more slipped his fingers inside his stomach flap, as if they were safest there. His voice, when he spoke, was pulled from deep in his throat.

"The dog's had a more affectionate welcome than her master."

Laura's eyes dropped, but unfortunately they fell to the sight of his palms tucked just inside his hip laces. She felt an unwanted heat pressing upward to steal across her cheeks. "She . . . she remembers her old spot," Laura managed in almost a whisper.

"Aye."

The unfamiliar term scarcely reached the far walls while she again fought the urge to explore the differences in him. She saw one dark hand slip into the open and reach for her elbow. "Rye, you can't—"

"Laura, I've been thinking of y'."

His fingers curled around her arm, but she pulled it safely out of reach and moved back a step while her eyes flew to his. "Don't!"

His hand hung in midair for a tense moment, then fell to his side. He sighed thickly, dropping his chin to stare at the floor. "I was afraid y'd say that."

She glanced nervously toward the alcove bed and whispered, "Josh is napping."

Rye's head came up with a jerk, and he, too, looked across the room. She watched an expression of longing cross his face. Again his blue eyes sought hers. "Can I see him?"

Indecision flickered in her eyes while she threaded her fingers tightly together. But finally she answered, "Of course."

He moved then, crossing the room with light steps that seemed to take eons of time before he stopped in front of the alcove bed and peered into its shadows. Laura remained where she was, following him with her gaze, watching Rye pause, hook a thumb into the top of his trousers again, and lean sideways from one hip. For a long moment he stood silent, unmoving. Then he reached into the recesses of the alcove to take the binding of Josh's small quilt between index and middle fingers. The fire burned cozily. The only sound was that of falling ash. A father studied his slumbering son.

Rye . . . oh, Rye . . .

The cry was locked inside Laura's throat, and her eyes were drawn into an expression of pain while she watched him slowly straighten and even more slowly look back over his shoulder at her. His blue gaze moved down to her stomach, and she realized both of her palms were pressed hard against it, as if she were only now in the throes of labor. Flustered, she dropped them to her sides.

"When was he born?" Rye asked softly.

"In December."

"December what?"

"Eighth."

Rye's eyes caressed the sleeping child again, then he turned away and moved with silent deliberation to the door of the new linter room. There he stopped again, looking in, his eyes moving across its interior to linger on the bed.

A queer mixture of feelings seemed to turn Laura's stomach over: familiarity, caution, yearning. She studied Rye's broad shoulders, covered by the sweater she had knit years ago, as they filled the bedroom doorway. He looked at once relaxed and tense as he stood contemplating her and Dan's bedroom, and Laura wondered if Rye had deliberately chosen to wear that particular sweater today. It strikingly emphasized his ruggedness, and the sight of him in it gripped her with a sudden flush of sensuality as she watched him slowly turn her way and take a slow walk around the edge of the keeping room, eyeing objects, running a finger along the edge of the mantel, taking in the new as well as the familiar. When he reached Laura again, he stood before her with that wide-legged stance of a seaman.

"Changes," he uttered in a broken voice.

"In five years they were inevitable."

"But all these?" Now his voice had taken on a harder note. Again he reached for her; again she avoided his touch.

"Rye, I went to see Ezra Merrill." Laura was grateful that her announcement distracted Rye, and he refrained from reaching again.

"You too? That makes two of y'."

''Two?'' She looked up, puzzled.

''It seems Dan visited Merrill yesterday.''

Yesterday, thought Laura. Yesterday?

At her look of consternation, Rye went on. ''He gave me the news this mornin' when I saw him at the countinghouse.''

''Then you know already?''

''Aye, I know. But I know that the law can't dictate how I feel.''

Rather than face his determined eyes, she turned away. But from behind he saw her lift a hand to touch her temple.

''This is such a muddled mess, Rye.''

''It appears the law can't dictate y'r feelings, either.''

She spun to face him again. ''Feelings are not what I'm speaking of, but legalities. I am his wife, don't you understand? You . . . you shouldn't even be here at this very minute!''

Her head was tipped slightly to one side, and her upper body strained toward him in earnestness. He spoke with deadly calm. ''Y' sound rather desperate, Laura.''

Immediately, she straightened. ''Rye, I have to ask you to leave and not to be seen here again until we can get this thing straightened out. Dan was . . . he was very upset last night, and if he should find you here again, I . . . I . . . '' She stammered to a halt, her eyes on the strong curve of his jawbone, where the new side-whiskers nearly met the thick turtleneck of his sweater, giving him a brawny and wholly unsettling appeal. ''Please, Rye,'' she ended lamely.

For a moment she thought he would raise his fist and shout at the heavens, releasing his tightly controlled rage. Instead, he relaxed—albeit with an effort—and agreed. ''Aye, I'll go . . . but the lad is asleep.''

His eyes flashed to the alcove bed, then back to her, and before she could prevent it, he'd taken a single long step forward and grasped the back of her head, commandeering it with one mighty hand while his mouth swooped over hers. She pressed her palms against the wool sweater, only to find his heart thundering within it. She strained to pull away, but his grasp was so relentless it pushed the whalebone hairpins into her scalp. His tongue had already wet her lips before she managed to jerk free. When she did, her lips escaped his with a frantic, sucking sound.

''Rye, this—''

''Shh . . .'' From violent to gentle, his quick change confused her as his admonition cut off her words. ''In a minute . . . I'll leave in a minute.'' Recklessly, he'd clasped the back of her neck and forced her forward, the action in direct contrast to his repeated, soft, ''Shh . . .''

She allowed herself to stay as she was, though rigidly, with his chin pressed against her forehead while his eyes sank shut. Beneath her fingers his heart still pounded, and she closed her fists about the rough, textured wool of his sweater, grasping and twisting it as if it could keep her from sinking. But both she and Rye were trembling now.

''I love y', Laura.'' The words rumbled from his throat while her knees went wobbly. ''Josh . . .'' She heard Rye swallow. ''Josh looks like my mother,'' he uttered thickly. Then, as suddenly as he'd demanded the kiss, he was gone, spinning away to jerk the door open with only one more word.

"Come!"

But Ship was already on her feet.

And Laura Morgan was left behind to wish desperately that she could follow that order as freely as Ship could.

Chapter 4

The following Saturday night, Joseph Starbuck's home was brightly lit with whale oil, appropriate for an occasion honoring the successful voyage of a whaleship.

When Laura Morgan stepped through the front door, it was into a fairyland of artificial brightness such as few Nantucket homes boasted at night. Chandeliers gleamed, reflecting off polished oak floors and the highly waxed banister of the staircase. On a refectory table in the main hall, smaller lanterns glimmered into the depth of a crystal punch bowl of persimmon beer beside another of syllabub, a rich mixture of sweet cream and wine. Around the edges of the room, small Betty lamps highlighted the array of colorful silk gowns whose skirts were held aloft by whalebone hoops, making the women appear to glide as if on wheels.

Dan had been taciturn and brooding all evening, ever since helping Laura lace her stays and hook her gown. He had looked up to find the whalebone corsets thrusting her breasts up higher than usual, helped along by the stiff boning that shaped the bodice of the dress itself. A sour look had overtaken his face and was still there.

The dress front was modest, topped by a stiff yoke of narrow pleating which swept from the crest of one shoulder to the other with scarcely a dip at the center. When she'd bought the dress, Laura had laughingly said there was no escaping whaling on Nantucket, for she even *looked* like a whaleboat! Indeed, the shadows of the pleating resembled the overlapped planking on a dory. But there was no mistaking Laura for anything except what she was—a shapely young beauty whose contours were ripe within her bodice.

Her muslin gown was interwoven with cream silk stripes between sprays of pink roses on a delicate background of tiny green leaves. Artificial roses of pink rode on the crests of her shoulders, from which the sleeves of the gown were also tightly pleated to the elbow before an enormous puff of muslin billowed out beneath a band of pink ribbon.

The dress set off her fine-boned fragility: the delicate jaw, chin, and nose, and an adorable mouth shaped like the leaf of a sweetheart ivy. Her dainty features made Laura's dark-lashed brown eyes appear even larger than they were, as did the style of her hair, most of which was pulled high onto the crown of her head in an intricate knot entwined with thin pink ribbons, while above her left ear nested another rose, from which fell a gathering of sausage-shaped curls. Around her face, tiny angel-wisps had been cut shorter than the rest and curled like an auburn halo about her delicate features.

Her femininity was further enhanced by the styles of the day, with their elongated waists and enormous skirts, which served to make the fat look fatter, the thin look emaciated, but the lucky ones, like Laura Morgan, look like a Dresden doll.

At the moment, however, Laura felt far from lucky. Her waist was pinched into a miserable little hourglass and felt as if it would surely snap in half a minute! A wide whalebone stay ran up the front of the dress and already it was digging into her stomach whenever she bent, and into the valley between her breasts each time she inhaled. Her discomfort had made her decidedly testy, to say nothing of light-headed.

Laura never went out for a social evening without silently cursing the rigging into which she was forced. But tonight's occasion demanded that she smile cordially and uncomplainingly, for it was a business dinner, Dan had said, meaning that Starbuck's more important employees had been invited, along with such honored guests as Captain Blackwell, of the *Omega,* and Christopher Capen and James Childs, the mason and carpenter whom Starbuck had contracted to build the Three Bricks for his sons.

The conversation seemed centered around the success of the *Omega* and the progress on the houses, which were well under way. Laura listened with half an ear to Annabel Pruitt, the wife of Starbuck's purchasing agent, who had a habit of releasing news even before the town newspaper did. Though it was of little interest to Laura that the bricks for the houses had come all the way from Gloucester, her attention was captured when the subject abruptly changed.

"They say Mr. Starbuck has offered Rye Dalton a substantial lay to sail on the *Omega* next time she goes out." Mrs. Pruitt closely watched the faces of Dan and Laura Morgan as she divulged this tidbit.

Laura felt Dan's fingers tighten on her elbow and suddenly scanned the hall in search of a fainting bench, that abominable invention created by men who'd never had to bear being trussed up like a Thanksgiving turkey! But in the next moment Dan's fingers dug in even harder, and Laura realized it was not the mere mention of Rye's name that had made her husband go stiff. He tugged on her elbow so sharply that the syllabub went sloshing in her glass.

"Why, Dan, whatever—" she began, jerking back to avoid soiling her dress, and sending the whalebone digging sharply into her stomach.

But in that instant, following the course of Dan's glare, the discomfort she endured to look so beautiful became suddenly justified. There, at the door, Rye Dalton was being greeted by the Starbucks. Laura's heart leaped. She could not help staring, for Rye was dressed like a fashion plate—no sweater or pea jacket in sight.

He wore stirruped pants of forest green with a matching tailcoat boasting a stiff, high collar, with the newest feature—notches—on its lapel. Long, tight sleeves dropped well below his wrist, half covering his bronze hands. His sea-tanned face was the color of a ripe chestnut above a pristine white stock wound tightly about his neck and tied in a small bow, half hidden behind his double-breasted jacket.

As a mallard finds its mate in a flock, so Rye found Laura in the throng of people that filled the room. His eyes met hers and sent a shaft of heat down her body. Forgotten were the pains in her stomach; instead, she was filled with pride at how she looked in the dress. As those blue eyes lingered on hers, then traveled down her body and back up, she realized her mouth was open, and snapped it shut.

They had not seen each other for four days, and she certainly hadn't expected him to be here tonight. Nor had she expected his eyes to seek her out so brazenly, nor the slight bow he gave her even before the footman reached for his beaver top hat.

Immediately, Laura hid her flaming cheeks behind her glass of syllabub, but not before Dan noted the exchange of glances between the two. With an acid look, he gripped Laura's elbow and turned her away from the door, circling her waist and leaving his hand there possessively, something rarely done here in public, in this city where Puritan founders had left their indelible mark.

Knowing Dalton watched their backs, Dan leaned intimately close to his wife's ear. "I didn't have any idea he'd be here tonight, did you?"

"Me? How could I have known?"

"I thought he might have told you." He watched her face carefully to see if he was right.

"I . . . I haven't seen him since Monday," she lied. She'd kissed him on Tuesday.

"If I'd known he'd be here, we wouldn't have come."

"Don't be silly, Dan. Living in the same town, we're bound to run into him now and then. You can't isolate me, so you'll just have to learn to trust me instead."

"Oh I trust you, Laura. It's him I don't trust."

Almost thirty minutes passed before the guests were called to dinner. By the time they entered the dining room, Laura had a backache from standing so rigidly and the beginnings of a headache from the tension. Try though she might to forget that Rye was in the room, she couldn't. It seemed each time she turned to visit with another guest, he managed to be in her line of vision, studying her from beneath those perfectly shaped eyebrows of his, smiling boldly when no one was looking. His hair was neatly trimmed now, but the new sideburns remained, bracketing his jaws in brawny appeal. Though she tried to keep from looking at him, she had little success, and once—she couldn't be sure—she thought he mimed a kiss to her, but he was lifting his glass at that moment, and the kiss, if it was one, became a sip.

He was in one of his devilish, teasing moods tonight. Laura remembered them well.

At dinner, as if her hostess had intentionally planned to compound Laura's misery, she and Dan were placed directly across the table from Rye and a talkative young blonde named DeLaine Hussey, whose forefathers, along with those of Joseph Starbuck, had settled the island.

Miss Hussey immediately engaged Rye in conversation about the voyage, sympathizing effusively over his bout with smallpox, studying the few marks left on his face, and claiming they'd done nothing whatever to mar his appearance. She followed this statement with a fluttery smile that made Laura wish the woman would get the pox herself! But Rye—damn him!—was lapping it up, grinning down at the woman, the grin enhanced by the pockmark that fell in the crease of his cheek and dimpled him beguilingly.

In no time at all Miss Hussey pursued a subject that raised Laura's temperature to that of the clam chowder she'd just been served. "The *Omega* was gone five years . . . that's a long time."

"Aye, it is."

Laura felt Rye's eyes upon her as she lifted a spoonful of steaming soup, but she carefully refrained from returning his glance.

"You don't know, then, about the group of women here on Nantucket who've organized and call themselves the Female Freemasons?" chirped the blonde across the way.

And Laura blew too hard on her soup, making some of it fly onto the table linen. DeLaine Hussey, she thought, had been aptly named! She'd been trying to get her claws into Rye for as long as Laura could remember, and she certainly wasn't wasting any time, now that word was out Rye had been refused admittance to the saltbox on the hill.

"No, ma'am," Rye was answering. "I've never heard of 'em."

"Ah, but you will now that the *Omega's* come in with full barrels."

"Full barrels? What do full barrels have t' do with a women's group?"

"The Female Freemasons, Mr. Dalton, are sworn to refuse to be courted by or to marry any man who has not killed his first whale."

Laura burned her tongue on the chowder and nearly overturned her water glass in her haste to cool her mouth.

Mr. Dalton, indeed! Laura thought. Why, the two of them had gone to school together. Just what did DeLaine Hussey think she was up to?

The servers came then to remove the chowder bowls and Laura realized she should not have eaten the entire helping, but she'd become preoccupied with the conversation and hadn't realized she was putting herself in jeopardy. Her restrictive whalebones were already causing extreme misery, but the servers were now bringing in a steaming veal roast ringed with glazed carrots and herbed potatoes.

Laura had no choice but to accept the main course when it came her turn. But the veal stuck in her throat, along with the flirtatious conversation continuing on the other side of the table.

The smitten Miss Hussey continued to delineate the doctrines of the chivalric order of island ladies devoted to loving only proven whalers, until Rye was forced to ask politely, "And are you a member of th' group . . . Miss Hussey?"

At that precise moment, Laura nearly choked on a piece of veal, for something soft and warm was working her skirts up and caressed her calf beneath the table.

Rye's foot!

"Indeed I am, Mr. Dalton," DeLaine Hussey simpered.

The gall of the man to do a thing like that while innocently smiling down at DeLaine Hussey! Why, he knew full well it was his and Laura's old playful signal that they wanted to make love when they got home!

While Rye's foot made shivers ripple through Laura's flesh, the doe-eyed Miss Hussey continued batting her sooty lashes and gazing devastatingly into Rye's eyes while pointedly asking, "Have *you* killed your first whale yet, Mr. Dalton?"

Rye laughed uninhibitedly, leaning back until his jaw lifted before he grinned engagingly at his table companion again. "Nay, Miss Hussey, I haven't, and y' well know it. I'm a cooper, not a boatsteerer," he reminded, using the official name of the harpooners.

At that moment Rye's toes inched up and curled over the edge of the chair between Laura's knees, all the while he smiled into DeLaine Hussey's eyes. This time Laura visibly jumped and a chunk of veal lodged in her throat, sending up a spasm of coughing.

Dan solicitously patted her back and signaled for the server to refill her water glass. "Are you all right?" he asked.

"F . . . fine." She gulped, struggling for composure while that warm foot brushed the insides of her knees, preventing her from clamping them shut.

The coughing, unfortunately, brought her hostess's attention to Laura's plate, and Mrs. Starbuck noted how little her guest had eaten and inquired if the food was all right. Thus, Laura felt compelled to lift yet another bite of veal and attempt to swallow it.

Just then Rye smiled nonchalantly at Laura and said, "Please pass the salt." He could see she was in misery: he remembered well enough her abhorrence of whalebone corsets.

To Laura's surprise, she then felt a *tap! tap! tap!* against the inside of one knee. And while across the table Rye and DeLaine Hussey engaged in a seemingly innocent conversation about coopering, Rye cut two pieces of his own veal, ate one, and covertly dropped the other on the floor, where the Starbucks' fluffy matched Persian cats immediately cleaned up the evidence.

Laura raised her napkin to her lips and smiled behind it. But she was grateful to Rye, for at the next possible opportunity she practiced the same sleight-of-hand he'd just demonstrated, which ultimately saved her from embarrassing either herself or her hostess—or both.

The meal ended with a rich rum-flavored torte, which neither of the cats liked—a barely perceptible shrug of Rye's shoulders made Laura again take smiling refuge behind her napkin—so she was forced to eat half her serving, which left her stomach in a perilous state.

By the time Rye chose to remove his foot, Laura was not only queasy but flustered. Their host and hostess were rising from their chairs when Laura could tell by the look on Rye's face that he was searching for his lost shoe. She let him suffer, slipping it further underneath her chair while up and down the table guests were getting to their feet and repairing to the main hall. Dan moved behind her chair, and for a moment she considered leaving the shoe where it was, but if it were spied there, it would convict her as well as Rye, so his scowl was rewarded a second later by the safe return of the shoe.

A string quartet played now in the main hall, and some couples danced while others visited. A small group of men stepped outside to smoke cigars, among them Joseph Starbuck and Dan, who reluctantly left Laura's side at his employer's request. But first he observed that Rye was still in the clutches of DeLaine Hussey, so he assumed Rye would have no chance to bother Laura.

Laura, meanwhile, did not need Rye Dalton to be bothered. She realized if she didn't soon ease her whalebone corsets she was going to either vomit or faint.

As soon as it was gracefully possible, she escaped through the back door, inhaling great gulps of night air. But the air alone did little to relieve her, for it was laden with fog tonight, and she nearly choked on the tang of tar, spread as it was beneath the fruit trees of Starbuck's orchard, to control canker worms. Picking up her skirts, she ran at a most unladylike clip between the apple trees, where the cloying scent of blossoms only worsened her nausea. She groped futilely for the row of brass hooks and eyes at the back of her dress, but knew full well there was no reaching them. Her mouth watered warningly. Tears stung her eyes. She clutched her waist and bent over, gagging.

At that moment cool fingers touched the back of Laura's neck and quickly began releasing the hooks while she broke out into a quivering sweat.

"What the hell're y' doin' in these things if y' can't tolerate them?" Rye Dalton demanded.

For the moment she was unable to answer, battling the forces of nature. But finally she managed to choke out a single word.

"Hurry!"

"Damn idiotic contraptions!" he muttered. "Y' should have more sense, woman!"

"Th . . . the laces . . . please," she gasped when the dress was open.

He yanked at the bow resting in the hollow of her spine, then jerked it free at last and began working his fingers up the lacings until Laura breathed her first easy breath in three hours.

"May you b . . . burn in hell, Rye D . . . Dalton, for ever bringing whalebones to shore and m . . . making women all over the world miserable!" she berated between huge gasps.

"If I burn in hell, might's well do it for a lot better reason than that," he said, moving close behind her, slipping his hand inside her loosened corset.

"Stop it!" She lurched away and spun on him while all her frustrations boiled to the surface. This incredible trap he'd caused by insisting on going whaling, the torture of these damned insufferable whalebones, the cozy little piece of flirtation she'd just been forced to witness—it all sparked an explosion of temper that suddenly raged out of control. "Stop it!" she hissed. "You have no right to sail in here after . . . after *five years* and act as if you'd never left!"

Immediately, his temper flared, too. "I left for *you,* so I could bring you—"

"I begged you not to go! I didn't want your . . . your stinking whale oil! I wanted my husband!"

"Well, here I am!" he shot back sarcastically.

"Oh . . ." She clenched her fists, almost growling in frustration. "You think it's so simple, don't you, Rye? Playing footsie under the table, as if the most important thing I have to decide is whether or not to take my shoe off. Well, you can see what a state it's put me in."

"And what about the state I'm in!"

She turned her back disdainfully. "I'm fine now. Thank you for your help . . . *Mister* Dalton," she retorted, imitating DeLaine Hussey, "but you'd better go back before you're missed."

"I did that so y'd see what I'm forced t' go through every time I see you and Dan together. It bothered y', didn't it—seeing your *husband* with another woman?"

Again she whirled to confront him. "All right . . . yes! It bothered me! But I realize now I have no right to be bothered by it. As I said before, you'd better go back before you're missed."

"I don't give a damn if I'm missed. Besides, all I'm doin' is standin' in an orchard visiting with my wife. What's wrong with that?"

"Rye, Dan won't like—"

At that moment Dan's voice came from just beyond the nearest row of apple trees.

"Laura? Are you out there?"

She turned toward the voice to reply, but Rye's hand found her elbow and he moved close, placing a finger over her mouth, breathing softly beside her ear, "Shh."

"I've got to answer him," she whispered while her heart drummed. "He knows we're out here."

He grabbed her head with both hands and brought her ear to his lips. "You do, and I'll tell him your corsets are loose because we were just enjoyin' a little roll beneath the apple trees."

She jerked away angrily, frantically scrabbling to retie her rigging. But it was futile, and Rye only stood by grinning.

"Laura, is that you?" came Dan's voice. "Where are you?"

"Help me!" she begged, turning her back on Rye as Dan's footsteps came closer. He was walking between the trees now; they could hear the branches snapping.

"Not on your life," Rye whispered.

In a panic she grabbed his wrist, picked up her skirts, and ran, pulling him along after her. Down the rows they went, ducking between trees, skimming silently through the fog-shrouded night, which buffered the sound of their passing. Foolish, childish thing to do! Yet Laura was unable to think beyond the fact that she could not let Dan discover her half undressed out here in the misty night with Rye.

The orchard was wide and long, stretching away in a maze of white-misted apple trees which gave way to quince, then to plum. The fog blanketed everything, obscuring the two who moved through it like specters. Laura's wide skirt might well have been only another explosion of apple blossoms, for the trees cowered close to the ground, protecting themselves from the incessant ocean winds, until they took on the same bouffant shape as a hooped skirt.

At last Laura stopped, alert, listening, one hand pressed against her heaving breasts to hold the dress up. Rye, too, listened, but they heard not the faintest strains of the music drifting from the house. They were surrounded by billows of white, lost in the swirling fog, alone in a private scented bower of quince, where they'd be neither seen nor heard.

She still clutched his wrist. Beneath her thumb she could feel his pulse racing. She flung the hand away and cursed, ''Damn you, Rye!''

But his good humor was back. ''Is that any way t' talk to the man who's just loosened your stays?''

''I told you I had to have time to think and work things out.''

''I've given y' five days . . . just what have y' worked out?''

''Five days—exactly! How can I get a mess like this worked out in five days?''

''So y' want to string me along and lead me out t' the apple orchard where we used t' do it right under Dan's nose even when we were kids?'' He moved closer, his breath coming heavy, too, after their run.

''That's not why I came out here,'' she protested, and it was true.

''Why, then?'' He put both wide hands on her waist to pull her closer. Immediately, she grabbed his wrists, but he would not be waylaid. He caressed her hipbones while his voice blended with the soft fog to muddle her. ''Remember that time, Laura? Remember how it was . . . with the sun on our skin and both of us so scared Dan would find us right there in the daylight, and—''

She clapped a hand over his mouth. ''You're not being fair,'' she pleaded, but the memory had been revived, as he'd intended, and already served Rye's purpose, for her breath was not easing. Instead, it came heavier and faster than when they'd first stopped running.

So he kissed the fingers with which she'd stifled his words. Immediately, she retracted them, freeing his lips to vow, ''I'll tell y' right now, woman, I've no intention of playin' fair. I'll play as dirty as I have to t' win y' back. And I'll start right here by soilin' your dress in this apple orchard if y' won't take the damn thing off.''

His hands pulled her against his hips again, then slid up her ribs and onto her back, finding the openings in her laces, pressing against her shoulder blades until her breasts touched his jacket.

She turned her mouth aside. ''If I kiss you once, will you be satisfied and let me go back?''

''What do y' think?'' he whispered gruffly, nuzzling the side of her neck, biting it lightly, sending goosebumps shivering across her belly.

''I think my husband will kill me if I don't get back to the house soon.'' But she inched her lips closer to his even as she said it.

''And I think *this* husband will kill y' if y' do,'' he said, almost at her mouth. He smelled of cedar and wine and the past. She recognized his aroma, and it prompted her response. The silence hemmed them in, so immense and total that within it their heartbeats seemed to resound like cannon shot. The first day when he'd kissed her, she'd been in shock. The second time he'd taken her by surprise. But now—if he kissed her now, if she let him, this one would be deliberate.

''Once,'' she whispered. ''Just once, then I have to go back. Promise you'll lace me up,'' she pleaded.

''Nay,'' he returned gruffly, breathing on her lips. ''No promises.''

Sensibly, she pulled back, but it took little effort for Rye to change her mind. He simply touched the corner of her mouth with his lips.

And the old thrill was back, as fresh and vital as always. He had that way about him, Rye did, that she'd tried to forget since being married to Dan. Call it technique, call it practice, call it familiarity—but they'd learned to kiss together, and Rye knew what Laura liked. He let their breaths mingle, then wet the corner of her mouth, dipping to taste before savoring fully. She liked to be aroused one tiny step at a time, and she waited now, her neck taut, her breathing labored, while he held her with one hand around the side of her neck, his thumb massaging the hollow beneath her jaw. The thumb circled lazily. Then came his tongue, wetting the perimeter of her lips with patient, faint strokes, as Rye sensed the fire building within her.

The memories came flooding back to Laura . . . being fifteen in a dory with lips tightly shut and eyes safely closed, being sixteen in a boathouse loft and knowing well the use of tongues; moving toward full maturity and learning together how a man touches a woman, how a woman touches a man to create impatience, then ecstasy.

As if he read her mind, Rye now murmured, ''Remember that summer, Laura, up in the loft above old man Hardesty's boathouse?''

And he took her back to those beginnings, pressing his mouth fully over hers, his tongue inviting hers to dance. His silky inner lips were just warm enough, just wet enough, just hesitant enough, just demanding enough, to wipe away today and take her back through the years to those first times.

She shivered. He felt the tremor beneath his palm on her neck and drew her against him, then slipped that warm, seeking palm within the dress that hung loosely from her shoulders. But when he would have pulled it down, she quickly flung her arms about his neck so that he couldn't. The dress was doing its intended job, for through spikes of whalebone and clumps of gathers there was little chance of his touching her intimately. The hoop was pressed tightly against his thighs and flared out behind her as if blowing in a hurricane.

But the hurricane blew not on her skirts but within her head and heart, for the kiss now had substance. It was a hot, whole giving of mouths, with neither holding back anything. Her tongue joined his and she knew the immediate shock of difference, as anyone knows who has kissed only one person for a long time, as she had Dan. It should have sobered her, reminded her she was not free to do these things with this man, but instead she welcomed it and realized that ever since she'd married Dan, she'd been comparing his kiss to this and finding it lacking.

That traitorous admission brought her somewhat to her senses, and she hoped fervently that Rye would be content with this kiss for now, because her resistance was fast slipping as he held her firmly and ran his hands along the exposed skin of her back, which was the only bareness he could reach.

He tore his lips away and spoke with savage emotion. ''Laura—my God, woman, does it give y' joy to torture me?'' He raised one hand and slid it along her arm, capturing one of her hands from the back of his neck, carrying it down, and placing it on his swollen body. ''I've been five years at sea and this is what it's done t' me. How long would y' make me wait?''

Shock waves sizzled through her body. She tried to pull free, but he held her palm where it had too long been absent, the heat of his tumescence insistent through the cloth of his trousers. Clutching the back of her neck, he drew her wildly against him once more, kissing her, his hot, demanding tongue stroking rhythmically in and out of her mouth, reminding Laura that it was he who had taught her these things in a boathouse loft years ago. Her hand stopped resisting and conformed to the shape of him, and he thrust against her caress, still pressing the back of her wrist and knuckles and fingers.

Against her will, she again compared him to the man who waited at the house for her now. Her palm moved up, then down, measuring, remembering, while Rye begged her with the motion of his body to seek the touch of his satin skin if she would not allow him to seek hers.

The fog curled its tendrils about their heads, and the seductive scent of blossoms filled the night. Their breathing scraped harshly with desire, like ocean waves rushing upon sand, then retreating.

"Please," Rye growled into her mouth. "Please, Laura-love. It's been so long."

"I can't, Rye," she said miserably, suddenly withdrawing her hand and covering her face with both palms, a sob breaking from her. "I can't . . . Dan trusts me."

"Dan!" he growled. "Dan! What about me?" Rye's voice trembled with rage. He grasped her arm and jerked her almost onto tiptoe. "I trusted you! I trusted y' t' wait for me while I sailed on that . . . that *miserable* whaleship and floundered in the stink of rancid oil and rottin' fish and ate flour with the weevils sifted out of it and smelled men's unwashed bodies day after day, and one of them my own!" His fingers closed tighter, and Laura winced. "Have y' any idea of how I longed for the smell of y'? I nearly lost my mind at the thought of it." But now he thrust her away almost distastefully. "Lyin' there adrift in the doldrums, at the mercy of a windless sky, while days and days passed and I thought of the wasted time when I could've been with you. But I wanted t' bring y' a better life. That's why I did it!" he raged.

"And what do you think I was going through?" she cried, her shoulders jutting forward belligerently, tears now coursing down her cheeks. "What do you think I suffered when I watched you stuffing clothes in your sea chest, when I saw those sails disappear and wondered if I'd ever see you alive again? What do you think it was like when I discovered I was carrying your baby and I got the news that that baby would never know his father?" Her voice shook. "I wanted to kill you, Rye Dalton, do you know that? I wanted to *kill* you because you'd *died on me!*" She laughed a little dementedly.

"But y' certainly wasted no time findin' someone t' take my place afterward, did y'!"

She clenched her fists and shouted. "I was pregnant!"

"With my child, and y' turned to him!" They stood almost nose to nose.

"Who else could I turn to? But you wouldn't understand! When's the last time your stomach swelled up like a balloonfish so you couldn't even walk without hurting or . . . or shovel a walk or carry wood or lift a water pail! Who do you think did all those things while you were gone, Rye?"

"My best friend," Rye answered bitterly.

"He was my best friend, too. And if he hadn't been, I don't know what I'd have done. He was there without being asked, whenever I needed him, and whether you want to believe it or not, it was as much because he loved you as because he loved me.''

''Spare me the dramatics, Laura. He was there because he couldn't wait t' get his hands on y', and you know it,'' Rye said coldly.

''That's a despicable thing to say, and *you* know it!''

''Are you denyin' that y' knew how he felt about y' all the years we were growing up?''

''I'm denying nothing. I'm trying to make you see what two people suffered at the news of your death . . . suffered together! After we heard that the *Massachusetts* had gone down, we got through those first days by walking the dunes where the three of us used to play, telling ourselves one minute that it couldn't be true, that you were still alive out there someplace, and the next minute telling each other to accept it—you'd never be back. But I was the weaker one by far. I . . . I told myself I was acting exactly like my mother, and I hated it, but the despair was worse than anything I'd ever known. I found I didn't care if I lived or died, and at times I felt the same about the child I carried. After the funeral was the worst . . .'' Her voice cracked with remembrance, and she shuddered. ''Oh God, that funeral . . . without a corpse . . . and me already awkward with your child.''

''Laura . . .'' He moved near, but she turned her back and went on.

''I couldn't have made it through that . . . that horror, if it weren't for Dan. My mother was perfectly useless, as you can well imagine. And she was no better when Josh was born. It was Dan who was my strength then, Dan who sat beside me through the first of my labor, then paced outside where you should have been pacing, then came to praise the baby and tell me he looked like you, because he knew those were the words I needed to give me the will to get strong again. It was your best friend who promised he'd always be there for Josh and me, no matter what. And I owe him for that.'' She paused a moment. ''You owe him.''

He studied her back, then stepped close and roughly began lacing up her stays.

''But *what* do I owe him?'' His hands stopped tugging. ''You?''

Laura shivered, unable to answer. What did they owe Dan? Certainly something better than stealing off into the night and indulging in sex play. Again Rye continued lacing.

''You've got to understand, Rye. He's been Josh's father since the day Josh was born. He's been my husband three times as long as you've been. I can't just . . . just fling him aside carelessly, without a thought for his feelings.''

At her back came one irritated tug, harder than the rest, then the tension disappeared around Laura's ribs as Rye fumbled. ''I'm not much good at this . . . I haven't had much practice.''

There was an icy insinuation in his tone. He was still angry with her, and with this seemingly unsolvable confusion into which their lives had been thrust. When he'd finally managed to close both corset and dress, his hands continued resting on her hips. ''So y' intend t' stay with him?''

Laura closed her eyes tiredly, inhaled deeply, no closer to solutions than Rye. ''For the time being.''

His warm hands slipped away. "And y' won't see me?"

"Not this way . . . not . . ." But she stammered to a halt, uncertain of her ability to resist him.

His anger was back, roiling just beneath the surface as he gritted his teeth. "We'll see about that . . . *Mrs. Morgan!*"

Then he spun and walked into the silent fog.

Chapter 5

The days that followed found Laura and Dan uncomfortable and distant. Since the night of the Starbucks' dinner, Dan had grown more and more stoical toward her, often wearing a wounded look that pricked Laura's conscience each time she glanced up and encountered it. She had not lied when he asked if she'd been with Rye that night, but Dan had seen her red-rimmed eyes and guessed the worst hadn't happened—not if there'd been tears. Yet those tears themselves told Dan that Laura still had feelings for Rye. And the tension grew.

On a warm golden evening in late May, when the sun hovered over the rim of the ocean like a ripe melon, Laura watched from the window above her zinc sink while Dan and Josh played together in the yard. Dan had made a pair of stilts and was patiently trying to teach Josh to walk with them. He held them upright, and Josh clambered up onto the footblocks once more while Dan supported him, keeping the sticks steady. But the minute Dan let go, Josh's legs spread apart like two halves of a wishbone. A single halting step, then the stilts went crashing to the ground in one direction and the boy in another, rolling over and over and over, playfully exaggerating, and Dan right with him, the two of them laughing joyously. They tumbled to a halt and Dan lay flat on his back, arms outflung while Josh straddled his chest as if he had Dan pinned. Then over they went in the other direction, and this time Dan pinned Josh, whose childish giggling drifted through the spring evening . . . the music of love.

The sun was behind the pair, turning their bodies to silhouette as Laura observed with a lump in her throat. Dan pulled Josh to his feet and brushed his clothes off, turning him around to tease with a playful spank on the boy's backside. Josh whirled around to get his giggling revenge, but in the next instant Dan's brushing slowed . . . then stopped . . . then his arms went around Josh and their two outlines melted into one.

Laura's heart expanded. Quick tears stung her eyes, seeing the desperation in that sudden embrace, the way Dan laid his cheek atop Josh's golden head, the way he hugged a little too tenaciously, and Josh squirming free, galloping toward the stilts once more while Dan knelt on the ground for a long moment, his eyes following the romping child.

He turned and looked down toward the house then, and Laura jumped back from the window, her throat constricting. Her eyes slid closed. Her fingers made a steeple before her mouth. How could I ever separate those two?

Later that night Laura and Dan made love, but she felt in his embrace that same desperation she'd seen in his clutching grasp of Josh earlier. He held her too hard. He kissed her too avidly. He apologized too profusely if he thought he'd done the smallest thing to displease her.

She wondered, after Dan at last fell into a restless sleep—would it ever be the same between them again? As long as Rye lived within touching distance, how could it be? Whether she saw Rye or not, kissed him or not, made love with him or not, he was there again, accessible, and this fact alone thwarted her and Dan's relationship.

Conscience-torn, Laura lay in the dark, the back of one wrist draped across her forehead, mouth dry, palms damp, willing her thoughts to take the straight and narrow.

But her reflections had a will of their own and would plague her with comparisons she had no right to be making. For what did it matter, the proportions of a man's body, the turn of his shoulder, the texture of his palm, the shape of his lips? None of this mattered. What mattered were his inner qualities, a man's values, the way he cared for a woman, worked for her, respected her, loved her.

But Laura wasn't fooling herself one bit. The physical comparisons were the ones that now brought her the most discontent. The undeniable truth was that Rye was the better lover and had the more desirable body. Deep in her heart she had recognized this during her years of marriage to Dan, but she had effectively suppressed the thought whenever they made love. But now Rye was back, and his superiority as a lover plagued her, causing great guilt each time she let the fact intrude between herself and the man to whom she was still wed.

Dan had always approached her almost as a supplicant approaches an altar, whereas she and Rye had always met on equal terms. She was no goddess, but a woman. She didn't want adulation, but reciprocation. Yes, there was a vast difference between making love with Dan and making love with Rye. With Dan it was sobering, with Rye intoxicating; with Dan it was mechanical, with Rye shattering; with Dan a ceremony; with Rye a celebration.

How could this be, and why should it matter? Yet it was . . . it did. Laura felt her body—only now, after Dan had left it—growing aroused at the memory of herself and Rye in the orchard with fog tendrils binding them closer and the scent of spring ripening in the damp night about them.

Oh, Rye, Rye, she despaired, you know me so well. We taught each other too well, you and I, to be able to live in the same town together and not be tempted.

Her hand rested on her stomach. She raised it to her breasts, finding them hard, tight peaks at the very thought of him. She pictured his lips, remembered that first time he'd kissed her . . . out in the bayberry patch up on Saul's Hill . . . and the first time he'd touched her here . . . and here. First times, first times . . . when they'd been trembling and afraid but burgeoning with sexuality as they treaded that fine line between adolescence and adulthood. It had begun with that innocent touch on his bare back . . .

They'd been swimming along the sandy beach at the head of the harbor near Wauwinet, ending, as always, by trudging along the place called the Haulover—a narrow stretch of sand separating the calm waters of the harbor from the pounding Atlantic, where fishermen often hauled over their dories from one side to the other.

She followed Rye through the reedy yellow-green beach grass that swept the strand and barred the intrusion of the mighty ocean from the quiet bay. To their left swept Great Point, crooking its narrow finger as if beckoning the ocean waves against it. But Rye gave it only a cursory glance before squatting in his customary way on the sand, hunching forward with his arms wrapped around his knees, searching the Atlantic for sails.

Grains of sand clung to his back, so Laura reached out and did as she'd done a hundred times before, whisking them off.

Only, this time he flinched and whirled around and shouted, ''Don't!'' Then he stared at her as if she'd committed some horrendous crime, while Laura gawked at him in owl-eyed amazement.

''All I did was brush the sand off.''

He glowered at her silently for several seconds, then abruptly jumped to his feet and ran as hard as he could across the beach toward the Coskata cedars while she watched him disappear and hugged her stomach, where a queer light feeling had settled.

It had never been the same after that. They were no longer three—Rye and Laura and Dan—but two plus one.

As children they'd played whaler the way mainland children play house. Laura was always the wife, Rye the husband, and Dan the child. Rye would plop a dry peck on her sunburned lips and stride off across the strand to his ''whaleship''—a beached skeleton of a rowboat that would never again split the brine—while she'd take Dan's hand and the two of them would wave goodbye, pretending that five minutes were five years, before Rye came striding back, some driftwood over his shoulder, the sailor home from the sea.

But those kisses didn't count.

The first time Rye really kissed Laura was long after those gamish pecks. Kissless years had gone by between then and the afternoon she'd brushed the sand from his back, but since that day, neither had thought of anything else.

Dan was with them, as usual, the next time they met to go clamming over at the creeks in the salt marsh at the harbor. They divided their catch, but Laura and Rye made excuses to linger together after Dan trudged off up the road past Consue Spring. Rye said he was going to help Laura carry her clams home, but when Dan was gone, he just stood there with his rake in his hand, nudging a buried shell up from the sand with his toe.

After a long silence, Laura asked, ''Wanna walk home along the road or on the commons?''

He looked up. The wind blew skeins of nutmeg-colored hair across her mouth, and he seemed to stare at it a long time before swallowing hard and answering in a falsetto, ''The commons.''

They headed west, across the sweep of land between Orange and Copper streets, toward the undulating terrain beside First Mile Stone, through the low hills toward the shearing pens at Miacomet. Fall had swept the island with her paintbrush, and they walked through gay patches of sweet fern, huckleberry, and trailing arbutus that covered the moorlands like a blazing carpet. Rutted footpaths led them through fragrant thickets of bayberry whose scent was heady when crushed beneath their soles. As if by mutual consent, they veered off the trail into a thick patch of the berries, to lend excuse for that which really needed no excuse.

Neither of them had a container for carrying berries, anyway.

Once off the path, Laura wondered how to get Rye to make the first move, for though they were in the concealing under-brush, he seemed to have lost his nerve. So she spilled her basket of clams, and when he knelt down to help her scoop them up, she managed to nudge his arm, and the touch of her autumn-warmed skin on his was all it took.

Their eyes met, wide and wondering and uncertain, fingers still trailing in the clams before finally touching, and clinging. They held their breaths while each leaned forward haltingly. Their noses bumped, then their heads tipped just enough, and it happened! Childish, dry, tongueless first kiss. But expertise lacking, emotion was not.

And that kiss led the way to others, kisses for the sake of which they filled that colorful autumn with countless walks through the bayberries, each kissing session growing more bold, until the touch of tongue upon tongue no longer sufficed.

But winter came, stripping the heath of color and cover. They lost their camouflage and found fewer times together. Miserably, they waited out the icy months until, in March, the mackerel started running and they at last found a place, an excuse.

That first time Rye touched Laura's breast she had not been wearing whalebones, for she yet had some growing to do. And neither had his hand grown to its full man's-width, nor had the blond hair sprouted on the back of it.

They'd been sitting in the dory facing each other, with their knees almost touching, pretending they were enjoying fishing when actually it was only keeping them from doing what they'd both thought about all winter.

Laura pulled her line in and dried her hands on her skirt, looking up to find Rye staring at her, his Adam's apple bobbing convulsively, as if he had a popcorn husk stuck on his tongue.

"I don't feel much like fishing," she admitted.

"Neither do I."

He licked his lips and swallowed once more, and without a word, she edged over and made room for him on her seat.

The boat rocked while he moved toward her and sat down without taking his eyes from her face. Her hands were freezing, clenched tightly between her knees.

When at last he kissed her, his nose and cheeks were cold, but his lips were as warm as that autumn day they'd first bumped noses on the blazing heath amid its scented colors. While his lips lingered on hers, Laura clamped her knees tighter upon the backs of her hands, wondering if Rye felt as grown-up as she did since the passing of winter. A moment later the touch of his tongue confirmed it, for it sought hers with a new insistence that made her turn on the seat and put both arms around him while she told him with her kiss how long the wait had been for her, too.

She felt Rye shiver, though he wore a bulky wool jacket to ward off the stiff March breeze. The dory rocked, swaying their bodies while their lips remained locked, bumping them first against each other, then tugging them apart.

At first she wasn't sure what Rye was doing, for her jacket was as bulky and cumbersome as his. But a moment later she realized his fingers were loosening the buttons. She jerked back, staring into his eyes.

''M . . . my hand is cold,'' he choked, voicing the first excuse he could think of.

''Oh.'' She gulped and let the rocking of the boat sway her against him, waiting, waiting for that first adult touch with the breathless eagerness of untutored youth. Then his hand slipped inside, where it was warm and secret and forbidden, and she knew they were doing wrong.

''Rye, we shouldn't,'' she protested.

''No, we shouldn't,'' he agreed hoarsely. But that didn't stop his hand from knowing its first of her, from learning the shape of her budding breasts through her dress, from discovering the way a woman's nipples grow rigid as they plead for more. As with all first times, it was more exploration than caress, a search for the differences that were making her woman, him man.

Laura's breath came jerky and fast. Her heart thumped madly beneath Rye's hand.

''Put your hand inside my jacket, Laura,'' he ordered, and she did his bidding for the first of many times to follow. She slipped her hand between jacket and sweater, and felt his ribs rising like sea swells, he was breathing so hard.

''Ouch! Not so hard!'' she exclaimed when his exploration of her nipple grew a little too insistent.

From that moment on they remained open and vocal about their sexuality.

When the weave of her linen chemise abraded her tender breast, she reached and pushed his exploring hand to her other breast, saying against his lips, ''That one's sore.''

Laura and Rye used the excuse of going mackerel fishing again two days later, but not until just before they made for shore did their lines get wet. They sat in the vast privacy of the open water, surrounded by Nantucket Bay, while the boat bobbed up and down and the sun came skipping up at them from the rippling sea. Only the inquisitive gulls observed the first time Laura followed Rye's instructions and slid her hands beneath his sweater to feel his warm, bare skin underneath.

There followed an excruciating week during which Josiah commanded all of Rye's time, for Rye was already a four-year apprentice and was nearly as adept at coopering as his father.

By the time Sunday came and Rye was free to be with Laura again, they both felt tense and desperate. Rye had planned all week where they would go to be alone. Old man Hardesty had a boathouse on the waterfront near Easy Street where he kept old lobster traps and seines. He'd given Rye free use of any of the abandoned equipment anytime Rye wanted it.

''Ma wants me to get her a couple lobsters for tomorrow,'' Rye said when he came to fetch Laura. ''Wanna come along with me over to old man Hardesty's and pick up a trap?''

''I suppose.''

They didn't look at each other along the way. Rye stalked with his hands in his pockets, whistling, while Laura watched her toes and tried to match her stride to his—impossible to do anymore since his legs had grown so long.

They climbed the steps of the silvery old boathouse, and at the top Rye stood back, holding the door open for her. She stopped with her hand on the rail, staring up at him: Rye had never bothered with courtesies in all his sixteen years! He looked up and nervously scanned the waterfront, then he shifted his feet, and she hurried up the steps.

Inside it was dry and dusty, cobwebs lacing the corners and junk everywhere. Coils of old rope lay on the floor, along with buckets of rusty clews, battered oars, and lanterns with missing side glass; trennels and tar pots, piggins and barrel rings. While Laura stood taking it all in, a calico cat jumped out of nowhere, startling her into a shriek.

Rye laughed and picked his way across the littered floor to pluck the cat from an old nail keg and bring her back to Laura. Standing close together, they scratched the cat, who purred contentedly between them as if happy that company had come to call. Both Laura and Rye studied the creature as she stretched her neck and squinted her eyes closed in ecstasy while their fingers moved on her fur but itched to move over each other.

Laced over the cat's back, their fingers touched, warm fur and warm flesh blending as they raised their eyes. For a long moment they stood still, the only movement the hammering of their hearts and the drifting of dust motes in the dry old loft. Rye leaned forward and Laura raised her lips, the kiss a gentle thing at first, until they lunged together and the cat squawked, making them leap apart and laugh self-consciously.

The cat took up her post on a barrel. She began to give herself a bath while Rye scanned the floor. He found an old mainsail rolled up and abandoned years earlier to mice and dust, and he tugged Laura's hand, leading her to it.

They knelt down, one on either side of the brittle, gray canvas, and together began smoothing it out. Sunlight slanted in through a single window, falling across their sail bed in an oblique slash of gold, while from below the lap and swash of waves continued lazily nudging the pilings of the building.

Rye looked down at the waiting canvas, then up at Laura. They were both on their knees, facing each other, afraid now, and hesitant. From outside came the cry of gulls, wheeling lazily above the wharf. On his knees, Rye moved to the center of the canvas, and after a moment Laura followed suit. She watched the sunlight play across his beautiful arched eyebrows and light the tips of his eyelashes to gold as they slid closed and he leaned forward to kiss her. He found her fingers and clasped them tightly, as if for courage. When the kiss ended, he sat back on his haunches, searching her eyes while he squeezed her fingers till she thought the bones would crack.

He swallowed, lowered his gaze to the center of her chest, rose again to kneeling height, and slowly began unbuttoning her jacket. She shuddered as he pushed it from her shoulders, and Rye looked up, startled.

''Are you cold, Laura?''

She hunched her shoulders and gripped the skirts in her lap. "No."

"Laura, I . . ." But he gulped to a stop, and she could see it was her turn to make a move.

"Kiss me, Rye," she said in a voice she'd never heard before, "the way I like it best." For by this time they had practiced it many ways.

He picked up her hands from her lap, gripping them tightly, and they met halfway, his tongue touching the seam of her lips even before they opened beneath his, her girl's ignorance clashing with her woman's intuition.

His hand found her breast across the vast distance that seemed to separate their bodies except for knees and lips. And for the first time ever, her hand nudged his toward the buttons at her throat, verifying that it was time. He hesitated, then shakily, inexpertly, opened the polished whalebone buttons all the way to her waist.

As if suddenly realizing what he'd done, he sat back on his haunches, staring into her eyes now with a frightened look in his own.

"It's okay, Rye. I want you to."

"Laura, it's different than just . . . just kissing, you know."

"How do I know?" she asked, experiencing her first heady recognition of the power of her feminine mystique, wielding it as surely as if she were an experienced woman of the world.

"You sure?" He gulped, still scared of all the unknowns.

"Rye, I didn't come up here to get any lobster trap. Did you?"

His lips were open, blue eyes wide and not a little frightened as he touched one shoulder inside her open dress, then the other, then carefully pushed the garment back to stare at her chemise.

The dark circles of her nipples showed against the linen cloth, and she followed the movement of his eyes from one to the other, then dropped her gaze to watch his hand reach for the streamer of the satin bow between her breasts. A moment later the cool air touched her bare skin as Rye pushed the chemise to her waist.

She held her breath, waiting for him to touch her, and when he didn't, her eyelids fluttered up to find his face red to the roots of his hair, while he stared as if struck dumb.

"Golly . . ." he muttered thickly, and she knew he was afraid to touch, now that he'd come this far. "Laura, you're so . . . so pretty."

Her face was red, too, but it ceased to matter when, a moment later, his scratchy wool sweater was pressed against her bare skin, then within seconds, it drifted back to make way for Rye's shaking hand.

His palm was damp with nervousness, but warm and already callused hard from working the drawknives. She wondered how it could possibly be wrong to let Rye touch her this way, because for the first time ever, she'd found justification for the growing pains she'd endured during the last year while her breasts had begun developing. At first he only brushed her breasts with callow timidity, but soon he explored the nipple with his fingertips, finding the hard little pebble of growth that would be there yet for some months.

It hurt, and though she only shrugged her shoulder away in response, he reacted as if she'd cried out in pain. He jerked his hand back, a stricken look on his face.

"Did . . . did I hurt you, Laura?"

"N . . . no, not really . . . just . . . I don't know."

He moved more cautiously after that, experimenting with great care until their kisses became wilder and it seemed their bodies could not press together hard enough, kneeling as they were.

He urged her backward, a little at a time, until she listed beneath the pressure of his chest and tumbled with him to the floor. Her arms twined up around his shoulders as he pressed his length against hers, and they kissed with the all-consuming fire that only first times ignite.

When at last he pulled away, she knew where his lips were headed, but lay very still, very cautious, her shoulder blades pressed solidly against the floor. His breath dampened her neck, stopping there a long, tremulous time before proceeding down, down, by inches, until his lips were at her breast. Once there, they only brushed the nipple, not so much as the dew of his breath dampening it, for his mouth was closed.

Her stomach and chest hurt, tight bands of expectancy and fear binding it strangely. But the urge to know, to understand this thing called growing up, made her touch his hair experimentally. And with that touch, his lips opened and she felt the sleek texture of his tongue stroking the bright rosebud not yet fully blossomed. A sound came from her throat and her shoulders lifted off the canvas as she was overcome with some new compulsion to reach toward him with her breast.

Liquid fire coursed through her veins. Her head fell back as he tasted her other nipple, and she felt her body go all limp and tense at once. His weight felt welcome as Rye lay across her body, and she learned with each new motion of his tongue why he had leaped up angrily and run away when she had brushed that sand from his shoulder the summer before.

Her eyes flew open as Rye suddenly sprang to his knees beside her, reaching for the bottom of his sweater, yanking it viciously over his head, then falling still a moment, again looking down at her for permission.

She had never seen hair on his chest before, but it was there now—a soft shadow of blond, sparkling in the light from the window, across the high square twin muscles of his chest. She reveled in discovery, moving her gaze downward eventually to the spot where his navel made a round, secret shadow, just above his waistline. He knelt before her with his knees apart, each of them satisfying curiosity for a moment before going any farther.

"Rye, you're all muscly," she said, amazed.

"And you're not," he said, unsmiling.

She could see—actually see!—the way his pulse pounded in the hallow of his throat, and wondered if hers did the same, for it seemed to be thrumming everywhere, in her temples, in her stomach, and in the secret part of her that now seemed the center of all feeling.

He fell toward her, one hand on each side of her head, and kneeling over her that way, kissed her before easing his bare, golden chest onto hers, their hearts thundering uncontrollably while hard muscle flattened soft.

There was wonder and astonishment then, feeling the difference between their textures, experimentally grinding those textures against one another in a touch that somehow proved silken.

Again he caressed her breasts. Again he kissed them, his tongue already dancing more masterfully on the puckered tips. She threaded her fingers through his hair, and she writhed in unknowing invitation, begging him to lay his full length over hers, for without it she felt incomplete and searching.

He bent a knee, lifted it, and pressed it on her leg while she sucked in a breath and held it. The knee passed heavily up her thigh, across the juncture of her legs, to her stomach, making her skirts whisper alluringly against her legs. The weight of that knee seemed to anchor her to earth, from which her body wanted to soar. Then, before long, a greater weight pressed her to the sail bed, for Rye shifted his hips to cover hers, lying flat on her now with not so much as a muscle moving while she marveled at how good it felt to know the curves and warmth of another this closely.

Then, somehow, her legs had parted and made a space where his knee fit securely, and he moved it against her in an altogether satisfying way that made her press and lift rhythmically against it.

When Rye's knee moved back and his weight slipped to one side, she felt his hand skimming along her skirt, raising layers of petticoats as he searched along the length of her leg. Her heart clamored crazily, and his breath beat like wild waves against her ear. His fingers touched the legband of her pantaloons, then moved higher . . . higher . . . until his palm covered the gentle swell between her legs, and she realized, horrified, that the linen fabric there was damp. She felt his hesitant surprise when he encountered the dampness, but when he pressed her hard, it felt wonderful and right and relieved some inner yearning even while Laura waited for the hand of Providence to reach out and smite her dead.

Instead, the hand of Rye Dalton explored her through the last barrier of linen, but when it ventured to the buttoned waist of her pantaloons, caution intruded. She caught his wrist and whispered shakily, "No more, Rye. I . . . I think we'd better get dressed. I have to go."

For a moment his eyes blazed down at her with an untamed intensity she'd never seen there before. She hadn't known he was holding his breath until it came out in a mighty gust that seemed to leave him weak. Immediately, he rolled to his knees, turning his back on her while yanking his sweater over his head. She pulled up her chemise, smoothed her skirts, and slipped her arms into her sleeves. He smoothed his hair, and his blue eyes met hers as he looked over his shoulder to find her buttoning her dress. His glance skittered away in self-consciousness. She studied his back a long time.

"Rye?"

"What?"

When she said nothing for a long moment, he looked over his shoulder again.

"Are we gonna go to hell now?"

They stared at each other, wide-eyed, for some seconds.

"I suppose so."

"Both of us, or just me?"

"Both of us, I think."

She experienced a sick feeling of dread in the pit of her stomach, for she didn't want Rye suffering in hell because of her.

"M . . . maybe if we don't ever do it again and if we pray real hard, we won't."

"Maybe." But his morose tone held little hope. He got to his feet. "I think we'd better go, Laura, and we'd better not come up here together anymore. I'll get those traps, and . . . and . . ." He half turned to find her sitting on her haunches, a look of dread on her face.

His words faded away. Below them, the old pilings of the boathouse creaked as the tide came in, while above them gulls reeled and screeched. Then suddenly they pitched together, holding each other tightly, their hearts hammering with this new awareness they didn't yet know how to handle.

"Oh, Rye, I don't want you to go to hell."

"Shh . . . maybe . . . maybe you don't for just one time."

Chapter 6

The next day in church, Rye avoided her eye all through services. Guilt was evident on his face, and it filled Laura with an awesome fear of retribution even while her mind was dominated by memories of what they'd done together. Furthermore, whenever she relived those moments, that liquid sensation began to build in her body and she was certain it alone was sinful. He avoided her in the churchyard, leaving her feeling bereft and abandoned while he walked off toward home without so much as a hello.

He kept away for nine days, but on the tenth, she went to Market Square to buy fresh haddock for her mother and was wending her way through the carts and drays when she saw Rye approaching. As he glanced up and saw her, his step faltered, but he continued in her direction until they met and he was forced to stop.

"Hi, Rye." She gave him her brightest smile.

"Hi."

Her heart fell to her feet, for he neither said her name nor met her eyes. "I haven't seen you for over a week," she said.

"I've been busy helping the old man." He studied something across the square.

"Oh." He seemed impatient, and she searched for something to keep him a minute longer. "Did you catch any lobsters in those traps?"

His gaze met hers fleetingly, then skittered away. "A few."

"You take the traps back yet?"

"No, I set 'em every morning and haul 'em at the end of the day."

"You gonna haul 'em today?"

His mouth pursed slightly, and he seemed reluctant to answer, but finally grunted, "Yeah."

"What time?"

"Four o'clock or so."

"You . . . you want some help?"

He looked at her from the corner of his eye, then turned his gaze toward Nantucket Bay. But instead of his usual bright invitation, he only shrugged. "I gotta go, Laura."

Her heart felt broken as she watched him walk off.

But she was waiting at the dory at four o'clock. When Rye spotted her, he came up short, but she stubbornly stood her ground. Neither said a word while she stooped to release the bow line and he the stern line. Neither did they talk while they headed out to collect the traps and haul them in. He had two good-sized lobsters, which he put in a burlap sack before heading again for shore.

When the dory bumped against the pilings, Rye hefted one of the traps up onto the wharf.

Laura looked up, surprised. "What you gonna do with that?"

He reached for the second trap and thumped it down beside the first, avoiding her eyes. "I've had 'em long enough. Time I return 'em to old man Hardesty's boathouse."

Her heart careened with a mixture of joy and foreboding.

Together they secured the dory, then each picked up a trap and they walked wordlessly side by side past old Cap'n Silas, who nodded and puffed his pipe without saying a word. When they'd passed him, they peered at each other guiltily but continued in the direction of the boathouse.

Inside, the boathouse was just as they'd left it, except today, with a shroud of fog at the windows, it seemed more secret and forbidden. Just inside the door Laura came to an abrupt halt, her fingers clinging to a bar of her lobster trap as it rested against her knees. She jumped and spun around when Rye dropped his trap with a clatter. He took hers and set it down, too, but when he straightened, neither of them seemed to know where to look. He slipped his hands inside the back waistline of his pants while she folded hers tightly together before her skirts.

"I gotta go," he announced abruptly. "My ma said to bring the lobsters home for supper." But the burlap bag lay forgotten near the door.

"I gotta go, too. My ma likes me to come and help her with supper."

He turned toward the door but had taken only three steps before she dared to speak the word that stopped him.

"Rye?"

He spun around and gave her a searching look that revealed what had possessed his thoughts for ten days now. "What?"

"Are . . . are you mad at me?"

His Adam's apple bobbed. "No."

"Well then, what's wrong?"

"I . . . I don't know."

Laura felt her chin tremble, and suddenly Rye's image seemed to grow wavery while she tried her hardest to keep the tears from showing. But Rye saw the glisten, and suddenly his lanky legs were covering the space between them, and a minute later she was crushed against his chest. The strength of his not-yet-adult arms was as powerful as that of any full-grown man as he pulled her hard against him, and she clung to his neck. Their kiss, too, held an adult intensity, and a wondrous letting go happened inside Laura when his tongue came into her mouth and circled hers, then licked the insides of her cheeks and made her own tongue arch so sharply that it ached sweetly.

Their lips broke apart and he hugged her close, rocking back and forth and dropping his face into the lee of her neck. Standing on tiptoe, she clung to him; he'd grown so tall in the past winter, they no longer matched in height.

"Rye, I was so scared when you wouldn't look at me in the square today." Her words were muffled against his thick brown sweater as he continued rocking her in a motion meant to pacify but that only inflamed. Laura pulled back to look at him. "Why did you act that way?"

"I don't know." His blue eyes appeared haunted.

"Don't ever do that again, Rye."

He only swallowed, then spoke her name in a strange, adult way. "Laura . . ."

Then she was pulled roughly against him again while they kissed and kissed, frightened of the needs of their bodies, yet hearkening to them nonetheless, for soon they were moving, hardly aware of their action, toward the canvas where they'd lain once before. By some unspoken agreement they went down on their knees, still kissing, then fell to their hips, then elbows, seeking that closeness they'd experienced and could not forget.

And this time when his hand slid beneath her skirts, Laura's limbs opened readily, anticipating the thrill of his intimate touch. As before, her body craved his exploration and blossomed at his caress. When his hand moved to the button of her pantaloons, she knew she should stop him, but was incapable. His palm slipped inside, exploring the warm surface of her stomach, then gingerly encountering the nest of new-sprung hair, hesitating at the threshold of femininity until she moved restlessly and made a soft sound in her throat.

Her heart felt as if it would explode with anxiety as she waited on the brink of the forbidden. But when at last his fingers slipped those final inches to discover the wherefore of her silken femininity, she jumped.

Immediately, he recoiled and withdrew. "Did I hurt you?" His blue eyes were wide with fright while carnality and morality waged war within her.

"N . . . no. Do it again."

"But what if . . ."

"I don't know . . . do it again."

When his inexperienced fingers plumbed her for a second time she did not jump, but closed her eyes and knew a great wonder. Naïvely he went on, far from mastering the touch yet, but needing not to master, only to explore.

"Rye," she whispered after some moments, "we're sure going to hell now."

"No we're not. I asked somebody about it, and it takes a lot more than this before you go to hell."

She pulled back sharply and shoved his hand away. "You . . . you asked somebody?" she repeated, horrified. "Who?"

"Charles."

She sighed with relief when he named an older, married cousin of his whom she scarcely knew.

"What did you ask him?"

"I asked him if he thought a man would go to hell for touching a woman."

"And what did he say?"

"He laughed."

"He laughed?" she parroted, amazed.

"Then he said if that was any man's idea of hell, he could do without heaven. And he told me . . ." Rye stopped in mid-sentence, and his hand moved toward that secret place again.

But she stopped it, demanding, "What did he tell you?" She saw Rye color and look away. Somewhere in the loft the cat made a soft sound.

At last Rye looked at her again and drew a deep breath. "How to do things."

She stared at him speechlessly and suddenly knew an overwhelming fright at these mysteries to which Rye was now privy.

She sat up abruptly. "It's getting close to supper time. Mother will be expecting me." Then she was on her feet and heading for the door before he could detain her. He sat up, too, raising one knee and draping an elbow across it. "Meet me here tomorrow after supper," he said quietly, studying her back as she hesitated with her hand on the doorknob.

"I can't."

"Why not?"

"We're going to Aunt Nora's."

"The next night, then."

"We're going to get in trouble, Rye!"

"No we're not."

"How do you know?"

"'Cause I found out from Charles."

But nothing made sense to Laura, for *trouble* was only a vague notion in her mind. When she'd said the word she'd only meant that by hanging around up here, they risked getting caught. But she sensed he meant something else.

"You afraid, Laura?" Rye asked.

"No . . . yes . . . I don't think I can come." Then she went out quickly and slammed the door.

But nature's curiosity ran rife through Laura's changing body. That night as she lay in bed, she recalled Rye's touch—his touch, oh his touch, what it had done to her!—and brushed her palms over her breasts, trying to recapture the exquisite sensation of Rye's rough fingers. But her own were somehow incompetent and left her wanting. She ran her fingers down to test the entrance to her virginity and found it sleek at the very thought of Rye. What would he teach her if she met him tomorrow night? So many mysteries, yet one thing was sure. Touching herself left her filled only with the longing to be touched instead by Rye. He'd be waiting at the boathouse, she knew, and the thought of advancing the next step with him filled her with queer feelings she both welcomed and resisted.

The following day crept by like a decade, but when at last the appointed time came, Laura was there before Rye, sitting on a rolled up tarp with the cat on her lap. When footsteps sounded on the outside stair, her heart hammered in trepidation. Suppose it was somebody else—old man Hardesty maybe, or . . . or . . .

But it was Rye, wearing a clean muslin shirt and black straight-legged pants with brass buttons, his hair freshly combed, his boots gleaming from an unaccustomed polishing.

This time their eyes met steadily, holding deep while he stood at the door, some ten feet distant from her perch. The evening shadows were long; only the lip of the window ledge was limned in gold. Already the loft felt secure and familiar.

''Hi,'' he greeted quietly.

A smile broke upon her face. ''Hi.''

Her heart thrilled at the sight of him. Her body welled with anticipation. But she scratched the cat's jaw with feigned poise while he crossed and sat down on the hard canvas roll beside her. His fingers, too, reached to stroke the cat and, as with that first time, touched Laura's accidentally, then not so accidentally until finally they stopped making excuses and clasped hands tightly, both of them staring at his thumb as it rubbed the base of hers.

With one accord their gazes were lifted and their eyes met, and Laura felt a great impatience to learn more of what Charles had told Rye. Her brown eyes were wide, her lips open with womanly waiting, while Rye squeezed her hand so hard she felt the soft skin bruise. He tipped his head aside and she lifted her face, eyelids closing as their lips met in a tender first hello, the fragile touch of a moth's wing against an evening leaf.

Rye pulled back his head and their eyes met again, filled with longing and uncertainty and the absolute awareness of sin.

''Laura,'' he croaked.

''Rye, I'm still scared.''

She flung her arms around his neck and felt his smooth jaw against her temple while they clung, perched like two gulls on a yardarm. He slid to the floor and tugged her along, both of them resting on their sides, facing each other while their eager lips and arms held fast. They kissed with fiery impatience, bringing their breasts and hips together as hard as nature allowed, until Rye's hand slowly moved from her shoulder blade to her breast, caressing it through thin spring cotton, making it bud like the lilacs outside their lofty nest. She rolled forward against his palm, then back, like a body being sucked and pushed by breakers on a shore, until finally his hand went down to her waist, where it lingered, garnering courage before finally drifting down her petticoats to lift them during long minutes of expectation.

Every inch of the way she knew she should stop him, remind him again of hell. But instead, she breathed harder and made the way clear and unencumbered. He touched her bare leg and she did nothing. He touched the hem of her pantaloons and still she did nothing. He unbuttoned the waist and she stretched acquiescently.

Then his hand slid down and her legs parted to accept his touch again. Her whole body felt liquid and hot, her pulse driven. Soft sounds came from Rye's throat, half groan, half accolade, until at last he spoke gruffly in her ear.

''You're supposed to touch me, too, Laura.''

Instinctively, she knew he meant in the same place he was touching her, but her fingers seemed spliced into the threads of his shirt. His lips rested on hers, then his tongue rode across her bottom lip and nuzzled toward her ear.

''Laura, don't be scared.''

But she was. She had come here knowing a little bit about what he might do to her, but nothing about a woman's part in all this. He kissed her ear, and she squeezed her eyes shut and bit her lower lip. He had asked Charles, hadn't he? Charles must know. She understood that boys were shaped differently than girls, but had never before questioned why. What would happen if she let her hand slide down? Would he grow wet, too? Then what? *How* should she touch him?

Her palm, resting on his ribs, grew damp. She held her breath and eased her hand to his hip, then stopped, afraid. He kissed her encouragingly, murmuring her name and nudging her hand until it began moving by degrees—until it halted with the backs of her knuckles touching the buttons of his fly. His hips began a series of slow undulations and she brushed lightly back and forth, feeling little except the woolen texture of his pants and the coolness of brass buttons.

Without warning his hand captured hers, turned it over, and pressed it hard against the brass buttons. Wild questions burst into her mind. Why wasn't he shaped as she'd thought men were shaped? What was this ridge which, even through wool and brass, she could tell was bigger than what her peeps at naked infants had led her to expect?

He held her hand firmly, playing it up and down before finally cupping it firmly against him, way down low, where his trousers felt warm and damp. Suddenly he rolled away and fell back against the tarp, eyes closed, legs outstretched. But he still held her wrist, guiding her hand up and down, up and down the mysterious ridge. Her fingertips grew brave and began exploring, counting buttons—one, two, three, four, five—the ridge stopped at the fifth button.

Rye rolled his head to face her, and opened his eyes. He licked his dry lips and she stared at his familiar blue eyes, which held an expression she'd never before encountered in them. She was sitting up now, higher than he, breathing hard through trembling lips, her own eyes wide and unsmiling, filled with discovery. His hand fell away and his hips began rising and falling rhythmically, and only when he felt her palm stay to complement the rhythm of his thrusts did his eyes close again.

She stared down at her hand, feeling the brass buttons grow warm as they scraped along her palm, watching Rye's stomach and ribs heaving torturously, as if he'd just completed a league's swim.

"Laura?"

The throaty word brought her eyes back to his with a snap.

"Kiss me while you do that."

She bent over him, and when their tongues met, hot and wet, his thrusting grew more pronounced. And then she felt his fingers circle her wrist again and haul her hand to the top button at his waist. Instinctively, she knew what he wanted of her and began to pull away. But he clapped a hand around the back of her neck and forced her to stay as she was.

She managed to free her mouth, shaking her head once and twisting free of his hand. "Rye, don't!"

"I did it to you. Don't you think I was scared, too?" His eyes seemed suddenly to blaze with anger while her clenched fist was held captive at his waist.

"I can't."

"Why not?"

"I . . . I just can't, that's all."

He braced himself up against the tarp, rolling slightly toward her, the anger now replaced by a new tone of encouragement. "Aw, Laura, come on, don't be scared. I promise nothing bad will happen." He bestowed fluttering touches of his lips upon her face until her fingers relaxed. He was rubbing the back of her hand softly, where it rested against the hard muscles of his stomach, just above his waistband. "Laura, don't you want to know what I feel like?"

Oh . . . she did, she did. But it was easier letting somebody touch you than being the one who touched. A moment later, though, he was releasing the brass buttons himself while her trembling palm still lay on his stomach and he half leaned over her, kissing her tenderly as if to reassure her it was all right. He raised his hip and pulled the tail of his shirt up, and its barrier was suddenly gone from between her palm and his skin. Then he found her wrist again and drew her hand down to something that was so hot, she flinched away. But relentlessly, Rye took her hand to his flesh again and covered her shaking fingers with his own, making a sheath of her hand into which his long, silken surprise slipped. My God, had there ever been skin so smooth or so hot? It was smoother than the tender flesh of his inner lip, which her tongue had grazed many times. It was hotter than the inside of his mouth, which she knew as well as her own. He held her fingers closed tightly and forced them to stroke up and down while her heart threatened to explode inside her body. I'm going to hell! I'm going to hell! But no threat of hell could tear her hand from his body now. She experimented, moving the silken skin with tender exploration, learning each ridge and hollow of the masculine shaft until he fell back in abandon, his hand now fallen away from hers. She looked down and saw what she held then for the first time. In the deepening shadows it appeared to be the color of the deepest of the cosmos in her mother's garden. Abashed at having viewed it, she felt the same color suffuse her face and tore her eyes away. But now Rye made a guttural sound at the crest of each stroke and a moment later his body began a frightful trembling, his hips seeming to shake in a way that scared Laura much more than anything that had happened so far. But when she would have pulled away, he held her, and a moment later something warm and wet cascaded over the back of her hand and between her fingers.

"Rye, oh Rye, stop!" Her voice was choked with fright. "Something's wrong. I think you're bleeding." She was afraid to look down and find out. It must be blood. What else could it be, warm and wet? She started to cry.

"Laura, shh . . ." They were lying on the floor, her head resting in the crook of his elbow, and he turned to pull her cheek beneath his lips. "Are you crying?"

"I'm scared. I think I hurt you."

"It's not blood, Laura . . . look."

But she was afraid to look down, sure now that when she did, she'd find her hand scarlet with Rye's blood. His blue eyes seemed so sure, looking deeply into hers, but her voice trembled and tears rolled down her temple.

"I . . . I told you I didn't want to . . . and now . . . now something awful has happened, I just know it."

Unbelievably, Rye smiled. Laura was incensed to think he could be smiling at a time like this.

"I said look, Laura. If you don't believe me, look."

She did at last. White. It was white and slick and had dampened a circle on the tarp between them.

Her eyes flew to his. "Wh . . . what is it?"

"It's what makes babies."

"Babies! Rye Dalton, how dare you put it on me if you knew that all the time!" Instinctively, she sat up, searching frantically for something with which to clean her hand so that one didn't start in her. At last she used her petticoat.

"Button your britches up, Rye Dalton, and don't you ever do that to me again. If I got a baby, my mother would kill me!" Disdainfully, she turned her back on him while fastening her buttons. When her clothing was all adjusted, she knelt with her hands clenched tightly between her knees, horrified to think of what he'd done to her.

On his knees, Rye moved close behind her. "Laura, haven't you ever heard how a woman gets pregnant?"

Her chin was trembling and the tears rolled freely. "No, never before tonight." Distressed by his thoughtlessness in jeopardizing her, she swung around angrily. "Why didn't you tell me before we . . . I . . . we did it?"

"Laura, I promise you you're not going to get pregnant. You can't."

"But . . . but . . ."

"That stuff's got to get inside you before you can get pregnant, but I wasn't inside you, was I?"

"Inside me?" Her puzzled eyes probed his.

"Haven't you ever seen animals do it, Laura?"

"Animals?"

"A dog or . . . or even chickens?" But her confused expression needed no further interpreting. It clearly spoke of ignorance.

"Do what?" No animal could do what they'd just done!

They knelt facing each other with their knees almost touching. Dusk had settled, so only the pale outlines of their faces were visible in the dusty old loft. His face wore an expression of deep tenderness.

He reached for her hand and placed it on his brass buttons. "This part of me goes into this part of you." He pressed his palm into her lap. "Then there are babies."

Her lips fell open. Her blue eyes were wide with disbelief. Could Rye be right? Her face burned, and she yanked her hand away from his.

"What happened in your hand has to happen inside your body, Laura. That's how a man gives a woman a baby." He touched her jaw, but she was too ashamed to look up at him. But he went on earnestly. "I promise I'll never do that to you, though, until after we're married."

Now her eyes flew to his. Her heart beat crazily and a flood of relief surged through her. "M . . . married?"

"Don't you think we should get married, Laura, after . . . well . . . after this?"

"M . . . married?" Her astonishment began to grow. "You want to marry me, Rye, really?"

His astonishment, too, blossomed into manly realization, then a grin. "Why, I can't imagine marrying anybody besides you, Laura."

"Oh, Rye!" Suddenly she was up against him, her arms about his neck, her eyes squeezed tightly shut at the thought of it. Until just this minute she hadn't thought of how awful it might have been *not* to marry Rye after what they'd done together. "I can't imagine marrying anybody besides you, either."

He held her, and they rocked back and forth while her face remained securely against his neck.

"Do you think that makes it all right . . . I mean . . . you know?" came her muffled question.

"Touching and stuff, you mean?"

"Mmm-hmm."

"I don't think husband and wives go to hell for touching."

She released a sign of relief, then backed away and looked eagerly into his face. "Rye, let's tell Dan."

"Tell Dan?"

"That we're going to get married."

Rye looked skeptical. "Not yet. We'll have to wait until my apprenticeship is served, Laura. Then, when I'm a master cooper, we can afford to live in a house of our own. I don't think we should tell Dan till then."

Slightly disappointed, she sank back on her heels. "Well . . . all right, if you think it's best."

But it was hard for Laura to keep from telling Dan the very next time they met, for she wanted to share her new joy—after all, the three of them had always shared everything.

It was a week later. An immense storm had blown up, and afterward, Laura and Dan went out together to scour the shingle for driftwood, a precious commodity here on Nantucket, where there was little wood to spare, since most was hauled over from the mainland. The coast along the south side of the island caught the worst of the Atlantic's wrath and also turned up the greatest rewards after storms. Laura and Dan were working their way eastward when they came upon Rye, standing some twenty yards away, across the wet, hard-packed shingle that was strewn with shells, kelp, and tidepools where small fish had been trapped. The storm itself had passed, but the skies were still low, with scudding gray clouds hemming in the island, making it a world apart.

Rye wore a heavy pea jacket, its collar turned up around the flaxen hair that whipped about his face in the wind. Laura, in a yellow slicker and red bandana, raised her arm to wave as soon as she saw him.

The three of them moved down the beach together after that, their burlap sacks scraping triple tracks as they dragged along. It was the first time Laura had seen Rye since the evening in the boathouse, and she immediately got that curious wanton feeling in the pit of her stomach and wondered how they could get rid of Dan. The natural way was to ask if his mother had anything good to eat, and when the answer was "gingerbread," they made Dan's house their first stop back in town.

By the time Laura and Rye left Dan's house, she felt ready to burst with impatience, yet he seemed calm and unaffected by the last two hours—the last seven days! But when they were moving down the street toward Josiah's, Rye did something he'd never done before: he took her sack from her and hoisted it over his shoulder with his own, refusing to heed her insistence that she could handle it herself. The waterlogged wood was as heavy as dead weight, and secretly Laura was pleased by Rye's chivalry. He even managed to open the door of the cooperage for her despite his burden.

Dropping the sacks just inside the door, he looked up when his mother called from overhead.

"Rye, is that you?"

He placed a finger over his lips in warning, and Laura bit off the greeting she'd been preparing to call up.

"It's me," he called. "I got some driftwood. Gonna make a fire and lay it around the fireplace to dry out."

It was Sunday, and the lower level of the cooperage was abandoned. The damp, windy clouds made the room shadowed and secret. As Laura and Rye stood silently staring at each other, they could hear the sounds of his parents moving back and forth above their heads. Then he dragged their two sacks over to the fireplace and began laying a fire. When it was crackling, he methodically began pulling wet driftwood from the sacks and arranging it in a circle on the dirt floor. When the bags were empty, he took them to the far wall and draped them over a tool bench. Returning to Laura, he silently reached for her slicker, and without a word she let him slip it from her shoulders. He pulled up one of the long shaving horses and positioned it near the hearth, where warmth already spread. The bench was four feet long, widened at one end to form a seat, the opposite end rising like a hunter's bow, forming the wooden clamp for holding the stave in place with a foot pedal. He swung a leg over and sat down at the wide end, then reached up a hand to Laura in invitation. Her gaze, of its own accord, dropped to his lap when he'd spread his knees wide to straddle the bench. Color flared in her face, and she diverted her gaze to his waiting hand, then placed her own in it, and let him pull her down to sit before him, her body at a right angle to his, with both knees touching only one of his thighs. He touched her face with his fingertips, seeming to search it avidly before kissing first one eyelid, then the other.

"I've missed you," he whispered so softly it might have been only the hiss of the fire.

"I've missed you, too." She snuggled against his pea jacket.

"You didn't tell Dan, did you?"

She shook her head, no.

"When I saw you together, I felt . . ." His whisper floundered, but his eyes were stormy, looking down into hers.

"What . . . tell me what you felt." Her hand lay on his chest. She felt his heart driving hard against it.

"Jealous," he admitted, "for the first time ever."

"Silly Rye," she whispered, and kissed his chin. "You never have to be jealous of Dan."

They kissed then, but in the middle of it the bracings overhead creaked, startling them apart. Their eyes turned toward the dark beamed ceiling, and they held their breaths. But no further sound came, and their eyes moved once again to each other. The fire was warm now, and Laura wondered why Rye hadn't removed his jacket. But with the next kiss she understood as he led her hand to the warmth between his open legs, hidden in the shadows behind his heavy garment, should anyone intrude.

"Laura . . ." he begged in a shaky whisper, "can I touch you again?"

"Not here, Rye. They'll catch us," she whispered.

"No they won't. They don't know you're here with me." He pulled her into his arms and slid her up firmly against his open legs, and she was immediately tempted.

"But what if they come?"

"Shh, just turn around here and lean back against me. We'll hear them coming, and if they do, go over and sit on the other shaving horse as if we were just warming up by the fire." He turned her until her back rested against his chest. "Swing your leg over," he ordered behind her ear.

Her leg went over the shaving horse and his hand up under her skirts, scarcely hesitating at the button before finding her feminine warmth with one hand and her breast with the other. She squirmed back against him, listening to his harsh breathing beside her ear, grasping his knees as the delight of sexuality kindled again at his touch. But when he touched a strangely sensitive spot, she jerked upright and sucked in a breath, trying to escape.

"Laura, don't pull away."

"I can't help it."

"Shh. Charles told me how to do something to you, but you have to sit still while I try it."

"Wh . . . what?"

"Shh . . ." he soothed, and again she settled back against him, but stiffly. He murmured softly in her ear, "Be still, Laura-love. Charles says you'll like it."

"No . . . no, stop, Rye, it . . . it . . ."

But her objections died aborning, and she leaned her head back against his shoulder as his touch seemed to rob her of the will to move or speak. Her breasts rose and fell deeply as his caress worked some sort of magic. And in a few short minutes she felt her body quicken with the same sort of rhythmic quaking Rye's had. Something tightened the tips of her toes, worked its way up the backs of her legs like creeping fire, and a minute later her body was convulsed by a series of inner explosions that stunned her, shook her, and brought a groan to her lips. Then Rye was clamping his free hand over her mouth to stifle the sound while, in the throes of ecstasy, she gripped his knees with her finger.

She tried to speak his name behind his palm, but he held her prisoner in a world so exquisite, her body was shattered with delight. The undulations grew, peaked, and were suddenly stilled.

She became foggily aware of a dim pain and realized Rye's teeth had clamped on her shoulder. She fell back into a panting near swoon, her limbs overcome by a tiredness such as she'd never imagined.

"Rye . . ." But his hand was still over her mouth. She reached to free her lips and whispered, "Rye . . . oh, Rye, what did you do?"

His voice shook. "Charles says . . ." He swallowed. "Charles says that's what you do if you don't want to have babies. Did you like it?"

"At first no, but then . . ." She pressed a kiss on his callused fingers. "Oh, then," she crooned, quite unable to express her new, soaring discovery.

"What was it like?"

"Like . . . like I was in both heaven and hell at once." But at the mention of hell, Laura sobered and straightened. Her voice became edged with guilt. "It's a sin, though, Rye. It's . . . it's what they call fornication, isn't it? I never knew what it meant before when—"

"Laura—" He swung her around by the shoulders, taking her jaw in both hands, rubbing her cheeks with his thumbs.

"Laura, we have to wait three years before we can get married."

Her brown eyes met his blue ones with a new understanding. "Yes, I know."

She knew also that morality weighed little against this newfound heaven-hell, for they had found a way . . . together. And they would be man and wife, just as they had pretended to be as children, when Rye had stalked off to sea with a kiss good-bye. Only there would be no good-byes after they were married, just hellos each morning, noon, and night.

And so they told themselves as they bounded through that wild, wicked, wonderful spring, pleasuring each other countless times without fulfilling the act of love. In the old boathouse, out in the dory, on the borders of Gibbs Pond within sweet groves of Virginia creeper, and in the stands of beech trees that grew in the protected shallows of the hilly heathlands, which became their playground.

They fled to privacy each chance they got, scattering herds of grazing sheep as they raced, laughing, across hilly pastures—carefree nymphs learning more and more about love as each day passed, running through the salt air of summer, bound for more of each other, yet never quite getting enough.

Chapter 7

The same memories had been plaguing Rye Dalton in the cooperage on Water Street; Laura was rarely absent from his thoughts. After the meeting with her in the orchard, he threw himself into his work with reckless zeal, pressing his body to limits he had no right to expect of it as two weeks passed, and then three, and he heard nothing from her.

But she was there before him even while he shaved away with a drawknife or hunched his shoulders over the howel or cranked the windlass about the resisting staves of a barrel to draw them in tight. She was there before him, her face beckoning, body bending. He saw her features in the grain of wood, imagined the outline of her breasts as he ran his fingers delicately along the bowed edge of a stave. When he wound the ropes of the windlass around the flaring barrel staves to cinch them together for banding with a hoop, he imagined her waist being tightly cinched by lacings, knowing it was Dan who did that daily.

And it was all he could do to keep from flinging the windlass aside and marching up the hill to claim her. But she had asked him for time, and though he wondered how much she would need, he'd do her bidding in the hope that she'd eventually come to a decision in his favor.

There was, for Rye, a modicum of contentment in being back at the cooperage again, toiling beside his father, bending to labor in the sweet-scented confines of the place where he'd grown up.

On foggy days there was always a fragrant blaze in the fireplace, with never an end of wood scraps to supply it. Josiah, when he finished a cedar pail, would set the tailings aside and dole them into the fire prudently, just often enough to provide a steady fragrance that wafted through the air like incense, to mingle with his pipe smoke.

On sunny days the wide double doors were thrown open to the street and the scent of lilacs drifted in to accent the aromas of wood, both wet and dry. There was a steady passing of townspeople, many of whom stepped inside for a brief greeting and to welcome Rye back. Everyone knew of the curious situation to which he had returned, yet not a soul mentioned it; they only watched and waited to see what would come of it.

The old man asked no questions either, but Josiah was shrewd enough to note the growing restlessness that made Rye jumpy and distracted. Tolerance was not Rye's long suit, and his father wondered how long it would take before things came to a head.

It was early June, a sparkling day of flawless blue sky and warm sun, when the old man took a midmorning break, shuffling to the open doorway to puff at his pipe and flex his back. ''Takin' that boy long enough to get back with them hoops,'' Josiah commented in his rich New England drawl. He spoke of his brother's boy, Chad Dalton, his newest apprentice, who was off to the smithy to fetch a pair of hoops. But now that Rye was back, the lad slacked off at times, taking advantage of his Uncle Josiah's good mood.

Rye didn't even look up, which scarcely surprised Josiah. His son was standing at the fixed blade of a five-foot-long jointer plane, drawing the edge of a stave across it. It took keen judgment, a steady hand, and your eyes on your work to shape every edge identical. No, it didn't bother Josiah that Rye didn't look up; what bothered him was that he didn't even seem to hear.

''Said it's takin' that boy long enough to get back with them hoops!'' Josiah repeated louder.

At last Rye's hands stilled and he glanced up, frowning. ''I heard you, old man, or is it y'r ears goin' bad?''

''Not a thing wrong with m' ears. Just don't like talkin' to m'self.''

''Boy's probably rollin' those hoops the opposite direction from Gordon's smithy—you know a boy and a hoop.'' Again Rye set to planing.

''Had in mind t' send him after some fresh oranges from the square—just come in from Sicily. Time he gets here, oranges'll be rottin' in the noon sun.'' Even from here Josiah could hear the calls of the vendors on Main Street Square, where the daily market was in full swing.

"Go get 'em yourself. Do y' good t' take a walk and get out of here for a few minutes."

Josiah, his back still to the cooperage, puffed his pipe and watched ladies pass with baskets over their arms. "Knees're a little stiff today—can't imagine why m' rheumatism's actin' up on a clear day like this." He scanned the flawless blue skies. "Must be foul weather blowin' in."

Behind him, Rye measured the shaped length of wood with a stave gauge. Ignoring the old man's hint, he studied it critically, found it to his liking, and took up a finished stave to compare the two. Finding them perfectly matched, he tossed them onto a completed stack and chose another rough-hewn piece to begin edging.

In the doorway, Josiah slipped his fingers between waistband and shirt back, rocked back on his heels, and complained to the azure sky, "Ayup! Sure could go for a fresh orange about now." A loud clatter sounded behind him as Rye flung the board down. Josiah smiled to himself.

"All right, if y' want me t' run to the damn market for your oranges, why don't y' just say so?"

Now Josiah turned his squint-eye back to his son. "Gittin' a little twitchy lately, ain't cha?"

Rye ignored him as he clumped across the cooperage and brushed around the older man with irritation in every step.

"Looks t' me like it's you needs gettin' outa here for a while, not me."

"I'm going! I'm going!" Rye barked.

When he stomped off up the street, Josiah smiled again, puffed his pipe, and muttered, "Ayup, y' sure are, boy—to-hell-in-a-rowboat crazy, and drivin' me right with y'."

Rye Dalton made an impressive sight storming along the cobbled street in close-fitting tan breeches and a drop-shouldered shirt of white cotton with wide sleeves gathered full at the wrist. The open collar left a deep vee of exposed skin behind the buttonless garment, and coarse gold hairs sparkled there against his dark flesh. Around his neck a red bandana was tied sailor fashion, the habit adopted from his shipmates and continued now, for the bandana was convenient for swabbing his temples when he sweated in the cooperage.

It was a warm morning, filled with the sounds of exuberant gulls and the grinding of wheels along the streets as Rye jumped around the tail of a passing wagon and leaped to the new, cobbled sidewalk. The wind ruffled his sun-streaked hair, whipped his full sleeves as he strode, long-legged and angry, toward Market Square.

Farmers were selling fresh flowers and butter from big-wheeled wooden carts. Fishermen peddled fresh cod, herring, and oysters while butchers kept fresh meat covered with heavy wet cloths in the backs of drays. At one end of the square, an auctioneer called out his gibberish as furniture and household items went up for sale.

Rye scanned the vendors until he spotted the bright splashes of citrus fruits—limes, lemons, and oranges piled in pyramids on the wagons, creating a tempting array of colors. The scent was heavenly, the fruit always coveted, for it was available only seasonally.

Rye took a long-legged step off the curb and took up a shiny-skinned orange, his mouth watering as he grudgingly admitted the old man was right—the fruit was tempting, and it was good to get out into the fresh air and activity of the market. There was a steady mingling of voices, the sharp staccato of the auctioneer, the indolent calls of wagon owners, and the musical hum of shoppers exchanging pleasantries, while over it all the gulls interjected their demands for scraps of fish, crumbs of bread, or anything else they might scavenge.

Rye squeezed the orange, selected another, and put it to his nose to sniff its pungent fruitiness, telling himself he'd be mellower to the old man; it wasn't Josiah's fault that Rye was in this damnable predicament. The old man had been more than patient with him during the past couple of weeks when Rye's temper flared or he became brooding and silent. He smiled now, in resolution, making his selections from the pyramid of fruit. He had chosen three flawless oranges when a voice at his elbow purred, "Why, Mr. Dalton, you out doing the daily marketing?"

"Miss Hussey . . . good morning," he greeted, turning at the sound of her voice. She peered up at him from beneath the crescent of a lavender bonnet brim, a becoming smile on her face.

"Aye, the old man had a cravin' and thinks I'm still an apprentice in knee-pants." He laughed indulgently.

She laughed, too, and turned to the selection of oranges for herself. "My mother sent me out for the same reason."

"I have t' admit they're temptin'. I can't wait t' peel one m'self." He grinned mischievously and angled her a glance. "'Course, don't tell the old man that or he'll have me runnin' down here every mornin' like a housemaid."

"If you had a wife, Mr. Dalton, you wouldn't have to worry about running to the market for oranges."

"I have a wife, Miss Hussey, but it doesn't seem t' do me much good."

It was out before he could stop it, but immediately he was sorry, for he'd brought a most unbecoming blush to DeLaine Hussey's cheeks, and he could see she was at a loss for something to say. She quickly became intense about her selection of oranges and refused to meet his eyes. He touched her hand briefly. "I apologize, Miss Hussey. Five years at sea, and I forget m' manners. I've made y' uncomfortable. That was a most indulgent thing for me t' say."

"It's true nevertheless. The whole town's wondering what she means to do about it, though, living up there in your house with your best friend . . ." But she stammered to a halt, her eyes widening in surprise as she stared at the woman and boy who'd quietly appeared on the other side of the wagon.

Rye noticed Laura a second too late, but immediately withdrew his hand from DeLaine Hussey's. Next to her overblown dressiness, Laura was a vision of feminine simplicity, standing in the sun with the brim of a becoming yellow bonnet angling over her face, a large satin bow caught just below one ear. Her dress was narrow-waisted, but she wore no billowing hoops today, and he couldn't help but wonder if she was pinched up in stays—she was thin enough that he could not tell by looking.

She held the hand of the boy tightly, and while Rye stared at Laura, he forgot everything but the welcome sight of her. Suddenly seeming to remember the presence of the other woman, he stepped back as if to acknowledge her, but before he could, Laura smiled and said, ''Hello, Miss Hussey. It's nice to see you again.''

In a pig's eyes, Laura thought all the while she beamed at the woman. She was very conscious that Rye's hand had been on DeLaine's.

''Hello,'' DeLaine replied shortly, a sour expression on her face.

''Hello, Rye,'' Laura said then, turning her bonnet brim up to him, hoping DeLaine Hussey could not tell the way her heart suddenly flew to her throat at the sight of him, tall and handsome and looking good enough to eat right along with those three oranges he held in his wide-spread palm. The sun tinted his blue eyes bluer and glanced off the narrow slit of exposed chest, turning it to rich gold behind the white shirt.

''Hello, Laura,'' he managed, oranges and DeLaine Hussey completely forgotten as he took in the face that had haunted him night and day.

Laura's expression instantly gave away her feelings, for her pink lips suddenly lost their smile and fell open slightly. Her eyes, refusing to obey her edict of caution, stared widely into his before fluttering to his bronze chest, then back up. And she'd squeezed Josh's hand so hard, he now squirmed and howled, then yanked free.

Reminded of the boy's presence, Rye smiled down at him. ''Hello, Josh.''

''You're the man with the funny name.''

''Aye, and do y' remember it?''

''It's Rye.''

''Aye, it is. So next time I'll expect a proper hello when I meet y'.''

But again he turned his eyes to Laura, and she could not resist asking sweetly, ''Are the two of you shopping for oranges?''

Rye colored deeply, the flush barely discernible on his face, which was already tanned to the shade of an old copper penny, darker than Laura ever remembered seeing it before the voyage of the *Omega*.

''Ah, no . . . well, I mean, yes, I was out buyin' oranges for Josiah.''

''And I was out buying oranges for my mother,'' Miss Hussey put in, a pinched expression about her mouth.

''And we was out buyin' oranges for Papa,'' Josh piped innocently.

At the word, Rye's mouth sobered, and he studied Laura's face.

DeLaine Hussey noted the exchange of glances, but remained stubbornly at Rye's side.

''Well, how about if we all have one now—my treat,'' Rye offered, unable to think of any other way to ease the tension.

''Mmm . . . I *like* oranges!'' Josh exclaimed, bright-eyed and eager.

''Then which one will it be?''

It was plain to Laura that Rye was suddenly as eager as Josh. He looked at the chubby hands that touched every orange as if it mattered a great deal which was chosen. And this first innocent encounter beneath the bright June sun in the bustling market square suddenly seemed representative of all the experiences of fatherhood Rye had missed. Laura hadn't the heart to deny him such a small joy. His eyes shone with delight when Josh finally picked an orange and plopped it into Rye's big hand with a ''There!'' as if he'd solved a great and important riddle.

Rye laughed, jubilant and handsome and capturing Laura's heart as she watched his dark, lean fingers tear into the orange skin for his son.

DeLaine Hussey, feeling a complete outsider in this little scene *en famille,* decided it was time to withdraw and aimed a flashing good-bye to Rye, and to Laura a nod so brisk it was undeniably rude.

No sooner was she out of earshot than Rye caught Laura's eye. "I've been wondering when I'd see you again," he said, extremely aware of the understatement, and quelling the urge to touch her.

"I come to the market every morning," she said.

"Every mornin'?" he repeated, cursing himself for wasting all these opportunities.

"Hey, hurry up, Rye!" Josh demanded, seeing that the peeling process had suddenly slowed while Rye and Laura indulged themselves with the sight of each other's faces.

"Aye-aye!" Rye snapped nautically, tearing his attention away from Laura long enough to finish the job. He handed half an orange to Josh, then began sectioning the rest, his eyes again on her.

She watched each dexterous movement of his fingers, the square nails separating the delicate filaments so expertly that not a drop of juice escaped. Hands, hands, she thought, there is no forgetting hands.

Just then one of his came toward her, offering a bright crescent of fruit. Her eyes flew to his. It was nothing, she thought, just a piece of an orange, so why was there a little drum tattooing the message through her veins that she was answering some unspoken innuendo as she reached breathlessly for Rye's offering?

Without taking his eyes from hers, he lifted a section of orange to his lips. They opened in slow motion to receive the ripe, plump fruit, and as he bit down, a succulent spurt of orange juice flew into the warm, summer air.

As if mesmerized, she answered by lifting her own delicacy, tasting old memories as she bit into its sweetness, her every sense heightened by awareness of the man before her.

In his turn he ate a second piece, and this time a sweet rivulet of juice drizzled down his chin, and her eyes followed it, unable to do otherwise.

Suddenly he laughed and broke the spell, Laura following suit, while he untied the red bandana from about his throat and wiped his chin, then offered it to her.

It smelled of salt and cedar and of him as she brushed her lips with it. He peeled another orange for Josh, whose eyes were too busy to note the looks being exchanged between his mother and the tall cooper.

"So y' come to the market every mornin'?" Rye asked.

"Well, almost. We come to get milk, Josh and I."

"And I carry it, too," Josh declared proudly, backhanding his orangy lips, making them both laugh down at him.

Something powerfully sweet swelled Rye's heart. He'd missed being this child's father, didn't even know if it was a great accomplishment for a four-year-old to safely carry a pitcher of milk. But it was heady learning, sharing such first revelations with the boy.

"You do!" Rye exclaimed, bending down to test Josh's biceps. "I can see why. Y've a fine set o' muscles in that arm. Y' must've been haulin' traps or pullin' rigging."

Josh laughed gaily. "I ain't old enough for that yet, but when I get big like my papa, I'm gonna be a whaler."

Rye's eyes flashed briefly to Laura's, then back to their son. "Whalers get mighty lonesome out there on the big ships, Josh, and sometimes they miss out on lots of fun, bein' gone so much of the time. Maybe you'd be better off bein' a clerk like . . . like y'r papa."

"Naw, I don't like it in the countinghouse. It's dark in there, and you can't hear the waves as good." Then, with typical childish caprice, Josh scarcely paused as he changed subject. "I wanna hear the auctioneer, Mama. Can I go over and listen to him?" He squinted up at her.

Aware of Rye suddenly turning pleading eyes to her, aware of her own heart thumping away in double time, Laura knew it was safer to keep Josh beside her, yet answered as her heart dictated. For what could happen out here in the middle of Market Square? "All right, but stay right there until I come for you, and don't go anywhere else."

"Aye-aye!" he answered, imitating Rye, then scampering away toward the lower end of the square.

Rye's gaze followed the boy. Softly, he said, "Ah, but he's bonny."

"Yes . . . yes, he is."

They were alone now, but hesitated to look at each other or say another word. Laura sought equilibrium in the oranges, turning to test them, selecting some to place in her drawstring bag. But while her hand moved from fruit to fruit, Rye's hovered beside it, doing likewise. He squeezed one, took it away, then squeezed another, but at last his hand fell still. A long motionless moment passed before Laura looked up to find his eyes upon her, full of her, taking their fill now as they hadn't been able to while Delaine and Josh had been with them.

His gaze moved up to the tiny springing curls beneath her bonnet brim, then to her lips, softly parted, and to her brown eyes, which seemed caught in his. "Jesus, but I've missed you," he breathed.

Her lips fell open further, and she stammered, "D . . . don't say that, Rye."

"It's the truth."

"But better left unsaid."

"And now I can be miserable thinking about the boy as well?"

But she was as miserable as he at the thought. She'd read his longing plainly enough in each glance he'd given Josh, each exchange of words they'd shared, and the small insignificant gift of peeled orange: a father's first offering to his son.

"Rye, I'm sorry."

"He's dreamin' of makin' the same mistakes I've made."

"He has a good fath . . . a good man to steer him."

"Aye, he does, and it cuts me t' the quick t' know it."

"Rye, please don't. You're only making it harder."

Momentarily, he glanced at the brick building across the square where even now Dan Morgan worked at his desk. "Have y' talked to him yet? Have y' told him . . . asked him . . ."

She shook her head, chin lowering, oranges suddenly becoming blurred by tears. "I can't. It would kill him to lose Josh now."

"And what about me? Josh is my son—have y' had a thought for what I'm feelin'?"

"I've had a thousand thoughts for what you're feeling, Rye." She raised tormented eyes and he saw tears sparkling on her lashes. "But if you could see the two of them together—"

"I have! I do! I see them in my nightmares, just the way they were the day I came home. But it doesn't alter the fact that I want t' be his father now, though it's four years late I'll be startin'."

"I've got to go, Rye. We've been together too long as it is. Dan is sure to find out about it."

"Wait!" He reached out quickly to stay her with a wide hand on her yellow sleeve. Shivers radiated through her from his touch. Reading her reaction in those brown, startled eyes, he immediately withdrew his hand. "Wait," he entreated more softly. "Will y' meet me here in the market tomorrow mornin'? I've somethin' to give y' . . . somethin' I made for y'."

"I can't accept gifts from you. Dan will ask questions."

"He'll know nothin' about this one. Please."

She looked up to find his face filled with pain and longing, just above hers, and wondered if it was not just a matter of time before she gave in to him—all the way in. She backed up a step, guilty for the thought, once again withdrawing to a safe distance, yet unable to deny his request. "We'd best not meet at the oranges again."

He glanced around, searching the crowded square. "Have y' planted y'r garden yet?"

"Most of it . . . not all."

"Do y' need seeds?"

"Parsnips."

"I'll meet y' by the flower carts. They sell seeds there, too."

"All right."

Their eyes clung for a last look.

"Y' won't disappoint me, now, will y', Laura-love?"

She swallowed, wanting nothing so much as to fling her arms about his neck and kiss him right here, and the whole square be damned.

"No, I won't disappoint you, Rye, but I must go now." She turned away, her heart knowing a delight it had not felt in years, that rapturous torture of first love happening all over again. The giddiness of secret meetings, of sharing small intimacies under the noses of others. How often they'd dared such things in years past. To do so again was dangerous, yet the idea seduced Laura in a way that made her feel more vibrant, more alive, then she'd been since Rye Dalton had sailed away.

When she'd taken a mere three steps, his voice came softly from behind her. "Bring the boy. I've known too little of him, too."

Without turning around, she nodded, then headed for the lower square.

Josiah noted the difference in Rye but offered no comment as his son sauntered into the cooperage, flipping three oranges up for grabs in quick succession, almost faster than Josiah could nab them. "There, y' old sea dog. Y' needn't worry about the scurvy catchin' up with y' now. Is the boy back yet?"

"Ayup, and gone again. I fear he's takin' advantage of me, but I've got a soft old heart, as y' well know, lettin' all m' help run out in the sun and leavin' me here to molder in the shadows of the place and carry on business without a bit o' help.'' Josiah chuckled softly.

''I've an errand for Chad t' run when he comes back, so keep him under y'r thumb next time he chooses t' darken the doorway for a minute.''

When Chad returned, Josiah pretended to pay no attention as Rye fished a penny from his pocket and ordered, ''I want y' to run t' the apothecary on Federal Street and fetch me as many sarsaparilla sticks as this will buy. And have one y'rself, but don't break the rest while y're dallyin' on the way back t' work.''

He had promised Laura that Dan wouldn't find out about what he had for her, but he'd said not a thing about any treat he might bring to Josh, knowing full well word of sarsaparilla sticks would reach Dan's ears. If he couldn't get Laura to make the first move toward separation from Dan, maybe he could get Dan to.

That night Rye opened his sea chest, still thinking of the sight of Laura and the boy standing in the sun against a backdrop of bright fruit and a pony cart filled with daisies, lilies, and tulips. It had been so unexpected, looking up to find her there after so many lonely days of searching faces on the streets each time he walked them.

How many times during the past five years had he thought of that face just as it had looked today, with its wide, bright eyes, delicate lips alluringly open, and that look about her that said she still felt the same?

Laura's face had been with him through the empty first days of the voyage while the weight of guilt for leaving her still lay heavy on his soul. It had accompanied him during endless hours of listening to the rush of the curling waters climbing the flared planking of the *Massachusetts*'s bow, washing the wooden knees of the figurehead, the only lady to make the voyage. It had been his reason to exult during the brief hours when a whale was hauled against the side of the ship and he sat on the quarterdeck sharpening spades while the second mate cut away blubber. The scent of her had been his sustenance while he erected barrels, with the sickening stench of half-decomposed blubber filling his nostrils as the trypot sizzled and spat on the deck, melting down fat in various stages of putrefaction. Laura had been the prayer on his lips during the terror-filled days rounding the Horn, when he was certain he would make her not a rich wife but a poor widow.

And during those fevered days of smallpox, when his senses dimmed, Laura had come to him in his delirium, giving him reason to fight for life.

Now, picking from his sea chest a small, flat piece of carved whalebone, he remembered how images of Laura's face and body had guided his hands as he'd filled the worst hours of all, those nerve-racking days considered the most excruciating by any man, be he deck hand or captain, who'd ever sailed a windjammer—the doldrums.

The doldrums, when the fickle wind denied them her breath, leaving the ship to drift motionlessly upon a merciless, windless sea. The doldrums, when the urge for home became agonizing. The doldrums, when wasted days only lengthened the voyage, profiting nothing, bringing a feeling of utter helplessness until tempers flared and vicious fights broke out on board.

He had shared the doldrums with shipmates who fought the lassitude with the only pastime available—scrimshaw. At first when Rye took up a knife to carve the whalebone, he was inept and impatient. The initial pieces he turned out were rough and hardly worth keeping, so he tossed them overboard. But he persisted, with the help of the others, and soon he produced a smooth splicing fid—a pin for separating the strands of a rope—then a walking stick. Next he tried a jewelry casket, and when it was finely polished, its etchings deep and true, the men started teasing him about making a busk, for they knew he'd left a wife ashore.

The busk was a foot-long strip of bone, fingernail-thick, that could be slipped into a casing along the front of a woman's bodice, like a batten on a sail. Its purpose was to uplift, it was extremely personal, and was meant to serve as a reminder to the woman who wore it that she must remain true to her seafaring man until he returned.

Yet for all their teasing, no skrimshander carved any piece as caringly as he did a busk, for in the end it became a vent for his loneliness and his hope for the journey's end.

When Rye finished the busk for Laura, it was smoother than anything he'd done before, and he polished the striated grooves with silicon carbide until it was as satiny as Laura's very breast. He'd carved on it an entwined design of Nantucket wild roses, among which he and Laura had played as children, adding gulls and a delicate scallop-edged heart. Then he deliberated long over the carved message, rephrasing the brief poem for weeks before deciding on the exact words.

Lifting the busk from his sea chest now, he read:

Until upon your rosy breast
My loving lips are fondly press't
Wear thee this token made of bone
And know I long for thee alone.

Never while he'd been carving the busk had Rye dreamed it would take on the poignant relevance it did now. He wondered if she'd bury it deep in some bureau drawer or wear it pressed secretly against her skin.

He thought of her sunlit face this morning beneath the brim of a yellow bonnet and recalled gay shafts of sunlight piercing a succulent section of orange, lighting it to near transparency as her straight white teeth broke it. He remembered her brown eyes and how they'd measured his awareness, and orange juice glistening on her lips. He thought of the way she'd clutched Josh's hand at first, then allowed Rye his first father's privileges.

And his heart swelled with hope.

Chapter 8

Sleep was impossible for Rye that night. Eagerness kept him tossing fitfully until finally, at four A.M., he pulled a thick turtleneck sweater over his head and found his boots in the dark, along with the cold nose of Ship, who woke at the sound of his rustling and came to investigate.

They crept out together to sit on the bottom step while Rye pulled on his boots and whispered, ''What do y' say we climb up the rock like we used to, old girl?''

Ship's tail answered, and her tongue lolled pink from the side of her mouth.

Rye scratched the dog's jaws, then got to his feet, whispering, ''Let's go, girl.''

They walked side by side through the somnolent town, the dog's warm bulk pressed against Rye's leg. The cobblestones were shiny and damp, but they soon left them behind for a sandy street that led eventually to the foot trails of Shawkemo Hills, which were still shrouded in fog as Rye and Ship made their way toward Altar Rock, the highest spot on the island.

They climbed up and sat side by side as they'd done a hundred times before, the rangy man folding his limbs, crossing his calves, and wrapping his knees with both arms, while beside him the dog sat on its haunches. Like a pair of monoliths, they awaited the spectacle they'd many times shared, and as it began the man rested a hand on the dog's back.

Summer was near her solstice, the dawn silent-still. In those last purple minutes before the sun intruded, the harbor lay like a mirror beneath tier upon tier of lavender mist. Between these foggy strata, the undulations of the island appeared like purple mountains whose feet were made of nothing more than the ocean's breath.

Then up stole the sun to peer over the sea's rim and cast her red-hazed eye over Nantucket, transforming those fog arms into lazy, pink limbs, now stretching, now flexing, now moving restlessly, yawning awake in ever widening chasms until the red-gold of morning spilled through.

The harbor's forest of masts was a study in stillness, each craft with its twin lying beside it on the glassy surface of the water.

And for that moment, at least, it seemed that all creatures of earth, sky, and sea waited, as did Rye and his dog—silent, respectful—paying homage to the spectacle of light and color that announced the day.

Then one by one the coots swam out, wrinkling the reflections of masts, spars, and stays in their search for silver minnows. The spotted sandpiper made her first run along the deserted shore, stopping to teeter in her drunken way, as if intoxicated, too, by the show just staged by morning.

Next came the gulls, lazy scavengers awaiting the first moving boat to follow, and with the gulls, their sisters—the terns—awaiting the first moving boat to lead.

Below Rye, the bell in the Congregational church tower tolled its peaceful wake-up peal over the harbor town, and a first catboat eased from its slip, then another and another, heading for the place called the ''cord of the bay,'' just inside the bar, where bluefish schooled now that June was here.

Rye lingered as long as he dared, till his spine grew numb and the dog's stomach growled, along with his own.

The scent of wood smoke drifted up from the fires of blacksmith, candle maker, tryworker, and baker. Soon the repetitive clang of the smith's hammer sounded from below, and the scent of ship's biscuits baking in beehive ovens told Rye he must go.

Reluctantly, he got to his feet and, followed by the yellow Labrador, made his way back down through the heathland to the quayside, where weathered wooden doors were now turned back as shops came to life. He passed the ropewalk, and from within came the rumble of steel wheels riding steel rails as the forming machine rolled backward, twisting yarns of manila into strands of rope. From inside the shop of a ship's carver came the soft rap of hammer on chisel, and farther up the street Rye nodded good morning to the clerk who was tacking up a sign in a window: ''Spermaceti Candles—Exceeding all Others in Beauty and Sweetness of Scent when Extinguished—Duration Double that of Tallow Candles.''

Ah, Nantucket—even though at times he felt trapped by it, he loved it just the same. He had forgotten the beauty of these intermingling sounds and smells and sights that seemed to symbolize the close correlation of all the island's livelihoods.

Rye stopped to buy a roll for his breakfast, ordering Ship to wait outside the shop until he emerged, eating a crispy bun. He offered one to the dog, and took another home for Josiah, who'd just arisen, his cold pipe already between his teeth, awaiting its first tamping of the day.

They set to work together, hooping a thirty-gallon wet barrel whose staves had been soaking overnight. They worked amiably now, for Rye's testy temper of the previous day seemed to have evaporated, replaced by a barely concealed eagerness that Josiah could not quite understand until later that morning, when Rye jogged up the steps to their lodgings above and then returned a few minutes later, whistling, in clean shirt and ducks, his hair neatly brushed.

Offhandedly, he announced, ''Those oranges took the edge off y'r tongue. I'll run out and get y' y'r day's supply.''

''Ayup, y' do that.'' The old one grinned around his pipestem.

This morning his grin was returned as Rye left the cooperage, again whistling, his step sprightly.

For both Laura and Rye it was a heady feeling, walking toward the square to meet. Innocent yet illicit, callow yet knowing; for though they'd been man and wife before and had shared the deepest intimacies of marriage, here they were plunged back to the beginning like sea-green children. As they approached the square from opposite sides, they were reckless spirits, straining toward that first glimpse of one another, hearts hammering, palms damp.

Laura picked out Rye with the canny instinct of a bufflehead diving for plankton. As his blond head moved toward her amid vendors, wares, and shoppers, she suppressed the urge to smile and wave, and the even greater one to hurry toward him.

It was hard to control the smile that wanted to burst over her face at the sight of him advancing, full sleeves luffing in the breeze, head bare to the June sun, his hair already coming in darker at the roots, and his eyebrows losing their bleached look even after so few weeks away from sea. And on his dark-skinned face she read the anticipation he, too, strained to conceal.

At his approach her heart went weightless, lifting with a fluttering expectancy every bit as poignant as during those long-ago days in the loft when they were learning together the thrill of first love.

''Hello,'' he said, as if it were not the most glorious day ever created.

''Hello,'' she answered, fingers trailing in a bin of parsnip seeds, as if parsnip seeds mattered in the least.

''It's nice to see you again.'' I love you! You're beautiful.

''And you.'' I cannot forget. I feel the same.

''Hi, Rye.'' It was Josh, looking up. The man went down on one knee, producing the sarsaparilla sticks.

''Hello, Joshua. Did y' come to hear the auctioneer again?''

Josh beamed, his eyes whipping from the candy to Rye's face, then back again as he answered, ''Aye.''

Rye laughed with fatherly ebullience. '' 'Aye,' is it? Yesterday it was 'yes.' ''

''I like aye better.''

Pleased, Rye gave the lad the treat and ordered, ''Well, be off with y', then. I'll keep an eye on y'r mother.''

Immediately, Josh darted away. Laura studied Rye as he knelt with an elbow braced on a knee, his full white sleeve drooping on a tight blue trouser leg.

Just then he looked up at her and slowly straightened to his full height to stand beside her and savor the look of her, her brown eyes agleam before her gaze dropped again to the parsnip seeds.

''I've brought it,'' he said softly, eyeing the square to make sure they were not being listened to or watched.

''Oh?'' She tipped her head aside and peered up at him, then back at the seeds. When she refrained from asking what the gift was, he teased her by delaying the giving.

''Y' have a lovely bonnet today.''

''Thank you.''

''And a lovely set o' curls peepin' around it.''

''Thank you.''

''And the prettiest mouth I've seen t'day.'' It tipped up at the corners while her cheeks nurtured roses.

''Thank you.''

''And I wouldn't mind kissin' it again as soon as possible.''

''Rye Dalton, stop that!'' She, too, looked around warily.

He laughed and captured her hand in the bin of parsnip seeds.

"What is it you've brought for me?" she couldn't resist asking at last.

He slipped the busk from inside his full sleeve and partially concealed the exchange under the seeds. Her color grew rosier as she hid it in her sleeve, unable to read what he'd written on it until she was alone.

"Oh, Rye, a busk!" Her eyelids flew up and she touched a fingertip to her throat.

"Will y' wear it?"

"I . . . it's very—"

"Personal," he finished.

"Yes." She demurely studied the seeds.

"And intimate."

"Yes."

She let her hand drift along to the bin of pumpkin seeds while he continued, "Like my feelings for you when I made it . . . like my feelings for you right now." He studied her forehead in the shadow of her bonnet, wishing she would meet his eyes again.

"Shh, Rye, someone will hear you."

"Aye, they well might, so tell me you'll wear it or I'll shout t' the square at large that Mrs. Daniel Morgan's got somethin' up her sleeve and it's a scrimshawed busk carved by Rye Dalton."

His willful teasing made Laura delight in being with him. Now she smiled prettily, raising her eyes, which had a teasing glint of their own. "And just what did you write on it?"

"What was on m' mind from the minute I sailed away from y'."

"Will it make me blush?"

"I hope so."

It did, when she got home later. She read the verse with a curious mingling of guilt and arousal; nevertheless, she secretly sewed the busk into its casing, where it rested intimately between her breasts through the days that followed. To have such words pressed against her skin did, indeed, keep her aware of Rye's wish to possess her again, and forbidden though it was to dwell on the thought, she did. She was woman, and carnal, and having the busk touch her was like having Rye touch her, tempt her, every minute of the day.

"I'm wearing it," she volunteered breathlessly the next time they met.

His eyes lit up with a knowing glint, and he lazily examined her bodice while the new dimple creased his right cheek. "Show me where."

She interlaced her fingers, folded her arms between her breasts, and rested her chin on her knuckles while all about them fishmongers sold 'blues.' "Here."

"How soon can I take it off y'?" he asked, raising her color to a very telling hue.

"Rye Dalton, you've not changed one bit."

"Thank God, no!" He laughed, then sobered only a little. "When?"

"You're harassing me."

"It's me bein' harassed. I want to take y' up into the bayberries and crush a few while I do what I wrote on that busk . . . and more." Her flustration was his only reward as she blushed prettily and turned away to buy butter.

There followed a heady string of sun-swelled days during which Rye and

Laura met that way, hearts, thoughts, and eyes communicating even before they reached each other across the square. They gave themselves these meetings as consolation, neither asking where the encounters were leading. They never touched—they couldn't. And they never met privately—they dared not. But their eyes spoke messages that voices could not, except on those rare days when they were gifted with a few sterling minutes alone. Then, the brief intimacies they spoke threatened to undo them.

Summer came on full, enticing them to roam the island's beloved floral landscape as they had years ago. In the village of Siasconset tame ivy thickened and greened upon the small silvery cottages of 'Sconset's narrow lanes while poison ivy climbed merrily up the trunks of scrub pines in the wilds. Bayberry and heather carpeted the heath while in the swamps and lowlands the wax myrtle glistened. The delicate lavender blossoms of the trailing arbutus, nicknamed the mayflower by the Pilgrims who'd first found it, gave way to the fragrant blooms of pasture roses. Marsh marigolds burst forth like droplets of sun fallen to earth while the higher slopes broke out in Solomon's seal and false spikenard.

Laura and Rye, meanwhile, hovered on the brink of accepting the invitation of the hills that seduced them with the promise of privacy. But before privacy became theirs, Dan Morgan paid a call at the cooperage.

Rye, his back to the door, was arranging the staves of a slack barrel into a temporary hoop when he heard Josiah say, ''Well, been some time since I seen you, young feller.''

''Hello, Josiah. You've been well, I hope.'' But Dan's eyes were on Rye, who continued working without turning around.

''Got no complaints. Business is good, fog's been scarce.''

Dan directed his glance back to Josiah. ''Working on the order for the *Omega*'s next voyage?''

''Aye, we are,'' the old man confirmed, then, following Dan's glance back to Rye, he decided it would be provident to quietly disappear for a while.

Silence fell as Rye set the final two staves in a wooden band that held them at the bottom while they flared out on top like the petals of a daisy.

''Could I talk to you a minute, Rye?'' Dan asked with strained courtesy.

The cooper glanced up briefly, then back down at his work. He took up a windlass to loop its rope about the petallike staves. ''Aye, go ahead.'' He began cranking the windlass handle and felt Dan move close behind him while the ropes began squeakily closing up the daisy petals.

''Word has it you've been seeing Laura in the square each day.''

''We've run into each other a time or two.''

''A time or two? That's not the way I've heard it.''

''Might have been a few times, come t' think of it.'' With each turn of the crank the staves cinched closer, the rope drawn as taut as the facial muscles of the visitor.

''I want it stopped!'' Dan ordered.

''We've talked in the square before a hundred watchful eyes and with the boy right there beside us.''

''People still talk—it's a small town.''

The staves were now joined, ballooning out at the middle. Rye reached for a permanent metal hoop, placed it around them, and tapped it down with mallet and drift. ''Aye, it is, and they all know she's my wife.''

''Not anymore she's not. I want you to stay away from her.''

At last Rye's hands fell still, and his eyes met Dan's. ''And what's she had t' say about that?''

Dan paled and his jaws tensed. ''What's between us is none of your business.''

''What's between y' is my son, and plenty of my business.'' This was one fact Dan Morgan could not deny and the one that sent fear piercing through him. His voice trembled slightly. ''You'd use him to try to get her away from me?''

Rye spun away angrily and flung the tools onto a high tool bench with a clatter. ''Damnit, what do y' take me for, Dan? He has no idea I'm his father. I've no wish to turn the boy against y', nor t' make him pick between us. She's only brought him t' the square so I could see a little of him, talk to him, get acquainted.''

''He tells me you bring him candy sticks, and the other day he showed me a whale's tooth he said you carved for him.''

''Aye, I gave it to him, I'll not deny it, but if y' were in my place, could y' keep yourself from doin' the same?''

Their eyes met, Rye's expression defensive, Dan's angry. Nevertheless a shaft of grudging guilt shot through Dan, followed by a lonely premonition of what it would be like if he himself were asked to withdraw as the boy's father. But he went on sternly.

''Since the day Josh was born, I've watched him grow up. I was there beside Laura that day while you were off to sea, where she'd begged you not to go. I was there for his christening, and when he got sick for the first time and she needed moral support and somebody to talk her fears away. And after we were married, I took my turn walking the floors with him at night when he got whooping cough and teeth and earaches and the . . . the hundred things that make babies cry! I was there for his first birthday, and every birthday after that, while you were off . . . *whaling!*'' Now Dan turned away. ''And I never once loved him less because he was yours. Maybe I loved him more because of it, wanting to make up to him for the fact that he'd . . . lost you.''

Rye glared at Dan's shoulders. ''So what do y' want now? My thanks, is it? Well, y've got 'em, but not the right to keep me from seeing him.''

Again Dan swung around angrily. ''And her along with him?''

Their eyes clashed while they faced off, one on each side of a half-made barrel, then suddenly Rye swung to work again, flipping the barrel over to begin hooping its other end. ''I said I expected you t' fight for her, so did y' expect any less of me? Be happy I haven't come up there t' claim that bed y' take her to—it belongs to me, too, y' know.''

The cruel barb stung, and immediately Dan retaliated. ''And I think it's all you want her for, judging from things I remember.''

''Damnit, man, you go too far!'' Rye Dalton roared, his fists bunching as he took one menacing step forward, the mallet still in his right hand.

''Do I? Do you think I was so ignorant I didn't know what the two of you did together all those times you ran off alone when we were sixteen? Do you think I didn't suffer, wanting her then while I watched her scamper after you as if I weren't even alive? But if you think I'll let her do it again, you're sorely mistaken, Dalton. She's mine now, and I paid dearly, waiting to have her to myself.''

Anger and embarrassment bubbled up in Rye, for like most who've stolen kisses, he never suspected others had guessed. ''I love her,'' he said unequivocably.

''You left her.''

''I'm back. Suppose we let her make the choice?''

''I'm her legal choice, and I intend to see to it these meetings stop.''

Almost nonchalantly now, Rye picked up a hand adz and began evening off the irregular ends of the staves. ''Y've a right t' try,'' he granted. ''Good luck.''

Having gained no more than he'd expected, Dan gave up, frustrated by the fact that Rye denied nothing and was waging a fair fight, frustrated even further by the fear that his rival might win. He turned on his heel and strode angrily out the door, swinging past Josiah, who sat indolently on an upturned keg out front.

When Josiah went back inside, he found Rye wielding the adz with a vengeance, all semblance of nonchalance now gone. The old man puffed on his pipe, watching wordlessly while the scowl on Rye's face warned that his temper was strained.

But it was nothing compared to the rage spawned later that day, when one Ezra J. Merrill appeared at the double doors and stepped diffidently inside. ''Good day, Josiah.'' He sounded nervous.

''Ezra.'' The grizzled cooper nodded. His eyes narrowed as he watched Ezra looking about for Rye, who was working in the rear of the shop. ''Somethin' I can do for y'?''

''Actually, I'm here to see Rye.''

''Well, there he is.''

Ezra cleared his throat and moved toward Rye, who stopped tapping a barrel bottom into place and looked back over his shoulder. ''Hello, Ezra.'' Rye turned, the hammer still in his hand. ''Need something made?''

Again Ezra cleared his throat. ''N . . . no, actually. I'm here in an official capacity. I've been hired by Dan . . . er, Daniel Morgan, that is, to act on his behalf.''

The hand holding the hammer tightened perceptibly upon its handle. Ezra's eyes shifted downward nervously, then back up.

''What the hell's he up t' now?''

''Are you the owner of a saltbox house at the end of the lane commonly called Crooked Record?''

Rye glanced at his father, then back at the lawyer. His eyebrows were drawn down into a scowl. ''Well, for God's sake, Ezra, you know as well as I do that I own that house. Everybody on the island knows I own it.''

Ezra Merrill's face was as red as an autumn apple. ''I've been authorized by Daniel Morgan to make you an offer of seven hundred dollars for the purchase of the house, exclusive of any furnishings within it that have been there five years or more, which you are free to take.''

The cooperage seemed to crackle in the silence before a storm.

"*You what!*" Rye growled, took a step toward Ezra, grinding the head of the hammer against his palm.

"I've been authorized to make you an offer—"

"The house is not for sale!" Rye barked.

"Mr. Morgan has instructed me to—"

"You go back and tell Dan Morgan my house is not for sale any more than my wife is!" Rye raged, now advancing on the retreating Ezra, whose mouth was pursed tightly while his eyes blinked rapidly in fright.

"You . . . I . . . shall I tell . . . er, Mr. Morgan, then, that you are rejecting his offer?"

The roof fairly shook as Rye Dalton backed the trembling attorney to the door, emphasizing his words with nudges of the steel hammer against Merrill's chest. "You tell Dan Morgan the goddamn house is not for sale and never will be so long as I draw breath. *Is that clear?*"

Rye watched the lawyer scurry up the street, clutching his hat to his balding head. Rye grasped the hammer so tightly, the hickory handle seemed to depress. Josiah merely puffed his pipe. Ship retreated to the shadows under the tool bench, whined once, laid her head on her paws, and kept a wary eye on her master.

Never in her life had Laura seen Dan as angry as he was that night after his confrontation with Rye. He waited until Josh was in bed before saying without preamble, "It's all over town that you've been meeting Rye in the square, as bold as brass."

"Meeting? I'd hardly call the exchange of hellos meetings."

"I saw him today, and he didn't deny it."

"You saw him—where?"

"At the cooperage. I had to swallow my pride and troop down there and demand that he stop courting my wife under the curious eyes of the entire town, and making a fool of me in the process!"

She colored and turned away. "Dan, you're exaggerating," she lied, the hidden busk seeming to scorch her skin as she spoke the words.

"Am I?" he snapped.

"Yes, of course. Josh and I have talked to him when we've gone to do the marketing, but nothing else . . . I assure you." She looked up entreatingly, and her voice softened as she appealed, "Josh is his son, Dan, his son. How can I keep—"

"Stop lying!" Dan shouted. "And stop using the boy to hide behind. I won't allow it, do you hear? He's not to be made a pawn while the two of you create a scandal right out in public!"

"Scandal? Who calls it a scandal—we've done nothing wrong!"

He wanted badly to believe her, but doubts ate at him, strengthened by things he suspected from their past.

"You've been . . . been doing *wrong* with him since—" His eyes narrowed on her accusingly. "Since when, Laura?" His voice turned silky. "When did it start with you and Rye? When you were fifteen? Sixteen? Or even before that?"

The blood drained from her face and she could think of no answer, could only stand before him appearing guilty as accused. She was stunned to think he'd known all these years yet had never said anything before.

''Don't,'' she begged in a tiny voice.

''Don't?'' he repeated, a hard edge to the word. ''Don't remind you of the times you left your . . . your *shadow* behind, thinking he didn't see the berry stains on your back when you came trooping down from the hills with your mouths still puckered, and you with your cheeks rubbed raw from his whiskers before he'd even learned how to shave.''

She turned away, chin dropping to her chest. ''I'm sorry you knew. We never meant to hurt you, but it has nothing to do with now.''

''Doesn't it?'' Dan grabbed her arm, forcing her to turn and face him. ''Then why do you turn away, blushing? What happened between you two out in the orchard the night of Joseph Starbuck's party? Why were you missing for so long without a trace? Why didn't you answer when I called to you? And how do you think I felt when I went back inside looking for you and found you still gone?''

''Nothing happened . . . nothing! Why won't you believe me?''

''Believe you! When I walk through the streets and people snicker behind my back?''

''I'm sorry, Dan, we . . . I . . .'' She choked to a stop.

He glowered at her stricken face, watching her swallow repeatedly in an effort to keep from crying. ''Yes, dear wife, we . . . you . . . what?''

''I didn't think of how it would look to others when they saw us together. I . . . I won't see him again, I promise.''

Immediately, Dan was sorry he'd jerked her around so roughly. Never in his life had he touched her without tenderness or caused fear to spring into her eyes. Forcing the picture of Rye Dalton from his mind, he clutched Laura tightly against his chest, sensing that he was losing her even as she vowed to be faithful. He buried his face in her neck while fear and passion coursed through him. Yet Josh was hers and Rye's, and Dan was muddled with guilt for denying Rye the right to his son.

''Oh God, why did he have to come back?'' Dan said thickly, holding Laura so tightly it seemed he would force the very flesh from her bones.

''Dan, what are you saying?'' she cried, struggling out of his arms. ''He's . . . he was a friend you loved. How can you say such a thing? Are you saying you wish he'd died?''

''I didn't mean I wanted him dead, Laura . . . not dead.'' With a horrified expression, Dan sat down heavily and dropped his face into his hands. ''Oh God,'' he groaned miserably, shaking his head.

Studying him, Laura, too, suffered. She understood the conflict of emotions that was changing Dan in ways that made him dislike himself. These same conflicts warred inside Laura at times, for she loved two men, each in a different way, yet enough to want to hurt neither.

''Dan,'' she said sadly, moving to rest her hands on his stooping shoulders, ''I'm very mixed up, too.'' Her eyes sparkled with unshed tears as he lifted his tortured face to hers. He willed her not to put voice to her feelings, but she went on, a note of growing weariness in each word as she crossed to the far side of the room and turned to face him.

"It would be a lie for me to say I feel nothing for him. What is between Rye and me is of a whole childhood's making. I can't cause it to disappear or pretend it never existed. All I can do is sort it out and try to make the right decision for . . . for four people."

Her words could have come from his lips and been equally true—what was between Dan and Rye was also of a whole childhood's making—but the realization only added to his wretchedness. Hearing it at last put into words made him realize that his place as Laura's husband was tenuous at best, for seven hundred dollars and a deed to this house were not necessarily the deed to her heart.

Dan contemplated her across the shadowed room. Her hands were gripped together tightly, her face a mask of torn emotions. Suddenly, he could not face the truth and made for the door, jerking his jacket from the hook and shrugging it on.

"I'm going out for a while."

The door slammed abruptly, leaving an absence so profound it seemed about to swallow Laura. It took several minutes before she believed he was actually gone, for he never went out in the evenings, except perhaps to take Josh for a walk or visit his parents. But tonight was different. Tonight Dan was escaping.

He was gone for two hours. Laura was waiting up for his return. When he came in, he stopped abruptly. "You're still up!" he exclaimed, surprised, a glint of hope lifting his brows.

"I needed your help with my laces," she explained.

The hope faded. He turned, hung his jacket on the coat tree, but his hand seemed to rest on the prong and hover there for several seconds, as if he were steadying himself.

Finally he turned, still near the door. "I'm . . . I'm sorry I kept you up."

"Oh, Dan, where did you go?" Her expression was grieved.

He stared at her absently for several seconds before his voice came, quiet and hurt. "Do you care?"

Pain darkened her eyes. "Of course, I care. You've never gone out like this before. Not . . . not angry."

He tugged the hem of his waistcoat down and came halfway across the room. "But I am angry," he said, with no apparent trace of that emotion. "Should I stay here and be? Would you prefer that?"

"Oh, Dan, let's just . . ." But she didn't know how to finish. Let's just what? Let's just go to bed and forget it? Let's just pretend everything is the same? That Rye Dalton doesn't exist?

As they studied each other, they both knew the reason her words had trailed away: there *was* no pretending. Rye was there between them every hour of the night and day.

Dan sighed tiredly. "Come," he said. "It's late. I'll help you get undressed so we can both get some sleep." His shoulders drooped as he crossed to Laura and turned her by an elbow toward the linter room.

Beside the bed, she presented her back to Dan, but when he stepped up behind her, she caught the smell of brandy on his breath. But Dan was no drinking man! Guilt swept her as his fingers moved down the row of hooks at her back.

When she was free of the dress, she stepped from it and waited. There followed a long, tense moment when nothing happened, and she knew his eyes were on her exposed back. Finally, he untied the stays and worked them loose, but when she bent forward to step out of the circlet of stiff whalebone, her backside bumped him and she realized he hadn't moved. She straightened and suddenly his arms circled her ribs, jerked her backward, and held her possessively. His mouth came down hard against the side of her neck while his tongue flavored her skin with brandy.

"Oh, Laura, don't leave me," he pleaded, cupping her breasts tightly, holding her firmly against his body.

Through the single layer of her pantaloons, she could feel his sexual arousal. The smell of his breath made her want to pull away, but she didn't. She covered the backs of his hands with her own and let her head tip back against his shoulder.

"Dan, I'm not leaving you. I'm here."

He ran his hand down the front of her, cradling the mound of womanhood in a tight, upward clutch that almost lifted her from the floor. "Laura, I love you . . . I've always loved you . . . you'll never know how much . . . I need you . . . don't leave me . . ." The litany went on and on, desperate, pleading words meant to inflame her, but filling her with pity instead. He unbuttoned her waistband and slid his hand over her bare stomach while she willed her body to respond. But there was only dryness, and she flinched when he touched her intimately. This recklessness was unlike Dan, and she realized the extent of his desperation. She told herself she must reassure him, but when he turned her in his arms and kissed her, the taste of brandy revolted her.

"Touch me," he begged, and she did, only to be reminded of Rye's so different body. The thought brought an immediate backlash of guilt, so she put more into her kisses and caresses than she felt. But the thought of Rye released the first faint sensation between her legs, so she went on thinking of him, to make this easier, even as Dan shed his clothes and blew out the light, then took her down. As his body moved over hers, she thought of orange sections—sweet, bright, and juicy—slipping between Rye's lips, leaving succulent droplets on his smiling mouth. She pictured Rye's tongue taking the droplets away, though it was Dan's tongue moving in her mouth. But at last her body was receptive, and his hips moved against hers for a brief time before he plunged hard and shuddered. It was over for him while it had scarcely started for her.

With Dan's body heavy on hers, Laura pictured the loft over old man Hardesty's boathouse, remembering all those times with Rye. And she wanted to weep. Oh, Rye, Rye, if only it were you beside me . . .

But as Dan settled into sleep, Laura was steeped with shame at her own duplicity, using thoughts of one man to arouse herself for another.

Chapter 9

The following day, Josiah said nothing when Rye went upstairs at the usual time, then came back down with fresh comb marks in his hair and his shirt tucked tightly into his waistband.

''I won't be gone long,'' the younger man said, setting off through the wide double doors with a confident step.

But he was gone longer than usual, having waited and watched and searched the square only to give up after thirty minutes. His booted feet clumped out a warning even before he strode angrily through the door of the cooperage, his lips narrowed tightly, a look of suppressed rage about him.

Josiah squinted behind his pipe smoke; his gaze followed Rye.

''So, she didn't show up t'day,'' he noted tersely.

Rye's fist came down like a battering ram on top of the tool bench. ''God-damnit, she's mine!''

''Not so's Dan's admittin'.''

''She wants t' be.''

''Aye, and what does it count for when the law's on Dan's side?''

''The law can free her, just as it tied her to him.''

Josiah's scowl nearly hid his blue-gray eyes beneath grizzled eyebrows. ''Divorce?''

Rye pierced his father with a look of determination. ''Aye, it's what I'm thinkin'.''

''On *Nantucket?*''

The two words needed no further embellishment. The rigid Puritanical beliefs of Nantucket's forefathers still clung; in his whole life Rye had never heard of any couple from the island divorcing.

With a sigh, he sank onto an upturned barrel, bending forward to twine his fingers into the hair at the back of his head while staring at the floor.

Josiah braced one handle of his drawknife on the floor, withdrew his pipe, and abruptly changed the subject. ''Been thinkin'. Y're not much good t' me lately, swingin' tools as if y'd like t' kill somebody, breakin' perfectly good staves and forgettin' y' left the wet ones out of the water.''

Rye looked up: his father never complained—Josiah was the most patient man Rye knew. Now his dry New England drawl continued.

''Be needin' t' set up our agreements with the mainlanders for our winter supply of staves.''

With no source of wood on Nantucket, Josiah got his rough-rived staves from the mainland farmers, whose wood supply was limitless and whose hands would otherwise have been idle during the long winter. Each spring a full year's supply of dimensional boards was delivered in exchange for finished barrels and pails, the arrangement benefiting both farmer and cooper.

"Best be gettin' over there and talk t' them Connecticut farmers." Here Josiah pointed his pipestem at Rye. "Thought y' might be talked inta goin' and gettin' the job done."

At Josiah's words, Rye's anger began losing sway.

Josiah bent his curly gray head over his work again, and the drawknife created more spiral shavings and the smoke wreathed and dissipated overhead. As if to himself, Josiah muttered, "If it was me sittin' on that barrel, I'd be thinkin' about chattin' with them mainland lawyers about what my rights was. Wouldn't take the word of Ezra Merrill that things was all cut 'n' dried."

Still leaning his elbows on his knees, Rye studied the old man's back. It flexed rhythmically as his burly forearms pulled, then retreated for a new bite at the cedar billet. Watching, mulling, Rye felt a softening about his heart. Silently, he unfolded, got to his feet, and crossed to stand behind his father, on whose tough, flexing shoulder Rye clasped a hand. Beneath his touch the muscles bunched and hardened as Josiah completed the stroke. Then, wordlessly, he let the knife rest and lifted his wise gaze to his son, who looked down at Josiah with eyes erased of anger. Josiah's lips pursed closed. They opened and a puff of smoke came out. Rye squeezed the shoulder and said quietly, "Aye, I'll go, old man. It's just what I need . . . thank you." Josiah nodded agreement, and Rye squeezed his shoulder once more before his hand fell away.

Laura heard that Rye had left the island, and it made it easier for her to keep her promise to Dan. But she felt as if her husband could see into the hidden recesses of her mind. More and more often she'd glance up to find him watching her with a look of consternation on his face, as if he had detected secret thoughts at work in his wife. It became an irritation to her to realize he had a right to mistrust her, for though in body she remained true to him, in her mind she again wandered the hills with Rye.

She owed Dan so much. He *had* been a good husband, and if possible, an even better father. He'd taught Josh how to fly a kite, how to walk on stilts, how to tell a gull from a tern, and how to handle the difficult quill pen. Why, already Josh was learning the alphabet, his shaky letters a constant inspiration for praise from Dan. The two spent long sessions bent over the trestle table with their heads side by side. And when the ink spilled, there was patience instead of anger; when the letters were inept, there was encouragement instead of criticism.

But most evenings when the lessons were over, Dan remained in the house only a short time before donning his coat and hat and heading toward the solace that alcohol seemed to provide. Then Laura would wander about the house restlessly, touching the countless luxuries Dan had bought for her—the zinc sink, the brass roasting kitchen before the fireplace, and at its top the clockjack for turning meat. Sometimes her fingers skimmed along the mantel as she paced the quiet room and stared at the pieces of whitewear that Dan had insisted upon her having so that she need not be constantly melting down and recasting the pewter, which was forever breaking or bending or springing holes.

Then he started bringing her presents, coming first with fragrant soap and discouraging her from the drudgery of making her own. When she protested, he made light of his gift, insisting it was inexpensive, since every candler on the island made it with the same materials and processes used in candle making. When a ship from France put in, he came home and presented her with a colorfully painted and varnished sugar box and tea caddy made of the new French toleware.

But she knew why he'd been bringing her gifts more and more often, and these constant offerings created an ever-growing sense of guilt within Laura. For even while she accepted them, she was wondering how to break away from the good life he'd provided her and her son, without bringing lasting hurt to all of them.

Rye returned from his trip to the mainland to find a check had been delivered—from Dan. House rent. Rye stubbornly refused to cash it, bellowing to Josiah that it'd be like accepting rent for Dan's use of Laura!

She, meanwhile, needed someone to talk to, someone who could help sort out the mixed emotions of a woman who pondered her duty to one man and resisted the temptation to seek out another man, whose busk was still pressed to her heart by day and whose image filled her dreams by night.

Laura discarded the possibility of going to have a talk with her mother. Her married friends, too, were out, for they were Dan's friends as well. That left Laura's sister, Jane, who lived on Madaket Harbor, a half-hour's walk to the west.

Jane's husband was a commercial fisherman who followed the seasonal schooling of fish on and about Nantucket—in March, the herring that crowded the island's channels, in April, the cod and haddock off the east end of the island. But now Laura knew John Durning's ketch would be out taking cod off Sankaty Head, so she and Jane could talk privately.

Laura took a warm hooded cloak and crossed the hills west of town paralleling the high cliffs along the island's inner curve, happy to be once again on the salty heath, though the day was overcast and threatened rain. With Josh skipping ahead, she followed Cliff Road as it bent between the strungout sections of Long Pond. As she approached the hills on the northwestern edge of the island and looked out beyond Madaket Harbor, Tuckernuck Island was scarcely visible through the dimming drizzle that was falling. She shivered and hurried on.

Jane's house was a weathered gray saltbox to which two linters had been added as her family grew, for Jane had six children, all under nine, and on any given day at least three extras seemed to be underfoot, until it seemed children squirted from between the wallboards! Jane managed the noise and fighting with surprising calmness, taking in stride the spats she was asked to arbitrate, the constant demands for food, and the cleaning up that inevitably followed the children's treats of milk and jam tarts.

The moment Laura walked into Jane's house, she knew it was a mistake to have chosen a rainy day for a confidential talk with her sister. The weather had chased all six of her nieces and nephews inside, and it seemed as if each had brought along a battalion of friends. Josh was in his glory, for he was immediately included in their game of hide-the-thimble, which sent the tribe scrambling to every corner of the keeping room, sometimes even across Laura's and Jane's laps, as the children probed the two women's pockets, their ears, their high-topped shoes, and even their chignons in search of the hidden thimble.

Jane laughed and abetted their scramblings by suggesting likely hiding places, while Laura grew more and more impatient. But just when it seemed that no chance would come to broach the subject, Jane herself introduced it.

"The whole island's talking about you and Rye . . . and Dan, of course."

"They are?" Laura looked up in surprise.

"They say you've been meeting Rye secretly."

"Oh, it's not true, Jane!"

"But you have seen him, haven't you?"

"Yes, of course I've *seen* him."

Jane studied her sister for a moment, then confided, "So have we. He looks wonderful, doesn't he?"

Laura felt herself color, and she knew Jane watched her closely as she went on.

"He stopped by here, brought some little things he'd carved for the children, though he didn't know we'd had the last three. Surprised him plenty to see us with enough to man a whaleboat." Jane chuckled, then her expression sobered as she leveled her hazel eyes on Laura. "He's been seen out walking the moors a lot, and they say he haunts the shore with that dog at his heels, looking like a lost dog himself."

The picture of a forlorn Rye walking the islands with Ship at his heels at last made Laura's face crumple. "Oh, Jane, what am I to do?" She covered her eyes, which were suddenly streaming tears.

A child came squealing past, but Jane ignored him for once and laid a sympathetic hand on her sister's hair. "What do you want to do?"

"I want to keep everyone from getting hurt," Laura sobbed miserably.

"I don't think that's possible, little one."

At the endearment, Laura grasped her sister's hand and held it against her cheek for a moment before lowering it to the tabletop, where she held it between them. "I have made them both miserable then, if what you say is true. Rye, wandering the hills with the dog, waiting for me to tell him yes, and Dan leaving the house every night to drink away his fear that I'll tell him no. And between them, Josh, who doesn't have any idea Rye is his father. I wish I knew what to do."

"You have to do what your heart tells you to do."

"Oh but, Jane, y . . . you haven't seen the look on Dan's face when he comes home at the end of the day bringing me another gift, hoping . . . oh, it's just awful." Again Laura dissolved into a pool of tears. "He's been so good to me . . . and to Josh."

"But which of them do you love, Laura?"

The red-rimmed eyes lifted. The trembling lips parted. Then she swallowed and looked down again. "I'm afraid to answer that."

Jane refilled Laura's teacup. "Because you love them both?"

"Yes."

Jane moved her hand across the tabletop and gently rubbed the back of Laura's. "I can't tell you what to do. All I can say is this: I was married already when . . . well, when you and Rye turned from children into adolescents. I saw you both growing up before my eyes. I watched what happened between the two of you, and the way Dan followed you with the same look he's probably got in his eyes now when he brings you gifts in an effort to win your love. Laura dear . . ." With a single finger Jane lifted Laura's trembling chin and looked into her troubled brown eyes. "I know how it was with Rye and you long before you married. I knew because John and I were so happily in love at the time that it was easy for me to recognize it in someone else. The two of you couldn't keep your eyes off each other—nor, I suspect, your hands either, when you were by yourselves. Would I be out of line to ask if your misery now's got something to do with that?"

"Jane, we haven't done anything since he's been back. He . . . we . . ." But Laura stumbled into silence.

"Ah, I see how it is. You want to."

"Dear God, Jane, I've fought it."

"Yes." Jane's pause was eloquent. "So Rye walks the hills with his dog, and you come to my kitchen to cry."

"But I was married to Rye for less than one year and to Dan for four. I *owe* Dan something!"

"And yourself—what do you owe yourself? The truth, at least? That if the false rumor of Rye Dalton's death had never reached Nantucket, you would no more have married Dan Morgan than you would've at the age of nineteen, when you chose Rye over him."

"But what about Josh?"

"What about him?"

"He loves Dan so much."

"He's young, resilient. He'd bounce back if he learned the truth.'

"Oh, Jane, if only I could be as . . . as sure as you."

"You're sure. You're just scared, that's all."

"I'm legally married to Dan. It would require a divorce."

"An ugly word. Enough to scare anyone raised in these Puritan parts, and enough to make the most benevolent of dogooders scorn you on the street. Is that what you're thinking?"

Laura shook her head tiredly and leaned her forehead on the heel of a hand. "I don't know what to think anymore. I had no idea everybody on the island has been watching Rye and me so closely."

Jane pondered for a long, silent moment, then squared herself in her chair, drummed on the tabletop with a palm in much the manner of a judge lowering a gavel, and mused, "They say Rye has become a familiar sight wandering the moors. If you were to run into him out there, who's to say it was no accident? And who'd be there to watch?"

"Why, Jane—"

But before Laura could say more the door opened and John Durning swept in, robust and big-voiced, booming a hello to his children and plopping a forthright kiss on his wife even before he slipped out of his yellow oilskins. With a smile and cheery hello for Laura, he stood behind Jane's chair and put his wide hands on the sides of her neck, kneading it with his thumbs while teasing, "And what's waiting at home to warm a man's body in weather like this?"

Jane craned around to grin up at him. "There's tea, among other things."

The affection between the two of them was so obvious, and the way they enjoyed each other and teased made Laura remember how it used to be with Rye when he'd come sweeping into the house. It had been like this—the smile, the bold caress, the words with second meanings. The simple events of every day had been enhanced to something sublime simply because they were shared.

If you were to run into him out there someplace, who's to say it was no accident?

And though it was undeniably tempting, Laura astutely avoided the moors after that day.

The sight of the listless, wandering Rye Dalton and his dog had indeed become familiar to the islanders. The pair could be seen at day's beginning and day's end, trekking along the myriad paths of the inner island or along any of its white, sandy shores, the man in the lead, the dog tramping faithfully at his heels.

In the dew-spattered dawns, their silhouettes were often etched against the colorful eastern sky as they sat atop Folger Hill or Altar Rock, the highest points of the island, with the panoramic view of the white-rimmed spit of land and the restless Atlantic beyond. Or if the dawn was murky, it was not uncommon for the old fishermen who lived in the tiny weatherbeaten cottages along 'Sconset's shores to see the pair emerge from the shrouds of mist at the ocean's edge, ambling listlessly, heads down, the man's hands buried deep in his trouser front, the dog giving the impression that were it possible, she'd have imitated her master's posture.

At other times the inseparable pair ran along the hard-packed shingle, Rye's heels digging deep into the flat-washed sand, his footprints disappearing as waves lapped behind him while Ship, with her tongue trailing from the side of her mouth, galloped just within the surf, keeping up with the man who seemed to run with a vengeance, his breath beating ragged while he pushed his body to its physical limits. Exhausted, they'd fall, panting, onto the sand flats, Rye lying supine, studying the deep sky, the dog searching the undulating horizons as if for sails.

Evenings, they could sometimes be seen standing on the high bluffs overlooking deserted Codfish Park, where in spring and fall, when the cod ran, fishermen hauled up their dories and lay their catch out to dry on the wooden "flakes" below.

Mornings, just after high tide had strewn the Atlantic's offerings on the island's southern shores, Rye and Ship often encountered kelp seekers, rummaging through the tide wrack for oarweed and tangle, though Rye would scarcely be aware that others occupied the same stretch of beach he haunted.

Other times, he and Ship picked their way around the boulders on Saul's Hill, scattering flocks of blackbirds which in days of old had been such a nuisance that each male islander was issued a quota he must kill before he was allowed to marry. "Ah, Ship," the man sighed, reaching blindly for the dog's head. "If only I could simply kill five hundred blackbirds and be free t' marry her."

A day came when not a breath of wind stirred, while the two stared at a nearly calm sea. Ship's ears suddenly perked up, and the hair along her spine bristled. She turned, alert, on guard, checking behind her for the source of the sudden, violent hissing sound that came out of nowhere. But there was naught to be seen, only an eerie sibilance as of something letting off a giant eruption of steam. The rare, unexplained sound emitted by the ocean was called a rut by the old-timers. Yet none knew its origin, only that it was sure to be followed by shrewish winds that would work their way east and bring rain.

And true to its prediction, before the day was out, the sky had lowered to a menacing greenish-gray. It found Rye and Ship watching the wild, broken waters of Miacomet Rip, where hidden currents tugged and sucked at the island's feet while the winds tore at the man's hair and whipped it about his head like spindrift.

There followed three days of punishing rain that lashed the island from the south and kept Rye and Ship indoors. On the fourth morning, though, the rain had disappeared, leaving in its wake a fogbank so dense it obscured even the scalloped curves of Coatue Peninsula's shores.

The three days' forced confinement had left Rye jumpy and irritable. Therefore, when in late morning of the fourth day the sun broke through and blue sky spread slowly from west to east, Josiah suggested Rye go up to Mill Hill and negotiate the exchange of barrels for flour that was periodically made between the cooper and the miller, Asa Pond.

Shortly after noon, Rye set out on the errand with Ship in tow, grateful to be free of the cooperage once again. The island looked crisp and fresh-washed after the rain. The cobblestones along Main Street shone brightly in the high sun, and along the narrower lanes gay splashes of red and coral geraniums spilled from windowboxes. Rye thought of the geraniums beside Laura's door and wondered if they bloomed, too, but with an effort he put her from his mind.

With Ship at his heels he walked past Sunset Hill, where the home of Jethro Coffin, one of the island's first settlers, had been standing for almost 150 years now. He passed along Nantucket Cliffs, beyond which the pale green waters marked the bar and the darker blue told of deeper waters in the sound beyond. Above, a pair of white mackerel gulls pursued a single black one, the ragged shred of their voices tossed aloft in the August afternoon.

He moved on toward the four "post" windmills of Dutch design that rode the breasts of four hills to the south and west of town. Asa Pond's mill had been built in 1746 of timbers taken from shipwrecks, but as it came into view over the hill, it appeared ageless, its four lattice-veined arms backed by new linen sails, now facing southwest, from which a gentle breeze blew. Like its sister mills, it was at once graceful and ungainly; graceful for its gently turning arms whose sails, like those of a windjammer, could be reefed in high winds; ungainly for its long tail pole extending from the rear, like the rump of an awkward beast squatting on the ground. This thick wooden spar projected from the structure and rested on a wheel by which the entire building could be turned to face windward. The wheel had worn a deep circular rut into the earth, and Rye now leaped over it, crossed the circle of grass, and climbed the ladder to the grinding floor high overhead.

Inside, the mill was adrift in bran- and corn-dust, ever present in the air as grain was poured down the hopper to the grinding wheel and meal was sifted by apprentices into varying grades of fineness. The elevated floorboards vibrated constantly from the thumping of wooden gears as giant pins meshed with oak pinions on the windlass drive. To Rye's nose the grain scent was pleasant, but he peered across the dust motes to find Asa with a handkerchief tied over his nose and mouth while he worked. The miller raised a hand in greeting and pointed to the doorway; the noise of the grating millstones and the thud of gears precluded speech. Following Rye back outside, Asa pulled the hanky from his face while they stood at the base of the building, conducting their business in the pleasant summer sun while the vanes creaked a quiet accompaniment.

Josh, too, had been restless and bored during the three days of inclement weather. As soon as the sky began clearing, he begged Laura to take him out bayberrying, one of his favorite things to do. When she patiently explained that the bayberries weren't quite ripe yet, Josh pleaded for another walk to Aunt Jane's. When that suggestion failed, he thought of his other favorite diversion, a trip to the mill, where he was sometimes allowed to ride aboard the spar while the oxen turned the building into the wind. But to this Laura answered almost gruffly, "No, I don't have time. The garden needs weeding, and right after the rain is the best time."

"But, Mama, Mr. Pond might—"

"Joshua!" She rarely called him Joshua.

Josh's mouth turned down and he hung around the garden while she worked, obviously bored, asking questions about June bugs and cabbage moths and baby cucumbers. He squatted between the rows, pointing an inquisitive finger at each weed that Laura touched, asking, "What's that one?" and "How can you tell it ain't a bedjtable?"

"I can just tell, that's all. I've been doing it a long time."

He watched her pull up a few more. "I could do that."

She scarcely looked up. "Why don't you just go play, Josh?"

"Papa would let me."

"Well, I'm not Papa, and I have a lot to do!" Laura went on weeding while Josh hung there beside her, his cheek now resting on a knee as he hummed tunelessly, poking in the dirt with one finger.

Laura moved farther down the row, and Josh continued to study her. A few moments later he came to squat beside her and proudly presented an uprooted plant. "Here, Mama, I can help . . . see?"

"Ohhh, Josh," she moaned, "you've pulled up a baby turnip."

"Oh." He stared at it disconsolately, then flashed a bright smile. "I'll put it back in!"

Impatiently, she retorted, "No, it won't work, Josh! Once it's pulled out, it'll wilt and die."

"It will?" Josh asked, mystified, and disappointed because he'd only intended to help.

"Yes, it will," she answered disgustedly before returning to her weeding.

Josh stood beside her a moment longer, studying the turnip green, which was already growing limp. "What's die?" he asked innocently.

Unbidden came the thought: die is what we thought your father did and why

I married somebody else. Upset with herself, impatient with him, she snapped, "Josh, just throw it away and go find something else to do! I'll never get done here if you keep pestering me with your everlasting questions!"

Josh's little mouth trembled and he pulled at his cheek with a dirty finger. Immediately, Laura hated herself for being so short with him when he'd only meant to help. This had happened more and more lately, and each time it did, she vowed not to let it happen again. She wanted to be like Jane, whose patience with her mob of children was close to saintly. But Jane was incredibly happy, and happiness made a difference! When you were happy you could handle things more easily. But Laura's growing tension sought a vent at some very unexpected times, and unfortunately her son often got the brunt of it. To make matters worse now, Laura realized Josh was right—Dan would have patiently shown him how to tell the weeds from the vegetables, regardless of how much efficiency he forfeited.

Josh was trying valiantly not to cry, but tears winked on his golden lashes as he studied the sad little turnip plant, wondering why his mama was so upset.

Laura sighed and sank back on her heels. "Josh darling, come here."

He dug his chin deeper into his chest as a tear went rolling, followed by another.

"Josh, Mama is sorry. You were just trying to help, weren't you, darling?"

He nodded his head forlornly, still looking at the earth.

"Come here before Mama cries, too, Josh." He lifted his teary eyes to her, dropped the turnip, and rushed into Laura's arms, hugging her fiercely, his sunny head buried in her neck. She knelt in the garden row holding Rye's son tightly against her apron front, just short of crying herself.

I am changing, she thought, in spite of my fight to preserve equanimity in my marriage. I'm becoming short-tempered with Josh and unhappy with Dan, and I'm not treating either one of them fairly. Oh, Josh, Josh, I'm sorry. If only you were old enough to understand how much I love your father but that I honestly love Dan, too. She closed her eyes, her cheek against her son's hair, his cheek pressed against her breast, where the busk was hidden even now. She rocked him gently, swallowing tears as she pushed him back to look down into his lovable face.

"You know, I really don't feel like weeding the garden at all. Suppose we take that walk up to the mill. I do need to order some flour from Asa."

"Really, Mama?" Josh brightened, tears forgotten just that quickly.

"Really." She tweaked his nose. "But you'll have to wash your hands and face first and comb your hair."

But he was already four rows away, jumping turnips, beans, peas, and carrots on his way to soap and water. "I bet I can beat you!" he hollered as he ran.

"I bet you can't!" And Laura, too, was up, skirts lifted, racing him through the backyard.

Chapter 10

It was a glorious day, the sky as blue as a jay's wing, a light breeze chasing through the grass. An afternoon hush lay on both land and sea, for few boats moved in the harbor below as Laura and Josh left the scallop-shell path and threaded their way toward the open moor and the gently rising hills beyond. Meadowlarks came to watch the mother and child passing, accompanying them with the sweetest music in all of summer. Field flowers seemed to be drying their cheeks as their faces arched toward the warm sun. Katydids droned lazily while an occasional gull wheeled overhead.

Josh stopped to examine an ant hill and Laura joined him, taking time to bask in the joy of watching him instead of the ants. His mouth formed an excited *O* and he exclaimed, "Look at that one! Look at the big rock he's carrying!" Laura laughed, and looked, and shrank for the moment into the miniature world of insects, where a grain of sand became a boulder.

In time they moved on up the sandy path. All around, the treeless hills were trimmed with creamy heads of Queen Anne's lace nodding in the breeze.

"Just a minute!" Laura called, and left the path to pick several stems of lace, adding a few brown-eyed Susans when they passed a patch, and later tucking wild yarrow into the bouquet.

"I see it! I see it!" Josh cried as the latticed vanes appeared at the crest of the hill. "Do you think Mr. Pond will let me ride the spar?"

"We'll have to see if the oxen are hooked to it today."

Laura was hatless and half-blinded as she turned her face toward the two-o'clock sun that formed an aureole behind the windmill. The vanes rotated slowly. And then a dark core seemed to separate itself from the sun and become distinct from it, and she shaded her eyes with a forearm to watch it take the shape of a man coming downhill in their direction.

He stopped when he saw them. Though she could not make out his face, she saw long, slender legs in calf-high boots and white sleeves billowing in the breeze. A moment later another dark shape moved around his ankles and stopped beside him. A dog . . . a big yellow Lab.

"Rye," she whispered, not realizing she had, the name coming to her lips as if in answer to a long-repeated prayer.

For a moment both man and woman paused, he with the grass feathering about his knees on the hill above her, she with skirts clutched in one hand and the shadow of a nosegay of wildflowers painting fernlike images across her features. The child scampered up the hill and the dog scampered down, but neither Rye nor Laura noticed. The breeze caught her pink calico skirt and held it abaft while two hearts soared and plunged.

Then Rye leaned forward and came down the hill at a dogtrot, half jumping, elbows lifting slightly as he took the decline with an eagerness that sent her hurrying upward, skirt caught up in both hands now. They met with Josh and Ship between them, exuberant child and overjoyed dog completely taken with each other, just as man and woman were. Josh fell to his knees while Ship wagged not only her tail but her whole body.

"Gosh, is he yours, Rye?" Josh asked, oblivious of all but the dog and the pink tongue he tried gaily to avoid.

"*She,*" Rye corrected, his eyes riveted on Laura.

"She," Josh repeated. "Is she yours?"

"Ayc, she's mine." the hlue eyes took in nothing but the face of the woman before him.

"Boy, I'll bet you really love her, don't you?"

"Aye, son, I love her," came the husky reply.

"You had her a long time?"

"Since I was a boy."

"How old is she?"

"Old enough t' know by now who she belongs to."

"Gee, I wish she was mine."

But to that came only the soft reply, "Aye."

There followed a long, trembling pause, filled only with the sigh of the wind in a woman's skirts and the shush-shush of whispering grass. Laura felt as if the field of wildflowers had just blossomed within her breast. Her lips were parted, and her heartbeat leaped wildly within her bodice of pink calico. The hills of Nantucket embraced them, and for that moment all else was wiped away.

And suddenly she had to touch him . . . just touch him.

She extended her hand to be shaken.

"Hello, Mr. Dalton. I didn't think I'd . . . we'd run into you out here."

His palm enfolded hers, held it like a treasure while he gazed into her eyes above the golden head of their son, frolicking at their feet.

"Hello, Laura. I'm glad y' did."

His palm was callused, hard, and familiar. "We're on our way up to the mill to order flour and bran."

He slipped his index and middle fingers between her cuff and the delicate skin of her inner wrist, then covered the back of the hand with his other. Her pulse raced wildly beneath his fingertips.

"And I was at the mill takin' an order for barrels."

"Well," she said, laughing nervously, "it seems everyone is out enjoying the sunny weather."

"Aye, everyone." Just then Josh scrambled to his feet, and only then did it strike them how long, how caressingly, they'd been holding hands. Immediately, Rye released hers. But Josh and Ship only leaped and cavorted in circles about them, leaving them to gaze at each other.

"Do you . . . do you come up this way often?" she questioned.

"Aye, Ship and I, we do a lot o' walkin'."

"So I've heard."

"And you?"

"Me?"

"Do y' come up this way often?"

"No, sometimes on the way to Jane's house is all."

"And when you order flour." He smiled into her eyes, and she smiled back. "And pick wildflowers."

She nodded and dropped her gaze to the cluster in her nervous hands.

"I stopped by Jane's myself one day," Rye said.

"Yes, she told me. It was nice of you to bring gifts for the children. Thank you."

There they stood, feeling as if they were smothering, talking of inconsequential things when there were a thousand things they wanted to tell each other, ask each other. Most overwhelming of all was the compulsion to touch. Laura let her gaze meander over his hair, his features. She wanted to reach up a fingertip and trace the new jutting line of the side-whiskers that followed his hard jaw. She wanted to thread her fingers through his thick rye-colored hair and say what was on her mind: *It's gotten darker since you've been back, but I like it better this way, the way I remember it.* She wanted to kiss each of the seven new pockmarks on his face and say, *Tell me about the voyage. Tell me everything.*

Josh interrupted their visual reverie to ask, "What's her name?"

Rye pulled his eyes away from Laura and went down on one knee—safer that way; in another moment he would have reached for Laura again, but this time it would have been for more than a handshake.

"Ship."

"That's a funny name for a dog, ain't it? You both got funny names."

Rye's rich laughter spilled across the flower-strewn field. "Aye, we both got funny names. Hers is really Shipwreck, 'cause that's where she came from. Found her swimmin' ashore when a bark piled up on the shoals."

The dog was taking swipes at Josh's face with her tongue, and he got her around the neck, giggling in delight. Then over they went, Josh on the bottom, eyes closed tightly while he giggled and the dog nuzzled and licked. Laura and Rye, too, joined in laughing as Josh curled up like an armadillo and the big Lab worried him.

Rye bent forward, resting an elbow on his knee, and smiled up at Laura. "If y' don't mind, Josh could stay here and play with Ship while you go on up and talk to Asa. We'll be waitin' when y' come back down."

She could no more have refused him than alter the changing of tides. Rye himself would have been invitation enough, kneeling in the strong sunlight, handsome and honed, with his shoulders slanted forward, sleeves flowing loosely as he held the back of one wrist with the opposite hand. His smiling eyes were raised to Laura, awaiting her answer.

Josh came out of his crouch to appeal, "Yeah, please, Mama! Just while you go up to the mill."

Laura teased, "What about riding the spar?"

"The oxes ain't hitched up anyway, so I wanna stay down here and play with Ship." The two rolled over in the long grass.

"All right. I'll be right back."

Her eyes met and held Rye's before he silently nodded. Then, seemingly of its own accord, her hand did a most surprising thing. It reached out to rest on the back of his neck—half on his hair, half inside his collar—while she passed behind him.

Rye's head snapped around and his elbow slipped from his knee, blue eyes smoldering in surprise. But she had turned and was already making her way up the hill. He watched her retreating form, the way her pink skirt bunched at the hip as she took long, high steps in her climb. When she disappeared over the crest of the hill, he returned his attention to Josh and Ship. They cavorted together until Ship tired and flopped down to pant.

Soon Josh flopped down, too, beside Rye and struck up a conversation. "How come you know my Aunt Jane?"

"I've lived on the island all my life. I knew Jane when I was a boy not much older than you."

"And Mama, too?"

"Aye, and your mama, too. We went t' school together."

"I get t' go to school, but not till next year."

"You do?"

"Uh-huh. Papa already bought me my hornbook, and he says he's gonna give his share of the firewood so I won't have to sit far away from the fire."

Rye laughed, but he knew it was true that those students whose parents donated firewood got the choicest seats, close to the fireplace. "Do y' think y'll like school?"

"It'll be easy. Papa's already taught me most of my letters."

Rye plucked a blade of grass and put it in the corner of his mouth. "Sounds like you get along real well with your papa."

"Oh, Papa's better'n just about anybody I know . . . 'cept Mama, o' course."

"O' course." Rye's gaze wandered up the hill momentarily, then back to his son. "Well, y're a lucky boy."

"That's what Jimmy says. Jimmy—" But Josh stopped, screwed up his face quizzically. "You know Jimmy?"

Rye shook his head, enchanted by the elfin child. He thought it best not to admit Jimmy Ryerson was a second cousin.

"Oh. Well, Jimmy, he's my best friend. I'll show him to you someday," Josh said matter-of-factly, "if you'll bring Ship along so Jimmy can see 'er, too."

"It's a deal." Rye stretched out on the grass while Josh continued.

"Well anyways, Jimmy, he says I'm lucky cause Papa made me stilts and he says I'm the onlyest one he knows that's got 'em. I let him use 'em sometimes, but Jimmy, he can't stand up too good on 'em—not like me, 'cause Papa, he taught me to get the sticks behind my—" Josh stretched an elbow over his head, rubbed his armpit, and strove to remember. "What do you call these things again?"

Rye controlled the urge to laugh, answering most seriously, "Armpits."

"Yeah . . . armpits. Papa, he says to put the sticks behind 'em and stick your butt out, but Jimmy, he falls over, cuz he holds the sticks in front of him, like this, all the time." Josh leaped to his feet to demonstrate. Then he dropped to his knees like quicksilver.

Delight filled Rye Dalton. The child was as lovable as his mother, quick-witted and spontaneous.

"Your papa sounds like a smart man."

"Oh, he's smarter 'n anybody else! He works at the countinghouse."

"Aye, I've seen him there." Rye plucked a new blade of grass. "Your papa and I went t' school together, too."

"You did?"

Josh's eyes were so like Laura's as they expressed surprise. "Aye."

Josh's expression became thoughtful before he asked, "Then how come you say aye and Papa says yes?"

" 'Cause I've been on a whaleship and heard the sailors sayin' it so much I don't remember startin' t' say it m'self."

"You talk funny, though." Josh giggled.

"Y' mean short-like? That's b'cause on a ship y' don't always have time t' give speeches. Y' got t' get things said fast or y're in trouble."

"Oh." And a moment later, "You like it on that whaleship? Was it fun?"

Rye's glance again swept the crest of the hill, then turned back to his son, finding an expression on the child's face that he sometimes encountered in his own mirror when he was thoughtful. " 'Twas lonely."

"Din't you take Ship along?"

Rye shook his head.

"Where'd she go?"

Rye reached for the Lab's big head and rested his hand on it. The dog opened lazy eyes and closed them again. It was difficult for the father to keep from giving the answer that was on his mind: *Ship lived with your mother at first, and maybe even with you when you were a baby. Maybe that's why you two like each other so much now. She remembers you.*

Instead, he said, "She went t' live with my father at the cooperage."

"Then I guess you *was* lonely," Josh sympathized.

"Well, I'm back," Rye said brightly, flashing the boy a smile.

Josh smiled, too, and piped, "You're nice. I like you."

Heady emotions sprang up within Rye at the boy's words, so impetuous, so honest. He wished he could be equally free, that he could hug this child and have him know the truth. Josh was a lovable sprite, untarnished, unspoiled. Laura and . . . and Dan had done a good job with him.

Laura stopped at the top of the hill as Josh and Rye came into view below. They were distant enough that Josh's childish laughter carried only faintly on the breeze, then Rye's could be heard more distinctly for a moment. They were stretched out on the grass alongside the dog. Rye lay on his side, ankles crossed, his jaw propped on a palm, chewing a blade of grass. Beside him, his son was sprawled with his head pillowed on the sleeping Lab, who'd collapsed beside her master with chin on paws, taking a breather. It was a scene of great repletion such as Laura had dreamed of countless times. The son she loved, beside his father, whom she also loved, and it took only herself to complete the family circle.

Again Jane's question came back to Laura. *Who's to know it wouldn't be an accident if you ran into him on the moors?*

She studied the man stretched out below her in a field of Queen Anne's lace. Who's to know? Who's to know? With the wind on her face, sun on her hair, and a heart dancing triple-time, she headed down the hill.

Laura knew the exact moment Rye saw her coming, though he lay as before, relaxed, only his blue eyes moving as they followed her progress. When she came within earshot, he shifted the blade of grass to the corner of his mouth to say, "Here comes your mother." Then, slowly, he uncrossed his ankles and sat up, rolling onto one buttock, lifting a knee, and draping a forearm over it.

"Do we hafta go yet? Do was hafta?" Josh pleaded, charging up the path to meet Laura, throwing himself into an enormous hug that pulled her skirts against her thighs.

She smiled down at him, ruffled his hair, but her eyes passed to Rye as she answered softly, "No, not yet."

The boy let go, and Laura moved to stand near Rye's outstretched foot. The hem of her skirt brushed his pant leg as his gaze drifted down the line of her shoulder, breast, and midriff, then rose once more to her brown eyes.

"Would y' like t' go for a walk around Hummock Pond?" he asked.

Instead of answering directly, Laura asked Josh, "Would you like to go for a walk around Hummock Pond?"

He spun toward Rye. "Is Ship coming, too?"

"Aye." The grass bobbed in the corner of Rye's mouth.

"Then, aye . . . me too!" the boy answered his mother.

She watched Josh and Ship scamper off ahead while Rye remained where he was, his eyes following the boy until Josh was safely out of hearing. Then he looked up at Laura and his gaze drew hers as the shore draws the surf. For a moment neither spoke, then Rye spit out the blade of grass. "I asked if *you'd* like to go for a walk around Hummock Pond," he said.

"More than anything else in the world," she answered simply.

He raised his palm. Her glance shifted from it to the child trudging up the hill, then back to the calluses. And without further hesitation she laid her hand in Rye's, and his strong fingers closed about hers as she tugged him to his feet.

Hummock Pond was one of a chain stretching north to south across the western center of the island. It was shaped like a lazy *J* whose lower curve extended to Nantucket's southern shore, where the pond's fresh water almost touched the briny Atlantic. As children, Rye and Laura had fished it for white and yellow perch, and he'd taught her how to bait her hook with angleworms. Years ago they'd picnicked in Ram Pasture and walked as they walked now, from North Head toward the ocean, which could be heard in the distance but not seen.

"I've dreamed about doing this with you and Josh," Rye said, just behind her shoulder.

"So have I. Only in my dreams you taught Josh to fish like you taught me."

"Y' mean he doesn't know how yet?"

"Not yet."

"Then y' haven't raised him proper." But his voice held a smile.

"He does all right with kites and stilts."

"Aye, he told me all about his stilts." His tone grew serious. "You and Dan've done a good job of it. He's a delightful child, Josh is."

They moved through a patch of white violets, the sun on their cheeks, conscious solely of how close they were, of how much closer they wanted to be. So much to say, so much to feel, so little time.

"I want Josh to know you, Rye, and to know you're his father."

"I, too. But I begin t' see the problem we'll have tellin' him. He loves the one he's got as much as I love my own."

The earth had grown tussocks here. Rye reached for her elbow to steady her. Red-winged blackbirds bobbed on thready reeds of cattail and sedge along the pond's marshy shore, scolding, holding tight while Rye, too, held tight to Laura's elbow as she leaped along to more even ground.

"But I do want us t' be a family," he wished aloud.

"So do I."

They held the thought and moved on slowly through the gift of afternoon, their time together at once luxuriant yet metered by the walk's length. They circled the pond's irregular shoreline, coming upon places where thick broom crowberry—mattress grass—invited them with its resilient cushion. But they could only walk, contenting themselves for the moment with an occasional touch of fingers or a meeting of eyes while the boy and the dog explored ahead.

The thrum of the ocean grew louder, its breakers now white feathers in the distance. Soon its boom surrounded them and they stood on the outwash before an ebbing tide that had scattered jellyfish, which the boy and dog found.

"Don't touch!" Rye called. "They sting!"

The dog knew and kept her distance. The boy waved back before moving on to the next find. Rye hid half his hands within his waistband while taking up that wide-legged stance he'd acquired on a listing deck. His expression was loving as he followed Josh. "There's so much I've missed. Just callin' out a small warnin' t' him that way becomes a joy t' me."

Their eyes met, a mingling of the sweet and the bitter in the exchange.

"When I heard you'd gone to the mainland, I thought you meant not to come back."

"I went t' contract for rough staves." He turned his eyes back to the ocean. "But while I was there, I spoke to a lawyer about this . . . this situation we're caught in. I'd hoped he'd tell me different, but it seems y' truly are Dan's wife."

Laura watched the rim of the world undulate far out on the horizon. "I've thought of divorcing him," she said softly, surprising even herself, for she hadn't meant to admit it.

She sensed Rye turn to her in surprise. "It's not often done."

"No, but it's not often a dead sailor returns from the bowels of the sea. They'd have to understand." She turned to search his face pleadingly. "How could I have known?" she asked with a plaintive note in each word.

"Y' couldn't."

They were on open sand with nothing but surf, a boy, and a dog visible for the white stretch of a mile. But resolutely, Rye refrained from taking her in his arms.

"Rye, does it bother you, what we'll be doing to Dan?"

"I try not t' think about him."

"He's taken to drinking almost every night."

"Aye, I've heard." His head moved sharply toward Miacomet Rip, and his face looked drawn.

"I feel as if I've forced him to start that," she said.

He turned back to her with a new intensity. "It's not our fault anymore than it's his. It's . . . providence."

"Providence," she repeated sadly.

He felt her slipping away and scowled down at her. "Laura, I can't . . ." he began, then his hand came up and worked across his unsmiling lips before he asked abruptly, "Will I have t' wait until then—until a divorce is granted?"

"No."

His eyes snapped to hers, but she was looking out at the horizon. "How long, then?"

"Until tomorrow," she answered quietly, still searching the sea.

His fingers closed on her elbow, and he gently turned her toward him. "I want to kiss you."

"I want to be kissed," she confessed. Not even when contemplating her first time with him had she known sexual impatience such as this. "But not here . . . not now."

His breath hissed out and he released her elbow. They turned and watched a sandpiper trotting the waves, eating sea fleas, and he understood her great trepidation at the decision she was making.

"I tried very hard to do the right thing. I kept away from you," she was saying. "But today, when I saw you coming down that hill . . ." She looked down at her feet. "I . . . I don't know anymore what's right and what's wrong."

"I know. It's the same with me. I keep walkin' in all my spare time, but I can't walk y' out of my system. Y're there in all the old spots we used t' haunt."

"I've thought of a way," she told the sandpiper.

"A way?" He looked at her askance.

"Josh has been begging to spend a day at Jane's."

"Will she suspect?"

"Yes, I think so. No, I know so."

"But—"

"She already knows how I feel. I've never been able to hide much from her. She's told me she knew about you and me and what we did together even before we were married. She'll help us now."

"What about . . . him?"

"I'll tell him tonight."

"Aye, and he'll come into the cooperage tomorrow morning and I'll have t' kill him t' keep from gettin' killed myself."

A smile touched her lips. "No, I won't tell him *that.* I mean I'll tell him I want to divorce."

Rye turned serious again. "Do y' want me there when y' tell him?"

She looked up into his face, his hair lifting like seaoats in the breeze. "I want you . . . everywhere I am. But, no. I'll have to do that part on my own."

He checked the beach in both directions. It was empty but for them. Josh was teasing the edges of waves as they crept up and back. Impulsively, Rye dipped his head and gave Laura a quick kiss.

"I'm sorry, I couldn't help it. I thought I'd been through hell on that whaleship, but I've never been through such hell in my life as the last ten weeks. Woman, when I get y' back, I'm never letting y' out o' my sight again."

"Rye, let's look for a place."

They smiled into each other's eyes, scarcely able to resist this craving.

"It should be easy. We know 'em all, don't we?"

A shiver of anticipation skimmed her arms. "Aye," she replied, low and sensuously. "Aye, we know them all, Rye Dalton."

He gave a sharp whistle between his teeth. The boy and dog perked up. "Come on! Let's head on!" he called.

They found a spot in the lee of Hummock Pond, where its south end looped around, almost closing in on itself. Here, within a sheltered woodlet of pine and oak, they found a secret clearing where bramble and briar seemed to have walled out the rest of the world. Upon these natural trellises wild grapes clung, creating an arbor of fluttering green tiers. Hip-high grass carpeted the glade while tiny wildflowers peeked through shyly. In spots the grass was flattened where deer had made their beds. Squirrels chased and chattered in the oaks. The wind was absent while the sun beat down on them, and on Ship and Josh, playing across the meadow.

"Here?" Rye asked, looking down at Laura.

"Here," she confirmed.

And their hearts raced, and they prayed for sun.

Chapter 11

Their prayers were answered, for the following day was as faultless and clear as a perfect diamond. Laura delivered Josh to Jane's house and arrived at the clearing first. Parting the grapevines, she ducked inside to stand motionless for a moment, listening. The afternoon was so still, she thought she could hear hammering from the shipyards four miles away. But maybe it was only the hammering of her own heart as she surveyed the woodsy oval before her—protected, private, perfect.

It smelled of grass and pine and time alone as Laura lifted her skirts to her ankles, then her face to the sun, eyelids closing, feeling only warmth and a sense of rightness upon her skin. She opened her eyes and turned in a slow circle, but all around were only shades of green enclosing her in a summer world of her own. She whirled faster, faster, arms flung wide in gay abandon, skirts twisting about her legs like a pinwheel.

He's coming! He's coming!

The thought of him tightened her chest and sent currents of anticipation to her limbs.

A movement flashed at the corner of her eye and she stopped twirling, the fingers of one hand moving to the underside of one breast as if to keep her heart confined within her body.

At the edge of the clearing Rye poised, the dog, as usual, coming to a halt beside the knees of her master. Blue eyes took in a vision in airy white dimity turning round and round while the shadow of a wide-brimmed straw hat flitted across her uplifted face. A mint-green ribbon fluttered from its crown, trailing over her shoulder and drifting to rest on the bare skin above the square-cut neckline of her bodice.

Their eyes met. Their senses thrummed while Laura remained totally unabashed at being caught in such a display of abandon, for she loved Rye too well to hide her impulses from him today.

He was dressed in tight tan breeches and a white muslin shirt that stood out strikingly against the green grape leaves behind him. One thumb was hooked in his waistband, the other in a drawstring bag slung over his shoulder.

He surveyed the waiting woman, neither smiling nor moving, but his heart drummed wildly. Laura, you came! You came!

Around her slim waist was tied a green satin ribbon to match that about her hat brim. Wide, white skirts, like a puffy cloud, were lifted by the grass while the bodice hugged Laura's ribs tightly and pressed firmly upward on breasts, which—even from a distance, Rye could clearly see—rose and fell more sharply at first sight of him.

He let the bag slip slowly to the ground, eyes riveted on Laura while he gave a soft command. "Stay."

Across the silence she heard him utter the word, and while the dog dropped to the ground to wait, Laura stood stalk still and breathless, as if the command were spoken for her.

He took a first slow step, then another, coming on deliberately, eyes never wavering from her. The grass whispered as his high boots brushed through it. Her heart clamored beneath the slim fingers still pressed to her breast. When he stood close, they drank in each other's faces for a long, silent moment before he lazily lifted a hand to the side of her ear, caught the green streamer in the crook of a finger, and trailed it slowly downward until he grazed the bare skin above her straining bodice.

"Satin," he said quietly, rubbing the back of the index finger up and down between her chest and the ribbon.

Beneath his knuckle her flesh rose and fell faster. She watched his eyes travel the path of the green streamer to the fullest part of her breast, then slowly back up to her lips. From low in her throat came a single, strained word. "Aye."

It brought an easy smile to his lips. "It's in my way." Still, he toyed with the skein of ribbon, brushing up and down, up and down, while the flutter of satin against her collarbone made goosebumps erupt along her arms. He stood so close, his shiny boots were buried within the mountainous billows of her skirts.

His eyes, as blue as the skies behind him, lingered on her every feature while hers traversed his face with its skin lit to nut-brown by the afternoon sunshine, his hair with its new sideburns making him seem partly stranger. Curiously, Laura's fingers still cupped her own breast. She could feel her hastened heartbeat there and wondered if he, too, detected it as he leaned slowly, knuckle slipping away to be replaced by his warm, open lips. Lightly, he touched the satiny skin of her collarbone, pushing the ribbon aside.

An ecstasy of emotions flooded Laura as her eyelids drifted shut and she touched his face for the first time. "Oh, Rye," she breathed, cupping his jaw, resting her lips against his hair. The scent of him was as she remembered, a mixture of cedar and his father's pipe tobacco and the flavor she thought of as sea breeze, knowing no other name for it.

He raised his head, seemingly unhurried, though within, he, too, knew great impatience. But it was too good to hurry, too fine, with Laura, to plunge through the luxury they'd been afforded in this golden afternoon.

"Turn around," he ordered gently, still having touched no more than that tantalizing bit of skin at her collarbone.

"But . . ." His lips were too inviting, his touch too enticing.

"Turn around," he said more softly, putting his wide brown hands on her tiny waist. She covered them with her own, turned away from him very slowly, scarcely able to breathe. His hands slipped from under hers and she felt the tug of the brass pin leaving her hat while he asked, "What am I wearing?"

"A white muslin shirt, the tan summer breeches you wore the day we ate oranges in the market, new black boots I've never seen before, and a whale's tooth on a silver chain in the open collar of your shirt."

"Ahh . . . very good. You get a reward." The hat was pulled from her head and rustled onto the grass at her side. His hands, spread wide, came back to span her ribs, as if she were a ballerina he was guiding in a spin. Then his lips touched the side of her neck above the scooped back neckline. She tilted her head to one side, luxuriating in the touch of his mouth on her skin.

"You're very stingy with your rewards, Mr. Dalton," she murmured, feeling as if her body would rebel if it couldn't soon know more of him than he chose to dole out in tantalizing deliberation.

"I seem to remember y' liked it lingery . . . or have y' changed? Do y' want it all at once?"

She laughed throatily, for her head was thrown back, the sun warm on her jaw as he bit the side of her neck and wet it with his tongue.

"Mmm, y' taste good."

"Like what?"

"Lilacs."

"Aye, lilac water." She moved sensuously. "You, too, get a reward." She knew he was smiling, though his face was buried in her neck and hers turned toward the Nantucket sky. She covered his hands with her own. For a moment neither of them moved but for his driving breaths against her shoulder and hers that raised their joined hands on her ribs. The backs of his hands were wider than hers, the fingers longer, the skin harder. She guided them slowly, slowly upward while the smile dissolved from her lips, which parted as she held his palms cupped tightly against both of her breasts. For a moment his breath stilled beside her ear and she pictured him with eyes closed as hers were, sunspots dancing in crazy, exhilarating patterns against her lids.

"Laura-love," he said gruffly as his hands started moving, caressing, relearning, while hers lingered on them, absorbing the very feel of his touch. "Am I dreaming or are y' really here at last?"

"I'm here, Rye, I'm here."

As they shared this first caress, the faraway notes of the bell in the church tower drifted across the meadow, chiming out the musical prelude to the hour, then the hour itself . . . one! . . . two! They had grown up to the chiming of that bell, had often gauged their waning time to it, and knew its message well.

"Two o'clock. How much time do we have?"

"Until four."

One hand left her breast and tipped her chin up. Twisting half-around, she met his lips at last over her shoulder. And as they kissed, each wished the bell had not rung. He dropped his hands to her waist and spun her around almost viciously. She looped one of her arms around his neck, the other around his ribs, while he held her so demandingly, the whalebones bit into her skin. His mouth blended with hers as their tongues possessed one another, thrusting and tasting, hungry for full intimacy. He grasped the sides of her head and slanted his mouth across hers in one direction, then another, low sounds coming from his throat, as if he were in pain. All pretense of nonchalance had disappeared with the ringing of the church bell, but it had left its reverberations within their bodies, which moved rhythmically against each other when he pulled the length of her against him.

He dropped to the earth, taking her with him, and fell across her lap in a billow of white dimity. Reaching an arm up, he hooked the back of her neck and bent her to him while she pressed kisses on his closed eyelids, his temple, the hollow beneath his nose, the corner of his mouth, and his throat. "Oh, Rye, I would know the smell of you if I were blindfolded. I could pick you out from all the men of this world with my nose alone." Without opening his eyes, he chuckled, letting her go on nuzzling and kissing her way around his face and hair.

"Mmm . . ." She made a humming sound of delight with her nose buried in the soft waves above his ear.

"What do I smell like?" he asked.

"Like cedar and smoke and salt."

He laughed again, then returned his mouth to hers for a long, ardent intermingling of tongues. She ran her hands along the firm muscles of his chest while he pressed his palm along the side of her breast, exploring with a long thumb until the nipple ached sweetly for release from its tight restraints.

She slipped her hand within his shirt. The chain was warm, the hairs silken, his nipple tiny-hard as her fingertips fluttered across it. His chest muscles tensed beneath her hand, then with a groan he turned his face toward her breasts, opening his mouth greedily against the dress front, forcing his warm breath through it before catching the fabric between his teeth and tugging it as he made inarticulate sounds deep in his throat.

"Are y' wearin' it?" He backed away, freeing his lips from the white dimity.

Their eyes met as with a single fingertip she traced the outline of a swooping sideburn, from the pulsebeat that rapped at his temple to the curve beneath his firm cheekbone. "Yes, I'm wearing it."

"I thought so. I could feel it."

"I've worn it every day since you gave it to me."

"Let me see." But he remained across her lap for a minute, studying her delicately pink cheeks and the brown eyes, heavy-lidded with anticipation. He braced up, resting a palm beside her hip, his eyes now on a level with hers. "Turn around," he ordered gently.

He moved back off her skirts to kneel behind her as the fabric rustled and puffed high, totally covering his thighs. Her hair was gathered in a cascade of ringlets, which she moved aside, presenting the nape of her neck. He touched it with his fingertips, sending shivers preceding his touch along the line of hooks down her vertebrae. She pictured his hands, tough and capable, hands that knew well how to control both oak and a woman's flesh. The contrasting pictures unleashed a rush of sensuality within Laura while he parted the dress down to her waist, then beyond.

The dress fell forward and she pushed it past her wrists, then, still sitting, reached for the button at the waistband of her petticoat. Watching, he pressed a hand to her shoulder blade, just above the corset, and stroked the soft hollow up the center of her back with his thumb. Dress and petticoats lay now like a newly blossomed lily, with Laura its pistil. Like a bee gathering nectar, he dipped his head to kiss her soft shoulder before straightening once more to free the laces along her back. Inch by inch they separated, revealing a wrinkled chemise. With a touch he urged her to stand, and she rose on shaky knees, resting a hand on his shoulder to steady herself as she stepped out of the cylinder of whalebone and buckram.

Rye raised his eyes, but she stood partially turned away from him, clad now in pantaloons and chemise. Strong, tan hands squeezed her hipbones, turning her slowly to face him while he gazed up, then reached for the ribbon between her breasts. But his hands stopped, then captured the backs of hers as he spoke into her eyes.

"You take it off. I want to watch y'. Out at sea, the picture of you undressing was the thing I remembered best." He turned one soft palm upward, then the other, leaving a lingering kiss in each before placing them at her laces. Then he sat back on his haunches, watching, remembering first times with her.

Slowly, Laura loosened the ribbons, and along with them a series of ricocheting feelings that made her feel wanton and shy, sinful and glorified, while his gaze remained steadily on her. She grasped the hem of the waist-length garment and worked it over her head, then dropped her arms to her sides, leaving the chemise dangling, forgotten, from her fingertips.

His eyes scanned her bare breasts, their dusky nipples exposed to the sun, then the criss-cross tracery of red lines on her skin. She watched, standing perfectly still, as his Adam's apple glided up and down before he rose to his knees, placing warm palms gently over her ribs to pull her near and kiss the imprint made by the busk along the center of her stomach and chest. Other impressions had been left by the whalebone stays on either side, and he treated them likewise, tracing each with the tip of his tongue, starting at the warm hollow beneath her breast, gliding down to her waist. His palms caressed her warm back, gathering her close against him as his lips at last covered a dark, sweet nipple.

Laura closed her eyes, adrift upon a liquid rush of desire, one hand seeking his hair, the other his shoulder, taking a fistful of shirt and twisting it tightly as he moved to her other breast, where he tugged and sucked, sending spasms of desire knifing through her limbs.

Rye clamped a strong arm about her hips, pulling her against his chest as he took his fill of this woman he'd wanted for five yearning years. Long, delighted minutes later, he leaned away to look up at Laura. She dropped her gaze to see him framed by her naked breasts, and smiled at the sight of his dark fingers stroking her white, soft flesh, shaping and reshaping it, a wonderous expression on his face. Unashamed, she watched and thrilled, letting the tide of emotions build.

''I thought I remembered perfectly, but y' were never this good in my memories. Aw, love, your skin is so soft.'' His tongue circled the outer circumference of one orb, then its crest, wetting a wide circle of skin. Then he sat back and watched as, the air touching it, evaporating, cooling, the nipple drew up tightly into a ripe, ready berry of arousal, which he again teased with tongue and teeth.

She reached over his shoulder to tug his shirttail free of his pants, needing to touch more than just his clothing. He sat back and obediently raised his arms while the shirt skimmed past ribs and wrists. Holding the garment, she plunged her face into the soft cloth to breathe deeply of his scent, which lingered there.

An impatient hand stole the shirt and flung it aside.

''Sit down,'' he ordered, the words rough-textured.

Immediately, Laura complied, dropping back onto ruffled pantaloons, bracing her palms on the grass behind. She watched in fascination while he lifted one foot and started removing her shoe. Over his shoulder it went before he peeled away her stocking and reached for her other foot.

He managed the second shoe without taking his eyes from her face, while she watched every movement of the arousing process, each shifting muscle of his hands undressing her. The second shoe and stocking joined their mates, then he held her foot in both hands, running a thumb over the sensitive instep. While he fondled the foot, his eyes traveled her disheveled hair, bare breasts, and pantaloons.

''Y're beautiful.''

''I have wrinkles on my belly.''

''Even y'r wrinkles are beautiful. I love every one of 'em.''

Sitting back on his haunches with knees widespread, he lifted her foot and kissed its arch, then the small hollow beneath her anklebone, while he watched her beguiling mouth drift open and her tongue catch between her teeth. He pressed the sole of her foot against the high, hard center of his chest, moving it in small circles while her eyes followed . . . silky-soft hair, hard muscle, the chain, and whale's tooth trailing on her bare toes.

Senses that had lain dormant for five years sprang to life in Laura while Rye gradually lowered her foot down the center of his chest to his hard belly, then to his waistline, settling it finally against the hot, hard hills of his tumescence. A shuddering breath fell from him and his eyes closed. She pressed her heel against him and he rocked forward on his knees while her fingers clutched handfuls of grass behind her. When he opened his eyes again, they were fraught with passion.

''I want y' more right now than I did in Hardesty's loft when we were sixteen.'' The heat of his body burned through his breeches while he soothed a hand over her ankle.

Elbows locked, she let her head drop backward, and her eyes drifted shut as she said chokily, ''I thought I'd never feel your hands on me again. I've wanted this since . . . since the day you sailed away from me. What's happening inside me now has never happened since that day . . . only with you.''

''Tell me what's happening.'' He moved sharply up beside her, bracing one hand on the grass, the other at last cupping the ripe readiness between her legs as he leaned over her, kissing her exposed throat.

But her only answer was an impassioned sound more expressive than any words she might have chosen as, with head slung back, palms braced firmly on the earth, she thrust her hips upward in invitation. He explored her through cotton pantaloons as he'd first done years ago, dipping his head to kiss the tip of her chin while she moved rhythmically against his hand.

''Let me see the rest of you,'' he begged against her throat.

She drew her heavy head up. ''In a minute.'' She pressed a palm against his breast until he went backward onto the grass, catching himself on his elbows, Laura's and his positions now reversed. ''Your boots.''

Unceremoniously, she took up his left foot, working assiduously at tugging the boot off. But her efforts proved futile. He couldn't help smiling as her face contorted with a grimace.

''Why do you wear . . . your . . . boots . . . so . . . tight?'' She grunted. ''They never . . . used to be.''

''They're new.'' He enjoyed every minute of her struggle, then she changed positions and his smile grew broader at the sight of her pink soles facing him, one on each side of his long leg.

''Laura, y' should see y'rself, sittin' there in nothin' but those ruffly pantaloons, pullin' at my boot like some hoyden.''

''It . . . won't . . . come . . .'' But just then the boot slipped off, nearly tumbling her backward. She laughed into his eyes and threw the boot over her shoulder, then ran her hands up inside the leg of his breeches to peel away his woolen sock.

''Did I make this?'' she asked, holding the stocking aloft.

''No, another woman did.''

''Another woman?'' Her eyebrows puckered.

His blue eyes twinkled mischievously. ''Aye, m' mother. An old pair I found in a chest at home.''

''Oh.'' Laura's smile was reborn as the sock sailed away, and she made quick work of the second boot and sock, which soon joined the others.

In a swift movement, Rye came up off the ground, tackling Laura with an arm around her waist, rolling her over and over on the grass until her hair was tumbled and her breasts heaved. Sprawled across the length of her body, he looked down into brown, eager eyes and a mouth across which a strand of hair had fallen during their tussle. His mouth slammed down across hers, heedless of the lock of hair, opening fully in a wild, voluptuous exchange of tongues while his left hand clamped the back of her head and his right kneaded a breast almost hurtfully. His knee came up hard between her legs and their bodies writhed together in reckless thrusts while they rolled to their sides, kissing with an unleashed ardor in which gentleness, for the moment, had no part.

Her fingers twisted in his hair and her eyelids shut out the blue sky background as he tore his mouth from hers and opened it on the breast, which he cupped high and hard, sending a sweet pain through her as she rejoiced, "Oh, Rye, Rye, is it really you at last?"

"Aye, it's me, with five years t' make up for." But his breath wheezed like a high wind and his chest heaved torturously as his blue eyes burned into her brown ones. Then suddenly she was released, and he sat up abruptly, straddling her hips as his hands roughly began jerking open the buttons of his breeches while his eyes blazed with the unmistakable fire of intent. Her own blazed an answer as she freed the single button at her side. Their eyes did not waver while he sat her straight and tall, like a rider in a saddle, then a moment later dismounted, swinging a knee back and pulling her to her feet all in one fluid motion.

Trousers and pantaloons drifted to the ground and a moment later they faced each other with but the distance of a glance between them, nature's children, dressed in no more than a whale's tooth and a criss-crossing of red lines, which even now were fading from her skin. Their eyes feasted for a brief time as they stood naked beneath a blue bowl of sunshine, surrounded by salt-scented grass and a wreath of grapevines.

When Laura and Rye's arms went about each other, the force nearly knocked the breath from their bodies. She felt her toes leaving the ground while he held her aloft, kissing her mouth, turning in a circle of ecstasy. Then she was struggling, squirming.

"Rye, put me down so I can touch you."

"You touch me, and I'm gone," he declared roughly. "Christ, it's been five years."

"Aye, love, I know. For me, too." His eyes pierced hers with a question, and she immediately realized she should not have admitted it. "Rye—" Her voice trembled. "—put me down . . . love me . . . love me . . ."

The trees tipped sideways as his hard brown arm slipped behind her knees to lift her, and a moment later Laura's shoulders were pressed to the grass. She looked at his face, framed by blue sky, then at his nodding tumescence, for which she immediately reached, then guided home. . . . He was solid velvet, she liquid, and his first thrust brought to Laura a bursting sensation of desire which this act had not brought since she'd last celebrated it with Rye. And then the beat began, rhythmic and fluent. And they ceased to be him and her and became simply them—one.

They arched together beneath the summer sun, which rained on his back as he moved, sending hovering shadow across her face and shoulders. The whale's tooth dangled across her breastbone to the hollow of her throat, then took up a pendulous tapping on her chin.

She lifted herself in reception to each thrust, watching Rye's pleasured face while he bared his teeth and sucked in great shuddering gulps of air. He hung his head to watch their bodies mingling, and her eyes followed. When his beat accelerated, the grass bit into her shoulders and her head was pressed back harder onto the earth. She closed her eyes and rode the swells with him, while his body beckoned her response. It built and it burned until the inward embraces began, forcing a throaty cry from her lips. He grunted as his climax neared, coming against her so hard she skittered beneath him along the earth, then unknowingly closed her fingers around the grass for a handhold.

She welcomed every inch of the force as her body quivered to its completion. His cry carried over the meadow as he spilled into her, and the final shudder sent sparkling beads of perspiration glinting on his shoulder.

He fell across her breasts, exhausted, and lay there panting until he felt silent laughter lifting her chest. He raised his weary head to meet her eyes. ''Look what we've done.'' She rolled her head to peer past his shoulder and along her hip.

He craned around to find in her hand a fistful of turf, pulled up by its roots. He smiled and checked her other hand. It, too, was clasping a clump of grass. Suddenly, she lifted both hands high off the ground and let the clods tumble from her fingers in a kind of jubilation, then flung her arms tightly about his shoulders. He rolled them to their sides, one hand reaching to brush off her palm.

''Was I too rough with y'?''

She smiled tenderly into his eyes. ''No, oh no, love. I needed it just as it was.''

''Laura . . .'' He cradled her gently, closing his eyelids against her hair. ''I love y', woman, I love y'.''

''I love you, Rye Dalton, just as I've loved you since I first knew what the word meant.''

They lay together with their heartbeats joined, letting the sun dry their skin. After several minutes, he rolled back his shoulder and flung an arm out, palm up. She did likewise, and they closed their eyes as they basked and rested. She lay on his left and with her right hand reached lazily to idle through the hair on his chest. Blindly, he reached for it and brought the fingertips to his lips before replacing it on his chest.

''Laura?''

''Hm?''

''What did y' mean before when y' said it'd been five years for y'?''

For a moment she didn't answer, but finally replied, ''Nothing. I shouldn't have said it.''

He studied the sky, where a single white cloud drifted. ''Dan doesn't take you all the way, does he?''

Immediately, she rolled near and covered his lips with her fingertips. ''I don't want to talk about him.''

He braced his jaw on a palm and lay on his side facing her. ''That's what y' meant, isn't it?'' He trailed the tip of a finger down between her breasts to her belly, and on to the nest of hair that held the warmth of the sun in its tangles, the warmth of him in its shelter. He watched goose pimples ride her skin, though her eyes were closed. He pressed the brown triangle. ''This is mine. It's always been mine, and the thought of him havin' it has kept me miserable every night that I've slept alone since I've been home. At least he didn't have it all.'' He kissed her chin lightly. ''I'm glad.''

Her eyes opened to his. ''Rye, I had no right to say it. I sh—''

His lips cut off her words. Then he lifted his head and stroked her jaw with a knuckle. "Laura, I taught you, you taught me. Learnin' together gave us rights."

But she didn't want to mar the day with any talk that might rob them of the smallest slip of joy. Brightly, she smiled, then studied his face, from hairline to chin. "Do you know what I've been wanting to do ever since you've been back?"

"I thought y' just did it." The dent appeared in his cheek.

"No, not that."

"What, then?"

"To explore each of these tiny pockmarks with the tip of my tongue, and to touch these—" she pressed both palms against his side-whiskers. "—like this."

With a smile, he fell onto his back, flipping her over on top of him. "Explore all y' like."

She wet each tiny mark, ending with the seventh, on his upper lip. Raising her head, she smoothed her palms over the side-whiskers, studying him, delight in her face. "I like these, do you know that? They're . . . very masculine. When I first saw you, they made you seem . . . well, almost like a stranger, somebody enticing but forbidden."

He lazily caressed her hipbones, then moved his hands down over her bare buttocks. "And do I still seem like a stranger?" he asked, grinning up at her.

"You're different in some ways." She flipped his lower lip down with an index finger, and let it slip closed again.

"How?"

"The way you stand, like the ship is going to yaw at any minute. And the way you talk. You used to talk just like I do, but now you say aye and nay and cut off the ends of words." She pouted and pondered. "Say, 'Laura darling.' "

"Laura darlin'," he repeated obediently.

"See? Laura, darli*nnn* . . ." She giggled, and he, too, laughed.

"Well, y' are my Laura darlin'," he said.

But she laughed again. "I fear it's there to stay, but it's charming, so I don't mind."

He gave her an affectionate slap on the rump. "Are y' hungry?"

"There y' go again, m' briny lad," she answered in her best imitation of a New England tar. "Aye, I'm rav'nous!"

He laughed, white teeth flashing in the sun, slapped her again, and demanded, "Then get up off me. I've brought food."

The next minute she was dumped away, and sat Indian-fashion while he strode off to where Ship lay guarding the drawstring bag. She watched the strong muscles of Rye's buttocks and thighs flexing as he crossed the clearing to retrieve his cache. The dog immediately sat up, alert. Rye went down on one knee, giving Ship a scratch and a muffled assurance of her master's affection. Then the two of them came back together with the bag of food.

Laura watched them, and as they drew near, raised up on her knees to greet Rye as if he'd been gone a long time. "Come here." She held her arms open and he walked flush against her. She pressed her face against his lower belly, then against his flaccid manhood before backing away and looking up at his face, which was bent to watch her smilingly. "You're a beautiful man. I could watch you walk naked across the grass forever and never turn my eyes away.'' He touched her face. ''I love you, Rye Dalton.'' Her arms tightened about his hips. His blue eyes smiled down at her with a fulfillment he hadn't known since his return.

''I love you, Laura Dalton.''

Ship's cold, wet nose divided them as she thrust it against Laura's bare side. Laura jumped back, scolding and laughing.

Rye laughed and dropped to the grass with a rough, affectionate graze of his palm on the dog's head. ''She's jealous.''

Laura watched as he worked the bag open. ''What do you have?'' she asked.

His hand plunged inside. ''Oranges!'' Up flew an orange, high above her head. She caught it with a lilt of laughter. ''For the lady who likes to share oranges with gentlemen in a most enticing way.'' His teasing grin brought a smirk to her lips.

''Oh, oranges. Perhaps you should have invited DeLaine Hussey today. I have the feeling Miss Hussey has wanted to get her hands on your oranges for years.''

''I only share my oranges with you.'' The dimple in his cheek was thoroughly engaging as he raised his eyes. Then it grew even deeper when he looked up to find her sitting back on her heels, breasts thrust forward and hidden impudently behind a pair of concealing oranges.

''And I only share my oranges with you,'' she returned innocently.

His wide brown hands came up to squeeze the fruit. ''Mmm . . . you have nice, ripe, firm oranges. I'd love sharing them.'' He dipped his head as if to sample with his teeth, but with one orange she rapped his cheek aside.

''Where are your manners, Rye Dalton! You have to ask politely first.''

He lunged at her then, knocking her backward in the grass, their laughter carrying over the meadow while Ship watched their antics with a lazy eye.

''I'll show y' the proper way t' share an orange, y' little minx!''

In their tussle one of the oranges went rolling, but he captured the other, subduing Laura finally until she ended up on her back, and he knelt over her with one powerful and well-placed knee pressing hard against her ribcage.

She pushed at it, laughing with utmost difficulty. ''Rye, I can't breathe.''

''Good.'' He ripped off a piece of orange peel. It landed on her cheek, and she twisted her head aside, laughing harder. ''First y' have t' peel the orange just so.'' Another piece of peel fell to her closed eye.

''Rye Dalton, you overgrown bully!''

''But only halfway, so y' have somethin' t' hang on to.''

Plop! This piece hit her on the nose, which she wrinkled as she pushed at his knee. ''Get off . . .''

He ignored her plea, letting her squirm away while calmly completing his chore. ''And when y' have the juiciest part exposed . . .'' The conqueror let another chunk of peel hit the vanquished on her upper lip. ''. . . you're ready t' share y'r orange.''

She was still pushing at his knee with her hands, but she bit her lip to keep from smiling. Lordly and lean, he held her down and kept his blue eyes on her mouth as he lifted the orange and sank his teeth into it. While he chewed, his lips all wet and sweet, she grew increasingly aware of his bold pose that left bare essentials hovering just above her. He tore into a second bite and lazily savored it, then swallowed.

"Y' want some?" he asked, arching a brow at her.

"Yes."

"Some what?"

"Some of your orange."

"Where're y'r manners, Laura Dalton? Y' have t' ask politely first."

"May I please have some of your orange?"

His eyes raked her body, from one breast, half-flattened by his knee, to the white flesh of her stomach, the triangle of hair, the flare of hips, then slowly back up to her face again. "I guess so."

The orange came slowly toward Laura's mouth, and she opened her lips slowly until at last the succulent flesh was pressed against her teeth, and she tore off a chunk with a twist of her head, all the while keeping her burning gaze on his deceptively fierce blue eyes. The pressure from his knee relaxed, and he began brushing it against her breast until the nipple rose up to meet the rough texture of the hair on his leg.

She swallowed, licked her lips, but left them parted and glistening. "Mmm . . . sweet," she murmured.

"Aye, sweet," came his throaty reply, while his eyes did queer things to her stomach.

"It's your turn," she said softly.

"Aye, so it is." His knee was gone from her breast. His dark hand moved above her, holding the orange. Its power was evident in the wide wrist, the blue veins on its back, the muscles corded from coopering these many years. Her eyes were polarized by the sight of his fingers slowly clenching about the orange. She started only slightly as the first cold droplet landed on her breast. She watched in soaring anticipation as his lean fingers squeezed, squeezed, sending the juice in a cool line down the valley between her breasts, to her navel, along her stomach, and down one thigh.

Then his head was slowly bending to her, his tongue tracing the sweet path of the juice, licking it from her while her eyelids slid shut and her heart went on a Nantucket sleighride.

He'd been five years at sea with a whaleship full of lusty men who'd had nothing more than talk and memory to buoy them over the course of the voyage. Rye Dalton had learned from listening.

And as he'd done in a loft above a boathouse and in a cooperage before a warming fire, he taught Laura new things about her own body. As he dipped his head to taste of her orange sweetness, he brought her a splendor of which she'd never dreamed. And later, he peeled a second orange and handed it to her while her eyes grew wide and she stared at his offering, then slowly, slowly reached to take it while he lay back on the grass and took his turn at splendor.

Chapter 12

The afternoon waned, and they were forced to regard the bell from the church tower as it chimed out each quarter hour. They lay on their backs, each with an ankle crossing an updrawn knee, their bare soles touching. Rye held Laura's hand, rubbing his thumb absently in her palm.

"Do you know what I did the night before you sailed?" she asked, smiling at the memory.

"What did y' do?"

"I put a black cat under a tub."

He laughed and pillowed his head on his free wrist. "Don't tell me y' believe that old wive's tale!"

"Not anymore, I don't. But I was so desperate, I'd try anything to keep you from sailing. But even the cat under the tub didn't bring anything resembling a strong enough headwind to keep your ship from leaving the harbor the next day, like it was supposed to."

He turned to study her. "Did y' miss me like I missed you?"

"It was . . . awesome. Terrible." A solemn moment of memory passed.

He shifted his weight and rolled onto his side, laying a hand on her stomach. "Y'r stomach is rounder . . . and y'r hips're wider."

"I've had your baby since you've been away."

"Why didn't y' have one of Dan's?"

The magic spell was broken. She sat up, curling her back and hugging her knees. "I said I don't want to talk about him."

Rye braced up on an elbow, studying her back. "Y' didn't tell him last night, did y'?"

She dropped her forehead onto her knees. "I . . . I couldn't. I tried, but I just couldn't."

"Do y' love him more than me, then?"

"No . . . no!" She turned with a quick flash of fire in her eyes, then once more presented her back. "Next to you he's . . . oh, Rye, don't make me say things that will only cause us both to feel guiltier than we already are."

"I don't like playin' him false any more than you do. But I won't have y' sleepin' with him nights and me days and not tellin' him it's over between y'."

"Rye, I know I promised, but . . . but there're Josh's feelings to consider, too."

He sat up and jerked distractedly at a tuft of grass. "And what about y'r feelin's for me? Do they count for nothin'? Do y' want me—us—t' settle for this, sneakin' up into the hills to make love once every month or so while Dan keeps remindin' you y' have an *obligation* t' him and the boy?'' Rye flung the grass away angrily.

''No,'' she answered in a tiny voice.

''What, then?''

Miserable, she had no answer. Rye stared at the ground, realizing he had the power to tell Dan the truth and be done with it, angry with himself for even having the thought because Laura trusted him not to do such a thing. His eyes moved down her bare spine, then to her arm as she reached for her clothing.

''Laura, if we keep on this way, it'll only get worse. I send y' home t' him, y' send me back t' my father, and everybody's miserable.''

''I know.''

As she slipped on the first article of clothing, the chimes rang again below. Rye, too, reached for his breeches. While donning them, he watched her reach for her chemise, pull it on, and began lacing its ribbons. Standing behind her, he could not resist asking, ''Laura, does he make love to y' often?''

She would not turn and face him. ''No.''

''Since I've been back?''

''Only a few times.''

Rye drew a shaky breath and ran a hand through his hair. ''I shouldn't have asked, I'm sorry,'' he said gruffly.

Her voice trembled, but her back remained turned upon him. ''Rye, with him it's never been like it is with you . . .'' She spun now to face him. ''Never!'' Her throat worked. ''I guess it's because I . . . I love him out of gratitude, not passion, and there's a world of difference between the two.''

''And y'll stay with him out o' gratitude, is that what y're sayin'?''

There were tears on her lashes now. ''I . . . I . . .''

Rye Dalton then spoke the hardest words he'd ever said. ''I won't string this out forever. Y'll have t' choose. And y'll have t' do it soon, else I'll be leavin' the island for good.''

She'd guessed something like this would happen. Yet how could she tell Josh? How could she tell Dan?

''Promise!'' Rye ordered, standing firmly before her, intensity in every rigid muscle of his body. ''Promise y'll tell him tonight. Then we'll go t' the mainland and begin divorce proceedin's immediately.'' At her hesitation, his words grew harsh. ''Woman, you tempt me in my dreams at night, when I walk the beaches with miles between us, and every wakin' hour of the day. T' me you're still my wife, and I've done what y' asked—I've given y' time t' break away from him. How much longer do y' think I can stand your livin' with him?''

Laura threw herself against Rye and their arms clung. ''I will tell him. Tonight. I promise on my love for you. It's always been you, always, since we were old enough to know the difference between boys and girls. In my heart the vow between you and me has never been broken, Rye. I love you.'' She backed away, took his cheeks in her palms, and said into his sea-blue eyes, ''I promise I will tell him tonight, and I'll meet you at the ferry tomorrow and we'll do as you said. We'll go to the mainland and begin divorce proceedings.''

He grasped the back of her hand and his eyes closed as he fiercely kissed her palm. "I love y', Laura. God, how I love y'."

"And I love you, Rye."

"I'll meet y' at the ferry."

She kissed his lips lightly. "At the ferry."

The promise was still fresh on Laura's lips as she walked up the scallop-shell path with Josh an hour later. As the house came into view, she immediately sensed something was amiss, for sitting on her doorstep was Josh's best friend, Jimmy Ryerson. But instead of leaping to his feet at the sight of Laura and Josh, Jimmy hunkered quietly, watching them approach.

"Hi, Jimmy!" Josh broke into an excited gallop.

"Hi." But Jimmy was all six-year-old business as he reported, "We can't play. I gotta tell your ma something and then you're supposed to come home with me."

"What is it, Jimmy?" Laura questioned, alarmed now, clasping his shoulder.

"They couldn't find you, and they said I was s'posed to sit here and wait till you come home and tell you to go down to Straight Wharf right away."

Laura's eyes flew toward the bay. "Who?"

Jimmy shrugged. "Everybody. They're all down there—your pa, too, Josh. They said your grampa's boat, it tipped over comin' across the bar, and they can't find him."

Laura's heart did somersaults. "C . . . can't find him?"

Jimmy shook his head.

"Oh no." The words were a whispered lament, and Laura's fingers covered her lips as she again looked down over the bay. Reactions tumbled through her in a swift succession: there's got to be some mistake . . . Zachary Morgan couldn't possibly have capsized, he knows these waters too well . . . they've all been looking for me . . . they'll know Rye was gone, too . . . where is Dan?

"How long have they been out looking?" she asked.

"I don't know." Jimmy shrugged again. "I been waitin' here a long time. They says I wasn't s'posed to—"

But Laura cut him off with a firmer grasp on his shoulder. She turned both him and Josh toward the path, ordering, "You go down to Jimmy's house and stay, like they said. And, Josh, you wait until Papa or I come for you. I've got to hurry down to the wharf and find him."

Josh's eyes widened. "Wh . . . what's the matter, Mama? Is Grampa all right?"

"I don't know, darling. I hope so."

Sensing tragedy, Josh suddenly balked. "I don't wanna go to Jimmy's house. I wanna come with you to find Grampa and Papa."

Though each passing second felt like an hour, Laura went down on one knee and brushed her son's hair back in a gesture of comfort. "I know you do, darling, but . . . it's best if you go with Jimmy. I'll try to come for you soon." She gave him a reassuring hug, forcing herself to appear calm for his sake while every muscle in her body was tensed to run.

At last Jimmy came to Laura's aid. "C'mon, Josh. My ma made poundcake and she said we could both have some when we got back."

The mention of poundcake at last put Josh's skepticism to rout, and he turned down the path toward Jimmy's house. Laura stared unseeingly at their backs for a moment, suddenly reluctant to make the journey down the hill herself. She pressed a hand to her lips, shut her eyes, thinking, No! no! This is all some . . . some silly little boy's mistake!

But a moment later she hiked up her skirts and flew like a windjammer before a gale—down the scallop-shell path, along the sandy lanes, onto the cobblestones that echoed the alarm of her running feet as she crossed deserted Main Street Square and ran on toward the blue water of the bay, where masts had come to harbor for the night. The closer she came to the wharves, the greater grew her terror, for she saw a crowd gathered there, all faces turned toward the bar, where nets were stretched between bobbing dories. She realized, too, that the wind had switched to the north, pushing the ocean before it. The bar, always treacherous, was more so when the winds blew northerly. Yet it seemed impossible that the bar could have wreaked disaster, for from here, the breakers did not look high enough to pose a threat.

Laura shouldered her way through the crowd. Murmurous voices trailed after her, and eyes watched her progress.

"Here she is now."

"They've found her."

"It's Laura."

Somber expressions turned her way as she lifted her skirts and edged toward the end of the wharf. Laura flashed pleading glances to one person after another while moving woodenly through the group, seeking a single face that did not reflect disaster. Her breath fell in bellowlike heaves after her headlong run, and her eyes were wide and sparkling with fear.

"Wh . . . where's Dan? What happened?"

A sympathetic hand touched her arm, but it seemed they'd all lost their tongues. Laura wanted to scream, shake someone, force at least one voice to speak!

"Where is Dan?" The words sounded strange, for her throat was tight with rising hysteria.

At last someone answered.

"He's out lookin' with the others." It was old Cap'n Silas who spoke. He surveyed the knot of people at the end of the wharf—the family—while Laura's knees turned to water and she put off going to them.

She clutched Cap'n Silas's wiry arm. "H . . . How long have they been looking?"

"Near two hours now. Y' mustn't fret, girl. All y' can do is wait with th' rest of us."

"Wh . . . what happened?"

Silas clamped his teeth hard on his cherrywood pipestem, turned rheumy eyes toward the waters of the bar, and replied tersely, "Pitchpoled."

"Pitchpoled?" Laura repeated disbelievingly. "But how? Was he alone?"

"With his brother Tom, as usual. But Tom was thrown clear. He's out there lookin', too."

Again Laura's eyes were drawn toward the searchers. Tom was out there looking, too? Searching for his own brother after the two had fished these waters together all their lives?

"But how?" Laura repeated, raising pleading eyes to Cap'n Silas. "How could a thing like that happen when they know every whim of these waters?"

"Overloaded 'er bow," Cap'n Silas answered flatly. He'd been a whaler for forty years, and after those forty had taken up his station as guardian of these wharves. He had seen everything that could happen along them. With the grim acceptance of one older and wiser, he'd come to understand that life and death meant little to the sea. If a man worked by it, he knew he might die by it. A fickle bitch, the sea.

"Good catch today," he went on, scanning the horizon. His voice was like the crackle of an old salt-caked tarpaulin. "Stayed out t' bring in a few more barrels, Tom said. Knew she was yawin', so they shifted a little weight to 'er stern before they hit the bar. But not enough. Wave caught 'er and flipped 'er end over end like a clown doin' handsprings." He puffed once on his pipe. "Tom was the only one surfaced afterwards."

On the calmest day there were breakers over Nantucket Bar. When the wind came in behind them, as it did now, the waves grew steep. Laura pictured Zach and Tom heading in, happy with their day's catch, when they misjudged the speed with which they climbed a wave; the bow, plummeting hard down the forward face of the wave while its succeeding crest nudged the underbelly of the schooner and flipped it stern over bow.

And now Tom Morgan was out there searching for his brother, and Dan Morgan for his father.

At last Laura could put it off no longer. She looked toward the end of the wharf. There, staring out over the water, was Dan's mother, Hilda, with a black shawl clutched tightly around her shoulders, as if to hold herself together. Beside Hilda stood Tom Morgan's wife, Dorothy, in much the same pose. The two women's shoulders almost touched as they stared out to sea. What went through their minds as they watched the hungry waters where brother searched for brother and son searched for father?

Laura looked at the spot at which the two women stared. The scene on the bar appeared to be nothing more momentous than a few fishermen putting out seining nets for minnows. From here the figures of the searchers appeared very tiny, and she could not make out which one was Dan. What was going through his mind out there in the boats when time after time the nets came up empty? And, my God, how long has he been hauling on them? For two hours, while Rye and I lay naked in a meadow, deceiving him? The first wave of guilt washed over Laura, leaving her stomach churning.

She studied the squared shoulders of the two women at the end of the wharf, thought of her afternoon with Rye, and silently cried, Dear God, what have I done?

Suddenly realizing she'd put off going to Hilda as long as she could, Laura approached her mother-in-law. Nantucket women had been schooled for generations to wait for their seafaring men with stiff backs, and as Laura lay her hand upon Hilda's shoulder, she felt that lesson incarnated: Hilda's back was as rigid as any whalebone.

"Hilda, I've just heard."

Hilda turned but seemed to maintain that same stoicism that Cap'n Silas managed. ''Dan's out there, and Tom, too, with the others. All we can do now is wait.'' The stiff back turned away.

Laura found herself clutching her arms just as Hilda and Dorothy clutched theirs, and tremors ran through her flesh as she squinted over the water toward Dan, besieged by memories of receiving the news of Rye's death. Oh, that corpseless death. No, Dan, no. Not again.

Feet shuffled behind Laura, and she turned to find Dan's older sister, Ruth, standing there with two cups of steaming coffee in her hands. Asperity was written on every muscle of Ruth's face as she assessed Laura's white dimity dress and broad-brimmed bonnet. Her eyes were red-rimmed and her mouth pinched in much more than grief. Even as she stared balefully at Laura, Ruth's lips pursed tighter and a knowing expression arched her eyebrows.

She pushed past Laura, handing the cups to her mother and aunt, elbowing her way as if to make it clear that *she* would do the comforting here!

Laura stepped back, but Ruth turned to confront her with slate eyes. ''We tried to find you. Dan was nearly out of his head.''

Laura swallowed, sickened further by the need to lie. ''I walked out to Jane's for the afternoon.''

Ruth made no effort to disguise her opinion of Laura's dress, which was totally inappropriate for a walk across the moors. The critical eyes raked from neck to hem, then back up. ''Well, you might have told Dan where you were going.''

''I . . . I thought he knew. Josh wanted to go out and spend the day with his cousins.''

But Ruth's expression told Laura she didn't believe a word of it.

Did they send someone out to Jane's looking for me? Would Jane have tried to cover for her?

Without another word, Ruth turned away, moving protectively to her mother's side, effectively shutting Laura out.

She knows! She knows! And if she knows, it won't be long before everyone on the island knows. Ruth will see to it. For the first time Laura scanned the faces on the wharf—DeLaine Hussey was there, and Ezra Merrill, and . . . and even Rye's cousin Charles! The whole town had seen her tardy arrival! Laura's insides trembled uncontrollably. She was shaken by guilt not only for the afternoon's act, but because she could stand here now more concerned with being found out than with the tragedy at hand.

No, that's not true, she told herself. You care about each of these people. Their sorrow is yours.

Yet Ruth Morgan had hit her mark. Laura felt tainted, outcast, and swamped by remorse. She stood removed from the trio of women, watching the pitiful spectacle on the water. Out near the bar, the searchers had pulled in their nets, hauled anchor, and were turning their bows toward shore. A muffled sound of despair came from Hilda Morgan's throat. She covered her mouth and watched the boats heading in and wept against Dorothy Morgan's shoulder.

Standing behind them, Laura felt helpless. She wanted to reach out and comfort Hilda, but Ruth and Dorothy still flanked her. Hilda, Hilda, I'm sorry. Have I been the cause of all this? I didn't mean to, I didn't mean to. Laura bit her lips to keep from crying as the boats came nearer and nearer. Let him be alive, she prayed, though she knew from the expressions of the approaching men that they had not found Dan's father, either dead or alive. Laura's eyes were dry as she picked out Dan's white face among the others. How will I answer when he asks where I was? With more lies?

As if she possessed some sixth sense, Ruth turned to pierce Laura with eyes that convicted and sentenced. But a moment later the reproachful stare moved to a point behind Laura's shoulder, where it remained fixed until at last Laura turned, too, to see what Ruth stared at.

There a few feet behind her stood Rye. He was still dressed in the clothes he'd worn this afternoon. His expression was somber as he looked from Laura to the approaching boat.

He found Dan among those on the water, and his gaze again returned to Laura. Already he sensed the direction her thoughts were taking, and he forced himself not to rush to her and say, Laura, Laura, it would have happened anyway. We are not to blame.

Suddenly aware that Ruth studied their silent exchange, Laura pulled her gaze away from Rye. But as she turned to await the search boats, Ruth's censuring eyes remained coldly assessing, until Laura felt transparent.

The dories drew nigh and Laura again found Dan's stricken face, the eyes empty and sunken, the skin deathly pale. He still wore the wool suit he'd donned that morning before leaving for the countinghouse, and the sight of it there among the ruggedly dressed men intensified Laura's feeling of guilt. She stared at his sleeves, wet to the elbows, and the wrinkled, ruined trousers, imagining Dan sitting at his desk on the high stool, looking up as someone approached with the horrifying news, then running home to tell her but finding the house empty. Had he paced the rooms in a frenzy, wondering where she was? Had he set out with the search party doubly forlorn because she wasn't there when he needed her? Had he tugged at those nets all afternoon with his suspicions of Laura and Rye adding weight to his grief?

The dejected men clumped tiredly onto the wharf only to face the next heartrending task, consoling the grief-stricken women. Dan lunged to his mother, taking her in his arms, pressing his cheek against her hair while she cried against him. Laura watched the mother seek strength from her son, the son sprung from the man the sea had claimed—father, husband, lost to both of them in life's inexorable cycle.

Laura hovered, tristful and uncertain, waiting for Dan to see her. When he did, he gave his mother over to the arms of his uncle, aunt, and sister and came to her. She saw his gaze move momentarily to Rye, still standing behind her, then she was clasped against his chest. She held him hard, awash with emotions—pity, shame, guilt, and love. Laura grasped him tightly while over the wharf drifted the awful sound of Hilda and Tom Dalton's weeping, though Dan made not a sound, only swallowed convulsively beside Laura's temple. He clung, arms trapping her in a crushing grip, while the town and Rye Dalton looked on.

At last Dan choked, "He's b . . . been sailing over that b . . . bar all his life," as if unable to comprehend how an incredible thing like this could have happened.

"I know, I know," was all Laura could manage. He rocked her back and forth while tears flooded her eyes.

"Where were you? I looked everywhere."

His question was like a thorn piercing her heart as she was forced to answer in a half truth. "I took Josh to Jane's."

"I was so . . ." He gulped to a stop, and she felt his body tremble. "I needed you." His eyes were pinched tightly closed, his cheek pressed against her hair.

"I'm here, I'm here," she reassured him, though half her heart was with the man who watched from a few paces away.

Dan opened his eyes to find Rye watching them. But friendships don't die as easily as Nantucket fishermen . . . and the gazes of the two men locked together with the joys of a thousand happy yesterdays come to revisit this sad today. Each felt the need to comfort and be comforted by those most familiar, those longest loved. And they were moved by forces quite beyond their control.

Dan released his hold on Laura. His heart thudded hard and heavy while the eyes of Rye Dalton remained burdened with deep sadness. They stood before each other, taut and straining, and it was Rye who took the first long step.

They met with a pining, silent agony, chest to chest, heart to heart, their competition for the woman who looked on arrested temporarily by the far greater importance of death. Clasping Dan tightly, Rye knew a confusion of emotions such as he'd never felt before: love and pity for this man, the need to solace him, and guilt for what he and Laura had done.

"Dan," he said thickly.

"Rye, I'm glad you're here."

The two separated. Rye placed a wide hand on Dan's shoulder. The wool of his jacket felt damp. "I'll wait with y' if y' want. He . . . he was good t' me . . . a good man."

Dan clamped a hand on Rye's hard forearm, pulling the comforting palm more firmly against his shoulder for a moment. "Yes, please. I think Mother would like it if you did . . . and . . . and Laura, too."

The onlookers shuffled their feet and glanced at each other self-consciously. They looked from Rye to Dan to the woman beside them. The face of Laura Dalton was a study in torment. Her hands were tightly clasped between her breasts. Tears trembled on her eyelids, then rolled down her cheeks as she watched the emotional exchange.

They turned then, Dan to Laura's side, and Rye to Hilda's. As Rye's arms went about Dan's mother, she wept against him. "R . . . Rye . . ."

"Hilda," was all he could manage as he spread a large brown hand on the gray knot of hair at the back of her head and held her firmly, silently, letting her weep.

The days turned back and Rye was a boy again, slamming in and out of Hilda's house on Dan's heels. He was fishing with Zachary, presenting Hilda with a fresh catch, and staying for supper when she'd cooked it. Then he and Dan were fetching water for dishes, at Hilda's orders, and being scolded equally when they spilled some on her clean floor. In those days Rye had only reached Hilda's shoulder; now she barely reached his. He swallowed and held her tight.

An awesome welling filled Laura's throat as she looked on. To the best of her knowledge, it was the first time Rye had spoken to Hilda since his return.

Laura remembered Hilda offering comfort at the news that Rye had been drowned without a trace. How ironic that it should now be he offering comfort to her when it appeared her husband had met the same fate.

Laura glanced at Dan to find him watching Rye and his mother with glistening eyes, his throat working convulsively.

At last Hilda moved out of Rye's arms, and the voice of Cap'n Silas seemed the only one to have a calming effect, perhaps because he had lived through scenes like this before and had learned to accept them.

''Tide'll turn in a couple hours or so. Y' can all go home till then. No sense waitin' here. Go home, have y'r supper.''

The crowd parted to make way for Tom and Dorothy Morgan, who turned to do as Silas suggested. They were followed by Ruth and Hilda. Behind them came Dan, flanked by Rye and Laura. The rest of the crowd dispersed, but when the trio came to the old worn benches on either side of the bait shack door, Dan turned to Cap'n Silas. ''Do you mind if we wait here? I'd rather.''

Seating himself on one of the benches, Cap'n Silas pointed toward the other one with his pipestem. ''Set yerself down.''

The three of them sat on the bench: Rye, Dan, and Laura. Their order had at last changed. For Laura there seemed some bizarre form of justice at work, that on this day when she and Rye had willfully betrayed Dan, they should now end up on either side of him, offering their united support and comfort. She held Dan's hand and rested her head wearily against the silvered boards of the bait shack wall while guilt made her dizzy and sick. If Zachary was dead, most certainly it was the great hand of justice reaching out to mete swift retribution and teach her a lesson. She squeezed Dan's hand tighter and waited for the tide to turn.

Sunset spilled over the island and bay. The sandpipers came in to nest while the piping plovers, with their dreary peeps, played their last evening song. The incessant carp of the gulls quieted at last as they settled on wharf piling and spar, fat-breasted and content. The wind disappeared, and the gentle lap of the water under the wharf seemed the world's only sound until the solemn notes of the vespers rang out from the Congregational bell tower.

Soon the tide would turn, but it would be grim either way—whether the body was borne in upon it or if it was not.

Laura's eyelids slid closed and she relived the horror of those days right after news of Rye's death had reached the island. Against her arm she felt the touch of Dan's sleeve. He sat utterly still, resigned. Now she would be the one to comfort him as he'd once comforted her. She opened her eyes to study his melancholy posture, hunched forward, elbows to knees, and Rye, too, came into view. Laura closed her eyes again and resigned herself to remaining with Dan as his wife.

When she lifted her eyelids it was to feel Rye's gaze on her, and she turned to find his head rested tiredly against the wall, his face turned her way. His arms were crossed on his chest, feet flat on the floor, and knees widespread while his somber blue eyes studied her. She read in those eyes the memories of the afternoon that came back with a haunting beauty. But there was hopelessness, too, in the mournful yet loving expression, and for long minutes she was unable to tear her gaze away. But then, of one accord, they turned their heads to face the bay again.

Just then Dan sighed. His shoulders lifted, then slumped, and he stared at the boards between his feet. Laura rested a palm on his back. Rye's eyes followed it. Dan looked back over his shoulder at Laura, then at the harbor again. As if seeking the comforting assurance that life still went on, he asked, "Where's Josh?"

Laura felt Rye's gaze move to her again as she answered, "He's at Jimmy's house."

"Did he have a good time at Jane's?"

It was all Laura could do to answer, "Yes . . . yes, he loves it there."

"What did they do today?"

Guiltily, Laura scoured her brain for a shred of the prattle that had hardly infiltrated her mind while she and Josh had walked home. She sensed Rye holding his breath, waiting for her answer, and suddenly remembered what Josh had said. "They made salt-water taffy."

From the corner of her eyes she saw Rye's shoulders wilt with relief as his eyelids drifted shut. Laura experienced a new agony at the duplicity she and Rye were practicing. Then, to her horror, Dan stretched, rubbed the back of his neck, and commented, "I don't know if it's the mention of something to eat or what, but I keep thinking I smell oranges."

Rye shot up off the bench while Laura's face burned, but Dan didn't turn around.

"Are you hungry, Dan?" Rye asked.

"No, I don't think I could eat if I tried."

But Rye went away just the same and returned with coffee, again taking up his place on the far side of Dan and keeping his eyes off Laura with an effort.

Twilight came on. They finished their coffee. Someone brought sandwiches, but nobody ate. Dan sighed again, rose from the hard bench, and walked aimlessly up the wharf to stare out over the water, his back to Rye and Laura while only the width of his absent shoulders separated them.

Soon he returned, took his place between them, and leaned back tiredly, then began speaking quietly. "I remember when the news came in that you were dead, Rye. Has Laura ever told you what a sea widow goes through?"

"Aye, a little. She said y'd got her through it."

A sound came from Dan's throat, a rueful half chuckle, while he shook his head tiredly, as if the memory must be cleared. Then he bent forward, again presenting a forlorn curve of shoulders to the two behind him while he went on in a heavy voice that seemed dredged up from the depths of despair.

"I was the one who got the job of going up to . . . to your house to tell Laura your ship had gone down. They sent me because the news came into the countinghouse and I was there working. And they knew, of course, that we were . . . we were best friends. I'll never forget how she looked that day when she opened the door." He paused, dropping his chin to his chest momentarily before he lifted it and stared vacantly across the harbor.

Laura wished Dan would lean back and cut off her view of Rye, but he didn't. Rye sat tensely, frowning at the back of Dan's neck.

"Do you know what Laura did when I broke the news to her?" When Rye remained silent, Dan glanced back over his shoulder briefly before facing away again. ''She laughed,'' he said sadly. ''She laughed and said, 'Don't be silly, Dan, Rye can't be dead. Why, he promised me he'd come back.' It would have been so much easier if she'd broken down and cried then and there, but she didn't. Not till months later. I suppose it was natural—her denial, I mean—especially since she had no corpse for proof.''

Laura's palms were damp. Her stomach felt cramped. She wanted to leap to her feet and escape, but she was forced to sit and listen while Dan went on.

''After that, every time a sail was sighted, she'd run to the wharves to wait, certain that the ship was bringing you back, still claiming there'd been some mistake. I can see her yet, hurrying down the square with that awful, too-bright smile pasted on her face, and me wondering what to do to get her to admit the truth and go on from there. I remember one evening when there were no sails at all, the first time I caught her haunting an empty harbor as if willing you to appear. I told her there were no sails, that she was deluding herself, that you were never coming back, that people were beginning to titter about poor, odd Laura Dalton who hounded the wharves waiting for her ghost husband. She slapped me . . . hard. But afterwards she burst into tears . . . for the first time.''

Stop, Dan, stop! Laura begged silently. Why are you doing this? To punish us? But again he went on.

''She stood there facing me defiantly with the tears running down her face, and she said, 'But don't you see, Dan, he's got to come back because . . . because I'm carrying his baby.' That's when I first understood why she'd continued to deny your death as long as she had.''

Laura stared at the harbor now, dry-eyed, recalling the vigils she'd spent here while willing the sea to return Rye to her. And it had . . . but too late. He sat now only a body's width away from her, but separated by a chasm as deep and wide as hell's while the soliloquy went on.

''I followed her one day—it was November, I think, with the beginning of a sleet storm coming out of the northeast. When I caught up to her, she was standing at the top of the cliffs, staring at the ocean as usual. But this time I could see she was resigned. God, she made a pitiful sight with the rain pouring down on her face and her not moving, as if she didn't know or didn't care it was there. She'd . . .'' Dan swallowed loudly. ''She was rounded out already, and when I told her she shouldn't be out there in that wind and rain, that she had to think about the baby, she said she didn't give a damn about the baby.''

Not one of the three moved so much as a muscle. Dan's back might have been carved of stone while the eyes of Rye and Laura remained riveted on it. His voice dropped to a scarcely audible murmur.

''This time I slapped *her*. It nearly killed me to do it. I . . . I thought she'd been standing there thinking about . . . about killing herself, and the baby with her.'' Dan dropped his face into his palms. ''Oh God,'' he muttered against his hands, and the silence grew crushing before he finally raised his face, drew a deep breath, and went on. ''That was weeks after the news of your death, but it was the first time she cried, I mean really broke down and cried like I knew she hadn't before. She said her heart had drowned with you. That was exactly how she said it—'my heart drowned with Rye'—but at least she'd finally admitted you had drowned.

''After that, she finally agreed we should have a funeral.'' At last Dan rested his shoulders and head against the building again. He closed his eyes, and he rolled his head tiredly from side to side. ''I never want to go through a thing like that again. There we were, praying for . . . for . . .'' But he seemed unable to go on.

After a long pause he cleared his throat. ''A funeral like that is hard on a woman. I don't want my mother to have to go through that.'' Then, abruptly, he rose, clumped down the echoing wharf, and stood staring out at Nantucket Bay, leaving the two behind him to wonder at his reason for delivering the painful recital.

At times it had sounded as if he were preparing himself to relinquish Laura to Rye, admitting he'd won her only by default. Yet at other times he seemed to be making it clear he was maintaining his claim on both her and Josh.

Rye Dalton interlaced his fingers across his belly. Inside, it fluttered from the vivid pictures Dan had drawn. Though his eyes were on the woeful figure before him, he was ever aware of Laura. He wanted to reach across the space that separated them and take her into his arms, kiss her eyelids, and soothe her for all she'd suffered over him. He needed very badly to touch her in an affirmation of life while they waited together for the verification of death. He loved her; she was the one he longed for, quite naturally, in this time of tragedy. Yet he could only sit with his hands pressed hard against his belly to keep them from reaching.

The mists came up, eerie fog fingers lending a ghostlike effect to the scene as the townspeople returned to the wharf with the uncanny timing of those who live by the tides. It was neap tide, that time of the lunar month when the difference between high and low tides is smallest. Did that mean the chance of a body washing in was better? Laura wondered. How odd that after living on the island all her life she didn't know the answer to that question. Would a body be bloated after being in the water for four or five hours? As she watched Hilda return with the others, Laura relieved the dread she had borne once before while imagining Rye's body, claimed by the sea, fed upon by fishes. She wanted to go to Hilda and comfort her, but there was no consoling this anguish. If a wife was spared the uncertainty of a bodyless death, she must then suffer the nightmare of viewing the unsightly, distorted corpse, or worse, a portion of it, should the fish have been hungry.

As the search party formed, their voices were hushed and respectful. They carried lanterns, now, that burned their precious whale oil—for such an occasion it could be spared. The hazy haloes of light refracting off the thick salt air seemed to bear witness to the fact that Nantucketers did indeed live *and die* by the whales.

Cap'n Silas dispersed them in parties of two and three to comb the length of the inner harbor. Again, Laura, Dan, and Rye moved together, paralleling the whispering waves as they'd done countless times in years past. The gulf stream had warmed the summer waters to a balmy seventy-two degrees, yet Rye was chilled by dread as he moved to his grisly task, wading barefoot through the shallows, wondering when his foot might strike a soft, inert lump. Dan and Laura were shuffling through the wet-packed sand of the tide wrack.

Rye carried the lantern as the three inched along, more slowly than any of the other searchers, for fear of being the ones to stumble upon the corpse. The lantern revealed a black shape ahead and the three halted, their eyes instinctively seeking one another. In the glow of the burning whale oil and surrounded by fog, their faces were mere glimmers.

"I'll check it," Rye said, clamping his jaw and moving ahead. When the wavering light fell on the dark mass, he sighed with relief and turned back to Dan and Laura. "It's just a log."

They advanced again through the fog-thwarted night, the two men and the woman who seemed, by tradition, both of theirs. And during the hours of the search they shared her equally, and she them, without thought of possessing or belonging. All enmity was, for the time, gone, displaced by the need to remain close, to support one another and draw sustenance for what lay ahead.

The body was found shortly after midnight, "neaped" on the shore after the tide had turned back to sea. The church bell signaled the message. At the sound of its muffled knell in the distance, three heads snapped up. Nobody moved. Rye stood yet in the water. Laura, still in her white dress with its hem gray and ruined, looked like a ghost beside Dan in his dark, shrunken suit.

Rye broke the silence. "They must have found him. We'd better go."

Yet they were reluctant to turn back. Waves slapped softly at Rye's ankles. The night air was thick and blanketing. The eerie bonging of the bell sent shivers up their spines.

Finally, Rye moved to Dan's side, placed a hand on his arm, and felt shudders there. "Are you all right?"

Dan seemed to be staring at nothing. "Let's just hope the sea returned a whole body."

Rye moved his hand to the side of Dan's neck and let the pressure of his palm speak a message too poignant for words. He turned, the lantern swinging squeakily on its hinges, and as if by some silent signal, Rye and Laura moved to flank Dan as together they made their way back, trudging desultorily through the fog, with shoulders often touching.

The sea had been generous. It had returned Zachary Morgan whole, undistorted. It was the living who felt distorted by the events of that day and that night, for in the moment just before parting, when Dan stood hollow-eyed, weaving as if ready to collapse, he reached a hand to Rye in thanks. As their palms touched and then clutched, they found themselves again roughly clinging while Laura stood in the shifting mists, watching.

Separating from Dan, Rye turned to her and ordered softly, "Take him home to bed. He needs some sleep." Speaking the words, Rye felt as if he, too, were drowning.

Laura's eyes were incredibly weary as she looked up at Rye. The tracks of tears painted colorless lines down her cheeks, reflecting the light from the lantern. Then suddenly she moved close, swirling about Rye like the night mists, her arms momentarily easing his pain as she pressed her cheek against his.

"Thank you, Rye."

Over her shoulder, Rye saw Dan looking on while a single, raspy word came to his own throat. "Aye." His hand touched the small of Laura's back for only a brief second, then she and Dan were gone, into the eerie fog that shut them away and left Rye isolated, alone.

Heaving his tired legs up the lonely steps to the loft above the cooperage, he pictured Laura and Dan going to bed together, comforting each other. He fell onto his own bed with a weary sigh, eyes sinking shut, wishing for arms to comfort him, too. The day's events passed before him in hazy review, and he rolled over, curling his body toward the wall.

Then without warning, Rye Dalton wept, anguished sobs of hopelessness and grief such as he had not known since he was a boy. Ship heard and came ambling across the dark loft to stand beside the bunk uncertainly, emitting a sorrowful whine of compassion. While her nostrils dilated, the dog turned questioningly toward the place where the old man lay. But there was no answer. Ship whined pitifully again, but the sounds from the bed continued and no loving hand reached out to assure. So she laid her chin on the warm back and whimpered while shudders lifted the ribs of her master, even after he at last slept in exhaustion.

Chapter 13

Zachary Morgan's funeral was held two days later. It was a flawlessly clear day, and gulls scolded from an azure sky while mourners pressed in a wide, deep circle around the grave. Laura's mother was there, along with Jane and John Durning and all their children. So was Josiah, as well as aunts, uncles, and cousins of both Dan and Rye—so many on the island were related. Friends, too, had come to pay last respects, among them DeLaine Hussey, the Starbucks, and everyone who worked at the countinghouse, which was closed for the afternoon.

Laura wore a black bombazine dress and a coal scuttle hat with a nubby veil that covered her face to the chin. She stood beside Dan and his family while Rye faced her from the opposite side of the grave. He stood in the traditional pose of funereal respect—feet spraddled, the palm of one hand clasping the back of the other over his lower abdomen. From behind her black veil, Laura studied his somber face while the rector's monotone drifted above the silent gathering. Then it, too, fell still, and the bombazine crackled as Josh shifted restlessly and pressed against Laura's legs. He jerked on her hand and she looked down.

''Are they gonna bury Grampa in the dirt?'' Josh asked plaintively, his voice carrying clearly across the silent graveside. ''I don't want Grampa to get buried in the dirt.'' Laura smoothed Josh's hair with a black-gloved hand, leaning over his head to whisper comforting words as the muffled sound of weeping increased upon the heels of his innocent question.

Straightening, Laura found Rye's gaze on her from across the grave. Josh started whimpering, and Rye looked at him with an expression of helplessness.

Beside Laura, Dan bent and picked up Josh in his arms, whispering something, while again Rye's gaze followed, fixing on the child's palm, which rested on Dan's cheek as the two exchanged words too soft to be heard across the grave. Laura leaned near them, her head close to Dan's as she rested a hand on Josh's small back, and they whispered. When she turned to attend the proceedings again, she found Rye still watching the three of them with the same wounded look. But she sensed Ruth observing every exchange of glances, so she dropped her eyes to the black-draped coffin with its spray of summer gladiolas and chrysanthemums from somebody's island garden.

The final prayers were intoned and the last hymn was sung. At a soft word from the minister, Rye and three others leaned to grasp the ropes while the weight of the coffin was released from wooden slats across the grave. Then the ropes creaked and the coffin swung slightly as it was lowered and finally touched the earth. Rye went down on one knee, pulling his rope up hand over hand, while Laura trained her eyes on that knee, battling against a new freshet of tears. As Rye again stood up, she blinked and saw the black fabric of his trouser leg now covered with a pale dusting of sand. The sight of it clinging there created a new surge of sorrow within Laura. She lifted her eyes behind the black veil with a look of desolation while the silence was broken by the soft sound of weeping, and Laura longed to go to Rye, to brush the sand from his knee and the agony from his brow. His eyes said a hundred things, but she understood one above all others: when? Now that this has happened—when?

She turned away, unable to offer even a reassuring glance, no matter how badly she wanted to. There was Hilda weeping as the first spadeful of dirt fell, and Dan with his eyes filled, too, and Josh, too young to understand, but forced to be here by rigid religious custom that Laura was helpless to change.

It was past midafternoon when the funeral party repaired to the home of Tom and Dorothy Morgan to share foods provided by friends and neighbors from all over the island. Blackclad matrons tended to setting out meats, pies, and breads on the trestle table in the keeping room, replenishing bowls, and constantly washing dishes and pewterware. Beer was abundant, for here on Nantucket it was as common a drink as water, being taken on every whaling voyage as a preventative for scurvy.

Tom Morgan's house was a saltbox like most on the island, consisting of a keeping room with two linters and a loft, scarcely enough room to hold the many who came to offer condolences. Rye stood in the yard with an overflow of men who drank beer, smoked pipes, and discussed news of the day. A Harvard graduate named Henry Thoreau had perfected a new gimmick called a lead pencil . . . some were saying there was danger of depleting the ocean of whales while others said such an idea was crazy . . . talk moved on to a discussion of the profits to be had by converting whaleships to haul ice from New England to the tropics.

But Rye's interest in the conversation died when he saw Laura step from the back linter, carrying a bucket. She crossed the yard to the sweep well and leaned over the rock coping to hook the rope handle in place. Rye quickly scanned the yard, looking for Dan, but finding him nowhere in sight, he excused himself and crossed to the sweep. It consisted of a long post, offset on a forked support that was anchored in the ground. It was weighted on its short end by a stone cradle, while the longer end of the pole hovered above the mouth of the well, making it easy to bring a full bucket up, but a struggle to get the empty bucket down. As Rye approached, Laura was leaning over the coping, straining on the rope.

"Let me help y' with that."

"Oh, Rye!" At the sound of his voice, Laura straightened with a snap. The rope slipped from her palms and the sweep pole flew into the air. She pressed a hand to her heart and quickly scanned the yard. Her coal scuttle hat was gone, the veil no longer shielding her face.

"Y' look tired, darlin'. Has it been bad?" One of Rye's hands closed on the rope, but he made no further move to lower it, looking instead into Laura's distressed eyes.

"I think you must not call me darling anymore."

"Laura—" He seemed about to drop the rope and take a step toward her.

"Rye, lower the bucket. People are watching us."

A quick glance confirmed it, so Rye tended to the task, forcing the pail down, hand over hand, until they heard it splash below.

"Laura, this doesn't change anything."

"How can you say that?"

"I still love y'. I'm still Josh's father."

"Rye, someone will hear."

The pail was back up. He rested a hand on its rope handle while it hung, dripping, above the mouth of the well, the sound echoing up to them in faraway musical blips while he filled his eyes with her. "Let them hear. There isn't a soul in this yard who doesn't know how I feel about y' and that y' were mine first."

The shadows beneath her eyes seemed to darken as she cast a furtive glance at the curious people who studied them. "Please, Rye," she whispered. "Give me the pail."

He reached above the well coping, and her eyes followed the strong muscles beneath the black suit jacket while his shoulders turned away and he hefted the pail. When he swung around he disregarded the hand that reached for the pail, turning toward the back linter, giving Laura no recourse but to follow at his side. He paused to let her move ahead of him, then followed into the cramped space containing ranks of wood and an assortment of wooden pails and tubs hanging on the wall. Inside, they were momentarily out of sight of either yard or house.

Laura glanced nervously toward the door leading into the keeping room from the rear, but it remained closed. "Rye, I can't—"

"Shh." His fingers touched her lips.

Their eyes met—troubled blue eyes fixed on worried brown ones.

The touch of his fingers on her flesh was like balm, but she forced herself to pull back. "Rye, don't touch me. It only makes it harder."

"Laura, I love y'."

"And don't say that . . . not now. Everything is changed, don't you see?"

His gaze roved over her face, studying the depths of her eyes, where he read things he did not want to read. "Why did this have t' happen now?" he asked miserably.

"Maybe it was a message to us."

His expression grew stern, and his voice was a hiss. "Don't say that—don't even think it! Zachary's death had nothin' to do with us, nothing!"

"Didn't it?" She studied him levelly.

"No!"

"Then why do I feel like I personally sent that boat bow over stern?"

"Laura, I knew that's what y' were thinkin' while we sat on the wharf beside Dan that night, but I won't have y' believin' such a thing." He still held the bucket in one hand while with his other he squeezed her upper arm, making the bombazine sleeve crackle in the confines of the linter.

"Don't you?"

Her eyes remained steadfastly on him, forcing him to admit the awful possibility. He wanted to answer no, but could not. The evening light bounced off the white shells outside the doorway, reflecting inside and lighting her face from below, giving her an ethereal glow, like an angel of judgment. She reached for the handle of the pail, but he refused to relinquish it. He studied her face, wanting her back worse than ever, now that he'd again had a taste of her body. Yet it was not her body alone he craved. He craved a return to things as they used to be, contentment, peace, sharing their home. And now their son. Yet Rye Dalton, even in the depths of his want, could not deny her words or force her to come back to him any sooner than she was ready. Their hands slipped close together on the rope, and he raised his free hand to touch her jaw.

"Is it so wrong for us t' want t' be together when we love each other?"

"What we did was wrong, Rye, yes."

His eyes took on a new pain. "How can y' call it wrong, Laura, knowing what it was like—what it always was like between us? How can y' walk away and st—"

The kitchen door suddenly opened.

"Oh, excuse me." Ruth Morgan confronted them with reproof in every unsmiling muscle of her face. "We were beginning to wonder if Laura dropped down the well, but I can see what's taken so long."

Rye flashed Dan's sister a look of sheer loathing, thinking that if she'd ever gone out and gotten herself frenzied with a man, she wouldn't have such a burr under her corsets when somebody else did. Ruth Morgan was nothing but a dried-up old maid who wouldn't know what to do with a man if she had one, Rye thought as he strode angrily into the keeping room and clapped the pail down.

The remainder of the day found Laura growing increasingly uncomfortable as Ruth Morgan's censure became more evident. At times she ostentatiously held her skirts from brushing Laura's hem as they moved about in the keeping room, clearing away dishes and foods. Rye did not leave, as Laura hoped he would. Instead, he was one of those who remained as night drew on and the men moved inside to continue drinking the everlasting beer. But Dan had already overindulged and had reached that maudlin stage of drunkenness accompanied by depression and self-pitying gibberish.

He sat at the trestle table in the keeping room, elbow to elbow with a group of others, his head slung low while his arms sometimes slipped clumsily off the table edge.

"The old man was always after me to be a fisherman." He swayed toward the companion at his left and looked blearily into the man's eyes. "Never liked the stink of fish, did I, Laura? Not like you and Rye." He twisted to pick her out where she sat with the women while Rye stood near the fireplace, looking on silently from behind Dan's back.

Laura rose. "Come, Dan, let's go home."

"Whatsa matter? Did Rye have t' leave?" Dan turned a loose, inebriated smile to the circle of men at the table, and brandished a floppy hand. "Party's over for my wife once Rye Dalton's not around anymore. Did I ever tell you—"

"You're drunk, Dan." Rye interrupted as he moved behind the slouched form. "Time to put your glass down and go home with Laura." He took the mug from Dan's hand and set it on the table with a decisive thud.

Dan twisted at the waist, turning watery eyes up at the man looming behind him. "Well, if it isn't my friend Rye Dalton, the one I share a wife with." He smiled crookedly.

Horrified, Laura saw everyone in the room look away uncomfortably. Feet shifted, sounding like thunder, then an awful silence hovered in the tense air.

"That's enough, Dan!" Rye spoke sharply, skewering the drunk man with a look of warning, ever aware of Laura waiting uncertainly behind them with Josh at her side, and of Ruth, standing in the dark corner of the room, her eyes snapping.

"I just wanted to tell the story of the three musketeers who grew up sharing everything. But I guess they all know it anyway." Dan's eyes went from man to man around the table, finally coming back to rest on Rye. "Yup! Guess they all know about it. No sense tellin' 'em what they already know. Where's that wife of ours, eh, Rye?"

Laura's face was poppy-red while Rye's looked thunderous. He stood stern and unmoving, scarcely holding himself back from plucking Dan to his feet and slamming a fist into him to shut him up.

"She's *your* wife, and she's waitin' for y' to gather yer wits and go home with 'er. Now put down the mug and stop makin' an ass o' yerself."

Murky eyes appealed to the circle of faces. "Am I making an ass of myself?"

Finally, one of the men suggested, "Why don't you do what Rye says? Go on home with Laura now."

Dan smiled stupidly at the tabletop, then nodded at it. "Yup, I guess you're right. 'Cause if I don't, my friend here will."

"Dan! Have y' forgotten y'r son is in the room?" Rye snapped, the anger growing more evident in each word.

"*My* son . . . now there's a subject I'd like to take up, too."

Rye waited no longer. With power spawned by rage, he clutched the shoulders of Dan's jacket and jerked him to his feet, sending the table screeching back as Dan's body jarred against it. Rye spun the limp form around and clutched Dan's lapels roughly, then ground out his next words through nearly clenched teeth. "Y'r *wife* is waiting for y' t' straighten up and take her and Josh home. Now are y' going t' do it, or do I have t' crack y' one to bring y' to your senses!"

Sobered somewhat, Dan yanked himself free of Rye's grip, shrugging his jacket back into place, then wavering a moment while trying to gather dignity that could not be restored in one so far gone.

"You always did have your way with her, Rye, starting when the two of you were—"

That was the last word Dan uttered. Rye's fist whistled out of nowhere and settled into Dan's stomach with a thud. A single grunt swooshed from Dan before he folded in half and slumped into Rye's arms.

Laura's hands flew to her mouth as Josh came to life, racing across the room, crying, "You hit my papa! You hit my papa! Put him down! Papa . . . Papa!" The pitiful little creature rushed to Dan's defense, but Rye bent down, put a shoulder to the inert stomach, and lifted the man onto his broad shoulder like a sack of potatoes. Before Laura could stop Josh, he'd fallen against Rye's stomach, punching him and yelling, "I hate you! I hate you! You hit my papa!"

It had happened so fast, Laura was stunned. But she finally moved, lurching forward to pull Josh away from Rye and calm him, then finally turn him toward the door.

Rye bounced Dan more comfortably onto his shoulder and spoke to a shocked Tom and Dorothy Morgan. "I apologize for the scene, but it's been a rough day for Dan. My condolences on the death of y'r brother." Then, turning to Laura, he ignored the curious onlookers, and ordered, "Come on, let's get him and the boy home."

They left the house without looking back, realizing that behind them speculation billowed. Rye's long legs strode along the cobblestones while Laura hurried to keep up. Josh was still crying, but she tugged him along by the hand.

"Why did he hit Papa?" Josh whimpered.

Rye stalked along without slowing or glancing at either Laura or Josh.

"Papa had too much beer," was all Laura could think of as explanation.

"But he hit him!"

"Hush, Joshua."

The heavy clump of Rye's heels led the way while Laura followed with her heart breaking and her son too young to comprehend any of it.

"And he put Grampa in that hole so they could bury him in the dirt."

"Joshua, I said hush!"

She yanked at Josh's hand and his head snapped. But when his accusations subsided into sniffling, tears brimmed in Laura's eyes and guilt tore at her insides. She leaned to scoop Josh into her arms and carry him the rest of the way home while he buried his wet face against her neck, clinging and confused.

When they reached the *Y* in the path, Rye stalked on ahead and she followed the sound of his footsteps up the scallop shells in the dark. At the door of the saltbox, Rye paused, letting her enter first. He stood with Dan's dead weight now creating an unbearable ache on his shoulder, listening as Laura found the tinderbox and lit the candles. As the light blossomed around them, her dark eyes sought Rye, then immediately she ordered Josh, "Get your nightshirt on, and I'll tuck you in in a minute."

She left him standing in the middle of the keeping room, watching as she led the way into the bedroom linter with a candle. Standing back, she watched Rye dump Dan's inert body on the bed. When he straightened, his eyes moved around the room from the bed to the partially opened door of the chifforobe where Laura's and Dan's clothing hung, to the small commode where her whalebone comb rested beside a pitcher and bowl. When his eyes at last came back to her, standing in the doorway with her hands clasped tightly against her bosom, Rye's expression was closed and stiff.

"You'd better take his clothes off."

Laura swallowed the lump in her throat and moved farther into the room. But there was little space, and as she neared the bed Rye was forced to step around her. He moved to the door as she bent over Dan and began removing his shoes.

From the doorway, Rye watched her lift one foot, then the other, and set Dan's shoes quietly on the floor beside the bed. She loosened his tie, then slipped it free and laid it on the commode. She freed the button at Dan's throat while Rye remembered those hands removing his own clothing such a short time ago in the meadow. He scowled as Laura sat on the edge of the bed and struggled to remove Dan's jacket, but his limp body refused to comply, and at last Rye ordered, "Leave him to me and go see to the boy."

She stood to face him again, and he saw tear-filled eyes and quivering lips. Then she brushed around him, holding her skirts well aside as she hurried out.

Rye removed Dan's coat, trousers, and shirt and managed to roll him beneath the covers into an unconscious, snoring heap. He studied Dan for a long minute, then—more slowly this time—he looked across the room. He stepped to the commode, picked up Laura's comb, and ran his thumbnail along its teeth. He brushed the back of his fingers along a towel hanging on a mirrored rack on the wall behind the pitcher. Swiveling slowly around, Rye confronted the chifforobe. With a single finger he slowly opened the carved mahogany door. It widened silently, and he removed his finger and slipped it inside his waistcoat pocket while his gaze glided over the contents of the chifforobe where her dresses hung beside Dan's shirts and suits. He reached out to finger the sleeve of the yellow dress she'd worn that first day he'd seen her in the market. He worked the fabric lightly between his fingertips, then wearily dropped his hand and sighed, deep and long. Glancing over his shoulder at the man sleeping behind him, Rye silently closed the chifforobe door before blowing out the candle and returning to the keeping room.

Laura was sitting on the edge of the alcove bed, tucking Josh in for the night. Rye told his feet to remain where they were, but the temptation was too great. With slow steps, he crossed to stand beside the bed and look down at Josh over Laura's shoulder. She leaned to kiss the child's face, which was still puffy and red from crying.

"Good night, darling."

But Josh's lip trembled, and he had eyes only for the man who hovered behind his mother. The accusing stare scored Rye's heart, but he submerged the hurt and moved a step nearer. As he did, his hips and stomach came lightly against Laura's back. He reached a hand over her shoulder and touched the boy's fine, soft bangs with a calloused finger while Josh's eyes remained wary and defensive.

"I'm sorry I hit your papa."

"You said you was his friend," the quavery little voice accused.

"Aye, and I am."

Laura watched the long, tanned finger slide away from the blond hair and retreat somewhere behind her, but she felt the warmth of Rye's body still pressing comfortingly against her back.

"I don't believe you." The little chin trembled. "And . . . and you put that box in the ground with my grampa in it."

"He's the one taught me t' fish when I wasn't much older than you. I loved him, too, but he's dead now. That's why we had t' put him in the ground."

"And I'll never see him again?"

Sadly, silently, Rye shook his head, assuming the role of father now, but with a pain he'd never imagined it might bring.

Josh dropped his gaze to the blanket over his chest, picking at it with an index finger. "I didn't think so, but nobody'd tell me for sure."

Rye felt a tremor run through Laura and lightly rested his palm on her shoulder. "That's because they didn't want t' hurt y' or make y' cry. They didn't think y'd understand, bein' y're only four."

"I'm almost five."

"Aye, I know. And that's old enough t' understand that y'r . . . y'r papa is going t' be very lonesome for his papa for a while. He's goin' t' need lots o' cheerin' up." Rye looked down at the top of Laura's head. "And y'r mama, too," he added with great tenderness.

Unable to stay there between the two of them and contain her tears a moment longer, Laura again leaned to kiss Josh. "Go to sleep now, darling. I'll be right here."

He turned over on his side, facing the wall, curling up into a little ball. But when he felt Laura's weight shift off his bed, he looked back over his shoulder. "Don't shut my doors, Mama."

"N . . . no, Josh, I won't."

She left the hinged doors wide and turned, wiping tears from her eyes. When she'd crossed to the far side of the room beyond Josh's range of vision, Rye remained where he was, studying the boy. From the bedroom came the sound of Dan's sonorous breathing, his repetitive soft snore the only sound in the dusky room. Rye looked at Laura's back, then tiredly crossed to stand behind her, studying the intricate coil of hair at the back of her neck, the tight stricture of her black mourning dress across her slumping shoulders. From behind, he covered her upper arms, chafing them gently, watching the tender hollow at the back of her neck as she dropped her face into her hands and wept softly.

"Aw, Laura-love," he uttered in a shaken whisper, pulling her back against his chest, feeling her shoulders shaking. She stifled her sobs into her palms, and he drew a handkerchief from his pocket and pressed it into her hands. He let her weep, feeling so much like weeping himself, but swallowing thickly, closing his eyes and rubbing her arms once again.

"Oh R . . . Rye, I feel so guilty, and I'm even more ashamed because I've been mourning as much for us as for Zachary."

He spun her around and crushed her against him. Her arms clung to his back as his head dropped down to her shoulder and they rocked together, solacing each other.

Josh heard his mother's sobs and slipped his feet over the edge of his alcove bed to stand beside it uncertainly, one hand still under the blankets while he watched the wide back of the man curving to hold her. He saw his mother's arms come up around Rye's neck, then the big man rocked her, the way she sometimes rocked Josh when he felt bad and cried. Josh studied them silently, perplexed, wondering whether or not he should be mad at Rye for hitting Papa like he had. It seemed like Mama would be mad at Rye . . . but she wasn't. Instead, she was hugging him and had buried her face in his neck just as Josh had buried his face against her when Laura carried him home tonight. Again he heard his mother's muffled sobs, and while the two rocked from side to side, the boy caught a glimpse of Rye's wide hand holding the back of his mother's head tight against him. He watched a moment longer, remembering how Rye had said his mother, too, would need cheering up. Then, silently, Josh lifted a knee to climb back into his bed again, to listen and wonder and decide that mamas, too, liked to be hugged.

Laura wept bitterly, allowing the full flood of grief to escape as it hadn't during the past three days.

"Laura . . . Laura . . ." Rye said against her hair.

"Hold me, Rye, oh hold me. Oh my darling, what you must have suffered through these last three days."

"Shh . . . hush, love," he intoned softly.

But she went on. "My heart broke for you when I saw you facing Dan at the end of the wharf, and . . . and when I saw you hold him in your arms and comfort him. And again along the beach while we were searching. Oh, Rye, I wanted to rush to you and hold you and tell you I loved you for what you were doing for him. He . . . he needed you so badly then. I sometimes think that fate keeps throwing the three of us together, knowing we all need each other."

"Damn fate, then. I've had all of it I can stand!" His voice shook as he held her near, running a hand along her back.

"Rye, I'm so sorry about Josh tonight. But he'll get over it and stop blaming you."

Rye backed away abruptly, gripping the sides of her head. "It's not them I care about. It's not them I need. It's you!" He gave her head one emphatic shake and their eyes delved deeply into each other's. Then he took her roughly against him again, breathing in the scent of her hair and skin, his voice a murmur of despair at her ear. "Why did this have t' happen now? Why now?"

"Maybe we've been made to pay for our sins."

"We did *not* sin! We are victims of circumstance, just like the others are. Yet we're the ones made t' suffer, t' stay apart, when it's none of our doing. We belong together, Laura, so much more than you and Dan do."

Her tears flowed afresh. "I know. But . . . but I can't leave him now, don't you see? How can I leave him at the worst time of his life, when he supported me through the worst time of mine? What would people say?"

"I don't give a damn what they'll say. I want y' back, and Josh along with y'."

"You know that's not possible, not now . . . not for a while."

Again he backed away. "How long?" His blue eyes were beginning to show anger.

"Until a decent period of mourning has passed."

"The mourning be damned! Zachary Morgan is dead, but must we pretend we died with him? We're alive, and we've wasted five years already."

"Please, Rye, please understand. I want to be with you. I . . . I love you so."

Suddenly Rye grew still. He studied her face in the dim light from the candle across the room. "But y' love him, too, don't y'?"

Her eyes dropped to Rye's chest, and when after a long silence she neither looked up nor answered, he moved his hands to span her throat, pressing his thumbs up against the underside of her jaw, forcing her to meet his gaze.

"Y' love him, too," he reiterated painfully.

"We both do, Rye, don't we?"

"Is that what it is?" He searched her brown eyes with their spiky, wet lashes while from the bedroom came the steady sound of Dan's snoring.

"Yes, that's why it hurts both of us so much to see him this way."

"Does he drink this much often?"

"More and more often lately, it seems. He knows how I feel about you, and he . . . he drinks to forget it."

"And so either way his turnin' to alcohol will bind y' t' him with guilt. If y' stay, he drinks because he knows y' want t' leave. And if y' leave, he drinks because y' did not stay."

"Oh, Rye, you sound so bitter. He's a far weaker man than you. Can't you take pity on him?"

"Don't ask me t' pity him, Laura. It's enough that I love him, God help my soul, but I will not pity him for usin' his weakness t' hold y'."

"It's not just that, Rye. This island is so small. What would people say if I walked away from him now? You saw the looks we got from Ruth today."

"Ruth!" Rye exclaimed in an exasperated whisper. "Ruth'd do well t' go out and spread her legs under a man so she'd know what hell you're goin' through!"

"Rye, please, you must not—"

He gripped her jaw and kissed her mouth with a battering assault of his own until he became aware of her working to free herself from the pressure of his thumbs. Then he hugged her to him, immediately repentant.

"Oh God, I'm sorry, Laura. It's just that I can't bear t' walk out of here and think of y' in that bed beside him when it should be you and me sharin' it as we used to."

"Six months," she said. "Can you bear it for six months?"

"Six months?" The words fell cold from his lips. "Y' may as well ask me t' bear it for six years. It would be as easy."

"It'll be no easier for me, Rye, you have to know that."

His thumbs brushed her cheeks, softly now, lovingly. "Tell me, is it possible you could be carryin' my baby now? Because I won't let y' stay with him if there's any chance of it whatsoever."

"No. It's the wrong time of month."

His haunted eyes roved her face. "Will y' let him make love to y'?"

She pulled away and turned her back on him. "Rye, why do you torture—"

‘‘Why?’’ He spun her around by an arm. His eyes were blazing. ‘‘Y’ do love him or, by God, you, too, would be tortured by the thought!’’

She clutched his forearms. ‘‘I pity him. I’ve betrayed him, and I owe him something for that.’’

‘‘And while y’re payin’ y’r debt, what if y’ become pregnant with his child? What will y’ do then? Plead for more time while y’ decide which of the two fathers y’ll grant y’r favors to next time?’’

She struck at him then, but he backed away just before her hand hit its mark.

Chagrined, she reached to touch his chest. ‘‘Oh, Rye, I’m sorry. Don’t you see, we’re angry at what we’re forced to do, not at each other? We strike out this way because we can’t strike out at the true cause of our trouble.’’

‘‘The true cause of our trouble is y’r obstinance, and y’ can end it with a single word—yes! Yet y’ choose not to.’’

He stalked toward the door.

‘‘Rye, where are you going?’’

He turned, lowering his voice when he caught sight of the alcove bed in the shadows behind her. ‘‘I’m leaving y’ to your drunken husband, who is not worthy of y’ yet somehow manages to keep y’ loyal even while he snores in that besotted state. Six months y’ ask for? All right, I’ll give y’ six months. But during that time, keep out of my sight, woman, or I’ll see t’ it y’ betray y’r husband again, and I won’t be fussy about where or when or who knows about it. The whole island can watch for all I care, and Ruth Morgan and her ilk can take lessons!’’

Chapter 14

Dan Morgan awakened the following morning to the sight of Laura lying beside him, still in her whalebone corsets. He groaned, remembering, and rolled to the side of the bed, where he sat clutching his head. He dug the heels of his hands into his eye sockets, then straightened gingerly, holding his stomach while he unfolded one muscle at a time. As he eased to his feet, the power of Rye Dalton’s fist made itself felt in every muscle of his torso.

At Dan’s soft groan, Laura awakened, bracing up on an elbow to ask sleepily, ‘‘Dan, are you all right?’’

He was ashamed to face his wife after the public insinuations he’d made yesterday. Glancing over his shoulder, Dan’s shame redoubled at the realization that he hadn’t even remained sober enough to help her out of her stays, but instead had left her to sleep in them like a freshly wrapped mummy.

He sank to the edge of the bed, again clutching the sides of his head and staring at the floor between his bare feet. ''Laura, I'm sorry.''

She touched his shoulder. ''Dan, this drinking has got to stop. It won't solve anything.''

''I know,'' he mumbled forlornly. ''I know.''

The back of his hair was mussed and flattened. She touched it reassuringly. ''Promise me you'll come home for supper tonight.''

He dropped his head farther forward and rubbed the back of it, brushing her touch away. Then his shoulders lifted as he sighed deeply. ''I promise.''

He got to his feet slowly, stretching his ribs and breathing carefully, then clumped out of the room to begin getting ready for work. They spoke little, but when he was ready to leave for the countinghouse, wearing the black armband of mourning on his left sleeve, Laura stepped up behind him and rested a hand on his shoulder.

''Don't forget . . . you promised.''

But all day long as Dan worked over his ledgers, the figures on the pages seemed to twine themselves into the shapes of Rye and Laura, and when he left work at the end of the day, Dan knew he could not go home without fortification.

So he turned back toward Water Street and entered the Blue Anchor Pub. The place was adorned with quarter boards bearing the names of old vessels, the most prominent from a long-gone ship called *The Blue Lady*. Whaling paraphernalia hung from the walls and from the open beams of the ceiling: harpoons, flensing knives, macrame, and scrimshaw. But best of all, kegs of beer and ale rested on their cradles at the rear of the room. Behind the kegs hung the personal tankards of the clientele who frequented the place, but since there was none with Dan's name, the alekeeper produced one of his own, offering his condolences by way of a free round of ''flip''—a powerful mixture of apple cider and rum. By the time Dan left for home, it was dark and long past the supper hour.

Laura looked up when Dan entered the keeping room. It took little more than a glance to know what had detained him. His movements were slow and deliberate as he hung up his beaver hat, then turned to stare at the table, where a single plate waited.

''I'm sorry, Laura.'' He slurred the words, weaving slightly, but making no move toward the trestle.

Laura stood behind a ladderback chair, clutching its top rung. ''Dan, I was so worried.''

''Were you?'' Silence fell heavily while he studied her with bleary eyes. ''Were you?'' he repeated, more quietly.

''Of course. You promised me this morning—''

He waved a hand as if shooing away a fly, tucked two fingers into his watch pocket, gazed at the ceiling, and swayed silently.

''Dan, you have to eat something.''

He gestured vaguely toward the table. ''Don't bother with supper for me. I'll just—'' His words trailed away listlessly, and he sighed. His chin dropped to his chest as if he'd fallen asleep on his feet.

Dear God, what have I done to him? Laura asked herself.

But the days that followed were to answer her tortured question only too plainly, for Dan Morgan was a wretched and torn man. And though he had promised to end his intemperance, his own personal tankard soon came to hang on the wall pegs behind the barrels at the Blue Anchor. Before long, his wife, waiting in the candlelit house on Crooked Record Lane, set aside her whalebone corsets and returned to the unbound freedom of only a chemise, for too many nights there was no one to help with her laces.

Summer drew to a close, and Laura filled her days with countless preparations for winter. The wild beach plums came ripe, and Laura took Josh with her to gather the fruit in baleen—whalebone—baskets, haul them home, and make mincemeat and preserves. But as she hurried back from her day on the moors, it was with a heartful of memories of Rye and to face an empty supper table, a lonely house, for Dan continued his late nights at the Blue Anchor.

Josh begged to go picking grapes next, and though Laura knew they hung in royal purple splendor in the best arbor on the island, she was reluctant to go there again and face more poignant memories. But the grapes were a ready source of provender for the making of jam, juice, and the dried, sugared sweetmeats called comfits, Josh's favorites, so at last Laura went. The sight of the arbor brought back a renewed surge of longing for Rye, but these thoughts were immediately followed by the now-familiar guilt that always came in their wake, especially that particular night, when Dan again appeared at supper and stayed home in the evening, lavishing time on Josh. Laura's spirits buoyed as Dan remained punctual and sober for several days. She put thoughts of Rye from her mind and strove to make their home the happy place it had once been.

But then one morning when Dan reached into the chifforobe for a fresh shirt, something fell to the floor—Laura's corset. He leaned to pick it up and held it in hands that were always slightly shaky these days. He stared disconsolately as he rubbed a thumb absently on a whalebone, then closed his eyes for a moment, wondering what was to become of his marriage. When he opened them, he saw part of a stay projecting from its cotton sheath. Haltingly, he reached to touch its smooth, rounded end, only to realize it was not just any whalebone but a busk. With growing dread he slipped it up until, word by word, the carving was revealed.

He stood a long time, head and shoulders drooping, as he read and reread the scrimshawed poem beneath his thumb. After some minutes he swallowed hard, then reeled on his feet as if Rye Dalton's fist had again leveled him. He pictured himself helping Laura cinch up the strings that had pressed Rye's words of love against her skin, and Dan suffered afresh the rending truth: Laura had never stopped loving Rye. Rye had always been and would always be her first choice.

"Dan, your breakfast is ready," Laura announced from behind him.

He dropped the corset, shut the chifforobe door, and spun around.

"Dan, what's wrong?" she said. He looked stricken and slightly ill. She glanced down to see what he held, but in his hands was only a clean shirt, and as he shrugged it on, he insisted nothing was amiss.

But after that, it was later than ever when Dan returned home at night.

September arrived. Dame school would soon open in the parlors across the island, thus several mothers planned a last squantum on the beach for a group of island children. Though it would be another year yet before Josh started school, he was included and went off exuberantly with Jimmy.

When the picnicking and games were over, the two boys went off by themselves. On their knees, they dug frantically after sandcrabs, which could bury themselves faster than any boy could dig them up. They laughed and sent sand flying behind them, knowing it was useless, but enjoying the pursuit for itself. Finally, Jimmy gave up, dropped back onto his haunches, and said, "I heard somethin' at your grampa's funeral that I bet you don't know."

"What?" Josh went on digging.

"I ain't supposed to tell you, 'cause when Mama found me standin' there listening to them ladies, she made me promise not to, and then she scooted me out so I couldn't hear no more."

Josh's interest was immediately diverted and he turned to his friend, bright with curiosity. "Yeah? What'd she say?"

Jimmy made a pretense of sifting sand through his fingers in search of small shells. "I wasn't gonna tell you, but then . . ." He squinted up at the younger boy, suddenly unsure of the wisdom of divulging the secret. But finally he went on. "Well, I got to thinkin', and if it's true what they said, well, you and me, we're cousints."

"Cousints?" Josh's eyes were round with surprise. "You mean like me and all of Aunt Jane's kids?"

"Uh-huh."

"You heard your mama say *that?*"

"Well, no, not exactly. She was talking to my Aunt Elspeth and they said your real pa ain't . . . well, the one you got, but that other man, Rye Dalton."

Josh was silent for a moment, then said disbelievingly, "They din't neither."

"They did too! They said Rye Dalton was your real pa, and if he is, then you and me are cousints, 'cause—"

"He ain't my pa!" Josh was on his feet now. "He can't be or my mama would know."

"He is too!"

"You liar!"

"What're you so mad about—gosh, I thought you'd like bein' my cousint!"

Josh was having a hard time keeping from crying. "It ain't true, you . . . you . . ." He searched for the worst word he knew. "You liar! Dummy! Poop!"

"I ain't no liar. Mr. Dalton, he's some cousint of my pa's, and that's why his name's even Rye, 'cause it's our last name, if you don't believe me!"

"Liar!" Josh scooped up a handful of sand and threw it in Jimmy's face, then spun and took off running.

"I'm gonna tell your ma you called me a poop, Josh Morgan! And anyway, I don't want to be your dumb old cousint!"

After the day of the picnic, Laura noticed an unusual reticence in Josh but attributed it to the fact that school had started and he was lost without his best friend, Jimmy. She knew, too, that he missed Dan's company in the evenings, and though she tried to make up for his absence, her heart was not totally in it, and Josh could not be cheered. He remained withdrawn and distant, at times almost angry. She tried to interest him in helping her with some of his favorite chores, but he showed no enthusiasm. When she finally invited him to go bayberrying and he refused this, too, Laura's concern grew. She waited for Dan one evening in hopes that he'd be sober enough to discuss the problem and offer some insight.

Dan was surprised to find her up when he came in. She was dressed in her nightgown and wrapper and came immediately to stand before him, working her hands together, her eyes sad and troubled. Her image grew fuzzy, then cleared, while through an alcoholic haze Dan thought, Why don't you just tell her she's free, Morgan? Why don't you just send her to Rye and be done with it? His eyes found hers and he knew the answer: because he loved her in a way she'd never fathom, and to give her up would be to give up his reason for living.

"Let me help you." Laura stepped close and reached to help Dan remove his jacket, but he brushed her hands aside.

"I c'n do it."

"Let me—"

"Get y'r goddamn hands off me!" he shouted, backing away, almost falling down.

She stiffened as if he'd slapped her. Her lips dropped open on a surprised breath, and tears glimmered in her eyes while she clutched her hands and backed a step away. "Dan, please—"

"Don't say it! Don't say anything, just leave me alone. I'm drunk. I j'st wanna go to bed. I j'st . . ." His knees were stiff as he swayed like a poplar in a summer breeze, staring at the floor between his feet.

For a horrifying moment Laura thought he was going to start crying, but suddenly he scooped her into his arms and held her tightly, clutching the back of her head while trying to maintain his balance.

"Oh God, how I love you." His eyes were squeezed tightly shut. His voice was wracked with emotion. "God help me, Laura, I wish Rye *had* been on that ship when it went down."

"Dan, you don't know what you're saying." His hold was unbreakable, and she was forced to remain where she was.

"I do. I'm drunk, but not so drunk I don't know what I've been thinking for weeks and weeks. Why did he have to come back? Why!"

But his cry became a maudlin appeal, and she remembered Dan turning to Rye at the end of the wharf, seeking his strength and comfort, and she understood his torture at the words he'd just spoken. "Go to bed, Dan. I'll blow out the candles and be in in a minute."

He released her and turned docilely toward the bedroom, deluged with shame at having put voice to such a heathen wish.

As she did every night, Laura went to peek in at Josh one last time before turning in. When he saw the flickering light approaching through the half-closed doors of his alcove, Josh shut his eyes and pretended to be asleep. But when she was gone, he lay in the dark, thinking about what he'd just heard, remembering the day he'd first seen Rye Dalton hugging Mama. Rye had said then that his name was Rye because his mother's name was Ryerson before she got married, and Jimmy had said the same thing. So could Jimmy be right? Josh remembered Rye hitting Papa . . . Rye hugging Mama . . . Rye making Mama smile on the hill by Mr. Pond's mill. He heard again the words his papa had just said. Papa wished Rye was dead! Dead . . . like Grampa. He tried to piece things together, but nothing fell into place. All Josh knew was that nothing had been the same since Rye came here. Papa never came home anymore, and Mama was sad all the time, and . . . and . . .

Josh could not understand any of it. So he cried himself to sleep.

It was a mellow day in mid-September when Laura invited Josh to join her in measuring and mixing the ingredients for potpourri, which the two of them had been carefully gathering and drying all summer.

Though he wistfully eyed the rose petals, citrus rinds, and spices, he jammed his hands into his pockets and hung his head. "Don't wanna."

Oh, Josh, Josh, what is it, darling?

"But you helped me last year, and we had such fun."

"Gonna go outside and play."

"But if you don't help me, the moths will eat holes in our things this winter." But Laura's effort at cajolery fell flat, for Josh only shrugged and reached for the latch.

Laura stared at the door a long time after he'd left, wondering how to bring him out of this uncharacteristic standoffishness. Her eyes wandered back to the fragrant collection on the table and the rose petals seemed to swim before her eyes. Leaning her forehead on her knuckles, she battled tears. As they often did at times like this, her thoughts turned to Rye, and she wished she could talk to him about Josh. The sight of the curled bits of orange and lemon rind and the perfume of the pungent collection mingled to remind her that each year at this time she was in the habit of walking down to the cooperage to fetch a bag of fragrant cedar chips to add to her potpourri, but this year she'd have to do without it.

Outside, Josh hunkered in the sun, poking listlessly at the scallop shells, wanting to go back in and join his mother, because mixing was the most fun—way more fun than scraping rind and plucking petals and all the hard stuff they'd done all summer. He looked toward the bay and his boyish lips tightened. Down there somewhere was Rye, and if it hadn't been for Rye, Josh would be inside right now doing one of his favorite things with his mother.

Rye was teaching his cousin, the apprentice, how to make the slats of a pail uniform when a small figure stopped in the doorway of the cooperage. Josh! Rye turned back to the task at hand, assuming Laura would appear next. But a full minute went by, and nobody joined the boy. He remained in the doorway, studying the interior of the cooperage and, more specifically, Rye himself. The cooper could feel the lad's eyes following each motion he made. Glancing up, he saw Josh's mouth drawn tight and a belligerent expression around his blue eyes.

"Hello, Josh," Rye greeted at last. When no reply came, he asked, "Y' down here all alone?"

Josh neither answered nor moved, but stood as before, antagonism written on every muscle of his face. Rye ambled toward the doorway, nonchalantly lifting two staves and comparing them. As he neared Josh, the boy defiantly stepped back. Outside, Rye glanced in both directions, but Laura was not in sight.

"Y'r mother know y're down here all alone?"

''She don't care.''

''Aw, lad, y're wrong there. Y'd better get back up home. She'll be worried about y'.''

Josh's small chin grew even more defiant. ''You can't tell me what to do. You . . . you ain't my papa.'' Before Rye could move, Josh rushed him, tears on his cheeks now. He hit Rye with his boyish fists, crying, ''You ain't neither my papa! You ain't! My papa is my papa, not you!'' And before Rye could recover from his stunned surprise, Josh wheeled and ran off up the street.

''Joshua!'' Rye called after him, but the child was gone.

''Damn!'' Rye stalked back into the cooperage and flung the pair of staves down with a clatter. His heart pounded and a film of perspiration sprang to his palms as he stood before the tool bench pondering what to do. Josh had been so angry, so hurt. He must have just found out, but if Laura was the one who'd told him, Rye was certain she'd have explained in a way that wouldn't have set the boy off this way. Suppose he didn't return home? He was disillusioned and upset right now, and Laura should know about it. But the last place on the island Rye should go was up to the house. Suddenly he spun around.

''Chad, I want y' to run an errand for me.''

''Yessir.''

Rye glanced around for paper, found none, and instead grabbed the first thing he could find: a flat clean scrap of cedar from the pail he'd been working. With a chunk of charcoal, he wrote, ''Josh knows,'' and signed it simply, ''R.''

''Y' know the house where Dan Morgan lives, up on Crooked Record Lane?'' Chad nodded. ''I want y' to run this up there and give it t' Mrs. Morgan. Nobody else, y' understand?'' Rye scowled.

''Yessir,'' Chad replied smartly.

''Good. Now be off with y'.''

Rye watched the boy head away, and a frown deepened between his eyebrows. He thought of the day he'd met Laura and Josh coming from the hill. *I like you,* the boyish voice came back. Rye stared into space, hearing the words again as he rubbed his stomach where Josh's fist had struck out against the truth. Rye's head dropped forward and a long sigh escaped. Would life ever be simple again? He wanted so little. The wife he loved, the son he'd lost out on, the home on the hill. He wanted only what was his.

Josiah watched his son's forlorn pose, then moved up behind Rye and clapped a hearty hand on his shoulder. ''Boy's not yet five years old. Too young t' reason things out. When he can, he'll judge y' for y'rself, not as the man who stole his father. Been a bit of a shock to him, I'd say. Give the lad some time.''

Though Rye seldom burdened Josiah with his cares, he now found himself somewhat shaken and very depressed. Still facing the door, still with his hand on his stomach, he said, ''There're days when I wish I'd never've been put off the *Massachusetts*.''

Josiah squeezed Rye's sturdy shoulder. ''Naw, son, don't say that.''

Rye looked back at his father and shrugged away his apathy. ''Y're right. I'm sorry, old man. Forget I said it.'' Then he turned back to work, forcing a cheerfulness he didn't feel.

* * *

When Josh burst into the house, Laura was unaware that he'd been gone from the yard. She straightened in surprise as the door slammed and Josh barreled across the room to fling himself, belly down, on his bed. Immediately, Laura was on her feet, scattering airy rose petals as she crossed to sit on the edge of the bed and smooth Josh's hair.

"Darling, what is it?"

But he only burrowed deeper into the pillow, weeping harder. When she attempted to turn him over, the boy pulled away. "Josh, is it something I've done? Please tell Mama what's made you so unhappy."

A muffled response came from the pillow while Josh's shoulders jerked pitifully.

Laura leaned low over him. "You what? Josh, come, darling, turn around here."

He lifted his head and sobbed, "I h . . . hate Jimmy!"

"But he's your best friend."

"I hate h . . . him anyway. He s . . . said all kind of st . . . stuff that ain't true!"

"Tell me what Ji—"

Just then Chad's knock interrupted, and Laura frowned in the direction of the door, brushed a staying hand across her son's shoulders, and went to answer. No sooner had she opened the door than Chad spit out, "Your little boy, he was down at th' cooperage, ma'am. Mr. Dalton, he says to give you this." Before Laura could say thank you, Chad had thrust the cedar scrap into her hand and was gone. She quickly read the message on the thin band of wood, then pressed it to her heart, glancing back at Josh, still crying on his bed. Oh, Josh, so this is what's been troubling you. Again she read the message, then, as tears burned her eyes, she pressed her nose against the pungent piece of cedar, searching for the right words. She closed her eyes, gathering composure. The piece of wood smelled like Rye, the clean, woodsy aroma that always clung to him. It seemed to drift to Laura now in a message of support while her heart throbbed with uncertainty.

Our son, she thought, swallowing the lump of love in her throat. Slowly, she moved to sit again beside the child, whose muffled sobs filled the alcove.

"Joshua—" She smoothed the blond locks on the back of his head, wondering what had taken place at the cooperage, wishing more than ever that Rye were here at this moment. "Darling, I'm so sorry. Please . . ." She forcibly turned the narrow shoulders over, and though Josh struggled to remain on his stomach, once she'd managed to get him turned, he flung his arms around her and clung. She pressed him close, resting her chin on his head. "Oh, Josh, don't cry."

"B . . . but Jimmy says Papa ain't m . . . my real papa."

"We'll talk about it, dear. Is that why you've been so quiet and upset with me lately?"

Josh's only answer was his continued sobbing, for he no longer knew who he should be angry at.

Laura sifted her fingers through Josh's angel-fine hair. "Your papa . . . Dan loves you very much. You know that, don't you?"

"B . . . but, Jimmy says R . . . Rye is my real papa, and he ain't! He ain't!"

Josh sat back and tried to look defiant, though his chin quivered and tears streamed everywhere.

Laura searched his watery blue eyes, groping through her mind for the least painful way to make Josh understand and believe the truth. "Did you go to the cooperage to ask him?"

"N . . . no."

"Then why?"

Josh's chin dropped and he shrugged.

Laura searched into her apron pocket, leaving the cedar piece in it, coming up with a handkerchief to dry her son's streaming eyes. "I'll tell you why Jimmy told you that, but you must promise to remember that I love you, and Dan does, too. Promise?" She tipped up his quivering chin.

After an uncertain nod, Josh let himself be gathered back against his mother while her voice went on comfortingly.

"Do you remember the first day you saw Rye? When you came home for dinner and found him kissing me? Well, that was . . . I don't even know how to tell you how important that moment was for me. You see, I had thought for a long time that Rye was dead, and because he was my . . . my friend since I was a child not much older than you are now, I was so, *so* happy to find him alive. You already know that all three of us were friends when we were little, your papa and Rye and me. We went to school together and pretty soon we were just like . . . oh, like three children playing follow the leader. Everywhere one of us went, the other two followed. Like you and Jimmy."

Laura pulled back to give her son a brief smile of reassurance, then tucked him where he'd been before. "Well, I was about fifteen years old when I discovered that I liked Rye in a different way than I liked Dan. And by the time I was sixteen, I understood that I loved Rye and he felt the same way about me. We got married as soon as we were old enough, and not long after that, Rye decided to go out whaling. I . . . I was very sad when he went, but he did it to earn money for both of us, and we planned that when he came back home, he'd never have to sail away again. But then the ship that Rye sailed on was sunk, and the news came back to Nantucket, and we all believed he'd drowned with the other men on the ship."

Josh pulled back and gazed up at his mother with wide, glistening eyes. "Drowned? You mean like . . . like Grampa?"

Laura nodded solemnly. "Yes, except we thought Rye was buried in the sea. We were very sad, Dan and I, because we both . . . well, we missed Rye very much."

Josh now centered his rapt attention on each word his mother said as she went on quietly.

"It was after I thought Rye was dead that I learned I was going to have a baby—that was you, of course." Laura held Josh's hand, gently rubbing the backs of his fingers. She looked directly into his blue eyes, which were so very much like Rye's. "Yes, darling, Rye is your real papa. But he went away not knowing you were going to be born, because you were still inside my stomach then. I felt sad when I thought he was dead, because he would never know about you, and you would never get to know him." Josh stared at her, showing no reaction for the moment. She pressed his hand between both of hers, continuing to caress it lovingly.

"Jimmy told you the truth. Rye *is* your real papa, but he's only one of them, because Dan was always there, taking care of you and me from the time you were born. He *chose* to be your papa, Josh, and you must always remember that. He knew you'd need one, and . . . and Rye wasn't here to take care of you and me, so we were . . . we were very lucky to have Dan, don't you think?" Laura tipped her head aside and touched Josh's cheek, but he dropped his eyes in confusion. "Nothing can ever change how much Dan loves you, do you understand, dear? That's the important thing. He was the only father you had until that day when Rye came back, and we found out he wasn't dead after all. But we all knew you would be confused and hurt if we told you, so we decided not to for a while. I . . . I'm sorry now that I put it off. It should have been me telling you, not Jimmy. And, darling, you mustn't blame Jimmy for any of this."

Josh looked up guiltily. "I . . . I called Jimmy a liar and a . . . a poop."

Laura stopped a tremulous smile before it could form. "You must have been very upset with him. But you must be sure to tell Jimmy you're sorry. It's not nice to call others bad names."

"So I . . . I got two papas?" Josh asked, trying to puzzle it out.

"I'd say so. And they both love you, too."

Josh seemed to digest that novel idea for a moment while staring at his knee. Then he looked up. "Do they love you, too?" he asked.

It was all Laura could do to keep her voice from trembling. "Yes, Josh, they do."

"Then are you married to both of 'em?"

"No, just to Dan." From her apron pocket, the scent of cedar drifted to Laura's nostrils as she battled emotions the story had managed to arouse within her.

"Oh." Again Josh seemed to mull, and soon he asked, "Did Rye know Papa helped me and you while he was gone?"

"Yes, he found out that day he came back and you saw him here."

"Then he shouldn't have hit Papa," Josh declared, as if coming to a firm decision.

Laura sighed, not knowing how to straighten out all the mistaken thoughts in Josh's young mind even as the child went on.

"And besides, after Rye came back, Papa started not coming home at night. I . . . I wish he'd come home for supper like he used to."

Unable to keep tears from forming, Laura hugged Josh close again to keep him from seeing her distress. "I know. So do I. But we have to be patient with him, and . . . and extra nice, too. Remember what Rye said? Papa needs an extra lot of cheering up, because it's a bad time for him right now, and we . . . we have to understand, that's all." What a large order for a child of four, thought Laura. How could he be expected to understand what she herself at times could not?

Yet there was a new peace within Laura now that Josh knew the truth about Rye. And later, as she and her son carefully measured and mixed the potpourri, Laura took the piece of cedar from her pocket and cut it into tiny pieces, which she added lovingly to the recipe. It seemed like a message of hope from Rye, one that would lie in her bureau drawer through the long winter ahead.

Chapter 15

It was often said that the commerce of the world would have come to a complete standstill without the lowly barrel stave. On a day in late September, there appeared at the cooperage a dapper little gentleman who knew well how highly honored the coopering craft was and understood that coopers were among the most respected and sought-after of tradesmen. As the visitor paused in the doorway, he produced a fine lawn handkerchief and wiped his nose, upon which perched a pair of oval wire-rimmed spectacles.

''G'dday,'' Josiah muttered around his pipestem, eyeing the stranger.

''Good day,'' came the nasal reply. ''I'm looking for the cooper, Rye Dalton.''

''That'd be m' son there.'' Josiah indicated Rye with the stem of his pipe.

''Ah, Mr. Dalton. Dunley Throckmorton is my name.'' He moved toward the rear of the cooperage, where Rye turned to meet the congenial handshake with a firm one of his own.

''G'dday, sir. Rye Dalton, and this is m' father, Josiah. What can we do for y'?''

''Don't let me stop you from your work. This world needs barrels, and I'd hate to be guilty of slowing down production for a moment.'' Throckmorton sniffed and burst out with a sneeze, after which he apologized. ''The weather on the sea-coast doesn't agree with me, I'm afraid.'' He dabbed his nose. ''Please, Mr. Dalton, please go on with what you were doing.''

Throckmorton watched as Rye went back to work on a partially constructed barrel, which had already been hooped and had its uneven ends trimmed off with a hand adz. Rye now set to work smoothing them with a sunplane. Throckmorton watched his powerful shoulders curve into his planing. The man had arms and hands of enviable strength, the kind America needed as its borders pushed westward.

''Tell me, Dalton, have you ever heard of the Michigan Territory?''

''Aye, I've heard of it.''

''A beautiful place, the Michigan Territory, a lot like here, with its snowy winters and mild summers, only without the ocean, of course. But it has the great Lake Michigan instead.''

''Aye?'' Dalton grunted almost indifferently, never missing a beat.

Throckmorton cleared his throat. ''Yes, a beautiful place, and all its land free for the taking.'' The visitor sensed Dalton's complacency and wondered what it would take to convince this young man to follow him into the frontier. He was of prime, child-producing age, which was vital to the future growth of newly established towns. And he knew his craft well, so could pass it on to others. A hearty, healthy, skilled young buck—Rye Dalton was exactly the kind of man Throckmorton sought. But competition for skilled coopers was keen.

''How's business, Dalton?''

Rye chuckled. ''Y' come askin' that of a barrel maker in a whalin' town? What do y' think those outgoin' whaleships put water and beer and flour and salt beef and herring in? And what do y' think they bring back blubber and oil in? How's business?'' He couldn't resist a second chuckle, for he had already guessed why Throckmorton was nosing around. ''We could turn off the lights o' the world if we stopped makin' barrels, Throckmorton. Business is boomin', as y've already guessed.''

Throckmorton knew it was true. Whale oil alone made up a large share of the commodities shipped to world markets in barrels. Still, he asked, ''Have you ever thought about leaving here?''

''Leave Nantucket?'' Rye only laughed in reply, and the visitor now employed his most convincing voice.

''Well, why not? There are other parts of the country where barrels are needed just as badly.''

Rye's muscles continued flexing as he laughed a second time. ''Somebody's got y' misinformed, man. Or haven't y' heard it's Yankee factories supplyin' the rest o' the country with everythin' from nails t' gunpowder? T' say nothin' of the Boston and Newport distilleries—and all shipped in barrels. Why, we could shut out more than the lights o' the world. We could keep it sober, and bring the triangle trade to a complete standstill.''

What Dalton said was true. Canary and Madeira—the ''wine islands''—shipped raw sugar and molasses to New England distilleries, which in turn shipped their rum and whiskey to Africa, whose slaves supplied labor to the Caribbean plantations, completing the triangle. And it all hinged on barrels produced along the northern seaboard, since the wood supplies of Europe were sorely depleted.

Throckmorton shook his head in surrender. ''I can't deny it, Dalton. What you say is true. Let me lay my cards on the table. It takes barrels to build new towns, and I've got a group of men and women who believe Michigan's the place to do it.'' Throckmorton paused for effect, then went on. ''We're forming up a group to leave Albany for the Michigan Territory in the spring, as soon as the Great Lakes open up, but we need a cooper.''

Rye's hands fell still on his work while he peered at the man from beneath lowered brows. ''Y' askin' me t' go to Michigan t' start up a town with y'?''

''I am.'' The dapper man gestured earnestly. ''We can't survive out there without barrels for flour, cornmeal, threshed grain, maple syrup, cider, soaking hams, and . . . and . . .'' Throckmorton released a distressed sigh. ''Even housewives need you for washtubs, pails, churns, dashers . . . why, you could be a rich man in no time, Dalton, and highly respected at that.''

Again Rye hunched over his work. ''I'm respected where I am, Throckmorton, and I have no hostile Indians t' contend with. If I wanted a change o' scenery bad enough t' leave Nantucket, why go to that godforsaken land? I could go t' the South and sell m' barrels for transportin' rice, indigo, tar, turpentine, rosin, sourghum—why, the list goes on and on. Why go with y' when the South's already civilized? I wouldn't have t' do without convenien—''

''Bah! The South!'' The small man clasped his hands behind his back and took up pacing like an incensed headmaster. ''What would you want in that wretched part of the country? No man accustomed to the . . . the healthy rigors of a brisk northern winter would be content in that hot, miserable climate!'' He gestured theatrically.

Rye smirked, erasing the expression when Throckmorton looked back at him. ''I didn't say I wanted t' live there. I was just pointin' out the fact that I can earn my livin' anywhere. I didn't spend seven years as an apprentice t' risk life and limb followin' a bunch of strangers into the wilderness. Besides, I'm content where I am.''

''Ah, but there's little challenge in this easy life, my boy. Think about having a hand in shaping America, extending its perimeter!''

The man was well chosen for his errand, thought Rye, who was enjoying this stimulating exchange more than he let on. Throckmorton was glib, and earnest to boot—a quite likable fellow, who aroused Rye's penchant for debate. The cooper found himself happily immersed in discussing the merits of the frontier versus civilization.

Still clasping his hands against his lower spine. Throckmorton studied him from beneath lowered brows. ''Tell me, Dalton, they say you've gone whaling. Is that true?''

''Aye, one voyage.''

''Ah! So you're the kind of man who seeks adventure and knows how to rough it, if need be.''

''Five years on a whaleship was enough roughin' it t' last me a lifetime, Throckmorton. Y're barkin' up the wrong tree.''

The visitor's spectacles turned toward the arresting sight of the cooper riding a croze cutter around the inner edge of the staves, beveling out the deep groove, called the chines, into which the barrel cap would be seated. Damn, the man knew his craft too well to let him slip away!

''How's your wood supply here, Dalton?''

''Y' know perfectly well we barter for our rough staves with the mainlanders.''

''Exactly!'' An index finger pointed to heaven for emphasis. ''Imagine, if you will, not this windblown island where the sea prunes every struggling tree to the height of the nearest hill, but a forest so thick and high you could make barrels until your hundredth year and never make a dent in your raw supplies.''

Rye could not restrain the grin that appeared on his face as the man looked upward and raised a hand, gesturing toward the ceiling beams as if he were standing in a verdant forest. Rye nodded and gave the shrewd man a point. ''Aye, y've got me there, Throckmorton. That'd be somethin', all right.''

As the cooper continued gouging out the chines, the other man pressed his advantage. ''The blacksmith we've found to go with us will have none of your advantage when it comes to raw materials. He'll have to have every ounce of iron shipped in from the East. Yet he's willing to take the risk.''

Rye looked up, surprised. ''Y've found a smithy?''

Throckmorton looked pleased. ''And a good one.'' Now his expression became the slightest bit smug.

Almost to himself, Rye muttered, ''I'd need a smithy.'' Then, remembering that Josiah was listening, he glanced in the old man's direction with almost a guilty cast to his eyes. Josiah gave no indication he'd heard Rye's remark, yet Rye knew he was taking in every word.

''We've found some fifty-odd people so far, among them all the necessary tradesmen the town will need to survive, except a cooper and a doctor. And I've no doubt I'll yet come up with a doctor this winter in Boston. As I said, the party is set to leave just after the spring thaws, as soon as the inland rivers open up.''

For just a moment the thought of making a fresh start in such a place as the Michigan Territory excited Rye's spirit of adventure. He was—it was true—a man who'd gone whaling, one of the greatest adventures a man could make. Yet the thought of leaving Nantucket gave him a sharp twinge of homesickness. He glanced again at Josiah, busy banding a hogshead, adjusting the pins through the holes of a temporary leather hoop like a man adjusts his belt. A puff of smoke drifted above the old man's head. The young cooper turned back to meet the earnest eyes behind the oval spectacles. ''I'm not for y', Throckmorton, though I appreciate the invitation. I have . . . family I wouldn't care t' leave behind.''

''Bring your father along,'' the agent said heartily. ''His knowledge would be as invaluable as yours. He could teach the young people far more than just coopering, I'll be bound. The West is a place where all ages are necessary—the old to bring experience, and the young to bring children. Tell me, Dalton,'' Throckmorton said, glancing around. ''Are you married? Have you a family?''

Dalton now stood erect, his croze forgotten in his left hand. The agent's eyes traveled down to check it and found there a gold wedding ring.

But Dalton's answer was, ''I'm . . . I'm not, sir, no.''

''Ah, well . . . a pity, a pity.'' But then the man gave a wily smile as he patted his waistcoat buttons as if preparatory to taking his leave. ''But then, there'll be young women making the trip, too.''

''Aye . . .'' the cooper said tonelessly.

Suddenly Josiah tipped the hogshead up on end and abandoned it to shamble across the dirt floor in his usual unhurried fashion, squinting and drawing on his pipe.

''Young man, if I was y'r age, y' could talk me inta goin' with y'. Specially on a day like this when the Little Gray Lady gits to givin' me twinges of the rheumatis'.'' He took the pipe from his mouth and rubbed its bowl thoughtfully. ''But m' son now—well, he ain't got no rheumatis' t' spur him on t' such *hiiigh* adventure.'' He drew the word out drolly as only a crusty New Englander can.

Rye's head snapped around. It sounded as though Josiah was issuing a challenge, though his eyes never touched his son as he went on with dry perspicacity.

''If y' was t' come back when his bones're creakin' and his hands gnarled and he's not good fer much anymore, y' might get him to take y' up on it then.''

Almost as if on cue, Throckmorton sneezed, reminding them how inclement the weather of Nantucket could be. When he'd dabbed his nose and tucked away his handkerchief, he shook hands with both men, first Josiah, then Rye, whose hand he clasped while delivering his final appeal.

"I ask you to think about it, Dalton. You have all winter to do so, and if you should decide to come along with us, I can be reached at the Astor in Boston. The party sets out from Albany on April fifteenth."

"Y'd better keep lookin', sir. I'm sorry." After a last hearty shake, Rye released the man's hand and a moment later he was gone.

Josiah buried his hands between his britches and his back shirttails, clasping his waistband and rocking back on his heels while air hissed softly into his pipestem. He concentrated on the doorway through which Throckmorton had just disappeared. "Notion's got some merit to it. Specially for a man caught in a sticky triangle's got him achin' like a horse 'ts thrown a shoe."

Rye scowled at his father. "Y're sayin' y'd have me go?"

"Ain't sayin' I would . . . ain't sayin' I wouldn't. I'm sayin' it's gettin' t' feel a mite crowded on this island, what with you and Dan Morgan both livin' on it full grown."

The old man's curious comments settled like a burr in Rye's thoughts as September gave way to October. Josiah was old; Rye couldn't leave him. But had the old man meant he'd actually consider going along? Though Rye puzzled over the conversation, he resisted bringing up the subject again, for talking about it lent the idea credence, and Rye wasn't at all sure he was prepared for that. There was Laura to consider, and Josh. But the thought of them presented the dizzying possibility of taking them along.

The first frosts came, and with them the most beautiful season on the island. The moors lit up with their autumn array of colors as out along Milestone Road vast patches of huckleberry turned bright red, then began softening to rust. Skeins of poison ivy thrilled the eye with their new hues of red and yellow. The scrub oaks turned the color of bright copper pennies and the bayberries turned gray, their skins like the texture of oranges. Ready for picking now, their fragrance was as spicy as any apothecary shop.

In the dooryards, mulberry bushes took fire and chrysanthemums put on their final show of the year, while the deepening frosts brought appropriate blushes to the cheeks of the island's apples.

Then the whole island took on a delicious fragrance, until it seemed the very ocean itself must be made of apple juice as wooden apple presses were brought into yards for cidering. The scent was everywhere, redolent and sweet. Cauldrons of peeled apples were boiled down into apple butter and jelly. Circles of white apple meat were strung up to dry until it seemed the ceiling beams in the keeping rooms of Nantucket would collapse beneath their weight.

In the house on Crooked Record Lane, baskets of bayberries waited for the cold days of December, when Laura would begin candle making. Overhead, the apple slices drooped like garlands between cheesecloth sacks filled with drying herbs—sage, thyme, marjoram, mint—filling the keeping room with an almost overwhelming essence.

Laura had delayed making apple butter until last. It was midafternoon when she hammered a scarred wooden lid onto the last wide-mouthed crock. Suddenly the cover cracked in half and one of the broken pieces dropped into her clean yellow fruit.

Tossing the hammer aside, she muttered an oath and fished the broken piece out, then licked it off before tossing it into the fire. Laura searched through her remaining wooden covers only to find that none fit the crock.

She glanced out the window at the bay, visible in the distance, and the forbidden thought crossed her mind. There was nothing to stop her—Josh was at Jane's for their annual pumpkin carving. Resolutely, Laura knelt down to try each wooden lid again. But still, none fit—no matter how she pushed, maneuvered, and jiggled.

Suddenly her hands fell still. She looked up at the window again. Scudding gray clouds with dark underbellies galloped across the skies like wild mustangs while the wind lifted loose mulberry leaves and threw them impatiently against the glass. Laura squeezed her eyes shut, slumped forward, and clasped her thighs as she sat on her haunches before the burning wooden cover. I must not go near him. I can put a plate over the crock.

But a minute later she was measuring the diameter of the container with a length of tatting string, then her apron was flying off to fall forgotten across a chair, and she was hurrying down the scallop-shell path toward the cooperage.

Its doors were closed now. She hesitated before opening them, to glance off down the street toward the quayside, where the large blue anchor hung over the door of the pub where she'd heard Dan spent most of his evenings. She shivered, drew her cape together, and stepped through the cross-buck doors into a place of bittersweet memory. It was shadowy, and fragrant with the smell of fresh-worked cedar, and warm from the fire blazing a welcome on the hearth.

Josiah was there, straddling his shaving horse, a curl of smoke twining through his grizzled gray eyebrows. He raised his head, relaxed his grip on the drawknife, then slowly leaned over to rest it against the horse. His benevolent gaze never left Laura as he swung to his feet and reached for his pipe, intoning in his familiar voice, ''Well hello, daughter.''

Always he had called her daughter that way, and the term now raised a wellspring of affection in Laura's breast as Josiah offered open arms.

She went against his woodsy-smelling flannel shirt, closing her eyes as the stubble on his chin abraded her temple. ''Hello, Josiah.''

He backed her away and smiled indulgently. ''I was beginnin' t' think this old cooperage'd never see y'r smile again.''

She turned to take it in. ''Ah, yes, it's been a long time, Josiah. It looks the same and smells just as good as ever.'' Her eyes fell to the other shaving horse and found it empty. A stab of disappointment knifed through her.

''Undoubtedly y're lookin' for my son.''

She turned quickly and assured Josiah a little too brightly, ''No . . . no . . . I . . . I've only come to order a lid for a crock.''

Josiah squinted, replaced the pipe between his teeth, and went on as if she hadn't spoken. ''He's stepped out for a minute, gone down t' Old North Wharf t' see about some hogsheads that's bein' packed aboard the *Martha Hammond*.''

Laura took refuge in the unoccupied shaving horse, turning to study it again, but she gave up her pretense to ask softly, "How is he?" Behind her she heard the soft sibilance of Josiah drawing on his pipe.

"Fair to middlin'. Better'n Dan, from what I hear."

Laura swung around, her face now drawn and pale. "I . . . I guess everybody on the island must know how Dan has been drinking since . . . since his father's death."

"Ayup." Josiah picked up a side ax and intently tested its edge with a horny thumb. "They're talkin', all right." Then he dropped the tool and swung onto his shaving horse again, turning his back to her and bending to work. "Been talkin' some about how that woman DeLaine Hussey finds excuses t' come pokin' around the cooperage every other day or so, too."

Laura spun around to gape at Josiah's flexing shoulders. "DeLaine Hussey?"

"Ayup."

"What does *she* want?"

Josiah smiled secretly at Laura's sudden, vitriolic response. "What does any woman want who dreams up excuses t' put herself in a man's vicinity?" Josiah let that sink in while he drew his knife toward his knees, shaving a wide white wood curl from the stave, then another and another. Next, he tested the concave curve with his fingers, running them time and again along the piece until he deemed it fit, and released it from the wooden jaws of the footclamp. "She came in t' buy a piggin for her mother, then she brought a basket of beach plums, than a batch of orange cookies."

"Orange cookies!"

Again Josiah smiled, though Laura could not see, for he'd kept his back to her. "Ayup. Tasty they was, too."

"O . . . orange cookies? She brought Rye orange cookies?"

"Ayup."

"What did he think about that?"

"Why, as I recall, he said he thought they was tasty, too. Seemed t' enjoy 'em tremendously. Then after that, I guess it was the cinnamon apples, then—let's see—oh, o' course. Then she came t' ask if he was goin' t' the clambake."

"What clambake?"

"Starbuck's annual clambake. Last o' the season. Whole island's bound t' be there. Didn't Dan tell y' about it?"

"He . . . he must've forgotten to mention it."

"Forgets a lot these days, Dan does. Even forgets t' go home at night and eat his supper, the way I've heard tell."

From the doorway a voice boomed. "Old man, y'r jaws're flappin'!"

Rye stood tall and stiff-shouldered at the entrance, dressed in high black boots, tight gray breeches, and a thick sweater that hugged his neck and emphasized the breadth of his shoulders. Laura felt her heart leap at the sight of him.

Rye glowered darkly at his father while Josiah, unflustered, only agreed amiably, "Ayup."

"I'd suggest y' put a lock on 'em!" his son returned none too gently, while Laura wondered how long he'd been listening.

The unflappable Josiah only inquired, "What took y' so long? Customer's waitin'."

Rye at last looked directly at Laura, but when his gaze drifted from her face down her arm, she realized she was standing beside his shaving horse, her fingers resting caressingly on the high arm of its clamp. She jumped and jerked her hand away, then crossed to Josiah's side, pulling the piece of tatting string from the pocket of her cape. "I told you it wasn't necessary for me to see Rye. You can do the work as well. All I need is a . . . a cover for a crock. This long."

Josiah squinted one blue-gray eye at the string in her palm, puffed once, twice, then turned away uninterestedly. "I don't do covers. He does." He gave a backward nod at Rye.

Helplessly, she stared at the string, thinking of DeLaine Hussey and Rye and a clambake. Laura was now utterly embarrassed for having come to the cooperage at all. But just then she sensed Rye at her elbow.

"When do y' need it?"

His voice was unemotional as a wide, familiar, callused palm came into Laura's range of vision, outstretched for the string. She handed it over, making certain not to touch him. "Whenever you get around to it."

"Will the end o' the week be soon enough?"

"Oh . . . certainly, but there's no need to rush."

He strode across the room and tossed the string onto the waist-high workbench, then stood with his back to the room, palms braced hard against the edge of the bench, far away from his sides. "Will y' come t' pick it up?" He stared out the window above the bench.

"I . . . yes, yes, of course."

"It'll be done."

His back was rigid. He neither turned nor spoke again, and Laura felt tears prickling at the backs of her eyelids. She presented a false, wavering smile to Josiah. "Well . . . it's been nice seeing you again, Josiah. And you, too, Rye."

The wide-held arms and stubborn shoulders didn't move. Her tears were now stinging, closer to overflowing, so Laura whirled and ran for the door.

"Laura!"

At Rye's bark, her feet didn't even slow. She jerked the door open while from behind her came a muffled curse, then, "Laura, wait!" But she swept outside and onto the street, leaving Rye to give chase in a long-legged stride. He shouldered through the door into the wind-wild day.

"Hove to, woman!" he ordered, grasping her elbow and forcing her to stop.

She swung around and yanked her elbow free. "Don't speak to me as if I'm the . . . the miserable whaleship that took you out to sea!"

"Why'd y' come here? Isn't it hard enough?" His eyes blazed down into hers.

"I needed a lid for a crock. This is the cooperage where one gets such things!"

"Y' could have got one at the chandlery as well."

"Next time I will!"

"I told y' t' keep out of my sight."

"Forgive me, Mr. Dalton, I had a temporary lapse of memory. You can be assured it won't happen again, unless, of course, it's absolutely unavoidable. In which case I would make sure I came with a basket full of *orange cookies* to pay for my wares."

His eyes took on a hooded look and he backed a step away from her, hooking his thumbs into his belt. ''The old man doesn't know when t' shut his trap.''

''I disagree. I found his conversation very . . . enlightening.''

Rye pointed a finger up the street, scowling angrily. ''It's all right for you t' live up there on the hill with him, but when it comes t' me and DeLaine Hussey, it's a different matter, is that it?''

''You may do exactly what you want with Miss DeLaine Hussey!'' She spat the words.

''Thank you, madam, I will!''

She had expected him to deny spending time with DeLaine. When instead he confirmed it, the pain seemed too great to bear. Haughtily, she looked down her nose, then lifted cold eyes to his and arched a single eyebrow. ''Have you taught her how to employ the shaving bench yet? I'm sure she'd find it delightful.''

For a moment Rye looked as though he wanted to strike her. His fingers bit into her arm, then he let her go, and a moment later he spun and strode angrily back to the cooperage, slamming the door behind him.

Immediately, Laura felt remorseful and wanted to run after him. But her angry words could not be recalled.

They were still echoing through her mind that night as she lay in bed, crying. Why did I say such a thing, oh why? He's right—I have no call to fault him for seeing DeLaine Hussey when I'm still living with Dan.

But there existed the very real possibility that DeLaine might eventually succeed in charming Rye, and it filled Laura with fear. Rye was lonely and miserable and more vulnerable than ever to a woman's advances. Laura remembered very clearly the night of the supper at the Starbucks' and DeLaine's flirtatious glances, as well as all that business about the Female Freemasons. There could be no doubt the woman had her sails set for Rye. In his forsaken state, how long could he resist the invitation of affection . . . and perhaps much more?

Chapter 16

The following day Laura's face looked as grim as the Nantucket skies as she set out for Jane's house to fetch Josh home. The open heathland was no longer a magic carpet of color. The sweet fern, Virginia creeper, and highbush blueberry had all succumbed to the ravages of frost, their golds and rusts now put aside. The huckleberry branches were no more than skeletal black fingers reaching bleakly toward the sky. The grapes that had formed a wall of green now shrouded the split-rail fences in barren tangles from which came the sharp, lonely bark of a pheasant who searched there for any last clinging berries. The double cart track of white sand wound through the hills before Laura with a singular loneliness common to late October. The sky was leaden and low, so heavy in places that it reached downward to lick at the barren moors that shivered as the wind picked up and moaned a lament for the passing of autumn. Soon the northers would bluster and blow, and the island would be battered by strong seas, then sealed off by ice and snow.

It seemed the world had taken on a brooding sadness to complement Laura's own. Her heart felt heavy, and she shuddered inside her woolen cape, drew the hood together tightly beneath her chin, and hurried on.

Jane took one look at her sister and said, "I'd better put on the tea. I think you can use it."

Half of Jane's brood had gone to school, leaving the house, for once, almost peaceful. A warm fire burned beneath the crane, and Josh came running with a welcome hug before Jane wisely bustled him and his cousins off into another room with a bowl of crisp-baked pumpkin seeds to nibble on. Then the two sisters settled across the table from each other, sipping strong mint-flavored tea.

"You look terrible," Jane opened frankly. "Your eyes are all swollen and your face is puffy."

"I had myself a good cry last night, that's why."

"Caused by which of the two men in your life?"

"The one I'm trying to avoid—Rye."

"Ah, Rye. I take it you've heard about DeLaine Hussey, then."

Laura's head snapped up in surprise. "Y . . . you know about it, too?"

Jane met her gaze steadily. "The whole island knows about DeLaine Hussey's unabashed pursuit of Rye. It shouldn't come as such a surprise to you that I've heard about it, too."

"Why didn't you tell me?"

"I haven't seen much of you. You've been hiding away down there, I suspect, so you wouldn't run into Rye."

Laura sighed. "You're right, I have been hiding away—scared to death of running into him someplace."

The room grew silent for a moment while Jane studied her sister's eyes. Beneath them were small swollen pillows of purple. "It's that strong between you two, is it?"

The truth was printed on each tired line of her face. "Yes, Jane, it is. I . . . we . . ." And without warning the tears came again. She covered her face with both hands and braced her elbows on the table. "Oh, Jane, I've met Rye alone, I've . . . I've *been* with him again, and it's made my life a living hell."

Jane placed a comforting hand on Laura's forearm, stroking it lightly with a thumb. "*Been* with him as a man and woman, you mean, in the fullest sense of the word." It was not really a question.

Behind her hands, Laura nodded her head wretchedly. Jane patiently waited for the fit of weeping to pass. When it had, she pressed a handkerchief into Laura's hands, and while Laura blew her nose, the two shared quavering smiles.

"Oh, Jane, you must think I'm terribly wicked, admitting that."

"No, dear, I don't. Not at all. I've told you before, I always knew how it was between you and Rye. Do you think I've been blind during all these years you've been married to Dan? I knew there was . . . well, something missing between you two. I only wondered when you'd admit it. Apparently, it took Rye's return for that to happen.''

''I tried to stay away from Rye, believe me, Jane, I did.'' Laura's haunted eyes pleaded for understanding. ''But I met him one day up in the hills when I'd gone to the mill to order flour. Josh was with me and . . . and seeing the two of them together, looking so much alike . . . I . . . well, he asked me to meet him and I did. The following day. That's the day I brought Josh here, the day when . . . when Zachary died.''

The full implication of Laura's words struck her sister, and Jane crooned sympathetically, ''Oh, Laura, no.''

Laura swallowed hard and nodded. She took a fortifying gulp of tea, then warmed her palms around the cup. ''I thought perhaps you'd guessed.''

''I suppose I did, about how difficult it was for you and Rye. But I had no idea it had happened that particular day.''

Laura studied her cup, remembering. ''Fateful, isn't it, that while Rye and I met and . . . and deceived Dan, he was out searching for his father on the bar.''

''Oh, Laura, you aren't saying you blame yourself for Zachary's death?''

Laura's eyes were etched with pain as she fixed them on her sister. ''Don't you understand? We were out there together, and when we returned to town, it was to the news that Zach was missing. The next time Rye and I saw each other was . . . was down at the wharf. But Dan was there, too, and . . . oh, Jane, I'll never forget the sight of Dan turning to Rye when he came in with the search party. He tried to . . . to resist going to him, but he couldn't. He needed comfort, and right there before the whole town, the two of them flung their arms around each other right after Rye and I had . . . oh, everything is so mixed up.'' Again Laura dropped her face into her hands. ''I feel so guilty!''

''I suppose that's natural, but to blame yourself for Zach's death is foolish. You're no more responsible for the fact that Zach drowned than you are for the fact that Rye Dalton *didn't!* I'll grant you the timing was unfortunate, but that's all I'll concede!''

''But you weren't there the night of the funeral when Dan was so drunk.''

''I wasn't there, but I heard about it.''

''Oh, Jane, it was dreadful. But it was true, everything he accused me of. I'm the one who's driven Dan to drink, and there's no way to cover up my feelings for Rye. I've vowed to stay away from him for six months, at least during the period of mourning. But Dan has guessed how I feel. He never comes home until late at night, then he stumbles in, too inebriated for us even to talk. And all the time I keep wondering, even after six months—if I divorce Dan and go to Rye, how can we face Dan then?''

Suddenly, Jane jumped to her feet, going to fetch more hot water for tea. ''You know the answer to that, Laura. You've always known. This island is not big enough for all three of you. It never has been.''

''N . . . not big enough?''

Jane replaced the kettle on the hearth, then turned and impaled her sister with a look that would force Laura to admit the truth. ''Hardly. It wouldn't matter which of the two you're married to. There's bound to be conjecture about the other, and you're bound to confront each other time and again and dredge up the past. Somebody will have to leave sooner or later."

"But Nantucket is our home, all three of ours!" Laura wailed.

Jane moved briskly back to her chair, but suddenly she looked ill at ease. Lifting her cup, she fixed her eyes on it as if reading its tea leaves. "There's been talk, Laura."

"Talk?" Laura looked puzzled.

"I can see you haven't heard."

"Heard what?"

"There's been a man visiting the island, named Throckmorton. He's an agent for a land company that's organizing a group of families to go to the Michigan Territory, come spring."

"M . . . Michigan?" Laura's brown eyes widened.

"Michigan." Jane swallowed a mouthful of tea. "To settle a new town there. And as you know, no town can survive without a . . . a cooper."

Laura's lips dropped open as realization dawned. "Oh no," she whispered.

"This man, this Mr. Throckmorton, has been seen at the cooperage more than once."

Foolishly, Laura looked toward the door, as if she could see the cooperage from where she sat. "Rye? Rye is planning to go to the frontier?" Laura's eyes again sought Jane's, hoping for denial.

"I don't know. I haven't heard that. All I've heard is that this Mr. Throckmorton has been sent to New England to drum up excitement, to seek skilled men, the kind of men necessary to carve out a living in the wilderness. They say a man can have all the land he wants. It's free for the taking. All he has to do is live on it and clear it and farm it for a year."

"But Rye is no farmer."

"Of course he isn't. I doubt that he'd homestead. He'd be going where his skill as a barrel maker would make him far more successful than farming."

"Oh, Jane!" Laura fairly wailed.

"I'm not saying it's true that Rye's going. I'm only saying what I've heard. I thought you should know."

Laura remembered Rye's stiff, forbidding pose the day before, how he'd turned his back on her, and her own impetuous words on the street. Could he be thinking of escaping Nantucket and its triangle of tension by simply turning to DeLaine Hussey and the frontier, accepting the challenge of both?

The thought haunted Laura continuously until the day when she returned to the cooperage to collect the lid she'd ordered. She fully intended to confront Rye and question him about his intentions for the future. But she was not to be given the chance, for when she arrived, it was to find only Josiah there. She had the distinct impression, though, that Rye had been on the watch for her and had hurriedly escaped to the lodgings overhead, for when she entered, Josiah was standing near the foot of the steps, looking up.

"Good morning, Josiah."

He nodded. "Daughter."

"I've come for my cover."

"Ayup. And it's ready."

He fetched it, handed it to her, then watched while she held it almost caressingly. She looked up directly. ''I . . . I wanted to talk to Rye. Is he here?''

The shrewd blue-gray eyes roved about the cooperage, but Josiah answered with deliberate evasiveness. ''Y' don't see him about anyplace, do y'?''

''No, Josiah, I don't *see* him,'' she replied pointedly.

''Then it'll be a bit difficult t' talk to him, won't it?''

''Is he deliberately avoiding me?'' she asked.

Josiah turned his back. ''Now, that I can't answer. Y'll have t' ask him next time y' see him.''

''Josiah, has there been a man named Throckmorton around here talking to Rye?''

''Throckmorton—well now, let's see . . .'' He scratched his chin thoughtfully. ''Throckmorton . . . mmm . . .''

''Josiah!'' she said with strained patience.

''Ayup. Come t' think of it, there has been.''

''What did he want?''

Josiah pretended to be busy cleaning the top of the tool bench, making a lot of racket as he rearranged tools. ''I don't listen to all the prattle of everybody who comes drifting in here t' talk t' that son o' mine. If I did, I wouldn't get a lick o' work done.''

''Where was Mr. Throckmorton from?''

''From? What do y' mean, from?''

''Was he from the Michigan Territory?''

Again Josiah scratched his grizzled chin, finally turning to face her, but assuming an expression of little concern. ''Well now, seems t' me I did hear him mention Michigan, not that I paid much attention.''

Laura's heart seemed to rattle against her ribcage. ''Thank you, Josiah. What do I owe you for the lid?''

''Owe me? Don't be silly, girl. Rye'd tar 'n' feather me if I tried t' take any money for it.''

Momentarily, her heart lifted, then she could not help asking as she looked down at the newly hewn cover. ''Did he make it or did you?''

Again the old one turned away. ''He did.'' At that moment Laura heard a floorboard creak overhead. She looked up at the ceiling and said loudly, ''Tell him thank you, Josiah, will you?''

''Ayup, I'll do that. I'll be sure t' do that.''

Several minutes later, Rye came down the steps and paused with his foot on the last riser, his palm resting on the upright post there.

''She's gone,'' Josiah grunted. ''No need for y' to skulk any longer. Y' weren't foolin' her, though. She knew y' was up there.''

''Aye, I heard her thankin' me.''

''Things've come to a fine pass when y' leave an old man t' tell lies to y'r woman,'' Josiah grumbled, ''and all the time y' hidin' over m' head like some sneak-thief.''

''If she were really my woman and mine alone, there'd be no need.''

''News of Throckmorton and his business here's got her scuttled.''

''Not enough to leave Dan, though.''

''How do y' know when y' wouldn't let her have her say?''

"If she'd decided, she'd have come up those steps and nothin' would have stopped her. I know Laura."

"Aye, I suspect y' do, though y' didn't see the look on her face when she mentioned Throckmorton. Who d' you suppose told 'er about him?"

"I haven't any idea, but the man's been talkin' to others besides me. Plenty on the island know his business here."

"And have y' been considerin' his offer?"

Rye's eyebrows drew together until they almost touched, but he didn't answer.

Josiah picked up a tool, turned his back and stepped to the grindstone, testing the dull blade with a thumb while asking nonchalantly, "Well, then have y' been considerin' the offer of that *hussy?*"

Rye jerked around to stare at his father's back. The way Josiah pronounced the word, it was questionable whether he meant it as a surname or a slur. "Aye, I'm takin' her up on it."

Josiah peered back over his shoulder to see Rye with a caustic smirk twisting one corner of his mouth.

"She makes a damn fine orange cookie."

"Humph!" The whine of the grindstone against steel cut off further conversation.

The final clambake of the season was held each year when the last of the winter stores had been put up and the beaches were not yet frozen. Cap'n Silas was the perennial tender of the firepit and could be seen each year on the day before the bake, gathering the indispensable rockweed from the stones and mussels on which it grew. Patiently, he filled burlap bags, each with nearly a hundred pounds of the yellowish-brown weed that contained small air sacs that flavored the food as the sacs burst. Bag after bag he dragged to the location of the clambake, heedless of the winds that gusted up to forty miles per hour—normal for this time of year. "We'll find a lee," he said, and they always did.

The hearty islanders thought little of braving the elements for a squantum such as this, the reward being the succulent scallops and clams that had been dug along Polpis Harbor and waited in baskets along with potatoes, squash, and cheesecloth bags stuffed with sausage, which would all be steamed along with the seafood.

On the day of this year's clambake, Rye and DeLaine Hussey arrived at the dunes in the late afternoon to find a large gathering already there and old Silas reigning over the building of the fire, ruling each step of the procedure like a despot. A shallow depression had been dug in the sand and was being lined with wood, then filled with rocks. "This is the tricky part," old Silas preached, as he did every year. "Got t' build y'r mound so's air c'n filter around every rock, else y'll get no draw t' heat 'em proper!"

DeLaine leaned close to Rye and whispered behind her hand. "Oh, thank heavens he told us!"

Rye chuckled silently, then drew his brows together in a mock scowl. "Got t' have good draw," he whispered back.

Rye Dalton had not been particularly anxious to spend the day with DeLaine Hussey, but her humorous remark seemed to loosen him up. She wasn't a bad-looking woman, and he realized he'd never spent enough time with her to know whether she had a sense of humor or not. It suddenly dawned on him that he knew very little about her. Standing now beside the pit in the buffeting winds, he made up his mind to enjoy the day as best he could. He was thankful the Morgan family, still in mourning, would not be joining the group.

Silas lit the fire, and true to his word, he'd laid it skillfully. Soon it spread and grew. Tankards of apple cider were warmed over it while the picnickers waited for Silas's final word that it was time to proceed. When the rocks began to crack and flake, he carefully spread them out and covered them with a layer of rockweed. On top of that went the food, then another layer of weed. Rye lent a hand as several men threw a tarpaulin over the mound, but this was the only role Silas assigned to anyone but himself. He took over again to weight the tarp with sand, sealing in the heat. At last the pit was steaming, and the crowd dispersed for the kite flying that had become traditional on this day.

As DeLaine and Rye ambled away from the fire, he studied her from the corner of his eye. She wore a simple bonnet of stiff blue silk that covered her to the ears. A caped woolen coat was buttoned high beneath her chin, and her hands were warmed by gray gloves. Rye turned up the collar of his pea jacket and resolved once again to enjoy himself.

They stood on a bluff with the wind at their backs and let out the kite to join the others that soared above the turgid ocean below. The breakers came pounding in, sending spray up toward the kite tails, which dipped and waggled, as if teasing the waves.

It had been years since Rye had flown a kite, and it brought a sharp smack of freedom as he watched the colorful triangle battle the wind, then crack smartly like a sail beneath a halyard. He looked up and watched the kite grow smaller. Suddenly, beside him, DeLaine laughed. He turned sharply to find her face tilted skyward as she held the string and felt it tug against her gloved hands.

"Did you know that when we were children I used to dream of doing this with you?"

"No," he answered, surprised.

She glanced at him. "I did. But you know what they say." Again she turned toward the kite. "Better late than never."

Rye could not think of a single thing to say, so he stood with his hands in his pockets, studying the kite.

DeLaine's voice was a deep contralto. "I used to envy Laura Traherne more than any other girl I knew."

Rye felt himself coloring, but DeLaine concentrated on the kite.

"She had you to follow everywhere, and such . . . such freedom, for a girl. I always envied her that freedom. While the rest of us were tucked away in our keeping rooms learning to tat and embroider, she was off running barefoot on the beaches." Now DeLaine turned and looked up at Rye's crisp jaw, outlined by the side-whiskers she'd longed to touch ever since she'd first seen them. "Am I embarrassing you, Rye? I don't mean to. It's all right, you know, that you love Laura."

His eyes flew to her face and found hers steady and assured.

"Everyone on this island knows how the two of you feel about each other. I just want you to know that I know, too, and it makes no difference to me. I intend to enjoy being with you because it's something I've wanted for a long, long time.''

Again Rye was speechless, his lips open in surprise.

Abruptly, Delaine became gay and lilting again. ''Tell me, Rye, have you seen Portugal?''

''Aye, of course.''

DeLaine pulled in a deep draft of air through flared nostrils and studied the faraway horizon. ''I've always wanted to see Portugal. It's out there—just imagine—I'm looking at it right now. I'd give anything to see it, or to see anyplace besides this stifling little island. I'm sick to death of it, and of the smell of whale oil and tar.''

''That's not the impression y' gave me the night y' brought up the Female Freemasons. Y' talked as if y' were proud of Nantucket and its . . . whalers.''

''Oh, that.'' She gave a self-deprecating grin. ''I was just saying that to see if I could get your attention, you know that. I couldn't care less if a man's killed a whale or not.'' The wind caught a wisp of her hair and blew it across her lips, and Rye quickly looked away. ''Tell me, Rye, is it true what they say, that you've been asked to go to the Michigan Territory, where they're settling a new town?''

He cast her a sidelong look, but she was studying him, so he quickly turned his attention to the waves below. ''I've been asked.''

''Oh how I envy you, *too,* being a man! Men have the freedom to make so many choices.''

''I haven't chosen t' leave Nantucket.''

''No, but you can if you want to. Just like you could choose to go whaling. I've been thinking about it a lot lately, about how women have to stand by idly and let the years march along while waiting for something to change the course of their lives. I thought about Laura and how different she was, flaunting convention and doing what she pleased, and I thought, DeLaine Hussey, it's time for you to do as *you* please! And so here I am, telling you things that no lady ought to tell a man. But I don't care anymore—I'm not getting any younger, and I'm still single, and . . . and I . . . I don't want to be.'' DeLaine's voice had grown soft, as if she were making wishes to herself. ''And I would give anything to be given the choice of starting a new life in a place like . . . like the Michigan Territory.''

Rye studied her profile while she studied the kite. My God, the woman was proposing marriage! ''DeLaine, I—''

''Oh, don't look so stricken, Rye, and don't bother saying anything. Let's just have a wonderful day and eat buckets of clams!'' She smiled brightly while he realized she was probably feeling quite chagrined at what she had just admitted. He had never before pondered the plight of a woman who wishes to marry but is never asked.

Without warning, the kite broke loose and soared away above the Atlantic.

''Oh look!'' DeLaine lifted a hand to touch the brim of her hat, which fluttered in the brisk wind. She laughed again and the sound was carried eastward, where a quartet of gulls swooped and called. ''It's heading for Portugal.'' The front of her coat lifted, too, and flapped against his trouser legs.

He smiled and took her arm, swinging back toward the fire. ''Portugal's got nothin' as good as Nantucket clams. Come on.''

They trudged back to the sunken pit, their moods once again carefree.

Cap'n Silas reversed the process he'd carefully overseen an hour before, removing the canvas in a great billow of steam, then pitching aside the limp seaweed whose tangy flavor lifted through the salt air.

Rye and DeLaine sat side by side on a blanket, eating succulent clams and scallops, tender vegetables, and spicy island sausage that never tasted quite as good when prepared in a roasting oven. They licked their lips and laughed and ran the backs of their hands across their chins and found themselves more at ease with each other as the evening wore on. When the meal was finished, nearly every man in the circle lit a pipe or a cigar.

''You don't smoke,'' DeLaine noted.

''Never had t', I just breathed the air m' father left behind.''

Again they chuckled, and Rye clamped his arms around his crossed and updrawn legs while DeLaine thought of how many years she had waited for this night.

It was dark by the time the charcoal had cooled, sending the islanders straggling back home along the beach. Though the wind had died with the coming of night, it was still cold, and now the damps crept in from the ocean to sneak down inside collars and up beneath petticoats.

Rye and DeLaine made their way back toward town silently. Now and then their shoulders bumped. She clutched the neck of her coat while watching the dark flare of her skirt on each step.

''Are y' cold?'' he asked, seeing her shiver.

''Isn't everyone on this island at this time of year?''

''Aye, and the worst is yet t' come.'' He had never touched DeLaine in a personal way before, but he draped an arm around her shoulders now, chafing her coat sleeve while their breaths created white clouds of mist on the night air.

They came to the streets of town, where an occasional lantern created a puddle of light in the murky darkness. DeLaine lived in a silvery clapboard house near the square, and as they reached its picket fence, Rye dropped his arm, opened the gate, and let her pass through before him. Her steps slowed as they neared the door, then she turned to face him.

''Rye, I've enjoyed every minute of it, and I'm sorry if—''

''There's no need t' be sorry about anything, Delaine.'' He studied her upturned face in the shadows. She was smaller than Laura, and her scent was different, spicy instead of floral. With a small jolt, he realized it was the first time he'd thought of Laura all evening.

DeLaine studied his face; he stood so near that her hem brushed his pantlegs. ''Rye, there is something I have wanted to do ever since that night at the Starbucks' dinner party. Would you mind very much if I . . . indulge myself?''

He wasn't at all sure he wanted to kiss DeLaine Hussey, but there was no way to avoid it gracefully. ''By all means,'' he replied quietly. But instead of rising up on tiptoe, she carefully removed one glove and raised her bare hand to embrace his cheek and the swooping side-whiskers.

''Why, they're soft!'' she exclaimed.

He chuckled as she ran the backs of her fingers over the opposite jaw, then tested the first one again, toying with the facial hair, running her fingertips over it.

"Of course they're soft. What did y' expect?"

"I . . . I don't know. They make your jaw look as hard as an anvil, and I just expected the whiskers would be . . . well, sharp."

Her palm had fallen still, but she did not withdraw it. It was very warm on Rye's cheek in the cool, damp night. "Have y' always been such an impetuous woman, DeLaine Hussey?"

"No, not always. I was taught, like all well-bred young misses, never to let my feelings show." But her fingertips trailed to the hollow of his cheek while her words died away into a whisper. The night was thick around them, while from the windows of the house candlelight painted their profiles a dim orange. "DeLaine, what y' said today . . . I've no way of knowing what—"

"Shh." She placed a single fingertip over his lips.

It, too, was warm and lingering, and the invitation was unmistakable in her touch and her eyes. He'd had no desire ever to kiss another woman except Laura. He had no intention of taking DeLaine Hussey to the Michigan Territory. But she was female, and yearning, and the finger on his lower lip gently glided across its width, and without warning Rye's blood set up a wild coursing through his loins.

What the hell, he thought. Try her.

He gently bit the tip of her index finger and reached for her waist with both hands. As he bent to press his mouth over hers, she raised up and lifted her arms, twining the fingers of the gloveless hand into the thick hair at the back of his head.

He had been manipulated by her all day long and Rye Dalton knew it, but for the moment it didn't matter. He was lonely and vulnerable and she tasted faintly of butter and smelled of sandalwood, and her mouth opened so willingly it surprised his own into doing the same. She made a soft sound in her throat and pressed herself close, until the front of her coat met the sturdy wool of his peajacket. DeLaine Hussey, he thought. Who ever would have guessed this would happen with her? She moved her mouth and head in gestures of invitation, slipping her palm into the warm recesses of his collar, and natural curiosity took over in Rye. He ran his hand up the bulky side of her coat to the place where her breast swelled beneath it, and she brought her midsection firmly against his. Again came a throaty sound of ardor, and his hand moved between them to unbutton first his own jacket, then her coat, before slipping both arms inside against her warm back.

Their bodies molded tightly together, and DeLaine Hussey felt the male hardness of the man she had coveted for years and years. Rye's palm slid to her breast and a shudder ran through her.

He felt it, and knew a small surge of satisfaction, remembering what she'd said this afternoon, how long she had had feelings for him. The breast was fuller than Laura's, and the feel of the mouth beneath his was different. But when her hips writhed once, he realized what he was doing. Comparing.

He broke the kiss and lifted his head, squeezing her waist inside the coat while pushing her slightly away. "DeLaine . . . I . . . listen, I'm sorry. I shouldn't have started this."

"Rye, I told you. It doesn't matter if Laura comes first with you—"

"Hey, hey," he said softly, drawing out the words, releasing her, and moving back a step. "Let's just leave it here for tonight, all right? My life is in a mess right now, and I have no business imposin' complications on y'."

"Imposing? Rye, you don't understand—"

"I do, but I'm not free t' . . ." He sighed and ran a hand through his hair while backing even farther away.

She suddenly looked down at her hands while pulling the glove back on. "I'm sorry I pushed, Rye." She looked up imploringly. "Forgive me?"

He relented and covered her upper arms with his palms. "There's nothin' t' forgive, DeLaine. I've enjoyed the day, too." He gave her a brief parting kiss, squeezed her arms, and said, "Good night, DeLaine."

"Good night, Rye."

He turned down the walk, and she heard the squeak of the picket gate before his footsteps echoed away into the blackness. Damn you, Laura Dalton Morgan! she thought. Isn't one man enough for you?

Chapter 17

November deepened, shrouding Nantucket with fog that seemed never ending. When it lifted, it was never for long: soon the wind would blow steadily from the southwest, and again the fog would appear as a gray line on the horizon, then race across the water to engulf the island like a windy cloak, and within ten minutes no one could see beyond twenty yards. The damp, frigid air sought a man's marrow, making fishermen bundle up like arctic whalers. But the fog was as much a part of life on Nantucket as was fishing itself, and those who gathered the provender of the Atlantic only dressed warmer and whistled softly between their teeth as they went about their work, accepting the whims of the weather.

Bass and bluefish were feeding off Rip Point, where the tides surged over the shoals, gouging and sucking at the shore in a froth of white water. John Durning, Tom Morgan, and others like them braved the elements daily, toiling at the nets until their chilled hands became bluer than the blues they caught.

Their boats, coming into the slips at the end of day, often appeared like spectral visions, gliding through the fog like silent ghost vessels. Then a voice would be heard calling hello, and another in answer, but it seemed no man ever stood in the spot from which a voice came, for the fog distorted the sounds and made them reverberate hollowly through the murky whiteness, like the disembodied utterances of wraiths.

During these bleak days, which Rye shared with Josiah, he thought about the coming of spring and the possibilities presented by the Michigan Territory. More and more he contemplated starting a new life there with Laura and Josh at his side. But would she truly leave Dan as she'd promised? And if so, could she possibly be legally divorced by that time? Perhaps she wouldn't consider leaving the island where she'd been born. There was no doubt in Rye's mind, however, that DeLaine Hussey would venture forth as his wife. Did he want her, though? Rye had the entire winter to answer that question for himself, but supposing he courted DeLaine and decided to marry her, there was the question of his father, who'd overtly demonstrated his distaste for her. Could the old man be persuaded to go to Michigan even if it were DeLaine going along as Rye's wife instead of Laura?

Rye and Ship took a walk one day to the house on Crooked Record Lane, but as they stood on the scallop-shell path, he knew it would be imprudent to knock on the door. He studied it, his hands buried deep, his hair covered by a woolen knit cap. Laura was inside, he knew, for the windows glowed through the gray day. But Josh was undoubtedly there, too, and as Rye studied the house that had once been his home, he felt again the pain he'd known that day the boy had flown at him, pummeling, crying, "You ain't neither my papa!" How many times since then had Rye wondered if Josh had accepted the truth yet? Countless times he'd cursed his own temper for flaring on that day Laura had come to order the lid, for he'd been so incensed, he hadn't even asked after the boy's well-being.

The wind shuddered through the barren leaves of the apple trees and sent the tall arborvitaes swaying against the linter, scraping the edge of the shingles with an eerie screech. Rye shivered.

Suddenly, he realized the foundation of the house had not been ballasted for the winter. So Dan's drinking was now affecting the way he carried out his responsibilities. Every house on the island was fortified against the drafts that seemed to creep and seep into every available crack during the cold months, and he was sure Dan had seen to it every winter during his absence. What an irony that it was Rye's turn to see to it in Dan's "absence."

With another glance at the window, Rye turned on his heel and made his way down to search out Cap'n Silas and ask if he knew someone who'd do the job.

The first snows fell; sleighs and bobsleds came to replace carriages and wagons. Across the undulating heathlands, ponds froze and small children skated with wooden runners strapped to their boots. Sometimes at night, fires could be seen near the frozen ponds where young people held skating parties. In keeping rooms, knitting needles clicked, turning out warm wool stockings.

A horse and bobsled delivered a load of kelp one day, much to Laura's relief, for though she'd piled the beds high with feather ticks, by morning the drafts had frozen the water in the bowl and left noses in nearly as bad a shape.

There came a day in early December when the fog rolled off across the Atlantic, leaving behind a churlish sky of clouds so gray they seemed to make dusk of day. The winds keened out of the northwest, delivering a stinging slap to the island.

Laura had set aside her bayberry-candle making until just such a day as this. When she rose that morning to the lowered clouds and blustering winds, she thrilled Josh by announcing that this was the day they would begin the task. Since Josh had patched up his friendship with Jimmy, he had softened toward Laura, too, and was now under foot, ''helping'' with the candle making. He sat at the trestle table with his mother, sorting through the first batch of berries, picking out twigs.

When they had enough, he begged, ''Can I scoop 'em in the kettle, Mama?''

In the process, bayberries dropped to the floor and rolled into hiding, followed by Josh, who scrambled on hands and knees to find them.

It was a slow, time-consuming process, making candles, and as Laura stirred the kettle over the fire, she was grateful for Josh's chatter.

''Will Papa be home tonight?'' he asked from his perch on a sturdy stool beside the crane.

''Of course Papa will be home. He comes home every night.''

''But I mean for supper.''

''I don't know, Josh.''

''He promised me I could have skates this year, and he said he'd teach me how to use 'em.''

''He did? When?''

Josh shrugged and looked into the brilliant coals beneath the kettle. ''Long time ago.''

Laura studied him. Poor darling Josh, she thought. Dan doesn't mean to disappoint you, and neither do I, but I'm running out of excuses for him.

''Maybe you should ask for skates for Christmas.''

But Josh's expression was forlorn. ''Christmas is so long to wait! Jimmy, he's already been skating twicet. He says I could go with him if I had skates.''

But Laura had no answer for her son. ''Come, would you like to stir the berries for a while?'' she suggested brightly.

''Could I!'' His eyes widened into blue pools of excitement.

''Pull your stool over here.''

He stood on the high stool with Laura's arm around his waist, ineptly stirring the gray-green nuggets that were already beginning to separate, sending a heady evergreen scent throughout the house. As the dark, blackish tallow rose to the surface, wax formed. This first rendering of tallow had to be cooled, skimmed off, strained, then melted down a second time, yielding an almost transparent wax ready for pouring into the molds. But long before the refining process was completed, Josh had tired of the activity, and lolled on his belly along one of the trestle benches.

At noon a driving rain began, and Laura looked up from her task of measuring and cutting wicks for the molds as the first droplets hit the window panes.

''A nor'wester,'' she remarked idly, happy to be inside in the warm house.

After the wicks were strung and the molds filled for the first time, Laura made a cup of hot tea and took a break before starting with the next batch of berries. Josh stood on a chair, peering out the window, and she wandered across the room to stand behind him. The rain had turned to sleet, glazing the surface of the snow and freezing on the limbs of the apple trees until they trebled in size and shimmered like ice-covered fingers.

"I wanna go skating," Josh lamented, pressing his nose against the window.

She ruffled his hair and watched the frosted limbs quake with the wind. "Nobody's skating today." Josh looked dejected and lonely, and for a moment Laura wished there was another child to keep him company. She wondered, if she'd been married to Rye all these years, how many there would be. "Come, Josh, you can help me sort through the next batch of berries for twigs."

"I don't like pickin' twigs," he decided now. "I wanna go skating."

"Joshua! Do you have your tongue on that window?"

He looked over his shoulder guiltily, and though he didn't answer, there were two melted spots in the ice on the pane. Laura couldn't help smiling. "Come on down from there. Let's make another batch of candles."

The weather worsened as the day wore on. The sleet covered everything with a dangerous sheet of ice before giving way to hard, dry snow that snaked ahead of the gale in undulating patterns across the slippery cobblestone streets.

Down in the harbor, not a boat moved. The rigging was draped with icicles that hung aslant, frozen by the winds at an odd angle, as if the earth's kilter had slipped awry. Gulls huddled beneath the piers, their feathers lifting as the wind buffeted their backs. Shopkeepers hunkered low, gripping their collars as they headed home at day's end.

Dan Morgan left the countinghouse, turning his collar high, too, and clamping a hand on his beaver hat as the wind threatened to carry if off to Spain. He bent low, making his way toward the Blue Anchor, already anticipating the warming effect of a hot rum toddy on this devil's day. Down below, the mainmasts of the windjammers rocked wildly as the water churned and billowed. Dan slipped once, caught himself, and shuffled more carefully toward his destination.

Inside the Blue Anchor, the fire roared and the smell of boiling shellfish permeated the air. But Dan disdained an offer of hot chowder, ordering the toddy instead and hunkering over the tankard after savoring the first taste of its welcome contents.

The tankard was emptied and refilled, and the usual gathering of indulgers clustered about the fire, reluctant to budge from their comfortable seats and face the snowy gale outside.

Ephraim Biddle came in, ordered himself a stiff one, and ambled over to Dan, commenting, "Got that load o' kelp around y'r house, just like y' ordered."

It was the first time it had occurred to Dan that he'd neglected to see about the kelp. "You did?"

"Well, didn't y' see it there, man?"

"Oh yes, of course."

Ephraim lifted his drink, swallowed heartily, then backhanded his lips. "Wull, I sh'd hope so. Cap'n Silas, he come on down by the shack and says he had two dollar f'r anybody'd do the kelpin' around y'r foundation, so I took th' two and did it."

"Rye," Dan muttered into his tankard, then added under his breath, "Rye

Dalton . . . damn the man.'' He took a deep draft of his toddy, clapped it down, and ordered, ''Another!''

The night settled in, and the elbows at the Blue Anchor pressed more heavily against the trestle tables. Outside, the anchor above the door complained as the wind buffeted and sent it creaking. The snow began gathering on the leeward sides of picket fences, leaving swales of exposed earth to the windward. In protected corners it clung to shingled walls, climbing high, inching up slowly until it rose in delicate spears of white that were oddly anomalous to the raging winds that sculpted such beauty. On the streets outside the pub, snow inched across the cobbles until its white shroud covered the dangerous ice hidden beneath it. In the belfry of the Congregational church, the wind pushed at the bell, sending out a dreary off-beat *clon-n-ng* that shivered away toward the bobbing boats on the harbor, where it mingled with the whistle of wind in the rigging.

The hour was half-past ten when Dan Morgan at last stumbled from his bench at the Blue Anchor and went weaving toward the door. Behind him only the alekeeper, Hector Gorham, and Ephraim Biddle wished Dan good night. With his back to the pair, Dan lifted a hand in a gesture of farewell, then stepped through the door into the howling night. He had not negotiated the first step along the street before his beaver hat was torn from his head and went sailing off toward Nantucket Harbor, first in the air, then spinning to earth and bouncing along on its brim as it went.

''Damnash'n,'' Dan mumbled as he turned to follow it, trying to focus on the black object that immediately tumbled beyond his range of vision. Giving the hat up for lost, he turned back toward home, battling his way against the wind that clawed at his coat front and sent it flapping open, though he clutched it time and again with one bare hand. ''Sh'd've brought m' gloves,'' he muttered to himself as he teetered along the streets, where the gale had managed to put out all the street lanterns, leaving the way black except for the shifting patterns of snow that whirled beneath Dan's feet.

Somewhere through his bleary mind came the realization that he had not buttoned his coat, and he was struggling to do just that when a fresh wall of wind struck him like a battering ram. His feet skidded, and he tried to regain his balance, but the force seemed to lift him as if by magic, flipping his body up, then dropping it to the cobblestones with the carelessness of a child examining a toy, then tossing it aside as if it were worthless after all. His head struck the bricks with a dull crack that made but the merest sound in the stormy night. The great-coat he'd been attempting to button as he went down was opened by the wind and left to flap against Dan's thighs, which were sprawled on the icy street. The hands without gloves rested palm up on the ice-covered bricks while snow gathered around his hair and covered the warm splotch of blood that quickly froze into a pool of red ice. Heedless of what it had done, the nor'wester meted out its wrath on the unconscious man and his island home, which had taught him well, through all his growing years, the bitterness of its merciless winters. He lay now supine and exposed, his breathing shallow as the snow hit his face and built up, as it had around the fences, drifting on his leeward side, swaling to the windward.

* * *

More than an hour later, Ephraim Biddle swallowed his last gulp, made a sound of resignation deep in his throat, and pushed himself off his cozy perch, reaching for the buttons of his jacket. ''There's no help f'r 'it but t' face th' long walk 'ome,'' he slurred. ''G'night, Hector,'' he mumbled to the alekeeper.

''G'night, Eph.'' Hector followed his last patron to the door gratefully, lowering the bar behind him.

Outside, Ephraim slogged up the street, muttering oaths as he bent low and balanced precariously on footing made all the more doubtful by his own inebriated state. The wind and snow drove down with a fury, and he clutched his collar, stooping even lower to protect his face from its wrath. When he stumbled against the inert body of Dan Morgan, he backed a step away, scanned the unmoving lump at his feet, and mumbled, ''Wh . . . what's this?'' A closer look revealed the shape of a man, and Ephraim bent on one knee, trying to clear his befuddled vision. ''Morgan? 'zat choo?'' He shook the limp arm. '' 'ey, Morgan, git up!'' But suddenly Ephraim sobered. ''Morgan?'' he said with a note of alarm. ''Morgan!'' He shook Dan harder, but to no avail. The man lay unmoving, unspeaking, while around him the snow already lay in drifts. ''Aw Jesus, no . . .'' Then Ephraim was on his feet again, running back toward the Blue Anchor, managing somehow to retain his footing on the icy cobbles, desperation keeping him upright.

Hector had already slipped the suspenders from his shoulders when a pounding came from below. ''Goddamn,'' he cursed, raising the suspenders once again and grudgingly taking the candle to light his way down the steps. ''I'm coming! I'm coming!''

''Hector! Hector!'' he heard through the door, as the pounding continued, harder. ''Hector, open up!''

The door swung open on a panic-stricken Ephraim Biddle. ''Hector, y've got t' come! I found Dan Morgan layin' dead in the street!''

''Oh God, no! I'll get my coat!''

Biddle waited by the door, shivering, afraid to make a move on his own now. When Hector returned, they leaned into the storm together, retracing Biddle's ever-fainter footprints to the motionless form lying in the snow. Without the slightest hesitation, Hector leaned and slipped his strong arms beneath the shoulders and knees of Dan Morgan, carried him back to the Blue Anchor, and lay him flat on a trestle table before the fireplace, where the coals had already been banked for the night.

''Is 'e dead?'' Biddle's eyes looked like those of an unfinished marble sculpture, two wide, deep, fearful depressions in his face.

Hector pressed his fingertips just below Dan's jaw. ''I can feel a pulse yet.''

''Wh . . . what we gonna do with 'im?''

''I don't know. I don't want him dyin' here, givin' the place a bad reputation.'' The alekeeper thought for a moment—Morgan's father was dead, and what could his mother or wife do? ''I'll get a quilt and stoke up the fire and you go down to the cooperage and get Rye Dalton. Tell him what's happened. He'll know what t' do.''

Biddle nodded as he made for the door with a wild look on his face. Never in his life had he had such a scare. He'd been spending evening after evening swilling with Morgan, and it was sobering in more ways than one to find his cohort brought so low by alcohol. Why—by the saints!—it coulda been me, Biddle thought.

Rye and Josiah were both in bed asleep when they were roused by a hammering from below.

''What the hell . . .'' Rye muttered as he braced up on an elbow and ran a hand through his hair in the dark.

Josiah's voice came from the opposite side of the room. ''Sounds like somebody's in a hurry f'r somethin'.''

''I'll go,'' Rye said, rolling to the edge of the bed, searching for the flint. When the wick caught, he quickly slipped on his pants, then made his way down the rough-hewn steps to the dark cavern of the cooperage below.

''Dalton, git up!''

''I'm comin'! I'm comin'!'' The door opened and Rye unceremoniously hauled Ephraim Biddle inside. ''Biddle, what the hell do y' want at this hour o' the night?'' Biddle's eyes looked like he'd been on more than a bad drunk.

''It's y'r friend Dan Morgan. He got drunk and fell down on the street, and we found him layin' there, all sprawled out and half froze to death.''

''Oh Jesus, no!''

''Hector says he's still got a pulse beatin', but—''

''Where is he?'' Already Rye was taking the steps two at a time, shouting back over his shoulder.

''Hector's got 'im layin' on a table at the Blue Anchor, but he don't know what t' do with 'im. Said t' come and fetch you and you'd know what we oughter do.''

''What is it?'' Josiah asked from his bed. Rye lunged across the room, yanking a sweater over his head, reaching for his pea jacket, mittens, and warm cap. ''Dan's been found out cold, in the storm someplace.''

Josiah, too, reached for his clothes now. ''Y' want me t' come?''

Ship whined and stood watching every motion of Rye, who roughly yanked on boots, then turned toward the stairs again.

''No, y' stay here and keep out o' the storm. I'll need a warm fire when I get back.'' Ship followed on the heels of his master, who ordered, ''Come on, Biddle,'' as he led the way out the door too hurriedly to take time to send the dog back inside.

Rye Dalton had rounded the Horn on a schooner. He knew the perils of an icy deck that tilted and pitched and threatened to toss men into the turbulent sea. Running across a flat cobblestone street was nothing for such a man. He hit the door of the Blue Anchor before Ephraim Biddle had scarcely found his footing. He stalked across the dim room toward the motionless form on the trestle table.

''Get 'im away from the fire!'' Dalton roared. ''Are y' daft, man?'' Without a pause, Rye pressed his weight against the edge of the trestle, sending it skittering away from the heat, then he reached to yank down the quilt with which the well-meaning Hector had covered Dan. ''Bring a candle!''

Hector jumped to follow the brisk order while Rye searched for one of Dan's hands. In the wavering candlelight, he immediately saw that Dan's fingers were frozen. With a quick snap he settled the quilt on the floor, then lifted Dan and lay him on it while he gave further orders.

''How long do y' think he was there?''

''An hour maybe, judging from when he left here.''

''Y' can't thaw out frozen flesh that fast or a man'll lose it, Hector!''

''I didn't—''

''Get over t' Doc Foulger and tell him t' meet me at my house—Dan's house, I mean—immediately. Dan'll need attention that only his wife can give him once the doc takes a look at these hands.'' Then Rye placed his own mittens on Dan's hands, his cap on Dan's head, wrapped the quilt around him as if he were an infant, hefted him off the floor, and strode toward the door. ''And send along a pint of the strongest brandy y' got with the doc. Now git y'r feet movin', Hector!'' Dalton didn't even pause to kick the door shut behind him as he shouldered through into the snow-swept night.

Laura was aroused from sleep by the sound of someone kicking the door. Thinking it was Dan, she swung her bare feet to the icy floor and hurried to the keeping room, where the mighty racket continued, as if Dan were trying to break the door down.

''Laura, open up!''

She realized it was Rye's voice in the same moment the wind knocked the door from her hand and sent it against the wall with a sound thud.

''Rye? What is it?'' He swept inside carrying something in his arms.

''Shut the door and light a candle, Laura.''

Even before she could move to obey his orders, Rye was clumping across the floor toward the bedroom doorway. The bulky shadow of Ship slipped inside, then the door cut off the wind and Laura groped her way toward the flint. In the dark she kicked over a basket of bayberries and heard them roll across the floor, but paid little heed as she called into the blackness, ''Rye, what happened?''

''Bring the candle in here. I need y'r help.''

''Rye, is it Dan?'' Laura's voice shook.

''Aye.''

The candle flared at last, and she moved toward the doorway with growing dread. Inside the bedroom, Rye had already placed Dan on the bed and was leaning over him, pressing his fingers to Dan's neck. Laura's stomach went weightless with alarm, then just as swiftly felt as if a lead ball were lying in it. Fear sent moisture to her palms as she hurried to the opposite side of the bed to lean over the unconscious man.

Josh came awake at the commotion and slipped over the edge of his bed to follow his mother to the doorway of the linter and observe the two, who were unaware of his presence.

''Oh, dear God, what's happened to him?''

''He got drunk at the Blue Anchor and fell down on his way home. Apparently he was lyin' there for an hour before Ephraim Biddle stumbled on him.''

''Is he alive?''

''Aye, but his fingers're frozen, and I don't know what else.''

Josh read the fear in his mother's face and sensed a great urgency in Rye as the two leaned across Dan from opposite sides of the bed. They hardly looked at each other. Instead, they both touched Dan as if they wanted him to wake up. Then Rye started taking off one of Dan's shoes like he was in a real hurry.

Laura pressed a palm to Dan's temple and forehead, trying to control the fear that made her hand tremble and tightened the muscles in her chest. She bit her lips and felt tears begin to swell as the fear of helplessness began to take hold. Laura Morgan, don't you go to pieces now! She dashed away the useless tears with the side of her hand, turned to Rye, and took command of her emotions. ''What do you want me to do?'' she asked with brisk intensity.

''Take off his socks. We have t' see if his toes are frozen, too.''

She peeled off the first sock to find the toes red but pliant.

''Thank God, they're not,'' Rye breathed, scanning the room now with an unemotional eye, his mind racing ahead. ''Doc Foulger is coming. We'll need a hammer and an awl, and y' can build up the fire out there a little at a time.'' Rye flung his jacket off and dropped it on the floor, then turned back to Dan. ''And bring an absorbent cloth and a small pitcher.'' Only then did Rye see the child, in his nightshirt, clinging to the doorframe, eyes wide with uncertainty and fear. As Laura headed for the keeping room, Rye issued one more order, but more gently. ''And keep the boy out there.''

''Josh, come. Do as Rye says.''

''Is Papa dead?''

''No, but he's very sick. Now you get back into your bed where it's warm and I'll—''

''But I wanna see Papa. Is he gonna die like Grampa?''

''Rye is taking care of Papa. Now please, Josh, just stay out of the way.''

Laura had little time to concern herself with Josh as she found the things Rye wanted. Neither had she time to wonder exactly what he wanted them for.

His voice came firmly from around the bedroom doorway. ''Laura, have y' got a small breadboard?''

''Yes.''

''Bring it!''

While she was reaching for it, Ship let out a single sharp bark, making Laura aware for the first time that the Lab lay on the rug at the door. Scarcely had she looked up before an impatient knock sounded, and the door was opened not by Dr. Foulger, but by the apothecary, Nathan McColl, carrying an alligator satchel.

McColl swept inside without a moment's pause. ''Where is he?''

''In there.'' Laura nodded toward the linter room, then followed McColl's black-caped shoulders through the doorway, her hands full of the items Rye had requested.

Rye straightened at the man's entrance, a deep frown lining his face. ''Where's the doc?''

''Stranded on the other side of the island. When Biddle couldn't find him, he had enough sense to come for me.''

Though doctors and apothecaries were authorized to practice almost identical methods, Rye had never trusted or liked McColl. But he had little choice now as the man stepped forward self-importantly.

McColl felt for a pulse, then examined one of Dan's hands. ''Frozen.''

"Aye, and not a minute t' waste before it thaws," Rye declared impatiently, reaching for the things Laura had brought.

"They can't be saved. We're better off concentrating on preventing the man from getting pneumonia."

Rye glared at McColl. "Can't be saved! Why, man, y're crazy! They can and *will* be saved if we act before they thaw!"

McColl allowed a smug expression to cross his face before glancing at the breadboard, hammer, and awl. "I take that to mean you know more about medicine than I do."

"Take it t' mean what y' will, McColl. Y've never been on a whaleship and seen a sailor's hands when he's pulled on the shrouds all night in an ice storm. What do y' think the captain does with frozen fingers? Chops 'em off?" Rye's face was stormy. "I'm not lettin' those fingers thaw without tryin' t' do what I can for 'em. If I can't save 'em, the pain'll be no worse either way. I could use a hand here." Rye moved toward the bed as if to place the equipment there, but McColl stepped forward to bar the way.

"If you're going to do what I think you're going to do, I'll have no part in it. I won't be held responsible for broken bones and infections that—"

"Out of the way, McColl! We're wastin' time!" Rye's expression was hard and angry as he counted precious seconds slip by.

"Dalton, I warn you—"

"Goddamnit, McColl, this man is my friend, and he earns his pay as an accountant—writin'! How can he do that without fingers? Now either lend me a hand or get the hell out of my way!" The order was issued at a near roar as Rye roughly shouldered the man aside and bent over the bed. "Laura?"

"Yes?" She stepped forward without hesitation.

Rye placed the breadboard on Dan's chest, then laid one hand on it, and at last met Laura's eyes. "Since McColl chooses not t' help me, I'll have t' ask you t'."

She nodded silently, suddenly dreading the task, for whatever Rye was planning seemed something hard to stomach. "Just tell me what to do, Rye."

He took a moment to give her a reassuring glance, then snapped at McColl, "Did y' bring the brandy?"

The man handed over the flask and looked down his nose superciliously. "I assumed it was meant to fortify you and Mrs. Morgan."

Rye ignored him. "Here, Laura, take the cork out and pour some into the pitcher. Then come and sit on the bed and hold Dan's hand steady." He covered the board with the absorbent cloth, and arranged Dan's hand on it, shifting the entire arrangement around until the fingers could lie flat.

"You'll end up breaking his bones, Dalton, I warn you."

Rye thought that if time were not of the essence, he'd take several seconds to wrap McColl's jaw around his knuckles! "Better a broken bone than a lost finger. The bones'll mend."

Laura held the pitcher ready now, but her face blanched and her eyes grew wide with apprehension. Rye paused and looked directly into them. "Y've got t' hold his fingers flat while I puncture 'em, then pour the brandy into the holes when I say. Can y' do that, darlin'?"

For a moment her eyes flickered, and she looked as if she might be sick. She swallowed, willing herself to take strength from Rye, to trust his decision, and finally she nodded.

"All right, sit down there. We've wasted too much time as it is."

She moved to the opposite side of the bed and sat down, watching as Rye carefully arranged the first of Dan's fingers flat on the surface of the board and looked up at her. "Hold it just like this." She pressed the finger onto the cloth, horrified at how stiff and cold it was. Nausea crept through her as she saw Rye take up the hammer and awl—a wooden-handled tool with a short point like an ice pick. He rested the sharp prick on Dan's fingertip and tapped the hammer once, twice. Laura felt the gorge rise in her throat as the tip sank into the frozen flesh.

"Damnit, Laura-love, don't y' faint on me now."

Her eyes flew up at the half-gentle, half-harsh words, and she found Rye sending his encouragement to her once again. "I won't. Just hurry."

The awl pierced the first finger three times, once on each of its inner pads, before Rye gave the order, "Pour."

The brandy ran into the holes and drizzled onto the white cloth, staining it a pale brown. Though McColl refused to help, he nevertheless stood by watching, fascinated by the process and by the endearments that passed from Rye Dalton to Laura Morgan. Behind him, a child stood in the doorway, watching too. Beside the child sat a dog, both of them so quiet nobody took notice as the tap of the hammer on the awl fell into the still room again and again, followed by the firm but quiet order, "Pour." The man on the bed remained blessedly unconscious, the alcohol in his bloodstream serving a totally useful purpose for the first time in his life: not only did it keep him from rousing, but it made it necessary for Rye to puncture the fingers fewer times than he'd otherwise have had to.

It was with great difficulty that Laura assisted Rye. Time and again she swallowed the clot of nausea that threatened. Tears made Rye's and Dan's hands swim before her, and she hunched a shoulder and blotted her eyes on her sleeve, took a firmer grip on her emotions, and steeled herself to hold the next finger.

Never once did Rye falter. His movements were steady and efficient with the tools as he tapped delicately, gauging the depth of each hole with great care. Not until the last finger had been bathed with brandy did Laura look up at Rye again. She was stricken to find his face ashen as he stared down at Dan. He opened his mouth and drew in a deep draft of air, as if battling for equilibrium, and suddenly he threw down the hammer and awl and spun from the room. A moment later, the outside door slammed.

Laura's eyes met McColl's, and suddenly she remembered how Rye had called her Laura-love. Then she saw Josh, whose chin was quivering as tears ran down his face. She scooped him up and hugged him close, kissing his hair, and comforting, "Shh, Joshua. Papa's going to be just fine. You'll see. There's no need to cry. We're going to take good care of Papa and make him teach you how to skate as soon as he's well again." She deposited Josh back in his own bed, then tucked him in, and whispered, "You try to sleep, darling. I . . . I've got to go to Rye."

She turned to grab a woolen shawl and stepped out into the howling night. Rye was sitting on the wooden step, slumped forward with his head on his crossed arms. Ship was there before him, whimpering softly, pacing back and forth and trying to nuzzle beyond his master's arms to his face.

''Rye, you must come back inside. You don't even have a jacket on.''

''In a minute.''

The wind lifted the fringe of Laura's shawl and slapped it across her face while snow streaked down and bit at her exposed skin. She hunkered down beside him and put her arm across his shoulders. He was shaking uncontrollably, though she realized it was not solely from the weather.

''Shh,'' she comforted as if he, too, were a child. ''It's over now, and you were magnificent.''

''Magnificent!'' he flung back. ''I'm shakin' like a damn baby.''

''You have a right to shake. What you did was hardly easy. Why, not even McColl had the nerve to do it. And me—why, if you hadn't been so sure and confident, I'd have fallen to pieces.''

He raised his head, wiping his cheeks with long palms as if exhausted. ''I've never done anythin' like that before in my life.''

His shudders continued beneath her arm, and she gently kissed the top of his head, tasting icy snow on his hair. ''Come on now. It won't do us any good if you catch pneumonia, too.''

With a shaky sigh he stood up, and she along with him. ''Just give me a minute, Laura. I'll be all right now. You go back in.''

She turned back toward the door, but his voice stopped her.

''Thank you for helpin'. I couldn't've done it alone.''

The wind moaned through the black dome of night sky as they were both stricken with the enormity of what they'd done. There had been no second thoughts. They had not *acted* so much as *reacted* when they saw that Dan needed them. It was like the day of Zach's death all over again. The three of them forever caught in a tapestry, woven into it like figures unable to change the course of their intertwined lives.

Chapter 18

When Rye Dalton stepped back inside, McColl was nowhere in sight. Laura had built up the fire and was heating water for tea. He stopped in the shadows near the door, and at the sound of his entry, Laura looked up, a teapot in her hands. During his preoccupation with Dan, Rye had scarcely noticed how Laura was dressed. But he paused now to note her wrapper of soft pink flannel, buttoned demurely from hem to high neck and belted around her middle, disguising her shape. On her feet were thick gray knit stockings. The fire danced and flickered, backlighting the outline of her hair, which was loosely braided in a single plait, with wisps flying free around her face. Their ends took on sparks of fire themselves as she stared into the shadows at Rye.

He shuddered and slipped his chilled fingers into the waist of his britches to warm them against his belly, but in that instant, while Laura poised and their eyes met, his body quivered from memory. It was the first time he'd been exposed to her, the Laura he remembered, moving about, doing familiar things, dressed in an intimate way. Almost as if she sensed his thoughts, she set the teapot on the table and turned to face the fireplace once again, the single braid swinging between her shoulder blades as she bent forward.

With a deep sigh, Rye pulled his errant thoughts back to the problem at hand; this was not the appropriate time for either memories or wishes.

He crossed the keeping room, but as he passed the alcove bed, he made out Josh, lying wide-eyed in the dimness, staring up at him. Still with his hands tucked against his belly, Rye paused, meeting the blue eyes of the child with an earnest gaze. Enough light slipped into the cavern above the bed that Rye could see fear and questions in the child's expression. He leaned sideways from the hip, lightly running a forefinger along the edge of the patchwork quilt covering the boy. ''Your pa . . .'' But the boy knew the truth now—there was no sense in trying to disguise it. Rye's voice was very low yet curiously rough as he began again. ''Dan is going t' get better, I promise y', son. Y'r mother and I'll see to it.''

The small chin quivered and tears suddenly glimmered on Josh's fair lashes as he tried not to cry. Then his childish voice trembled. ''H . . . he's got to, 'cause he . . . he promised t' teach m . . . me to skate.''

For the first time Rye, too, felt like crying. His chest went tight. His heart felt swollen. He dropped to one knee, adjusted the quilts beneath the boy's chin, and let his hand linger just a moment on the small chest. Through the layers of bedding he could feel shaken breaths being held tenuously. A surge of love welled up in Rye as he leaned to do what he had so often dreamed of doing. He placed a gentle kiss on his son's forehead. ''It's a promise, Joshua,'' he vowed against the warm skin that smelled different from any the man had ever been near—a child's scent, milky and mellow, and touched with the aroma of bayberry that clung to the room. ''But in the meantime, it's perfectly all right t' cry,'' Rye whispered. ''It'll make y' feel better and help y' get t' sleep.'' Even before Rye's words were out, Josh's tears spilled and his breath caught on a first sob. Realizing that Josh was chagrined at breaking down this way, Rye secretly added, ''I've cried plenty o' times m'self.''

''Y . . . you h . . . have?'' Josh tugged the quilts up to dry his eyes.

''Aye. I cried when I heard m' mother had died while I was out t' sea. And I cried when . . . ah well, there've been plenty o' times. Why, I nearly cried out on the step just now, but I figured if I did, the tears'd freeze and I'd be in a fix.''

Somehow during this conversation Josh's tears had abated. Rye touched the blond hair on his son's forehead. ''G'night now, son.''

''G'night.''

When Rye straightened and turned, he found Laura had been watching all the time. Her hands were clasped tightly together and her lower lip was caught in her teeth. She, too, appeared to be holding emotions in check, for her face reflected both tenderness and pain. Rye looked from her to the linter room doorway, from where McColl now watched them both. When Rye's glance shifted, Laura's did, too.

Flustered to find McColl observing something that was none of his business, Laura immediately sought to divert him. She crossed to pluck three mugs from their hooks on the wall and set them on the trestle.

At that moment Josh's voice came from behind Rye again. "Where's Ship?"

Rye turned. "Why, she's right here on the rug by the door."

"Could she come over here by me?"

Without hesitation, Rye ordered quietly, "Here, girl," and the dog ambled across the puncheon floor with clicking toenails. "Down," Rye ordered, and the Lab dropped to her stomach obediently.

Josh hung over the side of the bed to pet Ship's head, then looked up appealingly at his mother. "Couldn't she come up here with me, Mama, please?"

Rye could see the idea didn't agree with Laura, and put in quickly, "She's been trained that her place is beside the bed, not in it, Josh. But she'll stay right there and keep y' company."

"Will she be there when I wake up?"

Rye's blue eyes met Laura's brown ones across the firelit room. Then he turned back to his son. "Aye, she'll be there."

Again they both grew uncomfortably aware of the apothecary observing their every exchange. But then McColl cleared his throat and announced, "I'll need some boiling water."

Laura filled the teapot, then handed the simmering teakettle to him. "If you need more, I'll fill it again."

The apothecary answered with little more than a grunt before disappearing into the bedroom again. Laura and Rye sat down across from each other at the table, and she poured tea into two mugs. The fire snapped, and the wind howled around the windows, and from inside the bedroom came the sound of water being poured.

Rye had raised his cup to his mouth for the second time before some sixth sense warned him. He lurched to his feet, sending the bench scraping backward as he strode purposefully to the bedroom doorway, where he stopped short, his fists clenched.

"What the goddamn hell do y' think y're doin', McColl!"

His rage seemed to rival the force of the blizzard outside. Laura was beside Rye in a flash. She gaped in horror at the steam-heated glass cup McColl had placed upside down on Dan's exposed chest.

"We must restore his circulation . . ." McColl was lifting a second dome-shaped glass from the interior of the hot teakettle with metal tongs when both tongs and cup were suddenly smacked out of his hand and went flying across the room.

"Get the hell out, McColl!" Dalton roared, "and take y'r goddamn cuppin' with y'!"

Immediately, Rye spun toward the bed, searching for something to slip beneath the rounded lip of the cup to break the suction. He caught sight of the awl and quickly inserted its point beneath the thick-domed piece that was about the size of half a walnut shell, and handleless. Grabbing up the brandy-stained rag, he took the cup from Dan's skin, and as he did a little puff of steam came from beneath it. At the sight of the burn it had caused, Rye cursed, "Goddamn y', fool!"

"Fool!" The outraged apothecary glared at Dalton. "*You* call *me* the fool?" Cupping was as common a practice as pill-rolling, for the vacuum created beneath the steam-heated cups was believed to have the power to induce bad blood from incisions and cure respiratory ailments by stimulating the skin and drawing the blood to its surface. Thus, McColl's voice held a note of disdainful superiority as he scoffed, "People like you think you know more than trained men of medicine, Dalton. Well, I for one—"

"Trained men o' medicine! Y've burned him, man! *Needlessly burned him!*" Rye's face was a distorted mask of rage, and the power of his voice fairly shook the rafters.

"I did not invent the cure, Dalton, I only apply it."

"And enjoy every minute of it!" Rye's anger billowed afresh, for he knew that had he not stepped to the doorway when he did, McColl undoubtedly would have covered Dan's entire chest with the painful "cure-alls." Had the man shown any sign of compassion for the plight of his patient, Rye might have relented in his anger.

Instead, McColl only crossed to retrieve the cup from the floor, using his hanky to hold it as he headed toward Dalton to collect his bag. "The burns are an unfortunate side effect, but it's for the good of the patient in the long run," the apothecary stated smugly.

The sheer stupidity and pitilessness of such views was more than Rye could tolerate. Turning swiftly as McColl passed, the cooper suddenly pressed the hot cup he still held to McColl's cheek.

McColl jerked back, nursing the spot tenderly with his fingertips as it slowly turned red. His eyes snapped with hatred. "You're mad, Dalton," he growled. "First you call me in for help, then use your own queer methods and refuse to let me proceed with the accepted treatment, but I'll see that you pay for this . . . this insult!"

"How many more ways were y' plannin' t' torture him? I'm not the one who's mad, McColl, you are! You and all your kind who practice such atrocities in the name of medicine! And I did *not* send for y'. I sent for Doc Foulger, though I'm not too sure his methods're any less grisly than yours! How did it feel, McColl, huh? How do y' like bein' burned? Do y' think Dan here likes it any better than you do?" With each accusation Rye took another menacing step forward until he'd forced the apothecary back almost as far as the linter room doorway. There, Rye snarled, "Now take y'r fancy black bag with y' and get the hell out and never darken my door again!"

"B . . . but my cups!" McColl's wide eyes wavered toward the hot kettle still sitting on the bedside commode.

"Will stay right where they are!" Rye finished for him. "Out!" A shaking finger pointed the way.

McColl grabbed his cape, turned tail and ran.

A wide-eyed Laura, her face ashen, was bending over Dan, sickened by the unnecessary wound forced upon a man too ill to be able to object to such treatment.

As Rye turned back to her, he immediately noted that the circular burn was brilliant red and already beginning to blister. "Oh, Christ, would y' look at what that damn fool's done." Without pause, Rye strode out of the room and returned a moment later with a handful of snow, which he laid on the burn.

Immediately, it began melting, and Laura found the cloth with the brandy stains and dabbed away the rivulets as they formed.

"Oh, Rye, how could McColl do such a thing?" There were tears in her eyes.

The hand holding the snow shook yet with anger. "The man's an ass! He and all his ilk. What they get by with is criminal—leechin', cuppin', rowelin'—every last one of 'em should be made t' suffer their own *cures,* and they'd soon stop subjectin' others t' them."

"I'll mix up an ointment for it. How are Dan's fingers doing?"

Laura's question diverted Rye's attention, and his nerves stopped jumping. He checked Dan's fingers, which were warming now and beginning to bleed. He lifted his eyes to Laura's, and there was pain in the blue depths. "I won't lie to y', love. He'll do plenty o' sufferin' before this's over." Together they looked at the man on the bed, then at each other again.

"I know. But we'll be here to see him through it. Both of us."

The long lines of weariness at the sides of Rye's mouth were accented in the dim candlelight. And from where she stood, Laura made out each pockmark on his face as a round shadow while he answered.

"Aye, both of us."

A tremulous silence passed while they seemed to solemnize the vow, then Laura silently turned and left the room.

They wrapped Dan's hands in linen strips and covered them with a pair of mittens, then applied a balm of witch hazel to his burn, then covered it with a square of soft flannel before they bundled him in a feather tick and went back to the keeping room to wait.

Laura turned toward the fireplace to rewarm their tea, but she glanced over her shoulder at a soft word from Rye.

"Look."

Rye stood beside Josh's bed, gazing down into the alcove's shadows. Laura came up behind his broad shoulder and peered around to find Ship sound asleep at the foot of the bed, curled against Josh's feet, while the child, too, slumbered peacefully.

Rye turned his eyes from the bed to the woman beside him. She lifted her face, and for a moment he read peace there. He watched her coffee-colored eyes rove over his features, pausing on his hair, his eyes, lips, sideburns, and homing again to his eyes. Outside, the wind rattled the shutters while behind her a log broke and settled to the grate with a soft shush. More than anything in the world, Rye wanted simply to circle her with his arms and rest his cheek on top of her hair, close his eyes for a moment, and feel her face pressed against his collarbone. But he didn't. His thumbs remained hooked at his waist while he invented inanities to bridge the compelling moment.

"I'm sorry, Laura. I remember y' don't like dogs on y'r beds. Should I make 'er get down?"

"No. Josh needs her just as badly as . . ." She caught herself just in time before saying, *as I need you.* But Rye's sharp glance made her realize the words were clearly understood between them. Again she groped for something to say. "Thank you for coming, Rye."

"Y' don't have t' thank me, Laura, y' know that. Nothing could've kept me away when you or Dan needed me." He paused thoughtfully for a moment, then his mouth formed a rueful quarter-smile. "Funny, isn't it? Everyone on this island knows the truth of that. I was the first one they thought o' runnin' to when they found Dan, just like he was the first one they went runnin' to when I was supposed t've drowned."

They stood silent for a minute, once again pondering the reversal of the two men's roles in Laura's life, then she admitted, "I don't know what I'd have done without you. I would never have been able to stand up to McColl the way you did or know what was best for Dan."

Rye sighed and glanced toward the linter room doorway. "Let's *hope* we've done what's best for him." Then, looking down at Laura's hair, he asked, "Have y' got that tea ready?"

She led the way back toward the fireplace while Rye slumped to a bench at the trestle, and she placed two hot mugs on the boards, then sat down opposite.

Quite naturally, their thoughts roved backward five years to the last time they had shared this table. Laura looked up to find Rye watching her as he lifted the cup to his lips. He sipped, then the crease deepened between his eyes. He looked down into the cup. "The honey—you remembered." Again his blue-eyed gaze met hers over the cup.

"Why, of course I remembered. I must have fixed you tea with honey and nutmeg a hundred times."

The spicy, hot brew brought back at least as many memories now, but they knew it was dangerous to revive them. "When I was on the ship and the ice storms came on a night much like this, I'd think of sittin' with y' this way beside the fire, and I'd've given my entire lay t' have a cup o' y'r tea then."

"And I'd have given the same to be able to fix it for you," she added simply. It was the first time he had expressed regret over the choice he'd made. She tried to keep her eyes on anything except him, but it was as if they were unwilling to obey her wishes, and time and again, Laura's gaze got tangled up with his. They raised their mugs, drank deeply, and suddenly, beneath the table, Rye shifted his long legs and his knee bumped hers. Her knee jerked back to safety while he simultaneously sat up straighter.

For the first time Rye became fully aware of the pungent scent of bayberry permeating the room. He glanced toward the hearth, along the stones to one side, noting the candle forms, the baskets of berries, one of them spilled, the kettle and long-handled ladle for dipping the melted wax. Slowly, he turned back to look at her.

"Y've been makin' bayberry candles."

She nodded, her eyes flickering up, then quickly down again.

He let his eyelids drift closed, pulled in a deep lungful of evergreen-flavored air, and dropped his head back slightly. "Ahh . . ." The sound rumbled from his throat in a long syllable of satisfaction before he looked at Laura once again. "The memories that scent brings back." The perfume of the bayberries seemed to shift about his head like rich incense, bringing with it recollections of himself and Laura, younger then, seeking privacy in the bayberry thickets. And after they were married, there was the time she had made candles, and that night, in an orgy of excess, they had lit six of the fragrant tapers and placed them all around the bed, then pleasured each other within their circle of flickering golden light while the essence seemed to flavor their very skin.

Sitting now with that same smell filling their senses, the two were as aware of each other as man and woman as they'd ever been in their lives. The dancing firelight sent shifting highlights over their faces, and lit the sleeve of Laura's pink wrapper to a deep melon color. Her mug was empty, she had taken refuge in it so often, and she told herself to go get the kettle, to break this spell. But before she could, Rye lowered his right hand and laid it palm up on the table between them. Her gaze moved from his long fingers to his sea-blue eyes, which remained steadfastly on hers. Her heart tripped and thudded, and she clutched the handle of her mug while looking down again at the callused palm that waited in invitation.

''Don't worry,'' he said, low and gruff. ''I wouldn't do that t' Dan when he's lyin' unconscious. I just need t' touch y'.''

She moved her own hand slowly until it rested on his, then his fingers closed gently around hers and she searched for something proper to say, but so many intimate things came to mind instead.

''Rye, I got the message you sent about Josh. I meant to thank you for sending it that day I came to the cooperage to order the cover, but my temper got the better of me and I—''

''Laura, I'm sorry for what I said that day, and for not comin' downstairs the day y' came t' pick up the cover. I knew y' were down there, and I heard y' tellin' the old man y' wanted t' talk t' me.''

''Oh no, Rye, I'm the one who should apologize, for what I said that day about DeLaine Hussey. I realized later how unfair it was of me to put restrictions on you when I'm . . . well . . .'' She let the thought go unfinished, and asked instead, ''How did you find out that Josh knew you were his father?''

''He came t' the cooperage and denied it, then punched me in the stomach and took off, cryin'.''

Unconsciously, Laura covered Rye's hand with her free one. ''Oh, Rye, no.'' Her eyes were sad and her lips drooped compassionately.

''I could see he was terribly upset, and I worried about him day and night after that, wonderin' what was goin' through the little tyke's mind, and through yours. Then when y' came to the cooperage, I . . . I didn't even bother t' ask how he'd found out and how he was takin' it.''

''He found out from Jimmy . . .'' Laura relayed the happenings of that day, and as she finished, Rye was staring at their joined hands while his thumb stroked her knuckles.

''Did y' tell him about us? About the beginnin'?''

''I did. I tried to explain everything so that he'd understand, about our childhood and why you went on the voyage and what it was like when I thought you were dead, right up to the time you came back.''

''And what was his reaction?''

''He wanted to know if I was married to both of you, and if you both . . .'' But she decided it was wisest not to finish.

Rye shot her a sharp look, and Laura sensed that he knew, even though she hadn't said it. She understood intuitively that what Rye sought was some assurance that Josh was growing to accept the knowledge of his paternity. Laura's forehead showed lines of concern.

''Oh, Rye, his security has been so badly shaken. I can see changes in him as time goes on, and I believe he's coming to terms with the truth, but I really can't say what his feelings are. I think he's still very mixed up about all this.''

Rye sighed, then absently watched his mug as he moved it on the tabletop in circular motions.

Laura freed her hand and went to fetch the kettle once more. When she was again seated across from Rye, she purposely cradled her mug with both hands, gazing down into the wisps of steam as she stated quietly, ''So you've been seeing DeLaine Hussey.''

She looked up. Rye's face was somber, and he studied her as if trying to decide how to answer. At last he sat up straighter.

''Aye, I have . . . a few times.''

Her gaze dropped to the tabletop, where his hand rested. She concentrated on the back of it, where two engorged veins branched beneath the firm, brown skin. ''It hurt when I heard that,'' she admitted thickly.

''I didn't do it t' hurt y'. I did it 'cause I was lonely.''

''I know.''

''She kept comin' to the cooperage—''

''You don't have to explain, Rye. You're free to—''

''I don't feel free. I've never felt free of y'.''

Her heart raced with renewed feelings, and though she'd said there was no need to explain, she could not stop herself from asking, ''Did you enjoy being with her?''

''Not at first, but she . . . aw, what the hell, forget it, Laura.'' Rye looked away. ''She means nothin' to me, nothin' at all. When I kissed her, I—''

''You kissed her!'' Laura's startled eyes flew to his and her heart seemed to lurch.

''Y' didn't let me finish. When I kissed her, I found myself comparin' her to you, and when I realized what I was doin', I suddenly felt . . . I don't know what it was . . . disloyal, empty, I guess.''

''Yet you saw her again after that?''

''Aw, Laura, why are y' askin' such things?''

''Because DeLaine Hussey has had her eye on you for years.''

''I tell y', I've no designs on her, even though she all but asked me . . .'' But Rye abruptly halted and took a deep draft of tea.

''Asked you what?''

''Never mind.''

''Asked you what, Rye?'' Laura insisted.

His lips tightened, and he scowled, cursing himself for letting his tongue flap. Laura's lips dropped open as if her tea was too hot, but when he chanced a quick glance from beneath lowered brows, he found her face pinched with disapproval.

"What did she all but ask you, Rye?"

"Oh all right! T' marry her!" he admitted in exasperation.

In that instant, Laura tasted the bitterness Rye had been expected to swallow each time he saw her with Dan or thought of the two of them together. There was instantaneous jealousy tinged with a fine edge of anger at the idea that another woman could presume to make claim on the man she had considered *hers* most of her life. Laura's stomach did cartwheels and the color surged to her face.

"I told y', she means nothin' to me," Rye said.

"Is that why you've been considering leaving Nantucket and making a new start on the frontier with her—because she means nothing to you?" Laura was only groping in the dark, but she studied Rye carefully for his reaction. Her head seemed to go light and fuzzy when Rye failed to deny it.

Instead, he drained his cup, ran the back of his hand across his lips, and lurched to his feet. "You're tired, Laura. Why don't y' try to get some sleep and I'll sit up with Dan. If anything happens, I'll wake y'."

Laura felt suddenly bloodless and cold as Rye rounded the table, took her elbow, and urged her to her feet. Tell me I'm wrong. Oh, Rye, don't be considering such a thing.

But she knew he was, and they need not discuss it further for Laura to know *why* he was. Jane had come right out and said it: this island wasn't big enough for all three of them. And Rye was the one who was finally taking steps to give them all more space.

Laura lifted her eyes to him now as they stood in the bayberry-scented keeping room with the fire dwindling to lazily waving fingers of orange. The wind buffeted the house and snow hissed against the siding.

But though she still hoped he'd deny it, Rye only suggested, "Why don't you snuggle up beside Josh for a while? I think there's room for one more."

There was nowhere else in the house for her to lie. But though she didn't want to sleep, neither did she want to think. And she certainly didn't want to face the truth in Rye's blue eyes. Thus, when he turned her toward the alcove and nudged the small of her back, she resisted only halfheartedly as she whispered, "But you're tired, too."

"I'll wake y' t' sit watch if I get drowsy," he promised, and gave her a second nudge. She obediently crept to the bed, pulled back the covers, and slipped in, curling herself around Josh's warm little body. At her feet the dog's bulk pressed down on the quilts, but she pulled her knees up and faced the wall, scarcely caring or knowing how cramped the space was. She hugged Josh close and, behind her, heard Rye moving to take a chair into the linter room. She heard it thump lightly onto the floor, then a long, deep sigh.

She tried not to think about DeLaine Hussey proposing marriage and Rye talking to a stranger named Throckmorton. But behind her shuttered eyelids those images came and stayed and blended with that anomalous picture of Rye, propped on a chair at the bedside of Dan, whose life was now in Rye's safekeeping.

Chapter 19

The night winds howled and the wrath of a bitter Atlantic beat against the weathered cottages of Nantucket. In the linter room on Crooked Record Lane, Rye Dalton sat in a Windsor chair with his feet propped up on the bed, alternately dozing and stretching. Dan remained asleep, scarcely moving except for an occasional spasmodic twitch of his fingers inside the mittens. Rye leaned forward and placed a palm on Dan's forehead; it seemed hotter. Dan's left hand jerked again, and Rye wondered how long it would be before he woke up. When he did, the pain would be horrendous for him. Would Dan call out? Would Josh hear? Would Laura have to witness Dan's pain, too? Rye wished he could spare them.

He wrapped his left hand around his right, braced his elbows on his knees, and bent forward, resting his chin on cold knuckles and studying Dan. His breathing seemed to come with greater difficulty, and as Rye stared at the rise and fall of Dan's chest beneath the covers, his own thoughts meandered in disconnected fragments . . . my friend, I remember sharing your bunk when we were boys . . . why can't y' control y'r drinking . . . I love y'r wife . . . y' knew we were together that day Zachary died, didn't y'? . . . Jesus, man, look what y've done t' yourself . . . I don't really want t' be sittin' here, but my heart tells me I must . . . I will leave this island, come spring . . . there's no other way . . . easy, friend, don't move y'r hands that way . . . I wish dawn would come . . . I must go down and tell Hilda what's happened . . . Laura read the truth in my face . . . it'll kill part of me t' leave her, but . . . Josh had the best smell t' him . . . y'r breathin' seems worse . . . supposin' y' died, Dan . . .

The dark thought straightened Rye's spine, and he leaped from the chair, horrified at what had crossed his mind. He checked the time—five A.M. He'd been dozing, not fully responsible for the hazy wanderings of his mind. He stretched and made his way silently to the keeping room to add a log to the coals. When the wood caught and flared, he hunkered before it, elbows to knees, staring, thinking the awful thing again. Supposing Dan died . . .

After several long minutes he straightened, sighed, ran a hand through his hair, then ambled across to the alcove bed while massaging the back of his neck.

The three slept soundly, but the only one he touched was Ship, who sensed her master's presence and lifted a sleepy head, then stretched her feet straight out, quivered, and relaxed into sleep again. Rye's gaze caressed the curve of Laura's back, though she was covered by quilts to her chin. Her disheveled braid lay on the pillow and trailed over the quilt top, but as his hand gently slid from the dog's head, Rye resisted the urge to touch her and turned back to his vigil in the linter room.

He folded his long frame into the hard hoop-backed chair once again, but the room had grown chilly as the fire waned, and he wrapped his arms tightly across his chest, lifting his crossed calves again to the edge of the bed. He watched the rise and fall of Dan's chest and wondered if he imagined it had accelerated. But Rye's eyelids soon drooped, and the added log lent a small measure of warmth that seeped around the doorway, and soon he slept soundly with his chin digging into his chest.

Laura awakened and glanced back over her shoulder. The fire still burned and the blizzard still blew. She glanced at the windows, but they were dark, and as she turned the coverlets back and crept from the bed, a strange sound seemed to whisper an accompaniment to the chitter of snow on shingles. Josh did not stir as she silently slipped to her feet and crossed to the bedroom doorway.

Dan lay as before, on his back, covered to his neck, but with the mittened hands on top of the feather ticks, while Rye slumped beside the bed with his head drooping and his elbows propped loosely on the arms of the chair. The strident sound, she suddenly realized, was that of Dan's labored breathing. She inched nearer to the bed, gazing at his face, but it seemed to glow and fade in rhythm with the candle stub that guttered on the bedside table.

For nearly a full minute she stood utterly still, watching the quilt rise and fall, listening to the faint wheeze, trying to recall if his breathing had sounded like this before. She compared Dan's breathing to Rye's and found Rye's much slower and lacking the strident sound.

''Rye?'' She touched his shoulder. ''Wake up, Rye.''

''What?'' Disoriented, he opened his eyes and lifted his head. ''Laura?'' Still fuzzy from sleep, his head bobbed slightly before he jerked erect and ran his hands over his face. ''Laura, what is it?''

''Listen to Dan's breathing. Doesn't it sound strange?''

Immediately, Rye leaned forward and came to his feet, bending over Dan and placing his palm on the hot forehead. ''He's got a fever.''

''A fever,'' she repeated inanely, watching Rye's hand test the skin of Dan's neck, then slip to his chest.

''He's hot all over. Why don't y' fix a vinegar compress for his forehead?''

She left the room immediately to do as Rye suggested. When she returned and placed the cloth on Dan's head, his breathing seemed no worse. The candle was nearly out, and she fetched a fresh bayberry one, lighted it, and placed it in the holder, giving the room a renewed brilliance.

''I'll stay with him for a while. Why don't you go get some sleep?''

But Rye was wide awake again. ''It seems I did. And anyway, there's noplace for me t' lie, so I'll stay, too.''

He went into the keeping room and got another chair, which he placed on the opposite side of the bed from his. As they settled down across from each other, they both studied the man between them. The constant rush of his breathing grew more labored as dawn crept nearer. Dan's chest seemed to strain for each bit of air, and soon the sound of his inhalations became like that of a bellows with a piece of paper caught in its intake.

Laura lifted troubled eyes to Rye. He hunched forward with his lips pressed to his thumb knuckles, staring intensely at Dan's chest. As if he sensed her watching him, he glanced up. But her eyes skittered down; she was unable to look at him.

A pale thread of gray seeped over the windowsill, and with it the breathing of the man on the bed became more labored, carrying a distinct wheeze now.

This time it was Rye who looked up first. Laura raised her eyes, too, as if compelled by his gaze. Her eyes appeared larger than life-size, unblinking.

"I think he has pneumonia." The words fell from Rye's lips in a coarse, scratchy whisper that scarcely reached the opposite side of the bed.

"I think so, too," came her shaky reply.

Neither of them moved. Their eyes locked while between them the chest of the man lifted painfully, the new hissing sound whistling even more sibilantly with each breath that escaped his dry lips. Outside, a limb tapped the eaves, and in the other room their son rolled over and murmured in his sleep. On the walls of the linter room a bayberry candle cast two shadows while lifting its bittersweet and nostalgic fragrance above the bed they had once shared. For an instant they were transported back to a time when nothing stood between them. And somewhere in a place called Michigan, a new beginning waited for Laura and Rye Dalton. A place of high, green trees, where a cooper could make barrels for a hundred years and never run out of wood; a place where a boy could grow to manhood without reminders of the past; a place where not a soul knew their names or their histories; a place where a man and wife could build a log house and sleep in the same bed and shower each other with the love they were longing to share.

And in that moment of clarity, as Rye's and Laura's thoughts communed, as the pounding realization descended on them, their hearts hammered with the sheer magnitude of what they were considering. There was fear in their eyes as they understood with startling lucidity that this—all this!—could be theirs.

All they needed to do . . . was . . . *nothing.*

The solution to their problems. The obstacle removed. Fate taking over to give them back what it had robbed them of.

The cognizance struck them both at once. They saw comprehension settle, each in the other's eyes, while poised for that reckless moment in time.

Nothing. All we need do is nothing, and who would there be to blame us? There was Ephraim Biddle to swear he'd stumbled on an unconscious drunk in the snow, and if nobody would take the word of a drunk like Eph, there was Hector Gorham to verify the condition of Dan when he'd been laid out like a plank in the Blue Anchor. Even the confrontation between Rye and Nathan McColl was proof that Rye cared immensely for the outcome of his friend. And wouldn't the whole island know Doc Foulger was stranded somewhere on the far side of the island in this blizzard?

Like two wax mannequins, Rye and Laura stared at each other across Dan's struggling body, the list of justifications parading through their minds, each aware that this profound moment would change every moment that followed for the rest of their lives.

I love you, Laura, the somber blue eyes seemed to say.

I love you, Rye, the troubled brown eyes answered.

The moment lasted but several seconds, the realization smiting them swiftly, alarmingly, as they strained toward each other from the seats of the hard, wooden chairs.

Then suddenly, as if some wicked sorcerer's spell had at last been broken, they simultaneously flew to their feet, two blurs of motion.

"We have t' move him nearer the fire."

"I'll help you."

"No, y' get Josh and bring him in here. We'll switch beds. Y' have extra sheets, don't y'?"

"Yes."

"And plenty o' bayberries left t' boil down into wax?"

"More than enough!"

"And onions t' fry for a poultice?"

"Yes, and if that doesn't work, there's oil of eucalyptus and mint and mustard packs, and . . . and . . ."

Suddenly they halted, their eyes meeting with a new intense fire of dedication.

"He'll live, by God," Rye vowed. "He'll live!"

"He's got to."

The two sleeping bodies were interchanged without mishap. Josh's bed was ideal as a steam tent, with its hinged wooden doors. There they placed Dan, and while Laura rubbed eucalyptus oil on his chest, Rye built up the fire and unceremoniously dumped a basketful of berries into the iron kettle, then hung it on the crane. Laura made a thick poultice of fried onions and covered Dan's chest with it, while Rye worked to construct a makeshift funnel of linen sheets through which to direct the steam from the boiling bayberries into the opening of the alcove bed. They warmed bricks, wrapped them in blankets, and slipped them beneath the covers to keep Dan warm.

The pain in Dan's hands began infiltrating his semiconsciousness soon after the steam thickened above him. He moaned and tossed, and Laura drew her eyebrows together in concern. "How will he tolerate the pain?"

Scarcely looking up, Rye answered brusquely, "We'll keep him drunk. For once it'll do him more good than bad."

And they did.

Thus yesterday's bane became today's blessing. The analgesic quality of the liquor numbed Dan, and the lengthy time required to render clear candles provided a steady billow of aromatic steam that worked to loosen the congestion on Dan's chest. They forced him to drink brandy hourly, opening one of the hinged doors only briefly in an effort to keep the steam contained within. The combination of alcohol and the warm, steamy room was as effective as a narcotic in subduing Dan. He remained in a bleary stupor during the hours when the worst of his agony would otherwise have been sheer torture as his fingers burned and throbbed and his breathing turned to a thick rattle, followed by a racking cough that curled his shoulders and seemed to roll him into a tight ball as the expectorant did its work.

They waited for the first dread sign of dead skin on Dan's fingers: the flaking away of thin layers of flesh. None appeared. His fingertips were swollen and red, and obviously circulating healthy blood. When their worst fears were put to rout, Rye told Laura, ''I'll have t' go down t' let Hilda know. And Josiah, too. He'll be wonderin'.''

She took a moment to study him. Rye's beard had grown overnight, shadowing his chin and upper lip. His hair was messed and his eyes red. ''As soon as you've had something to eat. You look a little peaked yourself.''

''I can grab somethin' at the cooperage.''

''Don't be silly, Rye. The fire's hot, and I've thawed some fish.''

She fried him bass dipped in cornmeal, the way he liked it best, but as he sat for the first time at his own mealtime table, it was not under the circumstances he'd earlier imagined. Josh sat across from him, assessing all the goings-on, but once again keeping his distance from Rye. Laura tended the fragrant black broth that gurgled away on the hob and could not be abandoned for long. And from the alcove bed came the repetitive hacking of Dan, interspersed with an occasional weak moan or mumbled utterance too obscure to be distinguishable.

The storm had not abated by midmorning, when Rye was preparing to leave the house. Laura watched him as he stood near the door buttoning his jacket, pulling the knit cap low over his ears, and donning mittens. Skip stood at his knee, looking up and wagging her tail.

Rye turned to Laura. ''We'll be back soon. Is there anythin' y' need?''

For just a moment the spoon stopped moving in the bayberries and their eyes met.

Is there anything I need?

Her eyes lingered on his, but she was conscious of Josh studying them both and she only smiled and shook her head, continuing to stir.

In a flash of memory, Rye was swept back to the beginning of spring and a day when he'd stepped to this door and found her standing just where she was now, with a spoon in her hand like that. It would take discipline he was not sure he possessed to leave Nantucket for good.

He turned and pulled the door open, and a flat wall of snow collapsed and fell into the keeping room, for it was piled up hip-deep around the building. A delighted Josh came running to eat a handful as Rye stepped back and looked at the floor. ''The snow's made a mess—''

''I'll see to it.'' Already Laura was crossing the room with a broom. When she reached Rye's side, she looked into his eyes and murmured, ''Keep warm.''

''Aye.''

Then Ship made a dive into the world of white, and Rye followed, securing the door behind him.

The windows were running with steam that collected in corners and formed triangles of ice. Laura cleared a small spot on a pane, to watch Rye and Ship trudge through the drifts of snow, Rye taking giant steps and Ship resembling a dolphin leaping and surfacing on the ocean. She breathed a silent prayer of thanksgiving for having Rye here when she needed him, then turned back to sweep up the snow.

Josh took up sentry duty at the window, eager to have Ship back again. An hour later, he called, ''Mama, there's *two* people coming!''

''Two people?''

"I think it's Gramma!"

Laura crossed to stand behind Josh's chair and peer outside. It was Hilda Morgan who braved the elements with Rye and the dog. Laura opened the door and welcomed the distraught woman with a brief touch of cheeks. Snow and wind swirled inside, sending the fire dancing and ash lifting to the hearth in a backdraft.

"How is he?" Rye and Hilda inquired together as soon as the door was closed.

"There's not much change."

They stamped the curds of snow from their feet, and Hilda surveyed the makeshift tent around Dan. "It looks like you two have been busy," she noted while handing her coat to Laura, then she moved toward the alcove bed.

Hilda stayed until dusk. She proved to be a great help to Laura, taking turns with the bayberries, loading the forms with wicks, and helping with the pouring. She was an astute woman who immediately sized up the situation and read it correctly. Though Laura and Rye would have spared her the truth about how Dan had come to such a pass, Hilda was the antithesis of Dahlia Traherne, meeting life head-on instead of nursing self-delusions. She had deduced that Dan's drinking was responsible for his state, even before Josh informed her of all that had taken place here last night. She noted, too, the careful way Rye and Laura avoided looking at each other or crossing paths as they moved about the house.

But as the three of them paused in the late afternoon to share hot apple cider together before Hilda went back home, the woman surprised both Rye and Laura by forthrightly admitting, "My son is a fool. No one realizes that better than I. He knows perfectly well the two of you belong together, yet he refuses to admit it. I told him the day you came back, Rye, that if he kept Laura, it'd be against her wishes. I warned him—'Dan,' I said, 'you got to face reality. That boy is his, and that woman is his, and the sooner you come to terms with that, the better off you'll be.' "

She examined the surprised faces before her and went on crisply. "I'm not so blind I can't see what took place here. And I'm not too ignorant to figure out that you could just as easily have let him lose his fingers or wheeze himself to death. I only hope and pray that when he wakes up, he'll realize how much love it took—from the *both* of you—to do what you done for him." She reached across the table and covered one of each of their hands with her own, gave a firm squeeze, and added, "I thank you both from the bottom of my heart." Then, pretending to ignore their self-consciousness, she took a last gulp from her mug and pushed herself to her feet. "Now, I'd best get these old bones home through the snow before nightfall." Her tone changed to mock sternness. "Well, Rye Dalton, you gonna sit there all day, or you gonna see me safely to my door?"

To Rye's further amazement, Hilda said but one thing after that. They'd trudged through the snow with heads low against the gale-force winds, and when they reached Hilda's house, he hunched his shoulders, waiting for her to go inside so he could turn back toward home.

Hilda swung to face him. The wind licked her scarf and painted her nose bright red as she shouted above the storm, "That Hussey woman ain't for you,

Rye, just in case you was thinkin' she is.'' And with that, she opened the door and disappeared. Rye stared at the panel, dumbfounded. Was there anyone on this island who thought Laura belonged with Dan?

Rye made a sudden decision to stop at the cooperage again and let Josiah know how things were going. But as long as he was there, he took the opportunity to wash, shave, change his clothes, and comb his hair. Only then did he realize his loyal dog had remained with his son.

When he opened the door of the saltbox on the hill, the first thing he noticed was that Laura, too, had taken a few moments out for grooming. Her hair was wound into a neat nutmeg swirl at the back of her head, and she'd changed into a clean, simple dress of gray broadcloth, over which a white floor-length apron was tied. Rye hung up his jacket on the coat tree and stomped the snow from his trousers, and as he passed the table, noted it was set for three. Josh and Ship were preoccupied in a tug-of-war with a rag, and Laura was turning muffins out of a cast-iron form. For a moment Rye indulged in fantasizing that all was as it appeared—a man returning to his own abode, to a son, a dog, a wife who moved about their kitchen putting supper on their table. How ironic, Rye thought. It *is* what it appears, even though it isn't.

A restless movement from the alcove bed reminded Rye that Dan was there. ''How is he?''

''His coughing is worse, but it's looser.''

''Good . . . good.'' Rye stepped near the fire, extended his palms, and rubbed them together. Laura moved about, doing small domestic preparations at his elbow. Hilda's comments lingered fresh in their minds, and it suddenly seemed neither of them could look at one another.

''Wind might've gone down a little,'' Rye ventured.

''Oh, that's good news!'' She looked up brightly, then instantly turned away when she found his eyes on her.

Rye studied the fire. She had stopped boiling bayberries to make room on the hearth for supper. He looked back over his shoulder at the three places set at the table and counted the months, the years, he'd been waiting for this night.

''Josh, supper is ready. Come to the table,'' she called.

Rye turned from the hearth and stood uncertainly, watching Laura place the last of the serving bowls on the table, then settle Josh in his place.

Laura looked up to find Rye watching. In the subdued light of the candle and the fire glow, his pale blue irises looked like lustrous sapphires. ''Sit down, Rye,'' she urged softly.

His heart did a stutter-step, and suddenly he felt boyish, perhaps a little uncertain, like the first time after their marriage when she'd prepared a meal for him and called him to the table.

When they all were seated, she passed Rye a familiar tureen; it had been his grandmother's. He lifted the cover and found one of his favorites: thick nuggets of venison covered with rich brown gravy.

There was, Josh noted, something different about the way Rye and his mother looked at each other and the way Papa and Mama looked at each other. Though Josh understood Rye was his real papa, he still relegated the title to Dan only. But watching the exchange of glances between the two who sat at the table with him, he puzzled over his mother's pink cheeks and the cooper's satisfaction at each bite he took.

The meal was strained. What little there was of conversation was stilted and came to sudden stops until finally they forsook talk altogether. When supper was finished, Rye checked Dan, changed the dressing on his burn, and noted how Dan was now expectorating green phlegm—a good sign. He spread a square of flannel on his pillow, turned Dan onto his side, and propped several pillows behind his back.

''Why you doin' that?'' Josh asked.

''So he won't choke,'' Rye answered, and Josh wondered how a man could know so much, then added this newest detail to his growing list of observations of how carefully Rye and Mama took care of Papa. There were many things Josh noted about the tall cooper that puzzled him. There were many that intrigued him. Sometimes it took a great effort to keep from talking to him, but Josh still felt that to do so would be to divide his loyalty, and in his childish mind, this seemed wrong somehow.

Thus, the supper conversation had been thwarted by Josh's refusal to take part whenever Rye tried to include him. Also, there was a childish guilt at work within the boy for what he had said and done the day he'd run away to the cooperage.

Now, in the dim keeping room, Ship had finished her supper and Josh could not encourage the contented dog to play, so he watched guardedly as Rye crossed to the coat tree and extracted a piece of wood and a knife from the pocket of his jacket. Without a word, Rye placed a chair near the fireplace, sat down, stretched his legs out, and rested his heels on the hearth. He whistled softly between his teeth while the short knife bit into the wood and scraped off a loose curl that fell to his lap. But though Josh's interest was piqued, he remained guarded.

Another kettle of bayberries was hung on the crane, and Laura and Rye took turns tending them. In between times, Rye sat contentedly, whittling.

Josh was put to bed in the linter room, and as he kissed his mother, he inquired, ''Is Rye staying here tonight?''

''Yes. We have to take turns watching Papa.''

''Oh.'' Josh looked thoughtful for a moment, then asked, ''What's he makin'?''

Laura brushed the silky bangs back from his forehead and smiled. ''I don't know. Why don't you ask him?''

Josh seemed to think it over briefly, then posed a surprising question. ''How come you look at him funny all the time?''

Startled, Laura replied with the first words that came to her mind. ''I didn't know I did!''

When Laura returned to the keeping room, Rye had set aside his whittling and was stooping over Dan, checking him again. He straightened, unaware that Laura stood behind him, observing how he braced his back with one hand, his nape with the other, arching backward with a deep sigh.

''Rye, you haven't really slept for forty-eight hours.''

He snapped erect and turned. ''I'm doin' fine. And I slept some last night.''

''In that chair beside the bed?''

"There're berries left t' boil yet, and we'd best keep steamin' him at least till mornin'."

"You need some rest."

"Aye, then . . . in a while." Dan coughed. Rye turned to wipe his lips, then closed the hinged door so the steam could build up again.

Laura moved to the fireplace, doggedly taking up the spoon to stir the berries. She sensed Rye moving up quietly behind her. "You know—" She laughed tiredly. "I used to love this job, making bayberry candles. But I don't think I'll ever make another one as long as I live, once these are done."

She felt Rye's hands surround the tired muscles that sloped from her neck to her shoulders, and Laura's eyes sank shut, the spoon drifting to a stop. She sighed wearily, tipping her head back until it touched his hard chest.

"Laura," he murmured, gently turning her around.

"Oh, Rye . . ." She met his eyes for a moment, then closed her own and let herself rest against the hard bulk of his torso while his cheek pressed against her hair and their arms circled each other very loosely. The embrace was one of exhaustion rather than desire, a drawing of strength, an affirmation of support, and perhaps a consolation.

For a long time neither spoke. Laura rested her palms against the back of his sweater and felt its coarse knit texture beneath her cheek. Again she smelled the lingering essence of cedar trapped in the wool and, through it, felt the warmth of his body.

Rye breathed the scent of bayberry and turned his lips lightly against the silken skeins of her hair while his palm closed loosely over her upper arm, then rubbed reassuringly.

"He's goin' t' live," Rye murmured into her hair.

"Thank God," she said with a sigh of relief. Suddenly, Rye's knees trembled in sheer exhaustion. She felt it and backed away to observe his bloodshot eyes. "I've got a few good hours left in me yet. Please, Rye, will you rest? I'll wake you at midnight, I promise. Just go stretch out beside Josh."

Rye's brain could scarcely function, and he felt powerless to resist the temptation of closing his eyes and drifting into oblivion. And so he slept in his own bed for the first time in five years, though, again, not in the way of which he'd dreamed, not with Laura beside him. Rye slept instead with the gentle breath of his son falling peacefully against his wrist, which was flung out on the pillow between them.

He awakened in the deep of night, listening to the sounds of the storm losing strength and Josh's rhythmic breathing, then the persistent hack of Dan's coughing. Sitting up, Rye came alert, glanced back at Josh, then crept to the doorway on stockinged feet. It was well after three in the morning. The coals were glowing; a new batch of candles hung by their wick on a lathe resting between two chairs. A candle burned on the table beside Laura, who was slumped across the trestle with one arm flung out, fast asleep.

Dan's coughing subsided, and he mumbled incoherently, then fell still again. Rye went to the side of the bed, tested Dan's forehead, found it cooler. Then he turned to Laura, slipped his arms beneath her knees and back, and lifted her from the bench.

Her eyelids fluttered open, then slammed shut as if they were weighted. ''Rye . . .'' Her forehead dovetailed within the curve of his neck and her right hand lifted to curl about his collarbone while he carried her toward the bedroom. Incoherent, more asleep than awake, her voice came again, thick and muffled. ''Rye, I love you.''

''I know.'' He gently laid her down beside Josh and tenderly pulled the feather tick up around her ears.

Through her last vestiges of consciousness, Laura felt his warm lips pressed to her forehead as she snuggled into the bed that still held the warmth of his body.

The following day, Rye and Laura were revitalized as their vigil continued. One of them was always at Dan's side. When Rye took his turn, he often propped his feet up, took up the soft whistling and his whittling knife, pretending to be unaware of Josh's increasing interest in the project.

But as the mysterious object came to resemble an ice skate, Josh lost his will to remain stoic. He managed to creep nearer and nearer Rye's chair until finally, when his curiosity grew too great to contain, the child questioned, ''What you makin'?''

''What . . . this?'' Rye twisted the nearly finished skate back and forth in the air.

When his eyes fixed on the double runners, Josh nodded five times in succession—hard!

''Why, this's an ice skate.''

''For you?'' Josh's transfixed eyes grew even wider.

''Naw, I got a pair o' skates already.''

''Y' do?'' Josh could scarcely drag his eyes to Rye's face.

''I'm just passin' the time, like I used t' do on the ship, skrimshanding.'' Rye took another swipe at the wood with the blade, then he studied the results critically and suddenly started in surprise. ''Why, this skate looks like it's just about the size o' your foot, boy!'' It was all Rye could do to hold a straight face while Josh glanced down at his small feet, then back at the skate. ''Here, let's see.'' Rye leaned over to compare the skate to Josh's boot, and when the two complemented each other ideally, Rye mused, ''Mmm . . . seems t' me I heard y' had a birthday this week.'' Without looking, Rye sensed Laura's smile.

After that, Josh hung beside Rye's chair, asking questions, pointing, showing an interest in anything Rye had to tell about his years at sea. The cooper told him about the doldrums and how they were responsible for many a sailor taking up skrimshanding to pass the time. He described the Nantucket sleighride, that heart-stopping ride in a whaleboat just after the whale's been harpooned, when it tows the whalers through the boiling waters in a life and death struggle sometimes lasting for days. Eventually, Rye's stories came around to some of the tall tales exchanged by members of the New England Whalers' Liars Bench. Josh sat wide-eyed and eager through the fantastic yarns about the fabled deepwater sailorman Old Storm-along, who measured four fathoms from the deck to the bridge of his nose, took his whale soup in a Cape Cod dory, favored raw shark meat with the skin still on and ostrich eggs scrambled with their shells, then lay back after breakfast and picked his teeth with an oar of white oak—''Twenty-two feet long for good leverage!'' Rye ended, subduing a grin as he eyed Josh askance.

''Aw, you're just makin' that up!'' But Josh was grinning and eager for more of such spoondrift.

During those shared hours, as Rye entertained his son with brig yarns, he carefully slowed the speed of his whittling to extend the time while he got to know Josh better.

Toward the end of the third day, the funnel of sheets was taken down and the rations of whiskey stopped. The blizzard had run itself out, leaving a total accumulation of fourteen inches of snow over which Dr. Foulger's cutter delivered him safely from the far side of the island. He examined Dan and pronounced that there was nothing more he could do that had not already been done, but that Dan was definitely out of danger.

Laura and Rye had spoken of nothing personal since that first night. They sat now, on the fourth night of their vigil, on chairs pulled up facing the fireplace. Josh had been put to bed in the linter room, and Dan seemed to be resting more comfortably, the doors of the alcove bed open.

Laura was knitting a woolen stocking for Josh. Rye was pondering the fire, slumped down low in his chair with an ankle crossed over a knee.

The click of the needles went on and on in the silence until Rye hunched forward, resting elbows to knees. ''About the Michigan Territory . . .''

The needles stopped clicking. Laura held her breath. She looked up at the side of Rye's face, where the rough side-whiskers were burnished by the light of the fire as he stared into it.

Slowly, he turned to look back over his shoulder. ''I won't be goin' with DeLaine Hussey,'' he announced in a deep, quiet tone.

''Y . . . you won't?'' Laura's heart seemed to be slamming against her ribs hard enough to break them.

''I'll be goin' with you.''

The blood rushed to her face. Without thinking, she glanced at the open doors of the alcove bed while her heart thrummed on as if powered by some superhuman source. Her lips dropped open as she struggled for breath, then took up knitting with a new, frantic energy.

''That is, if y' think y' can leave this island.'' He continued studying her over his shoulder. Still she made the needles race. ''Will y' stop that infernal knittin','' he ordered with quiet impatience. Her hands fell to her lap, and her gaze followed. Rye sat back again, but did not touch her.

''Laura, we've paid our debt t' Dan. He's going t' live. But what about us?''

She looked up. Rye watched her intensely.

''I've been here with y' for three days and nights, and I've seen for myself what fools we've been t' let duty and guilt tell us what t' do. We belong together. I don't give a damn if it's here in this house on Nantucket or in some place we've never seen. All I know is, *you* are *home*. For me, home is where y' are. I love y', and I'm through apologizin' for it. I want no more misunderstandin's between myself and Dan. When he wakes up, I want t' be able to tell him the truth so we can all plan accordingly. Y' see, I've already written Throckmorton and agreed t' join his party. It leaves from Albany on April fifteenth, which means we'll have t' take the packet out of here at the end of March. That's only about three months from now, and there's a lot t' prepare for. I'm askin' y' for the first and last time, Laura. Will y' come with me t' Michigan in the spring, you and Josh?''

He did not smile. His eyes did not waver. His voice, though low, was steady, determined. She believed what he said . . . and what he didn't say: he would go in the spring with *or without* her. She knew in her heart that Rye was right. They had done the honorable thing. They'd saved Dan's life. But then, had there really been a choice? They both loved Dan, and they both always would. But Laura had learned in the past three days that love sometimes manifests itself in frightening and awesome ways.

She saw again the awl sinking into Dan's flesh, wielded by Rye's steady hand, then Rye's trembling shoulders when reaction set in. She heard the rage in his voice as he slapped the hot cup out of McColl's hand, felt again the pity of witnessing the unnecessary burn on Dan's chest. She relived the terror of that moment when her eyes had met Rye's across Dan's racked and wheezing body. Somehow during that emotionally charged instant when they'd considered letting Dan die, they'd both recognized the truth: they'd had to save Dan to save themselves.

Rye was still waiting for her answer. He studied her face while the weariness of their long fight for Dan's life was reflected in it. Yes, Dan would live, and so must they. There was only one answer Laura could give.

''Yes, I'll come with you, Rye. Both of us will come with you. But until then, we will not dishonor Dan in any way.''

''O' course not.''

Strangely enough, they agreed to these terms in the most businesslike voices. The time for hearts to sing was not now, while Dan still lay ill. There would be time for that later, as spring came, the season of rebirth.

Chapter 20

Dan Morgan awakened on the fourth morning after his fall. He opened his eyes to find himself in the strangest place—Josh's alcove bed. His hands hurt, as if each of his fingertips had been slammed in a door. He felt as if he were trying to breathe at a depth of twenty-five feet, with the water pressing painfully on his lungs. His tongue was stuck to the roof of his mouth as if he had a horrendous hangover, and the clanging in his head went on and on like a bell buoy on rough seas.

He turned his head gingerly. There beside the bed sat Rye.

"Well . . . hello," Rye greeted. He looked utterly relaxed, elbows resting on the arms of a Windsor chair, an ankle slung over a knee.

"Rye?" The word was a mere croak. Dan tried to lift himself up on his elbows, but failed.

"Rest easy, friend. Y've been through an ordeal."

Dan let his eyes blank out the bright daylight that hurt his already throbbing head. "What are you doing here?"

"Waitin' for y' t' wake up."

Dan lifted an arm that felt as heavy as waterlogged driftwood. He rested it across his forehead, but the movement made his fingertips throb anew. "Is there some water?" His voice cracked.

Immediately, Rye leaned over, slipping a hand beneath Dan's head to lift it as the blessedly cool drink soothed his parched throat. The effort left Dan aching and breathless. "What happened?" he managed to say when the weakness passed.

"Y' got roarin' drunk, fell off y'r damn feet in the worst blizzard t' hit Nantucket in ten years, hit y'r noggin on the cobblestones, and lay there till y'r fingers froze and y' caught pneumonia."

Dan opened his eyes and peered at Rye, who'd again settled back into the chair, his fingers laced over his belly. For all his brusque and scolding tone, there was a note of the old Rye once again in his voice. Somehow Dan sensed the animosity was gone. "I did it up good, did I?"

"Aye, y' did."

"How long ago was that?"

"Four days."

"Four! . . ." Dan turned his head too fast on the pillow and he grimaced at the resulting ache.

"I wouldn't move so fast if I was you. We've kept y' stewed t' the gills all that time, and y're bound t' have a hangover that'll put all y'r others t' shame."

"Where's Laura?"

"Out t' the market. She'll be back soon."

Dan lifted and examined the fingers of his right hand. "What did you do to these? They hurt like hell."

Rye chuckled. "Be happy y' still got 'em hooked to y'r arms. They'll heal."

"I take it you aren't wasting any sympathy on me, huh, Dalton?"

The corner of Rye's mouth quirked up. "None at all. Pullin' a trick like that, y' shouldn't by rights have either fingers *or* toes. Y' ought t' be six feet under, and y' damn well might be, except the ground was frozen so we didn't know where the hell we'd put y'."

In spite of his monumental aches and pains, Dan couldn't help smiling. He studied Rye carefully. "You've been here all that time?"

"Laura and I."

Dan was suddenly gripped by a spasm of coughing. Rye pressed a cloth into Dan's hand, then sat back again, waiting for the paroxysm to pass. When it had, Rye offered Dan another drink, this time of hot ginger tea laced with vinegar and honey. He gave Dan a moment to rest, then began speaking in a straightforward manner.

"Listen, Dan, I've got some things I want t' say before Laura comes back, and—granted, the time is not exactly appropriate, but it may be the only chance we'll have t' be alone." Rye pressed forward in his chair, absently chafing his knuckles together, frowning at the coral stitches on the patch-work quilt. Then he met Dan's eyes directly. "Y've nearly died here in the last few days, and it's all been y'r own doin'. I've watched it comin' on, you and y'r asinine drinkin', and there's not a soul on this island that'd be surprised if y'd frozen t' death where y' dropped." Rye leaned on his knees, scowling into Dan's eyes. "When're y' going t' see the light, man?" he demanded impatiently. "Y'r squanderin' y'r life! Wallowin' in self-pity and wastin' the most precious commodity that'll ever be given to y', y'r health!

"Now, I'm not sayin' y' haven't had reason to worry, but do y' know what y'r drinkin' does t' Laura? She's torn by guilt every time she sees y' stumblin' through that door, and the majority of it's not her fault.

"I'm bein' honest with y', man, and I'm trustin' y' to understand it's not because of the rivalry between us for Laura, but because I want t' see y' pick up y'r life and make somethin' of it again."

Rye's voice rumbled on as he studied his hands, joined between widespread knees. "When spring comes, I'm goin' to the Michigan Territory and Laura has agreed t' go with me . . . and Josh, too. Now y' can accept that and make a man o' yourself between now and then, or y' can go back down t' the Blue Anchor and drink y'rself into another stupor that lasts till spring. I don't care. For myself, I don't care. But I care for Laura, because if she leaves this island believin' she's the ruination of y'r life, it'll be a guilt she'll carry forever. I'm askin' y' to send her off without that burden. And the only way y' can do that is t' give up y'r drinkin' and . . . and . . ."

Suddenly, Rye exhaled a gushing breath and covered his face with both hands. "Goddamnit, I thought this'd be so simple . . ." He lunged to his feet, jammed his hands into the back waistline of his pants, and stood facing the trestle table.

His head dropped forward while Dan watched and felt a rush of something warm and nostalgic flood through him. It was the same feeling he'd had as he'd watched the *Massachusetts* sail away with Rye aboard.

The tall blond man turned back toward the alcove bed. "Damnit, Dan, I don't want t' hurt y', but I love that woman and we've done our damnest t' fight it, but some things can't be changed. I swear by all the saints in heaven, I haven't laid a hand on her while I've been in this house and I won't till spring. But then, I'm takin' her with me, married or not. But I want us t' go . . . if not with y'r blessin', at least without y'r scorn."

Something indefinable had changed between the two men. As Rye stood now beside Dan's bed, they each sensed the tether of lifelong sanguinity binding them together with a strength that superseded their rivalry for the same woman. They would both always love her, but—the realization hummed between them—they would both always love one another, too. To remain on this island together was to sentence themselves to certain hurt. The time had come for final separations. The pain in Dan's chest was, at that moment, more than just physical, and the softening of the expression in Rye's pale blue eyes did not quite disguise a sudden glitter there.

But at that moment the door opened and a rush of cold air ushered Laura and

Josh into the keeping room. Something in Rye's stance told the two Dan was awake.

Josh rushed to the bedside, hung over it on his belly, and cried happily, "Papa! Papa! You're awake!"

Laura was right behind him, leaning to touch Dan's brow. "Dan, thank God you've made it. We've been so worried." She smiled down tenderly, a wealth of concern etched on her brow, but lifting somewhat as she saw his revived color. "Josh, come. We mustn't bring the cold near Papa with our coats. Warm up by the fire first, then you can talk with him again, but only for a while. He's got to rest."

"But, Mama, I got to tell Papa about my skates and about how Rye brung him here and Mr. McColl tried to—"

"Later, Josh."

Dan noted Laura's swift interruption and how assiduously she sidestepped crediting herself or Rye for saving his life. But from Josh, Dan was to learn, during the days that followed, all that had transpired. The child painted the facts very vividly, until the information formed a concise picture of all Rye and Laura had done during the time he himself had been unconscious.

Dan's recovery was slow and painful. He was confined to bed for two weeks, racked by a cough that at times threatened to choke him. But he grew stronger as the days passed, and he had hours and hours to lie and ponder the curious fact that when he himself was in dire need, the islanders found Rye the natural one to turn to for help; the fact that when the local apothecary proclaimed his fingers lost, Rye refused to accept his word without a fight; the fact that when McColl would have covered his chest with vicious burns, Rye's anger raged out of control; the fact that for four nights and three days Rye and Laura had fought tenaciously to save his life. And had won.

Dan watched the two of them together, having plenty of time to do just that, for Rye came every day to carry wood and water for Laura, to bring fresh milk from town and greetings from the islanders and an analgesic balm for Dan's fingers and a potent medicine for his cough, though he offered no more alcoholic spirits, not even for medicinal purposes.

Dan's mother came every day, too, and from her Dan pieced together the few fragments of the story he was unable to glean from Josh.

Dan could not help but note the change in Josh's attitude toward Rye. The boy had clearly accepted Rye's daily presence in the house, and though it was Dan whom the child still refered to as Papa, there was a camaraderie between Rye and Josh that somehow had little to do with bloodlines.

There came a day in mid-December when Josh was hunkering crosslegged at the foot of Dan's bed and Laura was sitting in a chair nearby, hemming sheets.

"Papa, when will you teach me to skate?" Josh inquired.

Laura looked up and scolded gently, "Josh, you know that Papa's not well enough yet to go out in the cold air."

Dan had not questioned Laura about Rye's claim that she was going to the Michigan Territory in the spring, but by his closest count, this was the seventh sheet he'd seen her hemming. He watched the needle flash as she raised her hand and drew the thread tight. Then Dan turned back to Josh.

"Why don't you ask Rye to teach you to skate? He's a very good skater."

Laura looked up in surprise.

"He is?" Josh's voice went several notes higher whenever skating was mentioned.

"Oh, he's every bit as good as I am. We did plenty of skating together when we were boys."

"And Mama, too?"

Dan's eyes moved to Laura. "Yes, and Mama, too. She went everywhere we went, Rye and I."

There was no sting in Dan's words. Instead, he went on in a mellow tone, relating the story about the time they'd built a fire on the frozen surface of the pond and it melted the ice and fell through into the spring-fed water, nearly taking them all with it.

As Dan talked, Laura felt the breath catch in her throat, and a fierce gratitude grip her heart. Dan, oh, Dan, I understand the gift you are giving, and I know what it is costing you.

Though he would not meet her eyes, she knew Dan was aware of her studying him, listening to his every word. He was still talking when Rye arrived, to be immediately assaulted by Josh, who pitched himself against Rye's legs, looked up, and begged, "Will you take me skating, Rye? Will you?"

Rye glanced from Laura to Dan, then back down at the boy with the untamable rooster tail. Absently, Rye smoothed it down. "And whose idea was this?"

"Papa's. He said you and him skated all the time when you was little."

"Papa's, huh?" His eyes moved to the alcove bed where Dan was resting. "You sure about that?" Still with an eye on Dan, Rye started shrugging out of his jacket.

"Sure I'm sure. Just ask him!"

But just then Dan cleared his throat. "I . . . ahhh . . . I promised I'd teach him, but there'll be no getting out for me for a while, so I thought maybe . . . well—" Dan gestured with his palms.

Rye moved nearer the bed. Though he stood with thumbs hooked at his waist, it took an effort not to reach out and squeeze Dan's shoulder. "Say no more. I'll have him on the ice before the week is out."

Their eyes met and held, then wavered, and finally parted in the face of indomitable emotions that suddenly sprang up between them.

Before another hour was up, Laura found herself alone with Dan, for Josh had been so persistent, Rye had finally agreed to take him to the cooperage to pick up his own skates, then on to one of the island's many ponds to make use of the last couple of hours of daylight.

The house grew still when the two were gone, and Laura sensed Dan's eyes following her as she moved restlessly about the keeping room, folding sheets, putting away needle and thread, adding a log to the fire. It was the first time they'd been alone in the house in weeks. A spasm of coughing gripped Dan, and Laura turned toward him as she always did, offering a cup of soothing tea. When she brought it, he shifted into a sitting position with the pillows plumped behind his back, accepted the cup, then captured Laura's hand before she could escape.

"Sit down."

She perched on the edge of the alcove bed, and for a moment Dan kept her hand, rubbing it distractedly with his thumb, finally releasing it to hold his mug with both palms.

"Rye tells me he's going to the Michigan Territory with the first thaws and that you're going with him."

It was curious how calm Laura felt at this moment, after weeks of anticipating a great gush of guilt. "Yes, Dan, I am. I wish . . . I wish there was another answer I could give that wouldn't hurt you, but I believe it's time for honesty among all of us. Perhaps I should have told you two weeks ago, when Rye and I made the decision, but I was waiting for you to get stronger."

"I've got eyes, Laura. I've been watching you hem those sheets to take along."

She stared at her lap and groped for something to say. "They say it gets very cold in the Michigan Territory this time of year, and . . . and settlements are remote."

"So I've heard." His voice was deeper and gruffer than usual from days of coughing, but as he spoke now, the words were very quiet.

She looked up and met his eyes squarely. "We'll be taking Josh along with us, Dan."

"Yes, I know."

The room grew still. Outside, a soft snow had begun, but inside the fire glowed gold and pink. Dan's face was pale, but he was growing stronger each day, yet Laura understood—it took more than physical strength for Dan to face the truth.

"And I know why you sent him off with Rye—so the two of them could have some time alone, to get to know each other." She lightly touched the back of Dan's hand, which lay on the quilt. "Thank you."

For a moment Dan's eyes were tormented, then he quickly erased the drawn lines from his face, but continued gazing at Laura. "I know everything you two did," he said. "I know how Rye picked me up off the street and brought me here and saved my fingers, and how angry he got at McColl, and how the two of you tended the fires day and night to keep me from dying of pneumonia." His voice fell to a murmur. "Why did you do it?"

Her eyes caught and reflected the light from the fire and met Dan's with an openness and lack of guile that told the truth with an eloquence no words could convey. "Don't you know?" she breathed. But to say she loved him—they both loved him—would be to cause Dan unnecessary hurt, thus she only studied the play of emotions that turned his eyes soft with understanding.

"Yes . . . I guess I do."

Self-consciousness suddenly mushroomed between them, for the words need not be said to be felt. He took her hand, squeezed it in a grip that demonstrated surprising strength for a debilitated man. "Thank you," came his gruff words. For a moment they both concentrated on their joined hands.

"Don't thank me, Dan, just . . . just please don't jeopardize your life like that again." She beseeched him with her eyes. "Please, don't drink anymore."

"I've already promised Rye I won't."

She sighed and slumped her shoulders in relief. Then she gently withdrew her hand. ''Dan, there are some things, some *other* things, we must talk about that are very hard to say.''

''I think I know, Laura. I'm no fool. I don't need to sleep out here in this alcove bed anymore. I know the real reason why you and Josh sleep in there.'' He nodded toward the linter room.

Laura felt the blood press upward to paint her cheeks a discomfiting red. She nervously pleated and repleated the skirt over her knees, unable to lift her gaze to Dan as he went on.

''Laura, I found the busk a long time ago.''

''You did?'' Her eyes flew up and her face flared to an even brighter hue.

''I did.''

''Oh, Dan, I'm so sorr—''

He presented a palm to cut her short. ''We've been doing enough feeling sorry around here, don't you think? There's been you feeling sorry for me and Rye feeling sorry for you and me feeling sorry for myself, and Lord knows I've been the worst of the lot. At first when Rye came home, it was impossible for me to face the truth, then after I found that busk, I guess I knew this was inevitable.''

''This?''

''That I'd lose you to him.''

Hearing him voice it brought a great, crushing feeling to Laura's heart. He looked tired and beaten and for a moment the urge to protect was there again within her.

As Dan studied Laura, he saw a weariness to match his own. ''It's been hard on you, being caught in the middle. Most of the time I forgot that and thought only of myself.''

''Dan, I want you to know that I . . . I tried very hard to avoid Rye. You were so good to me, and you deserved—''

Again he silenced her with a movement of his hand. ''I know. Rye told me. He laid it all out in the open the day I woke up. I've thought a lot about it since then, and I realize you can't help your feelings any more than I can help mine. That's what I fought against for the longest time. But after I had seen the busk and had proof of your feelings—both of yours—I went to see Ezra Merrill and initiated divorce proceedings.''

Laura's teeth caught her lower lip and she stared at Dan in disbelief for several seconds. ''Y . . . you've already seen Ezra?''

Dan nodded. ''In September. I was angry at . . . at you and Rye. Oh hell, that's the only way I could make myself go talk to Ezra—if I got angry enough. But once I'd talked to him I wasn't able to carry through with it, and that's when I . . . well, I started staying at the Blue Anchor in the evenings. Then the rumor started about Rye and DeLaine Hussey and I got hopeful again and went back to Ezra and told him to stop everything.''

Laura's heart was thumping hard. She remembered the time Dan had manhandled her, venting his frustrations. Yes, it would have taken anger to make Dan act.

''Ezra, of course, knows the whole history of the three of us, and I suspect he had the foresight to guess exactly how unsettled the situation was. He said he'd already filed the proper papers and had explained the situation to Judge

Bunker, but he advised me that even though I wanted to withdraw the papers just then, maybe I ought to wait until . . . well, just wait and see. He said nothing would be acted upon without both of our signatures and an appearance before the judge, so we—''

Just then Dan was clutched by a spell of coughing that doubled him over. When he reclined against the pillows once more, he was winded. During the pause, Laura's mind reeled with questions, but finally Dan went on.

''The papers are still there, Laura, up at the town building, in probate court.''

Their eyes met, and unconsciously she counted the months until spring.

Dan's voice grew even more raspy as he went on. ''Even my own mother realizes I've held you against your wishes ever since Rye's return.''

There was no soothing response Laura could offer. She remembered very clearly the things Hilda Morgan had said.

''And do you know what else she told me?''

Laura only stared at Dan, not moving a muscle.

''She told me you and Rye had given me back my life and that it was time I gave you back yours.''

A poignant silence fell. A sense of impending ache settled between them. Faraway, a bell tolled as evening came on, and in the candlelit room all was silent but for his words hovering between them. ''Christmas being the season of giving, I thought it might be the appropriate time to . . . give you what I know you want most, Laura—your freedom.''

Laura felt a lump gathering in her throat. She swallowed, but the emotion could not be gulped away. No matter how badly she'd wanted her freedom, she'd never expected this overwhelming sense of loss at getting it.

Sensibly, Dan hurried on. ''As I said, the papers are still there, and the circumstances being what they are, Judge Bunker would never deny the dissolution of this marriage. He's known us all our lives, too.'' Dan cleared his throat, continuing with an assumed dispassion. ''Anyway, my mother said she'd welcome having a man around the house again to cook and do for, so as soon as I'm well enough, I'll be moving back there . . . until things can be properly settled in court.''

Laura was speechless. What could she possibly reply? Thank you? The noble gesture was painful enough for Dan without adding the insult of a gratuitous response. Then suddenly Laura felt as bereft as she knew Dan must be. The tears she had been trying to hold back became a deluge. Without warning, she was overcome and dropped her face into both palms while sobs jerked her shoulders. Though she'd neither planned nor anticipated this reaction, there could have been no more fitting response to Dan's words. The end of five married years that had been basically harmonious and loving deserved this moment of mourning.

She sat on the edge of the bed, crying softly for several minutes, and when the tears stopped, somehow Dan was holding her hand. With a gentle tug, he pulled her sideways until she fell into the shelter of his arm with her head tucked beneath his chin. There were no more words. But as they lay in silence, their unspoken thoughts became the requiem for all they'd shared, not only during the past five years, but for nearly two decades before that.

* * *

When Rye and Josh returned, Rye immediately noted the constrained atmosphere. He could see at a glance that Laura had been crying, and for a moment felt the clutch of dread weight his stomach. Josh scampered straight across the room to Dan, bubbling with excitement over his first skating lesson. Rye attempted to catch Laura's eye, but she assiduously avoided glancing his way, so with a worried scowl, Rye prepared to leave.

Dan's words stopped him at the door.

"Rye, I have a favor to ask."

The tall man turned back into the room. "Of course, anything."

"I hate to ask after all you've done already, but Laura goes out to Jane's every year a few days before Christmas to take her some bayberry candles and things and have a visit before the holidays. And I . . ." Dan raised his palms helplessly. "Well, of course I won't be able to take them this year, so I was wondering if you'd mind driving her and Josh out there one day soon."

Rye's glance swerved to Laura, but she was studying Dan with an expression warning she was having difficulty keeping from breaking into tears again. "Of course," Rye answered. "I'll rent a cutter and be here whenever Laura says."

At his words, Laura could no longer avoid meeting Rye's eyes. She thought that if this day didn't end soon, her heart would certainly crumble. It had been flooded with emotion so many times already, this seemed the final stroke that might shatter it. She wanted to cry out, Dan, don't be so damnably noble! Instead, she could only suffer an overwhelming sense of injustice for him and answer Rye. "Any day . . . whenever you can find the time."

"Tomorrow, then, at midafternoon?"

"We'll be ready."

The following day at the appointed time, Rye came to collect Josh and Laura in a sleek black cutter pulled by a gray and white piebald mare. With warmed bricks at their feet and a heavy sealskin fur across their laps, the three set out across the snow-covered moors. The breath of the horse billowed and formed a cloud that appeared the same color as both land and sky. The jingle of harness rang out with the clarity of a glockenspeil in the cold, cold air. As the runners of the vehicle sliced through the dry snow, they squeaked out an unending syllable and left behind a pair of tracks with hoofprints between.

There was room on the black leather seat for no more than two, thus Josh sat on his mother's lap, with both of his knees bumping Rye's left thigh. Josh did more talking than either his mother or father, and when he asked if he could hold the reins, Rye laughingly complied, settling the boy between his legs and placing the lines in Josh's smaller hands. The horse sensed the difference and turned a blinder sideways, then headed straight again, her trot never wavering as Rye kept a watchful eye.

With Josh seated between his spraddled thighs, Rye's warm leg now rested firmly against Laura's. The contact was thrilling, though neither turned or looked at the other.

When they reached Jane's house, Josh immediately scrambled from under the laprobe. But when Rye began shifting, Laura placed a hand on his forearm. "Josh, you run in and tell Aunt Jane we're here. Rye and I have to talk for a minute.'' Then Rye suspended Josh over the side of the rig by one arm and lowered him till his feet touched the ground.

When they were alone, Rye and Laura looked at each other fully for the first time.

''Hello,'' he murmured.

''Hello.'' Will I ever grow tired of looking into his pale blue eyes? she thought. Never . . . never.

''You were very sad yesterday.''

''Yes, I was.''

''Can y' tell me why?''

Against her thigh, his was pressed, warm, secure.

''I told Dan that I'd be leaving with you in the spring, and he told me that he was giving me a Christmas gift.'' She paused, knowing he had guessed what it was. ''He told me he is giving me my freedom. Mine and Josh's.''

The wisps of whitened breath ceased falling from Rye's nostrils for a long, long moment. Then he breathed again, a huge sigh. ''When?''

''He will be going to live at his mother's house as soon as he's well enough to make the move. As for legalities, he spoke to Ezra Merrill last September and filed divorce papers then. Right after he found the busk.''

Rye slowly turned to face forward, his sober expression anything but victorious. Laura laid her mittened hand on his forearm. The reins remained laced through the fingers of his leather gloves, but he seemed unconscious of the fact. ''He sent us out here today so we'd have a chance to tell Josh—both of us, together.''

Rye said nothing. He seemed to be staring at a point beyond the horse's head, then he sighed again and dropped his chin, and sat for a long moment, lost in thought. The horse shook her head and made the harness jingle, and it seemed to drag Rye from his reverie. ''Why don't I feel like celebratin'?'' he asked quietly.

She only squeezed his arm, for they both knew the answer to his question.

The visit to Jane's passed in a haze of distraction, for Laura's thoughts were on their ride home. When the three were again settled in the cutter, she felt apprehensive. Josh's acceptance was vital, and as she studied the back of his head, wrapped in a thick knit cap and a scarf whose fringes shimmied in rhythm to the hoofbeats, Laura closed her eyes, hoping.

''Joshua, Rye and I have something to tell you.''

Josh, with his ripe-apple cheeks and wind-reddened nose, turned to look up at her. Beneath the fur, Rye's leg flanked hers in firm support. ''Rye and I . . . well, we . . . we love each other very much, dear, and we never wanted to . . . to . . .''

When she faltered, Rye took over. ''I'm goin' t' marry your mother, come spring, and the three of us'll be goin' t' the Michigan Territory together, along with my father.''

For a moment Josh's face reflected his lack of comprehension. But when understanding dawned, it brought no smile. ''Is Papa comin' too?''

''No, Dan will stay here.''

''Then I ain't goin'!'' Josh declared stubbornly.

Laura's gaze skittered to Rye, then back to her son. ''I know it's hard for you to understand, Josh, but Rye is your real father, and when I marry him you'll be our son. You'll have to live where we do.''

"No, I don't want him to be my papa!" Josh stuck his lower lip out belligerently, and it began to tremble. "I wanna have the one I always had and live in our same house!"

Despair weighted Laura. "But wouldn't you like to go off on an adventure to the Michigan Territory, where you've never been before?"

"Is it far away?"

Laura was afraid to tell the truth, but knew a lie would only make matters worse, eventually. "Yes, it is."

"Do we have to take the ferry to get there?"

Oh, much more than the ferry, Josh, she thought, but answered only, "Yes."

"But then how could I see Jimmy?"

"Well . . . you wouldn't see him, but you'd make new friends where we lived."

"I don't want new friends. I wanna stay here with Jimmy and Papa and you." The belligerence had disappeared from Josh's face, and the tears he'd been valiantly trying to control whispered over his golden lashes and down his red cheeks.

Laura pulled him back against her and tucked his head beneath her chin. Holding Josh, she wondered how to make him understand, but suddenly she realized something Rye had said. She turned to look up at him.

"Josiah's going along—for sure?"

"Aye. He says his bones've had all they can take of this dampness and fog. Though I suspect he just doesn't want t' miss out on the adventure."

The idea of having Josiah along was pleasing, but still, it could not dispel the cloud cast over their plans by Josh's reluctance.

In an effort to win his son's approval, Rye now asked, "Would y' like t' drive the team again, Josh?"

But the boy only shook his head and burrowed closer against his mother. All the careful buildup of trust between father and son seemed to have been for naught. Lord, Laura thought, would things ever be easy? Would there forever be obstacles between her and Rye?

Chapter 21

It was an afternoon in late January, crisp but cloudy, when a wagon drawn by an aging sorrel mare pulled up at the foot of Crooked Record Lane and was loaded with the clothing and miscellany of Dan Morgan. It would have been easier for Laura had she conveniently planned to be absent from the house when Dan left it, but that would have been the coward's way out. Instead, she stood beside the dray while the last items were secured and Dan came around the tail end to stop before her and pull his gloves on tighter. He glanced at the house, then down at the icy bay, and once again needlessly tugged at his gloves.

"Well . . ." The word hung in the cold air like the ting of a bell in a winter woods.

"Yes, well . . ." She spread her palms nervously, then clutched them together.

"I'm not exactly sure what one says at a time like this."

"Neither am I," Laura admitted.

"Do I thank you again for saving my life?" He sounded not bitter, only resigned.

"Oh, Dan . . ." Suddenly she realized they were standing like wooden soldiers, and reached to lay a hand on his forearm. "Thanks aren't necessary, surely you know that."

He studied her right shoulder, and she his eyes. He glanced toward the house and spoke with false animation. "I fixed that loose hinge on the back door and put a shim under the leg of the dry sink so it won't rock anymore."

"Yes, thank you."

"And remember, if there's anything you need, just . . ." But if there was anything she needed, Rye would see to it from now on.

"I'll remember."

"Tell Josh I'm sorry I missed saying good-bye to him, but when he comes back from Jane's, I'll stop by and see him."

"I'll tell him."

"Good . . ." He fell silent for several long, long seconds. Then came the same word, scarcely audible. "Good." He squared his shoulders, but just then was hit by a spasm of coughing, the last lingering vestige of his illness.

"It's bad for you to be out in the cold any longer than necessary, Dan. You'd better go."

"You're right." His eyes found hers at last, and for a moment she thought he meant to kiss her. But in the end he only nodded formally, clambered aboard the dray and said simply, "Good-bye, Laura."

"Take care of yourself, Dan."

The dray moved off, and she watched Dan's back until a sharp shiver reminded her that she herself wore no gloves or hat. Clutching her cape, she stared at the ice-encrusted scallop shells while making her way back to the house. When the door closed behind Laura, she sighed and sank back against it, closing her eyes, feeling momentarily forlorn and guilty of something not exactly nameable. The silence of the house imposed itself on her and she opened her eyes, scanning the keeping room, noting the absence of Dan's humidor on the table, of his coat and hat from the tree beside the door, of his shaving strop from its peg.

But on the heels of her guilt came immense relief. Alone. How long had it been since she'd been alone? There was a rich healing revitalization in having time to oneself. No one to cook for. No one to answer to. Nobody whose chest needed poulticing or whose shoes needed tying or whose bruises needed kissing. No eyes to either meet or avoid.

Laura was suddenly grateful Josh was gone—they were all gone! Countless times she'd wondered how she'd feel at this moment. Never had she expected this weightless sense of release. When she was a girl she'd known an extraordinary amount of freedom, and having reveled in it as she had, Laura now became aware of how changed her life had become after marrying Rye, bearing Josh, and subsequently marrying Dan. There had always been someone around, someone either relying on her or on whom she relied. Now, for a short time, there was no one.

Laura felt reborn.

She put an extravagant three logs on the fire at once, poured a generous serving of apple cider and set it on the hob to heat, closed the door to the linter room, adding an extra coziness to the main room, dragged an upholstered wing chair from the far end of the keeping room to the hearth, replaced the spermaceti candle with one of bayberry, fetched a fat goose-down pillow and threw it onto the chair, flung her apron off and searched for something to read, coming up with a three-month-old copy of the *Fireside Companion* she'd never taken time to open.

Two hours later, when a knock sounded at the door, Laura was dozing in her cozy nest. She stretched, flexed, and reluctantly left the chair to pad across the room on stockinged feet.

Rye stood on the step, dressed as usual in his pea jacket and knit bobcap. ''Hello. Come t' do the chores.''

''Oh!'' Her eyes widened in surprise.

''Well, you goin' t' let me in or not? It's cold out here.''

''Oh, of course!'' She stepped back and closed the door as he entered and headed immediately for the water pail across the room. Halfway there, he caught sight of the chair, pillow, and book, her discarded shoes, the trestle table pushed away from its usual spot and positioned nearby with a bayberry candle and mug easily within reach.

Without a word, Rye took the pail and headed out back. When he returned, he lifted the filled pail to the dry sink, glanced at the alcove bed, then at the closed door of the linter room.

''Where's Dan?''

''Gone.''

''Gone?'' Rye glanced sharply at Laura. She seemed twitchy, standing on the far side of the trestle table as if intentionally keeping it between them.

''To his mother's.''

''For a visit?''

''No, for good.''

Rye's assessing gaze moved to the spot where the humidor used to be, then he boldly stalked to the door of the linter room and flung it open. She watched his eyes take inventory of the room before he spun again to face her. ''He moved out?''

Laura nodded silently.

''And where's Josh?''

''At Jane's.''

Without another word, Rye closed the bedroom door and strode out back to return in two minutes with an enormous armful of wood, which he deposited in the woodbox before heading out for another load. After the third trip the box was full, and he brushed the bark from his sleeves, then swung around with impatience emanating from every muscle of his body. ''The back path needs shovelin'. It won't take long.''

While he was gone, Laura put more cider to warm, added logs to the fire, and put a ring of spicy barley sausage on to cook.

When the back door opened again, Rye paused to ask, ''Is there anythin' else that needs doin' today?''

''No, that's all.''

He hesitated, watching her lift an arm to the mantle but keeping her back to him.

''I've put some sausage on to cook if you'd like to stay.''

''Is that an invitation?''

''Yes.'' She turned at last to face him squarely. ''To supper.'' The implication was clear. For a moment neither of them moved. Then Rye casually sauntered toward the fire while unbuttoning his jacket with one hand. He shrugged it off and flung it across the trestle table, eyeing the chair as he circled it.

''Looks like somebody's been spendin' a lazy afternoon here.'' He stopped beside the arm of the chair, leaned over from one hip, and picked up the magazine from atop the pillow.

''I confess. And it felt wonderful.''

With the tabloid in his hand, he next took stock of the candle, her cup, her apron tossed across the trestle beside his own jacket.

''Aye, I c'n see that.'' His mouth quirked up at one corner. ''Mind if I try it out?''

''Not at all. Just don't make yourself too comfortable.''

He plucked the pillow from the seat of the chair, took its place, and plopped the puffy thing onto his lap, watching Laura while she ladled hot cider.

''Here, I thought you could use this.'' She offered him the mug, but when he reached it was with both hands, taking the drink in one hand and her wrist in the other. Twisting around, he set the mug on the table, then tugged her toward his lap.

''I'll tell y' what I c'n use,'' She landed on the pillow with a soft plop. ''And it's not a cup o' cider.'' He still wore the navy blue knit bobcap. It rested against the tall back of the wing chair while his elbows indolently hooked its arms, and his palms contoured her waist.

''What, then?'' she asked in a voice no louder than the hiss of the fire.

His lips opened. His glance dropped to her mouth. His hard hands left her waist and traveled up Laura's sleeves to her shoulder blades before drawing her against his chest. She fell into the accommodating nest of his shoulder with a palm resting on Rye's heart, looking up into his face as he bent his head over her. Even before his lips touched hers, she felt the tumultuous hammering through his thick, cable-knit sweater. It was at first less than a kiss, rather, a reunion after their long separation, a hello again, as his mouth met hers lightly, lightly. The tip of his nose brushed her cheek, cold yet, as were the lips that moved in a silken exploration across her own while his warm breath created dew on her skin. Then her head was moving slowly from side to side in answer to the movements of his, with only the crests of their lips brushing, as if in reacquaintance. Their tongue tips met and passed, moving on to dampen the perimeters of their mouths. The kiss widened, deepened, and with an easy turn of her body Laura sought the thick cords of his neck, riding her palm inside the high turtleneck of his sweater while Rye slipped a hand beneath her knees and drew them over the arm of the chair.

Slowly, minute by minute, the ardor of the kiss grew until his tongue brushed the inner walls of her cheeks, and hers, his. Cradled in his arms, she felt the hand beneath her knees spread wide, then slide up along the underside of her thigh to her buttock, where it pressed, warm and firm, learning her contours once again as his moist, full kiss rocked her senses. Laura's hand moved from Rye's neck to his hair, and blindly she slid the knit cap away to thread her fingers into the thick strands at the back of his head.

Long moments later, when the first kisses and touches had ignited an emotional fire, Rye lifted his head to look into Laura's lambent brown eyes and whisper thickly, ''I can't believe we're really alone at last.''

She caressed his warm skull, shifting her fingers in his hair until the aroma of cedar seemed to lift from it. ''It's been five months, two weeks, and three days.''

''Is that all?''

''But, Rye, before you came I was—''

''Later. We'll talk later.'' His mouth descended to hers again and he shifted her weight in his arms, turning her so that one breast pressed against him, leaving the other free. She held her breath as he withdrew the arm from beneath her knees and slowly brushed it up her thigh, hip, and ribs until at last her resilient flesh was taken warm within his palm. A shudder of delight quaked through her limbs as he caressed her breast, squeezing, then releasing repeatedly while his tongue dipped into her mouth and hers played a circle dance around his. Through the cotton covering of her garments, his fingertips explored the projecting nipple until it stood up all the more boldly with desire.

Against her open mouth, he muttered, ''Let's go t' bed, darlin'.''

She shook her head in slow motion while his mouth followed. ''No, I tried to tell you—'' But his mouth closed tightly over hers, cutting off the words and inundating her with the wet, sleek texture of his tongue.

When he lifted his head again, it was to murmur, ''If y' won't say yes, I swear we'll do it right here in this chair.'' A trail of miniature kisses passed along the side of her nose.

''Mmm . . . that sounds wonderful,'' she approved throatily, and felt him smile against her neck. ''But we're not going to do it anywhere, not until I'm your wife.''

''You are my wife,'' he went on imperturbably, shifting their positions so that he could bend forward to cover her far breast with his mouth.

''No I'm not.''

''Mmm . . . y' smell good enough t' eat. Y've smelled like bayberries y'r whole life long. Did y' know that?'' he murmured, ignoring her protest.

She was draped over the arms of the chair like a dust cover, head slung back limply while his mouth took possession of the crest of her breast, deliberately wetting the fabric of her dress and camisole, then biting the engorged nipple until it sent up an incredible aching. He twisted his head from side to side, playfully ferocious as he tugged at her hidden flesh, until a guttural sound escaped Laura's throat and her hand sought his hair to urge more of the same.

But a moment later she insisted again, ''Rye, I'm not going to make love with you.'' With her head slung back, the words were strident and forced. She pulled herself up, finding some hidden source of resistance, until she sat on his lap again.

''Who're y' tryin' to fool?'' he questioned, still teasing the hardened nipple with the backs of his fingers. The point of flesh pressed outward against the wet circle on her dress front—it was silly to deny that she was tempted.

''I'm as human as you are. I could no more have stopped myself from kissing you than I could when we were sixteen. But I'm being honest with you, Rye.''

Still he didn't believe her, but grinned engagingly. ''Well, while you're bein' honest, do we have t' have this damn pillow between us?'' He manipulated her as if she were no heavier than a rag doll, lifting her up and jerking the pillow away to toss it onto the floor. Then he unceremoniously grasped one of her ankles and swung it across his stomach until she found herself straddling him in the chair with her most intimate parts settled obligingly against the bulging mound of his arousal.

''All right, where were we?'' he asked coolly. ''Oh yes, you were being honest with me and telling me that y've no intention of makin' love with me until you're legally divorced from Dan, is that it?'' But as he spoke, Rye tugged at the copious skirts of her dress and petticoats, which were pinned beneath her, hauling them hand over hand till she felt the lumpy hems scrape along her bottom, then slide free.

''Yes, that's it,'' she claimed, meaning it. But Laura sat on him now with only his trousers and her pantaloons between them. Unperturbed, he adjusted his hips, settling them more comfortably in the chair until his hardness and her softness fit together like two pieces of a jigsaw puzzle.

''Mmm . . .'' His hands slid beneath the billows of cotton and found her two ankles, pulling them against his hips, then continuing to caress them through her scratchy wool stockings. ''And y' intend t' hold out on me till March?''

''Exactly,'' she replied in the calmest voice she could muster while his mischievous eyes glowed, partly in amusement, partly in desire.

''Do y' mind if I test y'r will a little bit, Mrs. . . . ah, Morgan, is it?''

''Not at all,'' she answered with a firm smirk. ''Test away. As I said before, nothing more till we're married.'' She carelessly looped her wrists about his neck and laced her fingers together, accepting her bawdy pose with a blitheness Rye could imagine in no other woman.

''Y' know I'd never be one t' entice y' into doin' anythin' against y'r will.'' His warm palms slid up her calves to the shallows behind both knees, then back down, pushing the wool stockings to her ankles. He inserted thumbs and forefingers inside the ruched wool, caressing the hollows above her heels, then squeezing gently, massaging.

''I know.'' Tingles sizzled up her legs. He was, as he'd always been, the consummate lover, inventive, irresistible. He could stir her senses in ever-new ways, as he was doing now. Oh, Rye, I want to go the limit with you . . . but I can't and won't until he's truly gone from between us.

Rye tipped his head to one side, lolled back against the chair with a lopsided grin, and requested in a husky voice. ''Tell me again, then, what it was y' invited me t' stay for.'' But beneath her petticoat his hands slid to her hips, tipping them back slightly until she felt the warm knob of masculinity meeting the feminine pulsepoint that couched him.

Her eyelids slid closed. Her breath fell harshly. ''Sausage,'' she murmured, following his lead in precisely the fashion she knew he expected.

''Then maybe we ought t' eat. I think I smell it cookin'.''

Her eyelids fluttered open and her lips curved. ''You're a nasty man, Rye Dalton.''

''Aye, and don't y' love it. Come here.'' With total disregard for the state of her clothing, his arms tightened across her back—skirts and all—and he pulled her forward until their tongues met, as did their bodies, his lifting in invitation, hers pressing in answer. His right hand roved down her spine, caressing it through the rough cotton of her pantaloons, then sliding lower, around the curve of her buttocks, as she leaned forward, kissing him with an ardor that set their pulses pounding. When temptation was transformed to torture, they pulled apart and spoke simultaneously.

''Laura, let's go t' bed . . .''

''Rye, we have to stop . . .''

His hands squeezed her hips, but hers pressed his chest. Their eyes were so close together their lashes almost brushed.

''Y' mean it, don't y'?'' he questioned. ''Y' mean t' hold me off until y'r name is legally Dalton again?''

She backed farther away. ''I told you that when we started this.''

''Why?''

''Partly because of what happened the last time we made love, partly—''

''Y' mean Zach's death?''

When she nodded, his frustration at last surfaced. An expression of annoyance darkened his features. ''Laura, that's ridiculous!''

''Maybe to you, but—''

''And anyway, you're splittin' hairs!'' he interrupted. ''What's the difference between what we're doin' and what we want t' do? You're only justifyin' your actions, that's all.''

Singed because he'd hit on the truth, she immediately jumped from his lap and whisked her skirts down, facing him with the flares of embarrassment coloring her cheeks. ''Rye Dalton, don't you sit there accusing me when I'm the one that's trying to do the honorable thing here!''

''Honorable! Ha!'' Angry now, he sat sharply forward in his chair.

''Yes, honorable! We made a promise to each other not to dishonor Dan!''

''While he was in this house!''

''No, while he's still legally my husband. But you conveniently forget that now.''

''Because you've got me in the state of a . . . an appendix ready to rupture! I ache, damnit!''

Laura's frustrations of the past nine months had built up until now, without warning, they fought their way out. She stood before Rye's chair, little understanding that their tensions, both emotional and sexual, naturally sought release. Her temper blazed, then erupted in a rich, relieving spate of shouting.

''Oh you . . . you oversexed . . .'' She searched for an adequately scathing word. "... goat!" She pointed a shaking finger at the door. "Dan hasn't been gone half a day and you're right at my door to take his place. Well, did you ever stop to think that maybe I need a little time to myself, without one man pushing me to stay and the other pushing me to go! I'm sick and tired of both of you fawning over me like I'm some prize at a fair. And who asked you to come here anyway, Rye Dalton? I was sitting here just as contented as a calf in clover when you came charging in here, and ... and ... ooph!" It felt so wonderful to yell that she went one step farther and yanked him by the front of the sweater. "Get out of my chair! I was perfectly happy in it all by myself, so just *get out!*"

Rye was on his feet. They squared off almost nose to nose. "Oversexed goat!"

"Yes ... oversexed goat!"

"Y're onc to talk. I didn't see y' puttin' up much objection! And I did not come here t' claim y' like a prize at the fair! I came here t' do y'r chores, y' ungrateful hussy!"

"Hussy? ... Hussy! Don't you use that name on me, Rye Dalton, not when you've been fooling around with her while I was *unavailable*." Though she didn't know it, Laura looked very much the hussy with her fists on her hips, clothes wrinkled, voice raised.

"I never *fooled around* with DeLaine Hussey," he sneered.

"You expect me to believe that—a man with the *drive* you have?" She scooped the pillow off the floor and fluffed it with irate jerks.

"Maybe I should've! The lady was willin' enough!"

Laura gaped at Rye. Her mouth dropped open in surprise. "So you *were* fooling around with her! Damn you, Rye Dalton!" She threw the pillow at his head and he ducked too late. But when he straightened, he held it in a fist and swung it back at her, catching her on the side of the head, forcing her back a step.

"I scarcely touched the woman, fool that I am. Instead I remained *honorable* because of you, and what do I get for it but the sharp side of y'r tongue." The pillow was still clenched in his huge fist. He thrust it against her chest, letting go, and turning to scoop his hat off the floor.

She was nearly knocked off her feet, but recovered her balance in time to reach his jacket before he did. Instead of handing it to him, she swiped it at him. "With a tongue as sharp as mine, maybe I won't be wanted in the Michigan Territory."

He stood as still as a statue for several endless seconds. "Does that mean y' don't want t' go?"

"It'd serve you right if I didn't."

He shrugged into his jacket. "Suit y'rself. Y' can let me know when y'r mind's made up." He headed for the door. "Meanwhile, y' can find someone else t' do y'r daily chores. I got all I can handle down at the cooperage, gettin' ready for the trip, without wastin' my time up here where I'm not wanted."

The door slammed behind him.

Laura stood for a full minute, staring at it, wondering what had happened. Then, in utter childishness, she stuck her tongue out at the door. But a moment later she fell to her knees, burying her face in the pillow upon the seat of the chair, bawling and blaming him. You don't understand what I've been through, Rye Dalton! You don't have the vaguest notion what I need right now!

She howled to her heart's content and socked the pillow with a fury that felt wonderful! Cathartic!

But never for a moment did Laura doubt that she would leave this island with Rye in only nine short weeks.

Rye Dalton stormed down home, cursing all the way, calling her names he didn't mean, bellowing deprecations at women in general and her in particular, feeling masculine and self-righteous and thoroughly purged. He kicked at hunks of snow in his path, promised the Almighty that Laura Dalton would never feel his hardened member against her again—not if she begged till he was feeble and impotent—knowing even before he reached the cooperage that he didn't mean a word of it, and she'd damn well better be ready to make up for lost time when she was Mrs. Rye Dalton again!

Within a day's time they both came to understand what it was that had caused the irrational anger. The sexual tension and frustration had been building up for months, with a myriad of human emotions having been brought into play: desire, guilt, love, recrimination, hope, fear, impatience. And with at least two months to go before the situation could be resolved, their anger was a natural vent.

She stewed for a week.
He stewed for a week.
He felt revived.
She felt refreshed.
Damnit, but I love that woman, Rye Dalton agonized.
Lord in heaven, but I love that oversexed goat, Laura fumed.
I'll give her a couple weeks to realize what she's lost.
I'll give him a couple weeks to admit I was right.
Let her carry her own wood and water for a while!
Let him eat Josiah's cooking!
Three weeks till March.
Three weeks till March.
I wonder what she's doing.
I wonder what he's doing.
Sausage . . . (he smiled) . . . ah, what a woman.
Smelled it cooking, did he . . . (she smiled) . . . probably the steam off his own body.
Two weeks till March.
One week till March.
Damnit, but I miss her.
Wait till we're married, Rye Dalton. I'll make you pay for this misery!

They waited for the courts to set her free, and meanwhile, Josh remained belligerent, often scowling at Laura, angry because Dan was gone from the house. She grew sick and tired of looking at his lower lip protruding as if a weight were attached to it, and often had to keep herself from speaking out in self-defense when he watched her making preparations for Michigan and acted as if she was doing him some grave misdeed with every stitch she took, every item she stockpiled.

She readied an ample supply of clothing, for once they left the convenience of New England's mills, that commodity would become precious. She bought great hanks of yarn for socks and mittens and heavy cloth for sewing longer pants for Josh next winter. Garden seeds were carefully tucked into small cotton bags and packed between layers of clothing, where they could not freeze. She took inventory of her household goods, making decisions about which to take and which to abandon—any item made of wood was automatically left behind, for Rye could fashion a new one when they reached Michigan. It was glass and metal that would be precious on the frontier. She kept a growing list of necessities: needles, paper, ink, schoolbooks, mosquito netting, enough soap to last during their trip, lanolin, spices, herbs, medicinal ingredients, candle wicking, bedding, soft cotton for bandages, and wire—more simple home repairs were made with wire than anything else.

Meanwhile Rye, too, was preparing to leave. He and Josiah built up as large an inventory of barrels as possible, for when they left, the island would be without a cooper until one could be enticed away from the mainland. For their own use, special waterproof barrels were fashioned for that all-important commodity, gunpowder. Larger ones were constructed for clothing, and medium-sized barrels to carry their coopering tools. He purchased a new John H. Hall percussion rifle and bought molds for bullets. He made lists also, though his were concerned with survival and providing rather than with domestics: knives, spades, spare metal parts for harnesses, hoof trimmers (for horses would be necessary in Michigan), unguent, grease, and oil.

And Rye worried every day that the court would drag its feet and leave him and Laura in a quandary when it was time to leave. But then came the news that the hearing was scheduled six months to the day from the date Dan Morgan had first filed papers.

The probate court of the county of Nantucket, Commonwealth of Massachusetts, had been in existence since 1689. Throughout its history, it had dissolved many marriages by proclaiming missing seamen dead. But to the best of his knowledge, Judge James Bunker had never before heard of one being dissolved because a missing seaman was declared alive.

In his chambers on the second floor of the Town Building on Union Street, the Honorable Judge Bunker reviewed the case before him on this windy mid-March day in 1838, attempting to disassociate his personal knowledge of Rye Dalton, Dan Morgan, and Laura Dalton Morgan from the legal aspects to be considered. Bunker's Puritanical leanings made him averse to divorce. But in this case, knowing the history of the three and considering the bizarre set of circumstances cast upon them by fate, Judge Bunker found it impossible to do anything but grant the dissolution of the marriage.

As his gavel fell, its reverberations echoed through the high-ceilinged room. Ezra Merrill inserted the relatively few papers into a leather portfolio and reached for his greatcoat. Dan and Ezra shook hands and exchanged a few low words Laura couldn't hear, then the lawyer turned to her, wished her his best, and left.

In the ensuing silence, Laura met Dan's eyes with a wan smile.

"And so, it is done," he stated with an air of resignation.

"Yes, I—"

"Don't thank me, Laura. For God's sake, don't thank me."

"I wasn't going to, Dan. I was going to say I doubt that Judge Bunker has ever come up against a case like this before."

"Obviously not." Silence fell again. Dan reached for his coat, buttoned it slowly, then stared at the tips of his shoes while asking, "How soon will you be leaving?"

"At the end of the month."

He looked up. "Ah, that soon."

"Yes." The guilt she'd once felt was gone, but she hastened to add, "You'll want to spend a little time with Josh before we leave. I'll let you know exactly when that will be."

"Yes. Thank you."

Again that discomfiting silence settled between them. "Well then, I guess there's nothing left to do but go our separate ways. Shall we?" He turned, took her elbow in a courtly manner, but dropped it long before they reached the street.

They bid each other good-bye, and Laura turned toward home. Down below the shrill whistle of the steamboat *Telegraph* lifted with an ear-splitting shriek. The *ka-whoozh* of the whistle rattled the air again, and suddenly Laura's heart seemed to soar like the sound.

I'm free! I'm free! I'm free!

She stopped in the middle of the street, whirled around to see if she could spot the *Telegraph,* but though she couldn't see it, she knew it was picking up passengers at Steamboat Wharf, as it did every Monday, Wednesday, and Saturday. And one day soon it would take her away with Rye. All at once it came to her that she was totally free to go with him at last. She suddenly smiled at the memory of the spat they'd had. Good lord, Laura, you fool! You've never even asked him exactly what day you're leaving!

She turned and her feet flew up the street toward home. Her bonnet brim fluttered in the stiff March wind, and a thousand unasked questions danced through her mind. She'd never felt right about asking those questions of Rye, about discussing their plans while she was still Laura Morgan. But now she could ask Rye anything. As she hustled up the shell path to the house there was one—only one—question of utmost importance filling her pounding heart.

The message arrived at the cooperage late that afternoon, and Rye tossed a coin to Jimmy Ryerson, recognizing Laura's writing on the note. He took the stairs to the living quarters with great impatience and perched on the edge of his bunk while tearing the seal.

Dear Rye,

I'm sorry. Will you marry me anyway?

Love,

Laura

His face burst into an enormous smile. She's free! He let out a raucous whoop of joy and sent Chad up to the house with an immediate reply.

Dear Laura,

I'm sorry, too. I accept your proposal. Can I come and carry your water?
Love,
Rye

Dear Rye,

Stay away from me, you oversexed goat. It's not my water you're after.
All my love,
Laura

Dear Laura,

Then can I carry your wood? Or how about steaming up a sausage?
All my love,
The oversexed goat

Dear Rye,

Not until we're married. When do we leave? Everything is ready to be packed.
With love,
The ungrateful hussy
p.s. I need three big barrels, maybe four. But don't bring them, send them!

Dear Laura,

Am sending Chad with the first of four barrels. If you need more than four, let me know. We leave on the Albany packet, Thursday, March 30. What do you say to getting married by the captain?
I love you,
Rye

Dear Rye,

Yes, yes, yes! Everything is all ready. Have room left in one barrel for any of your clothes if you're short of space. When will I see you again?
I love you, too,
Laura

It was two days before they were due to leave when the final message was delivered to Laura's door. But this time it was delivered by Rye himself.

She answered the knock to find him not on the wooden step, but backed off about ten feet, standing on the scallop shells. ''Rye?'' Her heart seemed to stop up her throat at the sight of him. He was dressed in a rugged ecru sweater and the body-conforming sailor's breeches with belly flap and bell bottoms. On his tangled hair nested a Greek fisherman's hat of black cheviot wool, its shallow visor dipping at a jaunty angle across his tan brow. The rakish tilt of the cap set off his brawny handsomeness to great advantage, and as her dark eyes met those of sea-blue, Laura's face brightened into an enormous smile that was immediately reflected in Rye's.

"Hello, m'love." He swallowed, then said no more, only hooked his thumbs in his waist flap and gazed up at her as if he could not get his fill, the smile having softened into something far more eloquent upon his rugged features.

"I've missed you terribly," came her hearty admission.

"I've missed y', too."

"I'm sorry for the things I said."

"Aye, me too."

"Aren't we foolish?"

"Nay, just in love, wouldn't y' say?"

"Yes, I'd say." She smiled wistfully. Still he didn't move, so she invited, "Would you like to come in?"

"More than anything in the world." But his black boots remained firmly planted in the white shells.

"Well, then—"

"But I won't."

"Y . . . you won't?"

He shook his head slowly. A grin eased up along one side of his sculpted mouth. "Two more days . . . I'll wait."

She released a shuddering breath and glanced at the harbor, then back at him. "Two more days." Then she admitted, "I'm a little scared, Rye."

"So am I. But excited, too."

She let her eyes linger on his. "Aye, excited," she agreed softly, intentionally slipping into his nautical vernacular.

He cleared his throat and shifted his feet. "Well, Josiah's all ready t' go. How about Josh?"

"Josh has been treating me like I just kicked his dog. I don't know how he's going to act when it's time for good-byes." They thought of Jimmy Ryerson, Jane, Hilda . . . Dan. And for a moment shadows crossed over their faces.

"Aye, the good-byes're goin' t' be hard, aren't they?"

She nodded, then forced herself to smile, for his sake.

"Well, then . . ." He backed away two steps.

The closer it came to departure, the more the finality of the venture gave them pause. So many uncertainties lay ahead, miles to cross, dangers to face. And what would Josh's attitude be? But as brown eyes met blue, Laura and Rye drew from each other the reassurance that together they could conquer whatever the future might bring.

"I'll come for y' myself around nine on Thursday."

"We'll be ready."

Still he remained on the path below, gazing up into her deep brown eyes, reluctant to leave. Finally, with a small guttural sound in his throat, he crossed the distance between them and lifted the palm of her ringless left hand to his warm lips. "Josh'll come 'round," he reassured. Then he spun away and ran at a forced trot down the hill.

At that very moment, in a yard near the foot of the lane, Josh was on his knees on one side of a marble pit circled by a line drawn in the sand. Taking aim with a cat's eye balanced on his thumb, he suddenly straightened and looked across the circle at Jimmy.

"Hey, Jimmy?"

Jimmy Ryerson was counting the marbles in his cache and stopped at the interruption. "You made me lose count. What?" he demanded.

Josh scratched his head, leaving a gray smear of dirt on the blond hair, and finally asked the question that had been puzzling him for weeks. "What's a adventure?"

Chapter 22

The Little Gray Lady of the Sea was as good as her nickname on Thursday morning. A thin haze of fog covered the shoreline, and above the island, the sky was a somber iron gray. The town came awake to its never-changing sounds—the morning chimes of the Congregational church tower, the clang of the smith's hammer, the crackle of canvas catching wind, the *shushh* of waves beneath pilings, and the rumble of wooden wheels on cobblestones.

A pair of freight wagons pulled up before the gaping door of the cooperage, where only the fireplace and tool bench remained as before. Two stevedores jumped down and headed inside to begin rolling heavy barrels out and loading them. A gnarled old cooper with a head of hoary curls stood beside a long, lanky younger one, whose blond mane tangled about his face like beached kelp. A slow coil of blue smoke lifted above their heads as the younger man put his arm around the older one's shoulders, squeezing hard.

"Well, old man—"

A stretch of poignant silence slipped by.

"Aye, son, she's been a good ol' place."

They lifted their eyes to the rafters, the small window above the tool bench, the worn steps to the lodgings. The voice of a woman dear to both of them drifted back in memory, calling them to breakfast, to supper, to bed. Together they stood in the confines of the building that smelled of cedar and pipe smoke and always would.

Josiah removed the fragrant brier from his teeth and spoke quietly. "I'd like a few minutes alone with y'r mother. Go on now, get y'r woman."

Rye drew a deep, quivering breath, let his eyes pass one last, lingering time across the walls of the cooperage, then answered throatily, "Aye, then, we'll meet y' at the wharf." He squeezed the burly shoulders once more, then turned quickly toward the street.

With a long-legged leap, he mounted a wagon, gave a single sharp whistle, and peered back over his shoulder to find a large yellow Labrador bounding onto the scarred boards behind him. The dog jogged eagerly to the forward end of the wagon and rested her jaw over the back of the driver's seat, gave a few wags, and they set off.

At the bottom of Crooked Record Lane, the vehicle lurched to a stop while the man squinted up at a quaint little saltbox with silver-brown weatherbeaten shakes. A woman appeared at the door. She was dressed in a traveling cape of dove gray wool over a simple dress of lemon yellow gingham and a matching bonnet with a satin bow knotted just behind her left jaw.

She raised a gloved hand to wave in greeting, and a boy slithered around her skirts, caught sight of the lanky cooper, and stared at him with a surly expression. But at sight of the child, the dog broke loose and loped forward in her aging gait. The sullen look changed to one of surprise. The winsome eyes and mouth opened in dawning delight, and Josh could resist no longer. He came to meet the dog halfway, falling to his knees in the middle of the path, scrunching his blue eyes shut as the Lab bestowed a wet hello to the rounded curve of the boy's face.

"Ship! Ship!" Instinct made him begin to ask the man, "Is Ship . . ." Then, remembering, he turned to ask his mother instead. "Is Ship goin' with us?"

"Why don't you ask Rye?"

He looked up at the tall cooper he had once liked so much. "Is Ship goin' with us?" Josh asked at last.

Rye came near, dropped to one knee, and gave the dog's flat head an affectionate rumple. "Why, o' course she's goin' with us. Nobody should be without a watchdog where there're wolves and bears and raccoons t' raid the storehouse."

"W . . . wolves 'n' b . . . bears?" Josh's eyes widened. "Really?"

"Aye, but we won't have t' worry, not with Ship along."

"Is it really gonna be a adventure?"

"Aye, son. And have y' made up y'r mind yet if y'r goin' t' talk t' me while we make it, or are y' bound to keep a button on that lip?" Lowering his voice, Rye added, "It hurts y'r mother and me a lot, y' know. Especially y'r mother. She wants t' see you happy again, but she wants t' be happy, too." He paused, then declared softly, "We both love y', Josh."

Josh's eyes dropped to the dog. In a small voice, he said, "Jimmy, he said . . . well, he said your papa . . . well, if he's goin' along, he'll be my grampa."

Rye's expression softened, and his voice went lower. "Aye, son."

"And . . . and you'll be my father?"

From the doorway Laura watched, her heart filling her breast with wingbeats as the man in the dark breeches, light sweater, and jaunty black fisherman's cap bent near his son with one arm braced upon a knee.

''Aye, son. I am y'r father, as y've known for some time.''

Josh raised uncertain eyes, very much like those that looked down on him. ''Will I have to call you Papa?''

Rye swallowed, studying the piquant face of his son, realizing how difficult it was for the child to accept the sudden changes thrust upon his life. In a kind, caring voice, Rye answered, ''Nay, Joshua. I think there'll only be one man y'll ever think of as Papa. Nothin's goin' t' change that, you know. Y' can keep on lovin' Dan as much as y' ever did.''

''But I won't see him no more, will I?''

''Michigan's a long way from Nantucket, Josh. I'm afraid not. But maybe when y're grown up, Nantucket won't seem so far. Then y' can come back for a visit.''

Unmoving, Laura waited, willing the child to make peace with his father so that their lives might know their rightful share of contentment.

Josh was silent for a long time, hunkered before Rye half despondently. The dog took a desultory lick at Josh's chin, but he seemed unaware. At last he raised his eyes to the blue eyes in the tan face above him. In a very businesslike voice for a five-year old, he declared, ''I decided I'll call you Father.''

Their eyes searched, questioned, and Rye's body strained with repressed love for the boy. Suddenly they moved as one, Josh shooting to his feet, Rye's arms widening, and for three thundering heartbeats they were chest to chest as love had its irrepressible way.

Seeing father and son healing at last, Laura's eyes misted. Joy burst through her heart, and she thought now the best time to intrude upon the scene.

''Are you two going to stay down there all day or are you going to come up here and help me carry things out to the wagon?''

Josh backed away. Rye looked up toward the top of the path, then slowly got to his feet. Stretching his long legs into a calculatedly lazy stride, he began moving toward her while commenting in an undertone, ''Y'r mother's lookin' quite saucy t'day.''

The child looked up the long man beside him. ''What's saucy?''

But only Rye's rich laughter answered his son's question as they mounted the path together. At the step, Rye hooked one boot over its edge, leaned on the knee with both palms, and let his gaze rove over the floor-length cape and the long triangle of yellow gingham it revealed.

''And what are you laughing about, Rye Dalton?''

''Is that any way t' greet y'r groom on his weddin' day?''

Her jaw dropped. ''Today!''

''Aye, t'day. If I have t' commit mutiny t' get the captain t' perform the ceremony. That is, if we don't miss the Albany packet while we stand here yammerin'.''

With a gay smile she swung inside, followed by Rye, Josh, and Ship.

The house was stripped of all its former warmth and appeared forlorn now, its furnishings having been systematically rifled. Those that remained were to be sold by Ezra Merrill, and appeared sadly abandoned in the small rooms, which had been divested of all personal items. Rye avoided analyzing his surroundings, quickly tipping a barrel instead and shouldering it through the door. It was a day that would, by its very nature, repeatedly plunge them from optimistic joy to nostalgic sadness. The best they could do to get through the difficult moments of tugging memory was to put them behind as quickly as possible and look forward.

But when the last of the barrels was loaded and Rye returned to the house for the two black satchels that remained, he found Laura with her back to the door, running her gloved fingertips reminiscently along the edge of the fireplace mantel. Nearby, the doors to the alcove bed were opened, its tick and quilts gone, leaving it nothing but a hollow wooden box. Rye watched Laura's eyes turn to it and linger. Next she moved to the beckoning door of the linter room, and he stepped up quietly behind her shoulder. She glanced back at him, unsmiling, then together they gazed inside at the wooden bedstead.

"I'll make y' a new one," he promised softly, understanding that she truly did not pine to take the old one along, but that it deserved this moment of elegy. Upon it their marriage had been consummated. From it he had gone to sea. Upon it Joshua Dalton had been born. And to it Dan had come.

For the first time today, Rye touched her, in much the same fashion he had touched his father. "Come," he encouraged softly. "It's time t' go."

They turned from the bedroom doorway, crossed the keeping room with lagging steps that echoed in the still space where once their laughter had lilted. There was no laughter now. They stepped from the house, shut its door for the last time, closing it on a phase of their lives both sweet and sad. The stark white scallop shells clicked together in the familiar crunch that had meant home for so long. Halfway down the path, they turned one last time to impress the image of the little saltbox into their memories.

If it was difficult saying good-bye to their dwellings, the scene on the wharf was impossible. Everyone was there—Jane and John Durning and all six of their little stair-steps; Jimmy Ryerson and his parents; Dahlia Traherne; not only Hilda Morgan, but Tom and Dorothy as well; Chad Dalton and his parents, along with a large entourage of Dalton relatives—even Cousin Charles with his wife and three children. Joseph Starbuck had come, and Ezra Merrill and Asa Pond.

And standing in the background at the fringe of bravely smiling faces, looking as if she was trying to hold back tears, hovered DeLaine Hussey.

And, of course, there was Dan.

He was one of the last to arrive, and at first as he stole up quietly behind DeLaine, Rye and Laura were unaware of his presence. Laura was in the arms of Dahlia, who pressed a cluster of recipes into her daughter's palm. "These're your favorites from when you were a little girl." The tears started then and grew more insistent as Jane bestowed the next goodbye, a fierce hug in the middle of which she released a shattering sob beside Laura's ear. Rye was being passed from aunts to uncles while Josh and Jimmy Ryerson knelt one on either side of Ship, surrounded by Josh's cousins, all of them for the moment jealous of Josh's adventure, his acquisition of the dog, and the possible dangers of bears and wolves.

But then Cap'n Silas motioned the crowd to clear space for the stevedores to drive the wagons to the gangplank and unload them, and as the crowd parted, Rye and Laura glanced up the chasm to find Dan there, the thumbs and forefingers of both his hands slipped inside his vest pockets, a beaver hat on his head, and an expression of tight control on his face.

The eyes of the departing couple swerved to each other, then back to Dan, and a hush seemed to fall over the crowd before a self-conscious chatter swelled again.

The last of the barrels was loaded aboard the *Clinton,* and suddenly everyone winced as the deafening steam whistle blew over Steamboat Wharf.

The sudden jarring sound was so overwhelming it set Laura's heart thumping—or was the reaction caused by the sight of Dan, still hesitating twenty feet across the wharf, restraining himself just as she was?

But then Josh spied Dan and lurched to his feet, running the length of the wharf. He flung himself into the arms of the man who knelt down, then scooped the child up, and clung to him a last time while a woeful wail carried above the wharf.

"Papa . . . Papa . . ."

Cap'n Silas commanded, "All aboard!"

The steam whistle shrilled again while over Josh's shoulder Dan Morgan blinked and tried valiantly not to let his tears spill over.

Laura lifted pleading eyes to Rye, and even as her feet began moving, she felt Rye's hand grasping her elbow, hurrying her toward Dan. Dan set Josh on his feet and met Laura halfway. As her arms went around him, his hat was knocked onto the silvery boards of the wharf, but nobody seemed to notice. Rye's eyes had locked with those of DeLaine Hussey, and he nodded a silent good-bye while she pressed trembling fingers to her lips.

Laura felt Dan's heart slamming piteously hard against her breasts before she pulled back to look into his face. His lips were set grimly against his teeth, but his nostrils trembled while he blinked repeatedly. She lay a gloved hand on his cheek and managed two shaky words. "Good-bye, Dan."

He seemed unable to trust himself to speak. Then, to Laura's dismay, he suddenly pulled her against him once more and kissed her full on the mouth. When he put her away, her tears had wet his cheeks, and she realized Josh was standing alongside, looking up at all three of them.

Rye's hand met Dan's in a solid handshake, and their eyes joined in a last farewell.

"Take care of them, my friend."

"Aye, y' can be sure of it."

Their voices were unnaturally deep with emotion, and their four hands clung, gripping so hard the knuckles turned white.

From the gangplank, Cap'n Silas called, "Got a schedule t' keep. All aboard!"

Then Josh was on Rye's arm, looking back over his father's sturdy shoulder at his papa. Tears streamed down his freckled cheeks, and the rooster tail at the back of his blond head bobbed with each long-legged step that bore him away. Laura, too, felt Rye's commanding grip on her elbow and passed the sea of faces toward the boat with tears now blinding her completely.

They stood at the rail of the steam packet—Rye with Josh in his arms, Laura beside him, and Josiah on her far side. Ship whined and nudged between them, lunged up and caught her front paws on the port beam. There was a clunk and a lurch, then the cumbersome packet began to move, shivering to life with ponderous reluctance until the rhythmic clunk picked up speed and became the incessant heartbeat of the vessel.

Each of those at the rail had singled out a face on which to linger. For Josh it was Jimmy Ryerson, who waved one freckled hand and wiped his eyes with the other. For Laura it was Jane, who held her youngest and pressed a cheek against his hair. For Rye it was Dan, who had picked up his hat but seemed to have forgotten to put it on his head. But Josiah turned from the faces on the wharf to lift his gaze over the top of the bait shack and the candle shop beyond to the roof of a small wooden building scarcely visible in the distance. He dropped his hand to Ship's head and stroked it absently. The dog whined, raised doleful eyes to Josiah, then watched the shore slip away into the mists of Nantucket Harbor.

They remained at the rail for a long time, with eyes cast astern toward the little spit of land they loved. As they passed the shoals, the projecting fingers of Brant Point and Coatue seemed to want to pluck them back and hold them. But the *Clinton* headed into the sound toward the long tip of Cape Cod, chugging along steadily until Nantucket appeared no more than a pebble floating on the surface of the water before it dwindled, then disappeared altogether in a haze of distant fog.

Laura shivered, glanced up, and found Rye studying her.

"Well, would y' like t' see our quarters?"

Our quarters. If anything had the power to wrest Laura's dolorous thoughts from the place they'd just left, it was those two words.

"I guess I'd better, since we'll be spending two weeks in them."

The five passengers headed belowdecks. The *Clinton* was far less luxurious than the steamboat *Telegraph* would have been, for though it hauled a capacity of thirty passengers, the chief purpose of the Albany packet was transporting cargo, thus the accommodations could scarcely be called cabins. Rye led them to two rooms that were little more than partitioned spaces, offering thin-walled privacy but little else.

As he opened the door and stood back in the narrow companionway, Laura peered inside to find, to her dismay, a pair of single bunks, berthed one above the other, a small bench seat bolted to the wall, a tiny shelf above, and a whale-oil lantern swinging from the overhead beam. But her eyes were drawn to the sight of her suitcase sitting beside Rye's sea chest.

Before she could react, Josh pushed at his mother from behind. "Let me see!" He squeezed past and headed into the cubicle, but a restraining hand fell on his head and forced him into an abrupt about face.

"Not so fast there, young man! Y'rs is the next one!"

Laura's heart reacted with a flutter, and she wondered if Josh would put up any objection to being separated from her in the midst of all these strange surroundings and events. But she had little time to speculate, for there was a moment of confusion while she dipped inside the open door to let the three, plus Ship, pass along the companionway to the next door.

"Y' and Josiah will be sharin' this compartment," she heard, then poked her nose around the doorway to find a second cubicle identical to the first.

"Me and Josiah?" Josh looked up dubiously at Rye.

"Aye, y' and Josiah."

"Where's Mama gonna be?"

"Right next door." Rye nodded toward the first cabin.

"Oh."

At Josh's unenthusiastic grunt, Josiah spoke up in his slow New England drawl. "Got somethin' here I been meanin' t' show y', Joshua."

Josh's expression was skeptical as his glance passed from Rye to Laura. It was one of the weirdest moments of Laura's life, hoping for approval from her son to sleep with his father! But just then Josiah bent to retrieve a small wooden carton with airholes along its sides. He sat down on the lower berth and gave the container his full attention, carefully placing his hands on its cover as if it were a magician's box. Josh's attention was captured.

"What is it?" The boy moved nearer his grandfather's knee.

" 'Tain't much. Just a couple little companions f'r the long trip."

The wooden lid came up in Josiah's hands, and from within the box came a duet of *cheeps*.

"Chicks!" Already Josh was reaching eagerly, smiling and fairly squealing, "You mean we can keep 'em on the boat?"

"We'd better. The way I heard tell, there ain't many chickens in Michigan. Thought we'd best start up a flock right away so y'r mother'd have eggs f'r her cookin'."

Ship nosed forward and sniffed at the puff ball in Josh's hand. Already Josh seemed to have forgotten Rye and Laura. Josiah reached into his breast pocket and found a cold pipe, clamped it between his teeth while studying the boy, the chick, and the dog. He raised laconic eyes to Laura while continuing drolly, "Y' know, Joshua, I c'd use some help pamperin' them chicks, so I hope y'r mother don't mind if y' sleep in here with 'em."

Josh spun around and all but climbed Laura's skirts in enthusiasm. "Can I? Please, can I? Me and . . . me and Grampa, we got to take care of 'em and keep 'em warm and stuff, and make sure Ship don't eat 'em up!"

Rye and Laura laughed. She managed to catch Josiah's eye, found a charming twinkle there, and hoped he understood the wordless message of thanks she flashed.

"Yes, of course you can, Josh."

Immediately, he turned back to the box on Josiah's knees. "We gotta name 'em, don't we, Grampa?"

"Name them chickens? I never heard of no chickens with names!"

"Well, I can see you two don't need us, so we'll get settled next door." Rye took Laura's elbow and a shaft of fire seemed to sizzle up her arm. Josiah and Josh didn't even look up as they made their exit.

Inside their own cabin, the door was closed and all was silent but for the pulsating throb of the steam engine shimmying up through the floor. There was no porthole, only the oil lamp swaying on its hook, and Laura knew, to the exact highlight and shadow, what Rye's face would look like by its golden light should she turn and lift her eyes. But she stood facing the bunks, feeling him close behind her shoulder.

"It's not very fancy," he apologized, but she heard instead the note of tight control in his voice.

"When have I ever needed anything fancy?" She felt both of Rye's hands move up her back and circle her neck.

"Never," he said thickly. Then, as if he didn't trust himself, he dropped his hands from her.

"Were the chicks your idea?" she asked.

"Nay, my father gets the credit for that."

"Josiah is very astute."

"Aye."

She wanted to turn, but felt as shy as a violet blossom. Her heart was giving the engine some competition, throbbing so powerfully she thought surely it was her own pulse shaking the boards beneath the soles of her shoes.

Rye cleared his throat. "Well . . . I have t' talk t' the captain, so why don't you—"

"Josiah didn't dream up those chicks for nothing, Rye," she interrupted, turning at last to face him. "Don't you dare run off to the captain without—"

His mouth cut off her words, and she was in Rye's arms at last! His kiss was a rich, sensual welcome while his arms slipped within her cape to haul her up tight against his chest, and hers looped about his neck as her feet left the floor. Then Rye's warm, wet tongue was all over and around Laura's, and she whisked the cap from his head and held it in one hand while the other threaded his coarse hair.

He turned, backing her up against the cabin door, pressing the length of his body against hers while their kiss became a wild search for relief. She ran her tongue along the sleek texture of his teeth, then explored the moist depths of his mouth, missing none of its familiar landmarks.

He let her slip down only far enough that their stomachs and hips met and used his tremendous strength to wedge her between the door and his body, pressing so hard the breath was forced from her lungs. He was fully tumescent and wasted not a moment letting her know. His hips made figure eights as they ground against hers, thrusting the hard male ridge against the equally hard rise of her mons.

Desire sent a liquid rush of feeling to the part of her against which Rye pressed. She felt it, gloried in it, welcomed it! But Laura was impaled against the door, unable to transmit her own tacit message of arousal.

"Rye, put me down," she managed.

"If I do and my hands are free, there'll be no stoppin' them."

"I don't care."

"Yes y' do. Y' want t' get married first, so I'll put y' down, but then I'll go see the captain about arrangin' it, agreed?"

"Blast you, Rye Dalton," she murmured against his lips, provocatively inserting her tongue into his mouth between words. "What a time . . . for you to do . . . the proper thing."

"Agreed?" he repeated, moving his head back only far enough to escape her darting tongue.

"Oh all right, agreed."

She felt her toes regain the floor, and his hands steadied her for a moment while her skirt still clung to his trousers. He backed a step away and the skirt fell properly into place.

His voice seemed to throb like the engine while his impassioned blue eyes fixed upon hers. ''But I'm warnin' y', t'night will be a different matter.''

She rose up on tiptoe and placed the wool cap on his head, adjusted its narrow visor to a raffish angle, and studied her effort. ''It had better be,'' she rejoined softly.

They kissed once more, Rye's hands running possessively up her ribs while she touched his jaw. Then he put her away and backed off a step. ''I'll be back as soon as I can. Meanwhile, get y'rself ready for our weddin' . . . again. Only this time when he says *till death do us part,* y' can believe it.''

Then he turned and was gone.

She smiled at the door, then spun around. Her body felt combustible! This restraint was playing havoc with her composure. She took four deep breaths, but found it did little good, and at last ran a hand down the front of her skirt and clutched herself in an effort to quell the throbbing begun by his caress.

What time is it? Barely noon. How many hours to wait? Until at least eight o'clock, when we can respectably retire for the night. Goodness me, how will I last that long?

She removed her bonnet and cape and prowled about the small cabin, testing the mattress, pushing the suitcase and sea chest against the wall. There was no unpacking to do because no place was provided for the storage of extra clothes. Time crawled.

When Rye returned, he found Laura sitting on the edge of the lower bunk. She flew to her feet as he stepped inside, closed the door, and leaned back against it.

''Four o'clock,'' he announced without preamble.

''Four o'clock,'' she echoed like a litany.

''Aye. In the captain's cabin.'' His eyes assessed her yellow dress with an expression of strained forbearance.

''Well,'' she said breathlessly, raising her palms and glancing around as if expecting some diversion to come jumping out of the cabin walls.

He sucked in an enormous breath, let it out slowly while tilting his cap back beyond his hairline with a thumb. Then he heaved himself away from the cabin door, opened it, and stepped back. ''Let's go see how the chicks're doin'.''

Laura's knees felt watery from relief.

The four of them spent a pleasant half hour watching the chicks and the dog, who by now was less inquisitive and allowed the tiny yellow birds to be placed between her paws and even on her head.

Shortly after noon, a bell announced dinner, which was served in a long forward salon as lackluster as the rest of the craft. Tables and benches filled the room, and there was little space for the galley help to pass between them with the hot seafood chowder and hard dark bread that comprised the meal.

Laura sat next to Rye, scorchingly aware of every brush of his thigh against hers. The conversation around the table ran on brightly as passengers compared destinations and home ports. It was unnecessary to reveal that Laura and Rye were to be married that afternoon, for everybody took them to be a married couple, since Josh was with them, and Josiah, too.

In the afternoon, Rye left Laura in the cabin to rest if she wanted, while he excused himself, taking his suitcase next door. But she was keyed up so tightly it was impossible to relax. She found herself continuously checking the tiny gold pendant watch pinned near her collarbone, and finally, when it read three o'clock, she went next door to fetch Josh, ordering, much to the boy's dismay, that it was time for him to change clothes and get ready.

She had decided to wear the yellow dress, had recombed her hair into a flattering nutmeg top knot, but was nervously indecisive about whether or not to wear her bonnet.

"What do you think, Josh?"

But Josh was little help. He merely shrugged and wondered why his mother was acting as flappy as a fish out of water.

At ten to four, a knock sounded and Laura sucked in a quick breath and whispered, "You answer it, Josh!"

The door opened upon a freshly combed, freshly shaved Rye Dalton, decked out in the same splendid suit he'd worn the night of Joseph Starbuck's party. The green trousers clung to his thighs as the skin hugs a grape. The jacket delineated his shoulders' breadth and musculature with awesome precision. His sienna skin was temptingly foiled by the snowy ruffles that fell to his knuckles and the tightly wound stock that climbed his neck nearly to his side-whiskers.

"Are y' ready?"

I've been ready since I was fifteen.

Laura reined in her wild thoughts and managed to utter hoarsely, "Yes, both of us."

He nodded and stepped back from the door, through which Josh immediately began to precede his mother, only to be halted in midstride by his father's strong hand.

"Ladies first, young man."

They were joined in the companionway by Josiah, and the four made their way up to the main aft deck and the captain's quarters.

Captain Benjamin Swain was a burly mutton-chopped man with red cheeks and a raw scrape to his voice. He stepped back to allow them entrance, raspily welcoming, "Step inside! Step inside!" But he was surprised to see the shortest of the quartet, who followed on his mother's heels. "Well, now who have we here?"

Josh looked up. "Joshua Morgan, sir."

"Joshua Morgan, is it?"

Josh nodded, giving the captain no further enlightenment.

The ruddy-cheeked captain closed the door and cleared his throat with a thunderous rumble. "This is m' first mate, Dardanelle McCallister," Captain Swain announced. "Thought y' might need a witness."

Rye and the first mate shook hands. "Mr. McCallister, I thank y', but we won't be needin' y'. My father will act as witness."

"Ah, very well, sir, then I'll take m'self off to other duties."

Other introductions were made all around, and Laura's hand was crushed in the tight grip of the captain.

His cabin was the most luxurious part of the craft. It had rich walls of waxed teak and finely crafted fittings such as the belowdecks cubicles hadn't. A carved bedstead covered one end of the room while on another was a long pigeonholed desk and closed storage cabinet resembling a chifforobe. The center of the room was monopolized by a table over which were strewn maps, ledgers, a brass sextant, and compass. There was more space than their own cabins afforded, but still, with five people in this room, it was undeniably crowded.

Captain Swain motioned them to stand to one side of the desk while he stooped to fetch a Bible from its lower drawer.

Laura stood between Rye and Josiah, while Josh took up a place before them, with Rye's hands resting on the boy's shoulders. The captain began paging through the book, but before he found what he was looking for, Josiah leaned forward and whispered something in his ear. Rye and Laura exchanged curious glances but were left unenlightened as the whispered exchange continued, then the captain nodded his head, found his place, and looked up with a second clearing of his throat.

"All ready, then?"

Josh's rooster tail bobbed as he nodded enthusiastically. The captain puffed out his chest and began reading a simple prayer. Beside Laura, Rye's elbow seemed to quiver as it brushed hers. She stared at the gold buttons on the captain's protruding stomach. The prayer ended, and the rotund man dropped the book and extemporized.

"Y've come to me on this, the thirtieth day of March, eighteen thirty-eight, to join together as man and wife. Is that correct, Mr. Dalton?"

"That's correct."

"Is that correct, Miss Morgan?"

"That's correct—Mrs. Morgan."

The captain arched a brow. "Mrs. Morgan, yes," he amended. "And to the best of your knowledge, is there any reason why the Commonwealth of Massachusetts should not grant its seal to your wishes?" He looked first at Rye, then at Laura. In turn, they answered, "None."

"Marriage is a state into which you must enter with all intentions of making it last a lifetime. Do you both so intend? Mr. Dalton?"

"Yes, I do," Rye answered.

"Yes, I do," Laura answered.

"And it is also a state into which none should enter without the bond of love. Do you promise to love each other for the rest of your lives?"

"I promise . . ." Rye turned loving eyes on Laura, "for the rest o' my life."

"I promise," she echoed, meeting his blue eyes, "for the rest of my life."

"And who will witness this union?"

"I will," Josiah stated. "Josiah Dalton."

The captain nodded. "And who gives this woman?"

"I do," Josh piped up.

The captain quirked an eyebrow—obviously this was the part of the ceremony about which he'd been prompted. "And you are?"

"I'm Josh." He looked up over his left shoulder. "She's my mother." Then he looked up over his right. "And he's my father."

The captain forgot protocol. "What!"

Laura bit her lip to keep from smiling. Beside her, Rye colored and shuffled his feet.

"She's my mother and he's my father, and I give 'em permission to get married."

The captain gathered his wits and proceeded. "Very well, and are there any rings?"

There was a sudden flurry of activity as Laura pulled open the drawstring of a tiny reticule and the groom—to the captain's utter amazement—pulled a gold wedding band off his finger and handed it to his bride. Then they faced the captain as if nothing unusual were taking place here.

The captain's mouth hung open as he realized the groom would be wearing the same wedding ring again.

"You gonna marry 'em or not?" Josh asked, fidgeting now.

"Oh . . . oh, yes, where were we?"

"Are there any rings," Josh reminded the captain, who harrumphed in an effort to cover his confusion.

"Oh yes, so repeat after me while you're placing the ring on her finger. 'With this ring I take you, Laura Morgan, for my wife, forsaking all others, loving only you, till the end of our days on this earth.' "

Laura gazed at Rye's callused fingers holding the gold band on the appropriate knuckle. His own trembled, as did his voice while he repeated the words of the captain. Then he slipped the gold band onto her finger for the second time in her life.

She took Rye's left hand in hers and held the ring he'd just removed. It still held the warmth of his flesh, captured in the polished gold. She held it shakily while Captain Swain dictated the words again and her subdued voice repeated them.

"With this ring I take you, Rye Dalton, for my husband, forsaking all others, loving only you, till the end of our days on this earth."

She slid the ring on securely and her face lifted to find his pale blue eyes waiting as the captain sealed the union.

"By the power vested in me by the . . ." He took a moment to glance out the cabin window at the shoreline and verify their location. ". . . by the Commonwealth of Massachusetts, I now pronounce you man and wife."

"For once and for all," Josiah mumbled, smiling in satisfaction as his tall, strapping son bent over the woman who lifted her lips for his kiss. He watched the couple part, then break into two of the most beaming smiles Josiah had ever seen as they impetuously hugged each other one more time.

"Well, you goin' t' keep her all t' yourself or y' goin' t' let an old man get in on this?"

While Josiah hugged Laura, Rye shook hands with Captain Swain, but suddenly realized Josh's short stature put him well below the action. Rye leaned down and scooped the little one up.

"I think the bride deserves a kiss from her son." Perched on Rye's powerful arm, the child leaned to kiss his mother. The joy reflected in her face brought a bright smile to his face, too. Her laughter lilted through the cabin before she looked into Josh's eyes and spoke softly. "I think the groom deserves a kiss from his son, too."

For a moment Josh hesitated, his small hand resting at the back of Rye's collar, his other behind Laura's neck, uniting them into a trio. When he moved to touch his rosebud lips to Rye's for the first time, a current of joy swelled the man's heart. Josh straightened, and with their eyes so close together and so very much alike, the two studied each other. The moment seemed to stretch into eternity. Then suddenly Josh's hand left Laura and he flung both arms around Rye and buried his face in the strong neck that smelled of cedar. Rye's eyes closed as he breathed deeply to control the floodtide of emotion generated by the embrace.

The captain cleared his throat. "I believe a little toast is in order, after which I'd be honored to have you at my table for supper. I've asked the cook to see if he can't scratch up something besides stew for the occasion."

Laura and Rye might have been eating sawdust for all they cared. The conversation was sprightly, and the salon seemed much gayer than it had at noon, once Captain Swain announced to the other passengers that he'd had the honor of performing a marriage ceremony. But in spite of the chatter around them, Rye and Laura were conscious of only two things—each other and the time. It seemed to slog by on leaden feet. It took a conscious effort to keep from getting lost in each other's eyes. They were surrounded by people and were approached repeatedly by total strangers offering congratulations. Though it was impossible for Laura to check her pendant watch without being observed, she noted that, more and more often as the evening progressed, Rye pulled his watch out under cover of the table. Each time he snapped its cover shut and tucked it away in his vest, he would move his eyes to hers and she would feel the heat travel up her cheeks. Once as she listened to a female passenger relating an anecdote about a millinery store in Albany, Laura felt Rye's gaze and turned slightly to find him staring at her left hand, which was unconsciously fingering the pendant watch at her collarbone. She dropped the hand immediately and turned to pay attention to the woman. But Laura heard not a word the stranger said, for beneath the table Rye shifted his leg until a long, hard thigh pushed hard against hers, even as he turned to face the opposite direction and answer a man on his far side.

Several minutes later the leg shifted again, and Rye's heel began bouncing in an unconscious jitter of impatience. The motion quivered its way up Laura's leg and increased the heavy-hollow feeling of arousal deep within her.

At a point when she thought her patience couldn't hold out another second, Josh—bless him!—turned to Josiah and put a hand on his arm.

"Grampa, I think we better go check our chickens."

"Aye, I think y'r right, boy. Been lollygaggin' here long enough."

Beneath the table Rye's heel stopped jumping. He stretched his long form up off the bench with a feigned leisure that made Laura smile inwardly, then took her elbow to urge her to her feet. As if I need urging, she thought.

The handshakes and good nights seemed to take a monumental amount of time, but at last the group broke up and the Dalton party filed through the companionway to their quarters.

At Rye and Laura's door, Josiah stopped and gestured at them with the stem of his pipe. "Y' best sleep late in the mornin'. Don't worry about Josh and me . . ." His hand felt for Josh's shoulder, found it, and squeezed. "We'll be busy feedin' the animals."

Josh took the wide, gnarled hand and dragged his grandfather toward the next door. "C'mon, Grampa! Ship is whining!"

"'I'm comin', I'm comin." Josiah let the boy tug him away, knowing a sense of well-being he hadn't felt since the day his son sailed off on the whaleship *Massachusetts*.

Chapter 23

The latch clicked behind them. Laura paused in the middle of the room, Rye a foot from the door. Through the wall came the muffled sound of Josh greeting Ship enthusiastically, answered by two canine yips of excitement, then silence, but for the steady, throbbing beat of the steam engine that churned in the bowels of the boat. They'd left the lantern burning. It swung now above Laura's head, throwing her shadow across Rye's legs, up the wall, and back to his feet again.

Laura studied the narrow single bunks, comparing their inadequate length to Rye's, coming up short by a good six inches. She was slipping the drawstrings of her reticule from her wrist when Rye's low voice came from behind her.

"Mrs. Dalton."

She turned slowly to face him. He stood with feet planted wide apart, knees locked, one hand hanging loosely at his side while the other untied the stock at his throat.

"Yes, Mr. Dalton?" She tossed the reticule toward the bench without bothering to check where it landed. Her heart did a mating dance along her ribcage. Her breath was in short supply.

"Can I make love t' y' now?" He leisurely unwound the stock but let it hang loosely around his neck. Pushing his jacket front back, he hooked it with both wrists and rested wide hands on slim hips. His stance revealed why his foot had been jumping under the table earlier, though he stood now boldly, hiding nothing. The masculine ridge pressed outward up the center of his green trousers, and he watched her eyes travel down to it and back up to his mouth.

"I thought you'd never ask," came the husky reply.

They paused on the brink of forever, tarrying that last scintillating moment to relish the anticipation of the embrace before the embrace itself.

"Then come here and let's get started."

But they moved of one accord, meeting halfway, heart to heart, mouth to mouth, man to woman, in a union preordained by the years through which not even the frowns of fortune had been able to keep them apart. Their impatient tongues met, sleek, silken members joining husband to wife in an oral imitation of what was to follow. His kiss forced her head back against a solid shoulder as he bent low, savoring her taste, texture, and the ever-clinging essence of bayberry trapped in her clothing.

He smelled of fresh linen and the woodsy tang his body seemed to have captured from the furlongs of oak and cedar he'd shaped down through the years.

His body was warm, the flesh resilient within his clothing, as she slipped an arm between loose jacket and tight vest, contouring his wide ribs, then spreading her palm wide over the silk fabric that stretched taut across his shoulder blades as he bent into the embrace.

The months had been long, testing their rectitude time and again. But restraint was no longer necessary, hands need not delay. His moved to cup a waiting breast while hers measured and caressed the warm column of flesh along Rye's stomach.

A grum sound of passion rumbled from his throat while her answering murmur was swallowed by his kiss and the tongue that stroked the satin reaches of her mouth. Their hands began moving and delight to build.

When he moved his head at last, Rye's hand was atop Laura's, increasing the pressure and following her strokes. ''Ah, m' love, I was beginnin' t' think I'd never feel y' touch me again.'' His palm left her knuckles and moved down her yellow skirt, clasping the mound of femaleness hidden beneath layers of cotton. ''Or me you.''

His touch fired her blood and transformed the simple act of breathing into a most difficult labor.

''I thought supper'd never end,'' he uttered against her throat.

''I kept wanting to ask you what time it was.''

Rye's lips brushed Laura's and he straightened her with a deft sweep of an arm. Eyes as blue as the Atlantic's deep waters smiled into those as dark as rich loam. ''Time t' get y' out of that dress, Mrs. Dalton.''

''And you out of that suit, Mr. Dalton.''

He dimpled engagingly and scratched a sideburn. ''Aye, come t' think of it, it has grown a bit uncomfortable.''

''Then please allow me,'' she intoned sweetly, pushing his lapels back over his shoulders.

Obligingly, he turned his back and slipped from the jacket. She tossed it to the bench while he swung again to face her, unhooking the watch fob from its vest button while her eager fingers also moved to Rye's chest. His arm reached wide to place the watch more securely aside while she freed the vest buttons and nudged the garment from his shoulders, heedless of how it fell.

She was reaching for his collar button when her forearms were grasped firmly and held. ''What's y'r hurry, darlin'? You're gettin' ahead of me.'' His rough thumbs stroked the bare flesh of her inner arms, where pale veins seemed to throb beneath his touch. His eyes held blue sparks of impatience that put the lie to his words while he forcibly restrained himself from rushing. Keeping his eyes locked with hers, he kissed first the heel of her left palm, then of the right, before running his tongue lightly along the sensitive skin of her inner arm to the edge of her elbow-length sleeve. He placed her hands at her sides and lifted his own to the row of buttons running from the shallows of her throat to her hips. When the dress was open, he brushed it from her shoulders. It caught on the petticoats at her hips, where it lay forgotten while Rye delicately touched her beneath both earlobes with only the tips of his middle fingers, then ran them with agonizing slowness down the sides of her neck, along its sloping base to her shoulders, hooking the straps of her chemise and dragging them over the alluring curves.

While his fingertips made their journey, her eyelids trembled shut. A breath was captured and held deep within Laura as Rye's feather-light touch sent a hot arrow of fire down her belly. It seemed to pierce some vessel of liquid contained deep within her body, releasing it in a warm, sensual flow of desire and preparedness.

She shuddered and opened her eyes. His were deep and watchful, certain of what was happening within his bride as he sketched invisible tendrils around her collarbone, then over the soft, warm swell of her chest, ending at the lacy top of her chemise. Her hands came up beneath his, and with a single tug, the bow disappeared from between her breasts and the chemise lay reefed around her waist. She grasped the backs of his hands and filled their palms with her breasts, leaning against him with a pressure that still could not quell the almost painful aching in her flesh.

Again her eyelids dropped; her head was thrown slightly back and to one side as strained words whispered past her lips. "Rye, I've thought of this every day since last August. Kiss me, darling, please."

His head dropped forward, and warm lips opened over an ivory globe of flesh, which he lifted and reshaped until its pink tip thrust into his engulfing mouth. He suckled it, bathed it, and rolled the nipple between his teeth before they closed gently upon it. She moaned and grasped his shoulders, pulling back while his teeth held the aroused bud and stretched it. And when the sensations of pleasure bordered on pain, she lunged forward again, moving her shoulders sinuously, making his mouth seek and follow the nipple.

Suddenly he growled, grasping her hips and burying his face against her fragrant flesh, capturing the breast again and holding her still while his hands freed the button at her waist, then pushed chemise, pantaloons, petticoats, and dress into a lemon-colored billow at her ankles.

"Sit down. I'll take off your shoes."

She fell back with a soft plunk onto the cloud of garments and perched there like the pistil in the center of a yellow-and-white daffodil, while he knelt before her and quickly loosened the strings of her shoe, slipped it from her heel, and peeled off her stocking before at last looking up.

"The other one," he ordered, impatient now. It was caught in the waistband of the petticoat, but he freed it, then began baring the foot without a wasted motion.

While he deftly tugged at the strings, she caressed his hard thigh with her bare foot, studying the top of his hair as he bent over his task. "Have you any idea how badly I wanted to make love that day you had me on your lap in the chair?"

He looked up, surprised. "The day y' threw me out," he recalled.

"Yes, the day I threw you out," she said, then went on seductively, "I went to bed that night and pleasured myself."

His jaw dropped. A look of stunned disbelief held his face immobile. Then the shoe thudded to the floor. "After five years y're still full o' surprises."

She turned her knees to one side, rolled to a hip, and leaned nearer him with a palm braced on the floor. "Well, don't tell me you didn't do the same thing plenty of times all the years you were on that whaleship." While she spoke, her hand reached for the buttons of his trousers.

He manipulated his shirt buttons at the same time, grinning down into her face. "I won't deny it. But I thought of y' every time I did it." He grabbed the front panels of his shirt and, with an impatient jerk, thrust it from his shoulders. His grin grew bolder. "I don't think there'll be much need for self-pleasurin' in the future, d' you, Mrs. Dalton?"

"Oh, I hope not."

His trousers were unbuttoned, and he dropped flat onto his rump, began tugging at a long, black boot while her eyes caressed his face. The boot stuck. He muttered a curse, straining at it while she raised on both knees, grasped the ends of his stock in both hands, and hauled him close, then passed the tip of her tongue along his left eyebrow.

"This goddamn boot—" But just then it came free. Immediately, he hoisted the other one up while she went to work on his other eyebrow, nearly forcing him backward as she tantalized him, caressing his eyelids now with her moist tongue tip, moving to the side of his nose, and finally biting his upper lip.

"Do you need some help with that boot?" she murmured, closing her teeth on an unruly clump of side-whiskers, tugging gently before nuzzling her way toward his ear. Her tongue dipped inside, and Rye gave a vicious yank, sending the second boot flying across the room.

He spun on his hips, knocking her flat to the floor beneath him with her breasts crushed under the curled hair of his chest. He grabbed the sides of her head, plundering her mouth with his own, slipping his impatient tongue along her teeth, beneath her tongue, atop it, plunging it again and again with suggestive rhythm.

His disheveled trousers still clung about his hips, but her naked back was pressed to the raw wood of the cabin floor, through which the throb of the engine shuddered. She felt its beat drive up into her muscles while Rye adjusted himself until he fit securely against her length. Somewhere deep in the boat the valves of the steam engine plunged into the pistons and the steady thrum of its power reverberated through the wooden craft with a faint ongoing *ka-thunk, ka-thunk, ka-thunk.*

Laura's arms circled Rye's shoulders and her fingertips caressed each bone along his spinal column as far as they could reach, while Rye's hips began moving in rhythm with the powerful litany of the machinery that could be both felt and heard.

Their movements synchronized as she joined him in a cadence of thrust and ebb, then maneuvered one foot until it caught at the waistband of his pants and began working them down past his buttocks. He reached back to give a helping hand, and when the trousers shimmied from his heels, the soles of her feet silkily caressed the backs of his thighs and explored the hollows behind his knees.

He braced both forearms on the floor, cradling her head in his wide palms, dropping a garland of kisses across her face. "I love y' . . . Laura, Laura . . . all these years . . . I love y' . . ." His hips undulated, finding their complement within her own. Her body lifted in greeting while her fingertips slid along his skull and drew his head down above her own.

"Rye . . . it's always been you . . . I love you . . . Rye . . ." Her moist lips pressed his eyelids closed, adored his hollow cheek, and found his dear mouth once more, knowing its shape, its warmth, its treasure even before it closed over her own.

He rose.

She reached.

He poised.

She placed.

He pressed.

She parted.

He sank.

She surrounded.

To the uncountable and ceaseless rhythms of the universe, they added one more.

Her body opened like an oyster shell, and his silken strokes sought and grazed the pearl within, that precious jewel of sensuality whose arousal unleashed some magical force that fired Laura's limbs. She met each thrust with one of equal might, and together they reached for the reward they had earned with the long winter of solitude.

They were buoyed by love but powered by a lust as rich and demanding as their hale bodies deserved. Laura's teeth were bared as Rye drove into her with a puissance that soon set off the first pulsations deep within.

Unknowingly, she reached above her head, palms pressed flat against the cabin door as the explosions of feeling gripped her muscles. The sensations triggered a shuddering reaction and dotted the surface of her skin in a thousand tiny shivering pinpoints, as a breeze ruffles the smooth surface of a pond.

A growl sounded in Rye's throat as he lifted her higher, his wide hands spanning her hips while Laura's clasped her elbows above her head and the powerful muscles of his arms corded as tight as rigging under sail. He called out an unintelligible utterance of release as he lunged a last time, then shuddered against her, the hair over his forehead quivering for an interminable moment while his tense fingers left ten bloodless stamps of possession on her hips.

Then his arms went lax, his eyes slid shut, and his head dropped forward, open lips coming to rest on her shoulder.

Beneath them, the engine continued to throb. Above them, the lantern still swung. Beyond them, the two-tiered berths remained untouched. She brushed his damp shoulder to recall him from the lethargy into which he'd sunk.

"Rye."

"Hmm?" His weight was a gift that lay unmoving.

"Just Rye, that's all. I always want to say it . . . afterward."

The lips at her shoulder parted, pressed firmly in wordless accolade, and the tip of his tongue wet her skin.

"Laura Adele Dalton," he returned.

She smiled. He rarely used her middle name, because she disliked it. But hearing it now from her husband's lips, it took on a new note, sitting side by side with *Dalton.*

"Yes, Laura Adele Dalton forever."

They lazed in afterglow, thinking of it, until the boards beneath Laura spoke their piece.

"Rye."

His eyes opened and his head came up. "Hmm?"

"This floor is harder than the one in old man Hardesty's loft."

With a smile he pulled her up until she straddled him with their bodies joined. "Mmm, but it works good, doesn't it?"

She looped her arms around his neck and draped herself around him. "Wonderful."

"Y're wonderful. Y're better than wonderful. Y're . . . *stupendous.*"

She laughed silently against his chest. "Either stupendous or stupid. My hipbones are chapped, I think."

He laughed, rubbed the bruised parts, and warned, "Better get used t' it, woman."

She drew herself back and peered up impishly. "Oh, I brought lots of lanolin along."

Rye's teeth gleamed startlingly white behind his wide smile as he chuckled appreciatively. "Nevertheless, hang on, and we'll move t' more comfortable quarters." He locked his wrists beneath her buttocks and she her ankles behind his hips, and he struggled to his feet, then crossed to the bunks.

"Pull the blanket down," he murmured, kissing her jaw, and she leaned sideways in an effort to follow orders, but suddenly her eyes widened and she squirmed against him.

"Rye! You're slipping!"

"Aye, that's the general idea."

"Rye!"

But she squirmed again and they managed to stay together while he backed onto the lower bunk and fell, taking her with him. Unfortunately, when he stretched out, the space fell just short of accommodating his feet. He rolled them onto their sides and made himself as comfortable as possible.

"When we get t' Michigan, I'm goin' t' make us the biggest bed y've ever seen."

She snuggled against him, burying her nose in the thatch of gold hair on his chest. "This one's big enough to suit me."

"Ah no, we'll need an enormous bed for the lazy mornin's when all those young ones come pilin' in with us."

She reared back and stared. "All *what* young ones?"

"Why, all the young ones we're goin' t' have." He caressed her satin hip and buttock. "As often as I intend t' do this with y', I expect there'll be a pack of 'em in no time."

"And what do I have to say about that, Rye Dalton?"

He placed a lingering kiss on the end of her nose, another on the space between it and her upper lip, then on the lip itself. "If y' can say no, feel free to, m' love. But from the demonstration y' just put on on the floor down there, I'd say y' better get used t' knittin' booties."

"Demonstration!" She socked him one on the shoulder. "I did not put—"

His mouth cut off her words. He was smiling, nuzzling, spreading breathy warmth across her chin and lips. "Mmm . . . you were buckin' like an unbroke horse, now admit it, and I thought f'r a minute I'd have t' gag y' t' keep my father and Josh from hearin'."

"*I* was . . . well, what about you?"

"I was feelin' a little like a stallion m'self."

He hugged her close, she squeezed her legs tightly around his middle, and they laughed together. Once again silent, they lay entwined, listening to the beat of the engine, their breathing, an occasional creak of timbers. The lantern light fell across Laura's shoulder, gilding the bone structure of Rye's face, the tumbled hair across his forehead, the swooping whiskers on his cheek, his earlobe, his lips. Studying him, her heart swelled anew with love. She ran her fingertips along the outline of his upper lip, the expression in her eyes softening to reflect a profound depth of feeling.

"Rye, do you really want a lot of children?"

He didn't reply immediately, but looked into her brown eyes and into the past. His reply came softly. "I wouldn't mind. I've never seen y' carryin' my babe." He ran his hard palm across her stomach. "I've thought about it so many times, of how beautiful y'd be that way."

"Oh, Rye," she said almost shyly. "Women aren't beautiful when they're carrying babies."

"You'd be. I know you'd be."

Without warning her eyes stung. "Oh, Rye, I love you so much, and yes, I want lots of your babies."

He saw the tear, touched it with a fingertip, then placed the wet saltiness on his own lips. He drew a deep, uneven breath, spanned her cheek, ear, and jaw with one hand while his thumb stroked her chin. "Lau—" But his voice cracked, and the remainder of her name went unspoken. His strong arms pulled her once more against the hair of his chest, and beneath her ear she heard the racing beat of his heart. "I love y', Laura Dalton, but sometimes it seems like just those words don't say it all. I can't . . . I want . . ." But Rye found himself speechless in the face of an enormous tide of emotions. So he closed his eyes against her hair, his arms around her shoulders, and rocked her wordlessly.

She swallowed the thick knot of love that pushed high in her throat, understanding what he felt, overcome that for Rye it should be as magnificent as it was for her.

"I know, Rye, I know," Laura murmured. "Even now I can't quite believe you're here, you're mine, and we don't ever have to be apart again. I want to hurry, make up for lost time, crowd a thousand emotions into each minute I'm with you . . . and . . . and . . ." But neither could she adequately express this multitude of feelings.

His hand was heavy as it stroked her head. "Sometimes I feel like I don't know what t' do with it all. Like . . . like I'm a glass o' rich wine that's filled right up t' the top, and one more drop and I'm goin' t' spill over."

Words seemed suddenly pale and inadequate, none eloquent enough to relate the splendor they shared at that moment.

But Rye and Laura Dalton were mortal, and thus they held within their bodies the ideal manifestation of the emotion whose description eluded them. It needed no words. It required no verification. It simply happened, in all its wonder, in all its glory.

His body hardened, still within hers. And hers became liquid as it sheathed him. Their eyes, those windows of the soul, met and clung as she rose to meet him. She was lithe and passionate, and he, tensile and deep, while they moved harmoniously in the expression of love that supersedes all others. The act—this wondrous gift bestowed by nature—said all their hearts were feeling.

Rising and falling, like the engine that drove them through the Atlantic toward a new home, Laura understood fully what Rye had meant the day he'd asked her to go to the Michigan Territory. Home was not Nantucket, not Michigan. Home was the essence of love, one heart residing within another.

She felt the pulsations begin deep in her body and the last and longest possible reach of his body within her own, and beneath her palms his skin grew damp.

They shuddered.

They dissolved.

They were home.

Chapter 1

The wedding rehearsal was scheduled for 7:00 P.M. Winnifred Gardner opened the door of St. Alphonsus Catholic Church at ten after. Hoping to slip in unobtrusively, she was dismayed when a howling gust of March wind caught the door and whipped it out of her hand, then sent it thunking against the brick wall before swirling inside the vestibule, announcing her tardiness to everyone. Muttering a curse, she tried to hold the hair out of her eyes with one arm while recapturing the stubborn door with the other.

There must have been fifteen people in the vestibule, and every face turned to note her late arrival. Bride, groom, priest, servers, parents, groomsmen, ushers and bridesmaids all watched her rush in, breathless, smelling like old Earl Evvsvold's garage floor and looking as if her hair had been styled with his air hose.

Sandy Schaeffer—tomorrow's bride and Winnie's dearest friend—left Father Waldron's side and hurried forward, smiling.

"Winnie, you made it!"

"Sandy, I'm so sorry I'm late, but my car—"

Sandy waved away the explanation. "It's okay. The organist isn't here yet, either, so we've just been talking over the procedure before we walk through it." Sandy reached impulsively for Winnie's hand but had barely touched it before it was sharply withdrawn.

"Don't touch me! I stink like gas. Oh, I hate those pump-your-owns!" Winnie sniffed her fingers, grimaced and hid the hand inside her coat pocket just as a stocky brown-haired man joined them.

"There she is! The maid of honor." He plopped a platonic kiss on Winnie's cheek.

"Hi, Mick. Sorry I'm late. Everything went wrong tonight."

"No problem. We just got here ourselves."

Winnie assessed Sandy's prospective groom—a sturdy convivial man of Polish descent, who'd made his fiancée the happiest woman in Brooklyn Park,

Minnesota. There were times when Winnie envied them immensely for sharing "that certain something" so elusive and necessary to a truly special relationship. They laughed often, teased each other and shared so many common interests. Mick draped an arm around Sandy's shoulders and grinned down at her while Winnie began moving away toward the washroom.

But Mick stopped her and crooked a finger at someone. "Hey, Jo-Jo, come on over here." A man turned from his conversation with Mick's parents, raised an index finger, turned back to the couple to excuse himself and approached.

He clapped Mick's shoulder. "What's up, Ski, my man?"

Mick Malaszewski slapped his friend's shoulder and caught Winnie's elbow with his free hand. "I guess it's about time you two met. Jo-Jo, this is Winnifred Gardner, Sandy's maid of honor. Winnie, this is my best man and my best friend, Joseph Duggan."

Jo-Jo. How many times had she heard the name? A firm square hand captured Winnie's before she could warn him to beware of gas. But a moment later she forgot all about warnings, except that of her own heart as she heard again the pleasant tenor voice, rich with expressiveness.

"So this is Winnie. It's about time I met the woman I'm going to walk down the aisle with." He covered the top of her hand with his other and gave her a smile to match that in his voice.

He was nothing at all like what she'd expected. Not as tall, not as crude, not as brooding. Somehow the name Joseph Duggan had conjured up a tough thuggish sort, a longshoreman, maybe, with a wild Irish temper and a burly body. Instead, Jo-Jo was a toned and tapered five-feet-ten, had a head full of wild fluffy brown curls and the most twinkly eyes she'd ever encountered. His hand was dry, hard and very commanding. And as Winnifred placed her left hand atop his, she forgot the engagement ring upon it.

"Joseph," she said simply. "It seems as if we should have met years ago after all I've heard about you."

"I'll second that. I've heard plenty about you, too, and it appears none of it was quite true."

"Oh?" She cocked her head inquisitively.

"They've been holding out on me." For a moment his eyes flickered down to her mouth, then back up. Winnie suddenly realized how warm, personal and extended the handshake had become. She jerked free and leaped back a step.

"Oh, you're going to stink like gas! I'm sorry! I ran the pump over just a few minutes ago while I was filling my . . . my car, and I got it all over my hand and on my shoe and my cuff, and I was going straight to the ladies' room to get rid of the stench, but I never got the chance and—" she raked her hair with four fingers "—and the wind practically tore my hair out, roots and all. I have to . . . to comb it."

"A pity," he teased.

"A pity? Why, I look like a disaster, and I . . . I didn't—" She stumbled to a halt. *Winnifred Gardner, why ever are you prattling,* she thought while Joseph Duggan watched a becoming blush inch its way up one of the most charming chins he'd ever seen, then pass an exquisite mouth whose lips had dropped open in surprise. He lifted his eyes to her beguilingly disheveled hair. In the muted amber light it appeared to be the color of peanut butter. Large wide eyes stared at him momentarily before she did the most amazing thing: she blinked . . . but with only one eye! It was the most unusual nervous reaction he'd ever seen. And it *had* been a nervous reaction, and it *had* been a blink, not a wink. For a winking face uses more than an eye to flash its message. This was a blink, pure and simple, but he'd never in his life seen anyone do it so charmingly.

Her eyes flickered down to his Adam's apple, then away from him entirely, and he let his gaze wander downward. *Her name doesn't fit.* Winnifred Gardner sounds like a supercilious prude with lineage and laureateship. Instead, the woman before him seemed to blend the shyness of Winnie-The-Pooh with the conditioned body of Superwoman, and the whole bundle smelling like gas.

Joseph Duggan was enchanted.

"You have a few minutes yet. Father Waldron is still socializing over there."

Winnie clapped her mouth shut and whirled toward the hall leading to the washroom. Behind her, she heard Jo-Jo Duggan's voice chiding Sandy and Mick. "*Where* in the blazes have you been hiding her all these years?"

In the clean silent lavatory she doused her hands liberally with pink liquid soap and scrubbed furiously. After rinsing, she gave them a critical sniff and disgustedly began soaping again. This time she worked a thumb roughly over her knuckles in an effort to get rid of the smell. In the process she cut herself on her diamond ring. The swift sting of the soap in the cut brought her back to her senses.

Winnifred Gardner, act your age. He's just teasing. And obviously a flirt. He probably said what he did just to see how you'd react, and you came through with classic feminine witlessness!

Still, when she checked her reflection in the mirror, her cheeks held two bright patches of flustered blood, and her eyes were a little too sparkly, her lips quirked up in a grin that told how great it felt—witless or not—to be flirted with.

She removed her coat and caught it over one wrist, scrutinizing her dress. It was a pale mauve shapeless thing that came alive when its belt was cinched. She smoothed the wool over both hips and recalled Paul's words: "Well, well, a dress. What do you know about that?" If he hadn't prefaced his compliment with that wry remark, she wouldn't have become so piqued. But by the time he'd got around to adding, "You look great, darling," the effect had been ruined. Next he'd dropped his eyes to her high heels, given a mock-lurid grin followed by a growl as he buried his face in her neck, whispering his intentions, had she not had to leave at that moment. Still stung by his earlier remark, she'd pushed him away and given him a conciliatory kiss instead of the dressing down he deserved. It wasn't as if she *never* wore dresses!

Winnie pushed aside the memory, stooped to wipe the dull spot where the gas had splattered the toe of her black-patent high heel. She felt uncomfortable in both dress and heels, but what else was a woman supposed to wear in a church to practice walking on a white linen runner on the arm of a best man?

Back in the vestibule, Winnie felt his eyes following her as she slipped between Sandy's mother and father to greet them warmly, looping a hand through each of their arms.

"Why, Winnie, I didn't see you come in. Did the dress arrive?" Ann Schaeffer inquired.

''All hemmed properly and ready to go. And how about at your house? Any last-minute complications?''

''None. Everything's ready for tomorrow.''

''But I'll bet you're both exhausted.''

''I confess, we've—''

A shrill whistle cut through the vestibule and echoed in the cavernous nave beyond the open double doors: Mick calling attention to Father Waldron, who began filling everyone in on the opening part of the service. As he talked, he entered the main part of the church, and the wedding party followed.

Winnie moved toward the door, conscious that Joseph Duggan awaited there to escort her inside. She avoided his eyes until the last minute, then lifted her gaze to find him with a scintillating sparkle still in his eyes and the flirtatious expression on his lips. For the first time she realized why his buddies called him Jo-Jo. *That* name fit. While commandeering the coat from her arm, he gave her hair the once-over.

''I liked it better messy, Winnifred Gardner, and there was something a little offbeat and amusing about a girl wearing gasoline for perfume. But anyway, may I?'' He presented his right elbow in courtly fashion, still grinning devilishly as they moved inside.

''Thank you, and no thank you, Mr. Duggan. I'm not certain if I've just been insulted, laughed at or both. But I can walk perfectly well without your elbow while I'm deciding.''

His grin became dazzling, and without a glance aside he dropped her coat in the last pew, then took a rather deliberate grip on her elbow as they moved toward the front pews.

For the next five minutes Father Waldron outlined the procedures and rituals of the wedding service, explaining that both bride and groom had elected to walk up the aisle with their respective parents and have the attendants do so as pairs. Winnie had known this, of course, but had scarcely given it a second thought until now, seated on a hard wooden pew with Jo-Jo Duggan's knees sprawled wide, one of them only a scant inch from her own. He straightened, turned more fully in Father Waldron's direction and hung his wrist on the pew behind her.

Not only a flirt, but an *accomplished* flirt!

The door at the rear of the church slammed, and scampering footsteps clicked up the aisle, causing every head to turn.

There stood a birdlike woman, pulling black gloves from her fingers, clutching a portfolio against her coat front. ''I'm sorry, Father. I would have been here sooner, but somebody fed my cat beer and got it drunk and. . . .''

The rest was drowned out by laughter, and the twittery woman became more flustered. Father Waldron's voice echoed in the empty church. ''Lent just being over, the cat probably needed it, Mrs. Collingswood.''

Beside Winnie, Jo-Jo Duggan's chest shook with laughter, and his eyes glinted as if he himself might very well have pulled such pranks once or twice in his day and sympathized not with the cat, but with the prankster.

''We're ready for the music whenever you are, Mrs. Collingswood,'' Father advised benevolently.

''Oh . . . oh, certainly, Father.'' Her footsteps carried through the church again, then became a series of muffled thuds on the stairway at the rear. There followed a silence, the rustle of sheet music and a few testing notes.

Within minutes Winnie found herself walking beside Joseph Duggan toward the rear of the church. Father Waldron directed the proceedings like an elementary teacher at a school play, while everyone awaited instructions and cues.

Standing in the shadowed vestibule, Winnie covertly studied the best man more carefully. He was dressed casually, as were most of the men present. His Levi's were dark and new and creased. They fit snugly across lean hips and partially concealed clean new tennis shoes with a neat blue wave curling along their sides. Beneath a light-weight spring jacket he wore a button-down shirt of pale yellow. While listening to the priest, Duggan stood with feet widespread, firmly planted, both his hands slipped into his rear pockets. The stance pulled his open jacket aside, revealing a sturdy chest and hollow belly. Through the thin cotton of his right shirtfront she saw the dim image of a nipple. His other was hidden behind a breast pocket pressed flat against his chest. Father Waldron gestured, and Joseph Duggan's head swerved to follow the pointing finger. His profile was startlingly attractive, and she wondered why, for he had the kind of face that would still look seventeen when he was fifty, a vernal combination of features contrasting oddly with his physically fit five-feet-ten frame and the dense whiskers that must—she was sure—require two shaves a day if he had evening appointments. His nose was slightly upturned, rather short, and his forehead unmarked by frown line or blemish. The amber lights gilded the top of his girlish locks, which fluffed out just enough to obscure his hairline and touch the perimeter of his shiny forehead. For a moment Winnie wondered if she'd ever touched the hair of a man who possessed such curls. Not that she could recall. Paul's hair was feather cut to ultimate perfection, never out of place, always blow combed away from his face and held lightly in place with hair spray. She was accustomed to Paul's fastidious ways and found the breezy natural look of Joseph Duggan's unfettered curls arresting. She'd always thought curly-haired men rather effeminate looking. But there wasn't a square inch of Jo-Jo Duggan that was effeminate. Shorter by a good two inches than most men she'd dated, shorter than Paul by at least six, he had a sturdiness that compensated for the difference in height.

Perhaps it was the stance that caused her eyes to sweep his length and linger longer than was prudent: shoulders back, chest out, athletic, self-assured and perhaps a slight bit cocky.

Or maybe she gave him the twice-over simply because he was so different. Different from Paul.

He turned, caught her studying him and flashed a smile that transformed his face into a tableau of charm. He did it so effortlessly she wondered how many hearts he'd broken with no conscious intent. He smiled more with the right side of his mouth than the left, but with every volt of candle-power his eyes possessed. He had the most beautifully matched set of eyebrows she'd ever encountered, and when the lids beneath them lowered and crinkled at the corners, his smile was devastating. Bedroom eyes, some women called such as these, with their dark spiky lashes and that killing little flicker of teasing that would probably be present were he kissing the ring of the Pope of the Holy Catholic Church!

It glittered out of the nearly closed lids now as he turned and moved closer. "Looks as if you and I come fourth."

"Fourth?" She jerked awake, realizing she'd been preoccupied and had missed what Father Waldron was saying.

"In the wedding procession."

"Oh!"

"We head out when Jeanne and Larry get halfway up the aisle in front of us."

"Yes, I know." But she hadn't known. She'd been too busy assessing Jo-Jo Duggan to pay attention. "We'd better get behind them, then."

The vestibule was crowded, everyone conversing softly, when the talk was brought to a halt by the resounding chords of *Lohengrin's* Wedding March. The traditional song was a surprise in today's upbeat world where everything from the Beatles to John Denver was used as wedding music. The staunch fortissimo chords had a legend of power and tradition that vibrated not only through the ceiling over Winnifred Gardener's head, but right through her body.

Her head snapped up, and her eyes met those of Joseph Duggan.

"I think that's our song," he said, offering his elbow. The grin had softened but was still on his face, disarming. "This time you have no choice."

Her eyes dropped down to the cream-colored sleeve of his jacket, and a queer premonition joined the body vibrations already scintillating along her nerves in time to the music. *Touch him, and you're a goner.* The flower girl and ring bearer were being coaxed up the aisle, then the first pair of attendants had reached the halfway spot. Winnifred looped her hand on the crook of Joseph Duggan's arm and let him lead her to the double doors.

It was disconcerting, being so drawn to a total stranger. The sleeve of his jacket was cool, but as her hand rested upon it, the warmth of his skin seeped up and made her aware of how solid his flesh was within. He stood with feet firmly planted, watching the couple ahead, waiting. Winnie was on his left, thus it was her right ringless hand resting on his elbow. She experienced a discomfiting jolt of guilt at the thought that she was glad she didn't have to expose her left hand just yet. There was a smell about him she couldn't identify, something purifying, but not perfumed. A utilitarian soap, maybe, mixed with fresh air and the faint odor of dye, as if it were the first time he'd worn his blue jeans.

A twitch of his elbow made her look up into his face. "Ready?"

She nodded.

"On three, then, starting with the left."

They concentrated on the couple ahead. "One . . . two . . . three," she whispered. He pulled Winnie's hand against his ribs as they took their first step down the aisle.

It was the first time Winnie had been asked to act as a maid of honor. It was oddly disquieting. Why ever was she feeling so much like a bride? Programming, she supposed. Weren't all little girls programmed to respond to the song now beating upon her ears? Weren't they all taught to think of growing up in terms of "walking down the aisle"? Women's liberation had done virtually nothing to sway women's minds away from dreams of all that was traditional when it came to weddings.

She watched Jo-Jo Duggan's walk for the first time from the very distracting angle of top to bottom. His unblemished tennis shoes made not a sound, but his crisp jeans crackled slightly, and within them his thighs pressed as firmly as air against the inside of a balloon. To her surprise he strode not with the haughty athletic swagger she might have expected after his stance in the vestibule but instead moved with relaxed poise, almost as if strolling in time to the music instead of marching to it. He had superb rhythm.

''How am I doing?'' he whispered.

Her eyes flew up to find him grinning down at her.

''You must be a dancer.''

His grin shifted to a wince, and he whispered, ''Hardly.''

''Well, maybe you should be. You have impeccable timing.''

''Thank you, Ginger. Next time I'll bring my top hat and cane.''

She nudged his ribs and hissed, ''Shh. Not here, Fred.''

They'd reached the chancel rail and followed the verbal and hand directions of Father Waldron, separating and taking their places on either flank.

Turning to face the pews, Winnie watched Mick approach. She liked the fact that he and Sandy had chosen to walk up the aisle with their parents—Mick first, so he could be waiting when Sandy arrived to be given over from the arm of her father. She herself had never known a father and would be disinclined to walk up the aisle with her mother.

Just before Sandy reached the chancel, Winnie glanced across at Joseph and found his eyes resting steadily on her, as if they'd been there for some time. He smiled briefly, then looked away, and the rest of the instructions began. When they'd walked through the ritual of the bridal service itself, the attendants were instructed to file into the front pew, again in pairs, for the remainder of the Nuptial Mass.

Winnie and Joseph were seated side by side, their hips separated by a few scant inches of hard wooden pew. His upper arm brushed hers, and she felt him glance at her when she crossed her arms to end the contact.

''Are you Catholic?''

She looked up in surprise. ''Of course. Why?''

''Just wondering. I am, too, but I've never been too comfortable sitting through all this hoopla our church puts on at weddings. Reminds me of a carnival.''

She smiled at her lap, trying to imagine him sitting through it dressed in a tux and ruffles. Somehow the picture didn't fit.

Just then Father Waldron raised his voice toward the choir loft. ''And that will be my cue for you to begin the recessional, Mrs. Collingswood. Attendants, you'll come and take your places beside the new bride and groom before the final wedding march begins.''

They lined up along the front of the church again, and this time when the organ boomed its call to exit, Winnie and Joseph met in the center aisle with a chuckle, a smile and the sense of growing familiarity such routine practices often generate.

They walked through the entire service once more before the entourage again clustered in the vestibule, and Mrs. Malaszewski reminded everybody that the groom's supper would be served at their house as soon as everyone got back there.

"So you drove, huh?" Winnie found Joseph Duggan again at her side, this time holding her coat. Slipping it on, she wished she could say no, just to see what he'd suggest.

"Yes . . . remember the gas?"

"Yes, I remember. Too bad, or we could ride over to Mick's house together."

"Well, in any case, I'll see you there."

He opened the exterior door, and a blast of wind nearly knocked her back against his chest. Instinctively he took her elbow as they ran down the steps together, her coat flapping back across his thighs, and her hair slicked straight back from her face. In the parking lot he stopped her with a forceful pressure of his thumb in the hollow of her elbow.

"If you get there first, save me a place next to you."

The wind worked its way inside his jacket and ballooned it out. He dropped her elbow and reached to raise the zipper higher up his chest. The curls on the upper right-hand side of his skull were forced flat, while her own collar-length hair blew across her mouth and eye. She stood in the wind looking up at him, wondering what to reply, knowing she wasn't permitted to encourage him, yet answering, "And if you get there first, save a seat for me."

"It's a promise. Only don't comb your hair this time!"

"I. . . ." A strand of it whipped into her open mouth. "What?"

He'd started jogging away but turned and jogged backward five steps while calling, "I said don't comb your hair this time. It looked great when you first walked into church!"

Some off-tempo warning slanted through her heart. *Beware. He's an inveterate flirt and a practiced flatterer. And you're only walking up the aisle with him by accident. In three short months you'll be walking up the aisle for real!*

The groom's dinner turned out to be served buffet-style, but the dining-room table was extended as wide as it would go, and when Winnie took her plate and sat down, Joseph Duggan followed. He swung his leg over the seat of the chair as if it were a barbed-wire fence he was climbing over and deposited before himself a plate that needed sidecars to hold all the food he'd heaped upon it.

"Aw, you combed it," he chided, then sank his teeth into a slab of sliced ham.

"Mr. Duggan, do you always flirt with every girl you meet within five minutes of meeting her?"

"Was I flirting?"

"It's only a rough guess, because I'm really not up on the subject, but it felt like it to me."

"You're not up on the subject? A girl with your face and—" his eyes flickered downward, not quite reaching her breasts before starting up again "—hair?"

She ignored his continued flattery and commented, "Yes, I combed my hair. It looked like an explosion in a silo."

"Never." He assessed the subject of the discussion. "And it's pretty. A really pretty color and length."

She felt out of her league. "There you go again."

"You call that flirting?"

"Well, isn't it?"

He lifted a glass of milk, took three enormous swallows, ran a thumb along one corner of his mouth—and all without removing his eyes from her hair. When at last they dropped to hers, he replied, "No, just a compliment. I like your hair, okay? What are you so defensive about?"

It was the perfect opening. She lifted her left hand, pressed her thumb against the inner platinum band of the engagement ring so the stone stood out away from her fourth finger. "This."

His eyes dropped, and for a moment there was no change in his expression. "Oh, I see. Well, you can't blame a man for trying." She rested her hand on the edge of the table, and without warning he picked it up, studied the modest diamond at very close range and surprised her by carrying it to his mouth, tilting his head and pretending to bite the rock. Drawing back, he continued holding her hand while grinning engagingly. "Damned if it isn't real," he said softly.

She burst out laughing but left her hand where it was. Inadvertently his tongue had touched her fourth finger and left a tiny spot of skin damp at the knuckle. It seemed to burn now as he studied the diamond and fingered it with thumb and index finger. He glanced up and bestowed that teasing little-boy grin. "Some guys have all the luck."

Reluctantly she withdrew the hand and began eating again. But she could feel his eyes on her time and again in between the moments of attention he gave to his plate.

"So, when's your big day?" he asked.

"Only three months away. The third Saturday in June."

"Ah, a June wedding, no less."

"Yes, we've had the date picked out for almost a year."

"You and—?"

"Paul Hildebrandt."

"Paul Hildebrandt," he repeated thoughtfully, then filled his mouth with potato salad. When he'd swallowed, he studied her askance. "So, what's he like?"

"Oh, he's. . . ." She drew circles on her plate with a celery stick. "He's ambitious and extremely intelligent, and very easy on the eye." She sensed that Joseph Duggan had stopped chewing, so quirked a quick peek at him from the corner of her eye.

"Naturally," he grunted sardonically, "he would be good-looking."

"But then, maybe I'm biased. You'll meet him tomorrow, and you can see for yourself."

"He'll be at the wedding?"

"Yes, though he only knows Sandy and Mick through me. He wasn't part of my old college crowd. I met him after I graduated."

"From the University of Minnesota?"

"Uh-huh. I went there, too, at the same time as Sandy and Jeanne and Larry and some of the others."

"That makes you. . . ." He squinted an eye while doing mental calculations. "Twenty-four years old."

"Twenty-five. And how old are you?"

"Twenty-seven."

"And I take it you're not married, nor considering it?"

"Absolutely not."

"And there's no . . . girl friend coming with you tomorrow?"

"There's a *girl friend*—" he mimicked her pause perfectly "—but I'm not sure if she'll make it back in time. She's gone to South Dakota for a funeral."

"Nobody close, I hope."

"An aunt."

"Mmm. . . ."

They fell silent for a moment. Their plates were empty. Winnie carefully wiped her mouth and more carefully avoided eye contact with the man beside her. But after some moments curiosity got the better of her, and she turned to find he'd been sitting with an elbow propped on the table, jaw to knuckle, studying her for some time. Discomfited by his close scrutiny, she groped for a conversational diversion.

"What's her name?"

"I have no idea."

A puzzled frown puckered Winnie's eyebrows. "You have no idea what your girl friend's name is?"

He laughed and seemed to force himself out of a deep reverie long enough to stop staring. "Oh, I thought you meant her aunt. My friend's name is Lee Ann Peterson, but I wouldn't really call her a girl friend. We've been seeing each other, that's all."

"And what's she like?"

He squared his shoulders and pressed them against the cane-backed chair. "Like all the rest." Did he pronounce that rather wearily, she mused. "A little bit smart, but a lot more dumb. A little on the ball, but often vague. Not quite as mature as she should be for her age and kind of scatter-brained." He glanced at Winnie sharply, as if owing her an explanation. "These are only impressions, of course. I don't know her well enough."

"And what does she look like?"

He flashed his devilish grin. "She's got a great body."

Winnie felt herself blushing. He hadn't passed his eyes down her torso, but she felt as if he had, for comparison's sake.

"You're a body man, then?" she ventured, trying to cut him down with a note of cool disdain.

A wicked glint sparkled in his eye. "Yes, as a matter of fact, I am. You see I have this—"

"Spare me, Mr. Duggan." She lifted both palms and held her eyes closed for a full five disgusted seconds. "I'm not interested in the graphic details."

"You didn't let me finish . . . Miss Gardner. I was about to say I have this little shop in Osseo where I refurbish old cars. Two of my brothers are in it with me, and sometimes when we buy a wreck, there's plenty of bodywork to be done."

She covered her eyes and groaned, then peeked from behind her fingers. "I think I've been adequately put in my place."

"No, it was my fault. I deliberately made the comment about bodies. I'm sorry."

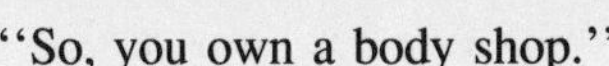

"So, you own a body shop."

He tipped his head aslant and puzzled silently. "Mmm . . . sort of, but not specifically. We do bodywork to earn money, but our labor of love is restoring classics."

"You mean like '57 Chevys?"

"No, mostly older, *classicker* than that. Right now I'm restoring a '54 Cadillac pickup."

"A Cadillac *pickup?* They never made pickups," she stated suspiciously.

"Oh, yes, they did. They used them as hearses for funerals. 'Flower cars,' they were called, and had rollers on the bed to roll the casket on."

"And where does one find such jewels?"

"In farmers' fields, at antique auctions, places like that. I bought this one from an old duffer up in Brooten, Minnesota, and it was in pretty decent condition. She's turning out to be a beauty—four hundred cubic inches and a V-8 engine, and—" Suddenly he cut himself off, then shrugged. "Well, you're not interested in that. I get carried away when it comes to cars."

She found it pleasant to be with a man who got carried away with something more understandable than computers. Duggan's eyes had danced with enthusiasm as he'd spoken of the collector's item he prized. But now he turned the conversation over to her.

"Tell me. What does the lucky Mr. Hildebrandt do?"

She was beginning to understand: flirting and flattery were second nature to this man. They scintillated from his eyes and rolled from his tongue with an effortless mindless ease. More than likely he was scarcely conscious of employing them so often. Ignoring his last ego tickler, she answered only the sensible portion of his remark.

"He's in computer work. They call him an 'optimizer.' He solves all the long-running problems nobody else has been able to solve. He's sort of a wizard, I guess you'd say."

"And how about you?"

But now she couldn't resist the temptation to tease. The subject was simply too opportune. "Well, I'm in bodywork, too." The grin had already begun climbing his attractive cheek when she hurried on. "But I work with human bodies. I'm a physical therapist at North Memorial Medical Center."

"An odd combination—a computer man and a physical therapist."

"No more odd than a body man and a—what is she again?"

"A hostess at a Perkins Pancake House."

"Ah," she breathed knowingly, laying a finger along her rounded cheek. "A hostess."

"Do I detect a supercilious note?"

Winnie was abashed to realize he had, so rushed to deny it. "Not at all. I was just . . . well, making small talk. After all, she. . . ." But suddenly Winnie had the surprising urge to tell the truth. She met Joseph Duggan's eyes directly, hoping she looked properly contrite. "Yes, I confess. I *was* being supercilious. I get it from my mother, whose main goal in life has been to succeed. And success to her is career. I find myself at times mirroring her—shall we call it, her middle-class disdain for the careerless multitudes? And when I catch myself at it, I hate it. But underneath I don't really think I'm as bigoted as I sound when I make comments like that. I sometimes think I've been programmed by mother to say things, whether I mean them or not.''

It was one of the first times she'd seen Joseph Duggan's face neither smiling nor teasing. It reflected only deep thought, then a straightforward study of her own face, ending with a glance at her forehead and hair. His deep brown eyes returned to her sapphire blue ones with a look of approval.

''You're remarkable.''

''I'm. . . .'' She chuckled and shook her head, glancing at her lap self-consciously, for this time she thought his compliment sincere. ''I'm not remarkable at all. I'm very ordinary and filled with flaws. That's only one of them I just foolishly blurted out.''

''Foolishly? I wouldn't call it foolish. I'd call it honest, and a little humble. Not many people assess their motives with that kind of clearheadedness. Is your . . . Paul Hildebrandt as honest as you?''

She met his eyes again, surprised at how she suddenly hated to recall that there was a Paul Hildebrandt while in this man's very enjoyable company. Guilt immediately followed, making her sing Paul's praises perhaps a little too vehemently. ''Oh, yes! He's not only honest, he's hardworking, successful and bound to give me an absolutely secure life.''

Joseph Duggan studied the clear-eyed blond woman whose first appearance had captivated him thoroughly. Throughout the pleasant meal with her that first impression had only been magnified. She *was* a remarkable woman—pretty, shapely, intelligent, the tiniest bit shy and the tiniest bit bold, honorable to her man and honest about herself.

But dammit, she was spoken for!

Chapter 2

Winnifred Gardner wasn't a morning person. She usually had to claw her way up from sleep like a person brushing thick spiderwebs aside while ducking through an abandoned building. The next morning, however, she came awake as if a light had been turned on directly above her face.

Joseph Duggan, she thought, staring straight at the ceiling. *You're going to see him again today! You're going to walk down an aisle with him. You're going to be photographed beside him. You're going to share the head table seated side by side with him. You're going to dance with him.* She smiled, recalling that he'd claimed to be no dancer. She found that hard to believe. He was one smooth mover was Joseph Duggan. In more ways than one, she suspected.

The thought brought her up sharply. Whatever was she doing, lying here at six in the morning, woolgathering about Joseph Duggan when she was engaged to marry Paul Hildebrandt in three months?

Paul. He'd promised to make it to the wedding today, and she was holding him to it! Why couldn't he get it through his flawlessly groomed head she didn't give a tinker's damn whether or not they had a furnished living room by the time they got married? Or even the house he'd insisted was a prerequisite. He was living in it already—so proud of the fact that he'd managed to provide it for her even before the big day. But the house wasn't enough for Paul. He'd taken on contract work to earn extra money for all the worldly goods he told her she deserved, and had installed a computer terminal in one of the three bedrooms, where he often worked Saturdays and evenings, rapping away at the keyboard that produced all the mysterious solutions to problems she could not grasp, in a language she could not understand and in methods that made her feel ignorant when he tried to explain them to her.

But he'd promised: today he'd be with her at the wedding *and* the dance.

With that reassuring thought she got up, concentrating on Paul and the pleasant surprise in store for him when he saw her in *the ultimate dress*. If he complimented her today—and he'd better—she promised herself she'd accept it at face value and not search for ulterior meanings.

The day was clear and sunny, but by ten in the morning the March winds had picked up again. The bridesmaids were all meeting at McLean's Beauty Shop to have their hair done into Gibson Girl hairdos.

When Winnie studied the finished results in the mirror, she knew instinctively Paul would glow with admiration when he saw her. He was as old-fashioned as a man could be when it came to women and femininity, and though it was often a burr under her saddle, preferring as she did casual clothing for her active personality, today Winnie could face him in a hairdo, hat and dress that would please him tremendously.

But—oh—it *was* a flattering hairdo. The style was chosen by Sandy to accommodate wide-brimmed straw hats, thus Winnie's streaked blond hair closely contoured her skull, lifting in the semidroopy Evelyn Nesbit coil that circled her entire head just within the hairline. She touched the puffy doughnut-shaped roll. Inside, a resilient "rat" added fullness. It felt foreign but not altogether alien. The dramatic change in her appearance made her smile at herself in the mirror and feel suddenly very, very impatient for two o'clock to arrive.

Shortly before noon Winnie stepped out of the bathtub, dried her freshly shaved legs, briskly toweled her belly, breasts and arms but stopped dead when she caught the reflection of her hair again in the mirror. She leaned closer, touched the loose tendril coiling upon her temple and decided to go the rest of the route and apply makeup in keeping with the same tradition as the hairdo.

But first she flapped a puffy mitt up one side of her body and down the other, liberally powdering her skin with the scent of Chanel No. 5, one of her few daily concessions to femininity. She was wild about the scent! She wondered what Joseph Duggan would think of it, but the sight of her naked puckered nipples made Winnie chide herself for caring *what* he thought. She had no business pondering the man's likes and dislikes, yet he'd been slipping into her mind, unbidden, all day.

Her new underwear—pure white—was again a nostalgic trip into the past, for the merry-widow bra cinched her waist and flared at the cutaway hips with boned stiffness that few modern-day women experience. But the confining strapless support garment was necessary, owing to the styling of the bridesmaids' dresses Sandy had chosen.

Winnie wasn't certain, when she'd finished applying her makeup, whether she'd done the right thing. The plum eyeshadow and darker penciled undershadings duplicated the look of the women pictured on old tin Coca-Cola trays, as did the apple-cheeked look she'd created with bright blush. But it was the lips she studied critically. She'd used cherry red lipstick and an applicator brush, etching the upper lip with exaggerated peaks, then narrowing the corners of her mouth until it took on the Cupid's pucker of Miss Clara Bow. Maybe Paul was right—she ought to dress up more often. It felt marvelous!

She slipped on an everyday dress and then packed up her gown, dyed-to-match high heels, hat, makeup and hair spray, and glanced out the window to find the wind still bending the leafless treetops at a forty-five-degree angle. With a silk scarf wrapped around her precious hairdo she ran out to the taxi she had called.

Racing up the steps toward the church door ten minutes later, she felt a thrill of anticipation—Joseph Duggan was probably inside already. Would she run into him in the vestibule the moment she stepped inside? Well, if so, at least she didn't smell like gasoline this time! But dammit, she didn't want him to see her with this scarf clutched around her head like a babushka.

But the vestibule was empty except for the florist's delivery man and one of the ushers, still clad in blue jeans and sneakers, his tux in a bag over his arm.

The two dressing rooms were situated just off the vestibule, and when Winnie opened the door to the women's, everything was excitement. Sandy was there already, as well as one of the bridesmaids, Jeanne, and right behind Winnie entered the other, a cousin named Jacqueline. Lighted mirrors reflected long plastic bags, women in half-clothed states and a bride with a bad case of the jitters.

"Oh, Winnie, thank God you're here! I've been higher than a North Dakota kite, worrying that everyone wouldn't get here on time or that the flowers would be late, or the photographer would forget his camera or—"

"All right, Sandra Schaeffer, calm down! None of the aforementioned calamities is going to happen. All of us are here now. The photographer is setting up his equipment inside, and the flowers are already in the vestibule."

As if on cue, there came a tap on the door, and a gray-haired woman poked her head inside. "Anybody in here getting married?" Then she swept in, bearing a broad flat green box, followed by a series of concealing purple bags, and before she left, the excitement had heightened considerably. Mothers and the flower girl soon arrived, adding to the festive nervousness.

The four young women donned their dresses, growing more fluttery and exhilarated with each passing minute.

Sandy was in pristine white, of course, but each of the others wore a different pastel hue: Jeanne's powder blue; Jacqueline's daffodil yellow; and Winnie's that most feminine of colors—pink.

Stepping into the ankle-length gown, Winnie caught the scent of Chanel, drifting up to her nostrils as she lifted first one foot, then the other, and slipped them inside the shimmery taffeta underlining over which the body of the dress was fashioned of organdy. Its skirt was pure vintage 1910, fitting snugly at the waist and hip, then flaring to a bell-shaped hemline that revealed her pink satin pumps with tiny straps across the instep, secured by a miniature pearl button on the outer side of each foot. The bodice of the dress was of simple spaghetti-strap styling, but its elegance was created by the loose transparent lace over-bodice that attached in a drooping fashion at the waist, then covered the chest to the throat. In the back it was hooked only once—at the nape—then gaped open in a long slit to the waist. Its sleeves were shaped much like the skirt—belled, loose and slightly slithery. The hat—that crowning touch—was of pink open-weave straw, a wide-brimmed leghorn style not entirely in keeping with the 1910 look, but utterly feminine. It had a pink silk rose nestled where crown met brim, and matching ribbons circling the crown, then streaming behind to the waist. While Sandy went gloveless and carried white gardenias, her attendants wore white gloves and held small wicker baskets of spring flowers whose colors coordinated with their outfits: one of purple iris, another of lemony jonquils, and the last—Winnie's—of blushing pink hyacinth whose fragrance was nothing short of overwhelming.

The two mothers, as well as grandmothers, nieces and flower girl, were all busy pinning on corsages. In the last-minute flurry Winnie caught a lingering glance at her own reflection.

It was crazy, she thought, standing here gawking at herself and wondering what Joseph Duggan would think when he caught sight of her, yet that's exactly what she was doing. The muse made her heart flutter as if *she* were the bride, and when the call came to exit to the nave for group pictures, she placed a hand over her heart, then realized her palm was sweating within her glove.

She picked him out with the surety of a wild bird seeking its life mate within a flock of thousands. Stepping out into the vestibule, she faced a cluster of masculine backs, most of which were garbed in jet black. Even from behind, Joseph Duggan stood out, identifiable by his well-proportioned build and those dark brown curls. He stood with one hand in his trouser pocket, the vented tail of his tuxedo jacket caught on his forearm, tugging it aside to reveal a wedge of taut black fabric stretched across his flat backside. He was speaking to another man, gesturing with his free hand, which was covered halfway to the knuckles by a tier of white ruffles that sprouted from beneath his black cuff. Another band of white showed above his collar, and the relaxed curve of his knee was accentuated by a narrow stripe of black satin that crooked down the side of his trouser leg. His hand clapped the other man on the shoulder, and he laughed. The sound seemed to shimmy its way between Winnie's thighs and her sleek underslip, raising little ripples of pleasure.

Mick approached the pair of men just then, appearing like a snowy swan among crows, dressed totally in white, his tuxedo jacket sporting knee-length tails at the rear. Yet Winnie scarcely afforded him a glance. Her eyes were fixed upon the black-clad figure of Joseph Duggan as he swung to face the groom, and the two clasped hands, exchanging words too low for her to hear across the murmurous distance between them. Mick drifted away, and Joseph turned in her direction, his eyes slowly scanning the vestibule.

He homed in on her as surely as she had him, his eyes advancing no farther once they found hers. Something tight and restricting gripped her chest. A weightless sense of expectancy buoyed her stomach, and her heart danced hollowly against her ribs. His lips dropped open, and his eyes swept to her feet and up again. The hand came slowly, slowly out of his pocket. Then he smiled, and something sizzling and exciting exploded in her heart. Oh, that smile! That wondrous killing smile! She *hadn't* imagined its brilliance. It was as blinding as ever.

He shouldered his way forward immediately, excusing himself as he rested his hand on a woman's shoulder, gently nudging her aside, all the while holding Winnifred in his gaze.

He approached with both hands extended, palms up. "My God, you look beautiful!"

She gripped the basket in one hand but gave him her other. He pressed it between both of his palms, and she watched in fascination as he bent forward to kiss it. But finding it clothed in the white glove, he kissed instead the back of her wrist, just above the cotton. His lips were warm, his breath moist, and the back of his head a dark mass of ringlets as he bent to her and lingered.

By the time he lifted his eyes and straightened, she was the color of the flowers in her basket.

"Why, thank you, kind sir. And you look—" she braved a hurried sweeping glance "—dashing!" She tried to keep her voice steady, but telltale tremors made it quiver.

"Are you afraid?" he asked and looked down at her hand, working it now between his own. "You're shaking." He galvanized her with his stunning eyes again while squeezing hard on her glove.

She withdrew reluctantly from his warm hold. "Oh, it's just . . . just excitement! Aren't you excited?"

His eyes danced mischievously—around, above, then into hers. "Absolutely," he returned softly. And she was forced to turn away when his dark brown pupils settled upon her bowed red lips and stayed there. He watched her relentlessly—she could feel it—even though he stood at ease, a hand again casually draped inside his trouser pocket. She was conscious of the faint scent of incense and that of candlewicks, and the ever-present aroma rising from the sweet spring flowers resting against her trembling stomach. When she could stand it no longer, she gave in to the irresistible compulsion and turned to study him, though common sense warned her not to.

Whatever Winn had expected him to be wearing, it was not black. Most groomsmen wore baby blue, gray or rich nutmegs these days. Yet she thought she would never again believe black a drab color after seeing it stretched across the muscles and limbs of Joseph Duggan. It set off the froth of snowy ruffles at his chest in an utterly masculine manner. The crisp black bow tie made his sturdy neck look even more manly, and the skintight stretch of black vest was as tempting as a shadowed haunted house, inviting exploration in much the same way as forbidden, yet compelling things are wont to do. Her eyes were drawn to the deep U-curve low upon his midsection, where black abutted white as he again held the left panel of his jacket back, hooked behind his ruffled wrist.

''Did what's-his-name see you dressed like this?'' he asked unsmilingly.

Her startled eyes swerved to his. ''Paul. His name is Paul. And no, he didn't.''

''So I take it he's not here yet.'' He glanced around, but his gaze returned to her as if there were no help for it.

''No, of course not. But he'll be here for the service.'' She fidgeted with the handle of her basket, suddenly wondering if the pancake hostess had made it back last night. ''Did what's-her-name see you dressed like that?''

''*Her* name is Lee Ann, and no, she didn't get back yet that I know of. And even if she had, she wouldn't have seen me. We don't live together if that's what you're asking. I live in an old house in Osseo with my two younger brothers.''

She felt the heat rising up her chest once again, staining her chin and cheeks. ''I wasn't asking that.''

''No, I suppose you weren't. But now you know just the same.'' Was it her imagination, or had his shoulders squared defensively? He had skewered her with a look that demanded she raise her eyes to his, but she took refuge in staring at the basket of hyacinth.

''Are you going to tell me, or not?'' he demanded quietly, studying her averted face.

Her eyes flew to his. ''Tell you what?''

''If you live with him.''

''I don't think it's any of your business.'' Then why was her heart flailing around like some wounded bird?

''You're absolutely right. But I'm asking, anyway.''

She considered lying just to set him in his place, but in the end couldn't. ''No, I don't. He lives in the house we'll be living in once we get married, and I live in my own town house on Shingle Creek Parkway.''

It hadn't been her imagination: he had straightened his shoulders, for now they relaxed noticeably as he released a pent breath.

''Everybody to the front of the church now, and we'll take the group pictures!'' Winnie nearly sighed aloud when the call of the photographer released them from the tension that seemed to dominate both her and Joseph Duggan today.

At the open double doors he touched the holy-water font and crossed himself, just as she did, but he did not offer his elbow. They walked in businesslike fashion up the aisle, just as all the others did, then submitted themselves for juggling, posturing, sucking in and holding breaths, presenting left shoulders to the viewfinder, then right shoulders, then backing off so the bride and groom could be photographed by themselves.

Winnie looked across the way to where the groom's attendants awaited further instruction. Joseph was staring at her as if puzzling something out, and she turned to whisper a trumped-up question in Jeanne's ear just so she wouldn't have to confront his eyes.

The photos at the altar were done, and the photographer herded them back to the women's dressing room where he shot the bride with her mother and father, with the flower girl and quite naturally with her maid of honor. There was the traditional pose of Sandy displaying her ring while Winnie lightly held the bride's palm and admired. But the photographer had asked her to remove her gloves, and she was devastatingly conscious of her own diamond winking up at her reprimandingly. The sequence of shots seemed to go on endlessly, while several of the groomsmen lingered in the doorway, watching. Joseph didn't even bother disguising his obvious fascination with her—he came right in and stood propped against the back wall, watching the session with keen interest.

There followed the old showing-off-of-the-garter shot, then the photographer bellowed, "Who's the best man and maid of honor?" Winnie's eyes sought Joseph's, and he boosted himself away from the wall. "I'd like a shot of the two of you together. Over here, against this simple background." And they found themselves nudged, pulled and manipulated into positions that pleased the photographer's compositional eye. There was one shot of Joseph bending over to sniff her hyacinths. In the middle of the pose he ruined it by sneezing—and everyone in the room burst out laughing, which managed to relieve some of the tension spinning between Joseph and herself. But it returned in full force when the photographer backed her up against Joseph's chest and asked him to place his hands on her waist.

To Winnie's surprise the man behind her not only spanned her hipbones with his hands but pulled her back flush against his trouser front. She had a flashing forbidden thought that she was nestled against him at a very accommodating height—and yes, he *was* several inches shorter than Paul, and she immediately felt the intimate difference.

The photographer asked her to lift her chin and turn her jaw slightly toward Joseph's. The juxtaposition of their faces brought her into the realm of his after-shave, a totally rich and masculine scent she'd never smelled before. Once, while they stood that way, she heard him swallow.

Then, to her relief the torture was over. The photographer went off to get the flower girl and ring bearer, and Winnie drifted out to the vestibule, trying unsuccessfully to put Joseph Duggan from her mind. But during the relatively short time between then and when they were hustled into hiding so the guests could convene, he remained in her mind's eye, whether within view or not.

The next time they met, the church was filled, the organ was rumbling overhead, and the vestibule was silent of even the most secret whispers. She was vividly aware of how intimately he had pulled her against himself only a few minutes earlier and found it extremely difficult to meet his eyes. She held back, waiting until the last possible moment to join him and take his arm. Finally he came across to her and silently reached for her elbow, a sober expression robbing his eyes of their customary glint.

The organ belted out the opening strains of *Lohengrin,* and he urged her into line behind the lead couples. She felt herself acquiescing with a stiffness that had somehow overcome her since the picture-taking episode. But when he released her elbow and found her hand, then tucked it securely into the folded warmth of his black sleeve, she knew a forbidden delight at the warmth radiating from inside the crisp gabardine.

The flower girl and ring bearer stepped onto the white runner, and she felt

Joseph cover her fingers on his arm, then squeeze them as he whispered, "I'm sorry, Winnie. I had no right."

If only he hadn't said that! If only he'd left things as they were! If only she could have walked up the aisle upon his arm with hostility simmering in her veins, everything might have been all right. But instead he had to go and apologize, and make her look up into his unsmiling brown eyes and see how genuinely he meant the apology. And it was at that precise moment it happened. Something fine and compelling and all-encompassing, a certainty that this day was destined to change them both in ways neither wanted nor welcomed.

Yet they were drawn to this place and time by forces beyond their control, with the organ playing a wedding march, and themselves clothed and coiffed in their regal best, stepping onto a white-lined center aisle, each of them trembling just a little and knowing beyond all certainty they should not be.

There is that about a wedding that compels and sweetens and woos like nothing except perhaps the sight of a newborn babe. It is as magnetic as the poles, as undeniable as gravity and as captivating as the quest for love. During the next hour and twenty minutes, while Winnifred Gardner and Joseph Duggan witnessed the marriage of their two dearest friends, murmured the vocal responses and heard the exchange of vows between bride and groom, that magnetic force worked upon them, drawing their thoughts solely to each other, trapped as they were in vulnerable roles.

The priest paused just before asking Sandy and Mick to repeat the vows after him and asked all married couples present to join hands and silently renew their own wedding vows, and reaffirm their own acts of faith.

For Winnifred and Joseph there were no spouses with whom to reaffirm vows. But their eyes locked and held, and bore no smiles, nor twinkles, nor hid the unquestionable fascination each held for the other. It was there. It had been born. And it flamed and burgeoned while the wedding vows were spoken. *To love . . . to cherish . . . all the days of my life. . . .*

Everything was different when they reached the vestibule this time. It was joyous, celebratory and spontaneous. The bride and groom received a broadside of kisses from their closest relatives, while attendants, too, became swept up in congratulatory embraces. Winnie was fleetingly aware of being ensconced in Pete Schaeffer's arms and of receiving a tearful kiss on her cheek from Ann, another from Sandy and still another from Mick. But it was the inevitable full-length hug from Joseph she carried away in memory.

In all the confusion she missed Paul somehow, but Joseph's arm contoured her shoulders nearly all the time, and momentarily he squeezed her waist and said, "I'll be right back for you."

Then he disappeared along with the other groomsmen, while the wedding guests spilled through the open double doors onto the sunny steps of the church portal. Then Joseph reappeared at her side, grabbing her hand and pulling her out on the heels of Sandy and Mick, through a spray of rice and smiles and cheers to a waiting line of cars out front.

Joseph ran, towing her along, but Winnie planted her feet and dragged on his arm at the sight that greeted her.

"Wh-what's this?"

Sandy and Mick were already packing her voluminous white skirts into the back seat of a square black automobile with a running board, bug-eye headlights and a rectangular rear window. Behind it there were three others, each at least fifty years old.

"Vintage automobiles. Come on!" Joseph tugged on her hand, and before she could get more than a fleeting glimpse of gleaming maroon paint and a spare tire mounted on the cowl just behind the high curved crown fender, she found herself whisked toward the car. Her foot was directed not to a running board—nothing that modern—but to an individual metal foot plate. Inside, the roof was high, and there was ample space for her wide-brimmed hat, though the car was only a two-seater. As her door was slammed, she turned to find herself confronting a horizontally split windshield, its top half hinged to create a wind deflector when pushed outward.

Joseph jogged around the hood with its distinguished ornament, then clambered up beside her, smiling and reaching to depress a button on the instrument panel, setting the engine to life.

It was difficult to keep from giggling in delight. The steering wheel jutted up at a stern awkward angle, and Joseph looked tall and proper and straight as the engine rumbled beneath the pleated leather seat. Winnie couldn't swing her head around fast enough to take it all in. Her eyes shone with excitement as she turned to her escort.

"Where in the world did you get this?"

"In my grandma's and grandpa's chicken coop."

"It's yours?"

"Since my grandma died, it is. I belong to a classic-car club, and I talked a few of the other members into offering their jitneys for the wedding today, but as you can see, they all agreed with one stipulation: that they drive them themselves."

The cars pulled away from the church, heading toward the main drag of Brooklyn Park, a wide four-lane commercial street named Brooklyn Boulevard. Winnie peered at the lead car. Through its rectangular rear window all she could see was Sandy's and Mick's heads—they were kissing. Craning around, she noted they were being followed by another shining vehicle of estimable age and condition, a stranger at its wheel. With a broad smile and an excited voice Winnie touched the wedge-shaped rear quarter window that gave the car a rakish roadster profile. Out the front she studied the rounded hood, the cowl lights on either side of the windshield and the tips of the side-mounted spare tires. She looked up to find mohair upholstery overhead and reached up to caress it in reaffirmation.

"Oh, this is absolutely beautiful! What is it?"

"A 1923 Haynes Sport Coupelet."

"I adore it! Why, it's perfect! I mean—" she shrugged expressively "—I feel as if we fit right in. I in my Gibson Girl hairdo and you in your elegant tuxedo. Straight out of *The Great Gatsby* or something. Except you really should have your dust coat and goggles."

He laughed—a deep rumble as smooth as the engine beneath them. "Oh, shoot, sugar pie, I forgot them at home. Next time."

"Where are we going?"

"Up and down Brooklyn Boulevard to toot and wave."

"Are we *really?*" Her voice rose excitedly.

"What's a wedding without a noisy procession?"

Just at that moment the lead car sounded a horn. It bleated out a raucous *a-oooga* before Joseph touched something on the dash that added to the blaring announcement of their coming. They passed Park Center High School, fast-food shops and gas stations and the city bank, while from the parking lots of McDonald's and Burger King teenagers turned from their prized vans and pin-striped Trans Ams to gawk in admiration at the procession of high-riding relics that paraded past.

They made an eye-arresting sight, chugging along with the sun gleaming off their vented side panels and spoke wheels: a 1932 Model B Ford in gleaming black; Joseph's own glistening '23 Haynes-55, whose original color he called "burgundy wine maroon"; a 1936 Plymouth in deep dark blue; a shiny black '22 Essex Coach with turtleback luggage compartment and drum headlights.

Laughter bubbled up in Winnie's throat as she saw heads snap around and mouths drop open all up and down Brooklyn Boulevard. She couldn't resist waving a hand at an awestruck teenager who was pointing a finger at them.

Turning, she beamed at Jo-Jo Duggan. "I suppose this was your idea."

"Mick's and mine. We decided to surprise you all."

"Oh, what fun! I've never ridden in anything like this before."

His eyes left the street for a moment to scan her lacy straw hat that threw dapples across her cheeks. "You look as classic as my car, Winnifred Gardner. Please wave some more to draw attention to the fact that I've drawn the prettiest girl in the wedding party."

It was uncanny, this wellspring of reaction his compliments unearthed. Perhaps it was the festive tenor of the day that made her respond so heartily with gay laughter and a tilt of her hat brim. Perhaps it was a release from the building tension surrounding her own wedding plans. Whatever it was, Winnie felt free and ebullient as they spent the next half hour riding proudly above the mundane modern vehicles going about their Saturday afternoon pursuits, looking too refined, too sleek and too powerful next to the charming '23 Haynes and its three contemporaries.

Winnie found herself totally relaxed as the minutes slipped by. She studied Joseph's profile as he told her stories about his grandfather, who had owned an auto dealership and had accepted this car as a trade-in during his early years but had never really driven it. Instead he had locked it in his chicken coop and allowed it to become his private obsession, coveted and polished, but never used. Only after the death of Joseph's grandmother three years ago had the car come out of mothballs—and then only on very special occasions and certainly never when the winter streets were spread with destructive salt.

The sun had turned warm. The sense of expanding familiarity and burgeoning acquaintanceship spun an ethereal web about the handsome man in his ruffles and tux and the dazzling young woman at his side.

Laughter came readily, and a certain amount of cavalier flirtation was inevitable. She found herself turning to glimpse his strong blunt fingers on the wheel with new interest, his jaw and mouth with forbidden curiosity.

"Isn't it odd that we've never met before?"

He turned, studied her silently, then nonchalantly returned his gaze to the open field beyond the city offices and the library on the outskirts of the suburb where it joined the corn and potato and gladiola fields at the edge of Hennepin County. The procession had broken up now, and the Haynes was purring along on its own.

''Yes, considering how long we've been friends with the bride and groom. I've known Mick since we were in elementary school, but then he went to the U and I went to Vo-Tech.''

''And I've known Sandy since high school.''

His eyes wandered back to her for a brief glittering second, then he looked away again. ''Well, now that we've met, Winnifred Gardner, there's nothing we can do about it, is there?''

It was a startling question and raised a shiver of apprehension up her arms. Yet she could not be tempted to indulge in spring fancy regarding this man. ''I think it's time we headed for the reception. It'll be starting in—do you have a watch?''

He lifted a hand from the wide thick steering wheel and pushed up a ruffled cuff to reveal a winking gold watch. The gesture was at once commonplace, yet captivating. It scared her, her gut reaction to such a simple movement.

''It's nearly four-fifteen.''

''We have to be at the reception hall by five, and I've left my street clothes in the changing room at the church.''

''We'd better head back, then.''

He pulled into a side road and wheeled into the start of a U-turn. She watched his neck as he craned to check the stretch of road behind them. When he turned suddenly and caught her studying him, she shifted her attention to view the rank and file of dried ivory cornstalks marching across an unplowed field to their right.

One car whisked past, then another. It grew silent, and she turned to see what was holding them up. But Joseph was no longer checking behind him for traffic. He was staring at her.

''We've lost the others,'' she announced unnecessarily.

''Just as well.'' His hand fell to the shifting lever between their knees, and he nudged it into neutral. ''Because there's something I've been wanting to do all afternoon.'' Her heart and blood sounded the alarm, but with a smooth commanding movement he slipped one arm around her shoulders, the other to her ribs, and pulled her close. He dipped his head to avoid the wide brim of her straw hat, still it all happened so fast she hadn't a thought of resisting until it was over.

He kissed her with a soft exploratory pressure that was rife with inquisitive speculation. His lips were hard, warm, and remained closed for the most part. The compelling contact lasted perhaps ten seconds, and during the last five her hand pressed his lapel more in surprise than resistance. Just before he pulled back, his lips parted to bestow a swift wet stroke of his tongue across her mouth, encountering the seam of her lips and the ivory texture of sleek teeth within. Her lips dropped open, but too late to encourage or to allow the kiss to become more intimate or lengthy.

His dark sparkling eyes were very close. His lashes caught chips of sun and threw them into her eyes. The brim of her hat touched his curls.

"Joseph . . ." she whispered upon the wings of surprise. "You mustn't do that." She treated him once again to that unconscious one-eyed blink that made him believe her the most charming creature he'd ever laid eyes upon.

"No one ever calls me Joseph. To my friends I'm Jo-Jo. To my brothers, Joey, and to most people, Joe. But I love the way you say it—Joseph."

Inanely she repeated her words of a moment ago, struggling for composure and a return of calm heart. "Joseph, you mustn't. . . ." Pressing his chest, she felt his heart thudding.

"I know. But you musn't move your lips along with the wedding vows when they're being pronounced and stare at a man with those irresistible blue eyes, either."

"I didn't. . . ." Again she blinked, a slow-motion flutter of a single eyelid that captivated him. But she tipped her head aside slightly as a newborn smile began to play upon her lips. "Did I?"

He dipped out from under the brim of her hat but kept one arm around her shoulders, his other hand gripping her upper arm, keeping her turned partially his way. The shadows from the wide-brimmed bonnet flickered beguilingly across her nose and forehead. A strand of hair rested in a gentle coil against her temple. He inserted his finger into the lazy curl, and it gripped him like the clinging finger of an infant. "And who were you thinking of as you whispered the words?"

Her lips parted, and the tip of her tongue peeked out to wet the full upper one, but she remained silent, staring up at him.

"Paul Hildegard?" he prompted.

"Hildebrandt," she corrected in a rather dazed breathless voice.

"Hildebrandt, then."

"No, not Paul Hildebrandt."

He touched the end of her nose with a fingertip. "How naughty of you, Miss Gardner, and only three months before your wedding to the man."

She pressed her palm firmly against his lapel and eased away. Though he released her, his shoulder still curved in her direction. "Who?" he insisted quietly.

She dropped her eyes to the flower basket on her lap. "I wasn't thinking of anyone. I was concentrating on the words. They're very beautiful."

His left hand moved. Its forefinger curled, then pressed lightly beneath her chin until she was forced to tip it up. For a moment his eyes danced merrily into hers, then he accused, "Why, you little liar."

"There are times, kind sir, when lying is the wisest choice."

His eyes darkened thoughtfully. He stroked the hollow beneath her lower lip with his thumb—slightly rough on her fine skin—then his hand fell away, and he turned to put the car into gear. The road was clear, and he headed back toward town.

"You're right, of course. So will you lie to him about what just happened?"

"I . . . there'll be no reason. He'd have no reason to ask."

"Was he there this afternoon?"

"Yes."

"And he'll be at the reception?"

"Yes."

"Then I'd better be careful around you, hadn't I?"

She didn't know what to reply or what to make of him. He was utterly direct. She'd never encountered a person as straightforward as he before. It seemed impossible to combat the barrage of reactions he could unleash by such blatant innuendos as his last. Even though such words rolled from his tongue as glibly as quicksilver and sounded like the practiced lines of an actor, he was devastating, this best man with whom she'd been paired for the day. And Winnie knew, she, too, had best watch her step.

"You'll be pleased to know Paul isn't the jealous type."

"What type is he?"

She mused while they cruised southward on Zane Avenue. "He's logical. Computer nuts tend to be that way. If he can't feed the facts into his terminal and come up with a black or white answer—either yes, there's reason to be jealous, or no, there's none—he'll take the logical sensible route and not be."

"God, he sounds like a bore."

"I should resent that, Joseph Duggan."

"And do you?" He turned to chart her expression as she answered.

It rattled Winnifred to realize she'd had to think for a minute before deciding. "Yes. Yes, I do!"

"Wonderful! That's the first sign of a healthy relationship between you and your fiancé that I've seen yet."

"Don't make assumptions. You don't know anything about our relationship since you've never even met him or seen us together."

"But I will on both counts before the day is over, won't I? What do you say we pick up this conversation at the end of it and see where we stand on the subject?"

"I'll be with him at the end of it, so don't wait around for me when the dance is over."

"In that case, remind me to steal a kiss sometime in the middle of the evening when he's not looking. The one I just got wasn't nearly good enough."

Her jaw dropped, and she smacked him on the arm. "Why, you arrogant, assuming . . . rake!"

His head dropped back, and he laughed with full-throated amusement. "*Rake?* God, I haven't heard that word since I saw my last Errol Flynn movie." With characteristic aplomb he captured her left hand and pressed it possessively to his thigh while she tried to yank it free. "Come on, don't get skittish. You look pretty enough for this rake to want to—what's the word—ravish? But I can hardly try it in the middle of a busy four-lane street in broad daylight, so let me console myself with your hand."

"That hand, Mr. Duggan, is wearing another man's engagement ring."

"And I'll turn you over to him as soon as we get to the reception. But in the meantime, quit pulling away."

She stopped resisting and let him hold her gloved hand palm down on his right thigh. His leg was firm and warm, and she knew she should withdraw, but it felt very pleasant, if very naughty, experiencing the flesh of a different man beneath her touch. He was much, much harder than Paul, and his thigh was larger in circumference, yet shorter in length. Realizing she'd been measuring the difference was unsettling. She tried to free her hand, but to no avail. He held it firm.

"Does he dance?" Joseph's eyes never left the road.

"Divinely."

"That won't work."

"What won't work?"

"I was thinking about stopping in there and catching a quick dancing lesson so I'd be one up on him in that department, anyway." He nodded toward a sign for the Gloria Allen Dance Studio as they passed it, then asked abruptly, "Does he smoke?"

"No."

"Mmm . . . we're even on that score. Is he rich?"

"He will be someday."

"Shot down again!" He eyed her askance. "Just how handsome is he?"

She growled suggestively, and he muttered a curse.

"Is he a good kisser?"

"Mmm . . . the best." She applied a slight pressure to his thigh for good measure.

"And how is he at—" His hand slipped from hers to clasp her thigh.

"Joseph Duggan, you cut that out!" She returned his hand to his own thigh, ignoring the pleasant tingle his teasing touch had brought.

They arrived at the church parking lot then. The other three cars were already there as Joseph pulled to a halt and killed the engine. He hooked an elbow through the steering wheel and turned to her.

"All right, then, a last resort—does he like dogs and cats and babies?"

"Babies, and that's all that matters." She was enjoying herself immensely by this time. They laughed lightheartedly, then Joseph threw a hand at the mohair upholstery overhead and barked in mock self-castigation, "God, is there anything the man hasn't got?"

She simpered, knowing she shouldn't. She gave him a coy pout, knowing she shouldn't. And even as the answer escaped her lips, she knew beyond a shred of doubt that she was shamelessly flirting. She peered up from beneath her darling hat brim and replied, "Yes . . . a 1923 Haynes."

Chapter 3

The wedding reception was held in a beautiful restored turn-of-the-century house with three stories of corniced gingerbread, wraparound porches, upstairs verandas, cupolas and a grand total of eight bay windows. It was called the Victorian Club, and inside was as evocative of a bygone era as was its immaculate white exterior and latticed backyard gazebo.

Arriving at the Victorian Club where all the wedding guests were waiting, Winnie experienced afresh the phantasmal sensation that for this day she was someone other than Winnifred Gardner, contemporary woman, careered, affianced. Indeed, everything today seemed to tug at Winnie's heart-strings and urge her into a fanciful state of déjà vu, as if she'd been dressed for the part intentionally by some omnipotent force so it could sweep her back to a time she formerly knew.

The four cars pulled to the curb in front of the stunning architectural eye-catcher, and as the wedding party disembarked from the high old-fashioned seats, laughter and gay badinage spilled into the warm afternoon.

Winnie reached for her door handle, but Joseph was right there to stop her with a quick hand on her arm. "Wait!" Immediately he was out his side and around to hers. The foot block was narrow, and as she turned in her seat to search it out with her high heel, Joseph's hands came up, catching her about the waist and swinging her down beside him. His hands were sure and lingered a bit longer than prudent. Was it her imagination, or had he intentionally swung her down too swiftly so her hip collided with his stomach? If so, he took scarcely a moment to savor the contact before turning her by an elbow toward the walk.

Merrymakers had noted their arrival, and a throng of them rushed from the house to encircle and accompany the bride and groom inside beneath a shower of rice, while Winnie and Joseph ran at their heels.

The house was decorated with lush antiques, its oaken floors varnished to a high gloss, and its ceiling-to-floor casement windows topped off by eyebrow sashes and decorated with antique sheer lace curtains that let the daylight stream inside. An elegant staircase curved up from the enormous central entry hall, and wide sliding double doors were rolled back on either side of the generous area, vastly expanding the space where the dancing would be done later. The dining room was at the rear of the house just off the kitchen, which was the only room closed off to guests, for it had been converted to meet modern standards of efficiency for the accommodation of large groups such as today's.

As Winnie stepped inside with Joseph's hand at the small of her back, she caught her breath at the setting. Something here called to her heart, and she turned to Joseph with an appreciative gaze in her eye. ''Isn't this place—'' she glanced up the thick red runner on the curved stairway ''—evocative? I was with Sandy when she first came to see it, and I was so afraid she might not choose it.''

''Yes, it's really beautiful.'' But his eyes made only a cursory swing past the ballroom-width entry and sweeping stair before returning to her as he spoke the words.

''Now, Joseph, you promised.''

''I did? What did I promise?'' His hand moved caressingly on her back.

''You said you had to watch yourself today, didn't you?''

''Ah, yes, but does that mean I can't admire the scenery?''

She laughed into his glinting eyes, then the two of them turned and ambled toward the rear of the hall, his hand still riding the shallows of her spine. ''Do you know what my first impression of you was when I met you last night?'' she asked, gazing at the ceiling's domed windows.

''No, what?'' He admired the arch of her neck as she looked up.

''That you are a consummate flirt, and that I should take everything you say with a grain of salt.''

It was his turn to laugh. ''Define the term *consummate,* if you will.''

She shrugged, thought about it for a second and made a vague gesture toward the heavens. ''Consummate . . . you know.'' Again she beamed him a grin. ''Perfect.''

''The perfect flirt? Is that how you see me?''

''You see? You're doing it again. Perhaps the word I should have chosen was *incorrigible* flirt.''

''I think I like consummate better. It sounds sexual, and it's nice to think one woman finds me perfect in some way.''

Just then a voice spoke behind them. ''Winnifred, dear, there you are.''

At the sound of Paul's voice Winnie spun around, pressing a hand to her thumping heart, wondering if he'd heard Jo-Jo's last remark, certain he'd seen Duggan's hand lingering on her waist. It took an effort to keep her voice light and lift her cheek for Paul's kiss while Jo-Jo looked on.

''Oh, hello, Paul. I'm sorry I missed you in the church lobby, but things were so hectic. We were swept outside before I could catch my breath.''

Jo-Jo Duggan watched as the tall perfectly groomed man slipped his hands around Winnie's ribs and dipped his head to kiss her briefly on the cheek. ''You . . . look . . . sensational, darling.'' As he straightened, his head caught the brim of her hat, and her hand flew up to hold it on.

''Do you like it?'' She smiled at the prepossessing man whose blond head towered above hers by a good ten inches.

''Like it!'' Hildebrandt backed off and ran his eyes down to her hem and back up again. ''I love it. The hair and the hat—'' he captured her hands and squeezed them for emphasis ''—and the dress.'' Once more his eyes dropped to assess her more feminine points while she wished Jo-Jo would politely refrain from watching every place Paul touched her and looked at her. ''You look ravishing.''

From the corner of her eye she saw Jo-Jo grimace, and felt a thrill ripple along her skin. She returned the pressure of Paul's hands and turned him toward her escort. ''Paul, I want you to meet the best man, Joseph Duggan. Joseph, this is my fiancé, Paul Hildebrandt.''

They shook hands. ''Hildebrandt.'' Joseph nodded.

''Hello,'' Paul greeted simply.

''So you're the lucky guy, huh?'' Jo-Jo transferred his amiable smile from Hildebrandt to the woman on his arm. ''She's been talking about you a lot while we were out doing the after-wedding joyride.''

''Oh-oh. I'm probably in trouble.''

''Not at all. Everything she said was highly complimentary.''

Hildebrandt's eyes rested on his betrothed, then made another tour of her appealing hairdo and hat. It suddenly irked Joseph Duggan to watch the man assessing her as if she were a pink-and-white striped parfait in a stem glass, and he'd just been given a spoon. Hildebrandt surprised Duggan by returning, ''Today it looks like you're the lucky man, escorting her when she's dressed like *that.*'' Then with scarcely a glance at Jo-Jo the suave executive type turned the maid of honor away by her arm. ''I'll bring her right back. I have to talk to her for a minute.''

Joseph watched the ''computer man'' commandeer Winnifred Gardner's elbow and appropriate her. Hildebrandt was dressed in an impeccable three-piece suit of proper navy blue, accompanied by the expected baby blue shirt and striped tie of muted wines and gray blues. His haircut looked like something out of *Gentleman's Quarterly,* and his shoes were polished like mirrors. As the pair turned away, Hildebrandt's arm slipped around Winnifred's shoulders, and he pulled her up tightly until she was tipped against his ribs and hip. Her face was raised and wearing a radiant smile as he spoke down at her, then she replied and together they laughed.

The sight of them that way made Duggan want to drive his fist into the wall.

''There's got to be some private corner where we can hide for a minute,'' Paul was saying.

''To what end, Mr. Hildebrandt?'' Winnie teased coquettishly.

He hauled her hip against his, and his hand rode higher up her side, almost to the armpit, fingertips extended toward her breast. ''Find me that corner and I'll show you.''

She laughed and they rounded a corner, then walked down a broad central hall and eventually came upon what must have been a butler's pantry in its day. Pushing open a swinging door, they found a long narrow room with built-in glass-doored cabinets on their left, bearing wide storage drawers for linens and silverware. There was another swinging door at the far side of the walk-through and to their right a broad window rising from a waist-high counter top to the twelve-foot ceiling. The blue sky beyond was framed by an arching tangle of ivy vines, bare of leaf now, but swollen with buds.

When the door swung closed behind them, Paul confiscated her basket of flowers, set it aside with careful deliberateness, then circled Winnie with both arms, pulling her securely against his body as he dropped his head to kiss her and pressed her hips back against the rounded edge of the ivory-painted cabinet below the window. ''Mmm . . .'' he murmured as his tongue slipped seductively into her mouth, which opened willingly. His head moved, and his hand pressed the side of her breast, then kneaded it firmly.

''Mmm . . .'' she echoed into his mouth, smiling beneath his open lips, running her hands over his smooth back.

He lifted his head and backed away only enough to see her but still held her prisoner between himself and the cabinet. "If you look even one-quarter this tantalizing on our wedding day, I'll have a hard time keeping my hands off you in front of the entire congregation."

She ran her fingertips demurely under both of his lapels. "Well, now, wouldn't that be something? The unflappable Paul Hildebrandt, losing control. I think I'd like that."

"I'm far from unflappable where you're concerned, and you know it."

She kissed his chin. "Not in public, you're not. Otherwise you would have kissed me back there in the entry instead of sneaking off into this pantry with me." Was it a subconscious wish to show Jo-Jo Duggan her fiancé desired her that made Winnie voice that comment? She pushed Duggan from her mind and lifted up on tiptoe, seeking Paul's mouth again. But in the middle of the kiss her hat began slipping, and she jerked free, both hands flying up to the long pearl-headed hat pin.

"Oh, shoot. We're not done taking pictures yet, so I have to keep this thing on and make sure my hair doesn't get messed. But I'll be able to get rid of it at the dance tonight, then we can take up where we left off here."

With characteristic seriousness Paul backed away from her and slipped a hand into his trouser pocket. "About the dance, Winnie. . . ."

Already her hands were on her hips—angrily. "Paul Hildebrandt, if you tell me you're not staying for the dance, I'm going to throw a fit right here and now!"

"Winnie, quiet down before somebody finds us in here. It isn't that I won't stay for the dance. I'll just have to leave a little bit earlier than I expected."

She tucked her lips against her teeth and made a pair of tough fists. "So what is it this time? Did the Almighty decree that he needed the lowly Mr. Hildebrandt to process some data before—"

"Winnie, you're being shrewish again."

"Shrewish!" She spun to face the window, presenting her back. "I have a right to be shrewish after you promised." She whirled again to face him. "You *promised.* You said we'd dance until the last dog was hung, and that nothing would make you miss it. So what came up?"

"Must you sound so antagonistic?"

She considered his question seriously. "Yes. Yes, I must, because I'm sick and tired of taking a back seat to your computers and your incessant late hours. It *is* your contract work again, isn't it?"

"They need it by Monday, and this extra money is going to come in so handy when we move into the house."

"Paul, how many times do I have to tell you, I don't care about the house. I can live with a card table and two chairs and a pair of fifteen-dollar bean bags! I don't *need* four thousand dollars' worth of carefully chosen decorator furniture. We'll have the rest of our lives to buy furniture. Now—especially tonight—I wanted to be ours."

"I know." His voice was repentant, and he slipped his hands inside the bell-shaped sleeves of her lace overdress, running them up past her elbows. "I know, Winnie, but I have . . . ideals. Goals. And one of them is seeing that you start with nothing but the best. Everything you deserve. You know I've given my solemn promise to your mother that I'd see to it."

But the subject of her mother was one Winnifred could not quite confront head-on in relationship to Paul Hildebrandt. If she voiced her true feelings on that score, she feared she'd sound neurotic, or at the very least, petulant. She dropped her head forward, staring at the crisp crease in Paul's trousers as she sighed deeply.

"Yes, I know," she replied wearily. She lifted her head. "I'm sorry I complain about it, but I . . . you . . ." How was it she always ended up feeling the one in error when this argument erupted between them again and again? His motives seemed very noble on the surface, and her complaints so juvenile, as if she were a spoiled child who demanded more attention after getting her just dole.

She circled his neck loosely with both hands. "Paul, I just wanted today to be special. I feel special, dressed up this way. And I know you'd like to see me dressed up more often than you do. I thought you'd want to be with me."

"I do. And I am." He kissed her nose and looped his hands loosely behind her back. "I can stay for a couple of hours."

"During dinner?"

He brightened and smiled. "Yes, during dinner and for a few dances."

She studied him with a new, disturbing insight, recalling Joseph Duggan's words: "That's the first sign of a healthy relationship between you and your fiancé that I've seen yet." Paul Hildebrandt was all the things a sane woman wanted in a husband. Hadn't her mother reiterated the fact time and again during the past two years?

She sighed again and leaned back against the cabinet edge, pulling him with her. His weight felt secure, pressing against her hips again. She pulled his head down, forgetting about the hat, commanding him to kiss her with a full exchange of tongues that grew into a greedy seeking of body pressure. Her hat fell off. She raised up higher, forcing her curves into his coves, wishing to assure him she would and could be content with a couple of hours with him.

"Paul, I love you," she said ardently against his neck. He smelled of Pierre Cardin cosmetics, as he always did—nothing but the best when it came to image, he always claimed. The clothes make the man. First impressions last longest. He was always clean, flawless and fragrant.

"I love you, too," he said, bracketing her face with his long tapered hands that were ever as immaculate as those of any dentist.

What's the matter with me tonight, she wondered. *Why am I assessing him so caustically when he has no outstanding faults? Am I searching for some all of a sudden, after what Jo-Jo Duggan intimated?*

"It's time I got back. They'll be seating the wedding party at the main table soon. I can't hold things up."

"Oh." A shadow crossed his handsome green eyes. "I guess that means I can't sit with you during dinner."

"I'll be seated next to the best man. But we can dance the first dance afterward, all right?"

"I'll mark your name on my program." He grinned, handed her her basket, and turned her toward the swinging door.

The main hall was emptying, but Joseph Duggan was waiting near the archway to the dining room. "Ah, there you are. They're seating the guests first, Hildebrandt, and they've already sent out the call." He noted Winnie's flushed face and that unmistakable swollen look of a woman who's just been well kissed. She'd had a faint sheen to her lips before slipping off with the computer man, but it was all gone now. He noted also a coolness as she told her fiancé, "I'll see you after dinner, Paul."

Hildebrandt left them and disappeared into the dining room. Winnie felt Duggan's eyes assessing her, missing nothing. He wore no grin this time as he advised, "You got a little bit messed in there. There's a hank of hair hanging from under the side of your hat, and you could use a touch of lipstick—for the camera, of course," he finished sardonically.

She felt a surge of color mounting her chest and bathing her chin, and bit back the sharp retort that it was none of his bloody business. "I left a small makeup bag in your car. Would you mind terribly running out to get it for me?"

"Not at all. What does it look like?"

"It's a lavender-flowered zipper bag about so big."

"Be right back." He turned and crossed the entry, but just before the door closed behind him, he paused and looked back with a frown on his face. It made her sizzling mad to feel his skewering eyes were reprimanding her.

When he returned, the crowd in the front hall had thinned even more. He thrust the bag into her hand, and she thrust her flower basket into his. Then he stood behind her shoulder—very, very close—watching her reflection as she faced a long ornate pier glass hanging on a wall to the left of the door.

She fished in the bag for a wand of lipstick, but when she found it, her hand trembled on its way to her lips. Joseph Duggan's brown eyes were relentless as they followed each move she made. She opened her mouth, pouted her lips toward the glass and began carefully outlining them.

"You have very beautiful lips. I like them better when they don't have that red crap on them and are left in their own natural shape."

The wand with its red tip trembled two inches from her mouth. Her eyes met Duggan's in the mirror, and she wanted to ask him please to forgo any further compliments tonight. She just wasn't in the mood anymore.

"Go ahead, princess, put it on, anyway. It'll take away that puffy look that tells what you and Hildegard were doing in the butler's pantry."

"Hildebrandt!" she spit and continued slashing the red hue on her lips.

"I beg your pardon," he returned silkily. "Hildebrandt." He raised his eyes to her hat. "And fix that hair, too . . . for the time being."

Rather than ask the obvious question, she jerked the hat pin free and handed him the hat by swatting it across his belly. He grinned as he added it to his collection of female frippery. It was beyond her why a frilly hat and a basket of pink hyacinth should enhance a man's masculinity as he held them in his wide blunt hands. She dropped her eyes from the reflection, feeling betrayed by two inanimate objects.

She lifted her arms to smooth the single strand of hair that had been jerked from its moorings, tucked it securely into the roll at the base of her neck, found a hidden hairpin and rammed it into place. Throughout the adjustments her chin rested on her chest, and her breasts jutted upward. She secretly peeked up to glimpse Joseph Duggan's eyes on her upturned focal spots, then wander to her bare arms, where the loose sleeves of her dress had slipped down to her shoulders as her elbows lifted to heaven. His gaze moved up and caught her watching him. One corner of his mouth tipped up slowly, and at the proper moment he reached around her with one arm and placed the hat against her stomach. When it touched her, something inside Winnifred Gardner went woozy.

"Thank you," she snapped sarcastically, jerking the hat from his fingers.

"Anytime, ma'am," he drawled. "If the damage is all repaired now, let's go. They're waiting for us, I'm sure."

Luckily the proceedings hadn't been held up, for Sandy had planned a rather unique substitute for the often disliked formal receiving line. Instead of forcing her wedding party to go through the polite ritual of making small talk to total strangers, she'd arranged for all dinner guests to be seated first, after which the members of the wedding party would be formally introduced and would make their entrance through the center aisle of the dining room toward the head table, where all the guests could see them and know exactly who each person was.

As Winnie and Joseph joined the others waiting at the entrance to the dining room, the announcer was calling, "I give you Mr. and Mrs. Michael Malaszewski!"

Joseph burst into applause, then bit his little fingers and shrilled an earsplitting whistle. Winnie clapped her hands over her ears and winced. He grinned, clapped louder and bellowed, "Way to go, Ski!"

The announcer called, "The maid of honor and the best man, Miss Winnifred Gardner and Mr. Joseph Duggan."

He postured a miniature bow, presented his elbow and invited, "Shall we, Miss Gardner?"

She forced a broad smile, laced her hand beneath his sleeve and followed his lead, conscious of Paul's eyes following as she and Joseph made for the head table. When the entire wedding party had been introduced, Joseph stepped behind her chair to pull it out solicitously. As he moved to his chair, she whacked her basket of flowers down between two candles, yanked her gloves off and slapped them down beside her silverware.

As soon as he was seated, he turned his full attention to her. "Well, I detect a bit of frost in the air."

"I'd rather not talk about it while one hundred wedding guests can watch everything that passes between us."

"You're angry with me."

"Yes, among other things."

"Then, I'm sorry. I didn't know you'd be so touchy about things like that. I shouldn't have teased."

"I'm not *touchy,* all right?"

"Then why are you throwing things around and pulling your mouth up like a purse string?"

She inhaled, closed her eyes for a second and forced her facial muscles to relax. "I'm not touchy. And I'm not quite as angry with you as I am with Paul, and I don't want to talk about it, if you don't mind."

"A lovers' quarrel? At a wedding? In a pantry? What could you possibly find to quarrel about when you were only gone five minutes?"

When she refused to answer but turned her head away from him, he searched out Paul Hildebrandt in a far corner of the room. "Mmm . . . your fiancé is looking pretty mellow and happy over there. Apparently *he's* not mad at *you.*"

She snapped her head back toward him. "Mr. Duggan, I said I didn't want to talk about it."

"All right, I'm versatile. What else would you like to talk about?" A white-clad waitress moved before them and offered to fill their stem glasses with champagne. He lifted his own glass and asked Winnie, "Champagne?" At her curt nod he held her glass, too, for filling. "There you are," he said amiably, offering it to her. Their discourse was sidetracked as Joseph declared, "I'd better do my duties as best man. We'll pick this up later."

He arose, raised his hands for silence and turned toward the bride and groom, lifting his glass. "Ladies and gentlemen, I think a toast is in order on this auspicious occasion. It goes without saying that we're all happy for you, Mick and Sandy, and each of us thanks you for inviting us to celebrate your great day along with you. It comes from the heart when I wish you a lifetime of love as rich as the love you're feeling today. May your blessings be many, your hardships be few." He lifted his glass momentarily higher. "To my friends Sandy and Mick Malaszewski." He drank, set his glass down, then moved between the bridal couple. Mick was on his feet, and the two men embraced, their arms wrapped securely around each other's shoulders. Then, as they clasped hands, they exchanged some private words too low for Winnie to catch. But they looked into each other's eyes, and for a moment she thought she saw an emotional glitter in both pairs of eyes. Again Joseph lifted his voice to the crowd. "And, as best man, I believe I'm entitled to what I'm about to take!" The wedding guests applauded as Joseph took Sandy's hand and prompted her to her feet. Then he wrapped her in his arms and planted a long firm kiss on her mouth before backing away and laughing into her rosy face. "Be good to him, you hear? I love that big galoot."

"I will," Sandy answered. "So do I."

Joseph nodded, released her hands and returned to his chair beside Winnie. By the time he refilled his glass and lifted it to hers, there was a warm appreciative glow where her anger had been. He was a man who loved and showed it, and voiced it. Unashamedly. How rare.

"I'd rather not spend the rest of the night with you mad at me, so let's have a toast to peace, okay, Miss Gardner?"

She touched the rim of her glass to his. "Pax," she agreed as the ting of crystal sounded faintly. "And I'm sorry, too. It really was never you I was upset with."

"Good." He drank, but his eyes never left hers as the rim of his glass tipped up, and her gaze remained steadily on his arresting dark eyes until she thought she saw the sparkle of the wine bubbles reflected in their brown irises. A vague nagging ache of tension seemed to disappear from between her shoulder blades now that they were on equable terms again.

Their dinner was served, and while they ate chicken breast and mushroom sauce on a bed of wild rice, they talked about nice safe subjects: his business, the vintage-auto club, her job at the hospital, the bride's and groom's refreshing flouting of tradition in planning this wedding.

"Did you know they're opening their own gifts tomorrow afternoon at Sandy's parents' house?"

"Yes, Mick told me. Will you be there?"

She looked up into his direct gaze. *Lord, but he has devastating eyes,* she thought. *I should answer an unqualified no and stick to it. There's no way I'll get Paul to come along, not when he has work to entice him.*

"Yes, will you?"

"Now I will."

They were playing cat and mouse, and she knew it. Yet she assuaged her immediate guilt feelings by telling herself being with him was "legal." She'd been paired off with him for the duration of the wedding, and wasn't tomorrow part of the ongoing celebration? Suddenly she realized she'd been staring into his eyes for too, too long and dropped hers to her plate, then quickly scanned the room to see if Paul was watching the head table. But he was immersed in conversation with someone else at his own.

"Miss Gardner?" Joseph paused expectantly, and she turned to find those inexcusably beautiful brown eyes still resting upon her. "What does he call you? Winnifred? Winnie?"

"Winnie, most of the time."

"Then would it be okay if I called you Winn?"

Her heart reacted in a way no heart of an engaged woman should react, and she wondered if people noted how often she and Joseph gazed into each other's eyes during the course of the meal.

The server interrupted just then. "Would either of you care for coffee?"

Winnie jumped at the chance to be diverted. "Yes . . . oh, yes, coffee, please." Too late she realized she hated coffee. *Maybe it'll sober me up and make me behave properly.*

"Winn?" The word sent her heart *ka-whumping* more erratically than before, and the tone of his voice compelled her to lift her eyes to his once more. "What did you two fight about?"

"It wasn't a fight exactly, just an ongoing difference between us. And I'm in the wrong about it, and I know it." She glanced at Paul and found him watching her. He raised a hand in silent salute, and she returned the hello, then dropped her eyes to the tablecloth. "You see, Paul is a very dedicated man. He has set goals for himself, for us, actually . . . things he wants us to own, to achieve. Only sometimes when he works overtime, I get . . ." She stopped, unsure of how to say it.

"You get?"

He touched the knuckle of her index finger where it was threaded through the handle of the coffee cup. At the brief contact she jerked back, sending the liquid sloshing to the rim of the cup. Alarmed, she looked up, striving to put Paul between herself and this very attractive man. "I get a little jealous of the time he spends with his computers. He has a terminal at home in the spare bedroom, and after his regular job he does contract work, programming on an independent basis during evenings and weekends. He does it because we've bought the house, and naturally there are fairly good-sized payments on it, plus he's bound and determined we'll have it totally furnished by the time I move in with him. So I should be grateful. I have a man who's got ambition and drive, I know. It's selfish of me to make demands on his time, I guess. But sometimes I. . . ." Again her eyes wandered to Paul, but she left the thought dangling.

"Sometimes you'd rather have his time than the money it can earn," Joseph filled in, leaning forward, resting an elbow on the table and turning his back to the room at large, shielding her from the eyes of her fiancé.

"Yes. I know it sounds absolutely ridiculous that a woman can be jealous of a . . . a panel of silicon chips, but. . . .'' Her eyebrows puckered and her lips trembled. ''Do you know they even give computers names? He's named his Rita. Rita, for God's sake! I mean, what kind of a man gives a woman's name to a hunk of metal and refers to her as *she* all the time?'' Her lips were trembling even more. ''And what kind of woman gets jealous of *her?*'' She was directly confronted by Jo-Jo Duggan's serious brown eyes, and to her horror she realized her own eyes were floating in tears. ''Oh, darn. . . .'' She felt utterly ridiculous to have admitted such a thing. She reached up to dash the salt away but had no handkerchief. ''I feel like a fool, getting all emotional over a thing like this, but he promised me he'd come to the wedding and dance all night. And I just love to dance, and I thought b-because I'm all d-dressed up and everything. . . .'' She stammered to a halt, more self-conscious than ever, after babbling on about such inconsequential and childish wishes.

Into her line of vision came a blurred hand, extending a clean folded handkerchief. ''Here, dry your eyes.''

She touched their inner corners gingerly and wiped the end of her nose. She lifted her face then, and there was Joseph Duggan only inches before her, unsmiling, watching her too carefully, still shielding her from the rest of the room. ''I'm sorry, Joseph. What a stupid thing to do, get all teary eyed because my man wants to work hard so he can buy me a houseful of furniture.''

''That's not the reason you're crying, and you know it.''

''It's not?''

''Hardly.''

''Then tell me why I am.''

''Because you're three months away from marrying a man, and all of a sudden you're discovering some very disturbing differences in values between the two of you. Deep differences. You like to dance, and he likes to talk to computers. But is that as deep as it goes?''

''Ye. . . .'' She'd been about to say yes but halted to give it some serious reflection. But, thinking, she decided it best not to dwell upon it. ''I want to have fun tonight, and this isn't helping. Can we talk about something else?''

''Of course. Are you all dried up now, so I can remove myself from between you and the curious multitude?''

She smiled and chuckled shakily, handed him his handkerchief and sniffed once. ''Yes. But I probably am in need of some makeup repair again. If you'll excuse me, I'll sneak back to the foyer and touch up my eyes.''

He immediately got to his feet and pulled her chair back. When she stood beside him, he detained her for a second with a hand on her arm. ''Winn, if it'll make you feel any better, I'll fill in for old Hildegard on the dance floor, inept as I am. You want to dance all night, you've got it, sweetheart. Two clubfeet and all.'' He glanced self-deprecatingly at his shoes, then straightened and gave her a teasing grin.

It was like a shot of revivifying sun.

''I think, Joseph Duggan, that you're a very nice man underneath all that flirting and teasing. And I'll hold you to it.''

They stood for a breathless moment, transfixed, staring at each other.

''Winn. . . .'' His fingers tightened on her arm. But his touch felt too welcome, too good, too exciting. She forced herself to turn and walk away.

Chapter 4

There's an old custom at Polish weddings that the groomsmen steal the bride sometime during the reception. When Joseph Duggan disappeared an hour later, Winnie missed him immediately. She'd danced with Paul, but now he was gone. She wandered from group to group, visiting with acquaintances, but the zest seemed to have fizzled out of the party once Joseph disappeared. She took her makeup bag to an upstairs bedroom, checked her mascara, refreshed her blush, but wiped all vestiges of the scarlet lipstick from her mouth and applied instead a soft pink, as luminescent as the recesses of a conch shell. She touched Chanel No. 5 to her wrists, neck and knees, then went back downstairs to wander around restlessly, listening to the music of the four-piece band that played in the large central hall.

It seemed forever before the front door swept open, and several laughing men crowded through, bearing the bride upon their shoulders. At the sight of Joseph Duggan the night suddenly regained its flavor. He spotted Winnie immediately and was crossing the hall toward her the moment the bride was lowered to the floor.

"I'm sorry I had to abandon you, but duty called." He captured her hand and towed her toward the area set aside for dancing. "But I do keep my promises for better or for worse. Come on, Twinkle Toes, let's make you happy again."

He swooped her into his arms, only to discover her wide hat brim forced them apart. She leaned back from the waist to smile up at him. "I was growing very impatient."

His engaging grin twinkled down at her. "So was I." He tightened his arm and settled her hips to his, but the hat brim still bothered. It nudged the crown of his forehead. He studied it with the look of a police inspector searching for clues, then stopped dancing, raised both hands and reached around her head. He knew where the hat pin was: he'd watched her remove and replace it earlier. When it slid free and the hat along with it, Winnie felt an unwarranted thrill of intimacy—after all, it was only a hat he'd taken off her, nothing more personal. Yet she liked the way he'd done it, without asking, without fumbling.

Unceremoniously he pulled her length back against his, immediately snuggling her close, resting his jaw against her temple while the hat rode lightly against her buttocks as he held it upon the small of her back. The faint brushing movements of the straw brim through her organdy dress brought shivers, and she imagined his blunt-fingered hand and ruffled cuff and how they must look with the hat suspended from them. Then she closed her eyes and simply enjoyed.

He hadn't the smooth expert grace of Paul on the dance floor, but he had superb timing and was content to nestle her against him and circle the floor with small unflamboyant steps. In his arms Winnie felt an immediate shock of difference. Joseph was shorter than Paul. Thus her face was closer to his, touching his; his muscles were firmer, and his hand wider, thicker, harder. His fingers were coarse. He had a workingman's hands, with texture and calluses, in contraposition to the soft warmth of the butt of his palm. He used a different brand of cosmetic than she was accustomed to smelling on a man's neck, for he radiated a pleasant mixture of herb, lime and something resembling cedar. His chin was coarser, and she felt a vague scratching from it against her temple and imagined before the night was over, her hairdo would be disheveled and flattened on that side. She thought again of his hair, but it was beyond her touch, unless she wanted to be so indiscreet as to reach up and feel it above his collar. She'd been wondering what it felt like—all those airy girlish ringlets—ever since she'd first seen it. But she danced in his arms content to know his other textures and scents, realizing they allured far more powerfully than a sensibly engaged woman ought to admit.

''You were gone so long.''

He backed away slightly and looked down into her eyes. ''Was I?''

Her heart fluttered. ''I . . . I was anxious to dance.''

''When I left, he was still here. Didn't the two of you dance?''

''Yes, for a little while, but he left shortly after you did.''

''Seems we didn't do such a hot job of spiriting the bride away without being noticed.''

''Oh, I noticed, all right.'' *Winnifred Gardner, now you're the one who's flirting.*

His hand moved caressingly on the hollow of her back, but he continued looking down into her eyes. ''You were right about him. He's tall, blond, handsome, immaculately groomed, well dressed, and I have to confess, I hung around just long enough to watch you two when the music started. He's a darn good dancer. You both are.''

''Well, that darn good dancer is laboring over a computer keyboard right now, so what good does he do me?''

''He may not be doing *you* any good, but I'll have to make it a point to thank old Hildegard for abandoning you the way he did. I couldn't be happier to fill in.'' Again he brought her up against his body, taking two dramatic swirls, then laughing into her ear when he lost his balance on the second and nearly sent them toppling. She laughed, too, enjoying the feel of her breast flattened to his.

''You were doing just fine before you started getting melodramatic, Joseph Duggan. I don't need Fred Astaire. You'll do very nicely.''

The next several songs were fast ones, and Jo-Jo Duggan gamely gyrated his hips and rocked his shoulders, thinking himself rather inept at the sport but enjoying himself immensely nevertheless, just because he was with the prettiest woman in the place.

''Whoever told you you aren't a good dancer?'' she queried.

''I can feel it. I don't need to be told.''

She glanced at his waist, shadowed within the open panels of his tuxedo jacket, then dropped her eyes a little lower. "Why, look at you. You have exquisite rhythm."

He lifted his chin and laughed at the ceiling, then gave her an open leer that passed from her breasts to her knees and back up again. "So do you, Winn Gardner, so do you."

After that last set of fast songs, he removed his tux jacket and left it hanging over the back of a chair. The back of his vest was made of sleek silk, and beneath it his musculature was easily felt. She moved into his arms when the music started again and gently explored his shoulder blades and the hollow between them. Around her waist his arm tightened, and she made a soft throaty sound and nestled more securely into his curves while he dropped his head until his lips rested just beside her right ear.

"Mmm . . . whatever that is you're wearing smells much better than the gasoline you wore last night."

She laughed. It felt wonderful, laughing against his firm chest, which lifted and fell against hers, while an answering chuckle rumbled deep within him.

"It's Chanel No. 5."

"I love it. Does it taste as good as it smells?"

"I don't know. Does yours?"

His fingers moved suggestively on her ribs. "Maybe we should both find out later, huh?"

"Uh-uh," she murmured against his neck. "Can't do that. I'm engaged to another man."

"Oh, that's right. Old Silicon Chip. The guy who left you here with me for safekeeping."

"Why is it I don't feel very safe around you?"

"I have no idea. I'm only filling in for your absentee fiancé. And with fresh reminders every fifteen minutes that you *are* promised to him, and you *do* wear his diamond." His hand left her waist and meandered upward to the small of her back, finding the vertical slit in the overbodice of her dress. His warm palm slipped inside and rode up to her bare shoulder blades, then down over the abbreviated back bodice, remaining inside the lace cover-up.

"What in blazes are you wearing under that dress?"

His point-blank question caught her by surprise, and she answered without thinking of the unsuitability of the subject. "Something old-fashioned and very hard to find these days."

"It feels like you're rigged out with two barrel staves." His hand explored her ribs and side, running down the long plastic stays that held up the foundation garment.

"It's called a merry widow."

Suddenly he lifted his head and met her eyes with his sparkling brown ones. "I wish you were," he whispered.

She cocked her head to one side. "What?"

"A merry widow. I wish you were a merry widow instead of a promised woman."

She came to her senses then, backing away a reasonable distance. But without the length of his warm body, hers felt cold and deprived.

"I think it's time we talked about something nice and safe and . . . neutral."

"You're right. How did you like the dinner?"

"I liked everything but the asparagus. How about you?"

"I liked everything including the asparagus."

That subject was shot. She groped for another, but her thoughts were taken up by him, his nearness, how much she was enjoying being with him. It seemed a long time since she'd laughed this readily or bantered this freely. Paul was so often serious or immersed and out of touch with earth. Winnifred had fleeting thoughts that it was wrong to enjoy another man's company this much. But when Pete Schaeffer asked her to dance, and she returned afterward to Joseph, it felt like home. Already he felt familiar and comfortable.

They danced another fast set, and after it their brows were damp, their breath short. She was fanning her face with an ineffectual hand, and he'd yanked his bow tie loose and stuffed it into his pocket, then rolled up the ruffled cuffs of his white shirt to the elbows.

"This is hot business, your kind of dancing," he chided good-naturedly.

"Whew! I'll say!"

"It's not too bad outside for March. In the fifties. Want to go out for a minute and cool off?"

"We'll probably catch pneumonia."

"We'll only stay a minute, and if you get shivery, we'll come back in. Or better yet, I'll grab my jacket." He retrieved it from the chair, and Winnie found herself crossing toward the great front door without having consciously made the decision to be alone with him.

Outside the moon was at its apex—it was nearly midnight. Stillness surrounded them, for it was too early in the year for frogs, crickets or any of the other night sounds that would bring midnight alive when summer came. They stood on the highest of three white steps, breathing deeply. Joseph slung his tuxedo jacket across his left shoulder, suspending it from two fingers. He scanned the dark star-dappled sky. Winnifred ran a hand up the back of her neck, lifting the tendrils of hair that had come loose. Her nape was damp and the air felt wonderful. Joseph turned, watching the outline of her face as she lifted it, hung her head back and let her eyes sink shut. God, she was lovely. He wondered if she ever had any doubts about her impending marriage; if Hildebrandt was too ignorant to see the dangers of letting a woman like her drift free on a night like this. Around a man like himself.

"Come on. . . ." He slid his hand from the soft inner curve of her left elbow down to her wrist and intertwined his fingers with hers. "Let's walk."

He held her hand loosely, and it would have taken the simplest movement for Winnie to withdraw, but it felt right, ambling down the steps, across the withered pale grass, around the side of the house with her hand innocently in Joseph Duggan's.

The lawn sprawled and rolled in two gentle undulations toward a small creek and a patch of woodland beyond. The Victorian Club had, in its prime, been a property of estate proportions, thus the grounds were measured in spacious acres. Here and there tall oaks lifted their bare branches toward the stars, and a line of evergreens created a black barrier against the slightly lighter hue of the night sky. They sauntered downhill. Winnie felt the heels of her shoes sinking into the grass at times, throwing her slightly off balance. Whenever she lurched, Joseph's fingers gripped hers more tightly.

Ahead of them the white latticed foundation of the gazebo clarified as they approached, its hexagonal rails and roof beckoning as they moved closer and closer. Again Winnie sensed the same queer time-lapse sensation. Déjà vu, perhaps, brought about by the fact that the gazebo, like so many other props today, was a hallmark of another time. In her slim-hipped dress and dated hairdo she felt as if she belonged in the nostalgic enclosure.

She shivered at the strong compulsion of yesteryear.

''Cold?''

She turned to meet his eyes but could make out only that he looked her way, for there were two deep shadows from which he studied her. *What is it about a man with a coat slung over his shoulder that way that's so alluring,* she wondered. The unhurried look of it, perhaps, or the sense that his pose meant he was at ease with her. But just then he pulled the jacket forward and placed it around her shoulders, leaving his arm there, too, to keep her warm. She was surrounded by that lime-cedar scent emanating from the jacket and by a sense of the forbidden, for she knew they were hovering on the brink of something neither of them felt it wisest to begin. They were not dancing now. His arm had no legitimate reason for encircling her.

But the yearning that beckoned to them both was too powerful to fight.

They watched their feet take slower and slower steps, lazy swinging steps in the fashion of idle lovers. They heard the crush of dried grass and within their heads the pounding of their own hearts.

Dammit, Duggan, don't kiss her. Once you do, you're in for a helluva problem.

He told you he had every intention of kissing you again. Will you let him? You must not, Winnifred Gardner. You must not.

The gazebo was made totally of wood. The steps were wide and echoed as Joseph and Winnie lifted their knees in unison, mounting the risers toward the elevated floor in lazy measured steps. Above them the peak of the hexagonal roof couched secret shadows. She looked up, shivered and held Joseph's jacket closed with one hand. Around them ran a hip-high railing supported by white columns and a half wall of lattices. A wooden bench ran around the five trellised sides of the structure. She began moving toward it, but his hand closed gently around the back of her neck. ''You'd better not. It's probably dirty, and you'll soil your dress.''

At his touch she inhaled sharply, then held her breath. She shrugged her shoulders, hoping he'd free her from the terrible sweetness of his touch. Instead, he began moving his fingers softly on the skin and hair that were so soft beneath his tough skin. Her neck was cool now as the night sipped up the beads of perspiration generated on the dance floor.

''Joseph . . . don't,'' she whispered, terrified of how much she wanted him to ignore her demand.

''In your opinion, does a man dishonor a woman by kissing her if she's already engaged to someone else?''

''Oh . . .'' she groaned and dropped her head backward, intending to shrug his hand away. Instead, the back of her skull touched his knuckles, and as her eyelids slid closed, she found her head moving as if to caress him. His fingers stroked her hairline, then just above—then just inside—the stiff collar of his jacket. She shuddered, and a shaft of liquid fire darted to her loins.

"Joseph, we shouldn't have come out here."

"I know," he agreed huskily.

"Then let's go back in. Quick, before it's too late."

"I'm right behind you. Just lead the way."

Her voice was strained and throaty as she remained where she was. "Joseph Duggan, you don't play fair."

"I'm not playing. I'm as serious as I've ever been in my life when I say something very, very special has happened to me since last night. When I looked up and saw you across the vestibule—"

She spun and covered his lips with her fingers. "Don't!" Her plea was shaken, her breathing harried. "Please, don't."

He jerked his head aside to free his lips but captured her hand and held it to his thudding heart. "Then why did you come out here with me?"

"I was hot."

"That makes two of us."

"Don't misconstrue wh—"

"You came out here for the same reason I did. You feel it, too, but now you're getting cold feet." His heart was ramming his chest walls like a jackhammer.

"You're right. I was wrong. Let's go ba—"

"No! Not yet!" He grabbed the lapels of his tuxedo jacket in both fists, jerked and lifted until she was forced onto tiptoe. But his voice lost its harsh bark and turned into a soft caress as he released the jacket and found her shoulders with his broad palms. "Not yet, Winn. I told you in the car I intended to do this again, and I meant it. But keep that jacket on tight if you know what's good for both of us."

She clung to it, turning the lapels inside, gripping them for dear life, covering her breasts with both arms while Joseph Duggan's hands slid to her shoulder blades and urged her close.

"Joseph, I'm eng—"

His warm mouth smothered the word and drove the fact from her mind. The kiss was gentle, exploratory and totally unhurried. It seemed to say, "Let's see what we think." He slanted his head aside, moving it in gentle circular nudges, licking her closed lips with a come-hither invitation until she could fight the urge no longer and opened her mouth tentatively. His tongue slipped immediately inside, and she hugged her chest tighter. His left arm pressed more firmly around her shoulder, his right moved caressingly until he spanned her lower skull commandingly, making her tip her head sideways to accommodate his wishes. When she refrained from moving her head seductively as he did, he moved it for her, gently gyrating it and forcing her mouth open more fully as the provocative seconds passed.

Within her mouth his tongue was sleek and seeking, circling hers, riding over it, under it, as if the world may as well go its way without them—this must be done and done properly. He delved and stroked, learning her every texture—from rough to smooth. She learned his, too: the wet velvet of his undertongue, the sharp edges of his teeth, the resilient softness of his inner cheeks and the hard ripples upon the roof of his mouth.

They became masters of exploration, overcome with a need to experience all they could of each other's mouths in lieu of taking further liberties.

As Joseph kissed Winn, his nostrils were filled with her flower-sweet scent. The taste of her was a surprise, rather like cinnamon, as if she'd been chewing spiced gum. As he enfolded her in his arms, he forced his kiss to remain gentle, swallowing the sounds of rising amourousness that wanted to murmur from his throat. The smooth cool texture of his own gabardine jacket across her shoulder blades created a desire to jerk it from her and feel her warm skin instead. But she clutched the lapels as ordered, and Joseph thought, thank God. *Thank God.*

He kissed the way he flirted—persuasively, skillfully, beguilingly. He was a head mover and a tongue teaser. A stroker. A talented refined stroker, she could tell already, though it was only her tongue receiving his rapt attention, only her shoulders he caressed. He'd had plenty of practice at this, she was certain. But maybe that's what made him so adept.

The hand on her neck was doing delightful things to the soft hollow up its center, then behind her left ear, and he'd managed to insert his fingers within the lace about her throat. But with its limited space the edge of the opening cut tightly at her Adam's apple, as if someone were tightening a single string about her neck.

She reached up to pull his hand away, for the cinching was making it more difficult than ever to breathe normally. But in the middle of the motion she changed her mind and did what she wanted to do more than anything else in the world at this moment: she flung her arms about his neck and sent the jacket falling to the dusty floor.

Surprised, he lifted his head for a second. His eyes were only two dim circles of shadow, but his breath was warm upon her nose. "Damn that man of yours," he muttered. "Doesn't he know better than to turn you loose on a night like this? Especially around a man like me?"

The reminder of Paul brought common sense rushing in, but before she could withdraw, Joseph embraced her again, tipping his head and meeting her lips with a series of brief plucking kisses, at the end of which he stroked the hollow beneath her lower lip with his tongue. Upon her back his hands wandered freely, inside the slitted lace, up her shoulder blade, under the spindly spaghetti strap, then back down, inside the dress top.

She trembled and tried again to pull away, but his head followed, and his tongue moved along the secret valley just inside her upper lip, tickling the sensitive frenulum, then sliding along her gums. She shuddered harder and raised up on tiptoe, wishing he'd tighten his grip around her waist. But he held her lightly, as if not trusting himself to totally eradicate the narrow space between their hips. She felt his hands shift, then both of them went to the nape of her neck, and he slipped the hook from the eye. Her lace drooped. He eased it forward and lifted both his hands to her elbows, forcing her to drop her arms from around his neck so the bodice could fall free, all the time nibbling and teasing her lips. When she stiffened and began to pull back sharply, he commanded her to stay, clasping the back of her head, pushing the lace overbodice down.

She felt his warm palms slide down the angles of her neck, across her shoulders, easing from them the thin straps that fluttered, then hung loose across her biceps.

She pressed a palm to his ruffles and freed her lips. ''Joseph, stop. This is madness.''

''Yes, I know. . . .'' He kissed the crest of her cheek. He nipped her earlobe. He whispered directly into her ear, ''Winn, you smell like heaven. Forgive me if I can't help wondering what you taste like.'' The tip of his tongue wet the skin just behind her ear. Goose bumps shimmied up her belly, and she dropped her jaw onto her collarbone to free her neck to his warm lips and tongue.

His fingertips skimmed up her bare arms, jumping over the straps, then finding her warmth again and riding it around the perimeter of her dress top to the back zipper.

''Joseph, please stop,'' she pleaded.

''In a minute . . . shh.''

Her head felt weightless, but her lower extremities suddenly grew as heavy as if she were experiencing labor pains. Everything surged and thrust against the juncture of her legs and left her wanting a corresponding upward pressure to relieve the burdensome weightiness. She felt the liquid musings of her body and heeded their warning, turning aside, backing away, denying herself the pleasure she knew could be found beneath Joseph Duggan's hands.

He clasped her elbow to stop her from running. ''You're not married to him yet.''

''But I'm promised. And I'm breaking that promise.''

''Maybe it should never have been made.''

''Don't try to justify this, Joseph. It's wrong.''

''I want to touch you.''

''I know, but if you do. . . .'' She left the thought dangling, but more explicit than if she'd completed it. She gasped faintly. ''Oh, Joseph . . . please don't. . . .'' But she was adrift in ecstasy, and her voice fell still as her head lolled slightly to one side and back. How could a single finger raise such stirrings of desire?

He slipped it inside the stiff cup of her merry widow and trailed it along, from just under her armpit to the heart-shaped dip at the center of the garment, not quite touching her nipple as he passed.

''You have wonderful skin. Hard, firm, toned—I love the feel of it. I'd begun to think there was no part of you that was soft, but I've found one soft place.'' The finger made its return journey but stopped at the nipple and bent the stiff cup downward as he rubbed the erect tip with the backs of his fingers only. ''Mmm . . . I spoke too soon.''

She was shriveled and goose bumped—it was cold in the March air, and what Joseph Duggan was doing wasn't helping matters at all. She conjured up a picture of Paul's face and backed away, taking Joseph's hand from her breast, folding it between her palms.

''Put my dress back the way you found it. I don't want to walk around with a guilt complex for the next three months.''

''Why should you feel guilty? Engagements are meant to give a man and woman time to decide if they've made the right choice. Maybe you're learning here."

"And maybe you're just justifying again."

His warm palms now contoured her ribs. "I'm enormously attracted to you, Winn Gardner. What should a man do about a thing like that? Let it go unexplored? What if—"

"And what if this were just a . . . a passing urge? It's part of the mood of a wedding, wouldn't you say? People get caught up by romance when they see a bride and groom walk down the aisle. They do as Rodgers and Hart put it—'falling in love with love.' And we were more susceptible than most because we walked down that same aisle ourselves."

"Winn, your first impression of me—"

"Shh. Let me finish. You and I are different today than we'd be on a normal day. We're wearing luscious clothes that carry us away from the present and sweep us to the past, just as the ride in your car did. At times today I've even experienced the weird feeling that I'm living in my second life, that I've been reincarnated, and this—" she gestured and looked up "—this gazebo and your Haynes and my Gibson Girl look are all part of the time in which I lived before. That's why it felt so familiar, returning to it again. But, Joseph, that's not true. You and I have to be more careful than most on a day like today. We have to see things for what they truly are." She slipped her spaghetti straps up. "You know what they say about spring and a young man's fancy, don't you?" She turned her jaw aside, not quite glancing back at him. He rested his hands on her hipbones.

"No, I've forgotten. What do they say?"

"You know perfectly well what they say, but I'll repeat it, anyway, since it applies. 'In the spring a young man's fancy lightly turns to thoughts of love.' "

He watched as she inserted her arms into the lace overbodice, dropped her chin to her chest and lifted her arms. Joseph moved to find hook and eye and close them. As he did, her fragrant hair brushed his nose, and it took stern discipline to obey her wishes. But he bent and retrieved his jacket from the floor and draped it across her shoulders again. She clutched it from inside as before, then turned to face him.

"I'm your spring fancy tonight, Joseph Duggan. And before either one of us gets carried away any further, I think we'd both better admit this is more mood than anything else."

He considered her words. She might very well be right. He'd never been affected by a woman quite this suddenly, quite this strongly. He was twenty-seven and had sampled his share of feminine companions, and the one before him now raised his sexual thermometer more rapidly than any he'd met. Was it the occasion? The hat? The hair? The dress? The car? Even his own tuxedo and ruffles and shiny shoes, so different from his usual mode of dress?

Yes, she probably was right. And if so, he had no business upsetting the equilibrium between herself and Hildebrandt.

He drew a deep breath, jammed his hands into his trouser pockets and stepped back.

"So . . ." he said, pulling in a jerky sigh.

Silence hovered between them.

"So," she repeated.

The air seemed detonated by repressed sexuality.

"So, I suppose you don't want to dance with me anymore, either?"

"I always want to dance. Shall we go back and join the others? I think we'll be safe enough inside now. And anyway, there's only about half an hour of music left, then we'll politely say goodbye and exit from each other's lives, as if today and tonight never happened. And in the meantime we'll only talk about nice safe subjects again. Agreed?"

He said nothing for a long time, then finally squared his shoulders and answered, "You're right. That's wisest. Should I apologize for what I just did? I don't want to."

"No, Joseph, no apology is necessary. You see—" she chuckled softly and perhaps a trifle sadly "—you're *my* spring fancy, too."

Then she turned, and her high heels sounded on the hollow floor as she crossed to the steps. He frowned, wishing she hadn't been so sensible. Then he checked his watch to find it was twelve-forty. He had only twenty minutes to come up with a reasonable excuse to keep her with him a little longer after the dance broke up.

Chapter 5

They returned to the dance floor, conscious of the fleeting minutes and wishing they had more of them. When the first song ended, Joseph turned from her, and she saw a slash of light gray angling across the back of his jacket.

"Joseph, you're marked."

Quickly he turned to face her. "I'm what?"

"Turn around again. Your jacket is dirty from the floor of the gazebo." He presented his broad back, and as she brushed it free of evidence, she wondered what his shoulders looked like inside the clothing. She was too aware of how hard his muscles were, of how trim his contours, especially down his lower half. He looked back over his shoulder and grinned.

"I could get used to this if you'd let me."

She stopped brushing, hand hanging in midair as he turned slowly to face her again, and she stared at the appendage as if wondering whose hand it was. Then she clutched it to her stomach.

"Safe subjects . . . remember?" she reminded him just as the music began again.

"Pick one," he ordered, reverting to a waltz position with six inches of space dividing their bellies.

She grabbed the first passing thought. "Where did you take the bride?"

"Out to Daytona."

"You mean the Daytona *Club?*"

"Yes."

"Why ever did you pick a place like that?"

"Because I'm a member, and it's a twenty-minute ride, and we had to keep her away an hour, anyway. So we went out there and had a drink."

"You're a member?" she asked, surprised.

"Yes."

"What do you play?"

"Tennis, racket ball, golf. Nearly everything. I like to keep in shape."

Her eyes grew round and glittery. "I do, too!"

"I could tell that from the condition of your muscles. You're as hard and smooth as a watermelon."

"So are you. What's your favorite?"

"Depends on the season. In the summer I like tennis because it's more active than golf. I play baseball, too, with my brothers. In the winter I do some jogging and play quite a bit of racket ball, again with my brothers."

"So do I—oh, not with my brothers, of course. I don't have any brothers. But Sandy and I play racket ball, or we used to, but I suppose that may change now that she's married. She and Mick will probably do that together from now on."

"What about old Hildegard? Doesn't he play with you?"

Was there a sexy glint in his eye, a note of sexual innuendo in the question? If so, she chose to ignore it.

"Occasionally. But he doesn't care for physical things. He likes to be neat and fragrant and unsweaty. He's a brain man. I'm a body woman."

Joseph Duggan's eyes made a tour of her face. He lingered longest upon her lips, then nestled her securely against his sturdy frame. Into her ear he said, "So tell me . . . what else don't you and the computer man have in common besides physical activity and the wonders of silicon chips?"

"Not much else. Only our taste in clothing."

"What?" He backed up and looked down at her breasts, then up at her hair. "What could he possibly not like about your taste in clothing?"

"Oh, I hardly ever dress like this, in all these feminine things. That's his main complaint. I'm active. I like sweat suits and blue jeans and tennis shoes and headbands. He says clothes make the man—or the person, rather. There are times when we get ready to go out, and I know he's disappointed when I show up in jeans and cowboy boots. I'm trying to get used to dressing in cuter things."

"Why should you?"

His question stunned her. It was the first time she'd bothered to probe the issue. She'd always felt it was a shortcoming in her, as a woman, that she preferred boyish clothes. Her mother had never failed to chide her for dressing like a *tomboy.*

"But, even *you* said you liked the way I'm dressed today."

"I love the way you're dressed today. But I'll bet you're sexy as hell in a pair of jogging shorts and running shoes with your ankles bare and your hair bouncing around free.'' His eyes lifted to it momentarily, then slid down again.

''When you say things like that, it makes me want to jump into my sweats and take a fast sprint around a blacktop track. That's the real me, not the one in this hairdo and merry-widow bra.''

''Then let's do it.''

''What?''

He dropped his arms from her waist and checked his watch. ''It's only five to one. That's early. There's got to be someplace in this city where we can find an empty jogging track that's got at least one streetlight shining on it. Let's go and burn it up. Whaddya say?''

''Are you serious?''

''Dead serious. I've been wracking my brain, trying to come up with some ingenious suggestion for something we can do together. It's almost time to call it a night here, and I find I haven't had my fill of you yet. I want to be with you a little longer. Can you think of anything safer for the two of us to do than jogging?''

She couldn't. A smile touched her lips, then lighted her eyes, and he thought he'd never seen a woman more beautiful. The hair at her right temple was roughened and pulled askew. Once again her lipstick was gone. But she had a beauty that surpassed superficiality. He wondered what she'd look like right after a shower, when all artifice was gone from her face and hair.

''You'd have to stop by my place so I can pick up some sweats.''

''And then you'd have to stop by mine so I can pick up some, too.''

The night suddenly sparkled with adventure. She didn't have to say goodbye to him yet! ''Let's.'' She smiled impishly.

''You're on!'' He grabbed her hand and towed her toward the table to collect her hat, flowers and makeup bag, and two minutes later they were pulling away from the curb in his '23 Haynes Sport Coupelet.

She crossed her left ankle over her right knee, took off the high heel and massaged her foot. ''Excuse me, but you have no idea how grossly uncomfortable dyed-to-match satin pumps can be, especially when you buy them for a wedding. You never have a chance to break them in because if you get a mark on them, it's there to stay.''

''You mean all this time your feet were aching, yet you kept me dancing without letup?''

''Well, I *do* love to dance.'' She angled him a cute smirk. ''But it's more fun in old shoes.''

''So take 'em off. We won't stand on formality around here.''

She eased off the other shoe and wriggled her toes. She stretched her legs as best she could on the angular old car seat. ''Ohh . . . that feels good.''

''Here, give me a foot,'' he ordered, one hand on the wheel, his eyes on the late-night streets where there was virtually no traffic. ''And tell me how to get to your house.''

''Take Brooklyn Boulevard to Shingle Creek Parkway and turn right. I live in a town house on the corner.'' The front seat of the old car was very narrow. She backed up against the door and plunked her heels on the car seat, then pushed her dress down between her up-drawn knees. He captured her left foot and rubbed it firmly, his hand slipping over the silky nylon, sending shivers up her calves.

''Don't lean against that door. These old cars weren't exactly built for safety.''

She curled her spine, dropped her head onto her knees and concentrated on the sensual feeling of his thumb massaging the arch of her foot. ''Mmm . . . you're very good at that, considering *I*'m the physical therapist.'' Her voice came muffled from the depths of her lap.

''That's right, I forgot you were. Well, maybe you can give me a rubdown after we run.''

She lifted her head and rested her chin on her crossed forearms, which still rested on her knees. ''I said I'm a therapist, not a trainer.''

He laughed and pressed her foot against his thigh, then left his warm hand covering it. Within five minutes they'd arrived at her house. She rummaged around on the floor of the car for all the trappings she'd dumped there at various times today. There was no interior light in the old flivver, but at last she'd gathered a stack of what she hoped was everything.

''Can I carry something?'' he offered.

''Yes, you can bring the plastic clothing bag with my other dress in it.'' She fished it off the floor, and while transferring the crooks of the hangers into his hand, their fingers touched. For a brief moment neither of them moved. Then she picked up her possessions and hurriedly opened her door. ''Come on in and see my house.''

There was a For Sale sign in the yard, and he looked back at it while she struggled to fit her key in the lock. ''I take it, it's your house that's up for sale.''

''Naturally. What would Paul and I do with two houses when he's trying to earn the money to furnish one?''

''No buyers yet?''

''No, the market's been in a slump, the realtors say. But I'm hoping to get more lookers now that spring is here.''

Inside she snapped on the entry light, and they faced an ordinary living room decorated in saffron yellow and white. The furniture was nondescript: a striped sofa in shades of brown, two director's chairs in yellow canvas, a table made from an enormous wooden spool—the kind steel telephone cable comes wrapped upon. A wine jug sat on the floor in one corner, sprouting dried bearded wheat and milkweed pods painted in horribly garish purple, red and royal blue. She caught him eyeing the ugly arrangement and offered, ''One of my younger patients gave those to me last year, and I haven't had the heart to throw them away. I know they're awful, but I love them in spite of it.'' She turned, and he watched the slit in the lace along the center of her back shift with each step as she walked away down a hall. Just before she reached what appeared to be her bedroom doorway, both elbows flew in the air, and she reached for the hook and eye at her nape. There followed a soft click as her bedroom door shut, then his long sigh as he ran a hand through his hair. He tried to keep his mind off what she was doing back there. He toured her living room, then the small efficient galley kitchen behind it—a cereal bowl in the sink with three Cheerios stuck to a glutinous puddle of milk, pencils sticking out of a mug that said

''Killer'' on its side, a tablet on which was written ''buy deodorant.'' He smiled and crossed to a sliding glass door hovering high above the dark yard. He slid it open and stepped out onto a small planked deck. Bracing his hands on the rail, he listened to the soft rush of Shingle Creek chortling in the dark.

She was the kind of woman he'd been searching for for a long time. At least, so far he thought so. Just his luck to find her and learn she was engaged to another man. He hoped Hildebrandt had more than silicon chips in his pants—she seemed like the kind who needed and deserved a mate who was all man, demanding and reciprocating. She had that way about her—the strong sure way she moved, walked, danced. She exuded a physicality. And she had the body of an athlete—toned, tensile, firm. Surely a body like that must be agile when it came to loving.

He stepped back inside and closed the sliding door. ''Are you decent?'' he called.

''Yes.''

''Can I come back there?''

A silent pause followed, then she called, ''Yes, come ahead.''

The doorknob clicked, the door swung open slowly, and Joseph Duggan leaned against the frame, his weight slung on one hip and his hands slipped inside his trouser pockets. His eyes swept her gray sweat pants and hooded shirt, then swerved to the bed where her merry widow lay like a plaster cast of the front half of her body. She snatched it up and stuffed it into a dresser drawer.

''Why aren't you and this computer man living together? Wouldn't it be cheaper?''

''I bought this town house two years ago because he said it'd be the wisest thing to do with my money at the time—an investment, you know? Then when we got engaged, he started looking for a house for both of us right away, and as soon as we found it, I put this one on the market. Unfortunately it hasn't sold, and I'm stuck here until it does.''

''Meaning you'd rather be living with him?''

She dropped to the foot of the bed and began pulling on tasseled white sport footlets and a pair of Adidas. ''You're very presumptuous, asking questions like that.'' Her eyes never left her feet.

''Sorry,'' he said with not the least hint of pique at her sharp retort. His eyes moved from item to item around the room: the rumpled bed, unmade, but with the spread tossed up, half covering the pillows; her panty hose; one discarded satin pump lying on its side with the tiny pearl against the saffron carpet; photographs stuck into the edge of an old-fashioned dressing-table mirror; a tangle of Ace bandages on a dresser top to his left, lying beside a black perfume bottle, a round white plastic container of body powder, a handful of change, a pair of theater-ticket stubs, a package of Big Red gum and a small plastic case with compartments numbered like days of the month.

He eased his shoulder nonchalantly away from the door frame and ambled over to the dresser, chose the black flask, uncapped it and took a deep sniff. He watched her pull on one tennis shoe while he smelled the perfume and admired the curve of her spine as she bent sharply from her perch on the mattress. Without a comment he placed the Chanel No. 5 back where he'd found it, then tinkered around, touching other things atop her dresser, observing that half the compartments in her birth-control pillbox were empty before moving on to the quaint scarred dressing table.

He knew very well she'd observed him inspecting her personal possessions, particularly the pills. And she knew he knew. He admired her for not leaping up and fussing about it in some artificially apologetic way.

"Is this you?"

She looked up to find his palms braced on the top of the dressing table, head cocked to one side as he studied a photo slipped between the mirror and its frame.

"Yours truly," she replied, reaching for her other shoe. He glanced back over his shoulder, still braced on the dresser, and gave her a disarming grin. "You were really cute in the pigtails. But what happened to all those freckles?"

"Luckily I outgrew them."

"Mmm, too bad," he mused, returning his attention to the photo and a string of others. "You played tennis in school?"

"Uh-huh."

"I played basketball and ran in track."

Her shoes were tied. She threw him a defiant look. "You don't seem tall enough to be a basketball player." She stood up, pulled her sweat shirt down at the waist, then reached around him to get a brush from the top of the dresser. He didn't move, only turned his head aside to watch her shoulder and breast brush close to his arm.

"I was one of those quick wily guards. What I lacked in height I made up for in speed."

"I'll bet." She smirked, and he finally straightened, then pulled out a small boudoir chair from under the kneehole of the dated dressing table, slung his leg over as if he were mounting a bronco and straddled it, facing her.

"I detect a wry note in that comment." He relaxed back, catching both elbows on the table behind him. The two top buttons of his shirt were freed, revealing a V of pale brown hair on his chest. His tuxedo jacket fell aside while the snowy ruffles of his jabot thrust forward, framed by the deep low U-shaped curve of his vest. The pose was unqualifiedly masculine. Unequivocally sexy. And it conjured up in Winnifred's mind the word "hombre." With his knees wide-spread on either side of the low delicate back of the diminutive chair, he looked more virile and tempting than ever. The black fabric of his trousers stretched taut across his groin.

She raised her eyes to find his had been watching the direction of her study, and she dredged up a comment to put him in his place because she herself was acutely discomfited by what she'd just seen.

"Short and fast, that describes you pretty well, I'd say."

"I'm tall enough to put you where you belong, and I can be as slow as the next man when the occasion merits."

"We *are* talking about basketball, aren't we, Mr. Duggan?"

"Are we?"

She was removing the hairpins from her coil when he answered the last question with one of his own. Her hand stilled in midair, and she treated him to the guileless single-eyed blink that fascinated him so. She did it with her left eye, again in slow motion, and he was certain she wasn't aware of the fact that she possessed this intriguing reflex, or that it showed up whenever she was tense or embarrassed.

Suddenly she seemed to realize she was staring at him, motionless, and began searching her hair once more for hairpins. She pulled out a handful while he watched her every movement, then indolently reached out a palm, waiting. She dropped the pins into his hand, stepped back a safe distance and began brushing her hair while he watched her as carefully as if she were poised prey.

''You have the most fascinating nervous reaction that I'll bet you're not aware of.'' She kept pulling the brush through her hair but made no reply. ''Did you know you sometimes blink only your left eye? In extremely slow motion?''

''I do?'' The brush stopped.

''You do. And it makes me want to do things I have no right to think about.''

Abruptly, almost angrily, he thrust himself forward, swung his leg over the chair back, stretched to his feet, but turned his back on her. When all was silent for a long minute, he glanced back over his shoulder and ordered harshly, ''Keep brushing, for God's sake, and let's get out of here!''

She couldn't help smiling at his smooth black shoulders, wondering if the reason he'd leaped off that chair was the one she thought—because if he hadn't, things were going to start showing any second.

''I'm ready. All I need is a sweatband. Excuse me.''

He whirled and jumped out of her way when he discovered her close behind him, waiting to get at a drawer of the dressing table. She stood only a scant foot from him while ducking down to see in the mirror, slipping a braided red headband over her disorderly hair. ''I'm a mess, but what the heck. All I'm going to do is run.''

Maybe not, he thought, but smiled at her refreshing acceptance of her rather unflattering state. She looked better to him now in her baggy sweat pants than she'd looked in her pink ankle-length dress. She looked approachable, messable and altogether feminine.

At his house they crept. ''Shh!'' he warned. ''My brothers are sleeping.'' He snapped on a dim light in an old crowded back entry. Basement stairs led straight ahead, and up one step to the left was a kitchen. It was as vintage as his cars, this house. It was built in the forties most likely and had as much class as a four-buckle overshoe. He'd said it was his grandparents' home, and she could see touches of the grandmother left behind: an ivy in a brass pot hanging by a chain above the kitchen sink; an old black cast-iron Dutch oven with a cover, sitting on a very dirty stove; a kitchen clock shaped like a red plastic teakettle. The floor was covered not in vinyl, but with linoleum—one-foot squares of red and gray straight from 1950. It was worn in front of the stove, and the black sublayer was beginning to show through. Linoleum, for heaven's sake! He left her to go upstairs, and she poked her head into a dark living room and heard the floorboards creaking overhead where Joseph rummaged for his athletic clothes. A bass voice mumbled something, and Joseph's answered—undoubtedly he'd roused one of his brothers. She heard what sounded like an ancient dresser drawer screeching as it resisted closing, then two thumps that might have been Joseph's dress shoes hitting the floor. She switched on a living-room lamp and perused the room: leftovers of grandma's. An overstuffed sofa with a matching chair, both of wear-like-iron nylon frieze; a step table with a bowl of peanut shells on it; an NFL magazine that was six months old and a stack of newspapers not much newer; an embroidered doily that needed washing and starching—or better yet, throwing away; a black-and-red wool lumberman's shirt and a disreputable-looking pair of work boots with leather strings and oily curled-up toes; ancient ecru-lace panel curtains—lace? Stucco walls. But upon them she saw the first touch she knew to be Joseph's: large color photos of vintage cars, framed in stainless steel and fronted with glass. There were five of them in the room, each one classier than the next. She was facing the largest of them when Joseph spoke just behind her shoulder.

"That's my dream. To own one of those babies one day."

She leaned forward and inspected the fancy English round hand at the bottom of the picture. "1932 Duesenberg Model SJ." She turned her head to watch his profile as he studied the picture with a reverence she found enlightening.

"When you get it, will you take me for a ride?"

His hand stole up and squeezed the side of her neck. "Honey, it's a date. I'll find you if you're findable by dry land."

She was suddenly saddened to think that if that day ever came, she couldn't go for the ride with him. She remembered the way he'd kissed her in the Haynes this afternoon, how he'd carefully dipped his head down to miss her hat brim, then had to dip back out again as he retreated. She thought of their encounter in the gazebo. And suddenly she wished he'd turn her around by the shoulders and kiss her again, without hat or hairdo to be careful of, with nothing more than their soft sweat suits between their two honed bodies. But instead, he only squeezed the side of her neck and spoke about the car before them.

"They say there were less than forty of those made. But they were the most prestigious car ever produced anywhere, and in their day had an exclusive reputation that put Rolls-Royce to shame. They'd deliver three hundred horsepower and perform like no other machine before or since. The SJ could top one hundred miles an hour in second gear! And she could go from a standstill to one hundred miles an hour in seventeen seconds. And you want to know something sad?"

She didn't, but he went on, still gazing at the picture. "The man she was named after was killed in an accident while driving one of these in 1932."

She lifted her face and half turned to look up at him. "In a way that's not as sad as it might have been. He died doing the thing he probably loved doing best in all the world."

His eyes met hers. "You're right, Winn. I never looked at it that way before. And he accomplished a lot in his life that was left for posterity—he and his brother had a lot to do with developing the Indy 500 into what it is today."

"You mean the Duesenberg is an American car?"

"As apple pie."

"It sounds German."

"They were immigrants, the Duesenberg brothers."

Joseph and Winnie stood for a minute longer in the dim light of the farmhouse-style living room with its peanut shells and work boots and its oddly contrasting 1932 Duesenberg.

"Well, good luck, Joseph Duggan," she said at last very quietly, her eyes on his prize, his dream.

He shook himself from his reverie and tugged on her neck. ''Come on, let's go run. I think I know just the place.''

They ran around the quarter-mile of Osseo Senior High School, only a few blocks from his house. They drove over in the Haynes and left it parked in the middle of the deserted parking lot. Silently they crossed the blacktop, made their way inside the chain-link fence surrounding the football field and track and peered at the white-painted lane lines that were barely visible in the deep night.

Then they were running side by side, puffing hard, their breathing coming in long controlled intakes and exhalations. There was only the sound of it and the slap of their rubber soles on the blacktop.

She thought of what a joy it was to run beside a man who enjoyed it as much as she.

He thought of what a damn fool old Hildegard was, to show no interest in sharing this with her.

She thought of what Joseph Duggan's legs must look like inside his navy sweat pants as the muscles flexed and stretched.

He pictured the curve of her buttocks, her flanks, her thighs reaching rhythmically along the track before him—naked.

She wondered if he'd ever get his Duesenberg.

He wondered if she'd really marry a silicon chip.

She wondered if he did this with the Perkins hostess.

He wondered who'd do this with her once she married the wrong man.

She thought she could run like this beside him forever.

He considered asking her to.

They'd circled the four-forty eight times when they approached the place from which they'd started.

''Want to go around again?'' he asked without breaking stride.

''No, I've had enough.''

They veered off the track, breathing hard, but not hurting. To their right rose a high set of metal bleachers, standing out like white ribs beneath the quarter moon that hung in the southwestern sky. They slowed to a cool-down pace and reverted to walking side by side, blowing and flexing and shaking their limbs. They padded on silent grass in the middle of the oval, heading for the break in the chain-link fence.

The city was silent—it was perhaps three o'clock in the morning. The only sound came from a diesel truck that rolled off down the highway beyond the far side of the football field, then all was still but for their labored breathing. They stopped on the black track—by now their eyes had grown accustomed to the darkness, and its white ribbons of paint stood out like writing on a blackboard.

She flexed forward at the waist, bracing her hands just above her kneecaps, hanging that way. He hung his hands upon his hipbones and leaned backward, blinking, then studying the stars. They both straightened at the same time, facing each other with nothing but three feet of night between them.

He saw her upraised face, bathed in star shine, and the hair upon her temples—damp tendrils clinging down her cheeks below the braided headband that crossed her forehead. Her breasts rose and fell rapidly. He could smell the vestiges of Chanel No. 5, brought again to life by her warm sweating body.

"Forgive me for doing this, Winn, but it's got to be done, so I'll know. . . ." His left arm circled her just beneath the ribs, and his right hooked over her opposite shoulder. He pulled her flush against his warm damp body, burying her lips beneath his in a kiss that was wholly different from that shared in the front seat of his Haynes or those exchanged in the gazebo. This was elemental, forceful, like two planets that have been reeling off orbit for several light years and finally collide in a shower of meteorites.

His mouth was open, hot and wet, and his tongue delved into her mouth with ripe demand for response. She gave it, satisfying her own need for this man, telling herself she would satisfy it no further, that this would surely be enough. But she had scarcely thrown her arms around his neck and back before she realized her mistake. This would never be enough—not with this man.

Their sweat suits were damp and scarcely concealed the firmness of the flesh beneath. Hers was equally as toned as his, equally as healthy. Holding her, kissing her with an almost frantic meeting of tongues, he slipped his hand up beneath the ribbed waistband, finding the small of her back damp and inviting. He ran his hand up, up, across the hard flesh just beneath her shoulder blades, collecting the sweet moisture from her skin as he went, moving left to right across the constricting band of her bra where it scarcely depressed the firm muscle.

She, too, slipped one hand beneath his shirt: warmth, dampness and rigid muscle greeted her caress. Their breathing, already labored from the two-mile run, became torturous now as their emotions swelled, and temptation brought their bodies to a fine-tuned peak of readiness.

And, Judas, he felt good. Hard, so hard. Against every surface that touched him, there was nothing less than hard. The soft moldable cotton of their garments conformed to their limbs, leaving little bulk between them to disguise how eagerly they strained toward one another. He stepped forward, placing one leg between hers, and their mutual height made the conformation of their bodies totally complementary. She followed his lead and widened her stance, allowing his hard thigh to press upward against the warm juncture of her legs, and answered the quest for familiarity by exploring him likewise, lifting a knee that was buttressed on either side by his firm thighs. Against the soft hollow beneath her hip, his urgency was transmitted by the thrust of his pelvis. It brought him undulating rhythmically against her, and she answered, in kind.

Inside her sweat shirt his hand went clear up to her neck, circling it, and threading fingers up into her scalp, which also was warm and damp, and exuded the scent of hair spray, not wholly unpleasant when combined with her own female scent.

Perhaps it was the scents that triggered the violent sexual reaction they both felt. Perhaps it was the sheer exertion of running that prompted them to seek something more that was totally physical. And certainly it was the romantic residuals of the wedding that put them in a frame of mind where each was eager to know and explore the other, after the countless times their eyes had met, their words had enticed, and their looks had conveyed both attraction and curiosity.

He broke away, ending the kiss with his mouth only, for it went ardently down the remainder of her body while his ragged voice rumbled near her ear.

"I knew it. Oh, God, I knew it."

"What?" Her own voice was slightly gruff and throaty. Her heart was thudding as if she were still pounding around the track at a full sprint.

"That it would be like this when I really kissed you and held you the way I've been wanting to." Suddenly he clasped her head in both hands, compelling her to stoop slightly. "Here . . . feel." Her cheek and ear were pressed against the wall of his chest which rose and fell with torturous speed while, inside, the vibrant force of his heart seemed as if it would crash its way through. He lifted her face, cradling her jaws, and held her that way while he kissed her mouth hard and sure. "That's what you do to me. It's been happening all day, since last night even, at certain times when I'd look at you and allow myself to fantasize."

No matter what she was feeling now, tomorrow, guilt would certainly outweigh any satisfaction she'd realize tonight if she let him continue this sexual foray. She removed his hands from her jaws and stepped back.

"I can't do this to Paul."

"You've never cheated on him?"

"Never. And I won't start now."

He studied her, scowling, then seemed to make a decision. "Good. I'm glad. I might not admire you as much otherwise."

She ran her fingers against her scalp, tipped her head back as if in pain and spun away from him. "Don't say things like that!"

"What? What did I say?"

"You know what you said—one minute loyal, the next untrue. It mixes me up."

"Winn." He pulled her hand down from her head and turned her to face him. "How are things, really, between you and him? If you're mixed up, it isn't because you just met and kissed me. It goes deeper than that."

"Don't probe. I don't like it. And furthermore, it's not healthy at this late date."

"Would it be better two years after you marry him? Or four years afterward, when you have two kids, maybe?"

She stiffened and her facial expression grew hard. "I have to go now. I'm really beat."

She turned toward the car. He watched the outline of her loose sweat suit grow indistinct as she moved away. He considered the countless complications this night might yet bring about for both of them. They'd begun already. She walked with her head down, hands in the warmer pocket across her belly. Her footsteps were tired, despondent. She opened the door of the Haynes and dragged herself up into the seat, then slammed the door.

He looked at the stars, at the blacktop, at the car, at his choices. It seemed there was only one.

When he sat beside her on the high seat, he laced his hands loosely over the steering wheel and stared straight out the two-piece windshield. "I'm sorry I've been ragging you about your relationship with Paul. I had no right. I'm a virtual stranger to you, and I've been drawing conclusions and making judgments ever since I met you. I just want you to know, though, that if you weren't... encumbered, I'd be pushing you full force from this day on, okay?'' He turned to find her with a sad expression on her face, staring at the break in the windshield. ''You're a dynamite lady, Winn Gardner. I hope he knows that.''

She turned, lifted her eyes to his hair and dropped them to his lips. Then she looked him steadily in the eye and said in a very soft voice, ''Please don't misconstrue this in any way. But there's been something I've wanted to do ever since I first met you. I want to do it just once to see what it feels like.'' She lifted a hand to his head, lightly touching the curls above his left ear. ''Why, it's soft!'' she exclaimed in a winsome voice.

''And what did you expect?''

''I don't know. I've just never known a man with natural curls before.''

It took a great effort for Joseph to keep his hands on the wheel; they clenched it now, no longer relaxed as they'd been a minute ago. Her touch was brief, innocent, but terribly sensual, and he thought if she didn't get her hands away, he'd lay her flat on the blacktop parking lot beside the car and see if he couldn't change her mind about cheating on old Silicon Chip.

''Don't!'' He pulled back, not jerking, not even forcefully. He simply retreated, and she understood: what she'd done was raising as much havoc with his libido as it was with her own. She tucked her hands between her knees and apologized. ''I'm sorry. Let's go.''

They remained quiet and solitary all the way back to her house. When they pulled up in her driveway, the car engine remained running, and they looked at each other. Neither of them was willing to call an end to their brief time together yet.

''Would you buy me breakfast?'' she asked, feeling foolish and as if she were goading him, when actually it was herself she seemed unable to stop punishing.

''I think I'd do almost near anything for you.''

''Then buy me breakfast and afterward wish me goodbye sensibly, without walking me to the door, and if we run into each other at the gift opening tomorrow, don't say more than hello.''

''You sure that's how you want it?''

''No. I'm sure that's how it's got to be.''

They ate apple pannekoekens at the Pannekoeken Huis, which was only a stone's throw from her town house. As they left the restaurant, the sun split the eastern sky with a bright wink of orange that spread and grew and tinted the rim of the world a brilliant combination of purple, heliotrope and lemon. He pulled up at the curb, and as she opened her door by herself, as she got out, he didn't look at her. When she stood on the street, holding onto the handle of the car door, she still waited.

''Goodbye, Joseph Duggan.''

''Goodbye, Winn Gardner.''

Both of them felt faintly ill as she watched the car drive up the street. He resolutely refrained from looking at her in the rearview mirror as long as he could stand it. But at last he lifted his eyes to see if she still stood in the street watching him drive away. But then he remembered. The Haynes was built before there were rearview mirrors.

Chapter 6

Winnifred awakened with a violent headache shortly past noon. *The gift opening,* she thought. *I can't face it.* She curled into a tight ball and shut her eyes again, reliving yesterday, feeling guilty for betraying Paul.

She called him five minutes later and came as close to begging as she ever had with him, but he said Sandy and Mick were actually her friends, and he'd prefer to stay home and finish the work he'd begun the day before. Then he added, "But have a good time, darling."

She considered calling Ann Schaeffer and offering her apologies, then going out for a long hard run to work off her frustration but felt it her duty as maid of honor to attend the gathering. She wore faded string-bean blue jeans and a white cotton-knit "Wallace Beery" shirt, the most unglamorous getup she could produce from her closet. She washed the hair spray from her hair and fluffed it with a blow dryer but left it free and uncurled, totally unspecial. She disdained all makeup except a pale application of lip gloss, chiefly because her lips were chapped from Joseph's rough chin, and the lanolin relieved them.

She was fifteen minutes late and expected to confront Joseph as she jogged down the steps to the Schaeffers' lower-level family room. But to her relief he wasn't there. Twenty or more people had arrived, and all the chairs were filled, so she took a seat on the floor near Sandy's feet. Sandy and Mick were just about to begin opening gifts, and Winnie was given the job of recording them in the wedding book.

She had written the eighth name and listed the gift when she looked up to find Joseph had just come in. Her heart went into overdrive, and her mouth watered. He was dressed much as he'd been the night of the rehearsal, in faded Levi's, the same new tennis shoes and same ivory jacket. His thumbs were hooked in his back pockets as he stood for a minute, saying hello, smiling at the group in general as his eyes passed from one person to another. When they came to her, they scarcely paused, and he gave a silent nod, then picked his way through the limited walking space and sat on the floor at the opposite end of the room from Winnie.

He followed her orders of the night before—to the max. He never again looked at her or spoke to her but visited most of the time with a pretty young woman named Connie, near whose chair he sat. There were times when Winnie thought she felt his eyes on her, especially when her attention was given to the book on her lap. But the two times she glanced his way, he was talking and laughing with Connie, who seemed more taken with him as the afternoon progressed.

The two of them walked out of the house together, and Winnifred followed, wondering at the deep sense of abandonment she felt while studying Joseph's back as he walked in front of her beside another woman. He laughed and Winnie's heart lurched. She felt empty and cast aside, wondering what the woman said that had amused him.

The two of them stood on the street beside a strange vehicle, and when Joseph's hand rested on the handle of the door, he looked over the woman's shoulder and saw Winnie, heading for her own car.

"Winn!" he called.

She came up short. Her heart lifted with hope. She hadn't time to ask herself for what.

"I found something of yours in the Haynes. Just a minute." He opened the door to the strange vehicle, and his head disappeared. When he turned, he held one of her pink high heels in his hand, its tiny pearl button winking a reminder in the waning Sunday afternoon. He lifted the shoe above his head and wagged it, walking toward her. They met in the center of the street; Connie remained where he'd left her, waiting.

Up close he looked and smelled wonderful. But he only handed her the shoe and said, "One's not much good, is it?"

"Thank you."

His back was already turning as he said, "It's okay," and waved with a negligent lifting of his knuckles.

He returned to Connie, and that's where he was when Winnie drove away. When she got home, she changed into her running clothes and ran until her body felt tortured.

Her life returned to normal in the weeks after the wedding. At least, as normal as life can be when you're less than three months away from your own wedding. She kept a list of things that needed checking, ordering or making, and crossed them off one by one: the florist, the organist, the singer, the garter, the pillow for the ring bearer.

She saw Paul several nights a week, usually at his place, and found it necessary to visit her mother once or twice a week concerning various details. At times Joseph Duggan entered her mind in a most distracting way. Then she'd put on her sweats and try to run him out of her system.

But it never seemed to work.

The one place he didn't manage to intrude was at the hospital. She loved her job and the people she worked with, and the patients, each of whom she considered a separate challenge.

The Physical Medicine and Rehabilitation Department of North Memorial Medical Center consisted of four systems: physical therapy; occupational therapy; cardiac rehab; and sports medicine, a relatively new and specialized facet of P.T. that was located in a separate building from the other three systems. But it was with those three housed within the main body of the hospital building that Winnifred worked.

She spent her days gaining the confidence of the patients to whom she was assigned, encouraging them with the often repeated phrase "You can" and making certain they never failed in the problem she assigned them for the day, be it raising a leg one inch higher than the previous day or touching an ear to a shoulder. It was one of the things she loved about being a physical therapist, the constant challenge of gauging each person's abilities and limits, and making certain she never expected more progress than their impaired bodies were ready for.

She worked with both inpatients and outpatients, seeing them once or twice a day until they were either released or had recuperated as much use of the affected body part as possible. Because she came to know each of them personally—their temperaments, personal histories, goals and fears—there was always a grave danger of becoming emotionally involved with them herself. Sympathy was fine and necessary, but when it grew too empathetic, it clouded judgment and affected a therapist's own emotions. Thus, they were taught from the start to beware of sympathetic involvement.

It was a gorgeous day in late April when Winnie was assigned a new patient. She met Meredith Emery shortly before noon, and from the first glance at the burn-scarred ten-year-old, something within Winn's heart trembled.

The child had been standing next to her father when the first match failed as he attempted to light a backyard barbecue. When he went inside for extra matches, he forgot to turn the gas jet down. The resultant explosion burned both of them badly, but the child suffered worse, simply because she was shorter, and the flame caught her at chest and neck level, scarring her face, too.

It was the frightened, lashless, eyebrowless eyes that caught at Winnifred's heartstrings from the very first moment she looked into them. The child's eyes must have been stunning before the accident—enormous, deep brown with large pupils and such wide-open lids. A poppet's eyes.

An orderly rolled Meredith Emery down to P.T. on a gurney, which was topped by a "rack" of canvas stretched onto an aluminum frame, much like an Indian litter. Winnifred met her at the door to the tank room and told the orderly she'd take over from there.

The child had been lightly sedated, but not enough so she wasn't capable of fear at yet another strange face, another strange stainless-steel facility, another new process for her small ravaged body.

"Hello, Meredith, my name is Winnifred. I'm going to be seeing you twice every day for as long as you're here, and together we're going to work on your arms and legs and toes and fingers and everything until you can move just like you did before and be able to run and play and go back to school. How does that sound?"

The wide doubtful eyes only stared.

"Meredith . . ." Winnie mused. "That's a rather big name for a girl. . . ." Winnifred checked her chart questioningly. "Ten? Are you ten?" She cocked her head closer to the level of the child's.

Meredith answered with an almost imperceptible nod.

"What do your friends call you?"

"Merry." The mouth was misshapen and drawn, and when it formed the words was transformed into a grotesque parody of a child's lips. Steeling herself, Winnifred ignored the pity that gripped her. "May I call you Merry? My name is kind of like yours, too—a little on the fancy side, kind of puts people off sometimes. So I'd like it if you'd call me . . . Winn.'' Where had it come from, this form of her name only Joseph Duggan used? She had never before encouraged people to call her by it, but now it soothed her as she looked down upon the unfortunate child.

Winn explained that because Merry's burns had been treated with sulfa and lanolin creams, they must be washed off to prevent infection, then she verbally attempted to prepare Merry for the sight that often terrified younger patients: the Hubbard tank. It was a stainless-steel monstrosity, shaped rather like a nine-foot-long four-leaf clover and equipped with a whirlpool. She explained that Merry could lie just as she was, and she and the orderly would attach four hooks to the corners of the rack, then lift her into the pool, rack and all, as if she were cargo being loaded aboard a ship.

But when the hooks were attached, and the motor began hoisting the child, she screamed and reached pathetically for Winn's hand.

''Nooo! Nooo!''

''Stop!'' Winn ordered immediately. The fissure in her heart widened, and she took the small hand, ordering the hoist to be lowered again. The thin hand clung. The lashless eyes cried. And Winn wanted to drop to her knees and cry herself. She soothed the child as best she could, rechecked her chart and made a quick decision.

''Have you been able to sit up yet, Merry?''

''They wouldn't let me.''

''Just a minute . . . I have another idea that you'll like better, but I'll be right back.'' Several minutes later, after receiving an okay from the child's doctor, Winn took Merry instead into a much smaller, less intimidating tub in which the child could sit instead of lie. Merry was strapped into the swivel chair of a device called a Century lift, and upon it was raised over the edge of the stainless-steel tub, then down inside.

When the ninety-eight-degree water touched her skin, the tiny body, which had had its chemistry so drastically upset, began to shudder violently. Merry howled and broke into tears, and begged to be taken from the tank, but it was necessary to keep her immersed and agitated by the water for a full five minutes.

They were five of the longest of Winnifred Gardner's life.

When they were up, the child was swathed in dry blankets and laid once more upon her rack and gurney to be returned to her room. But as she left, her eyes clung to Winn's, still filled with tears that made Winn wish to bend low and run a soothing hand over the little girl's hair. Only Merry had no hair. It, too, had been burned in the explosion.

When the gurney rolled away, Winn stood in the silent hall, watching the door through which it had disappeared. She sighed deeply, covered her cheeks with both hands and dug her fingertips into her eyes—they were filled with tears. *This is what they warned us about. I mustn't get emotionally involved. I mustn't.* But how was it possible not to feel anger and pity for a child such as Meredith Emery? Ten years old and already facing a trial more painful and defeating than many must face in a full lifetime.

At that moment Mrs. Christianson, the coordinator of P.T., stepped out of her office and paused beside the doorway.

"Winnifred?"

Winn turned around, her face burdened with pain.

"It's the child, isn't it?"

Winn roughly sieved her fingers through her hair. "Yes, it's the child. I'm not sure I can take this one, Sylvia."

"Of course you can. We all can when we have to. But sometimes it helps to discuss the case. We could go to lunch together."

"I think I'll pass today, if it's all right with you. I need something more than food right now."

Winn spent the next hour in the deserted rehab room, riding the stationary bike until her calves burned, then strapping weights onto her ankles and doing extended leg raises until her stomach and neck screamed for her to stop. Next she strapped the weights to her wrists and held them extended straight out from her sides until her facial muscles quivered and her pectoralis major felt ready to snap!

"What are you doing, Gardner?"

Winn dropped her arms and sank to her knees on the floor, panting, too breathless to answer.

Mrs. Christianson entered the gymnasiumlike room and stopped beside the hunkered figure. "No matter how hard you push yourself, you can't make up for it, you know that," came her sympathetic yet firm admonishment. Winn shook her head, still breathless. Her hair flew and stuck to her sweating forehead and cheeks, and she gripped her knees, trying to make sense out of such useless waste as that suffered by Meredith Emery. "The best I can do is offer to put someone else on the case if it gets to you. Will you let me know if it does?"

Winn nodded blindly. But the image of Merry's slim seeking hand lifting to her in entreaty filled the bleak depths of Winn's mind. She'd stick it out. That was the best thing she could do for the little girl.

That afternoon when Merry came back to P.T., Winn began a program of exercises whereby motion would be maintained—a flexion of the chin, rolling of the head, lifting of the arms—to prevent the child's skin from contracting and losing elasticity. She tried her hardest to instill confidence and optimism in Merry, but for the first time in her own career that sense of optimism was lacking in herself. The ten-year-old burn victim faced not only the enormous task of recovering motor movements and learning to live with a great deal of ongoing pain but would need to accept the horrendous fact that her appearance was defaced, then begin working upon the even more difficult assignment of attempting to regain a positive "body image."

At the end of the session Winn felt drained and depressed. How could anyone expect a ten-year-old to do all that?

The day had been one of the first ever when Winn wished to have any other career than the one she had. When she returned home, she immediately called Paul. She needed him equally as bad as Meredith Emery needed a physical therapist—perhaps worse.

"Paul, could you possibly break free to go to a movie or something tonight?"

"Oh, darling, I wish I could, but I've brought Arv home from the office because he's considering going into contract work, and he wanted to try out Rita and see what he thinks of her."

Rita again! Was that all the man could think of? Anger and jealousy immediately surfaced, but Winn bit back the accusation and asked as calmly as she could, ''Then could you make it an early evening with Arv and come over here afterward?''

''Is something wrong, Winnie?''

''Well . . . yes and no.''

''What is it, darling?'' To his credit he did sound terribly concerned.

''It's a patient at work.''

There followed a long pause. ''Oh.'' She heard his hesitation and understood. He never knew what to say to her when she spoke of the unfortunate, the accident victims, the aged, the diseased. These were repugnant to Paul in some odd indefinable way. They were not perfect, and he found it difficult to deal with imperfection of any kind. Paul Hildebrandt coped best when working within a tidy sphere. ''Well, just a minute, I'll ask Arv.'' Again a silence passed, then his voice came again. ''Listen, darling, I should be able to get over there in a couple of hours, okay?''

Disappointment welled. ''Okay,'' she said dejectedly, ''see you then.''

''And Winnie?'' He paused, then added, ''I love you.''

''I love you, too. See you as soon as you can make it.''

During those two hours Winn felt trapped in her own house. She simply did *not* want to be alone right now. She considered going over to her mother's but discarded the idea. Somehow her mother always managed to ruffle instead of soothe. She called Sandy but could sense her friend's impatience to get back to whatever she'd been taken from. Winn suggested they meet one day soon for a game of racket ball, but Sandy offered only a vague, ''Yeah, sure, maybe this weekend.'' At the sound of Sandy's distracted voice Winn wondered if perhaps Mick wasn't waiting in bed for his wife to finish her telephone conversation. At the thought she was chagrined, and felt awkward and excluded—from what, she did not know. Perhaps from the charmed circle of those who shared a part of each day with one special person of the opposite sex. If only Paul were here right now. What she needed most was to be held, petted and perhaps made love to . . . slowly, expertly.

Joseph Duggan's face appeared in her mind's eye, and it brought an inexplicable shaft of longing that momentarily overrode her lingering depression over Meredith Emery.

I wonder if he ever thinks of me. I wonder how he's getting along with his dim vague Perkins hostess. I wonder if, when she needs him, he answers her beck and call, maybe makes love to her slowly, expertly, then cradles her head against his chest and lets her talk it out while lying in his arms.

Winn put on her sweats and went for a run that nearly dropped her in her tracks, for she'd worked out so strenuously at noon and had been under so much stress all day she was virtually exhausted.

Paul never came. He called at nine-thirty and apologized, and said Arv had stayed later than expected and would Winnie like to talk about it now over the phone?

No, *Winn* definitely would not like to talk about it over the phone. And anyway, her run, her weariness and the five-hour lag time between the two phone calls had helped her overcome the pressing need she'd carried home from the hospital.

But it was back afresh the following day and each day that week as she worked with Merry during her two scheduled therapy sessions. The child was bright, and it was easy to tell she had been very happy before the accident. She spoke of things like ballet class, gymnastics and ten-speed bikes, all of which she'd have to forgo for a long time. One day she said, "Next summer we're going to go to Disneyland." But the following day when Winn checked the child's chart, she read that Merry had had a very bad night. At 2:00 A.M. her breathing had been interrupted, and oxygen had had to be brought in.

Standing with the clipboard braced against her stomach, Winn felt suddenly nauseous. She reread the charted information, and a premonition lifted the fine hairs along her back.

She's going to die.

That night when she called Paul, she didn't ask, she *told* him she was coming right over and needed to talk to him. But when she explained about Merry, he quietly encouraged her not to bring her troubles home from work. It's best if you leave the patients at the hospital, darling, he said. Yet when she walked into the house, she'd once again stolen him away from Rita. Winn closed her eyes and huddled against Paul's chest, cinching her arms around his back, wondering if he was moved at all by human plight. Or was he threatened by it? Was that why he could not let it infiltrate his very analytical mind? It could not be data processed. It could not be broken apart and analyzed on a green screen. Thus, perhaps it was beyond his concern.

He asked her if she'd stay that night, but she declined, dreaming up an excuse about it being somebody's birthday at work tomorrow and how she'd baked a cake that still needed frosting before she went to bed tonight.

Back at home she slumped onto the foot of her bed and fell back, supine, staring at the ceiling. She understood fully for the first time why every instructor she'd ever had in her college medicine courses had adamantly badgered their students about the pitfalls of becoming emotionally involved with their patients.

Not only will it be painful to you, should they die, but if they don't, you must make sure they never grow dependent upon you. The mark of a good therapist is knowing when to withdraw his or her support and make the patient stand alone.

Her head hurt. Her neck ached. She wished she were at work so she could stretch out on a table and have one of the other therapists give her a massage. She wished she had said yes to Paul's invitation to spend the night. But she'd felt oddly reluctant to sleep beside him after his failure to understand her need for a sympathetic ear and an understanding heart.

The name "Silicon Chip" came back to niggle.

Had Joseph Duggan been right? Was that all Paul Hildebrandt had for feelings—silicon chips?

She wondered, were she to call Joseph, and tell him she needed him, what would his response be? She somehow sensed he'd have the ready store of human compassion her fiancé seemed to lack.

She rolled to her side and curled up in a ball, blanking out the inviting idea of turning to Jo-Jo Duggan.

The next day Merry's chart showed she'd had another difficult night, and during her hydrotherapy session she had another even worse attack. When the child was returned to her room, Winn sought out Dr. Eldrid Childs, Merry's attending physician. She found him on the fourth floor, making rounds.

"It's about Meredith Emery, doctor," she explained.

"You're her therapist, aren't you?" The intelligent eyes met hers directly.

Winn nodded, then asked softly, "She's going to die, isn't she?"

He studied her silently, tapped the palm of one hand with the fingers of his other, then took her arm and walked her idly along the hall. "Yes, it looks that way. This morning it was more than a lung that failed. It was her kidneys." So often with explosion victims it was not the burns that got them but the resultant damage to vital organs that didn't always show up immediately.

Winn's eyes slid shut, and she struggled to keep from crying. *Next summer we're going to Disneyland.* She gulped at the lump in her throat, but it could not be swallowed away.

"You're involved in this one, huh?"

She nodded, keeping her eyes tightly closed. They were no longer walking.

"Sometimes we're wrong, Gardner. Sometimes they fool us."

She opened her eyes. He seemed to be swimming in a white lake of milk. "Yeah . . ." she grunted thickly. "Yeah, sure."

When her shift ended at 3:00 P.M., she faced her empty town house with the heaviest heart she'd ever borne. The child's eyes seemed to be staring at her from the bouquet of milkweed pods given her in a different time by another patient, but one who'd recovered.

She called Sandy's house, knowing perfectly well her friend was still at work, but thinking just by chance, if she'd stayed home today, the two of them could have a game of racket ball.

God, she needed to pound something, beat something, lash out and get even!

The house haunted. Outside it was spring, the season of renewed life, with robins nesting, angleworms squiggling and ants building doughnuts of sand. May was here. Trees were bursting with bloom.

Winn needed to be out there where the air was ripe with the promise of summer. She got in the car and drove. Unconsciously. Not caring where she went or whether she held up impatient drivers behind her. She was in an insulated bubble where hurt was temporarily held in abeyance.

She left Brooklyn Park behind and headed into the farm country north of the suburb, where farmers were planting their vast potato fields, and children were riding their bicycles in the driveways in the balmy late afternoon. She turned west off Douglas Drive and headed toward the old-fashioned water tower that lifted into the skyline ahead. Several minutes later she entered the quaint town of Osseo—population 2,906—by one of its lesser-used streets. Winn let her nose lead her, up one avenue and down another, searching for some sign she'd recognize, though she didn't know where it was or even if the business had a sign.

She found it on Second Avenue, two blocks off the main street of town, beside a gravel alley with grass beginning to sprout up its middle. It was a square brick building with old-fashioned double wood doors beside a windowless service door, and the sign said Duggan's Body Shop.

She stepped inside and found herself in a reception area of sorts, if it could be elevated to such a title. There was a desk made of oak, far older than his Haynes, and a nondescript pair of wooden chairs, a file cabinet, telephone and refrigerator, also very ancient, with rounded instead of squared corners. On the far side of the room an open doorway led to the shop beyond, and from it came the *screel* of an electric sander upon metal and the sound of someone whistling along as a country station played a Waylon Jennings song.

She stepped to the open doorway. The body shop had a cavernous ceiling, grease-stained concrete floors and a single line of windows up eight feet off the floor, plus another matching row at eye level across the dated double doors.

A man was leaning over at the waist, running the sander along the flank of an orangy-colored fender on a navy blue car. Two others were bending over another hoodless car, peering at its engine. Above them dangled a set of enormous chains with hooks at the ends, attached to the arm of a monstrosity that looked as if it might drop on their heads at any moment. The man on the left lifted his head, spied Winn and came over immediately, wiping his hands on a stained blue rag.

"Hi." His smile was Joseph's, but his eyes weren't nearly as pretty. "What can I do for you?" The rear end of the man she thought was Joseph was still protruding from the dismantled car.

"Is Joseph here?"

"Sure." He turned and bellowed over his shoulder. "Hey, Jo-Jo, somebody to see ya."

But Waylon was singing louder than Joseph's brother, and the sander was still whining. Brother Duggan crossed toward the bending figure in the washed-out blue jeans and called again, "Hey, Jo-Jo, there's a lady here to see you."

Joseph straightened halfway and looked over his shoulder. Winn's heart seemed to swell and thud while an awful constriction squeezed her chest. He straightened the remainder of the way very, very slowly, reaching blindly for a shop rag without taking his eyes from her. As he crossed the greasy floor, his smile grew broader with each step. Three feet before her, he stopped, wiping his hands. "Well, hello."

She had forgotten the magnetism of his incredible smile. "Hello, Joseph." Her heart was hammering so wildly it was difficult to speak in her customary tone of voice.

"What brings you to the thriving metropolis of Osseo?"

"Am I interrupting something important?"

"No. We're just jerking an engine. One's just like all the rest. It can wait." He shrugged and tossed the shop rag aside. He was dressed in filthy blue jeans and a soiled blue chambray shirt, a pair of boots that might have been those she'd seen in his living room. His hands were black and the nails lined with grease. He looked every bit as inviting as he had in his tux and ruffles.

"I probably should have called first, but I didn't really plan to stop here. I was just out driving and . . .'' She grew terribly self-conscious and gestured vaguely with one hand.

He glanced toward the windows in the double doors. ''You got car troubles or something?''

''No. I just wanted to talk to you. I thought maybe you could play a game of racket ball . . . or go out for a cup of coffee or . . . or something,'' she finished lamely.

He reached for her elbow, glanced at his dirty hand and thought better of it. With a jerk of his head he ordered her to follow. ''Hey, John, tell Tommy to turn that sander off. There's somebody I want you to meet.''

When she hesitated, Joseph turned, held out a hand as if to take her elbow, but didn't. His brothers came forward, and she saw again the sharp resemblance to Joseph in Tommy's smile. It was there in John's, too, that same contagiousness. ''This is the lady I told you about, the one I walked down the aisle with, Winn Gardner.'' Jo-Jo smiled at her while going on, ''And these are my kid brothers, Tommy and John.''

She extended her hand, realized too late it was the wrong thing to do, but kept it where it was while Tommy glanced at it, said, ''Hi, Winn'' and finally with a crooked smile grasped hers in his greasy hold before John did likewise.

''Hey, Jo-Jo, she's all right,'' Tommy approved.

''Damn right she's all right. But wipe the leer off your face, brother. She's spoken for, as I also told you.'' Without pause he informed them, ''I'm gonna knock off for the day, but you two get that cherry picker on this engine and get 'er hoisted up, then check to find out if those kingpins and bushing are in. If they've got 'em, leave a note on the kitchen table so I can pick 'em up in the morning. I might be late.'' Then he turned to Winn and said, ''Let's go.''

It had taken him less than three minutes to give the remainder of the day to her.

Outside he said, ''Well, this is a surprise.''

''For me, too.''

''You and old Hildegard have a fight or something?''

''No, not a fight.'' She glanced at him askance. ''But something.''

He glanced at her car, parked at the curb. ''I walk to work, since it's only a few blocks. Do you mind driving so we can stop by the house and I can wash up and get my sweats and racket?''

''Get in.''

He craned around to check his backside, then grinned at her across the hood of the car. ''My front side usually get dirtier than my back, so I shouldn't get your car seat dirty.''

They had just climbed in and slammed their doors when a rotund man came walking down the sidewalk, raised a hand and called, ''Hey, Joey!''

Joseph turned, then smiled and hooked an armpit over the window ledge. ''Hiya, Pa, what's up?''

From her side of the car Winn saw the man bend down, then in the window appeared a smiling face beneath a cap advertising ''John Deere.'' Into Joseph's lap he tossed a knotted plastic bag.

''Your mother says the rhubarb is ripe and sent me over to bring you some.

And who's this pretty little thing?'' His face was merry as he smiled at Winn, and she understood from whom Joseph inherited his charm.

Joseph awarded her a proud smile, informing his father, ''This is Winn Gardner, the lady I met at Mick's wedding. Remember I told you about her?''

''Oh, *she's* the one!'' Mr. Duggan doffed his cap. ''Well, nice to meet you, Winn. I'm Joey's dad.'' He thrust his hand across the front seat and shook hers.

''Nice to meet you, too, Mr. Duggan.''

''You takin' off for the day?'' he asked Joseph.

''Yeah, but the boys are inside.''

''Guess I'll go in and say hello and tell 'em ma sent the rhubarb.''

When he was gone, Winn's eyes dropped to the bag of pink and green fruit, then lifted to Joseph's face. He smiled and hefted the bag. ''Ma thinks we don't eat right since we moved out, and she keeps sending over our favorites.''

''They live close to you?''

''Yeah, right here in town. Pa works at the hardware store, Ma raises gardens and thinks she's still got to baby her boys.'' But he chuckled goodnaturedly and for a moment Winn envied him his very ordinary, but obviously caring family. There were more questions she wanted to ask about them, but while she drove, Jo-Jo changed the subject. She felt his eyes on her as he commented, ''I never thought I'd see you again. At least, not one on one.''

''I've had one of those days we'd all like to forget, and I needed something to take my mind off it. I tried calling Sandy, but she's still at work, and Paul was too, and my mother.'' She clutched the steering wheel and refrained from turning to look at him. ''I'm probably out of line, turning to you, but I was just driving and there was Osseo in front of me, and I thought of you and wanted . . . to . . . well. . . .'' Words finally failed and, anyway, explanations seemed suddenly phony.

''I'm glad,'' he said quietly, and pointed to a white house with red shingles and trim. ''That's it.'' She'd never seen it in daylight before. It was quaint and farmlike, and very much a grandma's house.

Inside, it was just as she remembered, except the kitchen stove had been cursorily cleaned, and the Dutch oven was nowhere in sight. The ivy hung in the west window above the kitchen sink, and the little red plastic clock read three-fifty-five. There was a bag of Taystee bread on the kitchen counter and a cluster of green grapes in the middle of the porcelain-topped table, not even in a bowl, just lying there with half their stems denuded.

The room was ugly. Homey. She loved it. From the red dotted Swiss curtains that had probably been hanging limply since years before his grandmother died, to the worn-off spots in the linoleum where she had undoubtedly stood while preparing hundreds of meals, Winn loved it all.

Jo-Jo uncapped a jar and took up a handful of something that looked like cold cream and began rubbing it into his hands. He turned on the kitchen faucet and scrubbed first his knuckles, then his nails with a small orange brush. She stood behind him, watching his blue shirt stretch tightly over his shoulders as he worked over the old-style double-width sink that had no divider, but a drain board off to one side.

He leaned down, opened a cabinet door and retrieved a square yellow plastic dishpan, then began filling it with water.

Glancing over his shoulder, he invited, ''Listen, if you'd rather wait in the living room, make yourself at home. I'm gonna wash up here quick and get rid of most of the grease smell, anyway.''

He turned to face the window while one-handedly unbuttoning the dirty blue shirt. He stripped it off and flung it across the cabinet top. Picking up a bar of soap, he bent forward and began scrubbing his face, neck, arms, armpits and stomach. He went at it as if in a great hurry and wasted no time being gentle with his own hide.

She stood in the archway leading to the living room, watching. When he leaned over the dishpan, the white elastic of his shorts peeped from beneath the waistband of his blue jeans. She caught a glimpse of hair under his arms and watched in fascination as the curls at the back of his neck grew wet and changed to a darker color. He turned on the water, cupped his hands and clapped them to his face about five times, snorting into the water to keep it from getting up his nostrils. It was like watching a dog charge out of a river and shake himself. Water flew everywhere, up onto the red curtains, across the faded gray linoleum lining the top of the cabinets and onto his dirty shirt there.

He straightened, groped beside his right hip for a towel that was strung through one of the drawer pulls and stood erect while beginning to dry his face.

When he turned, the towel was still covering his chin and jaws. He stopped dead, staring at her from above the towel. The pause was electric. Two droplets slid off his elbows, then he went on briskly toweling his arms and stomach. ''Oh, I didn't know you were still standing there.'' His eyes followed his hands, and so did hers. She noted the thick brown hair that covered his chest, the hard tough muscles, upper arms that had hourglass dips halfway to the elbow. ''I said you could go wait in the living room. I got a new print of a 1920 Essex, but I ran out of room to hang it on the wall. It's leaning beside the davenport. Tell me what you think.''

What she thought was that any woman who'd prefer looking at a 1920 Essex to Jo-Jo Duggan washing up would be an utter fool! The scent of Ivory soap was everywhere in the kitchen, and that other curiously lye-like aroma she'd detected about him the first night—she took it to be the solvent with which he washed his mechanic's hands.

It suddenly struck her that she'd run to Jo-Jo Duggan for more than one reason. He had been on her mind ever since she'd met him, and to deny it would be worse folly than marrying a man to whom she was not well suited.

She was studying the Essex when he clattered up the wooden steps that led off the end of the room just beside the kitchen archway. As he took the stairs two at a time, he called back, ''Where'd you have in mind to play racket ball?''

''Either my club or yours,'' she called back, casting her eyes about his living room, noting a tablet with some numbers scrawled on it, two old limp sofa pillows, two empty cans of Schlitz beer, a discarded white T-shirt—bits and pieces of Jo-Jo Duggan's life, the life of a simple workingman.

''Then let's go out to Daytona. I feel in the mood for the ride.''

He clattered back down the steps and appeared in the doorway with a navy blue duffel, his racket slipped into a sleeve upon its side. He wore a red jogging suit with a white stripe down each leg and each sleeve, white socks, and had his Adidas in his hand.

Her heart went off like a rocket.

"Let's go." He dazzled her with that high-voltage smile. "I'm all yours."

She had the crazy exhilarating feeling that he was. Or that he could be whenever she said the word.

Chapter 7

Daytona was a modest golf, tennis and racket-ball club nestled in the hills near a tiny village named Dayton, a scant half-hour ride west of Osseo. Old Highway 52 that led to it was once a major west-bound thoroughfare, but since the interstate had been built, it lazed in somnolence, its signs disappearing, its shoulders clothed in woods and grassland, dotted with cows and corncribs.

The afternoon sun lighted the hills to fresh spring green and reflected from the shimmering road surface. The air was fragrant. It was lilac time. Apple trees and wild plums were at their peak of blossom. The fragrant warmth of the spring day rejuvenated Winn's spirit. Bouncing along beside Joseph on the ancient cracked seat of an old pickup truck, she was loath to bring up the subject that had so disturbed her earlier in the day. It was too pleasant, too peaceful riding with Joseph, listening to some old Jim Reeves song—it seemed he was always surrounded by vintage of one sort or another—with the wind blowing in the lowered window, gently lifting the hair on her arm.

Winn sunk low, wedged a knee against the glove-compartment door and let her eyes sink closed. Joseph glanced at her lazy pose but said nothing. She had not brought up whatever it was she wanted to talk about, and that was fine with him. She looked sensational in the mint green jogging suit she'd produced when they detoured to her house. She was slumped low with her nape catching the top of the seat, hair loose and messed, and the breeze from the open window occasionally billowing it. As he studied her, a spirited gust caught a strand and whipped it across her lips. Without opening her eyes she hooked it with the crook of a little finger and pulled it aside. Immediately it blew back and she spit it out, then threaded it behind her ear.

Her eyes opened, and she indolently turned her head to find he'd been watching her. He smiled. She smiled back. Neither spoke as he drove on as before, with a wrist hooked languidly over the wheel, softly whistling "Four Walls" between his teeth.

At that moment Winn discovered something very wonderful: she could comfortably share silence with Joseph Duggan. There were at least a dozen men she knew, including Paul, who'd be chattering away a mile a minute. How pleasing it was to be with one today who was content to smile and whistle softly between his teeth, and let the true mellow voice of Jim Reeves do all the speaking.

Jo-Jo wondered what it was that was bothering her but decided not to probe. She'd get around to it whenever she was good and ready. In the meantime he was doing what he'd wondered if he'd ever have the chance to do again, what had kept him from readily falling asleep many nights since the wedding: he was simply being with her.

They passed Diamond Lake and soon turned the clattery old Chevrolet between two giant boulders, then rolled up the long gravel approach to the clubhouse that sat at the top of a hill. The golf links were verdant. Into the window came the smell of newly cut grass and fresh-turned loam from adjacent farms. On the club land itself were the ancient barn and farmhouse of those who'd owned the land previously.

When Jo-Jo and Winn stepped from the truck and slammed their doors, something fell off underneath it.

''Oops,'' he said with a slanting grin. ''This old heap isn't in quite as good a shape as the Haynes.''

''I wasn't going to ask where the Haynes was.'' Winn came around the truck to find him on one knee, bracing his palms on the gravel and peering underneath the truck's belly.

''This is my everydayer. New cars really don't do it for me. I like the old ones.'' He reached beneath the truck and withdrew a piece of tail pipe. ''They've got character.''

As he straightened, he was still grinning. She smiled down at the rusted hunk of metal in his hand. ''This one's character is a little loose, wouldn't you say?''

He tossed the piece onto the bed of the truck, clapped a rounded rear fender as if it were the flank of a horse, brushed off his palms and took her elbow. ''I love her just the same.''

But he was looking into Winn's eyes as he made the comment, and because his crinkle-eyed smile made her so very, very happy, and because his intentional double meaning made her far too giddy, she turned her eyes to the clubhouse as they approached.

Inside they passed a dining room with a field-rock fireplace in its center, and the bar where he'd brought Sandy when the groomsmen had stolen her. After Joseph signed them in at the desk, they parted to go to the locker rooms and check their tote bags.

He was waiting in the hall outside court number two, leaning back with one rubber sole against the wall, repeatedly flipping and catching a can of balls. As she walked toward him, he turned, and the can stopped doing cartwheels. He seemed to have forgotten he held it. His eyes made a quick scan of her length, and he slowly drew his hips away from the wall and smiled.

When she stood close before him, he grinned and said, ''Wow'' in a soft way that made her blush.

She had a healthy curiosity about his bared limbs, too, but felt it prudent to refrain from ogling. Once inside the racket-ball court, however, with the door closed behind them, there was ample opportunity for more than surreptitious glances without being detected. Assessing each other was almost unavoidable.

The court was a brightly lighted cell with a twenty-foot ceiling, poured-concrete walls, and a twenty-by-forty-foot hardwood floor. It was stark, bare and echoing. Every sound within it became amplified. As Joseph idly bounced the ball, it gave off an audible ping while expanding to its original shape. When he spoke, his voice seemed to reverberate from the walls.

"A little warm-up first?" He tugged on a short white leather glove.

"Yes. I haven't played for a good four weeks. I'll need it."

They looped cord handles around their wrists, spun them to take up the slack and gripped their rackets.

"Why four weeks?" he asked, bouncing a royal blue ball with his racket.

"Nobody to play with lately."

"How about Silicon Chip?"

"He's done it occasionally to please me. But I told you, he doesn't much care for sweat."

Joseph snatched the ball from the air, studied her expressionlessly for a moment, then turned away to face the front wall. Across the center of the court ran two parallel red lines five feet apart: the serving area. They stood just behind it as Joseph sent the ball bouncing off the front wall, giving her a direct easy return. Between them they made a total of eleven good returns before Winn missed.

She retrieved the ball and bounced it to him. As he nonchalantly juggled it above his head, bouncing it off the racket, he said, "You're pretty good, huh?"

"Good enough," she replied honestly. "But I haven't played against many men. You guys usually have the edge on power."

He turned away to the front again. "We'll see."

This time he gave her a more difficult serve, angling it so she had to cross behind him to return it from near the back wall. He didn't have time to turn around and watch her form before the ball sailed over his head and against the right sidewall. Then they concentrated on a volley of shots that lasted longer than the first. This time he missed.

She flicked the rolling ball up with the tip of her racket and gave him an impertinent grin. "You're pretty good, huh?"

"Damn right. And I don't give no quarter to no woman." His brown eyes danced mischievously.

"That's the way I like it."

"Volley?" he suggested.

"You're on."

She won the right to first serve, and as she walked to the red lines, his eyes skimmed down her lanky legs. With each step the muscles hardened and squared, but when she stood at ease, her limbs were shapely and feminine. She wore mint green athletic-style shorts trimmed with white cord around the notched legs. Her tank top was white and showed him the true spareness of the flesh across her ribs, for he'd never seen her in anything conforming before. Her tennis shoes were white with sturdy wedged soles, and as his eyes traveled down to them, he admired the shadows where her ankle tendons dove down into the shoes behind tiny white tassels.

Her first serve came whizzing off to his left, and he missed it completely. As a matter of fact, he moved a full second too late: he'd been engrossed with her shapely ankles.

She turned with a hand on her hip. ''Hey, you awake back there?''

''Yeah. Yeah . . . give me another one.''

She took three points before he executed a faultless roll-out shot, where the ball hit both floor and front wall at once, then rolled toward them as docilely as if a baby had pushed it with his chubby hands.

Winn swiveled to face Jo-Jo, raised one eyebrow and cooed, ''*Whooo-eee.* The man gets serious.''

''And the woman loses the serve.''

He now stood where she had, and Winn was the curious one. He wore white tennis-style shorts and a disreputable looking T-shirt of navy blue that said Dick's Bar on the back and looked as if it had been relieved of its sleeves and bottom half by somebody's dull hedge trimmer. The crudely slashed fabric curled back on his shoulders, and the armholes sagged halfway down his ribs. Six inches of bare stomach showed between navy shirt and white shorts, and it was remarkably tan for May, as were his sinewy legs above the calf-high socks. She was staring at the socks, one with a gold stripe around its top, the other with a purple, when his serve careered past her head. She completely ignored it and burst out laughing.

''Now who's asleep?''

''No fair, your socks broke me up!'' Her laughter resounded from the walls.

He rolled onto his heels, bringing his toes off the floor, and perused his hairy legs. ''What's the matter with them?''

''They don't match!'' She was still laughing.

''Naw, they never do. Not in a house where three men do their own laundry. *Clean* will do—*matched* we don't need.'' He grinned up at her. ''You ready to get serious now and stop laughing at my laundry?''

''Hit it,'' she returned.

They threw their total effort into racket ball then, and before the serve had changed twice, they'd quite forgotten to ogle each other. They were immersed in competition, concentrating on the reaching, running, reflexive joy of rivalry. They were well matched, and if physically Joseph had the edge, she was perhaps the more accurate shot. When he gained a point by charging up on a dying pigeon and slamming it off the back wall, she came back with a placement shot so deadly he missed it even after a belly dive. His legs were four inches longer, but hers were quicker. He'd perfected the difficult ceiling shot, and she missed it every time after it caromed from ceiling to front wall to floor, then always beyond her reach. But she had a keen feel for successfully sprinting to meet the ball a mere five feet before the front wall and softly finessing it so it dropped softly, two feet from the wall and fell dead, leaving Joseph no chance to charge forward and save the point.

They reveled in the exhilaration of pushing their bodies to great physical limits. The acoustical room was filled with the high magnified squeaks of their rubber soles on the hardwood floors, the slap of the ball, their grunts—and sometimes groans—and occasionally the clatter of a racket against concrete. They stretched their tensile limbs to their limits. They strained their bodies for the simple reward of beating the ball. They smashed and drove and sometimes watched a shot arcing over their heads, not knowing till the final second whether it would reach the back wall or fall that agonizing three inches from it. Their shirts became soaked and their limbs sheeny. His hair became curlier, and hers stringier. They smiled, teased, cried "I told you so" and sometimes, "Damn you!"

And he took the game 21-20.

They fell to their backs in the middle of the backcourt, panting, heaving, closing their eyes against the white fluorescent glare of caged lights overhead. Star bursts danced before their lids. Their hearts pounded against the cool boards beneath their shoulders. Their legs stuck to the floor. Their weary arms flopped straight out to the side, lifeless. They were in heaven.

He rolled his head to look at her. She was five feet away, but her lax fingers almost touched his.

"Hey, Gardner." She opened one eye and peeked at him. "You're good."

"So're you. But next time I'm gonna whip you, boy."

His laughter bounced off the walls like a well-executed Z-serve.

"My pleasure," he offered, then closed his eyes and rested again. A minute of pure silence passed. Their breathing was less labored. She pulled her shirt up, exposing her stomach, and rested a hand on it. He flexed a knee.

"Oh, God, I needed this." Her quiet admission whispered three times as it came back to them.

He rolled his head to look at her again. "Why?"

Meredith Emery came into her mind's eye. "Oh, Joseph, I've done the worst thing it's possible for a physical therapist to do. I've become empathetically involved with one of my patients."

"Who?" He studied her profile as she stared up at the overhead lights.

"Her name is Meredith Emery, and she's ten years old." He saw her swallow. "And she's the victim of an explosion."

Joseph hadn't guessed physical therapists worked with burn patients, and though he wanted to question her about it, he wisely kept silent.

"She has these enormous brown eyes that . . . that have no eyelashes anymore and no eyebrows, either. And her face has been scarred, and she's bald now. But she showed me her school picture when she had beautiful black hair down past her shoulders." She paused, took a deep gulp of air and went on. "She studied ballet and was a gymnast, too, and now she can't even touch her ear to her shoulder because her skin has lost so much elasticity she has to wear a splint to hold her chin up." A tear formed in Winn's eye and ran from its corner down her temple, disappearing within the droplets of perspiration already there.

Joseph inched nearer and took her outflung hand. She grasped his fingers so tightly his ring cut in almost painfully. Her ragged voice went on. "And next summer her family is all going to Disneyland . . . and . . . and. . . ." Suddenly Winn flung a forearm across her eyes and released one gulping sob that echoed from the high bright ceiling.

Joseph rolled to one hip and braced beside her on an elbow. "And?"

"And sh-she won't be g-going along b-because she's going to die." Winn began sobbing unrestrainedly then and attempted to roll away from Joseph, but he clasped her shoulder to keep her on her back.

"Winn . . . oh, Winn." He lifted her to a sitting position—they were hip to hip, facing each other—and wrapped his arms around her, cradling her against his chest, cupping the back of her damp hair while she clung to him and cried.

"Oh, J-Joseph, sometimes I d-don't understand why."

"I wish I could tell you, but I can't find any reason for the waste, either." He pressed her hair hard, contouring the back of her head. "God . . . only ten years old." He, too, sounded choked up.

"And she's b-been through such hell already. Pain and scars, and . . . and sh-she still fights with me when I tell her to—sh-she doesn't know that all the physical therapy is f-for nothing because she'll never l-live to see her limbs m-move as they did on the p-parallel bars." He kissed the side of her skull, then patted her back, feeling the pitiful heaving of her chest against his.

"Do her mother and father know?"

"I don't know. Her kidneys just failed today."

"What are they like? Do they love her a lot?"

"Oh, yes. She adores her mother and . . . and beams all over wh-when she talks about her father. At least her eyes look like they're beaming, but it's an . . . an awful sight when they don't have any lashes."

Joseph leaned back, grasped her temples in both hands and repeatedly pushed the hair back from her face, searching her eyes. "Maybe that's what it's all about . . . love. She had love, and she gave it, so her life wasn't for nothing, was it?"

Winn's eyes swam with tears. The skin beneath them was wet and shiny as he rested his thumbs there. Oh, God, she thought, why couldn't Paul have been this way when I needed him?

"Do you think so, Joseph?" She sat as still as the walls around them. He gazed into her sad wet eyes with their lashes stuck together, then lifted his gaze to her tawny hair and gently brought her forehead to his lips.

Meeting her eyes again, he assured Winn, "Yes, I think so. There's got to be a reason for all of this, and if it's not love, what else could there possibly be? You love her, too, and because you do, you needed to cry and so you came to me. And I think I could very easily fall in love with you. Maybe that's the reason . . . to bring us together."

"Joseph, you mustn't say that." Her voice was quiet, unchiding, as she probed his dark brown eyes with her troubled blue ones.

"But it's true."

"But there's still Paul."

"Yes . . . Paul." The pressure on her jaws increased as Joseph held her prisoner with his hands and eyes. "And why aren't you with him right now, crying on *his* shoulder? He's the one who should be comforting you at a time like this."

She pulled away and drew her knees up, looping them with both arms. "Paul has a hard time dealing with the fact of death or even disease. He sees perfection as the ultimate, I guess. The imperfect bodies I work with put him off, and he's uncomfortable talking about them."

"Did he try . . . this time?"

"He . . . I . . . no. I told you, he wasn't home when I tried to reach him. But when I first got Merry as a patient, I was upset one night and called him then."

"And what did he do?"

"We talked a little bit about it."

"Did he come over?"

She flashed him a warning glance. ''Don't judge him, Joseph. He has his own qualities. They may be different from yours or mine, but he has them just the same.''

''Such as?''

''Such as his supreme intelligence, his analytical mind, his . . . his tenacity. I mean, when Paul makes up his mind to do something, he does it, if it takes him a month or a year, he does it.''

''Such as providing you with a house and furniture?''

''Exactly. I'm the one at fault for wishing he'd—''

''Cut it out, Winn!'' he snapped.

''Cut *what* out?'' she snapped back.

''Rationalizing about your relationship with him. It stinks and you know it.''

''It does not stink! We get along wonderfully!''

''Oh, sure. That's why you came running to me instead of to him today. From what you tell me about him, he must have silicon chips for emotions!''

Her face colored deeply. ''You're overstepping, Joseph.''

''I'm pointing out what you already know but refuse to admit. The two of you have nothing in common except some goddam house *he's* living in without you! If you were engaged to me, I wouldn't be letting you flirt around with other men at wedding dances.''

''I didn't—'' But Joseph forged ahead.

''And your birth-control pills would be sitting in *my* bedroom. And your panty hose would be lying on *my* bedroom floor beside my jockstrap after we ended up every day with a rousing game of racket ball like the one we just played.''

She tried jumping to her feet, but he grabbed her wrist and held her where she was.

''Winn, sit still!'' he ordered, refusing to release her. ''How in blazes did you ever end up with somebody like him in the first place?''

She simmered for a long time while their eyes locked angrily. Her wrist strained against his grip, and at the precise moment she wrenched it free, she spit, ''My mother!''

His eyes widened in surprise. ''Your *what?*''

''My mother introduced me to him.'' Winn dropped her eyes, uncomfortable with the admission.

''Go on.''

''He was teaching a class on computers that she took, and the two of them discovered this great common interest in COBOL and FORTRAN.''

He screwed up his face. ''What?''

She waved an impatient hand. ''Oh, those are some high-level computer languages. Anyway, she told me she'd met this wonderful man.'' Winn stopped and shrugged.

''Then why didn't she marry him instead of you?''

Winn stiffened. The corners of her mouth pulled down, and she glared at Joseph. How unflinchingly he hit upon her most vulnerable spot. How many times had she submerged the very thought, believing it too touchy to allow herself to think, much less voice!

''I don't think that's funny, Joseph.''

''Why? Did I hit a nerve?''

"The nerve here is yours, and you're displaying plenty of it."

"It's nothing to be ashamed of. You wouldn't be the first woman who agreed to marry somebody because he was her parents' choice."

"That's not why I'm marrying him," she claimed, perhaps a little too emphatically.

"Then why are you? Did he sweep you off your feet—sexually?" Her mouth puckered tighter. He drove on, "Well, it's sure obvious you didn't fall for him because he shared your interests. Or your goals or your tastes! You've already told me enough about him to know you're like steam and he's like ice. They may both be made of the same element, but that doesn't mean they're anything alike, Winn, and you know it."

She crossed her forearms on her knees and dropped her forehead onto them. "I didn't come here so you could make me feel worse than I already did, but somehow you're managing it."

"I'm sorry, Winn." He rested a hand on her slumped shoulder, but she shrugged it away. "I didn't mean to make you upset, but so far the only thing I can name that the two of you do well together is dance, and he leaves you behind to do that with me? I should think you'd be the one picking out these gaping holes in your relationship, not me."

She raised her head wearily. "Don't you understand? Our wedding is only six weeks away."

His eyes pierced through her. "Yeah. Scary, isn't it?"

Winn did leap to her feet then and leaned over angrily to scoop the blue ball off the floor. She began bouncing it vehemently with the racket while presenting her rigid back. "Do you want to play another game or not?"

He glared at her shapely back, her erect shoulders and the irritation she displayed as she whapped the ball. He grew more than irritated. He was frustrated and angry that she refused to explore the mistake she was making in her choice of men just because of a few social commitments.

"You bet I do. And we'll see who whips who." She was standing in the serving lane when his answer bit the air just behind her shoulder. Then he went on, "I won the first match, Gardner. The serve is mine."

She felt properly chastised and not a little embarrassed. There were men who extended the courtesy of always letting ladies serve first. It had always peeved Winn. She'd win on her own merits or not at all. How dare Joseph Duggan imply that she was trying to grab an unearned advantage!

Wordlessly she retreated to the backcourt, leaving the serving lane to him. When the first ball came, it whistled off three surfaces before she reached it just in the nick of time. The volley was long and exhausting, and he took the point. Her ego was definitely stung, for she'd tried her hardest to take the initial point after their argument. As he bounced the ball preparatory to serving, she held her racket in a position that definitely stated, "Attack," leaning forward from the waist, rocking her hips from side to side, intensity written on every muscle of her face and stance.

The longer the game went, the better they both played. They were neck and neck at fifteen, and her lungs felt ready to explode. She felt a slight cramp in her right foot but shook it off, promising herself Joseph Duggan would lose this game, come hell or high water.

He slammed a power shot off the back wall, and she missed it.

She executed a beautiful pass shot and left him standing on the opposite side of the court from where the ball rebounded.

At nineteen all, the sweat was running down their legs, backs and bellies. Her bra was soaked, and the band of her shorts stuck to her skin. His shirt—what there was of it—was so dark with sweat she wondered why he bothered to pull at its shoulder to swab his forehead.

She served a deadly one that struck with the speed of a copperhead and took point twenty to tie him.

On his next attack he reached and leaped at a scorcher skimming no farther than a quarter inch away from the wall. But in his intensity he grew careless, leaped too hard and hit the concrete, then bounced off and landed with a thick thud, flat on his back.

He winced, bared his teeth, grabbed his right knee and rolled back and forth, sucking air.

She dropped her racket and ran, falling to her knees beside him. ''Joseph, I'm sorry. Oh, Judas, what is it? Is it your knee? Here, let me see.''

He rolled and winced all the more.

''Joseph, let go. See if you can straighten it.''

He felt her fingers on his arm and forced himself to lie back, releasing the knee and leaving it flexed while his foot rested on the floor. Her hands grasped the backside of his calf, then one of them eased over his shinbone, forcing him to straighten his leg. He gasped and arched his chest higher. She laid the leg on the cool floor, touched it exploringly here, there, there, there. She made him work it back and forth, gently probing the muscles, the kneecap.

His initial shot of pain eased slightly. ''Well, what do you think, doc?'' he asked.

''I think we'd better get some ice on it right away and, depending on how it feels within the next hour, have it X-rayed.''

She stood up, reached a hand down to help him. ''Can you use it?'' He could, but he limped. She wrapped his arm around her shoulder and together they hobbled back to the dressing rooms.

''If you shower, use cool water, not hot, and I'll meet you back here as quick as you can make it.'' He'd already pushed open the locker-room door. ''And Joseph?'' He stepped and looked back over his shoulder. ''I really am sorry.''

''It's not your fault, Winn. I was playing stupidly, with all body and no brains. I deserved it.''

She thought it best if he didn't drive the truck because it had a floor shift, and until they found out how serious his injury was, the leg definitely shouldn't be strained. She stalled the old rattle-trap three times before she'd even managed to back it out of its parking space. It chortled and chugged and nearly snapped their necks when she shifted from first to second.

But it made Joseph laugh. And when she heard him laugh, she was so relieved, she laughed, too. She talked him into letting her take him to North Memorial Medical Center, even though he said he didn't want to check into any emergency ward.

''All right, then I have another plan. But we'll have to sneak to do it.''

''Sneak?''

"Into P.T.—it should be deserted at this time of night—and we'll put an ice pack on your knee and wait to see if you think you need the X-ray."

"Why should you have to sneak when you work there?"

"Because I could get fired if we get caught. The hospital is liable if you're using their facilities, and unless you're officially admitted, they have no legal recourse if something happens to you on our equipment. But it won't. I'll see to it."

"But what if you get caught?"

She angled him a devilish corner-of-the-lip grin. "You'll be indebted to me for life."

A short time later they pulled up before the Abbott Street entrance, a back door used for patient pickup, which was deserted now at 7:00 P.M. and also was the closest route to Physical Medicine.

Just before Winn got out of the truck, Joseph reached out to lay his palm on the seat beside her. "Winn?"

She stopped and turned to him.

"I'm sorry. You were right. I overstepped."

Judas, but the man had eyes she couldn't get enough of. "We'll see," she answered cryptically, then the truck door slammed behind her.

It was quiet and dark in the rehabilitation room, and he stood in the doorway, interested in its every fixture simply because it belonged to her world, and he wanted to know as much about it and her as possible.

The room was like a narrow gymnasium with ceiling-to-floor windows at one end. Along the walls were various pieces of exercise equipment lined up: two sets of portable wooden stairs with handrails, two stationary bicycles, a refrigerator-freezer, low tables topped with blue mats, more mats on the floor and various ordinary wooden chairs.

She led the way to the far left end of the room. "Sit here," she ordered, "on the table." It was scarcely knee height and easy to fall back upon. She stood beside him and ordered him to stretch out on his back. He clasped his head as if about to do sit-ups and looked along his trunk to watch her untie and remove his tennis shoe, then the clean sock he'd put on only a half hour ago. He wore the red jogging suit again. He had six-inch zippers up each ankle. She slid the right one up, then pushed the pant leg past his knee until it drew tight around his thick thigh and stayed there.

Whatever he'd done, he'd done to the muscles just below his knee, and as she surrounded them with competent hands, she gently probed and tested.

"Relax," she ordered. "You're all tensed up with your head raised like that. I'm not going to hurt you."

He fell back flat and answered all her questions, telling her what each touch felt like. Her fingers were gentle and her palms soft as she explored the muscles below the knee, then the knee itself, and finally worked her way up his thigh, probing. He tried to concentrate on the discomfort, because her hand felt so good, and because he was having difficulty disassociating the therapist from the woman. Her hands skimmed over the hair-roughened surface of his leg all the way to the top of his thigh.

At last, when he thought he was in mortal danger from the wonderful feeling of her hands upon him, she dropped them. ''It's not a hamstring, and it's not a knee. I think it's your triceps surae.''

''My what?''

''Triceps surae, the muscles found in the lower leg. You may have pulled one or more when you fell after hitting the wall.''

''How can you tell?''

''Three things. Pain, heat—it's hot right here. . . .'' She touched a sensitive spot lightly. ''And swelling. You've got all three.'' She crossed to the refrigerator while he lay thinking about another swelling that she'd come awfully close to promoting. She returned with a flat pack that looked like a miniature inflated mattress and carefully wrapped it around his leg just below the knee and secured the Velcro patches.

''For the first forty-eight to seventy-two hours ice is best, then if it's still bothering you, we'll switch to heat.''

''We? Does that mean I'll see you again in the next couple days?''

She withdrew her hands from his leg immediately, then realized what she'd done and let her hands drop to her sides while sitting down on the edge of the table beside him, crossing her knees.

''If your leg is giving you pain, of course I'd be happy to help you work with it and save you the cost of outpatient care. But if it's not. . . .''

He reached to take one of her hands and twisted their fingers together.

''And if it's not?''

She studied him silently, and from nowhere came the appealing one-eyed blink that he could read so well by now.

''Joseph, you're an extremely attractive man.'' She rubbed the back of his hand with her thumb. ''But how many times in a woman's life does she meet an attractive man whom she must resist? Once I'm married, I'm not expecting never again to be face to face with men who raise my temperature a notch or two. It's bound to happen, but it's how I react to it that's important. I'm not denying I've . . . reacted to you. You're a very persuasive man, Joseph, and sexy to boot. But I'm involved in wedding plans that are so mind boggling I wouldn't even care to list all the people and dollars involved. My mother—'' again her thumb brushed his hand softly ''—well, my mother is a very frugal woman and always concerned about security—investing, saving, planning for the future. But this time she's throwing caution aside and going whole hog. Nothing's too good or too expensive for Pau—'' She caught herself in time and finished, ''For us.''

But Joseph heard her slip. ''Just make sure you aren't making a mistake, Winn.''

She dropped his hand, placed hers on her thighs and pushed herself up to her feet. ''There's no such thing as a sure bet, but I know mother will be ecstatic when I marry Paul, and he'll be terribly good to me, and I'll have all the security she always wanted for me.''

''All the security she never had?'' Joseph questioned.

Winn pondered silently, then answered, ''Yes. It's not hard to see through her. Security is her biggest hangup.''

''Because of your father?'' She had never mentioned her father.

''Yes.''

"Did he leave her?"

"It wasn't a question of his leaving. He never stayed long enough to leave. He got her pregnant while they were dating, then disappeared, and she never heard from him or saw him again. She's had a rough time making something of herself with me to raise and nobody else to rely upon. But she's a scrapper. She made it through business school and became a superb private secretary, and she didn't stop there. When things changed, when computers came along, she didn't rest on her laurels or make up her mind *she* wasn't going to go along with such upstart ideas. Instead she went to learn how to use them. And of course, that's when Paul became her teacher."

They fell silent again. But it was not a comfortable silence this time. Joseph wanted to tell her she was being a fool. She wanted to tell him to mind his own business.

At length, she picked a neutral subject. "How does your leg feel?"

"Numb."

"Good. Let's see it now."

She removed the ice pack and examined the leg again, had him flex it, stand on it, and judged it to have pulled muscles, not broken bones.

"I don't think you'll need an X ray. How does it feel when you walk?"

"Better since the ice."

"Good. Would you like to see the tank room where I work with Merry?"

"I'd love to."

She showed him around the rest of the Physical Medicine Department, but much of the time Joseph was thinking of other things than the Hubbard tank, traction units and treadmills. He wondered how she could be so sensitive to the needs of others, yet so ignorant of her own.

When they got back to his house, he tried to kiss her, but she pressed a hand to his chest and turned away.

"No, Joseph. My mind is made up."

"Can I call you?"

"No."

"I think you're making a mistake. I think you and I would be—"

"Don't say it."

"You think it's just spring fancy, but I don't."

"Goodbye, Joseph, I hope your leg gets better." She turned to her own car and practically ran the few steps to it before slamming herself inside its sanctuary, as if a mere enclosure of metal and glass could insulate her from the powerful force that compelled the two of them together.

He watched her back up and took a step toward the car as he thought he saw her start to cry. But before he could advance, she stepped on the gas and roared down the street.

Chapter 8

The shell pink invitations had been in Winn's possession for three weeks already. Proper bridal etiquette demanded they be mailed four to six weeks in advance. She had lists of addresses from both her side and Paul's, but it seemed there was always some other detail cropping up, some interruption just as she sat down to the task of doing the addressing.

Am I delaying because I think Joseph is right? But even the suggestion made her quail. Attempting to stop the tidal wave of fevered planning that advanced with deadly intent would be like trying to hold back a natural disaster. The plans gained momentum, force and inevitability as they rolled along. The planning of a wedding, Winn learned—much to her dismay—involved so many petty details they managed to detract from the main event, which was the marriage of a man and a woman.

Fern Gardner, for all her being totally inexperienced in such folderol, proved herself as capable and structured as a drill sergeant. Not an iota went unconsidered. She'd made a calendar listing the specific days by which each particular must be checked upon, each decision made, each person telephoned, each piece of frippery purchased. And Winn *did* consider much of it frippery. Had it been left entirely up to her, Winn would have elected a quiet wedding with a few close friends and relatives invited to her mother's house or anyplace simple and left all the grandstanding for those women much more suited to it.

Yes, she'd enjoyed dressing up and celebrating the day of Sandy's wedding, but for herself she preferred things much simpler. She was an artless woman of ordinary tastes and would have been much, much happier if all the silly special effects could have been side-stepped.

But Fern Gardner, self-made success, abandoned by her lover at age nineteen, mother of an illegitimate daughter, needed the reassurance and illusion of security attendant with a large flashy wedding. She had only one daughter and that one lucky enough to have attracted a man whom Fern had virtually handpicked. She wasn't about to stint on this most auspicious day of Winnifred's life.

Within the week following Winn's confrontation with Joseph Duggan, her mother called at least eleven times, always for some mindless noncruciality that made Winn grit her teeth while answering. The realtor called twice asking her to leave the house so he could show it in the evenings. At the hospital Meredith Emery brought brochures of Disneyland and asked how soon her hair would grow back. The furniture store called to say the new living-room sofa, chairs and tables had arrived, and Paul called to ask if they shouldn't take one evening to go out and choose lamps, pictures and also to buy one particular item he'd spied while out browsing on one of his lunch hours; a table-style chess set with inlaid two-toned wood top—perfect for a living-room accent piece.

"A chess set?" Winn echoed, dismayed.

"Not just a chess set. A very special chess set."

"But why?"

"I told you I'd give you another lesson when we had more time. I know you can get the hang of it."

"But, Paul, you know I'm no good at chess."

"You'll learn, darling. I have every confidence in you." He laughed lightly.

Suddenly she experienced a jagged flash of irritation. Unconsciously her back stiffened, and she coiled the telephone cord six times around her finger until it cut off the circulation.

"I'll make you a deal, Paul," she announced with a hard edge to her voice. "I'll come and look at your chess set if you'll agree that for every hour we spend playing it, we'll spend equal time playing racket ball."

A long silence followed, then his chuckle, more patronizing than humored. "Now, Winnifred, you know I'm all feet on the racket-ball court. I've never been a jock and never pretended to be. I'll leave the physical workouts to you."

She yanked the phone cord off her finger and rammed a kitchen chair with her foot till it slammed under the table with a resounding clatter. "Fine! Great! Then what do you say if one or two nights a week we each find somebody else to play our games with? You can find someone with an analytical mind to pore over your chess table with you, and I'll find somebody who likes to rap a ball around a racket-ball court." Naturally the picture of Joseph popped up, dressed in white shorts with his bare belly showing below a whacked-off T-shirt. "Paul, are you there, Paul? What do you say?" she hissed. "Maybe old Rita will oblige you, huh?"

"Winnifred, you're being unreasonable."

"Oh, am I? And what are you being?"

If there was one thing Paul Hildebrandt prided himself upon it was his ability to reason. The electric silence told Winn her words stung.

"It was just an idea, that's all. Naturally, if you're opposed to the chess table, we don't have to go look at it."

Suddenly the back of Winn's nostrils burned. She felt like dropping to her knees and bawling. He thought the issue here was a chess table! Judas priest! For a brilliant man he could be utterly dense.

"Well, what about going out to choose the lamps and other small items?" he was asking.

She opened her mouth wide, drew an enormous calming breath, ran four agitated fingers through her hair and said to the floor, "I don't care. I'd like to do it . . . whenever you want." But once the words were out, she realized one of the two statements had to be untrue. Which was true? Either she wanted to do it, or she didn't care.

"Day after tomorrow, then? I'll come and pick you up around seven."

"Fine," she answered despondently. "Seven."

''Good night, love. Get some good rest now. You seem a little high-strung lately, and it's probably all the last-minute details piling up.''

It was not the details and Winn knew it. The details were being handled with parliamentary punctiliousness by Fern Gardner, who only checked with her daughter as a matter of principle, not because Winn's approval was either sought or necessary. No, Winn's problem had nothing to do with details. It had to do with a curly-haired Irishman whose sexy eyes she could not forget, who played a wicked game of racket ball, drove rusty pickups and kissed like Prince Charming.

Within a half hour of Winn's hanging up after her conversation with Paul, Sandy called.

''Hi, kiddo, how're the wedding plans coming?''

Winn had to force herself not to vent her wrath upon her unsuspecting friend—after all, Sandy had no idea of the turmoil within Winn lately. ''Pretty well, considering mother's handling all the last-minute glitches with her usual steel-trap deadlines.''

''Oh-oh! Something's up.''

Winn sank onto the chair she'd earlier kicked so hard. ''No, nothing's up. It's just that I have other things on my mind besides wedding, wedding, wedding. But neither mother nor Paul seems concerned.''

''The little girl at the hospital?''

''Yes, among other things. She's dying and I—'' Winn drew a deep breath and battled the almost irresistible urge to tell Sandy everything, including her feelings for Jo-Jo Duggan, to be honest and open and ask her friend's opinion about the whole matter. But before she could broach the subjects, Sandy went on.

''Well, I have just the thing to take your mind off your troubles and put you in a happy frame of mind. I guess you know what it is. We've talked about it long enough.''

Winn covered her eyes and braced an elbow on the table. *Oh, no, not the shower.*

''It's the shower. I've just been waiting to hear from you until I put the date on the invitations. And it's getting awfully close. I think we'd better have it maybe week after next, or the week following that. Do you have your calendar handy?''

It was staring at Winn from a nail on the wall beside the telephone, and as she looked up at it, it suddenly became blurred by tears. Sandy was waiting for an answer, and here she sat, recalling how Paul had once walked up to that nail and said, ''I hope you don't plan to drive nails into the walls of our new house this way.'' If she wanted to drive a four-inch railroad spike into her wall, by God she'd drive it! On the ugly stucco walls of Jo-Jo Duggan's kitchen there hung a calendar with a picture of a tin lizzie, and a header advertising Duggan's Body Shop. Next time she was there, Winn promised herself to check and see what he'd hung it up with.

Apparently Winn took longer to mull over the shower than she'd realized, for Sandy's voice came across the wire once again. ''Winn, have you sent out your wedding invitations yet?''

"No, I've been working on them."

"Well, the shower invitations shouldn't really go out until after people get the ones for the wedding. Don't you think you should get going?"

Fern had called four days in a row to issue the same reprimand. Winn felt pressured and antagonized. "Yes, I'll make sure I have them out by the weekend if I have to stay home from work one day to finish addressing them." But at work Merry needed her, and she'd no more have deserted the child for a single precious day of her remaining life than Winn would have jumped at the chance to own a chess table of inlaid wood.

They chose two weeks from Saturday for the shower and agreed that Saturday would delay sending her invitations until midway through the following week, giving Winn enough time to get her own out first.

When Winn hung up the phone, she resolutely dragged out the box of pink envelopes and notes, the lists of addresses, her own phone book and a pen. She had addressed five when the phone rang again.

"Hello, Winn, this is mother."

What would it be this time? Had the apricot-rose crop failed in Florida? Winn bit back the sharp response and answered, "Hello, mother."

"Have you got the invitations in the mail yet?"

"No, but they're almost done," she lied.

"Winn, have you taken a look at the calendar lately? Those invitations should have been in the mail no later than last Saturday."

"I know, mother, I know."

"And now something else has come up. Perry Smith has just received word that he's being transferred to Los Angeles."

For a moment Winn was disoriented. She couldn't figure out what Perry Smith's transfer had to do with anything concerning her. Evidently her mother expected some moan of dismay that was not forthcoming, for her voice crackled with indignation. "Well, for heaven's sake, I should think there'd be some reaction from you. After all, there's not much time to find someone else to do the singing."

Oh, yes—Ramona Smith, Perry's wife, had agreed to do the music at the wedding and had already discussed the choice of songs with Winn.

"It's not the end of the world, mother. I'd be happy with just the organ, anyway. Mrs. Collingswood might be twittery, but she's wonderful when she touches a keyboard."

"Oh, Winnifred, don't be ridiculous. Whoever heard of a church wedding without vocal music? The songs are all chosen, and they've been planned into the entire service. Don't tell me you have no intention of asking someone else."

"I don't know any other singers, mother. I didn't even know this one. You found her."

"Well, it's imperative that we move fast on this."

Winn's temper snapped. "*You* move fast on it if you want to, mother. I've made all the fast moves I can stand for a while!"

Her mother's voice softened, but with an effort. "Darling, you're not yourself these days. Why, I swear you sound as if you really don't care about these decisions one way or another."

"Frankly, mother, I don't. If you want a different singer, get one. Tell him he can sing 'Betty Lou's Gettin' Out Tonight' for all I care. And hire a sequined chorus line to dance along with it!"

She could see her mother's stunned face and feel her hurt surprise at the rebuff. "Oh, Mother, I'm sorry. Please just do whatever you want and let me know, all right?"

Thirty minutes later Paul called again. "Your mother and I just had a long talk, Winnifred, and she tells me you just snapped at her and hurt her feelings, and have washed your hands of making decisions about the singer. Winnie, you really shouldn't treat your mother so . . . so. . . ." He ended with a sigh.

"So what?"

"You know. You're short with her all the time and find fault with everything she does when she's really bending over backward to facilitate matters and help us plan a very high-class wedding here."

"Maybe I didn't want a high-class wedding, Paul. Maybe I just wanted you to pay mother a few glass beads, open a vein, exchange blood with you and slip away to a tepee in the woods." Where had this caustic person come from? Winn was being unfair to Paul, and she knew it but couldn't seem to curb these cutting remarks. She felt him tightly controlling his anger.

"I understand, you're under a lot of pressure right now, so I'll excuse you for getting short with me, but I think you owe your mother an apology."

Dear God—it struck Winn—he's marrying me as much for the mother-in-law he'll inherit as he is for the bride he'll get. Still, she softened her tone. "Paul, do me a favor, will you? Call mother back, and you two discuss the singer and pick one. Will you do that for me, please?"

There followed a moment's pause while he decided how to handle this suddenly unreasonable fiancée of his. "Yes, I'll be happy to. My mother might have a name for us, too. I'll take care of it, darling."

"Thank you, Paul."

After hanging up, she addressed twenty-five more invitations, then dropped her head onto the tabletop and bawled as she'd been wanting to for days.

Her back ached. Her eyelids burned, and she felt like driving an entire box of nails into the kitchen wall, making a regular design of them all around the frame of the sliding glass door and maybe starting across the wall that abutted it. Instead, she left the invitations strewn all over the table, shucked off her clothes and dropped into bed. She was just dozing off when the phone rang—again!

She flung back the covers and stomped out to the kitchen, angry at being awakened and made to get out of bed.

"Hullo!" she growled.

"Hello," came the masculine voice she'd been trying her hardest to forget. Tears burned her eyes again. Her heart slammed against her chest. She covered her eyes with one hand and leaned her forehead against the cool glass of the sliding door in the dark.

"Are you alone?" he asked.

"What do you want, Joseph?"

"You."

The line hummed with a taut silence. Winn's feminine parts surged to life—nipples, stomach, inner reaches all pressing for contact with him.

"Don't," she begged in a voice very close to tears.

"I'm sorry, Winn. I complicate things for you, don't I?"

"Yes, oh, God, yes."

She heard him sigh as if close to defeat, yet unwilling to accept it quite yet. "Are the wedding plans progressing without a hitch?"

"Yes. I'm addressing the invitations."

"Oh." Again there followed a poignant silence. "Will you do me a favor, Winn? Will you send me one?"

"Jo-Jo," she sighed.

"Oh, I won't come. I'd just like one to keep."

"J—Joseph, you are b-being exceedingly unkind."

"Winn, are you crying?" He sounded anxious, as if he'd clutched the phone closer to his mouth.

"Yes, d-damn you, I'm crying."

"Why?"

"B-because! He wants to buy a chess table for the l-living room, and some w-woman I don't even know is m-moving to Los Angeles . . . and b-because Sandy wants to give me a sh-shower . . . oh, God, I don't know, Joseph. I only know I'm supposed to be happy, and I'm miserable."

"How's the little girl?"

"Oh, thank you for asking, darl—Joseph. Nobody else really cares how I feel about her around here. Sandy asked, but when I answered, she hurried on as if to avoid the subject, too."

Winn paused for breath, and his soft voice fell upon her ear. "Back up a minute, Winn. Start at the beginning of that."

"I . . . you don't make sense, Joseph Duggan." But he made perfect sense and she knew it.

"You were about to call me darling."

"No, I wasn't."

"Try it anyway and see how it feels." *Joseph Duggan, consummate flirt,* she thought. But she knew him to be far more than that now. His voice was odd as he asked, "Is that what you call Paul?" It was one of the only times she recalled Joseph referring to her fiancé by his correct name.

"No. He calls me darling. I call him Paul."

"We've got sidetracked. Tell me about the little girl, Winn."

Why did the name Winn sound more like an endearment from Joseph's lips than the term darling from Paul's?

She told him about Merry's lack of progress, about the brochures from Disneyland. She told him about the singer whose husband was being transferred to Los Angeles, about the argument with her mother, about the shower and the gift registration she was supposed to decide upon at a local department store, where she was expected to choose a china pattern she didn't give a damn about and crystal glasses she'd be uncomfortable drinking from. She told him she'd just made the final payment on Paul's wedding ring, and that her mother was harping about buying something called a unity candle that was to be used in the wedding service, though she herself didn't understand why it was necessary. And she ended by telling him Fern had now come up with the idea of providing limousine service on the day of the wedding.

''Limousine service!'' she cried, exasperated. ''Of all the phony things.''

''Your mother sounds as if she loves you very much.''

''My mother is putting on a show she wished for and never had herself. She's playing fairy godmother.''

''Then if you have to go through with it anyway, let her. Why do you agree with her one day and buck her the next? You're the one in the wrong, not her.''

''But she's railroaded me into all this . . . this circus stuff I never wanted.''

''Then why didn't you tell her a year ago when you should have instead of letting her believe it was what you wanted? Or is it really your mother you're upset about at all?''

''Joseph, I'm tired and I want to go to sleep.''

''And I'm frustrated and I want to see you again. Will you drive up to Bemidji with me this Saturday?''

She couldn't believe the man! Five weeks until her wedding, and he suggests she flit away with him like a carefree sprite. ''Bemidji! You want me to take off with you just like that and drive up to Bemidji?''

''Yes, to an auction sale.''

She was flabbergasted. ''An auction sale. Jo-Jo Duggan, you're crazy. I'm addressing my wedding invitations, and you invite me to an auction sale.''

''Yes. There's a '41 Ford on the billboard, and there'll be a swap meet, and I might be able to pick up a piece for my '54 Cadillac pickup I haven't been able to find. I thought we might drive it up there.''

''And what about Paul? Should I invite him to come along with us?''

''Sure. We'll put him in a coffin, and he can ride in the back.''

She gave a nasal snort of laughter before she could stop herself, then covered her nose with a hand. ''That's awful, Joseph!'' she scolded.

''With a comfortable pillow and blanket, of course,'' he added, ''not a satin lining. And a thermos of iced tea to keep him company for the long ride.''

She resisted the gravity of his teasing and became serious once again. ''Joseph, I have to go now.''

''My leg could use some of that attention you promised.''

''Goodbye, Joseph.''

''And I've signed up for dancing classes.''

''Goodbye, Joseph.''

''And I can't find anybody who's half as good as you on the racket-ball court, or who kiss—''

She forced herself to hang up gently. But she dreamed of his curls and crinkly eyes that night.

The prenuptial craziness continued the next day when Fern reminded Winn to send the caterers their time schedule and be sure not to forget to put return postage on the R.S.V.P. notes, and to tell her she'd found the perfect stem glasses for the toasting ceremony of the bride and groom. Winn shook her head as if she'd just been landed a right uppercut. They had to *buy* special glasses for *that?*

At eight that evening Winn sat at the kitchen table pouring on the steam to her addressing operation. A knock sounded, and Paul came in without waiting for her to answer.

''Winnie, darling, the most wonderful thing has come up!'' He swept into the kitchen and stepped behind her chair, grasping her shoulders while bending low to kiss her neck. ''I've been asked to go out to California for a week. The company is sending me on a tour of The Valley! Imagine that—*The Valley!*''

She knew by now there was only one ''valley'' in Paul's vocabulary. He referred to ''Silicon Valley,'' the world's foremost computer-manufacturing area.

''When?''

''I leave tomorrow for a week. There'll be tours of all the major computer-manufacturing plants and opportunities to learn about all the latest technological advances.'' The entire country knew that the area just south of San Jose had been in the vanguard of computer technology and was populated with brilliant young men and women whose genius in the field would see many of them millionaires in their thirties. Their expertise was so valued in the industry that the term ''The Valley'' was now recognized worldwide. Innovations came from The Valley so fast and radically that a computer was often obsolete almost before it rolled off the assembly line, bettered by its successor. Winn understood how the opportunity must excite Paul.

He urged her up from her chair. He kissed her ardently, then asked, ''Can you get along without me, darling? I know there's a lot going on, and I know I shouldn't be leaving you at this time, but it's the chance of a lifetime, Winnie.'' Seldom did his eyes dance like this. She looked into them and tried to conjure up even a quarter of the electric response generated by the mere sound of Joseph Duggan's voice crossing a telephone wire.

''Of course, I can get along without you for a week. All I really need to get done right now is the invitations, and you can't help me with them.''

''Oh, thank you, darling.'' He cupped the back of her head and lifted her toward his kiss—an excited, searching kiss—then wrapped her in both arms and pressed her body close to his. She clung and kissed him back with an almost violent twisting of her body against his, pressing and writhing against him. But it didn't work. She was forcing the issue, and when her body failed to respond as fully as she'd hoped, Winn realized Paul was stimulated as much by excitement over the trip to Silicon Valley as he was by his bride-to-be.

''Winnie,'' he groaned in her ear. ''Let's go to bed. God, it's so good to have you like this again. Something's been wrong for the last few weeks, and I haven't been able to put my finger on it. But tonight you're like you used to be.''

She kissed his jaw as she answered, ''No, Paul, not tonight.''

He drew back, hurt. ''But I'll be gone for a whole week.''

''I have my period.'' It was a lie, and she suffered the weight of guilt for it while he encircled her in his arms again, slipped his hands beneath her shirt and caressed her breasts while groaning into her ear.

''Damn!'' he murmured at last, forcing himself to release her.

She offered him a consolation that hardly eased her conscience. ''When you get back, we'll go out shopping for the lamps and buy you the chess table, too.''

''I love you,'' he declared gently.

His eyes were filled with admiration and gratitude, but he was as eager to leave as she was to have him go when he left a short while later.

After he was gone, she returned to her wedding invitations and attacked them almost frenziedly. She worked that night until midnight and the following night till ten-thirty when she became drowsy and got up to make a pot of coffee to help keep herself awake. She finished the last pink envelope around 1:30 A.M. and licked two hundred and twenty-five stamps before going to bed. She wondered if it was the taste of the glue that made her feel slightly nauseous.

On Friday morning—precisely four weeks and one day before the big event—she dropped the two hundred and twenty-five shell pink envelopes in the big drop box at the post office and breathed a shaky sigh of relief. Tonight when Paul called from California, she'd tell him. *Then* she'd feel excited.

At work she wrapped patients' limbs in hot packs, then put them through their various rehab exercises. She determined the resistance levels of those who rode the stationary bikes and decided how much weight to strap to those limbs needing strengthening. She gave massages, had a consultation with a doctor regarding a new patient to whom she was being assigned, went to lunch with two co-workers and told them she'd finally mailed her wedding invitations.

And at one o'clock that afternoon, Mrs. Christianson called Winn to her office and quietly announced that Meredith Emery had died.

Winnifred tried valiantly to control her tears.

"But she's due for her therapy at two o'clock," she said inanely, as if the reminder would bring the child back to life to meet the schedule.

Mrs. Christianson took Winn's hand, led her to the exercise room and forced her to sit on the edge of a table, then sat down behind her and started massaging Winn's shoulders and neck.

"You've got very close to this one, I know, Winnifred. And it's hard when you get close. Take the rest of the day off, then go out this weekend and do something wild and crazy to take your mind off it."

The woman's hands were superbly trained and exceedingly adept. She gently kneaded without pinching. But the pain couldn't be massaged away. It went too deep. Winn bent forward, braced her elbows to her knees and dug the heels of her hands into her eye sockets.

"Go home, Winnifred. Go home and take a run, then soak in a hot tub and call that man of yours and celebrate life with him instead of dwelling on death."

But Mrs. Christianson didn't know that man of hers was two thousand miles away, paying homage to a bloodless nerveless entity called "the computer."

Still, Winn followed her supervisor's advice. She put on her green shorts and sweat shirt and ran. She felt the overwhelming need to be outside where blossoms and fresh-cut grass gave testimony to the green resurrection of the world. She sucked in the fecund late May air and counted the number of people who were out planting their backyard gardens, and watched a pair of kites sailing far above her head, realizing two hearty and hale people held the other ends of the strings. She lifted a hand in greeting to every toddler on every tricycle she passed. She cut through a park where pet owners were out walking their dogs and through the parking lot of a small neighborhood grocery store where husbands were stopping to buy cartons of milk on their way home for suppers with wives and children. She steeped herself in life, clinging to each piece of evidence that it thrived, carrying those pictures with her while her legs pumped and stretched and passed the point of easy endurance. She ran on, feeling the heat build in her muscles, welcoming it as a reminder that she lived, panted, burned and ached.

Back at home she draped herself across the kitchen counter, pressing her hot cheek to its cool Formica surface, hardly able to stand for several minutes while her breath beat against her upthrown arm. When her heart had calmed and her breathing slowed, she stood beneath the pummeling hot shower before eating the most calorie-filled foods she had in the house—all starches and sugars and the forbidden junk she rarely put into the body she kept at its peak as a defense against all those she encountered daily who were not as lucky as she.

Paul called. She told him about Meredith Emery in as unemotional a voice as she could manage. He listened and offered a token response of sympathy before reminding her that it was best not to bring her worries home at the end of the workday, especially with a job like hers.

Rage grew within Winn that he, who spent night after night locked away from her, clattering the keyboard of a computer named Rita, should tell her not to bring her career-oriented concerns home at the end of the day!

In bed she tossed and flailed, and studied the black square of window and tried to cry but failed.

At 11:00 P.M. she gave in and called Joseph Duggan.

One of his brothers answered, then Joseph came on the line and grunted sleepily, "Yeah?"

"Joseph, it's Winn."

In the tiny house in Osseo, Joseph Duggan stood in his jockey shorts beside his grandmother's kitchen sink, which was piled high with dirty cups and plates, and pictured the woman whose voice now spoke in his ear. He pictured her as she'd looked the day he turned and found her watching him scrubbing up after work.

"Winn," he repeated, as if the name released a flock of white doves.

"Joseph, I need somebody tonight. I can't . . . oh, please, Joseph, can you meet me?"

"Anywhere. Anytime."

"Will I sound ridiculous if I ask you to play a game of racket ball at this hour of the night?"

"I'm already tying my Adidas."

"My club is open till midnight. It's closer than yours. I'll meet you there. Ask at the desk which court, and I'll tell them you're my guest."

"Let me go, so I can hurry."

He ran through the house searching frantically for anything to throw on, grabbing the first thing he found—a pair of sawed-off blue jeans and giving up when he couldn't find a shirt fast enough, so heading out without one, only his shoes in his hand, and his racket.

At the club he careered to a halt before the sleepy night-desk attendant and impatiently whacked a palm down beside the registration book. "What court is Winn Gardner in?"

"Number six."

He jogged down the long corridor and panted to a halt before the only court in which the lights were burning.

She was waiting in the middle of the floor, huddled, arms to knees and forehead to arms, facing the front wall. He stepped down onto the wooden floor and paused.

"Winn?"

Her head snapped up, and she spun around on her buttocks.

"Oh, Joseph, thank you for coming."

He crossed the distance between them with a strong muscular stride. "Don't you dare thank me for coming, Winn. Not me."

She swallowed hard and had an awful, belligerent set to her jaw as she rolled to her knees and looked up at him, standing above her. "Work me hard tonight, Joseph," she demanded sternly. "Don't give me no quarter. Promise?"

Their eyes clashed, and he wondered what this was all about but let her carry it to whatever end she desired without enlightening him in the meantime.

"I promise."

She leaped up and stripped her sweat shirt off almost angrily, flung it out into the hall and slammed the door. He watched, frowning as she strode to the center of the backcourt, dressed in a white T-shirt and green shorts.

"Serve!" she ordered, disdaining warm-ups, staring at the front wall almost as if she'd forgotten Joseph was there except as an instrument to do her bidding.

He strode to the serving lane and gave her what she wanted. He worked her like a slave driver, giving her everything he had. She smashed the ball with a vehemence that was awesome. She drove it and backhanded it, and all the time her teeth were clenched and her jaw bulging. She rushed forward to meet each oncoming ball as if her life depended upon meeting it in time. She was vicious and at times almost ugly in her grim fanaticism. But in that ugliness lurked a true beauty, that of the athlete who pushes her body to its physical limits. She arched her back to a torturous angle as she reached for high shots behind her head. She lunged with a pure surge of might and sometimes climbed two steps up the concrete walls in her frantic effort to wreak whatever vengeance she must upon a dumb blue sphere of rubber.

The sweat flowed freely. She swung at a shot and missed, then when the next serve came, cracked it dead center while gritting for emphasis, "God*damn* you!"

They played at the torturous pace for thirty minutes, then Joseph had to know. He stood at the serving line with his back to her and stubbornly refused to turn around while asking, "Did you send out the wedding invitations?"

"Yes!" she barked. "Serve, dammit!"

Joseph felt as if she'd stabbed him in the back with a broken blade.

They played fifteen minutes more, but now he was attacking each shot as recklessly, as angrily as she. Tonight it mattered not in the least who won or lost. It only mattered that they slammed the ball against the concrete walls and got even with the world's injustices and demands.

"*Why?*" he growled as his racket punished the innocent ball.

"Because I couldn't *stop* it!" She, too, performed an injustice to the game of racket ball with her next return.

"Is that why you're doing this?"

The whistling return he'd expected to fly past his ear never materialized. Instead, behind him all was silent. He whirled, white lipped now with fury. Dammit, he loved this woman! They stared each other down—she was poised as if to turn her racket on him while he gripped his own racket with a fist so tight it made veins bulge like blue rivers up his arms.

''Is that why?'' he demanded angrily.

''No!'' she bleated. Then, without warning, Winn Gardner collapsed to her knees, hugged her head and broke into a torrent of sobbing.

Jo-Jo's racket clattered to the floor. He was bending to her in less than a second, knee to knee, grasping her arms in a painful grip. ''Winn, please tell me what this is all about.''

Her hair was strewn and wild, for it had not been pampered after its last washing. It prodded the air around her face while her mouth yawned in anguish and tears streamed from her tormented eyes. Her fingers plucked at Joseph's chest as if searching for a shirt to grasp.

''Oh, God, Joseph, she died.''

And then he understood.

''Winn . . . Winn. . . .'' Gently he embraced her, kissing her temple, wanting to slip her inside his very body to protect her from further pain. ''I'm sorry, darling. I'm sorry.''

Her body jerked. Her arms clung. The salt of sweat and tears intermingled upon his neck as she buried her face there and wept. Incoherently she babbled out her sorrow while he quietly held her, understanding the meaning if not the words. Joseph and Winn were bound together wherever their bare skins touched by the sweat they'd forced from each other's bodies during the grueling combat of the past half hour. He ran his hands as far around her as he could and drew her in as if his arms were attached to a winch, and only she could release its catch. Their knees were widespread now, their stomachs and breasts molded flat together. Her hurt became his. And because she cried, his eyes misted, too.

When her sobbing grew terrifying, he plowed his hands through her hair and forced her head back, covering her mouth with his in a blessed surcease of solitariness. Their tongues, like the ball they had just battered, drove and smashed and volleyed, continuing to fight the fight of the living against the invincibility of death. Their heads moved as if they were fighting each other with their open mouths, when there was truly no fight at all, only enormous relief from tensions both emotional and sexual.

He pushed her back and fell with her onto the middle of the vast empty floor, covering her hard-muscled body with his own. His elbows struck the floor, then her head was cradled in his arms in a half awkward, half meshing embrace while their well-matched bodies fused. His hips shifted to one side, and a knee nudged hers open. She complied with profound defiance of everyone and everything save Joseph Duggan, placing her soles on the floor, widening her straddle until he was couched securely within her thighs, and she could freely and angrily thrust up against him.

At first their breaths were ragged, hers still shredded by the last vestiges of weeping. But soon they became conscious of the faint hum of the overhead lights in the otherwise still room. Neither their lips nor hips had separated when the writhing and lashing out stopped.

Their kiss grew tender, the movements of their heads mellowed into those of lovers exploring something wondrous. Her knees were still flexed, but they relaxed now, and one of them slipped down to lie flat against the floor while the other caressed his hip.

Combat became caress.

Grip became greeting.

Anger became accolade.

They moved as a wave moves upon the shore, one upon the other, slipping up to explore, cover, then receding to await the next nudge of nature.

His body was hard. He used it to encourage, to invite, but not to assault or punish. She lifted rhythmically in acceptance, and he backed away the shortest distance possible, only enough to see her wide blue eyes, filled with acceptance of the inevitable, and with something else, trembling, breathless loving.

''Joseph, what have I done?'' She spoke of the invitations, of course.

But he wouldn't have her asking of them now. ''You've made me fall in love with you. I love you, Winn. Take me home with you.''

''For the night, Joseph?'' she asked uncertainly.

''Yes, for the night, for only tonight if it's all I can have.''

''Yes, Joseph, oh, yes, darling. I think it's time I find out if you're right about a lot of things.''

He pushed himself from her, sat back on his haunches with one of his knees on either side of one of hers. Their eyes were polarized now, unable to break apart. He caught her hand and rolled to the balls of his feet, pulling her up with him.

Chapter 9

She stood in the shower, listening to the spray echo through the ceramic enclosure of the deserted locker room. Her eyes were closed, her face uplifted, slick palms working the bar of soap. She supposed the guilt would come later, but now there was nothing except sweet anticipation and a painful ache in the center of her chest from sexual suppression. How many weeks had it been since she'd met Joseph Duggan and recognized the vibrant carnality trembling between them? Only eight, yet as each of those weeks had passed, it'd left her more and more certain that her body pined for his.

She opened her eyes, stared at the nozzle of the shower, backed away from the warm liquid needles and ran the bar of soap around her neck and both breasts, down her belly, across her hips and down her legs. She disdained the cloth, using her own hands instead to cleanse her skin and feel the quivering nerve endings just beneath its surface. Her breasts felt engorged with eagerness, the nipples hard and pitted like steel thimbles.

Oh, I want him. When was the last time I felt this way? This ready? She had repressed all her bodily urgings for Joseph Duggan until, now, after the stimulus of lying beneath him, they retaliated. Tonight there would be no denial. Tonight . . . she gasped. And bent quickly to wash her legs and feet instead. Hurrying now. Hurrying.

Her shampoo smelled faintly of lily of the valley. She wrapped a towel turban fashion around her head and secured the loose end at her nape, then dressed in a pair of red nylon knit shorts and a simple white U-neck pullover, slipping these over panties only, no bra. She stuffed her shoes and socks into her tote bag and padded out barefoot to meet Joseph.

He was waiting outside the door to the locker room, barefoot, too, wearing nothing but the pair of faded cutoff denim shorts he'd worn on the court. Her eyes fell to them, then to his right hand in which he held a wad of something cotton and white—his underwear?

''I took off in such a hurry I didn't think about clean clothes,'' he explained. Oh, God—it *was* his underwear! Her dastardly eyes dropped to the fringe of the faded blue jeans. They were slightly stretched, untidy with drooping threads, and cut off so high that the tip of one white pocket peeped out at the leg line. His hard leg protruded from the soft blue cloth, creating an arresting contrast in textures and filling her imagination with what he must look and feel like naked inside the cutoffs.

The surge of sensuousness she'd experienced in the shower magnified a hundredfold. She raised her eyes and found him studying her breasts, obviously unbound within the scoop-neck shirt, and even as he looked, they started puckering. He swallowed and raised his eyes to the towel wrapped around her head.

When Winn spoke, her voice sounded as if she had strep throat. ''I forgot my brush, so I'll leave this on till I get home.'' But neither of them made a move toward the stairs leading up and out. Then, when they finally did, they jerked as if they'd got a load of buckshot in the tail.

Walking up the steps just ahead of him, she felt his eyes on her back, and the sensation was almost as palpable as a physical touch. In the lobby he slipped a hand along the bar of steel that crossed the heavy plateglass door at waist level. She saw nothing but his bare arm as he pushed the door wide and let her pass before him. His rusty pickup was parked next to her car in the deserted parking lot. Overhead a bluish light buzzed, and insects sent up a humming around it. Instinctively she headed for her own car, and just as she reached it, his hands clasped hers.

''Winn, if you'd like, I can leave my truck here so it won't have to sit in your driveway all night.''

His offer brought back reality: they had made one conscious choice, and one only. To become lovers for the night. Beyond that, nothing had been decided. If she told him to leave the pickup, their liaison took on overtones of sordidness and dishonesty. And though she didn't want to consider her relationship with Joseph Duggan in that light, there couldn't be another pickup like his old junker in the whole metro area. She was forced to make a choice.

"Yes, you can ride with me. I'll drive you back over here in the morning."

He dropped her hand, turned away and picked his barefooted way carefully around the tail of her car. He opened the back door, threw his racket and shoes inside, then slipped into the front seat beside her.

She lived only two miles from the club, and it took little time to drive that far along deserted Seventy-seventh Avenue. But when they reached the intersection at Highway 52, the light was red. As they sat, waiting for it to change, he studied her face, lighted to pink by the reflected glow, her eyes refracting a pair of red dots from the overhead traffic light. He sensed guilt coming to give her second thoughts and slid across the seat, put an arm around her shoulders and turned her face to him with the pressure of a single finger on her jaw.

"Winn, I won't be a hypocrite and tell you not to think of him. But when you do, and I know you will more than just once during the night, will you think of me, too, and remember that I love you?"

The light turned green in her eyes. She clutched the wheel and left her foot on the brake. *I love you, too, Joseph,* she thought but could not say it. To do so would be unfair to both of them. Instead she lifted her lips to his, touching his jaw with her fingertips—it was rough in contrast to the sleek satin of his mouth as his lips parted and the tip of his tongue greeted hers.

When the kiss ended, Winn said softly, "And I won't be a hypocrite and say I'm going to put him from my mind because he's there right now, and you know it."

"Then I'll do my best to get him out of it temporarily if you'll just drive on through this green light, Winn Gardner, and take us to someplace a little less public than the intersection of Highway 52 and Seventy-seventh Avenue."

But the light had turned red again, and they had a full three minutes more to blandish each other with lips and tongues.

At the town house the For Sale sign was still perched on the boulevard. The lights illuminated it momentarily, then arced around and a moment later died with the engine. Joseph turned to study Winn, but now that the moment was here, she was nervous. She opened her door, leaving him to do likewise and follow her up the sidewalk and the three steps leading to her front door.

There, he didn't reach to take the keys from her hand, but took her tote bag instead, leaving her with both hands free. Still she felt inept, and it seemed forever before she found the hole in the lock.

Finally the dead bolt clicked back, and she led the way inside into the dark recesses of her tiny front foyer and the living room, listening to the soft thunk of the door closing behind him, then the almost imperceptible *shush* of his bare feet on the carpet. She reached blindly and found his hand. He followed, recognizing the direction in which she led him, turning right along the short hall leading past the bathroom to her bedroom. Another right turn and he knew he was standing at the foot of her bed with the high dresser to his left and the old-fashioned dressing table to his right. Her fingers clutched his rather frantically now, and he felt her trembling.

Did she expect him to drop her on the bed in the dark, and afterward creep out like a clandestine debaucher? Did she think that if it happened under cover of darkness, it would be easier to forget later?

He slipped from her fingers and found the wall switch in the dark. A pair of matched boudoir lamps flashed on, reflecting themselves from the mirror of the ancient dressing table.

Winn's face was in shadow as she whirled to face Joseph. His hand was still on the light switch. ''If I'm going to have only one night with you, I certainly don't intend to have it in the dark. I want some memories to take away with me . . . of how you looked when you made love.''

She dropped her eyes to the floor, and he dropped his hand from the light switch. He leaned to set her bag on the floor, then paused expectantly, waiting for her to make some sign of invitation. Instead, she studied the carpet beneath her bare toes.

''I'm very nervous,'' she admitted. Her voice wasn't its usual calm self. It was high and pinched.

''So am I. Agreeing to go to bed together, then putting it off for the better part of an hour is a little nerve-racking, isn't it?''

She glanced up shyly—he was grinning warmly—and laughed nervously.

''I . . . I'm sorry this room is in such a mess. I'm afraid I'm not the best housekeeper. Other things always seem to come first.''

''At home my bed is made up only on the days when I change the sheets.'' He glanced at the tousled bed. Her sheets were white, the blanket army green and the spread a burnt orange—not exactly the boudoir of a vamp, yet it suited her.

With three unhurried steps he moved to stand before her, but when he reached to touch, she ducked aside and avoided him. Before the dressing table she reached up to remove the towel from her head. He took up a hipshot stance, hooked his thumbs in the back waistband of his shorts and watched as she bent forward at the waist, then rubbed her hair briskly. His eyes slid down the curve of her spine to the red knit shorts that magically rode up and down at the same time: up at the hem, revealing the gentle half-moon of skin where her white underwear stretched up to reveal a sliver of derriere, and dipping down at the waist as the elastic curved, revealing two knobs of her vertebrae thrown into shadowed relief.

Silently he moved up behind her and placed his hands on her waist. She jerked erect and met his eyes in the mirror, her own framed by a shock of wet wild hair. He heard the catch in her breath, then they both held motionless. When she realized how unsightly her hair looked, one hand came up to drive it back from her forehead.

Why, she's hiding. Of course. She felt vulnerable with her hair wet and tangled. No woman dreams of making love with a man for the first time looking less than perfect. Yet her fresh wet state seemed totally perfect for Winn Gardner.

He captured her hand and lowered it to her side.

''Sit down,'' he ordered softly. ''Let me.''

Her knees quivered as she stood transfixed by his stunning brown eyes in the mirror. Blindly she stepped around the tiny boudoir chair and lowered herself to it, feeling first with her hand to check her aim.

His eyes swerved away. ''Which brush? This one?'' A dark hand came into her range of vision, and she watched it select a brush from the three that lay on the vanity top.

"Yes."

It was a coarse plastic brush with a knob on the end of each bristle. As he lifted his hand, and the bristles bit into the hair at the top of her forehead, the knobs caught and forced her head back against his chest. Immediately his left hand came to press warmly against her forehead. "Tell me if I'm being too rough," he ordered, his eyes now on the top of her head while hers followed his every movement, mesmerized. Through her cold damp hair, his chest burned warm, then he backed away and completed the stroke, ending between her shoulder blades. He brushed slowly, lazily, and with each stroke her shirt grew wetter. An involuntary shiver shook her, and goose bumps skittered up her arms. Immediately he glanced up.

"Are you cold?"

"Yes."

He ran his hands down her arms, pulling her back against his stomach while his eyes locked with hers in the mirror.

"Your shirt is wet."

She swallowed, the ache of anticipation intensifying across her chest.

"Give me the towel again."

She handed it up, and he transferred his attention once more to her hair, folding it between two layers of terry cloth and drawing the remaining moisture from it before tossing the towel onto the floor, then giving her hair a final smoothing. She closed her eyes and lolled in the sensuous delight of the brush massaging her scalp, then tickling its way down her back.

"Put your arms up, Winn."

At his soft command her eyes fled to his, and she realized he was deliberately taking this one slow step at a time to give them longer to get used to each other. There was no hiding the fact that her breasts peaked up into two hard points, nor the fact that they were rising and falling with torturous rapidity as she obediently raised her arms above her head. He grasped the hem of her shirt, inverted it, peeling it up and over her elbows, leaving her torso naked, lighted by the lamps and exposed to his adoring eyes.

"You're beautiful, Winn," he breathed, "just as I pictured you." Her shoulders pressed firmly against his midsection, and she felt his hardness against the center of her back. His right hand still held the brush, but he seemed to have forgotten it. He slid both palms down around her neck, her collarbone, then outward to the top curves of both breasts, around their outer perimeter and finally to their soft lower swells, carefully avoiding the nipples, which stood out like twin rubies set in identical mounts. His eyes coveted them, but still he touched only the skin surrounding them. Her breasts were small, firm, conical, and she wondered how much space they would take up in his palms.

His hands continued to tantalize. She felt the smooth handle of the brush circle her skin, so much smoother than the rough fingertips that rode the paired curves, too, then slipped beneath them like mirrored images before lifting both breasts sharply, pointing her nipples more directly at their reflected faces high in the mirror.

"When I first met you, I wanted to do this. I told myself that someday I would, and that when I felt your flesh for the first time, it would be as hard and firm as mine is." He allowed her breasts to fall free, then ran one hand down to her ribs while stretching to set the brush on the tabletop. Then both hands were spanning her ribs, sliding down into the hollow above her navel as he dipped his head low and kissed her naked shoulder. ''Your skin is perfect, not soft like most women's. Whoever said soft skin was sexy?'' His thumbs circled and dug into the backside of her ribs as his hands rode back up and sheltered in the hollow just beneath both overhanging breasts again.

Will he never touch my nipples, she thought, wondering how long she could endure the agony of expectation. But still he didn't. He bit her shoulder tendon, and his tongue tickled it, making her give a one-shouldered shrug, followed by an involuntary shudder.

Against her skin he said, ''You smell too much like me from the soap at the club. All these weeks while I imagined you, I thought you'd smell the way you did the night of the wedding.''

Every word he said fueled her libido. He straightened. His palms cupped the lower halves of her breasts, his thumbs within a quarter inch of their crests now. ''Are you self-conscious, having me look at you this way?'' *Let her say no. Let her be proud of her well-cared-for body.*

''No,'' she whispered.

''Are you self-conscious looking at yourself this way?''

''No.'' She covered the backs of his hands with her own. ''Only impatient.'' Then she guided them up, up, until her distended nipples seemed to drill into his palms like diamond bits. She gently moved from left to right, her eyes sliding closed. Her shoulders shifted back and forth, too, and behind her she felt him moving in complementary motions.

''Oh, Joseph, Joseph, you make me so impatient.''

''I've been impatient for a good eight weeks. What's a few more minutes?''

Her eyelids lifted, and she met his gaze in the mirror. ''Have you? Have you really?''

His palms contoured the outer rims of her breasts while he gently twisted the nipples between thumb and forefinger, sending currents of tension zigging downward to meet the fire between her legs that seemed to connect the two disparate parts of her body.

''Right from the start. I wanted you that first night, I think, but after you talked me out of pressing the issue in the gazebo, I decided you just might be right. It might have been spring fancy and nothing more . . . what with you in your finery and me in mine, and everything setting the stage for romance. But even though I backed off, I didn't stop thinking about you, wanting to do what I'm doing right now, wondering how to go about wooing a woman with another man's ring on her finger.''

''Are you wooing me, Joseph?''

His one-sided smile brought the devil's sparkle to his eyes. ''What does it feel like to you?'' He bent to probe her ear with the warm wet point of his tongue.

''I thought we were having a one-night affair because I was in need of comfort.''

His hands flattened her milky white orbs with their tips pinched against the edges of his hands. ''Be honest with yourself, Winn. Yes, you needed me, but this has nothing to do with comfort. This is something we saw coming from the first time we laid eyes on each other, isn't it?''

She gasped slightly and arched her back against him. ''You're hurting me, Joseph.'' Her hands pulled at his.

Immediately his hold lightened. ''I'm sorry,'' he whispered gruffly. His head dropped down, and he kissed her shoulder again, then her jaw and the tip of her ear, caressing her breasts now with the consideration of a penitent. She tipped her head back until it rested on his bare shoulder and covered his hands again with her own, following his explorations with her fingers, which lined his and learned the texture of hard knuckles, hair and blunt nails.

Into her neck he murmured, ''Ah, Winn, I love you. This isn't just some crazy spring fever, this is the most terrible thing I've ever gone through in my life.''

Her heart seemed to swell and her blood raced. She wanted to confess her love, too, but in lieu of the words she was not allowed to say, she could only offer, ''I know, Joseph, I know. I've been going through the same misery.''

He forced her face to turn and lift, and kissed her with an ardency that fired her blood anew. His tongue tempted with provocative ministrations, circling, probing, riding along her teeth and within the most intimate confines where cheek met lip. He suckled her tongue the way she longed for him to suckle her breast, raising a deep yearning that beat against the inner walls of her femininity and made her arch back in delight and quest. She had to have more or die, it seemed. Unable to tolerate the constraint any longer, she swung up off the chair, then surprised both herself and him by ordering, ''Now you sit.'' She grabbed up the brush. ''What's good for the goose is good for the gander.''

Caught off guard by her sudden reversal of roles, just when he'd been about to make his move, he stood with his shoulders and chest heaving while the awesome power of his breath beat between them. His fists were clenched. The shadow in his navel became rhythmically wide, then narrow, wide, then narrow again.

Muscle by muscle he forced himself to relax, then with his dark eyes boring into hers, he swung onto the chair. But instead of facing the mirror, he faced her, straddling the small stool as he'd done once before, running his hands up the backs of her thighs, cupping her buttocks and pulling her up close. He pressed his face into the warm pillows of her breasts, but immediately she pushed his shoulders back, gaining her freedom.

''Not yet. I feel feminine and powerful when I make you wait, just as you made me wait. Let me hang onto it for a little while. Relax . . . close your eyes . . . please.''

He did. And stopped trying to claim her, resting his wrists on the low wire back of the chair, letting his relaxed fingers trail toward the floor. His shoulders slumped a little. His head relaxed and his lips parted slightly. Though his breathing was still pressured, the rest of him waited in apparent repose.

She adulated his hair with her eyes before doing what she'd thought of doing countless times. She lifted her fingers and threaded them through his curls. But his locks had coiled tightly as they'd dried, and only at the crown of his head was his hair still damp. So she brushed it, running the bristles back from his forehead to the base of his neck, then from his temples to the same spot. When she drove the brush through the curls, his chin lifted and his head was tugged backward. But his eyes stayed closed.

"The two things I loved first about you were your hair and your eyes. Even that first night I had the terrible urge to touch your curls, to smell them." She leaned forward and buried her nose in the soft strands, kissed his warm skull—his hair was the finest texture of any she'd ever felt, and as she sniffed its clean scent, his moist breath dampened the fullest part of her right breast. Still he remained docile, not grasping or nuzzling. Pleased, she returned to her delightful chore. She'd been brushing for a full minute when she felt his fingers behind her right knee. They brushed upward until they encountered her red knit shorts. Her breathing shattered, and she glanced down sharply only to find his eyelids still closed. His fingers glided slowly down to her knee again, then made the same titillating journey up and down her opposite leg. The brush continued drawing through his hair, but slower . . . slower . . . slower. . . .

His knuckles caressed her inner thigh and trailed upward to tease the tender flesh at the top of her leg. Then he treated the opposite limb to the sensual harbinger of things to come.

Her hand now lay still upon his head, the brush caught in his curls while the backs of his fingers brushed upward again and slipped within the elastic of her panties. But instead of retreating, his fingers continued moving up to her hip where they explored the hollow before making the leisurely journey back down again.

When they touched flattened hair, his fingers paused, and both Joseph and Winn opened their eyes. His head was thrown back, hers dropped forward. Neither of them saw a visible movement on the other.

He slipped his fingers fully within the white tricot garment and sent rivers within Winn's body flooding their banks. Her left eye blinked slowly. Her wrists fell limply across his shoulders, and her tongue stole out to wet her lips. His free hand found her back and drew her closer until she took a single step, and her knees came up against the back of the chair.

His warm wet tongue touched the bare skin of her stomach just above her waistband, and then his teeth grasped the elastic of her red shorts and worried it suggestively before he fell back again, gazing up at her blue aroused eyes.

He turned his exploring fingers over so the pads rested against her flesh, but still they encountered little, for Joseph reached from an awkward angle, sitting below her, straddling the chair as he did.

"Kneel down," he ordered in an odd, thick voice.

His hands pressed her hipbones, and without hesitation she dropped to her knees. His right hand splayed upon her back while his left slipped down inside the elasticized waists of both garments, searching for the object of his desire.

Then the brush dropped to the floor with a muffled thud as an agonized sound came from her throat.

His lips found hers, and she gripped his shoulders while his explorations took on a rhythm upon which she rode as if posting with the canter of a horse. A deep groan vibrated in his throat, and she slid one hand down his hard chest with its sleek covering of hair, passing a tiny nipple, then continuing down the wedge of hair that led to the brief strip of fabric covering his loins. When she caressed and measured him through the cutoffs, it was with zipper and placket adding to the fullness of his flesh.

His widespread legs gave her full access to him. She followed his example, slipping her fingertips up inside a frayed leg, encountering first the resilient texture of a soft masculine orb that was flattened by his shorts. He groaned and stretched backward, removing his lips from hers. But still, she couldn't reach. He moved sinuously, lifting his hips from the tiny chair, bracing against the dressing table on an elbow.

She reached for his waistband, and at the touch of her warm fingers on his stomach, he jerked in a breath and held it, creating slack between his flesh and the garment. The muscles of his stomach were like sculpted teak as she touched them with her knuckles while working the heavy metal button from its hole.

She thought about the white cotton he'd earlier clenched in his hands. She reached for the zipper and eased it down with agonizing slowness.

He jerked again as she touched him deliberately for the first time, but tentatively, almost shyly, with fingertips only, then he settled his hips back against the chair and waited. He lunged forward now in the chair, whispering harshly in her ear, "Winn . . . Winn . . . I've wanted you to touch me for so long."

She'd always thought it was women who voiced such yearnings, but his heavy breathing and words of encouragement made her realize he was different from most men. He was unashamed of admitting his vulnerability, and this pleased and excited Winn.

When her hand closed around him for the first time, he groaned and rammed one hand inside her back waistline, the other in the front, bracketing her like a saddle made of warm flesh, until his fingers met and nestled within her warm folds.

"Oh, Joseph, you're so good at this. I knew you'd be. I use to lie awake at night and imagine the different ways you'd touch me . . . oh!" She gasped and arched backward, and his tongue slipped into her mouth with a rhythmic imitation of the stimulation he was bestowing.

The upward pressure increased, taking her with it until she realized he had stood and bowed his legs around the tiny chair, then kicked it behind him, pulling her to her feet in front of him.

With a swift flexing of one knee, he took her shorts and panties down to the floor. When he raised up again her hands were waiting to skim down his ribs and shimmy his cutoffs over his hipbones. They hit the floor with a soft jingle of change from one pocket, and he stepped from them and swept both arms around her, as they'd been before, one along her center front, the other center back, resuming the sweet insinuation of which she'd not yet had her fill. Their mouths met with a voluptuous exchange of tongues while her hand stroked, caressed, explored.

"Easy, lady," he whispered gruffly into her mouth. "I'm about at my limit."

"So am I."

He lifted his head and smiled. "So soon?"

"Too soon?" she inquired diffidently.

"Mmm. . . ." His eyes caressed. "Not at all. Come here. . . ." His hair-spattered legs nudged her smooth ones until she came up against the foot of the bed and fell backward.

He dropped to his knees on the floor, parting her legs with his chest as he fell forward, spreading his hands wide across her ribs while kissing the soft valley at her waist. He pushed himself higher, driving his chest hard against the bony feminine structure that lifted to greet his flesh as it pressed.

Then at last—oh, sweet last—he kissed her breasts, taking turns, a kiss on the left, a kiss on the right. A lick across the left nipple, which lifted in frustration, and then across her right. She clutched the back of his head and would not allow him to move away, directing his mouth to the puckered tip that strained willingly against his tongue, which at last closed over it. Wide, wet, wonderful taking of what she offered, what he'd put off encountering until he, too, had known intense desire for it. He stroked the nipples with his pursed lips as if they had length, much as a clarinet player softens and plies the reed of his instrument before trying to force perfect notes from it.

But the perfect notes were forced from Winn's throat as ecstasy found voice. They were wordless notes of praise and heightened desire. She writhed beneath him and lifted her hips in invitation. But he pressed her flat, taking his time, leaving her breasts with the outward drawing and dampening strokes until the need for more was actual pain down the center of her body.

His warmth disappeared from her breast, and she opened her eyes to look down at him. He was studying her without smile, his eyes slightly somber in the mellow light from the dresser lamps. ''If I'm going to get you for only one night of my life, I want to have all of you. I don't want to look back and wish I'd done what I wanted to do.''

She braced up on both elbows, her blue eyes immersed in his intense brown ones. His pose announced his intentions, and her heart thrummed crazily as she wondered if she were adventurous enough for him. Yet she felt so right with him, her inhibitions waned before the power of his eyes. They were both exceedingly physical people—she should have guessed that in the love act he would be as physical as he was on a racket-ball court. She sensed him waiting for her approval and lifted a hand to caress the hair above his ear. He turned to bite her little finger and spoke with it still between his teeth.

''You still smell too much like me, and I want you to smell the way I remember you smelling. So, lay back, Winn, and indulge me, please, pretty lady.''

She paused uncertainly, then fell back, watching cautiously as he rose to his feet and crossed to her chest of drawers. From its top he took a round white plastic container upon which lay a white fuzzy puff. He slipped the cover off, then turned back toward the bed. Her eyes followed as he came to sit beside her, his knees hooked over the foot of the bed while he twisted at one hip, then fell back onto one elbow. He set the body powder on her far side, dipped the puff and said, ''Lift your chin for me.''

She did, letting her eyes drift closed as the scent of Channel No. 5 filled her nostrils. He fluffed it upon both of her breasts, her ribs. ''Lift your arms.'' She threw them lazily over her head and let erotic images drift across her mind, powered by the evocative scent. He dusted her armpits, then the arms themselves, replenished his supply and leisurely began an excursion down one leg, pushing himself to a sitting position, finally lifting her foot from the floor, bending forward to reach its instep. Her other leg and foot received the same attention before he bent her leg forward and kissed it lightly, then let it drop.

Once more he dipped the puff, applied a white cloud to her abdomen, and the soft hollow of her inner thighs. He leaned, gave her belly a lingering kiss, then ordered, "Roll over."

With hands still thrown above her head, she rolled. The soft tickle of the powder puff touched each inch of tensile skin as she turned her cheek into the rumpled bedding and relaxed. When he brushed the hollow behind one knee, she flinched and rubbed it with the opposite foot.

"Ticklish?"

"Mmm-hmm," she murmured into the bedspread.

"Mmm . . . interesting." He trailed only the finest tips of the puff along her hollows again, and she writhed and reached back to slap his hand away. He chuckled deep in his throat, then the mattress shifted, and she heard a light thump on the floor, the touch of plastic to plastic, and a moment of silence before his knees cracked.

His cool rough hands surrounded her left foot and bent it at the knee. Something warm—his nose—touched it, running from big toe to heel before he kissed and wet the arch, then lowered the foot again and ran a string of moist kisses up her calf, pausing longer at the hollow behind her knee before continuing along her firm thigh, over one buttock, which he bit lightly, then up its rise to her vertebrae. When he reached her neck, his knee was pressed between hers, and a palm rested on either side of her head.

"Winn, my beautiful Winn. If I do something you don't like, just stop me."

But she couldn't imagine putting a stop to heaven. He knew the female libido as he knew the angles of a racket-ball shot, anticipated Winn's every response, much as he could anticipate the caroms of a ball off walls, ceiling and floor.

He played her with an expertise she found at once appalling for all the practice it must have taken him to become so facile at it, and debilitating for how accurate he was about her most vulnerable spots.

He smoothed his hands over her shoulders, lowered his naked length upon her back and writhed his hips while slipping his hands beneath her to caress her flattened breasts. And all the while his tongue searched and teased her neck, her earlobe, her nape, the tendons below her arms, her waist, her buttocks, then down her legs until he knelt on the floor again.

With gentle but relentless hands he turned her over onto her back again. He kissed the insides of her knees, her thighs, bringing responses singing to the surface of her skin, plunging her into a new realm of wantonness where nothing mattered except that he bring ease to the awesome throbbing within her body.

When he touched her, she was unprepared for the fiery heat of it, and her hips leaped convulsively . . . once. Then her fingers took great fistfuls of the bedspread and twisted. And twisted. It was like nothing she'd ever experienced before, not only in its power to stimulate, but in its far greater meaning, the total giving over of one's self to another for that burning space of time. It was the epitome of vulnerability. The epitome of trust.

As she lifted to him, she heard his murmured wordless protestations of love. The pleasure was terrifying. And so intense at times she whimpered, hearing her throat creating sounds it had never made before.

She would realize much later that at one point while he stroked her ever closer to the brink of climax, her mind pictured a line of black powder with the sparkles of fire sizzling along at a steady relentless pace, burning its way closer and closer to the detonator, then reaching it at last and sending the earth into the sky.

''Jooooo-seffff . . .'' she growled in two elongated vowels of ecstasy as her body quivered and pulsated.

Then her hips collapsed. There were beads of perspiration on her face and along the center of her chest. Her throat hurt from the rasping cries he'd forced from it. She was lethargic, limp. She was sliding down the bed, drawn by strong hands that curled beneath her knees and tugged. When her hips reached the end of the mattress, Joseph's face appeared above her.

''Winn Gardner, I love you.'' His elbows trembled as he braced a palm on either side of her head, then his warm swollen lips pressed to hers. And she tasted of the sweet fragrance with which he'd earlier powdered her.

His rigid body hovered at the entrance to hers, and she reached to guide it within, offering her deepest self as his heart's ease. She learned a new wonder about this act of love: how magnificent it is to experience it in an already sated state. For while Joseph thrust above her, she was replete and aware, taking exploratory interest in each of his tensed muscles as they rippled along her ribs, corded at his inner elbow and bulged across his chest. Her palms hovered lightly on his buttocks, feeling them grow hollow, then round, with each driving stroke of man into woman. She contoured his hips and felt the smooth movements of meshing in his superbly toned body. His back—ah, his back, how warm and strong and tough it was as he undulated. She came to know its texture beneath her palms, then beneath her heels, beneath her calves. And once she reached the backs of her fingers to the soft masculine orbs that swayed against her as he rocked into her flesh, her light touch an accolade to the act they shared.

He was an exquisite male animal, a sensitive human being. He was more than her sexual nemesis. He was her love.

When he climaxed, he drove her a foot up the bed with the force of his final thrusts, and a magnificent animal sound escaped his gritted teeth.

Then he fell, exhausted, almost knocking the breath from her.

Chapter 10

''Winn, what are we going to do?'' The sheen had dried from his shoulders. He lay on his side, his troubled brown eyes probing hers.

''I don't know.''

''You can't marry him. You just can't.''

She closed her eyes and the lids trembled. She opened them, and he saw the turmoil she faced. A terrible hurt grabbed his heart like a giant fist, wringing.

"Could you really do this with me, then go back to him?"

"What other choice do I have?"

He lay with an elbow folded beneath an ear. With his free hand he caressed the side of her face, his fingertips delving the messed hair at her temple.

"I want to say, marry me, Winn, and I think that's what I want. But it's happened awfully fast. I need some time alone with you, more time than we've had. We both need it so we can explore the possibility. I'm twenty-seven. I've waited a long time to find the right woman, and I don't intend to make it a temporary commitment when I get married."

"Neither do I."

His thumb had been stroking her cheekbone but fell still. Their somber gazes grew too intense, and she closed her eyes to shut out his compelling face.

"Look at me!" His hand pressed hard in emphasis. She opened her eyes again. "I love you, Winn Gardner. But I don't want you to do the thing that's wrong for you. I've spent a lot of time sending out little digs about him and you, hinting that he's not right for you, not good enough for you. Is he?"

Her lips opened and she wet them. Her nostrils flared, and the hint of tears sparkled in the downward corners of her eyes. But she didn't know how to answer. How could Joseph think Paul had to measure up to *her* when she was the one who'd betrayed him? The strong hand left her cheek and brushed the hair back beside her ear, then fell to rest on the narrow space between their chins. "Tell me what he does to make you happy." She tried desperately to think of one single thing but could come up with no answers. "What about in bed?" Joseph pressed. "Has he ever done what I just did to you?"

Her eyelids became half-shuttered as she dropped her gaze. His knuckles pressed up on her chin, forcing her blue eyes and blushing cheeks to confront his direct gaze. "Has he?"

"No," she whispered.

"Has anyone?"

Her blush deepened. "No."

"The first time . . ." he mused wondrously. His forefinger measured the width of her lower lip, then slipped inside and touched her teeth. "Why with me?"

She tried to turn onto her back and shift her gaze to the ceiling, but he wouldn't let her. "Why did you let me?"

"Just because . . . because you . . . you tried it, and it . . . it felt right."

"You mean nobody else has ever tried it with you before?"

"There haven't been that many, Joseph."

"How many?"

"Four. You're my fifth."

"And who are the others?"

"My high-school steady and two others during college before I met Paul. And now you."

"And now me. . . ." At close range he saw that her eyes had startling aquamarine depths scattered within the surface blues. That unconscious single-lidded blink came at what—by now—he considered quite the appropriate time.

''On the day you dropped your wedding invitations into the mail, you allow me liberties you've never allowed even the man you're going to marry. Why?''

''Because I feel free and open with you, and at the moment it happened I felt committed. I wanted . . . it seemed. . . .'' She tried to cover her face with one hand, but he grasped the wrist and prevented it.

''Don't be ashamed before me . . . not ever, Winn. There's absolutely no reason to be. It seemed what?''

''I've read about it before and seen pictures, but it always seemed . . . perverted. And then with you it became. . . .'' She picked at the bedspread between their chins and finally lifted her eyes to his. Such eyes he had. She loved his eyes. ''Exalted,'' she finished quietly.

His intense eyes studied her somberly. He sighed—a wholesome sound—and kissed the bridge of her nose, between her eyes, then lay back, studying her again.

''And after that you could still marry him?''

Angrily now, she sat up, slipped from the end of the bed and crossed the hall to the bathroom, from where she informed him, ''You don't realize what all is involved, Joseph! You're not the one whose mother has hired caterers and cake decorators and florists and laid down big chunks of money as deposits for every service about to be rendered!''

He rolled to his back, cupped the back of his head in both hands and snorted at the ceiling. ''So it's the money?''

He heard the rush of water, then what sounded like the slam of a drawer. Her voice grew louder and closer as she reappeared and came to stand at the foot of the bed, still naked. ''Joseph, you don't quite understand about my mother. I'm a bastard she had to raise without a penny of help from anyone. She went through a pregnancy without a man and had me with no father to sign the birth certificate, and she's lived the twenty-five years since as frugally as it's possible to live. Security—that's always been her hang-up. And to her, money was the only security she could obtain, because she had no man for emotional security. So money came to mean a lot to her, and she slowly earned more and more of it but hoarded it very jealously.

''Until now. When I became engaged to Paul, she loosened the purse strings for the first time. She's giving me the kind of wedding she thinks is most socially acceptable. Can you imagine her chagrin if I were to go to her now, after the invitations have been sent, after the announcement has been put in the paper, after showers have been planned, and announce that I changed my mind?''

His eyes held none of their devilish twinkle now. They bored into her while he lay with his armpits exposed, his belly hollow. Unexpectedly he snapped up, stretching out a hand to her. ''Come here. Could we please continue this conversation tucked cozily under the sheets together instead of like cold angry strangers?''

Immense relief flooded her as she leaned to place her hand in his. He gave one hard tug, and she fell half on top of him. He held her upper arms tightly and informed her, ''I don't like arguing about it any more than you do, but we both knew it'd happen once we made love, didn't we?''

''Yes, I suppose we did.''

Their troubled eyes clung, and hers were on the verge of tears when he released her and ordered, ''Get in. I'm shivering.''

She crawled on hands and knees to the top of the bed, and he slipped in beside her, snuggling under the blankets and wrapping both arms around her, settling the top of her head just beneath his chin. She rolled on her side and circled his ribs with one clinging arm.

''Is it because I haven't asked you to marry me that you won't call it off with him?'' he asked.

''No, Joseph. It's the thought of canceling all the social obligations, all the commitments that scares me to death. I'd look like a fool, and that I could handle, but so would my mother and Paul, and they don't deserve that.''

''What other social commitments?''

She sighed and rolled away from him slightly. He wouldn't have it and pulled her back where she'd been. ''Tell me,'' he ordered.

She told him succinctly, listing everything she could think of: invitations, postage, caterers, personalized napkins, champagne, limousine, unity candle, photographer, jeweler, tuxedo rental, bridesmaids' dresses, bridal gown, registration book, ring bearer's pillow, garter, gifts for her attendants, organist, the singer and even the special stem glasses for the nuptial toasts. When she finished almost breathlessly, the hand that had been squeezing her shoulder fell limp onto the mattress.

''Oh, my God,'' he muttered.

She laughed, and it was such a relief. ''See, I told you.''

''You mean everybody goes through all that when they get married?''

''No. Only the stupid ones.''

''You mean you don't want any of it at all?''

''I always thought the perfect wedding would be to get married with only my favorite relatives and my best friends present, maybe in some pretty garden or field someplace when the lilacs are in bloom. Then maybe a quick dinner at my mother's house and slip away to the North Woods and sleep in a tent in two zipped-together sleeping bags for one solid week, with nothing but bears and raccoons and porcupines for company.''

His arm came around her again, caressing her naked back, her spine. ''Mmm . . .'' he murmured against her hair. ''Sounds perfect. Let's do it.''

''Jo-Jo, be serious!''

''I think I'm getting more serious by the minute. You and I find more in common the longer we know each other.'' He yawned all of a sudden.

She closed her eyes, wholly content, curled up against his warm naked limbs. ''Jo-Jo, I can't marry you,'' she said lazily. ''Besides, you said you haven't decided yet.''

''Did I?'' he murmured disinterestedly.

''Mmm-hmm.''

Her hand fell still in the midst of fanning across his chest. Beneath her fingers the rise and fall of his breathing became long and measured. The lights still burned. But neither cared. Their limbs grew liquid and their eyelids twitched. A gentle snore sounded through the room, and Winn's eyes flickered open. At the sight of his relaxed lips and face she smiled sleepily and curled up tighter into her pillow, her fists beneath her chin and her forearms pressed against his warm ribs.

His snoring grew a little louder, and she nudged him. "Roll over, Joseph."

"Wh—" His eyes flew open, disoriented.

"Roll over."

He rolled onto his right side, and she right behind him, circling his belly with an arm and pressed her body securely against his naked backside. There was no spot on earth she would rather be.

In the morning they awakened almost simultaneously and smiled at each other with the unaccustomed joy of greeting the face of the one each loved first thing in the day.

"I like sleeping with you." He lifted both arms above his head and posed like Charles Atlas, everything bulging and quivering from chin to waist.

"That's because I don't snore."

"Did I?"

"Just a little."

His arms hauled her close. "Mmm . . . I'll have to make up for it some way, won't I?"

"And also for the extra charge on my light bill."

He glanced back over his shoulder. "Oh, did we leave it on?"

"Mmm-hmm."

"You just wanted to check and make sure it was me with you if you woke up in the middle of the night with your hand on anything important."

"Yup!" she agreed, and they both laughed as he rolled her beneath him and braced up on both elbows.

"Come with me today," he urged.

"Where we goin'?"

"To the auction in Bemidji."

"Ohh, the auction. I'd forgotten."

He smiled into her eyes. "Will you come?"

She twisted one of his curls around her finger and smiled up at him very naughtily, then purred, "Try me, big boy."

"Oh, for shame!" he teased.

She looped her arms around his neck. "Well, you can't blame a girl for getting to like it, can you?"

"Winnifred Gardner, I'm shocked."

"Yeah, I can feel the shock absolutely *growing* on you."

"Oh, that. Well, you can't blame a boy for responding to the off-color innuendo of a fiery little sexpot who—"

"Fiery little sexpot!"

"Fiery little sexpot who keeps a cup in her kitchen with the nickname Killer on it."

"You take that back, Jo-Jo Duggan, or I'll make you sorry!" She yanked the curl.

"*Ow!* Watch it, Killer, you're askin' for it!" He got her by both wrists and showed her who was master here.

"Yes, Mr. Duggan, I am," she simpered.

He kissed her finally with a mock show of uncontrolled passion, writhing around as if he were swimming on top of her. She was laughing beneath his mouth, and her words came out muffled.

"Are you going to ravish me?"

"You bet, and you're going to love it."

"Am I supposed to fight you or cooperate?"

He mellowed. His squirming turned to undulation. He was assaulting her mouth, chin, throat, then breasts with breathtaking tenderness. "I never did care much for unwilling females."

"Have you had many . . . unwilling ones?"

His stubbled jaw was like a steel brush against her tender breast, and she loved it. "None."

"And what about the other kind? How many of them?"

He reared up, meeting her eyes. "My share. Does it bother you?"

She had a flippant remark on the tip of her tongue, but instead she cupped his face in both hands and spoke earnestly. "Oh, yes, Joseph Duggan, I hate every one of them for having you before I did. And I have no right."

"You have every right. After last night."

Tears sprang into her eyes, and her soft lips parted on a quick indrawn breath, not quite a sob, not quite a sigh. It had to be said. Feelings this strong simply must be voiced.

"God help me, Joseph, I love you."

"Then God help both of us, not just you."

This time when his body slipped inside hers, it was with great tenderness. Their coupling was totally different from the first time. It was rich with slowness, unfrenzied, almost studious. They watched each other, both faces and bodies, and loved with eyes, as well as the physical parts that joined. They neither spoke nor called out, for their union was not meant to ease, but to blend their spirits. And so it did. Only Joseph reached a climax, but it mattered little to Winn. This she could give, yet be the grateful one when it was over.

And this physical union, for all its simpleness—wholesomeness almost—was shattering.

"I love you," he vowed when it ended.

"And I love you," she answered. Then she cried.

They made a pact afterward that those would be the last tears of the day, that they'd be carefree, happy, and speak of no other people but themselves.

They spent the day going to Bemidji in Joseph's 1954 Cadillac pickup, a funereal gray monstrosity twenty-two feet long, with all its coffin rollers intact and sporting four doors, velour upholstery sumptuous enough to be used in any coffin and a roomy three feet of space behind the seat, from which the name "flower car" had been derived: the space for carrying the funeral flowers.

But the vehicle was luxurious to a fault. During much of the five-hour ride, Winn lay sprawled across the seat with the soles of her feet hanging out the window and her head snuggled in Joseph's lap.

Five miles outside of Bemidji they followed directions on the auction-sale billboard and parked the Caddy beside the narrow gravel road lined with cars on both sides for a quarter mile in either direction. They spent the day meandering the farmyard amid farmers wearing bib overalls and wives with their pin curls tied up in blue handkerchiefs knotted above their foreheads.

Joseph and Winn kept their promise. They forgot about all the outside forces working against them and enjoyed only each other, holding hands, laughing, occasionally dipping behind a large piece of machinery to exchange kisses. The '41 Ford was a rusted, wheelless heap that wasn't worth bidding on in Joseph's estimation, but they loved listening to the silver-tongued auctioneer calling the sale with mercurial glibness.

"Heep-hayy-o-what-am-I-bid-for-this-little-beauty-of-an-automobile-do-I-hear-five-hundred-to-start-five-hundred-five-hundred-do-I-hear-five-hundred-hayy-oo-take-the-safety-pins-off-your-pockets-folks-do-I-hear-four-fifty-she's-a-racy-little-number-just-needs-a-little-dip-in-penetrating-oil-do-I-hear-four-fifty-they-don't-make-'em-like-this-anymore-four-fifty-four-fifty-do-I-hear-four-fifty-to-start-all-right-we'll-do-this-the-hard-way-do-I-hear-four-hundred-to-start-four-hundred-what-am-I-bid-fooooour-fooooour. . . ."

Jo-Jo laughed. Winn joined him. It was utterly refreshing, holding hands in the sunshine, listening to the red-faced potbellied auctioneer plying his trade. Dogs and children scampered through the crowd, while housewives from neighboring farms poked and prodded amid the housewares on display, gleaning bits of the personal lives of those holding the sale from the oddments strewn across the yard: chairs, books, tables, pot-bellied stoves, doilies, pickling pots, carpet sweepers, bales of twine, dishes, hog feeders, treadle sewing machines, hay balers, scrolls of music from a roller piano and a claw-footed swivel organ stool with four amber marbles clutched in its feet.

"Imagine what we'll have strewn all over our yard when we're seventy years old and having an auction sale," Winn mused.

She and Joseph sauntered along between a line of blossoming honeysuckle bushes and a set of eight oak spoke chairs. He swung their hands between them. "Are we going to be seventy years old and having an auction sale?" He grinned down at her and kicked his feet out idly with each step.

"I said *imagine*."

"Oh . . . imagine. Okay, let's see. There'll be a whole truckload of old beat-up tennis shoes and an even bigger one of rackets, and ragbags full of grungy sweat pants and sweat shirts with the arms cut off."

"And the bellies," she put in.

"And the bellies," he seconded. "And what else?"

"And a yard full of your vintage cars, Joseph, all in mint condition, and we'll get rich, rich, rich from them and spend our eighties cruising oceans in the height of luxury."

"And there'll be a shed full of white plastic containers and white fluffy powder puffs."

"Oh, almost forgot them." She squinted an eye at the sun while peering up at him. "But why a whole shed full?"

"Because I'll have used up a lot of Chanel No. 5, powdering you every night for fifty years."

"*Every* night?"

"Every night."

"But, Joseph, you'll be seventy years old!"

He grinned luridly. "Imagine how good I'll be at it by then." He leaned down and bit her nose.

"We *are* talking about powdering, aren't we?"

"That, too."

"Quit talking dirty, old man, and tell me what else there'll be."

"Oh, the cribs and high chairs from when our kids were babies."

She jammed her hands into her hip pockets and confronted him belligerently. "Joseph, we are *not* selling our children's furniture, so just put the idea out of your head!"

"But why, my little flower?"

She sauntered on saucily. "Because we have our grandchildren coming to visit, silly. We'll have to leave the crib set up for them."

"Oh, of course, you're right, Killer. But can I sell that set of china with your nickname on it?"

"What set of china? It's only one cup."

"Well, I'm growing tired of the queer looks people give me when they see it sitting on the kitchen cabinet beside our liniment and Geritol. I always wonder if they think it belongs to *me!*"

They eyed each other, snickered, then snorted, then broke into gales of laughter while he tossed both arms around her and held her loosely, rocking back and forth at the sheer joy of enjoyment. Then he tugged her hand and sat down on one of the honorable-looking old kitchen chairs. "Come here." He pulled her down onto the chair next to his. Its seat was toasty warm from the sun beating down on it all afternoon. Around the honeysuckle hedge before them, bees buzzed and gathered pollen. Down the yard the auctioneer still called, his voice lifting to them faintly through the mellow butter yellow afternoon.

Joseph still held Winn's hand, sitting beside her on the heated wooden chair with an ankle draped casually across a knee.

"What?" she asked, mystified by his sudden shift of mood.

His rich brown eyes were partially hidden behind half-closed lids, their long lashes creating needlelike shadows upon his cheeks as he smiled at her and brushed a thumb lightly over the back of her hand.

"I just want to sit here a while and soak it in. And look at you."

And that's what they did . . . for a full thirty minutes. They sat in the sun on hard rung-backed chairs, facing a row of fragrant bushes, and looked at each other. Holding hands. Rubbing thumbs. Remembering. Wishing.

When did I last study any person this well, Winn thought. *When did I feel this rapport with another? When did it feel this right, just sharing the same sun with someone? What a stunning and good thing to do. How wise of Joseph to know the value of minutes like these.*

She partook to her heart's content.

I love this man's face, hair, form. I love his gaiety and earthiness, his lack of artifice. I love the sound of his laughter, the turn of his brow, the line of his jaw. I love the common ground we find. The time I spend with him has a quality none other holds for me. We relate, Joseph and I. With him would life be this good, always?

Only Joseph's unsmiling lips moved as he spoke. "You feel it, don't you?"

"Yes." There was no need to clarify.

''We could have it, you and I, I think.''

''I think so, too, Joseph.''

''But we made a pact, didn't we?''

''Yes, we did.''

So he removed his eyes from her precious face and—still holding her hand—bent forward to rest his elbows on his knees. She had promised no more tears. She lifted her face to the sun, hoping it might sip away the faint dampness that had gathered on her lashes. Joseph's callused thumb rubbed her knuckles, and she wanted to sit like this with him forever, wishing, until maybe the auctioneer might come by and ask, ''What am I bid for this man, this Joseph Duggan.''

And Winn would say, ''All that I have.'' And it would be that simple.

''It's a long drive home,'' he said quietly. ''Time we start back.''

She didn't lie with her head in his lap on their return trip, and he didn't claim to be sleepy. She sat most of the time close against his shoulder, her bare heels hooked over the edge of the seat, and her wrists looped around her ankles.

The ride was quiet. And long. And introspective. It screamed with unsaid things. Supper at a roadside restaurant was a failure, for neither was hungry, though they both ordered, then picked desultorily.

It was 11:00 P.M. when they pulled up in Winn's driveway. Joseph killed the engine, but neither of them moved. He stared at her front door.

At last he asked, ''Can I come in?''

''No, not tonight.''

He didn't ask why. He knew. Sighing, he slumped low in the seat and began kneading the bridge of his nose with his eyes shut.

''Joseph . . . I . . . thank you for—''

''Dammit!'' he growled angrily, interrupting, turning his face away from her, staring out the side window while holding his lower lip with thumb and forefinger.

She paused uncertainly, reached for the door handle, but at its first click his hand lashed out and grabbed her arm. ''What are you going to do?''

Her teary eyes met his across the broad seat. ''Think . . . long and hard.''

''And?''

''And I need time, Joseph. Promise me you won't call or try to see me until I contact you.''

''*Sit?* You expect me to sit doing nothing while you go back to him and make wedding plans?''

''Joseph, don't! You promised!''

''Yeah, well that's easier said than done.''

''Please don't ruin the end of a perfectly wonderful day.''

''It isn't over yet. I said I want to come in.''

''Joseph, this isn't—''

''All right, then!'' he snarled. ''I won't come in!'' In a flash he was across the seat, grabbing her roughly into his arms. ''There's plenty of room to do what we both want right here.'' His lips slammed onto hers, but halfway through the kiss she was gripping him violently and pulling him heavily against her breasts. She was both appalled and aroused by his anger, for she'd felt the wild frustration mounting within her body, just as he had, all the way home. It erupted now in a spate of pure animalism for both Winn and Joseph. Instead of fighting, she succumbed, clinging to his shoulders only momentarily before squirming down accommodatingly while he arranged his limbs upon hers with little gentleness or patience. His mouth was as hard as his arousal as he ground them simultaneously against her, gnashing her flesh with his lips and hips in an effort to quell the seething within. The punishing kiss lasted less than a minute before Joseph reared back, breath heaving harshly, and began jerking his shirt open. He yanked it out of his waistband while kneeling above her, one leg on the floor, the other angled across her body. Their eyes pierced, shameless in their intent while she, too, roughly unsnapped and unzipped her jeans, then together they stripped them down her right leg only, for they were too greedy to remove them entirely.

His clothing hadn't cleared his ankles before he threw his body down on hers. As he fell, he caught her behind a knee and forced the leg wide. Her foot caught the window ledge, and she used it for leverage, thrusting up to greet and welcome him, fully aroused now, both.

And so they sought restitution, he driving deep, she surging up to meet his oncoming force with an elemental need to settle the conflict between them that both knew could not be settled this way.

But it felt good. Fruitless as it was, it relieved. They pummeled each other, fingers gripping hips and buttocks almost painfully as he growled and she sobbed, and in the end, together, they cried out. An anguished, replete, wonderful, pitiable wail of gratification.

Her climax was devastating. His, awesome. And when their spent bodies lay tangled and sated, they understood perfectly what they had accomplished. And what they had not.

His voice, when at last he spoke, was thick with contrition, muffled in the collar of her blouse, which hung half on, half off her body.

''Oh, God, Winn, I'm sorry.''

''I am, too.''

''Why did I do that when I love you?''

''Why did I? I'm just as guilty as you are.''

''I'll never do it again, I swear, not in anger.''

Was he crying? My God, was he crying? ''Shh!'' she soothed. His skull was damp as she wove her fingertips into his hair. ''Shh.'' His arms tightened about her proprietarily. He lifted his head and spoke in a racked whisper.

''Did I hurt you, Winn?''

''No. I'm fine. A little messed, but fine.'' He rolled his shoulders back and groaned softly, squeezing his eyes shut and catching a hand in his hair.

She attempted to lighten his burden and make him smile. ''Did I hurt you?''

He gave a single mirthless huff of laughter and slowly eased himself off her, tugged up his jeans, lifted her legs across his lap and sat behind the wheel again. He crossed his arms on it, then lowered his head.

She withdrew her feet from his lap, arranged her clothing and threaded the fingers of both hands through her hair with an enormous sigh. He sat slumped over without moving.

''Joseph, I have to go in now.''

His head lifted slowly. His eyes looked tormented.

"I'll call you if and when I get myself freed from other commitments."

He sat silent and unmoving as black water. She leaned across the seat and placed her lips lightly on his, touched his chin and begged, "Don't blame yourself. It was both of us."

He swallowed. The sound was loud in the bleak silence.

"Goodbye, Joseph."

When she slipped away, he lurched, as if coming awake from a dream to find her truly escaping.

"Winn, wait!"

But the door slammed, and he watched her run to the house as fast as she could.

Chapter 11

During the following three days Winn learned things about crying she'd never known before. By Tuesday night she thought it might very well be possible to cry oneself to death. Sunday was spent alternately sobbing and drying up, running for the Kleenex box, then for ice cubes to soothe her stinging eyes. To make matters worse, Paul called, asking, "Where *were* you all day yesterday and last night?" And Winn was forced to make up a lie. To make matters additionally worse, Joseph called, too, ignoring her order to stay out of touch. His message was that he loved her and was despicably miserable and wanted to see her again. Though she managed to stave him off, she was deluged with fresh tears after she hung up.

Monday, with Merry gone from the hospital, Winn's gloom continued, camouflaged behind the cheeriness she forced for the benefit of the other patients. Monday night Paul called to say he missed her and would be home Wednesday at 4:00 P.M., and could she pick him up at the airport. She almost expected the ring that came just after nine. This time Joseph cursed at her, then apologized profusely, then called her Killer in the most heart-wrenchingly sweet voice she'd ever heard. "Hey, Killer . . . I love you, you know." Once more she cried herself to sleep.

At six-thirty the next morning Joseph called again. "Damnit, I didn't sleep a wink again last night! You *are* going to kill me yet, woman! Please tell me you aren't going to marry him."

Judas priest, what a wonderful way to start the day—crying again! She made it through eight hours at the hospital and returned to her town house exhausted, but had barely flopped to her back in the middle of the living-room floor when the phone pealed, and it was her realtor, asking if she could leave the house around seven so he could show it. To a couple who'd seen it before—a hopeful sign, he finished. With a sigh she told the realtor where she could be reached, but just as she was leaving the house, Joseph called again.

"Joseph, I can't talk. I've got to get out of the house so the realtor can show it. And this is a good prospect, too, 'cause it's the second time this party is looking at it."

He sounded desperate. "Winn, don't you dare sell that house!"

She squeezed her forehead in an effort to stop the tears that immediately began stinging. "Joseph, I have to go."

"Winn, please, I love y—" he was barking into the phone when she tenderly hung it up. She drove to her mother's house because she couldn't think of anywhere else to go where the realtor could reach her.

Before she was two steps inside her mother's kitchen, Fern Gardner demanded, "What in the world is wrong with you?"

"Nothing."

"With eyes like those . . . who are you trying to fool?" Fern took a grip on her daughter's chin and inspected at close range. "You look awful, dear."

"Thank you, mother," Winn replied sarcastically.

A knowing glint came into Fern's eyes. "Ah, you miss Paul, is that it?"

It was all Winn could do to keep from ruefully laughing. During the following hour, while Fern rambled on about how smoothly all the wedding preparations were going, Winn gritted her teeth and clamped her jaw. There were times when she wanted to scream at her mother to shut up. Finally she escaped to the bathroom, just to get away from the constant wedding prattle for a few minutes. There, locked in, she stared at herself in the mirror. *Tell her, you coward, tell her!* But the prospect of walking out there and dashing all her mother's bright hopes was daunting, to say the least. *What are you waiting for, Gardner? Your R.S.V.P.'s?* Winn's stomach hurt. At times she felt light-headed, and often her palms sweated. It struck her that this horrendous misery bore all the same symptoms as love.

Out in the living room the phone rang. "Winn, it's for you!" Fern called.

To Winn's dismay it was the realtor. He'd just received a firm offer on her house.

Winn, don't you dare sell that house! Winn, goddammit, I love you! Panic welled, and all of Winn's symptoms grew spontaneously worse. Stalling for time, she told the realtor she'd have to think about the offer and would get back to him either tonight or tomorrow. "It's a good offer," he reminded her. "I wouldn't wait too long to accept it." Winn hung up and stared at the wall.

"Did someone make an offer?"

"Yes."

Fern threw her hands in the air. "Hallelujah! It's as if fate stepped in just in the nick of time. Darling, I'm so happy for you and Paul."

That did it. The tears burst forth like a geyser, and Winn fell back into an upholstered armchair, covering her face with both hands, sobbing uncontrollably.

Fern couldn't have been more amazed. "Why, Winn, dear, what is it?" She bent to one knee and soothed the back of her daughter's head while the sobs shook Winn's shoulders.

"Oh, m-mother, it's the w-worst thing in the wo-world. It's so awf-awful that when I t-tell you, you're g-going to want to d-die."

Fern's dread billowed. "Are you sick? Is it some health problem or . . . or—"

Winn shook her head so hard the hair slashed Fern's face. Into her palms she sobbed, "It's wo-worse!"

"What could be worse?"

Winn lifted her streaming eyes and ran the back of one hand under her nose. "I c-can't m-marry Paul, mother. I d-don't love h-him."

Fern looked stricken. She turned as gray as Jo-Jo's funeral truck. Her mouth slacked, and she fell back as if landed a blow in the chest. She pressed a hand to her heart and spoke in a strained reedy voice. "You can't mean that!"

"I do. I mean every word of it." Winn tore out of her chair, heading for the kitchen Kleenex, then turned to find her mother still on her knees on the floor, stunned. "I don't love him, mother. I l-love somebody else." Now that it was out, Winn felt almost exultant.

"Somebody else!" Fern's face hardened, and she lurched to her feet angrily. "How dare you come to me three weeks before your wedding and tell me such a thing!"

"I don't know how I dare. It scared me all week, just thinking about it, but I decided it was either you or me, mother, and in the end I picked me."

"And what does that mean—you or me?" Fern spit.

"Either I can make you happy or I can make me happy. Mother, can't you see it's really you who admires Paul, not me?"

Two high spots of color appeared in Fern's outraged cheeks. "How dare you speak to me like that!"

Winn sighed and slumped. "Mother, sit down, please. There are so many things we should have talked about during the last year that we never did. About Paul, and me . . . and you . . . and even Rita."

Fern's chin snapped up. "Rita? You mean his computer?"

"Yes, his computer. Sit down, mother, please." At last Fern perched on the edge of the chair that matched Winn's. She crossed her knees stiffly and looked as if she'd just eaten a worm. "Mother, Paul and I have only one thing in common that I can think of. Dancing. And he'd rather stay home and punch his computer keys than do that with me. It's *you* who has things in common with him, not me. I should have realized that when you first introduced him to me. Now I do, and I can't go through with this marriage and take him as surrogate husband to make up for the one you never had."

Fern's lips pursed, but she refused to meet her daughter's eyes. "Are you intimating that I chose Paul for you because I couldn't have him for myself?"

"In a way, yes, but—" Fern spit out a pent breath and rocketed from her chair, presenting her back. "Not in a romantic way, mother, please understand. He's everything you ever wanted for me because he represents stability, security, all the things you had to fight for because you never had a husband. But those things aren't enough for me. I need someone who enjoys having fun, who laughs, who's physical, who . . . who. . . .'' Winn thought of Joseph, and it was as if a beam of sunshine shot into her head.

''I assume you think you've found him in this other man.''

''Maybe.''

Fern tossed a disdainful glance over her shoulder. ''And while you're deciding, what shall I do with all the guests who've been invited to your and Paul's wedding? What should I do with the gifts that have already started arriving here at the house? And the caterers and the flowers and the photographer and the gown?'' With each succeeding word Fern's voice grew sharper and higher until she was nearly shrieking. ''Do you know how much money this extravaganza has cost me!''

''Not exactly,'' Winn answered meekly, ''but I can imagine.''

Fern swung on her daughter, closing in. ''You don't get deposits back for those things, sweetheart!'' she declared with a sting in each word.

''I know, mother. But I'll pay you back, I promise.''

It was silent for a moment, then Fern snorted and turned away. ''You'll pay me back.'' She chuckled coldly. ''And you'll pay me back for the embarrassment I'll suffer every time I meet a friend on the street?''

''Mother, this isn't easy for me, either!''

''And what about Paul? Have you told him yet?''

''No.'' For the first time Winn's voice softened. ''I'll tell him tomorrow. I'm picking him up at the airport.''

''What a wonderful welcome home for him,'' Fern jeered.

Suddenly Winn felt sorry for her mother. ''Did losing my father turn you so hard and cynical that you can't be happy for me that I've at least made the discovery in time? Would you rather have had me marry Paul first and then find out it wouldn't work?''

Fern's shoulders seemed to wilt a little. She propped one hand across her stomach, dropped her face into the other. Wordlessly she shook her head.

''And you haven't asked me anything about Joseph, mother,'' Winn added softly.

''What does . . . *Joseph* do for a living?'' her mother obliged coldly.

''He runs a body shop.''

Fern raised one eyebrow, snorted softly and left the room.

But the worst was over. Winn had little doubt that telling Paul wasn't going to be nearly as hard as telling her mother. Oddly enough, it seemed Paul was less emotionally involved than Fern Gardner.

He came off the plane, beaming, with a clothing carrier slung over one shoulder. ''Winn, I've missed you.'' He gave her a kiss while they walked, and launched into a joyous recitation of the wonders of Silicon Valley.

''Do we have time for a cup of coffee?'' Winn asked before they headed for the luggage pickup.

''Sure. Anyway, there's so much I want to tell you.''

Odd, he didn't notice Winn's uncustomary distractedness while they sat over coffee in The Garden restaurant at Twin Cities International. He was carried away with exuberance. Winn felt extra guilty to have to prick his balloon, but by now all she wanted was to have it out in the open so she could start making restitution and get her life back on track.

After nearly thirty minutes Paul asked, ''How is everything back here?'' Only then did he notice the shadows in her expression. ''Something's wrong, isn't it?''

''Yes, Paul, something's very wrong. You aren't going to like it when I tell you, but I promised myself I would, immediately. It's bad news for us, and it's going to hurt you, I'm afraid. For that I'm sorry.''

He leaned forward and took her hands in his, studying her with a look of deep concern. ''What's wrong, Winn?''

She'd rehearsed it dozens of times. She took a deep breath, gripped his fingers and said straightforwardly, ''I want to call our wedding off.''

He blanched and went speechless for several seconds. ''Temporarily?'' he asked.

''No . . . permanently,'' she answered quietly, releasing his hands.

To Paul's great credit he reacted with poise in spite of the fact that his face went from bleached white to peony pink in a matter of five seconds. ''Oh . . . I see.'' When Winn remained silent, he amended, ''No, I don't see! I thought everything was so great between us.''

''Paul, answer me honestly. Which brings you greater—'' she searched for the proper term ''—*ongoing* joy—me or your work?'' He considered for a moment and turned a brighter red than before. ''See?'' she insisted, leaning forward. ''I'm not criticizing you for it. I'm telling you something we both should have recognized long ago. We joined forces because of mother, because you and she had so much in common that when she met you, she thought she just had to have you for me. But, Paul . . . I . . . I don't think I love you. I admire you. I respect you. But I don't love you.'' She paused, then asked, ''Will you be very, very honest and tell me if you really love me. Or did we fall together because it worked so smoothly, having the support of our parents as we did? And consider if you wouldn't enjoy me much, much more if I played chess and loved to tinker with computers myself, and enjoyed talking about them with you like mother does. Paul, that's the kind of woman you need. Somebody with an analytical mind that's as inquisitive as yours.''

''I can tell you've been thinking about this for a long time.''

''It's been . . . coming on for a few weeks, yes. But I was caught up in the crazy whirlwind preparations for the wedding and couldn't face telling the world—not to mention my mother—that I was canceling everything.''

''Can you really do that at this late date? What about all the invitations you sent out already?''

''I'll handle everything, Paul. And I'll make it clear whose fault it was.''

His eyebrows took on a frosty expression. ''Is there someone else, Winnie?''

This was the most difficult question of all, for Paul didn't deserve to be hurt. ''Yes, Paul, there is.''

He inhaled deeply, held the breath long, then released it in a giant *whoosh,* his shoulders sagging. ''Well, that settles that.''

''Paul, I'm terribly sorry. And if it's any consolation, mother is furious with me. She isn't even talking to me.'' Winn reached out and touched the back of his hand. ''Please don't take this in the wrong way, Paul, because I don't mean any disrespect, but it's too bad you and mother aren't closer to the same age. You'd make the most wonderful husband for her.'' Then she leaned across the table and kissed his cheek while Paul grew totally flustered and seemed unable to meet her eyes. That's when she knew she'd guessed right.

It was shortly after eight-thirty that evening when Winn Gardner stepped on the back stoop of Joseph Duggan's house. The radio was on in the kitchen. Tammy Wynette was belting out ''Stand By Your Man'' in her inimitable cracky voice, and water ran for a moment, then was turned off. Winn angled a peek through the screen and saw the left half of a Duggan back, dressed in a gold-and-black baseball uniform, shoeless, with a black cap pushed onto the back of his head, washing dishes. She waited until she was sure which Duggan it was, and when his profile appeared for a second, she smiled, opened the screen door silently and slipped inside. *Even his back turns me on,* she thought, watching as he rinsed a cup, set it on the drain board, then plunged his hands into the soapy water. The stretchy gold fabric of his breeches clung to his legs like an orange rind, displaying each dent and bulge. There was a grass stain on his left bun, and she smiled, picturing him as a boy, though loving him as a man. When at last she spoke, her voice was soft and quavery. ''Hiya, Jo-Jo.''

He spun around. Detergent bubbles flew from his fingertips and drifted to the floor. His stocking feet, in their black baseball leggings, were braced wide apart, like an outfielder waiting for a fly. There was a puff of dust on his right cheek, and his shirt was filthy, as if he'd managed a beauty of a slide, belly first. His conglomerate appearance was totally incongruous—the soiled virile athlete with his hands in soapsuds. He gaped at her as if she were a ghost, while she tried to act as if every cell in her body wasn't leaping to get at him. In the same trembling voice she asked, ''Need somebody to wipe for you?''

''Winn . . . my God . . . Winn.''

''Is that all you can say is Winn? After all I've been through today just to get out of one very fast-approaching wedding for you?''

In one leap he slammed against her, nearly knocking her breath out while taking her off her feet and against his chest, with both of his detergent hands leaving wet prints on the back of her yellow cotton blouse. ''Really? Oh, babe, really?'' But he didn't give her time to answer. His mouth crushed hers, wide and wet and celebratory as he whirled them both in a circle.

Her arms made a nest for his head, knocking the baseball cap askew while they kissed and kissed and kissed, moving their heads in impatient and wondrous circles, yet still unable to satiate themselves fast enough to believe it was real. When at last she drew her mouth back to say, ''Yes, really,'' her smile was as wide as center field, yet his was even wider. His beautiful bedroom eyes sparkled with the smile she loved, the one that half-closed them while his perfect teeth peeked from behind upturned lips. While he still held her aloft, she appropriated his black baseball cap and put it on her own head so she could get her fingers into that wonderful wealth of fine curls she loved so much.

''You really called it off?'' he demanded one more time.

''I really called it off. I told mother to cease and desist. I gave my apologies to Paul. I told the realtor to come and get his damned sign out of my yard and sent the buyers packing, then came to you as fast as my car could get me here.''

His mouth possessed hers again, and while they kissed, he let her slide down the front of him with very deliberate slowness. Her blouse caught on his uniform buttons and shimmied up her tummy, and his hands slid beneath it to caress her bare back and ribs.

Tommy Duggan, dressed in a uniform matching Jo-Jo's, turned the corner into the kitchen, came up short at the sight greeting him, folded his arms across his chest and leaned against the archway, smiling.

''Well, well, well,'' he drawled, ''what do we have here?''

Joseph's hands stayed right where they were while he craned around to look at his brother. Winn kept her arms around Jo-Jo's neck, unwilling to release him in spite of the interruption. ''What we have here is Killer Gardner, the woman who's made my life pure misery for the last two months.''

''She gonna join the team?'' Tommy inquired drolly, eyeing Joseph's cap that was too big for Winn's head and thus rested low against her ears.

Jo-Jo grinned down at her. ''Whaddya say, Killer, wanna join the Duggan team?''

She kissed him boldly on the mouth, ending with a loud smack. ''That depends. Who won tonight?''

Jo-Jo seemed unaware of his brother's presence as he smiled at the woman in his arms and rubbed her spine. ''Me.''

Tommy's eyes followed Joseph's hands, then he pulled his shoulder away from the doorway and picked up his own black hat from the kitchen table, settled its bill low over his eyes and remarked, ''Well, I can see I'm not needed around here. Might as well go join the guys at Dick's Bar.''

Then he slammed out the back door, and a minute later they heard his car start.

Alone again, Joseph and Winn gazed lovingly into each other's eyes, standing just where Tommy had left them, only now his hands were inside her waistband, caressing the slope of her spine. ''I can't believe you're here,'' he said in a gruff whisper, letting his eyes caress her face.

''Neither can I. The last four days have been absolute hell.''

This kiss was different. Deliberate, measured, beginning with the lazy lowering of Joseph's mouth to Winn's, the gradual intrusion of tongues, building in ardor as their hands started roaming each other's backs, shoulders, buttocks, breasts, until it was a total bodily clinging as they pressed yearningly against each other, as if never would they get enough . . . never.

He tore his mouth from hers long enough to utter, ''I was so scared I'd lose you, and there wasn't anything I could do about it.''

''I was scared, too.'' A hot weakening kiss cut her off for several seconds, then Joseph's face was on her neck, his hands releasing the catch of her bra while she went on. ''From the night of the wedding practice I've been scared. I fell for you so hard it terrified me. I thought you were a flirt, and flirts always seem insincere. Then I got to know you better and realized I was falling in love with you. . . .'' She clung to him harder. ''Oh, Joseph, you have no idea how awful it is to be engaged to one man and in love with another.''

His palm slid to ensconce her free breast in its warm curve. ''It can't be any worse than being the one on the outside, watching it happen. God, I felt so helpless!''

Again they kissed, allowing their bodies full greed. He caressed and toyed with her nipple until it stood out proudly, then ran his hand down the stomach of her white jeans, slipping down between her legs where it was warm and slightly damp.

Her hand, too, ran down his body. "Mmm . . . I like you in your baseball uniform. You can't hide anything from me in pants this tight."

"Who's trying to hide?"

"Not me."

"Me, either."

She rested her forehead against his nose, laughed then, and did her Mae West imitation: "*So, uh, tell me, big boy, where's your brother John?*"

"Up at Dick's Bar with the rest of the team, having a few beers."

"Wanna join them?" she teased, stroking him ardently now.

"Yeah, sure, I was thinking about it. Nothing a man loves better than a nice cold beer on a summer evening."

"Well, don't let me . . . uh, stop you." His eyes sparkled and crinkled at the corners. She'd never get enough of his eyes, not if they lived to be seventy. Or of the rest of him, for that matter.

"I'll head over there in a minute. There's something I've got to do first, though." He had her by both buns and was dancing her backward toward the archway and the stairway around the corner.

"How much time before your brothers get home?"

His tongue teased the corner of her mouth.

"They'll be gone till midnight." She felt him grin against her lips. "The beer's damn good at Dick's."

Her heels struck the bottom step and brought them both up short. With her arms looped about his neck she ordered huskily, "Hurry up, Jo-Jo Duggan. The past four days have seemed like years. Show me your bedroom."

He bent and picked her up like a sack of potatoes and took the steps at a leisurely pace while she caressed his backside. "I will. But I'll show you my bathroom first. I played a tough game and took a hard slide into home in the eighth inning. I'm dust from one end to the other."

The bathroom was Classic Grandma: no shower, but a tub with a rubber plug on the end of a chain. The room was painted aqua blue and trimmed with white swan decals on one wall, while that behind the vanityless sink was paneled with some marbly gray stuff that looked like plastic. There was a water heater in one corner and a clothes hamper next to the stool, and the floor was covered with pure unadulterated grade-B hardware-store linoleum, its worn spot covered with an aqua blue scatter rug.

But it mattered not in the least, for anywhere Joseph and Winn shared was their own private heaven. She watched him drop his dusty uniform in the hamper. Then the body that had taken a hard slide into home took a soft slide into the tub. And she came to know the texture of his slick, soapy skin both above and below the surface of the water.

Her Joseph. How she loved him. Kneeling beside the tub, with her eyes caught in his, she lifted her wet hand from the water and laid it on his cheek. His eyes were dark, lustrous, close to hers. "Joseph Duggan, I love you," she whispered thickly.

All was silent but for the soft blip of the ancient, dripping tap. Then he brought his hands from the water to her jaws. His wet thumbs caressed her lips before he gently eradicated the space between their mouths, kissing her gently, wonderingly, the touch filled with praise and promise.

''And I love you, Winn Gardner. Marry me.''

Her murmured agreement was lost in his kiss, but neither heard nor cared. For it could be no other way: the choice had never been theirs, not from the first night they'd met to walk down an aisle together.

The wedding invitations numbered twenty-two. Each was handwritten on plain typing paper, but not all in the same pen. Half were written in Winn's neat forward slant and half in Joseph's rather chicken-scratchy semi-legibility. They began with the words, ''Joseph Duggan and Winnifred Gardner invite you to join them in Elm Creek Park. . . .''

Joseph and Winn chose a Friday afternoon for their wedding. She wore a white summer dress of airy piqué, and fixed her hair in a Gibson Girl doughnut, trimming it with a simple sprig of baby's breath they found blooming in Joseph's grandma's garden.

Joseph and Winn rode out together in his Haynes a half hour before the scheduled time of the service to walk through the woods and gather a bouquet of brown-eyed Susans, wild buttercups and fragrant wild roses, conveniently abloom now in this month of roses.

The guests were waiting when they returned from their walk to the chosen spot, a grassy knoll in a break between the trees where birds were their only music and the grass their aisle. Around them were those they loved most dearly, including a surprised Sandy and Mick, Joseph's parents and brothers, as well as Fern Gardner, still in a state of shock, but present nevertheless.

The service lasted seven minutes and thirty-five seconds, approximately one-third the length of time it had taken most of the assembled to drive out from town.

When Winn kissed her mother's cheek, there was a radiant smile upon the bride's face. That smile was reflected upon the faces of several others close enough to hear the following words. ''Mother, I'd like you to meet my husband, Joseph Duggan.''

The two shook hands while Joseph spoke his first words to Fern. ''Mrs. Gardner, I promise to love your daughter and keep her ecstatic at least until we're seventy years old. After that it depends on whether she lets our grandchildren overrun us or not.''

Mr. and Mrs. Joseph Duggan honeymooned in a log cabin on Lake Bemidji. On their first afternoon there they went out fishing, something Winn had never tried before. With typical beginner's luck she caught the only fish of the day—a seven-pound walleyed pike. Within an hour, when the lake provided no more action, she lost all interest in the sport and asked Joseph to head the boat back to the cabin. There, inside, Jo-Jo warned, ''Hands off, Killer, I have to clean the fish first.''

''Throw him away.''

''But he's such a big one.''

"I caught one big one. I can catch another. . . ." Then she ran her hands down his body and giggled. "Oh-oh! Here comes one now!"

But in the end Joseph cleaned the walleye, and by the time he finished it was time for dinner. They ate at The Seasons, then returned to their private retreat amid the lakeshore pines. When they faced each other at the side of their bed, Winn felt oddly timid. Joseph was dressed in cotton pajama pants and she in a long white nightgown with tiny satin straps and a bow beneath her breasts. Her cheeks were flushed and his eyes sparkly. His callused hand reached for hers and gave one gentle tug.

"Come here, Mrs. Duggan."

She lifted her arms, and his closed about her, bringing their wispily clad bodies close. His neck smelled of the cedar after-shave she now knew so well. She closed her eyes against the warm skin there and slipped her fingers into his soft curls, cradling his head as her eyes drifted closed. "Mrs. Duggan," she repeated rapturously. "I really am." She backed away and found his eyes with her own. "I'm Mrs. Joseph Duggan."

He slipped one satin strap over a narrow shoulder. "From now till you're at least seventy," he replied with gruff tenderness.

Her fingers brushed the hair on his chest, trembling upon it. "And then?"

The second strap fell slack as he pushed it down. "And then. . . ." His eyes dropped to the satin bow as his fingers freed it. The gown shimmied into an ivory puddle at her feet. Just before his lips and arms claimed her Joseph chided raspily, "Don't ask foolish questions, my love."

"*In the spring a young man's fancy*
lightly turns to thoughts of love. . . ."

Alfred, Lord Tennyson
From the poem, *Locksley Hall*